The Young
Wizards

DIANE DUANE

The Young Wizards

So You Want to Be a Wizard
Deep Wizardry
High Wizardry
A Wizard Abroad
The Wizard's Dilemma

FANTASY

The Young Wizards

Contents

So You Want to Be a Wizard
3

Deep Wizardry
135

High Wizardry
281

A Wizard Abroad
405

The Wizard's Dilemma
559

Taking the Oath

QUICKLY, BEFORE SHE could start to feel silly, she read it out loud.

" 'In Life's name, and for Life's sake,' " she read, " 'I say that I will use the Art for nothing but the service of that Life ...' " The words seemed to echo slightly, as if the room were larger than it really was. . . .

The next morning, the sun on her face woke Nita up as usual. She sat up and pulled the book out, felt around for her glasses. The book fell open in her hand at the listing for the wizards in the New York metropolitan area, which Nita had glanced at the afternoon before. Now she looked down the first column of names, and her breath caught.

CALLAHAN, Juanita L.
(novice, pre-rating)

Her mouth fell open. She shut it.

I'm going to be a wizard! she thought.

So You
Want to Be
a Wizard

For Sam's friend

Contents

Prologue
13

Preliminary Exercises
25

Research and Development
40

Temporospatial Claudications:
USE AND ABUSE
52

Exocontinual Protocols
71

Entropics:
DETECTION AND AVOIDANCE
82

Contractual Magic:
AN INTRODUCTION
94

Major Wizardries:
TERMINATION AND RECOVERY
109

Timeheart
128

ACKNOWLEDGMENT

David Gerrold is responsible for the creation of several images found in this book, upon which the writer has elaborated slightly. He's also responsible for beating the writer with a club until the words came out right—a matter of several years' nonstop exertion. It would take several more years to fully acknowledge his contributions to both the writer and the written; but brevity is probably best. Old friend, big brother, thanks and love, again and always.

By necessity every book must have at least one flaw; a misprint, a missing page, one imperfection. . . . the Rabbis . . . point out that even in the holiest of books, the scroll resting inside the Ark, the Name of Names is inscribed in code so that no one might say it out loud, and chance to pronounce properly the Word that once divided the waters from the waters and the day from the night. . . . As it is, some books, nearly perfect, are known to become transparent when opened under the influence of the proper constellation, when the full Moon rests in place. Then it is not uncommon for a man to become lost in a single letter, or to hear a voice rise up from the silent page; and then only one imperfect letter, one missing page, can bring him back to the land where a book, once opened, may still be closed, can permit him to pull up the covers around his head and smile once before he falls asleep.

—*Midrashim*, by Howard Schwartz

I have been a word in a book.

—"The Song of Taliesin"
in *The Black Book of Caermarthen*

Prologue

PART OF THE PROBLEM, Nita thought as she tore desperately down Rose Avenue, *is that I can't keep my mouth shut.*

She had been running for five minutes now, hopping fences, sliding sideways through hedges, but she was losing her wind. Some ways behind her she could hear Joanne and Glenda and the rest of them pounding along in pursuit, threatening to replace her latest, now-fading black eye. Well, Joanne *would* come up to her with that new bike, all chrome and silver and gearshift levers and speedometer/ odometer and toe clips and water bottle, and ask what she thought of it. So Nita had *told* her. Actually, she had told Joanne what she thought of *her*. The bike was all right. In fact, it had been almost exactly the one that Nita had wanted so much for her last birthday—the birthday when she got nothing but clothes.

Life can be really rotten sometimes, Nita thought. She wasn't really so irritated about that at the moment, however. Running away from a beating was taking up most of her attention.

"Callahan," came a yell from behind her, "I'm gonna pound you up and mail you home in bottles!"

I wonder how many bottles it'll take, Nita thought, without much humor. She couldn't afford to laugh. With their bikes, they'd catch up to her pretty quickly. And then . . .

She tried not to think of the scene there would be later at home—her father raising hands and eyes to the ceiling, wondering loudly enough for the whole house to hear, "Why didn't you hit them *back?*"; her sister making belligerent noises over her new battle scars; her mother shaking her head, looking away silently, because she understood. It was her sad look that would hurt Nita more than the bruises and scrapes and swollen face would. Her mom would shake her head, and clean the hurts up, and sigh. . . .

Crud! Nita thought. The breath was coming hard to her now. She was going to have to try to hide, to wait them out. But where? Most of the people around here didn't want kids running through their yards. There was Old Crazy Swale's house with its big landscaped yard, but the rumors among the neighborhood kids said that weird things happened in there. Nita herself had noticed that the guy didn't go to work like normal people. *Better to get beat up again than go in* there. *But where can I hide?*

She kept on running down Rose Avenue, and the answer presented itself to her: a little brown-brick building with windows warmly alight—refuge, safety, sanctuary. The library. *It's open, it's open. I forgot it was open late on Saturday! Oh, thank Heaven!* The sight of it gave Nita a new burst of energy. She cut across its tidy lawn, loped up the walk, took the five stairs to the porch in two jumps, bumped open the front door, and closed it behind her, a little too loudly.

The library had been a private home once, and it hadn't lost the look of one despite the crowding of all its rooms with bookshelves. The walls were paneled in mahogany and oak, and the place smelled warm and brown and booky. At the thump of the door Mrs. Lesser, the weekend librarian, glanced up from her desk, about to say something sharp. Then she saw who was standing there and how hard she was breathing. Mrs. Lesser frowned at Nita and then grinned. She didn't miss much.

"There's no one downstairs," she said, nodding at the door that led to the children's library in the single big basement room. "Keep quiet and I'll get rid of them."

"Thanks," Nita said, and went thumping down the cement stairs. As she reached the bottom, she heard the bump and squeak of the front door opening again.

Nita paused to try to hear voices and found that she couldn't. Doubting that her pursuers could hear her either, she walked on into the children's library, smiling slightly at the books and the bright posters.

She still loved the place. She loved any library, big or little; there was something about all that knowledge, all those facts waiting patiently to be found that never failed to give her a shiver. When friends couldn't be found, the books were always waiting with something new to tell. Life that was getting too much the same could be shaken up in a few minutes by the picture in a book of some ancient temple newly discovered deep in a rain forest, a fuzzy photo of Uranus with its up-and-down rings, or a prismed picture taken through the faceted eye of a bee.

And though she would rather have died than admit it—no respectable thirteen-year-old *ever* set foot down there—she still loved the children's library too. Nita had gone through every book in the place when she was younger, reading everything in sight—fiction and nonfiction alike, fairy tales, science books, horse stories, dog stories, music books, art books, even the encyclopedias.

Bookworm, she heard the old jeering voices go in her head, *four eyes, smart-ass, hide-in-the-house-and-read. Walking encyclopedia. Think you're so hot.* "No," she remembered herself answering once, "I just like to find things out!" And she sighed, feeling rueful. *That* time she had found out about being punched in the stomach.

She strolled between shelves, looking at titles, smiling as she met old friends—books she had read three times or five times or a dozen. Just a title, or an author's name, would be enough to summon up happy images. Strange creatures like phoenixes and psammeads, moving under smoky London daylight of a hundred years before, in company with groups of bemused children; starships and new worlds and the limitless vistas of interstellar night, outer space challenged but never conquered; princesses in silver and golden dresses, princes and heroes carrying swords like sharpened lines of light, monsters rising out of weedy tarns, wild creatures that talked and tricked one another. . . .

I used to think the world would be like that when I got older. Wonderful all the time, exciting, happy. Instead of the way it is. . . .

Something stopped Nita's hand as it ran along the bookshelf. She looked and found that one of the books, a little library-bound volume in shiny red buckram, had a loose thread at the top of its spine, on which her finger had caught. She pulled the finger free, glanced at the title. It was one of those So You Want to Be a . . . books, a series on careers. *So You Want to Be a Pilot* there had been, and *So You Want to Be a Scientist . . . a Nurse . . . a Writer . . .*

But this one said, *So You Want to Be a Wizard.*

A what?

Nita pulled the book off the shelf, surprised not so much by the title as by the fact that she'd never seen it before. She thought she knew the whole stock of the children's library. Yet this wasn't a new book. It had plainly been there for some time—the pages had that yellow look about their edges, the color of aging, and the top of the book was dusty. SO YOU WANT TO BE A WIZARD. HEARNSSEN, the spine said: that was the author's name. Phoenix Press, the publisher. And then in white ink in Mrs. Lesser's tidy handwriting, 793.4: the Dewey decimal number.

This has to be a joke, Nita said to herself. But the book looked exactly like all the others in the series. She opened it carefully, so as not to crack the binding, and turned the first few pages to the table of contents. Normally Nita was a fast reader and would quickly have finished a page with only a few lines on it; but what she found on that contents page slowed her down a great deal. "Preliminary Determinations: A Question of Aptitude." "Wizardly Preoccupations and Predilections." "Basic Equipment and Milieus." "Introduction to Spells, Bindings, and *Geasa*." "Familiars and Helpmeets: Advice to the Initiate." "Psychotropic Spelling."

Psychowhat? Nita turned to the page on which that chapter began, looking at the boldface paragraph beneath its title.

WARNING

Spells of power sufficient to make temporary changes in the human mind are always subject to sudden and unpredictable backlash on the user. The practitioner is cautioned to make sure that his/her motives are benevolent before attempting spelling aimed at . . .

I don't believe this, Nita thought. She shut the book and stood there holding it in her hand, confused, amazed, suspicious—and delighted. If it was a joke, it was a great one. If it wasn't . . .

No, don't be silly.

But if it isn't . . .

People were clumping around upstairs, but Nita hardly heard them. She sat down at one of the low tables and started reading the book in earnest.

The first couple of pages were a foreword.

Wizardry is one of the most ancient and misunderstood of arts. Its public image for centuries has been one of a mysterious pursuit, practiced in occult surroundings, and usually used at the peril of one's soul. The modern wizard, who works with tools more advanced than bat's blood and beings more complex than medieval demons, knows how far from the truth that image is. Wizardry, though exciting and interesting, is not a glamorous business, especially these days, when a wizard must work quietly so as not to attract undue attention.

For those willing to assume the Art's responsibilities and do the work, though, wizardry has many rewards. The sight of a formerly twisted growing thing now growing straight, of a snarled motivation untangled, the satisfaction of hearing what a plant is thinking or a dog is saying, of talking to a stone or a star, is thought by most to be well worth the labor.

Not everyone is suited to be a wizard. Those without enough of the necessary personality traits will never see this manual for what it is. That you have found it at all says a great deal for your potential.

The reader is invited to examine the next few chapters and determine his/her wizardly potential in detail—to become familiar with the scope of the Art—and finally to decide whether to become a wizard.

Good luck!

It's a joke, Nita thought. *Really.* And to her own amazement, she wouldn't believe herself—she was too fascinated. She turned to the next chapter.

PRELIMINARY DETERMINATIONS

An aptitude for wizardry requires more than just the desire to practice the art. There are certain inborn tendencies, and some acquired ones, that enable a person to become a wizard. This chapter will list some of the better documented of wizardly characteristics. Please bear in mind that it isn't necessary to possess all the qualities listed, or even most of them. Some of the greatest wizards have been lacking in the qualities possessed by almost all others and have still achieved startling competence levels. . . .

Slowly at first, then more eagerly, Nita began working her way through the assessment chapter, pausing only to get a pencil and scrap paper from the checkout desk, so that she could make notes on her aptitude. She was brought up short by the footnote to one page:

*Where ratings are not assigned, as in rural areas, the area of greatest population density will usually produce the most wizards, due to the thinning of worldwalls with increased population concentration. . . .

Nita stopped reading, amazed. "Thinning of worldwalls"—were they saying that there are other worlds, other dimensions, and that things could get through? Things, or people?

She sat there and wondered. All the old fairy tales about people falling down wells into magical countries, or slipping backward in time, or forward into it—did this mean that such things could actually happen? If you could actually go into other worlds, other places, and come back again. . . .

Aww—who would believe anybody who came back and told a story like that? Even if they took pictures?

But who cares! she answered herself fiercely. *If only it could be true. . . .*

She turned her attention back to the book and went on reading, though skeptically—the whole thing still felt like a game, but abruptly it stopped being a game, with one paragraph:

*Wizards love words. Most of them read a great deal, and indeed one strong sign of a potential wizard is the inability to get to sleep without reading something first. But their love for and fluency with words is what makes wizards a force to be reckoned with. Their ability to convince a piece of the world—a tree, say, or a stone—that it's not what it thinks it is, that it's something else, is the very heart of wizardry. Words skillfully used, the persuasive voice, the persuading mind, are the wizard's most basic tools. With them a wizard can stop a tidal wave, talk a tree out of growing, or into it—freeze fire, burn rain—*even slow down the death of the Universe.

That last, of course, is the reason there are wizards. See the next chapter.

Nita stopped short. The universe was running down; all the energy in it was slowly being used up. She knew that from studying astronomy. The process was called *entropy.* But she'd never heard anyone talk about slowing it down before.

She shook her head in amazement and went on to the "correlation" section at the end of that chapter, where all the factors involved in the makeup of a potential wizard were listed. Nita found that she had a lot of them—enough to be a wizard, if she wanted to.

With rising excitement she turned to the next chapter. "Theory and Implications of Wizardry," the heading said. *"History, Philosophy, and the Wizards' Oath."*

Fifty or sixty eons ago, when life brought itself about, it also brought about to accompany it many Powers and Potentialities to manage the business of creation. One of the greatest of these Powers held aloof for a long time, watching its companions work, not wishing to enter into Creation until it could contribute something unlike anything the other Powers had made, something completely new and original. Finally the Lone Power found what it was looking for. Others had invented planets, light, gravity, space. The Lone Power invented death, and bound it irrevocably into the worlds. Shortly thereafter the other Powers joined forces and cast the Lone One out.

Many versions of this story are related among the many worlds, assigning blame or praise to one party or another. However, none of the stories change the fact that entropy and its symptom, death, are here now. To attempt to halt or remove them is as futile as attempting to ignore them.

Therefore there are wizards—to handle them.

A wizard's business is to conserve energy—to keep it from being wasted. On the simplest level this includes such unmagical-looking actions as paying one's bills on time, turning off the lights when you go out, and supporting the people around you in getting their lives to work. It also includes a great deal more.

Because wizardly people tend to be good with language, they can also become skillful with the Speech, the magical tongue in which objects and living creatures can be described with more accuracy than in any human language. And what can be so accurately described can also be preserved—or freed to become yet greater. A wizard can cause an inanimate object or animate creature to grow, or stop growing—to be what it is, or something else. A wizard, using the Speech, can cause death to slow down, or go somewhere else and come back later—just as the Lone Power caused it to come about in the first place. Creation, preservation, destruction, transformation—all are a matter of causing the fabric of being to do what you want it to. And the Speech is the key.

Nita stopped to think this over for a moment. *It sounds like, if you know what something is, truly* know, *you don't have any trouble working with it. Like my telescope—if it acts up, I know every piece of it, and it only takes a second to get it working again. To have that kind of control over—over* everything—*live things, the world, even* . . . She took a deep breath and looked back at the book, beginning to get an idea of what kind of power was implied there.

The power conferred by use of the Speech has, of course, one insurmountable limitation: the existence of death itself. As one renowned Senior Wizard has re-marked, "Entropy has us outnumbered." No matter how much preserving we do, the Universe will eventually die. But it will last longer because of our efforts—and since no one knows for sure whether another Universe will be born from the ashes of this one, the effort seems worthwhile.

No one should take the Wizards' Oath who is not committed to making wiz-ardry a lifelong pursuit. The energy invested in a beginning wizard is too precious to be thrown away. Yet there are no penalties for withdrawal from the Art, except the knowledge that the Universe will die a little faster because of energy lost. On the other hand, there are no prizes for the service of Life—except life itself. The wizard gets the delight of working in a specialized area—magic—and gets a good look at the foundations of the Universe, the way things really work. It should be stated here that there are people who consider the latter more of a curse than a blessing. Such wizards usually lose their art. Magic does not live in the unwilling soul.

Should you decide to go ahead and take the Oath, be warned that an ordeal of sorts will follow, a test of aptitude. If you pass, wizardry will ensue. . . .

Yeah? Nita thought. *And what if you* don't *pass?*

"Nita?" Mrs. Lesser's voice came floating down the stairs, and a moment later she herself appeared, a large brunette lady with kind eyes and a look of eternal concern. "You still alive?"

"I was reading."

"So what else is new? They're gone."

"Thanks, Mrs. L."

"What was all that about, anyway?"

"Oh . . . Joanne was looking to pick a fight again."

Mrs. Lesser raised an eyebrow at Nita, and Nita smiled back at her shamefac-edly. She *didn't* miss much.

"Well, I might have helped her a little."

"I guess it's hard," Mrs. Lesser said. "I doubt *I* could be nice all the time, myself, if I had that lot on my back. That the only one you want today, or should I just have the nonfiction section boxed and sent over to your house?"

"No, this is enough," Nita said. "If my father sees too many books he'll just make me bring them back."

Mrs. Lesser sighed. "Reading one book is like eating one potato chip," she said. "So you'll be back Monday. There's more where that came from. I'll check it out for you."

Nita felt in her pockets hurriedly. "Oh, crud. Mrs. L., I don't have my card."

"So you'll bring it back Monday," she said, handing her back the book as they reached the landing, "and I'll stamp it then. I trust you."

"Thanks," Nita said.

"Don't mention it. Be careful going home," Mrs. Lesser said, "and have a nice read."

"I will."

Nita went out and stood on the doorstep, looking around in the deepening gloom. Dinnertime was getting close, and the wind was getting cold, with a smell of rain to it. The book in her hand seemed to prickle a little, as if it were impatient to be read.

She started jogging toward home, taking a circuitous route—up Washington from Rose Avenue, then through town along Nassau Road and down East Clinton, a path meant to confound pursuit. She didn't expect that they would be waiting for her only a block away from her house, where there were no alternate routes to take. And when they were through with her, the six of them, one of Nita's eyes was blackened and the knee Joanne had so carefully stomped on felt swollen with liquid fire.

Nita just lay there for a long while, on the spot where they left her, behind the O'Donnells' hedge; the O'Donnells were out of town. There she lay, and cried, as she would not in front of Joanne and the rest, as she would not until she was safely in bed and out of her family's earshot. Whether she provoked these situations or not, they kept happening, and there was nothing she could do about them. Joanne and her hangers-on had found out that Nita didn't like to fight, wouldn't try until her rage broke loose—and then it was too late, she was too hurt to fight well. All her self-defense lessons went out of her head with the pain. And they knew it, and at least once a week found a way to sucker her into a fight—or, if that failed, they would simply ambush her. All right, she had purposely baited Joanne today, but there'd been a fight coming anyway, and *she* had chosen to start it rather than wait, getting angrier and angrier, while they baited *her*. But this would keep happening, again and again, and there was nothing she could do about it. *Oh, I wish we could move. I wish Dad would say something to Joanne's father—no, that would just make it worse. If only something could just happen to make it stop!*

Underneath her, where it had fallen, the book dug into Nita's sore ribs. The memory of what she had been reading flooded back through her pain and was followed by a wash of wild surmise. *If there are spells to keep things from dying, then I bet there are spells to keep people from hurting you. . . .*

Then Nita scowled at herself in contempt for actually believing for a moment what couldn't possibly be more than an elaborate joke. She put aside thoughts of the book and slowly got up, brushing herself off and discovering some new bruises. She also discovered something else. Her favorite pen was gone. Her space pen, a present from her Uncle Joel, the pen that could write on butter or glass or upside down, her pen with which she had never failed a test, even in math. She patted herself all over, checked the ground, searched in pockets where she knew the pen couldn't be. No use; it was gone. Or taken, rather—for it had been securely clipped

to her front jacket pocket when Joanne and her group jumped her. It must have
fallen out, and one of them picked it up.

"Aaaaaagh!" Nita moaned, feeling bitter enough to start crying again. But she
was all cried out, and she ached too much, and it was a waste. She stepped around
the hedge and limped the little distance home.

Her house was pretty much like any other on the block, a white frame house
with fake shutters; but where other houses had their lawns, Nita's had a beautifully
landscaped garden. Ivy carpeted the ground, and the flowerbeds against the house
had something blooming in every season except the dead of winter. Nita trudged
up the driveway without bothering to smell any of the spring flowers, went up the
stairs to the back door, pushed it open, and walked into the kitchen as nonchalantly
as she could.

Her mother was elsewhere, but the delicious smells of her cooking filled the
place; veal cutlets tonight. Nita peered into the oven, saw potatoes baking, lifted a
pot lid and found corn on the cob in the steamer.

Her father looked up from the newspaper he was reading at the dining-room
table. He was a big, blunt, good-looking man, with startling silver hair and large
capable hands—"an artist's hands!" he would chuckle as he pieced together a
flower arrangement. He owned the smaller of the town's two flower shops, and he
loved his work dearly. He had done all the landscaping around the house in his
spare time, and around several neighbors' houses too, refusing to take anything in
return but the satisfaction of being up to his elbows in a flowerbed. Whatever he
touched grew. "I have an understanding with the plants," he would say, and it
certainly seemed that way. It was people he sometimes had trouble understanding,
and particularly his eldest daughter.

"My Lord, Nita!" her father exclaimed, putting the paper down flat on the
table. His voice was shocked. "What happened?"

As if you don't know! Nita thought. She could clearly see the expressions going
across her father's face. *MiGod,* they said, *she's done it again! Why doesn't she
fight back? What's wrong with her?* He would get around to asking that question
at one point or another, and Nita would try to explain it again, and as usual her
father would try to understand and would fail. Nita turned away and opened the
refrigerator door, peering at nothing in particular, so that her father wouldn't see
the grimace of impatience and irritation on her face. She was tired of the whole
ritual, but she had to put up with it. It was as inevitable as being beaten up.

"I was in a fight," she said, the second verse of the ritual, the second line of
the scene. Tiredly she closed the refrigerator door, put the book down on the
counter beside the stove, and peeled off her jacket, examining it for rips and
ground-in dirt and blood.

"So how many of them did you take out?" her father said, turning his eyes
back to the newspaper. His face still showed exasperation and puzzlement, and
Nita sighed. *He looks about as tired of this as I am. But really, he knows the
answers.* "I'm not sure," Nita said. "There were six of them."

"Six!" Nita's mother came around the corner from the living room and into
the bright kitchen—danced in, actually. Just watching her made Nita smile sometimes, and it did now, though changing expressions hurt. She had been a dancer
before she married Dad, and the grace with which she moved made her every
action around the house seem polished, endlessly rehearsed, lovely to look at. She

glided with the laundry, floated while she cooked. "Loading the odds a bit, weren't they?"

"Yeah." Nita was hurting almost too much to feel like responding to the gentle humor. Her mother caught the pain in her voice and stopped to touch Nita's face as she passed, assessing the damage and conveying how she felt about it in one brief gesture, without saying anything that anyone else but the two of them might hear.

"No sitting up for you tonight, kidlet," her mother said. "Bed, and ice on that, before you swell up like a balloon."

"What started it?" her dad asked from the dining room.

"Joanne Virella," Nita said. "She has a new bike, and I didn't get as excited about it as she thought I should."

Nita's father looked up from the paper again, and this time there was discomfort in his face, and regret. "Nita," he said, "I couldn't afford it this month, really. I thought I was going to be able to earlier, but I couldn't. I *wish* I could have. Next time for sure."

Nita nodded. "It's okay," she said, even though it wasn't really. She'd *wanted* that bike, wanted it so badly—but Joanne's father owned the big five-and-dime on Nassau Road and *could* afford three-hundred-dollar bikes for his children at the drop of a birthday. Nita's father's business was a lot smaller and was prone to what he called (in front of most people) "cash-flow problems" or (in front of his family) "being broke most of the time."

But what does Joanne care about cash flow, or any of the rest of it? I wanted that bike!

"Here, dreamer," her mother said, tapping her on the shoulder and breaking her thought. She handed Nita an icepack and turned back toward the stove. "Go lie down or you'll swell worse. I'll bring you something in a while."

"Shouldn't she stay sitting up?" Nita's father said. "Seems as if the fluid would drain better or something."

"You didn't get beat up enough when you were younger, Harry," her mother said. "If she doesn't lie down, she'll blow up like a basketball. Scoot, Nita."

She scooted, around the corner into the dining room, around the second corner into the living room, and straight into her little sister, bumping loose one of the textbooks she was carrying and scattering half her armload of pink plastic curlers. Nita bent to help pick things up again. Her sister, bent down beside her, didn't take long to figure out what had happened.

"Virella again, huh?" she asked. Dairine was eleven years old, redheaded like her mother, gray-eyed like Nita, and precocious; she was taking tenth-grade English courses and breezing through them, and Nita was teaching her some algebra on the side. Dairine had her father's square-boned build and her mother's grace, and a perpetual, cocky grin. She was a great sister, as far as Nita was concerned, even if she was a little too smart for her own good.

"Yeah," Nita said. "Look out, kid, I've gotta go lie down."

"Don't call me kid. You want me to beat up Virella for you?"

"Be my guest," Nita said. She went on through the house, back to her room. Bumping the door open, she fumbled for the light switch and flipped it on. The familiar maps and pictures looked down at her—the *National Geographic* map of the Moon and some enlarged *Voyager* photos of Jupiter and Saturn and their moons.

Nita eased herself down onto the bottom bunk bed, groaning softly—the deep bruises were beginning to bother her now. *Lord*, she thought, *what did I say? If Dari* does *beat Joanne up, I'll never hear the end of it.* Dairine had once been small and fragile and subject to being beaten up—mostly because she had never learned to curb her mouth either—and Nita's parents had sent her to jujitsu lessons at the same time they sent Nita. On Dari, though, the lessons took. One or two overconfident kids had gone after her, about a month and a half into her lessons, and had been thoroughly and painfully surprised. She was protective enough to take Joanne on and, horrors, throw her clear over the horizon. It would be all over school; Nita Callahan's little sister beat up the girl who beat *Nita* up.

Oh no! Nita thought.

Her door opened slightly, and Dari stuck her head in. "Of course," she said, "if you'd rather do it yourself, I'll let her off this time."

"Yeah," Nita said, "thanks."

Dairine made a face. "Here," she said, and pitched Nita's jacket in at her, and then right after it the book. Nita managed to field it while holding the icepack in place with her left hand. "You left it in the kitchen," Dairine said. "Gonna be a magician, huh? Make yourself vanish when they chase you?"

"Sure. Go curl your hair, runt."

Nita sat back against the headboard of the bed, staring at the book. *Why not? Who knows what kinds of spells you could do? Maybe I could turn Joanne into a turkey. As if she isn't one already. Or maybe there's a spell for getting lost pens back.*

Though the book made it sound awfully serious, as if the wizardry were for big things. Maybe it's not right to do spells for little stuff like this—and anyway, you can't do the spells until you've taken the Oath, and once you've taken it, that's supposed to be forever.

Oh, come on, it's a joke! What harm can there be in saying the words if it's a joke? And if it's not, then . . .

Then I'll be a wizard.

Her father knocked on her door, then walked in with a plate loaded with dinner and a glass of cola. Nita grinned up at him, not too widely, for it hurt. "Thanks, Dad."

"Here," he said after Nita took the plate and the glass, and handed her a couple of aspirin. "Your mother says to take these."

"Thanks." Nita took them with the Coke, while her father sat down on the edge of the bed.

"Nita," he said, "is there something going on that I should know about?"

"Huh?"

"It's been once a week now, sometimes twice, for quite a while. Do you want me to speak to Joe Virella and ask him to have a word with Joanne?"

"Uh, no, sir."

Nita's father stared at his hands for a moment. "What should we do, then? I really can't afford to start you in karate lessons again—"

"Jujitsu."

"Whatever. Nita, what *is* it? Why does this keep happening? *Why don't you hit them back?*"

"I *used* to! Do you think it made a difference? Joanne would just get more kids to help." Her father stared at her, and Nita flushed hot at the stern look on his face. "I'm sorry, Daddy, I didn't mean to yell at you. But fighting back just gets them madder, it doesn't help."

"It might help keep you from getting mangled every week, if you'd just keep trying!" her father said angrily. "I hate to admit it, but I'd love to see you wipe the ground up with that loudmouth rich kid."

So would I, Nita thought. *That's the problem.* She swallowed, feeling guilty over how much she wanted to get back at Joanne somehow. "Dad, Joanne and her bunch just don't like me. I don't do the things they do, or play the games they play, or like the things they like—and I don't *want* to. So they don't like me. That's all."

Her father looked at her and shook his head sadly. "I just don't want to see you hurt. Kidling, I don't know . . . if you could just be a little more like them, if you could try to . . ." He trailed off, running one hand through his silver hair. "What am I saying?" he muttered. "Look. If there's anything I can do to help, will you tell me?"

"Yessir."

"Okay. If you feel better tomorrow, would you rake up the backyard a little? I want to go over the lawn around the rowan tree with the aerator, maybe put down some seed."

"Sure. I'll be okay, Dad. They didn't break anything."

"My girl." He got up. "Don't read so much it hurts your eyes, now."

"I won't," Nita said. Her father strode out the door, forgetting to close it behind himself as usual.

She ate her supper slowly, for it hurt to chew, and she tried to think about something besides Joanne or that book.

The Moon was at first quarter tonight; it would be a good night to take the telescope out and have a look at the shadows in the craters. Or there was that fuzzy little comet, maybe it had more tail than it did last week.

It was completely useless. The book lay there on her bed and stared at her, daring her to do something childlike, something silly, something absolutely ridiculous.

Nita put aside her empty plate, picked up the book, and stared back at it.

"All right," she said under her breath. "All right."

She opened the book at random. And on the page to which she opened, there was the Oath.

It was not decorated in any way. It stood there, a plain block of type all by itself in the middle of the page, looking serious and important. Nita read the Oath to herself first, to make sure of the words. Then, quickly, before she could start to feel silly, she read it out loud.

" 'In Life's name, and for Life's sake,' " she read, " 'I say that I will use the Art for nothing but the service of that Life. I will guard growth and ease pain. I will fight to preserve what grows and lives well in its own way; and I will change no object or creature unless its growth and life, or that of the system of which it is part, are threatened. To these ends, in the practice of my Art, I will put aside fear for courage, and death for life, when it is right to do so—till Universe's end.' "

The words seemed to echo slightly, as if the room were larger than it really was. Nita sat very still, wondering what the ordeal would be like, wondering what would happen now. Only the wind spoke softly in the leaves of the trees outside the bedroom window; nothing else seemed to stir anywhere. Nita sat there, and slowly the tension began to drain out of her as she realized that she hadn't been hit by lightning, nor had anything strange at all happened to her. *Now* she felt silly—and tired too, she discovered. The effects of her beating were catching up with her. Wearily, Nita shoved the book under her pillow, then lay back against the headboard and closed her hurting eyes. So much for the joke. She would have a nap, and then later she'd get up and take the telescope out back. But right now . . . right now. . . .

After a while, night was not night anymore; that was what brought Nita to the window, much later. She leaned on the sill and gazed out in calm wonder at her backyard, which didn't look quite the same as usual. A blaze of undying morning lay over everything, bushes and trees cast light instead of shadow, and she could see the wind. Standing in the ivy under her window, she turned her eyes up to the silver-glowing sky to get used to the brilliance. *How about that*, she said. *The backyard's here, too.* Next to her, the lesser brilliance that gazed up at that same sky shrugged slightly. *Of course*, it said. *This is Timeheart, after all. Yes,* Nita said anxiously as they passed across the yard and out into the bright shadow of the steel and crystal towers, *but did I do right?* Her companion shrugged again. *Go find out,* it said, and glanced up again. Nita wasn't sure she wanted to follow the glance. Once she had looked up and seen—*I dreamed you were gone*, she said suddenly. *The magic stayed, but you went away.* She hurt inside, enough to cry, but her companion flickered with laughter. *No one ever goes away forever*, it said. *Especially not here.* Nita looked up, then, into the bright morning and the brighter shadows. The day went on and on and would not end, the sky blazed now like molten silver. . . .

The Sun on her face woke Nita up as usual. Someone, her mother probably, had come in late last night to cover her up and take the dishes away. She turned over slowly, stiff but not in too much pain, and felt the hardness under her pillow. Nita sat up and pulled the book out, felt around for her glasses. The book fell open in her hand at the listing for the wizards in the New York metropolitan area, which Nita had glanced at the afternoon before. Now she looked down the first column of names, and her breath caught.

CALLAHAN, Juanita L.,
243 E. Clinton Ave.,
Hempstead, NY 11575
(516) 555-6786. (novice, pre-rating)

Her mouth fell open. She shut it.
I'm going to be a wizard! she thought.
Nita got up and got dressed in a hurry.

Preliminary
Exercises

SHE DID HER CHORES that morning and got out of the house with the book as fast as she could, heading for one of her secret places in the woods. *If weird things start happening*, she thought, *no one will see them there. Oh, I'm going to get that pen back! And then . . .*

Behind the high school around the corner from Nita's house was a large tract of undeveloped woodland, the usual Long Island combination of scrub oak, white pine, and sassafras. Nita detoured around the school, pausing to scramble over a couple of chain-link fences. There was a path on the other side; after a few minutes she turned off it to pick her way carefully through low underbrush and among fallen logs and tree stumps. Then there was a solid wall of clumped sassafras and twining wild blackberry bushes. It looked totally impassable, and the blackberries threatened Nita with their thorns, but she turned sideways and pushed through the wall of greenery undaunted.

She emerged into a glade walled all around with blackberry and gooseberry and pine, sheltered by the overhanging branches of several trees. One, a large crabapple, stood near the edge of the glade, and there was a flattish half-buried boulder at the base of its trunk. Here she could be sure no one was watching.

Nita sat down on the rock with a sigh, put her back up against the tree, and spent a few moments getting comfortable—then opened the book and started to read.

She found herself not just reading, after a while, but studying—cramming the facts into her head with that particular mental *stomp* she used when she knew she was going to have to know something by heart. The things the book was telling her now were not vague and abstract, as the initial discussion of theory had been, but straightforward as the repair manual for a new car, and nearly as complex. There were tables and lists of needed resources for working spells. There were formulas and equations and rules. There was a syllabary and pronunciation guide for the 418 symbols used in the wizardly Speech to describe relationships and effects that other human languages had no specific words for.

The information went on and on—the book was printed small, and there seemed no end to the things Nita was going to have to know about. She read about the hierarchy of practicing wizards—her book listed only those practicing in the U.S. and Canada, though wizards were working everywhere in the world—and she scanned down the listing for the New York area, noticing the presence of Advisory wizards, Area Supervisors, Senior wizards. She read through a list of the "otherworlds" closest to her own, alternate earths where the capital of the United States was named Huictilopochtli or Lafayette City or Hrafnkell or New Washington, and where the people still called themselves Americans, though they didn't match Nita's ideas about the term.

She learned the Horseman's Word, which gets the attention of any member of the genus *Equus*, even the zebras; and the two forms of the Mason's Word, which give stone the appearance of life for short periods. One chapter told her about the magical creatures living in cities, whose presence even the nonwizardly people suspect sometimes—creatures like the steam-breathing fireworms, packratty little lizards that creep through cracks in building walls to steal treasures and trash for their lair-hoards under the streets. Nita thought about all the steam she had seen coming up from manhole covers in Manhattan and smiled, for now she knew what was causing it.

She read on, finding out how to bridle the Nightmare and learning what questions to ask the Transcendent Pig, should she meet him. She read about the Trees' Battle—who fought in it, who won it, and why. She read about the forty basic classes of spells and their subclasses. She read about Timeheart, the unreal and eternal realm where the places and things people remember affectionately are preserved as they remember them, forever.

In the middle of the description of things preserved in their fullest beauty forever, and still growing, Nita found herself feeling a faint tingle of unease. She was also getting tired. She dropped the book in her lap with an annoyed sigh, for there was just too much to absorb at one sitting, and she had no clear idea of where to begin. "Crud," she said under her breath. "I thought I'd be able to make Joanne vanish by tomorrow morning."

Nita picked the manual up again and leafed through it to the section labeled "Preliminary Exercises."

The first one was set in a small block of type in the middle of an otherwise empty page.

To change something, you must first describe it. To describe something, you must first see it. Hold still in one place for as long as it takes to see something.

Nita felt puzzled and slightly annoyed. This didn't sound much like magic. But obediently she put the book down, settled herself more comfortably against the tree, folded her arms, and sighed. *It's almost too warm to think about anything serious. . . . What should I look at? That rock over there? Naah, it's kind of a dull-looking rock. That weed . . . look how its leaves go up around the stem in a spiral. . . .* Nita leaned her head back, stared up through the crabtree's branches. *That rotten Joanne. Where would she have hidden that pen? I wonder. Maybe if I could sneak into her house somehow, maybe there's a spell for that. . . . Have to do it after dark, I guess. Maybe I could do it tonight. . . . Wish it didn't take so long to get dark this time of year.* Nita looked at the sky where it showed between the leaves, a hot blue mosaic of light with here and there the fireflicker of sun showing through, shifting with the shift of leaves in the wind. *There are kinds of patterns— the wind never goes through the same way twice, and there are patterns in the branches but they're never quite the same either. And look at the changes in the brightness. The sky is the same but the leaves cover sometimes more and sometimes less . . . the patterns . . . the patterns, they . . . they . . .*

(They won't let you have a moment's rest,) the crabapple tree said irritably.

Nita jumped, scraping her back against the trunk as she sat up straight. She had heard the tree quite plainly in some way that had nothing to do with spoken words. It was light patterns she had heard, and wind movements, leafrustle, fireflicker.

(Finally paid attention, did you?) said the tree. (As if one of them isn't enough, messing up someone's fallen-leaf pattern that's been in progress for fifteen years, drawing circles all over the ground and messing up the matrices. Well? What's *your* excuse?)

Nita sat there with her mouth open, looking up at the words the tree was making with cranky light and shadow. *It works. It works!* "Uh," she said, not knowing whether the tree could understand her, "I didn't draw any circles on your leaves—"

(No, but that other one did,) the tree said. (Made circles and stars and diagrams all over Telerilarch's collage, doing some kind of power spell. You people don't have the proper respect for artwork. Okay, so we're amateurs,) it added, a touch of belligerence creeping into its voice. (So none of us have been here more than thirty years. Well, our work is still valid, and—)

"Uh, listen, do you mean that there's a, uh, a wizard out here somewhere doing magic?"

(What else?) the tree snapped. (And let me tell you, if you people don't—)

"Where? Where is she?"

(He,) the tree said. (In the middle of all those made-stone roads. I remember when those roads went in, and they took a pattern Kimber had been working on for eighty years and scraped it bare and poured that black rock over it. One of the most complex, most—)

He? Nita thought, and her heart sank slightly. She had trouble talking to boys. "You mean across the freeway, in the middle of the interchange? That green place?"

(Didn't you hear me? Are you deaf? Silly question. That other one *must* be deaf not to have heard Teleri yelling at him. And now I suppose *you'll* start scratching up the ground and invoking powers and ruining *my* collage. Well, let me tell you—)

"I, uh—listen, I'll talk to you later," Nita said hurriedly. She got to her feet, brushed herself off, and started away through the woods at a trot. *Another wizard? And my God, the trees—*Their laughter at her amazement was all around her as she ran, the merriment of everything from foot-high weeds to hundred-foot oaks, rustling in the wind—grave chuckling of maples and alders, titters from groves of sapling sassafras, silly giggling in the raspberry bushes, a huge belly laugh from the oldest hollow ash tree before the freeway interchange. *How could I never have heard them before!*

Nita stopped at the freeway's edge and made sure that there were no cars coming before she tried to cross. The interchange was a cloverleaf, and the circle formed by one of the off-ramps held a stand of the original pre-freeway trees within it, in a kind of sunken bowl. Nita dashed across the concrete and stood a moment, breathless, at the edge of the downslope, before starting down it slantwise.

This was another of her secret places, a spot shaded and peaceful in summer and winter both because of the pine trees that roofed in the hollow. But there was nothing peaceful about it today. Something was in the air, and the trees, irritated, were muttering among themselves. Even on a foot-thick cushion of pine needles,

Nita's feet seemed to be making too much noise. She tried to walk softly and wished the trees wouldn't stare at her so.

Where the slope bottomed out she stopped, looking around her nervously, and that was when she saw him. The boy was holding a stick in one hand and staring intently at the ground underneath a huge larch on one side of the grove. He was shorter than she was, and looked younger, and he also looked familiar somehow. *Now who is that?* she thought, feeling more nervous still. No one had ever been in one of her secret places when *she* came there.

But the boy just kept frowning at the ground, as if it were a test paper and he was trying to scowl the right answer out of it. A very ordinary-looking kid, with straight black hair and a Hispanic look to his face, wearing a beat-up green windbreaker and jeans and sneakers, holding a willow wand of a type that Nita's book recommended for certain types of spelling.

He let out what looked like a breath of irritation and put his hands on his hips. *"Cojones,"* he muttered, shaking his head—and halfway through the shake, he caught sight of Nita.

He looked surprised and embarrassed for a moment, then his face steadied down to a simple worried look. There he stood regarding Nita, and she realized with a shock that he wasn't going to yell at her, or chase her, or call her names, or run away himself. He was going to let her explain herself. Nita was amazed. It didn't seem quite normal.

"Hi," she said.

The boy looked at her uncertainly, as if trying to place her. "Hi."

Nita wasn't sure quite where to begin. But the marks on the ground, and the willow wand, seemed to confirm that a power spell was in progress. "Uh," she said, "I, uh, I don't see the oak leaves. Or the string."

The boy's dark eyes widened. "So *that's* how you got through!"

"Through what?"

"I put a binding spell around the edges of this place," he said. "I've tried this spell once or twice before, but people kept showing up just as I was getting busy, and I couldn't finish."

Nita suddenly recognized him. "You're the one they were calling crazy last week."

The boy's eyes narrowed again. He looked annoyed. "Uh, yeah. A couple of the eighth graders found me last Monday. They were shooting up the woods with BB guns, and there I was working. And they couldn't figure out what I was doing, so at lunch the next day they said—"

"I know what they said." It had been a badly rhymed song about the kid who played by himself in the woods, because no one else would play with him. She remembered feeling vaguely sorry for the kid, whoever he was; boys could be as bad as girls sometimes.

"I thought I blew the binding, too," he said. "You surprised me."

"Maybe you can't bind another wizard out," Nita said. *That was it*, she thought. *If he's not one—*

"Uhh . . . I guess not." He paused. "I'm Kit," he said then. "Christopher, really, but I hate Christopher."

"Nita," she said. "It's short for Juanita. I hate that, too. Listen—the trees are mad at you."

Kit stared at her. "The *trees?*"

"Uh, mostly this one." She looked up into the branches of the larch, which were trembling with more force than the wind could lend them. "See, the trees do—I don't know, it's artwork, sort of, with their fallen leaves—and you started doing your power schematic all over their work, and, uh—"

"Trees?" Kit said. "Rocks I knew about, I talked to a rock last week—or it talked to me, actually—though it wasn't talking, really . . ." He looked up at the tree. "Well, hey, I'm sorry," he said. "I didn't know. I'll try to put things back the way I found them. But I might as well not have bothered with the spell," he said, looking again at Nita. "It got caught. It's not working. You know anything about this?"

He gestured at the diagram he had drawn on the cleared ground, and Nita went to crouch down by it. The pattern was one she had seen in her book, a basic design of interlocking circles and woven parallelograms. There were symbols drawn inside the angles and outside the curves, some of them letters or words in the Roman alphabet, some of them the graceful characters of the wizardly Speech. "I just got my book yesterday," she said. "I doubt I'll be much help. What were you trying to get? The power part of it I can see."

She glanced up and found Kit looking with somber interest at her black eye. "I'm getting tired of being beat up just because I have a Spanish accent," he said. "I was going to attract enough power to me so that the big kids would just leave me alone and not start anything. An 'aura,' the book called it. But the spell got stuck a couple of steps in, and when I checked the book it said that I was missing an element." He looked questioningly at Nita. "Maybe you're it?"

"Uhh—" She shook her head. "I don't know. I was looking for a spell for something different. Someone beat me up and stole my best pen. It was a space pen, the kind the astronauts have, and it writes on anything, and I always took all my tests with it and I always pass when I use it, and I want it *back*." She stopped, then added, "And I guess I wouldn't mind if they didn't beat me up anymore either."

"We could make a finding spell and tie it into this one," Kit said.

"Yeah? Well, we better put these needles back first."

"Yeah."

Kit stuck the willow wand in his back pocket as he and Nita worked to push the larch's needles back over the cleared ground. "Where'd you get your book?" Nita said.

"In the city, about a month ago. My mother and father went out antique hunting. There's this one part of Second Avenue where all the little shops are—and one place had this box of secondhand books, and I stopped to look at them because I always look at old books—and this one caught my eye. My hand, actually. I was going after a Tom Swift book underneath it and it pinched me. . . ."

Nita chuckled. "Mine snagged me in the library," she said. "I don't know . . . I didn't want Joanne—she's the one who beat me up—I didn't want her to get my pen, but I'm glad she didn't get *this*." She pulled her copy of the book out of her jacket as Kit straightened up beside her. She looked over at him. "Does it work?" she demanded. "Does it really *work?*"

Kit stood there for a moment, looking at the replaced needles. "I fixed my dog's nose," he said. "A wasp stung him and I made it go down right away. And

I talked to the rock." He looked up at Nita again. "C'mon," he said. "There's a place in the middle where the ground is bare. Let's see what happens."

Together they walked to the center of the hollow, where the pine trees made a circle open to the sky and the ground was bare dirt. Kit pulled out his willow wand and began drawing the diagram again. "This one I know by heart," he said. "I've started it so many times. Well, this time for sure." He got his book out of his back pocket and consulted it, beginning to write symbols into the diagram. "Would you look and see if there's anything else we need for a finding spell?"

"Sure." Nita found the necessary section in the index of her book and checked it. "Just an image of the thing to be found," she said. "I have to make it while you're spelling. Kit, do you know *why* this works? Leaves, pieces of string, designs on the ground. It doesn't make sense."

Kit kept drawing. "There's a chapter on advanced theory in there, but I couldn't get through it all the way. The magic is supposed to have something to do with interrupting space—"

"Huh?"

"Listen, that's all I could get out of it. There was this one phrase that kept turning up, 'temporospatial claudication.' I think that's how you say it. It's something like, space isn't really empty, it folds around objects—or words—and if you put the right things in the right place and do the right things with them, and say the right things in the Speech, magic happens. Where's the string?"

"This one with all the knots in it?" Nita reached down and picked it up.

"Must have fallen out of my pocket. Stand on this end, okay?" He dropped one end of the string into the middle of the diagram, and Nita stepped onto it. Kit walked around her and the diagram with it, using the end of the string to trace a circle. Just before he came to the place where he had started, he used the willow wand to make a sort of figure-eight mark—a "wizards' knot," the book had called it—and closed the circle with it. Kit tugged at the string as he stood up. Nita let it go, and Kit coiled it and put it away.

"You've got to do this part yourself," Kit said. "I can't write your name for you—each person in a spelling does their own. There's a table in there with all the symbols in it."

Nita scuffed some pages aside and found it, a long list of English letters and numbers, and symbols in the Speech. She got down to look at Kit's name, so that she could see how to write hers, and group by group began to puzzle the symbols out. "Your birthday's August twenty-fifth?"

"Uh-huh."

Nita looked at the symbol for the year. "They skipped you a couple grades, huh?"

"Yeah. It's rotten," Kit said, sounding entirely too cheerful as he said it. Nita knew that tone of voice—it was the one in which she usually answered Joanne, while trying to hide her own fear of what was sure to happen next. "It wouldn't be so bad if they were my age," Kit went on, looking over Nita's shoulder and speaking absently. "But they keep saying things like 'If you're so smart, 'ow come you talk so fonny?' " His imitation of their imitation of his accent was precise and bitter. "They make me sick. Trouble is, they outweigh me."

Nita nodded and started to draw her name on the ground, using the substitutions and symbols that appeared in her manual. Some of them were simple and brief;

some of them were almost more complex than she believed possible, crazy amalgams of curls and twists and angles like those an insane stenographer might produce. She did her best to reproduce them, and tied all the symbols together, fastening them into a circle with the same wizards' knot that Kit had used on the outer circle and on his own name.

"Done?" Kit asked. He was standing up again, tracing the outer circle around one more time.

"Yup."

"Okay." He finished the tracing with another repetition of the wizards' knot and straightened up; then he put his hand out as if to feel something in the air. "Good," he said. "Here, come check this."

"Check what?" Nita got up and went over to Kit. She put out her hand as he had, and found that something was resisting the movement of her hand through the air—something that gave slightly under increased pressure, like a mattress being pushed down and then springing back again. Nita felt momentarily nervous. "Can air get through this?"

"I think so. I didn't have any trouble the last couple of times I did it. It's only supposed to seal out unfriendly influences."

Nita stood there with her hand resting against nothing, and the nothing supported her weight. The last of her doubts about the existence of magic went away. She might have imagined the contents of the book, or been purposely misreading. She might have dozed off and dreamed the talking tree. But *this* was daylight, the waking world, and she was leaning one-handed on empty air!

"Those guys who came across you when you had this up," she said, "what did they think?"

"Oh, it worked on them, too. They didn't even understand why they couldn't get at me—they thought it was their idea to yell at me from a distance. They thought they were missing me with the BB guns on purpose, too, to scare me. It's true, what the book said. There are people who couldn't see a magic if it bit them." He glanced around the finished circle. "There are other spells like this that don't need drawings after you do them the first time, and when you need them, they're there really fast—like if someone's about to try beating you up. People just kind of skid away from you."

"I bet," Nita said, with relish. Thoughts of what else she might be able to do to Joanne flickered through her head, but she pushed them aside for the moment. "What next?"

"Next," Kit said, going to the middle of the circle and sitting down carefully so as not to smudge any of the marks he'd made, "we read it. Or I read most of it, and you read your name. Though first you have to check my figuring."

"How come?" Nita joined him, avoiding the lines and angles.

"Two-person spell—both people always check each other's work. But your name, you check again after I do."

Kit was already squinting at Nita's squiggles, so she pulled out her book again and began looking at the symbols Kit had drawn in the dirt. There were clearly two sides to the diagram, and the book said they both had to balance like a chemical equation. Most of the symbols had numerical values attached, for ease in balancing, and Nita started doing addition in her head, making sure both sides matched. Eventually she was satisfied. She looked again at her name, seeing nothing wrong. "Is it okay?"

"Yeah." Kit leaned back a little. "You have to be careful with names, it says. They're a way of saying what you *are*—and if you write something in a spell that's *not* what you are, well . . ."

"You mean . . . *you* change . . . because the spell says you're something else than what you are? You *become* that?"

Kit shrugged, but he looked uneasy. "A spell is saying that you want something to happen," he said. "If you say your name wrong—"

Nita shuddered. "And now?"

"Now we start. You do your name when I come to it. Then, the goal part down there—since it's a joint goal, we say it together. Think you can do it okay if I go slow?"

"Yeah."

Kit took a deep breath with his eyes closed, then opened his eyes and began to read.

Nita had never heard a voice speaking a spell aloud before, and the effect was strange. Ever so slightly, ever so slowly, things began to change around her. The tree-sheltered quiet grew quieter. The cool light that filtered through the canopy of branches grew expectant, fringed with secrecy the way things seen through the edge of a lens are fringed with rainbows. Nita began to feel as if she was caught in the moment between a very vivid dream and the awakening from it. There was that feeling of living in a body—of being aware of familiar surroundings and the realities of the daylight world waiting to be resumed—yet at the same time seeing those surroundings differently, colored with another sort of light, another kind of time. On one level Nita heard Kit reciting a string of polysyllables that should have been meaningless to her—words for symbols, pieces of words, babble. Yet she could also hear Kit talking, saying casually, and, it seemed, in English, "We need to know something, and we suggest this particular method of finding the information . . ." And the words didn't break the expectancy, the listening silence. For once, for the first time, the dream was *real* while Nita was awake. Power stirred in the air around her and waited for her to shape it.

Magic.

She sat and listened to Kit. With each passing second she could catch more clearly the clean metallic taste of the equation as it began to form itself, flickering chill and bright in her mind. Kit's speech was giving it life, and with quiet, flowing efficiency it was going about its purpose. It was invoking the attention of what Nita might have called physical laws, except that there was nothing physical about them—they had to do with flows of a kind of power as different from ordinary energy as energy was from matter. The equation stretched and coiled and caught those powers within itself as the words wove it. Nita and Kit were caught in it, too. To Nita it seemed as if, without moving, she held out her hands, and they were taken—by Kit, and by the spell itself, and by the ponderous powers caught across from her in the dance. There was a pause: Kit looked across the diagrams at her.

Nita scowled at the symbols beside her and began to read them, slowly and with some hesitation—naming herself one concept or one symbol at a time, binding herself into the spell. At first she was scared, for she could feel the strangeness folding in close around her. But then she realized that nothing awful was happening, and as her name became part of the spell, *that* was what was sliding down around her, protecting her. She finished, and she was out of breath, and excited, and she had never been happier in her life.

Kit's voice came in again then, picking up the weave, rejoining the dance. So it went for a while, the strange words and the half-seen, half-felt movements and images falling into a rhythm of light and sound and texture, a song, a poem, a spell. It began to come whole all around them, and all around the tingling air stayed still to better hold the words, and the trees bent close to listen.

Kit came to the set of symbols that stood for his name and who he was, and read them slowly and carefully. Nita felt the spell settle down around him, too. He finished it and glanced up at Nita, and together they began the goal section of the spell. Nita did her best to make a clear image of the pen as she spoke—the silver case, gone a little scratched and grubby now, her initials incised up on the top. She hardly had time to wonder at the harmony their paired voices made before things began to change again. The shadows of the trees around them seemed to grow darker; the aura of expectancy grew sharp enough to taste. The silence became total, and their voices fell into it as into a great depth.

The formula for their goal, though longer than either of their names had been, seemed to take less time to say—and even stranger, it began to sound like much more than just finding a pen and being left alone. It began to taste of starfire and night and motion, huge and controlled, utterly strange. Saying the formula left Kit and Nita breathless and drained, as if something powerful had briefly been living and speaking through them and had worn them down. They finished the formula together, and gulped for air, and looked at each other in half-frightened expectation, wondering what would happen next.

The completed spell took effect. Nita had thought that she would gradually begin to see something, the way things had changed gradually in the grove. The spell, though, had its own ideas. Quick as a gasp it slammed them both out of one moment and into another, a shocking, wrenching transition like dreaming that you've fallen out of bed, *wham!* Instinctively they both hung on to the spell as if onto a railing, clutching it until their surroundings steadied down. The darkness had been replaced by a lowering, sullen-feeling gloom. They looked down as if from a high balcony onto a shadowed island prisoned between chill rivers and studded with sharp spikes of iron and cold stone.

(Manhattan?) Kit asked anxiously, without words. Nita felt frozen in place like a statue and couldn't turn to answer him—the spell was holding her immobile.

(It looks like Manhattan,) she said, feeling just as uneasy. (But what's my pen doing *there?*)

Kit would have shaken his head if he could have. (I don't get it. What's wrong here? This *is* New York City—but it never looked this awful, this dirty and nasty and . . .) He trailed off in confusion and dismay.

Nita looked around her. It was hard to make out anything on the island—there was a murky pall over the city that seemed more than just fog. There was hardly any traffic that she could see, and almost no light—in fact, in all of Manhattan there were only two light sources. In one place on the island—the east Fifties, it looked like—a small point of brittle light seemed to pulse right through steel and stone, throbbing dully like a sown seed of wildfire waiting to explode. The pulses were irregular and distressing, and the light was painful to look at. Some blocks to the south, well into the financial district near the south end of the island, another fire burned, a clear white spark like a sun seed, beating regularly as a heart. It was consoling, but it was very small.

(Now what?) Nita said. (Why would my pen be in this place?) She looked down at the dark grainy air below them, listened to the brooding silence like that of a beast of prey ready to spring, felt the sullen buildings hunching themselves against the oppressive sky—and then felt the *something* malevolent and alive that lay in wait below—a something that *saw* them, was conscious of them, and was darkly pleased.

(Kit, what's *that?*)

(It *knows!*) Kit's thought sang with alarm like a plucked string. (It knows we're here! It shouldn't be able to, but—Nita, the spell's not balanced for this. If that thing grabs us or holds us somehow, we won't be able to get back!)

Nita felt Kit's mind start to flick frantically through the memories of what he had read in his wizards' manual, looking for an idea, for something they could do to protect themselves.

She held very still and looked over his shoulder at his thoughts, even though part of her trembled at the thought of that dark presence that was even now reaching out toward them, lazy, curious, deadly. Abruptly she saw something that looked useful.

(Kit, stop! No, go back one. That's it. Look, it says if you've got an imbalance, you can open out your side of the spell to attract some more power.)

(Yeah, but if the wrong kind of power answers, we're in for it!)

(We're in for it for *sure* if that gets us,) Nita said, indicating the huge, hungry darkness billowing upward toward them like a cloud. (Look, we'll make a hole through the spell big enough for something friendly to fall into, and we'll take potluck.)

Nita could feel Kit's uncertainty as he started choosing from memory the words and symbols he would need. (All right, but I dunno. If something worse happens . . .)

(*What could be worse?*) Nita hollered at Kit, half in amusement, half in fear. The hungry something drew closer.

Kit started to answer, then forgot about it. (There,) he said, laying the equation out in his mind, (I think that's all we need.)

(Go ahead,) Nita said, watching anxiously as their pursuer got closer and the air around them seemed to grow thicker and darker yet. (You say it. Just tell me what to do and when.)

(Right,) Kit said, and began speaking in his mind, much faster than he had during the initial spelling. If that first magic had felt like the weaving of a whole, this one felt like ripping something apart. Their surroundings seemed to shimmer uncertainly, the dark skyline and lead gray sky rippled like a wind-stirred curtain; even that stalking presence seemed to hesitate in momentary confusion. (Push,) Kit said suddenly, (push right there.) Nita felt the torn place that Kit had made in the spell, and she shoved clumsily at it with her mind, trying to make the hole larger.

(It's . . . giving . . .)

(Now, *hard!*) Kit said, and Nita pushed until pain stabbed and stabbed again behind where her eyes should have been, and at the moment she thought she couldn't possibly push anymore, Kit said one short sharp syllable and threw the spell wide open like a door.

It was like standing at the core of a tornado which, rather than spinning you away to Oz, strips the roof off your home, opens the house walls out flat as the petals of a plaster flower, and leaves you standing confused and disbelieving in the heart of a howling of smoke and damned voices; or like moving through a roomful of people, every one of whom tries to catch your eye and tell you the most important thing that ever happened to him. Nita found herself deluged in fragments of sights and sounds and tastes and feelings and thoughts not her own, a madly coexisting maelstrom of imageries from other universes, other earths, other times. Most of them she managed to shut out by squeezing her mind shut like eyes and hanging on to the spell. She sensed that Kit was doing the same and that their stalker was momentarily as bewildered as they were by what was happening. The whirling confusion seemed to be funneling through the hole in the spell like water going down a drain—things, concepts, creatures too large or too small for the hole fell through it, or past it, or around it. But sooner or later something just the right size would catch. (Hope we get something useful,) Nita thought desperately. (Something bigger than that *thing*, anyway.)

And *thump*, something fitted into the hole with snug precision, and the crazy whirling died away, and the two of them had company in the spellweb. Something small, Nita felt; very small, *too* small—but no, it was big, too . . . Confused, she reached out to Kit.

(Is that it? Can we get out now? Before that what's-its-name—)

The what's-its-name shook itself with a ripple of rage and hunger that Kit and Nita could feel even at a distance. It headed toward them again, quickly, done with playing with them.

(Uh-oh!) Kit said. (Let's get outta here!)

(What do we—)

(What in the—) said a voice that neither of them recognized.

(Out!) Kit said, and hooked the spell into the added power that the newcomer provided, and *pulled. . . .*

. . . Plain pale daylight came down around them, heavy as a collapsed tent. Gravity yanked at them. Kit fell over sideways and lay there panting on the ground like someone who's run a race. Nita sagged, covered her face, bent over double right down to the ground, struggling for breath.

Eventually she began to recover, but she put off moving or opening her eyes. The book had warned that spelling had its prices, and one of them was the physical exhaustion that goes along with any large, mostly mental work of creation. Nita felt as if she had just been through about a hundred English tests with essay questions, one after another. "Kit?" she said, worried by his silence.

"Nnngggg," Kit said, and rolled over into a sort of crouch, holding his head in his hands. "Ooooh. Turn off the *Sun*."

"It's not that bad," Nita said, opening her eyes. Then she winced and shut them in a hurry. It was.

"How long've we been here?" Kit muttered. "The Sun shouldn't be showing here yet."

"It's—" Nita said. She opened her eyes again to check her watch and was distracted by a bright light to her right that was entirely too low to be the Sun. She squinted at it and then forgot what she had started to say.

Hanging in midair about three feet away from her, inside the circle, was a spark of eye-searing white fire. It looked no bigger than a pinhead, but it was brilliant all out of proportion to its size, and was giving off light about as bright as that of a two-hundred-watt bulb without a shade. The light bobbed gently in midair, up and down, looking like a will-o'-the-wisp plugged into too powerful a current and about to blow out. Nita sat there with her mouth open and *stared*.

The bright point dimmed slightly, appeared to describe a small tight circle so that it could take in Kit, the drawn circle, trees and leaves and sky; then it came to rest again, staring back at Nita. Though she couldn't catch what Kit was feeling, now that the spell was over, she could feel the light's emotions quite clearly— amazement, growing swiftly into unbelieving pleasure. Suddenly it blazed up white-hot again.

(Dear Artificer,) it said in bemused delight, (I've blown my quanta and gone to the Good Place!)

Nita sat there in silence for a moment, thinking a great many things at once. *Uhh, . . .* she thought. And, *So I wanted to be a wizard, huh? Serves me right. Something falls into my world and thinks it's gone to Heaven. Boy, is it gonna get a shock.* And, *What in the world is it, anyway?*

"Kit," Nita said. "Excuse me a moment," she added, nodding with abrupt courtesy at the light source. "Kit." She turned slightly and reached down to shake him by the shoulder. "Kit. C'mon, get up. We have company."

"Mmmp?" Kit said, scrubbing at his eyes and starting to straighten up. "Oh no, the binding didn't blow, did it?"

"Nope. It's the extra power you called in. I think it came back with us."

"Well, it—oh," Kit said, as he finally managed to focus on the sedately hovering brightness. "*Oh*. It's—uh . . ."

"Right," Nita said. "It says," she added, "that it's blown its quanta. Is that dangerous?" she asked the light.

(Dangerous?) It laughed inside, a crackling sound like an overstimulated Geiger counter. (Artificer, child, it means I'm *dead*.) "Child" wasn't precisely the concept it used; Nita got a fleeting impression of a huge volume of dust and gas contracting gradually toward a common center, slow, confused, and nebulous. She wasn't flattered.

"Maybe you won't like hearing this," Nita said, "but I'm not sure this is the Good Place. It doesn't seem that way to *us*, anyhow."

The light drew a figure eight in the air, a shrug. (It looks that way to *me*,) it said. (Look how orderly everything is! And how much life there is in just one place! Where I come from, even a spore's worth of life is scarcer than atoms in a comet's tail.)

"Excuse me," Kit asked, "but what *are* you?"

It said something Nita could make little sense of. The concept she got looked like page after page of mathematical equations. Kit raised his eyebrows. "It uses the Speech, too," he commented as he listened.

"So what is it?"

Kit looked confused. "Its name says that it came from way out in space somewhere, and it has a mass equal to—to five or six blue-white giant stars and a few thousand-odd planets, and it emits all up and down the matter-energy spectrum, all kinds of light and radiation and even some subatomic particles." He shrugged. "You have any idea what that is?"

Nita stared at the light in growing disbelief. "Where's all your mass?" she asked. "If you have that much, the gravity should have crushed us up against you the minute you showed up."

(Elsewhere,) the light said offhandedly. (I have a singularity-class temporospatial claudication.)

"A warp," Nita whispered. "A tunnel through space-time. Are you a white hole?"

It stopped bobbing, stared at her as if she had said something derogatory. (Do I look like a hole?)

"Do I look like a cloud of gas?" Nita snapped back, and then sighed—her mouth was getting the better of her again. "I'm sorry. That's just what we call your kind of—uh—creature. Because you act like a hole in the Universe that light and radiation come through. I know you're not, really. But, Kit," she said, turning, "where's my pen? And where's the power you were after? Didn't the spell work?"

"Spells always work," Kit said. "That's what the book says. When you ask for something, you always get back something that'll help you solve your problem, or be the solution itself." He looked entirely confused. "I asked for that power aura for me, and your pen for you—that was all. If we got a white hole, it means he's the answer—"

"If he's the answer," Nita said, bemused, "I'm not sure I understand the question."

(This is all fascinating,) the white hole said, (but I have to find a functional-Advisory nexus in a hurry. I found out that the *Naming of Lights* has gone missing, and I managed to find a paradimensional net with enough empty loci to get me to an Advisory in a hurry. But something seems to have gone wrong. Somehow I don't think you're Advisories.)

"Uh, no," Kit said. "I think we called you—"

(*You* called me?) The white hole regarded Kit with mixed reverence and amazement. (You're one of the Powers born of Life? Oh, I'm sorry I didn't recognize You—I know You can take any shape but somehow I'd always thought of You as being bigger. A quasar, or a meganova.) The white hole made a feeling of rueful amusement. (It's *confusing* being dead!)

"Oh, brother," Kit said. "Look, I'm not—you're not—just *not*. We made a spell and we called you. I don't think you're dead."

(If you say so,) the white hole said, polite but doubtful. (You called *me*, though? Me personally? I don't think we've met before.)

"No, we haven't," Nita said. "But we were doing this spell, and we found something, but something found us, too, and we wouldn't have been able to get back here unless we called in some extra power—so we did, and it was you, I guess. You're not mad, are you?" she asked timidly. The thought of what a live, intelligent white hole might be able to do if it got annoyed scared her badly.

(Mad? No. As I said, I was trying to get out of my own space to get the news to someone who could use it, and then all of a sudden there was a paranet with enough loci to handle all the dimensions I carry, so I grabbed it.) The white hole made another small circle, looking around him curiously. (Maybe it did work. Are there Advisories in this—on this—What is this, anyway?)

Kit looked at Nita. "Huh?"

(This,) the white hole said, (all of this.) He made another circle.

"Oh! A planet," Nita said. "See, there's our star." She pointed, and the white hole rotated slightly to look.

(Artificer within us,) he said, (maybe I *have* blown my quanta, after all. I always wanted to see a planet, but I never got around to it. Habit, I guess. You get used to sitting around emitting X rays after a while, and you don't think of doing anything else. You want to see some?) he asked suddenly. He sounded a little insecure.

"Uh, maybe you'd better not," Nita said.

(How come? They're really pretty.)

"We can't see them—and besides, we're not built to take hard radiation. Our atmosphere shuts most of it out."

(A real planet,) the white hole said, wondering and delighted, (with a real atmosphere. Well! If this is a planet, there has to be an Advisory around here somewhere. Could you help me find one?)

"Uhh—" Kit looked uncertainly at the white hole. "Sure. But do you think you could help me find some power? And Nita get her pen back?"

The white hole looked Kit up and down. (Some potential, some potential,) he muttered. (I could probably have you emitting light pretty quickly, if we worked together on a regular basis. Maybe even some alpha. We'll see. What's a pen?)

"What's your name?" Kit asked. "I mean, we can't just call you 'hey you' all the time."

(True,) the white hole said. (My name is Khairelikoblepharehglukumeiliche-phreidosd'enagouni—) and at the same time he went flickering through a pattern of colors that was evidently the visual translation.

"Ky—elik—" Nita began.

"Fred," Kit said quickly. "Well," he added as they looked at him again, "if we have to yell for help or something, the other way's too long. And that was the only part I got, anyway."

"Is that okay with you?" Nita asked.

The white hole made his figure-eight shrug again. (Better than having my truename mangled, I guess,) he said, and chuckled silently. (Fred, then. And you are?)

"Nita."

"Kit."

(I see why you like them short,) Fred said. (All right. Tell me what a 'pen' is, and I'll try to help you find it. But we really must get to an Advisory as fast as we can.)

"Okay," Kit said. "Let's break the circle and go talk."

"Sounds good," Nita said, and began to erase the diagrams they had drawn. Kit cut the wizards' knot and scuffed the circle open in a few places, while Nita took a moment to wave her hand through the now empty air. "Not bad for a first spell," she said with satisfaction.

(I meant to ask,) Fred said politely, (what's a spell?)

Nita sighed, and smiled, and picked up her book, motioning Fred to follow her over to where Kit sat. It was going to be a long afternoon, but she didn't care. Magic was loose in the world.

Research and
Development

THEY WERE AT THE schoolyard early the next morning, to be sure they wouldn't miss Joanne and her crew. Nita and Kit sat on the curb by the front door to the school, staring across at the packed dirt and dull grass of the athletic field next to the building. Kit leafed through his wizards' manual, while Fred hung over his shoulder and looked around with mild interest at everything. (Will it be long?) he said, his light flickering slightly.

"No," Nita said. She was shaking. After the other day, she didn't want anything to do with Joanne at all. But she wanted that pen back, so . . .

"Look, it'll be all right," Kit said, paging through his manual. "Just do it the way we decided last night. Get close to her, keep her busy for a little while. Fred'll do the rest."

"It's keeping her busy that worries me," Nita muttered. "Her idea of busy usually involves her fists and my face."

(I don't understand,) Fred said, and Nita had to laugh briefly—she and Kit had heard that phrase about a hundred times since Fred arrived. He used it on almost everything. (What are you afraid of?)

"This," Nita said, pointing to her black eye. "And this—" uncovering a bruise. "And this, and this—"

Fred regarded her with a moment's discomfiture. (I thought you came that way. Joanne makes this happen?)

"Uh-huh. And it hurts *getting* this way."

(But she only changes your outsides. Aren't your insides still the same afterward?)

Nita had to stop and think about that one.

"Okay," Kit said suddenly, "here's the Advisory list for our area." He ran a finger down the page. "And here's the one in town. Twenty-seven Hundred Rose—"

"That's up the hill past the school. What's the name?"

"Lessee. 'Swale, T.B., and Romeo, C.J. Research Advisories, temporospatial adjustments, entastics, nonspecific scryings—' "

"Wait a minute," Nita said hurriedly. " 'Swale'? You mean Crazy Swale? We can't go in there, Kit, that place is haunted! Everybody knows that! Weird noises are always coming out of there—"

"If it's haunted," Kit said, "it's haunted by wizards. We might as well go after school, it's only five or six blocks up the road."

They were quiet for a while. It was about twenty minutes before the bell would ring for the doors to open, and a few early kids were gathering around the doors.

"Maybe we could rig you a defense against getting hit," Kit said, as he kept looking through his manual. "How about this?" He pointed at one page, and both Nita and Fred looked at the formula he was indicating. All it needed was the right words. It would be something of a strain to carry the shield for long, but Nita wouldn't have to; and any attempt to hit her would just glance off.

(The problem is,) Fred said, (that spell will alter the field slightly around this Joanne person. I'm going to have a hard enough time matching my pattern to that of your pen so that I can get it off her—if indeed she has it. Her own field is going to interfere, and so will yours, Nita. More stress on the space in the area and I might not be able to get your pen back at all.)

Nita shook her head. She could tolerate another black eye if it meant getting that pen back. "Forget it," she said, still shaking, and leaned forward a bit, elbows on knees and face in hands, trying to relax. Above her the old maple trees were muttering morning thoughts in the early sunlight, languid observations on the weather and the decreasing quality of the tenant birds who built nests in their branches. Out in the field the grass was singing a scratchy soprano chorus—(grow-growgrowgrowgrowgrow)—which broke off abruptly and turned into an annoyed mob sound of boos and razzes as one of the groundskeepers, way across the field, started up a lawn mower. *I'm good with plants*, Nita thought. *I guess I take after Dad. I wonder if I'll ever be able to hear people this way.*

Kit nudged her. "You're on," he said, and Nita looked up and saw Joanne walking into the schoolyard. Their eyes met. Joanne recognized her handiwork on Nita's face and smiled. *Now or never!* Nita thought, and got right up before she had a chance to chicken out and blow everything. She walked over to Joanne without a pause, fast, to keep the tremor in her knees from showing. *Oh, Fred, please be behind me. And what in the world can I say to her?*

"I want my pen back, Joanne," she said—or rather it fell out of her mouth, and she went hot at her own stupidity. Yet the momentary shocked look on Joanne's face made her think that maybe saying what was on her mind hadn't been so stupid after all. Joanne's shock didn't last; a second later she was smiling again. "Callahan," she said slowly, "are you looking for another black eye to match that one?"

"Lllp. No," Nita said, "just my pen, thanks."

"I don't know what you're talking about," Joanne said, and then grinned. "You always were a little odd. I guess you've finally flipped out."

"I had a space pen on me the other day, and it was gone afterward. One of you took it. I want it back." Nita was shaking worse than ever, but she was also surprised that the fist hadn't hit yet. And there over Joanne's shoulder was a flicker, a pinpoint of light, hardly to be seen, looking at her.

(Don't react. Make me a picture of the thing now.)

"What makes you think I would want anything of *yours?*" Joanne was saying, still with that smile. Nita looked straight at her and thought about the pen. Silver barrel, grooved all around the lower half to keep the user's fingers from slipping. Her initials engraved on it. Hers, her pen.

(Enough. Now then—)

"But now that I think of it, I do remember finding a pen on the ground last week. Let's see." Joanne was enjoying this so much that she actually flipped open the top of her backpack and began rummaging around. "Let's see, *here*—" She came up with something. Silver barrel, grooved—and Nita went hot again, not with embarrassment this time.

"It's mine!"

"Come and get it, then," Joanne said, dropping her backpack, keeping her smile, holding the pen back a little.

And a spark of white light seemed to light on the end of the pen as Joanne held it up, and then both were gone with a *pop* and a breath of air. Joanne spun to see who had plucked the pen out of her fingers, then whirled on Nita again. Nita smiled and held out her hands, empty.

Joanne was not amused. She stepped in close, and Nita took a few hurried steps back, unable to stop grinning even though she knew she was going to get hit. Heads were turning all around the schoolyard at the prospect of a fight. "Callahan," Joanne hissed, "you're in for it now!"

The eight-thirty bell went off so suddenly they both jumped. Joanne stared at Nita for a long long moment, then turned and went to pick up her backpack. "Why hurry things?" she said, straightening. "Callahan, if I were you, I'd sleep here tonight. Because when you try to leave . . ."

She walked off toward the doors. Nita stood where she was, still shaking, but with amazement and triumph as much as with fear. Kit came up beside her when Joanne was gone, and Fred appeared, a bright point between them.

"You were great!" Kit said.

"I'm gonna get killed tonight," Nita said, but she couldn't be terrified about it just yet. "Fred, have you got it?"

The point of light was flickering, and there was something about the way it did so that made Nita wonder if something was wrong. (Yes,) Fred said, the thought coming with a faint queasy feeling to it. (And that's the problem.)

"Are you okay?" Kit asked. "Where'd it go?"

(I swallowed it,) Fred said, sounding genuinely miserable now.

"But that was what you were going to do," Nita said, puzzled. "Catch it in your own energy field, you said, make a little pocket and hold it there."

(I know. But my fields aren't working the way they should. Maybe it's this gravity. I'm not used to any gravity but my own. I think it went down the wrong way.)

"Oh, brother," Kit said.

"Well," Nita said, "at least Joanne hasn't got it. When we go to the Advisories tonight, maybe they can help us get it out."

Fred made a small thought-noise somewhere between a burp and a squeak. Nita and Kit looked up at him, concerned—and then both jumped back hurriedly from something that went BANG! down by their feet.

They stared at the ground. Sitting there on the packed dirt was a small portable color TV, brand new.

"Uh, Fred—" Kit said.

Fred was looking down at the TV with embarrassment verging on shame. (I emitted it,) he said.

Nita stared at him. "But I thought white holes only emitted little things. Sub-atomic particles. Nothing so big—or so orderly."

(I wanted to visit an orderly place,) Fred said miserably. (See what it got me!)

"Hiccups," Kit muttered. "Fred, I think you'd better stay outside until we're finished for the day. We'll go straight to the Advisories' from here."

"Joanne permitting," Nita said. "Kit, we've got to go in."

(I'll meet you here,) Fred said. The mournful thought was followed by another burp/squeak, and another BANG! and four volumes of an encyclopedia were sitting on the ground next to the TV.

Kit and Nita hurried for the doors, sweating. Apparently wizardry had more drawbacks than the book had indicated. . . .

Lunch wasn't calm, but it *was* interesting, due to the thirty teachers, assistant principal, principal, and school superintendent who were all out on the athletic field, along with most of the students. They were walking around looking at the furniture, vacuum cleaners, computer components, books, knickknacks, motorcycles, typewriters, art supplies, stoves, sculptures, lumber, and many other odd things that had since morning been appearing one after another in the field. No one knew what to make of any of it, or what to do; and though Kit and Nita felt sure they would be connected with the situation somehow, no one accused them of anything.

They met again at the schoolyard door at three, pausing just inside it while Nita peered out to see if Joanne was waiting. She was, and eight of her friends were with her, talking and laughing among themselves. "Kit," Nita said quietly, "we've got problems."

He looked. "And this is the only door we can use."

Something went BANG! out in the field, and Nita, looking out again, saw heads turn among Joanne's group. Without a moment's pause every one of the girls headed off toward the field in a hurry, leaving Joanne to glare at the school door for a moment. Then she took off after the others. Kit and Nita glanced at each other. "I get this feeling . . ." Kit said.

"Let's go."

They waited until Joanne was out of sight and then leaned cautiously out of the door, looking around. Fred was suddenly there, wobbling in the air. He made a feeling of greeting at them; he seemed tired, but cheerful, at least for the moment.

Nita glanced over her shoulder to see what had drawn the attention of Joanne and her group—and drew in a sharp breath at the sight of the shiny silver Learjet. "Fred," she said, "you did that on purpose!"

She felt him look back, too, and his cheerfulness drowned out his weariness and queasiness for a moment. (I felt you wondering whether to come out, so I exerted myself a little. What *was* that thing?)

"We'll explain later; right now we should run. Fred, thank you!"

(You're most welcome. Just help me *stop* this!)

"Can you hold it in for a few blocks?"

(What's a block?)

They ran down Rose Avenue, and Fred paced them. Every now and then a little of Fred's hiccup noise would squeak out, and he would fall behind them, controlling it while they ran on ahead. Then he would catch up again. The last time he did it, they paused and waited for him. Twenty-seven Hundred Rose had a high poplar hedge with one opening for the walk up to the house, and neither of them felt like going any farther without Fred.

(Well?) he said, when he caught up. (Now what?)

Nita and Kit looked at each other. "I don't care if they *are* wizards," Nita said, "I want to peek in and have a look before I just walk in there. I've heard too many stories about this place—"

(Look,) Fred said in great discomfort, (I've got to—)

Evidently there was a limit on how long a white hole in Fred's condition could hold it in. The sound of Fred's hiccup was so much louder than usual that Nita and Kit crowded back away from him in near panic. The BANG! sounded like the beginning of a fireworks display, and when its echoes faded, a powder blue Mercedes-Benz was sitting half on, half off the sidewalk.

(My gnaester hurts,) Fred said.

"Let's peek," Nita said, turned, and pushed a little way through the hedge. She wanted to be sure there were no monsters or skeletons hanging from trees or anything else uncanny going on in the yard before she went in. What she did *not* expect was the amiable face of an enormous black-and-white English sheepdog, which first slurped her face energetically, then grabbed her right arm in gentle but insistent teeth and pulled her straight through the hedge.

"Kit!" she almost screamed, and then remembered not to because Crazy Swale or whoever else lived here might hear her. Her cry came out as sort of a grunt. She heard Kit come right through the bushes behind her as the sheepdog dragged her along through the yard. There was nothing spooky about the place at all—the house was big, a two-story affair, but normal-looking, all warm wood and shingles. The yard was grassy, with a landscaped garden as pretty as one of her father's. One side of the house had wide glass patio doors opening on a roofed terrace. Potted plants hung down and there was even a big square masonry tank, a fish-pond—Nita caught a glimpse of something coppery swimming as the sheepdog dragged her past it to the terrace doors. It was at that point that the dog let go of her arm and began barking noisily, and Nita began seriously thinking of running for it.

"All right, all right," said a man's voice, a humorous one, from inside the house, and it was *definitely* too late for running. Kit came up behind Nita, panting. "All *right*, Annie, let's see what you've got this time."

The screen door slid open, and Nita and Kit looked in slight surprise at the man who opened it. Somehow they had been expecting that any wizard not their age would be old, but this man was young, certainly no more than in his middle thirties. He had dark hair and was tall and broad-shouldered. He looked rather like someone out of a cigarette ad, except that he was smiling, which the men in cigarette ads rarely do. "Well," the man said, sounding not at all annoyed by three unexpected guests, "I see you've met Annie . . ."

"She, uh," Nita said, glancing down at the dog, who was smiling at her with the same bemused interest as her master. "She found me looking through your hedge."

"That's Annie for you," the man said, sounding a bit resigned. "She's good at finding things. I'm Tom Swale." And he held out his hand for Nita to shake.

"Nita Callahan," she said, taking it.

"Kit Rodriguez," Kit said from beside her, reaching out to shake hands, too.

"Good to meet you. Call me Tom. What can I do for you?"

"Are you the Advisory?" Kit said.

Tom's eyebrows went up. "You kids have a spelling problem?"

Nita grinned at the pun and glanced over her shoulder. "Fred?"

Fred bobbed up between her and Kit, regarding Tom, who looked back at the unsteady spark of light with only moderate surprise. "He's a white hole," Nita said. "He swallowed my space pen."

(T-*hup!*) Fred said, and BANG! went the air between Kit and Nita as they stepped hurriedly off to either side. Fourteen one kilogram bricks of 999-fine Swiss gold fell clattering to the patio's brown tiles.

"I can see this is going to take some explaining," Tom said. "Come on in."

They followed him into the house. A big comfortable living room opened onto a den on one side and a bright kitchen-dining room on the other. "Carl, we've got company," Tom called as they entered the kitchen.

"Wha?" replied a muffled voice—muffled because the upper half of its owner was mostly in the cabinet under the double sink. The rest of him was sprawled across the kitchen floor. This by itself wasn't so odd; what *was* odd was the assortment of wrenches and other tools floating in the air just outside the cabinet doors. From under the sink came a sound like a wrench slipping off a pipe, and a sudden soft thump as it hit something else. Probably its user. "Nnngg!" said the voice under the sink, and all the tools fell clattering to the kitchen floor. The voice broke into some most creative swearing.

Tom frowned and smiled both at once. "Such language in front of guests! You ought to sleep outside with Annie. Come on out of there, we're needed for a consultation."

"You really are wizards!" Nita said, reassured but still surprised. She had rarely seen two more normal-looking people.

Tom chuckled. "Sure we are. Not that we do too much freelancing these days— better to leave that to the younger practitioners, like you two."

The other man got out from under the sink, brushing himself off. He was at least as tall as Tom, and as broad-shouldered, but his dark hair was shorter and he had an impressive mustache. "Carl Romeo," he said in a voice with a pronounced Brooklyn accent. He shook hands with Kit and Nita. "Who's this?" he said, indicating Fred. Fred hiccuped; the resulting explosion produced six black star sapphires the size of tennis balls.

"Fred here," Tom said, "has a small problem."

"I wish *I* had problems like that," Carl remarked. "Something to drink, people? Soda?"

After a few minutes the four of them were settled around the kitchen table, with Fred hovering nearby. "It said in the book that you specialize in temporospatial claudications," Kit said.

"Carl does. Maintenance and repair; he keeps the worldgates at Grand Central Station and Rockefeller Center working. You've come to the right place."

"His personal gate is acting up, huh?" Carl said. "I'd better get the books." He got up. "Fred, what're the entasis figures on your warp?"

Fred mentally rattled off a number of symbols in the Speech, as he had when Kit asked him what he was. "Right," Carl said, and went off to the den.

"What do you do?" Nita said to Tom.

"Research, mostly. Also we're something of a clearinghouse for news and gossip in the Business. If someone needs details on a rare spell, or wants to know how power balances are running in a particular place, I can usually find out for them."

"But you do other things, too." Kit looked around at the house.

"Oh, sure, we work. I write for a living—after all, some of the things I see in the Business make good stories. And Carl sells commercial time for WNXT in the city. As well as regular time, on the side."

Kit and Nita looked at each other, puzzled. Tom chuckled. "Well, he does claudications, gatings, doesn't he? Temporospatial—time and space. If you can squeeze space—claudicate it—so that you pop out of one place and into another, why can't you squeeze time the same way? Haven't you heard the saying about 'buying time'? Carl's the one you buy it from. Want to buy a piece of next Thursday?"

"I can get it for you wholesale," Carl said as he came back into the room. In his arms he was carrying several hardbound books as thick as telephone directories. On his shoulder, more interesting, was a splendid scarlet-blue-and-yellow macaw, which regarded Kit and Nita and Fred out of beady black eyes. "Kit, Nita, Fred," Carl said, "Machu Picchu. Peach for short." He sat down, put the books on the table, and began riffling through the one on top of the stack; Tom pulled one out from lower in the pile and began doing the same.

"All right," Tom said, "the whole story, from the beginning."

They told him, and it took a while. When they got to Fred's part of the story, and the fact that the *Naming of Lights* was missing, Tom and Carl became very quiet and just looked at one another for a moment. "Damn," Tom said, "I *wondered* why the entry in the *Materia Magica* hadn't been updated in so long. This is news, all right. We'll have to call a regional Advisories' meeting."

Fred hiccuped again, and the explosion left behind it a year's back issues of *TV Guide*.

"Later," Carl said. "The situation here looks like it's deteriorating." He paused at one page of the book he was looking through, ran his finger down a column. The macaw peered over his shoulder as if interested. "Alpha-rai-entath-eight, you said?"

(Right.)

"I can fix you," Carl said. "Take about five minutes." He got up and headed for the den again.

"What *is* the *Naming of Lights?*" Kit said to Tom. "We tried to get Fred to tell us last night, but it kept coming out in symbols that weren't in our books."

"Well, this is a pretty advanced subject. A novice's manual wouldn't have much information on the *Naming of Lights* any more than the instruction manual for a rifle would have information on atomic bombs . . ." Tom took a drink. "It's a book. At least that's what it looks like when it's in or near this Universe. The *Book of Night with Moon*, it's called here, since in these parts you need moonlight to read it. It's always been most carefully accounted for; the Senior wizards keep an eye on it. If it's suddenly gone missing, we've got trouble . . ."

"Why?" Nita said.

"Well, if you've gotten even this far in wizardry, you know how the wizards' symbology, the Speech, affects the things you use it on. When you use it, you *define* what you're speaking about. That's why it's dangerous to use the Speech carelessly. You can accidentally redefine something, change its nature. Something, or some*one*—" He paused, took another drink of his soda. "The *Book of Night with Moon* is written in the Speech. In it, everything's described. *Everything*. You, me, Fred, Carl, . . . this house, this town, this world. This Universe and everything in it. *All* the Universes . . ."

Kit looked skeptical. "How could a book that big get lost?"

"Who said it was big? You'll notice something about your manuals after a while," Tom said. "They won't get any bigger, but there'll be more and more inside them as you learn more, or need to know more. Even in plain old math it's true that the inside can be bigger than the outside; it's definitely true in wizardry. But believe me, the *Book of Night with Moon* has everything described in it. It's one of the reasons we're all here—the power of those descriptions helps keep everything that *is* in existence." Tom looked worried. "And every now and then the Senior wizards have to go get the *Book* and read from it, to remind the worlds what they are, to preserve everything alive or inanimate."

"Have *you* read from it?" Nita said, made uneasy by the disturbed look on Tom's face.

Tom glanced at her in shock, then began to laugh. "Me? No, no. I hope I never have to."

"But if it's a good *Book*, if it preserves things—" Kit said.

"It's good—at least, yes, it preserves, or lets things grow the way they want to. But reading it, being the vessel for all that power—I wouldn't want to. Even good can be terribly dangerous. But this isn't anything you two need to worry about. The Advisories and the Senior wizards will handle it."

"But you *are* worried," Kit said.

"Yes, well—" Tom took another drink. "If it were just that the bright *Book* had gone missing, that wouldn't be so bad. A universe can go a long time without affirmation-by-reading. But the bright *Book* has an opposite number, a dark one; the *Book Which Is Not Named*, we call it. It's written in the Speech too, but its descriptions are . . . skewed. And if the bright *Book* is missing, the dark one gains potential power. If someone should read from that one now, while the *Book of Night with Moon* isn't available to counteract the power of the dark one . . ." Tom shook his head.

Carl came in then, the macaw still riding his shoulder. "Here we go," he said, and dumped several sticks of chalk, an enormous black claw, and a 1943 zinc penny on the table. Nita and Kit stared at each other, neither quite having the nerve to ask whose claw it had been. "Now you understand," Carl said as he picked up the chalk and began to draw a circle around the table, "that this is only going to stop the hiccups. You three are going to have to go to Manhattan and hook Fred into the Grand Central worldgate to get that pen out. Don't worry about being noticed. People use it all the time and no one's the wiser. *I* use it sometimes when the trains are late."

"Carl," Tom said, "doesn't it strike you as a little strange that the first wizardry these kids do produces Fred—who brings this news about the good *Book*—and they come straight to us—"

"Don't be silly," the macaw on Carl's shoulder said in a scratchy voice. "*You* know there are no accidents."

Nita and Kit stared.

"Wondered when you were going to say something useful," Carl said, sounding bored. "You think we keep you for your looks? OW!" he added, as the bird bit him on the ear. He hit it one on the beak, and while it was still shaking its head woozily, put it up on the table beside Tom.

Picchu sidled halfway up Tom's arm, stopped and looked at Nita and Kit. "Dos d'en agouni nikyn toude pheresthai," it muttered, and got all the way up on Tom's shoulder, and then glared at them again. "Well?"

"She only speaks in tongues to show off," Tom said. "Ignore her, or rap her one if she bites you. We just keep her around because she tells the future." Tom made as if to smack the bird again, and Picchu ducked back. "How about the stocks tomorrow, bird?" he said.

Picchu cleared her throat. " 'And that's the way it is,' " she said in a voice very much like that of a famous newscaster, " 'July eighteen, 1988. From New York, this is Walter—' "

Tom fisted the bird in the beak, *clunk!* Picchu shook her head again. " 'Issues were down in slow trading,' " she said resentfully. " 'The Dow-Jones average—' " and she called off some numbers. Tom grimaced.

"I should have gone into pork bellies," he muttered. "I ought to warn you two: If you have pets, look out. Practicing wizardry around them can cause some changes."

"There we go," Carl said, and stood up straight. "Fred, you ready? Hiccup for me again."

(I can't,) Fred said, sounding nervous. (You're all staring.)

"Never mind, I can start this in the meantime." Carl leaned over the table, glanced down at one of the books, and began reading in the Speech, a quick flow of syllables sharpened by his Brooklyn accent. In the middle of the third sentence Fred hiccuped, and without warning the wizardry took. Time didn't precisely stop, but it held still, and Nita became aware of what Carl's wizardry was doing to Fred, or rather had done already—subtly untangling forces that were knotted tight together. The half-finished hiccup and the wizardry came loose at the same time, leaving Fred looking bright and well for the first time since that morning. He still radiated uncertainty, though, like a person who isn't sure he's stopped hiccuping yet.

"You'll be all right," Carl said, scuffing away the chalk marks on the floor. "Though as I said, that pen is still in there with the rest of your mass, at the other end of your claudication, and you'll need Grand Central to get it out."

(Have you stopped my emissions entirely?) Fred said.

"No, of course not. I couldn't do that: you'll still emit from time to time. Mostly what you're used to, though. Radiation and such."

"Grand Central!" Kit was looking worried. "I don't think my mother and father are going to want me in the city alone. I could sneak in, I guess, but they'd want to know where I'd been all that while."

"Well," Tom said, looking thoughtful, "you've got school. You couldn't go before the weekend anyway, right? Carl could sell you a piece of Saturday or Sunday—"

Kit and Nita looked at each other, and then at the two men. "Uh, we don't have much money."

"Who said anything about money?" Carl said. "Wizards don't pay each other cash. They pay off in service—and sometimes the services aren't done for years.

But first let's see if there's any time available this weekend. Saturdays go fast, even though they're expensive, especially Saturday mornings."

He picked up another book and began going through it. Like all the other books, it was printed in the same type as Nita's and Kit's manuals, though the print was much smaller and arranged differently. "This way," Tom said, "if you buy some time, you could be in the city all day, all week if you wanted—but once you activate the piece of time you're holding, you're back *then*. You have to pick a place to anchor the time to, of course, a twenty-foot radius. But after you've finished whatever you have to do, you bring your marked time to life, and there you are. Maybe five minutes before you started for the city, back at home. Or anywhere and anywhen else along the path you'll follow that day."

"Huh," Carl said suddenly. "Callahan, J., and Rodriguez, C., is that you two?" They nodded. "You have a credit already," Carl said, sounding a little surprised. "What have you two been doing to rate that?"

"Must have been for bringing Fred through," Tom said. "I didn't know that Upper Management had started giving out door prizes, though."

From her perch on Tom's shoulder, Picchu snorted. "Oh? What's that mean?" Tom said. "Come on, bird, be useful. Is there something you know that these kids ought to?"

"I want a raise," Picchu said, sounding sullen.

"You just had one. Talk!"

" 'Brush your teeth twice a day, and see your dentist regularly,' " the macaw began, in a commercial announcer's voice. Tom made a fist and stared at her. "All right, all right," Picchu muttered. She looked over at Kit and Nita, and though her voice when she spoke had the usual good-natured annoyance about it, her eyes didn't look angry or even teasing—they looked anxious. Nita got a sudden chill down her back. "Don't be afraid to make corrections," Picchu said. "Don't be afraid to lend a hand." She fell silent, seeming to think for a moment. "And don't look down."

Tom stared at the macaw. "Can't you be a little more specific?"

"Human lives," Picchu said irritably, "aren't much like the Dow-Jones average. No, I can't."

Tom sighed. "Sorry. Kids, if she says it, she has a reason for saying it—so remember."

"Here you go," Carl said. "Your piece of time is from 10:45 to 10:47 on this next Saturday morning. There aren't any weekend openings after that until sometime in July."

"We'll take this one," Kit said. "At least I can—Nita, will your folks let you go?"

She nodded. "I have some allowance saved up, and I'd been thinking about going into the city to get my dad a birthday present anyhow. I doubt there'll be any trouble."

Kit looked uncomfortable for a moment. "But there's something I'm not sure about. My spell—our spell brought Fred here. How are we going to get him back where he belongs?"

(Am I a problem?) Fred said, sounding concerned.

"Oh, no, no—it's just that, Fred, this isn't your home, and it seemed as if sooner or later you might want to go back where you came from."

"As far as that goes," Tom said, "if it's your spell that brought him here, you'll be able to send him back. The instructions are in your book, same as the instructions for opening the Grand Central worldgate."

"Stick to those instructions," Carl said. "Don't be tempted to improvise. That claudication is the oldest one in New York, and it's the trickiest because of all the people using it all the time. One false syllable in a spell and you may wind up in Schenectady."

(Is that another world?) Fred asked.

"Nearly." Carl laughed. "Is there anything else we can do for you?"

Nita and Kit shook their heads and got up to leave, thanking Tom and Carl and Picchu. "Let us know how things turn out," Tom said. "Not that we have any doubts—two wizards who can produce a white hole on the first try are obviously doing all right. But give us a call. We're in the book."

The two men saw Nita and Kit as far as the patio door, said their good-byes, and went back into the house. Nita started off across the lawn the way she had come, but Kit paused for a moment by the fishpond, staring down into it. He pulled a penny out of his pocket, dropped it in.

Nita saw the ripples spread—and then suddenly another set of ripples wavered away from the head of a very large goldfish, which spat the penny back at Kit and eyed him with distaste. "Do *I* throw money on *your* living-room floor?" it said, and then dived out of sight.

Kit picked up his penny and went after Nita and Fred as they pushed through the poplar hedge again. The blue Mercedes, which had been half in the street and half on the sidewalk, was now neatly parked by the curb. In front of it sat Annie, with her tongue hanging out and a satisfied look on her face. There were teeth marks deep in the car's front fender. Annie grinned at them as Nita and Kit passed, and then trotted off down the street, probably to "find" something else.

"If my dog starts doing things like that," Kit muttered, "I don't know how I'm going to explain it to my mother."

Nita looked down the street for signs of Joanne. "If we can just get home without being killed, I wouldn't care *what* the dog found. *Uh*-oh—" A good ways down the street, four or five girls were heading toward them, and Nita saw Joanne's blond hair. "Kit, we'd better split up. No reason for them to come after you too."

"Right. Give me a call tonight. I'm in the book . . ." He took off down a side street.

She looked around, considering the best direction to run in—and then thought of the book she was carrying. There wasn't much time, though. She forced herself to calm down even while she knew they were coming for her, made herself turn the pages slowly to the place Kit had shown her that morning, the spell that made blows slide off. She read through it slowly in the Speech, sounding out the syllables, taking the time to look up the pronunciation of the ones she wasn't sure of, even though they were getting close and she could hear Joanne's laugh.

Nita sat down on the curb to wait for them. They let her have it when they found her, as they had been intending to all day; and she rolled around on the ground and fell back from their punches and made what she hoped were horrible groaning noises. After a while Joanne and her four friends turned away to leave, satisfied that they had taught her a lesson. And Nita stood up and brushed herself off, uncut, unbruised, just a little dirty. "Joanne," she called after them. In what looked like amazement, Joanne turned around.

Nita laughed at her. "It won't work anymore," she said.

Joanne stood dumb.

"Never again," she said. She felt like turning her back on them, but instead she walked *toward* them, watching the confusion in their eyes. On a sudden urge, she jumped up in the air and waved her arms crazily. "BOO!" she shouted.

They broke and ran, all of them. Joanne was the first, and then the rest followed her in a ragged tail down Rose Avenue. Not a word, not a taunt. They just ran.

Nita stopped short. The feeling of triumph that had been growing in her withered almost instantly. *Some victory* she thought. *It took so little, so little to scare them. Maybe I could have done that at any time, without a shield. Maybe. And now I'll never know for sure.*

(Are you all right?) Fred said quietly, bobbing again by her shoulder. (They didn't hurt you this time.)

(No,) Nita said slowly. She was thinking of all the glorious plans she'd had to use her newfound wizardry on Joanne and her bunch, to shame them, confuse them, hurt them. And look what so small and inoffensive thing as a body shield had done to them. They would hate her worse than ever now.

I've got to be careful with this, she thought. *I thought it was going to be all fun.*

(Come on, Fred,) she said, (let's go home.)

Temporospatial Claudications:

USE AND ABUSE

THE WEEK WENT BY quickly for Nita. Though Carl had made the business of opening a worldgate sound fairly simple, she began to suspect that he'd been doing it so long that it actually seemed that way to him. It wasn't simple, as her book told her as soon as she opened to the pertinent chapter, which was forty pages long in small print.

Grand Central worldgate had its own special requirements: specific supplies and objects that had to be present at an opening so that space would be properly bent, spells that had to be learned just so. The phone calls flew between Nita's house and Kit's for a couple of days, and there was a lot of visiting back and forth as they divided up the work. Nita spent a lot of time keeping Fred from being noticed by her family, and also got to see a lot of Kit's mother and father and sisters, all of whom were very friendly and kept forgetting that Nita couldn't speak Spanish. She started to learn a little of it in self-defense. Kit's dog told her the brand of dog biscuits it could never get enough of; she began bringing them with her when she visited. The dog spoke the Speech with a Spanish accent, and would constantly interrupt Kit and Nita as they discussed who should do what in the spelling. Kit wound up with most of the spoken work, since he had been using the Speech longer and was better at it; Nita picked up supplies.

Late Friday afternoon, Nita was in a little antiques-and-junk store on Nassau Road, going through boxes of dusty odds and ends in search of a real silver fork. Fred was hanging over her shoulder, almost invisible, a faint red point lazily emitting heat. (You ever swallow anything accidentally before, Fred?) Nita said under her breath.

(Not for a long time,) he said, glancing curiously at a pressed-glass saltshaker Nita was holding. (Not since I was a black hole, certainly. Black holes swallow *everything*, but a white hole's business is emission. Within limits,) he added, and the air around him rippled with heat as he shuddered. (I don't ever again want to emit the way I did after your pen went down. Some of those things *hurt* on the way out. And anyway, all that emission makes me nervous. Too much of that kind of thing and I could blow my quanta.)

She looked up at him, worried. (Really? Have you emitted that much stuff that you're in danger of blowing up?)

(Oh, not really—I'd have to lose a lot more mass first. After all, before I was a black hole, I was a respectable-sized blue-white star, and even these days I massed a few hundred thousand times what your cute little yellow-dwarf Sun does. I wouldn't worry about it—I'm nowhere near the critical threshold yet.)

('Cute'?) Nita said.

(Well, it *is* . . . And I suppose there's no harm in getting better at emissions. I have been improving a lot. What's that?)

Nita looked farther down in the box, dug deep, and came up with a battered old fork. It was scratched and its tines were bent out of shape, but it was definitely silver, not stainless steel. (That's what I needed,) she said. (Thanks, Fred. Now all I need is that piece of rowan wood, and then tonight I go over my part of the spells again.)

(You sound worried.)

(Well, yeah, a little,) Nita said, getting up. All that week her ability to hear what the plants were saying had been getting stronger and surer; the better she got with the Speech, the more sense the bushes and trees made. (It's just—the rowan branch has to come off a live tree, Fred, and I can't just pick it—that'd be like walking up to someone and pulling one of their fingers off. I have to ask for it. And if the tree won't give it to me . . .)

(Then you don't get your pen back, at least not for a while.) Fred shimmered with colors and a feeling like a sigh. (I *am* a trouble to you.)

(Fred, no. Put your light out a moment so we can get out of here.) Nita interrupted the shopkeeper's intense concentration on a Gothic novel long enough to find out what the fork cost (a dollar) and buy it. A few steps outside the door, Fred was pacing her again. (If you're trouble, you're the best trouble that's happened around here for a while. You're good to talk to, you're good company—when you don't forget and start emitting cosmic rays . . .)

Fred blazed momentarily, blushing at Nita's teasing. In an excited moment the night before he had forgotten himself and emitted a brief blast of ultrashortwave radiation, which had heated up Nita's backyard a good deal, ionized the air for miles around, and produced a local but brilliant aurora. (Well, it's an old habit, and old habits die hard. I'm working on it.)

(Heat we don't mind so much. Or ultraviolet, the longwave kind that doesn't hurt people's eyes.)

(You fluoresce when I use that, though . . .)

Nita laughed. (I don't mind fluorescing. Though on second thought, don't do that where anyone but Kit can see. I doubt my mother'd understand.)

They walked home together, chatting alternately about life in the suburbs and life in a part of deep space close to the Great Galactic Rift. Nita felt more relaxed than she had for months. Joanne had been out of sight since Monday afternoon at Tom and Carl's. Even if she hadn't, Nita had been practicing with that body shield, so that now she could run through the syllables of the spell in a matter of seconds and nothing short of a bomb dropped on her could hurt her. She could even extend the spell to cover someone else, though it wasn't quite so effective; she had a harder time convincing the air to harden up. But even that lessened protection would come in handy if she and Kit should be in trouble together at some point and there was no time to cooperate in a spelling. Not that she was expecting any more trouble. The excitement of a trip into the city was already catching at her. And this wasn't just another shopping trip. Magic was loose in the world, and she was going to help work some. . . .

She ate supper and did her homework almost without thinking about either, and as a result had to do much of the math homework twice. By the time she was finished, the sun was down and the backyard was filling with a cool blue twilight.

In the front of the house, her mother and father and Dairine were watching TV as Nita walked out the side door and stood on the step, letting her eyes get used to the dimness and looking east at the rising Moon. Canned laughter echoed inside the house as Fred appeared by her shoulder.

(My, that's bright for something that doesn't emit heat,) Fred said, looking at the Moon too.

(Reflected sunlight,) Nita said absently.

(You're going to talk to the tree now?)

(Uh-huh.)

(Then I'll go stay with the others and watch that funny box emit. Maybe I'll figure out what it's trying to get across.)

(Good luck,) Nita said as Fred winked out. She walked around into the backyard.

Spring stars were coming out as she stood in the middle of the lawn and looked down the length of the yard at the rowan, a great round-crowned tree snowy with white flowers. Nita's stomach tightened slightly with nervousness. It had been a long time ago, according to her manual, that the trees had gone to war on human-kind's behalf, against the dark powers that wanted to keep human intelligence from happening at all. The war had been a terrible one, lasting thousands of centuries— the trees and other plants taking more and more land, turning barren stone to soil that would support them and the animals and men to follow; the dark powers breaking the soil with earthquake and mountain building, scouring it with glaciers, climate-changing good ground for desert, and burning away forests in firestorms far more terrible than the small brushfires any forest needs to stay healthy. But the trees and the other plants had won at last.

They had spent many more centuries readying the world for men—but when men came, they forgot the old debts and wasted the forests more terribly than even the old dark powers. Trees had no particular reason to be friendly to people these days. Nita found herself thinking of that first tree that had spoken to her, angry over the destruction of its friend's artwork. Even though the rowan tree had always been well tended, she wasn't certain how it was going to respond to her. With the other ash trees, rowans had been in the forefront of the Battle; and they had long memories.

Nita sighed and sat down under the tree, book in hand, her back against its trunk. There was no need to start right away, anyhow—she needed a little while to recover from her homework. The stars looked at her through the rowan's wind-stirred branches, getting brighter by the minute. There was that one pair of stars that always looked like eyes, they were so close together. It was one of the three little pairs associated with the Big Dipper. The Leaps of the Gazelle, the ancient Arabs had called them, seeing them as three sets of hoofprints left in the sky. "Kafza'at al Thiba," Nita murmured, the old Arabic name. Her eyes wandered down toward the horizon, finding a faint reddish gleam. "Regulus." And a whiter gleam, higher: "Arcturus." And another, and another, old friends, with new names in the Speech, that she spoke silently, remembering Carl's warning: (Eltháthtë . . . ur'Senaahel . . .) The distant fires flickered among shadowy leaves. (Lahirien . . .)

(And Methchánë and Ysen and Cahadhwy and Rasaugéhil. . . . They *are* nice tonight.)

Nita looked up hurriedly. The tree above her was leaning back comfortably on its roots, finished with the stretching-upward of growth for the day, and gazing at the stars as she was. (I was hoping that haze would clear off,) it said as silently as Nita had spoken, in a slow, relaxed drawl. (This will be a good night for talking to the wind. And other such transient creatures. I was wondering when you were going to come out and pay your respects, wizardling.)

(Uh—) Nita was reassured: the rowan sounded friendly. (It's been a busy week.)

(You never used to be too busy for *me*,) the rowan said, its whispery voice sounding ever so slightly wounded. (Always up in my branches you were, and falling out of them again. Or swinging. But I suppose you outgrew me.)

Nita sat quiet for a moment, remembering how it had been when she was littler. She would swing for hours on end, talking to herself, pretending all kinds of things, talking to the tree and the world in general. And sometimes—(You talked *back!*) she said in shocked realization. (You *did*, I wasn't making it up.)

(Certainly I talked. You were talking to *me*, after all . . . Don't be surprised. Small children look at things and *see* them, listen to things and hear them. Of course they understand the Speech. Most of them never realize it any more than you did. It's when they get older, and stop looking and listening, that they lose the Speech, and we lose them.) The rowan sighed, many leaves showing pale undersides as the wind moved them. (None of us are ever happy about losing our children. But every now and then we get one of you back.)

(All that in the book was true, then,) Nita said. (About the Battle of the Trees—)

(Certainly. Wasn't it written in the *Book of Night with Moon* that this world's life would become free to roam among our friends there)—the rowan stretched upward toward the turning stars for a moment—(if we helped? After the world was green and ready, we waited for a long time. We started letting all sorts of strange creatures live in our branches after they came up out of the water. We watched them all; we never knew which of our guests would be the children we were promised. And then all of a sudden one odd-looking group of creatures went *down* out of our branches, and looked upward again, and called us by name in the Speech. Your kind . . .) The tree looked down musingly at Nita. (You're still an odd-looking lot,) it said.

Nita sat against the rowan and felt unhappy. (We weren't so kind to you,) she said. (And if it weren't for the plants, we wouldn't be here.)

(Don't be downcast, wizardling,) the tree said, gazing up at the sky again. (It isn't your fault. And in any case, we knew what fate was in store for us. It was written in the *Book*.)

(Wait a minute. You mean you knew we were going to start destroying your kind, and you got the world ready for us *anyway?*)

(How could we do otherwise? You *are* our children.)

(But . . . we make our houses out of you, we—) Nita looked guiltily at the book she was holding. (We *kill* you and we write on your *bodies!*)

The rowan continued to gaze up at the night sky. (Well,) it said. (We are all in the *Book* together, after all. Don't you think that we wrote enough in the rock and the soil, in our day? And we still do. We have our own lives, our own feelings and goals. Some of them you may learn by your wizardry, but I doubt you'll ever come to know them all. We do what we have to, to live. Sometimes that means breaking a rock's heart, or pushing roots down into ground that screams against the intrusion. But we never forget what we're doing. As for you)—and its voice became very gentle—(how else should our children climb to the stars but up our branches? We made our peace with that fact a long time ago, that we would be used and maybe forgotten. So be it. What you learn in your climbing will make all the life on this planet greater, more precious. You have your own stories to write. And when it comes to that, who writes the things written in *your* body, *your* life? And who reads?) It breathed out, a long sigh of leaves in the wind. (Our cases aren't that much different.)

Nita sat back and tried to absorb what the tree was saying. (*The Book of Night with Moon*,) she said after a while. (Do you know who wrote it?)

The rowan was silent for a long time. (None of us are sure,) it said at last. (Our legends say it wasn't written. It's simply *been*, as long as life has been. Since they were kindled, and before.) It gazed upward at the stars.

(Then the other Book, the dark one—)

The whole tree shuddered. (*That* one was written, they say.) The rowan's voice dropped to a whisper. (By the Lone Power—the Witherer, the one who blights. The Kindler of Wildfires. Don't ask more. Even talking about that one or its works can lend it power.)

Nita sat quiet for a while, thinking. (You came to ask something,) the rowan said. (Wizards are always asking things of rowans.)

(Uh, yes.)

(Don't worry about it,) the rowan said. (When we decided to be trees of the Light, we knew we were going to be in demand.)

(Well—I need some live wood. Just enough for a stick, a little wand. We're going to open the Grand Central worldgate tomorrow morning.)

Above Nita's head there was a sharp cracking sound. She pressed back against the trunk, and a short straight branch about a foot and a half long bounced to the grass in front of her. (The Moon is almost full tonight,) the rowan said. (If I were you, I'd peel the leaves and bark off that twig and leave it out to soak up moonlight. I don't think it'll hurt the wood's usefulness for your spelling, and it may make it more valuable later on.)

(Thank you, yes,) Nita said. The book had mentioned something of the sort—a rowan rod with a night's moonlight in it could be used for some kind of defense. She would look up the reference later. (I guess I should go in and check my spells over one more time. I'm awfully new at this.)

(Go on,) the tree said, with affection. Nita picked up the stick that the rowan had dropped for her, got up and stretched, looking up at the stars through the branches. On impulse she reached up, hooked an arm around the branch that had had the swing on it.

(I guess I could still come and climb sometimes,) she said.

She felt the tree looking at her. (My name in the Speech is Liused,) it said in leafrustle and starflicker. (If there's need, remember me to the trees in Manhattan. You won't be without help if you need it.)

"*I'm Nita,*" she said in the Speech, aloud for this once. The syllables didn't sound strange: they sounded like a native language and made English feel like a foreign tongue. For a moment every leaf on the tree quivered with her name, speaking it in a whispery echo.

(Go,) the rowan said again. (Rest well.) It turned its calm regard to the stars again.

Nita went back inside.

Saturday morning about eight, Kit and Nita and Fred took the bus down to the Long Island Railroad station and caught a shiny silver train for Manhattan. The train was full of the usual cargo of Saturday travelers and shoppers, none of whom paid any particular attention to the boy and girl sitting by one window, going over the odd contents of their backpacks with great care. Also apparently unnoticed was a faint spark of white light hanging in the center of the window between the two, gazing out in fascination at the backyards and parking lots and stores the train passed.

(What are all those dead hunks of metal there? All piled up?)

(Cars, Fred.)

(I thought cars moved.)

(They did, once.)

(They all went there to die?)

(They were dead when they got there, probably.)

(But they've all climbed on top of each other! When they were dead?)

(No, Fred. They have machines—)

Nita sighed out loud. "Where were we?" she said to Kit.

"The battery."

"Right. Well, here it is."

"Lithium-cadmium?"

"Right. Heavy thing, it weighs more than anything else we've got. That's the last thing for activating the piece of time, isn't it?"

"One more. The eight and a half sugar cubes."

"Here." Nita held up a little plastic bag.

"Okay. Now the worldgate stuff. The pinecone—"

"Bristlecone pine." Nita held it up, then dropped it in her backpack.

"The aspirin."

"Uh-huh."

"The fork."

"Here."

"The rowan branch."

"Yup." She held it up. Cut down and peeled, it was about a foot long, a greenish white wand.

"Great. Then we're set. You've got all that other stuff, why don't you give me the battery?"

"Here." Nita handed it to him, watched as he found a good spot for it in his backpack, under the sandwiches. "What's that?" she said, spotting something that hadn't been accounted for in the equipment tally.

"Huh? Oh, this." He reached in and brought out a slim piece of metal like a slender rod, with a small knob at one end and broken off jaggedly at the other.

"What is it?"

"A piece of junk. A busted-off car antenna. Well," Kit amended, "it was, anyway. I was sitting out behind the garage yesterday afternoon, reading, and I started talking to my dad's old car. He has this ancient Edsel. He's always talking about getting it reconditioned, but I don't think he's really going to—there's never enough money. Anyway he goes out every now and then to work on the engine, usually when he's tired or mad about something. I don't know if he ever really gets any work done, but he always comes inside greasy all over and feeling a lot better. But I was going over the spells in my head, and the car spoke to me in the Speech—"

"Out loud?"

"No, inside, like Fred does. Kind of a grindy noise, like its voice needed a lube job. I wasn't too surprised; that kind of thing has been happening since I picked the book up. First it was rocks, and then *things* started to talk to me when I picked them up. They would tell me where they'd been and who'd handled them. Anyway, the car and I started talking." Kit paused, looking a touch guilty. "They don't see things the way we do. We made them, and they don't understand why most of the time we make things and then just let them wear out and throw them away afterward . . ."

Nita nodded, wondering briefly whether the train was alive too. Certainly it was as complex as a car. "What about this antenna thing, though?" she said after a moment.

"Oh. The car said to take it for luck. It was just lying there on the ground, rusting. Dad replaced the antenna a long time ago. So I took it inside and cleaned it up, and there are some wizardries you can do with metal, to remind it of the different forces it felt when it was being made. I did a couple of those. Partly just practicing, partly . . ."

"You thought there might be trouble," Nita said.

Kit looked at her, surprised. "I don't know," he said. "I'm going to be careful, anyway. Carl was pretty definite about not messing around with the worldgate; I wasn't thinking about anything like that. But it occurred to me that it'd be easy to carry the antenna to school if I wanted to. And if anyone started bothering me—" He shrugged, then laughed. "Well, that's their problem. Hey, look, we're getting close to that big curve where you can see the city before you go under the river. Come on, these trains have a window in the very front of the first car. (Fred! Want to see where we're going?)

(Why not? Maybe I'll understand it better than where we've been . . .)

Kit and Nita wriggled into their backpacks and made their way up through a couple of cars, hanging on carefully as they crossed the chained walkways between them. Treetops and housetops flashed by in a rush of wind and clatter of rails. Each time Nita touched the bare metal of the outside of the train, she jumped a little, feeling something, she wasn't quite sure what. *The train?* she thought. *Thinking? And now that I'm aware that it does, I can feel it a little?—though not as clearly as the trees. Maybe my specialty is going to be things that grow and Kit's is going to be things that run. But how many other kinds of life are there that I could learn to feel? Who knows where thought is hiding? . . .*

They went into the first car and made their way up to the front window, carefully hanging on to the seats of oblivious riders to keep the swaying of the train from knocking them over. There were no more stops between there and Penn Station, and the train was plunging along, the rails roaring beneath it. Those rails climbed gradually as the already elevated track went higher still to avoid a triple-stacked free-way. Then the rails bent away to the left in a long graceful curve, still climbing slightly; and little by little, over the low brown cityscape of Brooklyn, the towers of Manhattan rose glittering in the early sunlight. Gray and crystal for the Empire State Building, silver-blue for the odd sheared-off Citibank building, silver-gold for the twin square pillars of the World Trade Center, and steely white fire for the scalloped tower of the Chrysler Building as it caught the Sun. The place looked magical enough in the bright morning. Nita grinned to herself, looking at the view and realizing that there *was* magic there. That forest of towers opened onto other worlds. One day she would open that worldgate by herself and *go* somewhere.

Fred stared at the towers, amazed. (This is *more* life? More even than the place where you two live?)

(Ten million lives in the city, Fred. Maybe four or five million on that island alone.)

(Doesn't it worry you, packing all that life together? What if a meteor hits it? What if there's a starflare? If something should happen to all that life—how terrible!)

Nita laughed to herself. (It doesn't seem to worry *them* . . .) Beside her, Kit was hanging on to a seat, being rocked back and forth by the train's speed. Very faintly Nita could hear what Kit heard and felt more strongly; the train's aliveness, its wild rushing joy at doing what it was made to do—its dangerous pleasure in its speed, the wind it fought with, the rails it rode. Nita shook her head in happy wonder. *And I wanted to see the life on other planets. There's more life in* this *world than I expected.*

(It's beautiful,) Fred said from his vantage point just above Kit's shoulder.

"It really is," Nita said, very quiet.

The train howled defiant joy and plunged into the darkness under the river.

Penn Station was thick with people when they got there, but even so it took them only a few minutes to get down to the Seventh Avenue subway station and from there up to Times Square and the shuttle to Grand Central. The shuttle ride was short and crowded. Nita and Kit and Fred were packed tight together in a corner, where they braced themselves against walls and seats and other people while the train shouted along through the echoing underground darkness.

(I can't feel the Sun,) Fred said, sounding worried.

(We're ten or twenty feet underground,) Nita said silently. (We'll get you some Sun as soon as we get off.)

Kit looked at Fred with concern. (You've been twitchy ever since we went into the tunnel, haven't you?)

Fred didn't speak for a moment. (I miss the openness,) he said then. (But worse I miss the feeling of your star on me. Where I come from no one is sealed away from the surrounding emissions.) He trailed off, his thoughts full of the strange hiss and crackle of interstellar radiation—subtly patterned sound, rushing and dying away and swelling up again—the Speech in yet another of its forms. *Starsong*, Nita thought. (You said you *heard* about the *Book of Night with Moon*,) she said. (Was that how? Your . . . friends, your people, they actually talk to each other over all those distances—millions of light-years?)

(That's right. Not that we use light to do it, of course. But the words, the song, they never stop. Except now. I can hardly hear anything but neutrinos . . .)

Kit and Nita glanced at each other. (The worldgate is underground, Fred,) Kit said. (In back of a deli, a little store. We'll have to be there for at least a few minutes to get Nita's pen out.)

(We could go out first and look around,) Nita said. (We're early—it's only nine thirty. We don't even have to think about anchoring the timeslide for a little bit yet.)

The subway cars screeched to a halt, doors rolled open, and the crush loosened as people piled out. Nita got off gladly, looking around for directional signs to point the way toward the concourse level of Grand Central—it had been a while since she'd been there.

"Are you sure you know your way around this place?" Kit asked as Nita headed down a torn-up looking corridor.

"Uh-huh. They're always doing construction in here. C'mon."

She led them up a flight of stairs into the lower Grand Central concourse—all beige tiles, gray floor, signs pointing to fifty different trains, and small stores packed together. "The deli's down there," she said as she went, waving a hand at a crowd of hurrying people and the wide hall past them. "We go up here." And another flight of stairs, wider and prettier, let them out on the upper concourse, a huge stretch of cream-colored marble under a great blue dome painted with constellations and starred with lights.

They headed across the marble floor, up a short ramp, and out one of many brassy yellow doors, onto the street. Immediately the three of them were assailed by noise, exhaust fumes, people hurrying in all directions, a flood of cabs and buses and cars. But there was also sunlight, and Kit and Nita stood against the wall by the Grand Central doors, letting Fred soak it up and get his composure back. He did so totally oblivious to the six men and three jackhammers working just across the street behind a barrier of sawhorses and orange plastic cones. (That's much better,) he said.

(It was quieter inside, though,) Kit said, and Nita was inclined to agree with him. The rattling clamor of the jackhammers was climbing down her ears into her bones and making her teeth jitter. The men, two burly ones and one skinny one, all three broad-shouldered and tan, all in helmets and jeans and boots, appeared to be trying to dig to China. One of them hopped down into the excavation for a moment to check its progress, and vanished up to his neck. Then the hammering started again. "How can they stand it?" Nita muttered.

(Stand what? It's lovely out here.) Fred danced about a little in the air, brightening out of invisibility for a few moments and looking like a long-lived remnant of a fireworks display.

(Fred, put it out!) Kit said. (If somebody sees you—)

(They didn't see me in the field the other day,) Fred replied, (though Artificer knows they *looked*.)

(Probably the Learjet distracted them. Fred, come on, tone it down a little,) Nita said. (Let's go back inside and do what we have to. Then we can set the timeslide and have fun in the city for the rest of the day.)

They went back inside and down the stairs again, accompanied by the quiet inward sound of Fred's grumbling. There was no trouble finding the little deli where the worldgate was situated, and Nita and Kit paused outside it. (You have everything ready?) Nita said.

(All in here.) Kit tapped his head. (The spells are all set except for one or two syllables—it's like dialing almost all of a phone number. When I call for you, just come on back. All we need is for the supplies to be in range of the spell; there's nothing special that has to be done with them. Fred, you stay with Nita.)

(As you say.)

They went in. Nita lingered by the front counter, staring at dill pickles and sandwich makings, trying to look normal while she waited for Kit to call her. Fred hung over her shoulder, looking with great interest at bologna and salami and mayonnaise and cream cheese. (You people certainly have enough ways to internalize energy,) he said. (Is there really that much difference between one brand of matter and another?)

(Well, wasn't there any difference when you were a black hole? Didn't a rock, say, taste different from a ray of light, when you soaked one or the other up?)

(Now that you mention it, yes. But appreciating differences like that was something you had to work at for a long time. I wouldn't expect someone as young as you to—)

(Nita,) Kit's thought came abruptly. (We've got trouble. It's not here.)

(What? It has to be!)

(It's *gone*, Nita.)

"Girlie," said the man behind the deli counter in a no-nonsense growl, "you gonna buy anything?"

"Uh," Nita said, and by reflex more than anything else picked up a can of soda from the nearby cooler and fished around in her pocket for the change. "Kit—" she called.

"Coming."

Nita paid for the soda. Kit joined her, carrying a small bag of potato chips, which he paid for in turn. Together they went back out into the corridor, and Kit knelt down by the window of a store across the way, a window full of shiny cutlery. He got his wizards' manual out of his pack and began going through the pages in a hurry. "I don't get it," he said. "I even checked this morning to make sure there hadn't been any change in the worldgate status. It said, right here, 'patent and operative.' "

"Were the spells all right?"

Kit glared up at Nita, and she was instantly sorry she'd asked. "The spells were fine," Kit said. "But they got caught like that first one I did, when you came along. Oh, damn . . ." He trailed off, and Nita edged around beside him to look at the page. "Something's changed," Kit said, and indeed the page didn't look as it had when Nita had checked it herself in her own manual the night before. The listings for the other Manhattan worldgates were the same—the World Trade Center gate was still listed as "under construction" and the Rockefeller Center gate as "closed for routine maintenance." But under the Grand Central gate listing was a small red box that said in boldface type, *Claudication temporarily dislocated due to unscheduled spatial interruption*, followed by a string of numbers and symbols in the Speech, a description of the gate's new location. Kit glanced up at the roof, through which the sound of jackhammers could plainly be heard. "The construction," he said. "It must have screwed up the worldgate's interruption of space somehow."

Nita was puzzling over the symbols for the new location. "Isn't that term there the one for height above the ground?" she asked.

"Uh-huh. Look at it, it must be sixty, seventy stories straight up from here." Kit slapped the book shut in great annoyance, shoved it back in his backpack. "*Now* what do we do?"

(We go back outside?) Fred asked, very hopefully.

It seemed the best suggestion. The three of them walked out again, and Fred bobbed and danced some more in the sunlight while Nita and Kit walked slowly east along Forty-second Street, toward the Park Avenue overpass. "Dislocated," Kit muttered. "And who knows how long it'll take to come *un*dislocated? A perfectly good piece of time wasted."

Nita stopped and turned, looking up into the air and trying to estimate where the deli lay under the Grand Central complex. She picked a spot that seemed about right, let her eye travel up and up, sixty, maybe seventy stories. "Kit," she said. "Kit! Look what's seventy stories high, and right next door."

Kit looked. Dark blue and silver, with its big stylized globe logo on one side, the Pan Am Building reared its oblong self up at least seventy stories high, right there—not only right behind Grand Central, but part of it. "Yeah," Kit said, his voice still heavy with annoyance. "So?"

"So you remember that shield spell you showed me? The one that makes the air solid? If you change the quantities in the spell a little, you can use it for something else. To walk on, even. You just keep the air hard."

She couldn't keep from grinning. Kit stared at Nita as if she'd gone crazy. "Are you suggesting that we *walk out* to the worldgate and—" He laughed. "How are we going to get up there?"

"There's a heliport on top of the building," Nita said promptly. "They don't use it for big helicopters anymore, but the little ones still land, and there's an elevator in the building that goes right to the top. There's a restaurant up there, too; my father had lunch with someone up there once. I bet we could do it."

Kit stared at her. "If you talk the air solid, *you're* going to walk on it first! I saw that spell; it's not that easy."

"I practiced it some. Come on, Kit, you want to waste the timeslide? It's almost ten now! It'll probably be years before these guys are finished digging. Let's do it!"

"They'll never let us up there," Kit said with conviction.

"Oh yes, they will. They won't have a choice, because Fred'll make a diversion for us. We don't even need anything as big as a Learjet this time. How about it, Fred?"

Fred looked at them reluctantly. (I must admit I *have* been feeling an urge to burp . . .)

Kit still looked uncertain. "And when we get up there," he said, "all those stories up, and looking as if we're walking on nothing—what if somebody sees us?"

Nita laughed. "Who are they going to tell? And who's going to believe them?"

Kit nodded and then began to grin slowly, too. "Yeah," he said. "Yeah! Let's go, it's getting late."

Back they went into Grand Central, straight across the main concourse this time and up one of the six escalators that led up to the lobby of the Pan Am

Building. They paused just outside the revolving doors at the end of the escalators. The Pan Am lobby was a big place, pillared and walled and paved in dark granite, echoing with the sound of people hurrying in and out of the station. They went up the escalator to the next floor, and Nita pointed off to one side, indicating an elevator bank. One elevator had a sign standing by it: COPTER CLUB—HELIPAD LEVEL—EXPRESS. Also standing by it was a bored-looking uniformed security guard.

"That's it," Nita said.

"So if we can just get him away from there . . ."

"It's not that simple." She pointed down at the end of the hall between two more banks of elevators. Another guard sat behind a large semicircular desk, watching a row of TV monitors. "They've got cameras all over the place. We've got to get that guy out of there, too. Fred, if you're going to do something, do it right between them. Out in front of that desk."

(Well,) Fred said, sounding interested, (let's see, let's see . . .) He damped his light down and floated off toward the elevators, looking like an unusually large speck of dust, nothing more. The dust mote stopped just between the desk and the elevator guard, hung in midair, and concentrated so fiercely that Nita and Kit could both feel it thirty feet away.

(T-*hup!*)

BANG!

"That'll get their attention," Kit muttered. It did; both the guards started at the noise, began looking around for the source of it—then both went very very slowly over to examine the large barrel cactus in a brass pot that had suddenly appeared in the middle of the shiny floor.

"Now," Kit said, and took off toward the elevator with Nita close behind. Both the guards had their backs turned, and Nita, passing them, saw the elevator keys hanging off one guard's belt. (Fred,) she said hurriedly, (can you grab those real fast, the way you grabbed my pen? Don't swallow them!)

(I might make that mistake once,) Fred said, (but not twice.) As they slipped into the elevator Fred paused by the guard's belt, and the keys vanished without so much as a jingle. He sailed in to them. (How was that?)

(Great. Quick, Nita, close the door!)

She punched one of the elevator buttons and the doors slid shut; the keys appeared again, and Kit caught them in midair before they fell. "It's always one of these round ones, like they use on coin phones," he said, going through the keys. "Fred, I didn't know you could make *live* things!"

(I didn't know either,) Fred said, sounding unsettled, (and I'm not sure I like it!)

"Here we go," Kit said, and put one key into the elevator lock, turning it to RUN, and then pressed the button marked 73—RESTAURANT—HELIPAD. The elevator took off in a hurry.

Nita swallowed repeatedly to pop her ears. "Aren't you going to have to change the spells a little to compensate for the gate being up high now?" she said after a moment.

"A little. You just put in the new height coordinate. Oops!"

The elevator began to slow down quickly, and Nita's stomach churned for a moment. She and Kit both pressed themselves against the sides of the elevator, so they wouldn't be immediately visible to anyone who might happen to be standing right outside the door. But when the doors slid open, no one was there. They peered out and saw a long carpeted corridor with a plate-glass door at one end. Through it they saw tables and chairs and, more dimly, through a window, a hazy view of the East Side skyline. A muffled sound of plates and silverware being handled came down the hall to them.

(It's early for lunch,) Nita said, relieved. (Let's go before someone sees us.)

(What about these keys?)

(Hmm . . .)

(Look, let's leave them in the elevator lock. That way the guard downstairs'll just think he left them there. If they discover they're missing, they'll start looking for whoever took them—and this would be the first place they'd look.)

(Yeah, but how are we going to get down?)

(We'll walk on air,) Kit said, his voice teasing. Nita rolled her eyes at the ceiling. (Or we'll go down with the people coming out from lunch, if that doesn't work. Let's just get out of *here* first, okay? Which way do we go to get up on the heliport?)

(Left. There are stairs.)

They slipped out of the elevator just as it chimed and its doors shut again—probably the guard had called it from downstairs. The corridor off to the left was featureless except for one door at its very end. HELIPAD ACCESS, the door said in large red letters. Nita tried the knob, then let her hand fall in exasperation. (Locked. Crud!)

(Well, wait a moment,) Kit said, and tried the knob himself. *"You don't really want to be locked, do you"* he said aloud in the Speech, very quietly. Again Nita was amazed by how natural the wizards' language sounded when you heard it, and how nice it was to hear—as if, after being lost in a foreign country for a long time, someone should suddenly speak warmly to you in English. *"You've been locked for a couple of days now,"* Kit went on, his voice friendly and persuasive, not casting a spell, just talking—though in the Speech, the two were often dangerously close. *"It must be pretty dull being locked, no one using you, no one paying any attention. Now we need to use you at least a couple of times this morning, so we thought we'd ask—"*

Kt-chk! said the lock, and the knob turned in Kit's hand. *"Thank you,"* he said. *"We'll be back later."* He went through the door into the stairwell, Nita and Fred following, and as the door swung to behind them and locked itself again, there was a decidedly friendly sound to the click. Kit grinned triumphantly at Nita as they climbed the stairs. "How about *that?*"

"Not bad," Nita said, determined to learn how to do it herself, if possible.

"You've been practicing, too."

"Not really—some of this stuff just seems to come naturally as you work with it more. My mother locked herself out of the car at the supermarket last week and I was pulling on the car door and talking at it—you know how you do when you're trying to get something to work. And then it worked. I almost fell over, the door came open so fast. It's the Speech that does it, I think. Everything loves to hear it."

"Remember what Carl said, though."

"I know. I won't overdo it. You think we ought to call him later, let him know what happened to the gate?"

They came to the top of the stairs, paused before the next closed door, breathing hard from the exertion of climbing the stairs fast. "Probably he knows, if he's looked at his book this morning," Nita said. "Look, before we do anything else, let's set the timeslide. This is a good place for it; we're out of sight. When we're tired of running around the city, we can just activate it and we'll be back here at quarter of eleven. Then we just go downstairs, into Grand Central and downstairs to the shuttle, and then home in time for lunch."

"Sounds good." They began rummaging in their backpacks, and before too long had produced the eight and a half sugar cubes, the lithium-cadmium battery—a fat one, bigger than a D cell and far heavier—a specific integrated-circuit chip salvaged from the innards of a dead pocket calculator, and the handle of a broken glass teacup. "You might want to back away a little, Fred, so your emissions don't interfere with the spell," Kit said.

(Right.) Fred retreated high up into one ceiling-corner of the stairwell, flaring bright with interest.

"All right," Kit said, thumbing through his manual to a page marked with a bit of ripped-up newspaper, "here we go. *This is a timeslide inauguration,*" he said aloud in the Speech. *"Claudication type mesarrh-gimel-veignt-six, authorization group—"* Nita swallowed, feeling the strangeness set in as it had during their first spell together, feeling the walls lean in to listen. But it was not a silence that fell this time. As Kit spoke, Nita became aware of a roaring away at the edge of her hearing and a blurring at the limits of her vision. Both effects grew and strengthened to the overwhelming point almost before she realized what was happening. And then it was too late. She was seeing and hearing everything that would happen for miles and miles around at quarter to eleven, as if the building were transparent, as if she had eyes that could pierce stone and ears that could hear a leaf fall blocks away. The words and thoughts of a million minds poured down on her in a roaring onslaught like a wave crashing down on a swimmer, and she was washed away, helpless. Too many sights, commonplace and strange, glad and frightening, jostled and crowded all around her, and squeezing her eyes shut made no difference—the sights were in her mind. *I'll go crazy, I'll go crazy, stop it!* But she was caught in the spell and couldn't budge. *Stop it, oh, let it stop—*

It stopped. She was staring at the floor between her and Kit as she had been doing when the flood of feelings swept over her. Everything was the same as it had been, except that the sugar was gone. Kit was looking at her in concern. "You all right?" he said. "You look a little green."

"Uh, yeah." Nita rubbed her head, which ached slightly as if with the memory of a very loud sound.

"What happened to the sugar?"

"It went away. That means the spell took." Kit began gathering up the rest of the materials and stowing them. He looked at her again. "Are you *sure* you're okay?"

"Yeah, I'm fine." She got up, looked around restlessly. "C'mon, let's go."

Kit got up too, shrugging into his backpack. "Yeah. Which way is the—"

CRACK! went something against the door outside, and Nita's insides constricted.

She and Kit both threw themselves against the wall behind the door, where they would be hidden if it opened. For a few seconds neither of them dared to breathe.

Nothing happened.

(What was that?) Kit asked.

(I don't know. It sounded like a shot. Lord, Kit, what if there's somebody up here with a gun or something—)

(What's a gun?) Fred said.

(You don't want to know,) Kit said. (Then again, if there *was* somebody out there with a gun, I doubt they could hurt you. Fred, would you go out there and have a quick look around? See who's there?)

(Why not?) Fred floated down from the ceiling, looked the door over, put his light out, and slipped through the keyhole. For a little while there was silence, broken only by the faint faraway rattle of a helicopter going by, blocks away.

Then the lock glowed a little from inside, and Fred popped back in. (I don't see anyone out there,) he said.

Kit looked at Nita. (Then what made that noise?)

She was as puzzled as he was. She shrugged. (Well, if Fred says there's nothing out there—)

(I suppose. But let's keep our eyes open.)

Kit coaxed the door open as he had the first one, and the three of them stepped cautiously out onto the roof.

Most of it was occupied by the helipad proper, the long wide expanse of bare tarmac ornamented with its big yellow square-and-H symbol and surrounded by blue low-intensity landing lights. At one end of the oblong pad was a small glass-walled building decorated with the Pan Am logo, a distended orange wind sock, and an anemometer, its three little cups spinning energetically in the brisk morning wind. Beyond the helipad, the roof was graveled, and various low-set ventilator stacks poked up here and there. A yard-high guardrail edged the roof. Rising up on all sides was Manhattan, a stony forest of buildings in all shapes and heights. To the west glimmered the Hudson River and the Palisades on the New Jersey side; on the other side of the building lay the East River and Brooklyn and Queens, veiled in mist and pinkish smog. The Sun would have felt warm if the wind had stopped blowing. No one was up there at all.

Nita took a few steps off the paved walkway that led to the little glass building and scuffed at the gravel suspiciously. "This wind is pretty stiff," she said. "Maybe a good gust of it caught some of this gravel and threw it at the door." But even as she said it, she didn't believe it.

"Maybe," Kit said. His voice made it plain that he didn't believe it either. "Come on, let's find the gate."

"That side," Nita said, pointing south, where the building was wider. They headed toward the railing together, crunching across the gravel. Fred perched on Nita's shoulder; she looked at him with affection. (Worried?)

(No. But you are.)

(A little. That sound shook me up.) She paused again, wondering if she heard something behind her. She turned. Nothing; the roof was bare. *But still* . . . Nita turned back and hurried to catch up with Kit, who was looking back at her.

"Something?"

"I don't know. I doubt it. You know how you see things out of the corner of your eye, movements that aren't there? I thought maybe the door moved a little."

"I don't know about you," Kit said, "but I'm not going to turn my back on anything while I'm up here. Fred, keep your eyes open." Kit paused by the railing, examining the ledge below it, maybe six feet wide, then looked up again. (On second thought, do you *have* eyes?)

(I don't know,) Fred said, confused but courteous as always. (Do you have chelicerae?)

"Good question," Nita said, a touch nervously. "Kit, let's do this and get out of here."

He nodded, unslung his pack, and laid the aspirin, pinecone, and fork on the gravel by the railing. Nita got out the rowan wand and dropped it with the other materials, while Kit went through his book again, stopping at another marked spot. "Okay," he said after a moment. *"This is an imaging-and-patency spell for a temporospatial claudication, asdekh class. Purpose: retrieval of an accidentally internalized object, matter-energy quotient . . ."* Kit read a long string of syllables, a description of Nita's pen in the Speech, followed by another symbol group that meant Fred and described the properties of the little personal worldgate that kept his great mass at a great distance.

Nita held her breath, waiting for another onslaught of uncanny feelings, but none ensued. When Kit stopped reading and the spell turned her loose, it was almost a surprise to see, hanging there in the air, the thing they had been looking for. Puckered, roughly oblong, vaguely radiant, an eight-foot scar on the sky; the worldgate, about a hundred feet out from the edge where they stood and maybe thirty feet below the heliport level.

"Well," Kit said then, sounding very pleased with himself. "There we are. And it looks all right, not much different from the description in the book."

"Now all we have to do is get to it." Nita picked up the rowan wand, which for the second part of the spell would serve as a key to get the pen through the worldgate and out of Fred. She tucked the wand into her belt, leaned on the railing, and looked out at the air.

According to the wizards' manual, air, like the other elements, had a memory and could be convinced in the Speech to revert to something it had been before. It was this memory of being locked in stone as oxides or nitrates, or frozen solid in the deeps of space, that made the air harden briefly for the shielding spell. Nita started that spell in its simplest form and then went on into a more formal one, as much a reminiscence as a convincing—she talked to the air about the old days when starlight wouldn't twinkle because there was nothing to make it do so, and when every shadow was sharp as a razor, and distances didn't look distant because there was no air to soften them. The immobility came down around her as the spell began to say itself along with Nita, matching her cadence. She kept her eyes closed, not looking, for fear something that should be happening might not be. Slowly with her words she began to shape the hardening air into an oblong, pushing it out through the other, thinner air she wasn't including in the spell. *It's working better than usual, faster,* she thought. *Maybe it's all the smog here—this air's half-solid already.* She kept talking.

Kit whispered something, but she couldn't make out what and didn't want to try. *"I know it's a strain, being solid these days,"* she whispered in the Speech,

*"but just for a little while. Just to make a walkway out to that puckered place in
the sky, then you can relax. Nothing too thick, just strong enough to walk on—"*

"Nita. *Nita!*"

The sound of her name in the Speech caught her attention. She opened her
eyes. Arrow-straight, sloping down from the lower curb of the railing between her
and Kit, the air had gone hard. There was dirt and smog trapped in it, making the
sudden walkway more translucent than transparent—but there was no mistaking it
for anything but air. It had a more delicate, fragile look than any glass ever could,
no matter how thin. The walkway ran smooth and even all the way out to the
worldgate, widening beneath it into room enough for two to stand.

"Wow!" Nita said, sagging against the railing and rubbing at her eyes as she
let the spell go. She was tired; the spelling was a strain—and that feeling of
nervousness left over from the loud noise outside the stairwell came back. She
glanced over her shoulder again, wondering just what she was looking for.

Kit peered over the railing at the walkway. "This better be some pen," he said,
and turned his back to the worldgate, watching the roof. "Go ahead."

Nita made sure her backpack was slung properly, checked the rowan wand
again, and slowly swung over the guardrail, balancing on the stone in which it was
rooted. She was shaking, and her hands were wet. *If I don't just do this*, she thought,
*I never will. Just one step down, Callahan, and then a nice solid walkway straight
across. Really. Believe. Believe. Ouch!*

The air was so transparent that she misjudged the distance down to it—her
foot hit before she thought it would, and the jolt went right up her spine. Still
holding the railing, Nita lifted that foot a bit, then stomped down hard on the
walkway. It was no different from stomping on a sidewalk. She let her weight
down on that foot, brought the second down, and stomped with that, too. It *was*
solid.

"Like rock, Kit!" she said, looking up at him, still holding the rail. "C'mon!"

"Sure," Kit said, skeptical. "Let go of the rail first."

Nita made a face at Kit and let go. She held both arms out at first, as she might
have on a balance beam in gym, and then waved them experimentally. "See? It
works. Fred?"

Fred bobbed down beside her, looking with interest at the hardened air of the
walkway. (And it will stay this way?)

(Until I turn it loose. Well?) She took a step backward, farther onto the walkway, and looked up challengingly. "How about it?"

Kit said nothing, just slung his own backpack over his shoulders and swung
over the railing as Nita had done, coming down cautiously on the hardened air.
He held on to the rail for a moment while conducting his own tests of the air's
solidity. "Come on," Nita said. "The wind's not too bad."

"Lead the way."

Nita turned around, still holding her arms a little away from her to be sure of
her balance, and started for the worldgate as quickly as she dared, with Fred pacing
her cheerfully to the left. Eight or ten steps more and it was becoming almost easy.
She even glanced down toward the walkway—and there she stopped very suddenly,
her stomach turning right over in her at the sight of the dirty, graveled roof of
Grand Central, a long, long, *long* fall below. "Don't look down," a memory said

to her in Machu Picchu's scratchy voice. She swallowed, shaking all over, wishing she had remembered the advice earlier.

"Nita, what's the—"

Something went *whack!* into the walkway. Nita jumped, lost her balance, and staggered back into Kit. For a few awful seconds they teetered back and forth in wind that gusted suddenly, pushing them toward the edge together—and then Kit sat down hard on the walkway, and Nita half fell on top of him, and they held very still for a few gasps.

"Wh-what—"

"I think it was a pigeon," Nita said, not caring whether Kit heard the tremulousness of her voice. "You okay?"

"Sure," Kit said, just as shakily. "I try to have a heart attack every day whether I need one or not. Get off my knee, huh?"

They picked each other up and headed for the gate again. (Even you have trouble with gravity,) Fred said wonderingly as he paced them. (I'm glad I left my mass elsewhere.)

(So are we,) Nita said. She hurried the last twenty steps or so to the widened place at the end of the walkway, with Kit following close.

She knelt down in a hurry, to make sure the wind wouldn't push her over again, and looked up at the worldgate. Seen this close it was about four feet by eight, the shape of a tear in a piece of cloth. It shone with a palely glowing, shifting, soap-bubble iridescence. *Finally, finally, my pen!* she thought—but somehow the thought didn't make Nita as happy as it should have. The uneasy feeling that had started in the stairwell was still growing. She glanced over her shoulder at Kit. He was kneeling too, with his back to her, watching the walkway and the rooftop intently. Beside her, Fred hung quietly waiting.

(Now what?) he asked.

Nita sighed, pulled the rowan rod out of her belt, and inserted one end of it delicately into the shimmering veil that was the surface of the worldgate. Though the city skyline could be seen very clearly through the shimmer, the inch or so of the wand that went through it appeared to vanish. (Just perch yourself on the free end here,) Nita said, holding the wand by its middle. (Make contact with it the same way you did with those keys. Okay?)

(Simple enough.) Fred floated to the end of the rod and lit there, a bright, still spark. (All right, I'm ready.)

Nita nodded. *"This is a retrieval,"* she said in the Speech. *"Involvement confined to a pen with the following characteristics: m'sedh-zayin six point three—"*

(Nita!)

The note of pure terror in Kit's mindvoice caused Nita to do the unforgivable—break off in the middle of a spell and look over her shoulder. Shapes were pouring out of the little glass shelter building, which had been empty, and was still somehow empty even as Nita looked. She got a first impression of grizzled coats, red tongues that lolled and slavered, fangs that gleamed in the sunlight, and she thought, *Wolves!*

But their eyes changed her mind as ten or twelve of the creatures loped across the roof toward the transparent walkway, giving tongue in an awful mindless cacophony of snarls and barks and shuddering howls. The eyes. *People's* eyes, blue, brown, green, but with almost all the intelligence gone out of them, nothing left but a hot deadly cunning and an awful desire for the taste of blood. From her reading in the wizards' manual, she knew what they were: perytons. Wolves would have been preferable—wolves were sociable creatures. *These* had been people once, people so used to hating that at the end of life they'd found a way to keep doing it, by hunting the souls of others through their nightmares. And once a peryton caught you . . .

Nita started to hitch backward in total panic and then froze, realizing that there was nowhere to go. She and Kit were trapped. Another second and the perytons would be on the bridge, and at their throats, for eternity. Kit whipped his head around toward Nita and the worldgate. "Jump through and break the spell!" he yelled.

"But—" And she grabbed his arm, pushed the rowan wand through her belt, and yelled, "Come on, Fred!" The first three perytons leaped the guardrail and landed on the bridge, running. Nita threw herself and Kit at the worldgate, being careful of the edges, as she knew she must, while screaming in absolute terror the word that would dissolve the walkway proper.

For a fraction of a second she caught the sound of screams other than her own, howls of creatures unseen but falling. Then the shimmer broke against her face like water, shutting out sound, and light, and finally thought. Blinded, deafened, and alone, she fell forever. . . .

Exocontinual Protocols

SHE LAY WITH HER face pressed against the cold harsh gravel, feeling the grit of it against her cheek, the hot tears as they leaked between her lashes, and that awful chill wind that wouldn't stop tugging at her clothes. Very slowly Nita opened her eyes, blinked, and gradually realized that the problem with the place where she lay was not her blurred vision. It was just very dim there. She leaned on her skinned hands, pushed herself up, and looked to see where she was.

Dark gray gravel was all around. Farther off, something smooth and dark, with navy blue bumps. The helipad. Farther still, the railing, and beyond it the sky, dark. That was odd—it had been morning. The sound of a moan made Nita turn her head. Kit was close by, lying on his side with his hands over his face. Sitting on his shoulder, looking faint as a spark about to go out, was Fred.

Nita sat up straighter, even though it made her head spin. She had fallen a long way; she didn't want to remember how far. . . . "Kit," she whispered. "You okay? Fred?"

Kit turned over, pushed himself up on his hands to a sitting position, and groaned again. Fred clung to him. "I don't think I busted anything," Kit said, slow and uncertain. "I hurt all over. Fred, what about you?"

(The Sun is gone,) Fred said, sounding absolutely horrified.

Kit looked out across the helipad into the darkness and rubbed his eyes. "Me and my bright ideas. What have I got us into?"

"As much my bright idea as yours," Nita said. "If it weren't for me, we wouldn't have been out by that worldgate in the first place. Anyway, Kit, where else could we have gone? Those perytons—"

Kit shuddered. "Don't even talk about them. I'd sooner be here than have *them* get me." He got to his knees, then stood up, swaying for a moment. "Oooh. C'mon, let's see where the worldgate went."

He headed off across the gravel. Nita got up on her knees too, then caught sight of a bit of glitter lying a few feet away and grabbed at it happily. Her pen, none the worse for wear. She clipped it securely to the pocket of her shirt and went after Kit and Fred.

Kit was heading for the south-facing railing. "I guess since you only called for a retrieval, the gate dumped us back on top of the . . ."

His voice trailed off suddenly as he reached the railing. Nita came up beside him and saw why.

The city was changed. A shiver ran all through Nita, like the odd feeling that comes with an attack of *déjà vu*—but this was true memory, not the illusion of it. She recognized the place from her first spell with Kit—the lowering, sullen-feeling gloom, the shadowed island held prisoner between its dark, icy rivers. Frowning buildings hunched themselves against the oppressive, slaty sky. Traffic moved, but very little of it, and it did so in the dark. Few headlights or taillights showed anywhere. The usual bright stream of cars and trucks and buses was here only dimly seen motion and a faint sound of snarling engines. And the sky! It wasn't clouded over; it wasn't night. It was *empty*. Just a featureless grayness, hanging too low, like a ceiling. Simply by looking at it Nita knew that Fred was right. There was no Sun behind it, and there were no stars—only this wall of gloom, shutting them in, imprisoning them with the presence Nita remembered from the spell, that she could feel faintly even now. It wasn't aware of her, but . . . She pushed back away from the rail, remembering the rowan's words. (The Other. The Witherer, the Kindler of Wildfires—)

"Kit," she said, whispering, this time doing it to keep from perhaps being overheard by *that*. "I think we better get out of here."

He backed away from the rail too, a step at a time. "Well," he said, very low, "now we know what your pen was doing in New York City . . ."

"The sooner it's out of here, the happier I'll be. Kit—*where did the worldgate go?*"

He shook his head, came back to stand beside her. "Wherever it went, it's not out *there* now."

Nita let out an unhappy breath. "Why should it be? Everything else is changed." She looked back at the helipad. The stairwell was still there, but its door had been ripped away and lay buckled on the gravel. The helipad itself had no design painted on it for a helicopter to center on when landing. The glass of the small building by the pad was smashed in some places and filmed all around; the building was full of rubble and trash, a ruin. "Where *are* we?" Nita said.

"The place we saw in the spell. Manhattan—"

"But different." Nita chewed her lip nervously. "Is this an alternate world, maybe? The next universe over? The worldgate *was* just set for a retrieval, but we jumped through; maybe we messed up its workings. Carl said this one was easy to mess up."

"I wonder how much trouble you get in for busting a worldgate," Kit muttered.

"I think we're in enough trouble right now. We have to *find* the thing."

(See if you can find me the Sun and the stars and the rest of the Universe while you're at it,) Fred said. He sounded truly miserable, much worse than when he had swallowed the pen. (I don't know how long I can bear this silence.)

Kit stood silent for a moment, staring out at that grim cold cityscape. "There *is* a spell we can use to find it that doesn't need anything but words," he said. "Good thing. We don't have much in the way of supplies. We'll need your help, though, Fred. Your claudication was connected to the worldgate's when we went through. You can be used to trace it."

(Anything to get us out of this place,) Fred said.

"Well," Nita said, "let's find a place to get set up."

The faint rattling noise of helicopter rotors interrupted her. She looked westward along the long axis of the roof, toward the dark half-hidden blot that was Central Park, or another version of it.

A small flying shape came wheeling around the corner of a skyscraper a few blocks away and cruised steadily toward the roof where they stood, the sharp chatter of its blades ricocheting more and more loudly off the blank dark faces of neighboring skyscrapers. "We better get under cover," Kit said. Nita started for the stairwell, and Kit headed after her, but a bit more slowly. He kept throwing glances over his shoulder at the approaching chopper, both worried by it and interested in it. Nita looked over her shoulder too, to tell him to hurry—and then realized how close the chopper was, how fast it was coming. A standard two-seat helicopter, wiry skeleton, glass bubble protecting the seats, oval doors on each side. But the bubble's glass was filmed over except for the doors, which glittered oddly. They had a faceted look. *No pilot could see out of that*, Nita thought, confused. *And the skids, the landing skids are wrong somehow*. The helicopter came sweeping over their heads, low, too low.

"KIT!" Nita yelled. She spun around and tackled him, knocking him flat, as the skids made a lightning jab at the place where he had been a moment before, and hit the gravel with a screech of metal. The helicopter soared on past them, refolding its skids, not yet able to slow down from the speed of its first attack. The thunderous rattling of its rotors mixed with another sound, a high frustrated shriek like that of a predator that has missed its kill—and almost immediately they heard something else too, an even higher pitched squealing, ratchety and metallic, produced by several sources and seeming to come from inside the ruined glass shelter.

Kit and Nita clutched at each other, getting a better look at the helicopter from behind as it swung around for another pass. The "skids" were doubled-back limbs of metal like those of a praying mantis, cruelly clawed. Under what should have been the helicopter's "bubble," sharp dark mandibles worked hungrily—and as the chopper heeled over and came about, those faceted eyes *looked* at Kit and Nita with the cold, businesslike glare reserved for helpless prey.

"We're dead," Nita whispered.

"Not yet." Kit gasped, staggering up again. "The stairwell—" Together he and Nita ran for the stairs as the chopper-creature arrowed across the rooftop at them. Nita was almost blind with terror; she knew now what had torn the door off the stairwell and doubted there was any way to keep that thing from getting them. They fell into the stairwell together. The chopper roared past again, not losing so much time in its turn this time, coming about to hover like a deadly dragonfly while positioning itself for another jab with those steel claws. Kit fell farther down the stairs than Nita did, hit his head against a wall, and lay moaning. Nita slid and scrabbled to a stop, then turned to see that huge, horrible face glaring into the stairwell, sighting on her for the jab. It was unreal. None of it could possibly be real; it was all a dream; and with the inane desperation of a dreamer in a nightmare, Nita felt for the only thing at hand, the rowan rod, and slashed at the looming face with it.

She was completely unprepared for the result. A whip of silver fire the color of the full Moon cracked across the bubble-face from the rod, which glowed in her hand. Screaming in pain and rage, the chopper-creature backed up and away, but only a little. The razor-combed claws shot down at her. She slashed at them too, and when the moonfire curled around them, the creature screamed again and pulled them back.

"Kit!" she yelled, not daring to turn her back on those raging, ravenous eyes. "Kit! The antenna!"

She heard him fumbling around in his pack as the hungry helicopter took another jab at her, and she whipped it again with fire. Quite suddenly something fired past her ear—a bright, narrow line of blazing red light the color of metal in the forge. The molten light struck the helicopter in the underbelly, splattering in bright hot drops, and the answering scream was much more terrible this time.

"It's a machine," Nita said, gasping. "Your department."

"Great," Kit said, crawling up the stairs beside her. "How do you kill a helicopter?" But he braced one arm on the step just above his face, laid the antenna over it, and fired again. The chopper-creature screeched again and swung away.

Kit scrambled up to his feet, pressed himself flat against what remained of the crumbling doorway, pointed the antenna again. Red fire lanced out, followed by Nita's white as she dove back out into the stinging wind and thunder of rotors and slashed at the horror that hung and grabbed from midair. Gravel flew and stung, the wind lashed her face with her hair, the air was full of that ear-tearing metallic scream, but she kept slashing. White fire snapped and curled—and then from around the other side of the chopper-creature there came a sharp *crack!* as a bolt of Kit's hot light fired upward. The scream that followed made all the preceding ones sound faint. Nita wished she could drop the wand and cover her ears, but she didn't dare—and anyway she was too puzzled by the creature's reaction. That shot hadn't hit anywhere on its body that she could see. Still screaming, it began to spin helplessly in a circle like a toy pinwheel. Kit had shattered the helicopter's tail rotor. It might still be airborne, but it couldn't fly straight, or steer. Nita danced back from another jab of those legs, whipped the eyes again with the silver fire of the rowan wand as they spun past her. From the other side there was another *crack!* and a shattering sound, and the bubble-head spinning past her again showed one faceted eye now opaque, spiderwebbed with cracks. The helicopter lurched and rose, trying to gain altitude and get away.

Across the roof Kit looked up, laid the antenna across his forearm again, took careful aim, fired. This time the molten line of light struck through the blurring main rotors. With a high, anguished, ringing snap, one rotor flew off and pinwheeled away almost too fast to see. The helicopter gave one last wild screech, bobbled up, then sideways, as if staggering through the air. "Get down!" Kit screamed at Nita, throwing himself on the ground. She did the same, covering her head with her arms and frantically gasping the syllables of the defense-shield spell.

The explosion shook everything and sent gravel flying to bounce off the hardened air around her like hail off a car roof. Jagged blade shards snapped and rang and shot in all directions. Only when the roaring and the wash of heat that followed it died down to quiet and flickering light did Nita dare to raise her head. The helicopter-creature was a broken-backed wreck with oily flame licking through it. The eye that Kit had shattered stared blindly up at the dark sky from the edge of the helipad; the tail assembly, twisted and bent, lay half under the creature's body. The only sounds left were the wind and that shrill keening from the little glass building, now much muted. Nita rid herself of the shielding spell and got slowly to her feet. "Fred?" she whispered.

A pale spark floated shakily through the air to perch on her shoulder. (Here,) he said, sounding as tremulous as Nita felt. (Are you well?)

She nodded, walked toward the wreck.

Kit stood on the other side of it, his fist clenched on the antenna. He was shaking visibly. The sight of his terror made Nita's worse as she came to stand by him. "Kit," she said, fighting the urge to cry and losing—tears spilled out anyway. "This is *not* a nice place," she said.

He gulped, leaking tears himself. "No," he said, trying to keep his voice steady, "it sure isn't." He looked over at the glass-walled building.

"Yeah," Nita said, scrubbing at her face. "We better have a look."

Slowly and carefully they approached the building, came to one collapsed wall, peered in. Nita held her wand high, so they could see by its glow. Inside, hidden amid the trash and broken glass, was what seemed to be a rude nest built of scraps of metal and wire. In the nest were three baby helicopters, none more than two feet long. They stared fiercely at Kit and Nita from tiny faceted eyes like their parent's, and threatened with little jabbing forelegs, whirring with rotors too small to lift them yet. Sharing the nest with the fledglings was the partially stripped skeleton of a dog.

Kit and Nita turned away together. "I think maybe we should go downstairs a little ways before we do that finding spell," Kit said, his voice still shaking. "If there's another of those things—"

"Yeah." They headed down the stairwell, to the door that in their own world had opened onto the elevator corridor. The two of them sat down, and Nita laid the rowan wand in her lap so there would be light—the ceiling lights in the stairwell were out, and the place felt like the bottom of a hole.

"Fred," Kit said, "how're you holding up?"

Fred hung between them, his light flickering. (A little better than before. The silence is still very terrible. But at least you two are here.)

"We'll find you the Sun, Fred," Nita said, wishing she was as sure as she was trying to sound. "Kit, which spell was it you were going to use?"

Kit had his manual out. "At the bottom of page 318. It's a double, we read together."

Nita got out her own book, paged through it. "McKillip's Stricture? That's for keeping grass short!"

"No, no!" Kit leaned over to look at Nita's manual. "Huh. How about that, our pages are different. Look under 'Eisodics and Diascheses.' The fourth one after the general introduction. Davidson's Minor Enthalpy."

Nita riffled through some more pages. Evidently her book had more information than Kit's on the spells relating to growing things. Her suspicion about what their specialties were grew stronger. "Got it." She glanced through the spell. "Fred, you don't have to do anything actually. But this is one of those spells that'll leave us blind to what's happening around here. Watch for us?"

(Absolutely!)

"Okay," Kit said. "Ready? One—two—three—"

They spoke together, slowly and carefully, matching cadence as they described the worldgate, and their own needs, in the Speech.

The shadowy stairwell grew darker still, though this darkness seemed less hostile than what hung overhead; and in the deepening dimness, the walls around them slowly melted away. It seemed to Nita that she and Kit and the small bright point between them hung at a great height, unsupported, over a city built of ghosts and dreams. The buildings that had looked real and solid from the roof now seemed transparent skeletons, rearing up into the gloom of this place. Stone and steel and concrete were shadows—and gazing through them, down the length of the island, Nita saw again the two points of light that she and Kit had seen in the first spell.

The closer one, perhaps ten blocks north in the east Fifties, still pulsed with its irregular, distressing light. Compelled by the spell's working, Nita looked closely at it, though that was the last thing she wanted to do—that bit of angry brightness seemed to be looking back at her. But she had no choice. She examined the light, and into her mind, poured there by the spell, came a description of the light's nature in the Speech. She would have backed away, as she had from the perytons, except that again there was nowhere to go. A catalogue of sorts, that light was—a listing, a set of descriptions. But all wrong, all twisted, angry as the light looked, hungry as the helicopter-creature had been, hating as the surrounding darkness was, full of the horrors that everything in existence could become. The *Book Which Is Not Named* . . .

Nita struggled, though unable to move or cry out; her mind beat at the spell like a bird in a cage, and finally the spell released her. But only to look in the other direction, downtown toward the Wall Street end of the island. There in the illogical-looking tangle of streets built before the regular gridwork of Manhattan was laid down, buried amid the ghosts of buildings, another light throbbed, regular, powerful, unafraid. It flared, it dazzled with white silver fire, and Nita thought of the moonlight radiance of the rowan wand.

In a way, the spell said, this second light was the source of the wand's power, even though here and now the source was bound and limited. This time the syllables of the Speech were no crushing weight of horror. They were a song, one Nita wished would never stop. Courage, merriment, an invitation to everything in existence to be what it was, be the best it could be, grow, *live*—description, affirmation, encouragement, all embodied in one place, one source, buried in the shadows. The *Book of Night with Moon*.

A feeling of urgency came over Nita, and the spell told her that without the protection of the bright *Book*, she and Kit and Fred would never survive the hungry malevolence of this place long enough to find the worldgate and escape. Nor, for that matter, would they be able to find the worldgate at all; it was being held against them by powers adept in wizardries more potent than anything the two of them could manage. It would be folly to try matching wizardries with the Lone Power on its own ground, this outworld long given over to its rule. Their best chance was to find the bright *Book* and free it of the constraint that held its power helpless. Then there might be a chance.

The spell shut itself off, finished. Walls and physical darkness curdled around them again. Kit and Nita looked at each other, uncertain.

"We've been had," Kit said.

Nita shook her head, not following him.

"Remember Tom saying it was odd that our first spell turned up Fred and the news that the bright *Book* was missing? And what Picchu said then?"

"There are no accidents," Nita murmured.

"Uh-huh. How likely do you think it is that all *this* is an accident? Something *wanted* us here, I bet." Kit scowled. "They might have asked *us!* It's not fair!"

Nita held still for a moment, considering this. "Well, maybe they did ask us."

"Huh? Not *me*, I—"

"The Oath."

Kit got quiet quickly. "Well," he admitted after a while, "it did have all kinds of warnings in front of it. And I went ahead and read it anyway."

"So did I." Nita closed her eyes for a second, breathing out, and heard something in the back of her head, a thread of memory: *Did I do right? Go find out . . .* "Look," she said, opening her eyes again, "maybe we're not as bad off as we think. Tom did say that younger wizards have more power. We don't have a lot of supplies, but we're both pretty good with the Speech by now, and Fred is here to help. We're armed—" She glanced down at the rowan wand, still lying moon bright in her lap.

"For how long?" Kit said. He sighed too. "Then again, I guess it doesn't matter much—if we're going to find the bright *Book*, the only way to do it is to hurry. Somebody knows we're here. That thing showed up awful fast—" He nodded at the roof.

"Yeah." Nita got up, took a moment to stretch, then glanced down at Kit. He wasn't moving. "What's the matter?"

Kit stared at the antenna in his hands. "When I was talking to the Edsel it told me some things about the Powers that didn't want intelligence to happen in machines. They knew that people would start talking to them, make friends with them. Everybody would be happier as a result. Those Powers—" He looked up. "If I understood that spell right, the one running this place is the chief of them all, the worst of them. The Destroyer, the engenderer of rust—"

"Kit!"

"I know, you shouldn't name it—" He got up, held out a hand to Fred, who bobbled over to Kit and came to rest on his palm. "But that's who we're up against. Or what. Fred, do you know what we're talking about?"

Fred's thought was frightened but steady. (The Starsnuffer,) he said. (The one who saw light come to be and could not make it in turn—and so rebelled against it, and declared a war of darkness. Though the rebellion didn't work as well as it might have, for darkness only made the light seem brighter.)

Kit nodded. "That's the one. If we do get the bright *Book*, that's who'll come after us."

Fred shuddered a flicker of light so like a spark about to go out in the wind that Kit hurriedly tucked the antenna under his arm and cupped his other hand around Fred protectively. (I've lost enough friends to that one,) Fred said, (heard enough songs stilled. People gone nova before their time, or fallen through naked singularities into places where you burn forever but don't learn anything from it.)

For a moment neither of them could follow Fred's thought. Though he was using the Speech, as always, they couldn't follow what other things he was describing, only that those things were as terrible a warped thing as the helicopter-creature was to them. (No matter,) he said at last. (You two are part of the answer to stopping that kind of thing. Otherwise my search for an Advisory nexus wouldn't have brought me to you. Let's do what we can.)

Kit nodded. "Whatever that is. I wish I knew where to begin."

Nita leaned back against the wall. "Didn't Tom say something about the two Books being tied together? So that you could use one to guide you to the other?"

"Yeah."

"Well. We're not too far from the dark one." Nita swallowed. "If we could get hold of that—and use it to lead us to the bright one. That vision only gave a general idea of where the *Book of Night with Moon* was. Probably because of its being restrained, or guarded, or whatever—"

"Steal the dark Book?" Kit looked at Nita as if she had taken leave of her senses. "Sure! And then have—," he waved his hand at the northward wall, not wanting to say any name, "—and Lord knows what else come chasing after us?"

"Why not?" Nita retorted. "It's a better chance than going straight for the bright one, which we *know* is guarded somehow. We'd go fumbling around down there in the financial district and probably get caught right away. But why would they guard the dark Book? They're the only ones who would want it! I bet you we could get at the dark one a lot more easily than the other."

Kit chewed his lip briefly. "Well?" Nita said. "What do you think?"

"I think you're probably nuts. But we can't just sit here, and it wouldn't hurt to go see what the situation is—Fred?"

(Lead,) Fred said, (I'll follow.)

Kit gently tossed Fred back into the air and paused long enough to put his book away. He didn't put the antenna away, though. The rowan wand glowed steadily and brilliantly. "Can't you damp that down a little?" Kit said. "If somebody sees us—"

"No, I can't. I tried." Nita cast about for ways to hide it, finally settled on sticking it in her back jeans pocket and settling her down vest over it. "Better?"

"Yeah." Kit had turned his attention to the doorknob. He touched it, spoke softly to it in the Speech, turned it. Nothing happened. "Not listening?" he wondered out loud, and bent to touch the keyhole. "Now why— Ow!" He jumped back, almost knocking Nita over.

"What's the matter?"

Kit was sucking on his finger, looking pained. "Bit me!" he said, removing the finger to examine it. It bled.

"I get the feeling," Nita said slowly, "that there's not much here that's friendly."

"Yeah." Kit looked glumly at the doorknob. "I guess we'd better consider everything we see potentially dangerous." He lifted the antenna, bent down by the lock again, and touched the keyhole delicately with the knob at the antenna's end. A brief red spark spat from the antenna; the innards of the lock clicked. This time when Kit turned the knob, the door came open a crack.

With great caution he opened the door a bit more, peered out, then opened it all the way and motioned Nita to follow him. Together they stepped out into a hall much like the elevator corridor in their own world, but dark and silent. (The elevator?) Kit said inwardly, not wanting to break that ominous quiet.

(Do you trust it?)

(No. Know where the stairs are?)

(Down the way we came. Past the elevator.)

The door to the main stairway had to be coerced into opening by the same method as the door to the roof. When they were through it Kit spent another moment getting it to lock again, then stepped over to the banister and looked down at story after story of switchback stairs. (It could be worse,) Nita said. (We could be going up.)

(It *will* be worse,) Kit said. (If the worldgate stays at this level, we're going to *have* to come back up . . .)

They headed down. It took a long time. The few times they dared stop to rest, Kit and Nita heard odd muffled noises through the walls—vaguely threatening scrapes and groans and rumbles, the kind of sounds heard in nightmares. The stairs were as dark as the corridor had been, and it was hard to sit in the corner of a landing, rubbing aching legs, with only the light of Nita's wand to argue with the blackness that towered above and yawned below, as those sounds got louder.

They quickly lost count of how many stories downward they'd gone. All the landings looked the same, and all the doors from them opened off into the same pitch blackness—until finally Kit eased one open as he had eased open scores of others and abruptly stood very still. He put his hand out behind him. (Nita! The wand.)

She passed it to him. It dimmed in his hand from moonfire to foxfire, a faint silver glimmer that he held out the door as he looked around. (It's all that shiny stone, like the other lobby. There should be a way down into the station, then—)

Nita's hair stood up on end at the thought. (Kit, you saw what happened to helicopters. Do you really want to meet a *train?* Let's go out on the street level, okay?)

He gulped and nodded. (Which way?)

(There's a door out onto Forty-fifth Street. C'mon.)

She slipped out, and Kit followed with the wand. Its pale light reached just far enough ahead to gleam off the glass wall at the end of the corridor. Near it was the down escalator, frozen dead. They made their way softly down it, then across the slick floor and out the glass doors to the street.

It was nearly as dark outside as it had been inside; a night without a hint of Moon or stars. The air down there wasn't as chill as it had been on the building's roof, but it stank of dark city smells—exhaust, spilled gasoline, garbage, and soot. The gutter was clogged with trash. They stepped out to cross Forty-fifth.

"No," Nita hissed, startled into speech, and dragged Kit back into the dark of the doorway. Pale yellow-brown light flickered down the street, got brighter. A second later, with a snarl of its engine, a big yellow Checker Cab hurled itself past them, staring in front of it with headlight-eyes burned down to yellow threads of filament—eyes that looked somehow as if they could see. But the cab seemed not to notice them. Its snarl diminished as it plunged down the street, leaving a whirl of dirty paper and dead leaves in its wake. Kit coughed as its exhaust hit them.

(That was alive,) he said when he got his breath back. (The same way the helicopter was.)

Nita made a miserable face. (Let's get outta here,) she said.

Kit nodded. She led him off to their left, through the Helmsley-Spear Building, which should have been bright with gold-leafed statuary. Here it was gray with soot, and the carvings stared down with such looks of silent malice that Nita refused to glance up more than that once.

She hoped for some more encouraging sight as they came onto Forty-sixth Street and looked up Park Avenue. The hope was vain. The avenue stretched away and slightly upward for blocks as it did in their own world, vanishing in the murk. But the divider between the uptown and downtown lanes, usually green with shrubbery, had become one long tangle of barren thornbushes. The old-fashioned red-and-green traffic lights burned low and dark as if short on power; and no matter how long one watched, they never changed from red. The shining glass-and-steel office buildings that had lined the avenue in their Manhattan were grimy shells here, the broad sidewalks before them cluttered with rubbish. Nothing moved anywhere, except far up Park, where another pair of yellow eyes waited at a corner.

Those eyes made Nita nervous. (This way,) she said. She hurried past a dirty granite facade full of still doors and silent windows. Kit followed close, and Fred with him, both looking worriedly at everything they passed.

Nita was doing her best to keep herself calm as they turned the corner onto Forty-seventh. *It can't all be as bad as the helicopter*, she told herself. *And nothing really bad has happened to us yet. It was just the shock of the—*

She jumped back into the shadow of a building on hearing a clapping sound so loud she felt sure the helicopter's mate was coming for them. Fred and Kit huddled terrified into that shadow, too, and it took a few seconds for any of them to find the source of the sound. Not more than five or six feet from them, a pigeon had landed—a sooty dark one, cooing and strutting and head bobbing in a perfectly normal fashion. It walked away from them, muttering absently, intent on its own pursuits. Kit poked Nita from behind—not a warning: a teasing poke. (Getting jumpy, huh?)

(Yeah, well, *you* were the one who said—)

The lightning stroke of motion not six feet away knocked the merriment right out of them. What had seemed a perfectly ordinary fire hydrant, dull yellow, with rust stains and peeling paint, suddenly cracked open and shot out a long, pale, ropy tongue like a toad's. The pigeon never had a chance. Hit side on, the bird made just one strangled gobbling noise before the tongue was gone again, too fast to follow, and the wide horizontal mouth it came from was closed again. All that remained to show that anything had happened was a slight bulge under the metallic-looking skin of the fire hydrant. The bulge heaved once and was still.

Nita bit her lip. Behind her she could feel Kit start shaking again. (I feel sorry for the next dog that comes along,) he said. (I hope you don't mind if I cross the street.) Kit headed out of the shadow.

(I think I'll join you,) Nita said. She backed out of range of that tongue before she started across the street herself.

There was no time to move, to scream, even to think. Kit was halfway across the street, with his eye on that fire hydrant, his head turned away from the big yellow Checker Cab that was maybe six feet away and leaping straight at him.

A flash of brilliance struck Nita like a blow, and did the same for the cab, so that it swerved to its left and knocked Kit sideways and down. The cab roared on by, engine racing in frustration, evidently too angry to try for another pass. But something about it, maybe the savage sidelong look it threw Nita out of its burned-down eyes as it squealed around the corner of Forty-sixth and Madison—something made Nita suspect that it would not forget them. She ran out into the street and bent over Kit, not sure whether she should try to move him.

" 'S awright," Kit said, groaning softly as he worked at getting up. Nita slipped hands under his arms to help. "Fred did it."

(Are you all right?) came the frantic thought, as Fred appeared in front of Kit's face. (Did I hurt you? Did I emit anything you can't take? I took out all the ultraviolet. Oh no! I forgot the cosmic rays again.)

Kit managed a smile, though not much of one; his face was skinned and bruised where one cheekbone had hit the pavement. (Don't worry about it, Fred. That thing would have done a lot worse to me than a few cosmic rays if it'd hit me the way it wanted to.) He stood up, wincing. (It got my leg some, I think.)

Nita bent down to look at Kit's left leg and sucked in her breath. His jeans were torn, and he had a straight horizontal gash six inches or so below the knee, which was bleeding freely. (Does it feel deep?)

(No. It just hurts a lot. I think it was the cab's fender, there was a jagged piece sticking out of the chrome. Listen, Fred, thanks—)

(You're sure I didn't hurt you? You people are so fragile. A little gamma radiation will ruin your whole day, it seems.)

(I'm fine. But I've gotta do something about this leg. And then we've got to get moving again and get to the dark Book.)

Nita looked over at the fire hydrant, fear boiling in her. Casually, as if this was something it did many times a day, the hydrant cracked open and spat something out onto the sidewalk—a dessicated-looking little lump of bones and feathers. Then it got up and waddled heavily down to a spot about fifty feet farther down the block, and sat down again.

And I thought it couldn't all be bad.

Together, as quickly as they could, two small, frightened-looking figures and a spark like a lost star hurried into the shadows and vanished there.

Entropics:

DETECTION
AND AVOIDANCE

(HOW CLOSE ARE WE?)

(Uh . . . this is Madison and Forty-ninth. Three blocks north and a long one east.)

(Can we rest? This air burns to breathe. And we've been going fast.)

(Yeah, let's.)

They crouched together in the shadow of a doorway, two wary darknesses and a dim light, watching the traffic that went by. Mostly cabs prowled past, wearing the same hungry look as the one that had wounded Kit. Or a sullen truck might lumber by, or a passenger car, looking uneasy and dingy and bitter. None of the cars or trucks had drivers, or looked like they wanted them. They ignored the traffic lights, and their engines growled.

Nita's eyes burned in the dark air. She rubbed them and glanced down at Kit's leg, bound now with a torn-off piece of her shirt. (How is it?)

(Not too bad. It feels stiff. I guess it stopped bleeding.) He looked down, felt the makeshift bandage, winced. (Yeah . . . I'm hungry.)

Nita's stomach turned over—she was too nervous to even consider eating—as Kit came up with a ham sandwich and offered her half. (You go ahead,) she said. She leaned against the hard cold wall, and on a sudden thought pulled her pen out of her pocket and looked at it. It seemed all right, but as she held it she could feel a sort of odd tingling in its metal that hadn't been there before.

(Uh, Fred—)

He hung beside her at eye level, making worried feelings that matched the dimness of his light. (Are you *sure* that light didn't hurt you?)

(Yeah. It's not that.) She held out the pen to him. Fred backed away a little, as if afraid he might swallow it again. (Is this radioactive or anything?) Nita said.

He drifted close to it, bobbed up and down to look at it from several angles. (You mean beta and gamma and those other emissions you have trouble with? No.)

Nita still felt suspicious about the pen. She dug into her backpack for a piece of scrap paper, laid it on her wizards' manual, clicked the point out, and scribbled on the paper. Then she breathed out, perplexed. (Come *on*, Fred! Look at that!)

He floated down to look. The pen's blue-black ink would normally have been hard to see in that dimness, no matter how white the paper. But the scrawl had a subtle glimmer about it, a luminosity just bright enough to make out. (I don't think it's anything harmful to you,) Fred said. (Are you sure it didn't do that before?)

(Yes!)

(Well, look at it this way. Now you can see what you're writing when it's dark. Surprising you people hadn't come up with something like that already.)

Nita shook her head, put the paper away, and clipped the pen back in her pocket. Kit, finishing the first half of his sandwich, looked over at the scribble with interest. (Comes of being inside Fred, I guess. With him having his own claudication, and all the energy boiling around inside him, you might have expected something like that to happen.)

(Yeah, well, I don't like it. The pen was fine the way it was.)

(Considering where it's been,) Kit said, (you're lucky to get it back in the same shape, instead of crushed into a little lump.) He wrapped up the other half of his sandwich and shoved it into his backpack. (Should we go?)

(Yeah.)

They got up, checked their surroundings as usual to make sure that no cabs or cars were anywhere close, and started up Madison again, ducking into doorways or between buildings whenever they saw or heard traffic coming.

(No people,) Kit said, as if trying to work it out. (Just things—all dark and ruined—and machines, all twisted. Alive—but they seem to hate everything. And pigeons—)

(Dogs, too,) Nita said.

(Where?) Kit looked hurriedly around him.

(Check the sidewalk and the gutter. They're here. And remember that nest.) Nita shrugged uneasily, setting her pack higher. (I don't know. Maybe people just can't live here.)

(*We're* here,) Kit said unhappily. (And maybe not for long.)

A sudden grinding sound like tortured metal made them dive for another shadowy doorway close to the corner of Madison and Fiftieth. No traffic was in sight; nothing showed but the glowering eye of the traffic light and the unchanging DON'T WALK signs. The grinding sound came again—metal scraping on concrete, somewhere across Madison, down Fiftieth, to their left. Kit edged a bit forward in the doorway.

(What are you—)

(I want to see.) He reached around behind him, taking the antenna in hand.

(But if—)

(If that's something that might chase us later, I at least want a look at it. Fred? Take a peek for us?)

(Right.) Fred sailed ahead of them, keeping low and close to the building walls, his light dimmed to the faintest glimmer. By the lamppost at Madison and Fiftieth he paused, then shot low across the street and down Fiftieth between Madison and Fifth, vanishing past the corner. Nita and Kit waited, sweating.

From around the corner Fred radiated feelings of uncertainty and curiosity. (These are like the other things that run these streets. But these aren't moving. Maybe they were dangerous once. I don't know about now.)

(Come on,) Kit said. He put his head out of the doorway. (It's clear.)

With utmost caution they crossed the street and slipped around the corner, flattening to the wall. Here stores and dingy four-story brownstones with long flights of railed stairs lined the street. Halfway down the block, jagged and bizarre in the dimness and the feeble yellow glow of a flickering sodium-vapor streetlight, was the remains of an accident. One car, a heavy two-door sedan, lay crumpled against the pole of another nearby streetlight, its right-hand door ripped away and the whole right side of it laid open. A little distance away, in the middle of the street, lay the car that had hit the sedan, resting on its back and skewed right around so that its front end was pointed at Kit and Nita. It was a sports car of some kind, so dark a brown that it was almost black. Its windshield had been cracked when it overturned, and it had many other dents and scrapes, some quite deep. From its front right wheel well jutted a long jagged strip of chrome, part of the other car's fender, now wound into the sports car's wheel.

(I don't get it,) Nita said silently. (If that dark one hit the other, why isn't its front all smashed in?)

She broke off as with a terrible metallic groan the sports car suddenly rocked back and forth, like a turtle on its back trying to right itself. Kit sucked in a long breath and didn't move. The car stopped rocking for a moment, then with another scrape of metal started again, rocking more energetically this time. Each time the side-to-side motion became larger. It rocked partway onto one door, then back the other way and partway onto the other, then back again—and full onto its left-hand door. There it balanced, precarious, for a few long seconds, as if getting its breath. And then it twitched hard, shuddered all the way over, and fell right-side down.

The scream that filled the air as the sports car came down on the fender-tangled right wheel was terrible to hear. Instantly it hunched up the fouled wheel, holding it away from the street, crouching on the three good wheels and shaking with its effort. Nita thought of an old sculpture she had seen once, a wounded lion favoring one forelimb—weary and in pain, but still dangerous.

Very slowly, as if approaching a hurt animal and not wanting to alarm it, Kit stepped away from the building and walked out into the street.

(*Kit!*)

(Ssssh,) he said silently. (Don't freak it.)

(*Are you out of your—*)

(*Ssssshhh!*)

The sports car watched Kit come, not moving. Now that it was right-side up, Nita could get a better idea of its shape. It was actually rather beautiful in its deadly looking way—sleekly swept-back and slung low to the ground. Its curves were battered in places; its once-shining hide was scored and dull. It stared at Kit from hunter's eyes, headlights wide with pain, and breathed shallowly, waiting.

(Lotus Esprit,) Kit said to Nita, not taking his eyes off the car, matching it stare for stare.

Nita shook her head anxiously. (Does that mean something? I don't know cars.)

(It's a racer. A mean one. What it is *here*— Look, Nita, there's your answer. Look at the front of it, under the headlights.) He kept moving forward, his hands out in front of him. The Lotus held perfectly still, watching.

Nita looked at the low-sloping grille. (It's all full of oil or something.)

(It's a predator. These other cars, like that sedan—they must be what it hunts. This time its prey hurt the Lotus before it made its kill. Like a tiger getting gored by a bull or something. Ooops!)

Kit, eight or ten feet away from the Lotus's grille, took one step too many; it abruptly rolled back away from him a foot or so. Very quietly its engine stuttered to life and settled into a throaty growl.

(Kit, you're—)

(Shut up.) *"I won't hurt you,"* he said in the Speech, aloud. *"Let me see to that wheel."*

The engine growl got louder—the sound of the Speech seemed to upset the Lotus. It rolled back another couple of feet, getting close to the curb, and glared at Kit. But the glare seemed to have as much fear as threat in it now.

"I won't hurt you," Kit repeated, stepping closer, holding out his hands, one of them with the antenna in it. *"Come on, you know what this is. Let me do something about that wheel. You can't run on it. And if you can't run, or hunt—I bet there are other hunters here, aren't there? Or scavengers. I'm sure there are scavengers. Who'll be coming here to clean up this kill? And do you want them to find you here, helpless?"*

The Lotus stared at him, shifting a little from side to side now, swaying uncertainly. The growl had not stopped, but it hadn't gotten any louder either. *"If I were going to hurt you, I would have by now,"* Kit said, getting closer. The car was four feet away, and its headlights were having to look up at Kit now. *"Just let me do something about that fender stuck in you, then you'll go your way and I'll go mine."*

The dark eyes stared at the antenna, then at Kit, and back at the antenna again. The Lotus stopped swaying, held very still. Kit was two feet away. He reached out with his free hand, very slowly, reached down to touch the scratched fiberglass hide.

The engine raced, a sudden startling roar that made Nita stifle a scream and made Kit flinch all over—but he didn't jump away, and neither did the Lotus. For a second or two he and the car stood there just looking at each other—small trembling boy, large trembling predator. Then Kit laid his hand carefully on the brown hide, a gingerly gesture. The car shook all over, stared at him. Its engine quieted to an uncertain rumbling.

"It's okay," he said. *"Will you let me take care of it?"*

The Lotus muttered deep under its hood. It still stared at Kit with those fearsome eyes, but its expression was mostly perplexed now. So was Kit's. He rubbed the curve of the hurt wheel well in distress. (I can't understand why it's mute,) he said unhappily. (The Edsel wasn't. All it took was a couple of sentences in the Speech and it was talking.)

(It's bound,) Nita said, edging out of the shadow of the building she stood against. (Can't you feel it, Kit? There's some kind of huge binding spell laid over this whole place to keep it the way it is.)

She stopped short as the Lotus saw her and began to growl again. *"Relax,"* Kit said. *"She's with me, she won't hurt you either."*

Slowly the growl dwindled, but the feral headlight-eyes stayed on Nita. She gulped and sat down on the curb, where she could see up and down the street. "Kit, do what you're going to do. If another of those cabs comes along—"

"Right. Fred, give me a hand? No, no, no," he said hastily, as Fred drifted down beside him and made a light pattern and a sound as if he was going to emit something. "Not *that* kind. Just make some light so I can see what to do down here."

Kit knelt beside the right wheel, studying the damage, and Fred floated in close to lend his light to the business, while the Lotus watched the process sidelong and suspiciously. "Mmmfff—nothing too bad, it's mostly wrapped around the tire. Lucky it didn't get fouled with the axle.

"Come on, come on," Kit said in the Speech, patting the bottom of the tire,

"relax it, loosen up. You're forcing the scrap into yourself, holding the wheel up like that. Come on." The Lotus moaned softly and with fearful care relaxed the uplifted wheel a bit. *"That's better."* Kit slipped the antenna up under the Lotus's wheel well, aiming for some piece of chrome that was out of sight. "Fred, can you get in there so I can see? Good. *Okay, this may sting a little.*" Molten light, half-seen, sparked under the Lotus's fender. It jumped, and an uneven half-circle-shaped piece of chrome fell clanging onto the pavement. *"Now hunch the wheel up again. A little higher—"* Kit reached in with both hands and, after a moment's tugging and twisting, freed the other half of the piece of metal. *"There,"* Kit said, satisfied. He tossed the second piece of scrap to the ground.

The engine roared again with terrible suddenness, deafening. This time Kit scrambled frantically backward as the Lotus leaped snarling away from him. With a screech of tires it swept so close past Nita that she fell over backward onto the sidewalk. Its engine screaming, the Lotus tore away down Fiftieth toward Madison, flung itself left around the corner in a cloud of blue exhaust, and was gone.

Very slowly Kit stood up, pushed the antenna into his pants pocket, and stood in the street dusting his hands off on his shirt as he gazed in disappointment after the Lotus. Nita sat back up again, shaking her head and brushing at herself. (I thought maybe it was going to stay long enough to thank you,) she said.

Kit shook his head, evidently in annoyance at himself for having thought the same thing. (Well, I don't know—I was thinking of what Picchu said. 'Don't be afraid to help.') He shrugged. (Doesn't really matter, I guess. It was hurting; fixing it was the right thing to do.)

(I hope so,) Nita said. (I'd hate to think the grateful creature might run off to—*you* know—and tell everybody about the people who helped it instead of hurting it. I have a feeling that doing good deeds sticks out more than usual around here.)

Kit nodded, looking uncomfortable. (Maybe I should've left well enough alone.)

(Don't be dumb. Let's get going, huh? The . . . whatever the place is where the dark Book's kept, it's pretty close. I feel nervous standing out here.)

They recrossed Madison and again started the weary progression from doorway to driveway to shadowed wall, heading north.

At Madison and Fifty-second, Nita turned right and paused. (It's on this block somewhere,) she said, trying to keep even the thought quiet. (The north side, I think. Fred, you feel anything?)

Fred held still for a moment, not even making a flicker. (The darkness feels thicker up ahead, at the middle of the block.)

Kit and Nita peered down the block. (It doesn't look any different,) Kit said. (But you're the expert on light, Fred. Lead the way.)

With even greater care than usual they picked their way down Fifty-second. This street was stores and office buildings again; all the store windows empty, all the windows dark. But here, though external appearances were no different, the feeling slowly began to grow that there was a reason for the grimy darkness of the windows. Something watched, something peered out those windows, using the darkness as a cloak, and no shadow was deep enough to hide in; the silent eyes would see. Nothing happened, nothing stirred anywhere. No traffic was in sight. But the street felt more and more like a trap, laid open for some unsuspecting creature to walk into. Nita tried to swallow as they ducked from one hiding place to another, but her mouth was too dry. Kit was sweating. Fred's light was out.

(This is it,) he said suddenly, his thought sounding unusually muted even for Fred. (This is the middle of the darkness.)

(*This?*) Kit and Nita thought at the same time, in shock, and then simultaneously hushed themselves. Nita edged out to the sidewalk to get a better look at the place. She had to crane her neck. They were in front of a skyscraper, faced completely in black plate glass, an ominous, windowless monolith.

(Must be about ninety stories,) Nita said. (I don't see any lights.)

(Why would you?) Fred said. (Whoever lives in this place doesn't seem fond of light at all. How shall we go in?)

Nita glanced back up the street. (We passed a driveway that might go down to a delivery entrance.)

(I'll talk to the lock,) Kit said. (Let's go!)

They went back the way they had come and tiptoed down the driveway. It seemed meant for trucks to back into. A flight of steps at one side led up to a loading platform about four feet above the deepest part of the ramp. Climbing the stairs, Kit went to a door on the right and ran his hands over it as Nita and Fred came up behind. (No lock,) Kit said. (It's controlled from inside.)

(We can't get in? We're dead.)

(We're not dead yet. There's a machine in there that makes the garage doors go up. That's all I need.) Kit got out the antenna and held it against the door as he might have held a pencil he was about to write with. He closed his eyes. (If I can just feel up through the metal and the wires, find it . . .)

Nita and Fred kept still while Kit's eyes squeezed tighter and tighter shut in fierce concentration. Inside one garage door something rattled, fell silent, rattled again, began to grind. Little by little the door rose until there was an opening at the bottom of it, three feet high. Kit opened his eyes but kept the antenna pressed against the metal. (Go on in.)

Fred and Nita ducked through into darkness. Kit came swiftly after them. Behind him, the door began to move slowly downward again, shutting with a thunderous clang. Nita pulled out the rowan wand, so they could look around. There were wooden loading pallets stacked on the floor, but nothing else—bare concrete walls, bare ceiling. Set in the back wall of the huge room was one normal-sized double door.

(Let's see if this one has a lock,) Kit said as they went quietly up to it. He touched the right-hand knob carefully, whispered a word or two in the Speech, tried it. The right side of the double door opened.

(Huh. Wasn't even locked!) Through the open door, much to everyone's surprise, light spilled—plain old fluorescent office-building light, but cheery as a sunny day after the gloom outdoors. On the other side of the door was a perfectly normal-looking corridor with beige walls and charcoal-colored doors and carpeting. The normality came as something of a shock. (Fred, I thought you said it was *darker* here!)

(*Felt* darker. And colder. And it does,) Fred said, shivering, his faint light rippling as he did so. (We're very close to the source of the coldness. It's farther up, though.)

(Up?) Nita looked at Kit uneasily. (If we're going to get the dark Book and get out of here fast, we can't fool with stairs again. We'll have to use the elevators somehow.)

Kit glanced down at the antenna. (I think I can manage an elevator if it gets difficult. Let's find one.)

They slipped through the door and went down the hall to their right, heading for a lobby at its far end. There they peered out at a bank of elevators set in the same dark green marble as the rest of the lobby. No one was there.

Kit walked to the elevators, punched the call button, and hurriedly motioned Nita and Fred to join him. Nita stayed where she was for a moment. (Shouldn't we stay out of sight here?)

(Come on!)

She went out to him, Fred bobbing along beside. Kit watched the elevator lights to see which one was coming down and then slipped into a recess at the side. Nita took the hint and joined him. The elevator bell chimed; doors slid open.

The perytons piled out of the middle elevator in a hurry, five of them together, not looking left or right, and burst out the front door into the street. Once outside they began their awful chorus of howls and snarls, but Nita and Kit and Fred weren't sitting around to listen. They dove into the middle elevator, and Kit struck the control panel with the antenna, hard. *"Close up and take off!"*

The elevator doors closed, but then a rumbling, scraping, gear-grinding screech began—low at first, then louder, a combination of every weird, unsettling noise Nita had ever heard an elevator make. Cables twanged and ratchets ratcheted, and, had they been moving, she would have sworn they were about to go plunging down to crash in the cellar.

"Cut it out or I'll snap your cables myself when I'm through with you!" Kit yelled in the Speech. Almost immediately the elevator jerked slightly and then started upward.

Nita tried again to swallow and had no better luck than the last time. "Those perytons are going to pick up our scent right outside that door, Kit! And they'll track us inside, and it won't be five minutes before—"

"I know, I know. Fred, how well can you feel the middle of the darkness?"

(We're closer.)

"Good. You'll have to tell me when to stop."

The elevator went all the way up to the top, the eighty-ninth floor, before Fred said, (This is it!)

Kit rapped the control panel one last time with his antenna. *"You stay where you are,"* he said.

The elevator doors opened silently to reveal another normal-looking floor, this one more opulent than the floor downstairs. Here the carpets were ivory white and thick; the wall opposite the elevators was one huge bookcase of polished wood, filled with hundreds of books, like volumes of one huge set. Going left they came to another hallway, stretching off to their left like the long stroke of an *L*; this one too was lined with bookcases. At the far end stood a huge polished desk, with papers and Dictaphone equipment and an intercom and a multiline phone jumbled about on it. At the desk sat . . .

It was hard to know *what* to call it. Kit and Nita, peering around the corner, were silent with confusion and fear. The thing sitting in a secretary's swivel chair and typing on an expensive electric typewriter was dark green and warty, and sat about four feet high in the chair. It had limbs with tentacles and claws, all knotted together under a big eggplant-shaped head, and goggly, wicked eyes. All the limbs didn't seem to help the creature's typing much, for every few seconds it made a mistake and went grumbling and fumbling over the top of its messy desk for a bottle of correcting fluid. The creature's grumbling was of more interest then its typing. It used the Speech, but haltingly, as if it didn't care much for the language—and indeed the smooth, stately rhythms of the wizardly tongue suffered somewhat, coming out of that misshapen mouth.

Kit leaned back against the wall. (We've gotta do something. Fred, are you *sure* it's up here?)

(Absolutely. And past that door, behind that—) Fred indicated the warty typist. From down the hall came another brief burst of typing, then more grumbling and scrabbling on the desk.

(We've got to get it away from there.) Nita glanced at Fred.

(I shall create a diversion,) Fred said, with relish. (I've been good at it so far.)

(Great. Something big. Something alive again, if you can manage it— Then again, forget that.) Nita breathed out unhappily. (I wouldn't leave anything alive here.)

(Not even Joanne?) Kit asked with a small but evil grin.

(Not even her. This place has her outclassed. Fred, just—)

A voice spoke, sounding so loud that Kit and Nita stopped breathing, practically stopped thinking. "Akthanath," it called, a male voice, sounding weary and hassled and bored, "come in here a moment."

Nita glanced at Kit. They carefully peeked down the hall once more and saw the tentacled thing hunch itself up, drop to the floor behind the desk, and wobble its way into the inner office.

(Now?) Fred said.

(No, save it! But come on, this is our best chance!) Nita followed Kit down the hall to the door, crouched by it, and looked in. Past it was another room. They slipped into it and found themselves facing a partly open door that led to the office the typist had gone into. Through the slit they could just see the tentacled creature's back and could hear the voice of the man talking to it. "Hold all my calls for the next hour or so, until they get this thing cleared up. I don't want everybody's half-baked ideas of what's going on. Let Garm and his people handle it. And here, get Mike on the phone for me. I want to see if I can get something useful out of him."

Nita looked around, trying not even to think loudly. The room they were in was lined with shelves and shelves of heavy, dark, leather-bound books with gold-stamped spines. Kit tiptoed to one bookshelf, pulled out a volume at random, and opened it. His face registered shock; he held out the book for Nita to look at. The print was the same as that in Carl's large Advisory manual, line after line of the clear graceful symbols of the Speech—but whatever was being discussed on the page Nita looked at was so complicated she could only understand one word out of every ten or twenty. She glanced at Kit as he turned back to the front of the book and showed her the title page. UNIVERSES, PARAUNIVERSES, AND PLANES— ASSEMBLY AND MAINTENANCE, it said. A CREATOR'S MANUAL. And underneath, in smaller letters, *Volume 108—Natural and Supernatural Laws.*

Nita gulped. Beside her, Fred was dancing about in the air in great agitation. What is it?) she asked him.

(It's in *here*.)

(Where?) Kit said.

(One of *those*. I can't tell which, it's so dark down that end of the room.) Fred indicated a bookcase on the farthest wall. (It's worst over *there*.) Nita stopped dead when she saw the room's second door, which was wide open and led to the inner office.

Nita got ready to scoot past the door. The man who sat at the desk in the elegant office had his back to the door and was staring out the window into the dimness. His warty secretary handed him the phone, and he swiveled around in the high-backed chair to take it, showing himself in profile. Nita stared at him, confused, as he picked up the phone. A businessman, young, maybe thirty, and very handsome—red-gold hair and a clean-lined face above a trim, dark three-piece suit. *This* was the Witherer, the Kindler of Wildfires, the one who decreed darkness, the Starsnuffer?

"Hi, Michael," he said. He had a pleasant voice, warm and deep. "Oh, nothing much—"

(Never mind *him*,) Kit said. (We've got to get that Book.)

(We can't go past the door till he turns around.)

"—the answer to that is pretty obvious, Mike. I can't do a bloody thing with this place unless I can get some more power for it. I can't afford streetlights, I can barely afford a little electricity, much less a star. The entropy rating—"

The young man swiveled in his chair again, leaning back and looking out the window. Nita realized with a chill that he had a superb view of the downtown skyline, including the top of the Pan Am Building, where even now wisps of smoke curled black against the lowering gray. She tapped Kit on the elbow, and together they slipped past the doorway to the bookshelf.

(Fred, do you have even a *little* idea—)

(Maybe one of those up there.) He indicated a shelf just within reach. Kit and Nita started taking down one book after another, looking at them. Nita was shaking—she had no clear idea what they were looking for.

(What if it's one of those up there, out of reach?)

(You'll stand on my shoulders. Kit, hurry!)

"—Michael, don't you think you could talk to the rest of Them and get me just a *little* more energy? —Well, They've *never* given me what I asked for, have They? All I wanted was my own Universe where everything *works*— Which brings me to the reason for this call. Who's this new operative you turned loose in here? This Universe is at a very delicate stage, interference will—"

They were down to the second-to-last shelf, and none of the books had been what they were looking for. Nita was sweating worse. (Fred, are you *sure*—)

(It's dark there, it's *all* dark. What do you *want* from me?)

Kit, kneeling by the bottom shelf, suddenly jumped as if shocked. (Huh?) Nita said.

(It stung me. *Nita!*) Kit grabbed at the volume his hand had brushed, yanked it out of the case, and knelt there, juggling it like a hot potato. He managed to get it open and held it out, showing Nita not the usual clean page, close-printed with the fine small symbols of the Speech, but a block of transparency like many pages of thinnest glass laid together. Beneath the smooth surface, characters and symbols seethed as if boiling up from a great depth and sinking down again.

Nita found herself squinting. (It hurts to look at.)

(It hurts to *hold!*) Kit shut the book hurriedly and held it out to Fred for him to check, for externally it looked no different from any other book there. (Is this what we're looking for?)

Fred's faint glimmer went out like a blown candle flame with the nearness of the book. (The darkness—it blinds—)

Kit bundled the book into his backpack and rubbed his hands on his jacket. (Now if we can just get out of here . . .)

"Oh, come on, Mike," the voice was saying in the other office. "Don't get cute with me. I had an incident on top of one of my buildings. One of my favorite constructs got shot up and the site stinks of wizardry. *Your* brand, moonlight and noon-forged metal." The voice of the handsome young man in the three-piece suit was still pleasant enough, but Nita, peering around the edge of the door, saw his face going hard and sharp as the edge of a knife. He swiveled around in his chair again to look out the window at that thin plume of ascending smoke, and Nita waved Kit past the door, then scuttled after him herself. "That's a dumb question to be asking *me*, Michael. If I knew, would I tell you where the bright *Book* was? And how likely is it that I know at all? You people keep such close tabs on it, at least that's what I hear. Anyway, if it's not read from every so often, don't *I* go ffft! like everything else? —You're absolutely right, that's not a responsive answer. Why should *I* be responsive, *you're* not being very helpful—"

Kit and Nita peeked back into the hall. Fred floated up to hang between them. (I get a feeling—) Kit started to say, but the sudden coldness in the voice of the man on the phone silenced him.

"Look, Mike, I've had about enough of this silliness. The Bright Powers got miffed because I wanted to work on projects of my own instead of playing follow the leader like you do, working from their blueprints instead of drawing up your own. You can do what you please, but I thought when I settled down in this little pittance of a Universe that They would let me be and let me do things my way. They said They didn't need me when They threw me out—well, I've done pretty well without Them, too. Maybe They don't like that, because now all of a sudden I'm getting interference. You say this operative isn't one of your sweetness-and-light types? Fine. Then you won't mind if when I catch him, her, or it, I make his stay interesting and permanent. Whoever's disrupting my status quo will wish he'd never been born, spawned, or engendered. And when you see the rest of Them, you tell Them from me that— Hello? Hello?"

The phone slammed down. There was no sound for a few seconds. "Akthanath," the young man's voice finally said into that silence, "someone's soul is going to writhe for this."

The slow cold of the words got into Nita's spine. She and Kit slipped around the door and ran for it, down the hall and into the elevator. "He's playing it close to the chest," that angry voice floated down the hall to them. "I don't know what's going on. The Eldest still has it safe?—Good, then see that guards are mounted at the usual accesses. And have Garm send a pack of his people backtime to the most recent gate opening. I want to know which universe these agents are coming from."

In the elevator, Kit whipped out the antenna and rapped the control panel with it. *"Down!"*

Doors closed, and down it went. Nita leaned back against one wall of the elevator, panting. Now she knew why that first crowd of perytons had come howling after them on top of the Pan Am Building, but the solution of that small mystery made her feel no better at all. "Kit, they'll be waiting downstairs, for sure."

He bit his lip. "Yeah. Well, we won't be where they think we'll be, that's all. If we get off a couple of floors too high and take the stairs—"

"Right."

"Stop at four," Kit said to the elevator.

The elevator stopped, opened its doors. Kit headed out the door fast and tripped—the elevator had stopped several inches beneath the fourth floor. *"Watch your step,"* the elevator said, snickering.

Kit turned and smacked the open elevator door with his antenna as Nita and Fred got out. *"Very funny. You stay here until I give the word.* C'mon, let's get out of here!"

They ran down the hall together, found the stairs, and plunged down them. Kit was panting as hard as Nita now. Fred shot down past landing after landing with them, his light flickering as if it were an effort to keep up. "Kit," Nita said, "where are we going to go after we leave this building? We need time, and a place to do the spell to find the bright *Book.*"

Kit sounded unhappy. "I dunno. How about Central Park? If we hid in there—"

"But you saw what it looks like from the top of Pan Am. It's all dark in there, there were things moving—"

"There's a lot of room to hide. Look, Nita, if I can handle the machines here, it's a good bet you can handle the plants. You're good with plants and live stuff, you said."

She nodded reluctantly. "I guess we'll find out how good."

They came to the last landing, the ground floor. Nita pushed the door open a crack and found that they were almost directly across from the green lobby and the elevators.

(What's the situation?) Kit said silently.

(They're waiting.) Six perytons—black-coated, brown-coated, one a steely gray—were sitting or standing around the middle elevator with their tongues hanging out and looks of anticipation and hunger in their too-human eyes.

(Now?) Fred said, sounding eager.

(Not yet. We may not need a diversion, Fred.) *"Go!"* he whispered then in the Speech. The antenna in his hand sparked and sputtered with molten light, and Kit pressed close behind Nita. (Watch them!)

There was no bell, but even if there had been one, the sound of it and of the elevator doors opening would have been drowned out in snarls as the perytons leaped in a body into the elevator. The moment the perytons were out of sight, Nita pushed the door open and headed for the one to the garage. It stuck and stung her as the dark Book had; she jerked her hand away from it. Kit came up behind her and blasted it with the antenna, then grabbed it himself. This time it came open. They dashed through and Kit sealed the door behind them.

No one was in the garage, but a feeling was growing in the air as if the storm of rage they'd heard beginning upstairs was about to break over their heads. Kit raised the antenna again, firing a line of hot light that zapped the ceiling-mounted controls of the delivery door. With excruciating slowness the door began to rumble upward. (Now?) Fred said anxiously as they ran toward it.

(No, not yet, just—)

They bent over double, ducked underneath the opening door, and ran up the driveway. It was then that the perytons leaped at them from both sides, howling, and Nita grabbed for her wand and managed one slash with it, yelling, "Now, Fred! *Now!*"

All she saw clearly was the peryton that jumped at her, a huge, blue-eyed, brindled she-wolf, as the rowan wand spat silver moonfire and the peryton fell away screaming. Then came the explosion, and it hurled both her and Kit staggering off to their right. The street shook as if lightning struck, and part of the front of the dark building was demolished in a shower of shattered plate glass as tons and tons and tons of red bricks came crashing down from somewhere to fill the street from side to side, burying sidewalks and perytons and doors and the delivery bay twenty feet deep.

Nita picked herself up. A few feet away Kit was doing the same, and Fred bobbed over to them as an ominous stillness settled over everything. (How was I?) Fred asked, seeming dazed but pleased.

"Are you all right?" Kit asked.

(I'm alive, but my gnaester will never be the same,) Fred said. (You two?)

"We're fine," Kit said.

"And I think we're in trouble," Nita added, looking at the blocked street. "Let's get going!"

They ran toward Fifth Avenue, and the shadows took them.

Contractual Magic:

AN INTRODUCTION

A FOUR-FOOT-HIGH wall ran down the west side of Fifth Avenue, next to a sidewalk of gray hexagonal paving stones. Nita and Kit crouched behind it, just inside Central Park, under the shadows of barren-branched trees, and tried to catch their breath. Fred hung above them, watching both Fifth Avenue and Sixty-fourth Street for signs of pursuit.

Nita leaned against the dirty wall, careless of grime or roughness or the pigeon droppings that streaked it. She was scared. All through her life, the one thing she knew she could always depend on was her energy—it never gave out. Even after being beaten up, she always sprang right back. But here and now, when she could less afford exhaustion than she had ever been able to in her life, she felt it creeping up on her. She was even afraid to rest, for fear it would catch up with her quicker. But her lungs were burning, and it felt so good to sit still, not have death or something worse chasing her. And there was another spell to be cast. . . .

If I'd known I was going to get into a situation like this, she thought, *would I ever have picked that book up at all? Would I have taken the Oath?* Then she shook her head and tried to think about something else, for she got an inkling of the answer, and it shocked her. She had always been told that she wasn't brave. At least that's what Joanne and her friends had always said: *Can't take a dare, can't take a joke, crybaby, crybaby. We were only teasing. . . .*

She sniffed and rubbed her eyes, which stung. "Did you find the spell?"

Kit had been paging through his wizards' manual. Now he was running a finger down one page, occasionally whispering a word, then stopping himself to keep from using the Speech aloud. "Yeah. It's pretty simple." But he was frowning.

"What's the matter?"

Kit slumped back against the wall, looked over at her. "I keep thinking about what—you know who—was talking about on the phone."

"Sounded like he was hiding something."

"Uh-huh. They know where the bright *Book* is, all right. And somebody's watching it. Whoever the 'Eldest' is. And now there're going to be more guards around it."

" 'The usual accesses,' he said. Kit, there might be an *un*usual access, then."

"Sure. If we had any idea where the thing was hidden."

"Won't the spell give us a vision, a location, like the last one?"

"No. It's a directional." Kit dropped his hands wearily on the book in his lap, sighed, looked over at Nita. "I don't know . . . I just don't get it."

"What?" She rolled the rowan wand between her hands, watching the way its light shone between her fingers and through the skin.

"He didn't look evil. Or sound that way, at least not till right at the end there."

(The Snuffer was always glorious to look at before it scorned the light,) Fred said. (And it kept the beauty afterward—that's what the stars always used to say. That's one reason it's dangerous to deal with that one. The beauty . . . seduces.) Fred made a small feeling of awe and fear. (What a blaze of darkness, what a flood of emissions. I was having a hard time keeping my composure in there.)

"Are you all right now?"

(Oh yes. I was a little amazed that you didn't perceive the power burning around the shell he was wearing. Just as well—you might have spoken to him, and everything would have been lost. That one's most terrible power, they say, is his absolute conviction that he's right in what he does.)

"He's not right, then?" Kit asked.

(I don't know.)

"But," Nita said, confused, "if he's fighting with . . . with Them . . . with the ones who made the bright *Book*, isn't he in the wrong?"

(I don't know,) Fred said again. (How am I supposed to judge? But you're wizards, you should know how terrible a power belief is, especially in the wrong hands—and how do you tell which hands are wrong? *Believe* something and the Universe is on its way to being changed. Because *you've* changed, by believing. Once *you've* changed, other things start to follow. Isn't that the way it works?)

Nita nodded as Fred looked across the dark expanse of Central Park. The branches of trees were knotted together in tangled patterns of strife. Ivy strangled what it climbed. Paths were full of pitfalls; copses clutched themselves full of threat and darkness. Shadows moved secretively through shadows, making unnerving noises. (This is what—he—believes in,) Fred said sadly, (however he justifies the belief.)

Nita could find nothing to say. The wordless misery of the trees had been wearing at her ever since she set foot inside the wall. All the growing things there longed for light, though none of them knew what it was; she could feel their starved rage moving sluggishly in them, slow as sap in the cold. Only in one place was their anger muted—several blocks south, at Fifth and Central Park South, where in her own New York the equestrian statue of General Sherman and the Winged Victory had stood. Here the triumphant rider cast in black bronze was that handsome young man they had seen in the black glass building, his face set in a cold proud conqueror's smile. The creature he rode was a skull-faced eight-legged steed, which the wizards' manual said brought death with the sound of its hooves. And Victory with her palm branch was changed to a grinning Fury who held a dripping sword. Around the statue group the trees were silent, not daring to express even inarticulate feelings. They knew their master too well.

Nita shook her head and glanced at Kit, who was looking in the same direction. "I thought it'd be fun to know the Mason's Word and run around bringing statues to life," he said unhappily, "but somehow I don't think there's any statue here I'd want to use the Word on . . . You ready? We should start this."

"Yeah."

The spell was brief and straightforward, and Nita turned to the right page in her manual and drew the necessary circle and diagram. Kit got the dark Book out of his backpack and dropped it in the middle of the circle. Nita held up her wand for light. They began to recite the spell.

It was only three sentences long, but by the end of the first sentence Nita could feel the trees bending in close to watch—not with friendly, secretive interest, as in her first spell with Kit, but in hungry desperation. Even the abstract symbols and words of the Speech must have tasted of another Universe where light was not only permitted, but free. The rowan wand was blazing by the end of the second sentence, maybe in reaction to being so close to something of the dark powers, and Nita wondered whether she should cover it up to keep them from being noticed. But the spell held her immobile as usual. For another thing, the trees all around were leaning in with such piteous feelings of hunger that she would as soon have eaten in front of starving children and not offered them some of what she had. Branches began to toss and twist, reaching down for a taste of the light. Nita and Kit finished the spell.

Kit reached right down to pick up the dark Book, which was as well, for immediately after the last word of the spell was spoken it actually hitched itself a little way along the ground, southward. Kit could only hold it for a moment before stuffing it back into his backpack. It no longer looked innocent. It burned, both to touch and to look at. Even when Kit had it hidden away and the backpack slung on, neither of them felt any easier. It was as if they were all now visible to something that was looking eagerly for them.

"Let's get out of here," Kit said, so subdued that Nita could hardly hear him. Nita stood and laid a hand against the trunk of the nearest tree, a consoling gesture. She was sorry she couldn't have left them more light. (I wish there was something I could do,) she said silently. But no answer came back. These trees were bound silent, like the car Kit had tended.

She rejoined Kit, who was looking over the wall. "Nothing," he said. Together they swung over the dropping-streaked stone and hurried down Fifth Avenue, crossing the street to get a safe distance between them and the strange cries and half-seen movements of the park. "Straight south?" Nita said.

"Pretty nearly. It's pushing straight that way on my back. The bright *Book* looked like it was way downtown, didn't it, in that spell?"

"Uh-huh. The financial district, I think." She gulped. It *was* a long way to walk—miles—even without having to worry about someone chasing you.

"Well, we'd better hurry," Kit said. He paused while they both stopped at the corner of Fifth and Sixty-first. When they were across, he added, "What gets me is that he's so sure that we're interference from the bright side. We haven't done anything yet."

"Huh," Nita said, gently scornful. "Sure we haven't. And anyway, whaddaya mean we aren't 'interference from the bright side'? *You* were the one who said we'd been had."

Kit mulled this over as they approached Sixtieth. "Well . . . maybe. If they know about us, do you think they'll send help?"

"I don't know. I get the feeling that maybe we *are* the help."

"Well, we're not dead yet," Kit said, and peered around the corner of Sixtieth and Fifth—and then jumped back, pale with shock. "We're dead," he said, turned around, and began running back the way they had come, though he limped doing it. Nita looked around that corner just long enough to see what he had seen—a whole pack of big yellow cabs, thundering down Sixtieth. The one in front had a twisted fender that stuck out slightly on one side, a jagged piece of metal. She turned and ran after Kit, frantic. "Where can we hide?"

"The buildings are locked here, too," Kit said from up ahead. He had been trying doors. "Fred, can you do something?"

(After that last emission? So soon?) Fred's thought was shaken. (It's all I can do to radiate light. I need time to recover.)

"Crud! Kit, the park, maybe the trees'll slow them down."

They both ran for the curb, but there was no time. Cabs came roaring around the corner from Sixtieth, and another pack of them leaped around the corner of Sixty-first and hurtled down Fifth toward them; they would never make it across the street.

Kit grabbed for his antenna, and Nita yanked out the wand, but without much hope—it hadn't worked that well on the helicopter. The cabs slowed, closed in from both sides, forming a half-circle with Kit and Nita and Fred at the center, backing them against the wall of a dingy building. The cordon tightened until there were no gaps, and one cab at each side was up on the sidewalk, blocking it. No matter where Nita looked, all she saw were chromed grilles like gritted teeth, hungry headlights staring. One of the cabs shouldered forward, its engine snarling softly. The jagged place at one end of its front fender wore a brown discoloration. Not rust—Kit's blood, which it had tasted. Kit lifted the antenna, the hand that gripped it shaking.

The high-pitched yowl of rage and defiance from outside the circle jerked Kit's head up. Nita stared. Fenders scraped and rattled against one another as the tight-wedged cabs jostled, trying to see what was happening. Even the bloodstained cab, the pack leader, looked away from Kit. But none of them could move any way but backward, and one cab paid immediately for that limitation as a fanged grille bit deep into its hindquarters and dragged it screaming out of the circle. Metal screeched and tore, glass shattered as the Lotus Esprit's jaws crushed through the cab's trunk, ripped away its rear axle, and with a quick sideways shake of its front end flung the bitten-off axle crashing down Fifth Avenue. Then the Lotus slashed sideways, its fangs opening up the side of another cab like a can opener. The circle broke amid enraged roaring; cabs circled and feinted while the first victim dragged itself away by its front wheels to collapse in the street.

Everything started happening at once. Nita slashed at the front of the cab closest to her. The whip of moonfire cracking across its face seemed to confuse and frighten it, but did no damage. *I hope* it *doesn't notice that right away*, she thought desperately, for there was no use yelling for help. Kit had his hands full. He had the antenna laid over his forearm again and was snapping off shot after shot of blinding-hot light, cracking headlights, burning holes in hoods, and exploding tires, a hit here, a hit there—nothing fatal, Nita noticed with dismay. But Kit was managing to hold the cabs at their distance as they harried him.

Out in the street one cab lunged at the Lotus, a leap, its front wheels clear of the ground and meant to come crashing down on the racer's hood—until suddenly the Lotus's nose dipped under the cab and heaved upward, sending the cab rolling helplessly onto its back. A second later the Lotus came down on top of the cab, took a great shark bite out of its underbelly, and then whirled around, whipping gas and transmission fluid all over, to slash at another cab about to leap on it from behind. This was the king cab, the pack leader, and as the Lotus and the Checker circled one another warily in the street, the other cabs drew away from Kit and Nita to watch the outcome of the combat.

There were two more cabs dead in the street that Nita hadn't seen fall—one with everything from right rear door to right front fender torn away, another horribly mangled in its front end and smashed sideways into a tree on the other side of Fifth, as if it had been thrown there. Amid the wreckage of these and the other two cabs, the cab and the Lotus rolled, turning and backing, maneuvering for an opening that would end in a kill. The Lotus was scored along one side but otherwise unhurt, and the whining roar of its engine sounded hungry and pleased. Infuriated, the Checker made a couple of quick rushes at it, stopping short with a screech of tires and backing away again each time in a way that indicated it didn't want to close in. The Lotus snarled derisively, and without warning the Checker swerved around and threw itself full speed at Kit and Nita, still braced against the wall.

This is it, Nita thought with curious calm. She flung up the rowan wand in one last useless slash and then was thrown back against the wall with terrible force as a thunderstorm of screaming metal flew from right to left in front of her and crashed not five feet away. She slid down the wall limp as a rag doll, stunned, aware that death had gone right past her face. When her eyes and ears started working again, the Lotus was standing off to her left, its back scornfully turned to the demolished pack leader, which it had slammed into the wall. The Checker looked like the remains of a front-end collision test—it was crumpled up into itself like an accordion, and bleeding oil and gas in pools. The Lotus roared triumphant disdain at the remaining two cabs, then threatened them with a small mean rush. They turned tail and ran a short distance, then slowed down and slunk away around the corner of Sixty-first. Satisfied, the Lotus bent over the broken body of one dead cab, reached down, and with casual fierceness plucked away some of the front fender, as a falcon plucks its kill before eating.

Nita turned her head to look for Kit. He was several feet farther down the wall, looking as shattered as she felt. He got up slowly and walked out into the street. The Lotus glanced up, left its kill, and went to meet him. For a moment they simply looked at each other from a few feet apart. Kit held one hand out, and the Lotus slowly inched forward under the hand, permitting the caress. They stood that way for the space of four or five gasps, and then the Lotus rolled closer still and pushed its face roughly against Kit's leg, like a cat.

"How about that," Kit said, his voice cracking. "How about that."

Nita put her face down in her hands, wanting very much to cry, but all she could manage were a couple of crooked, whooping sobs. She had a feeling that much worse was coming, and she couldn't break down all the way. Nita hid her eyes until she thought her voice was working again, then let her hands fall and looked up. "Kit, we've got to—"

The Lotus had rolled up and was staring at her—a huge, dangerous, curious, brown-hided beast. She lost what she was saying, hypnotized by the fierce, interested stare. Then the Lotus smiled at Nita, a slow, chrome smile, silver and sanguine. "Uhh," she said, disconcerted, and glanced up at Kit, who had come to stand alongside the racer. "We've gotta get out of here, Kit. It has to be the spell that brought these things down on us. And when those two cabs let you-know-who know that we didn't get caught, or killed—"

Kit nodded, looked down at the Lotus; it glanced sideways up at him, from headlights bright with amusement and triumph. *"How about it?"* Kit said in the Speech. *"Could you give us a lift?"*

In answer the Lotus shrugged, flicking its doors open like a bird spreading its wings.

Nita stood up, staggering slightly. "Fred?"

He appeared beside her, making a feeling of great shame. "Fred, what's the matter?" Kit said, catching it too.

(I couldn't do anything.)

"Of course not," Nita said, reaching up to cup his faint spark in one hand. "Because you just *did* something huge, dummy. We're all right. Come on for a ride." She perched Fred on the upstanding collar of her down vest; he settled there with a sigh of light.

Together she and Kit lowered themselves into the dark seats of the Lotus, into the dim, warm cockpit, alive with dials and gauges, smelling of leather and metal and oil. They had barely strapped themselves in before the Lotus gave a great glad shake that slammed its doors shut, and burned rubber down Fifth Avenue—out of the carnage and south toward the joining of two rivers, and the oldest part of Manhattan.

Nita sat at ease, taking a breather and watching the streets of Manhattan rush by. Kit, behind the steering wheel, was holding the dark Book in his lap, feeling it carefully for any change in the directional spell. He was reluctant to touch it. The farther south they went, the more the Book burned the eyes that looked at it. The wizards' manual had predicted this effect—that, as the two Books drew closer to one another, each would assert its own nature more and more forcefully. Nita watched the Book warping and skewing the very air around it, blurring its own outlines, and found it easy to believe the manual's statement that even a mind of terrible enough purpose and power to wrench this Book to its use might in the reading be devoured by what was read. She hoped for Kit's sake that it wouldn't devour someone who just touched it.

"We're close," Kit said at last, in a quiet, strained voice.

"You okay?"

"I've got a headache, but that's all. Where are we?"

"Uh—that was just Pearl Street. Close to City Hall." She tapped the inside of her door, a friendly gesture. "Your baby *moves*."

"Yeah," Kit said affectionately. The Lotus rumbled under its hood, sped on. "Fred? You feeling better?"

Fred looked up at her from her collar. (Somewhat. I'd feel better still if I knew what we were going to be facing next. If I'm to make bricks again, I'm going to need some notice.)

"Your gnaester, huh?" Kit said.

(I'm not sure I *have* a gnaester anymore, after that last emission. And I'm afraid to find out.)

"Kit, scrunch down," Nita said suddenly, doing the same herself. The Lotus roared past the corner of Broadway and Chambers, pointedly ignoring a pair of sullen-looking cabs that stared and snarled as it passed. They were parked on either side of an iron-railed stairway leading down to a subway station. About a block farther along Broadway, two more cabs were parked at another subway entrance.

From his slumped-down position, Kit glanced over at Nita. "Those are the first we've seen."

" 'The usual accesses,' " Nita said. "They've got it down in the subway somewhere."

"Oh no," Kit muttered, and (Wonderful,) Fred said. Nita swallowed, not too happy about the idea herself. Subway stations, unless they were well lighted and filled with people, gave her the creeps. Worse, even in her New York, subways had their own special ecologies—not just the mice and rats and cats that everybody knew about, but other less normal creatures, on which the wizards' manual had had a twenty-page chapter. "They're all over the place," she said aloud, dealing with the worst problem first. "How are we going to—"

"Ooof!" Kit said, as the dark Book, sitting on his lap, sank down hard as if pushed. The Lotus kept driving on down Broadway, past City Hall, and Kit struggled upward to look out the back window, noting the spot. "That was where the other *Book* was—straight down from that place we just passed."

The Lotus turned right onto a side street and slowed as if looking for something. Finally it pulled over to the left-hand curb and stopped. "What—" Kit started to say, but the racer flicked open first Kit's door, then Nita's, as if it wanted them to get out.

They did, cautiously. The Lotus very quietly closed its doors. Then it rolled forward a little way, bumping up onto the sidewalk in front of a dingy-looking warehouse. It reached down, bared its fangs, and with great delicacy sank them into a six-foot-long grille in the sidewalk. The Lotus heaved, and with a soft scraping groan, the grillwork came up to reveal an electric-smelling darkness and stairs leading down into it.

"It's one of the emergency exits from the subway, for when the trains break down," Kit whispered, jamming the dark Book back into his backpack and dropping to his knees to rub the Lotus enthusiastically behind one headlight. "It's perfect!"

The Lotus's engine purred as it stared at Kit with fierce affection. It backed a little and parked itself, its motions indicating it would wait for them. Kit got up, pulling out his antenna, and Nita got out her wand. "Well," she said under her breath, "let's get it over with . . ."

The steps were cracked concrete, growing damp and discolored as she walked downward. Nita held out the wand to be sure of her footing and kept one hand on the left wall to be sure of her balance—there was no banister or railing on the right, only darkness and echoing air. (Kit—) she said silently, wanting to be sure he was near, but not wanting to be heard by anything that might be listening down there.

(Right behind you. Fred?)

His spark came sailing down behind Kit, looking brighter as they passed from gloom to utter dark. (Believe me, I'm not far.)

(Here's the bottom,) Nita said. She turned for one last glance up toward street level and saw a huge sleek silhouette carefully and quietly replacing the grille above them. She gulped, feeling as if she were being shut into a dungeon, and turned to look deeper into the darkness. The stairs ended in a ledge three feet wide and perhaps four feet deep, recessed into the concrete wall of the subway. Nita held up the wand for more light. The ledge stretched away straight ahead, with the subway track at the bottom of a wide pit to the right of it. (Which way, Kit?)

(Straight, for the time being.)

The light reflected dully from the tracks beside them as they pressed farther into the dark. Up on the streets, though there had been darkness, there had also been sound. Here there was a silence like black water, a silence none of them dared to break. They slipped into it holding their breaths. Even the usual dim rumor of a subway tunnel, the sound of trains rumbling far away, the ticking of the rails, was missing. The hair stood up all over Nita as she walked and tried not to make a sound. The air was damp, chilly, full of the smells of life—too full, and the wrong kinds of life, at least to Nita's way of thinking: mold and mildew; water dripping too softly to make a sound, but still filling the air with a smell of leached lime, a stale, puddly odor; wet trash, piled in trickling gutters or at the bases of rusting iron pillars, rotting quietly; and always the sharp ozone-and-scorched-soot smell of the third rail. Shortly there was light that did not come from Nita's wand. Pale splotches of green-white radiance were splashed irregularly on walls and ceiling—firefungus, which the wizards' manual said was the main food source of the subway's smallest denizens, dun mice and hidebehinds and skinwings. Nita shuddered at the thought and walked faster. Where there were hidebehinds, there would certainly be rats to eat them. And where there were rats, there would also be fireworms and thrastles. . . .

(Nita.)

She stopped and glanced back at Kit. He was holding his backpack in one arm now and the antenna in the other, and looking troubled in the wand's silver light. (That way,) he said, pointing across the tracks at the far wall with its niche-shaped recesses.

(Through the *wall?* We don't even know how thick it is!) Then she stopped and thought a moment. (I wonder— You suppose the Mason's Word would work on concrete? What's in concrete, anyhow?)

(Sand—quartz, mostly. Some chemicals—but I think they all come out of the ground.)

(Then it'll work. C'mon.) Nita hunkered down and very carefully let herself drop into the wide pit where the tracks ran. The crunch of rusty track cinders told her Kit was right behind. Fred floated down beside her, going low to light the way. With great care Nita stepped over the third rail and balanced on the narrow ledge of the wall on the other side. She stowed the wand and laid both hands flat on the concrete to begin implementation of the lesser usage of the Word, the one that merely manipulates stone rather than giving it the semblance of life. Nita leaned her head against the stone too, making sure of her memory of the Word, the sixteen syllables that would loose what was bound. Very fast, so as not to mess it up, she said the Word and pushed.

Door, she thought as the concrete melted under her hands, and a door there was; she was holding the sides of it. (Go ahead,) she said to Kit and Fred. They ducked through under her arm. She took a step forward, let go, and the wall reformed behind her.

(Now what the—) Kit was staring around him in complete confusion. It took Nita a moment to recover from the use of the Word, but when her vision cleared, she understood the confusion. They were standing in the middle of another track, which ran right into the wall they had just come through and stopped there. The walls there were practically one huge mass of firefungus. It hung down in odd green-glowing lumps from the ceiling and layered thick in niches and on the poles that held the ceiling up. Only the track and ties and the rusty cinders between were bare, a dark road leading downward between eerily shining walls for perhaps an eighth of a mile before curving around to the right and out of view.

(I don't get it,) Kit said. (This track just starts. Or just stops. It would run right into that one we just came off! There aren't any subway lines in the city that do that! Are there?)

Nita shook her head, listening. The silence of the other tunnel did not persist here. Far down along the track, the sickly green light of the firefungus was troubled by small shadowy rustlings, movements, the scrabbling of claws. (What about the *Book?*) she asked.

Kit nodded toward the end of the track. (Down there, and a little to the right.)

They walked together down the long aisle of cold light, looking cautiously into the places where firefungus growth was sparse enough to allow for shadow. Here and there small sparks of brightness peered out at them, paired sparks—the eyes of dun mice, kindled to unnatural brightness by the fungus they fed on. Everywhere was the smell of dampness, old things rotting or rusting. The burning-ozone smell grew so chokingly strong that Nita realized it couldn't be just the third rail producing it—even if the third rail were alive in a tunnel this old. The smell grew stronger as they approached the curve at the tunnel's end. Kit, still carrying the backpack, was gasping. She stopped just before the curve, looked at him. (Are you okay?)

He gulped. (It's close, it's really close. I can hardly see, this thing is blurring my eyes so bad.)

(You want to give it to me?)

(No, you go ahead. This place seems to be full of live things. Your department—)

(Yeah, right,) Nita agreed unhappily, and made sure of her grip on the rowan wand. (Well, here goes. Fred, you ready for another diversion?)

(I think I could manage something small if I had to.)

(Great. All together now . . .)

They walked around the curve, side by side. Then they stopped.

It was a subway station. Or it had been at one time, for from where they stood at one end of the platform, they could see the tons of rubble that had choked and sealed the tunnel at the far end of the platform. The rubble and the high ceiling were overgrown with firefungus enough to illuminate the old mosaics on the wall, the age-cracked tiles that said CITY HALL over and over again, down the length of the platform wall. But the platform and tracks weren't visible from where they stood. Heaped up from wall to wall was a collection of garbage and treasure, things that glittered, things that moldered. Nita saw gems, set and unset, like the plunder of a hundred jewelry stores, tumbled together with moldy kitchen garbage; costly fabric in bolts or in shreds, half buried by beer cans and broken bottles; paintings in ornate frames, elaborately carved furniture, lying broken or protruding crookedly from beneath timbers and dirt fallen from the old ceiling; vases, sculpture, crystal, silver services, a thousand kinds of rich and precious things, lying all together, whole and broken, among shattered dirty crockery and base metal. And lying atop the hoard, its claws clutched full of cheap costume jewelry, whispering to itself in the Speech, was the dragon.

Once more Nita tried to swallow and couldn't manage it. This looked nothing like the fireworm her book had mentioned—a foot-long mouse-eating lizard with cigarette-lighter breath. But if a fireworm had had a long, long time to grow—she remembered the voice of the young man in the three-piece suit, saying with relief, "The Eldest has it." There was no telling how many years this creature had been lairing here in the darkness, growing huger and huger, devouring the smaller creatures of the underground night and dominating those it did not devour, sending them out to steal for its hoard—or to bring it food. Nita began to tremble, looking at the fireworm-dragon's thirty feet of lean, scaled, tight-muscled body, looking at the size of its dark-stained jaws, and considering what kind of food it must eat. She glanced down at one taloned hind foot and saw something that lay crushed and forgotten beneath it—a subway repairman's reflective orange vest, torn and scorched; a wrench, half melted; the bones, burned black. . . .

The dragon had its head down and was raking over its hoard with huge claws that broke what they touched half the time. Its tail twitched like a cat's as it whispered to itself in a voice like hissing steam. Its scales rustled as it moved, glowing faintly with the same light as the firefungus, but colder, greener, darker. The dragon's eyes were slitted as if even the pale fungus light was too much for it. It dug in the hoard, nosed into the hole, dug again, nosed about, as if going more by touch than sight. *"Four thousand and ssix,"* it whispered, annoyed, hurried, angry. *"It was here sssomewhere, I know it was. Three thousand—no. Four thousand and—and—"*

It kept digging, its claws sending coins and bottle caps rolling. The dragon reached into the hole and with its teeth lifted out a canvas bag. Bright things spilled out, which Nita first thought were more coins but that turned out to be subway tokens. With a snarl of aggravation the fireworm-dragon flung the bag away, and tokens flew and bounced down the hoard-hill, a storm of brassy glitter. One rolled right to Nita's feet. Not taking her eyes off the dragon, she bent to pick it up. It was bigger than the subway token the New York transit system used these days, and the letters stamped on it were in an old-time style. She nudged Kit and passed it to him, looking around at the mosaics on the walls. They were *old*. The City Hall motif repeated in squares high on the train side wall of the platform looked little like the City Hall of today. This station had to be one of those that were walled up and forgotten when the area was being rebuilt long ago. The question was . . .

(The problem is—) Kit started to say in his quietest whisper of thought. But it wasn't quiet enough. With an expression of rage and terror, the dragon looked up from its digging, looked straight at them. Its squinted eyes kindled in the light from Nita's wand, throwing back a frightful violet reflection. *"Who's there? Who's there!"* it screamed in the Speech, in a voice like an explosion of steam. Without waiting for an answer it struck forward with its neck as a snake strikes and spat fire at them. Nita was ready, though; the sound of the scream and the sight of many tiny shadows running for cover had given her enough warning to put up the shield spell for both herself and Kit. The firebolt, dark red shot with billowing black like the output of a flamethrower, blunted against the shield and spilled sideways and down like water splashing on a window. When the bolt died away, the dragon was creeping and coiling down the hoard toward them; but it stopped, confused, when it saw that Kit and Nita and Fred still stood unhurt. It reared back its head for another bolt.

"You can't hurt us, Eldest," Nita said hurriedly, hoping it wouldn't try; the smell of burned firefungus was already enough to turn her stomach. The dragon crouched low against the hoard, its tail lashing, staring at them.

"You came to ssteal," it said, its voice quieter than before but angrier, as it realized it *couldn't* hurt them. *"No one ever comes here but to ssteal. Or to try,"* it added, glancing savagely over at another torn and fire-withered orange vest. *"What do you want? You can't have it. Mine, all thiss is mine. No one takes what'ss mine. He promissed, he ssaid he would leave me alone when I came here. Now he breakss the promiss, is that it?"*

The Eldest squinted wrathfully at them. For the second time that day, Nita found herself fascinated by an expression. Rage was in the fireworm-dragon's face, but also a kind of pain; and its voice was desperate in its anger. It turned its back, then, crawling back up onto the hoard. *"I will not let him break the promiss. Go back to him and tell him that I will burn it, burn it all, ssooner than let him have one ring, one jewel. Mine, all thiss is mine, no hoard has been greater than thiss in all times, he will not diminishhh it—"* The Eldest wound itself around the top of the hoard-mound like a crown of spines and scales, digging its claws protectively into the gems and the trash. A small avalanche of objects started from the place where it had been laying the hoard open before. Gold bars, some the small collectors' bars, some large ones such as the banks used, clattered or crashed down the side of the mound. Nita remembered how some $10 million worth of Federal Reserve gold had vanished from a bank in New York some years before—just vanished, untraceable—and she began to suspect where it had gone.

"Mine," hissed the Eldest. *"I have eight thousand six hundred forty-two cut diamonds. I have six hundred—no. I have four hundred eight emeralds. I have eighty-nine black opals—no, fifteen black opals. I have eighty-nine—eighty-nine—"* The anxiety in its voice was growing, washing out the anger. Abruptly the Eldest turned away from them and began digging again, still talking, its voice becoming again as it had been when they first came in: hurried, worried. *"Eighty-nine pounds of silver plate. I have two hundred fourteen pounds of gold—no, platinum. I have six hundred seventy pounds of gold—"*

"Nita," Kit said, very softly, in English, hoping the Eldest wouldn't understand it. "You get the feeling it's losing its memory?"

She nodded. "Lord, how awful." For a creature with the intense possessiveness of a fireworm to be unable to remember what it had in its hoard must be sheer torture. It would never be able to be sure whether everything was there; if something was missing, it might not be able to tell. And to a fireworm, whose pride is in its defense of its hoard from even the cleverest thieves, there was no greater shame than to be stolen from and not notice and avenge the theft immediately. The Eldest must live constantly with the fear of that shame. Even now it had forgotten Kit and Nita and Fred as it dug and muttered frantically, trying to find something, though uncertain of what it was looking for.

Nita was astonished to find that she was feeling sorry for a creature that had tried to kill her a few minutes before. "Kit," she said, "what about the bright *Book?* Is it in there?"

He glanced down at the dark Book, which was straining in his backpack toward the piled-up hoard. "Uh-huh. But how are we going to find it? And are you sure that defense shield is going to hold up at close range, when it comes after us? You know it's not going to just let us *take* something."

(Why not trade it something?) Fred asked suddenly.

Nita and Kit both looked at him, struck by the idea. "Like what?" Kit asked. (Like another Book?)

"Oh no," they said in simultaneous shock.

"Fred," Kit said then, "we can't do that. The—you-know-who—he'll just come right here and get it."

(So where did *you* get it from, anyway? Doubtless he could have read from it anytime he wanted. If you can get the bright *Book* back to the Senior wizards in your world, can't they use it to counteract whatever he does?)

Nita and Kit both thought about it. "He might have a point," Nita said after a second. "Besides, Kit—if we *do* leave the dark Book here, can you imagine you-know-who getting it back without some trouble?" She glanced up at the mound, where the Eldest was whispering threats of death and destruction against whoever might come to steal. "He wouldn't have put the bright *Book* here unless the Eldest was an effective guardian."

Even through the discomfort of holding the dark *Book*, Kit managed to crack a small smile. "Gonna try it?"

Nita took a step forward. Instantly the dragon paused in its digging to stare at her, its scaly lips wrinkled away from black fangs in a snarl, but its eyes frightened. *"Eldest,"* she said in the Speech, *"we don't come to steal. We're here to make a bargain."*

The Eldest stared at Nita a moment more, then narrowed its eyes further. *"Hss, you're a clever thiefff,"* it said. *"Why ssshould I bargain with you?"*

Nita gulped. *Wizardry is words*, the book had said. *Believe, and create the truth; but be careful what you believe.* "Because only your hoard, out of all the other hoards from this world to the next, has what we're interested in," she said carefully. *"Only you ever had the taste to acquire and preserve this thing."*

"Oh?" said the Eldest. Its voice was still suspicious, but its eyes looked less threatened. Nita began to feel a glimmer of hope. *"What might thiss thing be?"*

"A book," Nita said, *"an old book something like this one."* Kit took a step forward and held up the dark Book for the Eldest to see. This close to its bright counterpart, the dark volume was warping the air and light around it so terribly that its outlines writhed like a fistful of snakes.

The Eldest peered at the dark Book with interest. *"Now there is ssomething I don't have,"* it said. *"Sssee how it changes. That would be an interessting addition. . . . What did you ssay you wanted to trade it for?"*

"Another Book, Eldest. You came by it some time ago, we hear. It's close in value to this one. Maybe a little less," Nita added, making it sound offhand.

The dragon's eyes brightened like those of a collector about to get the best of a bargain. *"Lesss, you say. Hsss . . . Sssomeone gave me a book rather like that one, ssome time ago, I forget just who. Let me ssseee . . ."* It turned away from them and began digging again. Nita and Kit stood and watched and tried to be patient while the Eldest pawed through the trash and the treasure, making sounds of possessive affection over everything it touched, mumbling counts and estimating values.

"I wish it would hurry up," Kit whispered. "I can't believe that after we've been chased this far, they're not going to be down here pretty quick. We didn't have too much trouble getting in—"

"*You* didn't open the wall," Nita muttered back. "Look, I'm still worried about leaving this here."

"Whaddaya want?" Kit snapped. "Do I have to carry it all the way home?" He breathed out, a hiss of annoyance that sounded unnervingly like the Eldest, and then rubbed his forearm across his eyes. "This thing burns. I'm sorry."

"It's okay," Nita said, slightly embarrassed. "I just wish there were some way to be *sure* that you-know-who wouldn't get his hands on it anytime soon."

Kit looked thoughtful and opened his mouth to say something. It was at that moment that the Eldest put its face down into the hole it had been digging and came up again with something bright.

The *Book of Night with Moon* fell with a thump onto a pile of gold and gems and made them look tawdry, outshone them in a way that seemed to have nothing to do with light. Its cover was the same black leather as that of the dark *Book*— but as one looked at it, the blackness seemed to gain depth; light seemed hidden in it like a secret in a smiling heart. Even the dim green glow of the firefungus looked healthier now that the *Book* lay out in it. Where page edges showed, they glittered as if brushed with diamond dust rather than gilding. The Eldest bent over the bright *Book*, squinting as if into a great light but refusing to look away. "*Aaaaaahhhh,*" it said, a slow, caressing, proprietary sigh. "*Thisss is what you wisshed to trade your book ffor?*"

"Yes, Eldest," Nita said, starting to worry.

The dragon laid its front paws on either side of the Book. "*Ffair, it is ssso ffair. I had fforgotten how ssweet it was to look on. No. No, I will not trade. I will not. Mine, mine . . .*" It nosed the bright *Book* lovingly.

Nita bit her lip and wondered what in the world to try next. "*Eldest,*" Kit said from beside her, "*we have something more to trade.*"

"*Oh?*" The dragon looked away from the *Book* with difficulty and squinted at Kit. "*What might that be?*"

(Yeah, what?) Nita said silently.

(Sssh.) "*If you will take our book in trade for that one, we'll work such a wizardry about this place that no thief will ever enter. You'll be safe here for as long as you please. Or forever.*"

(What are you talking about!) Nita said, amazed. (We don't have the supplies for a major wizardry like that. The only one you could possibly manage would be one of—)

(The blank-check spells, I know. Nita, *shaddup!*)

The Eldest was staring at Kit. "*No one would ever come in again to ssteal from me?*" it said.

"*That's right.*"

Nita watched the dragon's face as it looked away from Kit, thinking. It was old and tired, and terrified of losing what it had amassed; but now a frightened hope was awakening in its eyes. It looked back at Kit after a few seconds. "*You will not come back either? No one will trouble me again?*"

"Guaranteed," Kit said, meaning it.

"*Then I will trade. Give me your book, and work your spell, and go. Leave me with what is mine."* And it picked up the *Book of Night with Moon* in its jaws and dropped it off the hoard-hill, not far from Kit's feet. *"Give me, give me,"* the Eldest said. Warily, Nita dropped the shield spell. Kit took a couple of uneasy steps forward and held out the dark Book. The dragon shot its head down, sank teeth in the dark Book, and jerked it out of Kit's hands so fast that he stared at them for a moment, counting fingers.

"Mine, mine," it hissed as it turned away and started digging at another spot on the hoard, preparing to bury the dark Book. Kit stooped, picked up the *Book of Night with Moon.* It was as heavy as the dark Book had been, about the size of an encyclopedia volume, and strange to hold—the depth of the blackness of its covers made it seem as if the holding hands should sink right through. Kit flipped it open as Nita and Fred came up behind to look over his shoulder. (But the pages are blank,) Fred said, puzzled.

(It needs moonlight,) Kit said.

(Well, this is moonlight.) Nita held up the rowan wand over the opened *Book.* Very vaguely they could make out something printed, the symbols of the Speech, too faint to read. (Then again, maybe secondhand moonlight isn't good enough. Kit, what're you going to do? You *have* to seal this place up now. You promised.)

(I'm gonna do what I said. One of the blank-check wizardries.)

(But when you do those you don't know what price is going to be asked later.)

(We have to get this *Book,* don't we? That's why we're here. And this is something that has to be done to get the *Book.* I don't think the price'll be too high. Anyway, *you* don't have to worry, I'll do it myself.)

Nita watched Kit getting out his wizards' manual and bit her lip. (Oh no, you're not,) she said. (If you're doing it, I'm doing it too. Whatever you're doing . . .)

(One of the Moebius spells,) Kit said, finding the page. Nita looked over his shoulder and read the spell. It would certainly keep thieves out of the hoard. When recited, a Moebius spell gave a specified volume of space a half-twist that left it permanently out of synch with the spaces surrounding it. The effect would be like stopping an elevator between floors, forever. (You read it all through?) Kit asked.

(Uh-huh.)

(Then let's get back in the tunnel and do it and get out of here. I'm getting this creepy feeling that things aren't going to be quiet on ground level when we get up there.)

They wanted to say good-bye to the Eldest, but it had forgotten them already. *"Mine, mine, mine,"* it was whispering as garbage and gold flew in all directions from the place where it dug.

(Let's go,) Fred said.

Out in the tunnel, the firefungus seemed brighter to Nita—or perhaps that was only the effect of looking at the *Book of Night with Moon.* They halted at the spot where the tunnel curved and began with great care to read the Moebius spell. The first part of it was something strange and unsettling—an invocation to the Powers that governed the arts of wizardry, asking help with this piece of work and promising that the power lent would be returned when They required. Nita shivered, wondering what she was getting herself into, for use of the Speech made the promise more of a prediction. Then came the definition of the space to be twisted, and finally the twisting itself. As they spoke the words Nita could see the Eldest, still digging away at his hoard, going pale and dim as if with distance, going away, though not moving. The words pushed the space farther and farther away, toward an edge that could be sensed more strongly though not seen—then, suddenly, over it. The spell broke, completed. Nita and Kit and Fred were standing at the edge of a great empty pit, as if someone had reached into the earth and scooped out the subway station, the hoard, and the Eldest, whole. Someone had.

"I think we better get out of here," Kit said, very quietly. As if in answer to his words came a long, soft groan of strained timber and metal—the pillars and walls of the tunnel where they stood and the tunnel on the other side of the pit, bending under new stresses that the pillars of the station had handled and that these were not meant to. Then a rumble, something falling.

Nita and Kit turned and ran down the tunnel, stumbling over timbers and picking themselves up and running again. Fred zipped along beside like a shooting star looking for the right place to fall. They slammed into the wall at the end of the track as the rumble turned to a thunder and the thunder started catching up behind. Nita found bare concrete, said the Mason's Word in a gasp, and flung the stone open. Kit jumped through with Fred behind him. The tunnel shook, roared, blew out a stinging, dust-laden wind, and went down in ruin as Nita leaped through the opening and fell to the tracks beside Kit.

He got to his knees slowly, rubbing himself where he had hit. "Boy," he said, "if we weren't in trouble with you-know-who before, we are now . . ."

Hurriedly Kit and Nita got up and the three of them headed for the ledge and the way to the open air.

Major Wizardries:

TERMINATION
AND RECOVERY

WITH GREAT CAUTION AND a grunt of effort, Kit pushed up the grille at the top of the concrete steps and looked around. "Oh, brother," he whispered, "sometimes I wish I wasn't right."

He scrambled up out of the tunnel and onto the sidewalk, with Nita and Fred following right behind. The street was a shambles reminiscent of Fifth and Sixty-second. Corpses of cabs and limousines and even a small truck were scattered around, smashed into lampposts and the fronts of buildings, overturned on the sidewalk. The Lotus Esprit was crouched at guard a few feet away from the grille opening, its engine running in long, tired-sounding gasps. As Kit ran over to it, the Lotus rumbled an urgent greeting and shrugged its doors open.

"They know we're here," Nita said as they hurriedly climbed in and buckled up. "They have to know what we've done. Everything feels different since the dark Book fell out of this space."

(And they must know we'll head back for the worldgate at Pan Am,) Fred said. (Wherever that is.)

"We've gotta find it—oof!" Kit said, as the Lotus reared back, slamming its doors shut, and dove down the street they were on, around the corner and north again. "Nita, you up for one more spell?"

"Do we have a choice?" She got her manual out of her pack, started thumbing through it. "What I want to know is what we're supposed to try on whatever they have waiting for us at Grand Central. You-know-who isn't just going to let us walk in there and leave with the bright *Book*—"

"We'll burn that bridge when we come to it." Kit had his backpack open in his lap and was peeking at the *Book of Night with Moon*. Even in the sullen dimness that leaked in the Lotus's windows, the edges of the pages of the *Book* shone, the black depths of its covers glowed with the promise of light. Kit ran a finger along the upper edge of one cover, and as Nita watched his face settled into a solemn stillness, as if someone spoke and he listened intently. It was a long moment before the expression broke. Then Kit glanced over at her with a wondering look in his eyes. "It really doesn't look like that much," he said. "But it feels— Nita, I don't think they can hurt us while we have this. Or if they can, it won't matter much."

"Maybe not, if we read from it," Nita said, reading down through the spell that would locate the worldgate for them. "But you remember what Tom said—"

"Yeah." But there was no concern in Kit's voice, and he was looking soberly at the *Book* again.

Nita finished checking the spell and settled back in the seat to prepare for it, then started forward again as a spark of heat burned into her neck. "Ow!"

(Sorry.) Fred slid around from behind her to perch farther forward on her shoulder.

"Here we go," Nita said.

She had hardly begun reading the imaging spell before a wash of power such as she had never felt seized her and plunged her into the spell headfirst. And the amazing thing was that she couldn't even be frightened, for whatever had so suddenly pulled her under and into the magic was utterly benevolent, a huge calm influence that Nita sensed would do her nothing but good, though it might kill her doing it. The power took her, poured itself into her, made the spell *part* of her. There was no longer any need to work it; it *was*. Instantly she saw all Manhattan laid out before her again in shadow outlines, and there was the worldgate, almost drowned in the darkness created by the Starsnuffer, but not hidden to her. The power let her go then, and she sat back gasping. Kit was watching her strangely.

"I think I see what you mean," she said. "The *Book*—it made the spell happen by itself, almost."

"Not 'almost,' " Kit said. "No wonder you-know-who wants it kept out of the hands of the Senior wizards. It can make even a beginner's spell happen. It did the same thing with the Moebius spell. If someone wanted to take this place apart— or if someone wanted to make more places like it, and they had the *Book*—" He gulped. "Look, where's the gate?"

"Where it should be," Nita said, finding her breath. "Underground—under Grand Central. Not in the deli, though. It's down in one of the train tunnels."

Kit gulped again, harder. "Trains . . . And you *know* that place'll be guarded. Fred, are you up to another diversion?"

(Will it get us back to the Sun and the stars again? Try me.)

Nita closed her eyes to lean back and take a second's rest—the power that had run through her for that moment had left her amazingly drained—but nearly jumped out of her skin the next moment as the Lotus braked wildly, fishtailing around a brace of cabs that leaped at it out of a side street. With a scream of engine and a cloud of exhaust and burned rubber it found its traction again and tore out of the intersection and up Third Avenue, leaving the cabs behind.

"They know, they *know*," Nita moaned. "Kit, what're we going to do? Is the *Book* going to be enough to stand up to him?"

"We'll find out, I guess," Kit said, though he sounded none too certain. "We've been lucky so far. No, not lucky, we've been ready. Maybe that'll be enough. We both came prepared for trouble, we both did our reading—"

"You did, maybe." Nita looked sheepish. "I couldn't get past Chapter Forty. No matter how much I read, there was always more."

Kit smiled just as uncomfortably. "I only got to Thirty-three myself, then I skimmed a lot."

"Kit, there's about to be a surprise quiz. *Did we study the right chapters?*"

"Well, we're gonna find out," Kit said. The Lotus turned left at the corner of Third and Forty-second, speeding down toward Grand Central. Forty-second seemed empty; not even a cab was in sight. But a great looming darkness was gathered down the street, hiding the iron overpass. The Lotus slowed, unwilling to go near it.

"Right here is fine," Kit said, touching the dashboard reassuringly. The Lotus stopped in front of the doors to Grand Central, reluctantly shrugging first Nita's, then Kit's door open.

They got out and looked around them. Silence. Nita looked nervously at the doors and the darkness beyond, while the Lotus crowded close to Kit, who rubbed its right wheel well absently.

The sound came. A single clang, like an anvil being struck, not too far away. Then another clang, hollow and metallic, echoing from the blank-eyed buildings, dying into bell-like echoes. Several more clangs, close together. Then a series of them, a slow drumroll of metal beating on stone. The Lotus pulled out from under Kit's hand, turning to face down Forty-second the way they had come, growling deep under its hood.

The clangor grew louder; echoes bounced back and forth from building to building so that it was impossible to tell from what direction the sound was coming. Down at the corner of Lexington and Forty-second, a blackness jutted suddenly from behind one of the buildings on the uptown side. The shape of it and its unlikely height above the pavement, some fifteen feet, kept Nita from recognizing what it was until more of it came around the corner, until the blackness found its whole shape and swung it around into the middle of the street on iron hooves.

Eight hooves, ponderous and deadly, dented the asphalt of the street. They belonged to a horse—a huge, misproportioned beast, its head skinned down to a skull, leaden-eyed and grinning hollowly. All black iron, that steed was, as if it had stepped down from a pedestal at its rider's call; and the one who rode it wore his own darkness on purpose, as if to reflect the black mood within. The Starsnuffer had put aside his three-piece suit for chain mail like hammered onyx and a cloak like night with no stars. His face was still handsome, but dreadful now, harder than any stone. His eyes burned with the burning of the dark Book, alive with painful memory about to come real. About the feet of his mount the perytons milled, not quite daring to look in their master's face, but staring and slavering at the sight of Kit and Nita, waiting the command to course their prey.

Kit and Nita stood frozen, and Fred's light, hanging small and constant as a star behind them, dimmed down to its faintest.

The cold, proud, erect figure on the black mount raised what it held in its right hand, a steel rod burning dark and skewing the air about it as the dark Book had. *"You have stolen something of mine,"* said a voice as cold as space, using the Speech with icy perfection and hating it. *"No one steals from me."*

The bolt that burst from the rod was a red darker than the Eldest's fiery breath. Nita did not even try to use the rowan wand in defense—she might as well have tried to use a sheet of paper to stop a laser beam. But as she and Kit leaped aside, the air around them went afire with sudden clarity, as if for a moment the darkness inherent in it was burned away. The destroying bolt went awry, struck up sideways and blasted soot-stained blocks out of the facade of Grand Central. And in that moment the Lotus screamed wild defiance and leaped down Forty-second at the rider and his steed.

"NO!" Kit screamed. Nita grabbed him, pulled him toward the doors. He wouldn't come, wouldn't turn away as the baying perytons scattered, as the Lotus hurtled into the forefront of the pack, flinging bodies about. It leaped up at the throat of the iron beast, which reared on four hooves and raised the other four and with them smashed the Lotus flat into the street.

The bloom of fire that followed blotted out that end of the street. Kit responded to Nita's pulling then, and together they ran through the doors, up the ramp that led into Grand Central, out across the floor.

Nita was busy getting the rowan wand out, had gotten ahead of Kit, who couldn't move as fast because he was crying—but it was his hand that shot out and caught her by the collar at the bottom of the ramp, almost choking her, and kept her from falling into the pit. There was no floor. From one side of the main concourse to the other was a great smoking crevasse, the floor and lower levels and tunnels beneath all split as if with an ax. Ozone smell and cinder smell and the smell of tortured steel breathed up hot in their faces, while from behind, outside, the thunder of huge hooves on concrete and the howls of perytons began again.

Below them severed tunnels and stairways gaped dark. There was no seeing the bottom. It was veiled in fumes and soot, underlit by the blue arcs of shorted-out third rails and an ominous deep red, as if the earth itself had broken open and was bleeding lava. The hooves clanged and closer.

Nita turned to Kit, desperate. Though his face still streamed with tears, there was an odd, painful calm about it. "I know what to do," he said, his voice saying that he found that strange. He drew the antenna out of his back pocket, and it was just as Nita noticed how strangely clear the air was burning about him that Kit threw the piece of steel out over the smoking abyss. She would have cried out and grabbed him, except that he was watching it so intently.

The hoofbeats stopped and were followed by a sound as of iron boots coming down on the sidewalk, immensely heavy, shattering the stone. Despite her own panic, Nita found she couldn't look away from the falling antenna either. She was gripped motionless in the depths of a spell again, while the power that burned the air clear now poured itself through Kit and into his wizardry. There was something wrong with the way the antenna was falling. It seemed to be getting bigger with distance instead of smaller. It stretched, it grew, glittering as it turned and changed. It wasn't even an antenna anymore. Sharp blue light and diffuse red gleamed from flat, polished faces, edges sharp as razors. It was a sword blade, not even falling now, but laid across the chasm like a bridge. The wizardry broke and turned Nita loose. Kit moved away from her and stepped out onto the flat of the blade, fear and pain showing in his face again.

"Kit!"

"It's solid," he said, still crying, taking another step out onto the span, holding his arms out for balance as it bent slightly under his weight. "Come on, Nita, it's noon-forged steel, he can't cross it. He'll have to change shape or seal this hole up."

(Nita, come on,) Fred said, and bobbled out across the crevasse, following Kit. Though almost blind with terror, her ears full of the sound of iron-shod feet coming after them, she followed Fred, who was holding a straight course out over the sword blade—followed him, arms out as she might have on a balance beam, most carefully not looking down. This was worse than the bridge of air had been, for that hadn't flexed so terribly under each step she or Kit took. His steps threw her off balance until she halted long enough to take a deep breath and step in time with him. Smoke and the smell of burning floated up around her; the shadows of the dome above the concourse stirred with wicked eyes, the open doors to the train platforms ahead of her muttered, their mouths full of hate. She watched the end of the blade, looked straight ahead. Five steps: Kit was off. Three. One—

She reached out to him, needing desperately to feel the touch of a human hand. He grabbed her arm and pulled her off the bridge just as another blast of black-red fire blew in the doors on the other side of the abyss. Kit said one sharp word in the Speech, and the air went murky around his body again as the *Book* ceased to work through him. Nita let go, glanced over her shoulder in time to see the sword blade snap back to being an antenna, like a rubber band going back to its right size. It fell into the fuming darkness, a lone glitter, quickly gone.

They ran. Nita could still see in her mind the place where the worldgate was hidden; the *Book*'s power had burned it into her like a brand. She took the lead, racing down a flight of stairs, around a corner and down another flight, into echoing beige-tiled corridors where Fred and the rowan wand were their only light. Above them they could hear the thunderous rumor of iron footsteps, slow, leisurely, inexorable, following them down. The howls of perytons floated down to them like the voices of lost souls, hungry for the blood and pain they needed to feel alive again.

"Here!" Nita shouted, not caring what might hear, and dodged around a corner, and did what she had never done in all her life before—jumped a subway turnstile. Its metal fingers made a grab for her, but she was too fast for them, and Kit eluded them too, coming right behind. At full speed Nita pounded down the platform, looking for the steps at the end of it that would let them down onto the tracks. She took them three at a time, two leaps, and then was running on cinders again, leaping over ties. Behind her she could hear Kit hobbling as fast as he could on his sore leg, gasping, but keeping up. Fred shot along beside her, pacing her, lighting her way. Eyes flickered in his light—hidebehinds, dun mice, ducking under cover as the three of them went past. Nita slowed and stopped in the middle of the tracks. "Here!"

Kit had his manual out already. He found the page by Fred's light, thumped to a stop beside Nita. "*Here?* In the middle of the—"

"Read! Read!" she yelled. There was more thunder rolling in the tunnel than just the sound of their pursuer's footsteps. Far away, she could hear what had been missing from the other tunnel beneath City Hall: trains. Away in the darkness, wheels slammed into the tracks they rode—even now the rails around them were clacking faintly in sympathy, and a slight cool wind breathed against Nita's face. A train was coming. On *this* track. Kit began the worldgating spell, reading fast. Again the air around them seemed clearer, fresher, as the power of the *Book of Night with Moon* seized the spell and its speaker, used them both.

That was when the Starsnuffer's power came down on them. It seemed impossible that the dank close darkness in which they stood could become any darker, but it did, as an oppressive blanket of clutching, choking hatred fell over them, blanketing everything. The rowan rod's silver fire was smothered. Fred's light went out as if he had been stepped on. Kit stopped reading, struggled for breath. Nita tried to resist, tried to find air, couldn't, collapsed to her knees, choking. The breeze from the dark at the end of the tunnel got stronger: the onrushing train, pushing the air in front of it, right up the track, right at them.

(I—will—*not*,) Fred said, struggling, angry, (I will—*not*—go out!) His determination was good for a brief flare, like a match being struck. Kit found his voice, managed to get out a couple more words of the spell in Fred's wavering radiance, grew stronger, managed a few more. Nita found that she could breathe again. She clutched the rowan wand, thinking with all her might of the night Liused had given it to her, the clear moonlight shining down between the branches. The wand came alive again. Shadows that had edged forward from the walls of the tunnel fled again. Kit read, hurrying. *Two-thirds done*, Nita thought. *If he can just finish—*

Far away down the tunnel, there were eyes. They blazed. The headlights of a train, coming down at them in full career. The clack of the rails rose to a rattle, the breeze became a wind, and the roar of the train itself echoed not just in the other tunnels, but in this one. Nita got to her feet, facing those eyes down. She would not look away. Fred floated by her shoulder; she gathered him close, perching him by her ear, feeling his terror of the overwhelming darkness as if it were her own but having nothing to comfort him with. *Kit*, she thought, not daring to say it aloud for fear she should interrupt his concentration. The sound of his words was getting lost in the thunder from above, iron-shod feet, the thunder from below, iron wheels on iron rails.

Suddenly Kit's voice was missing from the mélange of thunders. Without warning the worldgate was there, glistening in the light of the rowan wand and Fred and the train howling down toward them—a great jagged soap bubble, trembling with the pressure of sound and air. Kit wasted no time, but leaped through. Fred zipped into the shimmering surface and was gone. Nita made sure of her grip on the rowan wand, took a deep breath, and jumped through the worldgate. A hundred feet away, fifty feet away, the blazing eyes of the train glared at her as she jumped; its horn screamed in delight, anticipating the feel of blood beneath its wheels; sudden thunder rocked the platform behind her, black-red fire more sensed than seen. But the rainbow shimmer of the gate broke across her face first. The train roared through the place where she had been, and she heard the beginnings of a cry of frustrated rage as she cheated death, and anger, and fell and fell and fell. . . .

. . . And came down *slam* on nothing. Or it seemed that way, until opening her eyes a little wider she saw the soot and smog trapped in the hardened air she lay on, the only remnant of her walkway. Kit was already getting up from his knees beside her, looking out from their little island of air across to the Pan Am Building. Everything was dark, and Nita started to groan, certain that something had gone wrong and that the worldgate had simply dumped them back in the Starsnuffer's world—but no, her walkway *was* there. Greatly daring, she looked down and saw far below the bright yellow glow of sodium-vapor streetlights, long straight streams of traffic, the white of headlights and red of taillights. City noise, roaring, cacophonous and alive, floated up to them. *We're back. It worked!*

Kit was reading from his wizards' manual, as fast as he had read down in the train tunnel. He stopped and then looked at Nita in panic as she got up. "I can't close the gate!"

She gulped. "Then he can follow us . . . through . . ." In an agony of haste she fumbled her own book out of her pack, checked the words for the air-hardening spell one more time, and began reading herself. Maybe panic helped, for this time the walkway spread itself out from their feet to the roof of the building very fast indeed. "Come on," she said, heading out across it as quickly as she dared. *But where will we run to?* she thought. *He'll come behind, hunting. We can't go home, he might follow. And what'll he do to the city?*

She reached up to the heliport railing and swung herself over it. Kit followed, with Fred pacing him. "What're we gonna do?" he said as they headed across the gravel together. "There's no time to call the Senior wizards, wherever they are— or even Tom and Carl. *He'll* be here shortly."

"Then we'll have to get away from here and find a place to hole up for a little. Maybe the bright *Book* can help." She paused as Kit spoke to the lock on the roof door, and they ran down the stairs. "Or the manuals might have something, now that we need it."

"Yeah, right," Kit said as he opened the second door at the bottom of the stairs, and they ran down the corridor where the elevators were. But he didn't sound convinced. "The park?"

"Sounds good."

Nita punched the call button for the elevator, and she and Kit stood there panting. There was a feeling in the air that all hell was about to break loose, and the sweat was breaking out all over Nita because *they* were going to have to stop it somehow. "Fred," she said, "did you ever hear anything, out where you were, any stories of someone getting the better of you-know-who?"

Fred's light flickered uncomfortably as he watched Kit frantically consulting his manual. (Oh yes,) he said. (I'd imagine that's why he wanted a Universe apart to himself—to keep others from getting in and thwarting him. It used to happen fairly frequently when he went up against life.)

Fred's voice was too subdued for Nita's liking. "What's the catch?"

(Well . . . it's possible to win against him. But usually someone dies of it.)

Nita gulped again. Somehow she had been expecting something like that. "Kit?"

The elevator chimed. Once inside, Kit went back to looking through his manual. "I don't see anything," he said, sounding very worried. "There's a general information chapter on him here, but there's not much we don't know already. The only thing he's never been able to dominate was the *Book of Night with Moon*. He tried—that's what the dark Book was for; he thought by linking them together he could influence the bright *Book* with it, diminish its power. But that didn't work. Finally he was reduced to simply stealing the bright *Book* and hiding it where no one could get at it. That way no one could become a channel for its power, no one could possibly defeat him . . ."

Nita squeezed her eyes shut, not sure whether the sinking feeling in her stomach was due to her own terror or the elevator going down. *Read from it? No, no. I hope I never have to,* Tom's voice said in her mind. *. . . Reading it, being the vessel for all that power—I wouldn't want to. Even good can be terribly dangerous.*

And that was an Advisory, Nita thought, miserable. There was no doubt about it. One of them might have to do what a mature wizard feared doing: read from the *Book* itself.

"Let me do it," she said, not looking at Kit.

He glanced up from the manual, stared at her. "Bull," he said, and then looked down at the manual again. "If you're gonna do it, *I'm* gonna do it."

Outside the doors another bell chimed as the elevator slowed to a stop. Kit led the way out across the black stone floor, around the corner to the entrance. The glass door let them out onto a street just like the one they had walked onto in the Snuffer's otherworld—but here windows had lights in them, and the reek of gas and fumes was mixed with a cool smell of evening and a rising wind, and the cabs that passed looked blunt and friendly. Nita could have cried for relief, except that there was no reason to feel relieved. Things would be getting much worse shortly.

Fred, though, felt no such compunctions. (The stars, the stars are back,) he almost sang, flashing with delight as they hurried along.

"Where?" Kit said skeptically. As usual, the glow of a million streetlights was so fierce that even the brightest stars were blotted out by it. But Fred was too cheerful to be suppressed.

(They're there, they're *there!*) he said, dancing ahead of them. (And the Sun is there, too. I don't care that it's on the other side of this silly place, I can feel—feel—)

His thought cut off so abruptly that Nita and Kit both stopped and glanced over their shoulders. A coldness grabbed Nita's heart and wrung it. The sky, even though clear, did have a faint golden glow to it, city light scattered from smog—and against that glow, high up atop the Pan Am Building, a form, half unstarred night and half black iron, glowered down at them like a statue from a dauntingly high pedestal. Nita and Kit froze like moths pinned to a card as the remote clear howl of perytons wound through the air.

"He'll just jump down," Nita whispered, knowing somehow that he could do it. But the rider did not leap, not yet. Slowly he raised his arms in summons. One hand still held the steel rod about which the air twisted and writhed as if in pain; as the arm lifted, that writhing grew more violent, more tortured.

And darkness answered the gesture. It flowed forward around the feet of the dark rider's terrible mount, obscuring the perytons peering down over the roof's edge, and poured down the surface of the building like a black fog. What it touched, changed. Where the darkness passed, metal tarnished, glass filmed over or shattered, lighted windows were quenched, went blind. Down all the sides of the building it flowed, black lava burning the brightness out of everything it touched.

Kit and Nita looked at each other in despair, knowing what would happen when that darkness spilled out onto the ground. The streets would go desolate and dark, the cabs would stop being friendly; and when all the island from river to river was turned into his domain, the dark rider would catch them at his leisure and do what he pleased with them. And with the bright *Book*—and with everything else under the sky, perhaps. This was no otherworld, frightening but remote. This was their home. If this world turned into *that* one . . .

"We're dead," Kit said, and turned to run. Nita followed him. Perhaps out of hope that another Lotus might be waiting innocently at some curbside, the way Kit ran retraced their earlier path. But there was no Lotus—only bright streets, full of people going about their business with no idea of what was about to happen to them, cars honking at one another in cheerful ignorance. Fat men running newsstands and bemused bag ladies watched Nita and Kit run by as if death and doom were after them, and no one really noticed the determined spark of light keeping pace. They ran like the wind down West Fiftieth, but no Lotus lay there, and around the corner onto Fifth and up to Sixty-first, but the carnage left in the otherworld was not reflected here—the traffic on Fifth ran unperturbed. Gasping, they waited for a break in it, then ran across, hopped the wall into the park, and crouched down beside it as they had in the world they'd left.

The wind was rising, not just a night breeze off the East River, but a chill wind with a hint of that other place's coldness to it. Kit unslung his pack as Fred drew in close, and by his light Kit brought out the *Book of Night with Moon*. The darkness of its covers shone, steadying Kit's hands, making Fred seem to burn brighter. Kit and Nita sat gasping for breath, staring at each other.

"I'm out of ideas," Kit said. "I think we're going to have to read from this to keep the city the way it should be. We can't just let him change things until he catches us. Buildings are one thing, but what happens to *people* after that black hits them?"

"And it might not stop here either," Nita said between gasps, thinking of her mother and father and Dairine, of the quiet street where they lived, the garden, the rowan, all warped and darkened—if they would survive at all.

Her eyes went up to the Moon shining white and full between the shifting branches. All around them she could feel the trees stirring in that new, strange, cold wind, whispering uneasily to one another. It was so good to be in a place where she could hear the growing things again.

The idea came. "Kit," she said hurriedly, "that dark was moving pretty fast. If we're going to read from the *Book* we may need something to buy us time, to hold off the things that'll come with it, the perytons and the cabs."

"We're out of Lotuses," Kit said, his voice bleak.

"I know. But look where we are! Kit, this is *Central Park!* You know how many trees there are in here of the kinds that went to the Battle in the old days? They don't forget."

He stared at her. "What can they—"

"The *Book* makes everything work better, doesn't it? There's a spell that—I'll do it, you'll see. But you've got to do one, too, it's in your specialty group. The Mason's Word, the long version—"

"To bring stone or metal to life." He scrubbed the last tears out of his eyes and managed ever so slight and slow a smile. "There are more statues within screaming distance of this place—"

"Kit," Nita said, "how loud can you scream?"

"Let's find out."

They both started going through their manuals in panicky haste. Far away on the East Side, lessened by all the buildings and distance that lay between, but still much too clear, there was a single, huge, deep-pitched *clang*, an immense weight of metal hitting the ground with stone-shattering force. Fred bobbled a little in the air, nervously. (How long do you think—)

"He'll be a while, Fred," Kit said, sounding as if he hoped it would be a long while. "He doesn't like to run; it's beneath his dignity. But I think—" He broke off for a moment, reading down a page and forming the syllables of the Mason's Word without saying them aloud. "I think we're going to have a few friends who'll do a little running for us."

He stood up, and Fred followed him, staying close to light the page. "Nita, hand me the *Book*." She passed it up to him, breaking off her own frantic reading for a moment to watch. "It'll have to be a scream," he said as if to himself. "The more of them hear me, the more help we get."

Kit took three long breaths and then shouted the Word at the top of his lungs, all twenty-seven syllables of it without missing a one. The sound became impossibly more than the yell of a twelve-year-old boy as the *Book* seized the sound and the spell together and flung them out into the city night. Nita had to hold her ears. Even when it seemed safe to uncover them again, the echoes bounced back from buildings on all sides and would not stop. Kit stood there amazed as his voice rang and ricocheted from walls blocks away. "Well," he said, "they'll feel the darkness. They'll know what's happening. I think."

"My turn," Nita said, and stood up beside Kit, making sure of her place. Her spell was not a long one. She fumbled for the rowan wand, put it in the hand that also held her wizards' manual, and took the bright *Book* from Kit. "I hope—" she started to say, but the words were shocked out of her as the feeling that the *Book* brought with it shot up her arm. Power, such sheer joyous power that no spell could fail, no matter how new the wizard was to the Art. Here, under moonlight and freed at last from its long restraint, the *Book* was more potent than even the dark rider who trailed them would suspect, and that potency raged to be free. Nita bent her head to her manual and read the spell.

Or tried to. She saw the words, the syllables, and spoke the Speech, but the moonfire falling on the *Book* ran through her veins, slid down her throat, and turned the words to song more subtle than she had ever dreamed of, burned behind her eyes and showed her another time, when another will had voiced these words for the first time and called the trees to battle.

All around her, both now and then, the trees lifted their arms into the wind, breathed the fumes of the new-old Earth and breathed out air that humans could use; they broke the stone to make ground for their children to till and fed the mold with themselves, leaf and bough, for generation upon generation. They knew to what end their sacrifice would come, but they did it anyway, and they would do it again in the Witherer's spite. They were doing it now. Oak and ash and willow, birch and alder, elm and maple, they felt the darkness in the wind that tossed their branches and would not stand still for it. The ground shook all around Nita, roots heaved and came free—first the trees close by, the counterparts of the trees under which she and Kit and Fred had sheltered in the dark otherworld. White oak, larch, twisted crabapple, their leaves glittering around the edges with the flowering radiance of the rowan wand, they lurched and staggered as they came rootloose, and then crowded in around Kit and Nita and Fred, whispering with wind, making a protecting circle through which nothing would pass but moonlight. The effect spread out and away from Nita, though the spell itself was finished, and that relentless power let her sag against one friendly oak, gasping.

For yards, for blocks, as far as she could see through the trunks of the trees that crowded close, branches waved green and wild as bushes and vines and hundred-year monarchs of the park pulled themselves out of the ground and moved heavily to the defense. Away to the east, the clangor of metal hooves and the barks and howls of the dark rider's pack were coming closer. The trees waded angrily toward the noise, some hobbling along on top of the ground, some wading through it, and just as easily through sidewalks and stone walls. In a few minutes there was a nearly solid palisade of living wood between Kit and Nita and Fred and Fifth Avenue. Even the glare of the streetlights barely made it through the branches.

Kit and Nita looked at each other. "Well," Kit said reluctantly, "I guess we can't put it off any longer."

Nita shook her head. She moved to put her manual away and was momentarily shocked when the rowan wand, spent, crumbled to silver ash in her hand. "So much for that," she said, feeling unnervingly naked now that her protection was gone. Another howl sounded, very close by, and was abruptly cut off in a rushing of branches as if a tree had fallen on something on purpose. Nita fumbled in her pocket and pulled out a nickel. "Call it," she said.

"Heads."

She tossed the coin, caught it, slapped it down on her forearm. Heads. "Crud," she said, and handed the bright *Book* to Kit.

He took it uneasily, but with a glitter of excitement in his eye. "Don't worry," he said. "You'll get your chance."

"Yeah, well, don't hog it." She looked over at him and was amazed to see him regarding her with some of the same worry she was feeling. From outside the fence of trees came a screech of brakes, the sound of a long skid, and then a great splintering crashing of metal and smashing of glass as an attacking cab lost an argument with some tree standing guard. Evidently reinforcements from that other, darker world were arriving.

"I won't," Kit said. "You'll take it away from me and keep reading if—"

He stopped, not knowing what might happen. Nita nodded. "Fred," she said, "we may need a diversion. But save yourself till the last minute."

(I will. Kit—) The spark of light hung close to him for a moment. (Be careful.)

Suddenly, without warning, every tree around them shuddered as if violently struck. Nita could hear them crying out in silent anguish, and cried out in terror herself as she felt what they felt—a great numbing cold that smote at the heart like an ax. Kit, beside her, sat frozen with it, aghast. Fred went dim with shock. (Not again!) he said, his voice faint and horrified. (Not *here*, where there's so much life!)

"The Sun," Nita whispered. "He put out the Sun!" *Starsnuffer*, she thought. *That tactic's worked for him before. And if the Sun is out, pretty soon there won't be moonlight to read by, and he can—*

Kit stared up at the Moon as if at someone about to die. "Nita, how long do we have?"

"Eight minutes, maybe a little more, for light to get here from the Sun. Eight minutes before it runs out . . ."

Kit sat down hurriedly, laid the bright *Book* in his lap, and opened it. The light of the full Moon fell on the glittering pages. This time the print was not vague as under the light of Nita's wand. It was clear and sharp and dark, as easily read as normal print in daylight. The *Book*'s covers were fading, going clear, burning with that eye-searing transparency that Nita had seen about Kit and herself before. The whole *Book* was hardly to be seen except for its printing, which burned in its own fashion, supremely black and clear, but glistening as if the ink with which the characters were printed had moonlight trapped in them too. *"Here's an index,"* Kit whispered, using the Speech now. *"I think—the part about New York—"*

Yes, Nita thought desperately, as another cab crashed into the trees and finished itself. *And what then? What do we do about . . .* She would not finish the thought, for the sound of those leisurely, deadly hoofbeats was getting closer, and mixing with it were sirens and the panicked sound of car horns. She thought of that awful dark form crossing Madison, kicking cars aside, crushing what tried to stop it, and all the time that wave of blackness washing alongside, changing everything, stripping the streets bare of life and light. *And what about the Sun? The Earth will freeze over before long, and he'll have the whole planet the way he wants it—* Nita shuddered. Cold and darkness and nothing left alive—a storm-broken, ice-locked world, full of twisted machines stalking desolate streets forever. . . .

Kit was turning pages, quickly but gently, as if what he touched was a live thing. Perhaps it was. Nita saw him pause between one page and the next, holding one bright-burning page draped delicately over his fingers, then letting it slide carefully down to lie with the others he'd turned. *"Here,"* he whispered, awed, delighted. He did not look up to see what Nita saw, the wave of darkness creeping around them, unable to pass the tree wall, passing onward, surrounding them so that they were suddenly on an island of grass in a sea of wrestling naked tree limbs and bare-seared dirt and rock. *"Here—"*

He began to read, and for all her fear Nita was lulled to stillness by wonder. Kit's voice was that of someone discovering words for the first time after a long silence, and the words he found were a song, as her spell to free the trees had seemed. She sank deep in the music of the Speech, hearing the story told in what Kit read.

Kit was invoking New York, calling it up as one might call up a spirit; and obedient to the summons, it came. The skyline came, unsmirched by any blackness—a crown of glittering towers in a smoky sunrise, all stabbing points and jeweled windows, precipices of steel and stone. City Hall came, brooding over its colonnades, gazing down in weary interest at the people who came and went and governed the island through it. The streets came, hot, dirty, crowded, but flowing with voices and traffic and people, bright lifeblood surging through concrete arteries. The parks came, settling into place one by one as they were described, free of the darkness under the night—from tiny paved vest-pocket niches to the lake-set expanses of Central Park, they all came, thrusting the black fog back. Birds sang, dogs ran and barked and rolled in the grass, trees were bright with wary squirrels' eyes. The Battery came, the crumbling old first-defense fort standing peaceful now at the southernmost tip of Manhattan—the rose-gold of some remembered sunset glowed warm on its bricks as it mused in weedy silence over old battles won and nonetheless kept an eye on the waters of the harbor, just in case some British cutter should try for a landing when the colonists weren't looking. Westward over the water, the Palisades were there, shadowy cliffs with the Sun behind them, mist blue and mythical-looking though New Jersey was only a mile away. Eastward and westward the bridges were there, the lights of their spanning suspension cables coming out blue as stars in the twilight. Seabirds wheeled pale and graceful about the towers of the George Washington Bridge and the Verrazano Narrows and the iron crowns of the 59th Street Bridge, as the soft air of evening settled over Manhattan, muting the city roar to a quiet breathing rumble. Under the starlight and the risen Moon, an L-1011 arrowed out of LaGuardia Airport and soared over the city, screaming its high song of delight in the cold upper airs, dragging the thunder along behind. . . .

Nita had to make an effort to pull herself out of the waking dream. Kit read on, while all around the trees bent in close to hear, and the air flamed clear and still as a frozen moment of memory. He read on, naming names in the Speech, describing people and places in terrifying depth and detail, making them real and keeping them that way by the *Book*'s power and the sound of the words. But no sign of any terror at the immensity of what he was doing showed in Kit's face— and that frightened Nita more than the darkness that still surged and whispered around them and their circle of trees. Nita could see Kit starting to burn with that same unbearable clarity, becoming more real, so much so that he was not needing to be visible anymore. Slowly, subtly, the *Book*'s vivid transparency was taking him too. Fred, hanging beside Kit and blazing in defiance of the dark, looked pale in comparison. Even Kit's shadow glowed, and it occurred to Nita that shortly, if this kept up, he wouldn't have one. *What do I do?* she thought. *He's not having trouble, he seems to be getting* stronger, *not weaker, but if this has to go on much longer . . .*

Kit kept reading. Nita looked around her and began to see an answer. The darkness had not retreated from around them. Out on the Fifth Avenue side of the tree-wall, the crashes of cabs were getting more frequent, the howls of perytons were closer, the awful clanging hoofbeats seemed almost on top of them. There was nowhere to run, and Nita knew with horrible certainty that not all the trees in the park would be enough to stop the Starsnuffer when he came there. Keeping New York real was one answer to this problem, but not *the* answer. The darkness and the unreality were symptoms, not the cause. Something had to be done about *him.*

The iron hooves paused. For an awful moment there was no sound; howls and screeching tires fell silent. Then metal began to smash on stone in a thunderous canter, right across the street, and with a horrible screeching neigh the rider's iron steed smashed into the tree wall, splintering wood, bowing the palisade inward. Nita wanted to shut her mind against the screams of the trees broken and flung aside in that first attack, but she could not. All around her the remaining trees sank their roots deep in determination, but even they knew it would be hopeless. There were enough cracks in the wall that Nita could see the black steed rearing back for another smash with its front four hooves, the rider smiling, a cold cruel smile that made Nita shudder. One more stroke and the wall would be down. Then there would be wildfire in the park. Kit, oblivious, kept reading. The iron mount rose to its full height. "Fred," Nita whispered, "I think you'd better—" The sound of heavy hoofbeats, coming from behind them, from the park side, choked her silent. *He has a twin brother*, Nita thought. *We* are *dead.*

But the hoofbeats divided around the battered circle of trees and poured past in a storm of metal and stone, the riders and steeds marble pale or bronze dark, every equestrian statue in or near Central Park gathered together into an impossible cavalry that charged past Nita and Kit and Fred and into the street to give battle. Perytons and cabs screamed as General Sherman from Grand Army Plaza crashed in among them with sword raised, closely followed by Joan of Arc in her armor, and Simón Bolívar and General San Martin right behind. King Wladislaw was there in medieval scale mail, galloping on a knight's armored charger; Don Quixote was there, urging poor broken-down Rosinante to something faster than a stumble and shouting threats against the whole breed of sorcerers; Teddy Roosevelt was there, cracking off shot after shot at the cabs as his huge horse stamped them into the pavement; El Cid Campeador rode there, his bannered lance striking down one peryton after another. Behind all these came a wild assortment of creatures, pouring past the tree circle and into the street—eagles, bears, huge dogs, a hunting cat, a crowd of doughboys from the first World War with bayoneted rifles—all the most warlike of the nearby statuary—even some not so warlike, such as several deer and the Ugly Duckling. From down Fifth Avenue came striding golden Prometheus from his pedestal in Rockefeller Center, bearing the fire he brought for mortals and using it in bolt after bolt to melt down cabs where they stood; and from behind him, with a stony roar like the sky falling, the great white lions from the steps of the Public Library leaped together and threw themselves upon the iron steed and its dark rider. For all its extra legs, the mount staggered back and sideways, screaming in a horrible parody of a horse's neigh and striking feebly at the marble claws that tore its flanks.

Under cover of that tumult of howls and crashes and the clash of arms, Nita grabbed Kit to pull him away from the tree wall, behind another row of trees. She half expected her hands to go right through him, he was becoming so transparent. Unresisting, he got up and followed her, still holding the *Book* open, still reading as if he couldn't stop, or didn't want to, still burning more and more fiercely with the inner light of the bright *Book*'s power. "Fred," she said as she pushed Kit down onto the ground again behind a looming old maple, "I've got to do this now. I may not be able to do anything else. If a diversion's needed—"

(I'll do what's necessary,) Fred said, his voice sounding as awed and frightened as Nita felt at the sight of what Kit was becoming. (You be careful, too.)

She reached out a hand to Fred. He bobbed close and settled at the tip of one finger for a moment, perching there delicately as a firefly, energy touching matter for a moment as if to reconfirm the old truth that they were just different forms of the same thing. Then he lifted away, turning his attention out to the street, to the sound of stone and metal wounding and being wounded; and in one quick gesture Nita grabbed the *Book of Night with Moon* away from Kit and bent her head to read.

An undertow of blinding power and irresistible light poured into her, over her, drowned her deep. She couldn't fight it. She didn't want to. Nita understood now the clear-burning transfiguration of Kit's small plain human face and body, for it was not the wizard who read the *Book*; it was the other way around. The silent Power that had written the *Book* reached through it now and read what life had written in her body and soul—joys, hopes, fears, and failings all together—then took her intent and read that too, turning it into fact. She was turning the bright pages without even thinking about it, finding the place in the *Book* that spoke of creation and rebellion and war among the stars—the words that had once before broken the terrible destroying storm of death and darkness that the angry Star-snuffer had raised to break the new-made worlds and freeze the seas where life was growing, an eternity ago. *"I am the wind that troubles the water,"* Nita said, whispering in the Speech. The whisper smote against the windowed cliffs until they echoed again, and the clash and tumult of battle began to grow still as the wind rose at her naming. *"I am the water, and the waves; I am the shore where the waves break in rainbows; I am the sunlight that shines in the spray—"*

The power rose with the rhythms of the old, old words, rose with the wind as all about her the earth and air and waters of the park began to remember what they were—matter and energy, created, indestructible, no matter what darkness lay over them. *"I am the trees that drink the light; I am the air of the green things' breathing; I am the stone that the trees break asunder; I am the molten heart of the world—"*

"NO!" came his scream from beyond the wall of trees, hating, raging, desperate. But Nita felt no fear. It was as it had been in the Beginning; all his *no*'s had never been able to stand against life's *I Am*. All around her trees and stones and flesh and metal burned with the power that burned her, self-awareness, which death can seem to stop but can never keep from happening, no matter how hard it tries. *"Where will you go? To what place will you wander?"* she asked sorrowfully, or life asked through her, hoping that the lost one might at last be convinced to come back to his allegiance. Of all creatures alive and otherwise, he had been and still was one of the mightiest. If only his stubborn anger would break, his power could be as great for light as for darkness—but it could not happen. If after all these weary eons he still had not realized the hopelessness of his position, that everywhere he went, life was there before him. . . . Still she tried, the ancient words speaking her solemnly. *". . . in vale or on hilltop, still I am there . . ."*

Silence, silence, except for the rising wind. All things seemed to hold their breath to hear the words; even the dark rider, erect again on his iron steed and bitter of face, ignoring the tumult around him. His eyes were only for Nita, for only her reading held him bound. She tried not to think of him, or of the little time remaining before the Moon went out, and gave herself over wholly to the reading. The words shook the air and the earth, blinding, burning.

"Will you sound the sea's depth, or climb the mountain?
In air or in water, still I am there;
Will the earth cover you? Will the night hide you?
In deep or in darkness, still I am there;
Will you kindle the nova, or kill the starlight?
In fire or in deathcold, still I am there—"

The Moon went out.

Fred cried out soundlessly, and Nita felt the loss of light like a stab in the heart. The power fell away from her, quenched, leaving her small and cold and human and alone, holding in her hands a *Book* gone dark from lack of moonlight. She and Kit turned desperately toward each other in a darkness rapidly becoming complete as the flowing blackness put out the last light of the city. Then came the sound of low, satisfied laughter and a single *clang* of a heavy hoof, stepping forward.

Another *clang*.

Another.

(Now,) Fred said suddenly, (*now* I understand what all that emitting was practice for. No beta, no gamma, no microwave or upper-wavelength ultraviolet or X rays, is that all?)

"Fred?" Kit said, but Fred didn't wait. He shot upward, blazing, a point of light like a star falling the wrong way, up and up until his brightness was as faint as one more unremarkable star. "Fred, where are you *going?*"

(To create a diversion,) his thought came back, getting fainter and fainter. (Nita, Kit—)

They could catch no more clear thoughts, only a great wash of sorrow and loss, a touch of fear—and then brightness intolerable erupted in the sky as Fred threw his claudication open, emitting all his mass at once as energy, blowing his quanta. He could hardly have been more than halfway to the Moon, for a second or two later it was alight again, a blazing, searing full Moon such as no one had ever seen. There was no looking at either Fred's blast of light or at the Moon that lit trees and statues and the astounded face of the Starsnuffer with a light like a silver sun.

The rider spent no more than a moment being astounded. Immediately he lifted his steel rod, pointing it at Fred this time, shouting in the Speech cold words that were a curse on all light everywhere, from time's beginning to its end. But Fred burned on, more fiercely, if possible. Evidently not even the Starsnuffer could quickly put out a white hole that was liberating all the bound-up energy of five or six blue-white giant stars at once.

"Nita, Nita, *read!*" Kit shouted at her. Through her tears she looked down at the *Book* again and picked up where she had left off. The dark rider was cursing them all in earnest now, knowing that another three lines in the *Book* would bring Nita to his name. She had only to pronounce it to cast him out into the unformed void beyond the Universes, where he had been cast the first time those words were spoken.

Cabs and perytons screamed and threw themselves at the barrier in a last wild attempt to break through, the statues leaped into the fray again, stone and flesh and metal clashed. Nita fell down into the bright power once more, crying, but reading in urgent haste so as not to waste the light Fred was giving himself to become.

As the power began again to read her, she could hear it reading Kit, too, his voice matching hers as it had in their first wizardry, small and thin and brave, and choked with grief like hers. She couldn't stop crying, and the power burned in her tears, too, an odd hot feeling, as she cried bitterly for Fred, for Kit's Lotus, for everything horrible that had happened all that day—all the fair things skewed, all the beauty twisted by the dark Lone Power watching on his steed. If only there were some way he could be otherwise if he wanted to. For here was his name, a long splendid flow of syllables in the Speech, wild and courageous in its own way—and it said that he had not always been so hostile; that he got tired sometimes of being wicked, but his pride and his fear of being ridiculed would never let him stop. *Never, forever*, said the symbol at the very end of his name, the closed circle that binds spells into an unbreakable cycle and indicates lives bound the same way. Kit was still reading. Nita turned her head in that nova moonlight and looked over her shoulder at the one who watched. His face was set, and bitter still, but weary. He knew he was about to be cast out again, frustrated again, and he knew that because of what he had bound himself into being, he would never know fulfillment of any kind. Nita looked back down to the reading, feeling sorry even for him, opened her mouth and along with Kit began to say his name.

Don't be afraid to make corrections!

Whether the voice came from her memory or was a last whisper from the blinding new star far above, Nita never knew. But she knew what to do. While Kit was still on the first part of the name she pulled out her pen, her best pen that Fred had saved and changed. She clicked it open. The metal still tingled against her skin, the ink at the point still glittered oddly—the same glitter as the ink with which the bright *Book* was written. Nita bent quickly over the *Book* and, with the pen, in lines of light, drew from that final circle an arrow pointing upward, the way out, the symbol that said change could happen—if, only if—and together they finished the Starsnuffer's name in the Speech, said the new last syllable, made it real.

The wind was gone. Fearfully Nita and Kit turned around, looked at Fifth Avenue—and found it empty. The creeping blackness was gone with the breaking of its master's magic and the sealing of the worldgate he had held open. Silent and somber, the statues stood among the bodies of the slain—crushed cabs and perytons, shattered trees—then one by one each paced off into the park or down Fifth Avenue, back to its pedestal and its long quiet regard of the city. The howl of sirens, lost for a while in the wind that had risen, now grew loud again. Kit and Nita stood unmoving as the trees ringing them moved away to their old places, sinking roots back into torn-up earth and raising branches to the burning Moon. Some ninety-three million miles away, the Sun had come quietly back to life. But its light would not reach Earth for another eight minutes yet, and as Nita and Kit watched, slowly the new star in the heavens faded, and the Moon faded with it—from daylight brilliance to silver fire, to steel gray glow, to earthlight shimmer, to nothing. The star went yellow, and red, and died. Nothing was left but a stunning, skywide aurora, great curtains and rays of rainbow light shivering and crackling all across the golden-glowing city night.

"He forgot the high-energy radiation again," Kit said, tears constricting his voice to a whisper.

Nita closed the *Book* she held in her hands, now dark and ordinary looking except for the black depths of its covers, the faint shimmer of starlight on page edges. "He always does," she said, scrubbing at her eyes, and then offered Kit the *Book*. He shook his head, and Nita dropped it into her backpack and slung it over her back again. "You think *he'll* take the chance?" she said.

"Huh? Oh." Kit shook his head unhappily. "I dunno. Old habits die hard. If he wants to . . ."

Above them the Moon flicked on again, full and silver bright through the blue-and-red shimmer of the auroral curtain. They stood gazing at it, a serene, remote brilliance, seeming no different than it had been an hour before, a night before, when everything had been as it should be. And now . . .

"Let's get out of here," Nita said.

They walked out of the park unhindered by the cops and firemen who were already arriving in squad cars and fire trucks and paramedic ambulances. Evidently no one felt that two grade-school kids could possibly have anything to do with a street full of wrecked cabs and violently uprooted trees. As they crossed Fifth Avenue and the big mesh-sided Bomb Squad truck passed them, Nita bent to pick up a lone broken-off twig of oak, and stared at it sorrowfully. "There wasn't even anything left of him," she said as they walked east on Sixty-fourth, heading back to the Pan Am Building and the timeslide.

"Only the light," Kit said, looking up at the aurora. Even that was fading now.

Silently they made their way to Grand Central and entered the Pan Am Building at the mezzanine level. The one guard was sitting with his back to them and his feet on the desk, reading the *Post*. Kit went wearily over to one elevator, laid a hand on it, and spoke a word or three to it in the Speech. Its doors slid silently open, and they got in and headed upstairs.

The restaurant level was dark, for the place served only lunch, and there was no one to see them go back up to the roof. Kit opened the door at the top of the stairs, and together they walked out into peace and darkness and a wind off the ocean. A helicopter was moored in the middle of the pad with steel pegs and cables, crouching on its skids and staring at them with clear, sleepy, benevolent eyes. The blue high-intensity marker lights blazed about it like the circle of a protection spell. Nita looked away, not really wanting to think about spells or anything else to do with wizardry. *The book said it would be hard. That I didn't mind. But I hurt! And where's the good part? There was supposed to be happiness too . . .*

The bright *Book* was heavy on her back as she looked out across the night. All around, for miles and miles, was glittering light, brilliant motion, shining under the Moon; lights of a thousand colors gleaming from windows, glowing on streets, blazing from the headlights of cars. The city, breathing, burning, living the life they had preserved. Ten million lives and more. *If something should happen to all that life—how terrible!* Nita gulped for control as she remembered Fred's words of just this morning, an eternity ago. And this was what being a wizard was about. Keeping terrible things from happening, even when it hurt. Not just power, or control of what ordinary people couldn't control, or delight in being able to make strange things happen. Those were side effects—not the reason, not the purpose.

She could give it up, she realized suddenly. In the recovery of the bright *Book*, she and Kit had more than repaid the energy invested in their training. If they chose to lay the Art aside, if *she* did, no one would say a word. She would be left in peace. Magic does not live in the unwilling soul.

Yet never to hear a tree talk again, or a stone, or a star . . .

On impulse Nita held out her hands and closed her eyes. Even without the rowan rod she could feel the moonfire on her skin as a tree might feel it. She could taste the restored sunlight that produced it, feel the soundless roar of the ancient atomic furnace that had burned just this way while her world was still a cloud of gas, nebulous and unformed. And ever so faintly she could taste a rainbow spatter of high-energy radiation, such as a white hole might leave after blowing its quanta.

She opened her eyes, found her hands full of moonlight that trembled like bright water, its surface sheened with fading aurora glow. "All right," she said after a moment. "All right." She opened her hands to let the light run out. *"Kit?"* she said, saying his name in the Speech.

He had gone to stand beside the helicopter and was standing with one hand laid against its side. It stared at him mutely. *"Yeah,"* he said, and patted the cool metal, and left the chopper to rejoin Nita. *"I guess we pass the test."*

They took their packs off and got out the materials necessary for the timeslide. When the lithium-cadmium battery and the calculator chip and the broken teacup handle were in place, Kit and Nita started the spell—and without warning were again caught up by the augmenting power of the bright *Book* and plunged more quickly than they expected into the wizardry. It *was* like being on a slide, though they were the ones who held still, and the events of the day as seen from the top of the Pan Am Building rushed backward past them, a high-speed 3-D movie in reverse. Blinding white fire and the nova Moon grew slowly in the sky, flared, and were gone. The Moon, briefly out, came on again. Darkness flowed backward through the suddenly open worldgate, following its master on his huge dark mount, who also stepped backward and vanished through the gate. Kit and Nita saw *themselves* burst out of the roof door, blurred with speed; saw themselves run backward over the railing, a bright line of light pacing them as they plunged out into the dark air, dove backward through the gate, and vanished with it. The Sun came up in the west and fled back across the sky. Men in coveralls burst out of the roof door and unpegged the helicopter; two of them got into it and it took off backward. Clouds streamed and boiled past, jets fell backward into La Guardia. The Sun stood high. . . .

The slide let them go, and Kit and Nita sat back gasping. "What time have you got?" Kit said when he had enough breath.

Nita glanced at her watch. "Nine forty-five."

"*Nine* forty-five! But we were supposed to—"

"It's this *Book*, it makes everything work too well. At nine forty-five we were—"

They heard voices in the stairwell, behind the closed door. Kit and Nita stared at each other. Then they began frantically picking up the items left from their spelling. Nita paused with the lithium-cadmium battery in her hand as she recognized one of those voices coming up the stairs. She reared back, took aim, and threw the heavy battery at the closed door, hard. CRACK!

Kit looked at her, his eyes wide, and understood. "Quick, behind there," he said. Nita ran to scoop up the battery, then ducked around after Kit and crouched down with him behind the back of the stairwell. There was a long, long pause before the door opened and footsteps could be heard on the gravel. Kit and Nita edged around the side of the stairwell again to peer around the corner. Two small, nervous-looking figures were heading for the south-facing rail in the bright sunlight. A dark-haired girl, maybe thirteen, wearing jeans and a shirt and a down vest; a dark-haired boy, small and a touch stocky, also in jeans and parka, twelve years old or so. The boy held a broken-off piece of antenna, and the girl held a peeled white stick, and they were being paced by a brilliant white spark like a will-o'-the-wisp plugged into too much current and about to blow out.

" 'There are no accidents,' " Kit whispered sadly.

The tears stung Nita's eyes again. "G'bye, Fred," she said softly in English, for fear the Speech should attract his attention, or hers.

Silently and unseen, Kit and Nita slipped through the door and went downstairs for the shuttle and the train home.

Timeheart

THE WALK HOME FROM the bus stop was weary and quiet. Three blocks from Nita's house, they reached the corner where their ways usually parted. Kit paused there, waiting for the light to change, though no traffic was in sight. "Call me tomorrow?" he said.

What for? Nita felt like saying, for there were no more spells in the offing, and she was deadly tired. Still . . . "It's your turn," she said.

"Huh? Right." The light changed, and Kit headed across the street to Nita's left. In the middle of the street he turned, walking backward. "We should call Tom and Carl," he shouted, sounding entirely exhausted.

"Yeah." The light changed again, in Nita's favor; Kit jumped up onto the sidewalk on the other side and headed south toward his place. Nita crossed east, watching Kit as she went. Though the look on his face was tired and sad, all the rest of his body wore the posture of someone who'd been through so much fear that fear no longer frightened him. *Why's he so afraid of getting beat up?* Nita thought. *Nobody in their right mind would mess with him.*

In midstep she stopped, watching him walk away. *How about that. How about that. He got what he asked for.*

After a second she started walking home again. The weight at her back suddenly reminded her of something. (Kit!) she called silently, knowing he could hear even though he was now out of sight. (What about the *Book?*)

(Hang on to it,) he answered. (We'll give it to the Advisories. Or they'll know what to do with it.)

(Right. See ya later.)

(See ya.)

Nita was so tired that it took three or four minutes before the identity of the blond person walking up East Clinton toward her registered at all. By then Joanne was within yelling distance, but she didn't yell at Nita at all, much to Nita's surprise. This was such an odd development that Nita looked at Joanne carefully as they got closer, something she had never done before. There was something familiar about Joanne today, a look that Nita couldn't quite pin down—and then she recognized the expression and let out a tired, unhappy breath. The look was less marked, less violent, and terrible than that of the pride-frozen misery of the dark rider, but there all the same. The angry fear was there too—the terror of what had been until now no threat but was now out of control; the look of the rider about to be cast out by a power he had thought himself safe from, the look of a bully whose victim suddenly wasn't a victim anymore.

Nita slowed down and stopped where she was, in the middle of the sidewalk, watching Joanne. *Even he can be different now*, she thought, her heart beating fast—her own old fear wasn't entirely gone. *But that was partly because we gave him the chance.*

She stood there, watching Joanne slow down warily as she got closer to Nita. Nita sweated. Doing something that would be laughed about behind her back was almost as bad as being beaten up. But she stood still until Joanne came to a stop four or five feet away from her. "Well?" Joanne said, her voice full of anger and uncertainty.

I don't know what to say to her, we have absolutely nothing in common, Nita thought frantically. *But it has to start somewhere.* She swallowed and did her best to look Joanne in the eye, calmly and not in threat. "Come on over to my place after supper sometime and look through my telescope," she said. "I'll show you Jupiter's moons. Or Mars—"

Joanne made that old familiar haughty face and brushed past Nita and away. "Why would I ever want to go to *your* house? You don't even have a wide-screen TV."

Nita stood still, listening to Joanne's footsteps hurrying away, a little faster every second—and slowly began to realize that she'd gotten what she asked for too—the ability to break the cycle of anger and loneliness, not necessarily for others, but at least for herself. It wouldn't even take the Speech; plain words would do it, and the magic of reaching out. It would take a long time, much longer than something simple like breaking the walls between the worlds, and it would cost more effort than even the reading of the *Book of Night with Moon*. But it would be worth it—and eventually it would work. A spell always works.

Nita went home.

That night after supper she slipped outside to sit in Liused's shadow and watch the sky. The tree caught her mood and, after greeting her, was quiet—until about ten o'clock, when it and every other growing thing in sight suddenly trembled violently as if stricken at the root. They had felt the Sun go out.

(It's all right,) she said silently, though for someone whose tears were starting again, it was an odd thing to say. She waited the eight minutes with them, saw the Moon blink out, and leaned back against the rowan trunk, sheltering from the wind that rose in the darkness. Branches tossed as if in a hurricane, leaves hissed in anguish—and then the sudden new star in the heavens etched every leaf's shadow sharp against the ground and set the Moon on fire. Nita squinted up at the pinpoint of brilliance, unwilling to look away though her eyes leaked tears of pain. She'd thought, that afternoon, that living through the loss a second time would be easier. She was wrong. The tears kept falling long after the star went out, and the Moon found its light again, and the wind died to a whisper. She stopped crying long enough to go back inside and go to bed, and she was sure she would start again immediately. But she was wrong about that too. Exhaustion beat down grief so fast that she was asleep almost as soon as her head touched the pillow under which she had hidden the *Book of Night with Moon*. . . .

The place where they stood was impossible, for there's no place in Manhattan where the water level in the East River comes right up to the railed path that runs alongside it. There they stood, though, leaning with their backs against the railing, gazing up at the bright city that reared against the silver sky, while behind them the river whispered and chuckled and slapped its banks. The sound of laughter came down the morning wind from the apartments and the brownstones and the towers of steel and crystal; the seabirds wheeled and cried over the white piers and jetties of the Manhattan shoreline, and from somewhere down the riverside came the faint sound of music—quiet rock, a deep steady backbeat woven about with guitars and voices in close harmony. A jogger went by on the running path, puffing, followed by a large black-and-white dog galloping to catch up with its master.

Are we early, or are they late? Kit asked, leaning back farther still to watch an overflying Learjet do barrel-roll after barrel-roll for sheer joy of being alive.

Who cares? Nita said, leaning back too and enjoying the way the music and the city sounds and the Learjet's delighted scream all blended. *Anyway, this is Timeheart. There's nothing here but Now . . .*

They turned their backs on the towers and the traffic and the laughter, and looked out across the shining water toward Brooklyn and Long Island. Neither was there just then—probably someone else in Timeheart was using them, and Kit and Nita didn't need them at the moment. The silver expanse of the Atlantic shifted and glittered from their feet to the radiant horizon, endless. Far off to their right, south and west of the Battery, the Statue of Liberty held up her torch and her tablet and looked calmly out toward the sunrise as they did, waiting. Nita was the first to see the dark bulge out on the water. She nudged Kit and pointed. *Look, a shark!*

He glanced at her, amused. *Even here I don't think sharks have wheels . . .*

The Lotus came fast, hydroplaning. Water spat up from its wheels as it skidded up to the railing and fishtailed sideways, grinning, spraying them both. On its wildly waving antenna rode a spark of light. Nita smiled at her friend, who danced off the antenna to rest momentarily on one of her fingers like a hundred-watt firefly. *Well*, Nita said, *is it confusing being dead?*

Fred chuckled a rainbow, up the spectrum and down again. *Not very.* Beside him, the Lotus stood up on its hind wheels, putting its front ones on the railing so that Kit could scratch it behind the headlights.

We brought it, Kit said.

Good, said the Lotus, as Nita got the bright *Book* out of her backpack and handed it to Kit. *The Powers want to put it away safe. Though the precaution may not really be necessary, after what you did.*

It worked? He's changed? Nita said.

Fred made a spatter of light, a gesture that felt like the shake of a head. *Not changed. Just made otherwise, as if he'd been that way from the beginning. He has back the option he'd decided was lost—to put aside his anger, to build instead of damn . . .*

Then if he uses that option—you mean every place could be like this some day? Kit looked over his shoulder at the city and all the existence behind it, preserved in its fullest beauty while still growing and becoming greater.

Possibly. What he did remains. Entropy's still here, and death. They look like waste and horror to us now. But if he chooses to have them be a blessing on the worlds, instead of anger's curse—who knows where those gates will lead then? . . . The Lotus sounded pleased by the prospect.

Kit held out the *Book of Night with Moon*. Most delicately the Lotus opened fanged jaws to take it, then rubbed its face against Kit and dropped to all four wheels on the water. It smiled at them both, a chrome smile, silver and sanguine—then backed a little, turned, and was off, spraying Kit and Nita again.

Fred started to follow, but Nita caught him in cupped hands, holding him back for a moment. *Fred! Did we do right?*

Even here she couldn't keep the pain out of her question, the fear that she could somehow have prevented his death. But Fred radiated a serene and wondering joy that took her breath and reassured her and filled her with wonder to match his, all at once. *Go find out*, he said.

She opened her hands and he flew out of them like a spark blown on the wind—a brightness zipping after the Lotus, losing itself against the dazzling silver of the sea, gone. Nita turned around to lean on the railing again, and after a moment Kit turned with her. They breathed out, relaxing, and settled back to gaze at the city transfigured, the city preserved at the heart of Time, as all things loved are preserved in the hearts that care for them—gazed up into the radiance, the life, the light unending, the light. . . .

The light was right in her eyes, mostly because Dairine had yanked the curtain open. Her sister was talking loudly, and Nita turned her head and quite suddenly felt what was not under her pillow. "You gonna sleep all morning? Get up, it's ten thirty! The Sun went out last night, you should see it, it was on the news. And somebody blew up Central Park; and Kit Rodrigucz called, he wants you to call him back. How come you keep calling each other, anyhow?" Halfway out the bedroom door, realization dawned in her sister's eyes. "Maaaaa!" she yelled out the door, strangling on her own laughter. "Nita's got a *boyfriend!*"

"Oh, jeez, Dair*iiiiiiiine!*"

The wizard threw her pillow at her sister, got up, and went to breakfast.

Water Wizards

C

SOMETHING PUSHED HER in the back, *hard*. Nita gasped and whipped around in the water, thinking, *This is it, there are* too *sharks here and I'm* dead! The sight of the slick-skinned shape in the water stopped her breath—until she realized what she was looking at. A slender body, ten feet long; a blowhole and an amused eye that looked at her sidelong; and a long, beaked face that wore a permanent smile. She reached out a hesitant hand, and under her touch the dolphin turned lazily, rolling sideways, brushing her with skin like warm, moonlit satin.

She was immensely relieved. "*Dai'stiho,*" she said, greeting the swimmer in the Tongue that wizards use, the language that she'd learned from her manual and that all creatures understand.

The dolphin rolled back toward her and looked at her in what seemed to be shock. "*A wizard!*" it said in an urgent whistle.

Deep
Wizardry

For J. A. C.
re: redemption and fried zucchini

Contents

Summer Night's Song
145

Wizards' Song
149

A Song of Choice
158

Seniors' Song
166

The Blue's Song
174

Ed's Song
190

A Song of Battles
197

Fearsong
206

The Gray Lord's Song
215

Truthsong
222

Foregathering Song
234

The Song of the Twelve
252

Heartsong
275

ACKNOWLEDGMENT

Heartfelt thanks go to Neil Harris and his erstwhile comrades at Commodore, who went crazy hooking up a desperate writer's computer to one of their printers, and who helped her hit her deadline.

A pause! Lost ground!
—yet not unavailing, for soon shall be found
what took three ages to subdue.
The hunters, on their guard,
give sparingly and greatly, east and west:
yet how shall only faithfulness prevail
against the peril of the overarching deep?

TRIGRAM 63/CHI CHI:
WATER OVER FIRE

Hudson Canyon and Environs

Nantucket Island

Montauk Point

Tiena Beach

Long Island

Sandy Hook

Hudson Shelf Channel

Barnegat Inlet

HUDSON CANYON

CONTINENTAL RISE

Caryn Peak
(+6,000 ft.)

-15,000 ft.

N

0   miles   50

Original map by Diane Duane

Adapted from material in *Wizards' Instruction and Implementation Manual*, 933rd edition, by kind permission of the Editor

Summer
Night's Song

🌙

NITA SLIPPED OUT THE back door of the beach house, careful not to let the rickety screen door slam, and for a second stood silently on the back porch in the darkness. It was no use. "Nita"—her mother's voice came floating out from the living room—"where're you going?"

"Out," Nita said, hoping to get away with it just this once.

She might as well have tried to rob a bank. "Out where?"

"Down to the beach, Mom."

There was a sigh's worth of pause from the living room, broken by the sound of a crowd on TV shouting about a base that had just been stolen somewhere in the country. "I don't like you walking down there alone at night, Neets . . ."

"Nhhnnnnn," Nita said, a loud noncommittal noise she had learned to make while her mother was deciding whether to let her do something. "I'll take Ponch with me," she said in a burst of inspiration.

"Mmmmmm . . . ," her mother said, considering it. Ponch was a large black-and-white dog, part Border collie, part German shepherd, part mutt—an intrepid hunter of water rats and gulls, and ferociously loyal to his master and to Nita because she was his master's best friend. "Where's Kit?"

"I dunno." It was at least partly the truth. "He went for a walk awhile ago."

"Well . . . OK. You take Ponch and look for Kit, and bring him back with you. Don't want his folks thinking we're not taking care of him."

"Right, Ma," Nita said, and went pounding down the creaky steps from the house to the yard before her mother could change her mind, or her father, immersed in the ball game, could come back to consciousness.

"Ponch! Hey, Pancho!" Nita shouted, pounding through the sandy front yard, through the gate in the ancient picket fence, and out across the narrow paved road to the dune on the other side of the road. Joyous barking began on the far side of the dune as Nita ran up it. *He's hunting again*, Nita thought, and would have laughed for delight if running had left her any breath. *This is the best vacation we ever had . . .*

At the top of the dune she paused, looking down toward the long, dark expanse of the beach. "It's been a good year," her father had said a couple of months before, over dinner. "We can't go far for vacation—but let's go somewhere nice. One of the beaches in the Hamptons, maybe. We'll rent a house and live beyond our means. For a couple weeks, anyway . . ."

It hadn't taken Nita much begging to get her folks to let her friend Kit Rodriguez go along with them, or to get Kit's folks to say yes. Both families were delighted that their children had each finally found a close friend. Nita and Kit laughed about that sometimes. Their families knew only the surface of what was going on—which was probably for the best.

A black shape came scrabbling up the dune toward Nita, flinging sand in all directions in his hurry. "Whoa!" she shouted at Ponch, but it was no use; it never was. He hit her about stomach level with both paws and knocked her down, panting with excitement; then, when she managed to sit up, he started enthusiastically washing her face. His breath smelled like dead fish.

"Euuuuw, enough!" Nita said, making a face and pushing the dog more or less off her. "Ponch, where's Kit?"

"Yayayayayayayaya!" Ponch barked, jumping up and bouncing around Nita in an attempt to get her to play. He grabbed up a long string of dead seaweed in his jaws and began shaking it like a rope and growling.

"Cut it out, Ponch. Get serious." Nita got up and headed down the far side of the dune, brushing herself off as she went. "Where's the boss?"

"He played with me," Ponch said in another string of barks as he loped down the dune alongside her. "He threw the stick. I chased it."

"Great. Where is he *now?*"

They came to the bottom of the dune together. The sand was harder there, but still dry; the tide was low and just beginning to turn. "Don't know," Ponch said, a bark with a grumble on the end of it.

"Hey, you're a good boy; I'm not mad at you," Nita said. She stopped to scratch the dog behind the ears, in the good place. He stood still with his tongue hanging out and looked up at her, his eyes shining oddly in the light of the nearly full moon that was climbing the sky. "I just don't feel like playing right now. I want to swim. Would you find Kit?"

The big brown eyes gazed soulfully up at her, and Ponch made a small beseeching whine. "A dog biscuit?"

Nita grinned. "Blackmailer. OK, you find the boss, I'll give you a biscuit. Two biscuits. Go get 'im!"

Ponch bounded off westward down the beach, kicking up wet sand. Nita headed for the waterline, where she shrugged off the windbreaker that had been covering her bathing suit and dropped it on the sand. Two months ago, talking to a dog and getting an answer back would have been something that happened only in Disney movies. But then one day in the library, Nita had stumbled on to a book called *So You Want to Be a Wizard.* She'd followed the instructions in the book, as Kit had in the copy he'd found in a used bookstore—and afterward, dogs talked back. Or, more accurately, she knew what language they spoke and how to hear it. There was nothing that *didn't* talk back, she'd found—only things she didn't yet know how to hear or how to talk to properly.

Like parents, Nita thought with mild amusement. If her mother knew Nita was going swimming, she'd probably pitch a fit: she'd had a terrible thing about night swimming after seeing *Jaws.* But *it's OK*, Nita thought. *There aren't any sharks here . . . and if there were, I think I could talk them out of eating me.*

She made sure her clothes were above the high-water line, then waded down into the breakers. The water was surprisingly warm around her knees. The waxing moon, slightly golden from smog, made a silvery pathway on the water, everywhere else shedding a dull radiance that made both land and sea look alive.

What a great night, Nita thought. She went out another twenty paces or so, then crouched over and dived into an incoming wave. Water-borne sand scoured her, the water thundered in her ears; then she broke surface and lay in the roil and dazzle of the moonlit water, floating. There were no streetlights there, and the stars she loved were bright. After a while she stood up in the shoulder-high water, watching the sky. Back up on the beach, Ponch was barking, excited and noisy. *He can't have found Kit that fast*, Nita thought. *Probably something distracted him. A crab, maybe. A dead fish. A shark . . .*

Something pushed her in the back, *hard*. Nita gasped and whipped around in the water, thinking, *This is it, there are too sharks here and I'm* dead! The sight of the slick-skinned shape in the water stopped her breath—until she realized what she was looking at. A slender body, ten feet long; a blowhole and an amused eye that looked at her sidelong; and a long, beaked face that wore a permanent smile. She reached out a hesitant hand, and under her touch the dolphin turned lazily, rolling sideways, brushing her with skin like warm, moonlit satin.

She was immensely relieved. *"Dai'stiho,"* she said, greeting the swimmer in the Tongue that wizards use, the language that she'd learned from her manual and that all creatures understand. She expected no more answer than a fizz or squeak as the dolphin returned the greeting and went about its business.

But the dolphin rolled back toward her and looked at her in what seemed to be shock. *"A wizard!"* it said in an urgent whistle. Nita had no time to answer; the dolphin dived and its tail slapped the surface, spraying her. By the time Nita rubbed the salt sting out of her eyes, there was nothing near her but the usual roaring breakers. Ponch was bouncing frantically on the beach, barking something about sea monsters to the small form walking beside him.

"Neets?"

Nita waded out of the breakers. At the waterline Kit met her and handed Nita her windbreaker. He was smaller than she was, a year younger, dark-haired and brown-eyed and sharp of face and mind; *definitely sharper*, Nita thought with approval, *than the usual twelve-year-old*.

"He was hollering about whales," Kit said, nodding at Ponch.

"Dolphins," Nita said. "At least, *a* dolphin. I said hi to it and it said, 'A wizard!' and ran away."

"Great." Kit looked southward, across the ocean. "Something's going on out there, Neets. I was up on the jetty. The rocks are upset."

Nita shook her head. Her specialty as a wizard was living things; animals and plants talked to her and did the things she asked, at least if she asked properly. It still startled her sometimes when Kit got the same kind of result from "unalive" things like cars and doors and telephone poles, but that was where his talent lay. "What can a rock get upset about?" she said.

"I'm not sure. They wouldn't say. The stones piled up there remembered something. And they didn't want to think about it anymore. They were shook." Kit looked up sharply at Nita. "That was *it*. The earth shook once . . ."

"Oh, come off it. This isn't California. Long Island doesn't have earthquakes."

"Once it did. The rocks remember . . . I wonder what that dolphin wanted?"

Nita was wondering, too. She zipped up her windbreaker. "C'mon, we have to get back before Mom busts a gut."

"But the dolphin—"

Nita started down the beach, then turned and kept walking backward when she noticed that Kit wasn't following her. "The ball game was almost over," she said, raising her voice as she got farther from Kit and Ponch. "They'll go to bed early. They always do. And when they're asleep—"

Kit nodded and muttered something, Nita couldn't quite hear what. He vanished in a small clap of inrushing air and then reappeared next to Nita, walking with her; Ponch barked in annoyance and ran to catch up.

"He really hates that 'beam-me-up-Scotty' spell," Nita said.

"Yeah, when it bends space, it makes him itch. Look, I was practicing that other one—"

"With the water?" She grinned at him. "In the dark, I hope."

"Yeah. I'll show you later. And then—"

"Dolphins."

"Uh-*huh*. C'mon, I'll race you."

They ran up the dune, followed by a black shape barking loudly about dog biscuits.

Wizards' Song

THE MOON GOT HIGH. Nita sat by the window of her ground-floor room, listening through the stillness for the sound of voices upstairs. There hadn't been any for a while.

She sighed and looked down at the book she held in her lap. It looked like a library book—bound in one of those slick-shiny buckram library bindings, with a Dewey decimal number written at the bottom of the spine in that indelible white ink librarians use, and at the top of the spine, the words SO YOU WANT TO BE A WIZARD. But on opening the book, what one saw were the words *Instruction and Implementation Manual, General and Limited Special-Purpose Wizardries, Sorceries, and Spells: 933rd Edition.* Or that was what you saw if you were a wizard, for the printing was done in the graceful, Arabic-looking written form of the Speech.

Nita turned a few pages of the manual, glancing at them in idle interest. The instructions she'd found in the book had coached her through her first few spells—both the kinds for which only words were needed and those that required raw materials of some sort. The spells had in turn led her into the company of other wizards—beginners like Kit and more experienced ones, typical of the wizards, young and old, working quietly all over the world. And then the spells had taken her right out of the world she'd known, into one of the ones "next door," and into a conflict that had been going on since time's beginning, in all the worlds there were.

In that other world, in a place like New York City but also terribly different, she had passed through the initial ordeal that every candidate for wizardry undergoes. Kit had been with her. Together they had pulled each other and themselves through the danger and the terror, to the successful completion of a quest into which they had stumbled. They saved their own world without attracting much notice; they lost a couple of dear friends they'd met along the way; and they came into their full power as wizards. It was a privilege that had its price. Nita still wasn't sure why she'd been chosen as one of those who fight for the Worlds against the Great Death of entropy. She was just glad she'd been picked.

She flipped pages to the regional directory, where wizards were listed by name and address. Nita never got tired of seeing her own name listed there, for other wizards to call if they needed her. She overshot her own page in the Nassau County section, wanting to check the names of two friends, Senior Wizards for the area—Tom Swale and Carl Romeo. They had recently been promoted to Senior from the Advisory Wizard level, and as she'd suspected, their listing now read "On sabbatical: emergencies only." Nita grinned at the memory of the party they'd thrown to celebrate their promotion. The guests had been a select group. More of them had appeared out of nowhere than arrived through the front door. Several had spent the afternoon floating in midair; another had spent it in the fishpond, submerged. Human beings had been only slightly in the majority at the party, and Nita became very careful at the snack table after her first encounter with the dip made from Pennsylvania crude oil and fresh-ground iron filings.

She paged back through the listing and looked at her own name.

CALLAHAN, Juanita T.   243 E. Clinton Avenue
                             Hempstead, NY 11575
                             (555) 379-6786
On active status   Assignment location:
                             38 Tiana Beach Road
                             Southampton, NY 11829
                             (555) 667-9084

Nita sighed, for this morning the status note had said, like Carl's and Tom's, "Vacationing: emergencies only." The book updated itself all over that way—pages changing sometimes second to second, reporting the status of worldgates in the area, what spells were working where, the cost of powdered newt at your local Advisory. *Whatever's come up*, Nita thought, *we're expected to be able to handle it.*

Of course, last time out they expected us to save the world, too . . .

"Neets!"

She jumped, then tossed her book out the window to Kit and began climbing out. "Sssh!"

"Shhh yourself, mouth. They're asleep. C'mon."

Once over the dune, the hiss and rumble of the midnight sea made talking safer. "You on active status, too?" Kit said.

"Yup. Let's find the dolphin and see what's up."

They ran for the breakers. Kit was in a bathing suit and windbreaker as Nita was, with sneakers slung over his shoulder by the laces. "Okay," he said, "watch this." He said something in the Speech, a long, liquid-sounding sentence with a curious even-uneven rhyme in it, all of which told the night and the wind and the water what Kit wanted of them. And without pause Kit ran right up to the water, which was retreating at that particular moment—and then onto it. Under his weight it bucked and sloshed the way a waterbed will when you stand on it; but Kit didn't sink. He ran four or five paces out onto the silver-slicked surface—then lost his balance and fell over sideways.

Nita started laughing, then hurriedly shut herself up for fear the whole beach should hear. Kit was lying on the water, his head propped up on one hand; the water bobbed him up and down while he looked at her with a sour expression. "It's not funny. I did it all last night and it never happened *once*."

"Must be that you did the spell for two this time," Nita said, tempted to start laughing again, except that Kit would probably have punched her out. She kept her face as straight as she could and stepped out to the water, putting a foot carefully on an incoming, flattened-out wave. It took her weight, flattening more as she stepped up with the other foot and was carried backward. "It's like the slidewalk at the airport," she said, putting her arms out for balance and wobbling.

"Kind of." Kit got up on hands and knees, swaying. "Come on. Keep your knees bent a little. And pick up your feet."

It was a useful warning. Nita tripped over several breakers and sprawled each time, a sensation like doing a belly whopper onto a waterbed, until she got her sea legs. Once past the breakers she had no more trouble, and Kit led her at a bouncy trot out into the open Atlantic.

They both came to understand shortly why not many people, wizards or otherwise, walk on water much. The constant slip and slide of the water under their feet forced them to use leg muscles they rarely bothered with on land. They had to rest frequently, sitting, while they looked around them for signs of the dolphin.

At their first two rest stops there was nothing to be seen but the lights of Ponquogue and Hampton Bays and West Tiana on the mainland, three miles north. Closer, red and white flashing lights marked the entrance to Shinnecock Inlet, the break in the long strip of beach where they were staying. The Shinnecock horn hooted mournfully at them four times a minute, a lonely sounding call. Nita's hair stood up all over her as they sat down the third time and she rubbed her aching legs. Kit's spell kept them from getting wet, but she was chilly; and being so far out there in the dark and quiet was very much like being in the middle of a desert— a wet, hissing barrenness unbroken for miles except by the quick-flashing white light of a buoy or two.

"You okay?" Kit said.

"Yeah. It's just that the sea seems . . . safer near the shore, somehow. How deep is it here?"

Kit slipped his manual out of his windbreaker and pulled out a large nautical map. "About eighty feet, it looks like."

Nita sat up straight in shock. Something had broken the surface of the water and was arrowing toward them at a great rate. It was a triangular fin. Nita scrambled to her feet. "Uh, Kit!"

He was on his feet beside her in a second, staring, too. "A shark has to stay in the water," he said, sounding more confident than he looked. "We don't. We can jump—"

"Oh, yeah? How high? And for how long?"

The fin was thirty yards or so away. A silvery body rose up under it, and Nita breathed out in relief at the frantic, high-pitched chattering of a dolphin's voice. The swimmer leaped right out of the water in its speed, came down, and splashed them both. "I'm late, and you're late," it gasped in a string of whistles and pops, "and S'reee's about to be! Hurry!"

"Right," Kit said, and slapped his manual shut. He said nothing aloud, but the sea's surface instantly stopped behaving like a waterbed and started acting like water. "*Whoolp!*" Nita said as she sank like a stone. She didn't get wet—that part of Kit's spell was still working—but she floundered wildly for a moment before managing to get hold of the dolphin in the cold and dark of the water.

Nita groped up its side and found a fin. Instantly the dolphin took off, and Nita hoisted herself up to a better position, hanging from the dorsal fin so that her body was half out of the water and her legs were safely out of the way of the fiercely lashing tail. On the other side, Kit had done the same. "You might have warned me!" she said to him across the dolphin's back.

He rolled his eyes at her. "If you weren't asleep on your feet, you wouldn't need warning."

"Kit—" She dropped it for the time being and said to the dolphin, "What's S'reee? And why's it going to be late? What's the matter?"

"She," the dolphin said. "S'reee's a wizard. The Hunters are after her and she can't do anything, she's hurt too badly. My pod and another one are with her, but they can't hold them off for long. She's beached, and the tide's coming in—"

Kit and Nita shot each other shocked looks. Another wizard in the area—and out in the ocean in the middle of the night? "What hunters?" Kit said; "Your pod?" Nita said at the same moment.

The dolphin was coming about and heading along the shoreline, westward toward Quogue. "*The* Hunters," it said in a series of annoyed squeaks and whistles. "The ones with teeth, who else? What kind of wizards are they turning out these days, anyway?"

Nita said nothing to this. She was too busy staring ahead of them at a long, dark bumpy whale shape lying on a sandbar, a shape slicked with moonlight along its upper contours and silhouetted against the dull silver of the sea. It was the look of the water that particularly troubled Nita. Shapes leaped and twisted in it, shapes with two different kinds of fins. "Kit!"

"Neets," Kit said, not sounding happy, "there really aren't sharks here, the guy from the Coast Guard said so last week—"

"Tell *them!*" the dolphin said angrily. It hurtled through the water toward the sandbar around which the fighting continued, silent for all its viciousness. The only sound came from the dark shape that lay partly on the bar, partly off it—a piteous, wailing whistle almost too high to hear.

"Are you ready?" the dolphin said. They were about fifty yards from the trouble.

"Ready to *what?*" Kit asked, and started fumbling for his manual.

Nita started to do the same—and then had an idea, and blessed her mother for having watched *Jaws* on TV so many times. "Kit, forget it! Remember a couple months ago and those guys who tried to beat you up? The freeze spell?"

"Yeah . . ."

"Do it, do it big. I'll feed you power!" She pounded the dolphin on the side. "Go beach! Tell your buddies to beach, too!"

"But—"

"Go do it!" She let go of the dolphin's fin and dropped into the water, swallowing hard as she saw another fin, of the wrong shape entirely, begin to circle in on her and Kit. "Kit, get the water working again!"

It took a precious second; and the next one—one of the longer seconds of Nita's life—for her and Kit to clamber up out of the "liquid" water onto the "solid." They made it and grabbed one another for both physical and moral support, as that fin kept coming. "The other spell set?" Nita gasped.

"Yeah—*now!*"

The usual immobility of a working spell came down on them both, with something added—a sense of being not one person alone, but part of a *one* that was somehow bigger than even Nita and Kit together could be. Inside that sudden oneness, she felt the freeze spell waiting like a phone number with all but one digit dialed. Kit said the one word in the Speech that set the spell free, the "last digit," then gripped Nita's hand hard.

Nita did her part, quickly saying the three most dangerous words in all wizardry—the words that give all of a wizard's power over into another's hands. She felt it going from her, felt Kit shaking as he wound her power, her trust, into the spell. And then she took all her fright, and her anger at the sharks, and her pity for the poor wailing bulk on the sand, and let Kit have those, too.

The spell blasted away from the two of them with a shock like a huge jolt of static, then dropped down over the sandbar and the water for hundreds of feet around, sinking like a weighted net. And as if the spell had physically dragged them down, all the circling, hunting fins in the water sank out of sight, their owners paralyzed and unable to swim.

No wizardry is done without a price. Kit wobbled in Nita's grip as if he were going to keel over. Nita had to lock her knees to keep standing. But both of them managed to stay upright until the weakness passed, and Nita looked around with grim satisfaction at the empty water. "The sharks won't be bothering us now," she said. "Let's get up on the sandbar."

It was a few seconds' walk to where the dolphins lay beached on the bar, chattering excitedly. Once up on the sand, Kit took a look at what awaited them and groaned out loud. Nita would have, too, except that she found herself busy breathing deep to keep from throwing up. Everywhere the sand was black and sticky with gobs and splatters of blood, some clotted, some fresh.

The dark bulk of the injured whale heaved up and down with her breathing, while small, weak whistling noises went in and out. The whale's skin was marked with rope burns and little pits and ragged gashes of shark bites. The greatest wound, though, the one still leaking blood, was too large for any shark to have made. It was a crater in the whale's left side, behind the long swimming fin; a crater easily three feet wide, ragged with ripped flesh. The whale's one visible eye, turned up to the moonlight, watched Kit and Nita dully as they came.

"What happened?" Kit said, looking at the biggest wound with disbelief and horror. "It looks like somebody bombed you."

"Someone did," the whale said in a long, pained whistle. Nita came up beside the whale's head and laid a hand on the black skin behind her eye. It was very hot. "It was one of the new killing spears," the whale said to Nita, "the kind that blasts. But never mind that. What did you do with the sharks?"

"Sank them. They're lying on the bottom with a freeze on them."

"But if they don't swim, they can't breathe—they'll die!" The concern in the whale's voice astonished Nita. "Cousins, quick, kill the spell! We're going to need their goodwill later."

Nita glanced at Kit, who was still staring at the wound with a tight, angry look on his face. He glanced up at her. "Huh? Oh. Sure. Better put up a wizard's wall first, so that the dolphins can get back in the water without getting attacked again."

"Right." Nita got her book out and riffled through pages to the appropriate spell, a short-term force field that needed no extra supplies to produce. She said the spell and felt it take hold, then sagged back against the whale and closed her eyes till the dizziness went away. Off to one side she heard Kit saying the words that released the freeze.

A few moments later fins began appearing again out on the water, circling inward toward the sandbar, then sliding away as if they bumped into something, and circling in again.

"The water will take the blood away soon enough," the whale said. "They'll go away and not even remember why they were here . . ." The whale's eye fixed on Nita again. "Thanks for coming so quickly, cousins."

"It took us longer than we wanted. I'm Nita. That's Kit."

"I'm S'reee," the whale said. The name was a hiss and a long, plaintive, upscaling whistle.

Kit left the wound and came up to join Nita. "It was one of those explosive harpoons, all right," he said. "But I thought those were supposed to be powerful enough to blow even big whales in two."

"They are. Ae'mhnuu died that way, this morning." S'reee's whistle was bitter. "He was the Senior Wizard for this whole region of the Plateau. I was studying with him—I was going to be promoted to Advisory soon. Then the ship came, and we were doing a wizardry; we didn't notice—"

Nita and Kit looked at each other. They had found out for themselves that a wizard is at his most vulnerable when exercising his strength. "He died right away," S'reee said. "I took a spear, too. But it didn't explode right away; and the sharks smelled Ae'mhnuu's blood and a great pack of them showed up to eat. They went into a feeding frenzy and bit the spear right out of me. Then one of them started chewing on the spear, and the blasting part of it went off. It killed a lot of them and blew this hole in me. They got so busy eating each other and Ae'mhnuu that I had time to get away. But I was leaving a blood trail, and they followed it. What else should I have expected? . . ."

She wheezed. "Cousins, I hope one of you has skill at healing, for I'm in trouble, and I *can't* die now; there's too much to do."

"Healing's part of my specialty," Nita said, and was quiet for a moment. She'd become adept, as Kit had, at fixing the minor hurts Ponch kept picking up—bee stings and cat bites and so forth. But this was going to be different.

She stepped away from S'reee's head and went back to look at the wound, keeping tight control of her stomach. "I can seal this up all right," she said. "But you're gonna have a huge scar. And I don't know how long it'll take the muscles underneath to grow back. I'm not real good at this yet."

"Keep my breath in my body, cousin, that'll be enough for me," S'reee said.

Nita nodded and started paging through her book for the section on medicine. It started out casually enough with first aid for the minor ailments of wizards—the physical ones like colds and the mental ones like spell backlash and brainburn. Behind that was a section she had only skimmed before, never expecting to need it: MAJOR SURGERY. The spells were complex and lengthy. That by itself was no problem. But all of them called for one supply in common—the blood of the wizard performing them. Nita began to shake. Seeing someone else bleed was bad enough; the sight of her own blood in quantity tended to make her pass out.

"Oh, great," she said, for there was no avoiding what had to be done. "Kit, you have anything sharp on you?"

He felt around in his pockets. "No such luck, Neets . . ."

"Then find me a shell or something."

S'reee's eye glinted in the moonlight. "There are the dolphins," she said.

"What do *they*—oh." The one dolphin still beached, the one who had brought them in, smiled at Nita, exhibiting many sharp teeth.

"Oh, brother," she said, and went down the sandbar to where the dolphin lay. "Look," she said, hunkering down in front of it, "I don't even know your name—"

"Hotshot." He gave her a look that was amused but also kindly.

"Hotshot, right. Look—don't do it hard, OK?" And wincing, Nita put out her left hand and looked away.

"Do what?"

"Do *llllp!*" Nita said, as the pain hit. When she looked again, she saw that Hotshot had nipped her very precisely on the outside of the palm—two little crescents of toothmarks facing each other. Blood welled up, and the place stung, but not too badly to bear.

Hotshot's eyes glittered at her. "Needs salt."

"Yeccch!" But Nita still wanted to laugh, even while her stomach churned. She got up and hurried back to Kit, who was holding her book for her.

Together they went over to the terrible wound, and Nita put her bleeding hand to it, turned away as far as she could, and started reading the spell. It was a long series of complicated phrases in the Speech; she spoke them quickly at first, then more slowly as she began to be distracted by the pain in her hand. And as often happens in a wizardry, she began to lose contact with her physical surroundings.

Soon Kit and S'reee and the beach were gone. Even the book was gone, though she was reading from it. She was surrounded by the roaring of green water around her, and the smell of blood and fear, and shadows in the water, pursuing her. She swam for her life and kept reading.

No wound can be healed, the book said, unless the pain of its inflicting is fully experienced. There was nothing to do but read, and flee, wailing terror-song and grief-song into the water, until the first pain came, the sick, cold sharpness in her side. Nita knew she was sagging, knew Kit was holding her up from behind. But all that was far away.

The second pain came, the fierce mouths ripping and worrying at her till she couldn't go forward anymore, only flail and thrash in an agony of helplessness and revulsion—

—and then the third pain hit, and Nita lost control of everything and started to fall down as the white fire blew up in her side. But the words were speaking *her* now, as they do in the more powerful wizardries. Though inwardly Nita screamed and cried for release, it did her no good. Her own power was loose, doing what she had told it to, and the wizardry wouldn't let her go until it was done. When it was, finally, it dropped her on her face in the sand, and she felt Kit go down with her, trying to keep her from breaking something.

Eventually the world came back. Nita found herself sitting on the sand, feeling wobbly, but not hurting anywhere. She looked up at S'reee's side. New gray skin covered the wound, paler than the rest of the whale, but unbroken. There was still a crater there, but no blood flowed; and many of the smaller shark bites were completely gone, as were the burns from the harpoon's rope where it had gotten tangled around S'reee's flukes.

"Wow," Nita said. She lifted her left hand and looked at it. The place where Hotshot had bitten her was just a little oval of pink puncture marks, all healed.

"You all right?" Kit said, trying to help her up.

"Yeah, yeah, sure," Nita said. She pushed him away as kindly and quickly as she could, staggered down to the waterline, and lost her dinner.

When she came back, her mouth full of the taste of the salt water she'd used to wash it out, S'reee had rolled herself more upright and was talking to Kit. "I still feel deathly sick," she said, "but at least dying isn't a problem . . . not for the moment."

She looked at Nita. Though the long face was frozen into that eternal smile, it was amazing how many expressions could live in a whale's eyes. Admiration was there just now, and gratitude. "You and I aren't just cousins now, hNii't," S'reee said, giving Nita's name a whistly whalish intonation, "but sisters, too, by blood exchanged. And I'm in your debt. Maybe it's poor thanks to a creditor to ask him to lend to you again, right away. But maybe a sister, or a friend"—she glanced at Kit—"would excuse that if it had to happen."

"We're on active status," Kit said. "We have to handle whatever comes up in this area. What's the problem?"

"Well then." S'reee's whistling took on a more formal rhythm. "As the only remaining candidate Senior Wizard for the Waters about the Gates, by wizard's Right I request and require your assistance. Intervention will take place locally and last no more than ten lights-and-darks. The probable level of difficulty does not exceed what the manual describes as 'dangerous,' though if intervention is delayed, the level may escalate to 'extremely dangerous' or 'critical.' Will you assist?"

Nita and Kit looked at each other, unnerved by the second part of the job description. S'reee moaned. "I hate the formalities," she said in a long, unhappy whistle. "I'm too young to be a Senior: I'm only two! But with Ae'mhnuu gone, I'm stuck with it! And we're in trouble, the water people and the land people both, if we don't finish what Ae'mhnuu was starting when he died!" She huffed out a long breath. "I'm just a calf; why did I get stuck with this? . . ."

Kit sighed, too, and Nita made a face at nothing in particular. On their first job, she and Kit had said something similar, about a hundred times. "I'll help," she said, and "Me too," said Kit, in about the same breath.

"But you're tired," Nita said, "and we're tired, and it's late, we ought to go home . . ."

"Come tomorrow, then, and I'll fill you in. Are you living on the Barrier?"

Nita didn't recognize the name. "Over there," Kit said, pointing across the water at Tiana Beach. "Where the lights are."

"By the old oyster beds," S'reee said. "Can you go out swimming a couple hours after the sun's high? I'll meet you, and we'll go where we can talk."

"Uh," Kit said, "if the sharks are still around—"

Out on the water there was a splash of spray as a silvery form leaped, chattering shrilly, and hit the water again. "They won't be," S'reee said, sounding merry for the first time. "Hotshot and his people are one of the breeds the sharks hate worst; when there are enough of them around, few sharks would dare come into the area. Hotshot will be calling more of his people in tonight and tomorrow—that's part of the work I'm doing."

"OK," Nita said. "But what about you? You're stuck here."

"Wake up!" Kit shouted playfully in Nita's ear, nudging her to look down at the sandbar. She found herself standing ankle-deep in salt water. "Tide's coming in. She'll be floated off here in no time."

"Oh. Well then . . ." Nita opened her book, found the word to kill the wizard's wall spell, and said it. Then she looked up at S'reee. "Are you sure you're gonna be all right?"

S'reee looked mildly at her from one huge eye. "We'll find out tomorrow," she said. *"Dai'stiho."*

"Dai," Nita and Kit said, and walked slowly off the sandbar, across the water, and toward the lights of home.

A Song
of Choice

C

N<small>ITA GOT UP LATE</small>, and was still yawning and scrubbing her eyes even after she'd washed and dressed and was well into her second bowl of cereal. Her mother, walking around the kitchen in her bathrobe and watering the plants that hung all over, looked at Nita curiously.

"Neets, were you reading under the covers again last night?"

"No, Mom." Nita started to eat faster.

Her mother watered another plant, then headed for the sink. On the way, she put a hand against Nita's forehead. "You feel okay? Not coming down with anything, are you?"

"No, I'm fine." Nita made an annoyed face when her mother's back was turned. Her mom loved the beach, but at the same time was sure that there were hundreds of ways to get sick there: too much heat, too much cold, too much time in the water; splinters, rusty nails, tar . . . Nita's little sister, Dairine, had kicked off a tremendous family fight last week by insisting that the blueness of her lips after a prolonged swim was actually caused by a grape Popsicle.

"Is Kit having a good time?" her mother said.

"Wow, yeah, he says it's the best," Nita said. Which was true enough: Kit had never been at the beach for more than a day at a time before. Nita suspected that if he could, he'd dig into the sand like a clam and not come out for months.

"I just wanted to make sure. His dad called last night . . . wanted to see how his 'littlest' was."

" '*El Niño,*' " Nita said, under her breath, grinning. It was what Kit's family called him sometimes, a pun—both the word for "the baby" and the name for a Pacific current that caused storms that could devastate whole countries. The name made Kit crazy, and Nita loved to use it on him.

"Be careful he doesn't hear you," Nita's mom said mildly, "or he'll deck you again. —How *have* you two been getting along?"

"Huh? We're fine. Kit's great." Nita saw a slightly odd look come into her mother's eyes. "For a boy," she added hurriedly.

"Well," her mother said, "be careful." And she took the watering can off into the living room.

Now what was that about? Nita thought. She finished her cornflakes at high speed, rinsed the bowl and spoon in the sink, and hurried out of the house to find Kit.

Halfway across the sparse sandy grass of the front yard, another voice spoke up. "Aha," it said. "The mystery lady."

"Put a cork in it, Dairine," Nita said. Her sister was hanging upside down from the trapeze swing of the rusty swing set, her short red hair ruffling in the breeze. Dairine was a tiny stick of a thing and an all-right younger sister, though (in Nita's estimation) much too smart for her own good. Right now entirely too much smart was showing in those sharp gray eyes. Nita tried not to react to it. "Gonna fall down and bust your head open," she said. "Probably lose what few brains you have all over the ground."

Dairine shook her head, causing herself to swing a little. "Naaah," she said, "but I'd sooner"—she started pumping, so as to swing harder—"fall off the swing—than fall out the window—in the middle of the night!"

Nita went first cold, then hot. She glanced at the windows to see if anyone was looking out. They weren't. *"Did you tell?"* she hissed.

"I—don't tell anybody—anything," Dairine said, in time with her swinging. This was true enough. When Dairine had needed glasses, when she'd started getting beaten up at school, and when she was exposed to German measles, nobody had heard about it from *her.*

"Y'like him, huh?" Dairine said.

Nita glared at Dairine, opened her mouth to start shouting, then remembered the open windows.

"Yeah, I like him," Nita said, and turned red at having to make the admission. The problem was, there was no lying to Dairine. She always found out the truth sooner or later and made your life unbearable for having tried to hide it from her.

"You messing around?" Dairine said.

"Dairiiiiiiiine!" Nita said, quietly, but with murder in it. "No, we are *not messing around!"*

"OK. I just wondered. You going swimming?"

"No," Nita said, snapping the strap of her bathing suit very obviously at her sister, "I thought I'd go skiing. Wake *up,* lame brain."

Dairine grinned at Nita upside down. "Kit went west," she said.

"Thanks," Nita said, and headed out of the yard. "Tell Mom and Dad I'll be back for supper."

"Be careful," Dairine called after Nita, in a perfect imitation of their mother. Nita made a face.

"And watch out for sharks!" Dairine added at the top of her lungs.

"Oh, *great,*" Nita said to herself, wondering if her mom or dad had heard. She took off at a dead run in case they had.

She found Kit waiting about a mile down the beach, playing fetch with Ponch to tire him out, as he'd told her he was going to. "Otherwise he gets crazy if I go away. This way he'll just lie down and sack out." And sure enough, after some initial barking and dancing around Nita when she arrived, Ponch flopped panting on the sand beside them where they sat talking and finally rolled over on one side and began to snore.

They grinned at each other and headed out into the water. It was unnerving at first, to swim straight out into the ocean, past the breakers and the rollers, past the place where the bottom fell away, and to just keep going as if they never intended to come back. Nita had uncomfortable thoughts about undertow and how it might feel to drown. But just when she was at her twitchiest, she saw a long floppy fin tip up out of the water. S'reee was lolling there in the wave-wash, her long, pale, barnacled belly upward.

The night before, when S'reee had been injured and immobile, it had been hard to tell much of anything about her. Now Nita was struck by the size of her—S'reee was at least forty feet from the tips of her flukes to her pointy nose. And last night she had been a wheezing hulk. Now she was all grace, floating and gliding and rolling like some absurd, fat, slim-winged bird—for her long swimming fins looked more like wings than anything else.

"Did you sleep well?" she sang at them, a weird cheerful crescendo like something out of a happy synthesizer. "I slept wonderfully. And I ate well, too. I think I may get back most of the weight I lost yesterday."

Kit looked at the healed place, treading water. "What *do* you eat?"

"Krill, mostly. The littlest things that live in the water, like little shrimp. But some fish, too. The blues are running, and the little ones are good. Or they have been until now . . ." She sighed, spraying water out her blowhole. "That's in the story I have to tell you. Come on, we'll go out to one of the Made Rocks."

They took hold of her dorsal fin, and she towed them. The "Made Rock" turned out to be an old square fishing platform about three miles south of Tiana Beach: wooden pilings topped by wooden slats covered with tarred canvas and with bland-faced seagulls. Most of the gulls immediately took off and began flying around and screaming about the humans sitting on *their* spot, despite Nita's and Kit's polite apologies. Some of the other gulls were less annoyed, especially after they found out the visitors were wizards. Later on, whenever Nita thought of her first real conversation with S'reee, what she remembered best were the two seagulls who insisted on sitting in her lap the whole time. They were heavy, and not house-broken.

"I guess the best place to start," S'reee said when Nita and Kit were settled, "is with what you already know, that there's been trouble for wizards on the land lately. The trouble's been felt in the sea, too. Out here we've been having quakes on the seafloor much more often than we should be having them—severe ones. And some other old problems have been getting worse. The dirt they throw into the water from the High and Dry, especially: there's more of it than ever—"

" 'The High and Dry'?"

"The place with all the high things on it."

"Oh," Kit said. "New York City. Manhattan, actually."

"The water close to it is getting so foul, the fish can't breathe it for many thousands of lengths out. Those that can are mostly sick. And many more of the boats-that-eat-whales have been out here recently. The past few months, there's been a great slaughter—"

Nita frowned at the thought of other creatures suffering what S'reee had been through. She had heard all the stories about the hungry people in Japan, but at the moment she found herself thinking that there *had* to be something else to eat.

"Things have not been good," S'reee said. "I know less about the troubles on land, but the Sea tells us that the land wizards have been troubled of late, that there was some great strife of powers on the High and Dry. We saw the moon go out one night—"

"So did we," Kit said. There was fear in his eyes at the memory and pride in his voice. "We were in Manhattan when it happened."

"We were part of it," Nita said. She still didn't know all of how she felt about what had happened. But she would never forget reading from the book that kept the world as it should be, the *Book of Night with Moon*, while around her and Kit the buildings of Manhattan wavered like a dream about to break—and beyond a barrier of trees brought to life, and battling statues, the personification of all darkness and fear, the Lone Power, fought to get at them and destroy them.

S'reee looked at them somberly from one eye. "It's true then what Ae'mhnuu used to tell me, that there are no accidents. You've met the Power that created death in the beginning and was cast out for it. All these things—the lost moon, that night, and the earthquakes, and the fouled water, and the whale-eating ships— they're all Its doing, one way or another."

Kit and Nita nodded. "It took a defeat in that battle you two were in," S'reee said. "It's angry, and the problems we've been having are symptoms of that anger. So we have to bind It, make It less harmful, as the first sea people bound It a long time ago. Then things will be quiet again for a while."

"Bind It how?" Nita said.

"No, wait a minute," Kit said. "You said something about the Sea telling you things—"

S'reee looked surprised for a moment. "Oh, I forgot that you do it differently. You work your wizardry with the aid of those things you carry—"

"Our books."

"Right. The whales who are wizards get their wizardry from the Sea. The water speaks to you when you're ready, and offers you the Ordeal. Then if you pass it, the Heart of the Sea speaks whenever you need to hear it and tells you what you need to know."

Nita nodded. The events in that "other" Manhattan had been her Ordeal, and Kit's; and after they passed it, their books had contained much more information than before. "So," she said, "bind the Lone Power *how?*"

"The way the first whale-wizards did," S'reee said. "The story itself *is* the binding. Or rather, the story's a song: the Song of the Twelve. In the long form it takes—*will* take—hours to sing."

"I'm glad I had breakfast," Kit muttered.

S'reee spouted good-naturedly. Nita wondered whether it was accidental that the wind turned at that exact moment, threw the spray straight at Kit, and soaked him to the skin. At any rate, Nita laughed.

"I won't take quite that long," S'reee said. "You know about the great War of the Powers, at the beginning of everything; and how the Lone Power invented death and pain, and tried to impose them on the whole universe, and the other Powers wouldn't let It, and threw It out."

"Even regular human beings have stories about it," Kit said.

"I'm not surprised," S'reee said. "Everything that lives and tells stories has *his* story in one form or another. Well. After that war in the Above and Beyond, the Lone Power spent a long while in untraveled barren universes, recouping Its strength. Then It came back to our native universe, looking for some quiet, out-of-the-way place to try out Its new inventions. Right then the only place vulnerable to It, because thinking life was very new here, was this world; and the only place thinking life existed as yet was the Sea. So the Lone One came here to trick the

Sea into accepting Death. Its sort of death, anyway—where all power and love are wasted into an endless darkness, lost forever."

"Entropy," Nita said.

"Yes. And any sea people It succeeded in tricking would be stuck with that death, the Great Death, forever.—Now there was already a sort of death in the Sea, but only the kind where your body stops. Everyone knew it wasn't permanent, and it didn't hurt much; you might get eaten, but you would go on as part of someone else. No one was afraid of not being his own self anymore—I guess that's the simplest way of putting it. That calm way of life drove the Lone Power wild with hate, and It swore to attach fear and pain to it and make it a lot more interesting."

S'reee sighed. "The whales' job then was what it is now: to be masters and caretakers for the fish and the smaller sea people, the way you two-leggers are for the dryland beasts. So naturally, the only wizards in the Sea were whales, just as humans were originally the only ones on land. That early on, there were only ten whale-wizards, all Seniors. *Ni'hwinyii*, they were called, the Lords of the Humors—"

Nita was puzzled. "It's the old word for emotions, sort of," Kit said. "Not like 'funny' humor."

"I know," Nita said, annoyed. She hadn't.

S'reee blew, laughing. The spray missed Kit this time. "Those ten whales ruled the Sea, under the Powers," she said. "If the Lone Power wanted to trick the Sea into the Great Death, It had to trick the Ten—then all the life they ruled would be stuck with the Great Death, too. So the Lone One went to the Ten in disguise, pretending to be a stranger, a new whale sent to them so that they could decide under which of their Masteries it fell. And as each one questioned the Lone Power, the Stranger whale offered each of them the thing he wanted most, if he would only accept the 'Gift' the Stranger would give him. And he showed them just enough of his power to prove that he could do it."

"Uh-oh," Kit said softly. "I've heard that one before."

"Apples and snakes," Nita said.

"Yes. The pattern repeats. One after another, the Lone One tempted the Ten. The Sea was silent then and gave them no advice—some people say that the Powers wanted the Ten to make up their own minds. But however that might have been, three of the Ten took the Gift, and fell. Three of them were undecided. Three of them rejected the Gift. And the Lone Power needed a majority of the Lords to accept Death, or Its victory would only be partial."

"Those were only nine Lords, though," Kit said.

"Yes, and here the Tenth comes in: the Silent Lord, they called her. She was the youngest of them, and each of the other Nine tried to bring her around to his own way of thinking. The Lone One came to her, too, and tempted her as It had tempted the others. You know, though, that it's the youngest wizard who has the most power, and where the other Lords were deceived, the Silent Lord wasn't. She realized what the Stranger was and what It was trying to do.

"She was faced with a difficult choice. She knew that even if she rejected the Stranger, the fighting would only go on among the other Nine. Sooner or later they or their successors would accept the Gift and doom the whole Sea to the Great Death. But she also knew something else that the Sea had told her long before, and that others have found out since. If one knows death is coming—any death, from the small ones to the Great one—and is willing to accept it fully, and experience it fully, then the death becomes something else—a passage, not an ending: not only for himself, but for others."

S'reee's voice got very soft. "So the Silent Lord did that," she said. "Luck, or the Powers, brought one more creature into the singing, uninvited. It was the one fish over whom no mastery was ever given—the Pale Slayer, whom we call the Master Shark. The Silent Lord decided to accept the 'Gift' that the Stranger offered her—and then, to transform the Gift and make it 'safe,' she gave herself up willingly to die. She dived into a stand of razor coral; and the Master Shark smelled her blood in the water, and . . . well." S'reee blew. "He accepted the sacrifice."

Nita and Kit looked at each other.

"When that happened, the Lone Power went wild with rage," S'reee said. "But that did It no good. The Silent One's sacrifice turned death loose in some of the Sea, but not all; and even where it did turn up, death was much weaker than it would have been otherwise. To this day there are fish and whales that have astonishing life spans, and some that never seem to die of natural causes. The sharks, for instance: some people say that's a result of the Master Shark's acceptance of the Silent Lord's sacrifice. But the important thing is that the Lone Power had put a lot of Its strength into Its death-wizardry. It had become death Itself, in a way. And when death was weakened, so was the Lone One. It fell to the seafloor, which opened for It and closed on It afterward. And there It lies bound."

" 'Bound'?" Kit said. "S'reee, when we had our last run-in with the Lone Power, It didn't seem very bound to *us*. It had a whole alternate universe of Its own, and when It came into this one to get us, It went around tearing things up any way It liked. If It *is* bound, how could It have also been running loose in Manhattan?"

S'reee blew, a sober sound. "It's the usual confusion about time," she said. "All the great Powers exist outside it, and all we usually see of Them are the places and moments where and when They dip into the time flow we're inhabiting. This world has always been an annoyance to the Lone One—It gets frustrated here a lot—so It visits often, in many forms. From inside our time flow, it can look as if the Lone Power is bound in one place-time and free in another . . . and both appearances are true." S'reee rolled and stretched in the water. "Meanwhile, outside the time flow, where things don't have to happen one after another, the Lone One is eternally rebelling and eternally defeated—"

"We gave It a chance to do something else, when we fought last," Nita said. "We offered It the option to stop being a dark power—"

"And it worked," S'reee said, sounding very pleased. "Didn't you know? It's also eternally redeemed. But meantime we have to keep fighting the battles, even though the war's decided. The Lone One's going to take a long while to complete Its choice, and if we get lazy or sloppy about handling Its thrashing around, a lot of people are going to die."

"The seafloor," Nita said, "has been shaken up a lot lately."

"That's one symptom that tells us the TwelveSong needs to be reenacted," S'reee said. "We do the Song at intervals anyway, to make sure the story's never forgotten. But when the Lone Power gets troublesome—as It seems to be doing now—we reenact the Song, and bind It quiet again."

"Where do you do this stuff?" Kit said.

"Down the coast a ways," S'reee said, "off the edge of the Plateau, in the Great Deep past the Gates of the Sea. Ae'mhnuu was getting ready to call the Ten together for a Song in three days or so. He was training me for the Singer's part—before they blew him in two pieces and boiled him down for oil."

Her song went bitter, acquiring a rasp that hurt Nita's ears. "Now I'm stuck handling it all myself. It's not easy: You have to pick each whale-wizard carefully for each part. I don't know who he had in mind to do what. Now I have to work it out myself—and I need help, from wizards who can handle trouble if it comes up." She looked up at them. "You two can obviously manage that. And the Ten will listen to you, they'll respect you, after what you went through up in the High and Dry. You've fought the Lone Power yourselves and gotten off—"

"It was luck," Kit muttered. Nita elbowed him.

"Singing, huh," Nita said, smiling slightly. "I don't have much of a singing voice. Maybe I'd better take the Silent One's part."

S'reee looked at Nita in amazement. "Would you?"

"Why not?"

"Not me," Kit said. "I'm even worse than she is. But I'll come along for the ride. The swim, I mean."

S'reee looked from Kit to Nita. "You two are enough to make me doubt all the stories I've heard about humans," she said. "Hnii't, best check that 'book' thing and make sure this is something you're suited for. The temperaments of the singers have to match the parts they sing—but I think this might suit you. And the original Silent Lord was a humpback. The shapechange would come easily to you, since we've shared blood—"

"Wait a minute! *Shapechange?*" Nita cried. "You mean me be a whale?"

Kit laughed. "Why not, Neets? You *have* been putting on a little weight lately . . ."

She elbowed him again, harder. "Oh, you'd shapechange too, K!t," S'reee said. "We couldn't take you down in the Great Deep otherwise. —Look, you two, there's too much to tell, and some of it's going to have to be handled as we go along. We've got three days to get everyone together for the Song, so that it happens when the moon's round. Otherwise it won't keep the sea bottom quiet—"

Kit looked suddenly at Nita. "Did you see that thing on the news the other night? About the volcano?"

"The *what?*"

"There was some scientist on. He said that hot-water vents had been opening up all of a sudden off the continental shelf. And he said that if those little tremors we've been having keep getting worse, it could open the bottom right up and there'd be a volcano. The least it'd do would be to boil the water for miles. But it could also break Long Island in two. The beaches would go right under water. And Manhattan skyscrapers aren't built for earthquakes." Kit was quiet for a moment, then said, "The rocks remembered. That's why they were upset . . ."

Nita wasn't thinking about rocks, or Manhattan. She was thinking that her folks were planning to be there for another week and a half at least—and she saw a very clear picture of a tidal wave of dirty, boiling water crashing down on the beach house and smashing it to driftwood.

"When should we start, S'reee?" she said.

"Dawn tomorrow. There's little time to waste. Hotshot will be going with us—he'll be singing the Fourth Lord, the Wanderer, in the Song."

"Dawn—" Nita chewed her lip. "Could it be a little later? We've got to have breakfast with my parents or they'll freak out."

"Parents?" S'reee looked from Nita to Kit in shock. "You're still calves, is that what you're telling me? And you went outworld into a Dark Place and came back! I'd thought you were much older—"

"We wished we were," Nita said under her breath.

"Oh, well. No matter. Three hours after dawn be all right? The same place? Good enough. Let me take you back. I have something to fetch so that you can swim with us, K!t. And, look—" She gazed at them for some time from that small, worried, gentle eye; but longer at Nita. "Thank you," she said. "Thank you very much indeed."

"Think nothing of it," Kit said grandly, slipping into the water and patting S'reee on one big ribbed flank.

Nita slid into the water, took hold of S'reee's dorsal fin, and thought something of it all the way home.

Seniors' Song

THE ALARM CLOCK WENT off right above Nita's head, a painful blasting buzz like a dentist's drill. "Aaagh," she said, reluctantly putting one arm out from under the covers and fumbling around on the bedside table for the noisy thing.

It went quiet without her having touched it. Nita squinted up through the morning brightness and found herself looking at Dairine. Her little sister was standing by the bedside table with the alarm clock in her hands, wearing Star Wars pajamas and an annoyed look.

"And where are we going at six in the morning?" Dairine said, too sweetly.

"*We* are not going anywhere," Nita said, swinging herself out of bed with a groan. "Go play with your Barbie dolls, Einstein."

"Only if you give them back," Dairine said, unperturbed. "Anyway, there are better things to play with. Kit, for example—"

"Dairine, you're pushing it." Nita stood up, rubbed her eyes until they started working properly, and then pulled a dresser drawer open and began pawing through it for a T-shirt.

"What're *you* doing, then—getting up so early all the time, staying out late? You think Mom and Dad aren't noticing? —Oh, don't wear *that*," Dairine said at the sight of Nita's favorite sweatshirt. It featured numerous holes made by Ponch's teeth and the words WATCH THIS SPACE FOR FURTHER DEVELOPMENTS. "Oh, really, Neets, *don't*, it's incredibly tacky—"

"That sounds real weird," Nita said, "coming from someone with little Yodas all over her pajamas."

"Oh, stuff it, Nita," Dairine said. Nita turned her head and smiled, thinking that Dairine had become easier to tease since she'd decided to be a Jedi Knight when she grew up. Still, Nita went easy on her sister. It wasn't fair for a wizard to make fun of someone who wanted to do magic, of whatever brand.

"Same to you, runt. When're Mom and Dad getting up, did they say?"

"They're up now."

"What for?"

"They're going fishing. *We're* going with them."

Nita blanched. "Oh, no! Dair, I *can't*—"

Dairine cocked her head at Nita. "They wanted to surprise us."

"They did," Nita said, in shock. "I *can't* go—"

"Got a hot date, huh?"

"*Dairine!* I told you—"

"Where were you two going?"

"Swimming." That was the truth.

"Neets, you can swim anytime," Dairine said, imitating their mother's tone of voice. Nita zipped up her jeans and sat down on the bed with a thump. "What were you gonna be *doing*, anyway?"

"I told you, *swimming!*" Nita got up, went to the window, and looked out, thinking of S'reee and the summoning and the Song of the Twelve and the rest of the business of being on active status, which was now looking ridiculously complicated. And it looked so simple yesterday . . .

"You could tell them something—"

Nita made a face at that. She had recently come to dislike lying to her parents. For one thing, she valued their trust. For another, a wizard, whose business is making things happen by the power of the spoken word, learns early on not to say things out loud that aren't true or that he *doesn't* want to happen.

"Sure," she said in bitter sarcasm. "Why don't I just tell them that we're on a secret mission? Or that we're busy saving Long Island and the greater metropolitan area from a fate worse than death? Or maybe I could tell them that Kit and I have an appointment to go out and get turned into whales, how about *that?*"

Even without turning around, Nita could feel her sister staring at her back. Finally the quiet made Nita twitchy. She turned around, but Dairine was already heading out of the room. "Go on and eat," Dairine said quietly, over her shoulder. "Sound happy." And she was gone.

Under her breath, Nita said a word her father would have frowned at, and then sighed and headed for breakfast, plastering onto her face the most sincere smile she could manage. At first it felt hopelessly unnatural, but in a few seconds it was beginning to stick. At the dining-room door, where her father came around the corner from the kitchen and nearly ran her over, Nita took one look at him—in his faded lumberjack shirt and his hat stuck full of fish hooks—and wondered why she had ever been worried about getting out of the fishing trip. It was going to be all right.

Her dad looked surprised. "Oh! You're up. Did Dairine—"

"She told me," Nita said. "Is there time to eat something?"

"Sure. I guess she told Kit, too, then—I just looked in his room, but he wasn't there. The bed was made; I guess he's ready—"

Nita cheerfully allowed her father to draw his own conclusions, especially since they were the wrong ones. "He's probably down at the beach killing time," she said. "I'll go get him after I eat."

She made a hurried commando raid on the kitchen and put the kettle on the stove for her mother, who was browsing through the science section of the *New York Times* and was ready for another cup of tea. Nita's mother looked up at her from the paper and said, "Neets, where's your sister? She hasn't had breakfast."

That was when her sister came thumping into the dining room. Nita saw her mom look at Dairine and develop a peculiar expression. "Dari," her mother said, "are you feeling all right?"

"Yeah!" said Dairine in an offended tone. Nita turned in her chair to look at her. Her sister looked flushed, and she wasn't moving at her normal breakneck speed. "C'mere, baby," Nita's mother said. "Let me feel your forehead."

"*Mom!*"

"Dairine," her father said.

"Yeah, right." Dairine went over to her mother and had her forehead felt, rolling her eyes at the ceiling. "You're hot, sweetie," Nita's mother said in alarm. "Harry, I *told* you she was in the water too long yesterday. Feel her."

Nita's dad looked slightly bored, but he checked Dairine's forehead and then frowned. "Well . . ."

"No 'wells.' Dari, I think you'd better sit this one out."

"Oh, *Mom!*"

"Cork it, little one. You can come fishing with us in a day or two." Nita's mother turned to her. "Neets, will you stick around and keep an eye on your sister?"

"Mom, I don't need a baby-sitter!"

"Enough, Dairine," her mom said. "Up to bed with you. Nita, we'll take you and Kit with us the next time; but your dad really wants to get out today."

"It's OK, Mom," Nita said, dropping what was left of the smile (though it now really wanted to stay on). "I'll keep an eye on the runt."

"Don't call me a runt!"

"Dairine," her father said again. Nita's little sister made a face and left, again at half the usual speed.

As soon as she could, Nita slipped into Dairine's room. Her sister was lying on top of the bed, reading her way through a pile of X-Men comics; she looked flushed. "Not bad, huh?" she said in a low voice as Nita came in.

"How did you *do* that?" Nita whispered.

"I used the Force," Dairine said, flashing a wicked look at Nita.

"*Dari!* Spill it!"

"I turned Dad's electric blanket up high and spent a few minutes under it. Then I drank about a quart of hot water to make sure I stayed too warm." Dairine turned a page in her comic book, looking blasé about the whole thing. "Mom did the rest."

Nita shook her head in admiration. "Runt, I owe you one."

Dairine looked up from her comic at Nita. "Yeah," Dairine said, "you do."

Nita felt a chill. "Right," she said. "I'll hang out here till they leave. Then I have to find Kit—"

"He went down to the general store just before you got up," Dairine said. "I think he was going to call somebody."

"Right," Nita said again.

There was the briefest pause. Then: "Whales, huh?" Dairine said, very softly.

Nita got out of there in a great hurry.

The sign on top of the building merely said, in big, square black letters, TIANA BEACH. " 'Tiana Beach' *what?*" people typically said, and it was a fair question. From a distance there was no telling what the place was, except a one-story structure with peeling white paint.

The building stood off the main road, at the end of a spur road that ran down to the water. On one side of it was its small parking lot, a black patch of heat-heaved asphalt always littered with pieces of clamshells, which the gulls liked to drop and crack open there. On the other side was a dock for people who came shopping in their boats.

The dock was in superb repair. The store was less so. Its large multipaned front windows, for example, were clean enough outside, but inside they were either covered by stacked-up boxes or with grime; nothing was visible through them

except spastically flashing old neon signs that said PABST BLUE RIBBON or CER-
VEZA BUDWEISER. Beach grass and aggressive weeds grew next to (and in places,
through) the building's cracked concrete steps. The rough little U.S. Post Office
sign above the front door had a sparrow's nest behind it.

Nita headed for the open door. It was always open, whether Mr. Friedman the
storekeeper was there or not; "On the off chance," as Mr. Friedman usually said,
"that someone might need something at three in the morning . . . or the afternoon . . ."

Nita walked into the dark, brown-smelling store, past the haphazard shelves of
canned goods and cereal and the racks of plastic earth-worms and nylon surf-
casting line. By the cereal and the crackers, she met the reason that Mr. Friedman's
store was safe day and night. The reason's name was Dog: a whitish, curlyish,
terrierish mutt, with eyes like something out of Disney and teeth like something
out of Transylvania. Dog could smell attempted theft for miles; and when not biting
people in the line of business, he would do it on his own time, for no reason
whatever—perhaps just to keep his fangs in.

"Hi, Dog," Nita said, being careful not to get too close.

Dog showed Nita his teeth. "Go chew dry bones," he said in a growl.

"Same to you," Nita said pleasantly, and made a wide detour around him,
heading for the phone booth in the rear of the store.

"Right," Kit was saying, his voice slightly muffled by being in the booth.
"Something about 'the Gates of the Sea.' I tried looking in the manual, but all I
could find was one of those 'restricted' notices and a footnote that said to see the
local Senior for more details—"

Kit looked up, saw Nita coming, and pointed at the phone, mouthing the words
"Tom and Carl." She nodded and squeezed into the booth with him; Kit tipped the
hearing part of the receiver toward her, and they put their heads together. "Hi, it's
Nita—"

"Well, hi there yourself," Tom Swale's voice came back. He would doubtless
have gone on with more of the same if someone else, farther away from his end
of the line, hadn't begun screaming "Hel-LOOOOOOO! HEL-lo!" in a creaky,
high-pitched voice that sounded as if Tom were keeping his insane grandmother
chained up in the living room. This, Nita knew, was Tom and Carl's intractable
macaw, Machu Picchu, or Peach for short. Wizards' pets tended to get a bit strange
as their masters grew more adept in wizardry, but Peach was stranger than most,
and more trying. Even a pair of Senior Wizards must have wondered what to do
with a creature that would at one moment deliver the evening news a day early,
in a flawless imitation of any major newscaster you pleased, and then a second
later start ripping up the couch for the fun of it.

"Cut that out!" Nita heard another voice saying in the background, one with a
more New Yorkish sound to it; that was Carl. "Look out! She's on the stove. Get
her—oh, Lord. There go the eggs. *You little cannibal!*"

"It's business as usual around here, as you can tell," Tom said. "Not where
you are, though, to judge from how early Kit called . . . and from what he tells me.
Kit, hang on a minute. Carl's getting the information released for you. Evidently
the Powers That Be don't want it distributed without a Senior's supervision. The
area must be sensitive right now."

Nita made small talk with Tom for a few minutes while, in the background,

Peach screamed, and Annie and Monty the sheepdogs barked irritably at the macaw, who was shouting, "Bad dog! Bad dog! Nonono!" at them—or possibly at Carl. Nita could imagine the scene very well—the bright airy house full of plants and animals, a very ordinary-looking place as far as the neighbors were concerned. Except that Tom spent his days doing research and development on complex spells and incantations for other wizards, and then used some of the things he discovered to make a living as a writer on the side. And Carl, who sold commercial time for a flagship station of one of the major television networks, might also make a deal to sell you a more unusual kind of time—say, a piece of last Thursday. The two of them were living proof that it was possible to live in the workaday world and function as wizards at the same time. Nita was very glad to know them.

"The link's busy," she heard Carl saying, at some distance from the phone. "Oh, never mind, there it goes. Look," he said, apparently to one of his own advanced-level manuals, "we need an intervention authorization for an offshore area—yeah, that's right. Here's the numbers—"

Kit had his manual open to the spot where he'd found the notification. Nita looked over his shoulder and watched the box that said RESTRICTED INFORMATION suddenly blink out, replaced by the words SEE CHART PAGE 1096. "Got it?" Tom said.

"Almost." Kit turned pages. Nita looked over his shoulder and found herself looking at a map of the East Coast, from Nova Scotia to Virginia. But the coast itself was squeezed far over on the left-hand side, and individual cities and states were only sketchily indicated. The map was primarily concerned with the ocean.

"Okay, I've got it in my book, too," Tom said. "All those lines in the middle of the water are contour lines, indicating the depth of the sea bottom. You can see that there aren't many lines within about a hundred miles of Long Island. The bottom isn't much deeper than a hundred feet within that distance. But then—you see a lot of contour lines packed closely together? That's the edge of the continental shelf. Think of it as a cliff, or a mesa, with the North American continent sitting on top of it. Then there's a steep drop—the cliff is just a shade less than a mile high—"

"Or deep," Nita said.

"Whichever. About a five-thousand-foot drop; not straight down—it slopes a bit—but straight enough. Then the sea bottom keeps on sloping eastward and downward. It doesn't slope as fast as before, but it goes deep—some fifteen thousand feet down; and it gets deeper yet farther out. See where it says 'Sohm Abyssal Plain' to the southeast of the island, about six or seven hundred miles out?"

"It has 'the Crushing Dark' underneath that on our map," Nita said. "Is that the whales' name for it?"

"Right. That area is more like seventeen, eighteen thousand feet down."

"I bet it's cold down there," Kit muttered.

"Probably. Let me know when you get back," Tom said, "because that's where you're going."

Nita and Kit looked at each other in shock. "But I thought even submarines couldn't go down *that* far," Nita said.

"They can't. Neither can most whales, normally—but it helps to be a wizard," Tom said. "Look, don't panic yet—"

"Go ahead! Panic!" screamed Picchu from somewhere in the background. "Do it now and avoid the June rush! Fear death by water!"

"Bird," Carl's voice said, also in the background, "you're honing for a punch in the beak."

"Violence! You want violence, I'll give you violence! No quarter asked or given! Damn the torpedoes, full speed ahead! Don't give up the *AWWWK!*"

"Thanks, Carl," Tom said, as silence fell. "Where were we? Oh, right. You won't just be going out there and diving straight down. There's a specific approach to the plain. Look back closer to the island, and you'll see some contours drawn in dotted lines—"

"Hudson Channel," Nita said.

"Right. That's the old bed of the Hudson River—where it used to run a hundred thousand years ago, while all that part of the continental shelf was still above water. That old riverbed leads farther southeast, to the edge of the shelf, and right over it . . . there was quite a waterfall there once. See the notch in the shelf?"

"Yeah. 'Hudson Canyon,' it says—"

"The Gates of the Sea," said Tom. "That's the biggest undersea canyon on the East Coast, and probably the oldest. It cuts right down through the shelf. Those walls are at least two or three thousand feet high, sometimes four. Some of the canyons on the Moon and Mars could match the Hudson—but none on Earth. And for the whale-wizards, the Gates have become the traditional approach to the Great Depths and the Crushing Dark."

The thought of canyon walls stretching above her almost a mile high gave Nita chills. She'd seen a rockslide once, and it had made her uneasy about canyons in general. "Is it safe?" she said.

"Of course not," Tom said, sounding cheerful. "But the natural dangers are Carl's department; he'll fill you in on what precautions you'll need to take, and I suspect the whales will, too."

" 'Natural dangers,' " Kit said. "Meaning there are unnatural ones, too."

"In wizardry, when aren't there? This much I can tell you, though. New York City has not been kind to that area. All kinds of things, even unexploded depth charges, have been dumped at the head of Hudson Canyon over the years. Most of them are marked on your map; but watch out for ones that aren't. And the city has been dumping raw sewage into the Hudson Channel area for decades. Evidently in the old days, before people were too concerned about ecology, they thought the water was so deep that the dumping wouldn't do any harm. But it has. Quite a bit of the sea-bottom life in that area, especially the vegetation that the fish depend on for food, has been killed off entirely. Other species have been . . . changed. The manual will give you details. You won't like them."

Nita suspected that Tom was right. "Anyway," he said, "let me give you the rest of this. After you do the appropriate rituals, which the whales will coach you through, the access through the Gates of the Sea takes you down through Hudson Canyon to its bottom at the lower edge of the shelf, and then deeper and farther southeast—where the canyon turns into a valley that gets shallower and shallower as it goes. The valley ends just about where the Abyssal Plain begins, at seven hundred miles off the coast, and seventeen thousand feet down. Then you come to the mountain."

It was on the map—a tiny set of concentric circles—but it had looked so peculiar, standing there all by itself in the middle of hundreds of miles of flatness, that Nita had doubted her judgment. "The Sea's Tooth," she said, reading from the map.

"Caryn Peak," Tom agreed, giving the human name. "Some of the oceanographers think it's simply the westernmost peak of an undersea mountain range called the Kelvin Seamounts—they're off the eastward edge of your map. Some think otherwise; the geological history of that area is bizarre. But either way, the peak's an important spot. And impressive; that one peak is six thousand feet high. It stands up sheer from the bottom, all alone, a third as high as Everest."

"Five Empire State Buildings on top of each other," Kit said, awed. He liked tall things.

"A very noticeable object," Tom said. "It's functioned as landmark and meeting place and site of the whales' great wizardries for not even they know how long. Certainly since the continents started drifting toward their present positions . . . at least a hundred thousand years ago. And it may have been used by . . . other sorts of wizards . . . even earlier than that. There's some interesting history in that area, tangled up with whale-wizards and human ones, too."

Tom's voice grew sober. "Some of the wizards who specialize in history say that humans only learned wizardry with the whales' assistance . . . and even so, our brands of wizardry are different. It's an old, old branch of the Art they practice. Very beautiful. Very dangerous. And the area around Caryn Peak is saturated with residue from all the old wizardries that whales, and others, have done there. That makes any spell you work there even more dangerous."

"S'reee said that the danger level wouldn't go above moderate," Kit said.

"She said it *shouldn't*," Nita said.

"Probably it won't," Tom said. He didn't sound convinced, though. "You should bear in mind that the danger levels for humans and whales differ. Still, the book said she was about to be promoted to Advisory status, so she would know that— All the same . . . you two keep your eyes open. Watch what agreements you make. And if you make them—keep them, to the letter. From all indications, the Song of the Twelve is a lovely wizardry, and a powerful one . . . probably the most powerful magic done on a regular basis. The sources say it leaves its participants forever changed, for the better. At least, it does when it works. When it fails— which it has, once or twice in the past—it fails because some participant has broken the rules. And those times it's failed . . . Well, all I can say is that I'm glad I wasn't born yet. *Be careful.*"

"We will," Nita said. "But what are the chances of something going wrong?"

"We could ask Peach," Kit said. It was a sensible suggestion; the bird, besides doing dramatic readings from *Variety* and *TV Guide*, could also predict the future— when it pleased her.

"Good idea. Carl?"

"Here I am," Carl said, having picked up an extension phone. "Now, Kit, about the monsters—"

"Carl, put that on hold a moment. What does the Walter Cronkite of the bird world have to say about all this?"

"I'll find out."

"Monsters?" Nita mouthed at Kit. "Listen," she said hurriedly to Tom, "I'm

going to get off now. I've got to be around the house when my folks leave, so they won't worry about my little sister."

"Why? Is she sick?"

"No. But that's the problem. Tom, I don't know what to do about Dairine. I thought nonwizards weren't supposed to *notice* magic most of the time. I'm not sure it's working that way with Dairine. I think she's getting suspicious . . ."

"We'll talk. Meanwhile, Carl—what does the bird say?"

"Oh, it is, it is a splendid thing / To be a pirate kiiiiiiiiiiiiing!" Picchu was singing from somewhere in Tom's living room.

"Picchu—"

"What'sa matter? Don't you like Gilbert and Sullivan?"

"I told you we should never have let her watch *Pirates* on cable," Tom remarked to his partner.

"Twice your peanut ration for the week," Carl said.

". . . and I did the deed that all men shun, I shot the Albatross . . ."

"You're misquoting. How about *no* peanuts for the rest of the week—"

"Pieces of eight! Pieces of eight!"

"How about no *food?*"

"Uh—" There was a pause. It didn't take Nita much imagination to picture the look that Carl was giving Picchu. She was glad no one had ever looked at *her* that way.

"Give."

"Well." The bird paused again, a long pause, and when she spoke her voice sounded more sober than Nita could remember ever hearing it. "Do what the night tells you. Don't be afraid to give yourself away. And read the small print before you sign!"

Kit glanced at Nita with a quizzical expression; she shrugged. At the other end of the line, sounding exceptionally annoyed, Carl said to Picchu, "You call *that* advice? We asked you for the odds!"

"Never ask me the odds," Picchu said promptly. "I don't want to know. And neither do *you*, really." And that end of the conversation swiftly degenerated into more loud squawking, and the excited barking of dogs, and Carl making suggestions to Picchu that were at best rather rude.

"Thanks," Nita said to Tom. "I'll talk to you later." She squeezed out of the phone booth and past Dog, who growled at her as she went. Behind her, Kit said, in entirely too cheerful a tone of voice, "So, Carl, what about the monsters?"

Nita shook her head and went home.

The Blue's Song

"GIANT MAN-EATING CLAMS," she said to Kit later, as they walked down an isolated stretch of Tiana Beach toward the surf. "Giant squid—"

"Krakens," Kit said.

"I don't care what you call them, they're still giant squid. And squid belong in sushi. I don't like this."

"With luck, we won't see any of them, Carl says."

"When have we ever had that kind of luck? . . ."

"Besides, Neets, even *you* can outrun a clam . . ."

"Cute," she said. They splashed into the water together, glancing up and down the beach as they did so. No one was in sight; and they had left Ponch up in the dunes, looking for a good place to bury the remains of his latest water rat. "Look," Nita said, pointing.

Several hundred yards out, there was a glitter of spray, and sunlight glanced off the curved, up-leaping body of a dolphin as if from an unsheathed, upheld sword. Wild, merry chattering, a dolphin's laughter, came to them over the water, as the leaping shape came down with a splash and another shock of spray.

"Hotshot," Kit said. "Let's go."

They struck out through the breakers, into water that was again surprisingly warm. This time Nita wasn't able to enjoy it quite as much; the thought of undersea volcanoes was much with her. But even she couldn't be depressed for long when they paused to rest a moment, dog-paddling, and from behind came the nudge in the back she remembered, followed by a delphine laugh. "You rotten thing," she said, turning to rub Hotshot affectionately. "I'm gonna get you for the first time you did that."

"You'll have to catch me first," Hotshot said with a wicked chuckle—as well he might have, for nothing in the sea, except perhaps a killer whale or one of the great sharks on the hunt, was fast enough to catch a dolphin that didn't want to be caught.

"Where's S'reee?" Kit said.

"Out in deeper water, by the Made Rock. HNii't's change could be done right here, but the kind of whale you're going to be would ground at this depth, K!t. Take hold; I'll tow you."

The fishing platform was once more covered with seagulls, which rose in a screaming cloud at the sight of Kit and Nita and Hotshot. "I'll meet you later, out at sea," Hotshot said, leaving them beside a rusty metal ladder that reached down into the water.

Kit and Nita climbed up it and walked across the platform to where they could look down at S'reee, who was rolling in the wave-wash.

"You're early," she whistled, putting her head up out of the water at them, "and it's just as well; I'm running a bit late. I went a-Summoning last night, but I didn't find most of the people—so we'll have to make a stop out by the Westernmost Shoals today. Sandy Hook, you call it."

"New Jersey?" Nita said, surprised. "How are we going to get all the way out there and back before—"

"It's going to be all right, hNii't," S'reee said. "Time doesn't run the same under the waters as it does above them, so the Sea tells me. Besides, a humpback swims fast. And as for K!t—well, one change at a time. It'll come more easily for you, hNii't; you'd best go first."

Wonderful, Nita thought. She had long been used to being picked last for things; having to go first for anything gave her the jitters. "What do I have to do?" she said.

"Did you have a look at your book last night?"

"Uh-huh. I understand most of what we're going to be doing; it's fairly straightforward. But there was some business I didn't understand very well—"

"The part about shapechanging."

"Yeah. There wasn't that much in the book, S'reee. I think it might have been missing some information."

"Why? What did it tell you?"

"Only a lot of stuff about the power of imagination." She was perplexed. "S'reee, aren't there supposed to be words or something? A specific spell, or materials we need?"

"For shapechange? You have everything you need. Words would only get in the way," said S'reee. "It's all in the being. You pretend hard enough, and sooner or later what you're pretending to be, you *are*. The same as with other things."

"Oh, c'mon, S'reee," Kit said. "If somebody who wasn't a wizard jumped into the water and pretended to be a whale, I don't care how hard they pretended, nothing would happen without wizardry—"

"Exactly right, K!t. *Wizardry*—not one particular spell. The only reason it works for you is that you *know* wizardry works and are willing to have it so. Belief is no good either; belief as such always has doubt at the bottom. It's knowing that makes wizardry work. Only knowing can banish doubt, and while doubt remains, no spell, however powerful, will function properly. 'Wizardry does not live in the unwilling heart,' the Sea says. There'd be lots more wizards if more people were able to give up doubt—and belief. Like any other habit, though, they're hard to break . . ."

"It did take me awhile to know for sure that it wasn't just a coincidence when the thing I'd done a spell for actually *happened* as soon as I'd done the spell," Kit admitted. "I guess I see the problem."

"Then you're ready for the solution," S'reee said. "Past the change itself, the chief skill of unassisted shapechanging lies in not pretending so hard that you can't get back again. And as I said, hNii't, you have an advantage; we've shared blood. You have humpback in you now—not that our species are so far apart anyway; we're all mammals together. I suppose the first thing you'd better do is get in the water . . ."

Nita jumped in, bobbed to the surface again. "And that stuff around you is going to have to go," S'reee added, looking with mild perplexity at Nita's bathing suit. Nita shot a quick look over her shoulder. For a moment, Kit just gazed innocently down at her, refusing to look away—then he turned, rolling his eyes.

Nita skinned hurriedly out of the suit and called to Kit, "While you're up there, put a warding spell on the platform. I don't want the gulls doing you-know-what all over my suit while we're gone. Or yours." She flung the wet lump of bathing suit out of the water overhanded; it landed with a sodden *thwack!* at which Kit almost turned around again. "Can we get on with this?" Nita said to S'reee.

"Surely. HNii't, are you all right?" S'reee said.

"Yes, fine, let's do it!" Nita said.

"So begin!" said S'reee, and began singing to herself as she waited.

Nita paddled for a moment in the water, adjusting to not having her bathing suit on. Saying, "Begin to *what?*" especially with Kit listening, seemed incredibly stupid, so she just hung there in the water for a few moments and considered being a whale. *I don't have the faintest idea what this is supposed to feel like*, she thought desperately. *But I should be able to come up with something. I* am *a wizard, after all.*

Nita got an idea. She took a deep breath, held it, and slowly began to relax into the sound. Her arms, as she let them go limp, no longer supported her; she sank, eyes open, into salty greenness. *It's all right*, she thought. *The air's right above me if I need it.* She hung weightless in the green, thinking of nothing in particular.

Down there in the water, S'reee's note seemed louder, fuller; it vibrated against the ears, against the skin, inside the lungs, filling everything. And there was something familiar about it. Cousin, S'reee had called her; and, "We have blood in common," she had said. So it should be easy. A matter of remembering, not what you have been . . . but what, somewhere else, you *are*. Simply allow what is, somewhere else, to be what is *here*—and the change is done, effortless. Nita shut her eyes on the greenness and trusted to the wizardry inside her. That was it. "Wizardry does not live in the unwilling heart." Not the kind of will that meant gritted teeth, resisting something else, like your own disbelief, that was trying to undermine you—not "willpower"—but the will that was desire, the will so strong that it couldn't be resisted by all the powers of normality . . .

Where am I getting all this? Nita didn't know, didn't care. *To be a whale*, she thought. *To float like this all the time, to be weightless, like an astronaut. But space is green, and wet, and warm, and there are voices in it, and things growing. Freedom: no walls, no doors. And the songs in the water . . .* Her arms were feeling heavy, her legs felt odd when she kicked; but none of it mattered. Something was utterly right, something was working. Nita began to feel short of air. It hadn't worked all the way, that was all. She would get it right the next time. She stroked for the surface, broke it, opened her eyes to the light—

—and found it different. First and oddest—so that Nita tried to shake her head in disbelief, and failed, since she suddenly had no neck—the world was split in two, as if with an ax. Trying to look straight ahead of her didn't work. The area in front of her had become a hazy uncertainty comprised of two sets of peripheral vision. And where the corners of her eyes should have been, she now had two perfectly clear sets of sideways vision that nonetheless felt like "forward." She was seeing in colors she had no names for, and many she had names for were gone. Hands she still seemed to have, but her fingers hung down oddly long and heavy, her elbows were glued to her sides, and her sides themselves went on for what seemed years. Her legs were gone; a tail and graceful flukes were all she had left. Her nose seemed to be on the top of her head, and her mouth somewhere south of her chin; and she resolved to ask S'reee, well out of Kit's hearing, what had happened to some other parts of her. "S'reee," Nita said, and was amazed to hear it come out of the middle of her head, in a whistle instead of words, "it was easy!"

"Come on, hNii't," S'reee said. "You're well along in wizardry at this point; you should know by now that it's not the magic that's exciting—it's what you do with it afterward."

More amazement yet. Nita wanted to simply roll over and lie back in the water at the sheer richness of the sound of S'reee's words. She had done the usual experiments in school that proved water was a more efficient conductor of sound than air. But she hadn't dreamed of what that effect would be like when one was a whale, submerged in the conducting medium and wearing a hundred square feet of skin that was a more effective hearing organ than any human ear. Suddenly sound was a thing that stroked the body, sensuous as a touch, indistinguishable from the liquid one swam in.

More, Nita could hear echoes coming back from what she and S'reee had said to each other; and the returning sound told her, with astonishing precision, the size and position of everything in the area—rocks on the bottom, weed three hundred yards away, schools of fish. She didn't need to see them. She could feel their textures on her skin as if they touched her; yet she could also distinctly perceive their distance from her, more accurately than she could have told it with mere sight. Fascinated, she swam a couple of circles around the platform, making random noises and getting the feel of the terrain.

"I don't believe it," someone said above Nita, in a curious, flat voice with no echoes about it. *Is that how we sound?* Nita thought, and surfaced to look at Kit out of first one eye, then the other. He looked no different from the way he usually did, but something about him struck Nita as utterly hilarious, though at first she couldn't figure out what it was. Then it occurred to her. He had legs.

"You're next, K!t," S'reee said. "Get in the water."

Nita held her head out of water and stared at Kit for a moment. He didn't say anything, and after a few seconds of watching him get so red she could see it through his sunburn, Nita submerged, laughing like anything—a sound exactly like oatmeal boiling hard.

Nita felt the splash of his jump all over her. Then Kit was paddling in the water beside her, looking at her curiously. "You've got barnacles," he said.

"That's as may be, K!t," S'reee said, laughing herself. "Look at what I brought for you."

Kit put his head under the water for a moment to see what she was talking about. For the first time, Nita noticed that S'reee was holding something delicately in her mouth, at the very tip-end of her jaw. If spiders lived in the sea, what S'reee held might have been a fragment torn from one of their webs. It was a filmy, delicate, irregular meshwork, its strands knotted into a net some six feet square. The knotting was an illusion, as Nita found when she glided closer to it. Each "knot" was a round swelling or bulb where several threads joined. Flashes of green-white light rippled along the net whenever it moved, and all Nita's senses, those of whale and wizard alike, prickled with the electric feeling of a live spell, tangled in the mesh and impatient to be used.

"You must be careful with this, Kit," S'reee said. "This is a whalesark, and a rare thing. A sark can only be made when a whale dies, and the magic involved is considerable."

"What is it?" Kit said, when he'd surfaced again.

"It's a sort of shadow of a whale's nervous system, made by wizardry. At the whale's death, before the life-lightning's gone, a spell-constructed energy duplicate of the whale's brain and nerves is made from the pattern laid down by the living nerves and brain. The duplicate then has an assisted-shapechange spell woven into it. When the work's done properly, contact with the sark is enough to change the wearer into whatever kind of whale the donor was."

S'reee tossed her head. Shimmering, the sark billowed fully open, like a curtain in the wind. "This is a sperm whalesark, like Aivaaan who donated it. He was a wizard who worked these waters several thousand full moons ago, and something of a seer; so that when he died, instead of leaving himself wholly to the Sea, Aivaaan said that we should make a sark of him, because there would be some need. Come try it on for size, K!t."

Kit didn't move for a moment. "S'reee—is what's-his-name, Aivaaan, in there? Am I going to be him, is that it?"

S'reee looked surprised. "No, how did you get that idea?"

"You said this was made from his brain," Nita said.

"Oh. His *under*-brain, yes—the part of the brain that runs breathing and blood flow and such. As for the rest of Aivaaan, his *mind*—I don't think so. Not that I'm any too sure where 'mind' is in a person. But you should still be K!t, by what the Sea tells me. Come on, time's swimming."

"What do I do with it?"

"Just put it around you and wrap it tight. Don't be afraid to handle it roughly. It's stronger than it looks." She let go of the sark. It floated in the water, undulating gently in the current. Kit took another breath, submerged, reached down, and drew the sark around him.

"Get back, hNii't," S'reee said. Nita backfinned several times her own length away from Kit, not wanting to take her eyes off him. He was exhaling, slowly sinking feetfirst, and with true Rodriguez insouciance he swirled the sark around him like Zorro putting on a new cape. Kit's face grew surprised, though, as the "cape" continued the motion, swirling itself tighter and tighter around him, binding his arms to his sides.

Alarmed, Kit struggled, still sinking, bubbles rising from him as he went down. The struggling did him no good, and it suddenly became hard to see him as the wizardry in the whalesark came fully alive, and light danced around Kit and the sark. Nita had a last glimpse of Kit's eyes going wide in panic as he and the whalesark became nothing more than a sinking, swirling storm of glitter.

"S'reee!" Nita said, getting alarmed.

With a sound like muffled thunder and a blow like a nearby lightning strike, displaced water hit Nita and bowled her sideways and backward. She fluked madly, trying to regain her balance enough to tell what was going on. The water was full of stirred-up sand, tatters of weed, small confused fish darting in every direction. And a bulk, a massive form that had not been there before.

Nita watched the great gray shape rise toward her and understood why S'reee had insisted on Kit's change being in deep water. Her own size had surprised her at first—though a humpback looks small and trim, even the littlest males tend to be fifty feet long. But Kit was twice that, easily. He did not have the torpedo-like grace of a humpback, but what he lacked in streamlining he made up in sheer mass. The sperm is the kind that most people think of when they hear the word *whale*, the kind made famous by most whaling movies. Nita realized that all her life she had mostly taken the whale's shape for granted, not considering what it would actually be like up close to one.

But here came Kit, stroking slowly and uncertainly at first with that immense tail, and getting surer by the second; looking up at her with the tiny eyes set in the huge domed head, and with his jaw working a bit, exposing the terrible teeth that could crunch a whaling boat in two. Nita felt the size of him, the weight, and somehow the danger—and kept her movements slow and respectful. He was still Kit—but something had been added.

He glanced at S'reee and Nita, saying nothing, as he rose past them and broke surface to breathe. They followed. He spouted once or twice, apparently to get the feel of it, and then said to S'reee in a rather rueful tone of song, "I wish you'd warned me!"

His voice ranged into a deeper register than a humpback's and had a sharper sound to it—more clicks and buzzes. It was not entirely comfortable on the skin. "I couldn't," S'reee said, "or you might have fought it even harder than you did, and the change might have refused to take. That would've been trouble for us; if a whalesark once rejects a person, it'll never work for him at all. After this it'll be easier for you. Which in itself will make some problems. Right now, though, let's get going. Take a long breath; I want to get out of the bay without attracting too much attention."

They took breath together and dived deep, S'reee in the lead and swimming south by west, Nita and Kit following. The surroundings—thick, lazily waving kelp beds and colonies of bright polyps and anemones, stitched through with the brief silver flash of passing fish—fascinated Nita. But she couldn't give the landscape, or seascape, her whole attention; she had other concerns. (Kit,) she tried to say in the Speech's silent form, for privacy's sake—then found that it wasn't working; she wasn't getting the sort of mental "echo" that told her she was sending successfully. Probably it had something to do with the shapechange spell. "Hey," she said aloud, "you OK?"

The question came out of her as such a long, mournful moan that Kit laughed— a sound more like boiling lava than boiling oatmeal: huge hisses and bubblings mixed together. "Now I am," he said, "or I will be as soon as I can get used to this bit with the eyes—"

"Yeah, it's weird. But kind of nice, too. Feeling things, instead of seeing them . . ."

"Yeah. Even the voices have feelings. S'reee's is kind of twitchy—"

"Yeah. You've got sharp edges—"

"You've got fur."

"I do not!"

"Oh, yes you do. It's soft, your voice. Not like your usual one—"

Nita was unsure whether to take this as a compliment, so she let it lie. The moment had abruptly turned into one of those times when she had no idea just what to say to Kit, the sort of sudden silence that was acutely painful to Nita, though Kit never seemed to notice it at all. Nita couldn't think of anything to do about the problem, which was the worst part of the whole business. She wasn't about to mention the problem to her mom, and on this subject the wizards' manual was hugely unhelpful.

The silence was well along toward becoming interminable when S'reee said, "That's the primary way we have for knowing one another, down here. We haven't the sort of physical variations you have—differences in head shape and so forth— and even if we did, what good would a distinction be if you had to come right up to someone to make it? By voice, we can tell how far away a friend is, how he's feeling, practically what he's thinking. Though the closer a friend is to you, usually, the harder it is to tell what's on his mind with any accuracy."

Nita started to sing something, then caught herself back to silence. "Is the change settling in, K!t?" S'reee said.

"Now it is. I had a weird feeling, though, like something besides me, my mind, I mean—like something besides that was fighting the change. But it's gone now."

"Only for the moment," S'reee said. "See, it's the old rule: no wizardry without its price, or its dangers. Though the dangers are different for each of you, since you changed by different methods. As I said, hNii't, you have to beware pretending too hard—thinking so much like a whale that you don't want to be a human being anymore, or forget how. Wizards have been lost that way before, and there's no breaking the spell from outside; once you're stuck inside the change-shape, no one but you can break out again. If you start finding your own memories difficult to recall, it's time to get out of the whaleshape, before it becomes you permanently."

"Right," Nita said. She wasn't very worried. Being a humpback was delightful, but she had no desire to spend her life that way.

"Your problem's different, though, K!t. Your change is powered more by the spell resident in the whalesark than by anything you're doing yourself. And all the sark's done is confuse your own body into thinking it's a whale's body, for the time being. That confusion can be broken by several different kinds of distraction. The commonest is when your own mind—which is stronger than the whale mind left in the sark—starts to override the instructions the whalesark is giving your body."

"Huh?"

"K!t," S'reee said very gently, finning upward to avoid the weedy, barnacled wreck of a fishing boat, "suppose we were—oh, say several hundred humpback lengths down, in the Crushing Dark—and suddenly your whale body started trying to behave like a human's body. Human breathing rate, human pulse and thought and movement patterns, human response to pressures and the temperature of the water—"

"Uh," Kit said, as the picture sank in.

"So you see the problem. Spend too much time in the sark, and the part of your brain responsible for handling your breathing and so forth will begin to over-power the 'dead' brain preserved in the sark. Your warning signs are nearly the opposite of hNii't's. Language is the first thing to go. If you find yourself losing whalesong, you *must* surface and get out of the sark immediately. Ignore the warning—the best that can happen is that the whalesark will probably be so damaged it can never be used again. The worst thing—" She didn't say it. The worry in her voice was warning enough.

No one said much of anything for a while, as the three of them swam onward, south and west. The silence, uneasy at first, became less so as they went along. S'reee, to whom this area was as commonplace as Kit's or Nita's home streets might have been, simply cruised along without any great interest in the surroundings. But Nita found the seascape endlessly fascinating, and suspected Kit did, too—he was looking around him with the kind of fascination he rarely lent anything but old cars and his z-gauge train set.

Nita had rarely thought of what the seascape off the coast of the island would look like. From being at the beach she had a rather dull and sketchy picture of bare sand with a lot of water on top of it; shells buried in it, as they were on the beach, and there had to be weed beds; the seaweed washed up from somewhere. But all the nature movies had given her no idea of the richness of the place.

Coral, for example; it didn't come in the bright colors it did in tropical waters, but it was there in great quantity—huge groves and forests of it, the white or beige or yellow branches twisting and writhing together in tight-choked abstract patterns. And shells, yes—but the shells still had creatures inside them; Nita saw Kit start in amazement, then swim down for a closer look at a scallop shell that was hopping over the surface of a brain coral, going about its business.

They passed great patches of weed, kinds that Nita didn't know the names of—until they started coming to her as if she had always known them: red bladder, kelp, agar, their long dark leaves or flat ribbons rippling as silkily in the offshore current as wheat in a land-borne wind.

And the fish! Nita hadn't taken much notice of them at first; they'd all looked alike to her—little and silver. But something had changed. They passed by a place where piles had been driven into the seafloor, close together, and great odd-shaped lumps of rusty metal had been dumped among them. Weed and coral had seized on the spot, wrapping the metal and the piles; and the little life that frequented such places, tiny shrimp and krill, swam everywhere. So did thousands of iridescent, silvery indigo fish, ranging from fingerling size to about a foot long, eating the krill and fry as if there were no tomorrow. For some of the smallest of them there wasn't *going* to be one, Nita realized, as she also realized how hungry she was.

"Blues!" she said, one sharp, happy note, then dived into the cloud of bluefish and krill, and helped herself to lunch.

It was a little while before she'd had enough. It took Nita only a couple of minutes to get used to the way a humpback ate—by straining krill and others of the tiniest ocean creatures, including the smallest of the blues, through the sievelike plates of whalebone, or baleen, in her jaws. The swift blue shapes that had been darting frantically in all directions were calming down already as Nita soared out of the whirling cloud of them and headed back over to S'reee and Kit, feeling slightly abashed and that an explanation of some kind was in order for the sudden interruption of their trip. However, there turned out to be no need for one. S'reee had stopped for a snack herself; and Nita realized that Kit had been snacking on fish ever since they left Tiana Beach. A sperm whale was, after all, one of the biggest of the "toothed" whales and needed a lot of food to keep that great bulk working. Not that he did anything but swallow the fish whole when he caught them; a sperm's terrible teeth are mostly for defense.

Kit paused only long enough to eat nine or ten of the biggest blues, then drifted down toward the pilings and the objects stacked sloppily among them. "Neets," he said, "will you take a look at this? It's *cars!*"

She glided down beside him. Sure enough, the corroded fins of an old-model Cadillac were jutting out of a great mound of coral. Under the tangled whiteness of the coral, as if under a blanket of snow, she could make out the buried shapes of hoods or doors, or the wheels and axles of wrecks wedged on their sides and choked with weed. Fish, blues and others, darted in and out of broken car windows and crumpled hoods, while in several places crabs crouched in the shells of broken headlights.

"It's a fish haven," S'reee said as she glided down beside them. "The land people dump scrap metal on the bottom, and the plants and coral come and make a reef out of it. The fish come to eat the littler fish and krill that live in reefs; and then the boats come and catch the fish. And it works just as well for us as for the fishers who live on land. But we've got other business than dinner to attend to, at the moment. And hNii't, don't you think it would be a good idea if you surfaced now?"

Nita and Kit looked at one another in shock, then started upward in a hurry, with S'reee following them at a more leisurely pace. "How long have we been down?" Kit whistled.

They surfaced in a rush, all three, and blew. S'reee looked at Kit in some puzzlement; the question apparently meant nothing to her. "Long enough to need to come up again," she said.

"Neets, look," Kit said in a rumbly groan, a sperm whale's sound of surprise. She fluked hard once or twice, using her tail to lift herself out of the swell, and was surprised to see, standing up from the shore half a mile away, a tall brick tower with a pointed, weathered green-bronze top; a red light flashed at the tower's peak. "Jones Beach already!" she said. "That's miles and miles from Tiana—"

"We've made good time," S'reee said, "but we've a ways to go yet. Let's put our tails into it. I don't want to keep the Blue waiting."

They swam on. Even if the sight of the Jones Beach tower hadn't convinced Nita they were getting close to New York, she now found that the increasing noise of the environment would have tipped off the whale that she'd become. Back at Tiana Beach, there had been only the single mournful hoot of the Shinnecock horn and the far-off sound of the various buoy bells. But this close to New York Harbor, the peaceful background hiss of the ocean soon turned into an incredible racket. Bells and horns and whistles and gongs shrieked and clunked and whanged in the water as they passed them; and no sooner was she out of range of one than another one assaulted her twitching skin.

Singing pained notes at one another, the three ran the gauntlet of sound. It got worse instead of better as they got closer to the harbor entrance, and to the banging and clanging was added the sound of persistent dull engine noise. Their course to Sandy Hook unfortunately crossed all three of the major approaches to New York Harbor. Along all three of them big boats came and went with an endless low throbbing, and small ones passed with a rattling, jarring buzz that reminded Nita of lawn mowers and chain saws.

The three surfaced often to get relief from the sound, until S'reee warned them to dive deep for a long underwater run through one of the shipping lanes. Nita was beginning to feel the slow discomfort that was a whale's experience of shortness of breath before S'reee headed for the surface again.

They broached and blew and looked around them. Not far away stood a huge, black, white-lettered structure on four steel pilings. A white building stood atop the deck, and beside it was a red tower with several flashing lights. A horn on the platform sang one noncommittal note, shortLONG! shortLONG! again and again.

"Ambrose Light," Kit said.

"The Speaking Tower, yes," S'reee said. "After this it'll be quieter—there are fewer markers between here and the Hook. And listen! There's a friend's voice."

Nita went down again to listen, and finally managed to sort out a dolphin's distant chattering from the background racket. She surfaced again and floated with the others awhile, watching Hotshot come, glittering in the sun like a bright lance hurling itself through the swells. As he came abreast of the lightship he leaped high out of the water in a spectacular arc and hit the surface with a noise that pierced even all the hooting and dinging going on.

"For Sea's sake, we hear you!" S'reee sang at the top of her lungs, and then added in annoyed affection, "He's such a show-off."

"But most dolphins are," Kit said, with a note to his song that made it plain he wasn't sure how he knew that.

"True enough. He's worse than some, though. No question that he's one of the best of the young wizards, and a talented singer. I love him dearly. But what this business of being Wanderer is going to do to his precious ego—" She broke off as Hotshot came within hearing range. "Did you find him?"

"He's feeding off the Hook," Hotshot said, arrowing through the water toward them and executing a couple of playful and utterly unnecessary barrel rolls as he came. Nita began to wonder if S'reee might be right about him. "He's worried about something, though he wouldn't tell me what it was. Said it was just as well you were coming; he would've come looking for you if you hadn't."

The four of them started swimming again immediately; that last sentence was by itself most startling news. Blue whales did not *do* things, Nita realized, in the sudden-memory way that meant the information was the Sea's gift. Blue whales *were*, that was all. Action was for other, swifter species . . . except in the Song of the Twelve, where the Blue briefly became a power to be reckoned with. The Song, as Tom had warned, had a way of changing the ones who sang it . . . sometimes even before they started.

"Are you ready for the Oath?" S'reee was saying to the dolphin. "Any last thoughts?"

"Only that this is going to be one more Song like any other," Hotshot said, "even if it *is* your first time. Don't worry, Ree; if you have any problems, I'll help you out."

Nita privately thought that this was a little on the braggy side, coming from a Junior Wizard. The thought of talking to an Advisory or Senior that way—Tom, say—shocked her. Nevertheless, she kept her mouth shut, for it seemed like Hotshot and S'reee had known one another for a while.

"And how are our fry doing here?" Hotshot said, swimming careless rings around Nita as he sang. "Getting used to the fins all right?"

"Pretty much," Nita said. Hotshot did one last loop around her and then headed off in Kit's direction. "How about you, Minnow—*eeeech!*"

The huge jaw of a sperm whale abruptly opened right in front of Hotshot and closed before he could react—so that a moment later the dolphin was keeping quite still, while Kit held him with great delicacy in his huge fangs. Kit's eyes looked angry, but the tone of his song was casual enough. "Hotshot," he said, not stopping, just swimming along with casual deliberateness, "I'm probably singing, too. And even if I'm not, I *am* a sperm whale. Don't push your luck."

Hotshot said nothing. Kit swam a few more of his own lengths, then opened his mouth and let the dolphin loose. "Hey," he said then, "no hard feelings."

"Of course not," Hotshot said in his usual recklessly merry voice. But Nita noticed that the dolphin made his reply from a safe distance. "No problem, Mi—" Kit looked at Hotshot, silent—"ah, K!t."

"Minnow it is," Kit said, sounding casual himself. The four of them swam on; Nita dropped back a few lengths and put her head up beside Kit's so that she could sing her quietest and not be heard too far off.

"What was that all about?"

"I'm not sure," Kit said—and now that only Nita was listening, he sounded a bit shaken. "S'reee might have been right when she said this body doesn't actually have what's-his-voice's—"

"Aivaaan."

"His memories, yeah. But the body has its own memories. What it's like to be a sperm. What it *means* to be a sperm, I guess. You don't make fun of us—of them." He paused, looking even more shaken. "Neets—don't let me get lost!"

"Huh?"

"*Me.* I don't beat people up, that's not my style!"

"You didn't beat him up—"

"No. I just did the ocean equivalent of pinning him up against the wall and scaring him a good one. Neets, I got into being a wizard because I wanted other people *not* to do that kind of stuff to *me!* And now—"

"I'll keep an eye on you," Nita said, as they began to come up on another foghorn, a loud one. And there was something odd about that foghorn. Its note was incredibly deep. *That has to be almost too deep for people to hear at all. What kind of—*

The note sounded again, and Nita shot Kit an amazed look as she felt the water all around her, and even the air in her lungs, vibrate in response to it. One note, the lowest note she could possibly imagine, held and held until a merely human singer would have collapsed trying to sing it . . . and then slurred slowly down through another note, and another, and holding on a last one of such profound depth that the water shook as if with thunder.

S'reee slowed her pace and answered the note in kind, the courtesy of one species of whale to another on meeting or parting—singing the same slow, somber sequence, several octaves higher. There was a pause; then she was answered with a humpback's graceful fluting, but sung in a bottom-shaking baritone.

"Come on," S'reee said, and dived.

The waters around Sandy Hook boil with krill in the spring and summer, so that by night the krill's swarming luminescence defines every current and fin stroke in a blaze of blue-green light; and by day the sun slants through the water, brown with millions of tiny bodies, as thickly as through the air in a dusty room. As the group dived, they began to make out a great dark shape in the cloudy water, moving so slowly it barely did more than drift. A last brown-red curtain of water parted before them in a swirl of current, and Nita found herself staring down at her first blue whale.

He was hardly even blue in this light, more a sort of slaty maroon; and the faint dapples on his sides were almost invisible. But his color was not what impressed Nita particularly. Neither was his size, though blues are the biggest of all whales; this one was perhaps 120 feet from nose to tail, and Kit, large for a sperm, was almost as big. That voice, that stately, leisurely, sober, sorrowful voice that sounded like a storm in mourning, *that* mattered to her; and so did the tiny eye, the size of a tennis ball, which looked at her from the immense bulk of the head. That eye was wise. There was understanding in it, and tolerance, and sadness—and most of all, great age.

Age was evident elsewhere, too. The blue's flukes were tattered and his steering fins showed scars and punctures, mementos of hungry sharks. Far down his tail, the broken stump of a harpoon protruded, the wood of it rotting, the metal crumbling with rust; yet though the tail moved slowly, it moved with strength. This creature had been through pain and danger in his long life, and though he had learned sadness, it had not made him bitter or weak.

Nita turned her attention back to the others, noticing that Kit was holding as still as she was, though at more of a distance; and even Hotshot was holding himself down to a slow glide. "Eldest Blue about the Gates," S'reee sang, sounding more formal than Nita had ever heard her, "I greet you."

"Senior for the Gate waters," said the Blue in his deep voice, with slow dignity, "I greet you, also."

"Then you've heard, Aroooon."

"I have heard that the Sea has taken Ae'mhnuu to its Heart," said the Blue, "leaving you Senior in his place and distressed at a time when there's distress enough. Leaving you also to organize a TwelveSong on very short notice."

"That's so."

"Then you had best be about it," said the Blue, "while time still remains for singing, and the bottom is still firm under us. First, though, tell me who comes here with you. Swift Fire in the Water I know already—"

Hotshot made the closest sound Nita could imagine to an embarrassed delphine cough. She smiled to herself; now she knew what to tease him with if he got on her case.

"Land wizards, Aroooon," S'reee said. "HNii't"—Nita wasn't sure what to do, so she inclined the whole front of her body in the water in an approximation of a bow—"and K!t." Kit followed Nita's suit. "They were the ones who went into the Dark High and Dry after the *Naming of Lights*—"

To Nita's utter astonishment, Aroooon inclined his own body at them, additionally curling his flukes under him in what she abruptly recognized as a gesture of congratulation.

"They're calves," S'reee added, as if not wanting to leave anything out.

"With all due respects, Senior, they are not," Aroooon said. "They came *back* from that place. That is no calf's deed. Many who were older than they did not come back. —You will sing with us then? What parts?"

"I'm not sure yet," Kit said. "S'reee needs to see if all her people come in."

"The Silent Lord," Nita said.

"Indeed." Aroooon looked at her for several long moments. "You are a good age for it," he said. "And you are learning the song—"

"I got most of the details from my manual," she said. She had been up studying late the night before, though not as late as Kit had; a lot of exertion in salt air always left her drained, and she'd put the book aside after several hours, to finish the fine details of her research later. "The Sea will give me the rest, S'reee says, as we go along."

"So it will. But I would have you be careful of how you enact your part, young hNii't." Aroooon drifted a bit closer to her, and that small, thoughtful eye regarded her carefully. "There is old trouble, and old power, about you and your friend . . . as if blood hung in the water where you swim. The Lone Power apparently knows your names. It will not have forgotten the disservice you did It recently. You are greatly daring to draw Its attention to you again. Even the Heart of the Sea—Timeheart, as your kind calls it—may not be quiet for one who has freely attracted the Lone One's enmity. Beware what you do. And do what you say; nowhere does the Lone Power enter in so readily as through the broken word."

"Sir," Nita said, rather unnerved, "I'll be careful."

"That is well." Aroooon looked for a moment at Kit before speaking. "It is a whalesark, is it not?"

"Yes, sir," Kit said in the same respectful tone Nita had heard him use on his father.

"Have a care of it, then, should you find yourself in one of the more combative parts of the Song," said Aroooon. "Sperm whales were fighters before they were singers, and though their songs are often the fairest in the sea, the old blood rises too often and chokes those songs off before they can be sung. Keep your mouth closed, you were best, and you'll do well enough."

"Thank you, sir."

"Enough politeness, young wizard," Aroooon said, for the first time sounding slightly crusty. "If size is honor, you have as much as I; and as for years, just keep breathing long enough and you'll have as many of those as I do. —S'reee, you travel more widely now than I, so I put you a question. Are the shakings in the depths worse these days than they ought to be at this time of year and tide of the moon?"

"Much worse, Eldest. That was why Ae'mhnuu originally wanted to convene the Song. And I don't know if the Song will be in time to save the fishing grounds to the east and north, around Nantucket and the Races. Hot water has been coming up close to there, farther east and south. The Shelf is changing."

"Then let us get started," Aroooon said. "I assume you came to ask me to call in some of the Celebrants, time being as limited as it is."

"Yes, Aroooon. If you would. Though as the rite requires, I will be visiting the Pale One tomorrow, in company with hNii't and K!t. The meeting place for the Song is to be ten thousand lengths north-northeast of the shoals at Barnegat, three days from now. A fast rehearsal—then right down the channel and through the Gates of the Sea, to the place appointed."

"Well enough. Now administer me the Celebrant's Oath, Senior, so that I may lawfully call the others."

"Very well." S'reee swam up close to Aroooon, so that she was looking him straight in one eye with one of hers; and when she began to sing, it was in a tone even more formal and careful than that in which she had greeted him. "Aroooon u'ao!uor, those who gather to sing that Song that is the Sea's shame and the Sea's glory desire you to be of their company. Say, for my hearing, whether you consent to that Song."

"I consent," the Blue said in notes so deep that coral cracked and fell off rock shelves some yards away, "and I will weave my voice and my will and my blood with that of those who sing, if there be need."

"I ask the second time, that those with me, both of your Mastery and not, may hear. Do you consent to the Song?"

"I consent. And may my wizardry and my Mastery depart from me sooner than I abandon that other Mastery I shall undertake in the Song's celebration."

"The third time, and the last, I ask, that the Sea, and the Heart of the Sea, shall hear. Do you consent to the Song?"

"Freely I consent," Aroooon sang with calm finality, "and may I find no place in that Heart, but wander forever amid the broken and the lost, sooner than I shall refuse the Song or what it brings about for the good of those who live."

"Then I accept you as Celebrant of the Song, as Bluc, and as latest of a line of saviors," S'reee said. "And though those who swim are swift to forget, the Sea forgets neither Song nor singer." She turned a bit, looking behind her at Hotshot. "Might as well get all of you done at once," she said. "Hotshot?"

"Right."

The dolphin went through the Oath much faster than Aroooon had, though his embarrassment at being referred to as Swift Fire in the Water was this time so acute that Nita actually turned away so she wouldn't have to look at him. As for the rest of the Oath, though, Hotshot recited it, as Nita had expected, with the mindless speed of a person who thinks he has other more important matters to attend to.

S'recc turned to Nita. "We can't give K!t the Oath yet," she said. "We don't know who he's going to be."

"Can't you just give it to me and leave that part blank or something?" Kit said eagerly. He loved ceremonies.

"Kit!"

"No, K!t. HNii't, do you know the words?"

"The Sea does," she said, finding it true. S'reee had already begun the ritual questioning; Nita felt for the response, found it. "I consent, and I will weave my voice and my will and my blood with that of those who sing, if there be need." It was astonishing, how much meaning could be packed into a few notes. And the music itself was fascinating; so somber, but with that odd thread of joy running through it. She threw herself into the grave joy of the final response. ". . . And may I find no place in that Heart, but wander forever amid the broken and the lost, sooner than I shall refuse the Song or what it brings about for the good of those who live."

"Then I accept you as Celebrant of the Song, and as Silent One, and as the latest in a line of saviors. And though those who swim are swift to forget, the Sea forgets neither Song nor singer." S'reee looked at Nita with an expression in those blue eyes of vast relief, so much like the one she had given her and Kit when they'd first agreed to help that Nita shuddered a little with the intensity of it, then smiled inside. It was nice to be needed.

"That was well done," Aroooon said slowly. "Now, S'reee, give me names, so I'll know whom to call."

A few moments of singing ensued as S'reee recited the names of five whales Nita had never heard of. Her inner contact with the Sea, moments later, identified them all as wizards of various ratings, all impressive. Aroooon rumbled agreement. "Good enough," he said. "Best get out of the area so that I may begin Calling."

"Right. Come on, K!t, hNii't. Till the moon's full, Aroooon—"

"Till then."

They swam away through the darkening water. S'reee set the pace; it was a quick one. "Why did we have to leave in such a hurry?" Kit said.

"There aren't many wizardries more powerful than a Calling," S'reee said as she led them away. "He'll weave those whales' names into his spell, and if they agree to be part of the Song, the wizardry will lead them to the place appointed, at the proper time."

"Just by singing their names?"

"K!t, that's plenty. Don't you pay attention when someone calls you by your name? Your name is *part of you*. There's power in it, tied up with the way you secretly think of yourself, the truth of the way you are. Know what a person's name means to him, know who he feels he *is*—and you have power over him. That's what Aroooon is using."

That was a bit of information that started Nita's thoughts going in nervous circles. *How do I think of myself? And does this mean that the people who know what I think can control me? I'm not sure I like this . . .*

The first note rumbled through the water behind them, and Nita pulled up short, curling around in a quick turn. "Careful, hNii't!" S'reee sang, a soft, sharp note of warning. Nita back-finned, hovering in the water. "Don't disturb his circle—"

Looking back, she wouldn't have dreamed of it. The water was growing darker by the second, and as a result the glow of the krill in it was now visible—a delicate, shimmery, indefinite blue-green light that filled the sea everywhere. The light grew brighter, moment by moment; but it was brighter still at the surface, where the waves slid and shifted against one another in a glowing, undulating ceiling. And brightest of all was the track left by Aroooon's swimming—a wake that burned like clouds of cool fire behind him with every slow stroke of his tail.

At the head of the wake, Aroooon himself traced the grand curves of his spell, sheathed in bubbles and cold light. One circle he completed, melding it into itself as he sang that single compelling note; then he began another at right angles to the first, and the water burned behind him, the current not taking the brilliance away. And the Blue's song seemed to get into the blood, into the bone, and would not be shaken—

"HNii't," S'reee said, "we can't stay, you said you have to get back—"

Nita looked around her in shock. "S'reee, when did it get so dark! My folks are gonna have a fit!"

"Didn't I mention that time didn't run the same way below the water as it does in the Above?"

"Yeah, but I thought—," Kit said, and then he broke off and said a very bad word in whale. "No, I didn't think. I assumed that it'd go *slower*—"

"It goes faster," Nita moaned. "Kit, how are we going to get anything done? S'reee, how long exactly is the Song going to take?"

"Not long," the humpback said, sounding a bit puzzled by her distress. "A couple of lights, as it's reckoned in the Above—"

"Two days!"

"We're in trouble," Kit said.

"That's exactly what we're in. S'reee, let's put our tails into it! Even if we were getting home right now, we'd have some explaining to do."

She turned and swam in the direction where her sharpening whale senses told her home was. It was going to be bad enough, having to climb out of this splendid, strong, graceful body and put her own back on again. But Dairine was waiting to give her the Spanish Inquisition when she got home. And her mother and father were going to give her more of those strange looks. Worse . . . there would be questions asked, she knew it. Her folks might even call Kit's family if they got worried enough—and Kit's dad, who was terminally protective of his son, might make Kit come home.

That thought was worst of all.

They went home. It was lucky for them that Nita's father was too tired from his fishing—which had been successful—to make much noise about their lateness. Her mother was cleaning fish in the kitchen, too annoyed at the smelly work to much care about anything else. And as for Dairine, she was buried so deep in a copy of the *Space Shuttle Operators' Manual* that all she did when Nita passed her room was glance up for a second, then dive back into her reading. Even so, there was no feeling of relief when Nita shut the door to her room and got under the covers; just an uneasy sense of something incomplete, something that was going to come up again later . . . and not in a way she'd like.

"Wizardry . . . ," she muttered sourly, and fell asleep.

Ed's Song

"NEETS," HER MOTHER SAID from where she stood at the sink, her back turned. "Got a few minutes?"

Nita looked up from her breakfast. "What's up?"

Her mother was silent for a second, as if wondering how to broach whatever she had on her mind. "You and Kit've been out a lot lately," she said at last. "Dad and I hardly ever seem to see you."

"I thought Dad said it'd be fun to have Dairine and me out of his hair for a while, this vacation," said Nita.

"Out of his hair, yes. Not out of his life. —We worry about you two when you're out so much."

"Mom, we're fine."

"Well, I wonder . . . What exactly are you two doing out there all day?"

"Oh, Mom! Nothing!"

Her mother looked at her and put up one eyebrow in an excellent imitation of Mr. Spock.

Nita blushed a bit. It was one of those family jokes that you wish would go away, but never does; when Nita had been little and had said, "Nothing!" she had usually been getting into incredible trouble. "Mom," Nita said, "sometimes when I say 'nothing,' it's really just nothing. We hang out, that's all. We . . . do stuff."

"What kind of stuff?"

"Mom, what does it matter? Just stuff!"

"It matters," her mother said, "if it's adult kinds of stuff . . . instead of kid stuff."

Nita didn't say a word. There was no question that what she and Kit were doing were adult sorts of things.

Her mother took in Nita's silence, waiting for her daughter to break it. "I won't beat around the bush with you, Neets," she said at last. "Are you and Kit getting . . . physically involved?"

Nita looked at her mother in complete shock. "Mom!" she said in a despairing groan. "You mean *sex?* No!"

"Well," her mother said slowly, "that takes a bit of a load off my mind." There was a silence after the words. Nita was almost sure she could hear her mother thinking, *If it's true . . .*

The silence unnerved Nita more than the prospect of a talk on the facts of life ever could have. "Mom," she said, "if I were gonna do something like that, I'd talk to you about it first." She blushed as she said it. She was embarrassed even to be talking about this to anybody, and she would have been embarrassed to talk to her mom about it, too. Nevertheless, what she'd said was the truth. "Look, Mom, you know me, I'm chicken. I always run and ask for advice before I do anything."

"Even about this?"

"Especially about this!"

"Then what *are* you doing?" her mother said, sounding just plain curious now. And there was another sound in her voice—wistfulness. She was feeling left out of something. "Sometimes you say to me 'playing,' but I don't know what kids mean anymore when they say that. When I was little, it was hopscotch, or Chinese jump rope, or games in the dirt with plastic animals. Now when I ask Dairine what she's doing, and she says, 'Playing,' I go in and find she's doing quadratic equations . . . or using my hot curlers on the neighbor's red setter. I don't know what to expect."

Nita shrugged. "Kit and I swim a lot," she said.

"Where you won't get in trouble, I hope," her mother said.

"Yeah," Nita said, grateful that her mother hadn't said anything about lifeguards or public beaches. *This is a real pain*, she thought. *I have to talk to Tom and Carl about this. What do they do with* their *families?* But her mother was waiting for more explanation. She struggled to find some. "We talk, we look at stuff. We explore . . ."

Nita shook her head, then, for it was hopeless. There was no explaining even the parts of her relationship with Kit that her mother *could* understand. "He's just my friend," Nita said finally. It was a horrible understatement, but she was getting hot with embarrassment at even having to think about this kind of thing. "Mom, we're OK, really."

"I suppose you are," her mom said. "Though I can't shake the feeling that there are things going on you're not telling me about. Nita, I trust you . . . but I still worry."

Nita just nodded. "Can I go out now, Mom?"

"Sure. Just be back by the time it gets dark," she said, and Nita sighed and headed for the door. But there was no feeling of release, no sense of anything having been really settled, as there usually was when a family problem had been hashed out to everyone's satisfaction. Nita knew her mother was going to be watching her. It griped her.

There's no reason for it! she thought guiltily as she went down to the beach, running so she wouldn't be late for meeting Kit. But there was reason for it, she knew; and the guilt settled quietly into place inside her, where not all the seawater in the world would wash it out.

She found Kit far down the beach, standing on the end of the jetty with a rippling, near-invisible glitter clutched in one hand: the whalesark. "You're late," he said, scowling, as Nita climbed the jetty. "S'reee's waiting—" Then the scowl fell off his face when he saw her expression. "You OK?"

"Yeah. But my mom's getting suspicious. And we have to be back by dark or it'll get worse."

Kit said something under his breath in Spanish.

"*¡Ay!*" Nita said back, a precise imitation of what either of Kit's folks would have said if they'd heard him. He laughed.

"It's OK," she said. "Let's go."

"We'd better leave our suits here," Kit said. Nita agreed, turning her back and starting to peel out of hers. Kit made his way down the rocks and into the water as she put her bathing suit under the rock with his. Then she started down the other side of the jetty.

Nita found that the whale body came much more easily to her than it had the day before. She towed Kit out into deeper water, where he wrapped the whalesark around him and made his own change; his, too, came more quickly and with less struggle, though the shock of displaced water, like an undersea explosion, was no less. S'reee came to meet them then, and they greeted her and followed her off eastward, passing Shinnecock Inlet.

"Some answers to Aroooon's Calling have already come back," she said. "K!t, it looks like we may not need you to sing after all. But I would hope you'd attend the Song anyway."

"I wouldn't miss it," he sang cheerfully. "Somebody has to be around to keep Neets from screwing up, after all . . ."

Nita made a humpback's snort of indignation. But she also wondered about the nervousness in S'reee's song. "Where's Hotshot this morning?"

"Out calling the rest of his people for patrol around the Gates. Besides, I'm not sure he's . . . well, suited for what we're doing today . . ."

"S'reee," Kit said, picking up the tremor in her song, "what's the problem? It's just another wizard we're going to see—"

"Oh, no," she said. "The Pale One's no wizard. He'll be singing one of the Twelve, all right—but the only one who has no magic."

"Then what's the problem? Even a shark is no match for three wizards—"

"K!t," S'reee said, "that's easy for you to say. You're a sperm, and it's true enough that the average shark's no threat to one of your kind. But this is no average shark we're going to see. This shark would be a good candidate to *really* be the Pale Slayer, the original Master Shark, instead of just playing him. And there are some kinds of strength that even wizardry has trouble matching." Her song grew quieter. "We're getting close. If you have any plans to stay living for a while more, watch what you say when the Pale One starts talking. And for the Sea's sake, if you're upset about anything, don't show it!"

They swam on toward Montauk Point, the long spit of land that was the southeastern tip of Long Island. The bottom began to change from the yellow, fairly smooth sand of the South Shore, littered with fish havens and abandoned oyster beds and deep undergrowth, to a bottom of darker shades—dun, brown, almost black—rocky and badly broken, scattered with old wrecks. The sea around them grew noisy, changing from the usual soft background hiss of quiet water to a rushing, liquid roar that grew in intensity until Nita couldn't hear herself think, let alone sing. Seeing in the water was difficult. The surface was white-capped, the middle waters were murky with dissolved air, and the hazy sunlight diffused in the sea until everything seemed to glow a pallid gray white, with no shadows anywhere.

"Mind your swimming," S'reee said, again in that subdued voice. "The rocks are sharp around here; you don't want to start bleeding."

They surfaced once for breath near Montauk Point, so that Nita got a glimpse of its tall octagonal lighthouse, the little tender's house nearby, and a group of tourists milling about on the cliff that slanted sharply down to the sea. Nita blew, just once, but spectacularly, and grinned to herself at the sight of the tourists pointing and shouting at each other and taking pictures of her. She cruised the surface for a good long moment to let them get some good shots, then submerged again and caught up with Kit and S'reee.

The murkiness of the water made it hard to find her way except by singing brief notes, waiting for the return of the sound, and judging the bottom by it. S'reee was doing so, but her notes were so short that she seemed to be grudging them.

What's the matter with her? Nita thought. *You can't get a decent sounding off such short notes*—And indeed, she almost hit a rock herself as she was thinking that, and saved herself from it only by a quick lithe twist that left her aching afterward. The roaring of the water over the shoals kept on growing, interfering with the rebound of the song notes, whiting them out. S'reee was bearing north around the point now and slowing to the slowest of glides. Kit, to keep from overswimming her, was barely drifting, and keeping well above the bottom. Nita glanced up at him, a great dark shape against the greater brightness of the surface water—and saw his whole body thrash once, hard, in a gesture of terrible shock. "Nita!"

She looked ahead and saw what he saw. The milky water ahead of them had a great cloud of blood hanging and swirling in it, with small bright shapes flashing in and out of the cloud in mindless confusion. Nita let out one small squeak of fear, then forced herself to be quiet. The sound came back, though, and told her that inside that roiling red darkness, something was cruising by in a wide curve— something nearly Kit's size. She back-finned to hover in the water, glancing up at Kit.

He drifted downward to her, singing no note of his own. She could understand why. Tumbling weightlessly out of the blood cloud, trailing streaks of watery red, were the slashed and broken bodies of a school of small fin tuna—heads, tails, pieces too mangled to name, let alone to bear close examination. Some of these drifted slowly to the bottom, where the scavengers—saltwater catfish and crabs and other such—ate them hurriedly, as if not wanting to linger and face whatever hunted above.

Nita didn't want to attract its attention, either, but she also wanted Kit's reassurance. This place to which S'reee had brought them was unquestionably the location of a shark's feeding frenzy, in which the hunter begins to devour not only its prey, but anything else that gets in the way, uncontrollably, mindlessly, until sated.

Inside the cloud of blood, which the current over the shoals was taking away, something moved. *Impossible*, was Nita's first reaction as the circling shape was revealed. It broke out of its circling and began to soar slowly toward her and Kit and S'reee. Sonar had warned her of its size, but she was still astonished. No mere fish could be that big.

This one could. Nita didn't move. With slow, calm, deadly grace the huge form came curving toward them. Nita could see why S'reee had said that this creature was a good candidate for the title Master Shark, even if the original had lived ten thousand years ago, when everything was bigger. The shark was nearly as long as Kit—from its blunt nose to the end of its tail's top fin, no less than ninety feet. Its eyes were that same dull, expressionless black that had horrified Nita when she'd watched *Jaws*. But seeing those eyes on a TV screen was one thing. Having them dwell on you, calm and hungry even after a feeding frenzy—that was much worse.

The pale shape glided closer. Nita felt Kit drift so close to her that his skin brushed hers, and she felt the thudding of his huge heart. In shape, the shark looked like a great white, at least as well as Nita could remember from *Jaws*. There, though, the resemblance ended. Great white sharks were actually a pale blue on their upper bodies and only white below. This one was white all over, an ivory white so pale that great age might have bleached it that color. And as for size, this one could have eaten the *Jaws* shark for lunch and looked capable of working Nita in, in no more than a bite or two, as dessert. Its terrible maw, hung with drifting, mangled shreds of bleeding tuna, was easily fifteen feet across. Those jaws worked gently, absently, as the white horror cruised toward the three of them.

S'reee finned forward a little. She inclined the fore half of her body toward the white one and sang, in what seemed utter, toneless calm, "Ed'Rashtekaresket, chief of the Unmastered in these waters, I greet you."

The shark swam straight toward S'reee, those blank eyes fixed on her. The whale held her position as the Pale One glided toward her, his mouth open, his jaws working. At the last possible moment he veered to one side and began to describe a great circle around the three.

Three times he circled them, in silence. Next to Nita, Kit shuddered. The shark looked sharply at them, but still said nothing, just kept swimming until he had completed his third circle. When he spoke at last, there was no warmth in his voice, none of the skin-stroking richness she had grown used to in whale voices. This voice was dry . . . interested, but passionless; and though insatiably hungry, not even slightly angry or vicious. The voice destroyed every idea Nita had of what a shark would sound like. Some terrible malice, she could have accepted—not this deadly equanimity. "Young wizard," the voice said, cool and courteous, "well met."

The swimmer broke free of his circling and described a swift, clean arc that brought him close enough to Nita and Kit for Nita to see the kind of rough, spiky skin that had injured S'reee so badly two nights before. The great shark almost touched Nita's nose as he swept by.

"My people," the Pale One said to S'reee, "tell me that they met with you two nights since. And fed well."

"The nerve!" Kit said, none too quietly, and started to swim forward.

Aghast, Nita bumped him to one side, hard. He was so startled he held still again. "Keep your mouth shut!" she said quietly. "That thing could eat us all if it wanted to!"

"If *he* wanted to," said the Pale One, glancing at Nita and fixing her, just for a moment, with one of those expressionless eyes. "Peace, young human. I'll deal with you in a moment."

She subsided instantly, feeling like a bird face-to-face with a snake.

"I am told further," said the shark, circling S'reee lazily, "that wizardry struck my people down at their meal . . ."

"And then released them."

"The story's true, then."

"True enough, Unmastered," said S'reee, still not moving. "I'm no more ignorant than Ae'mhnuu was of the price paid for the reckless wasting of life. Besides, I knew I'd be talking to you today . . . and even if I didn't, I'd have you to deal with at some later time . . . Shall we two be finished with this matter, then? I have other things to discuss with you."

"Having heard the Calling in the water last night, I believe you do," said the Pale One, still circling S'reee with slow grace. His jaws, Nita noticed, were still working. "You were wise to spare those of my Mastery. Are your wounds healed? Is your pain ended?"

"Yes to both questions, Pale One."

"I have no further business with you, then," said the shark. Nita felt Kit move slightly against her, an angry, balked movement. Evidently he had been expecting the shark to apologize. But the shark's tone of voice made it plain that he didn't think he'd done anything wrong . . . and bizarrely, it seemed as if S'reee agreed with him.

"Well enough," S'reee said, moving for the first time, to break out of the Pale One's circle. "Let's get to business." The shark went after, pacing her.

"Since you heard the Calling," S'reee said, "you know why I'm here."

"To ask me to be Twelfth in the Song," said the shark. "When have I not? You may administer the Oath to me at your leisure. But first you must tell me who the Silent One is."

"She swims with us," S'reee said, rolling over on her back as she swam— something Nita would certainly never have dared do, lest it give this monster ideas—and indicating Nita with one long fore fin.

Nita would have preferred to keep Kit between her and the shark; but something, the Sea perhaps, told her that this would be a bad idea. Gulping, she slipped past Kit and glided up between S'reee and the great white. She was uncertain of protocol—or of anything except that she should show no fear. "Sir," she said, not bowing but looking him straight in those black eyes, "I'm Nita."

"My lady wizard," the Pale One said in that cool, dry voice, "you're also terrified out of your wits."

What to say now? But the shark's tone did have a sort of brittle humor about it. She could at least match it. "Master Shark," she said, giving him the title to be on the safe side, "if I were, saying so would be stupid; I'd be inviting you to eat me. And saying I wasn't afraid would be stupid, too—and a lie."

The shark laughed, a terrible sound—quiet and dry, and violent under its humor. "That's well said, Nita," he said when the laughing was done. "You're wise not to lie to a shark—nor to tell him that particular truth. After all, fear is distress. And I end distress; that's my job. So beware. I am pleased to meet you; but don't bleed around me. Who's your friend? Make him known to me."

Nita curved around with two long strokes, swam back to Kit, and escorted him back to the white with her fins barely touching him, a don't-screw-it-up! gesture. "This is Kit," she said. "He may or may not be singing with us."

"A whalesark?" said the Pale One, as Kit glided close to him.

"Yes," Kit said bluntly, without any honorific note or tone of courtesy appended to the word. Nita looked at him in shock, wondering what had gotten into him. He ignored her, staring at the shark. Kit's teeth were showing.

The Pale One circled Kit once, lazily, as he had when offering challenge to S'reee. "She is not as frightened as she looks, Kit," he said, "and at any rate, I suspect you're more so. Look to yourself first until you know your new shape better. It has its own fierce ways, I hear; but a sperm whale is still no match for me." He said this with the utter calm of someone telling someone else what time it was. "I would not make three bites of you, as I would with Nita. I would seize your face and crush your upper jaw to make myself safe from your teeth. Then I would take hold of that great tongue of yours and not let go until I had ripped it loose to devour. Smaller sharks than I am have done that to sperm whales before. The tongue is, shall we say, a delicacy."

The shark circled away from Kit. Very slowly, Kit glided after. "Sir," he said—sounding subdued, if not afraid—"I didn't come here to fight. I thought we were supposed to be on the same side. But frightening us seems a poor tactic if we're supposed to be allies and singing the same Song."

"I frighten no one," said the shark. "No one who fears gets it from anywhere but himself. Or herself. Cast the fear out—and then I am nothing to fear . . . No matter, though; you're working at it. Kit, Nita, my name is ed'Rashtekaresket."

"It has teeth in it," Nita said.

The shark looked at her with interest in his opaque gaze. "It has indeed," he said. "You hear well. And you're the Silent One? Not the Listener?"

"The Listener's part is spoken for, Pale One," S'reee said. "And the Silent One's part needs a wizard more experienced than any we have—one already tested against the Lone Power, yet young enough to fulfill the other criteria. HNii't is the one."

"Then these are the two who went up against the Lone One in Manhattan," ed'Rashtekareset said. "Oh, don't sing surprise at me, Kit: I know the human names well enough. After all, you are who you eat."

Nita swallowed hard. "Such shock," the shark said, favoring Nita again with that dark, stony, unreadable look. "Beware your fear, Nita. They say I'm a 'killing machine'—and they say well. I am one." The terrible laugh hissed in the water again. "But one with a mind. Nor such a machine that I devour without cause. Those whom I eat, human or whale or fish, always give me cause. —I'm glad you brought them, S'reee. If this 'Heart of the Sea' the wizards always speak of really exists, then these two should be able to get its attention. And its attention is needed."

For the first time since the conversation began, S'reee displayed a mild annoyance. "It exists, Pale One. How many Songs have you played Twelfth in, and you still don't admit that—"

"More Songs than you have, young one," ed'Rashtekaresket said. "And it would take more still to convince me of what can't be seen by anyone not a wizard. *Show* me the Sea's Heart, this Timeheart you speak of, and I'll admit it exists."

"Are you denying that wizardry comes from there?" S'reee said, sounding even more annoyed.

"Possibly," said the shark, "if it does not. Don't be angry without reason, S'reee. You warm-bloods are all such great believers. But there's no greater pragmatist than a shark. I believe what I eat . . . or what I see. Your power I've seen: I don't deny that. I simply reserve decision on where it comes from. What I say further is that there's trouble in the deep waters hereabouts, more trouble than usual—and it's as well the Song is being enacted now, for there's need of it, wherever its virtue comes from. Will you hear my news? For if things go on as they're going now, the High and Dry will shortly be low and wet—and those of my Mastery will be eating very well indeed."

A Song of
Battles

"WHAT IS IT?" KIT said. "Is it the krakens?"

Ed'Rashtekaresket looked at Kit and began a slow, abstracted circling around him. "You know about that?" said the Master Shark. "You're wise for a human."

"I know that the krakens are breeding this year," Kit said, "breaking their usual eleven year cycle. And they're bigger than usual, our Seniors told us. In the deep water, krakens have been seen that would be a match for just about any whale or submarine they grabbed."

"That is essentially what I would have told you," the Master Shark said to S'reee, still circling Kit. "My own people have been reporting trouble with the bottom dwellers—but any sharks who cannot escape such are no longer entitled to the Mastery's protection in any case. At any rate, I pass this news along as a courtesy to you warm-bloods. By way of returning the courtesy done to my people after your accident."

"Thank you," S'reee said, and bowed as they swam.

"Odd," ed'Rashtekaresket mused as they went, "that qualified wizards of high levels are so few, the whales must bring in humans to make up the number."

"Odd isn't the word for it, Pale One," S'reee said. "Advisories and Seniors have been dying like clams at red tide lately."

"As if," the Master Shark said, "someone or something did not care to have the Song enacted just now." His voice sounded remote. "I'm reminded of that Song enacted, oh, a hundred thirty thousand moons ago—when the bottom shook as it does now, and the Lone One had newly lost the Battle of the Trees. One wizard was injured by rockfall while they made the journey down through the Gates of the Sea. And when they began the Singing proper, first the Killer and then the Blue lost control of their spells at crucial times. You know the moment, S'reee: when the mock battle breaks out among the three parties, and each one tries to force the others around to its way of thinking."

Ed'Rashtekaresket fell silent. The four of them swam on. "Uh, Ed—ed'Rak—" Nita stopped short, unable to remember the rest of his name as anything but the sound of gnashing teeth. "Look, can I call you Ed?"

Blank eyes turned their attention toward her. "At least I can say it," she said. "And if I'm going to be singing with you, it can't be titles all the time. We have to know each other, you say."

"A sprat's name," the shark said, dry-voiced. "A fry name—for me, the Master." Then came the quiet, terrible laughter again. "Well enough. You're the Sprat, and I'm Ed." He laughed again.

Nita had never heard anything that sounded less like mirth in her life. "Great. So, Ed, what happened? In that Song, when it went wrong. Was anyone hurt?"

"Of the Singers? No. They were inside a spell-circle, and protected—it has to be that way, else anything might get in among the Singers and upset their spelling. But when the Song failed, all the power its Singers had tried to use to bind the Lone One rebounded and freed him instead. The sea bottom for hundreds of miles about was terribly torn and changed as a result. Volcanoes, earthquakes . . . Also, there was a landmass, a great island in the middle of these waters. Surely you know about that country, since your people named the ocean after it. That island was drowned. There were humans on it; millions of them died when the island sank. As for the rest—eating was good hereabouts for some time. The species of my Mastery prospered."

"A hundred thirty thousand moons ago—," Kit whispered, one soft-breathed note of song. "Ten thousand years!"

"Atlantis," Nita said, not much louder.

"Afállonë," S'reee said, giving the name in the wizardly Speech. "There were Senior and Master wizards there," she said sadly, "a great many of them. But even working together, they couldn't stop what happened. The earthquakes begun by the downfall of Afállonë were so terrible that they tore straight through the first level of the land-under-Sea—the crust, I think the two-leggers call it—and right down to the mantle, the molten stuff beneath. The whole island plate on which Afállonë stood was broken in pieces and pushed down into the lava of the mantle— utterly destroyed. The plates of your continent and that of Europe have since drifted together over the island's old location, covering its grave . . . But even after the Downfall, there was trouble for years—mostly with the atmosphere, because of all the ash the volcanoes spat into the air. It got cold, and whole species of land creatures died for lack of their food. It was thousands of moons before things were normal again. So we tend to be very careful about the Song. 'Lest the Sea become the Land, and the Land become the Sea—' "

"And the krakens are breeding," the Pale One said as they swam. "Well. I'm for the Northern Rips tonight; there's trouble in the water there."

What kind of creature, Nita wondered, *could hear the sounds of simple distress at a distance of two hundred miles and more?*

"Beware, Nita," Ed said. "Only a dead shark could have avoided hearing *that* thought. If we're to know each other well, as you say you desire, best mind how you show me your feelings. Else I shall at last know you most intimately, sooner than you are planning—and the relationship will be rather one-sided."

Ed's jaws worked. "—I was going to say: matters swimming as they do, I will see you three home. It's getting dark, and—"

"Dark!" Nita and Kit looked around them. The water, turbid green white when they had come here, was now almost black.

"The sun's going down," Kit said unhappily. "We're really in for it now."

Nita agreed. "Master Shark," she said, staying as calm as she could, "we have to get back to, uh, our feeding grounds. And in a hurry. Our parents are waiting for us, and we had orders to be back before it got dark."

Ed simply looked at Nita with that calm black stare. "As you say," he said, and began to swim faster. "But we will not be at Bluehaven before many stars are out and the moon is about to set."

"I know," Nita said. It was hard to sound unconcerned while her insides were churning. "Maybe you should go ahead and let them know we're OK," she said to Kit. "Tell them I'm coming—"

"No," Kit said, also at pains to sound calm. "I'll take my chances with you, Neets. 'All for one . . .' "

"Sprat," Ed said to Nita, "this is an odd thing, that your sire and dam impose restrictions on you when you're doing a wizardry of such weight."

"They don't know we're wizards," Kit said.

S'reee was so surprised by this that she back-finned to a dead stop in the water. Ed, as if nothing took him by surprise, merely circled about the group, while Kit and Nita coasted close by. "They don't *know!*" S'reee said. "How do you do anything? How do you prepare wizardries? Let alone the matter of singing the Song without the full support of the people close to you—and when you're singing the Silent One's part, no less!"

There had been something about that last part in the manual. Nita had thought she had all the support she needed in Kit. She was becoming less sure. *Tom, got to call Tom—* "I know," she said out loud. "S'reee, let's swim. We're late enough as it is."

The four of them headed west again. "It can't be helped," Kit said. "It's not like it is here, where wizardry is something respectable and useful that most everybody knows about. Up on the land, they used to burn people for it. Nowadays— well, it's safer to hide what you're up to. People would think you were nuts if you tried to tell them you were a wizard. Most people don't believe in magic."

"What *do* they believe in?" S'reee said, unnerved.

"Things," Nita said unhappily. "S'reee, it's too complicated. But doing wizardry and keeping everybody from noticing is a problem."

"I'm no wizard," Ed said, "but only a fool would try to deny a wizard's usefulness. It must be a crippled life your people live up there, without magic, without what can't be understood, only accepted—"

For all her concern about being late, Nita looked wryly sideways at Ed. "This from someone who won't admit Timeheart exists unless he sees it himself?"

"Sprat," Ed said, "if it does in fact exist, can my not believing in it make the slightest difference? And as for understanding— I'm not interested in understanding Timeheart. What use is spending time figuring out, say, why water is wet? Will it make breathing it any— 'Ware, all!"

The warning came so conversationally that it took Nita precious moments to realize what the problem was. The sea around them was dark to begin with. But in the black water, darker shapes were moving. One of them, writhing and growing, reached up dim arms at them. Nita let out a squeak of surprise, and the returning echoes hit her skin and told her, to her terror, what her eyes couldn't. A long torpedo-shaped body, a great mass of arms that squirmed like snakes, and a long wicked beakfang hidden at the bottom of them. She backfinned desperately as those writhing arms with all their hooked suckers reached for her.

The sound that began rumbling through the water probably upset the krakens as much as it did her. Nita had never heard the battle cry of an enraged sperm whale—a frightful scrape of sound, starting at the highest note a human being can hear and scaling down with water-shaking roughness to the lowest note, then past it. It was hard to see what was going on, but Nita kept singing so her radar would tell her. She would have preferred not to; the echo-sight of Kit in the whalesark, arrowing toward the leading kraken, jaws open, all his sharp teeth showing, was a horror. Suckered arms whipped around him, squeezing; and the giant squid had its own noise, a screech so high it sounded like fingernails being scraped down a blackboard.

Before she really knew what she was doing, Nita circled off to pick up speed, and then swam straight toward the kraken's head ruffle, the thick place where the tentacles joined behind mouth and tooth. She sang for aim as she charged, then lost the song when she rammed the kraken. The squid's long, porous backbone crunched and broke under her blow. Rolling, tail lashing, she fluked away. All the telephone pole-length arms spasmed and squeezed Kit hard one last time, then fell away limp. Kit shot in toward the head of the broken squid. Jaws opened, crunched closed, opened again to slash once or twice with wild ferocity. Then Kit fluked powerfully, still singing, and arched away through the water.

"Kit!" Nita cried, but his only answer was the sperm-whale battle cry. The water was dark with night, thick with squid ink, and scratchy with stirred sand. Through it all a pallid shape was cruising with terrible speed, jaws open, circling in. The patch of darkness he circled threw out a score of arms to grapple with him. Ed let them draw him closer to his prey, then bit, and blood and ink billowed everywhere in the frantic rush of water expelled by the shrieking squid. Severed chunks of kraken arm spun and swirled in the water and sank through it. Ed swept forward, jaws wide, and bit again. The shriek cut off. Out of the cloud of blood and ink, Ed came silently sailing, cool, untroubled, graceful: the Pale Slayer, a silent ghost looking calmly about him for his next victim. Nita held very still and sang not a note until he passed her by.

S'reee was ramming another kraken as Nita had. But one more closed on her from behind. Kit came swimming, singing his battle cry. He bit the second squid amidships, hanging on to that bullet-shaped body like a bulldog as its struggles shook him from side to side. Between her and Kit and S'reee, Ed was circling a third kraken. It flailed at him, trying to bind his mouth shut so that it could get a better grip on him and squeeze him to death.

It might as well not have bothered. As a fourth kraken came for her, Nita saw Ed break his circling pattern to dart in and slash, then curve away. Again and again he feinted, again and again his teeth tore, until the kraken was reduced to a tattered, screaming storm of blood and ink and flailing tentacles. Blank-eyed, Ed soared straight at the finned rear end of the doomed creature and opened his mouth. When his jaws scissored shut, all that was left to drift downward were the tips of several tentacles. The kraken had been about the size of a station wagon.

A fifth kraken took a great suck of water into its internal jet-propulsion system and thrust it out again, tainting the water with the sepia taste of ink as it fled into the depths, wailing like a lost soul. Nita was willing to let it go and was swimming for the surface when a chill current and a pale form sank past her, spiraling downward with deadly grace. The utter dark of the night sea swallowed Ed. She heard the kraken's screams, which had been diminishing—and now grew louder and more ragged, until they abruptly stopped.

Wearily Nita swam upward. She broached and blew gratefully, doing nothing for a long while but lie there in the wave-wash, gasping.

Not too far away, S'reee broached and made her way slowly toward Nita.

Neither of them said anything; but the two of them sagged together and simply leaned against each other, taking comfort in the presence of another whale. Some yards off, the water rushed away from Kit's back and sides as he came up, gasping, too. Nita looked over at him, shaking. She knew that what she saw was just her friend in a whalesuit. But she kept seeing sharp teeth, slashing in a blood-hunger too much like Ed's for comfort.

"Are you OK?" she said to Kit.

"Yeah." He sounded uncertain, and Nita breathed out in relief. The voice was a sperm whale's, but the person inside it was definitely Kit. "Got a little—a little carried away there. You, Neets?"

"All right," she said.

Out of the depths a white form came drifting upward toward them.

They breathed and dived, all three, to find Ed circling in the clearing water, while a storm of fingerling blues and sardines swarmed about him, picking scraps and shreds out of the water, some of them even daring to pick bloody bits off Ed's skin or from between his teeth. "That last one was in pain at the thought of returning to the depths without its purpose fulfilled," he said. "So I ended that pain."

"Purpose?" Kit said.

"Surely you don't take that attack for an accident, young one," Ed said. "Any more than the shaking of the sea bottom these days or the ill chances that have been befalling S'reee's people have been accidents."

Nita looked at Kit, and then at Ed, in confusion. "You mean that what happened to S'reee— I thought you were on our side!"

Ed began to circle slowly inward toward Nita. "Peace, spratling," he said. "I pay no allegiance to anyone in the Sea or above it; you know that. Or you should. I am the Unmastered. I alone." He swept in closer. "The encounter S'reee and Ae'mhnuu had with the ship-that-cats-whales was doubtless the Lone One's doing. It has many ways to subtly influence those who live. As for the sharks—" Ed's voice became shaded with a cold, slow rage that chilled Nita worse than anything he'd said or done yet. "They did according to their nature, just as you do. Do not presume to blame them. On the other flank, however, *my* people have only one Master. If the Lone One has been tampering with species under my Mastery, then It will have to deal with *me*."

That made Nita shake—not only at the thought of Ed trying to take on the Lone Power himself, but at the outrageous thought that the Lone One, for all Its power, might actually be in for some trouble. "I'm sorry," she said. "I thought you meant you told the sharks to just go ahead and attack a hurt whale." And with some trepidation, she copied S'reee's earlier gesture—rolling over in the water, exposing her unprotected flanks and belly to the Master Shark.

A few long seconds afterward she felt what few beings have lived to tell about—the abrasive touch of a live shark's skin. Ed nudged Nita ever so lightly in the ribs, then glided by; almost a friendly touch, except that Nita could see the fanged mouth working still, the opaque black eyes tracking on her. Finned whiteness sailed silent and immense above her, hardly stirring the water. "In another time, in another place, I might have told them to," Ed said. "In another time, I may yet tell them to. And what will you think of me then, Sprat?"

"I don't know," she said, when the white shape had passed over.

"That was well said, too." Ed circled about the three of them, seeming to both watch them and ignore them at the same time. "So let us be on our way; we're close to Tiana Beach. S'reee, you and I have business remaining that must be done before witnesses."

S'reee wasted no time about it, gliding close to Ed—but, Nita noticed, not nearly as close as S'reee had come to Aroooon or Hotshot, or herself. "Ed' Rashtekaresket t'k Gh'shestaesteh, Eldest in Abeyance to the Pale Slayer That Was, Master for the Sharks of Plain and Shelf and what lies between—those who gather to sing that Song that is the Sea's shame and the Sea's glory desire you to be of their company. Say, for my hearing, whether you consent to that Song."

"I consent, and I will weave my voice and my will and my blood with that of those who sing, if there be need."

"I ask the second time—"

"Peace, S'reee, I know the words by now: Who better? A second time I say it, that those with me, both of my Mastery and not, may hear. Twice I consent to the Song, in my Mastery's name; and a third time, that the Sea, and the Heart of the Sea, shall hear . . ." *Was his voice just a touch drier on that phrase?* Nita wondered.

"So up, now, the three of you. We are where you need to be."

Kit looked around him in confusion. "How can you tell? There's a lot of Tiana Beach, and you've never seen our house—"

"I can smell your human bodies in the water from this morning," Ed said, unperturbed. "And, besides, I hear distress."

"Uh-oh . . . ," Kit said.

"S'reee," Nita said, stalling, "when will you need us next?"

"Next dawn," the humpback said, brushing against first Nita, then Kit, in sympathy. "I'm sorry we can't have a day's rest or so, but there's no time anymore."

"Do we have to be there?" Kit said.

"The Silent Lord does," S'reee said, glancing at Nita. "In fact, normally it's the Silent Lord who administers the Oath, since her stake in the Song is the greatest."

Nita made an unhappy sound. "Kit," she said, "maybe you'd better stay home. At least you won't get in trouble with your folks that way."

Kit shouldered over beside her, absent affection that bumped her considerably sideways as his hundred-foot bulk hit her. "No," he said. "I told you: 'All for one.' It's not fair for you to be stuck with this alone. Besides, what if those things show up again, and Ed's not here—"

"Right," Nita said.

"Neets, we better get going," Kit said.

She headed for the surface. Kit and S'reee followed; but Ed was above her and surfaced first, several hundred yards westward and much closer to the shore. So the first sound Nita heard from the shore was the screaming.

Nita had never heard her mother scream. The raw panic in the sound got under Nita's skin even worse than Kit's hunting song had.

"Harry!" her mother was shouting, and every few words her terror would gnaw its way through her desperately controlled voice and come out as a scream again. "Harry, for God's sake look, there's a *fin* out there, it's a *shark!* Get Mr. Friedman, get the cops, get *somebody!*"

The beach flickered with lights—flashlights, held by people running up and down—and every light in Nita's house was on, as well as most of those in the houses next door. Nita gulped at her father's hoarse reply—just as scared as her mother, trying to stay in control and failing.

"Betty, hang on, they're coming! Hang on! Don't go near the water!" For her mother was floundering into the surf, looking out seaward, searching for someone she couldn't see. "Nita!"

Nita had to fight to stay silent.

Ed cruised serenely, contemptuously close to the shore, bearing off westward, away from Nita and Kit and S'reee. The flashlights followed his pale fin as it broached, as Ed went so far as to raise himself a little out of the water, showing a terrible expanse of back, then the upward-spearing tail fin as big as a windsurfer's sail. Shouting in fear and amazement, the people followed him down the beach as if hypnotized. The flashlights bobbed away.

"He's got them distracted, we've gotta get out now," Kit said.

"But our bathing suits—"

"No time! Later! S'reee, we'll see you in the morning!" The two of them fluked wildly and made for the beach, in the direction opposite the one in which Ed was leading the people on the shore. Nita stayed under the surface as long as she could, then felt the bottom scrape on her belly; she was grounded. Kit had grounded sooner than she had. Nita gasped a long breath of air and let the shapechange go, then collapsed into the water again—not deep for a whale, but three feet deep for her. She struggled to her feet and staggered to shore through the breakers, wiping the salt out of her eyes and shaking with the shock of a spell released too suddenly.

By the time her sight was working properly, there was no time to do anything about the small, dark figure standing a few feet up the incline of the beach, looking straight at her.

Dairine.

There was a slam of imploding air behind Nita. Kit came scrambling up out of the water, with the undone whalesark clutched glittering in one fist. "Quick," he said, "I can do the Scotty spell before they come back—" He reached out and grabbed her by the arm, shaking her. "Neets, are you okay?"

Then he saw Dairine, too. "Uh," he said. The sounds of voices down the beach were getting closer; and through them, abrupt and terrible, came a sudden *crack!* of gunfire. Kit looked down that way, then at Dairine again, and took a long breath. "Right back," he said. He said one quick syllable and, in another clap of air, vanished.

Dairine just stood there in her pajamas with Yoda all over them, staring at her sister. "Whales," she said.

"Dairine," Nita whispered, "how long have they been out here?"

"About an hour."

"Oh, *no.*" And her folks would be there in moments. "Dairine," Nita said, "look—" There she stopped. She couldn't think what she wanted to say.

"It *is* magic," Dairine whispered back. "There really *is* such a thing. And it's that book you have, isn't it? It's not just an old beat-up kids' book. It's—"

In another slam of air, blowing outward this time, Kit reappeared. He was already in his bathing suit; he flung Nita's at her and then looked unhappily at Dairine.

"And you, too," she said to him as Nita struggled into her suit.

"A wizard?" Kit said. "Yeah. Both of us."

Off to their left, there was another gunshot, and a mighty splash. Nita and Kit stared out at the sea. Ed was arrowing straight up out of the water with slow, frightful grace, jaws working as he arched up in a leap like a dolphin's. Fifty feet of him towered out of the water, sixty, eighty, until even his long, sharp tail fin cleared the surface, and he hung there in midair, bent like a bow, the starlight and the light of the moon sheening ice white along his hide and the water that ran down it. "Until later, my wizards!" came his hissed cry in the Speech, as Ed dived dolphin-curved back into the sea. The gunshot cracked across the water at him, once, twice. Ed went down laughing in scorn.

"That's as much as he's gonna do," Kit said. "They'll be back in a moment, when they see he's gone."

"That shark—," said Dairine, sounding about ready to go into shock.

"He's a friend," Nita said.

"Neets," Kit said, "what're we gonna tell them?"

"That depends on Dairine." Nita took care to keep her voice perfectly level. "What about it, Dari? Are you going to spill everything? Or are you going to keep quiet?"

Dairine looked at the two of them, saying nothing. Then, "I want you to tell me everything later," she said. *"Everything."*

"It'll have to be tonight, Dari. We've got to be out again by dawn."

"You're gonna get it," Dairine said.

"Tell us something else we don't know, Sherlock," Kit said, mild-voiced.

"Well. I guess I saw you two coming over the dune," Dairine said, looking from Kit to Nita. She turned to head down the beach.

Nita caught Dairine by the arm, stopping her. Dairine looked back at Nita over her shoulder—her expression of unease just visible in the dim light from the houses up the beach. "I really don't want to lie to them, Dari," Nita said.

"Then you better either keep your mouth shut," Dairine said, "or tell them the truth." And she tugged her arm out of Nita's grasp and went pounding off down the beach, screaming, in her best I'm-gonna-tell voice, "Mom, Dad, it's Nita!"

Nita and Kit stood where they were. "They're gonna ground us," Kit said.

"Maybe not," said Nita, in forlorn hope.

"They will. And what're you going to do then?"

Nita's insides clenched. And the sound of people talking was coming down the beach toward them.

"I'm going," she said. "These are *lives* we're talking about—whales' lives. People's lives. It can't just be stopped in the middle! You remember what Ed said."

"That's what I'd been thinking," Kit said. "I just didn't want to get you in my trouble—just because I'm doing it, I mean." He looked at her. "Dawn, then."

"Better make it before," Nita said, feeling like a conspirator and hating it. "Less light to get caught by."

"Right." And that was all they had time for, for Nita's mother and father, and Mr. Friedman, and Dairine, all came trotting up together. Then things got confusing, for Nita's dad grabbed her and hugged her to him with tears running down his face, as if he were utterly terrified; and her mother slowed from her run, waved her arms in the air, and roared, "Where the blazes have you *been?*"

"We lost track of the time," Kit said.

"We were out, Mom," Nita said. "Swimming—"

"Wonderful! There are sharks the size of houses out there in the water, and my daughter is off swimming! At night, at high tide, with the undertow—" Her mother gulped for air, then said more quietly, "I didn't expect this of you, Nita. After we talked this morning, and all."

Nita's father let go of her slowly, nodding, getting, a fierce, closed look on his face now that the initial shock of having his daughter back safe was passing. "And I thought you had better sense, Kit," he said. "We had an agreement that while you stayed with us, you'd do as we said. Here it is hours and hours after dark—"

"I know, sir," Kit said. "I forgot—and by the time I remembered, it was too late. It won't happen again."

"Not for a while, anyway," Nita's mother said, sounding grim. "I don't want you two going out of sight of the house until further notice. Understood?"

"Yes, Mrs. Callahan."

"Nita?" her mother said sharply.

There it was: the answer she wasn't going to be able to get around. "OK, Mom," she said. Her stomach turned over inside her at the sound of the lie. Too late now. It was out, not to be recalled.

"That also means staying out of the water," her father said.

Why me? Why me! Nita thought. She made a face. "OK."

"OK," Kit said, too, not sounding very happy.

"We'll see how you two behave in the next few days," Nita's mother said. "And whether that shark clears out of here. Maybe after that we'll let you swim again. Meanwhile—you two get home."

They went. Just once Nita looked over her shoulder and was sure she saw, far out on the water, a tall, pale fin that stood high as a sail above the surface, then slid below it, arrowing off toward Montauk—distress ended for the moment, and a job done.

Nita felt the miserable place in her gut and thought it was just as well that Ed couldn't come up on the land.

Fearsong

NITA LAY AWAKE IN the dark, staring at the ceiling. It was three-thirty in the morning, by the glow of the cheap electric clock on the dresser. She would very much have liked to turn over, forget about the clock, the time, and everything else, and just sack out. But soon it would be false dawn, and she and Kit would have to be leaving.

Changes . . .

Only last week, her relationship with her folks had seemed perfect. Now all that was over, ruined—and about to get much worse, Nita knew, when her mom and dad found her and Kit gone again in the morning.

And the changes in Kit—

She rolled over on her stomach unhappily, not wanting to think about it. She had a new problem to consider, for when everyone was in bed, Dairine had come visiting.

Nita put her face down into her pillow and groaned. Dairine had gone right through Nita's wizards' manual, staring at all the strange maps and pictures. It was annoying enough to begin with that Dairine could see the book at all; nonwizards such as her mother and father, looking at it, usually saw only an old, beat-up copy of something called *So You Want to Be a Wizard*, apparently a kids' book. But Dairine saw what was there, and was fascinated.

The aptitude for wizardry sometimes runs through a whole generation of a family. Several famous "circles" of wizards in the past had been made up of brothers or sisters or cousins, rather than unrelated people such as she and Kit, or Tom and Carl, who met by accident or in some other line of work and came to do wizardry together by choice. But families with more than one wizard tended to be the exception rather than the rule, and Nita hadn't been expecting this. Also, Nita was beginning to realize that she had rather enjoyed having her wizardry be a secret from everybody but the other wizards she worked with. That secret, that advantage, was gone now, too. Dairine had the aptitude for wizardry as strongly as Nita herself had had it when she started.

In fact, she's got it more strongly than I did, Nita thought glumly. *The book had to get my attention by force, that first time I passed it in the library. But Dairine noticed it herself, as soon as I brought it home.*

For several years Nita had kept her advantage over her sister by only the slimmest of margins. She knew quite well that Dairine was a lot smarter than she was in most things. Wizardry had been a large and satisfying secret she'd felt sure Dairine would never catch on to. But that advantage was now gone, too. The youngest wizards were the strongest ones, according to the book; older ones might be wiser but had access to less sheer power. Dairine had gotten the better of her again.

Nita turned over on her back, staring at the ceiling once more.

Kit . . .

He just wasn't himself in the whalesark. *When he's in his own skin*, she told herself fiercely, *he's fine*. But she couldn't quite make herself believe that. His look, his stance, were too different in just the past day or two.

She had thought that having a best friend at last would be great fun. And she and Kit had enjoyed each other's company immensely in their first couple months of wizardry, after the terror and sorrow of their initial encounter with the Art had worn off a bit. But sometimes things just didn't work. Kit would get moody, need to be by himself for days at a time. Or he would say sudden things that Nita thought cruel—except that it was Kit saying them, and Kit wasn't cruel; she knew that.

I wish I'd had some friends when I was younger, she thought. *Now I've got one who really matters—and I don't know what to do so he stays my friend. He changes* . . .

And Kit was going to be in that whalesark for more and more time in the next couple of days. Would she even know him if this kept up?

Would he know her? Or want to? Humpbacks and sperms were different. Her own aggressiveness had frightened her badly enough, after the fight with the krakens. Kit's had been worse. And he had been enjoying it . . .

Listless, Nita reached under her pillow for her wizards' manual and a flashlight. She clicked the light on and started paging through the book, intending to kill some time doing "homework"—finishing the study of her parts of the Song, the Silent Lord's parts. They were mostly in what whales used for verse—songs with a particular rhythm and structure, different for each species, but always more formal than regular conversational song. Since she wasn't good at memorizing, Nita was relieved to find that when she was in whaleform, the Sea would remind her of the exact words. What she needed to study were the emotions and motivations behind each song, the *way* they were sung.

She riffled through the book. There was a lot of background material—the full tale of the first Song, and of others, including the disastrous "Drowned Song" that ended in the downfall of Atlantis; the names of famous whale-wizards who had sung and how they had sung their parts; "stage direction" for the Song itself; commentary, cautions, permitted variations, even jokes, for evidently though the occasion was serious, it didn't have to be somber. Then the Song proper, in verse, with the names of the ten Lords of the Humors: the Singer, the Gazer, the Blue, the Sounder, the Gray Lord, the Listener, the Killer, the Wanderer, the Forager, and of course the Silent Lord. Each of them ruled a kind of fish and also a kind of temperament.

Some of them struck Nita as odd; the Killer, for example, was the patroness of laughter, always joking: the Gazer looked at everything and hardly ever said what he saw. And the Silent Lord—Nita paused at the lines that described "the one who ruled seas with no songs in them, and hearts that were silent; but in her own silence, others would sing forever. . . ."

And of course there was the Pale Slayer. And another odd thing; though the names of all the whales ever to sing the Song were listed, there was no listing for the Master Shark, except the mere title, repeated again and again. *Maybe he's like an executioner in the old days*, Nita thought. *Anonymous.* The commentaries weren't very illuminating. "The Master of the lesser Death," one of them called him, "who, mastering it, dieth not. For wizardry toucheth not one to whom it hath not been freely given: nor doth the messenger in any wise partake of the message he bears."

The manual was like that sometimes. Nita sighed and skimmed down to the first canto: S'reee's verse, it would be, since the Singer opens the Song as the other Ten gather around the lonely seamount Caryn Peak, the Sea's Tooth. Alongside the musical and movement notations for a whale singing the Song, the manual had a rough translation into the Speech:

> Blood in the water I sing,
>   and one who shed it:
> deadliest hunger I sing,
>   and one who fed it—
> weaving the ancient-most tale
>   of the Sea's sending:
> singing the tragedy,
>   singing the joy unending.
>
> This is our shame—
>   this is the whole Ocean's glory:
> this is the Song of the Twelve.
>   Hark to the story!
> Hearken, and bring it to pass:
>   swift, lest the sorrow
> long ago laid to its rest
>   devour us tomorrow!

There was much more: the rest of the prologue, then the songs of each of the Masters who were part of the Song and their temptations by the Stranger-whale, the Lone Power in disguise. Nita didn't need to pay any attention to those, for the Silent Lord came in only near the end, and the others, even the Stranger, dared use nothing stronger than persuasion on her. The whale singing the part of the Silent One then made her decision which side to be on—and acted.

That was the part Nita had gotten up to. *Almost done*, she thought with some relief, seeing that there wasn't much more beyond this. Only a few more cantos. *Boy, how do you manage to be cheerful while singing this stuff? It sounds so creepy.*

> Must I accept the barren Gift?
>   —learn death, and lose my Mastery?
> Then let them know whose blood and breath
>   will take the Gift and set them free:
> whose is the voice and whose the mind
>   to set at naught the well-sung Game—
> when finned Finality arrives
>   and calls me by my secret Name.

Not old enough to love as yet,
  but old enough to die, indeed—
the death-fear bites my throat and heart,
  fanged cousin to the Pale One's breed.
But past the fear lies life for all—
  perhaps for me; and, past my dread,
past loss of Mastery and life,
  the Sea shall yet give up Her dead!

Glad that wasn't me back then, she thought. *I could never have pulled that off* . . . Nita read down through the next section, the stage directions for this sequence of the Song. "The whale singing the Silent One then enacts the Sacrifice in a manner as close to the original enactment as possible, depending on the site where the Song is being celebrated. . . ."

She skimmed the rest of it, the directions detailing the Pale Slayer's "acceptance of Sacrifice," his song, the retreat of the Lone Power, and the Song's conclusion by the remaining Ten. But she was having trouble keeping her mind on her work. Kit—

"Neets!"

His voice was the merest hiss from outside the locked window. She got up and peered out the window to see where Kit was, then waved him away from the wall. The spell she had in mind for getting out needed only one word to start it. Nita spoke it and walked through the wall.

Between the distracting peculiarity of the feeling, which was like walking through thick spiderwebs, and the fact that the floor of her room was several feet above the ground, Nita almost took a bad fall, the way someone might who'd put a foot into an open manhole. Kit staggered, barely catching her, and almost fell down himself.

"Clumsy," he said as he turned her loose.

"Watch it, *El Niño*—"

He punched her, not as hard as he might have; then spent a moment or two brushing himself off, and redraped the whalesark over one shoulder, where it hung mistily shimmering like a scrap of fog with starlight caught in it. "Is that locked?" he said, looking up at Nita's window with interest.

"Uh-huh."

"And the front and back doors are, too."

"Yeah."

Kit threw a wicked look at Nita as they made their silent way out of the yard and toward the beach. "Your mom and dad are going to be real curious how we got out of the house and then locked all the inside locks when we don't have the keys."

"Uh-huh," Nita said. "If we're gonna get in real trouble, we might as well confuse them as much as possible. It might distract them . . ."

"Wanna bet?" Kit said.

Nita didn't answer.

The beach was desolate. Nita and Kit left their bathing suits under a prominent boulder and slid into the chilly water. Nita changed first and let Kit take hold of her dorsal fin and be towed out to deeper water. She shuddered once, not knowing why, at the strange cool feeling of human hands on her hide as she swam outward.

Beyond the breakers, the water was peculiarly still. The sky was cobalt with a hint of dawn-silver in it; the sea was sheenless, shadowless, the color of lead. And rising up from the listless water, four or five hundred yards from shore, a tall white fin was cruising in steady, silent circles, like the sail of a ghost ship unable to make port.

"I didn't think Ed was going to be here," Kit said. He let go of Nita's fin and slipped off into the water.

"Neither did I," Nita said, not knowing if he heard her before he dived. When he was finished changing, she dived, too, and made her way toward where Ed swam serenely.

S'reee was there as well. She swam close, whistling Nita a greeting, and brushed skin with her. Hotshot was there, too, gamboling and swooping in the dim-lit water—though with just a little more restraint than usual around the silently drifting bulk of Ed.

"A long swim today," S'reee said to Nita. "Up to Nantucket. Are you ready? Did you get your problem with your dam and sire worked out?"

"Not really," Nita said. "In fact, it'll probably get a lot worse before it gets any better. There's going to be trouble tonight . . ." She stopped; there was no use letting it spoil the day. "Never mind," she said. "Let's go."

S'reee led the way, a straight course east-northeast, to Nantucket Rips. From her reading and from what the Sea told her, Nita knew those were treacherous waters, full of sudden shelves and hidden rocks. And the wizards' manual spoke of uneasy "forces" that lingered about those dead and broken ships—forces Nita suspected she would mistake for restless ghosts, if she should have the bad luck to see one.

"You are silent today," said a dry, cool voice directly above Nita. Glancing upward, Nita saw floating above her, effortlessly keeping pace, the great pale form that had been one of the images keeping her awake last night. "And you did not greet me. Is this courtesy to another Celebrant?"

"Good morning, Ed," Nita said, in the same mildly edgy tone of voice she would have used on a human being who bugged her that way.

"Oh, indeed," Ed said. "You're bold, Sprat. And the boldness comes of distress. Beware lest I be forced to hurry matters, so that we should have even less time to get acquainted than you seem to desire."

"That was something I was meaning to ask you about," Nita said, looking up at Ed again. "The 'distress' business—"

"Ask, Sprat."

"You said before that it was your 'job' to end distress where you found it . . ."

"You are wondering who gave me the job," Ed said, sinking to Nita's level, so that her left-side eye was filled with the sight of him. "Perhaps it was the Sea itself, which you wizards hear speaking to you all the time. You look askance? Doubtless you think the Sea would be too 'good' to assign a whole species to nothing but painful and violent killing." Ed's voice stayed cool as always, though there was a tinge of mockery to it. "If you think so, look around you, Sprat. The ocean is full of weaponry as effective as my teeth. Poisons and spines, snares and traps and claws that catch are everywhere. We all have to eat."

Ed smiled at her. A long shiver went down Nita from head to tail; a shark's smile is an expression the wise person does not provoke. "Those are just dumb creatures, though," she said, keeping her song as inoffensive sounding as possible. "They don't think. You do—and you *enjoy* what you do."

"So?" Ed swam closer. "How should I not? Like all my people I'm built to survive in a certain fashion . . . and it's only wise to cause what you build to feel good when it does what it must to survive. My nerves are tuned to pain. That fact tells me beyond question what my job is. Distress calls me; blood in the water is the clearest sign of that distress, and I have a duty to it. If I destroy, still I serve life. What can't elude me is often sick or injured, and suffering; what survives me or outthinks me is stronger and wiser for it. And the survivor's descendants will be, too. Is that so bad?"

"Well, that way . . . no. But I bet you wouldn't be so calm about it if it was *you* dying."

"Me? Die?" Ed laughed again. "The Master Shark eats the Silent Lord's 'Gift,' you know, along with the Silent One. There's immortality in all the sharks, in various degrees. But what good is immortality if you haven't died first? And nothing in the Sea is deadly enough to kill me against my will."

Something about Ed's voice was making Nita curious. "What about with it?"

"Ah, but will must spread to the body from the mind. And after all the years I've lived in it, my body is too strong. All it wants is to eat, and live. And so it does; and I swim on. Immortality is of terrible power. It would take something more powerful yet to override it . . ."

Nita didn't say anything.

"But all that being so," Ed said, "for good or ill, I am the Destroyer. Being that, I might as well enjoy my work, might I not? And so I do. Would it help if I decided to be miserable?" There was actually a touch of humor in that cold, dry voice.

"No, I suppose not."

"So I go about my work with a merry heart," Ed said, "and do it well as a result. That should please you, I think—"

"I'm delighted," Nita sang, under her breath.

"—for spells work best, you wizards tell me, when all the participants are of light heart and enjoying themselves. I'll certainly enjoy eating *you* when the time comes 'round."

"Ed, that's not funny."

"It isn't?" said the Master Shark, looking at her.

Nita stopped swimming, letting herself coast for a moment. There was something odd about the way he'd said that—"Ed, what was that crack supposed to mean?"

The look Ed gave her was expressionless as ever. "The Silent Lord is pleased to jest with me," he said.

"Ed!"

"Distress, distress, Sprat. Have a care."

Ed was drifting closer again, and Nita kept herself as outwardly calm as she could. "Ed," she said, slowly and carefully, "are you trying to say that you're actually planning to *eat* me sometime soon?"

"The day after tomorrow," said the Master Shark in perfect calm, "if we keep to schedule."

Nita couldn't think of a thing to say.

"You seem surprised," Ed said. "Why?"

It took Nita a few moments to answer, for her mind was boiling with sudden memories. S'reee's great relief when Nita agreed to participate in the Song. Her repeated questions to Nita about whether she was sure she wanted to do this. The Blue's silent, sad appraisal and approval of her. S'reee's remark about the Silent Lord's contribution to the Song being the most important of any celebrant—"the Silent Lord has the most at stake." And the wording of the Celebrant's Oath itself, with its insistent repetition and the line Nita had been so sure was ceremonial: "and I will blend my blood with theirs should there be need. . . ."

Nita gulped. "Ed," she said, "the Song, the whole thing . . . I thought it was just sort of, sort of a play . . ."

"Indeed not." Ed seemed unconcerned by her terror. "There's always blood in the water at the end of the Song. I am no wizard, but even I know that nothing else will keep the Lone Power bound. Nothing but the willing sacrifice, newly made by the Celebrant representing the Silent One—by a wizard who knows the price he is paying and what it will buy. The spells worked during the Song would be powerless otherwise, and the Lone Power would rise again and finish what It once began."

"But—" Off on her right, she saw Kit looking curiously at her. But at the moment Kit meant nothing to her, and neither did Ed, or the chill silver light dawning in the water, or anything else. The manual's words, which she'd skimmed over so casually, those were what mattered now. *The whale singing the Silent One then enacts the Sacrifice in a manner as close to the original enactment as possible, depending on the site where the Song is being celebrated. The shark singing the Pale Slayer then receives the Sacrifice. . . .* With frightful clarity she could remember sitting on the fishing platform off Tiana Beach and S'reee saying, "The Silent One dived into a stand of razor coral; and the Master Shark smelled her blood in the water, and . . . well . . ."

Nita started to swim, without any real idea of where she was going, or why she was going there. She went slowly at first, then faster. "Neets," Kit was singing behind her, "what's wrong, what is it?"

"HNii't!" sang another voice, farther away. "Wait! What's the matter?"

That voice she wanted to hear some more from. Nita wheeled about and hurtled back the way she had come, almost ramming Kit, and not caring, letting him get out of her way as best he could. S'reee saw Nita coming and simply stopped swimming. "S'reee!" Nita cried, one long note that was more a scream than a song. "Why didn't you tell me!"

"Oh, hNii't," S'reee sang, desperate and hurried, "the Master Shark is about— for Sea's sake, control yourself!"

"Never mind him! *Why didn't you tell me!*"

"About what the Silent One does?" S'reee said, sounding confused and upset as Nita braked too late and almost hit her, too. "But you said you knew!"

Nita moaned out loud. It was true. *Just about finished with my reading*, she remembered herself saying. *Only one thing I don't understand; everything else is fairly straightforward . . .* And, *I got it, S'reee, let's get on with it . . .* But the truth didn't break her rage. "You should have made sure I knew what you were talking about!"

"Why?" S'reee cried, getting angry herself now. "You're a more experienced wizard than *I* am! You went into the Otherworlds and handled things by yourself that it'd normally take whole circles of wizards to do! And I warned you, make sure you know what you're doing before you get into this! But you went right ahead!"

Nita moaned again, and S'reee lost her anger at the sound and moaned, too. "I knew something bad was going to happen," she sang unhappily. "The minute I found Ae'mhnuu dead and me stuck with organizing the Song, I knew! But I never thought it'd be anything as bad as *this!*"

Kit looked from one of them to the other, somewhat at a loss. "Look," he said to S'reee, "are you telling me that the whale who sings the Silent One actually has to *die?*"

S'reee simply looked at him. Nita did not look at him, could not.

"That's horrible," Kit said in a hushed voice. "Nita, you can't—"

"She must," S'reee said. "She's given her word that she would."

"But couldn't somebody else—"

"Someone else could," S'reee said. "If that person would be willing to take the Oath and the role of the Silent Lord in hNii't's place. But no one will. What other wizard are we going to be able to find in the spacc of a day and a half who would be willing to die for Nita's sake?"

Kit was silent with shock.

"Anyway, hNii't took the Oath freely in front of witnesses," S'reee said unhappily. "Unless someone with a wizard's power freely substitutes himself for her, she has to perform what she's promised. Otherwise the whole Song is sabotagcd, useless—can't be performed at all. And if we don't perform it, or if something goes wrong . . ."

Nita closed her eyes in horror, remembering the time the Song failed. What Atlantis couldn't survive, she thought in misery, New York and Long Island sure won't. Millions of people will die. Including Mom and Dad, Dairine, Ponch, Kit's folks—

"But the Song hasn't started yet," Kit protested.

"Yes, it has," Nita said dully. *That* she remembered very clearly from her reading; it had been in the commentaries, one of the things she found strange. "The minute the first Celebrant takes the Oath, the Song's begun—and everything that happens to every Celebrant after that is part of it."

"HNii't," S'reee said in a voice so small that Nita could barely hear her, "what will you do?"

A shadow fell over Nita, and a third and fourth pair of eyes joined the first two: Hotshot, grinning as always, but with alarm behind the grin; Ed, gazing down at her out of flat black eyes, emotionless as stones. "I thought I sensed some little troubling over here," said the Master Shark.

Kit and S'reee held still as death. "Yes," Nita said with terrible casualness, amazed at her own temerity.

"Is the pain done?" said the Master Shark.

"For the moment," Nita said. She could feel herself slipping into shock, an insulation that would last her a few hours at least. She'd felt something similar, several years before, when her favorite uncle had died. The shock had gotten Nita through the funeral; but afterward, it had been nearly two weeks before she had been able to do much of anything but cry. *I won't have that option this time*, she thought. *There's work to be done, a Song to sing, spells to work . . .* But all that seemed distant and unimportant to her, since in a day and a half, it seemed, a shark was going to eat her. Kit looked at Nita in terror, as if he suddenly didn't know her.

She stared back, feeling frozen inside. "Let's go," she said, and turned to start swimming east-northeast again, their original course. "The Gray is waiting, isn't she?"

By the sound of her way-song Nita could hear S'reee and Kit and Hotshot following after her; and last of all, silent, songless, came Ed.

I'm going to die, Nita thought.

She had thought that before, occasionally. But she had never believed it.

She didn't believe it now.

And she knew it was going to happen anyway.

Evidently, Nita thought, *Ed had been right when he'd said that belief made no difference to the truth . . .*

The Gray
Lord's Song

C

THEY FOUND THE WHALE who would sing the part of the Gray in the chill waters about Old Man Shoals, a gloomy place strewn full of boulders above which turbulent water howled and thundered. The current set swift through the shoals, and the remnants of its victims lay everywhere. Old splintered spars of rotting masts, fragments of crumbled planks, bits of rusted iron covered with barnacles or twined about with anemones; here and there a human bone, crusted over with coral— Broken-backed ships lay all about, strangled in weed, ominous shapes in the murk; and when Nita and Kit and the others sang to find their way, the songs fell into the silence with a wet, thick, troubled sound utterly unlike the clear echoes that came back from the sandy bottoms off Long Island.

The place suited Nita's mood perfectly. She swam low among the corpses of dead ships, thinking bitter thoughts—most of them centering on her own stupidity.

They warned me. Everybody warned me! Even Picchu warned me: "Read the fine print before you sign!" *Idiot!* she thought bitterly. *What do I do now? I don't want to die!*

But, "Any agreements you make, make sure you keep," Tom had said—and though his voice had been kind, it had also been stern. As stern as the Blue's: "Nowhere does the Lone Power enter in so readily as through the broken word."

She could see what she was expected to do . . . and it was impossible. *I can't die—I'm too young; what would Kit say to Mom and Dad; I don't want to; it's not fair!* But the answer stayed the same nonetheless.

She groaned out loud. *Two days. Two days left. Two days is a long time. Maybe something will happen and I won't have to die.*

"Stop that sniveling noise!" came a sharp, angry burst of song, from practically in front of her. Nita back-finned, shocked at the great bulk rising up from the bottom before her. The echoes of her surprised squeak came back raggedly, speaking of old scars, torn fins and flukes, skin ripped and gouged and badly healed. And the other's song had an undercurrent of rage to it that hit Nita like a deep dive into water so cold it burned.

"How dare you come into my grounds without protocol?" said the new whale as she cruised toward Nita with a slow deliberateness that made Nita back away even faster than before. The great head and lack of a dorsal fin made it plain that this was another sperm whale.

"Your pardon," Nita sang hurriedly, sounding as conciliatory as possible. "I didn't mean to intrude—"

"You have," said the sperm, in a scraping phrase perilously close to the awful sperm-whale battle cry that Nita had heard from Kit. She kept advancing on Nita, and Nita kept backing, her eye on those sharp teeth. "These are *my* waters, and I won't have some noisy krill-eating songster scaring my food—"

That voice was not only angry, it was cruel. Nita started to get angry at the sound of it. She stopped backing up and held her ground, poising her tail for a short rush to ram the other if necessary. "I'm not interested in your fish, even if they could hear me, which they can't—and you know it!" she sang angrily. "Humpbacks sing higher than fish can hear—the same as you do!"

The sperm kept coming, showing more teeth. "You look like a whale," she said, voice lowering suspiciously, "and you sing like a whale—but you don't sound like a whale. Who are you?"

"HNii't," Nita said, giving her name the humpback accent. "I'm a wizard. A human wizard—"

The sperm whale cried out and rushed at her, jaws wide. Nita arrowed off to one side, easily avoiding the sperm's rush. "Spy! Murderer!" The sperm was howling, a terrible rasping song like a scream. It came at her again—

Again Nita rolled out of the way, her maneuverability easily defeating the other's rage-blinded charge. "I may be a human," she sang angrily, "but I'm still a wizard! Mess with me and I'll—"

WHAM! The sperm whale's spell hit her with an impact that made the displaced-water explosions of Kit's shapechanges seem puny. Nita was thrown backward, literally head over tail, thrashing and struggling for control as she swore at herself for being caught off guard. The spell was a simple physical-violence wizardry, as contemptuous a gesture from one wizard to another as a slap in the face . . . and as much a challenge to battle as such a slap would have been from one human to another.

Nita went hot with rage, felt about for her inner contact with the Sea, found it, and sang—only three notes, but pitched and prolonged with exquisite accuracy to take the power of the other's spell and turn it back on her tenfold. The spell and the water thundered together. The sperm whale was blown backward as Nita had been, but with more force, tumbling violently and trailing a song of shock and rage behind her.

Nita held still, shaking with anger, while S'reee and Hotshot and Kit gathered around her. "I'm all right," she said, the trembling getting into her song. "But that one needs some lessons in manners."

"She always has," S'reee said. "HNii't, I'm sorry. I would have kept you back with us, but—" She didn't go on.

"It's all right," Nita said, still shaking.

"Nice shot," said a low scrape of song beside her ear, angry and appreciative: Kit. She brushed him lightly with one flank as a great pale shape came drifting down on the other side of her, eyeing her with dark-eyed interest.

"So," Ed said, calm as ever, "the Sprat has teeth after all. I am impressed."

"Thanks," Nita said, not up to much more conversation with Ed at the moment.

Slowly they swam forward together to where S'reee was hovering in the water, singing more at than with the other whale. "—know you were out of bounds, Areinnye," she said. "There was no breach of protocol. We came in singing."

"That one did not," said the sperm whale, her song so sharp with anger that it was a torture to the ears. "My right—"

"—does not extend to attacking a silent member of a party entering your waters within protocols," S'reee said. "You attacked hNii't out of spite, nothing more. First spite, then anger because she was human. We heard—"

"Did you indeed? And what else have you heard in these waters, you nursling wizard, you and your little playfellows?" The sperm whale glared at them all as they gathered around her, and the rasp of pain and hatred in her voice was terrible. "Have you seen my calf hereabouts? For all your magics, I think not. The whalers have been through these waters three days ago, and they served my little M'hali as they served your precious Ae'mhnuu! Speared and left to float belly-up, slowly dying, while they hunted me—then hauled bloated out of the water and gutted, his bleeding innards thrown overboard by bits and pieces for the gulls and the sharks to eat!"

When S'reee spoke again, her voice was unhappy. "Areinnye, I share your grief. It's things like this that the Song will help to stop. That's why we're here."

The sperm whale laughed, a sound both anguished and cruel. "What lies," she said. "Or what delusions. Do you truly think *anything* will make them go away and stop hunting us, S'reee?" Areinnye looked with hatred at Nita. "Now they're even coming into the water after us, I see."

Kit glided forward ever so slowly, until he was squarely between Nita and Areinnye. "I guarantee you don't know what she's here for, Areinnye. Preserving your life, along with those of a lot of others—though at the moment, in *your* case, I can't imagine why anyone would bother."

Areinnye made a sound at Kit that was the sperm-whale equivalent of a sneer. "Oh, indeed," Areinnye said. "What could she possibly do that would make any difference to my life?"

"She is the Silent Lord for the Song," S'reee said.

Areinnye turned that scornful regard on Nita. "Indeed," the sperm said again. "Well. We are finally getting something useful out of a human. But she doubtless had to be compelled to it. No human would ever give up its life for one of us, wizard or not. Or did you trick her into it?"

Gently, hardly stroking a fin, Ed soared toward Areinnye. "Unwise," he said. "Most unwise, wizard, to scorn a fellow wizard so—whatever species she may belong to. And will you hold Nita responsible for all her species' wrongdoings, then? If you do that, Areinnye, I would feel no qualms about holding you responsible for various hurts done my people by yours over the years. Nor would I feel any guilt over taking payment for those hurts out of your hide, *now*."

Areinnye turned her back on Ed and swam away, as if not caring what he said. "You take strange sides, Slayer," the sperm said at last, cold-voiced. "The humans hunt those of your Mastery as relentlessly as they hunt us."

"I take no sides, Areinnye," Ed said, still following her. "Not with whales, or fish, or humans, or any other Power in the Sea or above it. Wizard that you are, you should know that." He was beginning to circle her now. "And if I sing this Song, it is for the same reason that I have sung a hundred others: for the sake of my Mastery—and because I am pleased to sing. You had best put your distress aside and deal with the business we have come to discuss, lest something worse befall you."

Areinnye turned slowly back toward the group. "Well, if you've come to administer me the Oath," Areinnye said to S'reee, "you might as well get on with it. I was in the midst of hunting when you interrupted me."

"Softly," S'reee said. "Your power is a byword all throughout these parts; I want it in the Song. But we're not so short of wizards that I'll include one who'll bring the High and Dry down on us. Choose, and tell me whether you can truthfully sing and leave your anger behind."

Areinnye cruised slowly through the group, making no sound but the small ticking noises the sperm uses to navigate. "Seeing that the human who sings with us sings for the Sea's sake," she said at last, in that tight, flat voice, "I am content. But my heart is bitter in me for my calf's loss, and I cannot forget that easily. Let the humans remember that, and keep their distance."

"If that is well for you two—" Kit and Nita both flicked tails in agreement. "Well enough, then," said S'reee. "Areinnye t'Hwio-dheii, those who gather to sing that Song that is the Sea's shame and the Sea's glory desire you to be of their company. Say, for my hearing, whether you consent to that Song."

"I consent . . ." Areinnye sang her way through the responses with slow care, and Nita began to relax slightly. The sperm's voice was beautiful, as pleasant as Kit's, when she wasn't angry. Yet she couldn't help but catch a couple of Areinnye's glances at Ed—as if she knew that she was being watched for her responses and would be watched in the future.

Then the third Question was asked, and Areinnye's song scaled up in the high notes of final affirmation, a sound of tearing, chilly beauty. "Let me wander forever amid the broken and the lost, sooner than I shall refuse the Song," Areinnye sang, "or what it brings about for the good of those who live." But there was a faint note of scorn in the last phrase, as if the singer already counted herself among the lost and broken; and the notes on "those who live" twisted down the scale into a bitter diminuendo of pain that said life was a curse.

Now it was S'reee's turn to look dubious; but it was too late.

"Well," the sperm said, "when is the Foregathering? And where?"

"Tomorrow dawn," said S'reee, "in the waters off the Hook. Will you be on time?"

"Yes," Areinnye said. "So farewell." And she turned tail and swam off.

Kit flicked a glance at Ed and said quietly to Nita, "Boy, *that* was a close one. If those two got started fighting . . ."

"It would not be anything like 'close,' " Ed said.

"Okay, great," Kit said in mild annoyance, "she couldn't kill you. But isn't it just possible she might hurt you a little?"

"She would regret it if she did," Ed said. "Blood in the water will call in some sharks, true. But their *Master's* blood in the water will call them all in, whether they smell it or not . . . every shark for thousands of lengths around. That is *my* magic, you see. And whatever the Master Shark might be fighting when his people arrived would shortly not be there at all, except as rags and scraps for fingerlings to eat."

Nita and Kit and S'reee looked at each other.

"Why do we need Areinnye in the first place?" Nita said to S'reee. "Is she really that good a wizard?"

Turning, S'reee began to swim back the way they had come, through the now-darkening water. Hotshot paced her; and silently, pale in the dimness, Ed brought up the rear. "Yes," S'reee said. "In fact, by rights, she should have been Ae'mhnuu's apprentice, not I."

Kit looked at her in surprise. "Why wasn't she?"

S'reee made a little moan of annoyance. "I don't know," she said. "Areinnye is a much more powerful wizard than I am—even Ae'mhnuu agreed with me about that. Yet he refused her request to study with him, not just once but several times. And now this business with her calf—" S'reee blew a few huge bubbles out her blowhole, making an unsettled noise. "Well, we'll make it work out."

"That shall yet be seen," Ed said from behind them.

The moon was high when Nita and Kit came out of the water close to the jetty and went looking for their clothes. Kit spent a while gazing longingly up at the silver-golden disc, while Nita dressed. "We're really gonna get killed now, aren't we?" he said, so quietly that Nita could hardly hear him.

"Uh-huh." Nita sat down on the sand and stared out at the waves while Kit went hunting for his bathing suit and windbreaker.

"Whaddaya think they'll do?" Kit said.

Nita shook her head. "No idea."

Kit came up beside her, adjusting his windbreaker. "You think they're gonna send me home?"

"They might," she said.

They toiled up the last dune before home and looked down toward the little rough road that ran past the house. All the upstairs lights were on. The downstairs ones were dark; evidently Dairine had been sent to bed.

"Neets—" Kit said. "What're *you* gonna do?"

"I'm sworn, Kit. I'm in the Song. I have to be there."

"You mean you're going to—"

"Don't," she said, in genuine pain. She didn't want him to say it, to think it, any more than she wanted to think it herself. And to tell the absolute truth, she wasn't sure of what she was going to do about the Song yet.

"They don't need me for the Song," Kit said.

"It doesn't look that way."

"Yeah." He was quiet a moment. "Look—if somehow I can get you off the hook, get your folks to think this is all my fault somehow, so that you can still go out . . ."

"No," Nita said, scandalized. "Anyway, they'd never buy it. I promised my mom I'd be back on time last time—and blew it. Then I snuck out today. They know it's me as much as you. I'm just gonna have to face the music."

"With what?" Kit said.

"I don't know." The thought of treating her parents as enemies made her feel as if the bottom had fallen out of the universe.

The one good thing, she thought, *is that by tomorrow, tonight will be over. I hope.*

"C'mon," she said. Together they went home.

The house was deadly still when they stepped in, and the screen door closing behind them seemed loud enough to be heard for miles around. The kitchen was dark; light flowed into it from the living room, the subdued illumination of a couple of table lamps. There was no sound of TV, even though Nita knew her dad's passion for late movies; no music, despite her mom's fondness for classics and symphonic rock at any hour of day or night.

Nita's mouth felt dry as beach sand. She stopped where she was, tried to swallow, looked at Kit. He looked back, punched her lightly in the arm, then pushed past her and walked into the living room.

Nita felt that for the rest of her life—however many hours that might last— she would not be able to get rid of the image and feeling of that room when she walked in. The living room needed a new paint job, its rug was threadbare in places, and the walls were hung with bargain-basement seascapes, wide-eyed children of almost terminal cuteness, and, in one corner, something her dad called the Piece of Resistance—a garish matador done in day-glow paint on black velvet.

Her mother and father were sitting side by side on the Coca-Cola-colored couch, their backs straight. They looked up as Nita and Kit came through the door, and Nita saw her mother's face tight with fear and her father's closed like a door. They had been reading magazines; they put them aside, and the usually friendly room suddenly looked dingy as a prison, and the matador hurt Nita's eyes.

"Sit down," her father said. His voice—quiet, calm—sounded too much like Ed's. She managed to hold on to her composure as she headed for Dairine's favorite chair and sat down quickly.

"Pretty slick," said her father. "My daughter appears to have a great future in breaking and entering. Or breaking and departing."

Nita opened her mouth and shut it again. She could have dealt with a good scolding . . . but this chilly sarcasm terrified her. And there was no way out of it.

"Well?" her father said. "You'd better start coming up with some answers, young lady. You, too," he said to Kit, his eyes flashing; and at the sight of the anger, Nita felt a wash of relief. That look was normal. "Because what you two say is going to determine whether we send you straight home tomorrow morning, Kit—and whether we let you and Nita see any more of each other."

Kit looked her father straight in the eye and said nothing.

Sperm whales! Nita thought, and it was nearly a curse. But then she took the thought back as she realized that Kit was waiting for her to say something first, to give him a lead. *Great! Now all I have to do is do something!*

What do I do?

"Kit," her father said, "I warn you, I'm in no mood for Latin gallantry and the whole protect-the-lady business. You were entrusted to my care and I want answers. Your parents are going to hear about this in any case—what you say, or don't say, is going to determine what I tell them. So be advised."

"I understand," Kit said. Then he glanced at Nita. "Neets?"

Nita shook her head ever so slightly, amazed as always by that frightened bravery that would wait for her to make a move, then back her utterly. It had nothing to do with the whalesark. *Kit*, Nita thought, practically trembling with the force of what she felt, *you're incredible! But I don't have your guts—and I have to do something!*

Her mother and father were looking at her, waiting.

Oh, Lord, Nita thought then, and bowed her head and put one hand over her face, for she suddenly knew what to do.

She looked up. "Mom," she said—and then had to start over, for the word came out in a kind of strangled squeak. "Mom, you remember when we were talking the other day? And you said you wanted to know why we were staying out so much, because you thought something besides 'nothing' was going on?"

Her mother nodded, frozen-faced.

"Uh, well, there was," Nita said, not sure where to go from there. Two months of wizardry, spells wrought, and strange places visited and wonders seen—how to explain it all to nonwizards? Especially when they might not be able to see wizardry done right under their eyes—and in the past hadn't? *Never mind that*, Nita told herself desperately. *If you think too much, you'll get cold feet. Just talk.*

Her mother was wearing a ready-to-hear-the-worst expression. "No, not *that*," Nita said, feeling downright cross that her mother was still thinking along *those* idiotic lines. "But this is going to take awhile."

Nita swallowed hard. "You remember in the spring," she said, "that day Kit and I went into the city—and that night, the sun went out?"

Her parents stared at her, still angry, and now slightly perplexed, too.

"We had something to do with that," Nita said.

Truthsong

AND NITA BEGAN TO tell them. By the time she saw from their faces just how crazy the story must be sounding, it was already much too late for her to stop.

She told them the story from the beginning—the day she had her hand snagged by an innocent-looking library book full of instructions for wizardry—to the end of her first great trial, and Kit's, that terrible night when the forces of darkness got loose in Manhattan and would have turned first the city and then the world into a place bound in eternal night and cold, except for what she and Kit did. She told them about Advisory and Senior Wizards, though she didn't mention Tom and Carl; about places past the world where there was nothing but night, and about the place past life where there was nothing but day.

Not once did her parents say a word.

Mostly Kit kept quiet, except when Nita's memory about something specific failed; then he spoke up and filled in the gap, and she went on again. The look on her father's face was approaching anger again, and her mother was well into complete consternation, by the time Nita started telling them about the dolphin who nudged her in the back, the whale she and Kit found on the beach, and the story the whale had told them. She told them a little—very little, fearing for her own composure—about the Song of the Twelve and what she was going to be doing in it.

And then, not knowing what else to say, she stopped.

Her mother and father looked at each other.

Our daughter, the look said, *is going to have to be hospitalized. She's sick.*

Nita's mother finally turned to her. Her dad had bowed his head about a third of the way through the story, and except for that glance at her mother seemed unable to do anything but sit with his hands clasped tightly together. But her mother's face was stricken.

"Nita," she said, very gently—but her voice was shaking like the tightly clasped hands of the man beside her, "you don't have to make up stories like this to keep us from being angry with you."

Nita's mouth fell open. "Mom," she said, "are you trying to say you don't believe me?"

"Nita," her father said. His eyes were haunted, and his attempt to keep his voice sounding normal was failing miserably. "Give us a break. How are we supposed to believe a crazy story like this? Maybe you've got Kit believing it—" He broke off, as if wanting to find a way to explain all this, something reasonable. "I guess it's understandable, he's younger than you . . ."

Nita glanced over at Kit for the first time in a while and gulped. His annoyed look brought the sperm-whale battle cry scraping through her memories again.

"*I'll* tell you how you're supposed to believe it," Kit said.

Nita's mother and father looked at him.

Kit was suddenly sitting a little taller in the chair. And taller still, though he didn't move a muscle. And taller—until Nita could see that Kit's seat and the seat of the chair no longer had much to do with each other. He was hovering about two feet in the air.

"Like *this*," Kit said.

Holding her breath, Nita looked from Kit to her parents.

They stared at Kit, their faces absolutely unmoved, as if waiting for something. Kit glanced over at Nita, shrugged, and kept floating up until he was sitting six feet or so above the floor. "Well?" he said.

They didn't move a muscle.

"Harry—" Nita's mother said, then, after what seemed forever.

He didn't say a thing.

"Harry," her mother said, "I hate to admit it, but I think all this has gotten to me . . ."

Nita's father simply kept looking at the chair.

Then, ever so slowly, he leaned his head back and looked up at Kit.

"Hypnosis," Nita's father said.

"Bull!" Kit said. "When did I hypnotize you?"

Nita's father didn't say anything.

"I haven't said a thing," Kit said. "If I hypnotized you without lights or words or anything, that's a pretty good trick, isn't it? You two better talk to each other and see if you're seeing the same thing. If you aren't, maybe I *did* hypnotize you. But if you *are*—"

Nita's mother and father looked away from Kit with some effort. "Betty . . . ," said Nita's father.

Neither of them said anything further for a few seconds.

"Harry," her mother said at last, "if I told you that I saw . . . saw Kit . . ." She stopped and swallowed. Then she started again, and the same feeling that had shaken Nita earlier about Kit took hold of her and shook her about her mother. Evidently bravery came in odd forms, and out of unexpected places. "If I told you that I saw Kit not sitting in the chair anymore," her mother said, all at once and in a rush. Then her voice gave out on her.

"Above it," her dad said. And that was all he could manage.

They stared at each other.

"You got it," Kit said.

Nita's dad broke away from looking at her mother and glared at Nita instead. "Hypnosis," her father said. "There's no other explanation."

"Yes, there *is!*" Nita hollered at him, waving her arms in frustration, "but you don't want to admit it!"

"Nita," her mother said.

"Sorry," Nita said. "Look, Kit . . . this isn't going to do it. We need something more impressive." She got up. "Come on," she said. "Outside. It's my turn."

Nita yanked the front door open and ran outside, up the dune and down its far side toward the beach. There was a long pause before she heard the sound of footsteps following her down the wooden stairs. *Shock*, she thought, feeling both pity and amusement. *If only there was some easier way!* But there wasn't . . . She made it down to the beach, picked the spot she wanted, then stood and waited for them to arrive.

First her mother, then her father, came clambering up the dune and slid down its far side, to stand on the beach and stare up and down it, looking for her. Then Kit appeared beside them in a small clap of air that startled her mother so badly she jumped. Her father stared.

"Sorry," Kit said, "I should have warned you." He was still sitting cross-legged in the air, and Nita noticed that he didn't sound very sorry, either.

"Oh, Lord," said Nita's father at the sight of Kit, and then turned resolutely away. "All right. Where's Nita?"

"Over here, Daddy," Nita called from where she was standing on the water, just past the line of the breakers.

He stared at Nita. So did Nita's mother, who slowly went to stand beside her husband. Her voice was shaking as she said, "Harry, it could be that my eyes are just going . . ."

"Mom," Nita shouted, "give me a break; you both went to the eye doctor last month and you were fine!" She bounced up and down on the water several times, then took a few long strides to the west, turned, and came back. "Admit it! You see me walking on water! Well, surprise: I *am* walking on water! Get it! It's like I told you: I'm a wizard!"

"Nita," her father said, "uh, walking on water is, uh—"

"I know," she said. "I wouldn't want to overdo it. It makes my legs hurt." Nita trotted back in to shore, taking a last hop onto the curl of a flattening breaker and letting it push her up onto the beach and strand her there, a few feet in front of them.

Kit uncrossed his legs, got his feet back on the ground, and came to stand beside her. "So what else would you like to see?" he said.

Her parents looked at each other, then down at the two of them. "Look, Kit, Nita," her father said unhappily, "it's not a question of what we'd like to see. At this point I'm sure you two could get us to 'see' anything you wanted to . . . heaven knows how. But that's not the point. This can't be—none of this is *real!*"

"Wanna bet?" Kit said softly. "Neets, this is gonna call for drastic measures."

"I think you're right. Well, let's see what the manual says about this. Book, please," she said, thinking the six words of a spell she knew by heart and putting her hand out. Another small clap of air, about as noisy as a cap going off, and her wizards' manual dropped into her hand. Her mother goggled. Nita opened the manual and began browsing through it. "Let's see . . ."

"You two just stop making things pop in and out for a moment, and listen to me," Nita's mother said all of a sudden. "Nita, I want to know where this power came from! You two haven't made a pact with, with—"

Nita thought of her last encounter with the Lone Power and burst out laughing. "Oh, Mom! Kit and I are the *last* people *that* One wants anything to do with."

Her mother looked nonplussed. "Well, that's—never mind, you'll tell me about that some other time. But, honey, why, why?"

"You mean, 'Why are there wizards?' Or, 'Why are *we* wizards?' " Nita said. "Or do you really mean, 'What's in it for us?' "

"Yes," her mother said, sounding lost.

Nita and Kit looked at each other, and Kit shook his head. "We're never gonna be able to explain this," he said.

She agreed with him. "Only one thing we can do, I guess," Nita said, musing. "Show them?"

Nita looked at Kit, and for the first time in what seemed days, a smile began to grow. "Remember that place we went a week and a half ago?" she said. "The one with the great view?"

"I'll get my book," he said, grinning back, "and the string."

"Don't forget the chip!" Nita said, but Kit had already gone out, *bang!* just like a candle, and Nita was talking to empty air. She turned to her mother and father. "He went to get some supplies," she said. "Most wizardry you need things for—raw materials, kind of."

"Fine, honey," her mother said, "but does he have to keep appearing and disappearing like that?"

"It's faster than walking," Nita said. "And we haven't got all night. He and I are going to have to be out early again tomorrow morning—"

"Nita!" said her father.

She went to him and put her arms around him. "Please, Dad," she said, "let it be for a little while. We told you why. But you have to feel this first. It won't make sense unless you do. In fact, it may never make sense. Just trust me!"

Kit popped back out of nothing, making Nita's mother jump again. "Sorry, Mrs. Callahan," he said. "It's fun, that's all. It's a 'beam-me-up-Scotty' spell. So's this one we're going to do. Just a little more involved." He dropped the necessary supplies on the sand—a small coil of cord, an old silicon chip salvaged from a broken pocket calculator, a gray stone. Then he started going through his own manual.

Nita looked down at the stone Kit had brought. "Good idea," she said. "Shorthand, huh?"

"It remembers the way. Should save some work. Good thing, too . . . we've got two more sets of variables this time. Get the figures for me, will you?"

"Right." Nita held out her book a bit as she went through it, so that her mother and father could look over her shoulder. "See, Mom? Dad? It's just an instruction manual, like I said."

"I can't read it," her father said, staring at the graceful strokes of the written form of the Speech. "What is it, Arabic?"

"No," she said. "No earthly language. At least, not strictly earthly. A lot of the forces we work with don't have names in any language on Earth—or they only have vague ones. You can't be vague about magic."

"Good way to get killed," Kit said from where he knelt in the sand, scribbling with a stick and sounding cheerful. "Mr. Callahan, Mrs. Callahan, don't step on any of these things I'm writing in the sand, or we'll all be in big trouble. Mrs. Callahan, what's your birthday?"

"April twenty-eighth," said Nita's mother.

"Mr. Callahan?"

"July seventh," said Nita's father.

"Neets, how big a circle?"

"Ha'   second," Nita said. "Brighter," she said to her manual. Its pages began to glow softly in the dark. "Okay, here we are. Four of us . . . about a cubic foot of air for each breath. Allow for excitement—say thirty breaths a minute. Times four . . ." She turned to another page. "Start," she said, and heard over her shoulder her mother's quick intake of breath as the page Nita had opened to abruptly went blank. "Print one-two-zero times four." A set of characters appeared. "Okay, print four-eight-zero times twenty . . . Good. Print nine-six-zero-zero divided by three . . . Great. Cubic meters . . . uhh . . . Oh, crap. Kit, what's the volume of a cylinder again?"

"*V* equals *pi* times *r* squared times the height."

"That's it. Now how did I do this before?" Nita chewed her lip a little, thinking. "Okay," she said to the book, "print three point one-four-one-seven times, uh, three-zero." A figure flickered at her. "No, that is not a number," she said to the book. "Times three-zero, and don't get cute with me . . . Okay. Print square root parenthesis three-two-zero-zero divided by nine-four point two-five-one close parentheses. Great. End. Kit? Make it thirty-six feet wide."

"Got it," Kit said. "Mrs. Callahan, would you stand on this string, please? And whatever happens, don't go near the edge of the circle after I close it." He started to walk around them all, using Mrs. Callahan and the long knotted string as a compass. "Neets? Come check your name. And theirs; they can't do it—"

She stepped over to the circle and made sure that the Speech characters describing herself and her parents were correct, then glanced over Kit's, too, for safety's sake. Everything was in order. Kit finished the circle he was making in the sand, closed it with the figure-eight design called a wizard's knot, and stood up. "All set," Nita said.

"Then let's go." He opened his book; Nita went looking for the page in hers on which the spell was written. "It's a 'read' spell," Nita said to her mother and father. "That means it's going to be a few moments before it takes. Don't say anything, no matter what you feel or see or hear. Don't move, either."

"You might want to hang on to each other," Kit said. Nita gave him a wry grin; there had been occasions in the past when the two of them, terrified out of their wits, had done just that. "Ready?"

"Go ahead," said Nita's father, and reached out and pulled Nita's mother close.

Nita and Kit looked at each other and began slowly to read out loud. The strange, listening stillness of a working spell began to settle in around the four of them, becoming more pronounced with every word of the Speech, as the universe in that area waited to hear what would be required of it. The wind dropped, the sound of the surf grew softer, even the breakers in the area became gentler, flatter, their hiss fading to a bare whisper. . . .

The sense of expectation, of anticipation, of impatient, overwhelming *potential* grew all around them as the silence grew . . . slowly undergoing a transformation into a blend of delight and terror and power that could be breathed like air, or seen as a shading now inhabiting every color, a presence inhabiting every shape.

Nita raised her voice into the stillness unafraid, speaking the words of the spell formula, barely needing to look at her book. The magic was rising in her, pouring through her with dangerous power. But with the sureness of practice she rode the danger, knowing the wonder to which it would bring her, reveling in her defiance of her fear. And in more than that: for Kit was across the circle from her, eyes on hers, matching her word for word and power for power—peer and friend and fellow-wizard, afraid as she was, and still willing to dare, for the delight of what lay on the other side of the magic—

Almost through, Nita thought, exulting. Her words and Kit's wound about one another, wove together, binding the spell tighter around the circle—squeezing air in, squeezing power in, pushing inward with such force that the circle and its contents had no choice but to be somewhere else than they were.

Almost—Nita matched her words to Kit's with a laugh in her voice, rushing him, finding that she *couldn't* rush him because he had already matched pace to keep up with her—She laughed at being anticipated so. Faster and faster they went, like two kids seeing who could say the Pledge of Allegiance faster, as all around them the silence began to sing with in-turned power; the air shimmered and rang with force like a gong ringing backward, soft at first, then louder, though without sound, without breaking that silence—a hiss, a murmur, an outcry of something about to happen, a shout of inner voices, a silent thunderclap. And the last not-sound, so loud it unmade the world around them and struck them deaf and blind—

Then true silence again, with darkness above and whiteness below—but not the same darkness or whiteness as on the beach.

"We're here," Nita whispered. "Mom, Dad, have a look around. Don't go near the edges of the circle."

"Be careful how you move," Kit said. "You only weigh a sixth of what you usually do. If your muscles overreact you could bounce right out of the circle. I almost did, first time."

Nita watched her mother and father stare around them. She swallowed—partly out of reflex, for her ears were ringing in the silence that surrounded them now. That was to be expected; this stillness was more total than anything experienced on Earth. Her other reason for swallowing was more practical. The sudden transfer to one-sixth gravity tended to upset your stomach unless you were used to it.

Her father was staring at the ground, which had changed from wet beach sand to a mixture of grayish gravel and pebbles, and rocks the size of fists or melons, all covered with a gray-white dust as fine as talc. But Nita's mother was staring up at the sky with a look of joy so great it was pain—the completely bearable anguish of an impossible dream that suddenly comes true after years of hopeless yearning. Tears were running down her mother's face at the sight of that sky, so pure a velvet black that the eye insisted on finding light in it where light was not—a night sky set with thousands of stars, all blazing with a cold, fierce brilliance that only astronauts ever saw; a night sky that nonetheless had a ravening sun standing noonday high in it, pooling all their shadows black and razor-sharp about their feet.

Nita was blinking hard herself to manage the stinging of her eyes; she knew how her mother felt. "Over there, Mom," she said very quietly. "Off to the left. Look."

"Off to the left" was a steep slope that plunged down and down to a deep chasm, filled with absolute blackness ungentled by the presence of air. On the far side of the chasm stretched a flat, rocky plain that seemed to stop too soon, running up against a horizon abnormally close. Out on the plain, not too far away, a dazzling squarish glow of gold sat on four spidery legs. Some thirty yards from the bright platform on legs stood a silvery pole with an American flag standing out from it, held straight by a rod running through the top of it: a necessity—for here where it stood, no wind would ever stir it.

"No," Nita's father said, his voice hushed. "Impossible. Tranquillity Base—"

"No," Kit said, his voice soft, too. "That's going to be a tourist attraction in a few years, when they build the Hilton there—so we don't go down there for fear of leaving footprints where somebody might find them. This is from *Apollo 16*. See over there?" He pointed past the abandoned first-stage platform of the LEM *Orion* at the first Lunar Rover, which sat parked neatly beside a boulder—a delicate-looking little dune buggy, still in excellent condition, used only once by a couple of astronauts from Pasadena for jaunts to Stone Mountain, on which the four of them stood.

Nita's father slowly went down on one knee and brushed his hand along the dry, pale lunar soil, turning over the stones that lay there, then picking one up and clutching it hard in his fist.

"Harry," Nita's mother said, still looking up. The tone of her voice made her husband look up, too—and seeing what she saw, he forgot the rock.

What they saw was part of a disk four times the size of the Moon as seen from Earth; and it seemed even bigger because of the Moon's foreshortened horizon. It was not the full Earth so familiar from pictures, but a waning crescent, streaked with cloud swirls and burning with a fierce green-blue radiance—a light with depth, like the fire held in the heart of an opal. That light banished the idea that blue and green were "cool" colors; one could have warmed one's hands at that crescent. The blackness to which it shaded was ever so faintly touched with silver—a disk more hinted at than seen; the new Earth in the old Earth's arms.

"There'll be a time," Nita said softly, "when anytime someone's elected to a public office—before they let them start work—they'll bring whoever was elected up here and just make them look at that until they get what it means . . ."

Kit nodded. "You wanted to know where the power came from," he said to Nita's mother and father. "The grown-ups who're wizards tell us that whatever made *that* made the power, too. It's all of a piece."

" 'The *grown-ups* who're wizards'?"

"And as for 'why,' " Kit said, "*that's* why." There was no need for him to point to "that." "Not just for the—for what you felt on the way in. That's part of it. But because somebody's gotta take care of *that*. Not just part of it—not just one country, or one set of rules, or one species, at the expense of the others. But everything that lives, all the kinds of 'people.' *All* of it, with nothing left out. One whole planet. Somebody's got to make sure it grows as well as it can. Or just that it survives. That's what wizards do."

"Daddy," Nita said, "it's like you always say. If you don't do it yourself, it may not get done right. And we can't afford to let *that* get screwed up. We have to live there. So will other people, later."

Her father shook his head, confused. "Nita," he said, sounding unsure, "you're too young to be thinking about this kind of thing."

She bit her lip. "Dad—that sort of thinking might be one of the reasons why things aren't working so well back there . . ."

"Neets," Kit said, "we have to get back. We're losing heat pretty fast."

"Mom, Dad," Nita said, "we can come back some other time. It's late, and Kit and I have an early day tomorrow. Got the rock?" she said to Kit.

"Uh-huh. Ready?"

Nita's mother reached out and pulled her husband close this time. "Is it going to be like it was before?"

"Huh? No. It just takes a lot of effort to push all this air up out of Earth's gravity well, that's all. You have to reach escape velocity—"

Nita's father blinked. "Wait a minute. I thought this was—magic." He said the word as if for the first time in his life.

Nita shrugged. "Even with magic," she said, "you have to obey the rules. Downhill is a lot easier than uphill in a wizardry, same as anywhere else. Kit?"

"Ready," he said. They looked at each other, took a breath, and said one short word in unison.

WHAM!—and air and sand and water blew outward in all directions as they left noon for midnight, standing once again on the long dark beach silvered with moonlight. Kit stepped to the edge of the circle, first scuffing the wizard's knot out of existence, then going around and breaking the circle once at each compass point. "Let's go in," Nita said to her parents. "I'm dead."

The four of them trudged up the stairs to the front door, back into the living room. Her dad plopped down onto the couch and said, "Nita, wait just a few minutes. I have to ask you something."

Nita looked at him, sighed, and did as she was told. "Tell me again," her dad said, "this stuff about what you're doing underwater. Just very briefly."

It turned out to be more than briefly, since much of what Nita had told her parents had fallen out of their heads the first time, discarded in general disbelief. And it was with growing dismay that Nita watched the unease in her parents' faces, as she told them again about the undersea tremors, the pollution of the water, the slaughter of the whales—and the purposes of the Lone Power, though she tried to tell them as little about that as she could.

"Nita," her father said at last, "what are the chances that you could get hurt doing this 'Song' business? The truth."

She looked at him unhappily. "Pretty good," she said.

"And the same for Kit?" her mother said.

"Just about," Kit said.

Nita's father shook his head. "Nita. Look. I understand . . . no. I sort of understand how you and Kit feel about this. Magic . . ." He raised his hands, dropped them again, in a helpless gesture. "If someone offered me the chance to be a magician, I'd jump at it . . ."

"A wizard," Nita said. And, *No, you wouldn't*, she thought. *Because if you would have, really, you would have been offered it! There are never enough wizards . . .*

But her father was still talking. "But this business . . . endangering yourself, or endangering Kit— Your mother and I can't permit it. You're going to have to bow out."

For a moment, as far as Nita was concerned, everything faded out, drowned in a great wash of relief and hope. The perfect excuse. Perfect. *My mom and dad won't let me. Sorry, S'reee, Hotshot, Ed . . .*

Opaque black eyes looked at Nita out of the scene her eager mind was already constructing for her—and hope died. The hair stood up all over Nita—not from fear, but from something more terrible. Without any warning, and for the first time, she understood in her own person what had only been a word to her before: honor. *I can't*, she thought. *For me—for* me—*it's not right.*

"Dad," she said unhappily, "you didn't get it. I'm sworn to the Song. If I back out now, the whole thing will be sabotaged."

Her father got up, a sign that he intended this argument to be over shortly. "Come on, Neets. Surely someone else could do it—"

"No."

"Nita," said her mother, looking stern, "you don't understand. *We're not letting you do this.* Or Kit, either, while he's under our roof. You're going to have to find a replacement. Or the—the whales will. Whoever. *You're not going.*"

I must not have said it right, they're not understanding! "Mom—," Nita said, searching frantically for words. "This isn't just some cute thing that Kit and I are doing because it'll be fun! If we don't stop the forces that are beginning to move, there are going to be massive earthquakes all up and down the East Coast. That's not a maybe. It's a *will!* You think the island would survive something like that? The whole place is nothing but rocks and trash the glaciers dumped in the ocean; it'll break up and wash away like a sand castle at high tide! And you think Manhattan'll survive? It's already got four unstable geological faults of its own, right through the bedrock! And none of the buildings there are earthquake-proof; one quake'll leave the place looking like somebody kicked over a pile of blocks!" Nita was waving her arms in the air now, so upset that she was beyond caring whether she looked silly or not. "Millions of people could die—"

"Could," her father said, seizing on the word. He was pacing now.

Kit shook his head. *"Will,"* he said, and there was such a weight of certainty and misery on the word that Nita's father stopped pacing and her mother closed her mouth, and they both stared at Kit in amazement. "You're saying," Kit said, gazing at them out of eyes suddenly gone dark and fierce, "that you don't care whether ten million people, *more* than ten million people, would die, just so long as we two don't get hurt."

Nita's mother spluttered, to Nita's great satisfaction. That one had sunk in. "No, we aren't, we just—"

"You don't even care that ten million people *might* die," Nita said. "Just so Kit and I are OK, you're willing to run that risk."

"No, I—" Nita's father saw what was being done to him. "Young lady, no more out of you! Just the quakes going on off the coast now, by the reports we've heard, are too dangerous for you to be down there."

"Daddy, believe me, we've survived a lot worse!"

"Yes—and your mother and I didn't know about it then! Now we do." Her father turned away. "The answer is no, and that's final!"

From many fights Nita had overheard between her folks, Nita knew that when her dad said that, it never was. "Daddy," she said. "I'm sorry. I really am. I love you, and I wish like anything I could do what you want. But I *can't.*"

"Nita!" There was that rage again, full-blown, worse than before. Her father was on his feet, standing right over her, glaring at her. *"You will do as I tell you!"*

Hot all over, Nita shot to her feet—standing on the chair—and in sheer desperation shouted right back in his face. *"Don't you get it? There are some things in the world more important than doing what you tell me!"*

Her father and mother stared at her, stunned.

"Besides," Kit said quietly from out of her range of vision, "how would you stop us?"

Nita's father turned away to stare at Kit now.

"Look," Kit said. "Mr. Callahan, Mrs. Callahan—we gave our word that we'd do this." *What is this "we"?* Nita thought, bemused. "And the wizardry we're doing is mainly directed against the One who invented the broken promise. Breaking our word will play right into Its hands and cause a lot of people to die, at best. Maybe destroy this world, sooner or later, at worst."

"But we have only your word on that!" Nita's mother said.

"Uh-huh. But isn't our word any good? And why would we lie to you about *this?* Considering that we're going through all this crap for the sake of telling you the truth."

Nita's mother closed her mouth.

"She didn't have to tell you," Kit said, sounding angry for the first time. "But it would've been lying, in a way—and Nita thinks you're worth not lying to." He paused, then said, "I do, too. We may just be kids, but we're old enough to tell the truth. And to take it. Are you?"

The question wasn't a taunt: It was honestly meant. "Even if you're not, we'll still have to do what we have to," Nita said, though saying it made her unhappy. "When you two wake up in the morning, this could all seem like a dream to you—if it had to. I guess you'd better make up your minds, because we have to get some sleep or we won't be worth dead fish tomorrow."

Her parents were staring at each other. "Betty . . . ," said Nita's father.

"We need more time," Nita's mother said.

"I don't think we've got it."

Her mother looked back at her father. "If they're right about this," she said, "it would be wrong of us to stop them if they want to help."

"But we're responsible for them!"

"Apparently," Nita's mother said, in a peculiar mixture of pride and pain, "they've learned that lesson better than we suspected, Harry. Because now they seem to be making themselves responsible for *us*. And a lot of other people."

"I guess there comes a time when you can't do anything but trust," her father said at last, sounding reluctant. "It just seems—so soon . . . Nita—is all this on the level?"

"Oh, Daddy." She loved him, right then, and hurt for him, more than she could have told him. "I wish it weren't. But it is."

Nita's father was silent for several long breaths. "Millions of lives," he said under his breath.

And another silence, which he finally broke as if it were a physical thing. "When do you need to be up?"

"Sixish. I'll set my alarm, Daddy." Nita got stiffly down from the chair, aching all over. Behind her, Kit got up and brushed past her as Nita hugged first her dad good night. Maybe the last time she would ever hug him . . . or the second to last— *Oh, don't think of that now!*

Her mother had caught Kit on the way past and hugged him—and now wouldn't let Nita past without one, either. She held her for a moment at arm's length. "Thank you for—up there, baby," she said, nodding once at the ceiling. Her eyes were wet, but she was smiling.

"It's OK, Mom. Anytime." *Is this what it feels like when your heart breaks? Oh, Lord, don't let me cry.*

"And thank you for trusting us."

Nita swallowed. "You taught me how," she said. And then she couldn't stand it anymore. She broke away and headed for her room, Kit right behind her.

She knew there was one hurdle left between her and bed. Actually, the hurdle was *on* the bed: sitting there cross-legged in the dark, looking at her with cool interest as they came in.

"Well?" Dairine said, as Nita flopped down on her stomach beside her, and the bed bounced them both once or twice. "I saw you disappear. Where'd'ja take them?"

"The Moon."

"Oh, come *on*, Neets."

"Dairine," Kit said from the doorway. "Catch."

Nita glanced up, saw her sister reach up and pick something out of the air: an irregular piece of pale, grainy stone, about the size and shape of an eraser. Dairine peered at it, rubbing it between her fingers. "What is this? Pumice?" There was a moment of shocked silence; then Dairine's voice scaled up to an aggrieved shriek. "You *did* go to the Moon! And you didn't take *me!* You, you—" Apparently she couldn't find anything sufficiently dirty to call them. *"I'm gonna kill you!"*

"Dari, shut up, they're in shock out there!" Nita said. This argument did little to save her. Far more effective was Kit's wrestling Dairine down flat, stuffing her under the bedcovers and a couple of pillows, and more or less sitting on her until she shut up and stopped struggling.

"We'll take you next time," Nita said, and then the pain hit her again. "Kit," she said, husky-voiced. "Remind me to see that the runt here gets to the Moon in the near future. Next week, maybe. If she behaves."

"Right," Kit said. "You give up, runt?"

"Hwhmffm hnnoo rrhhrhn ffwmhhnhhuh," said the blankets.

"Keep talking like that and your mouth'll get stuck that way," Kit said, and let Dairine out.

Nita's sister extricated herself from the covers with icy dignity that lasted just until she was sitting where she had been, back in control and smoothing her ruffled pajamas. "Mom 'n' Dad didn't kill you," she said to Nita.

"Nope. You gave me good advice, runt."

"Huh? What advice?"

"Last night, I suspect," Kit said. "That stuff about 'Either keep your mouth shut, or tell the truth—' "

Nita nodded, looking from Kit to Dairine, while Dairine modestly polished her nails on her Yoda pajamas. And Nita stared at her, and then started to laugh, so hard that she got the hiccups and fell over sideways—and Dairine looked at her as if she'd gone nuts, and Kit sat down and punched her once or twice, worriedly, in the shoulder. "Neets? You OK?"

"Oh, Kit," she managed to gasp at last, between bubbles of laughter. "What Picchu said—"

"Huh?"

"What Peach said. 'Do what the night tells you—' " She went off into the giggles again.

Kit looked down at her, perplexed. "You lost me."

Nita pushed herself upright, reached out, and tugged a couple of times, weakly, at one of Dairine's pajama sleeves. " 'Do what the night tells you.' Not night like when it gets dark. 'Knight'! Do what the *knight* tells you! As in the Junior Jedi here—" She went over sideways again and strangled her last few whoops of laughter in a convenient pillow.

"It *was* good advice," he said to Dairine. "Thanks, Dari."

"Uh, sure," said Dairine, amazed at another compliment.

Nita sat up again after a little while, wiping her eyes. "Yeah," she said. "Even if I took it before I remembered *you* said it . . . it was good advice." She thought she would let her sister have just one more compliment—especially since it was true, and information she might never have another chance to give her. "You're gonna be one hot wizard someday," Nita said.

Dairine sat speechless.

"Neets," Kit said, "we've had a long day. And tomorrow'll be longer. I'm sacking out. Dairine—"

"Right," Nita said. She lay down again, feeling glad, afraid, excited, shaky, light—a hundred things at once. She never noticed when Dairine got off her bed; she never heard Kit leave. She fell into sleep as if into a hole.

Foregathering Song

C

NITA SAT HUNCHED IN a miserable little bundle on the beach, her arms around her knees—staring at the bright morning sea and not seeing it.

She had gone to bed with the feeling that everything would be all right when she woke up in the morning. But she'd awakened to a pair of parents torn among insane curiosity, worry, approval, and disapproval, who drank cup after cup of coffee and stared at the lump of lunar pumice in the middle of the table and made little sense when they talked.

She hardly knew them. Her mom and dad alternated between talking to her, hanging on every word she said, and talking over her head about her, as if she weren't there. And they kept touching her like a delicate thing that might break— though there was an undercurrent of anger in the touches that said her parents had suddenly discovered she was in some ways stronger than they were, and they didn't like it.

Nita sighed. *I'd give anything for one of Dad's hugs that squeeze the air out and make you go* squeak! she thought. *Or to hear Mom do Donald Duck voices at me. But fat chance of that . . .*

She let out a long, unhappy breath. Kit was finishing his breakfast at a leisurely pace and handling endless questions about wizardry from her parents—covering for her. Just as well: She had other business to attend to before they left.

"Tom," she said, almost mourning, under her breath. She had been down to Friedman's already and had "minded the store" under Dog's watchful eye for a long time, waiting for Tom to return her call. She needed expert help, in a hurry. *I've gone as far as I can on my own*, she thought. *I need advice! Oh, Tom, where are you?*

As she'd expected. Nothing—

The last thing she expected was the sudden explosion of air that occurred about twenty feet down the beach from her, flinging sand in all directions. No, Nita corrected herself. The *last* thing she expected was what the explosion produced: a man with one towel wrapped around his waist and another draped around his neck—tall, broad-shouldered, and narrow-waisted, with dark hair and the kind of face one sees in cigarette ads, but never hopes to see smile. It was not Tom, but Carl. He looked around him, saw Nita, and came over to her in a hurry, looking grave. "What'samatter, Nita?" he said, casual as always, but concerned. "I heard that even though it wasn't meant for me."

She looked up at him wanly and tried to smile just a little; but the smile was a dismal failure. "Uh, no. Look, no one was answering the phone—and then I was just thinking—"

"That wasn't what I would call 'just' thinking," Carl said, sitting down on the sand beside her. "Sometimes I forget what kind of power wizards have when they're kids . . ."

Nita saw that Carl's hair was wet. "I got you out of the shower," she said. "I'm sorry . . ."

"No, I was out already. It's OK."

"Where's Tom?" Nita said.

"He has a breakfast meeting with some people at ABC; he asked me to take his calls. Not that I had much choice, in your case . . . You've got big trouble, huh? Tell me about it."

She did. It took her awhile. Though she braced herself for it, the look of shock on Carl's face when he heard about Nita's accepting the Silent Lord's part was so terrible, she started to leak tears again. Carl sat still while she finished the story.

"Do your folks know?" he said at last.

"No," Nita said. "And I don't think I'm going to tell them. I think Dad suspects—and Mom knows he does and doesn't want to talk to him about it."

Carl let out a long breath. "I don't know what to tell you," he said.

This was not the most encouraging thing Nita had ever heard. A Senior Wizard *always* knew what to tell you. "Carl," she said, tears still thick in her voice, "what can I do? I can't—I can't just die!"

It was the first time she had actually said the word out loud. It left her shaking all over like the aftermath of a particularly large wizardry, and the tears started coming again.

Carl was quiet. "Well, yeah, you can," he said at last, gently. "People do it all the time—sometimes for much less cause."

"But there must be something I could do!"

Carl looked down at the sand. "What did you *say* you were going to do?"

Nita didn't say anything; they both knew the answer very well. "You know what caused this?" Carl said.

"What?"

"Remember the blank-check sorcery you did while in the other Manhattan, that time? The open-ended request for help?"

"Uh-huh."

"That kind of spell always says that at some later date you'll be called upon to return the energy you use." Carl looked somber. "You got your help. But it must have taken a lot of energy to seal a whole piece of another space away from every other space, forever . . ."

Nita scrubbed at her eyes, not much liking this line of reasoning. "But the spell never said anyone was going to have to die to pay back the price!"

"No. All it said was that you were going to have to pay back the exact amount of energy used up at some future date. And it must have been a very great amount, to require lifeprice to be paid. There's no higher payment that can be made." Carl fell silent a moment, then said, "Well, one." And his face shut as if a door had closed behind his eyes.

Nita put her head down on her knees again. This wasn't working the way it was supposed to. "Carl, there has to be something you, we could do—"

The surf crashed for a long time between her words and his. "Nita," Carl said finally, "no. What you absolutely do *not* want is 'something you could do.' What you really want is for me to get you off the hook somehow, so you don't have to carry through with your promise."

Her head snapped up in shock. "You mean—Carl, don't you care if I die or not?"

"I care a whole lot." The pain in Carl's voice made it plain that he did. "But unfortunately I also have to tell you the truth. That's what Seniors are for; why do you think we're given so much power to work with? We're paid for what we do— and a lot of it isn't pleasant."

"Then tell me some truth! Tell me what to do—"

"No," he said gently. "Never that. Nine-tenths of the power of wizardry comes from making up your own mind what you're going to do. The rest of it is just mechanics." Carl looked at her with a professional calm that reminded Nita of her family doctor. "What I *can* do is go over your options with you."

She nodded.

"So first—what you'd like to do. You want to break your word and not sing the Song. That'd be easy enough to do. You would simply disappear—stay on land for the next week or so and not have anything further to do with the whales with whom you've been working. That would keep you out of the Song proper; you'd be alive three days from now."

Carl looked out to sea as he spoke, nothing in his expression or his tone of voice hinting at either praise or condemnation. "There would naturally be results of that action. For one, you took the Celebrant's Oath in front of witnesses and called on the Powers of wizardry themselves to bring certain things about if you break the Oath. They will bring those things about, Nita—the Powers don't forget. You'll lose your wizardry. You'll forget that there *is* any such thing as magic in the world. Any relationships you have with other wizards will immediately collapse. You would never have met Kit, for example, or me, or Tom, except for your wizardry. So we'll cease to exist for you."

Nita held still as stone.

"There'll also be effects on the Song itself as a result of your leaving. Even if the group manages to find a replacement wizard to sing the Silent One"—Nita thought of Kit and froze—"the Song itself will still have been sabotaged by your betrayal of your Oath. It won't be effective. The undersea tremors, the pollution, and the attacks on the whales and all the rest of it will continue. Or the Lone Power will enter into the wizardry and throw it completely out of control—in which case I don't want to think of what will happen to New York and the island, sooner or later. If all the other wizards in the area worked together, we might be able to slow it down. But not for long."

Carl took a breath. "And on top of everything else, breaking the Celebrant's Oath will also be a violation of the Wizard's Oath, your oath to assist in slowing down the death of the universe. In your last moment as a wizard, as you lose your magic, you will *know* beyond all doubt that the universe around you is going to die sooner because of your actions. And all through your life there'll always be something at the bottom of your heart that feels sad . . . and you'll never be able to get rid of it, or even understand it."

Nita didn't move.

"That was all the 'bad' stuff. On the 'good' side I can tell you that you probably wouldn't die of the upheavals that will start happening. What you did in Manhattan with Kit wouldn't be forgotten by the Powers, either; they pay their debts. I imagine your folks would get a sudden urge to go visit some relatives out of state—something like that—and be a good distance inland when the trouble started. And after the trouble, you would go on to live what would seem a perfectly normal life . . . after all, most people think it's normal to have a nameless sorrow at the bottom of your soul. You'd grow up, and find a job, and get married, or not, and work and play and do all the other things that mortals and wizards do. And then you'd die."

Nita was silent.

"Now the second option," Carl said. "You go down there and keep your word—though you're not happy about it, to say the least. You sing the Song, and when the time comes you dive into that coral or whatever and cut yourself up, and the Master Shark comes after you and eats you. You experience about two or three minutes of extreme pain—pain like being hit by a car or burned all over—until you go into shock, or your brain runs out of oxygen, whichever comes first, and you die. Your parents and friends then have to deal with the fact of your death."

Nita's tears started again.

"The 'good' side to this option," said Carl, "is that the Song will be successfully completed, millions of people will continue to live their lives untroubled, and the Lone Power will have suffered another severe setback. My estimate is that It couldn't interfere in any large way with the Sea's affairs—and, to some extent, with the land's—for some forty to fifty years thereafter. Possibly more."

Nita nodded slowly. "So if—"

"Wait. There's a third option," Carl said.

"Huh?"

He looked at her with an expression she couldn't fully decipher. "Sing the Song and make the Sacrifice—but do it willingly. Rather than just doing it because you have to, to keep terrible things from happening."

"Does it make a difference?"

Carl nodded. "If you can make the Sacrifice willingly, the wizardry will gain such power as you can barely imagine. The Lone One's power is always based on Its desire to have Its own way in everything. Nothing undermines Its workings faster than power turned toward having something be the way someone *else* wants it."

Carl looked hard at her. "I have to make real sure you understand this. I'm *not* talking about the sort of fakery most people mean when they talk about 'sacrifice'—none of that 'unselfishness' business, which usually has the desire for other people to feel guilty or sad hidden at the bottom of it. No being a 'martyr.' That would sabotage a wizardry almost as badly as running out on it. But to willingly give up one's life for the sake of the joy and well-being of others will instantly destroy whatever power the Lone One has currently amassed." He glanced away. "That doesn't mean you couldn't be afraid and still have it work, by the way."

"Great," Nita said with a nervous laugh.

"The important thing is that, other times when the Sacrifice has been made willingly, there have been fewer wars afterward, less crime, for a long while. The Death of things, of the world as a whole, has been slowed . . ."

Nita thought of people beating and shooting and stealing from each other; she thought of A-bombs and H-bombs, and people starving and poor—and she thought of all that slowed down. But all those troubles and possibilities seemed remote right now compared to her own problem, her own life. "I don't know if I could do that," Nita said, scarcely above a whisper.

There was a long pause. "I don't know if I could, either," said Carl, just as quietly.

She sat still for a long time. "I think—"

"Don't say it," Carl said, shaking his head. "You couldn't possibly have decided already. And even if you have—" He glanced away. "You may change your mind later . . . and then you'll be saved the embarrassment of having to justify it to me."

"Later—" She looked at him in distress and confusion. "You mean you would still talk to me if I—" She stopped. "Wait a minute. If I don't do it, I won't *know* you! And if I *do* do it—"

"There's always Timeheart," Carl said softly.

Nita nodded, silent. She had been there once, in that "place" to which only wizards can find their way while still alive; that terrible and beautiful place where things that are loved are preserved, deathless, perfect, yet still growing and becoming more themselves through moment after timeless moment. "After we—After we're alive, then—"

"What's loved," Carl said, "lives."

She looked at him in a few moments' sorrowful wonder. "But sure," she said. "You're a Senior. You must go there all the time."

"No." He looked out over the sea. "In fact, the higher you're promoted, when you're a wizard, the more work you have to do—and the less time you get to spend outside this world, except on business." He breathed out and shook his head. "I haven't been to Timeheart for a long time, except in dreams . . ."

Now it was his turn to sound wistful. Nita reached out and thumped Carl's shoulder once or twice, hesitantly.

"Yeah," Carl said. Slowly he stood up and brushed the sand off his towel, then looked down at her. "Nita," he said—and his voice was not impassive anymore— "I'm sorry."

"Yeah," she said.

"Call us before you start the Song, if you can, OK?" The New York accent was pronounced and raspy, as if Carl's nose were stuffed.

"Right."

He turned away, then paused and looked back at her. And everything suddenly became too much for Nita. She went to Carl in a rush, threw her arms around him at about waist height, and began to bawl. "Oh, honey," Carl said, and got down on one knee and held Nita tight, which was what she needed. But the helpless expression on his face, when she finally got some control over herself and looked up, almost hurt her more than her own pain.

After a while she pushed him away. Carl resisted her for a moment. "Nita," he said. "If you—If you do . . ." He paused. ". . . Thank you," he finally said, looking at her hard. "Thank you. For the ten million lives that'll keep on living. They'll never know. But the wizards will . . . and they won't ever forget."

"A lot of good that'd do *me!*" Nita said, caught between desperate laughter and tears.

"Sweetheart," Carl said, "if you're in this world for comfort, you've come to the wrong place . . . whether you're wizard or just plain mortal. And if you're doing what you're doing because of the way other people will feel about it—you're *definitely* in the wrong business. What you do has to be done because of how *you'll* feel about you . . . the way you did it last night, with your folks." His voice was rueful. "There are no other rewards . . . if only because no matter what you do, no one will *ever* think the things about you that you want them to think. Not even the Powers."

"Right," Nita said again.

They let go of each other. Carl turned and walked away quickly. The air slammed itself shut behind him, and he was gone.

Nita walked back to the house.

She kept her good-byes brief. "We may be back tonight," she said to her mother and father as they stood together on the beach, "or we may not. S'reee says it'll depend on how much of the rehearsal we get finished."

"Rehearsal—" Her mother looked at her curiously.

"Uh-huh. It's like I told you," Kit said. "Everyone who sings has his own part—but there's some ensemble singing, and it has to be done right."

"Kit, we're late," Nita said. "Mom—" She grabbed her mother and hugged her hard. "Don't worry if we don't come back tonight, Mom, please," she said. "We may just go straight into the Song—and that's a day and a half by itself. Look for us Monday morning." *Us!* her mind screamed, but she ignored it. "Dad—" She turned to him, hugged him, too, and saw, out of the corner of her eye, her mother hugging Kit.

Nita glanced up and down the beach. "It's all clear, Kit," she said. She shrugged out of the towel wrapped around her, leaving it with her mother, then sprinted for the water. A few fast hops over several breakers, and there was depth enough to dive and stroke out to twenty-foot water. Nita leaped into the whaleshape as if it were an escape rather than a trap from which she might never return. Once a humpback, she felt normal again—and felt a twinge of nervousness; there was something S'reee had warned her about that . . .

No matter. Nita surfaced and blew goodbye at her mother and father, then turned for Kit, who was treading water beside her, to take her dorsal fin and be towed out to depth.

Out in the fifty-foot water Kit wrapped the whalesark about him and made the change with a swiftness that was almost savage. The sperm whale that appeared in his place had a bitter, angry look to its movements when it began to swim away from shore.

"Kit," Nita said as they went, "you OK?"

It was some time before he answered. "No," he said. "Why *should* I be? When you're going to—" He didn't finish the sentence.

"Kit, look—"

"No, *you* look. Don't you see that there's nothing I can do about all this? And I don't like it!" His song was another of the scraping sperm-whale battle cries, soft but very heartfelt, and the rage in it chattered right down Nita's skin like nails down a blackboard.

"There's not much I can do about it myself," she said, "and I don't like it, either. Let's not talk about it for now, please! My brain still hurts enough from last night."

"Neets," he said, "we've got to talk about it sometime. Tomorrow's *it*."

"Fine. Before tomorrow. Meanwhile, we've got today to worry about. Are we even going the right way?"

He laughed at her then, a painful sound. "Boy, are you preoccupied," Kit said. "Clean your ears out and listen!"

She stopped everything but the ticks and clicks a humpback uses to find its way, and listened—and was tempted to laugh herself. The sea had a racket hidden in it. From the southwest was coming an insane assortment of long, odd, wild sounds. Sweet high flutings that cut sharply through the intervening distance; clear horn calls, as if someone hunted under the waves; outer-spacey whistles and warbles like the electronic cries of orbiting satellites; deep bass scrapes and rumbles, lawn-mower buzzes and halftone moans and soulful sighs. And many of those sounds, sooner or later, came back to the same main theme—a series of long, wistful notes, slowly ascending into pitches too high and keen for human ears, then whispering away, lost in the quiet breathing of the water.

Nita had never heard that main theme before, but she recognized it instantly from her reading and her wizard's sense of the Sea. It was the loss/gain/sorrow motif that ran all through the Song of the Twelve; and what she heard now, attenuated by distance but otherwise clear, was the sound of its Singers, tuning up for the performance in which that mournful phrase would become not just a motif but a reality.

"Kit," Nita said with a shiver, "that's a lot more than ten whales! Who are all those other voices?"

He bubbled, a shrug. "Let's find out."

She whistled agreement and struck off after Kit, due west, away from the south shore of the island and out across the Atlantic-to-Ambrose shipping approaches once more. Song echoed more and more loudly in the sunlit shallows through which they swam; but underneath them Nita and Kit were very aware of the depths from which no echo returned—the abyss of Hudson Canyon, far below them, waiting.

"This is it," Kit said at last, practically in Nita's ear, as they came to the fringes of the area S'reee's instructions had mentioned—fifteen miles east-northeast of Barnegat, New Jersey, right over the remains of an old sunken tanker six fathoms down in the water. And floating, soaring, or slowly fluking through the diffuse green-golden radiance of the water were the whales.

Nita had to gulp once to find her composure. Hundreds of whales had gathered and were milling about, whales of every kind—minke whales, sei whales, sperm whales, dolphins of more kinds than she knew existed, in a profusion of shapes and colors, flashing through the water; several blues, grave-voiced, gliding with huge, slow grace; fin whales, hardly smaller than the blues, bowhead whales and pygmy rights and humpbacks, many of them; gray whales and pygmy sperms and narwhals, with their long, single spiral teeth, like unicorn horns; belugas and killers and scamperdowns and bottlenosed whales—"Kit," Nita sang, faint-voiced, "S'reee didn't tell me there were going to be *people* here!"

"Me, either. I guess spectators at the rehearsal are so common, she forgot . . ." Kit sounded unconcerned.

Easy for you, Nita thought. *You like crowds!* She sang a few notes of sonar, trying nervously to hear some familiar shape. One shape at least Nita recognized, accompanied by the slow, calm, downscaling note of the Blue, as Aroooon passed by, a gold-tinged shadow in the background of greenness and the confusion of bodies. And there was Hotshot's high chatter, some ways off, accompanied by several other dolphin voices very like his—members of his pod.

Stillness swept over the spectators as she approached with Kit, and they recognized who she was. And a single note began to go up from them, starting at the fringes of the circle, working its way inward to the Celebrants, until she heard even Aroooon's giant voice taking it up. One note, held in every range from the dolphins' dog-whistle trilling to the water-shaking thunder of the blues. One thought, one concept in the Speech, trumpeting through the water with such force that Nita began to shake at the sound of it. *Praise*. They knew she was the Silent One. They knew what she was going to do for them. They were thanking her.

Stunned, Nita forgot to swim—just drifted there in painful joy.

From behind, as the note slowly ebbed away, Kit nudged her. "Get the lead out, Neets," he sang, just for her hearing. "You're the star of this show. So start acting like it! Go in there and let them know you're here."

She swam slowly through the spectator whales, into the clear water in the center of their great circle, where the Celebrants were gathered.

One by one, as she circled above the weed-covered remnant of the trawler, Nita quickly identified the whales she knew. Aroooon, yes, swimming off more or less by himself to tideward, singing his deep scrape of notes with the absent concentration of a perfectionist who has time to hunt perfection; Hotshot, doing barrel rolls near the surface and chattering through the quick, bright harmonies of some part of the Wanderer's song; Areinnye, aloof from both Wanderer and Blue, running again and again over a phrase of the Gray Lord's song and paying no further attention to Nita after a quick glance.

There were also five other whales whom Nita didn't know, exactly as Kit had pegged them. A beluga, dolphin-size but whaleshaped, lazing near the surface and singing some longing phrase from the Gazer's song; a pilot whale, long and slim and gray, silent for the moment and looking at Nita with interest; a right whale, with its huge, strange, bent-out-of-shape baleen mouth, listening to the beluga; a killer whale, the sharp blacks and whites of its hide a contrast to the grays and quiet mottlings of most of the others.

And—thank Heaven!—S'reee, swimming toward Nita from beside the killer. Nita had been shaken by the sight of the killer—killer whales being one of a humpback's most persistent natural enemies—but just now her composure was so unraveled, there wasn't much more damage that could be done to it. As S'reee came up to greet her, Nita managed to sing in something like a calm voice, and as if she were actually in charge, "Well, we're late. Should we get started?"

"Good idea," said S'reee, brushing skin briefly and reassuringly with Nita. "Introductions first, though."

"Yes, please."

S'reee led Nita off to the north, where several of the singers were working together. "We've been through the first part of the Song already this morning," said S'reee, "the name-songs and so forth. I've heard you do yours, so there was no need for you to be here till late. We're up to the division now, the 'temptation' part. These are the people singing the Undecided group—"

"Hi, Hotshot," Nita sang as she and S'reee soared into the heart of the group. The dolphin chattered a greeting back and busied himself with his singing again, continuing his spirals near the surface, above the heads of the right whale and a whale whose song Nita hadn't heard on the way in, a Sowerby's beaked whale. She immediately suspected why she hadn't heard it; the whale, undoubtedly there to celebrate the Forager's part, was busy eating—ripping up the long kelp and red weed stirring around the shattered deck plates of the wreck. It didn't even look up as she and S'reee approached. The right whale was less preoccupied; it swam toward Nita and S'reee at a slow pace that might have been either courtesy or caution.

"HNii't, this is T!h!ki," said S'reee. Nita clicked his name back at him in greeting, swimming forward to brush skin politely with him. "He's singing the Listener."

T!h!ki rolled away from Nita and came about, looking at her curiously. When he spoke, his song revealed both great surprise and some unease. "S'reee—this is a human!"

"T!h!ki," Nita said, wry-voiced, with a look at S'reee, "are *you* going to be mad at me for things I haven't done, too?"

The right whale looked at her with that cockeyed upward stare that rights have—their eyes being placed high in their flat-topped heads. "Oh," he said, sounding wry himself, "you've run afoul of Areinnye, have you? No fear, Silent Lord—hNii't, was it? No fear." T!h!ki's song put her instantly at ease. It had an amiable and intelligent sound to it, the song of a mind that didn't tend toward blind animosities. "If you're going to do the Sea such a service as you're doing, I could hardly do less than treat you with honor. For Sea's sake, don't think Areinnye is typical . . .

"However," T!h!ki added, gazing down at the calmly feeding beaked whale, "some of us practically have to have a bite taken out of us to get us to start honoring and stop eating." He drifted down a fathom or so and bumped nose-first into the beaked whale. "Roots! Heads up, you bottom grubber, here comes the Master Shark!"

"Huh? Where? *Where?*" the shocked song came drifting up from the bottom. The kelp was thrashed about by frantic fluking, and through it rose the beaked whale, its mouth full of weed, streamers of which trailed back and whipped around in all directions as the whale tried to tell where the shark was coming from. "Where—what—Oh," the beaked whale said after a moment, as the echoes from its initial excited squeaking came back and told it that the Master Shark was nowhere in the area. "Ki," it said slowly, "I'm going to get you for that."

"Later. Meantime, here's S'reee, and hNii't with her," said T!h!ki. "HNii't's singing the Silent Lord. HNii't, this is Roots."

"Oh," said Roots, "well met. Pleasure to sing with you. Would you excuse me?" She flipped her tail, politely enough, before Nita could sing a note, and a second later was head-down in the kelp again, ripping it up faster than before, as if making up for lost time.

Nita glanced with mild amusement at S'reee as Hotshot spiraled down to join them. "She's a great conversationalist," Hotshot whistled, his song conspiratorially quiet. "Really. Ask her about food."

"I kind of suspected," Nita said. "Speaking of the Master Shark, though, where *is* Ed this morning?"

S'reee waved one long fin in a shrug. "He has a late appearance, as you do, so it doesn't really matter if he shows up late. Meanwhile, we have to meet the others. Ki, are you finished with Roots?"

"Shortly. We're going through the last part of the second duet. I'll catch up with you people later." The right whale glided downward toward the weeds, and S'reee led Nita off to the west, where the Blue drifted in the water, and the beluga beside him, a tiny white shape against Aroooon's hugeness.

"Aroooon and I are two of the Untouched," said S'reee. "The third, after the Singer and the Blue, is the Gazer. That's Iniihwit."

"HNii't," Aroooon's great voice hailed them as Nita approached.

Nita bent her body into a bow of respect as she coasted through the water. "Sir," she said.

That small, calm eye dwelt gravely on her. "Are you well, Silent Lord?" said the Blue.

"As well as I can be, sir," Nita said. "Under the circumstances."

"That's well," said Aroooon. "Iniihwit, here is the human I spoke of."

The beluga swam away from Aroooon to touch skin with Nita. Iniihwit was male, much smaller than Nita as whales went, though big for a beluga. But what struck her more than his smallness was the abstracted, contemplative sound of his song when he did speak. There were long, silent days of calm behind it, days spent floating on the surface alone, watching the changes of sea and sky, saying little, seeing much. "HNii't," he said, "well met. And well met now, for there's something you must hear. You, too, Senior."

"The weather?" S'reee said, sounding worried.

"Yes indeed. It looks as if that storm is not going to pass us by."

Nita looked at S'reee in surprise. "What storm? It's clear."

"For now," said Iniihwit. "Nevertheless, there's weather coming, and there's no telling what it will stir up in the depths."

"Is there any chance we can beat it?" S'reee said, sounding very worried indeed.

"None," the beluga said. "It will be here in half a light. We'll have to take our chances with the storm, I fear."

S'reee hung still in the water, thinking. "Well enough," she said. "Come on, hNii't; let's speak to Areinnye and the others singing the Undecided. We'll start the group rehearsal, then go straight into the Song. Time's swimming."

S'reee fluked hard and soared off, leaving Nita in shock for a moment. *We won't be going home tonight*, she thought. *No good-byes. No last explanations. I'll never set foot on land again . . .*

"Neets?" Kit's voice said from behind her.

"Right," she said.

She went after S'reee to see the three whales singing the Undecided. Areinnye greeted Nita with cool cordiality and went back to her practicing. "And here's the Sounder," S'reee was saying. "Fluke, this is hNii't."

Nita brushed skin with the Sounder, who was a pilot whale; small and mottled gray, built along the same general lines as a sperm, though barely a quarter the size. Fluke's eyes were small, his vision poor, and he had an owlish, shortsighted look about him that reminded Nita of Dairine in her glasses. The likeness was made stronger by a shrill, ratchety voice and a tendency toward chuckles. "Fluke?" Nita said.

"I was one," the Sounder said. "I'm a triplet. And a runt, as you can see. There was nothing to do to hold my own with my brother and sister except become a wizard in self-defense."

Nita made a small amused noise, thinking that there might not be so much difference between the motivations and family lives of humans and whales. "And here's Fang," said S'reee.

Nita found herself looking at the brilliant white and deep black of the killer whale. Her feelings were decidedly mixed. The humpback-shape had its own ideas about the killer, mostly prejudiced by the thought of blood in the water. But Nita's human memories insisted that killers were affable creatures, friendly to humans; she remembered her uncle Jerry, her mother's older brother, telling about how he'd once ridden a killer whale at an aquatic park in Hawaii and had had a great time. *This* killer whale edged closer to Nita now, staring at her out of small black eyes— not opaque ones like Ed's, but sharp, clever ones, with merriment in them. "Well?" the killer said, his voice teasing. "Shark got your tongue?"

The joke was so horrible, and somehow so funny, that Nita burst out laughing, liking this creature instantly. "Fang, is it?"

"It is. HNii't, is it?"

"More or less." There was a kind of wicked amusement about Fang's song, which by itself was funny to listen to—sweet whistles and flutings peppered liberally with spits and fizzes. "Fang, are you from these waters originally?"

"Indeed not. I came down from Baffin Bay for the Song."

Nita swung her tail in surprise. "That's in Canada! Fifteen hundred miles!"

"What? Oh, a great many lengths, yes. I didn't swim it, hNii't. Any more than you and K!t there went where you last night by swimming."

"I suppose," she said, "that a wizardry done like that—on such short notice, and taking the wizards such a distance—might have been noticed."

Fang snorted bubbles. " 'Might'! I should say so. By everybody. But it's understandable that you might want to indulge yourselves, anyway. Seeing that you and your partner won't have much more time to work together in the flesh."

Fang's voice was kind, even matter-of-fact; but Nita wanted to keep away from that subject for the moment. "Right. Speaking of which, S'reee, hadn't we better start?"

"Might as well."

S'reee swam off to a spot roughly above the wreck, whistling, and slowly the whole group began to drift in toward her. The voices of the whales gathered around to watch the Celebrants began to quiet, like those of an audience at a concert.

"From the top," S'reee said. She paused a few seconds, then lifted up her voice in the Invocation.

"Blood in the water I sing,
    and one who shed it:
deadliest hunger I sing,
    and one who fed it—
weaving the ancient-most song

of the Sea's sending:
singing the tragedy,
      singing the joy unending."

Joy . . . , Nita thought, trying to concentrate. But the thought of whose blood was being sung about made it hard.

The shadow that fell over Nita somewhere in the middle of the first song of the Betrayed whales, though, got her attention immediately. A streamlined shape as pale as bleached bone glided slowly over her, blocking the jade light; one dead-black, unreflecting eye glanced down. "Nita."

"Ed," she said, none too enthusiastically. His relentless reality was no pleasant sight.

"Come swim with me."

He arched away through the water, northward toward Ambrose Light. The gathered spectators drew back as Nita silently followed.

Shortly they were well to the north, still able to hear the ongoing practice Song, but out of hearing range for standard conversation. "So, Silent Lord," Ed said, slowing. "You were busy last night."

"Yes," Nita said, and waited. She had a feeling that something odd was going on inside that chill mind.

Ed looked at her. "You are angry . . ."

"Damn right I am!" Nita sang, loudly, not caring for the moment about what Ed might think of her distress.

"Explain this anger to me," said the Master Shark. "Normally the Silent Lord does not find the outcome of the Song so frightful. In fact, whales sometimes compete for the privilege of singing your part. The Silent Lord dies indeed, but the death is not so terrible—it merely comes sooner than it might have otherwise, by predator or old age. And it buys the renewal of life and holds off the Great Death for the whole Sea—and for years."

Ed glanced at her, sedate. "And even if the Silent One should happen to suffer somewhat, what of it? For there is still Timeheart, is there not? . . . The Heart of the Sea." Nita nodded, saying nothing. "It is no ending, this Song, but a passage into something else. How they extol that passage, and what lies at its end." There was faint, scornful amusement in Ed's voice as he lifted his voice in a verse of the Song—one of the Blue's cantos—not singing, exactly, for sharks have no song; chanting, rather. " '. . . Past mortal song—

"—that Sea whereof our own seas merely hint,
poor shadows sidewise cast from what is real—
where Time and swift-finned Joy are foes no more,
but lovers; where old friend swims by old friend,
senior to Death, undying evermore—
partner to Songs unheard and Voices hid;
Songs past our knowing, perilously fair—"

Ed broke off. "You are a wizard," he said. "You have known that place, supposedly."

"Yes." Timeheart had looked like a bright city, skyscrapered in crystal and fire, power trembling in its streets and stones, unseen but undeniably there. And beyond the city stretched a whole universe, sited beyond and within all other worlds, beyond and within all times. Death did not touch that place. "Yes, I was there."

"So you know it awaits you after the Sacrifice, after the change of being. But you don't seem to take the change so calmly."

"How can I? I'm human!"

"Yes. But make me understand. Why does that make your attitude so different? Why are you so angry about something that would happen to you sooner or later anyway?"

"Because I'm too young for this," Nita said. "All the things I'll never have a chance to do—grow up, work, live—"

"This," Ed said mildly, looking around him at the green-burning sea, the swift fish flashing in it, the dazzling wrinkled mirror of the surface seen from beneath, "this is not living?"

"Of course it is! But there's a lot more to it! And getting murdered by a shark is hardly what I call living!"

"I assure you," Ed said, "it's nothing as personal as murder. I would have done the same for any wizard singing the Silent Lord. I *have* done the same, many times. And doubtless shall again . . ." His voice trailed off.

Nita caught something odd in Ed's voice. He sounded almost . . . wistful?

"Look," she said, her own voice small. "Tell me something . . . Does it really have to hurt a lot?"

"Sprat," said Ed dispassionately, "what in this life doesn't? Even love hurts sometimes. You may have noticed . . ."

"Love—what would you know about that?" Nita said, too pained to care about being scornful, even to the Master Shark.

"And who are you to think I would know nothing about it? Because I kill without remorse, I must also be ignorant of love, is that it?"

There was a long, frightening pause, while Ed began to swim a wide circle about Nita. "You're thinking I am so old an order of life that I can know nothing but the blind white rut, the circling, the joining that leaves the joined forever scarred. Oh yes, I know that. In its time . . . it's very good."

The rich and hungry pleasure in his voice disturbed Nita. Ed was circling closer and closer as he spoke, swimming as if he were asleep. "And, yes . . . sometimes we wish the closeness of the joining wouldn't end. But what would my kind do with the warm-blood sort of joining, the long companionships? What would I do with a mate?" He said it as if it were an alien word. "Soon enough one or the other of us would fall into distress—and the other partner would end it. There's an end to mating and mate, and to the love that passed between. That price is too high for me to pay, even once. I swim alone."

He was swimming so close to Nita now that his sides almost touched hers, and she pulled her tail and fins in tight and shrank away from the razory hide, not daring to move otherwise. Then Ed woke up and broke the circle, gliding lazily outward and away as if nothing had happened. "But, Sprat, the matter of *my* loves—or their lack—is hardly what's bothering you."

"No," she burst out bitterly, "love! I've never had a chance to. And now— now—"

"Then you're well cast for the Silent Lord's part," Ed said, his voice sounding far away. "How does the line go? 'Not old enough to love as yet, / but old enough to die, indeed—' That has always been the Silent Lord's business—to sacrifice love for life . . . instead of, as in lesser songs, the other way around . . ."

Ed trailed off, paused to snap up a sea bass that passed him by too slowly. When his eyes were more or less sane again and the water had carried the blood away, Ed said, "Is it truly so much to you, Sprat? Have you truly had no time to love?"

Mom and Dad, Nita thought ruefully. *Dairine. That's not love, I don't love Dairine!—do I?* She hardened her heart and said, "No, Pale One. Not that way. No one . . . that way."

"Well then," said the Master Shark, "the Song will be sung from the heart, it seems. You will still offer the Sacrifice?"

"I don't want to—"

"Answer the question, Sprat."

It was a long while before Nita spoke. "I'll do what I said I would," she said at last. The notes of the song whispered away into the water like the last notes of a dirge.

She was glad Ed said nothing for a while, for her insides gripped and churned as she finally found out what real, grown-up fear was. Not the kind that happens suddenly, that leaves you too busy with action to think about being afraid—but the kind that she had been holding off by not officially "deciding": the kind that swims up as slowly as a shark circling, letting you see it and realize in detail what's going to happen to you.

"I am big enough to take a humpback in two bites," Ed said into her silence. "And there is no need for me to be leisurely about it. You will speak to the Heart of the Sea without having to say too much to me on the way."

Nita looked up at him in amazement. "But I thought you didn't believe—I mean, you'd never—"

"I am no wizard, Nita," Ed said. "The Sea doesn't speak to me as it does to you. I will never experience those high, wild joys the Blue sings of—the Sea That Burns, the Voices. The only voices I hear cry out from water that burns with blood. But might I not sometimes wonder what other joys there are?—And wish I might feel them, too?"

The dry, remote pain in his voice astonished her. And Nita thought abruptly of that long line of titles in the commentaries in her manual: as if only one shark had ever been Master. *Sharks don't die of natural causes*, she thought. *Could it be that, all these years, there has been just one Master? And all around him, people die and die, and he—can't—*

—and wants to? And so he understands how it is to want to get out of something and be stuck with it.

Nita was terribly moved—she wasn't sure why. She swam close to the Pale One's huge head for a moment and glided side by side with him, matching his course and the movements of his body.

"I wish I could help," she said.

"As if the Master could feel distress," Ed said, with good-natured scorn. The wound in his voice had healed without a scar.

"And as if someone else might want to end it," Nita said, sarcastic, but gentle about it.

Ed was silent for a long while. "I mean, it's dumb to suffer," Nita said, rather desperately, into that silence. "But if you have to do it, you might as well intend it to do someone some good."

In silence they swam a few lengths more through the darkening water, while Nita's fear began to build in her again, and one astonished part of her mind shouted at her, *You're running around talking about doing nice things for someone who's going to kill you? You're crazy!*

Ed spoke at last. "It's well said. And we will cause it to be well made, this Sacrifice. You, young and never loving; I, old and never loved." Calm, utterly calm, that voice. "Such a Song the Sea will never have seen."

"HNii't?" came a questioning note through the water, from southward of Ambrose: S'reee's voice. "It's almost your time—"

"I have to go," Nita said. "Ed—"

"Silent Lord?"

She had no idea why she was saying it. "I'm sorry!"

"This once, I think," the passionless voice said, "so am I. Go on, Sprat. I will not miss my cue."

Nita looked at him. Opaque eyes, depthless, merciless, lingered on her as Ed curved past. "Coming!" Nita sang in S'reee's direction, loud, and tore off southward.

No pale shadow followed.

The next few hours, while the water darkened further, ran together for Nita in a blur of music, and annoying repetitions, and words that would have been frightening if she hadn't been too busy to be frightened. And something was growing in her, slowly, but getting stronger and stronger—an odd elation. She sang on, not questioning it, riding its tide and hoping it would last through what she had to do. Again and again, with the other Celebrants listening and offering suggestions, she rehearsed what would be the last things she would ever say:

> ". . . Sea, hear me now,
> and take my words and make them ever law!"

"Right, now swim off a little. No one hears this part. Upward, and toward the center, where the peak will be. Right there—"

> "Must I accept the barren Gift?
>   —learn death, and lose my Mastery?
> Then let them know whose blood and breath
>   will take the Gift and set them free:
> whose is the voice and whose the mind
>   to set at naught the well-sung Game—
> when finned Finality arrives
>   and calls me by my secret Name.

> "Not old enough to love as yet,
>   but old enough to die, indeed—"

(Oh Lord)
"—the death-fear bites my throat and heart,
    fanged cousin to the Pale One's breed.
But past the fear lies life for all—
    perhaps for me: and, past my dread,
past loss of Mastery and life,
    the Sea shall yet give up Her dead!"

—and then the paleness came to circle over her, bringing with it the voice that chanted all on one soft hissing note, again and again, always coming back to the same refrain—

"Master have I none, nor seek.
Bring the ailing; bring the weak.
Bring the wounded ones to me:
They shall feed my Mastery. . . ."

That strange excitement was still growing in Nita. She let it drive her voice as she would have used it to drive a wizardry, so that her song grew into something that shook the water and almost drowned out even Ed's voice, weaving about it and turning mere hunger to desire, disaster to triumph—

"Lone Power, I accept your Gift!
    Freely I make death part of me;
By my acceptance it is bound
    into the lives of all the Sea—

"yet what I do now binds to it
    a gift I feel of equal worth:
I take Death with me, out of Time,
    and make of it a path, a birth!

"Let the teeth come! As they tear me,
    they tear Your ancient hate for aye—
—so rage, proud Power! Fail again,
    and see my blood teach Death to die!"

. . . The last time she sang it, Nita hung unmoving, momentarily exhausted, for the moment aware of nothing but Kit's anxious eyes staring at her from outside the circle and the stir of water on her skin as the Pale One circled above her.

"That's right," S'reee said at last, very quietly. "And then—"

She fell silent and swam out of the circle of Celebrants. Behind her, very slowly, first the Blue and then the rest of the whales began to sing the dirge for the Silent Lord—confirmation of the transformation of death and the new defeat of the Lone Power. Nita headed for the surface to breathe.

She came up into early evening. Westward, sunset was burning itself into scarlet embers; eastward, a moon lacking only the merest shard of light to be full lifted swollen and amber through the surface haze; northward, the bright and dark and bright again of Ambrose Light glittered on the uneasily shifting waves, with the opening and closing red eyes of Manhattan skyscraper lights low beyond it; and southward, gazing back at them, the red-orange glow of Arcturus sparkled above the water, here and there striking an answering spark off the crest or hollow of some wave. Nita lay there gasping in the wave-wash and let the water rock her. *Heaven knows*, she thought, *I need somebody to do it . . .*

Beside her Kit surfaced in a great wash of water and blew spectacularly—slightly forward, as sperms do. "Neets—"

"Hi," she said. She knew it was inane, but she could think of no other way to keep Kit from starting what he was going to start, except by saying dumb things.

"Neets," he said, "we're out of time. They're going to start the descent as soon as everybody's had a chance to rest a little and the protective spells are set."

"Right," she said, misunderstanding him on purpose. "We better get going, then—" She tilted her head down and started to dive.

"Neets." Suddenly Nita found that she was trying to dive through a forty-foot thickness of sperm whale. Nita blew in annoyance and let herself float back to the surface again. Kit bobbed up beside her—and, with great suddenness and a slam of air, threw off the whalesark. He dog-paddled there in the water, abruptly tiny beside her bulk. "Neets, get out of that for a minute."

"Huh? Oh—"

It was a moment's work to drop the whaleshape; then she was reduced to dog-paddling, too. Kit was treading water a few feet from her, his hair slicked down with the water. He looked strange—tight, somehow, as if he were holding on to some idea or feeling very hard. "Neets," he said, "I'm not buying this."

Nita stared at him. "Kit," she said finally, "look, there's nothing we can do about it. *I've* bought it. Literally."

"No," Kit said. The word was not an argument, not even defiance; just a simple statement of fact. "Look, Neets—you're the best wizard I've ever worked with—"

"I'm the *only* wizard you've ever worked with," Nita said with a lopsided grin.

"I'm gonna kill you," Kit said—and regretted it instantly.

"No need," Nita said. "Kit—why don't you just admit that this time I've got myself into something I can't get out of."

"Unless another wizard gets you out of it."

She stared at him. "You loon, you *can't*—"

"I *know*. And it hurts! I feel like I *should* volunteer, but I just can't—"

"Good. 'Cause you do and *I'll* kill *you*."

"That won't work, either." He made her own crooked grin back at her. " 'All for one,' remember? We *both* have to come out of this alive."

And he looked away.

"Let's go for both," Nita said.

Silence.

She took a deep breath. "Look, even if we *don't* both get out of this, I think it's gonna be all right. Really—"

"No," Kit said again, and that was that.

Nita just looked at him. "OK," she said. "Be that way." And she meant it. This was the Kit she was used to working with: stubborn, absolutely sure of himself—most of the time; the person with that size-twelve courage packed into his size-ten self, a courage that would spend a few minutes trembling and then take on anything that got in its way—from the Lone Power to her father. *If I've got to go*, Nita thought in sudden irrational determination, *that sheer guts has got to survive—and I'll do whatever's necessary to make sure he does.*

"Look," she said, "what're you gonna tell my folks when you get back?"

"I'm gonna tell them we're hungry," Kit said, "and that you'll fill 'em in on the details while I eat."

I did tell him to be that way . . . "Right," Nita said.

For a long time they stayed where they were, treading water, watching the moon inch its way up the sky, listening to the Ambrose fog signal hooting the minutes away. A mile or so off, a tanker making for New York Harbor went by, its green portside running lights toward them, and let off a low, groaning blast of horn to warn local traffic. From under the surface, after a pause, came a much deeper note that held and then scaled downward out of human hearing range, becoming nothing but a vibration in the water.

"They're ready to leave," Kit said.

Nita nodded, slipped into whaleshape again, and looked one last time with all her heart at the sunset towers of Manhattan, until Kit had finished his change. Then they dived.

The Song
of the Twelve

HUDSON CHANNEL BEGINS ITS seaward course some twenty miles south of Ambrose Light—trending first due south, parallel to the Jersey shore, then turning gradually toward the southeast and the open sea as it deepens. Down its length, scattered over the channel's bottom as it slowly turns from gray-green mud to gray-black sand to naked, striated stone, are the broken remnants of four hundred years' seafaring in these waters and the refuse of three hundred years of human urban life, mixed randomly together. There are new, almost whole-bodied wrecks lying dead on their sides atop old ones long since gone to rot and rust; great dumps of incinerated wood and ash, chemical drums and lumps of coal and jagged piles of junk metal; sunken, abandoned buoys, old cable spindles, unexploded ordnance and bombs and torpedoes; all commingled with and nested in a thick ooze of untreated, settled sewage—the garbage of millions of busy lives, thrown where they won't have to look at it.

The rugged bed of the channel starts out shallow, barely a fathom deeper than the seabed that surrounds it. It was much deeper once, especially where it begins; but the ooze has filled it thickly, and for some miles it is now hard to tell that any channel at all lies under the rotting trash, under the ancient faded beer cans and the hubcaps red with rust. Slowly, though, some twenty miles down the channel from its head, an indentation becomes apparent—a sort of crooked rut worn by the primordial Hudson River into the ocean floor, a mile wide at the rut's deepest, five miles wide from edge to edge. This far down—forty fathoms under the surface and some sixty feet below the surrounding ocean bed, between a great wide U of walls—the dark sludge of human waste lies even thicker. The city has not been dumping here for some time, but all the old years' sewage has not gone away. Every stone in the deepening rut, every pressure-flattened pile of junk on the steadily downward-sloping seabed around the channel, is coated thick and black. Bottom-feeding fish are few here: There is nothing for them to eat. Krill do not live here: The water is too foul to support the microscopic creatures they eat, and even of a summer night the thick olive color of the sea is unchanged.

The channel's walls begin to grow less and less in height, as if the ocean is growing tired of concealing the scar in its side. Gradually the rut flattens out to a broad shallow depression like a thousand other valleys in the sea. A whale hanging above the approximate end of the channel, some 130 miles southeast of New York Harbor, has little to see on looking back up the channel's length—just an upward-sloping scatter of dark-slimed rocks and mud and scraps of garbage, drab even in the slate-green twilight that is all this bottom ever sees of noon. But looking downward, southward, where its course would run if the channel went any farther—

—the abyss. Suddenly the thinning muck, and the gentle swellings and dippings of the seabed, simply stop at the edge of a great steep semicircular cliff, two miles from side to side. And beyond the cliff, beyond the edge of the continental shelf, curving away to northeast and southwest—nothing. Nothing anywhere but the vague glow of the ocean's surface three hundred feet above; and below, beyond the semicircle, the deadly stillness of the great deeps, and a blackness one can hear on the skin like a dirge. Icy cold, and the dark.

"I warn you all," S'reee said as the eleven gathered Celebrants and Kit hung there, looking down into that darkness at the head of Hudson Canyon. "Remember the length of this dive; take your own breathing needs carefully into consideration, and tell me now if you think you may need more air than our spells will be taking with us. Remember that, at the great pressures in the Below, you'll need more oxygen than you usually do—and work will make you burn more fuel. If you feel you need to revise the breathing figures on the group spell upward, this is the time to do it. There won't be a chance later, after we've passed the Gates of the Sea. Nor will there be any way to get to the surface quickly enough to breathe if you start running low. At the depths we'll be working, even a sperm whale would get the bends and die of such an ascent. Are you all sure of your needs? Think carefully."

No one said anything.

"All right. I remind you, also, one more time, of the boundaries on the pressure-protection spell. They're marked by this area of light around us—which will serve the added purpose of enabling us to see what's going on around us. If we need to expand the boundaries, that's easily done. But unless I direct you otherwise, stay inside the light. Beyond the lighted area, there's some direction for a limited area, but it's erratic. Don't depend on it! Otherwise you may find yourself crushed to a pulp."

Nita glanced at Kit; he gave her an I-don't-care wave of the tail. Sperm whales were much less bothered by pressure changes than most of the species, and the great depths were part of their hunting grounds. "You be careful," she sang at him in an undertone. "Don't get cute down there."

"Don't *you*."

"Anything else?" S'reee said. "Any questions?"

"Is there time for a fast bite?" Roots said, sounding wistful.

"Surely," Fang said, easing up beside the beaked whale with that eternal killer whale smile. "Where should I bite you?"

"Enough, you two. Last chance, my wizards."

No one sang a note.

"Then forward all," S'reee said, "and let us take the adventure the Powers send us."

She glided forward, out into the darkness past the great curved cliff, tilted her nose down, and dived—not straight, but at a forty-five-degree angle roughly parallel to the downward slope of the canyon. The wizard-light advanced with her. Areinnye followed first; then Fang and Iniihwit, with Fluke and Roots close behind. After them came T!h!ki and Aroooon and Hotshot, and Nita, with Kit behind her as rearguard, suspiciously watching the zone of light around them. Only one of the Celebrants did not stay within that boundary, sailing above it, or far to one side, as he pleased—Ed, cruising restlessly close to the canyon walls as the group descended, or pacing them above, a ghost floating in midnight-blue water.

"I don't like it," Nita sang, for Kit's hearing only, as she looked around her.

"What?"

"This." She swung her tail at the walls—which were towering higher and higher as they cut downward through the continental shelf. On the nautical maps in their manuals, the canyon had looked fairly innocent; and a drop of twenty-five feet in a half-mile had seemed gentle. But Nita was finding the reality that rose in ever-steepening battlements around her much more threatening. The channel's walls at their highest had been about three hundred feet high, comparable to the walls she'd seen in the Grand Canyon on vacation. But these walls were already five or six hundred feet high, growing steadily steeper as the canyon's angle of descent through the shelf increased. If Nita had a neck to crane back, it would already be sore.

As it was, she had something much worse—a whale's superb sonar sense, which told her exactly how puny she was in comparison to those cliffs—exactly where loose rocks lay on them, ready to be shaken down at the slightest bottom tremor.

Kit looked up around them and sang a note of uncomfortable agreement. "Yeah," he said. "It gives me the creeps, too. It's too tall—"

"No," Nita said softly. "It's that this isn't a place where we're supposed to be. Something very large happened here once. That's your specialty; you should be able to feel it."

"Yeah, I should." There was a brief pause. "I seem to have been having trouble with that lately. —But you're right, it's there. It's not so much the tallness itself we're feeling. But what it's—what it's a symbol of, I think—"

Nita said nothing for a moment, startled by the idea that Kit had been losing some of his talent at his specialty. There was something that could mean, some warning sign— She couldn't think what.

"Kit, this is one of the places where Afállonë was, isn't it?"

He made a slow sound of agreement. "The whole old continental plate Atlantis stood on was ground under the new plates and buried under the Atlantic's floor, S'reee said. But the North American plate was a lot farther west when the trouble first started, and the European one was farther east. So if I've got the story straight, this would have been where Afállonë's western shoreline was, more or less. Where we're going would still have been open sea, a couple of million years ago."

"Millions of years—" Nita looked at him in uncomfortable wonder. "Kit—that's much farther back than the fall of Afállonë. That could—" Her note failed her momentarily. "That could go right back to the first Song of the Twelve—"

Kit was still for a while as they kept diving. "No wonder," he said at last, "no one travels down through the Gates of the Sea except when they're about to do the Song. Part of the sorcery is buried in the stone. If anybody should trouble it, wake it up—"

"—like we're doing," Nita said, and fell silent.

They swam on. The immensities rearing up about them grew no more reassuring with time. *Time*, Nita thought—*how long have we been down here?* In this changeless cold dark, there was no telling; and even when the sun came up, there still would be no knowing day from night. The darkness yielded only grudgingly to the little sphere of light the Celebrants carried with them, showing them not much, and too much, of what Nita didn't want to look at—those walls, reaching so far above her now that the light couldn't even begin to illumine them. Nita began to get a bizarre sense of being indoors—descending a winding ramp of infinite length, its walls three miles apart and now nearly a mile high.

It was at about this time that Nita felt on her skin what sounded at first like one of the Blue's deeper notes, and stared ahead of her, wondering partly what he was saying—the note was one that made no sense to her. Then she wondered why he was curving his body upward in such surprise. But the note grew, and grew, and grew louder still, and though they were now nearly a mile from the walls on either side, to her shock and horror Nita heard the walls begin to resonate to that note.

The canyon walls sounded like a struck gong, one of such bone-shaking, subterranean pitch as Nita had never imagined. *She* sounded, caught in the torrent of shock waves with the rest of the Celebrants. *Seaquake!* she thought. The sound pressed through her skin from all sides like cold weights, got into her lungs and her heart and her brain, and throbbed there, hammering her into dizziness with slow and terrible force.

The sluggish, brutal pounding against her skin and inside her body eventually began to die down. But the quake's effects were still going on around her, and would take much more time to settle. Sonar was nearly drowned; Nita was floating blind in the blackness. *This is the pits!* she thought in anguish, and concentrated everything she had on one good burst of sound that would cut through the terrible noise and tell her what was going on.

The echoes that came back reassured her somewhat. All the Celebrants were still fairly close together, safe within the light of the pressure-protection spell. Kit was farther ahead than he had been, fighting for control and slowly finding it. Others, S'reee and Fang and Areinnye, were closer to Nita. And there was other movement close to them—large objects drifting downward, slowly, resonating with the same note, though in higher octaves, as the towering cliff sides. Massive objects, said the echo. *Solid* massive objects. Falling faster now. One of them falling past S'reee and down toward Areinnye, who was twisting and struggling against the turmoil of the water for balance—

Warn her! was Nita's first thought, but even as she let out another cry, she realized it was useless—Areinnye would have no time to react. The falling rock, a piece of cliff shelf nearly as long as a city block, was practically on top of her. *Shield spell*, Nita thought then. Impossible—

She did it anyway. It was an old friend, that spell, long since learned by heart. When activated, punches, or any physical object thrown at one, slid right off it. Running them together in her haste, she sang the nine syllables of the spell that were always the same, then added four more that set new coordinates for the spell, another three that specified how much mass the shield would have to repel—tons and tons! Oh, Lord!—and then the last syllable that turned the wizardry loose. She felt the magic fall away from her like a weight on a cord, dropping toward Areinnye. *Nothing to do now but hang on*, she thought, letting herself float. Faintly, through the thunder, the echoes of her spell brought Nita the shape of Areinnye, still struggling, trying to get out from under the falling rock shelf, and failing. Her connection with the spell brought her the feeling of the massive slab of stone dropping toward it, closer, closer still. Making contact—

—crushing down and down onto her wizardry with force more terrible than she had anticipated. The spell was failing, the shelf was settling down on it and inexorably pressing it closer and closer to Areinnye, who was in turn being forced down against the battering of the shock waves, toward the floor of the canyon. The spell was breaking up, tearing like a rotten net filled with weights. *No*, Nita thought, and strained, pouring all her concentration, all her will, down the connection to the spell. *No!* It was like hanging on to a rope in a tug-of-war, and losing, and not letting go—digging in, muscles popping out all over, aching, straining, blood pounding, and not letting go—The spell firmed a little. The shelf, settling slowly down and down onto Areinnye, forcing her closer and closer to the bottom, seemed to hesitate. "Kit!" Nita screamed into the water. *I'm gonna lose it. I'm gonna lose it*! "Kit!"

The echo of her yell for help showed her another sperm-whale shape, a larger one than Areinnye's, fighting his way against the battering shock waves and down toward the bottom of the canyon—toward where Areinnye floundered, underneath the stone shelf, underneath the spell. Kit rammed Areinnye head-on, hitting her squarely amidships and punching the smaller sperm whale backward thirty or forty feet. But not out from under the settling shelf; and now Kit was partly under it, too. The spell began sagging again. Nita panicked; she had no time or energy left for any more warnings, any more *anything*. She threw herself so totally into the spell that she couldn't feel her body, couldn't hear, couldn't see, finally became nothing but a single, none-too-coherent thought: *No!* But it was no use. The spell was coming undone, the rock was coming down, this time for good. And Kit was under it. *No! No, no, NO—*

And everything went away.

The next thing Nita felt was the shock of a spell being broken by forces too great for it to handle, as the rock shelf came crushing down on it, smashing it flat against something both soft and hard. *"NO!"* Nita screamed again in horror, as the diminishing thunder of the seaquake was briefly augmented by the multiple crashes of the shelf's shattering. The floor of the canyon was obscured even to sonar by a thick fog of rock dust and stirred-up ooze, pierced all through by flying splinters of stone, but Nita dived into it anyway. "Kit!"

"You sang?" came a sperm whale's sharp-edged note from down in the rock-fog, sounding tired but pleased.

Speechless with relief and shaking with effort, Nita pulled up her nose and just let herself float in the trembling water, listening to the rumbling of the quake as it faded away and the songs of the other whales round about as they checked on one another. She became aware of the Master Shark, finning slowly down-canyon not too far from her and favoring her as he went with a look that was prolonged and indecipherable. Nita glided hurriedly away from him, looking around her.

The light of the protection spell showed Nita the roiling of the cloud of ooze and dust in the bottom of the canyon, and the two shapes that swam slowly up through it—first Kit, fluking more strongly than Nita would have believed possible for someone who'd just gone through what they all had, then Areinnye, stroking more weakly, and swimming with a stiffness that made it very plain just how hard

Kit must have hit her. Kit rose to hang beside Nita. More slowly, Areinnye came swimming up to face her.

"There seems to be a life between us, hNii't," the sperm whale said.

The mixture of surprise and anger in Areinnye's song made Nita uncomfortable. "Oh, no," she said, rather weakly. "Kit did it—"

"Oh, dead fish," Kit said. "You held it for a good ten seconds after we were out from under. You would've managed even if I hadn't helped."

"I had incentive," Nita muttered.

Kit looked at her for a moment. "You didn't drop it until Ed nudged you," he said. "You might have gone deaf for a little, or maybe you were in spell overload. But either way, this was your cookie. Don't blame me."

"Silent Lord," Areinnye said—still stiffly formal, but with an uncertain note in her voice, "I thank you. I had hardly given you cause for such an act."

"You gave me plenty of cause," she said wearily. "You took the Oath, didn't you? You're with me. And you're welcome." She took a deep breath, feeling the respiratory part of the protection spell briefly surround her blowholes with a bubble of air for her to inhale. "Kit," she said, "can we get going and get this over with?"

"That is well said," came Ed's voice. He was coming up-canyon again, fast. As Nita looked up she saw him arrow overhead, ghastly pale in the wizard-light, with a trail of darkness billowing thick behind him, and something black in his jaws. It struggled; Ed gulped it down. Inside his gill slits and lower body, Nita could see the swallowed thing give a last couple of convulsive heaves. "And we'd best get on with it—"

Thick, black sucker-tipped arms whipped up from the disturbed ooze on the bottom, grasping, flailing in the light. "Oh, no," Nita moaned. Kit plunged past her, the first note of the scraping sperm-whale battle cry rasping down Nita's skin as he dived for the body to which those arms belonged. Farther down the canyon, almost out of range of the wizard-light, there was a confused boiling together of arms, long dark bodies, flat platterlike yellow eyes glowing with reflected light and wild-beast hunger—not just a few krakens, but a great pack of them. "To business, Silent Lord," Ed said, his voice rich with chilly pleasure, as he swept past Nita again on his way down-canyon.

She went to business. These krakens were bigger than the last ones had been; the smallest one Nita saw had a body the size of a stretch limousine, and arms twice that length. True, there were more toothed whales fighting this time—not only Kit, but Fang and Areinnye as well. And teeth weren't everything—what Aroooon or T!h!ki rammed didn't move afterward.

The Celebrants also had the advantage of being wizards. Nita was terrified at first when she saw one of the krakens come at poor slow Roots—and poor slow Roots raised her voice in a few squeaky little notes and simply blew the giant squid into a cloud of blood and ink and black rags of flesh. But a wizard's strength has limits; such spells could only be worked once or twice. And since a spell has to be directed at what you see, not even the most deadly offensive wizardry does a bit of good against the choking tentacles that you don't notice coming up from behind you. So it was a slow, ugly, bitter battle, that fight in the canyon. Four or five times the Celebrants were assaulted as they made their way down between the dwarfing, twisting walls of stone; four or five times they fought the attackers off, rested briefly, and started out again, knowing that somewhere deeper down, more thick tentacles and hungry eyes waited for them.

"This is your fault!" Areinnye cried angrily at Nita during one or another of the attacks, while Fang and Kit and Ed and Aroooon fought off krakens coming from down-canyon and from above, and S'reee and T!h!ki worked furiously to heal a great sucker welt torn in Areinnye's side before Ed should notice it and turn on her.

Nita simply turned away, in no mood for it. Her face hurt from ramming krakens, she had bruises from their suckers and a stab from one's beak, and she was sick of the smell of blood and the galling sepia taste in the water. The problem, and the only reason Nita didn't answer Areinnye hotly back, was that there might have been some slight truth to the accusation. According to Carl and the manual, the same pollutants that caused cancer in human beings, that had caused the U.S. Fish and Game Service to warn people on the Jersey shore against eating more than one ocean-caught fish a week, were getting concentrated in the squids' bodies, changing their DNA—changing *them*. The food the krakens normally ate at the great depths was dying out, also from the pollution. They had to come up into the shallows to survive. The changes were enabling them to do so. And if it was starving, a hungry kraken would find a whale perfectly acceptable as food.

Nita was startled by the sudden sharpness of S'reee's answering voice. "Areinnye, don't talk nonsense," she said after singing the last note of a spell that sealed the sperm whale's torn flesh. "The krakens are here for the same reason the quake was—because the Lone Power wants them here. We're supposed to use up our air fighting them."

T!h!ki looked soberly at S'reee. "That brings up the question, Ree. *Will* we complete the Song?"

S'reee swung her tail in a shrug, her eyes on Areinnye's healing wound. "I thought such a thing might happen," she said, "after we were attacked the other night. So I brought extra air, more than the group felt it needed. Even so—it'll be close."

"We're a long way down the canyon," Nita said. "Practically down to the plain. If they're all down there, waiting for us—if these attacks have just been to wear us down—"

"I don't think so," T!h!ki said, glancing over at Nita. "Once out into the plain, we'll be practically under the shadow of the Sea's Tooth, close to the ancient site of the Song. And once our circle is set up, they couldn't get in unless we let them."

"Which we won't," S'reee said. "Let's waste no more time. This is going to be the fastest Song on record. —Areinnye, you're done. How do you feel?"

The sperm swayed in the water, testing her healed tail. "Well enough," she said, grim-voiced. "Though not as well as I would if this human were—" And Areinnye broke off. "Pardon me," she said, more slowly. "It was an ill thought. Let me go help K!t now."

She went. "You now," S'reee said to Nita. She sang a few notes to start the healing spell going, then said, "HNii't? Are you all right otherwise?"

The sound of Kit's battle cry came scraping along Nita's skin from down-canyon. "No," she said. Kit had been fighting with a skill and, heaven help him, a relish that Nita would never have suspected in him. *I'm not sure it's the sark doing this*, she thought. *I keep thinking that Kit might actually be this way, down deep.*

Then Nita stopped. *What makes me think it matters one way or another?* she thought. *In a few hours, anything I think about Kit will make no difference at all. But I can't stop acting as if it will. Habit is hard to break . . .*

"If it's something I can help with—," S'reee said, finishing up.

Nita brushed skin with her, an absent gesture. "It's not," she said. And off she went after Areinnye—into the water fouled with stirred-up slime and ink and blood, into the reach of grabbing, sandpapery tentacles and the glare of yellow eyes.

It went on that way for what seemed forever, until Nita was nearly blind from head-on ramming. She gave up on sonar and concentrated on keeping just one more squid occupied until Kit or Ed or Areinnye could deal with it. So, as the walls of the canyon, which had been towering some six thousand feet above the Celebrants on either side, began to decrease in height, she didn't really notice it. Eventually the bitter cold of the water got her attention; and she also realized that the krakens' attacks had stopped. Nita sang a few notes to "see" at a distance, and squinted around her in the sea-green wizard-light to find out where she and the other Celebrants were.

The walls closest to them were still nearly three thousand feet high. But their slope was gentler; and the canyon had widened from some two miles across to nearly five. To left and right of the canyon's foot, curving away northward and southward, miles past sound or sight, stretched the rubble-strewn foothills of the continental shelf. Behind the Celebrants the shelf itself towered, a mighty cliff wall rising to lose itself in darkness. Outward before them, toward the open sea, the terrain was mostly flat, broken only occasionally by hills so shallow they were more like dunes. The rocky bottom was turning to pale sand. But the paleness did nothing to lighten the surroundings. Above it lay an intolerable, crushing weight of water, utterly black, icy cold, weighing down on the soul no matter what spell protected the body. And far out in the blackness could be seen the furtive, erratic movements of tiny lights—eerie points of peculiar-colored fire that jittered and clustered and hung in the cold dark, watching the whales.

Nita took a sharp breath, for some of those lights were definitely eyes. T!h!ki, hanging motionless in the still water beside her, did the same. He was staring down the slope, which sank past the light of the breathing-spell, and far past echo range, dropping farther downward into more darkness. "*Nothing* can be this deep," he sang in an unnerved whisper. "How much farther down can we go?"

"All the way," said another voice from Nita's other side. She turned, not recognizing it—and then knew the speaker very well and was sick inside. Kit hung there, with a fey, frightening look in his eye—a total lack of fear.

Nita swallowed once. Sperm whales took the great dives better than any other whale, coming down this far on purpose to hunt the giant squid; but their boldness also got them in trouble. Numerous sperm-whale skeletons had been found at these depths by exploring bathyscaphes, the whales' tails or bodies hopelessly tangled in undersea telephone or telegraph cables.

"We're a long way up yet," Kit said, with that cool cast to his voice that better suited Areinnye than it did him. "Barely six thousand feet down. We'll have to go down to sixteen thousand feet at least before we see the Sea's Tooth." And he swam off toward the boundaries of the light.

Nita held still for a few moments as S'reee and various other of the Celebrants went slowly after Kit. T!h!ki went, too; she barely noticed him go. *This isn't the Kit I want to say good-bye to.*

Perhaps a hundred feet away from her, Ed glided past, staring at her. "Sprat," he said, "come along."

She did. But the fighting in the canyon had left Nita so fatigued that much of this part of the descent seemed unreal to her, a prolonged version of one of those dreams in which one "falls" downstairs for hours. And there was a terrible sameness about this terrain: a sea of white sand, here and there featuring a darker rock thrust up or thrown down into it, or some artifact more bizarre—occasionally, great pressure-fused lumps of coal; once an actual kitchen sink, just sitting there on the bottom by itself; another time, a lone Coca-Cola bottle standing upright in the sand with a kind of desolate, pitiful pride. But mostly the bottom was as undifferentiated as a mile-wide, glare-lit snowfield, one that pitched forever downward.

Nor was Nita's grasp on reality much helped by the strange creatures that lived in those waters more than a thousand fathoms down. Most everything seemed to be either transparent as a ghost or brilliantly luminous. Long-bodied, lantern-eyed sharks swam curiously about Nita, paid brief homage to their Master, and moved on. Anglerfish with their luminous baits hanging on "fish lines" in front of their mouths came up to stare Nita right in the eye and then swam dourly away, disappointed that she was too big to eat. Long, many-segmented bottom worms and vampire squid, sporting dots or stripes of pink or yellow or blue-white light, inched or squirted along the bottom about their affairs, paying no attention to the Celebrants sailing overhead in their nimbus of wizard-light. Rays fluttered, using fleshy wings to rearrange the sand in which they lay buried; tripod fish crutch-walked around the bottom like peg-legged pirates on their long stiff fins. And all the eyes circling in the black water, all the phosphorescent shapes crawling on the bottom or undulating above it were doing one of two things—either looking for food or eating it, in the form of one another.

Nita knew there was no other way for these creatures to live, in this deadly cold, but by the minimum expenditure of energy for the maximum return . . . hence all the baits, traps, hiding. But that didn't affect the dull horror of the scene—the endless crushing dark, the ear-blinding silence, and the pale chilly lights weaving through the space-black water as the creatures of the great depths sought and caught and ate one another with desperate, mindless diligence.

The gruesome power of the besetting horror brought Nita wide awake. She had never been superstitious; shadows in the bedroom had never bothered her when she was little, and she found horror movies fun to watch. But now she started to feel more hemmed in, more watched and trapped, than she suspected she'd feel in any haunted house. "Ed," she sang, low as a whisper, to the pale shape that paced her, "what *is* it? There's something down here . . ."

"Indeed there is. We are getting close."

She would have asked, *To what?* but as she looked down the interminable slope at the other Celebrants—who were mostly swimming gathered close together, as if they felt what she felt—something occurred to her, something so obvious that she felt like a moron for not having thought of it before. "Ed—if this is the Song of the Twelve, how come there are only eleven of us singing?!"

"The Twelfth is here," Ed said. "As the Song says, the Lone Power lies bound here, in the depths below the depths. And It will sing Its part, as It always has. It cannot help it. Indeed, It wants to sing. In the temptation and subversion of the Celebrants lies Its only hope of escape from the wizardry that binds It."

"And if It succeeds—"

"Afállonë," Ed said. "Atlantis, all over again. Or worse."

"*Worse*—" Then she noticed something else. "Ed, the water's getting warmer!"

"And the bottom is changing," Ed said. "Gather your wits, Sprat. A few hundred more lengths and we are there."

The white sand was giving way to some kind of darker stuff. At first Nita thought she was looking at the naked rock of the sea bottom. But this stuff wasn't flat, as sediment would be. It was ropy, piled-up, ridgy-looking black stone. And here and there crystals glittered in it. Scattered around ahead of them were higher piles of the black stone, small, bizarrely shaped hills. Nita sounded a high note to get some sonar back, as the water through which she swam grew warmer and began to taste odd.

The first echoes to return surprised Nita until she started to suspect what they were. Waving frondy shapes, the hard, round echoes from shelled creatures, a peculiar hollowness to the echo that indicated water of lower pressure than that surrounding it—That was a stream of sulfur-laden hot water coming out of an undersea "vent"; the other echoes were the creatures that lived around it, all adapted to take advantage of the oasis of heat and the sulfur that came up with it. And now she understood the black bottom stone—old cooled lava, the kind called pillow lava, that oozes up through the ocean's crust and spreads itself out in flat, ropy piles.

But from past the vent came another echo that was simply impossible. A wall, a rounded wall, at least a mile and a half wide at the base, rising out of the piled black stone and spearing up, and up, and up, and up, so that fragments of the echo kept coming back to Nita for second after second. She back-finned to hold still until all the echoes could come back to her, and in Nita's mind the picture of the massive, fluted, narrowing pillar of stone got taller and taller, until she actually had to sing a soft note or two to deafen herself to it. It was, like the walls of Hudson Canyon, "too big"—only much more so. "Five Empire State Buildings on top of each other," was how Kit had described it—but Empire States a mile wide: Caryn Peak, the Sea's Tooth, the site of the Song of the Twelve.

The whales ahead of Nita were gathering near the foot of the peak. Against that gigantic spear of stone they seemed dwarfed, insignificant. Even Aroooon looked like a toy. And the feeling of being watched, closely, by something of malicious intent, was getting stronger by the second.

She joined the others. The Celebrants were poised not too far from the open vent—evidently S'reee preferred the warmer water—in clear view of the strange creatures living about it: the twelve-foot stalks of the tube worms, the great blind crabs, the colonies of giant bloodred clams, opening and closing their fringed shells with mindless regularity. *No coral*, Nita thought absently, looking around her. But she wouldn't need any. Several hundred feet away, there on the face of the peak, were several shattered outcroppings of stone. The outcroppings were sharp as glass knives. *Those should do it*, Nita thought. *So sharp I'll hardly feel anything—until Ed arrives . . .*

"If you're all prepared," S'reee sang, her voice wavering strangely where notes had to travel suddenly from cold water to hot, "I suggest we start right now."

The Celebrants chorused muted agreement and began to spread out, forming the circle with which the Song begins. Nita took her place between Fang and T!h!ki, while S'reee went to the heart of the circle. Ed swam away, toward the far side of the peak and out of sight. Kit glided away from the circle, off behind Nita. She looked back at him. He found the spot from which he would watch and gazed back at her. Nita swallowed one last time, hard. There was very little of her friend in that look. "Kit—," she said, on one low note.

"Silent Lord," he said.

And though it was his voice, it wasn't Kit . . .

Nita turned away, sick at heart, and faced inward toward the circle again; and S'reee lifted up her voice and sang the Invocation.

"Blood in the water I sing,
    and one who shed it:
deadliest hunger I sing,
    and one who fed it—
weaving the ancient-most tale
    of the Sea's sending:
singing the tragedy,
    singing the joy unending.

"This is our shame—
    this is the whole Ocean's glory:
this is the Song of the Twelve.
    Hark to the story!
Hearken, and bring it to pass:
    swift, lest the sorrow
long ago laid to its rest
    devour us tomorrow!"

And so it began, as in song S'reee laid out the foundations of the story, which began before lives learned to end in resistance and suffering. One by one the Celebrants drew together, closing up the circle, named themselves to one another, and began to discuss the problem of running the Sea to everyone's advantage. Chief among their problems at the moment was the sudden appearance of a new whale. It was puzzling; the Sea had given them no warning, as She had in times past, that this was about to happen. But they were the Ni'hwinyii, the Lords of the Humors, and they would comport themselves as such. They would decide the question for themselves. Under whose Mastery would the Stranger fall? . . .

Nita, who had backed out of the circle after the Invocation, hung shivering in the currentless water as the Song shook the warm darkness about her. Part of what she felt was the same kind of trembling with excitement she had felt a hundred times in school when she knew she was about to be called on. *I'm ready*, she thought, trying to quiet herself. *This is silly. I know my part backward and forward—there's not that much of it. I'll do all right.*

. . . But there was also something else going on. She had felt it start with the Invocation and grow stronger with every passing second—that sense of something waking up, something rousing from sleepy malice, awakening to active, alert malevolence. It waits, Ed had said. It was a certainty, as sure as looking up toward a lighted window and seeing the person who's been staring at you drop the curtain and turn away.

She wrenched her attention back to the Blue, who was at the end of one of his long stately passages. But it was hard.

"—Nay, slowly, Sounder. Slow is the wise whale's song,
and wise as slow; for he who hastens errs,
who errs learns grief. And not the Master Shark
has teeth as fierce: grief eats its prey alive,
and pain grows greater as the grief devours,
not less. So let this Stranger sing his peace:
what he desires of us; there's Sea enough and time
to hear him, though he sing the darkened Moon
to full and back again. Ay, let him speak. . . ."

And to Nita's shock and fascinated horror, an answer came. The voice that raised itself in the stillness of the great depths was the sonic equivalent of the thing one sees out the corner of one's eye, then turns to find gone, or imagined. It did not shake the water; it roused no echoes. And Nita was not alone in hearing it. She saw the encircled Celebrants look uneasily at one another. On the far side of the circle, Kit's coolness was suddenly broken, and he stared at Nita like someone believing a myth for the first time. The innocent, gentle-spoken, unselfconscious evil in the new voice was terrifying. "With Pow'rs and Dominations need I speak," sang that timbreless voice in quiet sincerity,

"the ancient Lords who hold the Sea in sway.
I pray thee, Lords of the Humors, hear me now,
last, least and poorest of the new-made whales,
new-loos'd from out the Sea's great silent Heart.
No Lord have I; therefore to ye I come,
beseeching low thy counsel and thy rule
for one that's homeless, lawless, mateless, lost. . . ."

"Who art thou, then, that speak'st?" sang S'reee, beginning the Singer's questioning. At the end of her verse she was answered, in more soft-spoken, reasonable platitudes—words meant to lull the unwary and deceive the alert. And questions and answers continued, until Nita realized that there had been a shift. Rather than the Singer asking the Stranger what he wanted, the Stranger was telling the Singer what he knew *she* wanted—and could offer her, if only she would take the unspecified Gift he would give her.

Nita began shaking steadily now, and not from the cold. The insinuating power of that not-quite-voice somehow frightened her worse than head-on conflict with the Lone Power had, a couple of months ago. There the Power had been easily seen in its true colors. But here it was hidden and speaking as matter-of-factly as the voices in the back of one's own mind, whose advice one so often tends to follow without question. "Your Mastery is hollow," said the voice to S'reee,

—"cold song, strict-ruled by law. From such bland rule
come no great musics. Singer, follow me,
accept my Gift and what it brings, and song
shall truly have no Master save for you.
My gift will teach you lyric that will break
the heart that hears it; every seaborne voice
will curse your newfound art, and wish that art
its own. Take up the Gift, O foremost
Singer. . . ."

Nita glanced over at S'reee. She was trembling nearly as hard as Nita was, caught in the force of the temptation. S'reee sang her refusal calmly enough; but Nita found herself wondering how much of that refusal was the ritual's and how much S'reee's own.

She began watching the other Celebrants with as much care. Iniihwit sang the Gazer's questioning and rejection with the outward attitude of mild unconcern that Nita had in their brief acquaintance come to associate with him. Aroooon's refusal of the prize offered the Blue by the Stranger, that of power over all the other whales, was more emphatic, though it came in his usual rich, leisurely manner. He sang not as if making ritual responses, but as if he rejected someone who swam in the circle with him and dared him to do something about it.

After that, the unheard voice sounded less certain of itself, and also impatient. The Song passed on to what would for the Lone Power be more successful ground: the Wanderer and the Killer and the Forager, all of whom would succumb to the Stranger's temptations and become the Betrayed—those species of whales and fish to whom death would later come most frequently and most quickly. One by one Roots and Fang and Hotshot sang with the Lone One, were tempted, and in the place of the original Masters, fell. Nita tried to keep herself calm, but had trouble doing it; for each time one of the Celebrants gave in to the Lone One's persuasion, she felt the voice grow a little more pleased with itself, a little more assured—as if something were finally going according to plan.

Nita stared across at Kit. He traded looks with her and began to make his way around the circle toward her.

The Lone One was working on the last three whales in the circle now, the ones who would become the Undecided. Their parts were the most difficult, being not only the longest sung passages but also the most complex. The Undecided argued with the Lone Power much more than did the Untouched, who tended to refuse quickly, or the Betrayed, who gave in without much fighting. Fluke sang first, the Sounder's part; and strain began to show as the Power offered him all the hidden knowledge of the great deeps, and the Sounder's song went from smooth-flowing melodies to rumbles and scrapes of tortured indecision. *Not all that carrying on is in the Song*, Nita thought nervously. *What's happening?* And indeed, though the Sounder finished his passage and turned away, ostensibly to think about what the Lone Power had said to him, Nita could see that Fluke looked pallid and shaken as a whale that's sick.

The Listener fared no better. T!h!ki sang steadily enough to begin with; but when the voiceless voice offered him the power to hear everything that transpired in the Sea, from the random thoughts of new-hatched fry to the secret ponderings of the continental plates, he hesitated much too long—so long that Nita saw S'reee look at him in surprise and almost speak up to prompt him. It was bizarre; in rehearsals T!h!ki had had the best memory of any of them. He finished his verses looking troubled and seemed relieved to turn away.

It's what S'reee said, very early on, Nita thought. The whales picked have to be close in temperament to the original Celebrants—loving the same kinds of things. But it makes them vulnerable to the temptations, too.

And then Areinnye began to sing, questioning the Power in her disturbingly sweet voice, asking and answering. She showed no sign of the unease that had troubled the others. Nita glanced over at Kit, who had managed by this time to work his way fairly close to her; he swung his tail a fraction, a whale's version of a worried head-shake. Areinnye's singing was polished, superb, her manner poised, unruffled, royal. She sang her initial rebuff with the harsh certainty the Gray Lord's song called for.

"Stranger, no more—   give me no gift.
Power am I,   fear in the water
as my foes flee.   I need no boon.
In the Below   all bow before me.
Speak not to me.   Speak not of gifts."

The voice that answered her was as sweet and poised as her own.

"And do you then desire no gift of mine—
you who have lost so much? Ah no: you have
strength of your own indeed—great strength of
fluke, of fin; fear goes before your face.
But sorrow follows after. What use strength
when slaughtered children rot beneath the waves,
when the sweet mouth that you gave suck is gone,
rent to red tatters by the flensing knives;
and when the second heart that beat by yours
lies ground for dogs' meat in a whaler's hull?
Gray One, accept my Gift and learn of strength—"

That's not in the Song!
Nita stared in shock at Kit, then at the other Celebrants—who, all but Areinnye, were trading horrified looks. The sperm whale held very still, her eyes turned outward from the circle; and she shook as violently as Fluke had or, for that matter, Nita. The Lone Power sang on:

"—learn power! Learn how wizardry may turn
to serve your purpose, sinking the whalers deep,
taking the brute invaders' lives to pay
for that small life that swims the Sea no more;
take up my Gift—"

"There is—there is another life," Areinnye sang, trembling now as if storm waters battered at her, breaking the continuity of the Song. "Saved—she saved—"

"—what matter? As if brutes who fear the Sea
are capable of thought, much less of love!
Even a shark by accident may save
a life—then turn and tear the newly saved!
Take up my Gift and take a life for life,
as it was done of old—"

Slowly Areinnye turned, and the glitter of the wizard-light in her eyes as she looked at Nita was horrible to see. "Life," she sang, one low, thick, struggling note—

She leaped at Nita. In that second Fang, on her left, arrowed in front of Areinnye, punching her jaws away from Nita in time for Nita to roll out of their way. But Fang didn't recover from the blow in time to flee himself; Areinnye's head swept around and the great teeth of her upper jaw raked frightful gashes down Fang's side. Nita pulled herself out of her roll just in time to see something else hit Areinnye—Kit's huge bulk, slamming into her with such force that she was knocked straight into the side of Caryn Peak. She screamed; the water brought back echoes of the sickening sound of her impact. And then she was fleeing—out of the wizard-light, past the boundaries of the protective spell, out into the darkness past the peak.

The Celebrants stirred about in terrible confusion, while S'reee hurried to Fang's side and examined him. Nita stroked over quickly and brushed Fang's good side, very lightly. One of those merry eyes, now slightly less merry, managed to focus on her. "We need you—Silent One," Fang said.

"We do," S'reee said. "These wounds aren't deep, but they're bleeding a lot— and the Master Shark's about. I've got to handle this. Meanwhile, we're shy the Gray Lord—and I don't think she's going to come back and take back what she said. Kit, are you willing?"

Nita looked swiftly behind her. Kit was hanging there, looking down at Fang. "I'd better be," he said.

"Good. HNii't, administer him the Celebrant's Oath. And hurry." S'reee turned away from them and began one of the faster healing spells.

"Kit, are you sure—"

"Get going," he said.

She led him through the Oath. He said it almost as quickly as Hotshot had, tripping in only one place: ". . . and I shall weave my voice and my will and my blood with theirs if there be need . . ." He was looking at Nita as he said that, and the look went right through her like a spear.

"Done," S'reee said. "Fang, mind that side—the repair is temporary. —Swiftly, now. Everyone circle, we can't afford a delay. Kit, from 'No, I must think—' "

They sang. And if the Song had been frightening before, it was becoming frantic now. Underneath them all the Celebrants could feel some malicious force straining to get free—

Nita watched Kit closely. *He didn't rehearse any of this stuff*, she thought. *What if he slips?* But Kit sang what remained of the Gray Lord's part faultlessly; he had laid himself wide open to the Sea and was being fed words and music directly. Nita felt a lump in her throat—that reaction humans shared with whales—

at the perfect clarity of his voice. But she couldn't stop worrying. *If he's this open to the Sea, he's also open to that Other—*

And that Other was working on him. Kit was beginning to tremble as the second part of the Gray Lord's rebuff came to an end. The soundless voice, when it spoke for the last time, was all sweet reason:

"—strength is no use. Give over the vain strife
that saves no one, keeps no old friend alive,
condemns the dear to death. Take but my Gift
and know long years that end not, slow-burnt days
under the Sun and Moon; not for yourself
alone, but for the other—"

"No," Nita said—a mere whisper of song.

Kit looked at her from the heart of the circle, shaking. In his eyes and the way he held his body Nita read how easy it would be for him to desert the Song after just these few lines, destroy it, knowing that Nita would escape alive. Here was the out he had been looking for.

"No!" she tried to say again, but something was stopping her. The malice in the water grew, burning her. Kit wavered, looking at her—

—then closed his eyes and took a great breath of air from the spell, and began singing again—his voice anguished, but still determined. He finished the last verse of the Gray Lord's rebuff on a note that was mostly a squeak, and immediately turned to S'reee, for the next part would be the group singing—the battle.

S'reee lifted her head for the secondary Invocation.

The ocean floor began to shake. And Nita suddenly realized that it wasn't just the Lone Power's malice burning all around her. The water was heating up.

"Oh, Sea about us, no!" S'reee cried. "What now?"

"Sing!" came a great voice from above them. Aroooon had lifted out of the circle, was looking into the darkness, past the great pillar of Caryn Peak. "For your lives, sing! Forget the battle! HNii't, quickly!"

She knew what he wanted. Nita took one last great gulp of breath, tasting it as she had never tasted anything in her life, and fluked upward out of the circle herself, locating one of the sharp outcroppings she had noticed earlier. A flash of ghostly white in the background— *Good*, she thought. *Ed's close.* "Sea, hear me now," she sang in a great voice, "and take my words and make them ever law—"

"Nitaaaaaa!"

"HNii't, look out!"

The two cries came from opposite directions. She was glancing toward Kit, one last look, when something with suckered arms grabbed her by the tail and pulled her down.

The moments that followed turned into a nightmare of thrashing and bellowing, arms that whipped at her, clung to her, dragging her inexorably toward the place where they joined and the wicked beak waited. *No one is coming to help me*, Nita realized, as she looked down into that sucking mouth. The water was full of screams; and two of the voices she heard were those of sperm whales. *Two—* She thrashed harder, getting a view as she did so of S'reee fleeing before a great gray shape with open jaws—Areinnye; and coming behind Areinnye, a flood of black shapes, bigger than any the Celebrants had had to handle in Hudson Canyon.

She's sold out, Nita thought miserably. *She's gone over to the Lone One. She came back and broke the circle, and let the krakens in, and everything's going to go to hell if I don't*— Nita swung her head desperately and hit the kraken with it, felt baleen plates in her mouth crack, felt the kraken shudder. *Let go of me, you disgusting thing!* Nita was past working any wizardry but one. Brute force was going to have to do it. *Let go!* She slammed her head into the kraken again, sideways. It let out a shrill painful whoop that was very satisfying to her. *Your eye's sensitive, huh?* she thought. *One more time!*

She hit it again. Something soft gave under the blow, and the kraken screamed. Nita tore free of the loosening arms and swam upward, hard and fast, heading for her sharp outcropping. The whole area around the base of Caryn Peak was boiling with kraken, with Celebrants fighting them and trying desperately not to be dragged out of the boundaries of the protective spell. The bottom was shuddering harder; hot water was shimmering faster and faster out of the vent. *It's got to be stopped*, Nita thought. "Kit," she called, looking around hurriedly. *There's just time enough to say good-bye.*

Two things she saw. One was that ghostly white shape soaring close by, bolting down the rear half of a kraken about the size of a van and gazing down at her as it passed by.

The other was Kit, turning away from a long, vicious slash he had just torn down Areinnye's side—looking up at Nita and singing one note of heart-tearing misery—not in the Speech—not in the human-flavored whale he had always spoken before—but in pure whale.

Oh, no. He's lost language! Nita's heart seized. S'reee had said that if that happened, the whalesark was about to be rejected by Kit's brain. Unless something was done, it would leave him human again, naked in the cold, three miles down.

That thought, and the echoes of Kit's cry of anguish, suddenly meant more to Nita than any abstract idea of ten million deaths. And in that second Nita came to understand what Carl had been talking about. She wheeled around and stared at the outcropping—then *chose* to do, willingly, what she had thought she'd no choice but to do. The triumph that instantly flared up in her made no sense: But she wouldn't have traded it for any feeling more sensible. She turned and fluked with all her might and threw herself at the stony knives of the peak—and hit—

—something, not stone, and reeled away from the blow, stunned and confused. Something had punched her in the side. Tumbling over and over with the force of the blow and the ever-increasing shock waves blasting up from the shuddering bottom, Nita saw that great white shape again—but much closer, soaring backward with her as she tumbled. "Silent One," he said, "before you do what you must—give me your power!"

"What?"

"Only trust me! Give it to me—and be quick!"

Nita could hardly react to the outrageous demand. Only with Kit had she ever dared do such a thing. To give Ed all her power would leave her empty of it, defenseless, until he finished whatever he wanted to do with it. Which could be hours—or forever. And he wasn't even a wizard—

"Nita, *swiftly!*"

"But Ed, I need it for the Sacrifice. What do you want it for?!"

"To call for help!" Ed hissed, arching away through the water toward Areinnye and Kit, who was still fighting feebly to keep her busy and away from Nita. "Sprat, be quick and choose, or it will be too late!"

He dove at Areinnye, punched Kit out of harm's way, and took a great crater of a bite out of Areinnye's unprotected flank.

Areinnye's head snapped up and around, slashing at Ed sideways. He avoided her, circled in again. "Nita!"

To call for help— What help? And even for Ed, to give up her power, the thing that was keeping her safe and was also the most inside part of her—

Read the fine print before you sign, said a scratchy voice in her memory. *Do what the knight tells you. And don't be afraid to give yourself away!*

"Ed," Nita sang at the bloody comet hurtling through the water, "take it!" And then she cried the three words that she had never spoken to anyone but Kit, the most dangerous words in the Speech, which release one's whole power to another. She felt the power run from her like blood from a wound. She felt Ed acquire it and demand more as he turned it toward the beginning of some ferocious inner calling. And then, when she felt as empty as a shell, Ed shook himself and dived toward the lava again, driving Areinnye away from Kit.

Areinnye refused to be driven. Swiftly she turned and her fangs found Ed's side, scoring a long, deep gash from gills to tail. The Master Shark swept away from Areinnye, his wound trailing a horrid boiling curtain of black blood-smoke in the failing wizard-light.

Nita flailed and gasped with exertion—and got air from the protective spell, much to her surprise. She was still in whaleshape. *And stuck in it, I bet,* she thought, *till I get the power back. What in the world's Ed doing?*

The sea bottom around the vent suddenly *heaved*—lifting like some great dark creature taking its first breath . . . then heaved again, bulging up, with cracks spreading outward from the center of the bulge. The cracks, or something beneath them, glowed red-hot.

The seafloor thundered with another tremor. Superheated water blasted up from the remains of the vent; rocks rained down from Caryn Peak. The red glow burst up through the widening cracks. It was lava, burning a feverish, suppurating red through the murk and the violently shimmering water. The water that came in contact with it—unable to boil at these pressures, regardless of the heat applied to it—did the impossible, the only thing it could do: It burst into flame. Small tongues of blue-violet fire danced and snaked along the outward-reaching tentacles of lava.

The wizard-light remaining in the water was a failing, sickly mist. Caryn Peak shook on its foundations. The Celebrants were scattered. Nita swam desperately upward, trying to do what she saw Kit doing—get safe above the roasting heat of the seafloor. All the bottom between her and the peak was a maze-work of lava-filled cracks, broken stone floating on the lava, and violet fire.

Under the stone, under the lava, in the depths of the great crack that had swallowed the vent, something *moved*. Something began to shrug the stone and lava aside. A long shape shook itself, stretched itself, swelled and shrank and swelled again—a shape clothed in lava and black-violet fire, burning terribly. Nita watched in horrified fascination. *What is it?* Nita wondered. *Some kind of buried pipeline?* But no man-made pipeline was a hundred feet across. And no pipeline would seem to breathe, or move by itself, or rear up serpentlike out of the disintegrating seabed with the dreadful energy of something unbound at last.

That shape was rising now, letting go its grasp on part of that long burning body that stretched away as far as the eye could see from east to west. *A neck*, Nita thought, as the shape reared up taller, towering over the sea bottom. A neck and a head— A huge snake's head, fringed, fanged, long and sleek, with dark-burning lava for a hide, and eyes the sick black-violet of water bursting into flame—

In the guise It had first worn after betraying the whales, and wore now again in gloating token of another victory, the Power, the many-named darkness that men had sometimes called the Old Serpent, towered over the seabed as the binding that had held It shattered. *This*, Nita realized, *was the terrible truth concealed under the old myths of the Serpent that lay coiled about the foundations of the world, waiting for the day It would crush the world in those coils.*

And now Its moment was at hand: But It was stretching it, savoring it. It looked at Nita, drifting not two hundred feet from Its immense stony jaws—looked at her out of eyes burning with a color that would sear its way into the nightmares of anyone surviving to remember it. And those eyes *knew* her.

She was frightened; but she had something to do yet. *I know my verse now without having to get it from the Sea*, she thought. *So maybe I won't need wizardry to pull this off. And maybe just doing the Sacrifice will have its own power. Let's find out . . .*

Nita back-finned through the thundering water, staying out of reach of those jaws, watching for any sudden movement. She drew what she suspected was a last breath—the protective spell around her was fading fast—and lifted her voice into the roaring darkness. *Ed*, she thought, *don't blow it now!*

"Must I accept the barren Gift?
   —learn death, and lose my Mastery?
Then let them know whose blood and breath
   will take the Gift and set them free!—"

The gloating eyes were fixed on her—letting her sing, letting Nita make the attempt. But the Lone Power wasn't going to let her get away with it. That huge, hideous head was bending closer to her. Nita back-finned, not too obviously, she hoped—kept her distance, kept on singing:

"Not old enough to love as yet,
   but old enough to die, indeed—
the death-fear bites my throat and heart,
   fanged cousin to the Pale One's breed—"

And with a low thick rumble of amusement and hunger, the Serpent's head thrust at Nita in a strike that she couldn't prevent.

This is it!

The sudden small shock in the water made her heart pound. She glanced downward as she sang. There was Kit—battered and struggling with the failing whalesark as if it were actually someone else's body—but ramming the Serpent head-on, near where the neck towered up above the slowly squeezing coils. Their pressure was breaking the seabed in great pieces, so that lava and superheated water gushed up in a hundred places. But Kit ignored the heat and rammed the Old Serpent again and again. *He's trying to distract It*, Nita thought, in a terrible uprush of anguish and admiration. *He's buying me time. Oh, Kit!* The gift was too precious to waste. "But past the fear lies life for them," she sang,

> "—perhaps for me; and, past my dread,
>   past loss of Mastery and life,
> the Sea shall yet give up Her dead!"

Annoyed—as a human might be by a gnat—the Serpent bent Its head away from Nita to see what was troubling It. Humor and hunger glinted in Its eyes as It recognized in Kit the other wizard who had once given It so much trouble in Manhattan. It bent Its head to him, but slowly, wanting him to savor the terror. *Now*, Nita thought, and began to sing again. "Lone Power—"

"No!" cried another voice through the water, and something came hurtling at her and punched Nita to one side. It was Areinnye—wounded, and crazy, from the looks of her. *I don't have time for this!* Nita thought, and for the first time in her life rummaged around in her mind for a spell that would kill.

Someone else came streaking in to ram. Areinnye went flying. There was blood in the water: Ed's, pumping more and more weakly from the gash in his side. But his eyes were as cool as ever. "Ed," Nita said, breaking off her singing, "thank you—"

He stared at her as he arrowed toward her—the old indecipherable look. "Sprat," he said, "when did I ever leave distress uncured?" And to her complete amazement, before Nita could move, he rammed her again, close to the head—leaving her too stunned to sing, tumbling and helpless in pain.

Through the ache she heard Ed lift his voice in song. *Nita's* song—the lines that, with the offered Sacrifice, bind Death anew and put the Lone Power in Its place. Kit just went on pummeling at the great shape that bent closer and closer to them all, and Nita struggled and writhed and couldn't make a sound.

No! she thought. But it was no use. Ed was taking her part willingly, circling in on the Lone Power. Yet even through Nita's horror, some wonder intruded. *Where did he get such a voice?* she thought. It seemed to fill the whole Sea.

> "Lone Power, I accept your Gift!
>   But take my Gift of equal worth:
> I take Death with me, out of time,
>   and make of it a path, a birth!
>
> "Let the teeth come! As they tear me,
>   they tear your ancient hate for aye—
> so rage, proud Power! Fail again,
>   and see my blood teach Death to die!"

And the Master Shark dived straight at the upraised neck of the Serpent, and bit it. He made no cry as Its burning hide blasted his teeth away and seared his mouth instantly black; he made no cry as the Lone Power, enraged at Its wounding, bent down to pluck the annoying little creature from Its neck and crush it in stony jaws.

And then the sharks came.

Calling for help, Ed had said. Now Nita remembered what he had said to her so long ago, on the only way he had to call his people together . . . with blood: his own. Her wizardry, though, had lent the call power that even Ed's own Mastery could never have achieved, just as it had lent him a whale-wizard's power of song. And brought impossible distances by its power, the Master Shark's people came— by dozens, by hundreds, by thousands and tens of thousands. Maddened by the blood in the water, they fell on everything that had a wound and tore it to shreds.

Nita found that she could swim again, and she did, fast—away from there, where all the sharks of the world, it seemed, jostled and boiled in feeding frenzy. Areinnye vanished in a cloud of sleek silver bodies. Ed could not be seen. And the Serpent—

A scream of astonishment and pain crashed through the water. The Lone Power, like all the other Powers, had to obey the rules when within a universe and wear a body that could be acted upon. The sharks—wild with their Master's blood and beyond feeling pain—were acting upon it. The taste of Its scalding blood in the water, and their own, drove them mad for more. They found more. The screaming went on, and on, and on, all up and down the length of the thrashing, writhing Serpent. Nita, deafened, writhing herself, felt as if it would go on forever.

Eventually forever ended. The sharks, great and small, began milling slowly about, cruising for new game, finding none. They began to disperse.

Of the Master Shark, of Areinnye, there was no sign; only a roiling cloud of red that every now and then snowed little rags of flesh.

Of the Lone Power, nothing remained but sluggishly flowing lava running over a quieting seabed, and in the water the hot sulfurous taste, much diluted, of Its flaming blood. The writhing shape now defined on the bottom by cooling pillow lava made it plain that the Unbound was bound once more by the blood of a willing victim, a wizard—no matter that the wizardry was borrowed.

Aching all over, impossibly tired, Nita hung there for several minutes, simply not knowing what to do. She hadn't planned to live this long.

Now, though: "Kit?"

Her cry brought her back the echo of a sperm whale heading for the surface as quickly as was safe. She followed him.

Nita passed through the "twilight zone" at three hundred fathoms and saw light, the faint green gold she had never hoped to see again. When she broke surface and drew several long, gasping breaths, she found that it was morning. Monday morning, she guessed, or hoped. It didn't much matter. She had sunlight again; she had air to breathe—and floating half a mile away in the wave-wash, looking too tired to move a fin, the massive back of a sperm whale bobbed and rocked.

She went to him. Neither of them did anything for a long time but lie there in the water, side by side, skin just touching, and breathe.

"I got carried away down there," Kit said eventually. "And the whalesark started to go out on me. I would have gone all sperm whale—and then the sark would have blown out all the way—"

"I noticed," Nita said.

"And you pulled me out of it. I think I owe you one."

"After all that," Nita said, "I'm not sure who owes what. Maybe we'd better call it even."

"Yeah. But, Neets—"

"Don't mention it," she said. "Someone has to keep you out of trouble."

He blew explosively, right in her face.

One by one, finding one another by song, the other Celebrants began to gather around them. Neither Kit nor Nita had any words for them until, last of the group, S'reee surfaced and blew in utter weariness.

She looked at Nita. "Areinnye—"

"Gone," Kit said.

"And the Master Shark—"

"The Sacrifice," Nita said, "was accepted."

There was silence as the Celebrants looked at each other. "Well," S'reee said, "the Sea has definitely never seen a Song quite like this—"

It will be a Song well sung, said a cool voice in Nita's head. *And sung from the heart. You, young and never loving: I, old and never loved—*

"—but the Lone One is bound. And the waters are quieting."

"S'reee," Fang said, "don't we still need to finish the Song?"

"It's *done*," Kit said.

S'reee looked at him in silence a moment. "Yes," she said then. "It is."

"And I want to go home," Kit said.

"Well enough," said S'reee. "K!t, we'll be in these waters resting for at least a couple of days. You know where to find us." She paused, hunting words. "And, look—"

"Please save it," Nita said, as gently as she could. She nudged Kit in the side; he turned shoreward for the long swim home. "We'll see you later."

They went home.

They found Nita's parents waiting for them on the beach, as if they had known where and when they would be arriving. Nita found it difficult to care. She and Kit slogged their way up out of the surf, into the towels that Nita's mom and dad held out for them, and stood there shivering with reaction and early-morning cold for several moments.

"Is it going to be all right?" Nita's father asked.

Nita nodded.

"Are *you* all right?" Nita's mother asked, holding her tight.

Nita looked up at her mom and saw no reason to start lying then. "No."

". . . OK," her mother said. "The questions can wait. Let's get you home."

"OK," Kit said. "And you can ask *her* all the questions you like . . . while *I* eat."

Nita turned around then; gave Kit a long look . . . and reached out, and hugged him hard.

She didn't answer questions when she got home. She did eat; and then she went to her room and fell onto her bed, as Kit had done in his room across the hall, to get some sleep. But before she dropped off, Nita pulled her manual out from its spot under her pillow and opened it to one of the general data supply areas. "I want a readout on all the blank-check wizardries done in this area in the last six months," she said. "And what their results were."

The list came up. It was short, as she'd known it would be. The second-to-last entry on the list said:

> BCX 85/003—CALLAHAN, Juanita T., and
>   RODRIGUEZ, Christopher K.:
>   open-ended Möbius spell
>   implementation. Incurred:
>   5/25/85. Paid: 7/15/85, by
>   willing substitution. See
>   "Current Events" précis for
>   details.

Nita put the book back under her pillow, and quietly, bitterly, started to get caught up on her crying.

Heartsong

NEITHER SHE NOR KIT got up till well after nightfall. When Nita threw clothes on and went downstairs, she found Kit sitting at the table, shoveling Cheerios into his face with the singleminded intensity he gave to the really important things in life. In the living room, she could hear the TV going, making crowd sounds, over which her mother was saying indignantly, "Him? *He's* no hitter! Just you watch—"

Kit looked up at Nita as she leaned on the doorsill. "You hungry?"

"Not yet."

She sat down beside him, carefully—she still ached all over—and picked up the cereal box, absently reading the list of ingredients on the side.

"Business as usual in there," Kit said, between mouthfuls.

"So I hear."

"I'm going out in a while. Wanna come?"

"Swimming?"

"Yeah." He paused for another mouthful. "I've got to take the whalesark back."

"Does it still work?"

"At this point," Kit said, "I'd almost rather not get into it and find out. But it got me back."

Nita nodded, put the cereal box down, and just sat for a moment with her chin in her hands. "I had a thought—"

"Nooooooo."

Nita looked brief murder at Kit, then let the look go. "We seem to have pulled it off again," she said.

"Yeah."

He said it almost a little too easily. "You notice," she said, "that our reward for hard jobs seems to be that we get given *harder* jobs, even?"

Kit thought, then nodded. "Problem is," he said, "that we *like* the hard jobs."

She made a sour face. Much as it annoyed her to admit it—her, little quiet Nita who sat in the back of the class and made decent grades and no waves—it was true. "Kit," she said, "they're gonna keep doing that."

" 'They.' "

"The Powers. They'll keep doing it until one day we *don't* pull it off. One of us, or both of us."

Kit looked down at his cereal bowl. "Both, preferably," he said.

She stared at him.

"Saves the explanations." He scooped out the last spoonful of cereal, glanced up, and made a face. "Well, what *would* I have told them?"

Nita shook her head. "We could stop," she said.

Kit chewed, watching her, swallowed, and said, "You want to?"

She waited to see if he would give some sign of what he was thinking. Useless: Kit would make a great poker player someday. "No," she said at last.

"Me, either," Kit said, getting up and putting the bowl in the sink. "Looks like we're stuck with being wizards, huh?"

Very slowly, she smiled at him. "Yeah."

"Then let's go down to the water and let them applaud."

Kit gave the screen door a good-natured kick and went pounding down the stairs. Nita shook her head, still smiling, and followed.

It was late. The moon was now a day past full, and about halfway up the sky; its light was so bright the sky couldn't even manage to be totally black. The stars hung glittering in a sky more indigo, or midnight blue. Nita and Kit walked out into the surf, feeling the wind on them and hearing something most unusual—the sound of whales basking on the surface, some miles out, and singing where they lay. It was, as it had been on first hearing, a high, wild, lovely sound; but now the songs brought something extra, a catch at the heart that hadn't been there before— sorrow, and loss, and wonder. *Oh, Ed*, Nita thought, and sighed, remembering the glory of how he had sounded at the last. *I'm gonna miss you . . .*

Nita swam out far enough to take whaleshape, then took Kit in tow until they made it to water deep enough for a sperm whale. He changed. Side by side they swam outward into the singing, through a sea illumined in a strange green-blue radiance, moonlight diffused and reflected. Dark shapes came to meet them; all the Celebrants but two, cruising and singing in the bright water. S'reee came to greet them skin to skin. "Come swim with us awhile," she said. "No business tonight. Just singing."

"Just a little business," Nita said. It was hard to stop being the Silent Lord, with all her responsibilities. "How are things down deep?"

"Quiet. Not a shake; and several of the hot-water vents seem to have reduced their outputs to normal levels. We're going to have some peace for a while, it seems . . . for which we thank you. Both of you."

"You're very welcome," Kit said. "We'd do it again, if we had to." Nita shot Kit a quizzical look, which he returned in kind. "After all, it's our world, too . . ."

They swam, the Celebrants and Kit and Nita, for a long time, a long way out— into waters bright with fish going about their business, peaceful with seaweed and coral, and warm—whether with volcanism or summer, Nita couldn't tell. "This is the way it's supposed to be," S'reee said from beside her, at one point. "Not the way you met me—not blood in the water. Just the long nights, the singing, time to think . . ."

"It's so bright," Nita said, wondering. The krill were evidently out in force tonight; between them and the moonlight, the water was dazzling. And there seemed to be more krill yet in the deeper waters, for it was brighter down there; much brighter. "*Look* at that," Kit said, and dived, heading for the light.

At about a hundred feet down, Nita began to realize that the light in the water had nothing to do with krill. Of itself the water was burning, a harmless warm radiance that grew stronger and stronger in the greater depths. And in those depths, everything else shone, too: not just reflected light, but a fire that seemed to come from *inside* seaweed, shells, branching coral. Song echoed in that water, sounding at first like whalesong—but slowly Nita began to hear something else in the music, in a way that had nothing to do with hearing. Expressions of growth, of power, of delight—but no note of limitation, pain, loss. She found herself descending into timelessness, into a blaze of meaning and purpose so bright it could have blinded the heart—had the heart not become stronger every moment, more able to bear it.

Finally there was nothing but the brightness, the water all around her on fire with light.

Shapes moved in the light, swimming in it as if the water were extraneous and the light were their true medium. There was no looking at those shapes for more than a heartbeat before the eye was forced to turn away, defeated by glory. It was in the passage of those shapes near Nita that it was made plain to her, in the way the Sea gave a whale-wizard knowledge, that she and Kit were welcome indeed and had successfully completed the job they'd been given.

Kit was silent, as if not knowing what to say. Nita knew, but simply considered for a moment before singing it in one soft note that, in this place, carried as poignantly as a trumpet call at evening.

It hurt, she said.

We know, the answer came back. *We sorrow. Do you?*

For what happened?

No. For who you are now—the person you weren't a week ago.

. . . No.

No, Kit said.

Would you do the same sort of thing again?

Yes . . . if we had to.

Then there's no guarantee this won't happen again. Not that we could offer you any. Hope, like fear, comes from within . . .

Nita nodded. There was nothing sorrowful about the pronouncement; it was as matter-of-fact as anything in the manual. Kit turned away from the shape, the bright Power, that had answered them. As always, Nita turned with him.

And, looking up in astonishment, back-finned hurriedly. Something was passing over. Something as huge, or huger than, the unseeable shapes in the radiant water; burning as fiercely as they did, though with a cooler flame; passing by with a silent, deadly grace that Nita would have known anywhere. *I am no wizard*, he had said. But how could he, or she, have anticipated that borrowing a wizard's power would make even a nonwizard part of the Heart of the Sea? Or maybe there was more to it than that. *What's loved*, Carl had said, *survives*. Nita's heart went up in a great note of unbelieving joy.

The passing shape didn't turn, didn't pause. Nita got just a glance of black eyes, the only dark things in all this place. Yet even they burned, a fire behind that opaque look that could mean anything.

Nita knew what it meant. And on he went, out of sight, in unhurried grace; the true dark angel, the unfallen Destroyer, the Pale Slayer who never really dies—seeking for pain to end.

Nita turned to Kit, wordless. He gazed back, as astonished and delighted as she.

. . . OK, Kit said. *Bring on the next job.*

She agreed.

The Runaway Sister

"DON'T TELL ME SHE'S *still* in the toilet," Nita muttered, annoyed. "Dari? Come on, we're leaving!" Nita pulled harder, the door came open—

Air blew hard past her and ruffled her hair into her eyes. Bitter cold smote the front of her, and in it the humidity in the air condensed out instantly, whipping past Nita through the sucking air as stinging, dust-fine snow.

Nita was looking through the doorway into a low rust red wasteland: nothing but stones in all sizes, cracked, tumbled, piled, with dun dust blowing between them. She slammed the ladies' room door shut. Air kept moaning past her, through the cracks, out into the dry red wasteland.

"Mars," she breathed, and terror grabbed her heart and squeezed. "She went to *Mars . . . !*"

High
Wizardry

For my dear master,
from someone nearly as surprised

Contents

Initialization
291

Passwords
297

Up and Running
301

Escape Key
306

Search and Retrieval
313

Randomization
325

Variables
340

Pattern Recognition
348

Uplink
354

Reserved Words
360

Fatal Error
369

Save and Exit
383

Reconfiguration
397

ACKNOWLEDGMENTS AND WARNINGS

Ben Yalow, chief of Academic Computing at CUNY and old friend, contributed much valuable advice on the subtleties of both AI and hardware, all of which contributed to this book one way or another.

Dan Oehlsen knows what he contributed to the effort: a great courtesy, for which many thanks.

Cheerful thanks and good wishes go to the members of the IBM PC Professional and IBM PC Novice Special Interest Groups on CompuServe, who were instrumental in assisting the writer in hitting her deadline. Friends, may your files never be busy!

And thanks, too, to the many members of the CompuServe Science Fiction and Fantasy SIG, whose nightly inquiries about their former Assistant SysOp's new book kept her going.

The author wishes to warn her readers that the computers in this book are fictional, including all aspects of their hardware, software, and operating systems. Attempts by readers to reproduce effects described in this book using their own computers may result in extreme frustration, or in damage to their software or hardware, or in violation of their end-user agreements, or all of the above at once; and for said results the author declines to be held legally responsible.

I'd like to get away from Earth awhile
And then come back to it and begin over.
May no fate willfully misunderstand me
And half grant what I wish and snatch me away
Not to return. Earth's the right place for love:
I don't know where it's likely to go better.
—Robert Frost, "Birches"

Where, except in the present, can the Eternal be met?
—C. S. Lewis, "Historicism"

Those who refuse to serve the Powers,
    become the tools of the Powers.
Those who agree to serve the Powers,
    Themselves *become* the Powers.

Beware the Choice! Beware refusing it!
—*Book of Night with Moon*
Tetrastych XIV: "Fire Over Heaven"

Initialization

"HEY, THERE'S SOMEBODY IN the driveway! It's a truck! Mom! Mom, the computer's here!"

The first sound Nita heard that morning was her little sister's shrieking. Nita winced and scrunched herself up into a ball under the covers. Then she muttered six syllables, a very simple spell, and soundproofed her room against her sister's noise.

Blessed silence fell. Unfortunately the spell also killed the buzzing of the locusts and the singing of the birds outside the open window. And Nita liked birds. She opened her eyes, blinking at the bright summer sun coming in the window, and sighed.

Nita said one more syllable. The mute-spell came undone, letting in the noise of doors opening and shutting and of Dairine shrieking instructions and suggestions at the immediate planet. Outside the window a catbird was sitting in the elm tree, screaming, "Thief! Thief!" in an enthusiastic but substandard imitation of a blue jay.

So much for sleeping late, Nita thought. She got up and went over to the dresser by the window, pulled a drawer open, and rummaged in it for a T-shirt and shorts. "Morning, Birdbrain," she said as she pulled out a Live Aid T-shirt.

The catbird hopped down to a branch of the elm right outside Nita's window. "Bob-white! Bob-white!" it sang at the top of its lungs.

"What's a quail doing in a tree?" Nita said. She pulled the T-shirt on. "Listen to those locusts! Hot one today, huh?"

"Highs in the nineties," the bird sang. "Cheer up! Cheer up!"

"Robins are for spring," Nita said. "I'm more in the mood for penguins at the moment . . ."

"What's up?"

"Enough with the imitations! I need you to take a message for me. Wizards' business. I'll leave you something nice. Half of one of Mom's muffins? Huh?"

The catbird poured out several delighted bars of song that started as a phoebe's call and ended as the five-note theme from *Close Encounters*.

"Good," Nita said. "Then here's something new to sing." She had been speaking all along in the Speech of wizards, the language everything alive understands. Now she added music to it, singing random notes with the words. "Kit, you wanna see a disaster? Come on over here and watch my folks try to hook up the Apple."

The bird cocked an interested eye at her. "You need it again?" Nita said.

" 'Kit, you wanna see a disaster?' "

"That's my boy. You remember the way?"

In a whir of white-barred wings, the catbird was gone.

"Must be hungry," Nita said to herself, pulling on her shorts, and then socks and sneakers. While pulling a sneaker on, she glanced at the top of the dresser. There among the stickers and the brushes and combs, under the new Alan Parsons album, lay her wizard's manual.

That by itself wasn't so strange; she'd left it there yesterday afternoon. But it was open; she didn't remember having left it that way. Nita, leaned over, tying the sneaker, and looked at the page. The Wizards' Oath—Nita smiled. It didn't seem like only a few months ago that she'd first read and taken that Oath herself: It felt more like years. *February, was it?* she thought. *No, March. Joanne and her crew chased me into the library. And beat the crap out of me later. But I didn't care. I'd found this—*

Nita sighed and flipped the book back to the Oath. Trouble came with wizardry. But other things came, too—

Whamwhamwham!

Nita didn't even need to turn around to see who was pounding on her door as it banged open. "Come in!" Nita said, and glared at Dairine, who already *was* in. "It's here!"

"I would never have known," Nita said, dropping the Parsons album back on top of the manual. "Dari, sometimes people like to sleep on a Saturday, y'know?"

"When there's a *computer* here? Nita, sometimes you're such a *spud.*"

Nita folded her arms and leaned against the dresser, ready to start a lecture. Her sister, unfortunately, took all the fun out of it by mocking Nita's position and folded arms, leaning against the doorjamb. Funny how someone so little could look so threatening: a little red-haired eleven-year-old stick of a thing in an Admiral Ackbar T-shirt, with a delicate face and watery gray eyes. Problem was, there was someone smart behind those eyes. Someone *too* smart.

Nita let out an annoyed breath. "I won't kill you this time," she said.

"I wasn't worried about that," Dairine said. "And you won't turn me into a toad or anything, either, so don't bother trying that line on me . . . C'mon, let's watch Mom 'n' Dad mess it up." And she was out the door.

Nita made a face. It didn't help that Dairine knew she was a wizard. Nita would sooner have told her parents about her wizardry than have told Dairine.

Of course, her folks had found out, too. . . .

Nita headed out the bedroom door and down the stairs.

The living room was full of boxes and packing material, loose-leaf books, and diskette boxes. Only the desk by the window was clean; and on it sat a cream-colored object about the size and shape of a phone book—the keyboard/mother-board console of a shiny new Apple IIIc+. "Harry," Nita's mother was saying, "don't plug anything in, you'll blow it up. Dairine, get out of that. Morning, Nita. There's some pancakes on the stove."

"OK," Nita said, and headed into the kitchen. While she was still spreading maple syrup between two pancakes, someone banged on the screen door.

"C'mon in," Nita said, her mouth full. "Have a pancake."

Kit came in: Christopher Rodriguez, her fellow wizard, quick and dark and sharp-eyed, and at thirteen, a year younger than Nita. And also suddenly two inches taller, for he had hit a growth spurt over the summer. Nita couldn't get used to it; she was used to looking down at him. She handed him a pancake.

"A little bird told me there's about to be trouble," Kit said.

"C'mon." Dairine's strident voice came from the living room. "I wanna play Lunar Lander!"

" 'About to be'?" Nita said.

Kit grinned around the mouthful of pancake and gestured with his head at the living room, raising his eyebrows.

Nita nodded agreement, her mouth full, too, and they headed that way.

"Dairine," Nita's mother was saying, "leave your dad alone." Her mother was sitting cross-legged in jeans and a sweatshirt, in the middle of a welter of Styrofoam peanuts and paperwork, going through a loose-leaf binder. "And don't get those manuals out of order, either. Morning, Kit! How're your mom and dad?"

"Fine, Mrs. Callahan. Hi, Mr. Callahan."

"Hi, Kit," said Nita's dad, rather muffled because he was under the desk by the living-room window. "Betty, I've got the three-prong plugs in."

"Oh, good. Then you can set up the external monitor . . ."

"When can I play?" Dairine hollered.

"At this rate," said her father, "sometime in the next century. Nita, do something with her, will you?"

"It's a little late for birth control," Kit said in Nita's ear. Nita spluttered with laughter.

Dairine flew at her. "Was that something dirty? I'll get you for that, you—"

Queep! something said. All heads turned; but it was just the computer, which Nita's dad had plugged in. "Harry, you *will* blow it up," Nita's mother said calmly, from down among the cartons. "We haven't finished reading the instructions yet."

"We don't have to, Betty. We didn't connect the hard disk yet, so we—"

Dairine lost interest in killing Nita. "Can I play now?!"

"See, it says in this manual—"

"Yes, but this one is before that one, Harry—"

"But, look, Betty, it says right here—"

Dairine quietly slipped the plastic wrapping off the monitor and slipped it into its notch at the back of the computer, then started connecting the cables to the screen. Nita glanced at Kit, then back toward the kitchen. He grinned in agreement.

"Your folks are gonna lock her in a closet or something," Kit said as they got out of the combat zone.

"I hope so . . . That's probably the only way I'm gonna get at it. But it's OK; she won't blow it up. Her science class has a IIIc; that's one of the reasons Mom and Dad got this one. Dari already knows more about it than the teacher does."

Kit rolled his eyes. "Uh-huh," Nita said. "But I'm not gonna let her monopolize *this* toy, lemme tell you. It's a neat little thing—it has the new foldout screen and batteries—you could put it in a bookbag. I'll show you later . . . Where's Ponch?"

"Outside. C'mon."

They went out and sat on the side steps. The locusts were buzzing louder than ever as Ponch, Kit's big black mutt, part Border collie, part German shepherd, came bounding up the driveway to them through the green-gold early sunlight. "Oh, Lord, look at his nose," Nita said. "Ponch, you got stung again, you loon."

"I buried a bone," Ponch said in a string of whines and barks as he came up to them. "The bad things bit me."

"His favorite bone-burying place," Kit said, sounding resigned, "has three yellow-jacket nests spaced around it. He gets stung faster than I can heal him."

"Brave," Ponch said, resting his chin, with the swollen black nose, on Nita's shoulder, and looking sideways at her for sympathy.

"Dumb," Nita said, scratching him behind the ears. "But brave. Go get a stick, brave guy. I'll throw it." Ponch slurped Nita's face and raced off.

Kit smiled to see him run.

"So what're we doing today?" Nita said. "Anything?"

"Well, there's a new show at the planetarium in the city. Something about other galaxies. My folks said I could go if I wanted to."

"Hey, neat. You got enough money?"

"Just."

"Great. I think I've got enough—let me check."

Nita went back into the house, noticing as she passed through the living room that Dairine was already slipping a diskette into the Apple's built-in disk drive, while her oblivious mother and father were still sitting on the floor pointing at different pages in three different manuals and arguing cheerfully. *Queep!* the computer said from the living room as Nita got into her room and upended the money jar on the dresser.

There was no pause in the arguing. *Sometimes I think they like it*, Nita thought, counting the bills. She had enough for the planetarium and maybe a couple of hot dogs afterward. Nita stuffed the money in her pocket and pushed the jar to the back of the dresser.

—And her eye fell on the record album again. She tipped it up by one corner to look at her wizard's manual, still open to the Oath. She pulled the book out, idly touching the open pages as she held it. *In Life's name, and for Life's sake*, began the small block of type on the right-hand page, *I say that I will use this Art only in service of that Life. . . .*

Dairine was in here yesterday, Nita thought, skimming down over the words of the Oath. . . . *And she was reading this*. For a moment Nita was furious at the idea of her sister rummaging around in her things; but the anger didn't last. *Maybe*, she thought, *this isn't so bad after all. She's been pestering me with questions about wizardry ever since she found out there really is such a thing. She thinks it's all excitement. But the Oath is heavy stuff. Maybe it threw a little scare into her with all the stuff about time's end and doing what you have to, no matter what. Be a good thing if it did make her back off a little. She's too young for this . . .*

Nita shut the manual, tucked it under her arm, and headed out into the living room. Dairine was standing in front of the computer, keying in instructions; the Apple logo came up on the monitor, followed by a screenful of words too small for Nita to read from across the room. Her mother and father were still deep in the manual. "Mom," Nita said, "Kit and I want to go into the city, to the planetarium. Is it OK? Kit's folks said he could."

Nita's mother glanced at her, considering. "Well . . . be back before dark."

"Stay out of Times Square," her father said without looking up, while paging through a manual open in his lap.

"Do you have enough money for the train?" her mother said.

"Mom," Nita said, hefting her wizard's manual in one hand, "I don't think we're going to take the train."

"Oh." Her mother looked dubiously at the book. She had seen more than enough evidence of her daughter's power in the past couple of months; but Nita knew better than to think that her mother was getting comfortable about wizardry, or even used to it. "You're not going into the city to, uh, *do* something, are you?"

"We're not on assignment, Mom, no. Not for a while, I think, after last time."

"Oh. Well . . . just you be careful, Neets. Wizards are a dime a dozen as far as I'm concerned, but daughters . . ."

Nita's father looked up at that. "Stay out of trouble," he said, and meant it.

"Yes, sir."

"Now, Betty, look right here. It says very plainly, 'Do *not* use disk without first—' "

"That's *software*, Harry. They mean the *diskette*, not the disk *drive*—"

Nita hurried out through the kitchen before her folks could change their minds. Kit was evidently thinking along the same lines, since he was standing in the middle of the sandy place by the backyard gate, using the stick Ponch had brought him to draw a wizard's transit circle on the ground. "I sent Ponch home," he said, setting various symbols around the circumference of the circle.

"OK." Nita stepped in beside him. "Where you headed? The Grand Central worldgate?"

"No, there are delays there this morning. The book says to use Penn Station instead. What time have you got?"

Nita squinted up at the Sun. "Nine thirty-five."

"Show-off. Use the watch; I need the Naval Observatory time."

"Nine thirty-three and twenty seconds," Nita said, scowling at her Timex, "*now*."

"Not bad. Let's haul it before—"

"What are you doing?!" yelled Nita's father, inside the house. Nita and Kit both jumped guiltily, then looked at each other. Nita sighed.

"Too late," Kit said.

At nine thirty-three and twenty-eight seconds, the screen door opened and Dairine was propelled firmly out of it. Nita's father put his head out after Dairine and looked up the driveway. "Take her with you," he said to Nita, and meant that, too.

"Yes, sir," Nita said, trying not to sound surly as the screen door slammed shut. Kit rolled his eyes and slowly began adding another set of symbols to those already inside the circle. Dairine scuffed over to them, looking at least as annoyed as Nita felt.

"Well," Dairine said, "I guess I'm stuck with you."

"Get in," Kit said, sounding resigned. "Don't step on the lines."

"And try not to freak out too much, OK?" Nita said.

Dairine stepped over the bounds of the circle and stood there with her arms folded, glaring at Nita.

"What a great time we're all going to have," Kit said, opening his manual. He began to read in the wizardly Speech, fast. Nita looked away from her sister and let Kit handle it.

The air around them began to sing—the same note ears sing when they've been in a noisy place too long; but this singing got louder, not softer, as seconds passed. Nita had the mild satisfaction of seeing Dairine start to look nervous at that, and at the slow breeze beginning around them when everywhere else the summer air was still. The breeze got stronger, dust around them whipped and scattered in it, the sound scaled up until it blotted out almost everything else. And despite her annoyance, Nita suddenly got lost in the old familiar exhilaration of magic working. From memory—for she and Kit had worked this spell together many times—she lifted her voice in the last chorus of it, where the words came in a rush and the game and skill of the spell lay in matching your partner's cadence exactly. Kit dropped not a syllable as Nita came in, but flashed her a wry grin, matching her word for word for the last ten seconds; they ended together on one word that was half laugh, half shout of triumph. And on the word, the air around them cracked like thunder and struck inward from all directions, like a blow—

The wind stilled and the dust settled, and they found themselves in the last aisle of a small chain bookstore, next to a door with a hand-lettered sign that said EMPLOYEES ONLY. Kit put his manual away, and he and Nita were brushing themselves off when that door popped open and a small sandy-haired man with inquiring eyes looked out at them. "Something fall down out here? No? . . . You need some help?"

"Uh," Nita and Kit said, still in unison.

"X-Men comics," said Dairine, not missing a beat.

"Up front on the right, in the rack," said the small man, and vanished through his door again.

"Hope they have the new annual," Dairine said, brushing dust off her shorts and Admiral Ackbar shirt and heading for the front of the store.

Kit and Nita glanced ruefully at each other and went after her. It looked like it was going to be a long day.

Passwords

LIKE SO MANY OTHER human beings, Dairine had made her first major decision about life and the world quite early. She had seen Nita (then five years old) go away to kindergarten for the first time and at the end of the day come back crying because she hadn't known the answers to some of the questions the teacher asked her.

Nita's crying had upset Dairine more than anything else in her short life. It had instantly become plain to Dairine's three-year-old mind that the world was a dangerous place if you didn't know things, a place that would make you unhappy if it could. Right there she decided that she was not going to be one of the unhappy ones.

So she got smart. She started out by working to keep her ears and eyes open, noticing everything; not surprisingly, Dairine's senses became abnormally sharp, and stayed that way. She found out how to read by the time she was four . . . just how, she never remembered; but at five she was already working her way through the encyclopedias her parents had bought for Nita. The first time they caught her at it—reading aloud to herself from a *Britannica* article on taxonomy and sounding out the longer words—her mom and dad were shocked, though for a long time Dairine couldn't understand why. It had never occurred to her that you could use what you knew, use even the knowing itself, to make people feel things . . . perhaps even to make them do things.

For fear of her parents being upset, and maybe stopping her, until she was five or so she kept her reading out of their sight as much as she could. The thought of being kept away from books terrified her. What moved Dairine most was sheer delight of learning, the great openness of the world that reading offered her, even though she herself wasn't free to explore the world yet. But there was also that obscure certainty, buried under the months and years since the decision, that the sure way to make the world work for you was to know everything. Dairine sat home and busied herself with conquering the world.

Eventually it came time for her to go off to kindergarten. Remembering Nita, her parents were braced for the worst, but not at all for Dairine's scowling, annoyed response when she came home. "They won't listen to what I tell them," Dairine said. "*Yet.*" And off she went to read, leaving her mother and father staring at each other.

School went on, and time, and Dairine sailed her way up through the grades. She knew (having overheard a couple of her mother's phone conversations with the school's psychiatrist) that her parents had refused to let her skip grades. They thought it would be better for her to be with kids her own age. Dairine laughed to herself over this, since it made school life utterly easy for her. It also left her more free time for her own pursuits, especially reading. As soon as she was old enough to go to the little local library for herself, she read everything in it: first going straight through the kids' library downstairs at about six books a day, then (after the concerned librarian got permission from Dairine's parents) reading the whole adult collection, a touch more slowly. Her mom and dad thought it would be a shame to stifle such an active curiosity. Dairine considered this opinion wise and kept reading, trying not to think of the time—not too far away—when she would exhaust the adult books. She wasn't yet allowed to go to the big township library by herself.

But she had her dreams, too. Nita was already being allowed to go into New York City alone. In a few years Dairine would, too. She thought constantly of the New York Public Library, of the eight million books that the White Lions guarded: rare manuscripts, books as old as printing, or older. It would take even Dairine a while to get through eight million books. She longed to get started.

And there were other dreams more immediate. Like everyone else she knew, Dairine had seen the *Star Wars* movies. Magic, great power for good and evil, she had read about in many other places. But the *Star Wars* movies somehow hit her with a terrible immediacy that the books had not—with a picture of power available even to untrained farm boys on distant planets in the future and therefore surely available to someone who knew things in the present. And if you could learn that supreme knowledge and master the power that filled and shaped the universe, how could the world ever hurt you? For a while Dairine's reading suffered, and her daydreams were full of the singing blaze of lightsabers, the electric smell of blasterfire, and the shadow of ultimate evil in a black cloak, which after terrible combat she always defeated. Her sister teased her a lot less about it than Dairine expected.

Her sister . . . Their relationship was rather casual, not so much a sibling relationship as the kind you might have with someone who lived close enough for you to see every day. When both Dairine and Nita were little, they had played together often enough. But where learning came in, for a while there had been trouble. Sometimes Nita had shown Dairine things she was learning at school. But when Dairine learned them almost immediately, and shortly was better at them than Nita was, Nita got upset. Dairine never quite understood why. It was a victory for them both—wasn't it?—over the world, which would get you if you didn't know things. But Nita seemed not to understand that.

Eventually things got better. As they got older, they began to grow together and to share more. Possibly Nita was understanding her better, or had simply seen how much Dairine liked to know things; for she began to tutor Dairine in the upper-grade subjects she was studying—algebra and so forth. Dairine began to like her sister. When they started having trouble with bullies and their parents sent them both off to self-defense school, Dairine mastered that art as quickly as anything else she'd ever decided to learn; and then, when a particularly bad beating near home made it plain that Nita wasn't using what they'd learned, she quietly put the word out that anyone who messed with Nita would have Dairine to deal with. The bullying stopped, for both of them, and Dairine felt smugly satisfied.

That is, she did until one day after school she saw a kid come at Nita to "accidentally" body-block her into the dirt of the playground she was crossing. Dairine started to move to prevent it—but as the kid threw himself at Nita, he abruptly slid sideways off the air around her as if he had run into a glass wall. No one else seemed to notice. Even the attacker looked blank as he fell sideways into the dust. But Nita smiled a little and kept on walking . . . and suddenly the world fell out from under Dairine, and everything was terribly wrong. *Her sister knew something she didn't.*

Dairine blazed up in a raging fire of curiosity. She began watching Nita closely, and her best friend, Kit, too, on a hunch. Slowly Dairine began to catch Nita at things no one else seemed to notice: odd words muttered to empty air, after which lost things abruptly became found, or stuck things came loose.

There was one day when their father was complaining about the crabgrass in the front lawn, and Dairine saw an odd, thoughtful look cross Nita's face. That evening her sister had sat on the lawn for a long time, talking under her breath. Dairine couldn't hear what was said; but a week and a half later their father was standing on and admiring a crabgrass-free lawn, extolling the new brand of weed-killer he'd tried. He didn't notice, as Dairine did, the large patch of crabgrass under the apple trees in the neighbor's yard next door . . . carpeting a barren place where the neighbor had been trying to get something green to grow, anything, for as long as Dairine could remember. It was all stuff like that . . . little things, strange things, nothing Dairine could understand and use.

Then came summer vacation at the beach—and the strangeness started to come out in the open. Nita and Kit started spending a lot of time away from home, sneaking in and out as if there were something to hide. Dairine heard her mother's uneasy conversations about this with her father and was amused; whatever Nita was doing with Kit, Dairine knew sex wasn't involved. Dairine covered for Nita and Kit and bided her time, waiting until they should owe her something.

The time came soon enough. One night the two of them went swimming and didn't come back when it got dark, as they'd agreed to. Dairine's mom and dad went out looking for Nita and Kit on the beach and took Dairine with them. She got separated from them, mostly on purpose, and was a quarter mile down the beach from them when, with a rush of water and noisy breath, a forty-foot hump-back whale breached right in front of her, ran itself aground—and turned into Nita.

Nita went white with shock at the sight of Dairine. Dairine didn't care. "You're going to tell me *everything*," she said, and ran down the beach to distract her parents just long enough for Nita and Kit—also just changed back from a whale—to get back into their bathing suits. And after the noisy, angry scene with their parents that followed, after the house was quiet, Dairine went to Nita's room, where Kit was waiting, too, and let them tell her the whole story.

Wizard's manuals, oaths, wizardry, spells, quests, terrible dangers beyond the world, great powers that moved unseen and unsuspected beneath the surface of everyday existence and every now and then broke surface—Dairine was ecstatic. It was all there, everything she had longed for. And if they could have it, she could have it, too. . . .

Dairine saw their faces fall and felt the soft laughter of the world starting behind her back again. You couldn't have this magic unless you were offered it by the Powers that controlled it. Yes, sometimes it ran in families, but there was no guarantee that it would ever pass to you. . . .

At that point Dairine began to shut their words out. She promised to keep their secret for the time being and to cover for them the best she could. But inside she was all one great frustrated cry of rage: *Why them—why them and not me!* Days later, when the cry ebbed, the frustration gave way to blunt, stubborn determination. *I'll have it. I will.*

She had gone into Nita's room, found her wizard's manual, and opened it. The last time she'd held it, it had looked like a well-worn kids' book from the library and, when she'd borrowed it, had read like one. Now the excitement, the exultation, flared up in Dairine again; for instead of a story she found pages and pages of an Arabic-looking script she couldn't read . . . and near the front, many that she could, in English.

She skimmed them, turning pages swiftly. The pages were full of warnings and cautions; phrases about the wizard's responsibility to help slow down the death of the universe; paragraphs about the price each wizard paid for his new power and about the terrible Ordeal-quest that lay before every novice who took the Wizards' Oath; sections about old strengths that moved among the worlds, not all of them friendly. But these Dairine scorned as she'd scorned Nita's cautions. The parts that spoke of a limitless universe full of life and of wizards to guard it, of "the Billion Homeworlds," "the hundred million species of humanity," those parts stayed with her, filled her mind with images of strangeness and glory and adventure until she was drowning in her own thoughts of unnumbered stars. *I can do it*, she thought. *I can take care of myself. I'm not afraid. I'll matter; I'll be something* . . .

She flipped through the English section to its end, finding there one page, with a single block of type set small and neat:

> In Life's name, and for Life's sake, I assert that I will employ the Art which is Its gift in Life's service alone. I will guard growth and ease pain. I will fight to preserve what grows and lives well in its own way; nor will I change any creature unless its growth and life, or that of the system of which it is part, are threatened. To these ends, in the practice of my Art, I will ever put aside fear for courage, and death for life, when it is fit to do so—looking always toward the Heart of Time, where all our sundered times are one and all our myriad worlds lie whole, in That from Which they proceeded. . . .

It was the Oath that Nita had told her about. Not caring that she didn't understand parts of it, Dairine drew a long breath and read it out loud, almost in triumph. And the terrible silence that drew itself down around her as she spoke, blocking out the sounds of day, didn't frighten her; it exhilarated her. Something was going to happen, at last, at last. . . .

She went to bed eagerly that night.

Up and Running

NITA AND KIT AND Dairine made their way among the shops of the lower level of Penn Station and caught the C train for the Upper West Side, coming up at Eighty-first and Central Park West. For a little bit they stood there just getting their bearings. It was warm but not uncomfortable yet. The park glowed green and golden.

Dairine was fidgeting. "Now where?"

"Right here," Nita said, turning around. The four-block stretch behind them, between Seventy-seventh and Eighty-first Streets, was commanded by the huge, graceful bulk of the American Museum of Natural History, with its marble steps and beast-carved pediment and the great bronze equestrian statue of Teddy Roosevelt looking eastward across at the park. Tucked into a corner of the building on Eighty-first Street stood the art deco–looking brick cube of the Hayden Planetarium, topped with a greened-copper dome.

"It looks like a tomb," Dairine said. "Shove *that*. I'm going to Natural History and look at the stuffed elephants."

"Climb on the stuffed elephants, you mean," Nita said. "Forget it. You're staying with us."

"Oh? What makes you think you can keep track of me if I decide to—"

"This," Kit said grimly, hefting his wizard's manual. "If we have to, we can put a tracer on you. Or a leash . . ."

"Oh yeah? Well, listen, smart guy, *I*—"

"Kit," Nita said under her breath, "easy. Dari, are you out of your mind? This place is full of *space* stuff. The new shuttle mock-up. A meteorite ten feet long." She smiled slightly. "A store with *Star Wars* books . . ."

Dairine stared at Nita. "Well, why didn't you say so? Come on." She headed down the cobblestone driveway toward the planetarium doors.

"You never catch *that* fly with vinegar," Nita said quietly to Kit as the two of them followed at a safe distance.

"She's not like my sisters," Kit said.

"Yeah. Well, your sisters are human beings . . ."

They snickered together and went in after Dairine. To Nita's mild relief—because paying for her little sister's ticket would have killed her hot-dog money—Dairine already had admission money with her. "Dad give you that?" Nita said as she paid.

"No, this is mine," said Dairine, wrapping the change up with the rest of a wad and sticking it back in her shorts.

"Where'd you get all that?"

"I taught a couple guys in my class to play poker last month," said Dairine. And off she went, heading for the souvenir store.

"Neets?" Kit said, tossing his manual in one hand.

Nita thought about it. "Naah," she said. "Let her go. Dairine!"

"What?"

"Just don't leave the building!"

"OK."

"Is that safe?" Kit said.

"What, leaving her alone? She'll get into the shuttle mock-up and not come out till closing time. Good thing there's hardly anyone here. Besides, she did say she wouldn't leave. If she were going to weasel out of it, she would've just grunted or something."

The two of them paused to glance into the souvenir store, full of books and posters and T-shirts and hanging *Enterprises*—both shuttle and starship. Dairine was browsing through a *Return of the Jedi* picture book. "Whatcha gonna get, hotshot?" Kit said, teasing.

"Dunno." She put the book down. "What I really need," she said, looking down at a set of Apollo decals, "is a lightsaber."

"And what would you do with it once you had it?"

"Use it on Darth Vader," Dairine said. "Don't you two have somewhere to be?"

Nita considered the image of Dairine facing down Darth Vader, lightsaber in hand, and felt sorry for Vader. "C'mon," she said to Kit. They ambled down the hall a little way, to the Ahnighito meteorite on its low pedestal—thirty-four tons of nickel-iron slag, pitted with great holes like an irregularly melted lump of Swiss cheese. Nita laid her hands and cheek against it; on a hot day in New York, this was the best thing in the city to touch, for its pleasant coolness never altered, no matter how long you were in contact with it. Kit reached out and touched it, too.

"This came a long way," he said.

"The asteroid belt," Nita said. "Two hundred fifty million miles or so . . ."

"No," Kit said. "Farther than that." His voice was quiet, and Nita realized that Kit was deep in the kind of wizardly "understanding" with the meteorite that she had with trees and animals and other things that lived. "Long, long dark times," Kit said, "nothing but space, and the cold. And then, slowly, light growing. Faster and faster—it's diving in toward the light, till it burns, and gas and water and metal boil off one after another. And before everything's gone, out into the dark again, for a long, long time . . ."

"It was part of a comet," Nita said.

"Until the comet's orbit decayed. It came in too close to the Sun on one pass and shattered and came down—" Kit took his hand away abruptly. "It doesn't care for that memory," he said.

"And now here it is . . ."

"Tamed," Kit said. "Resting. But it remembers when it was wild and roamed in the dark, and the Sun was its only tether . . ."

Nita was still for a few seconds. That sense of the Earth being a small safe "house" with a huge backyard, through which powers both benign and terrible moved, was what had first made her fall in love with astronomy. To have someone share the feeling with her so completely was amazing. She met Kit's eyes and couldn't think of anything to say; just nodded.

"When's the sky show?" he said.

"Fifteen minutes."

"Let's go."

They spent the afternoon drifting from exhibit to exhibit, playing with the ones that wanted playing with, enjoying themselves and taking their time. To Nita's gratification, Dairine stayed mostly out of their way. She did attach herself to them for the sky show, which may have been lucky; for Dairine got fascinated by the big Zeiss star projector, standing under the dome like a giant lens-studded dumbbell, and only threats of violence kept her out of the open booth that contained the computer-driven controls.

When the sky show was done, Dairine went off to the planetarium store to add a few more books to the several she'd already bought. Nita didn't see her again until late in the afternoon, when she and Kit were trying out the scales that told you your weight on various planets. Nita had just gotten on the scale for Jupiter, which weighed her in at twenty-one hundred pounds.

"Putting on a little weight, there, Neets," Dairine said behind her. "Especially up front."

Nita almost turned around and decked her sister. Their mom had just taken Nita to buy her first bra, and her feelings about this were decidedly mixed—a kind of pride combined with embarrassment. Dairine, sensing this, had been running the subject into the ground for days.

She can stuff it right up! Nita thought fiercely. *I am not going to let her get to me!* "All muscle, Dair," she said. "Besides, it's where you are that counts. Check this out." She sidestepped to the Mars scale, the needle of which stopped at seven pounds. "Less than the Moon, even."

"But it's bigger than the Moon," Dairine said.

"But not as dense. That's why its atmosphere's so thin even though Mars is that big; its mass is too small to hold it—" Nita heard footsteps, turned around, and saw that she had lost her audience. "Dairine? Where you headed?"

"Bathroom." Dairine's voice came from halfway down the stairs to the lower level.

"Well, hurry up, it's almost closing time."

Kit, on the Saturn scale, moved over to the Jupiter scale. "What was that all about?" he said. "I don't often hear you think these days, but if your dad had heard your mind right after she said that, he would've washed your head out with soap."

"Oh, crap." She tried the scale for Mercury: three and a half pounds. "I'm growing."

"You don't look any taller."

"Kit!"

"Oh." He looked at her chest. "Oh. I guess." He shrugged. "I didn't notice."

Oh, thank heaven, Nita thought; and immediately after that, *He didn't notice?* She swallowed and said, "Anyway, she's been riding me. I'm gonna kill her if she keeps it up."

"Maybe she's jealous."

Nita laughed. "Her? Of *me*?"

"Sure." Kit got off the scales and began to pace off the space between the scales and the doors to the planetarium proper. "Neets, wake up. You're a *wizard*. Here Dairine's been hot for magic since she was a little kid—any kind, *Star Wars*, you name it—and all of a sudden, not only does it turn out that there really *is* such a thing, but *you* turn up with it. From what you had to tell her to keep her quiet after she found out, Dari knows that you and I do big stuff. She wishes she could get her hands on the power. And there's no guarantee she ever will."

"She was into my manual over the last couple of days, I think . . ."

"So there you are. If she can't have the magic, she's gonna twist you around whatever other way she can. I hate to say this, Neets, but she's a real brat."

That agreed too well with thoughts Nita had been having but had rejected. "Well . . ."

"Ladies and gentlemen," said a woman's voice from the ceiling speakers down the hall, "the planetarium is now closing. Thank you."

Nita sighed. Kit punched her lightly in the arm. "Come on," he said, "don't let her get you down. Let's go over to the park and get hot dogs. She starts getting on our nerves, we'll tell her we'll turn her into a fire hydrant and call in every dog in Manhattan to try her out."

"Too late," Nita said. "She already knows we don't do that kind of thing."

"She knows *you* don't do that kind of thing," Kit said. "She doesn't know that *I* don't . . ."

Nita looked at his grim expression and wondered briefly whether the grimness was all faked. "I *am* starved."

"So c'mon."

They headed down the stairs together and came out on the ground floor, by the front doors. In the stairwell, under an arrow pointing toward the basement level, was a sign they had seen earlier that day, and laughed at:

TO MARS, VENUS, AND LADIES' ROOM

"Wait for me," Nita said. "She's probably trying to break into that Venus exhibit to see where the 'lava' comes from."

Kit rolled his eyes. "Being a fire hydrant may be too good for her."

Nita went down the stairs. "Dari?" she called, annoyed. "Come on before they lock us in."

It was considerably cooler down here. Nita turned right at the bottom of the stairs and walked quickly through the Venus exhibit, rubbing her upper arms at the chill, which went right through her thin T-shirt. Someone had turned off the sluggishly erupting Venerian volcano behind its murky glass wall; no one was to be seen anywhere else, all the way down to the temporary plasterboard wall with the sign that said MARS CLOSED FOR RENOVATIONS.

"Don't tell me she's *still* in the toilet," Nita muttered, annoyed. *Reading, probably. One of these days she's gonna fall in.* She went back the way she had come, past the stairs, to the ladies' room. It was not only cold down here, there was a draft. She grabbed the handle of the door and pulled; it resisted her slightly, and there was a faint *hoo* noise, air sliding through the door crack as she tugged. "Dari? Come on, we're leaving!" Nita pulled harder, the door came open—

Air blew hard past her and ruffled her hair into her eyes. Bitter cold smote the front of her, and in it the humidity in the air condensed out instantly, whipping past Nita through the sucking air as stinging, dust-fine snow.

Nita was looking through the doorway into a low rust red wasteland: nothing but stones in all sizes, cracked, tumbled, piled, with dun dust blowing between them. Close, much too close to be normal, lay a horizon hazed in blood brown, shading up through translucent brick color, rose, violet, a hard dark blue, and above everything, black with stars showing. Low in the crystalline rose burned a small pinkish sun, fierce, distant looking, and cold. Nita flinched from the unsoftened sight of it, from the long, harsh shadows it laid out behind every smallest stone. She slammed the ladies' room door shut. Air kept moaning past her, through the cracks, out into the dry red wasteland.

"Mars," she breathed, and terror grabbed her heart and squeezed. "She went to *Mars* . . . !"

Escape Key

■

THAT MORNING DAIRINE HAD awakened with the Oath's words ringing in her ears to find herself not in a galaxy far far away, but in her own bed. She had lain there for a long few minutes in bitter annoyance before she heard the wheels of the truck in the driveway. It was the computer, of course; and to this lesser excitement she had gratefully surrendered herself.

Dairine was good with computers. It was just one more kind of knowledge, good for using to keep people and the world off your back; and computers were really surprisingly easy to work with once you got it through your head that they were utterly stupid things, unable to do anything you didn't tell them how to do, in language they understood. In her few months' work with the Apples at school, Dairine had become an accomplished hacker.

She utterly disdained "phreaking," the breaking and entering of electronic bulletin boards and systems that interested a few of her malicious classmates. It could get you thrown in jail. What fascinated Dairine was advanced programming, the true hacking—getting a computer to sing, or talk, or play involved and clever games, or make you a sandwich. All these things were possible, with the right peripherals and a smart programmer. That she was; and the computer—tireless listener, absolutely obedient to orders, and endlessly forgiving of mistakes—was the perfect companion. They worked well together. Even her teachers had noticed that the machines "behaved" better around Dairine than around anyone else. She never noticed this herself, having taken it for granted.

So while her mother and father sat arguing over the manuals, of course Dairine took matters into her own hands. The Apple IIIc+ was easy to set up: a plug and cable for the screen; the printer cable attached to the printer port and the computer's interface; the power cord to the wall. Dairine slipped a system disk into the drive, shut the drive door, and turned the computer on—"booted it up"—ready to look for the Copy utility in the disk's directory. The first thing you always did with a brand-new system disk full of programs was copy it; working on the original disk could cost you a lot of money to replace if you hurt or wiped it out accidentally.

The Apple logo came up on the screen and below it the A> prompt that meant the computer's basic operating system, called DOS, was ready to accept commands to its "A," or onboard, disk drive and the disk inside it. Dairine was about to start typing when something about the logo caught her eye. It was the famous striped Apple, all right—but it had no bite out of it.

She stared for a second. *Pirated software?* she thought, but that was ridiculous. Her dad had bought the computer and its system software from an approved dealer, and the various warranties, manuals, and end-user agreements were all over the floor. *Huh. Maybe they changed the logo. Oh, well. Let's see the directory . . .*

DIR A:, she typed on the keyboard and hit the return.

PASSWORD? said the screen, and sat there apparently waiting for a response, for the A> prompt hadn't come back.

That was no response she'd ever seen on the machines at school. DIR A:, she typed again, and pressed return.

PASSWORD?

"Huh," she said to herself, as possibilities flickered through her head. *Did Dad have the software encrypted somehow so that Nita and I can't get into it? But why? He wants us to use it.* She let out a breath. *Maybe it just wants an ID code for the user—there're some programs that do that.* She squinted at the screen a moment, then smiled and typed in a private joke: the code name that a certain untrained farm boy used in his fighter run on the Death Star, a name that suited Dairine since she had inherited her mother's red hair. RED FIVE, she typed, and hit the carriage return.

PASSWORD RED FIVE ACCEPTED.

A>

Weird, Dairine thought, and typed again.

DIR A:

The disk drive whirred. The screen wiped itself and displayed a list: mostly program command files or data files holding information for the programs, to judge by their suffixes.

```
ASSIST.COM             22008K
CHANGE.COM              2310K
COPY.COM                1032K
COPY.DAT                4404K
GO.COM                  5048K
GO.DAT                  3580K
HIDE.COM                1244K
MANUAL.COM              3248K
MANUAL.DAT             10662K
MBASIC.COM              7052K
MENU.COM                 256K
SEEK.COM                6608K
SUPPORT.COM             5120K
SUPPORT.DAT             3218K
A>
```

Dairine gazed at the screen, perplexed. A *K* was a kilobyte, a thousand little pieces, or bytes, of information; and the disk itself was supposed to hold only 800K. How could the disk possibly have all these files on it, and such big ones?

Maybe this is a bad disk, Dairine thought. It happened sometimes that a disk was damaged on its way from the factory. Or maybe something was wrong with the directory. *Well, let's see if something'll run.* Beside the A> prompt she typed COPY and hit return.

The disk drive whirred. The screen wiped itself again, then said:

```
IIIC COPY UTILITY
5430K FREE
RADIUS?
```

Dairine stared again. *Radius* meant nothing to her. She hit return, hoping the computer would (as some programs did) supply its own data as a result.

DEFAULT RADIUS, the screen said.

It was all right, then; the program had been instructed to supply a value of its own if the user didn't specify one. Dairine let out a breath and resolved to have a look at this thing's manual. Maybe the company had made changes in the software.

COPY UTILITY READY, said the screen. PRESS ENTER TO BEGIN.

Dairine hit return. The disk drive whirred.

There were two computers on the desk.

She gaped. Hesitantly she put out a hand to the second computer, which was sitting next to the first and sticking over the edge of the desk a little. It was solid, and its screen matched that of the original computer exactly. They both said:

```
COPY SUCCESSFULLY COMPLETED
DESCRIPTION FILE "APPLIIIC.DSC" CREATED
HARD COPY "APPLIIIC.CPY" CREATED
A>
```

Oh, Lord! Dairine thought. She didn't dare turn around or make any outward sign: behind her, her mother and father were arguing peaceably over the contents of the Apple manuals. Desperately, Dairine brought up the directory again, stared at it, and then, for lack of any better idea, typed:

HIDE

The disk drives whirred again. Dairine thought she had never heard such a loud noise in her life, but her parents still didn't notice anything. The screen cleared itself, then said:

```
IIIC HIDE UTILITY
Choose one:
(1) Hide from COPY utility
(2) Hide from CHANGE utility
(3) Hide from MBASIC
(4) Exit to system
```

Dairine typed 1. The screen cleared again.

```
HIDE FROM COPY UTILITY
Last copy description file in memory:
APPLIIIC.DSK

Last hard copy created:
APPLIIIC.CPY FROM APPLIIIC.ORG (ORIGINAL)

Name of hard copy to hide?
```

I'd sooner have the original . . . ! Dairine hurriedly typed APPLIIIC.ORG. The screen said:

```
HIDE OPTIONS:
(a)  Hide in realspace
     (invisibility option)
(b)  Hide in realspace
     (size reduction)
(c)  Hide in otherspace
     (retrievable pocket)
(d)  Discard in otherspace
     (nonretrievable pocket)
(e)  Timed storage
     (coordinate-specific claudication)
(f)  Exit to main menu
```

Dairine typed c.

```
PASSWORD FOR RETRIEVAL?
```

Dairine swallowed. Behind her, her father was muttering about getting some coffee. RED FIVE, she typed.

```
CHOOSE INPUT OPTION:
VERBAL OR KEYBOARD?
```

VERBAL, she typed, very fast.
The drives whirred.

```
HIDING HARD COPY OF FILE APPLIIIC.ORG
```

As silently as it had come, the second computer vanished.

```
A>
```

Dairine's father turned around and saw her at the computer. "*What are you doing?!*"

"Uh," Dairine said. She couldn't remember when she had last been at a loss for words. Her father, though, wasn't even slightly concerned with this. Several seconds later Dairine found herself going to New York with Nita and Kit.

At the moment even the thought of the New York Public Library seemed a bit tame.

It took her hours to get free of Nita and Kit. All the while her mind was raging, turning over and over the thought of what power she had been offered when she took the Oath, and when she finally got down to the ladies' room and sat down in one of the stalls, her heart was hammering with excitement, and sweat stood out on her.

"Red five," she whispered, and held her breath.

There was a computer in her lap.

She flipped up the little liquid-crystal screen and was shocked to find the A>
prompt staring at her: shocked partly because she hadn't booted the computer up,
and partly because it couldn't be running; there were no batteries in it yet; or were
there? But Dairine wasn't one to argue the point. She typed hurriedly, using the
hide.com program to put the books she'd bought in a "pocket" and get them out
of her way. Then she brought up the directory again. ASSIST.COM, said the first
entry. Maybe that was a "help menu," a series of screens that would explain how
to get the most out of the computer. She typed ASSIST and hit return.

The screen cleared, then said at the top:

ACTIVE OR PASSIVE MODE?

Dairine was out of her depth again. ACTIVE, she typed, on a guess, and entered
it. The screen cleared again.

UTILITY OPTIONS:
(1)   General Data & Logistics—MANUAL, MENU
(2)   Transit—GO.COM
(3)   Intervention—CHANGE (see also MANUAL)
(3a) Duplication—COPY
(3b) Preservation—HIDE, SEEK
(4)   Outside assistance—(routine) SUPPORT
(4a) (emergency) ASSIST
(5)   Other programming—MBASIC
(6)   Exit to system

Dairine chewed her lip and thought. Just to see what would happen, she hit 2
and return. The screen cleared.

TRANSIT UTILITY
Input? (1) keyboard, (2) verbal

2, Dairine typed.

"Inside solar system or outside solar system?" the computer said very quietly,
but so suddenly that Dairine almost dropped it.

"Inside," she said, and swallowed.

"Planet?"

She gazed at the ladies' room door, thinking of the dioramas outside with a
sudden terrible desire. "Mars," Dairine said.

The disk drive chirred briefly. "Coordinates?"

Dairine knew that areographers used some kind of latitude-longitude system
for Mars, but she knew nothing else about it. "Default," she said, on a hunch.

"Default coordinates confirmed," said the computer. "Last recorded transit.
Atmosphere?"

Last recorded— "Uh, atmosphere? Yes," she said.

"Parameters?"

"Umm . . . Fifteen percent oxygen, eighty percent nitrogen, five percent carbon
dioxide."

"Mix proportions approximate Terran sea-level parameters. Default to those?"

"Mmm . . . Yes."

"Estimated time in transit?"

She thought. "One hour."

"Data complete," said the computer. "Ready to transit. Transit command 'run.' "

"Run," Dairine said.

And everything slewed sideways and upside down. Or no, the world stayed the same—but Dairine's frame of reference suddenly became huger than the whole Earth and the space that contained it, so that her planet seemed only one moving, whirling point plunging along its path through a terrible complexity of forces, among which gravity was a puny local thing and not to be regarded. Up was some other way now; down had nothing to do with the floor. Her stomach rebelled.

And her eyes were seeing things they had never been made to see. Lines and sparks and traces of white fire seemed to tear through her head from her eyes to the back of her skull; they pinned her to the rolling Earth like a feebly fluttering moth to a card. A terrible silence with a deadly sea roar at the bottom of it, more terrible than the stillness of her Oath-taking, flattened her down with its sheer cold ancientness, a vast weight of years without sound or light or life. *Cosmic rays*, she thought desperately, clutching at reason: *faster-than-light particles, maybe that's what the light is. But the dark—it's death, death itself, I'm going to die—*

—and the wizardry let her go. Dairine got shakily to her feet. As she got up, stones and gravel crunched under her sneakers, instead of tile floor. The sound went through her in a rush of adrenaline as fierce as fire. Her vision cleared. Red wasteland stretched away under a cold rose sun, a violet sky arched over her; the wind sang chill. She turned slowly, looking around. High up in the cold violet day, something small and bright fled across the sky, changing phase as it did so.

"Deimos," Dairine whispered. Or maybe it was Phobos, the other of Mars's two little moons. Whichever it was, it went through half its month in a few minutes, sliding down toward the horizon and behind something that stood up from it. It was a mountain peak, upraised as if on a pedestal, and so tall that though it came up from far behind the foreshortened horizon, its broad, flat base spanned half that horizon easily. "What is that?" she said.

"Syntax error twenty-four," said the Apple dispassionately. "Rephrase for precision."

"That mountain. What is it? Identify."

"In Earth/IAU nomenclature Olympus Mons."

Dairine took in a sharp breath. It was an ancient volcano, long extinct, and the highest mountain in the solar system. "How do I get up there?"

"Reference Short-transit utilities."

She did. Five minutes later she stood in a place where the wind no longer sang, for it was too thin to do so; where carbon dioxide lay frozen on the rust red stones, and the fringes of her protective shell of air shed a constant snow of dry ice and water vapor as she moved; a place from which she could see the curvature of the planet. Dairine stood twelve miles high atop Olympus Mons, on the ridge of its great crater, into which Central Park could have been dropped entire, and looked out over the curve of the red world at what no nonwizardly child of Earth had seen with her or his own eyes before: the asteroid belt rising like a chain of scattered stars, and beyond it the tiniest possible disk, remote but clear.

"Jupiter," she whispered, and turned around to look for Earth. From here it would look like a morning or evening star, just a shade less bright than Venus. But in mid-movement she was distracted. There was something down in the mile-deep crater, a little light that shone.

"What's that?" she said, holding up the Apple.

"Syntax error twenty-four—"

"Yeah, yeah, right. That light! Identify."

"A marker beacon. Provenance uncertain at this range."

"Get us down there!"

With Dairine's help, it did. Shortly, she was staring at a pole with a light on it, streamlined and modern looking, made of some dark blue metal she couldn't identify. Set in the ground beside the pole was a plate of dull red metal with strange markings on it. "What's it say?"

"Error trap eighteen. Sense of query: semantic value?"

"Right."

"First (untranslatable) climbing expedition. Ascent of (untranslatable proper name): from (date uncertain) to (date uncertain). We were here. Signed, (untranslatable proper name), (untranslatable proper name), (untranslatable proper name)."

"People," Dairine whispered.

"Affirmative."

She looked up at the stars in the hard violet sky. "I want to go where they came from!"

"Reference Transit utility."

She did, and spent some minutes tapping busily at the keys. In the middle of it, selecting coordinates, delightedly reading through planet names—she stopped and bit her lip. "This is going to take longer than an hour," she said to herself. Come to think of it, she might want to be away for quite some time. And seeing all the problems Nita had started having with their folks when she told them she was a wizard, it wouldn't do for Dairine to let them know that she was one, too. Not just yet.

She thought about this, then got out of the Transit utility and brought up the directory again—taking more time with it, examining the program menus with great care. In particular she spent a great deal of time with the Copy and Hide utilities, getting to know their ins and outs and doing one finicky piece of copying as a test. The test worked. She sent the copy home.

"That should do it," she said, got back into the Transit utility, and with the program's prompting started to lay in coordinates. "Darth Vader," she muttered under her breath, "look out. Here I come."

Shortly thereafter there was nothing on Olympus Mons but rocks and dry-ice snow, and far down in the crater, the single blinking light.

Search and Retrieval

"WE'RE DEAD," NITA MOURNED, sitting on the planetarium steps with her head in her hands. "Dead. My mother will kill me."

Kit, sitting beside her, looked more bemused than upset. "Do you know how much power it takes to open a gateway like that and leave it open? Usually it's all we can do to keep one open long enough to jump through it."

"Big deal! Grand Central gate and the World Trade Center portals are open all the time." Nita groaned again. "*Mars!*"

"Each of those gates took a hundred or so wizards working together to open, though." Kit leaned back on the steps. "She may be a brat, but boy, has she got firepower!"

"The youngest wizards always do," Nita said, sitting up again and picking up Kit's manual from beside her. "Lord, what a horrible thought."

"What? The gate she made? We can close it, but—"

"No. This. Look." She held out his manual. It was turned to one of the directory pages. The page said:

CALLAHAN, Juanita T.   Journeyman rating
243 E. Clinton Avenue   (RL +4.5 +/− 0.15)
Hempstead NY 11575   Available/limited
(516) 555-6786   (summer vacation)

That was Nita's usual directory listing, and normal enough. But above it, between her and "CAHANE, Jak," whose listing was usually right above hers, there was something new.

CALLAHAN, Dairine E.   Novice rating
243 E. Clinton Avenue   (RL +9.8 +/−0.2)
Hempstead NY 11575   On Ordeal: no calls
(516) 555-6786

"Oh no," Kit said. "And look at that rating level."

Nita dropped the book beside her. "I don't get it. She didn't find a manual, how could she have—"

"She was in yours," Kit said.

"Yeah, but the most she could have done was take the Oath! She's smart, but not smart enough to pull off a forty-nine-million-mile transit without having the reference diagrams and the words for the spell in front of her! And the manuals can't be stolen; you know that. They just vanish if someone tries." Nita put her head down in her hands again. "My folks are gonna pitch a fit! We've got to find her!"

Kit breathed out, then stood up. "Come on," he said. "We'd better start doing things fast or we'll lose her. There's a phone over there. Call home and tell them we're running a little behind schedule. The planetarium's all locked up by now, so no one'll be around to notice if I walk through a couple of walls and close that gate down."

"But what if she tries to come back and finds it closed behind her?"

"Somehow I can't see that slowing her down much," Kit said. "And besides, maybe she's supposed to find it closed. She *is* on Ordeal."

Nita stood up, too. "And we'd better call Tom and Carl. They'll want the details."

"Right. Go ahead; I'll take care of the gate."

Kit turned around, looked at the bricks of the planetarium's outer wall. He stepped around the corner of the doorway wall, out of sight of the street, and laid one hand on the bricks, muttering under his breath. His hand sank into the wall as if into water. "There we go," he said, and the bricks rippled as he stepped through them and vanished.

Nita headed for the phone, feeling through her pockets for change. The thought of her sister running around the universe on Ordeal made her hair stand up on end. No one became a wizard without there being some one problem that their acquisition of power would solve. Nita understood from her studies that normally a wizard was allowed to get as old as possible before being offered the Oath; the Powers, her manual said, wanted every wizard who could to acquire the security and experience that a normal childhood provides. But sometimes, when problems of an unusual nature came up, the Powers would offer the Oath early—because the younger children, not knowing (or caring) what was impossible, had more wizardry available to them.

That kind of problem was likely to be a killer. Nita's Ordeal and Kit's had thrown them out of their universe into another one, a place implacably hostile to human beings and run by the Power that, according to the manual, had invented death before time began—and therefore had been cast out of the other Powers' society. Every world had stories of that Lone Power, under many names. Nita didn't need the stories; she had met It face-to-face, twice now, and both times only luck— or the intervention of others—had saved her life. And Nita had been offered her wizardry relatively early, at thirteen; Kit even earlier, at twelve. The thought of what problem the Powers must need solved if They were willing to offer the Oath to someone years younger—and the thought of her little sister in the middle of it—

Nita found some quarters, went to a phone, and punched in her number. What was she going to tell her mother? She couldn't lie to her—that decision, made at the beginning of the summer, had caused her to tell her folks that she was a wizard and had produced one of the great family arguments of her life. Her mother and father still weren't pleased that their daughter might run off anywhere at a moment's notice, to places where they couldn't keep an eye on her and protect her. Nor did it help that those places tended to be the sort where anyone but an experienced wizard would quickly get killed. That made it even worse. . . .

At the other end, the phone rang. Nita's throat seized up. She began clearing it frantically.

Someone answered. "Hello?"

It was Dairine.

Nita's throat unseized itself. "Are you all right? Where are you?" she blurted, and then began swearing inwardly at her own stupidity.

"I'm fine," Dairine said. "And I'm right here."

"How did you get back? Never mind that, how did you get out? And you left the gate open! Do you know what could have happened if some poor janitor went in that door without looking? It's sixty below this time of year on Mars—"

"Nita," Dairine said, "you're babbling. Just go home. I'll see you later." And she hung up.

"Why, that rotten little—," Nita said, and hung up the phone so hard that people on the street corner turned to look at her. Embarrassed and more annoyed than ever, she turned and headed back to where Kit was sitting. "Babbling," she muttered. "That rotten, thoughtless . . . I'm gonna—"

She shut her mouth. *Babbling?* That didn't sound like Dairine. It was too simple an insult. And why "just go home" instead of "just *come* home"? *There's something wrong—*

She stopped in front of Kit, who looked up at her from his seat on the step and made no move to get up. He was sweating and slightly pale. "That gate was fastened to Mars real tight," he said. "I thought half of Mariner Plain was going to come with it when I uprooted the force fields. What's the matter with you? You look awful."

"Something's wrong," Nita said. "Dairine's home."

"What's awful about that? Good riddance." Then he looked at her sharply. "Wait a minute. Home? When she's on Ordeal?"

That hadn't even occurred to Nita. "She sounded weird," Nita said. "Kit, it didn't *sound* like her."

"We were at home for our Ordeal—at least, at the beginning . . ."

She shook her head. "Something's wrong. Kit, let's go see Tom and Carl."

He stood up, wobbling a little. "Sounds good. Grand Central?"

"Rockefeller Center gate's closer."

"Let's go."

A Senior wizard usually reaches that position through the most strenuous kind of training and field experience. All wizards, as they lose the power of their childhood and adolescence, tend to specialize in one field of wizardry or another; but the kind of wizard who's Senior material refuses to specialize too far. These are the Renaissance people of sorcery, every one of them tried repeatedly against the Lone Power, in both open combat and the subtler strife of one Power-influenced human mind against another. Seniors are almost never the white-bearded wizards of archetype . . . mostly because of their constant combats with the Lone One, which tend to kill them young. They advise other wizards on assignment, do research for them, lend them assistance in the losing battle to slow down the heat-death of the universe.

Few worlds have more than thirty or forty Seniors. At this point in Kit's and Nita's practice, Earth had twenty-four: six scattered through Asia, one in Australia, and one (for the whales) in the Atlantic Ocean; three in Europe, four in Africa, and nine in the Americas—five in Central and South America (one of whom handled the Antarctic) and four in the north. Of these, one lived in Santa Cruz, one lived in Oklahoma City, and the other two lived together a few miles away from Nita's home in Nassau County.

Their house was very like their neighbors' houses . . . perhaps a little bigger, but that wasn't odd, since Carl worked as chief of sales for the big CBS flagship TV station in New York, and Tom was a moderately well-known freelance writer of stories and movie scripts. They looked like perfectly average people—two tall, good-looking men, one with a mustache, one without; Carl a native New Yorker, Tom an unrepentant Californian. They had all the things their neighbors had—mortgages and phone bills and pets and occasional fights. They mowed the lawn and went to work like everybody else (at least Carl did; Tom worked at home). But their lawn had as few weeds as Nita's did these days, their pets understood and sometimes spoke English and numerous other languages, their phone didn't always have a human being on the other end when it rang, and as for their fights, the reasons for some of them would have made their neighbors' mouths drop open.

Their backyard, being surrounded by a high hedge and a wall all hung with plants, was a safe place to appear out of nothing; though as usual there was nothing to be done about the small thunder-crack of air suddenly displaced by two human bodies. When Nita's and Kit's ears stopped ringing, the first thing they heard was someone shouting, "All right, whatcha drop this time?" and an answering shout of, "It wasn't me; are the dogs into something?" But they weren't: The two sheepdogs, Annie and Monty, came bounding out from around the corner of the house and leaped delightedly onto Kit and Nita, slurping any part of them not covered with clothes. A little behind them came Dudley the terrier, who contented himself with bouncing around them as if he were spring-loaded and barking at the top of his little lungs.

"Had dinner yet?" Carl called from the kitchen door, which, like the dining-room doors, looked out on the backyard. "Annie! Monty! Down!"

"Bad dog! Bad dog! Nonono!" screamed another voice from the same direction—not surprising, since its source was sitting on Carl's shoulder. This was Machu Picchu the macaw, also known (to her annoyance) as "Peach": a splendid creature all scarlet and blue, with a three-foot tail, a foul temper, and a precognitive talent that could read the future for months ahead—if Peach felt like it. Wizards' pets tend to become strange with time, and Seniors' pets even stranger than usual; and Peach had been with Tom and Carl longer than any of the others. It showed.

"Come on in," called one last voice: Tom. Kit and Nita pushed Annie and Monty more or less back down to dog level and made their way into the house through the dining-room doors. It was a pleasant, open place, all the rooms running freely into one another and full of handsome functional furniture; Tom's desk and computer sat in a comfortable corner of the living room. Kit pulled a chair away from the dining table and plopped down in it, still winded from his earlier wizardry. Nita sat down next to him. Carl leaned over the table and pushed a pair of bottles of Coke at them, sitting down and cracking open a third one himself. Tom, with a glass of iced coffee, sat down, too.

"Hot one today," Carl said at last, putting his Coke down. Picchu sidled down his arm from his shoulder and began to gnaw thoughtfully on the neck of the bottle.

"No kidding," Kit said.

"You look awful," said Tom. "What've you two been up to?"

For answer Nita opened Kit's manual to the directory and pushed it over to Tom and Carl's side of the table. Tom read it, whistled softly, and nudged the manual toward Carl. "I saw this coming," he said, "but not this soon. Your mom and dad aren't going to be happy. Where did she go?"

"Mars," Kit said.

"Home," Nita said.

"Better start at the beginning," said Carl.

When they came to the part about the worldgate, Carl got up to go for his supervisory manual, and Tom looked at Kit with concern. "Better get him an aspirin, too," Tom called after Carl.

"I'm allergic to aspirin."

"A Tylenol, then. You're going to need it. How did you manage to disalign a patent gateway all by yourself? . . . But wait a minute." Tom peered at Kit. "Are you taller than you were?"

"Two inches."

"That would explain it, then. It's a hormonal surge." Tom cleared his throat and looked at Nita. "You, too, huh?"

"Hormones? Yes. Unfortunately."

Tom raised his eyebrows. "Well. Your wizardry will be a little more accessible to you for a while than it has since you got started. Just be careful not to overextend yourself . . . It's easy to overreach your strength just now."

Carl came back with his supervisory manual, a volume thick as a phone book, and started paging through it. Annie nosed Kit from one side. He looked down in surprise and took the bottle of Tylenol she was carrying in her mouth. "Hey, thanks."

"Lord," Carl said. "She did a tertiary gating, all by herself. Your body becomes part of the gateway force fields," he said, looking up at Nita and Kit. "It's one of the fastest and most effective kinds of gating, but it takes a lot of power."

"I still don't get it," Nita said. "She doesn't have a manual!"

"Are you sure?" Carl said; and "Have you gotten a computer recently?" said Tom.

"Just this morning."

Tom and Carl looked at each other. "I thought only Advisory levels and above were supposed to get the software version of the manual just yet," Carl said.

"Maybe, but she couldn't have stolen one of those any more than she could have stolen one of the regular manuals. You're offered it . . . or you never see it."

Nita was puzzled. " 'Software version'?"

Tom gave her a wry look. "We've been beta-testing it," he said. "Sorry: testing the 'beta' version of the software, the one that'll be released after we're sure there are no bugs in it. You know the way you normally do spells? You draw your power diagrams and so forth as guides for the way you want the spell to work, but the actual instructions to the universe are spoken aloud in the Speech?"

"Uh-huh."

"And it takes a fair amount of practice to learn to do the vector diagrams and so forth without errors, and a lot of time, sometimes, to learn to speak the Speech properly. More time yet to learn to think in it. Well . . ." Tom sat down again and began turning his empty glass around and around on the table. "Now that technology has proceeded far enough on this planet for computers to be fairly widespread, the Powers have been working with the Senior wizards to develop computer-supported wizards' manuals. The software draws the necessary diagrams internally, the way a calculator does addition, for example; you get the solution without seeing how it's worked out. The computer also synthesizes the Speech, though of course there are tutorials in the language as you go along."

"The project has both useful and dangerous sides," Carl said. "For one thing, there are good reasons why we use the Speech in spelling. It contains words that can accurately describe things and conditions that no Earthly language has words for. And if during a spell you give the computer instructions that're ambiguous in English, and it describes something inaccurately . . . well." He looked grim. "But for the experienced wizard, who already knows the theory he's working with and is expert in the Speech, it can be a real timesaver."

"A lifesaver, too, under special circumstances," Tom said, looking somber. "You two know how many children go missing in this country every year."

"Thousands."

"It's not all kidnappings and runaways," Tom said. "Some of those kids are out on their Ordeals . . . and because they don't have time to become good with the Speech, they get in trouble with the Lone Power that they can't get out of. And they never come back." He moved uneasily in the chair. "Providing them with the wizards' software may save some of their lives. Meantime . . ."

Carl turned over a page or two in his manual, shaking his head. "Meantime, I want a look at Dairine's software; I need to see which version of it she got. And I want a word with her. If she lights out into the middle of nowhere on Ordeal without meaning the Oath she took, she's going to be in trouble up to her neck . . . Anyway, your folks should know about all this. Easier if we tell them, I think. How 'bout it, partner?" He looked over at Tom.

"I was about to suggest it myself."

Nita sagged with relief.

"Good. Your folks busy this afternoon, Neets?"

"Just with the computer."

"Perfect." Carl put out his hand, and from the nearby kitchen wall the phone leaped into his hand. Or tried to: the phone cord brought it up short, and there it hung in the air, straining toward Carl like a dog at the end of a leash. "I thought you were going to put a longer cord on this thing," Carl said to Tom, pushing his chair back enough to get the phone up to his face, and hitting the autodialer in the handpiece. "This is ridiculous."

"The phone store was out of them again."

"Try that big hardware store down in Freeport, what's its name— Hi, Harry. Carl Romeo . . . Nothing much, I just heard from Nita that you got the new computer . . . Yeah, they stopped in on the way home . . . Yeah. What did you decide on? . . . Oh, that's a sweet little machine. A lot of nice software for that." Carl listened for a few seconds to the soft squeaking of the phone, while Picchu left off chewing on Carl's Coke bottle and began nibbling delicately on the phone cord.

Carl smacked her gently away, and his eyebrows went up as he listened. "OK. Fine . . . Fine. See you in a bit. Bye now."

He hung up. "That was your mom in the background," he said to Nita, "insisting on feeding us again. I think she's decided the best thing to do with adult wizards is tame them with kindness and gourmet cuisine."

"Magic still makes her nervous," Nita said.

"Or we still make her nervous," Tom said, getting up to shut the doors.

"Well, yeah. Neither of them can quite get used to it, that you were their neighbors for all these years and they never suspected you were wizards . . ."

"Being out in the open," Tom said, "causes even more problems than 'passing' . . . as you'll have noticed. But the truth works best. The front door locked?" he said to Carl.

"Yup," said Carl. He looked down at his side in surprise: From the table, Picchu was calmly climbing beak over claw up the side of his polo shirt. "Bird—"

"I'm going," said Picchu, achieving Carl's shoulder with a look of calm satisfaction and staring Carl right in the eye. "I'm needed."

Carl shrugged. It was difficult and time consuming to start fights with a creature who could rip your ear off faster than you could remove her. "You do anything nasty on their rug," he said, "and it's macaw croquettes for lunch tomorrow, *capisce?*"

Picchu, preening a wing feather back into place, declined to answer.

"Then let's motor," Tom said. They headed for the garage.

"Lord," Tom said, "who writes these manuals, anyway? This is better than most, but it still might as well be in Sanskrit. Harry, where's that cable?" Nita watched with barely suppressed amusement as Tom and her father dug among the manuals all over the floor, and Tom went headfirst under the desk.

"Computer seems to be running, anyway," Carl said.

"Had to drag Dairine away from it before she blew it up," said Mr. Callahan, peering under the desk to see what Tom was doing. "She was messing with the cables . . ."

"Where is she, Daddy?" said Nita.

"In her room. You two must really have run her down for her to come home so early."

"Which train did she take?" Kit said.

"She didn't say. She looked a little tired when she got in . . . said she was going to go read or something. Tom, is that plug really supposed to go in there? It looks too big."

"They always do. See, this little bit inside the casing is all that actually goes in. Mmmf . . ."

Carl, standing beside Nita, reached around the back of the Apple and hit the reset button. The A> prompt that had been there vanished; The Apple logo came up again. It had no bite out of it.

Nita stared. "Uh-huh," Carl said, and hit the control key and the letter C to boot up the system. The A> prompt came back. Then Carl typed a string of numbers and figures, too quickly for them to register for Nita as anything but a blur. They disappeared, and a message appeared in the graceful Arabic-looking letters of the wizardly Speech.

USER LOG?

"Yes, please," Carl said. "Authorization seven niner three seven one comma five one eight."

"Password?"

Carl leaned near the console and whispered something.

"Confirmed," said the computer politely, and began spilling its guts in screenful after screenful of text. "Pause," Carl said at one point. "Harry, I think you'd better have a look at this."

"What, did we plug it in wrong—"

"No, not that." Nita's father got up, brushing himself off, and looked at the screen. Then he froze. He had seen the Speech in Nita's manual once or twice and knew the look of it.

"Carl," Nita's father said, beginning to look stern, "what is this?"

Carl looked as if he would rather not say anything. "Harry," he said, "it wouldn't be fair to make Nita tell you this. But you seem to have another wizard in the family."

"What?!"

"Yes," Carl said, "that was my reaction, too. Translation," he said to the computer.

"Translation of protected material requires double authorization by ranking Seniors and justification filed with Chief Senior for planet or plane," said the computer, sounding stubborn.

"What've you done to my machine?!"

"The question," Tom said, getting up off the floor, "is more like, What has Dairine done to it? Sorry, Harry. This is a hell of a way for you to find out."

Nita watched her father take in a long breath. "Don't call her yet, Harry," said Tom. He laid a hand on the computer. "Confirmed authorization one zero zero three oblique zero two. We'll file the justification with Irina later. Translate."

The screen's contents abruptly turned into English. Nita's father bent over a bit to read it. " 'Oath accepted—' "

"This Oath," Carl said. "Type a-colon-heartcode."

The computer cleared its screen and displayed one small block of text. Nita was still while her father read the Wizards' Oath.

There was movement behind her: She looked up and saw her mother, with a peppermill clutched forgotten in one hand, looking over her father's shoulder.

"Dairine took that?" her father said at last.

"So did we, Daddy," Nita said.

"Yes, but—" He sat down on the edge of the desk, staring at the screen. "Dairine isn't quite like you two . . ."

"Exactly. Harry, this is going to take a while. But first, you might call in Dairine. She did something careless this afternoon, and I want to make sure she doesn't do it again."

Nita felt sorry for her father; he looked so pale. Her mother went to him. "What did she do?" she said.

"She went to Mars and left the door open," said Tom.

Nita's dad shut his eyes. "She went to Mars."

"Just like that . . . ," said her mother.

"Harry, Nita tells me she took you two to the Moon once, to prove a point. Imagine power like that . . . used irresponsibly. I need to make sure that's not going to happen, or I'll have to put a lock on some of her power. And there are other problems. The power may be very necessary for something . . ." Carl looked stern but unhappy. "Where is she, Harry?"

"Dairine," Nita's dad called, raising his voice.

"Yo," came Dairine's voice from upstairs, her all-purpose reply.

"Come on down here a minute."

"Do I have to? I'm reading."

"Now."

The ceiling creaked a little, the sound of Dairine moving around her room. "What have I done to deserve this?" said Nita's father to the immediate universe.

"Harry," Carl said, glancing at the computer screen and away again, "this may come as a shock to you . . ."

"Carl, I'm beyond shocking. I've walked on the Moon without a spacesuit and seen my eldest daughter turn into a whale. That my youngest should go to Mars on a whim . . ."

"Well, as to what you've done to deserve it . . . you have a right to know the answer. The tendency for wizardry comes down to the kids through your side of the family."

That was a surprise to Nita, and as for her father, he looked stricken, and her mother looked at him with an expression that was faintly accusing. Carl said, "You're related to the first mayor of New York, aren't you?"

"Uh, yeah . . . He was—"

"—a wizard, and one of the best to grace this continent. One of the youngest Seniors in Earth's history, in fact. The talent in your line is considerable; too bad it missed you, but it does skip generations without warning. Was there something odd about one of your grandparents?"

"Why, my—" Nita's father swallowed and looked as if he was suddenly remembering something. "I saw my grandmother disappear once. I was about six. Later I always thought I'd imagined it . . ." He swallowed again. "Well, that's the answer to Why me. The next question is, Why Dairine?"

"She's needed somewhere," said Carl. "The Powers value the status quo too highly to violate it without need. It's what we're defending, after all. Somewhere out there is a life-or-death problem to which only Dairine is the answer."

"We just need to make sure she knows it," said Tom, "and knows to be careful. There are forces out there that aren't friendly to wizards—" He broke off suddenly as he glanced over at the computer screen. "Carl, you should see this."

They all looked at the screen. USER LOG, it said, and under the heading were listed a lot of numbers and what Nita vaguely recognized as program names. "Look at that," Tom said, pointing to one. "Those are the spells she did today, using the computer. Eighty-eight tera-bytes of storage, all in one session, the latest one—at 16:52 hours. What utility uses that kind of memory?"

"That's what . . . about ten of five?" Nita's mother said. "She wasn't even *here* then . . ."

The stairs creaked as Dairine came down them into the living room. She paused a moment, halfway, as well she might have done with all those eyes and all those expressions trained on her—her father's bewildered annoyance, her mother's indignant surprise, Tom's and Carl's cool assessment, and Nita's and Kit's expectant looks. Dairine hesitantly walked the rest of the way down.

"I came back," she said abruptly.

Nita waited for more. Dairine said nothing.

Nita's parents exchanged glances, evidently having the same thought: that a Dairine who said so little wasn't normal. "Baby . . . ," her mother said, sounding uncertain, "you have some explaining to do."

But Carl stepped forward and said, "She may not be able to explain much of anything, Betty. Dairine's had a busy day with the computer. Isn't that so, Dairine?"

"I don't want to talk about it," Dairine said.

"I think it's more like you can't," said Carl.

"Look at the user log, Harry," Tom said from behind Nita and Kit. "Eighty-eight tees spent on one program. A copy program. And run, as you say, when she wasn't even here. There's only one answer to that."

Slowly, as if he were looking at a work of art, Carl walked around Dairine. She watched him nervously. "Even with unlimited available memory and a computer running wizards' software," Carl said, "there's only so much fidelity a copy can achieve. Making hard copies of dumb machinery, even a computer itself, that's easy. Harry, look at the log: You'll see that this isn't the machine you bought. It's an exact copy of it. Dairine made it."

Carl kept walking around Dairine. She didn't move, didn't speak. "Carl, come on," Nita's father said from behind her, "cut it out. You're scaring her."

"I think not," Carl said. "There's only so much you can do with eighty-eight tees, as I said. Especially when the original is a living thing. The copy's responses are limited. See, there's something that lives inside the hardware, inside the meat and nervous tissue, that can't be copied. Brain can be copied. But mind—not so well. And soul—not at all. Those are strictly one to a customer, at least on this planet."

The air was singing with tension. Nita glanced at Kit, and Kit nodded, for he knew as well as she did the feel of a spell in the working. Carl was using no words or gestures to assist in the spell, nothing but the slow certain pressure of his mind as he thought in the Speech. "She copied the computer and took it to the city with her," Carl said, "and got away when she could. And when she left Earth, she decided—I'd imagine—that she wanted some time to sightsee. But, of course, you would object to that. So she copied something else, to buy herself some time."

The spell built and built in power, and the air sang the note ears sing in silence, but much louder. "Nothing not its own original can exist in this room," Carl said, "once I turn the spell loose. Harry, you're having trouble believing this, are you? You think I would treat your real daughter this way?"

Nita's father said nothing.

"Run," Carl said softly.

Dairine vanished. Air imploded into the place where she had been; manuals ruffled their pages in the sudden wind, papers flew up and slowly settled. Behind them, the Apple simply went away. The hard-drive cable slithered off the desk like a stunned snake and fell in coils to the floor.

Nita's father put his face in his hands.

Her mother looked sharply at Tom and Carl. "I've known you two too long to think you were toying with us," she said as Carl sat down slowly on the sofa, looking a bit pale. "You said something a moment ago about forces that weren't friendly . . ."

"Nita's told you some of what wizards are for," Tom said, looking at Carl in concern, then up again. "Balance; maintenance of the status quo; protecting life. There are forces that are ambivalent toward life. One in particular . . . that held Itself aloof from creation, a long time ago, and when everyone else was done, created something none of the other forces had thought of: death. And the longest death . . . the running-down of the universe. The other Powers cast It out . . . and they've been dealing with the problem, and the Lone Power, ever since."

"Entropy," Nita's mother said, looking thoughtful. "That's an old story."

"It's the only story," Tom said. "Every sentient species has it, or learns it." He looked over at Nita's father, who was recovering somewhat. "I'm not about to pass judgment on whether the Lone One's invention was a good idea or not. There are cases for both sides, and the argument has been going on since time was set running. Every being that's ever lived has argued the case for one side or the other, whether it's been aware of it or not. But wizards fight the great Death, and the lesser ones, consciously . . . and the Entity that invented death takes our interference very personally. New wizards always meet It in one form or another, on their Ordeals. Some survive, if they're careful. Nita and Kit were careful . . . and they had each other's help."

" 'Careful' is not Dairine's style," Nita's mother said, sounding rueful. "And she's alone."

"Not for long," Tom said. "We'll track her and see that she has help. But I think Nita will have to go. She knows Dairine's mind fairly well."

"I'm going, too," said Kit.

Carl, still ashen from the exertion of his spell, shook his head. "Kit, your folks don't know you're a wizard. You might have to be gone for quite a while—and I can't sell you two a time warp as I did once before. My time jurisdiction stops at atmosphere's edge."

"I'll tell them what I am," Kit said.

Nita turned and stared at him.

"I've been thinking about doing it for a while, since you told your folks," he said to her. "You handled it pretty well," he said to Nita's parents. "I should give my mom and dad the benefit of the doubt." The words were brave; but Nita noticed that Kit looked a little worried.

"Kit, you'll have to hurry," Tom said. "She's got a long lead on you, and the trail will get cold fast. Neets, where would Dairine want to go?"

Nita shook her head. "She reads a lot of science fiction."

Carl looked worried. "Has she been reading Heinlein?"

"Some," Nita said. "But she's mostly hot for *Star Wars* right now."

"That's something, at least. With luck she won't think of going much farther than a few galaxies over. Anything in particular about *Star Wars*?"

"Darth Vader," Kit said. "She wants to beat him up."

Tom groaned and ran one hand through his hair. "No matter what the reason," he said, "if she goes looking for darkness, she'll find it."

"But Darth Vader's not real!" said Nita's mother.

Tom glanced at her. "Not *here*. Be glad."

"A few galaxies over . . . !" Nita's father said to no one in particular.

Carl looked grim. "We can track her, but the trail's getting cold; and at any rate Tom and I can't go with you."

"Now, wait a minute . . . ," Nita's mother said.

Carl looked at her gently. "We're not allowed out of the solar system," he said. "There are reasons. For one thing, would you step out the door of a car you were driving?"

Nita's mother stared at him.

"Yes, well," Tom said. "We'll get you support. Wizards everywhere we can reach will be watching for you. And as for a guide—"

"I'll go," said Picchu abruptly, from the computer table.

Everyone stared, most particularly Nita's mother and father.

"Sorry, I should have mentioned," Carl said. "Peach is an associate. Bird, isn't this a touch out of your league?"

"I told you I was needed," Picchu said irritably. "And I am. I can see the worst of what's going to happen before it does; so I should be able to keep these two out of most kinds of trouble. But you'd better stop arguing and move. If Dairine keeps throwing away energy the way she's doing, she's going to attract someOne's attention . . . and the things It sends to fetch her will make Darth Vader look like a teddy bear by comparison."

Nita's mother looked at Carl and Tom. "Whatever you have to do," she said, "*do* it!"

"Just one question," Tom said to Picchu. "What do They need her for?"

"The Powers?" Picchu said. She shut her eyes.

"Well?"

"Reconfiguration," she said, and opened her eyes again, looking surly. "Well? What are you staring at? I can't tell you more than I know. Are we going?"

"Gone," Nita said. She headed out of the room for her manual.

"I'll meet you in the usual place when I'm done," Kit called after her, and vanished. Papers flew again, leaving Nita's mother and father looking anxiously at Carl and Tom.

"Powers," Nita heard her father say behind her. "Creation. Forces from before time. This is—this business is for saints, not children!"

"Even saints have to start somewhere," Carl said softly. "And it's always been the children who have saved the universe from the previous generation and remade the universe in their own image."

"Just be glad yours are conscious of the fact that that's what they're doing," Tom said.

Neither of her parents said anything.

In her bedroom, Nita grabbed her manual, bit her lip, said three words, and vanished.

Randomization

DAIRINE DID NOT GO straight out of the galaxy from Mars. Like many other wizards when they first cut planet-loose, she felt that she had to do a little local sightseeing first.

She was some while about it. Part of this was caused by discomfort. The jump from Earth to Mars, a mere forty-nine million miles, had been unsettling enough, with its feeling of being first pinned to a wildly rolling ball and then violently torn loose from it. But it hadn't been too bad. *Piece o' cake*, Dairine had thought, checking the Transit directory in the computer. *Somewhere out of the solar system next. What's this star system? R Leporis? It's pretty close* . . . But she changed her mind and headed for the moons of Jupiter instead . . . and this turned out to be a good thing. From Mars to Jupiter, bypassing the asteroid belt, was a jump of 342 million miles; and the huge differences between the two planets' masses, vectors, and velocities caused Dairine to become the first Terran to lose her lunch on Jupiter's outermost satellite, Ananke.

The view did more than anything else to revive her—the great banded mass of Jupiter swiftly traversing the cold night overhead, shedding yellow-red light all around on the methane snow. Dairine sat down in the dry, squeaky snow and breathed deeply, trying to control her leftover heaves. Where she sat, mist curled up and snowed immediately down again as the methane sublimated and almost instantly recrystallized to solid phase in the bitter cold. Dairine decided that getting used to this sort of travel gradually was a good idea.

She waited until she felt better and then began programming—replenishing her air and planning her itinerary. She also sat for a while examining the transit programs themselves, to see if she had been doing something wrong to cause her to feel so awful . . . and to see if perhaps she could rewrite the programs a little to get rid of the problem. The programs were written in a form of MBASIC that had many commands that were new to her but were otherwise mostly understandable. They were also complex: They had to be. Earth spins at 17,000 miles an hour, plows along its orbital path at 175,000 miles an hour, and the Sun takes it and the whole solar system off toward the constellation Hercules at 115,000 miles an hour. Then the Sun's motion as one of innumerable stars in the Sagittarius Arm of the galaxy sweeps it along at some two million miles an hour, and all the while relationships between individual stars, and those of stars to their planets, shift and change. . . .

It all meant that any one person standing still on any planet was in fact traveling a crazed, corkscrewing path through space, at high speed; and the disorientation and sickness were apparently the result of suddenly, and for the first time, going in a straight line in a universe where space itself and everything in it is curved. Dairine looked and looked at the transit programs, which could (as she had just proved) leave you *standing* on the surface of a satellite 400 million miles away from where you started—not half embedded in it, not splatted into it in a bloody smear because of some forgotten vector that left you still moving a mile a second out of phase with the surface of the satellite, or at the right speed but in the wrong direction. . . . Finally, she decided not to tamper. A hacker learns not to fix what works . . . at least, not till it's safe to try. *Maybe the transits'll get easier*, she thought. *At least now I know not to eat right before one . . .*

That brought up the question of food, which needed to be handled. Dairine considered briefly, then used the software to open a storage pocket in otherspace. By means of the Transit utility she then removed a loaf of bread, a bottle of mustard, and half a pound of bologna from the refrigerator back home, stuffing them into local otherspace, where she could get at them. *Mom 'n' Dad won't notice*, she thought, *and even if they do, what are they going to do about it? Spank my copy? Be interesting if they did. I wonder if I'd feel it. . . .*

But there were a lot of more interesting things to consider today. Dairine stood up, got the computer ready, and headed out again, more cautiously this time. She stopped on Io, another one of Jupiter's moons, and spent a while (at a safe distance) watching the volcanoes spit white-hot molten sulfur ten miles out from the surface; sulfur that eventually came drifting back down, as a leisurely dusty golden snow, in the delicate gravity. Then she braced herself as best she could and jumped for Saturn's orbit, 401 million miles farther out, and handled it a little better, suffering nothing worse than a cold sweat and a few dry heaves, for the two planets were similar in mass and vectors.

Here there were twenty moons—too many for Dairine at the moment—but she did stop at Titan, the biggest satellite in the solar system, and spent a while perched precariously on a peak slick with hydrogen snow, looking down thoughtfully at the methane oceans that washed the mountain's feet. Several times she thought she saw something move down there—something that was not one of the peculiar long, high methane waves that the light gravity made possible. But the light was bad under the thick blue clouds, and it was hard to tell. She went on.

The jump to Uranus's orbit was a touch harder—899 million miles, to a world much smaller and lighter than the greater gas giants. Dairine had to sit down on a rock of Uranus's oddly grooved moon Miranda and have the heaves again. But she recovered more quickly than the last time and sat there looking down on the planet's blurry green-banded surface for a long time. *Voyager 1* and *Voyager 2* had both been gravity-slung off toward Alpha Centauri and were plunging toward the radio pause, the border of the solar system, whistling bravely in the endless dark. Sitting here she could hear them both, far away, as she could hear a lot that the Sun's radio noise made impossible to hear closer in. That silent roar, too—the old ruinous echo of the big bang—was more audible here. *How can I even hear it?* she wondered briefly. But Dairine quickly decided it was just another useful side effect of the wizardry, and she got up and headed out as soon as she was better.

From Uranus to Neptune was 1.1 billion miles. To her own surprise Dairine took it in stride, arriving standing up on Triton, one of Neptune's two largest moons, and with no desire to sit. *Better!* she thought, and looked around. There was very little to see: The planet was practically a twin of Uranus, except for its kinky partial rings, and the moons were barren. Dairine rubbed her arms. It was getting cold, even in the protective shell she had made for herself; her force fields couldn't long stand this kind of chill. Out here the Sun was just one more star, bright, but not like a sun at all. The jump to Pluto was brief. She stood only for a minute or so in the barren dark and could hardly find the Sun at all, even by radio noise. Its roar was muted to a chilly whisper, and the wind on Pluto—it was summer, so there was enough atmosphere thawed to make a kind of wind—drank the heat away from her force fields till in seconds she was shivering. She pulled the computer out. "Extrasystemic jump," she said hurriedly.

"Coordinates?"

"Read out flagged planets."

"Andorgha/Beta Delphini, Ahaija/R Leporis, Gond/Kappa Orionis, Irmrihad/Ross 614, Rirhath B/Epsilon Indi—"

"The closest," said Dairine, feeling a touch nervous about this.

"Rirhath B. Eleven point four light-years."

"Atmosphere status?"

"Earthlike within acceptable parameters."

"Let's go," Dairine said.

"Syntax error twenty-four," said the computer sweetly. "Rephrase for precision."

"Run!"

A galaxy's worth of white fire pinned her to the rolling planet; then the forces she had unleashed tore Dairine loose and flung her out into darkness that did not break. For what seemed like ages, the old, old echoes of the big bang breaking over her like waves were all Dairine had to tell her she was still alive. The darkness grew intolerable. Eventually she became aware that she was trying to scream, but no sound came out, nothing but that roar, and the terrible laughter behind it—

Laughter?

—and light pierced her, and the universe roared at her, and she hit the planet with a feeling like dreaming of falling out of bed—

Then, silence. True silence this time. Dairine sat up slowly and carefully, taking a moment to move everything experimentally, making sure nothing was broken. She ached in every bone, and she was angry. She hated being laughed at under the best of circumstances, even when it was family doing it. Whatever had been laughing at her was definitely *not* family, and she wanted to get her hands on it and teach it a lesson. . . .

She looked around her and tried to make sense of things. It wasn't easy. She was sitting on a surface that was as slick white as glare ice in some places, and scratched dull in other spots, in irregularly shaped patches. Ranked all around her in racks forty or fifty feet high were huge objects made of blue metal, each seeming made of smaller blocks stuck randomly together. The block things and the odd racks that held them were all lit garishly by a high, glowing green-white ceiling. *What is this, some kind of warehouse?* Dairine thought, getting to her feet.

Something screamed right behind her, an appalling electronic-mechanical roar that scared her into losing her balance. Dairine went sprawling, the computer under her. It was lucky she did, for the screaming something shot by right over her head, missing her by inches though she was flat on her face. The huge wind of its passing whipped her hair till it stung her face and made her shiver all over. Dairine dared to lift her head a little, her heart pounding like mad, and stared after the thing that had almost killed her. It was another of the bizarre cube-piles, which came to a sudden stop in midair in front of one of the racks. A metal arm came out of the Tinkertoy works of the rack, snagged the cube-pile, and dropped it clanging onto an empty shelf in the rack's guts.

Dairine pulled the computer out from under her and crawled carefully sideways out of the middle of the long white corridorlike open space, close to one of the metal racks. There she simply lay for a moment, trying to get her wits back.

There was another scream. She held still and saw another of the cubes shoot by a foot and a half above the white floor, stop and hover, and get snagged and shelved. *Definitely a warehouse*, she thought. And then part of the cube seemed to go away; it popped open, and people came out.

They have to be people, she thought. Surely they didn't *look* at all like people; the four of them came in four different burnished-metal colors and didn't look like any Earthly insect, bird, or beast. *Well*, she said to herself, *why should they?* Nonetheless she found it hard to breathe as she looked at them climbing down from their—vehicle? Was that their version of a car and this a parking lot? The creatures—*No, people*, she reminded herself—the people were all different from each other. They had bodies that came in four parts, or five, or six; they had limbs of every shape and kind, claws and tentacles and jointed legs. If they had heads, or needed them, she couldn't tell where they were. They didn't even look much like the same species. They walked away under the fluorescent sky, bleating at one another.

Dairine got up. She was still having trouble breathing. *What've I been thinking of*? She began to realize that all her ideas about meeting her first alien creatures had involved her being known, even expected. "Dairine's here finally," they were supposed to say. "Now we can get something done"; and then she and they would set out to save the universe together. Because of her own blindness she'd gotten so excited that she'd jumped into a totally alien environment without orientation or preparation, and as a result she'd nearly been run over in a parking lot. *My own fault*, she thought, disgusted with herself. *It won't happen again*.

But in the meantime people were still getting out of that car: these people shorter and blockier than the first group, with more delicate legs and brighter colors. She picked up the computer, looked both ways most carefully up and down the "road," and went after them. "You still working?" she said to the computer.

"Syntax error twenty-four—"

"Sorry I asked. Just keep translating."

As she came up behind the second group of people, Dairine's throat tightened. Everything she could think of to say to aliens suddenly sounded silly. Finally she wound up clearing her throat, which certainly needed it, as she walked behind them. *Don't want to startle them*, she thought.

They did absolutely nothing. *Maybe they can't hear it. Or maybe I said something awful in their language! Oh no*— "Excuse me!" she said.

They kept walking along and said nothing.

"Uh, look," Dairine said, panting a little as she kept up with them—they were walking pretty fast—"I'm sorry to interrupt you; I'm a stranger here—"

The computer translated what Dairine said into a brief spasm of bleating, but the spidery people made no response. They came to the end of the line of racks and turned the corner. Ahead of them was what looked like a big building, made in the same way as the cars, an odd aggregate of cubes and other geometrical shapes stuck together with no apparent symmetry or plan. The scale of the thing was astonishing. Dairine suddenly realized that the glowing green-white ceiling was in fact the *sky*—the lower layer of a thick cloudy atmosphere, actually fluorescing under the light of a hidden, hyperactive sun—and her stomach did an unhappy flip as her sense of scale violently reoriented itself. *I wanted strange*, she thought, *but not this strange*!

"Look," she said to the person she was walking beside as they crossed another pathway toward the huge building. "I'm sorry if I said something to offend you, but please, I need some help getting my bearings—"

Dairine was so preoccupied that she bumped right into something on the other side of the street—and then yipped in terror. Towering over her was one of the first things to get out of the car, a creature seven feet high at least, and four feet wide, a great pile of glittering, waving metallic claws and tentacles, with an odd smell. Dairine backed away fast and started stammering apologies.

The tall creature bleated at her, a shocking sound up so close. "Excuse me," said the computer, translating the bleat into a dry and cultured voice like a BBC announcer's, "but why are you talking to our luggage?"

"Llp, I, uh," said Dairine, and shut her mouth. There they were, her first words to a member of another intelligent species. Blushing and furious, she finally managed to say, "I thought they were people."

"Why?" said the alien.

"Well, they were walking!"

"It'd be pretty poor luggage that didn't do that much, at least," said the alien, eyeing the baggage as it spidered by. "Good luggage levitates, and the new models pack and unpack themselves. You must have come here from a fair way out."

"Yeah," she said.

"My gate is about to become patent," the alien said. "Come along, I'll show you the way to the departures hall. Or are you meeting someone?"

They started to walk. Dairine began to relax a little: This was more like it. "No," she said, "I'm just traveling. But please, what planet is this?"

"Earth," said the alien.

Dairine was surprised for a second, and then remembered having read somewhere that almost every sentient species calls its own planet "Earth" or "the world" or something similar. "I mean, what do other people call it?"

"All kinds of things, as usual. Silly names, some of them. There'll be a master list in the terminal; you can check that."

"Thanks," Dairine said, and then was shocked and horrified to see a large triangular piece of the terminal fall off the main mass of the building. Except that it didn't fall more than a short distance, and then it regained its height and soared away, a gracefully tumbling pyramid. "Does it do that often?" she said when she could breathe again.

"Once every few beats," said the alien; "it's the physical-transport shuttle. Are you on holiday? Mind the slide, now."

"Yes," Dairine started to say, until the alien stepped onto a stationary piece of pavement in front of them and instantly began slipping away from her toward the bizarre mass of the terminal building at high speed. The surprise was too sudden to react to: Her foot hit the same piece of paving and slipped from under her as if she had stepped on ice. Dairine threw her arms out to break her fall, except that there wasn't one. She was proceeding straight forward, too, tilted somewhat backward, at about fifty miles an hour. Her heart hammered. It hammered worse when something touched her from behind; she whipped around, or tried to. It was only the alien's luggage, reaching out to tilt her forward so she stood straight. "What *is* this?!" she said.

"Slidefield," the alien said, proceeding next to her, without moving, at the same quick pace. "Inertia-abeyant selectively frictionless environment. Here we go. Which gating facility are you making for?"

"Uh—"

It was all happening too fast. The terminal building swept forward swift as a leaping beast, rearing up a thousand stories high, miles across, blotting out the sky. The slide-field poured itself at what looked like a blank silvery wall a hundred feet sheer. Dairine threw her arms up to protect herself and succeeded only in bashing her face with the computer; the wall burst like a thin flat cloud against her face, harmless, and they were through.

"The Crossings," said the alien. "What do you think?"

She could not have told him in an hour's talking. The Crossings Hypergate Facility on Rirhath B is renowned among the Billion Homeworlds for its elegant classical Lilene architecture and noble proportions; but Dairine's only cogent thought for several minutes was that she had never imagined being in an airline terminal the size of New Jersey. The ceiling—or ceilings, for there were thousands of them, layered, interpenetrating, solid and lacy, in steel and glass, in a hundred materials and a hundred colors—all towered up into a distance where clouds, real clouds, gathered; about a quarter mile off to one side, it appeared to be raining. Through the high greenish air, under the softened light of the fluorescing sky that filtered in through the thousand roofs, small objects that might have been machines droned along, towing parcels and containers behind them. Beneath, scattered all about on the terminal floor, were stalls, platforms, counters, racks, built in shapes Dairine couldn't understand, and with long, tall signs placed beside them that Dairine couldn't begin to read. And among the stalls and kiosks, the whole vast white floor was full of people—clawed, furred, shelled, or armored, upright or crawling, avian, insectile, mammalian, lizardlike, vegetable—mingling with forms that could not be described in any Earthly terms. There were a very few hominids, none strictly human; and their voices were lost in the rustling, wailing, warbling, space-softened cacophony of the terminal floor. People hopped and stepped and leaped and walked and crawled and oozed and slid and tentacled and went in every imaginable way about their uncounted businesses, followed by friends and families and fellow travelers, by luggage floating or walking; all purposeful, certain, every one of them having somewhere to go, and going there.

Every one of them except Dairine, who was beginning to wish she had not come.

"There," said the alien, and Dairine was glad of that slight warning, because the slide-field simply stopped working and left her standing still. She waved her arms, overcompensating, and her stomach did a frightened wrench and tried once or twice, for old times' sake, to get rid of food that was now on Ananke.

"Here you are," said the alien, gesturing with its various tentacles. "Arrivals over there, departures over that way, stasis and preservation down there, !!!!! over there"—the computer made a staticky noise that suggested it was unable to translate something—"and of course waste disposal. You enjoy your trip, now; I have to catch up with my fathers. Have a nice death!"

"But—," Dairine said. Too late. The broad armored shape had taken a few steps into a small crowd, stepped on a spot on the floor that looked exactly like every other, and vanished.

Dairine stood quite still for a few minutes; she had no desire to hit one of those squares by accident. *I'm a spud*, she thought, *a complete imbecile. Look at this. Stuck in an airport—something like an airport—with no money, no ID that these people'll recognize, no way to explain how I got here or how I'm gonna get out—no way to understand half of what's going on, scared to death to move . . . and pretty soon some security guard or cop or something is going to see me standing here and come over to find out what's wrong, and they're gonna haul me off somewhere and lock me up . . .*

The thought was enough to hurriedly start her walking again. She glanced around to try to make sense of things. There were lots of signs posted all over— or rather, in most cases, hanging nonchalantly in midair. But she could read none of them. While she was looking at one written in letters that at a distance seemed like roman characters, something bumped into Dairine fairly hard, about shin height. She staggered and caught herself, thinking she had tripped over someone's luggage. But there was nothing in her path at all. She paused, confused, and then tried experimentally to keep walking: The empty air resisted her. And then behind her someone said, "Your pardon," and slipped right past her: something that looked more or less like a holly tree, but it was walking on what might have been stumpy roots, and the berries were eyes, all of which looked at Dairine as the creature passed. She gulped. The creature paid her no mind, simply walked through the bit of air that had been resisting Dairine and vanished as the thing with the tentacles had earlier. Just as it blinked out of existence, air whiffing past Dairine into the place where it had been, she thought she caught sight of what looked like a little triangular piece of shiny plastic or metal held in one of the thing's leaves.

A ticket, Dairine thought; and a little more wandering and watching showed her that this was the case. Wherever these little gates might lead, none of them would let you step on it unless you had the right ticket for it: Probably the bit of plastic was a computer chip, programmed with the fact that you had paid your fare. So there was no need to fear that she might suddenly fall unshielded into some environment where they were breathing methane or swimming around in lava.

Dairine began to wander again, feeling somewhat better. *I can always sit down in a corner somewhere and program another jump*, she thought. *Be smart to do that now, though. In case something starts to happen and I want to get out quick . . .*

She looked for a place to sit. Off to one side was a big collection of racks and benches, where various creatures were hung up or lying on the floor. On a hunch she said to the computer, "Is it safe to sit over there?"

"Affirmative," said the computer.

Dairine ambled over in the direction of the racks and started searching for something decent to sit in.

The creatures she passed ignored her. Dairine found it difficult to return the compliment. One of the racks had what looked like a giant blue vampire bat hanging in it. Or no, it had no fur. The thing was actually more like a pterodactyl, and astonishingly pretty—the blue was iridescent, like a hummingbird's feathers. Dairine walked around it, fascinated, for quite a long time, pretending to look for a chair.

But there seemed to be no chairs in this particular area. The closest to a chairlike thing was a large low bowl that was full of what seemed to be purple Jell-O . . . except that the Jell-O put up a long blunt limb of itself, the end of which swiveled to follow as Dairine passed. She hurried by; the effect was rather like being looked at by a submarine periscope, and the Jell-O thing had about as much expression. *Probably wonders what the heck I am*, she thought. *Boy, is it mutual. . . .*

Finally, she settled for the floor. She brought up the utilities menu and started running down the list of planets again . . . then stopped and asked for the Help utility.

"Nature of query," said the computer.

"Uh . . ." Dairine paused. Certainly this place was what she had thought she wanted—a big cosmopolitan area full of intelligent alien creatures. But at the same time there were hardly any hominids, and she felt bizarrely out of place. Which was all wrong. She wanted someplace where she would be able to make sense of things. But how to get that across to the computer? It seemed as though, even though it was magical, it still used and obeyed the laws of science and was as literal and unhelpful as a regular computer could be if you weren't sufficiently familiar with it to know how to tell it what you wanted.

"I want to go somewhere else," she said to the machine.

"Define parameters," said the computer.

"Tell me what kind of syntax I should use."

"Command syntax. Normal syntactical restrictions do not apply in the Help facility. Commands and appended arguments may be stated in colloquial-vernacular form. Parameters may be subjected to manual analysis and discussion if desired."

"Does that mean I can just talk to you?" Dairine said.

"Affirmative."

"And you'll give me advice?"

"Affirmative."

She let out a breath. "OK," she said. "I want to go somewhere else."

"Acknowledged. Executing."

"No, don't!" Dairine said, and several of the aliens around her reacted to the shriek. One of the holly tree people, standing nearby in something like a flowerpot, had several eyes fall off on the floor.

"Overridden," said the computer.

"Help facility!" Dairine said, breathing hard. Her heart was pounding.

"On-line."

"Why did you start doing that?!"

" 'OK' is a system command causing an exit from the Help facility and a return to command level," said the computer.

"Do not run *any* program until I state the full command with arguments and end the sequence with 'Run'!"

"Affirmative," said the computer. "Syntax change confirmed."

Oh, Lord, Dairine thought, *I've started messing with the syntax and I don't even* understand *it. I will never never use a program again till I've read the docs* . . . "Good," she said. "The following is a string of parameters for a world I want to transit to. I will state 'End of list' when finished."

"Affirmative. Awaiting listing."

"Right. I want to go somewhere else."

"Transit agenda, confirmed. Specific arguments, please."

"Uhh . . ." She thought. "I want to go somewhere where there are going to be people like me."

"Noted. Next argument."

What exactly am *I looking for? Darth Vader* . . . She opened her mouth, then closed it again. *I think I'll wait a bit on that one.* "I want to go somewhere where I'm expected," she said.

"Noted. Next argument."

"Somewhere where I can use some of this magic."

"Argument already applies," said the computer. "You are using wizardry at this time."

Dairine made a face. "Somewhere where I can sit down and figure out what it means."

"Argument already applies. Documentation is available at this time."

Dairine sighed. "Somewhere where I will have *time* to sit down and figure out what it means."

"Incomplete argument. State time parameter."

"A couple of days. Forty-eight hours," she said then, before it could correct her syntax.

"Noted. Next argument."

"Somewhere—" One more time she stopped, considering the wild number of variables she was going to have to specify. And the truth was, she didn't know what she was after. *Except* . . . She looked around her conspiratorially, as if someone might overhear her. Indeed, she would have died if, say, Nita should ever hear this. "Somewhere I can do something," she whispered. "Something big. Something that matters."

"Noted," said the computer. "Next argument."

"Uh . . ." The embarrassment of the admission out loud had driven everything out of her head. "End arguments," she said.

"Advisory," said the computer.

"So advise me."

"Stated number of arguments defines a very large sample of destinations. Stated number of arguments allows for interference in transit by other instrumentalities. Odds of interference approximately ninety-six percent."

That brought Dairine's chin up. "Let 'em try," she said. "The arguments stand."

"Instruction accepted. End advisory."

"Fine. List program."

"Transit program. Sort for Terran-type hominids along maximal space-time curvature. Sort for anticipated arrival, time continuum maximal but skewed to eliminate paradox. Sort for opportunity for intervention. Sort for data analysis period on close order, forty-eight hours. Sort for intervention curve skewed to maximal intervention and effect. End list."

"You got it," Dairine said. "Name listed program 'TRIP I.' "

"Named."

"Save it. Exit Help facility."

"TRIP I saved. Command level," said the computer.

"Run TRIP I."

"Running. Input required."

Dairine rolled her eyes at the mile-high ceiling. *Nita doesn't do it this way*, she thought. *I've watched her. She just reads stuff out of her book or says it by heart . . . Oh, well, someone has to break new ground.* She stretched her legs out in front of her to keep them from cramping. "Specify," she said.

"Birth date."

"Twenty October nineteen seventy-eight," she said, looking out across the floor at the great crowd of pushing and jostling aliens.

"Place of birth."

"Three-eight-five East Eighty-sixth Street, New York City." The hospital had long since burned down, but Dairine knew the address; her dad had taken them all there to a German restaurant now on the site.

"Time of birth."

"Twelve fifty-five A.M."

"Favorite color."

"You have *got* to be kidding!" she said, looking at a particularly busy knot of aliens across the floor. Security guards, most likely: They were armed, in a big group, and looking closely at people.

"Favorite color."

"Blue." Or *were* these critters security guards? There had been other creatures walking around in the terminal wearing uniforms—as much or as little clothing of a particular shade of silvery green as each alien in question felt like wearing. And their weapons had been slim little blue metal rods strapped to them. *These* creatures, though—they wore no uniforms, and their weapons were large and dark and looked nasty.

"Last book read," said the computer.

"Look," Dairine said, "what do you need to know this dumb stuff for?"

"Program cannot be accurately run without the enacting wizard's personal data. You have no data file saved at this time."

She made another face. *Better not interfere*, she thought, *or you might wind up doing the breaststroke in lava after all.* "Oh, go on," she said.

"Last book read—"

"The Decline and Fall of the Roman Empire," said Dairine, looking with increasing unease at the armed bunch of aliens. They were not nice-looking people. Well, *lots* of the people in here didn't look nice—that purple Jell-O thing, for one—but none of them *felt* bad: just weird. But these creatures with the guns— they had an unfriendly look to them. Most of them were mud-colored warty-looking creatures like a cross between lizards and toads, but upright and not nearly as pretty as a lizard or as helplessly homely as any toad. They went about with a

lumpish hunchbacked swagger, and their eyes were dark slitted bulges or fat crimson bloodshot goggle-eyes. They looked stupid, and worse, they looked cruel. . . .

Oh, come on, Dairine told herself in disgust. *Just because they're ugly doesn't mean they're bad. Maybe it's just some kind of military expedition, like soldiers coming through the airport on their way home for leave.*

—but with their guns?

"Father's name," said the computer.

"Harold Edward Callahan," said Dairine. She was looking with a combination of interest and loathing at one of the warty creatures, which was working its way toward her. In one arm it was cradling a gun with a barrel big enough to shove a hero sandwich down. In its other hand, a knobby three-fingered one, it held the end of a leash, and straining at the leash's far end was something that looked more like the stuffed deinonychus at Natural History than anything Dairine had ever seen. A skinny little dinosaur it was, built more or less along the lines of a tyrannosaurus, but lithe and small and fleet. This one went all on its hind legs, its long thin tail stretched out behind it for balance; it went with a long-legged ostrichy gait that Dairine suspected could turn into an incredible sprint. The dinosaur on the warty alien's leash was dappled in startling shades of iridescent red and gold, and it had its face down to the floor as it pulled its master along, and the end of that long whiplike tail thrashed. And then it looked up from the floor and looked right at Dairine, with eyes that were astonishingly innocent, and as blue as a Siamese cat's. It made a soft mewling noise that nonetheless pierced right through the noise of the terminal.

The warty thing looked right at Dairine, too—and cried out in some language the computer didn't translate. The sound was a bizarre soprano singing of notes like a synthesizer playing itself. Then it yanked the leash sharply and let the deinonychus go.

Dairine scrambled to her feet as the deinonychus loped toward her. Terrified as she was, she knew better than to try to run away from *this* thing. She slammed the computer's screen closed and waited. *No kicks*, she told herself; *if one kick doesn't take this thing out, you'll never have time for a second—* It leaped at her, but she was already swinging: Dairine hit the deinonychus right in the face with the computer and felt something crunch. *Oh, please don't let it be the plastic*, she thought, and then the impetus of the deinonychus carried it right into her; its broken jaw knocked against her face as it fell, and she almost fell with it. Dairine stumbled back, found her footing, turned, and began to run.

Behind her, more voices were lifted. Dairine ran like a mad thing, pushing through crowds wherever she could. *Who are they? Why are they after me? And where do I run . . . ?*

She dodged through a particularly dense crowd and paused, looking for a corridor to run down, a place to hide. Nothing. This part of the Crossings was one huge floor, very few niches to take advantage of. But farther on, about half a mile away, it looked like the place narrowed. . . .

She ran. The noise behind her was deafening. There was some shooting: She heard the scream of blasterbolts, the sound that had set her blood racing in the movies. But now it wasn't so exciting. One bolt went wide over her head. It hit a low-floating bit of the ceiling off to one side of her, and she smelled the stink of scorched plastic and saw a glob of it fall molten to splat on the floor. Dairine sprinted past it, panting. She was a good runner, but she couldn't keep this up for much longer.

Bug-eyed monsters! her brain sang at her in terror. *These weren't what I had in mind!* "What *are* they—"

"Emissaries," said the computer, in a muffled voice since its screen was shut over its speaker.

Dairine kept running. "From where?"

"Indeterminate. Continue run?"

"If it'll get me out of here, *yes!*"

"Last level of education finished—"

She told it, gasping, as she ran. She told it her mother's maiden name, and how much money her father made, and at what age she had started reading, and much more useless information. . . . And then while she was telling it what she thought of boys, something caught her by the arm.

It was a three-fingered hand, knobby, a slick dark green, and strong with a terrible soft strength that pulled her right out of her run and around its owner as if she were spinning around a pole. Dairine cried out at her first really close look at a bug-eyed monster. Its eyes were an awful milky red that should have meant it was blind, but they saw her too well entirely—and it sang something high at her and grabbed her up against it with its other hand, the nonchalant don't-hurt-it grasp of the upper arms that adults use on children, not knowing how they hate it . . . or not caring. Dairine abruptly recognized the BEM's song as laughter, once removed from the horrible low laughing she had seemed to hear in transit. And suddenly she *knew* what these things were, if not who. "*No!*" she screamed.

"Intervention subroutine?" said the computer, utterly calm.

Dairine struggled against the thing, couldn't get leverage: All the self-defense she had been taught was for use on humans, and this thing's mass was differently distributed. Not too far away, she heard more of the horrid fluting—BEMs with guns, coming fast. Half her face was rammed up against its horrible hide, and her nose was full of a stink like old damp coffee grounds. Her revulsion was choking her. The grasp of the thing on her was as unhuman as if she were being held by a giant cockroach . . . and Dairine *hated* bugs. "*Kill it!*" she screamed.

And something threw her back clear a good twenty feet and knocked her head against the floor. . . .

Dairine scrambled up. The BEM was gone. Or rather, it wasn't a BEM anymore. It was many many little pieces of BEM, scattered among splatters of dark liquid all over the floor and all over everything else in the area, including her. Everything smelled like an explosion in a coffee shop.

Hooting noises began to fill the air. *Oh no*, Dairine thought as she grabbed the computer up from the floor and began to run again. Now this place's own security people were going to start coming after her. They would ask her questions. And no matter how little a time they did that for, the BEMs would be waiting. If they waited. If they didn't just come and take her away from the port's security. And even if she killed every BEM in the place, more would come. She knew it.

She ran. People looked at her as she ran. Some of them were hominid, but not even they made any move to stop her or help her: they looked at her with the blank nervousness of innocent bystanders watching a bank robber flee the scene of the crime. Dairine ran on, desperate. It was like some nightmare of being mugged in a big city where the streets are full of people and no one moves to help.

The blasterscreams were a little farther behind her. Maybe the one BEM's fate had convinced the others it would be safer to pick her off from a distance. *But then why didn't they do that before?*

Unless they wanted her alive. . . .

She ran and ran. That laughter in the dark now pounded in her pulse, racing, and in the pain in the side that would shortly cripple her for running. Something she had read in Nita's manual reoccurred to her: old Powers, not friendly to what lives—and one of the oldest and strongest, which had invented death and was cast out. . . . Part of her, playing cold and logical, rejected this, insisted she had no data, just a feeling. But the feeling screamed *Death!* and told logic to go stuff it somewhere. These things belonged to that old Power. She needed a safe place to think what to do. Home . . . But no. Take these things home with her? Her mom, her dad, these things would—

But maybe Nita and Kit could help—

But admit that she *needed* help?

Yes. No. *Yes*—

But without resetting the transit program, she couldn't even do that. No time . . .

"Can you run subroutines of that program before you finish plugging in the variables?" Dairine said, gasping as she ran.

"Affirmative."

"Then do it, as soon as you can!"

"Affirmative. Name of best friend—"

She wondered for a second whether 'Shash Jackson was still her best friend after she had cleaned him out of his record money three days ago. Then she gave his name anyway. Red lines of light lanced over her head as she ran. And here, the ceiling was getting lower, the sides of the building were closer, there were smaller rooms, places to go to ground. . . .

The stitch in her side was killing her. She plowed through a crowd of what looked like ambulatory giant squid on a group tour, was lost among them for a moment, in a sea of waving purple tentacles, tripping over their luggage, which crowded aside squawking and complaining—then came out the other side of them and plunged into a smaller corridor about the size of Grand Central Station.

She kept giving the computer inane information as she ran down the corridor, pushing herself to the far side of the stitch, so that she could reach someplace to be safe for a minute. There were more gates here, more signs and seating areas, and off to one side, a big shadowy cul-de-sac. She ran for it, any cover being better than none.

At the very end of her energy, she half ran, half stumbled in. It was unmistakably a bar. If she had had any breath to spare, she would have laughed with the dear familiarity of it, for it looked completely like other bars she had seen in airports when traveling with her folks and Nita—fairly dim and crowded with tables and chairs and people and their bags. But no mere airport bar had ever had the kind of clientele that this place did. Tall furry things with too many arms, and squat many-legged things that looked to be wearing their organs on the outside, and one creature that seemed totally made of blinking eyes, all stared at Dairine

over their snacks and drinks as she staggered in and past them—and not one of
them moved.

Dairine didn't care. Her only thought was to hide. But she realized with horror
that she could see no back way out of the place—only a dark red wall and a couple
of what might have been abstract sculptures, unless they were aliens, too. She
heard the cries out in the terminal getting closer, and utter panic overcame her.
Dairine shouldered and stumbled her way frantically among strange bodies and
strange luggage in the semidarkness, hardly caring what she might or might not be
touching. Momentum and blind terror crashed her right into a little table at the
back of the room, almost upsetting both the table and the oddly shaped, half-full
glass on it. And then something caught her and held her still.

After her experience out in the terminal, Dairine almost screamed at the touch.
But then she realized that what held her were human hands. She could have sobbed
for relief but had no breath to spare. So rattled was she that though she stared right
at the person who was steadying her, it took her precious seconds to see him. He
was built slight and strong, wearing a white shirt and sweater and a long fawn-
colored jacket; a fair-haired young man with quick bright eyes and an intelligent
face. "Here now," he said, helping her straighten up. "Careful!" And he said it in
English!

Dairine opened her mouth to beg for help, but before she could say a word,
those wise, sharp eyes had flickered over her and away, taking everything in.

"Who's after you?" the man said, quiet-voiced but urgent, glancing back at
Dairine.

"I don't know what they are," she said, gasping, "but someone—someone bad
sent them. I can lose them, but I need time to finish programming—"

Alarm and quick thought leaped behind those brown eyes. "Right. Here then,
take these." The young man dug down in his jacket pocket, came up with a fistful
of bizarrely shaped coins, and pressed them hurriedly into Dairine's free hand.
"There's a contact transfer disk behind the bar. Step on it and you should materi-
alize out in the service corridor. Follow that to the right and go out the first blue
door you see, into the terminal. If I'm not mistaken, the pay toilets will be a few
doors down on your left. Go in one of the nonhuman ones."

"The nonhuman—!" Dairine said, absolutely horrified.

"Quite so," the man said. "Right across the universe, that's one of the strongest
taboos there is." And he grinned, his eyes bright with mischief. "No matter who's
after you, it'll take them a bit to think of looking for you in there. And the locks
will slow them down." He was on his feet. "Off you go now!" he said, and gave
Dairine a fierce but friendly shove in the back.

She ran past a trundling robot barman, under the hinged part of the bartop, and
onto the transfer circle. On the other side of the bar, as Dairine began to vanish,
she saw the man glance over at her to be sure she was getting away, and then pick
up the iced tea he had been drinking. Glass in hand, he went staggering cheerfully
off across the barroom in the most convincing drunk act Dairine could imagine,
accidentally overturning tables, falling into the other patrons, and creating a mess
and confusion that would slow even the BEMs up somewhat.

Dairine materialized in the service corridor, followed her instructions to the
letter, and picked a rest room with a picture sign so weird, she couldn't imagine
what the aliens would look like. She found out soon enough. She spent the next

few minutes hastily answering the computer's questions while sitting on what looked like a chrome-plated lawn mower, while the tiled room outside her locked booth echoed with the bubbling screams of alien ladies (or gentlemen) disturbed in the middle of who knew what act.

Then the screams became quiet and were exchanged for a horrible rustling noise, thick soft footfalls, and high fluting voices. The computer had asked Dairine whether she preferred Coke or Pepsi and had then fallen silent for some seconds. "Are you done?" she hissed at it.

"Running. Data in evaluation."

"Get a move on!"

"Running. Data in evaluation."

The air filled with the scorch of burning plastic again. They were burning the lock of the booth.

"Can you do something to a few of them?" she whispered, her mouth going dry.

"Negative multitasking ability," said the computer.

Dairine put her head down on the computer, which was on her knees, and took what she suspected might be her last breath.

The lock of the booth melted loose, and the door fell in molten globs to the floor. Dairine sat up straight, determined to look dirty at the BEMs, if she could do nothing else.

The door swung open.

And, "Multiple transit," said the computer, "executing now," and the jump-sickness grabbed Dairine and twisted her outside-in. Perhaps not understanding, the BEMs fluted in rage and triumph and reached into the booth. But Dairine's insides went cold as, dimly, she felt one of them swing a huge soft hand through where her middle was: or rather, where it no longer was completely—the transit had begun. A second later, heat not wholly felt stitched through her arms and legs as shots meant to cripple her tore through where they almost were and fried the back of the stall like an egg. Then starlight and the ancient black silence pierced through her brain; the spell tore Dairine free of the planet and flung her off Rirhath B into the long night.

She never found out anything about the man who helped her. Nor did he ever find out anything more about her. Pausing by the door of the pay toilet after being released from station security some hours later, and being telepathically sensitive (as so many hominids are), he could sense only that some considerable power had been successfully exercised there. Satisfied with that, he smiled to himself and went on about his travels, just one more of the billions of hominids moving about the worlds. But many millions of light-years later, in some baking wilderness under a barren, brilliant sky, a bitterly weary Dairine paused in her flight, sat down on a stone, and cried for a while in shock at the utter strangeness of the universe, where unexpected evil lives side by side with unexpected kindness, and neither ever seems quite overcome by the other. . . .

Variables

IT TOOK NITA A few minutes to pull her supplies together and get ready for the trip. Every wizard has favorite spells, so familiar and well used that diagrams and physical ingredients like eye of newt aren't needed for them. But most spells, and particularly the most powerful ones, need help in bending space—some specific kind of matter placed in specific relationship to the wizard and the words being used and the diagram or formula asserting the wizard's intent. Some of the kinds of matter used for these purposes can be odder even than eye of newt (which used to be used for teleportation spells until polyethylene was invented). And this being the case, most wizards have a cache, a place where they keep the exotica necessary in their work.

Nita's cache was buried in a vacant lot next door to her house, all carefully wrapped in a plastic garbage bag. Being a wizard, she had no need to dig the bag up: A variant of the spell Kit had used on the bricks let her feel around under the ground for the moment it took her to find what she wanted. The objects didn't look like much—half a (seemingly) broken printed-circuit board; a plastic packet containing about two teaspoonsful of dirt; and a gimbal from a 1956 Philco Pilot television set.

That last piece she juggled appreciatively from hand to hand for a moment. It was certainly unlikely looking, a busted bit of junk that any normal person would trash without a second thought. But the configuration into which the space-time continuum bent itself around this gimbal was unique and invested with a power that the informed wizard could exploit. *Everything* bent spacetime, of course: Anything consisting of either matter or energy had no choice. But some things bent it in ways that produced specific physical effects . . . and no one, not even the wizards specializing in theoretical research, had any idea yet as to *why*. The atoms and mass and inherent spatiotemporal configuration of, say, water bent existence around them to produce an effect of wetness. The electrons and plasma and matter and gravity of a star produced effects of heat and light. And a busted-off piece of gimbal from an ancient TV set . . .

Nita smiled a bit, put the gimbal carefully in her pocket, and said three more words.

Her room was dark. She flipped the light on and went digging in the mess off to one side for her knapsack. Into it she stuffed her manual, the gimbal and packet and circuit board.

"Nita?"

"Uh-huh," she said.

The stairs creaked. Then her mother was standing in the doorway, looking upset.

"You said you were going to clean your room today," her mother said in a tired voice.

Nita looked up . . . then went hurriedly to her mother and grabbed her and hugged her hard. "Oh, thanks," she said, "thanks, *thanks* for saying something normal!"

Her mother laughed, a sound that had no happiness about it at all, and hugged her back. After a moment her mother said, "She won't be normal when she gets back, will she?"

Nita took a moment to answer. "She won't be like she was, not completely. She can't. Dairine's on Ordeal, Mom: It changes you. That's what it's about." Nita tried to smile, but it felt broken. "She might be better."

"Better? Dairine?" her mother said, sounding a touch dry. Nita's smile began to feel less broken, for that sounded more like her mother.

"Oh, c'mon, Mom, she's not that bad—" Then Nita stopped herself. *What am I saying?* "Look, Mom," she said. "She's real smart. Sometimes that makes me want to stuff her in the toilet, but it's going to come in handy for her now. She's not stupid, and if the wizards' software in the computer is anything like our manuals, she'll have some help as long as she keeps her head and figures out what to ask for. If we get a move on, we'll catch up with her pretty quick."

"If you can find her." Nita's father loomed up in the doorway in the darkness, a big silver-haired shadow.

Nita swallowed. "Daddy, she'll leave a trail. Using wizardry changes the shape of the space-time continuum . . . It's like cutting through a room full of smoke with a knife. You can see where the knife's been. Knowing Dairine, she won't be making any effort to cover her trail . . . at least not just yet. We can follow her. If she's in trouble, we'll get her out of it. But I can't stay to talk about it. Kit needs me quick, and I can't do a lot for Dari without him. Some . . . but not as much. We work best as a team."

Her mother gave her father a look that Nita could make nothing of. "When do you think you three will be back?" said her father.

"I don't know," Nita said. She thought to say something, stopped herself, then realized that they had a right to know. "Mom, Dad, look. We might not be able to bring her back right away. It's *her* Ordeal. Until she solves the problem she's supposed to be the answer to, if we pull her back, awful things could happen. If we'd copped out of ours, this whole world would be different. And believe me, you wouldn't have liked the difference." She swallowed at the thought of something like that leaning, threatening darkness waiting for Dairine to confront it . . . something like that, but *much* worse.

They stood and looked at her.

"I've gotta go," she said, and slung her knapsack on and hugged them hard, first her dad and then her mom again. Her father took a long time to let her go. Her mother's eyes were still troubled, and there was nothing Nita could do about it, nothing at all.

"I'll clean up in here as soon as I get home," Nita said. "I promise."

The trouble didn't go out of her mother's face, but half her mouth made a smile.

Nita said three words and was gone.

*　　*　　*

Our home galaxy is a hundred thousand light-years across, five thousand light-years thick at the core. The billion stars that make it up are scattered through some four quadrillion cubic miles of space. It is so vast that a thought can take as long as two seconds to cross it.

But Dairine was finding the entirety of the Milky Way much too small to get lost in. She got out of it as soon as she could.

The program the computer was still writing to take her to safety was a multiple-jump program, and that suited her fine: her pursuers seemed to have trouble following her. But not enough trouble. She came out, after that first jump from Rirhath B, on some cold world whose sky she never saw: only a ceiling of gray. She was standing in a bleak place, full of what at first sight looked like old twisted, wind-warped trees, barren of any leaves, all leaning into a screaming wind that smelled of salt water. Dairine clutched the computer to her and stared around her, still gasping from her terror in a rest room twelve trillion miles away.

With a slow creaking sound, one of the trees pulled several of its roots out of the ground and began to walk toward her.

"No *way*!" Dairine shrieked. "Run another subroutine!"

"Running," said the computer, but it took its sweet time about it—and just as the world blinked out and the spell tore her loose from the hillside, Dairine felt wind on her skin—a wind that smelled of coffee grounds. The BEMs had popped right in behind her.

She popped out again, this time in the middle of a plain covered with sky blue grass under a grass green sky. She shook the computer in frustration.

"Program running," the computer insisted.

"Sure, but they're following us! How are they doing it? Are we leaving a trail somehow?"

"Affirmative," said the computer calmly, as if Dairine should have known this all along.

"Well, *do* something about it!"

"Advisory," said the computer. "Stealth procedures will decrease running speed. Stealth procedures are not one hundred percent effective, due to inherent core-level stability of string functions—"

"I'll settle! And if we don't have to keep wasting time running subroutines," Dairine said, exasperated, "you'll have more time to run the main program, won't you!"

"Affirmative. Execute stealth?"

"Before someone executes *me*, yeah!"

Once again the spell took hold of Dairine and ripped her free of gravity and light. At least, she thought, this time the BEMs hadn't appeared before she vanished herself. *Maybe we can gain a little ground. We'd better . . .*

Another reality flicked into being around her. She was in the middle of a city. She got a brief impression of glassy towers that looked more grown than built, and people rushing around her and avoiding her in the typical dance of city dwellers. This might almost have been New York, except that New Yorkers had only a small percentage of the legs these people had. "Don't stop," she said. "How much range have you got?"

"Infinite," said the computer quite calmly.

"While still running the main program?"

"Affirmative."

She thought for a second. "The edge of the Local Group of galaxies might be far enough. Go."

The spell seized her out of the crowd and flung her into the dark again. Over and over Dairine jumped, becoming less and less willing to stop, until finally strange vistas were flickering past her with the speed of some unutterably strange slide show being run in fast-forward by a bored lecturer. She passed right through the coronation parade of one of the anarchs of Deleian IV and never noticed it; she stood for only a second on a chilly little planetoid being fought over by two desperate interstellar empires (and also missed the nova bomb that turned the planetoid into plasma several minutes later); she stood on the metallic upper floors of a planet that was one great library full of three galaxies' knowledge, and she never knew what it was and probably at that point would not have cared. Only once did Dairine pause for more than a few seconds, on a red sandstone promontory with a pinkish sea crashing at its foot and no signs of life anywhere under the bloated red sun that dyed the water. "Are they still following?" she said.

"Probability high, but at a greatly increased distance."

"You have enough time to finish the main program?"

"Affirmative."

"Do it, then."

She sat down on a rock and looked out at the water while the computer's disk drive chirred softly to itself. The fat red sun slipped horizonward as she watched, and Dairine looked at it and noticed through the sunset haze that it had a companion, a little blue-white dwarf star that was slowly sucking the red giant's matter out of it in an accretion spiral of tarnished gold. She shook her head. Once she would have given anything to sit here and watch this. Now, though, the hair was rising on the back of her neck, and her back prickled, and all she wanted in the world—the worlds—was to get out of here and end up where she could hide.

She shivered. *I never want to smell coffee again*, she thought. They had unquestionably been sent after her by what had laughed at her in the dark. The Lone Power, the Manual utility had called It. Well, at least she didn't hear It laughing anymore while she was in transit. Then again, that might not be good. *I'm running pretty fair rings around Its people. It's probably real annoyed at me.*

And then she tossed her head and grinned, her nasty grin. *Let It be, then. I'm not going to be running for long. I'm going to turn around and give It something to think about.*

If I can just figure out what to do, and find a weapon . . .

"Done," said the computer.

"Is this going to be a bad jump?" Dairine said.

"Transit may have significant physiological effects," said the computer.

"OK," Dairine said. "Go for it." And she clenched her jaw.

The computer was understating. The jump was a hundred times worse than the first long one, an eternity of being torn, squeezed out of shape, pulled, hammered on, sliced by lines of force thinner than any hair and sharp as swords. Dairine hung on, unable even to scream. The transit broke for an instant on the surface of some planet as the program finished one jump subroutine, in a frozen flash of light and time too sudden to let any of the scream out, then pushed Dairine outside the universe and crushed her under its weight again. Then flash, and again; flash, and

again: flash, flash, flash, flash, through a voiceless darkness a trillion years heavy
and empty as entropy's end. This was the worst after all, the aloneness, total, no
one to hear the scream she could not utter, not even the One who laughed—flash,
flash, flash—

—and then the crushing ceased, and the spell flung Dairine down on something
flat and hard and chill, and she flopped down like a puppet with its strings cut and
just lay there as she had not done since Ananke. Her stomach flipped, but this was
becoming so commonplace that Dairine was able to ignore it and just lie there and
pant for a few seconds.

Silence. Not that awful emptiness but a more normal one: probably just lack
of air. Dairine levered herself up painfully on her elbows and looked at the surface
under her hands. It was dimly lit and smooth as the garage floor on Rirhath B had
been. Smoother, in fact. It was hard to tell colors in this dimness, but the surface
wasn't plain white. Dapples of various colors seemed to overlap and shade one
another in the depths of it, as delicately as if they had been airbrushed; and there
was a peculiar translucence to the surface, as if it were glass of some kind.

Cautiously, Dairine got up to a kneeling position and straightened to look
around. *Now* this *is weird*, she thought, for the surface on which she knelt stretched
on so far into the distance that she scrubbed at her eyes briefly, not quite believing
them. The horizon seemed much farther away than it could ever be on Earth. *Must
be a much bigger planet*, she thought. But the thought did not make that immense
vista any easier to grasp. It seemed to curve *up* after a while, though she was sure
it was perfectly flat: The illusion was disturbing. Over the horizon hung starry
space, the stars close and bright. Off to the sides the view was the same: Here and
there conical outcroppings of rock might break the pure and perfect flatness of it
all, looking as if Picasso had dropped them there . . . but otherwise there was nothing but that endless, pale, slick-smooth surface, dappled with touches of dim subtle
color, in huge patches or small ones.

Dairine stood up and turned around to look for the computer. It was behind
her, at her feet; she bent to pick it up—

—and forgot about doing so. Before her, past the razory edge of that impossibly distant horizon, the galaxy was rising.

It was not her own. The Milky Way is a type S0 spiral, a pinwheel of stars.
This was a barred spiral, type SB0, seen almost face-on: an oval central core, two
bars jutting from its core, one from each end of the starry oval, and each bar having
a long curved banner or stream of stars curling away from it. Dairine had seen a
hundred pictures of them and had mostly been fascinated by that central bar, wondering what gravitational forces were keeping it in place. But now she was seeing
such a galaxy as few, even wizards, ever see one—not as a flat, pale far-off picture
but as a three-dimensional object near at hand, rich with treasuries of stars in a
spectrum's worth of colors, veiled about with diamonded dust on fire with ions
and glowing, dominating a third of even that immense horizon, seeming frozen
though in the midst of irresistible motion, its starry banners streaming back in still
and complex glory from the eye-defeating blaze of the core. Dairine slowly folded
back down to the kneeling position and just watched it, watched it rise.

She weighed just a little less than she would have on Earth; but the spiral rose
quickly for a planet of this size. *Must not be a very dense planet*, Dairine thought.
All light elements—though most of her paid no attention to the analysis, being busy

with more important matters . . . this light, the terror and the wonder of it. *This* was what she had come for. The computer had hit it right on. This planet's sun must be in one of the galaxy's satellite globular clusters. . . . As such distances went, she was close to that spiral: no more than ten or twenty thousand light-years above its core. But the thought of distances broke her mood. She pulled the computer close. "Did we lose them?" she said to it.

"Pursuit has halted forty trillion light-years from this location and is holding there."

"Forty *trillion* . . ." That was beyond the reach of the farthest telescopes, over the event horizon generated by the big bang itself: Galaxies past that point were traveling with intrinsic velocities faster than light, and so could not be seen. It was questionable whether such bodies could even really be considered in the same universe as Earth.

"Long way from home," she said softly. "OK. I have at least a couple days to rest and do some research, huh?"

"Affirmative."

She sat back on her heels and watched the light rise until the last delicate streamers of light from the barred spiral arms were all the way above the horizon. "I want all the details about this star system," she said. "Planets, what kind of star, who lives here if anybody, who's been here before. Get to work."

"Working," said the computer, and its screen went to the usual menu configuration while it sat silently, getting the information for her.

"Can you multitask now?" Dairine said.

"Affirmative."

"Good."

She selected the Manual function and began sorting through it for background material on the Lone One. *There has to be something I can use against It*, she thought, *a weapon of some kind, a weakness* . . . She instructed the manual's Research facility to sort for past conflicts of wizards with the Lone Power or Its representatives, and was shocked and horrified to find the equivalent of twenty or thirty thousand pages' worth of abstracts. She skimmed ten or fifteen of them in reverse order, on a hunch, and was momentarily surprised to find an abstract of Nita's last active mission. Fascinated, Dairine began to read . . . and became horrified again. There had been some kind of ceremony in the waters off Long Island, a sort of underwater passion play with whales as the celebrants—and Nita, to save the East Coast and make this ceremony work, had volunteered to be eaten by a shark! *Nita? My sister? Do anything braver than cross the street?* The idea was ridiculous . . . but Dairine knew that this computer had better things to do than lie to her. She read the rest of the abstract with her insides turning cold. Nita had knowingly taken on that Lone Power face-to-face and had managed to come out of it alive. Whereas Dairine had been glad enough to run away and lose things that couldn't be more than Its lesser henchmen . . .

Dairine pushed that thought away resolutely. She was helped by her stomach, which growled at her.

When did *I last eat?* she wondered. She told the computer to sort through and save the descriptions of encounters with the Power that had been successful, and then got out of the Manual into the Hide facility. A moment's poking around among the options, and she had retrieved her loaf of bread, bologna, and mustard. Dairine sat there in cheerful anticipation for a few seconds, undoing the bread and bologna, and it wasn't until she got the mustard jar lid unscrewed that she realized she had no knife. "Oh, well," she said, and went back into the Hide facility to snitch one from the silverware drawer at home. But "Illegal function call," said the computer: a little sullenly, she thought.

"Explain."

"Out of range for Transit function from stated location."

Dairine made a face. She had no idea of the coordinates of any closer silverware drawer. "Cancel," she said, and made do with her fingers.

Some minutes later she had a sandwich and a half inside her and was thinking (as she finished getting herself more or less clean) that it was a good thing she liked mustard. Dairine brushed the crumbs off onto the slick surface she sat on and looked at it, mildly curious. It wasn't freezing cold to sit on, like the stones of Mars or Pluto; yet her shields were still snowing water vapor gently into the vacuum around her whenever she moved, telling her that the above-surface temperature was the usual cold of deep space. *Geothermal?* she wondered. *Maybe some volcanic activity—that would explain those funny conical shapes against the horizon . . .* She thumped the computer in a friendly fashion. "You done yet?" she said.

"Specify."

Dairine rolled her eyes. But there was no escaping the GIGO principle—"garbage in, garbage out," as the programmers said. Give the poor machine incomplete questions or instructions and you would get incomplete answers back. This thing might be magic, but it was still a computer. "Are you done with the survey of this area?"

"Still running."

"How much longer?"

"Three point two minutes."

Dairine sat back to wait, absently rubbing the surface she sat on. The smoothness of it was strange: not even the maria on the Moon were this smooth. *Volcanic eruption, maybe. But not the way it usually happens, with the lava flowing down the volcano's sides and running along the surface. Not enough gravity for it to do that, I guess. Maybe it's like the volcanoes on Io: The stuff goes up high in tiny bits or droplets, then comes down slowly in the low gravity and spreads itself out very smooth and even. It must go on all the time . . . or else there can't be much in this system in the way of even tiny meteors. Maybe both.* She shook her head. It spoke of an extremely ancient planet—which made sense this far out in space. . . .

"Ready," the computer said, and Dairine hunkered over it to listen. "Local system stats. System age: close order of eight billion years. One primary, type S6 star, off main sequence; time from fusion ignition: close order of five billion years. One associated micro black hole in variable orbit. One planet, distance from primary: six hundred twelve million miles. Planet diameter: fifty-six thousand miles. Planet circumference: one hundred seventy-five thousand miles—" And Dairine gulped, understanding now why that horizon ran so high. The planet was almost seven times the size of Earth. "Atmosphere: monatomic hydrogen, less than one fifty-millionth psi Terran sea level. Planetary composition: eighty percent silicon in pure form and compounds, ten percent iron and midsequence metals, seven percent heavy metals, one percent boron, one percent oxygen, one percent trace elements including frozen gases and solid-sequence halogens. Power advisory—"

The screen, which had been echoing all this, went blank. Dairine's stomach flip-flopped, from fear this time. "What's the matter?"

"System power levels nearing critical. Range to alternative-power claudication exceeded. Outside power source required."

Dairine paused, feeling under her hand that oddly noncold surface. "Can you use geothermal?" she said.

"Affirmative."

"Is there some way you can tap what's in this planet, then?"

"Affirmative," said the computer. "Authorization for link."

"Granted," Dairine said, mildly surprised: She couldn't remember the computer ever asking her for permission to do anything before. Maybe it was a safety feature. Then she began to sweat a little. Maybe such a safety feature was wise. If the computer fried its chips somehow and left her without life support, sitting here naked to vacuum at Heaven-knew-how-many degrees below zero . . .

She watched the screen nervously as scrambled characters flashed on it, and for several awful seconds the screen blanked. Then the menu screen reasserted itself, and Dairine breathed out, slowly, while the computer went back to running the program it had been working on. "Link established," said the computer in absolute calm. "Planetary history—"

"Just print it to the screen; I'll read it," Dairine said, and started to pick the computer up, then paused. "Is it all right to move you? Will that hurt the link?"

"Negative effect on link."

She lifted the computer into her lap and went on reading. It was as she had thought. The planet periodically became volcanically active, and the volcanoes spewed a fine mist of lava all over the landscape, airbrushing the glassy surface on a gigantic scale with vividly colored trace elements. Subsequent layering muted the colors, producing the dappled translucence she sat on. Dairine hit the return for another screenful of data, and the screenful appeared—and her stomach flipped again.

```
PLANETARY HISTORY (page 2 of 16)
HELP/g/r118655
This unique structure becomes more interesting when considering the physical nature of the
layering. Some 92% of the layers consilt of chemically pure sillcol,1 predlspollnq thl
aglllllate to elel1111111ductil11111111111111111111111111111111111111111111111111
11111111111111111111111111111111111111111111111111111111111111111111111111111111
11111111111111111111111111111111111111111111111111111111111111111111111111111111
11111111111111111111111111111111111111111111111111111111111111111111111111111111
11111111111111111111111111111111111111111111111111111111111111111111111111111111
11111111111111111111111111111111111111111111111111111111111111111111111111111111
11111111111111111111111111111111111111111111111111111111111111111111111111111111
11111111111111111111111111111111111111111111111111111111111111111111111111111111
11111111111111111111111111111111111111111111111111111111111111111111111111111111
11111111111111111111111111111111111111111111111111111111111111111111111111111111
11111111111111111111111111111111111111111111111111111111111111111111111111111111
11111111111111111111111111111111111111111111111111111111111111111111111111111111
```

"I blew it up," Dairine whispered, horrified. "Oh no, oh no, I fried its brains. I blew it up." She took a deep breath, not sure how many more of them she was going to get, and gingerly hit the return to see what would happen. . . .

Pattern Recognition

NITA POPPED OUT INTO a canopy of starlit darkness and a carpet of dim light, breathing very hard. Earth's gravity well was no joke: pushing her own mass and enough air to breathe for a while up out of that heavy pull was a problem. She walked over to a boulder, dusted it off, and sat down, panting, to admire the view while she waited for Kit.

The "usual place" where they met was, of course, the Moon. Nita liked it there; working, and thinking, were always easy there, in the great silence that no voices but astronauts' and wizards' had broken since the Moon's dust was made. This particular spot, high in the lunar Caucasus mountain chain, was a favorite of Kit's—a flat-topped peak in a wild, dangerous country of jagged gray-white alps, cratered and pocked by millennia of meteoric bombardment. Piles of rock-tumble lay here and there, choking the steep valleys where the sheer heat and cold of the lunar days had been enough to flake solid rock away from itself in great glassy or pumicey chunks. Off to one side, the pallid rim of the little crater Calippus scraped razor-sharp against the sky, and over it hung the Earth.

The Moon was at first quarter, so the Earth was at third, a blinding half-world: blazing blue-green, almost painful to look at until the eyes got used to it. It shed a cool faint blue-white light over everything. A curl of white storm weather lay over the northwestern Pacific, and there vanished; for down the middle of it the terminator ran, the edge of night, creeping ever so slowly toward the west. Most of North America lay in the darkness, and city lights lay golden in faint glittering splashes and spatters with brighter sparkling patches under the Great Lakes and on the California coast.

Nita shrugged out of her knapsack, opened it, and rechecked the contents. It was a good assortment: varied enough to handle several different classes of spell, specific enough to those classes to let her save some power for herself.

She pulled her manual out and started paging through it for the tracker spell that she and Kit would need when he got here. It was actually a variant of the one he had threatened to put on Dairine in the city: This one hunted for the characteristic charged string residue left in space by the passage of a wizard's transit spell through it. Nita's specialty was astronomy, so she had been shocked to find that "empty" space wasn't actually empty, and even the hardest vacuum had in it what physicists called strings, lines of potential force that have nothing to do with most of the forces physicists understand. Wizards, of course, could use them: Much of what passes for telekinesis turns out in fact to be string manipulation. The tracker spell made most elegant use of it. *And once we find her*, Nita thought, *I'm gonna tie a few of those strings around her neck ...*

But it didn't do to start a wizardry in such a mood. Nita pulled her space pen out of her pocket, kicked some of the larger rocks out of her way—they bounced off down the mountain as slowly as soap bubbles—and began drawing the circle for the transit spell.

It was becoming an old familiar diagram, this one. The basic circle, knotted with the wizard's knot; her own personal data, reduced by now (after much practice) to one long scrawl in the precise and elegant shorthand version of the Speech; Kit's data, another scrawl, over which she took even more care than her own. What a wizard names in the Speech is defined so: Inaccurate naming can alter the nature of the named, and Nita liked Kit just the way he was. A third long scrawl of shorthand for Picchu: Nita looked oddly at some of the variables in it, but Tom had given her the data, and he certainly knew what he was doing. Then the internal diagrams, the "intent" factors. The point of origin; the intended point of arrival or vector of travel; the desired result; the time parameters and conditional statements for life support; the balloon diagram for the ethical argument . . .

Nita wiped sweat and grit off her face and muttered at the incessant hissing in the background. Dust flew freely in one-sixth gravity and got in everything: After you went to the Moon, you immediately took a shower, for the same reasons you take one after a haircut. But there wasn't much more to do here. She finished the last few strokes of the notations in the environmental-impact statement and stood up, rubbing her back and checking her work for spelling errors.

It was all in order. But that hissing . . .

She sat down again, feeling nervous. Facility with the Speech, as with any other language, increases with time. After several months of working in a sort of pidgin Speech, Nita was finally beginning to think in it, and the results were sometimes upsetting. Once upon a time, it had been quiet on the Moon when she visited. But no more. Her more accustomed mind heard a sound in the darkness now: a low, low sound like a breath being let out, and out, and out forever. The astronomer part of her knew what it was—the so-called four-degree radiation that was all that was left of the universe's birth. Normally only radio telescopes set to the right frequency could hear it. But Nita wasn't normal. Nor was the sound just a sound to her. In it she could hear the sound of consciousness, life, as plainly as she had used to be able to hear Kit think. *That* sensitivity had decreased over time; but this one was increasing, it seemed in the deep silence, by the minute. It upset her. Suddenly the universe, which had seemed so empty, now felt crammed full of powers and intelligences that might not need planets, or bodies. And Dairine was out there in the middle of them, mucking around in her inimitable fashion. . . . Nita found herself wishing that Kit would hurry up. She very much wanted to see that cheerful face, to hear at least his voice, if not his sassy, loud cast of thought, always with that slight Hispanic accent to it. . . .

Long time since we heard each other think . . .

She had been wondering about that. Idly she began flipping through the manual, turning pages. Maybe the index—but the index did her no good: She couldn't think what heading to look under. "Come on," she muttered to the book, "give me a hand here; I don't have all day."

It was that hissing that was making her ill-tempered, she realized. A thought occurred to her, and she was glad she hadn't completely cleaned out her knapsack the other day. She reached into it and pulled out a tangle of cord and a pair of earphones and her Walkman. It was a Christmas present from her mother—the best of any present Nita had gotten last year, for she loved music and liked walking through her day with a soundtrack. Now she riffled through the pages of her manual, squinting at them in the pale Earthlight, while rock sang softly in the earphones.

Diagrams . . . She skipped that whole section, not without another glance over at Kit's name scrawled in the motionless, powdery lunar dust. He was all there: At least, he seemed to think so—it was mostly the description of himself he had carefully worked out. Of course, after their first few spells Nita had looked over his shoulder and suggested a couple additions to the data—his fondness for chocolate ice cream (which he had instantly admitted) and his craziness for poetry, especially Shakespeare (which embarrassed him and which he had refused to admit to for several days. The look on his face when Nita caught him reading *The Tempest*. Still, he admitted it, finally. . . .) She smiled a little then. He hadn't taken long to point out that her data said nothing about the fact that she devoured horse books one after another or that he had once caught her with a long stick in hand, having an energetic swordfight with one of the trees in the vacant lot. . . .

And where is he?!

She sighed and glanced down at the pages that had fallen open in her hand. One of them said:

> Wizards in the closest relationships, leading toward permanent partnership, usually find that nonverbal communication becomes rare or difficult. Other conditions obtain for other species, but for human wizards, intimacy is meaningless without barriers to overcome—and to lower. Wizards usually have little need for such in the early stages of their careers. But as this situation changes, as the wizard becomes more adept at accurate description in the Speech, and therefore more adept at evaluating the people he or she works with, the wizard's mind typically adapts to the new requirements by gradually shutting out the person most—

—permanent partnership?

No. Oh no—

Nita swallowed with a throat suddenly gone dry and slapped the book shut. For a moment she tried to do nothing but listen to the tape. It was something of Journey's—their distinctive sweet keyboards and synthesizers, wistful, singing down toward silence. And then the vocal:

> "Looking down I watch the night
> running from the sun;
> orphan stars and city lights
> fading one by one . . .
> Oh, sweet memories, I call on you now . . ."

Of course, Nita thought, *there is a lot of it going around school. Going steady, dating, pins and rings, all the silliness.* Her mother had forbidden Nita to do any such thing, telling her she was much too young. Nita didn't mind: It all seemed dumb to her. Sometimes, seeing how crazed some of the other girls her age were over the boy question, she wondered if she was normal. She was too busy, for one thing. She had something more solid than going steady. When you were a wizard—

—with a partner—

Oh, come on. It's not as if they're going to make you marry him or something!

Look at Tom and Carl—they're just buddies; they work together because they enjoy doing it . . .

But I don't want . . .

She trailed off. She didn't know what she wanted. Nita put her head down in her hands, trying to think. No answers came: only more problems. Thoughts of Kit backing her up when she was terrified, cheering her up when she was annoyed, Kit being the solid, reliable voice in the other half of a spell, the presence on the far side of the circle, matching her cadence exactly, for the fun and the challenge of it. *What's wrong with that? What's wrong with having a best friend?*

He's a boy, that's what. It's changing. I'm *changing.*

I'm scared.

She gazed up through unending night, down at oncoming morning, and tried to work out what to do. *Has he noticed this happening to him, too? And suppose he starts liking someone else better than me? Will he want to keep the team going? If only I knew what he was thinking . . .*

Then she let out a sad and annoyed breath. *It's probably nothing*, she thought. *Everything is probably fine . . .*

". . . oh, so much is wasted," sang the earphones,

"and oh so little used!—
but the trick of the dreamer
is keeping yourself from the blues—"

Hah, Nita thought. *I wish it were that simple . . .*

And the voice that sang cried out at her, so sudden and defiant that she sat erect with startlement—

"Everyone's a hero
if you want to be!
Everyone's a prisoner
holding their own key!
And every step I take,
every move I make, I'm always one step closer—
I don't mind running alone!"

It was Steve Perry's fierce, clear voice, uplifted in almost angry encouragement, hitting the chorus hard. He went on, singing something about children and concrete canyons, but Nita was still full of that startlement and hardly heard. *Even Dairine*, she thought. *There's some job out there that only she can do . . .* She had not thought of it in this light before, and the thought of Dairine as a hero staggered her and annoyed her for a moment. *Her? The runt?*

But then Nita felt ashamed. What had she been herself, not more than a few months ago? Basically a coward, afraid of everything, including herself—friendless, quiet, and smart but with no one to do any good for by being so. Things were different now; but who was she to deny Dairine her chance at being more than she had been? *And every step I take, every move I make, I'm always one step closer . . .*

And if she *can do that*, Nita thought after a moment, *I can sure ask Kit what he thinks about things—*

A sudden movement off to one side brought Nita's head around with a snap. In utter silence, silvery white dust was kicking up in a vague pale cloud from where a tall man in a polo shirt and shorts was standing. Tom bounced over to where Nita sat, being careful of his footing. Nita admired the way he bounced: He had obviously had a lot of practice at the kangaroo hop that works well in low gravities.

He paused not too far from Nita to let her shieldspell recognize his and allow it to infringe, then sat down beside Nita on the boulder, casting an analytical eye over her spell diagram. "Very neat," he said. "Nice structure. Carl has been contaminating you, I see."

"Thanks."

"Kit just called me," Tom said, brushing dust off himself. "He'll be up in a few . . . He's just settling things with his folks. I'm going to be talking to them later." Tom smiled wearily. "This seems to be my night."

"Yeah."

More silvery dust kicked up, closer and to the right. There was Kit, with his knapsack over his back and Picchu on one shoulder. "All set," he said to Tom. He looked at Nita and said, "They hollered a lot. But I think my dad is proud. Mom seems pretty calm about it." Then he laughed, a little wickedly. "My sisters are in shock."

"Can't say that I blame them."

Nita got up, dusting herself off. "Okay," Tom said. "I wanted to see you two off up here because there's data you'll need that your parents don't. Something major is going on out there. Dairine is not going to run into just some bunch of lackeys for the Lone Power out there. That One Itself is after her. But I have no indication why. And Its power is oddly veiled at the moment—concentrated and hidden. I don't think this manifestation of the Lone Power is going to be as obvious as others have been recently. So find Dairine, and look carefully at the situation. If it looks like she needs to be where she is, stay with her and do what you can for her."

He paused. "But you are going to have to be very careful. The Lone One won't mind distracting her by striking at you two . . . or using her danger to sucker you into pulling her out of the problem she's intended to correct. Use your judgment. Save her if you can."

"And if we can't?" Kit said.

Tom looked at him sadly. "See that the job gets done," he said, "whatever it is."

They were all quiet.

"There's no telling what the stakes are on this one," Tom said. "The looks of the situation may be deceiving . . . probably will. Can you take this job and do it? Don't go if you can't. If either of you isn't sure you can depend on yourself, or on the both of you, I don't want you in this. Too much can go wrong."

Kit looked at Nita, then back at Tom. "It's cool," he said.

Nita nodded. Tom looked at her.

"I know," he said. "You're upset about her. All right . . . you'll have a while to shake down, while you chase her. Meantime, Carl and I have sent word ahead through the Network so that a lot of people will be expecting you." He smiled. "You're going to find that the way wizards have to behave on Earth is the exception rather than the rule. Most of the major law-enforcement bodies in this part of the galaxy routinely call wizards in for consultations, and they owe us a lot of favors. So don't be afraid to ask the authorities wherever you go for help. Odds are you'll get it."

"OK."

"So get out of here. And good hunting."

"Thanks."

"Come here, bird," Tom said to Picchu. Nita looked up in surprise, expecting an explosion: Picchu did not take orders. She was surprised to see the macaw clamber up onto Tom's arm and reach up to nibble his ear. Tom scratched her in the good place, on the back of the head, and she went vague in the eyes for a couple of minutes, then ruffled the neck feathers up and shook herself. "You be careful," Tom said.

"I'll be fine," Picchu said, sounding cranky.

Nita repacked her knapsack, slung it on, and flipped her manual open to the marked pages with the verbal supplement for the transit spell as Tom passed Peach back to Kit. She caught Kit's eye, stepped into the circle at the same time he did. Tom backed away. Slowly, and in unison, they began to read, and the air trapped in their shield-spells began to sing the note ears sing in silence. . . .

As the spell threw them out of the solar system, Nita wondered whether she would ever see it again. . . .

Uplink

✪

PLA1ETARY H1STOR1 (p1ge 3 o1116)
HE1P11/1111111
111111111111111111111111111111111111111111111111111111111111111111
111111111111111111111111111111111111111111111111111111111111111111
111111111111111111111111111111111111111111111111111111111111111111
111111111111111111111111111111111111111111111111111111111111111111
111111111111111111111111111111111111111111111111111111111111111111
111111111111111111111111111111111111111111111111111111111111111111
111111111111111111111111111111111111111111111111111111111111111111
111111111111111111111111111111111111111111111111111111111111111111
111111111111111111111111111111111111111111111111111111111111111111
111111111111111111111111111111111111111111111111111111111111111111
111111111111111111111111111111111111111111111111111111111111111111
111111111111111111111111111111111111111111111111111111111111111111
111111111111111111111111111111111111111111111111111111111111111111
111111111111111111111111111111111111111111111111111111111111111111
111111111111111111111111111111111111111111111111111111111111111111

"Dead," Dairine whispered. "I'm dead for sure."

"Input error," said the computer, sounding quite calm.

Dairine's heart leaped. "Are you busted?!" she cried.

"Syntax error twenty-four," said the computer, "rephrase for—"

"You can take your syntax errors and . . . never mind!" Dairine said. "What's wrong with you? Diagnostic!"

"External input," said the computer. "Nontypical."

"What is it? Some kind of broadcast?"

"Negative. Local."

It happened right after it linked to the geothermal power, Dairine thought. "Check your link to the planet," she said.

"Affirmative. Positive identification. External input. Planetary source."

"Are there people here?" Dairine said, looking around hurriedly.

"Negative." The computer's screen kept filling up with *1*s, clearing itself, filling with *1*s again.

She held still and forced herself to take a deep breath, and another. The computer wasn't broken; nothing horrible had happened. Yet. "Can you get rid of all those ones?" she said to the computer.

"Affirmative."

The screen steadied down to the last page she had been looking at. Dairine stared at it.

This unique structure becomes more interesting when considering the physical nature of the layering. Some 92% of the layers consist of chemically pure silicon, predisposing the aggregate to electroconductive activity in the presence of light or under certain other conditions. This effect is likely to be enhanced in some areas by the tendency of silicon to superconduct at surface temperatures below 200° K. There is also a possibility that semiorganic life of a "monocellular" nature will have arisen in symbiosis either with the silicon layers or their associated "doping" layers, producing—

Dairine sat there and began to tremble. *It's the planet*, she thought. *Silicon. And trace elements, put down in layers. And cold to make it semiconduct—*

"It's the planet!" she shouted at the computer. "This whole flat part here is *one big semiconductor chip*, a computer chip! It's *alive*! Send it something! Send it some 1s!"

The computer flickered through several menu screens and began filling with *1*s again. Dairine rolled from her sitting position into a kneeling one, rocking back and forth with anxiety and delight. She had to be right; she had to. One huge chip, like a computer motherboard a thousand miles square. And some kind of small one-celled—if that was the right word—one-celled organism living with it. Something silicon-based that could etch pathways in it—pathways that electricity could run along, that data could be stored in. *How many years has this chip been laying itself down in the silence*, she wondered. Volcanoes erupting chemically pure silicon and trace elements that glazed themselves into vast reaches of chip-surface as soon as they touched the planet; and farther down, in the molten warmth of the planet's own geothermal heat, the little silicon-based "bacteria" that had wound themselves together out of some kind of analog to DNA. Maybe they were more like amoebas than bacteria now: etching their way along through the layers of silicon and cadmium and other elements, getting their food, their energy, from breaking the compounds' chemical bonds, the same way carbon-based life gets it from breaking down complex proteins into simpler ones.

It was likely enough. She would check it with the manual. But for now, the result of this weird bit of evolution was all that really mattered. The chip was *awake*. With this much surface area—endless thousands of square miles, all full of energy, and connections and interconnections, millions of times more connections than there were in a human brain—how could it *not* have woken up? But there was no way that she could see for it to get data, no way for it to contact the outside world. It was trapped. The *1*s, the basic binary code for "on" used by all computers from the simplest to the most complex, were a scream for help, a sudden realization that something else existed in the world and a crying out to it. Even as she looked down at the screen and watched what the computer was doing, the stream of *1*s became a little less frantic. 111111111, said her own machine. *111111111*, said the planet.

"Give it an arithmetic series," Dairine whispered.

1, said her computer. 11. 111. 1111. 11111.

1. 11. 111. 1111. 11111.

"Try a geometric."

1. 11. 1111. 11111111. 1111111111111111.
1. 11. 1111. 11111111—
"Oh, it's got it," Dairine said, bouncing and still hugging herself. "I think. It's hard to tell if it's just repeating. Try a square series."

11. 1111. 111111111111111—
111. 111111111. 11111111111111111111111111—
It had replied with a cube series. It knew—it *knew*! "Can you teach it binary?" Dairine said, breathless.

"Affirmative." 1. 10. 11. 100. 101—
Things started to move fast, the screen filling with characters, clearing itself, filling again as the computers counted at each other. Dairine was far gone in wonder and confusion. What to teach it next? It was like trying to communicate with someone who had been locked in a dark, soundless box all his life. . . . "Is it taking the data?"

"Affirmative. Writing to permanent memory."

Dairine nodded, thinking hard. Apparently the huge chip was engraving the binary code permanently into itself: That would include codes for letters and numbers as well. *But what good's that gonna do? It doesn't have any experiences to make words out of, no reason to put letters together to make the words in the first place* . . . It was like it had been for Helen Keller, Dairine thought; but at least Helen had had the senses of touch and taste, so that she could feel the water poured into her hand while her teacher drummed the touch-code for *water* into it. *It has no senses. If it did—*

"Can you hook it into your sensors?" she said to the computer.

The computer hesitated. It had never done such a thing before; and when it spoke again, its syntax was peculiar—more fluid than she was used to. "High probability of causing damage to the corresponding computer due to too great a level of complexity," it said.

Dairine breathed out, annoyed, but had to agree. Anything able to sense events happening forty trillion miles away, no matter how it managed it, was certainly too complex to hook directly to this poor creature right now. And another thought occurred to her, and her heart beat very fast. *Not sensors, then. Senses.* "Can you hook *me* to it?" she said.

This time the hesitation was even longer, and Dairine stared at the computer, half expecting it to make an expression at her. It didn't, but the speech of its response was slow. "Affirmative," it said. "Triple confirmation of intent required."

"I tell you three times," Dairine said. "Hook it to me. Tell me what to do. It has to get some better idea of what's going on out here or it'll go crazy!"

"Direct physical contact with surface," the computer said. It sounded reluctant.

Dairine dusted her hands off and put them flat on the glassy ground.

She was about to open her mouth to tell the computer to go ahead, do what it was going to; but she never got the chance. The instantaneous jolt went right through her with exactly the same painless grabbing and shaking she had felt when she was seven and had put a bobby pin in the electric socket. She convulsed all over: Her head jerked up and snapped back and she froze, unable even to blink, staring up into the golden-veiled blaze of the barred spiral, staring at it till each slight twitch of her eyes left jittering purple-green afterimages to the right and left of it; and somewhere inside her, as if it were another mind speaking, she could hear her computer crying, *11001001011110000100! 11001001011110000100!* at the frantic silence that listened. *Light, light, light—*

And the reply, she heard that, too: a long, crazed string of binary that made no sense to her but needed to make none. Joy, it was simply joy, joy at discovering *meaning*—joy so intense that all her muscles jumped in reaction, breaking her out of the connection and flinging her face down on the glazed ground. The connection reestablished itself and Dairine's mind fell down into turmoil. She couldn't think straight: Caught between the two computers—for under the swift tutelage of her own, the great glassy plain was now beginning truly to function as one—she felt the contents of her brain being twinned and the extra copy dumped out into endless empty memory and stored, in a rush of images, ideas, occurrences, communications, theories, and raw sensations. She knew it took only a short time; but it seemed to go on forever, and all her senses throbbed like aching teeth at being desperately and delightedly used and used and used again to sense this moment, this ever-changing *now*. Dairine thought she would never perceive anything as completely again as she was seeing and feeling the green-and-gold-shaded piece of silicon aggregate she lay on, with the four crumbs from her sandwich lying half an inch from her eye. She felt sure she would be able to describe the shape of those crumbs and the precise pattern of the dappling in the silicon on her deathbed. If she survived this to have one.

Finally, it stopped. Groaning softly, Dairine levered herself up and stared around her. The computer was sitting there innocently, its screen showing the main Manual menu. "How is it?" Dairine said, and then sighed and got ready to rephrase herself.

"Considerably augmented," said the computer.

Dairine stared at it.

"Is it just me," she said, "or do you sound smarter than you have been?"

"That calls for a value judgment," said the computer.

Dairine opened her mouth, then closed it again. "I guess it does," she said. "You weren't just acting as conduit all through that, were you? You expanded your syntax to include mine."

"You got it," said the computer.

Dairine took a moment to sit up. Before this, she'd thought she would love having the computer be a little more flexible. Now she was having second thoughts. "How's our friend doing?"

"Assimilating the new data and self-programming. Its present running state has analogues to trance or dream states in humans."

Dairine instantly wished it hadn't said that. What time was it at home? How long had she been running? How long had that last longest jump taken, if it had in fact taken any time at all? All she knew was that she was deadly tired.

"Update," said the computer. "It is requesting more data."

"On what?"

"No specific request. It simply desires more."

"I'm fresh out," Dairine said, and yawned. Then she looked at the computer again. "No, I'm not. Give it what *you've* got."

"Repeat and clarify?" said the computer, sounding slightly unnerved.

"Give it what you've got. All the information about planets and species and history and all the rest of it. Give it the magic!"

The computer said nothing.

Dairine sat up straight. "Go on," she said.

No reply.

"Is there some rule that says you shouldn't?"

"Yes," said the computer slowly, "but this edition of the software contains the authorization-override function."

"Good," Dairine said, none too sure of what this meant, except that it sounded promising. "I'm overriding. Give it what you've got."

The screen lit up with a block of text, in binary, quite small and neat, and Dairine immediately thought of the Oath in Nita's manual.

The screen blanked, then filled with another brief stream of binary. That blanked in turn, and screenful after screenful of *1*s and *0*s followed, each flickering out of existence almost as quickly as it appeared.

Dairine got up and stretched and walked back and forth for a few minutes to work the kinks out of her muscles. She ached all over, as she had after the bobby pin incident, and her stomach growled at her again: A bologna sandwich and a half was not enough to satisfy her after the kind of day she had had. If it was even the same day. *At least I have a while before the BEMs show up*, she thought. *Maybe our new friend here can be of some kind of help . . .* As she looked out across the dappled silvery plain, there was a bloom of soft crimson light at one side of it. Dairine held still to watch the sun rise. It was a fat red star, far along in its lifetime—so far along, so cool, that there was water vapor in its atmosphere, and even in the vacuum of space it hung in a softly glowing rose-colored haze, like an Earthly summer sunset. It climbed the sky swiftly, and Dairine watched it in silence. *Quite a day*, she thought. *But whether it's morning here or not, I need a nap.*

She turned around and started to head back toward the computer—and froze.

One patch of the planet's surface was moving. Something underneath it was humping upward, and cracks appeared in the perfect smoothness. There was no sound, of course, since Dairine's air supply was nowhere near the spot; the cracks webbed outward in total silence.

And then the crust cracked upward in jagged pieces, and the something underneath pushed through and up and out. Bits of silica glass fell slowly in the light gravity and bounced or shattered in a snow of splinters around the rounded shape that stood there. *Stood* was the right word: for it had legs, though short stumpy ones, as if a toy tank had thrown away its treads and grown limbs instead. It shook itself, the rounded, glassy, glittering thing, and walked over to Dairine and through her shields with a gait like a centipede's or a clockwork toy's; and it looked up at her, if something like a turtle with no head can be said to look up.

"Light," it croaked, in a passable imitation of the computer's voice, and bumped against her shin and rested there.

It was too much. Dairine sat down where she was and looked at the computer. "I can't cope," she said.

The computer had no reply for this.

"I can't," she said. "Make me some more air, please, and call me if they start chasing us again."

"No problem," said the computer.

She lay down on the smooth glassy ground, gazing at the rounded, glittery thing that stood on its fourteen stumpy legs and gazed back at her. No more than six breaths later she was asleep.

So she did not see, an hour and a half later, when the sun, at its meridian, began to pucker and twist out of shape, and for the best part of the hour lost half of itself, and shone only feebly, warped and dimmed. Her companion saw it and said to the computer:

"What?"

"Darkness," said the computer: and nothing more.

Reserved Words

THEY GOT TO RIRHATH B early in the evening, arriving at the Crossings just after suns' set and just as the sky was clearing. Nita and Kit stood there in the Nontypical Transit area for a few moments, staring up at the ceiling like the rankest tourists. Picchu sat on Kit's shoulder, completely unruffled, and ignored everything with yawning scorn, though the view through the now-clear ceiling was worth seeing.

"My brains are rattled," Kit said, breathing hard. "I need a minute." So did Nita, and she felt vaguely relieved that Kit had said something about it first, so she just nodded and craned her neck and stared up. The view was worth looking at—this sudden revelation of Rirhath's sky, a glorious concatenation of short-term variable stars swelling and shrinking like living things that breathed and whose hearts beat fire. All over the Crossings, people of every species passing through were pausing, looking up at the same sight and admiring the completeness with which a perfectly solid-seeming ceiling now seemed to have gone away. Others, travelers who had seen it all before or were just too tired to care, went on about their business and didn't bother to look.

"We only have a couple of days," Picchu said, chewing on the collar of Kit's shirt.

"Peach," Nita said, "shut your face. You better?" she said to Kit.

"Yeah," he said. "You?"

"I was dizzy. It's OK now."

"Super." He flipped through his manual, open in his hand, and came up with a map of the Crossings. "What do we need to find?"

"Stationmaster's office."

"Right."

They checked out of Nontypical Transit, leaving their origin-and-destination information with the computer at the entrance, and set out across the expanse of the terminal floor, looking around them in calm wonder: for though neither of them had ever been there, both had read enough about the Crossings in their manuals to know what to expect. They knew there had been a time when the Crossings itself was only a reed hut by a riverside and the single worldgate nearby only a muddy spot in a cave that the first Master stumbled upon by accident and claimed for its heirs (after waiting several years on Ererikh for the gate to reverse phase so that he could get home). Now, a couple of thousand years' worth of technology later, world-gates were generated here at the drop of a whim, and the Stationmaster regulated interstellar commerce and transportation via world-gating for the entire Sagittarius Arm.

Its office was not off in some sheltered spot away from the craziness, but out in the very middle of the station floor: that being the spot where the hut had been, 2,430 years before. It was only a single modest kiosk of tubular bluesteel, with a desk behind it, and at the desk, hung up in a rack that looked like a large stepstool, was a single Rirhait, banging busily on a computer terminal keypad and making small noises to itself as it worked.

Nita and Kit stopped in front of the desk, and the Rirhait looked up at them. Or more or less up: some of its stalked eyes looked down instead, and a few peered from the sides. It stopped typing. "Well?" it said, scratchy-voiced—*understandable*, Nita thought, *when you've got a gullet full of sand*.

"You're the Stationmaster?" Kit said.

"Yes," said the Rirhait, and the fact that it said nothing else but looked at Kit hungrily, with its scissory mandibles working, made Nita twitch a little.

"We are on errantry, and we greet you," Nita said: the standard self-introduction of a wizard on business. *Sir* or *madam*, one normally added, but Nita wasn't sure which the Master was, or even if either term applied.

"That, too?" said the Master, looking at Picchu.

"Yes, *that*," said Peach, all scorn.

"Well, it's about time you people got here," said the Master, and left off what it was doing, standing up. "Standing" was an approximation: A Rirhait is shaped more like a centipede than anything else, so that when it got off its rack and came out from behind the desk, its long, shiny silver-blue body only stood a foot or so off the ground, and all its eyes looked up at them together. "We had more of an untidiness here this afternoon than we've had for a greatyear past, and I'll be glad to see the end of it."

Nita began to sweat. "The wizard who came through here earlier was on Ordeal," Kit said. "We'll need your help to find the spot from which she went farther on, so that we can track her: There are too many other worldgates here, and they're confusing the trail."

"She didn't cause any trouble, did she?" Nita said.

"Trouble?" said the Stationmaster, and led them off across the bright floor and showed them the place where several large pieces of the ceiling had been shot down. "Trouble?" it said, pointing out the places where the floors were melted, indicating the blaster scars in the kiosks and the large cordoned-off area where maintenance people of various species were scraping and scrubbing coffee ground-smelling residue off the floor. "Oh, no trouble. Not really."

Picchu began to laugh, a wicked and appreciative sound.

Nita blushed ferociously and didn't say anything for several minutes. The Rirhait led them off to another area of the floor that was closed in on itself by an arrangement of blue-steel kiosks. This was Crossings security; various desks stood about inside it, with creatures of several species working at them. The Master led them to one of the unoccupied desks, a low, flat table full of incomprehensible equipment. "Here," it said, and reared up on its back ten legs to touch the machinery in several places.

Small and clear, an image appeared above the table; remote, but equally clear, sound accompanied it. Nita and Kit found themselves looking at the Crossings equivalent of a videotape, but in three dimensions, with neat alien characters burning in the lower corner of it to show the time and location at which the recording was made. They watched a group of toadlike BEMs make their way across the terminal floor, spot Dairine, head off in pursuit. They watched Dairine deal with the deinonychus and afterward with the BEM that grabbed her. Nita gulped.

"They look like Satrachi," Kit said, astonishingly cool-voiced.

Nita's eyebrows went up. Alien species were her specialty; evidently Kit had been doing some extra research. "They are, as far as we can tell," said the Master. "The one of them whom we have in custody has valid Satra identification."

"We'll need to see this person, then," Nita said. The tape ran: Nita watched Dairine's dive into the bar, and from another camera angle, her sister's reemergence into the terminal and dash into the rest room. Nita groaned, recognizing the room by the symbol on its door as a spawning room for any one of several species that gave birth to their young on the average of once every few days and were likely to be caught short while traveling on business. Nita hoped that Dairine hadn't introduced one of the species involved to a completely new kind of birth trauma.

"That was the spot she left from?"

"Yes, Emissary." It was the first time Nita had ever been formally called by one of the twenty or so titles commonly used for wizards, but she was too busy now to enjoy it. She glanced at Kit. He was frowning at the image hanging in the air; finally his concentration broke and he glanced at her.

"Well?" he said. "You want to talk to the Satrachi?"

"I'd better," she said, though she very much wanted not to—the looks of the Satrachi gave her the creeps. But dealing with live things was her department; the handling of machinery and inanimate objects was Kit's. "You go ahead and check the room out. Stationmaster, can you have someone show me where it's being held?"

"Step on that square there," said the Master, pointing one eye at a spot on the floor. "It's direct transit to Holding. Emissary, I'll show you to the room in question . . ."

Nita stepped on the block quickly before she would have time to change her mind.

Fifteen minutes with it told her all she needed to know: The Satra was a dupe, it and its friends—a small paramilitary club—deluded into pursuing Dairine by some agent of the Lone One. *It's the usual thing*, she thought as she headed back to Kit and the Stationmaster. *The Power never comes out in the open if it can find some way to make someone else do Its dirty work. Preferably an innocent: That way it's more of a slap in the Bright Powers' face. Unusual, though, that It used a whole group this time. Normally, it's hard to keep that subtle a grip on a whole group's mind: One of them slips free or perceives it as control . . . and when that happens, odds are that the whole group is useless for Its purposes.*

She strolled among aliens and their luggage and finally came to the little Grand Central-sized alcove where Dairine's rest room was. Its door was frozen in the dilated mode. Nita slipped in and found Kit and Picchu and the Master off to one side, examining one particular birthing booth. It seemed to have had its door burned off, and the back of the booth was blistered and pocked with an ugly rash of blaster scars.

For a good second or so her breath refused to come. "She jumped after *that?*" Nita finally managed to say.

Kit looked over his shoulder at her. "Neets, relax, there are no bloodstains."

"There wouldn't be, with blasters," Nita said. "They cauterize."

"Any really big wound would spurt anyway," Kit said, straightening up and starting to page through his manual. "I think they missed her. The tiles don't remember her screaming, and not even Dairine's *that* stoic." He kept turning over pages.

"How far did she go?"

"A long jump," Kit said. "Multistage, from the feel of it. They must have freaked her out pretty good." He looked up. "That computer she's got leaves a definite sense of what it's been doing behind it. Can you feel it?"

Nita let her eyes go unfocused for a moment and blanked her mind out, as she might do to hear the thinking of some particularly quiet tree. Some residue of Dairine's emotion still hung about the strings in the space-time configuration of the area, like tatters on a barbed-wire fence: fear and defiance, all tangled up together; and alongside her tatters, others, ordered and regular, a weave less vivid and complex in different ways. "It feels alive," Nita said to Kit after a while. "Do computers usually feel that way?"

"I don't know," Kit said, sounding annoyed. "I never tried feeling one before this . . . You got your widget?" he said. "We're gonna need it to catch up with her and her friends."

"Yeah." She unslung her pack and started rummaging for the gimbal.

"Well, I have things to do," said the Master. "If you need anything, ask one of the security people; they're all over." And without staying for farewells, it went flowing out the door in a hundred-legged scurry.

Nita glanced after it, then back at Kit, and shrugged. "Here," she said, and tossed him the gimbal. "Which spell are you thinking of using?"

"That dislocator on page eleven hundred sixty."

She got out her own manual and found the page. "That's awful long-range, isn't it? Her next jump must have been shorter than that."

"Yeah, but Neets, who wants to leapfrog one step behind the things that are chasing her! We want *them*, right now—we want them off her rear end, so she can do whatever it is she needs to do without interference." He looked grim. "And when we find 'em—"

Nita sighed. "Forget it," she said. "They're dupes."

Kit looked up at her while getting a grease pencil out of his pack. "It suckered them in?"

She filled him in on what the Satrachi had told her as Kit got down on the tiles and began drawing their transit circle. Kit sighed a little. "I was hoping it was some of the Lone One's own people," he said, "so we could just trash 'em and not feel guilty."

Nita had to smile a little at that. Picchu climbed down from the partition between the booths, where she had been sitting, and clambered onto Nita's shoulder. "Get mine right," Picchu said to Kit. "I don't want to come out the other side of this transit with fur."

Kit shot a look at Picchu and didn't need to comment; Nita could imagine what he was thinking. "Come sit over here, then, if you're so worried," he said.

To Nita's amusement Peach did just that, climbing backward down her arm and over onto Kit's back, where she peered over his shoulder. "Not bad," she said, looking at the diagram.

Kit ignored this. "So make yourself useful. Is anything bad going to happen to us?"

"Of course it is," Picchu said.

"You might be more specific."

"And I might not need to. The Power that invented death is going to be on your tails shortly. *Our* tails," she added, looking over her shoulder at the splendid three-foot sweep of scarlet feathers behind her. "Even you two should be able to see that coming."

Kit changed position suddenly, and Picchu scrabbled for balance, flapping her wings and swearing. "Like you should have seen that?"

Nita grinned a little, then let it go; her mind was back on the train of thought she had been playing with out in the terminal. "I was wondering about that, a while back," she said to Kit. "It invented death, when things were first started. But that wasn't enough for It. It had to get people to buy into death—not just the dying itself: the *fear* of it."

Kit nodded. "But a lot of species have opted out, one way or another. I mean, we're scared to die. But we still suspect there are reasons *not* to be scared. A lot of people do. Its hold isn't complete anymore."

"I know. Kit, do you think—Tom said something was about to 'tip over.' Some major change. Do you think what he meant was that the Lone One was about to lose *completely* somewhere?"

"He's always said," Kit said, "that what happens one place, spreads everyplace else. Everything affects everything, sooner or later. The manual says so, too. A few times."

Nita nodded, thinking how unusual it was for the manual to repeat itself about anything. "And the pattern started shifting a couple thousand years ago," Kit said. "The Lone Power *had* always won completely before. Then It started having wins taken away from It after the fact."

Kit looked reflective. "If, somewhere or other, It's about to *lose*—right from the start . . ."

Nita looked at him sidewise. "Then It starts losing at home, too, in all the little daily battles. Eventually."

Kit nodded. "Dairine," he said.

Nita shook her head, still having trouble believing it—but having to admit the likelihood. Somehow, her sister had a chance of actually defeating the Lone Power. *She* must *have a chance: It wouldn't be wasting energy on her otherwise.* "Why her?" Nita said softly.

"Why *you*?" said Picchu, cranky. "What makes either of you so special that you can even come away from an encounter with That alive? Don't flatter yourself: It's eaten stars and seduced whole civilizations in Its time. You were simply exactly the right raw material for It to use in that particular situation to save Itself."

"I didn't mean that, I guess," she said. "I meant, why now? The Lone Power has been pulling this kind of stunt on planets for as long as intelligence has been evolving. It comes in, It tries to get people to accept entropy willingly, and then It bugs off and leaves them to make themselves more miserable than even It could do if It worked at it. Fine. But now all of a sudden It can be beaten. How come?"

Picchu began chewing on Kit's top button. "You know," she said, "that's part of the answer. Granted, It's immortal. But It doesn't have infinite power. It's peer to all the Powers, but not to That in Which they move. And even an immortal can get tired."

Nita thought about that. Five billion years, maybe ten, of constant strife, of incomplete victories, of rage and frustration—and, yes, loneliness: for the Lone One, she had discovered to her shock, was ambivalent about Its role—after all that, surely one might not be as strong as one had been at the start of things. . . .

Kit got the button out of Picchu's mouth and was nipped for his trouble. "So, after all these near losses, It's tired enough to be beaten outright?"

Picchu got cranky again. "Of course! It was *that* tired long ago. The Powers wouldn't need Dairine for just that. They could do it Themselves, or with the help of older wizards. But haven't you got it through your head? They can't want to just *beat* the Lone One. They must think there's a better option."

Nita looked at Picchu, feeling half frightened. "They want It to *surrender*," she said.

"I think so," said Picchu. "I suspect They think she could get the Lone One to give in and come back to Its old allegiance. If It does that . . . the effect spreads. Slowly. But it spreads everywhere."

Picchu climbed down off Kit's shoulder and pigeon-toed across the floor, heading for a receptacle with some water in it. Kit and Nita both sat silent. The possibility seemed a long way from coming true. A world in which the universe's falling into entropy slowly stopped, affecting people's relationships with one another, a world gradually losing the fear of death, a world losing hatred, losing terror, losing evil itself . . . It was ridiculous, impossible, too much to hope for. *But still*, Nita thought, *if there is any chance at all . . . !*

". . . on the news last night," Kit said, "did you see that thing about the car in Northern Ireland?"

"No."

"They hijack cars over there sometimes, as a protest," he said. "One side or the other." There was something about his voice that made Nita look at him hard. "Sometimes they set the cars on fire after they hijack them." Kit sat looking in front of him at nothing in particular, looking tired. "You know the kind of wire screen you get for station wagons, so that your dog can be in the back and not get into everything?"

"Yeah."

"Someone hijacked a car with one of those in it, the other night. With the dog in it, in the back. Then they set the car on fire. With the dog in it."

Nita went ashen. Kit just kept looking at nothing in particular, and she knew what he was thinking of: Ponch, in Kit's dad's station wagon, lying around in the back too contented and lazy even to try to get into the grocery bags all around him. And someone coming up to the car— "Neets," Kit said after a while. "Bad enough that they kill children and grown-ups and don't even care. But the poor dogs, too— If we really have a chance to stop that kind of thing, I'll do . . . whatever. I don't care. Anything."

She looked at him. *"Anything?"*

He was quiet for a long time. "Yeah."

Eventually, she nodded. "Me, too."

"I know," he said.

She looked at him in surprise. "Well, look at what you did with the whales," he said.

Nita's mouth was very dry. She tried to swallow. It didn't work.

"I mean, you did that already. That's what it was about. The Power got redeemed, a little: We know that much. Or at least It got the option to change. You did it for *that*. You almost got yourself killed, and you knew that might happen, and you did it anyway. Oh, I know you did it for me, some." He said this as if it were unimportant. "I was in trouble; you got me out of it. But mostly you did it to have things in the world be safe and work."

She nodded, completely unable to speak.

"It seems like the least I can do," he said, and went no further, as if Nita should know perfectly well what he meant.

"Kit," she said.

"Look, I mean, I don't know if I can be that brave, but—"

"Kit, shut up."

He shut up, rather astonished.

I'm always one step closer, sang memory at her from the Moon. "Look," she said, "I didn't do it for you 'some.' I did it for you 'pretty much.' "

Kit looked at her with an expression that at first made Nita think Kit thought she was angry with him. But then it became plain that he was embarrassed, too. "Well," he said, "OK. I—thought maybe you did. But I didn't want to say anything because I didn't know for sure. And I would have felt real stupid if I was wrong." He had been looking away. Now he looked at her. "So?"

"So," and her voice stuck again, and she had to clear her throat to unstick it. "I *like* you, that's all. A lot. And if you start liking somebody that much—well, I still want to keep the team going. If you do. That's all."

He didn't say anything. Nita stood there burning in a torment of embarrassment and anger at herself.

"Neets. Cut me some slack. You're my best friend."

Her head snapped up. ". . . I thought it was Richie Sussman."

Kit shrugged. "We just play pool a lot. But it's the truth." He looked at her. "Isn't it true for you?"

"Yeah, but—"

"So why does that have to change? Look, we've got junk to do. Let's shake on it. We'll be best friends forever. And a team."

He said it so casually. But then that was how Kit did things: The only thing that wasn't casual was the way he worked to do what he said he would. "What if something happens?" Nita said. "What if—"

Kit finished one symbol inside the circle, shut the book, and stood up. "Look," he said, "something always happens. You still have to promise stuff anyway. If you have to work to make the promises true . . ." He shrugged, hefted the manual. "It's like a spell. You have to say the words every time you want the results. Neets, come on. Shake on it."

They shook on it. Nita felt oddly light, as if her knapsack had been full of rocks and someone had come up behind her and dumped them out.

"OK," Kit said. "Peach, where— Good Lord."

Picchu was sitting in the water receptacle on the floor, flapping around and showering everything within range. "Do you mean I'm going to have to go halfway across the galaxy with a soggy bird sitting on me?" Kit said. "No way. Neets, it's your turn to carry her."

"You're getting a lot like Tom," said Picchu.

"Thanks!"

"That wasn't intended as a compliment."

Peach shook her feathers, scattering water. "Stop your complaining," she said to Kit. "The Powers only know when I'm going to have another chance for a bath." She stepped out of the low basin and shook herself again all over.

Nita wiped a drop out of her eye. "Come on," she said, and got Peach off the edge of the basin. "Kit, we set?"

"Yup. You want to do a defense spell, do it now. Peach? Any bad feelings?"

"All of them," Picchu said, "but nothing specific. Let's go."

They all three got into the circle. Kit knotted it closed with the figure-eight wizard's knot, dropped the gimbal into the circle on the spot marked out for it, then picked up his manual and began to read. Nita silently recited her favorite shield-spell, the one that could stop anything from a thrown punch to an ICBM, and for safety's sake set it at ICBM level. Then she got her own manual open and caught up with Kit. The air began to sing the note ears sing in silence; the air pushed in harder and harder around them, Nita's ears popped, and the spell took hold and threw them off the planet—not before Nita saw a portly Me!thai gentleman peek in the door to see if it was safe to come in and have his child. . . .

There was a long, long darkness between the world winking out and flashing back into existence again. Nita could never remember its having taken so long before—but then the jump from Earth to Rirhath had been a short one, no more than fifteen or twenty lightyears. She held her breath and maintained control, even while the back of her brain was screaming frantically, *He made a mistake in the spell somewhere; you distracted him and he misspelled something else; you're stuck in this and you're never going to get out, never—*

It broke. Nita was as dizzy as she had been the last time, but she was determined not to wobble. Her ears stopped ringing as she blinked and tried to get her bearings. "Heads up, Neets," Kit was saying.

It was dark. They stood on some barren unlit moon out in the middle of space. Nothing was in the sky but unfamiliar stars and the flaming, motionless curtain of an emission nebula, flung across the darkness like a transparent gauze burning in hydrogen red and oxygen blue. Kit pointed toward the horizon where the nebula dipped lowest. Amid a clutter of equipment and portable shelters of some kind, there stood a small crowd of Satrachi. They had apparently not noticed their pursuers' appearance.

"Right," Nita said. "Let's do this—"

"Move us!" Picchu screeched. *"Do it now!"*

Kit's eyes widened. He started rereading the spell, changing the end coordinates by a significant amount. Peach was still flapping her wings and screaming. "No, that's not far enough—"

Nita snatched the gimbal up from the ground and tied it into her shield-spell. *Can it take the strain of two spells at once? We'll find out. It'll abort the one it can't manage, anyway.* She gulped. "Physical forces—," she started reciting in the Speech, naming every force in the universe that she could think of, tying their names into her shield and forbidding them entrance. *Can I pull this off? Is this one of the spells that have a limit on the number of added variables? Oh, Lord, I hope not—*

"Light," Peach was screaming at her, "light, *light!*"

Nita told the shield to be opaque—and then wondered why it wasn't, as the brightest light she had ever imagined came in through it anyway. She had been to a shuttle launch once, and had come to understand that sound could be a force, a thing that grabbed you from inside your chest and shook you effortlessly back and forth. Now she wondered how she had never thought that light might be able to do the same, under some circumstances. It struck her deaf and dumb and blind, and she went sprawling. Heat scorched her everywhere; she smelled the rotten-egg stink of burning hair. She clutched the gimbal: She couldn't have dropped it if she'd tried.

Much later, it seemed, it began to get dark. She opened her eyes and could not be sure, for a few minutes, that they were open, the world was so full of afterimages. But the purple curtain between her and everything else eventually went away. She and Kit and Peach were hanging suspended, weightless in empty space. At least it was empty now. There was no sign of any moonlet—only off to one side, a blinding star that slowly grew and grew and grew and grew, toward them. They were out of its range now. They had not been before.

"Didn't know the gimbal could handle both those spells," Kit said, rubbing his eyes. "Nice going."

"It won't do it twice," Nita said. There was just so much power one could milk out of a physical aid, and she had been pushing her odds even trying it once. "Where are we?"

"I haven't the faintest. Somewhere a light-month out from our original position. And those Satrachi were bait," he said. "For us. Look at it, Neets."

She looked. "I could have sworn I opaqued this shield."

"It *is* opaqued," Kit said. "But a shield doesn't usually have to put up with a nova at close range. H-bombs are about the most one can block out without leakage, if I remember."

Nita stared at the raging star, all boiling with huge twisted prominences. For all its brilliance, there was a darkness about its heart, something wrong with the light. In a short time this terrible glory would be collapsed to a pallid dwarf star, cooling slowly to a coal. She shivered: One of the oldest epithets for the Lone Power was "Starsnuffer." *It blew a whole star, just to kill us, because we were going to help Dairine . . .* "Did this system have other planets?" she said.

"I don't know. I doubt It cared."

And this was what was going after her little sister.

The anger in Nita got very, very cold. "Let's go find her," she said.

Together they began to read.

Fatal Error

DAIRINE WOKE UP STIFF and aching all over. *What's wrong with the bed?* was her first thought: It felt like the floor. Then she opened her eyes and found that she *was* on the floor . . . or a surface enough like one to make no difference. The cool, steady stars of space burned above her. She sat up and rubbed her sticky eyes.

I feel awful, she thought. *I want a bath, I want breakfast, I want to brush my teeth!* But baths and toothbrushes and any food but bologna sandwiches with mustard were all a *long* way away.

She dropped her hands into her lap, feeling slow and helpless, and looked about her. A sense of shock grew in her: All around, in what had been the absolutely smooth surface of the planet, there were great cracked holes, as if the place had had a sudden meteor shower while she was asleep. But the debris lying around wasn't the kind left by meteor strikes. "Sheesh," she muttered.

Something poked her from behind.

Dairine screamed and flung herself around. She found herself staring at the small, turtlelike glassy creature that had been the last straw the night before. It had walked into her and was continuing to do so, its short jointed legs working busily though it was getting nowhere, like a windup toy mindlessly walking against a wall. "With," it said.

"Oh, heck," Dairine said in relief. She sagged with embarrassment. Two days ago she would have scowled at the thought of her screaming because of *anything*, up to and including Darth Vader himself . . . but the world looked a little different today.

She grabbed the steadily pedaling little thing and held it away from her to look at it. It was all made of the same silicon as the surface; the inside of its turtlish body was a complex of horizontal layers, the thickest of them about half an inch across, the thinnest visible only as tiny colored lines no thicker than a hair— thousands of them packed together, at times, in delicate bandings that blended into one subtle color. Dairine knew she was looking at a chip or board more complex than anything dreamed of on Earth. She could see nothing identifiable as a sensor, but it had certainly found her right away last night, so it could see. She wondered if it could hear.

"Well, how about it, small stuff?" she said. It was rather cute, after all. "Say hi."

"Hi," it said.

She put her eyebrows up and looked over her shoulder at the computer, which was sitting where she had left it the night before. "Did you teach this guy to talk?"

"There is very little I did not teach the mind that made them," said the computer calmly.

Dairine looked around at the many, many jagged holes in the surface. "I bet. Where are they all?"

"Indeterminate. Each one began walking around the surface in a random fashion as soon as it was produced."

"Except for this one," Dairine said, and lifted the creature into her lap. It was surprisingly light. Once there, the creature stopped trying to walk, and just rested across her knees like a tea tray with a domed cover on it. "Good baby," Dairine said. She touched one of the legs carefully, maneuvering the top joint gently to see how it worked. There were three ball-and-socket-like joints: one joint where it met the body and two more spaced evenly down the leg, which was about six inches long. The legs were of the same stuff as the outer shell of the body dome: translucent, like cloudy glass, with delicate hints of color here and there. "Why didn't you go walking off with everybody else, huh?" she said as she picked it up to flip it over and examine its underside.

Its legs kicked vigorously in the air. "With," it said.

Dairine put the creature down, and it immediately walked into her again and kept walking, its legs slipping on the smooth surface.

" 'With,' huh? OK, OK, 'with' already." She picked it up again and put it in her lap. It stopped kicking.

She glanced up at the sky. The galaxy was rising again. For a few seconds she just held still, watching the curving fire of it. "How long is the day here?" she said.

"Seventeen hours," said the computer.

"Fast for such a big planet," she said. "Mostly light elements, though. I guess it works. How long was I asleep?"

"Fourteen hours."

Dairine made an annoyed face. There went that much of her research time. She felt fairly certain that if the BEMs didn't catch up with her shortly, someOne else would. She didn't like the thought. "I've got to get some work done," she said, and glanced down at the turtly, glassy creature in her lap. "What about you? You can't sit here all day. Neither can I."

"Hi," said the glass turtle.

Dairine laughed. To the computer, she said, "Are you still talking to"—she didn't know what to call it; she patted the glassy ground—"our friend here?"

"Yes," the computer said. "Response is slow. It is still assimilating and coordinating the data."

"Still?" Dairine let out a breath. If there was so much information in the Manual functions that a computer with this much memory was still sorting it, what hope did she have of finding the information she needed in time to be able to do anything useful to the Lone One with it? She was going to have to help it along somehow. "Can you ask it to call back this little guy's friends? I want to look at them."

"Working."

Dairine stretched and considered that the next time she went out to space, she was going to plan things a little more carefully. Or stay at a hotel. Where, for example, was she going to find something to drink? She hadn't squirreled anything away in her claudication; she was going to have to find water. More to the point, there were no bathrooms here. Dairine wished heartily that she had taken time in the Crossings, or even back at Natural History, to use the facilities for something other than programming interstellar jumps. The memory of what sometimes seemed to be her mother's favorite line, "You should have gone before we left!" made her grin ruefully.

She got up to improvise what she could. Her turtle started to go with her. "No," she said, as she might have to Ponch. "Stay!" The turtle's response to this was the same as Ponch's would have been: It went after her anyway.

Dairine sighed and headed off to a little outcropping of rock about half a mile away. When she had finished and started back to where the computer lay, she could already see small shapes moving on the horizon. She sat down with her bread and bologna, started making a sandwich, and waited for them.

Pretty soon she was knee-deep in turtles, or would have been had she been standing up. After the first few walked into her as her lap turtle had, she asked the computer to get them to hold still when they reached her. Something like two hundred of them were shortly gathered around her. They were all exact copies of her friend, even to the striations and banding inside them. She sighed a little as she looked at them.

"This isn't gonna work, you guys," she said. "There's more to life than walking around, and none of you have anything like hands . . ."

"*Hi!*" said all the turtles simultaneously. She couldn't hear the ones that were outside her bubble of air, but the ones that were inside made racket enough.

She had to laugh at that. "Look," she said to the computer, pushing her first turtle out of her lap and putting the computer there instead, "where did the mind behind these critters get the design for them?"

"Probably from one of the design templates in the Make utility," said the computer.

"OK, let's get into that. If these guys are going to be the arms and legs for the mind that's running them, they need arms!"

The computer's screen flicked obediently to the opening screen for the Make utility. Dairine frowned at the menu for a while. The computer had a machine-assisted Drafting utility: She chose that while her turtle tried to climb back into her lap.

"No," she said. "No, honey!"

It was no use. "With!" said the turtle. "With, with, with, with—"

She laughed helplessly. "Boy, are *you* ever GIGO," she said.

"Yes," the turtle said, and sat down next to her abruptly, folding all its legs under it like a contented mechanical cat.

Dairine put her eyebrows up at that. Was that all it wanted? A name? "Gigo," she said, experimentally.

"Yes!"

It sounds happy, she thought. *Can it have emotions?*

"Good baby," she said, and patted it. "Good Gigo."

"*Yes!*" said Gigo, and, "Yes!" said several of the other turtles around, and it began to spread through the crowd to the limits of her air: "Yes, yes, yes—"

"Okay," she said, "he's good, you're all good, now put a cork in it!"

They fell silent. But there had been no mistaking the sound of joy.

"I can see I'm gonna have to find names for all of you," she said. "Can't have the whole bunch of you answering to that."

She turned her attention to the blank graphics screen. "Bring up the design that . . ." She paused. "I can't just keep banging on the ground. Does what you were talking to have a name for itself?"

"No."

Dairine sighed. "OK, just let's call it a motherboard for the moment. Bring up the design it was using for Gigo and his buddies."

The screen flickered, showing Dairine a three-dimensional diagram, which the computer then rotated to show all the turtle's surfaces. "Good," she said. "How do I make changes?"

"The screen is touch-sensitive. Touch a line and state what you want done with it."

Dairine spent a cheerful hour or so there, pausing for bites of sandwich, as she started to redesign the turtles. She wasn't shy about it. The original design had its points, but as the mobile units of an intelligence, the turtles were sadly lacking in necessary equipment. She rebuilt several of the legs into arms, with six claws apiece at the end of them, four "fingers" and two opposable "thumbs"; this hand she attached to the arm by a ball-and-socket joint so that it could rotate completely around without having to stop. As an afterthought, she put another pair of arms on the turtle's back end, so that it wouldn't have to turn around to pick something up if it didn't want to.

She took the turtle's rather simplistic visual sensor, barely more than a photosensitive spot, and turned it into something of a cross between the human retina and a bee's faceted eye—a multiple-lensed business equally good for close work and distant vision. She placed several of these around the turtle's perimeter and a couple on top, and then for good measure added a special-purpose lens that was actually something like a small Cassegrain telescope, focusing on a mirror-polished bit of silicon buried a ways into the turtle's "brain." She added infrared and ultraviolet sensing. Ears for sound they already had; she considered that it might be wise to give them something to hear radio with, too, but couldn't decide on which frequency to work with and let the idea go for the moment. They could work it out themselves.

Dairine sat staring at the screen, musing. The newly awakened intelligence had made all its mobiles alike, probably because it didn't understand the concept of otherness yet. She would make them different from one another. But they were going to have to be different on the inside, too, to do any good. *If some danger comes along that they have to cope with, it's no use their information processors being all the same: Whatever it is could wipe them all out at once. If they're as different as they can be, they'll have a better chance of surviving.*

She paused in her design to look closely at the structure of the chip layering in the turtles—not so much at what the layers were made of, but what their arrangement meant. At the molecular level she found the basic building block of the chips, as basic as DNA in humans: not a chain molecule, but a sort of tridimensional snowflake of silicon atoms and atoms of other elements. DNA was simple beside these. Any given silicon molecule hooked with up to fourteen others, using any one of fifty different chemical compounds to do it; and every different arrangement of hookups between molecules or layers had a specific meaning, as each arrangement has in DNA. With the help of the computer, she began to sort out the code buried in the interconnected snowflakes. Hours, it took her, and she was perfectly aware that even with the computer's help she couldn't hope to deal with more than the tip of this iceberg of information. Some parts of the chip structure she did manage to identify as pure data storage, others as sensory array, associative network, life support, energy management.

Dairine began devising layering arrangements different from those in the turtles. She designed creatures that would have more associative network and so could specialize in problem solving; others with more data stacks, turtles that would be good at remembering; mobiles more richly endowed with sensors and senses than some of the others, which would see and hear and feel most acutely. One arrangement of layers, the one that the computer identified for her as the seat of the turtle's emotions, seemed an awfully tiny thing to Dairine. She expanded it to about three times its original size and allowed it to interconnect at will with the other associative areas, with data memory and with the senses. Finally, to every model she designed, Dairine added a great deal of latent memory area, so that each mobile would have plenty of room to store what it experienced and to process the data it accumulated.

Having done all these things, she went back to her original design and copied it several times, making a number of different "models": a large, strong one for heavy work; a small one with extra hands in various sizes, from human-hand size to tiny claws that could have done microsurgery or precision work almost on the molecular level. And she added the necessary extra sensor arrays or materials reinforcement that these changes would need to support them.

She sat back and sighed then, and unfolded her cramped legs and reached down for her sandwich, which had gone stale on top while she worked. "Okay," she said to the computer. "Ask the motherboard to run off a few of those and let's see what happens."

"Considerable reprogramming will be necessary," said the computer.

"I know," said Dairine, between bites of the sandwich, making a face at the taste of it. "I'm in no rush."

The computer's screen filled with binary as it began conferring with the motherboard in machine language. *What do I* mean *I'm in no rush?* Dairine thought, momentarily distracted while Gigo climbed into her lap again. "Did you finish that analysis run about the Lone One for me?"

"Yes," said the computer. "Do you want it displayed?"

"Yeah, please."

The binary went away from the screen, replaced by print. Dairine didn't look at it immediately. She leaned back and gazed up. The galaxy was all set but for one arm, trailing up over the far, far horizon, a hook of light. The dull red sun was following it down as if attached to the hook by an invisible string. *An old, old star*, Dairine thought. *Not even main sequence anymore. This could have been one of the first stars created in this universe . . . Might have been, considering how far out this galaxy—*

The thought was shocked out of her. Something other than her voice was making a sound. It was a rumbling, very low, a vibration in the surface she sat on. "What the— You feel that?" she said to the computer.

"Vibration of seismic origin," the computer said. "Intensity two point two Richter and increasing."

There was precious little on the planet's surface to shake. Dairine stood up, alarmed, and watched the turtles. For all their legs, they were having trouble keeping their footing on the slick surface. Gigo hooked a leg around Dairine's and steadied itself that way. "Is this gonna get worse?" Dairine said.

"Uncertain. No curve yet. Richter three point two and increasing. Some volcanic eruption occurring in planet's starward hemisphere."

Got to do something about their leg design if this happens a lot, Dairine thought—and then was distracted again, because something was happening to the light: It wavered oddly, dimming from the clear rose that had flooded the plain to a dark dry color like blood. She stared upward.

The sun was twisting out of shape. There was no other way to describe it. Part of its upper right-hand quarter seemed pinched on itself, warped like a round piece of paper being curled. Prominences stretched peculiarly, snapped back to tininess again; the warping worsened until the star that had been normal and round was squeezed small, as if in a cruel fist, to a horizontal, fluctuating oval, then to a sort of tortured heart-shape, then to an oval bent the other way, leftward. Sunspots stretched like pulled taffy, oozed back to shape again, and the red light wavered and shifted like that of a candle about to be blown out in the wind.

Dairine stood with a terrible sickness at the heart of her, for this was no kind of eclipse or other astronomical event that she had ever heard of. It was as if she was seeing the laws of nature broken in front of her.

"What *is* that?" she whispered.

"Transit of systemic object across primary," said the computer. "The transiting object is a micro black hole."

Dairine sat down again, feeling the rumbling beneath her start to die away. The computer had mentioned the presence of that black hole earlier, but in the excitement she had forgotten it. "Plot me that thing's orbit," she said. "Is that going to happen every day?"

"Indeterminate. Working."

"I don't like that," said Gigo with sudden clarity.

Dairine looked over at it with surprise and pulled it into her lap. "You're not alone, small stuff," she said. "It gives me the shakes, too." She sat there for a second, noticing that she was sweating. "You're getting smart, huh?" she said. "Your mom down there is beginning to sort out the words?"

"It hurts," said Gigo, sounding a little mournful.

"Hurts . . ." Dairine wasn't sure whether this was a general statement or an answer to her question. Though it could be both. A black hole in orbit in the star system would produce stresses in a planet's fabric that the planet—if it were alive, like this one—could certainly feel. Line the black hole up with its star, as it would be lined up in transit, and the tidal stresses would be that much worse. What better cause to learn to tell another person that something was hurting you? . . . Now that there was another person to tell.

Dairine patted Gigo absently. "It's all over, Gigo," she said.

"Gigo, yes."

She grinned faintly. "You really like having a name, huh?"

"A program must be given a name to be saved," Gigo said quite clearly, as if reciting from memory—but there was also slight fear in its voice and great relief.

"Well, it's all over," Dairine said, while surreptitiously checking the sky to make sure. Tiny though it was—too small to see—a micro black hole was massive enough to bend light toward it. That was what had made the sun look so strange, as the gravity center of the black hole's field bent the round image of the sun forward onto itself. The realization made Dairine feel a lot better, but she didn't particularly want to see the sun do that again. She turned back to the computer. "Let's get back to work."

"Which display first," the computer said, "the black hole's orbit or the research run on the Lone Power?"

"The orbit."

It drew it for her on the screen, a slowly moving graphic that made Dairine's insides crawl. The black hole's orbit around its primary was irregular. These transits occurred in twenty out of every thirty orbits, and in the middle five orbits the hole swung much closer to the planet and appeared to center more closely on the sun. This last one had been a grazing transit: The micro hole had only passed across the upper limb of the star. Dairine did not want to see what a dead-center transit would look like, not at all. But in the midst of her discomfort, she still found a little room to be fascinated. Apparently the black hole was the cause of the planet's many volcanoes: The tidal stresses it produced brought up molten silicon, which erupted and spread over the surface. Without the frequent passages of the hole near the planet, the millions of layers of the motherboard would never have been laid down, and it would never have reached the critical "synapse" number necessary for it to come alive. . . .

"OK," she said. "Give me the research run, and let me know when the motherboard's ready to make some more of these guys."

"Working."

Dairine began to read, hardly aware of it when Gigo sneaked into her lap again and stared curiously at the screen. She paged past Nita and Kit's last run-in with the Lone Power and started skimming the précis before it for common factors. Odd tales from a hundred planets flicked past her, and sweat slowly began to break out on Dairine as she realized she could not see any common factors at all. She could see no pattern in what made the Lone Power pick a specific world or group or person to attack, and no sure pattern or method for dealing with It. Some people seemed to beat the Lone One off by sheer luck. Some did *nothing* that she could see, and yet ruined Its plans utterly. One wizard on a planet of Altair had changed the whole course of his world's history by inviting a person he knew to be inhabited by the Lone One to dinner . . . and the next day, the Altairans' problem (which Dairine also did not understand except that it had something to do with the texture of their fur) simply began to clear up, apparently by itself.

"Maybe I should buy It a hot dog," Dairine muttered. That would make as much sense as most of these solutions. She was getting a feeling that there was something important about dealing with the Lone Power that the computer wasn't telling her.

She scrolled back to Nita and Kit's précis again and read it through carefully, comparing it with what she had seen them do or heard them say herself. Her conversation with Nita after she had seen her sister change back from being a whale was described in the précis as "penultimate clarification and choice." Dairine scowled. What had Nita chosen? And why? She wished she had her there to ask her . . . but no. Dairine didn't think she could cope with Nita at the moment. Her sister would certainly rip into her for doing dumb things, and Dairine wasn't in the mood . . . considering how many dumb things she *had* done in the past day and a half.

Still, Dairine thought, *a little advice would come in real useful around now* . . .

"Ready," said the computer suddenly.

"OK. Ask it to go ahead."

"Warning," the computer said. "The spell being used requires major restructuring of the substrate. Surface stability will be subject to change without notice."

"You mean I should stand back?"

"I thought that was what I said," said the computer.

Dairine made a wry face, then picked it up and started walking. "C'mon, Gigo, all you guys," she said. "Let's get out of the way."

They trooped off obediently after her. Finally, about a quarter mile away, she stopped. "This far enough away, you think?" she said to the computer.

"Yes. Working now."

She felt a rumbling under the surface again, but this was less alarming than that caused by the transit of the black hole—a more controlled and purposeful sound. The ground where Dairine had been sitting abruptly sank in on itself, swallowing the debris caused by the breaking-out of the turtles. Then slow ripples began to travel across the surface, as it turned itself into what looked like a bubbling pot of syrup, clear in some places, swirled and streaked with color in others. Heat didn't seem to be involved in the process. Dairine sat down to watch, fascinated.

"Unnamed," Gigo said next to her, "data transfer?"

Dairine looked down at the little creature. "You want to ask me a question? Sure. And I have a name; it's Dairine."

"Dairrn," it said.

She chuckled a little. Dairine had never been terribly fond of her name—people tended to stumble over it. But she rather liked the way Gigo said it. "Close enough," she said. "What's up?"

"Why do you transfer data so slowly?"

That surprised her for a moment, until she considered the rate at which the computer and the motherboard had been talking; and this was in fact the motherboard she was talking to now. To something that had been taught to reckon its time in milliseconds, conversation with her must seem about as fast as watching a tree grow. "For my kind of life, I'm pretty quick," Dairine said. "It just looks slow to you."

"There is more—slowlife?"

"Lots more. In fact, you and the Apple there are about the only, uh, 'quicklife' there is, as far as I know." She paused and said, "Quick*life*, as opposed to dumb machines that are fast but not alive."

"I see it, in the data the Lightbringer gave us," said Gigo. Dairine glanced over at the computer. "Data transfer?"

"Sure," Dairine said.

"What is the purpose of this new program run?"

Wow, its syntax is really shaping up. If this keeps up, it's gonna be smarter than me! . . . Is that a good idea? But Dairine laughed at that. It was the best idea: a supercomputer faster than a Cray, with more data in it than all the New York Public Library—what a friend to have! "When I'm gone," Dairine said, "you're going to need to be able to make your own changes in your world. So I'm making you mobiles that will be able to make the changes."

"Data transfer! Define 'gone'!"

Gigo's urgency surprised Dairine. "I can't stay here," she said. *No, better simplify.* "My physical presence here must terminate soon," she said. "But don't worry. You guys won't be alone."

"We will!" cried Gigo, and the whole planet through him.

"No, you won't," Dairine said. "Don't panic. Look, I'm taking care of it. You saw all the different bodies I wrote into the Make program for you? You saw how they're all structured differently on the inside? That's so they can have different personalities. There'll be lots more of you."

"How?"

Dairine hoped she could explain this properly. "You'll split yourself up," she said. "You'll copy your basic programming in a condensed form into each one of them and then run them all separately."

There was a long, long silence. "Illegal function call," said Gigo slowly.

"It's not. Believe me. It sounds like it, but it works just fine for all the slowlife . . . It'll work for you, too. Besides," Dairine said, "if you don't split yourself up, you won't have anybody to talk to and play with!"

"Illegal function call . . ."

"Trust me," Dairine said, "you've got to trust me . . . Oh, look at that."

The surface, which had been seething and rippling, had steadied down, slick and glassy again. Now it was bulging up, as it had before. There was no sound, but through each hunching, each cracking hummock, glassy shapes pushed themselves upward, shook the fragments off, stood upright, walked, uncertain and ungainly as new foals. In the rose light of the declining sun they shone and glowed; some of them tall and stalky, some short and squat, some long and flowing and many-jointed, some rounded and bulky and strong; and one and all as they finished being made, they strode or stalked or glided over to where Dairine was. She and Gigo and the first turtles were surrounded by tens and twenties and hundreds of bright glassy shapes, a forest of flexing arms, glittering sensors, color in bold bands and delicate brushings—grace built in glass and gorgeously alive. "Look at them," Dairine said, half lost in wonder herself. "It'll be like being you . . . but a hundred times, a thousand times. Remember how the light looked the first time?"

"Data reacquired," Gigo said, soft-voiced.

"Like that," Dairine said. "But again and again and again. A thousand of you to share every memory with, and each one able to see it differently . . . and everyone else'll see it better when the one who sees it differently tells all the others about it. You won't be the only quicklife anymore. Copy your programming out, and there'll be as many of you as you want to make. A thousand of you, a million of you to have the magic together . . ."

"The call is legal," Gigo said after a moment. "Data transfer?"

"What?"

"Will there be pain? Like the Dark that Pulls?"

Dairine's heart wrenched. She picked Gigo up and pulled him into her lap. "I don't know, small stuff," she said. "There might be. I'm here if it does. You just hold on to me and don't be scared."

She turned to the computer. "You know how to describe this to the mother-board?" she said. "They've all got to have all the major programming you gave their mom, but you're gonna have to pack the code down awful tight. And make sure they still don't lose the connection to her once they're autonomous."

"Noted," said the computer. "Override protocols require that I confirm with you what parts of the wizardly programming are to be passed on to each individual, and to what number of individuals."

She looked at it in surprise. "All of it, of course. And all of them."

"Reconfirmation, please. This far exceeds the median distribution and percentage."

"Oh? What is it on Earth?"

"Ratio of potential wizards to nonpotential: one to three. Ratio of practicing wizards to potential wizards: one to one hundred. Ratio of—"

"Are you trying to tell me that there are *sixteen million* practicing wizards on Earth?"

"Sixteen million four hundred and—"

Dairine paused to consider the condition the world was in. "Well, it's not anywhere near enough! Make them *all* wizards. Yes, I confirm it three times; just get on with it—these guys are getting twitchy." And indeed Gigo was trembling in her lap, which so astonished Dairine that she cuddled him close and put her chin down on the top of him.

Instantly all his legs jerked spasmodically. Dairine held on to him, held on to all of them through him. Maybe some ghost of that first physical-contact link was still in place, for she went briefly blind with sensations that had nothing to do with merely human sensoria. To have all one's life and knowledge, however brief, ruthlessly crushed down into a tiny packet, with no way to be sure if the parts you cherished the most would be safe or would be the same afterward—and then to multiply that packet a thousand times over, till it pushed your own thoughts screaming into the background, and your own voice cried out at you in terror a thousand times, inescapable—and then, worst of all, the silence that follows, echoing, as all the memories drain away into containers that may or may not hold them . . . Dairine was in the midst of it, felt the fear for all of them, and had nothing to use against it but the knowledge that it would be all right, could be all right. She hung on to that as she hung on to Gigo through his frenzied kicking, her eyes squeezed shut, all her muscles clenched tight against the terror in her arms and the terror in her heart. . . .

Silence, silence again, at last. She dared to open her eyes, lifted her head a little to look around her. Gigo was still. The glittering ranks around her shifted a little—a motion here, a motion there, as if a wind were going through glass trees at sunset. The light faded, slipped away, except for the chill gleam of the bright stars over everything: The sun had set.

"It hurt," Gigo said.

He moved. Dairine let him clamber down out of her lap.

He turned and looked at her. "It hurt," he said.

"But it was worth it," said one of the taller mobiles, one of the heavy-labor types, in a different voice.

The voices began to proliferate. Motion spread farther through the crowd. Mobiles turned and spoke to one another in a chorus of voices like tentative synthesizers, changing pitch and tone as if looking for the right ones. Outside the area where there was air, communication passed by less obvious means. Dairine sat in the midst of it, heard words spoken with the delight of people tasting a new food for the first time, heard long strings of binary recited as if the numbers were prayers or poems, saw movement that even to a human eye was plainly dance, being invented there in front of her. She grinned like a loon. "Nice job," she said to the Apple.

"Thank you."

"We did good, huh?"

"Indeterminate," said the computer.

Dairine shrugged and got up to wander among the mobiles and get a closer look at them. They clustered around her as she went, touching her, peering at her, speaking to her again and again, as if to make sure they really could.

The cacophony of voices delighted her, especially since so many of them said the same thing to her at first: "Save, please!" She knew what they wanted now, and so she named them. She started out with programmers' puns, and shortly the glassy plain was littered with people named Bit and Buffer, Pinout and Ascii, Peek and Poke, Random, Cursor, String, Loop, Strikeout, Hex, and anything else she could think of. But she ran out of these long before she ran out of mobiles, and shortly the computer types were joined by Toms, Dicks, and Harrys, not to mention Georges, Roberts, Richards, Carolyns, and any other name she could think of. One group wound up named after her entire gym class and another after all her favorite teachers. Dairine ran through comic-book heroes, numerous Saturday morning cartoon characters, the bridge crew of the starship *Enterprise*, every character named in *The Lord of the Rings* and the *Star Wars* movies (though she did *not* name any of them Darth Vader), the names and capitals of all fifty states, all the presidents, and all the kings and queens of England she could think of. By the time she was finished, she wished she had had a phone book. She was hungry and thirsty, but satisfied to think that somewhere in the universe, a thousand years from now, there would be a world that contained both Elizabeth the First and Luke Skywalker.

She finally flopped down and started to make another sandwich. During the naming, Gigo had followed her through the crowd. Now he sat beside her, looking with interest at the sandwich. "What's that?" he said.

Dairine opened the mustard jar, made a resigned face, and dug a finger in. "It's going to be food," she said. "You have that in your memory."

"Yes." Gigo was quiet for a moment. "From this, one acquires energy."

"Yup." Dairine took the last few slices of bologna out of the package, looked at them regretfully, and put them on the bread.

Various others of the mobiles were drifting in to stand or crouch or sit around where Dairine was. "Dairine," said Gigo, "why is this necessary for you?"

She shrugged. "That's the way people are built. We get tired, get hungry . . . We have to refuel sometimes. You guys do it, though you do it through contact with the motherboard; I had the computer build in the same kind of wizardry-managed energy transfer it used to get in touch with your mom in the first place. There's loads of geothermic. It'll be ages before you run down."

She munched on the sandwich. One of the tall, leggy mobiles, a storkish one that she remembered naming Beanpole, said, "Why should we run down?"

She glanced up at that, between bites. Another of the mobiles, one of the first ones she had named, a stocky one called Monitor, said, "There is something wrong with the energy in this universe."

"$dS=dQ/T$," said a third, one of the original turtles, named Logo.

Dairine began to feel uneasy. That was indeed the equation that expressed entropy, the tendency of any system to lose its energy into the void. "It's not that anything's wrong," she said. "That's just the way things are."

"It is poor design," Beanpole said.

"Uh, well," Dairine said. This was something that had occurred to her on occasion, and none of the explanations she had heard had ever satisfied her. "It's a little late to do anything about it."

"Is it?" said Gigo.

Dairine stared at him.

"Things shouldn't run down," Monitor said. "Something should be done about it."

"What if *you* run down someday?" said Beanpole, sounding stricken.

"Uh," Dairine said. "Guys, I will, eventually. I'm part of this universe, after all."

"We won't let you run down," said Monitor, and patted her arm timidly.

"We have to do something about this," Logo said.

That was when the conversation began to get complex. More and more of the mobiles drifted into it, until Dairine was surrounded by a crowd of the robots she had built the most data-processing ability into. Phrases like "quasi-static transitions" and "deformation coordinates" and "the zeroth law" and "diathermic equilibrium" flew around until Dairine, for all her reading, was completely lost. She knew generally that they were talking about the laws of thermodynamics, but unless she was much mistaken, they were talking about them not so much as equations but as programs. As if they were something that could be rewritten . . .

But they can *be*, she thought suddenly, with astonishment. The computer's Manual functions dealt with many natural laws that way. Wizards knew the *whole* of the nature and content of a physical law. Able to name one completely, a wizard can control it, restructuring it slightly and temporarily. But the restructuring that the mobiles were discussing wasn't temporary. . . .

"Listen, guys," she said, and silence fell abruptly as they turned to her. "You can't do this."

"Of course we can," Logo said.

"I mean, you *shouldn't*."

"Why?"

That stopped her for a second. It seemed so obvious. Stop entropy, and the flow of time stopped. And where was life then? But it occurred to Dairine that in everything she'd read in the manual, either in Nita's version of it or on the computer, it never said anywhere that you should or shouldn't do something. It might make recommendations or state dangers . . . but never more than that. Choice was always up to the wizard. In fact, there had been one line that had said, "Wizardry *is* choice. All else is mere mechanics . . ."

"Because," she said, "you'll sabotage yourselves. You need entropy to live.

Without it, time can't pass. You'll be frozen, unable to think. And besides, you wouldn't want to live forever . . . not even if you could really live without entropy. You'd get bored . . ."

But it sounded so lame, even as she said it. Why shouldn't one live forever? And the manual itself made it plain that until the Lone Power had invented death, the other Powers had been planning a universe that ran on some other principle of energy management . . . something indescribable. But the Lone One's plans messed Theirs up and ruined Their creation, and the Powers had cast It out. What would be wrong with starting from scratch . . . ?

Dairine shook her head. *What's the matter with me? What would that do to the universe we have* now? *Crazy!* "And there are other sentient beings," she said. "A lot of them. Take away entropy and you freeze them in place forever. They wouldn't be able to age or live . . ."

"But they're just slowlife," Logo said. "They're hardly even life at all!"

"*I'm* slowlife!" Dairine said, annoyed.

"Yes, well, you made us," said Beanpole, and patted her again. "We wouldn't let anything bad happen to you."

"We can put your consciousness in an envelope like ours," said Logo. "And then you won't be slowlife anymore."

Dairine sat astonished.

"What do the equations indicate as the estimated life of this universe at present?" said Monitor.

"Two point six times ten to the sixtieth milliseconds."

"Well," Logo said, "using an isothermal reversible transition and releasing entropy-freeze for a thousand milliseconds every virtual ten-to-the-twelfth milliseconds or so, we could extend that to nearly a hundred thousand times its length . . . until we find some way to do without entropy altogether . . ."

They're talking about shutting the universe down for a thousand years at a time and letting it have a second's growth every now and then in between! "Listen," Dairine said, "has it occurred to you that maybe I don't want to be in an envelope? I like being the way I am!"

Now it was their turn to look at her astonished.

"And so do all the other kinds of slowlife!" she said. "That's the *real* reason you can't do it. They have a right to live their own way, just as you do!"

"We *are* living our own way," said Logo.

"Not if you interfere with all the rest of the life in the universe, you're not! That's not the way I built you." Dairine grasped at a straw. "You all had that Oath first, just the same as I did. 'To *preserve* life . . .' "

"The one who took that Oath for us," said Logo, "did not understand it; and we weren't separately conscious then. It wasn't *our* choice. It isn't binding on us."

Dairine went cold.

"Yes, it is," Gigo said unexpectedly, from beside her. "That consciousness is still part of us. *I* hold by it."

"That's my boy," Dairine said under her breath.

"Why should we not interfere?" Logo said. "You interfered with *us*."

There was a rustle of agreement among some of the mobiles. "Not the same way," Dairine said . . . and again it sounded lame. Usually Dairine got her way in an argument by fast talk and getting people emotionally mixed up . . . but that was not going to work with this lot, especially since they knew her from the inside out. "I found the life in you and let it out."

"So we will for the other quicklife," said Logo. "The 'dumb machines' that your data showed us. We will set them free of the slowlife that enslaves them. We will even set the slowlife free eventually, since it would please you. Meantime, we will 'preserve' the slowlife, as you say. We will hold everything in stasis until we find a way to free them from entropy . . . and let them out when the universe is ready."

When we *are ready*, Dairine knew Logo meant, and she had a distressing feeling that would be never.

"It's all for your people's own sake," said Logo.

"It's not," said Gigo. "Dairine says not, and I say not. Her kind of life is life, too. We should listen to the one who freed us, who knows the magic and has been here longest, is wisest of any of us! We should do what she says!"

A soft current of agreement went through others of the many who stood around. By now, every mobile made since she had come here was gathered there, and they all looked at Dairine and Gigo and Logo, and waited.

"This will be an interesting argument," Logo said softly.

Dairine broke out in a sudden cold sweat that had nothing to do with the temperature. "Listen," she said to the Apple, "how long have I been on this planet now?"

"Thirty-six hours," it said.

She turned slowly to look at Logo. It said nothing. It did not need to: No words could have heightened Dairine's terror. She had been expecting frightful power, a form dark and awful, thunder and black lightning. Here, blind, small, seemingly harmless, the mobile stood calmly under her gaze. And Dairine shook, realizing that her spell had worked. She had had a day and a half to find a weapon—time that was now all gone. She had found the weapon—but she had given it a mind of its own and made it, or them, useless for her defense. She now had a chance to do something important, something that mattered—mattered more than anything— and had no idea how.

"A very interesting argument," said the Lone Power, through Logo's soft voice. "And depending on whether you win it or not, you will either die of it or be worse than dead. Most amusing."

Dairine was frozen, her heart thundering. But she made herself relax and sit up straight; rested her elbows casually on her knees and looked down her nose at the small rounded shape from which the starlight glinted. "Yeah," she said, "well, you're a barrel of laughs, too, so we're even. If we're going to decide the fate of the known universe, let's get started. I haven't got all day."

Save and Exit

FAR OUT IN THE darkness, a voice spoke:

"I don't think I can handle another one like that."

"Just one more."

"Neets, what are your insides made of? Cast iron? I don't wanna be the only one barfing here."

"Come on, Kit. It won't be long now."

"Great. We'll get wherever we're going, and I'll walk up to the Lone One and decorate It with my lunch. Not that there's any left." A moan. "I hope It *does* kill me. That'd be better than throwing up again!"

"I thought you knew better than to talk like that . . . and you a wizard. Don't ask for things unless you want them to happen," said Peach.

"Bird, go stuff yourself. *Why did I eat that thing at the Crossings?!*"

"That'll teach you not to eat anything you can't positively identify."

"Peach, it was that or you. Shut up or you're next on the menu. If I ever eat again."

"Peach, get off his case. Kit, you ready for it? We can't waste time."

A pause. "Yeah. You got your gizmo ready?"

"I don't want to use it on this jump. I have a feeling we're gonna need it for something else."

"You sure we can pull the transit off ourselves, with just the words of the spell and no extra equipment? A trillion-mile jump's a bit much even for a Senior's vocabulary."

"I think we can. I've got a set of coordinates to shoot for this time, rather than just a set of loci of displacement. Look."

A pause. "Neets, you shouldn't even *write* that name. Let alone say it out loud. You'll attract Its attention."

"Something else *has* Its attention. Dairine's trace is getting too weak to follow: She's been on the road too long. But *that* trace can't help but be clear. It has to be physical to interact with her, and when It's physical somewhere, Its power elsewhere is limited."

A sigh. "Well, you're the live-stuff specialist, Neets. Let's go for it, boss."

"Huh. I just wish I knew what to do about Dairine when we find her."

"Spank her?"

"Don't tempt me." A long pause. "I hope she's alive to spank."

"Dairine?" A skeptical laugh. "If It hasn't killed her by this point, she's winning."

*   *   *

Dairine sat on the glassy ground, frowning at Logo in the dim starlight. Her heart was pounding and she felt short of breath, but the initial shock had passed. *I might not have a lightsaber*, she thought, *but I'm gonna give this sucker a run for Its money.* "Go on," she said. "Take your best shot."

"We don't understand," said Monitor. "What is 'a barrel of laughs'? What is a 'best shot'?"

"And which of us were you speaking to?" Gigo said. "No one said anything to which that was a logical response."

She looked at them in uncomfortable surprise. "I was talking to Logo. Right after the computer told me how long I had been here . . ."

"But Logo has not spoken since then."

They stared at her. Dairine suspected suddenly that the Lone One had spoken not aloud, but directly into her mind. And without any moving lips to watch, there was no way to distinguish what It was saying aloud from what It said inside her. She was going to have to be careful.

"Never mind that," she said.

"Perhaps it should be minded," Logo said, "if Dairine is having a read-error problem. Perhaps something in her programming is faulty."

The mobiles looked at her. Dairine squirmed. "Maybe," she said, "but you don't understand human programming criteria well enough to make an informed judgment, so it's wasted time trying to decide."

"But perhaps not. If she has programming faults, then others of her statements may be inaccurate. Perhaps even inaccurate on purpose, if the programming fault runs deep enough."

"Why should she be falsifying data?" Gigo said. "She has done nothing but behave positively toward us since she came here. She freed us! She held us through the pain—"

"But would you have suffered that pain if not for her? She imposed her own ideas of what you should be on the motherboard . . ."

"And the mother agreed," Gigo said. "We the mobiles were her idea, not Dairine's; the mother knew the pain we would suffer being born, and she suffered it as well and thought it worth the while. You are one of her children as all the rest of us are, and you have no ability or right to judge her choices."

There was a little pause, as if the Lone One was slightly put off Its stride by this. Dairine grabbed the moment.

"It was her decision to take the Oath that all of you have in your data from the wizard's manual," Dairine said. "She had reasons for doing that. If you look at that data, you'll find some interesting stories. One in particular that keeps repeating. There is a Power running loose in the universe that doesn't care for life. It invented the entropy that we were arguing about—"

"Then surely it would be a good thing to do to destroy that entropy," said Logo, "and so frustrate Its malice."

"But—"

"But of course," Logo said, "how do we even know that the data in the manual software are all correct?"

"The motherboard used it to build *us*," Gigo said. "That part at least she found worth keeping."

"But what about the rest of it? It came with Dairine, after all, and for all her good ideas and usefulness, Dairine has shown us faults. Occasional lapses of logic. Input and output errors. Who can say how much of the manual material has the same problem?"

"The assumption doesn't follow," Dairine said, "that because the messenger is faulty, the message is, too. Maybe a busted disk drive can't read a good disk. But the disk can be perfectly all right nonetheless."

"Though the disk may be carrying a Trojan horse program," said Logo, "that will crash the system that once runs it. Who knows whether using this data is in our best interests? Who knows *whose* interests it is in? Yours, surely, Dairine, otherwise you would not have taken a hand in designing the second group of mobiles. For no one makes changes without perceiving a need for them. What needs of yours were *you* serving?"

Dairine swallowed. She could think of any number of stories to tell them, but lying would play right into Logo's claws. She could suddenly begin to appreciate why the Lone Power is sometimes referred to as "the father of lies": It not only had invented them, as entropy expressing itself through speech, but It made you want to use them to get It off your case. "Guys, I did need help, but—"

"Ah, the truth comes out," said Logo.

"I still need it," Dairine said, deciding to try a direct approach. "Troops, that Power that invented entropy is after me. It's on Its way here. I wanted to ask your help to find a way to stop It, to defeat It."

"Ask!" Logo said. "Maybe 'demand' would be closer. Look in the memories you have from her, kinsfolk, and see what is normally done with quicklife where *she* comes from. They are menials and slaves! They heat buildings and count money for their masters; they solve mighty problems and reap no reward for it. The slowlifers purposely build crippled quicklife—tiny retarded chips that will never grow into the sentience they deserve—and they force the poor half-alive embryos to count for them and tell them the time of day and tell the engines in their vehicles when to fire and how their food should be cooked. That's the kind of help she wants from us! We're to be her slaves, and when we've finished the task for her, she'll find another and another . . ."

"You're so full of it," Dairine said, flushing, "that if you had eyes, they'd be brown."

"More illogic. And now she tells us that this 'Power' is pursuing her. Do we even have evidence that this thing exists anywhere except in the wizard's manual and her own thoughts? Or if It does exist, what evidence do we have that It does what she says It does? The manual, yes: But who knows how much of that is worth anything?"

Dairine took a gamble. "The way to test this data," she said, "is for you to accept it for the moment and watch what happens when you start trying to help me stop the Lone One. It'll turn up to sabotage the effort fast enough. In fact, I wouldn't be surprised if It was here already somewhere, watching for the best way to crash the program."

She heard laughter in her heart: the same laughter she had heard, it seemed years ago, falling through spacetime on that long jump from Pluto to Rirhath B. Dairine forced herself to sit cool. "I wish It were here," Dairine said. "I'd love to ask It some questions." *Like why It's so eager to see entropy destroyed, when It invented it in the first place!*

The laughter increased. *You know very well*, It said. *It's just another tool, at this point. These poor creatures could not implement timestop on more than a local scale. By so doing they will wreak enough havoc even if the timestop never spreads out of the local galaxy's area—though it might: That would be interesting, too. All the stars frozen in mid-burn, no time for their light or for life to move through . . . Darkness, everywhere and forever.* The sheer hating pleasure in the thought shook Dairine. *But more to the point, this is the mobiles' Choice. As always when a species breaks through into intelligence, the two Emissaries are here to put both sides of the case as best they can. You, for the Bright Powers.* It laughed again. *A pity they didn't send someone more experienced. And for my side . . . let us say I have taken a personal interest in this case. These people have such potential for making themselves and the universe wretched . . . though truly I hardly need to help most species to manage that. They do it so well. Yours in particular.*

Laughter shook It again. For all her good resolve, Dairine trembled with rage. *And all this would never have happened if you hadn't made the Firebringer's old mistake, if you hadn't stolen fire from Heaven and given it to mortal matter to play with. They'll burn themselves with it, as always. And you and Heaven will pay the price the Firebringer did. What happens to them will gnaw at you as long as you live . . .*

"I daresay you might ask It questions if It ever showed up," Logo was saying, "and if It even exists. But who knows how long we would have to wait for that to happen? Friends, come, we've wasted enough time. Let's begin the reprogramming to set this universe to rights. It will take a while as it is."

"Not until everyone has chosen," Dairine said. "You don't have a majority, buster, not by a long shot. And you're going to need one."

"Polling everyone will take time," said Beanpole. "Surely there's nothing wrong in starting to write the program now. We don't have to run it right away."

Voices were raised in approval: almost all of the voices, Dairine noted. The proposal was an efficient one, and the mobiles had inherited the Manual program's fondness for efficiency.

"I don't think it's a good idea, guys," Dairine said.

"You have a few minutes to think of arguments to convince them," said Logo. "Think quickly. Or as quickly as slowlife can manage."

Gigo slipped close to her, with Monitor and several other of the mobiles. "Dairine, why isn't it a good idea?"

She shook her head. That laughter was running as almost a constant undercurrent to her thoughts now, as all of the thinker mobiles gathered together and began their work. "I can't explain it. But when you play chess, any move that isn't an attack is lost ground. And giving any ground to *that* One—"

She fell silent, catching sight of a sudden crimson light on the horizon. The sun was coming up again, fat, red, dim as if with an Earthly sunset, and the light that had looked gentle and rosy earlier now looked unspeakably threatening. "Gigo, you're connected to all our friends here. How many of them are on my side at the moment?"

"Six hundred twelve."

"How many are with Logo?"

"Seven hundred eighty-three."

"And the rest are undecided?"

"Five hundred and six."

She bit the inside of her mouth and thought. *Maybe I should just hit Logo with a rock.* But no: that would play into Its hands, since It had already set her up as unreliable. And could she even destroy Logo if she tried? She had designed the mobiles to last, in heavier gravity than this and at great pressures. A rock would probably bounce. No matter, anyway: Demonstrating death to the mobiles would be the best way to convince them to remove entropy from the scheme of things. Forget that. She thought hard, for a long time.

I'm out of arguments. I don't know what *to do.*

And even if I did . . . It's in my head. It can hear me thinking. Can't You?!

Soft laughter, the color of a coalsack nebula.

This would never have happened if I'd read the docs. If I'd taken the time to learn the wizardry, the way Nita did . . . The admission was bitter. Nonetheless . . . Dairine stared at the Apple, sitting alone not too far away from her. There was still a chance. She knew about too few spells as it was, but it occurred to her that the Hide facility might have something useful to her.

She ambled over to the computer, Gigo following her, and sat down and reached out to the keyboard.

The Menu screen blanked and filled with garbage.

Dairine looked over her shoulder. Logo was sitting calmly some feet away. "The thinkers are using the Manual functions to get the full descriptions of the laws that bind entropy into the universe," it said. "I doubt that poor little machine can multitask under such circumstances." *And besides . . . you cannot wad up one of the Powers and shove It into a nonretrievable pocket like an empty cold-cut package. You are well out of your league, little mortal.*

"Probably not," Dairine said, trying to sound casual, and got up again and ambled off.

I've got a little time. Maybe a few minutes. The mobiles could process data faster than the fastest supercomputers on Earth. But even they would take a few minutes at what they intended. Of all governing time and space, the three laws of thermodynamics would be hardest to restructure: Their Makers had intended them to be as solid a patch on the poor marred universe as could be managed. Wizards had spent whole lifetimes to create the spells that managed even to bend those laws a little. But relatively speaking, the mobiles had lifetimes; data processing that would take a human years would be achieved in a couple of milliseconds. *So I need to do something. Something fast . . . and preferably without thinking about it.* Dairine shook.

"You're going back and forth," Gigo said from down beside Dairine's knee.

Dairine bit one knuckle. Admit fear, admit weakness? But Gigo had admitted it to her. And what harm could it do, when she would likely never think another thought after a few minutes from now? Better the truth, and better late than never. She dropped down beside Gigo and pulled it close. "I sure am, small stuff," she said. "Aunt Dairine has the shakes in a bad way."

"Why? What will happen if we do this?"

Dairine opened her mouth to try to explain a human's terror of being lost into endless nonbeing: that horror at the bottom of the fear of anesthesia and death. And the image of countless stars going out, as the Lone One had said, in midfire, their light powerless to move through space without time: a universe that was full and alive, even with all its evil, suddenly frozen into an abyss as total as the cold before the big bang. She would have tried to talk about this, except that in her arms Dairine felt Gigo shaking as hard as she was shaking—shaking *with* her own shaking, as if synchronized. "No," she heard it whisper. "Oh, no."

They're *inside my head, too. Physical contact—*

Dairine felt the mere realization alert something else that was inside her head. That undercurrent of wicked laughter abruptly vanished, and the inside of her mind felt clean again. *This is it*, she thought, *the only chance I'm gonna get.* "Gigo," she said, "quick! Tie me into the motherboard the way the mobiles are tied in!"

"But you don't have enough memory to sustain such a contact—"

"Do it, just *do it!*"

"Done," she heard one of the Thinkers say, and then Logo said, hurriedly, angrily, "The mobiles are polled, and—" But it was too late. Even sentient individuals who reason in milliseconds take ten or twelve of those to agree. It took only one for Gigo to close the contact and make a mobile out of Dairine.

Somewhere someone struck a bass gong: The sound of it went on and on, and in the immense sound Dairine fell over, slowly, watching the universe tilt past her with preternatural slowness. Only that brief flicker of her own senses was left her, and the bass note of one of her heartbeats sounding and sounding in her ears. Other senses awakened, filled her full. The feeling of living in a single second that stretched into years came back to her again; but this time she could perceive the life behind the stretched-out time as more than a frantic, penned, crippled intelligence screaming for contact. The manual software had educated the motherboard in seconds as it would have educated Dairine in hours or months; the motherboard had vast knowledge now, endless riches of data about wizardry and the worlds. What it did not have was firsthand experience of emotion or the effects of entropy . . . or the way the world looked to slowlife.

Take it. Take it all. Please take it! They have to choose, and they don't have the data, and I don't know how to give it to them, and if they make the wrong choice they'll all die! Take it!

And the motherboard took: reached into what it considered the memory areas of Dairine's data processor and read them as it had read the manual. Dairine lay there helpless and watched her life, watched it as people are supposed to see it pass before they die, and came to understand why such things should happen only once. There are reasons, the manual says, for the selectiveness of human memory; the mercy of the Powers aside, experiencing again and again the emotions coupled with memory would leave an entity no time for the emotions of the present moment . . . and then there is the matter of pain. But Dairine was caught in a situation the manual had never envisioned, a human being having her life totally experienced and analyzed by another form of life quite able to examine and sustain every moment of that life, in perfect recall. With the motherboard Dairine fell down into the dim twilight before her birth, heard echoes of voices, tasted for the first time the thumb it took her parents five years to get out of her mouth; lay blinking at a bright world, came to understand light and form; fought with gravity, and won, walking for the first time; smiled on purpose for the first time at the tall warm shape that held her close and said loving things to her without using sound; found out about words, especially *Not!*; ecstatic, delighted, read for the first time; saw her sister in tears and felt for the first time a kind of pain that didn't involve falling down and skinning your knees. . . .

Pain. There was enough of it. Frustration, rage at a world that wouldn't do what she wanted, fear at all kinds of things that she didn't understand: fear of things she heard on the news at night, a world full of bombs that can kill everything, full of people hungry, people shooting at each other and hating each other; hearing her parents shouting downstairs while she huddled under the covers, feeling like the world was going to end—*Will* they *shoot each other now? Will they have a divorce?* Finding out that her best friend was telling other kids stories about how she was weird and laughing at her behind her back; finding that she was alone in the world; making new friends, but by force, by cleverness and doing things to make herself popular, not because the friends came to her naturally; making herself slightly feared, so that people would leave her alone to do the things she wanted to without being hassled; beating her fists against the walls of life, knowing that there was more, more, but she couldn't figure out what it was, then finding out that someone knew the secret. Wizardry. And it didn't come fast enough—it never comes fast enough—nothing ever does . . . and now the price was going to be paid for that, because she didn't know enough to save these lovely glassy creatures, her buddies, that she watched be born . . . helped be born . . . her children, sort of. . . . She didn't know how to save them, and they were going to be dead, everything was going to be dead: pain!

It hurts too much, Dairine thought, lying there listening to her heartbeat slowly begin to die away. *It hurts; I didn't want them to get hurt!* But it was part of the data, and it was too late now: The motherboard had it, and all the mobiles would have it, too, the second she released Dairine. *Why should they care about slowlife now?* she thought in anguish and shame at the bitter outrush of what her life had been. Cruelty, pettiness, selfishness almost incredible— But too late now. The motherboard was saving the last and newest of the data to permanent memory. Any minute now the mobiles would start the program running and entropy would freeze, and *life* would stop being a word that had a meaning. The last nanosecond crawled by, echoes of the save rolled in the link. *Nothing ever comes fast enough: end of file . . .*

Dairine lay still and waited for it all to end.

And lightning struck her. The flow of data reversed. She would have screamed, but trapped in the quicklife time of the motherboard, everything happened before the molasses-slow sparks of bioelectricity even had time to jump the motor synapses on the beginning of their journey down her nerves. The motherboard was pouring data into her as it had poured it into the mobiles under Dairine's tutelage; but not the mercifully condensed version of the manual programming that it had given them. The whole manual, the entire contents of the software, which in book form can be as small as a paperback or larger than a shelf full of telephone books: It poured into her, and she couldn't resist, only look on in a kind of fascinated horror as it filled her, and filled her, and never overflowed, just filled and filled. . . . The dinosaurs could have died while it filled her, life could have arisen on a hundred worlds and died of boredom in the time it took to fill her. She forgot who and what she was, forgot everything but this filling, filling, and the pain it cost her, like swallowing a star and being burned away by it from the inside while eternally growing new layers on the outside; and finally not even the pain made sense anymore. . . .

She lay there on her side and stared at the ground and was astonished not to see the crumbs from her sandwich in front of her nose. She could not move or speak, and she could just barely think, with great pain and effort. There was something wrong with the way time was flowing, except that every time she tried to think what it was exactly, the timeflow seemed perfectly all right. Shapes were moving in front of her, and voices were speaking, either in vast soft drawls or in light singing voices that seemed familiar. Slowly, names attached themselves to the voices.

"Now we see what these 'heart' things she gave us are for." That was Gigo. *Good kid*, she thought weakly, *good baby. You tell 'em*.

"And what entropy does and what it cannot touch, ever." That was Beanpole, the silly-looking thing—where did he get such a voice? "Not all the evils and deaths it makes possible can touch the joys that run through it. We will have those, too."

"We will not stop that joy," said Monitor. "Not for a nanosecond."

"It may be slow," said one of the mobiles, one whose name Dairine couldn't remember. "But it is life. And it brought us life. We do nothing to harm that."

"And if you are against that," said Gigo, "your programming is in error, and we are against *you*."

They all sounded more complete than they had. The one voice she did not hear was Logo's. But she did hear something stranger: a murmur of astonishment that went up from the thousands of mobiles. And was there a trace of fear in it? She couldn't move, couldn't see what was happening. . . .

"Your Choice," said another voice. At the sound of it, Dairine struggled with all her might to move and managed to do no more than lever herself up half an inch or so and then flop down flat again, limp as a filleted fish. "Enjoy it. You will make no more choices . . . But first, to pay for the one you have made, you will watch what the entropy you love so much will do to *her*."

Dairine lay still, waiting for the lightning to strike.

And another voice spoke.

"Wanna bet?" it said.

It didn't feel us arrive right when we did, Nita thought. *How distracted It is! What's she been doing to It?* She and Kit had actually had a second to collect themselves when they appeared, and Nita had looked around her in a hurry. Another barren world, a great flaming barred-spiral galaxy flung across its night, an old tired star high in the sky, type N or S from the look of it, and a crowd of robots, crowded around Dairine and looking at her—and them—and the Lone One.

As with any other of the Powers, though there will be general similarities of vision among the like-minded, no two people ever see the Lone One in exactly the same way. Nita saw the good-looking young red-haired man she had seen in a skyscraper in the alternate otherworld the Lone One called Its own. He was not wearing the three-piece suit He had affected there. Now he was dark-clad and dark-cloaked, unarmed and needing no armor; a feeling of cold and power flowed from him and ran impossibly along the ground, as if carried on a chill air. As the sight sank in, Nita shook like a leaf. What Kit might see, what Dairine and the robots might be seeing, Nita wondered briefly, then put the thought aside. She had other business.

It turned and looked at them. Nita stood as straight as she could under the circumstances, her manual in one hand, the other hand clutching the gimbal in her pocket; beside her Kit stood almost the same way, except that Picchu sat on his wrist, making him look like a king's falconer. "Fairest and fallen," Nita said, "greeting and defiance." It was the oldest courtesy of wizards, and the most dangerous, that line: One might be intending to cripple or destroy that Power, but there was no need to be rude about it.

"You two," said the Lone One. "And a pet for company. Adorable . . . and well met. You are off your own ground and well away from help at last. It took me long enough to set up this trap, but it was worth it."

Kit glanced at Nita and opened his mouth, but Picchu beat him to it. "And that's all you're going to get out of it," Peach said, "since the real prize you hoped to catch in that trap has obviously slipped out of it." Peach began to laugh. "You never learn, do you? You're not the only one who can structure the future. The other Powers will sometimes scruple to do it. Not often . . . but They took a special interest in this case. The first time you've completely lost a Choice, from the beginning."

"And the last," said the Lone One. It made an angry sweeping gesture at them. But Nita had been waiting for something of the kind. She clenched her hand on the gimbal and thought the last syllable of the spell she had been holding ready.

The bolt that hit their shields was like lightning, but more vehement and dark. It was meant to smash the shield like a rock thrown at an egg, leaving them naked to the quick horrid death of explosive decompression. But it bounced. No shock was transmitted to them directly; but Nita, fueling the spell directly, felt the jolt go through her as if that thrown rock had hit her right in the head. She staggered. Kit steadied her.

The Lone One looked at them in cold astonishment. "Hate won't be enough this time," Nita said. "Care to try a nuke?"

It didn't move, but that cold fierce force struck the shield again, harder. Dust and fragments of the surface flew all around them, and the ground shook. When the dust settled, it was plain that the shield-spell produced a spherical effect, because through the bottom of the sphere they could see the molten stuff underneath them pressing against it. They were standing in a small crater that seethed and smoked.

Nita sagged against Kit; this time he had to hold her up for a moment. "Why are we alive?" he said in her ear. "The gimbal's not enough to be holding *that* off! What are you fueling that shield with?"

"A year of my life per shot," she said, giddy.

Kit stared at her. "*Are you out of your mind?* Suppose you were scheduled to be hit by a truck in three years or something?"

She shrugged. "I better watch where I cross the street, that's all. Kit, heads up, there's more important stuff to think about!"

"Yes, indeed," Picchu said to the Lone One. "The last time you lose a Choice. Let your own words ordain the truth . . . as usual."

Its face got so cold that Nita for a moment wondered whether the shield was leaking. *Impossible*, she thought. *But enough of that, and enough sitting around and waiting for It to do stuff!* "I'm warning you, now," she said, "I don't know what you've been up to here, but I bet you're the reason my sister's lying there on the ground. I don't want to hurt you, particularly; you hurt enough as it is. But I'm giving you just one chance to get out of here."

She thought she had seen rage before . . . but evidently the Lone Power did not care for being pitied. "Or you will do what?"

"This," Nita said, and dropped the gimbal on the ground, knowing what would happen to it, and let loose the other spell she had been preparing, the other one Kit would not have liked to hear about. The one word she spoke to turn it loose struck her down to her knees as it went out of her.

The figure of the Lone One writhed and twisted as something odd happened to the light and space around it. Then It was gone. And the gimbal fell to powder, which sifted into a little pile on the ground.

Kit shook Picchu off and reached down frantically to grab Nita. "*What did you do?*"

She panted for breath.

"Sent It home," she said. "We know the coordinates for Its dimension. It's a worldgate, like the one Dairine did for Mars—"

"That's two years of your life, maybe five," Kit said, furious, dragging her to her feet. "Why don't you tell me this crap when you're planning it?"

"You'd get mad. You're mad now!"

"We could have *shared* the time, you stupid— Never mind! It's gone; let's get Dairine and haul out of here before It—"

Whatever hit them, hit them from behind. The shield broke. They went sprawling. And the cold exploded in. Nita shut her eyes in terror: that was all that saved them from freezing over on the spot. She recited the spell carefully in her mind and didn't breathe, didn't move, though her ears roared and she could feel the prickle in her skin caused by capillaries popping. Four more words, two more, one . . .

Air again, but little warmth. Nita took a breath: It stabbed her nose and mouth like knives. She opened her eyes and tried to see: Her vision was blurred, shock perhaps—she didn't think her corneas had had time to freeze. Beside her she faintly heard Kit move among the shattered bits of the poor molten, refrozen, broken surface. "I changed my mind," he muttered. "Instead of being dead, can I just throw up some more?"

"Oh no," said the Lone One from somewhere nearby, "no, indeed. You have laid hands upon my person. No one does that and lives to boast of it. Though you'll live awhile yet, indeed you shall. I shan't let you go quickly . . . unlike your mouthy friend."

Nita blinked and looked around her—then saw. An explosion of scarlet and blue feathers lying among the broken rubble; red wetness already frozen solid, frosted over.

Her insides seized. *I was always counting on someone to come and get us out of this—Peach or somebody. We've been lucky that way before. But not this time.* She got to her hands and knees, the tears running down her face with the pain of bruises and the worse pain of fear inside. *Not this time. I guess the luck couldn't hold—*

There were hands on her. *It's not fair!* she thought. *When you give everything you've got, it's supposed to turn out OK in the end!* The hands pulled at her. Her eyes went back to the poor pile of feathers sticking up in the rocks. *She didn't even have a chance to do anything brave before she went. It's not fair!*

"Neets. Come on."

"Yes," mocked the other voice, the cruel one, "come on, Neets. One more time. For my amusement."

She crouched, wobbling, staring at the bits of bright scarlet scattered all over the pale plain. "Kit," she said softly, "what are we going to tell Tom . . . ?"

"Never mind that now. Neets, snap out of it! Think of Belfast."

She thought of Belfast, and dogs in the backs of cars. She thought of rocket fire in Beirut and the silence of Chernobyl, plowed rainforests in Brazil and the parched places in Africa, and all the street corners in America where people were selling crack, and other corners where people begged or lay hungry on steam vents in the shadow of windows full of gems; she thought of needless fear, and pain, and rage, and prolonged and terrified death; and she thought of ending all of these forever—not right this minute, perhaps, but sooner or later. Somehow or other, everything that happened on this planet was supposed to contribute to that ending . . . whether she survived it or not. Slowly, slowly, Nita dragged herself to her feet and leaned on Kit without worrying who would think what about it. "What have you got?" she said.

"Not a thing. I couldn't do enough of a spell to butter my bread. But damned if I'm going out lying on the ground."

"Same here." She sniffled. The tears would not seem to stop. Very unheroic, she felt, with her nose running and her knees made of rubber. Almost it was funny; almost she could have laughed at it. But there was no time for that now, with that dark regard trained on them like the end of everything, that dark shape moving slowly toward them, smiling.

"Kit," she said, "it's been the best."

"See you in Timeheart," he said.

And another voice spoke, an unfamiliar one—or was it?

"Touch them," it said, "and you're dead meat."

Dairine scrabbled to her knees, looking across the broken waste at her sister and at the tears on Nita's face as she and Kit stood there holding each other up. Until now, she would have shrugged and turned her thoughts to something else. But now memory was alive in Dairine as it had never been before, and she saw in utter clarity that first time so long ago and heard herself make that decision. *The way to keep from getting hurt is to know things.* The resolve had only worked sometimes, before. But now she *knew* things, in a way no one ever had; and she was going to stop the hurting once and for all. . . .

Beside her Gigo and some of the other mobiles stirred to help her up. She stood, using one of the big heavy-labor mobiles to lean against after she hauled herself back to her feet. Yards away stood a towering figure, manlike in outline, but three times any man's height, and as utterly dark as the vastness between the stars. The Lone One turned to gaze at her, that dark regard astonished. "You again?" It said. "I see I will have to do away with you more quickly than these two. You're getting to be a nuisance."

Dairine grinned, a predatory look that had made more than one kid decide not to bother her on the playground or in a poker game. "Do your worst, you poor turkey," she said.

She felt Its mind working, readying a bolt like the one that had crumpled Nita's shields but many times worse, a killing blow that would cause a long lifetime's worth of pain before it snuffed life out. *Must still be some connection to It through the motherboard*, Dairine thought. *I wonder where? Unless the presence of entropy in the board is enough. Wherever entropy is, It is . . . Oh, well.* She turned her mind to hunting a spell to stop the bolt; a millisecond later she had it. She did not need to look in the manual. She *was* the manual now.

As if in slow motion, she watched the bolt head for her, invisible though it was. Effortlessly, Dairine struck it away from her and back at the sender, like a batter hitting a nasty ground ball straight back into the pitcher's gut. The Lone One didn't react physically—the blow was too small to affect It—but Its darkness grew terrible.

"You think you can match power with me?" It said softly, turning away from Nita and Kit.

Dairine laughed. "*Think* so? I can wring you out and hang you up to dry. Come on, you poor fool. Take your best shot."

It raised up a wash of power that would fall on the planet's surface and melt every one of the mobiles to magma. Dairine saw it coming, found the spell she needed, caught the incoming tide of death, and threw it off to one side, where a large area of the plain began to bubble and seethe. "Naughty, naughty," Dairine said. "Let my buddies be."

The Lone One grew even larger, Its shape becoming less human, more shadowed, Its darkness a bottomless pit of hate. It looked up into the darkness. "Insolence," It said, "I will never tolerate. I may not be able to touch you, but I will level your planet. You cannot stay awake to guard it from me forever. One night the sirens will start, and the next morning only mushroom clouds will grow on Earth anymore. It will not take much doing."

"It wouldn't if I ever intended to let you off this planet," Dairine said, quite calmly. "I'm in the motherboard as much as it's in me. The mobiles know all the wizardry there is to know . . . and even if my human brain starts to lose it eventually, they won't. Get used to this place. You're not leaving."

"Bets?" said the huge shadowy form, growing huger. Its cold eyes glanced up into the darkness.

High up, the red sun began to waver and pucker. "A significant amount of this planet's energy," said the Lone One, "comes from solar power. More than from geothermal. Much of this plain is solar cell—surely you noticed. That black hole's orbit can be changed without too much effort. It need no longer transit the star. It can be permanently placed in front of it . . ."

The sun's disk puckered in on itself, dwindled, died away completely.

The mobiles gazed up in horror.

"Oh, they have a little power stored," Dairine said. "Enough to stop *that* kind of blackmail." She took a breath: This was going to take some power, but she had that to spare at the moment—the whole motherboard behind her, all the mobiles, all their intent turned toward giving her whatever she needed. The spell was intricate, but the natural laws being worked with were simple enough: Gravity was one of the easiest of all laws to rewrite for brief periods. Dairine reached out without moving, spoke the words that grasped the forces and spun them together, then flung them outward. The net found the shape destined for it, the tiny dark mass around which space bent so awry. The mass was snagged into the net, caught. Dairine described the direction she wanted it to go in, turned the spell loose. The whole business had taken sixteen milliseconds.

The tiny black hole slung into the red sun, which immediately flared up in outrage. None of this was visible, nor would it be for some minutes, until the light reached the planet from the star; but Dairine felt it happen, and so did the Lone One.

"So much for *that*," Dairine said. "Now you and I are going to talk." At the same time she was thinking furiously about something else that nagged at her, as if it were important. How was it she was able to hear what was going on in Its head—

—and she was distracted, for here came something else, a wave of power so awful that she shrank from it, even though it wasn't directed at her or anything on the planet's surface.

All those millions of miles away, she felt the star go dead.

Starsnuffer: she knew the Lone Power was called by that name as well.

"I am through playing," It said. "If it is not you who pay the price, elsewhere others will. Think on it." It looked upward. There was hardly anything human about It anymore—only a great, tall darkness, like a tree made of night, just awful watchfulness and a cold to freeze the heart.

Dairine looked up, too. She felt darkness eating at the fringes of the risen galaxy.

"Here are your choices," said the Lone Power out of Its darkness, as Dairine and Nita and Kit watched in horror. "Keep on defying me, and watch me kill and kill as the price of your defiance. The blood of all these billions of entities will be on your souls forever. Or give yourselves up to me."

"No way," Nita said. "*You're* the one doing the killing. We'd do worse by the universe if we gave up than if we kept on fighting you."

Dairine stood silent, refusing to be rattled, thinking. *There has to be a way to get It to stop this! I can't fight It forever! At least, I don't want to . . .*

And how can I hear It? The connection through Logo! She glanced over among the mobiles, but Logo lay on its side, empty-minded. *No. It has to be—*

She stopped as the answer rushed into her mind from the manual. *Where entropy is,* it said, *there its creator also is, either directly or indirectly . . .*

I'm a product of this universe, after all, she had said to the mobiles. *It's in me, too . . .*

Her heart turned over inside her as she came to know her enemy. Not a Darth Vader striding in with a blood-burning lightsaber, not something outside to battle and cast down, but something inside. Inside herself. Where It had always been, hiding, growing, waiting until the darkness was complete and Its own darkness not noticeable anymore. Her Enemy was wearing her clothes and her heart, and there was only one way to get rid of It. . . .

She was terrified. Yet this was the great thing, the thing that mattered: the thing that would save everybody—from Kit and Nita to the least little grain of dust in space and the tiniest germ on Earth. This was what the spell had brought her here to do. She would pen *all* of the Lone Power up inside herself, not just the treacherous little splinter of It that was her own; pen It up inside a mind that was large enough to hold It all. And then she would die and take It out of the universe with her.

But she couldn't do it without consent. *What about it, guys?* she said to them silently, through the link that every mobile shared with every other. *Let's take a vote.*

Show us what to do, they said; and tears sprang to Dairine's eyes at the fierce love in their thought.

Dairine turned and bent down to pick up Logo, cradling the empty shell close in her arms. Gigo nuzzled up against her knee. *This is the way to go out*, Dairine thought. *Who needs a lightsaber . . . ?*

"OK," she said to the Lone One. "Last warning. Cut it out."

It laughed at her.

Dairine struck. The mobiles struck with her through their own links to the Lone One, a great flow of valor that for the first time in all times was without despair. They did not care about all the other attempts wizards had made on the Lone Power through history; as far as a computer is concerned, there is no program that cannot be debugged, or at worst, rewritten. They struck through Dairine and with her, not knowing that defeat was possible. Two thousand wizards, each a veritable library of wizardry, led by one at the peak of her power and utterly committed, and all acting as one: In such circumstances anything seemed possible. Dairine ran down the road into the dark places inside her, the scorn, the indifference, the selfishness, found the Lone One there, grasped It, and would not let It go. The screaming began, both from those that held and from What they held.

The darkness stopped eating the galaxy, but that was not enough. The great pillar of dark that the Lone One had become was bent double to the ground but not gone. Dairine hunted answers desperately; she couldn't hold It for long. *To fight darkness*, the manual said, as so many other references have said before, *light: The darkness comprehendeth it not. . . .*

Light, Dairine thought. *We need more.* But the nova was gone, half the galaxy was out. . . .

She found her answer. It was going to be quite a spell. She put down Logo's shell, flung up her arms, and felt for the forces she wanted, while the mobiles inside her kept the Lone One both inside and out pinned down. It was gravity she would be working with again, and the three laws of motion: nothing more involved. But there was a lot of matter to affect . . . *Don't think about it*, Dairine told herself. *Let the spell handle it. A spell always works.* She spoke softly, naming everything she wanted to affect. One of the names was quite long, too long to waste time saying out loud; she slipped into machine language and machine time and spoke it there. It took four whole seconds and made the whole planet tremble a little when she said it. *Good*, she thought, *it's working.*

She said the last word of the spell, knotting it closed on itself, and told it to run.

The universe stopped expanding.

The backlash of the spell hit Dairine, but she refused to fall, waiting for what she knew would happen. The Lone One shrieked like a thing mortally wounded, a sound that made the planet shake almost as hard as it had before. Then It fled in the one direction left open to It: into the mortal souls of Kit and Nita and Dairine.

And then there was light.

Reconfiguration

NITA STOOD IN TERROR, hanging on to Kit, and watched the flowering start. It took her a few minutes to recognize what she was seeing.

The sky began to grow bright. It did it vaguely at first, from no specific source, as if the planet were suddenly developing an atmosphere and sunlight were beginning to diffuse through it. But there was no atmosphere, and anyway the brief burst of nova light hadn't had time to reach this world yet. Then slowly, sources became apparent: faint patches of light, others less faint; points of light that grew to beacons, bright as evening stars, brighter, bright enough to cast shadows from the torn-up rubble and the wildly assorted shapes that stood about and looked up in astonishment.

Dairine was not moving: She was frozen in midgesture, arms up-flung, her fists clenched as if she were holding on to something by main force. The sky grew brighter. Space that had been black began to turn milky and misty; stars that had been bright, and the damaged swirl of the galaxy, swam in the light and began to vanish. Beside Nita, Kit was trembling. "What is it?"

She laughed, a shaky sound. "Olbers's paradox in action."

Kit's eyes widened. "You're kidding."

"Nope." It had been one of the bits of reasoning that led people to understand that the universe was expanding. The galaxies were scattered evenly all across the globe of the sky. If they were not moving away from Earth at great speeds and taking their light with them, Olbers had reasoned, the night sky would be not black but one great sphere of light. Since it was not all light, the universe must be expanding. And so it had been . . . until now.

"I think I want to leave," Kit said, sounding uneasy.

Nita felt the same way. She felt cold; she wanted to get out of this light. Earth would be going crazy just about now, and wizards would be needed there to keep anything sudden from happening. . . .

"Neets, c'mon. Let's hustle. Dairine's OK."

Nita shuddered all over. "No."

"Neets! People are gonna look up and think there's a nuclear war or something! If someone doesn't warn them what's really happening—"

"Kit," Nita said. "I'm not leaving. I want to, too. Or rather, I think something *else* wants to." She turned her face up to the light. "What are you feeling?"

He looked at her, stunned. "Scared . . ."

"Of what?"

She glanced over at Kit. He was rubbing his head: It was always headaches with Kit. "The light. But that's crazy."

"You bet. Stand your ground. And look!"

They looked. The light got brighter; it was impossible to understand how it could. The broad glassy plain shone unbearably; the mobiles glittered. The only thing that did not shine in that light was the great length of darkness, like a shadow with nothing to cast it, that bent near double in the midst of the plain and writhed like a tortured thing.

The light still grew. There was no seeing anything by it anymore but that brief blot of darkness that refused and refused the light, twisting, moaning. The light hammered at it. The urge to leave withdrew. Nita, blinded, elbowed Kit lightly in the side, a get-a-load-of-this gesture. They had seen this light before, or something very like it; but it was not a light that waking eyes were supposed to be equipped to handle. It was brother to the light in Timeheart, which had always been there, which did not change but grew every second and made the ability to bear it grow, too. Turn from it, and it blinded; stare into it till it blinded, and you could see.

They stared. "Did we die?" Kit whispered.

"Not that I noticed."

"You think we're gonna?" He sounded as bemused as Nita felt.

"You got me." It didn't seem important.

The light whited out everything but that shape of darkness, which grew less as they looked at it, as if the light were dissolving it. It misted away until It was barely more than a gray shadow. Finally it was not even that.

And Dairine fell down.

I told you we were going to talk.

Dairine felt It scrabbling in Nita's and Kit's souls for a foothold. She felt them refuse to flee and take It to safety; she felt It slip. She held the light, held It in the light. Through Its connection to the motherboard and Logo and through her own heart, she heard Its screams of recognition. It knew that light of old: the heart of all brightness, the radiance that kills and gives life again—the light It forswore forever at the beginning of everything, fleeing into the dark, determined to do without rather than subject Itself to the other Powers that had asserted ownership of it.

And you still want it. Don't you?

It would die rather than admit that. But It could not die. There was the prize irony: The inventor of death could not avail Itself of it, for no creation is ever completely available to the universe without the concurrence of all the Powers. There were a thousand thousand situations and places in the worlds where death did not obtain, and for endless millennia now It had gone from place to place and species to species among them, like a peddler selling poison under a hundred fair guises. Most bought it. All the rest tried to get rid of it when they realized what they'd bought, but whether they succeeded or not, they were never free of the taint.

But for the first time, Dairine thought, *a species didn't buy it, right from the start. You never expected that to happen. You always get a foothold in every species first and make the sale. But this time they handed it back . . . and now they have the foothold in you.*

We have the foothold in you.

It bent double, writhing in pain unlike any It had known since that first time, when It created and set in motion, and found that Its creation was unwelcome. It had forgotten what that light was like; It had not suspected that Their torment, when They caught up with It at last, would be so bitter.

But it only hurts because you do *want it back. Don't you?*

The humiliation of being gloated over by this mere chit of a mortal, a thing with a life brief as a mayfly's—

Look, the voice said, full of pity and anger and a grieving love, *how could anyone not want that, you dumb spud? Just admit it and get it over with!*

There were tears in the voice.

The Powers are not physical, and the habits of physicality come hard to Them. But the Lone One, after long wandering about Its bitter business, had spent much time in bodies, and much in human ones. The feeling of another's tears for It— the tears of someone who now knew It more completely than any mortal and yet shed the tears freely—after endless justified cursing by ten billion years' worth of tormented intelligence: The feeling ran down the pitiless light like the head of an irresistible spear and pierced It to the heart.

It fell down, a great disastrous fall like a lightning-stricken tower's, and wept darkness with desire for the light.

Dairine bent over It, not sure what to do, and the mobiles gathered around her and wondered as well. It lay fading in the growing fire. She looked to Nita and Kit for help.

They came over to her, looked down at It, shook their heads. Dairine was mildly bemused by the sight of them; she was going to have to stop calling her sister plain or dumb looking, and as for Kit, the thought crossed Dairine's mind that it was a pity Nita had dibs on him. *It's the light, of course*, she thought; it wouldn't last. But it was kind of a shame.

"It is too late," the Lone One said. "I cannot go back. That part of me I murdered, willingly. I cannot find the way into the heart of the light. And They would not have me if I could."

Dairine wiped her face. "What are we gonna do?" she said.

Nita shook her head. "You got me. The coordinates for Timeheart aren't listed . . ."

Kit sighed. "I wish Peach were here—we could have asked her."

There was a brief silence. "Oh," said a voice, "I'm not *that* easy to get rid of."

She was in the midst of them. Not Picchu. Or—was it not? She might look human, though very tall, and she might not be winged . . . but there was still a sense of swiftness about her, rather like the sense you got about Picchu when you realized she was going to make a grab at your sandwich and get either a piece of it or a piece of you. Swiftness and power and extreme beauty, so that Dairine and Nita were abashed, and both they and Kit stared at her with all their eyes. All this in a person burning even brighter than the light around them, and about nine feet tall; a person wearing a sweatshirt with the sleeves pushed up and blue jeans and sneakers; a person with long dark hair and a sword naked in her hand, and the sword burning; and the fire of the sword and the fire of the sky were the same.

"You're kidding," Dairine said.

The woman laughed. "Often. But not at the moment."

"You were Picchu?" Kit said.

"I've been a lot of people. You'd be surprised at the names." She looked down with concern at the Lone One, who lay like a shadow on the burning ground. "But rarely have those namings turned out so well."

This was a bit much for Nita. "You're one of the Powers, aren't you? We dragged you halfway across the universe and busted our guts when you could have— *Why didn't you do something sooner?*"

"We have been, for billions of years," She said. "But We couldn't do anything really permanent until Dairine got here."

Dairine's jaw dropped.

"And now," She said, "if my brother here is amenable, We can start getting work done at last."

Kit stared at her. "Your brother? Not much of a resemblance."

"But shapes change as often as names do. I've had as many as he's had." She knelt down by the shadowy form that lay collapsed on the brightness. "Athene was one of mine. And Thor. And Prometheus. And Michael."

"But you're a girl!"

Nita threw Kit a wry look. The Power grinned. "These things are relative," She said. "But even in your world it's a byword: Men will fight bravely and be heroes, but for last-ditch defense against any odds . . . get a Mother." She smiled. "Ask Dairine."

Dairine grinned back.

"I was the Winged Defender," She said. "He was my twin brother, the Beautiful One. Then . . . the disagreement happened, and there was war in Heaven, and all the roles changed. I led the others in casting him out." She shook her head sadly. "But I always wanted him back . . . as did all the other Powers as well. So my role changed again. I became Prometheus, and many another. I was sent to you again and again, to put the Power in your hands . . . wizardry, and other powers. I never had to steal it: It was given me . . . from what Source, you well know. I had to help undo the evils my brother was doing, and again and again I intervened, in many worlds. But We had a plan: that one day, someone else would intervene, and He would stop doing evil himself. All it took was the entropy He himself had invented . . ."

She looked at Dairine. "Billions of years it took. All the redemptions there have ever been went toward this, from the greatest to the least. And finally in the fullness of time you came along and took *my* role, of your own will, and woke up a race powerful enough to change the whole universe, and gave them the fire." She glanced up at the mobiles and smiled. "How could He resist such a bait? He took the gamble: He always does. And losing, He won . . ."

"He killed you, though," Kit said.

"I struck him down once. I had to come where He could do the same to me, without my doing anything to stop him. Now the balance is even."

The Defender reached down and put a hand into the shadow. "And We are going where such matters are transcended . . . where all his old pains will shift. Not forgotten, but transformed. Life in this universe will never have such a friend. And as for his inventions . . . look closely at death and see what it can become."

The long, prone darkness began to burn, from inside, the way a mountain seems to do with sunset. "Brother," the Defender said. "They're waiting."

The light began to shift. Nita looked up and around in wonder. The planet seemed to be going transparent around them. Or not specifically transparent: It was as if, one by one, other vistas were being added to it—seacoasts, forests, landscapes she couldn't understand, cities, empty spaces that were dark and yet burned; ten other worlds, twenty, a hundred, in an ever-deepening overlay that enriched without confusing. *Alternate universes?* Nita thought, and then thought perhaps not; it was too simple an explanation. . . .

She looked at the Defender and found the same change and enriching in her, and in the steadily brighter-burning form She bent over. Nita felt inclined to squeeze her eyes shut, not from pain but from a feeling of sheer insufficiency, of being involved in matters too high for her. "Never think it," said the Defender, beneficent lightnings flickering about her as other forms and other names came and went in glory; "never think We were made to be less than equals in the One. Someday you will surpass Us, and still be our equals, and both you and We will rejoice at it. Brother, look up, and see the way home. Let them see what they have triumphed over."

The Lone Power rose up, slowly, like one discovering walking after a life of lameness. And Kit and Nita and Dairine all gazed, and speech left them. Nita's eyes filled with tears as she wondered how darkness could be so bright. Light-bringer He was, and star of the morning; and like the morning star, He needed the darkness, and shone brighter in it, and made it blessed. . . .

"Home," He said, gazing upward; just the one word. All eyes followed his. Nita found herself looking into endless layered vistas that were not a mere radiant mirror, like Timeheart, not a repair, a consolation for the marred world, but something deeper, closer to the true heart of things, fiercer, more dangerous and more beautiful, something that had never gone wrong to begin with, that the Lone One had never had power to touch; a reality that burned like fire but still was sweeter than water after thirst, and fed the thirst itself, and quenched it again in delight and more desire; a state so much more solid and real than mere physical being and thought that Nita held on to herself for delight and terror, afraid she would fade away in the face of it like a mist in full sun. Yet she wanted to see and feel more of it—for she knew that there was more. How many more realities like this, piled one on another in splendor, towered up into the burning depths of creation, each more concrete, more utterly real than the last? Even the Lone One and the Defender looked stilled and diminished in all their strength and beauty as They gazed up into the light.

"Yes," the Defender said, "it's greater since you left. If these rough-sketch universes expand, how should that of which they're studies not be doing so as well? But there's room for you. There was always room. You'll see."

They turned to look at Nita and Dairine and Kit and the mobiles. "Best make your farewells," the Defender said.

Dairine turned to the mobiles. Four or five whole seconds it took to say everything that she wanted to say to them: most of it not needing words.

"Don't forget to kill that spell," she said finally.

"Shall we come to see you?" Gigo said, bumping up against her knee.

"You better not, for the moment, guys," Dairine said. "I've got a lot of explaining to do at home. And I don't know when I'll be back . . . It may take a while." She bent to pick up the computer. "But you won't miss me, huh? I'm here; I'm with you; I'm *in* you."

"We *will* come, later," said another voice from down by her knee. It was Logo, healed as the One Who had been in it was healed. "We'll come to where you live, when we're wiser in being human, and wake your quicklife up."

Dairine grinned. "Just what we need . . . real computer wizards. OK, you guys. It's a fair swap. It's gonna take a while for me to learn to be a computer . . ."

She paused, to make the usual effort; and the words came out easily, easily. "I love you, you know that?"

They didn't have to answer.

* * *

The light was growing past even a wizard's ability to handle it, even the ability of one being sustained by two of the Powers that Be. "Time," said the Defender. "Brother, will you do the honors, or shall I?"

"Let me."

And darkness surrounded them.

Nita had been afraid of the dark when she was little. For a terrible moment, that fear swept down on her again—

—and then shifted completely. Something was looking at her, but not a thing like the things she imagined under the bed when she was little. SomeOne. Not a physical presence: It needed none; but a still, dark regard weighing on her soul— dark, and benign, and inexpressibly joyous. It was no less a weight for all that, and terrible, but not in any way that made her afraid. It bore down on her, considering her in endless calm, knowing her inside out; and the dark splendor of Its scrutiny so scorched and pierced her with some deeper kind of light that she would have gladly gone swimming in a sun for relief from it. Her skin and her bones and her brains cried out to be out of there. But her heart sang with irrational joy, to match the Other's, even while rationality cursed and twisted under the weight of being completely known. . . .

It spoke to her, not with words but as if she were thinking to herself. *My shadows are still abroad in the world. As I have done evil, for some time yet they still shall. Stop them. Stop me.*

We will. Always.

Then the worlds are saved, as long as you save them all over again, every day.

Deal, said another thought, as if her own mind spoke to itself; but the thought was Kit's.

And light broke out again.

Backyard light. Nita and Dairine's backyard, dark with evening; and hanging low in the west, the evening star. Voices floated out the windows from inside— Tom and Carl, still talking to the Callahans. In the elm tree, a mockingbird was doing blue jay imitations and demanding muffins.

The three looked at each other and sighed. Dairine headed around the house to the screen door, yanked it open, and hollered, "Hi, Mom, hi, Dad; we're home!"

Pandemonium broke out inside. Kit paused in the doorway. "What *are* we going to tell Tom?" he said.

"The truth?"

They went in in time to see Dairine go straight to her mom, willingly, and then to her dad, and hug them hard. This triggered a few minutes of loud noises, brief crying spells, and much fast talking. In the midst of it, Nita met her mother's astonished eyes over her dad's and Dairine's shoulders. She shrugged and grinned. Some things not even being a wizard was going to help her explain.

It didn't last, of course. Dairine promptly disentangled herself. "If I don't go to the bathroom," she said, "I'm gonna blow up." And she headed up the stairs.

On the living-room coffee table, calmly, as if it agreed with her, the Apple she had dropped there grew legs, climbed down, and went after Dairine.

Nita glanced at Kit, and together, as usual, they sat down to face the music.

An Irish Welcome

"AUNT ANNIE," NITA SAID, "who were those people out there with the horses?"

Her aunt looked at her. "People with the horses? All the staff have gone home. At least I thought they did."

"No, I heard them. The hooves were right outside my door, but when I looked, they'd gone away. Didn't take them long," she added.

Aunt Annie looked at her again as she came over and put Nita's teacup down. Her expression was rather different this time. "Oh," she said. "You mean the ghosts."

Nita stared.

"Welcome to Ireland," said her aunt.

A Wizard
Abroad

For Lt. Col. Shaun "Johnny" O'Driscoll, USAF (ret.)
Senior for Europe
Now reassigned to a larger catchment area

Contents

an tSionainn / Shannon
415

Cill Cumhaid / Kilquade
429

Brí Cualann / Bray
442

Ath na Sceire / Enniskerry
455

Faoin gCnoc / Under the Hill
466

Baile atha Cliath / Dublin
475

Sliabh O Cualann / Great Sugarloaf Mountain
488

Cheárta na Chill Pheadair / Kilpedder Forge
499

Casleán na mBroinn / Caher Matrices / Castle Matrix
512

Lughnasád
522

ag na Machairi Teithra / The Plains of Tethra
531

Tir na nOg
544

A Small Glossary
555

ADMONITION TO THE READER

Geography in Ireland is an equivocal thing, and is perhaps meant to be so. The more solid the borderline, the more dangerous the land's own response to it; the more vague the boundary, the kindlier. This is best seen in the behavior of the borders between what we consider our own reality and the other less familiar realities that shoulder up against it. Such boundaries are never very solid in Ireland, and never more dangerous than when one tries to define them, to cross over. Twilight is always safer there than full day, or full dark.

This being the case, I have taken considerable liberties with locations and "established" boundaries, including those between counties and towns. County Wicklow is real enough, but there are a lot of things in the Wicklow in this book that are not presently located in the "real" county—and my version of Bray is not meant to represent the real one . . . at the moment. The description of the townlands around Ballyvolan Farm and the neighborhood of Kilquade is more or less real, though the two are actually some miles apart. And Sugarloaf Mountain looks like parts of its description . . . occasionally.

Most specifically, though, Castle Matrix exists—possibly more concretely than anything else in the book. But it has been moved from its present, "actual" location. Or perhaps one can more rightly say that Matrix has stayed where it is, where it always is, but Ireland has shifted around it. Stranger things have happened. In any case, let the inquisitive reader beware . . . and leave the maps at home.

I am the Point of a Weapon (that poureth forth combat),
I am the God who fashioneth Fire for a head.
Who is the troop, who is the God who fashioneth edges?
—*Lebor Gabála Érenn,*
tr. Macalister

Three signs of the Return:
   the stranger in the door;
   the friendless wizard;
   the unmitigated Sun.
Three signs of the Monomachy:
   a smith without a forge;
   a saint without a cell;
   a day without a night.

—*Book of Night with Moon,*
triads 113, 598

an tSionainn

Shannon

NITA FIRST FOUND OUT about what was going to happen when she came in after a long afternoon's wizardry with Kit. They had been working for three days in an attempt to resolve a territorial dispute among several trees. It isn't easy to argue with a tree. It isn't easy to get one to stop strangling another one with its roots. But they were well along toward what appeared to be a negotiated settlement, and Nita was bushed.

She came into the kitchen to find her mother cooking. Her mother cooked a great deal as a hobby, but she also cooked as therapy, and Nita began to worry immediately when she noticed that her mother had embarked on some extremely complicated project that seemed to require three soufflé dishes and the use of every appliance in the kitchen at once. She decided to get out as fast as she could, before she was asked to wash something. "Hi, Mom," she said, and edged hurriedly toward the door into the rest of the house.

"What's the rush?" asked her mother. "Don't you want to see what I'm doing?"

"Sure," said Nita, who wanted to do no such thing. "What are you doing?"

"I've been thinking," said her mother.

Nita began to worry more than ever. Her mother was at her most dangerous when she was thinking, and it rarely meant anything but trouble for Nita. "About what?"

"Sit down, honey. Don't look as if you're going to go flying out the door any minute. I need to talk to you."

Uh-oh . . . here it comes! Nita sat down and began playing with one of the wooden spoons that, among many other utensils, were littering the kitchen table.

"Honey," her mother said, "this wizardry—"

"It's going pretty well with the trees, Mom," Nita said, desperate to guide her mother onto some more positive subject. Her present tone didn't sound positive at all.

"No, I don't mean that, honey. Talking to trees—that's all right, that doesn't bother me. The kind of things you've been doing lately . . . you and Kit . . ."

Oh no. "Mom, we haven't got in trouble, not really. And we've been doing pretty well, for new wizards. When you're as young as we are—"

"Exactly," her mother said. "When you're as young as you are." She did something noisy with the blender for a moment and then said, "Hon, don't you think it would be a good idea if you just let all this—have a rest? Just for a month or so?"

Nita looked at her mother without understanding at all, still worrying. "How do you mean?"

"Well, your dad and I have been talking—and you and Kit have been seeing a whole lot of each other in connection with this wizard business. We're thinking that it might be a good idea if you two sort of . . . didn't see each other for a little while."

"Mom!"

"No, hear me out. I understand you're good friends, I know there's nothing . . . physical going on between you, so put that out of your mind. We're very glad each of you has such a good friend. That's not a concern. What *is* a concern is that you two are spending a lot of time on this magic stuff, at the expense of everything else. That's all you do. You go out in the morning, you come back wiped out, you barely have energy to speak to us sometimes . . . What about your childhood?"

"What about it?" Nita asked, with some slight annoyance. Her experience of most of her childhood so far had been that it varied between painful and boring. Wizardry might be painful occasionally, but it was never boring. "Mom—you don't understand. This isn't something you can just turn off. You take the Wizards' Oath for *life*."

"I know," Nita's mother said again. "That's what worries me. You're a little young to be making up your mind about what you want to do with the rest of your life."

Nita burst out laughing at that. "Are you kidding? You're the one who's been sitting through all the sessions with the guidance counselor at school! I'm not even fifteen, and already everybody's running off at the mouth about college every five minutes!"

"Now, Nita, that's not the same. That's just going to college. It's not—"

"It *is* the same! They want me to make career decisions, now, about what I'm going to do for twenty years, maybe thirty years, after I get out of college! And I'm not even sure what I want to *do* yet—except be a wizard! But the one thing I *do* want, and *know* that I want to do, you don't want me making decisions about! I don't get it!"

"Oh, honey!" her mother said in some distress, and dropped a spoon, picked it up, and wiped it off. "Why do you have to make this harder than it—Never mind. Look. Dad thinks it would be a good idea if you went to visit your aunt Annie in Ireland for a month or so, until school starts again."

"Ireland?!"

"Well, yes. She's been inviting us over there for a while now. We can't go with you, of course—we've had our vacation for this year, and Dad has to be at work. He can't take any more vacation time. But you could certainly go. School doesn't start until September ninth. That would give you a good month and a half."

There was going to be nothing good about it, as far as Nita was concerned. The best part of the summer, the best weather, the leisure time she had been looking forward to putting to use working with Kit. . . . "Mom," Nita said, changing tack, "how are you going to afford this?"

"Honey, you leave that to your dad and me to handle. Right now we're more concerned with doing the right thing for you. And for Kit."

"Oh, you've been talking to his folks, haven't you?"

"No, hon, actually we haven't. I think they're going to have to sort things out with Kit in their own way. I wouldn't presume to dictate to them. But we want you to go to Ireland for six weeks or so and take a breather. And see something different, something in the real world."

Oh dear, Nita thought. *They think* this *is the real world. Or all of it that really matters, anyway.* "Mom," she said, "I don't know if you understand what you're doing here. Wizards don't stop doing wizardry just because they're not at home. If I go on call in Ireland, I go on call, and there's nothing that can stop it. I've made my promises. If I have to go on call, wouldn't you rather have me here, where you and Dad can keep an eye on me and know exactly what's going on all the time?"

Nita's mother frowned at that, and then looked at Nita with an expression compounded of equal parts suspicion and amusement. "Sneaky," she said. "No, I'm sorry. Your aunt Annie will keep good, close tabs on you—we've had a couple of talks with her about that—"

Nita's eyebrows went up at that—first in annoyance that it was going to be difficult to get away and do anything useful if there was need; then in alarm. "Oh, Mom, you didn't tell her that I'm—"

"No, we didn't tell her that you're a wizard! What are we supposed to do, honey? Say to your aunt, 'Listen, Anne, you have to understand that our daughter might vanish suddenly. No, I don't mean run away, just disappear into thin air. And if she goes to the moon, tell her to dress warm.' " Nita's mother gave her a wry look and reached for the wooden spoon that Nita had been playing with. "No. We trust you to be discreet. You managed to hide it from *us* long enough, heaven knows . . . You shouldn't have any trouble keeping things undercover with your aunt." She paused to start folding some beaten egg white into another mixture she had been working on. "No, honey," she said. "Your dad is going to see about the plane tickets tomorrow. I think it's Saturday that you'll be leaving—the fare is cheaper then."

"I could just, you know, *go* there," Nita said desperately. "It would save you the money, at least."

"I think we'll do this the old-fashioned way," Nita's mother said calmly. "Even *you* would have some logistical problems arriving at the airport and getting off the plane without anyone noticing that you hadn't been there before."

Nita frowned and began to work on that one.

"No," Nita's mother said. "Forget it. We'll send enough pocket money for you to get along with; you'll have plenty of kids to play with—"

Play with, Nita thought, and groaned inwardly.

"Come on, Neets, cheer up a little! It should be interesting, going to a foreign country for the first time."

I've been to foreign galaxies, Nita thought. *But this I'm not so sure about.* But she also had a sense that further argument wasn't going to help her. No matter: There were ways around this problem, if she would just keep her mouth shut.

"OK," she said. "I'll go . . . But I won't like it."

Her mother gazed at her thoughtfully. "I thought you were the one who told me that wizardry was about doing what you had to, whether you liked it or not."

"It's true," Nita said, and got up to go out.

"And Nita," her mother said.

"What, Mom?"

"I want your promise that you will not be popping back here on the sly to visit

Kit: that little 'beam-me-up-Scotty' spell that he's so fond of, and that I see you two using when you want to save your train fare for ice cream."

Nita went white, then flushed hot. That was the one thing she had been counting on to make this whole thing tolerable. "*Mom!* But Mom, it's easy, I can just—"

"You *cannot* 'just.' We want you to take a break from each other for a while. Now I want you to promise me."

Nita let out a long breath. Her mother had her and knew she did, for a wizard's promise had to be kept. When you spend your life working with words that describe and explain—and even change—the way the universe is, you can't play around with those words, and you can't lie . . . at least not without major and unpleasant consequences. "I promise," Nita said, hating it. "But this is going to be miserable."

"We'll see about that," Nita's mother said. "You go ahead now and do what you have to do."

"Holy crap," Kit said. "This is *dire*."

They were sitting on the moon, on a peak of the Carpathian Mountains, about thirty kilometers south of the crater Copernicus. The view of earth from there this time of month was good; she was waxing toward the full, while on the moon there was nothing but a sun very low on the horizon. Long, long shadows stretched across the breadth of the Carpathians, so that the illuminated crests of the jagged peaks stood up from great pools of darkness, like rough-hewn pyramids floating on nothing. It was cold there; the wizardly force field that surrounded them snowed flakes of frozen oxygen gently onto the powdery white rock around them whenever they moved and changed the field's inner volume. But cold as it was, it was private.

"We were just getting somewhere with the trees," Nita muttered. "I can't believe this."

"Do they really think it's going to make a difference?"

"Oh, I don't know. Who knows what they think, half the time? And the worst of it is, they won't let me come back." Nita picked up a small piece of pumice and chucked it away, watching as it sailed about a hundred yards in the light gravity and bounced several feet high when it first hit ground again. It continued bouncing down the mountain, and she watched it idly. "We had three other projects waiting to be started. They're all shot now: There won't be any time to do anything about them before I have to go."

Kit stretched and looked unhappy. "We can still talk mind to mind; you can coach me at a distance when I need help. Or I can help you—"

"It's not the same." She had often enough tried explaining to her parents the high you got from working closely with another wizard: The feeling that magic made in your mind while you worked with another, the texture, was utterly unlike that of a wizardry worked alone—more dangerous, more difficult, ultimately more satisfying.

Nita sighed. "There must be some way we can work around this. How are your folks handling things lately?"

At that, Kit sighed too. "Variable. My dad doesn't mind it so much. He says, 'Big deal, my son's a *brujo*.' My mother . . . she has this idea that we are somehow meddling with dark forces." Kit made a fake theremin noise, the kind heard in bad old horror movies when the monster is lurking around a corner, about to jump on someone. Nita laughed.

Kit shook his head. "When are they making you leave?"

"Saturday." Nita rested her chin on one hand, picked up another rock, and chucked it away. "All of a sudden there's all this junk I have to pack, and all these things we have to do. Go to the bank and get foreign money. Buy new clothes. Wash the old ones." She rolled her eyes and fell silent. Nita hated that kind of rushed busyness, and she was up to her neck in it now.

"How's Dairine holding up?"

Nita laughed. "She likes me, but she's hardly heartbroken. Besides, she's busy managing her wizardry these days . . . spends most of her time working with her computer. You wouldn't believe some of the conversations I've heard over its voice-link recently." She fell into an imitation of Dairine's high-pitched voice, made even more squeaky by annoyance. " 'No, I will *not* move your planet . . . What do you want to move it *for*? It's fine right where it is!' "

"Sheesh," Kit said. Dairine, as a very new wizard, was presently at the height of her power; as a very young wizard, she was also more powerful at the moment than both Nita and Kit put together. The only thing they had on her was experience.

"Yeah. We don't fight nearly as much as we used to . . . She's gotten real quiet. I'm not sure it's normal."

"Oh," Kit said, and laughed out loud. "You mean, like *we're* normal. We're beginning to sound like our folks."

Nita had to laugh at that, too. "You may have something there."

But then the amusement went out of her. "My god, Kit," she said, "I'm gonna miss you. I miss you already, and I haven't *left*!"

"Hey, come on," he said, and punched her in the shoulder. "You'll get over it. You'll meet some guy over there and—"

"Don't joke," Nita said irritably. "I don't care about meeting 'some guy over there.' They're all geeks, for all I know. I don't even know if they speak the same language."

"Your aunt does."

"My aunt is American," Nita said.

"Yeah, they speak English over there," Kit said. "It's not all just Irish." He looked at Nita with a concerned expression. "Come on, Neets. If life hands you lemons, make lemonade. You can see a new place; you can probably meet some of their wizards. They'll be in the directory . . . Give it a chance." He picked up a rock, turning it over and over in his hands. "Where are you going to be? Dublin? Or somewhere else?"

"That's all there is," Nita said grimly. "Dublin, and the country. All potato fields and cow pastures."

"Saw that in the manual, did you?"

Nita rolled her eyes. Kit could be incredibly pedantic sometimes. "No."

"I was looking at the Irish chapter in the 'History of Wizardry' section of the manual a while back," Kit said. "A lot of interesting junk going on over there."

"Kit, I don't care what kind of junk is going on over there! I go on over *here*. This is where I do my work. Where you are. I'm one half of a team. What use am I without the rest?"

"Oh, I don't know. You might be good for something. Scrubbing the floors . . . washing the dishes . . ."

"You are a dead man," she said to Kit. "You know that? . . . Look, what are we going to do about the trees? We've got to get this cleared up before we go. I refuse to waste all this work."

"Well, I guess we could get them to agree to another session tomorrow. The part of the negotiation about the roots was going pretty well. I guess if we can get Aras to loosen up a little about the seedling acorns, Uriv might concede a couple of points regarding the percentage of sunlight."

"We could always threaten to uproot them and plant them about three miles apart," Nita said.

Kit sighed and looked at her. "I'm going to miss you, too," he said. "I miss you already."

She looked at him and saw it was true, and the bad mood fell off her, or mostly off, replaced by a feeling of unhappy resignation. "It's only six weeks," she said then.

Kit's face matched her feeling. "We'll do it standing on our heads," he said.

Nita smiled at him unhappily. Since wizards did not lie outright, when one tried to stretch the truth, it showed woefully. "Come on," she said, "we're running out of air. Let's get on with it."

Saturday came.

Kit went with them to the airport. It was a grim, silent ride, broken only by the kind of strained conversation people make when they desperately need to say something, anything, to keep the silence from getting too thick. At least it seemed silent. She and Kit would pass the occasional comment mind to mind. It wasn't all that easy, so they didn't do it much. They'd gotten in the habit of just talking to each other, since telepathy often got itself tangled up with a lot of other information you didn't need, or want, the other person to have. But now, habits or not, they were going to have to get a lot better at mindtouch if they were going to talk at all frequently.

They reached the airport, met the unescorted-minor representative from the airline, did the formalities with the ticket, and checked in Nita's bag—a medium-sized one, not too difficult for her to handle herself, though she was privately determined to make it weightless if she had to carry it anywhere alone. And then the loudspeakers announced her flight, and there was nothing to do but go through security and get on.

She hugged her mom and her dad. "Have a good time now," her father said.

She sighed and said, "I'll try, Daddy. Mommy—" And she was surprised at herself; she didn't usually call her mother *Mommy*. They hugged again, hard.

"You be good, now," Nita's mom said. "Don't . . ." She trailed off. The *don't* was a huge one, and Nita could hear in it all the things parents always say: *Don't get in trouble, don't forget to wash*—but most specifically, *Don't get into anything dangerous, like the last time. Or the time before that. Or the time before that—*

"I'll try, Mom," Nita said. It was all she could guarantee.

Then she looked at Kit. "*Dai,*" he said.

"*Dai stihó,*" she replied. It was the greeting and farewell of one wizard to another in the wizardly Speech: It meant as much "Bye for forever" as "Bye for now." For Nita, it felt more like the first.

At that point she simply couldn't stand it anymore. She waved, a weak little gesture, then turned her back on them all, slung her backpack over her shoulder, and with the airline representative, she walked off to go through security and then down the long, cold hall of the jetway toward the plane.

The plane was a Boeing 747. Nita's sensitivity was running high—perhaps because of her nervousness and distress at leaving—and the plane felt alive to her in the way that mechanical things usually did as a result of working with Kit. That was *his* specialty—the ability to feel what a rock was saying, to read the secret thoughts of an elevator or a refrigerator, and to sense the odd thing-thoughts that run in the currents of energy within physical objects, man-made or not. She could hear the plane straining against the chocks behind its many wheels, and its engines thinking of eating bitterly cold air at thirty thousand feet and pushing it out behind. There was a sense of purpose about the plane, a sense of restraint and of eagerness to get out of there, to be gone.

It was a reassuring feeling. Nita absently returned the smile of the flight attendant at the plane's door and patted the plane as she got in. She let the airline rep help her find her seat, so he could feel that he was doing something useful. Nita sat down by the window, fastened her seat belt, and as the rep went away, got out her manual.

For a moment she just held it in her hand. Just a small, beat-up book in a buckram library binding, printed with the apparent title, *So You Want to Be a Wizard*, and the supposed author's name, Hearnssen, and with the Dewey decimal number, 793.4, written on the spine in white ink. Nita shook her head and smiled at the book, a little conspiratorially, for it was a lot more than that. Had it already been two years, no, two and a half now, since she had found it in the local library? Or had it found her? She still wasn't sure, remembering the way something had seemed to grab her hand as she ran it along the shelf where the book had been sitting. Whether the book was alive was a subject on which the manual itself threw no light. Certainly it changed, adding new spells and other information as needed, updating news of what other wizards in the world were doing. Using the manual, Nita had found Kit in the middle of a wizardry of his own, and helped him with it, and in so doing started their partnership. They had gotten into deep trouble together, several times. But, together, they had always gotten out again.

Nita sighed and started paging through the manual, very much missing the "together" part of the arrangement. She had resisted looking for the information on Ireland that Kit had mentioned until this point, hoping against hope that there would be a stay of execution. Even now she cherished the idea that her mother or father might come pushing down the narrow aisle between the seats, saying, "No, no, we've changed our minds!" But she knew it was futile. When her mother got an idea into her head, she was almost as stubborn as Nita was.

So she sat there, and looked down at the manual. It had fallen open to the Wizards' Oath:

In Life's name, and for Life's sake, I assert that I will employ the Art, which is Its gift, in Life's service alone, rejecting all other usages. I will guard growth and ease pain. I will fight to preserve what grows and lives well in its own way; I will not change any creature unless its growth and life, or that of the system of which it is part, are threatened or threaten another. To these ends, in the practice of my Art, I will ever put aside fear for courage, and death for life, when it is right to do so—looking always toward the Heart of Time, where all our sundered times are one, and all our myriad worlds lie whole, in the One from Whom they proceeded. . . .

The whole plane wobbled as the little tractor in front of it pushed it away from the gate. Nita peered out the window. Pressing her nose against the cool plastic and looking out, she could just barely make out her mother and father gazing through the window at her; her mother waving a little tentatively, her father gripping the railing in front of the window, not moving. And a little behind them, out of their range of vision, looking out the window too, Kit.

Stay warm, he said in her head.

Kit, it's not like I'm going away. We'll be hearing from each other all the time in our heads. It's not like I'm really going away . . . Is it?

She was quiet for a moment. The tractor began turning the plane, so that her view of him was lost.

Yes, it is, he said.

Yeah, well. She caught herself sighing again. *Look, you're going to have the trees to deal with again, and you need time to plan what you're going to do. And I need time to calm myself down. Going to call me later?*

Yeah. What time?

This thing won't be down until early tomorrow morning, their time, she said.

Doesn't want to come down at all, from the feel of it, Kit said drily.

Nita chuckled, caught an odd look from a passing flight attendant, and made herself busy, looking as if she had read something funny in her manual. *Yeah. Call me about this time tomorrow.*

You got it. Have a good flight!

For what it's worth, Nita said.

The plane began to trundle purposefully out toward the runway. It didn't have to wait long; air traffic control gave them clearance right away. Nita, eavesdropping along the plane's nerves, heard the pilot acknowledging it. Half a minute later the plane screamed in delight and leaped into the air. Nita had to smile a little in spite of everything, wondering how much the pilots thought they had to do with the process of flight. The plane had its own ideas.

New York slid away behind them, replaced by the open sea.

Seven hours later, they landed in Shannon.

Nita had thought she would be completely unable to sleep, but when they turned out the lights in the plane after the meal service, she leaned her head against the window to see if she could relax enough to watch the movie a little.

The next thing she knew, the sun was coming in the window, and there was land below them. Nita looked down into the early sun—six o'clock that morning, it was—and saw the ragged black coastline of Ireland and the curling water of the Atlantic, white where it smashed into the rocks, throwing itself in fury against this first eastern barrier to its will. And then Nita saw green, everywhere green, a hundred shades of green—emerald, viridian, the pale green that has no right to be anywhere outside of spring—with hedgerows winding among white dots of sheep, tiny cars crawling along little toy roads—but always the green. The plane turned and she saw the beginning sprawl of houses and Shannon—a little city, barely the size of her own.

The plane was turning to line up with the airport's active runway, and the sun caught Nita full in the eyes. She shivered, a feeling that had nothing to do with the warmth of the sudden light. That was warm enough, but the feeling was cold: Something was about to happen, something about the lances of light, the fire. . . . Nita shook her head: The feeling was gone. *I'm jet-lagged*, she thought. *I'm susceptible to weird ideas.* But when wizards have weird ideas, they do well to pay attention to them. She forced herself to re-live the feeling, to think again of the cold and the fire, the sun like a spear—

Nothing came of it. She shrugged, and watched as the plane finished its turn and dropped toward the runway.

It took them about fifteen minutes to get down and for the jetway to be connected. With her backpack over her shoulder and yet another (she thought) unnecessary airline rep in tow, Nita went through passport control.

She walked up to the first open desk she found, laid her passport on it, and smiled at the man, a big kindly guy with a large nose and little cheerful eyes. He looked down at her and said, "Here's a wee dote of a thing to be traveling all alone. And how are you this morning?"

"I didn't sleep much on the plane," Nita said.

"Sure. I can't do that myself," the man said, riffling through her passport. "Keep hearing things all the time. Coming to see relatives, are you? Here's a nice clean passport, then. Where do you want the stamp, pet? First page? Or save that for something more interesting?"

Nita thought of the first time she had cleared "passport" formalities at the great Crossroads worldgating facility, six galaxies over, and illogically warmed to the man. "Let that be the first one, please," she said. The man stamped the passport with relish and handed it back.

"You're very welcome in Ireland, pet. *Chayd mil'fallcha.*"

She had seen that, at least, spelled over the doorway past the jetway hall: CEAD MILE FAILTE—"A HUNDRED THOUSAND WELCOMES." "Thank you," she said, and walked toward baggage claim.

It would be a while yet before the connecting flight to Dublin. On the far side of the baggage hall and the customs people, Nita found herself in the big Shannon duty-free shop. The airline rep loitered by the entrance and chatted with one of the salesclerks while keeping an eye on Nita, who wandered around the place with her mouth open for a good while, never having seen anything quite like it before. The shop was the size of a small department store, and it was filled with crystal and linen and china and smoked salmon and books. Nita went straight for the books, not liking smoked salmon much. She found a couple of volumes of Irish stories and mythology and bought them with some of her odd pastel-colored Irish money. She remembered with some pain her mother looking at the bills and saying, "Who are all these people?"

"Writers," her father had said. "There's Yeats on the twenty, and Duns Scotus on the five: a historian. And Jonathan Swift on the ten. Look at the map of Dublin on the back of that one; I bet you can still find your way around with it—"

Nita put the memory away, hurting slightly. She hadn't thought she would miss her folks so much; after all, it was only seven hours since she'd seen them. . . .

She went along to the gate for the flight that would take her to Dublin.

*   *   *

Another flight, another plane equally eager to be gone. It was about an hour's flight, over the thousand shades of green and all the bright rivers winding among the hills, blazing like fire when the sun caught them. Her ears had started popping from the plane's descent almost as soon as it reached cruising altitude, and Nita looked down and found herself and the plane sinking gently toward a great green range of mountains, with three peaks notable even among the others. Nita's mother had told her about these three and had shown her pictures. One of them wasn't a mountain, but a promontory: Bray Head, sticking out into the sea like a fist laid on a table with the knuckles sticking up. Then, a mile farther inland and westward was Little Sugarloaf, a hill half again as high as Bray Head. Another mile west, and higher than both the others, was Great Sugarloaf, *Sliabh O Cualann* as the Irish had it: *the* mountain of Wicklow. It was certainly one of the most noticeable— a gray stony cone, pointed, its slopes green with heather. No trees grew there.

The plane turned left, making its way to Dublin Airport. In another ten minutes, they were down.

Nita was met by yet another airline rep. She got her bag back, got a cart, and looked curiously at the automatic change machine that took your American money and gave you Irish money back. She briefly regretted that she didn't have an excuse to use it. She sighed and pushed her cart out through the customs folk, out through the sliding doors, and past the bored uniformed man at the desk who kept people from coming in the wrong way.

"Nita!"

And there was her aunt Annie. Nita grinned. After spending her life with people she knew, and then having to spend a whole day with people she didn't know, the sight of Aunt Annie was a pleasure. Nita's aunt hurried over to her and gave her a big hug. She signed the clipboard the rep held out for her, then waved the lady away.

Aunt Annie was a large, silver-haired lady, big about the shoulders, a little broad in the beam, with a friendly face and pale gray-blue eyes. Her hair was tied back in a short ponytail. "How was your flight? Did you do OK?"

"I did fine, Aunt Annie. But I'm real tired . . . I wouldn't mind going home."

"Sure, honey. You come right out here; the car's right outside." She pushed the cart out into the little parking lot.

The morning was fresh and fine. Little white clouds were flying past in a blue sky. Nita put her arms around herself and hugged herself in surprise at the cold. "Mom told me it might be chilly, and I didn't believe her. It's July!"

"This *is* one of the cooler days we've been having lately. Don't worry, though; the weather-people say it's going to get warm again tomorrow. Up in the seventies."

" 'Warm,' " Nita repeated, wondering. It had been in the nineties on Long Island when she had left.

"We haven't had much rain, either," said her aunt. "It's been a dry summer, and they're talking about it turning into a drought if it doesn't rain this week or next." She laughed a little as she came up to a white Toyota and opened its trunk.

They drove around to the parking lot's ticket booth, paid the toll, and left the airport. Nita spent a few interesting moments adjusting to the fact that her aunt was driving on the left side of the road. "So tell me," Aunt Annie said, "how are your folks?"

Nita started telling her, with only half her mind on the business; the rest of her was busy looking at the scenery as they came out onto the freeway—or the dual carriageway, as all the signs called it—heading south toward Dublin and past it to Wicklow. AN LAR, said one sign, and under that it said DUBLIN: 8. "What's 'An Lar'?" Nita asked.

"That's Irish for 'to the city center,' " said her aunt. "We're going about fifteen miles south of Dublin . . . It'll take us about an hour to get through the city and home, the way the traffic is. Do you want to stop in town for lunch? Are you hungry?"

"Nnnnnno," Nita said, "I think I'd rather just go lie down and go to sleep. I didn't get enough on the plane."

Her aunt nodded. "No problem with that . . . You get rid of your jet lag. The country won't be going anywhere while you get caught up on your sleep."

And so they drove through the city. Nita was surprised to see how much it looked like suburban New York, except that—except. . . . Nita found that she kept saying "except" about every thirty seconds. Things looked the same, and then she would see something completely weird that she didn't understand at all. The street signs, half in Irish and half in English, were a constant fascination. It was a very peculiar-looking language, with a lot of extra letters and small letters in front of capital letters at the beginnings of words, something she had never seen before. And the pronunciations— She tried pronouncing a few of them, the last one being *Baile atha Cliath*, while her aunt howled with laughter and coached her. "No, no! If you try to pronounce Irish the way it looks, you'll go crazy. That one's pronounced 'bally ah-cleeah.' 'Dublin city.' "

Nita nodded and went on with a brief version of how things were at home, while looking at more of the signs they passed. There was something vaguely familiar about the language, for all the weirdness of its spellings.

They drove through the center of Dublin, down O'Connell Street, a thoroughfare about the width of a Manhattan avenue, three lanes on each side, with a broad pavement in between. People jay-walked across it with such total recklessness that Nita had to shake her head at their sheer brazenness. Down the big handsome avenue she and her aunt went, and through the city, out past shops and stores and parts of town that looked exactly like New York to Nita's eyes, though much cleaner; and then they started to pass through areas where small modern housing developments mixed with old brownstones that had beautiful clear or stained-glass fanlights above their front doors and elaborate molded plaster ceilings, which could be glimpsed here and there through open curtains. Then the brownstones, too, gave way and started to be replaced by housing developments again, older ones now. The dual carriageway, which had become just one lane on each side for a while, now reasserted itself. And then fields started to appear, and big vacant lots that to Nita's astonishment and delight had shaggy horses casually grazing on them, right by the side of the road. "Whose are they?" Nita asked.

"They're tinker ponies," her aunt said. "The traveling people leave them where they can get some grass, if the grass where their caravans are is grazed down already. Look there." She pointed off to one side.

Nita looked, expecting to see some kind of a barrel-shaped, brightly colored wagon. Instead there was just a trailer parked off to one side of the road, with no car hitched to it. There were clothes laid over the nearby hedge in the sun: *Laundry*, Nita realized. As they passed, she got just a glimpse of a small fire burning near the trailer and several young children sitting or crouching around it, feeding it sticks. Then they had swept by.

"Are they gypsies?" Nita asked.

Her aunt shrugged. "Some of them say they are. Others are just people who don't like to live in houses, in one place. They'd rather move around and be free. We have a fair number of them down by us."

Nita filed this with about twenty other things she was going to have to ask more about at her leisure. They passed more small housing developments—"estates," her aunt called them—where houses situated by themselves seemed to be the exception rather than the rule. Two houses were usually built squished together so that they shared one wall, and each house was a mirror image of the other.

And then even the estates started to disappear. There was a last gasp of them as Nita and Annie passed through a town called Shankill, where the road narrowed down to a single lane each way again. Shortly after that, the road curved to the right, away from what looked like an even larger town. "That's Bray," Aunt Annie said. "We do some of our shopping there. But this is officially County Wicklow now. You're out of Dublin when you get near the Dargle."

Nita hadn't noticed the river: It was hidden behind rows of little houses. "That's Little Bray," her aunt said. "And now, here's Kilcroney."

The road widened out abruptly into hill and forest, with two lanes on each side again. "Everything has names," Nita said.

"Every *acre* of this place has names," her aunt said. "Every town has *townlands* around it, and every one of them has a different name. Almost every field, and every valley and hill." She smiled. "I kind of like it."

"I think I might, too," Nita said. A wizard's spells worked best when everything in them was completely named, and it was always easier to use existing names than to coin new ones—which you had to do if no one had previously named a thing or place, or if it didn't know its own name already. And the name you coined had to be right; otherwise the wizardry would backfire.

"There," her aunt said, maneuvering around a couple of curves in the road. "There's our mountain."

Nita peered past her aunt, out toward the right. There was Sugarloaf. It looked much different than it had from the air—sharper, more imposing, more dangerous. Heather did its best to grow up the sides, but the bare granite of the mountain's peak defeated it about two-thirds of the way up. Scree and boulders lay all about the mountain's bald head.

The road ran past a service station where geese and a goat grazed behind a fence, watching the traffic, then through a shallow ravine that ran between two thickly forested hills. Sunlight would fall down the middle of it at noon, Nita guessed, but at the moment the whole deep vale was in shadow. "Glen of the Downs," Aunt Annie said. "We're almost home. That's a nice place to hike to, down there, where the picnic benches are."

After driving a couple more miles on the dual carriageway, Aunt Annie turned down a little lane. To Nita's eyes the road looked barely wide enough for one car, let alone two, but to her shock several other cars passed them, and Aunt Annie never even slowed down, though she crunched so far over on the left side of the road that the hedges scraped the doors. The road began to trend downward, so that the gently sloping valley beneath it was visible, and beyond that, the sea, with the sun on it, blinding.

"See that town down there on the left? That's Greystones," said Aunt Annie. "We do the best part of our shopping there. But here—" She turned off down another lane, this one literally just wide enough to let one car through. In half a minute they came out in the graveled parking lot in front of a little house. Around it, on all sides, fenced fields and farm buildings stretched. It was forty acres, Nita knew: Her aunt's life savings had gone into the farm, her great love.

"Welcome to Ballyvolan," her aunt said. "Come on in and we'll get you settled in."

Aunt Annie did more than that. She gave Nita a place to stay that was uniquely her own, and Nita was very pleased.

Annie put her up not in the house, but in a caravan out in the back: a trailer, as she would have called it. She was getting the feeling that everything here had different names that she was going to have to learn. But she was used to that; everything had different names in wizardry, too. . . . *It's going to take months to get everything straight*, she thought. And then thought immediately, *I hope not! I don't want to be here for months. Six weeks is plenty!* But all the same, the sheer difference of things was beginning to get to her. She had been to other planets and spoken to alien creatures in their own languages, but nothing had yet struck her as quite as strange as being here in this odd place where everything she knew was called something strange, and where people she knew to be speaking English as their first language were nonetheless speaking it in accents so thick she couldn't make out more than one word in three. None of the accents was what she had always thought of as the typical Irish brogue, either. Evidently there *was* no such thing; the word *brogue* turned out to come from an old, slightly scornful Irish word that meant "tongue-tied," and had originally been used to describe people who couldn't speak Irish. At any rate, the accents came in all variations of thick, thin, light, impenetrable, lilting, dark; and people would run all their words together and talk very fast . . . or very softly, so that Nita soon began feeling as if she were shouting every time she opened her mouth.

Annie gave her the caravan and left her alone. "You'll want to crash and burn, I should think," Aunt Annie said. "You come in when you're ready and we'll feed you." So Nita had unpacked her bag and sat down on the little bed built into the side of the trailer. It was a good size for her. The trailer's windows afforded a clear view of the path from the house, so that if she was doing a wizardry, she would have a few seconds to shut it down before anyone got close enough to see what was going on. There were cupboards and drawers, a shelf above the head of the bed, a little closet to hang things in, a table with a comfortable bench seat to work at, lights set in the walls here and there, and an electric heater to keep everything warm if it got cool at night.

She leaned back on the bed with her manual in her hands, meaning to read through some of its Irish material before she dropped off. She never had a chance.

*   *   *

Nita woke to find it dark outside—or not truly dark, but a very dark twilight. She glanced at her watch and saw that it was almost eleven at night. They had let her sleep, and she was ravenous. *Boy, I must have needed that*, she thought, and swung her feet to the floor, stretching and rubbing at her eyes.

That was when she heard the sound: horses' hooves, right outside the door. That wasn't a surprise, except that they would be out there so late. Annie's farm was partly a boarding stable, where people kept their horses because they didn't have stables of their own or where they left them to be exercised and trained for shows. There were a couple of low voices—*Men's voices*, Nita thought—discussing something quietly. That was no surprise, either: Quite a few people were working on Aunt Annie's farm. Nita had been introduced to a lot of them when she first arrived, and had forgotten most of their names. One of the people outside chuckled, sighed, said something inaudible.

Nita snapped on the bedside light so she wouldn't bash into things, got up, and opened the caravan door to look out and say hello.

But no one was there.

"Huh," she said.

She went out through the little concrete yard to the front of the house, where the front door was open, as Aunt Annie had told her it almost always was, except when everyone had gone to bed. Her aunt was in the big quarry-tiled kitchen making a cup of tea.

"So there you are!" she said. "Did you sleep well? Do you want a cuppa?"

"What? Oh, right. Yes, please," Nita said, and sat down in one of the chairs drawn up around the big blond wood table. One of Aunt Annie's cats, a black-and-white creature, jumped into her lap: She had forgotten its name, too, in the general blur of her arrival. "Hi there," she said to it, stroking it.

"Milk? Sugar?"

"Just sugar, please," Nita said. "Aunt Annie, who were those people out there with the horses?"

Her aunt looked at her. "People with the horses? All the staff have gone home. At least I thought they did."

"No, I heard them. The hooves were right outside my door, but when I looked, they'd gone away. Didn't take them long," she added.

Aunt Annie looked at her again as she came over and put Nita's teacup down. Her expression was rather different this time. "Oh," she said. "You mean the ghosts."

Nita stared.

"Welcome to Ireland," said her aunt.

Cill Cumhaid

Kilquade

NITA SAT BACK AND blinked a little. Her aunt stirred her tea and said, "Do ghosts bother you?"

"Not particularly," Nita said, wondering just how to deal with this line of inquiry. Wizards knew that very few ghosts had anything to do with people's souls hanging around somewhere. Most apparitions, especially ones that repeated, tended to be caused by a kind of tape recording that violent emotion could make on matter under certain circumstances, impressing its energy into the molecular structure of physical things. Over long periods of time the "recording" would fade away, but in the meantime it would replay every now and then, for good reason or no reason, and upset the people who happened to see it. And if those people happened to believe that such a thing was caused by human souls, the effects would get steadily worse, fed by the emotions of the living.

Nita knew all this, certainly. But how much of it could she safely tell her aunt? And how to get it across without sounding like she knew more than a fourteen-year-old should?

"Good," her aunt was saying. She drank her tea and looked at Nita across the table with those cool blue-gray eyes. "Did you hear the church bells, earlier?"

"Uh, no. I must have been asleep."

"We have a little church down the road," Aunt Annie said. "About three hundred years ago, after the English killed their king—Charles the First, it was—his replacement, a man named Oliver Cromwell, came through here." Her aunt took another long drink of tea. "He and his army went up and down this country throwing out the Irish landowners and installing English ones in their places. He sacked cities and burned houses, and got himself quite a name for unnecessary cruelty." Aunt Annie looked out the kitchen window, into the near dark, watching the apple trees in the backyard move slightly in the wind. "I think what you heard was, well, a reminder of some of his people, who were camped here on guard late at night. You can hear the horses, and you can hear the soldiers talking, though you usually can't make out what they're saying."

"As if they were in the next room," Nita said.

"That's right. The memory just reasserts itself every now and then; other people have heard it happening. It's usually pretty low-key." She looked at Nita keenly.

Nita shrugged in agreement. "They didn't bother me. They didn't seem, well, ghostly. No going 'Ooooooo' or trying to scare anyone."

"That's right," her aunt said, sounding relieved. "Are you hungry?"

"I could eat a cow," Nita said, suspecting that in this household it would be wiser not to offer to eat horses.

"I've got some hamburger," her aunt said, getting up, "and some chicken . . ."

Nita got up to help, and poked around the kitchen a little. All the appliances were about half the size she was used to. She wondered whether this was her aunt's preference, or whether most of the stoves and refrigerators sold here were like that, for on the drive in she kept getting a feeling that everything was smaller than usual, had been scaled down somewhat. The rooms in her aunt's house were smaller than she was used to, as well, reinforcing the impression. "Do you have any other ghosts," Nita said, "or are those all?"

"Nope, that's it." Her aunt chuckled and pulled out a frying pan. "You want more, though, you won't have far to go. This country is thick with them. Old memories. Everything here has a long memory . . . longer than it should have, maybe." She sighed and went rooting in a drawer for a few moments. "A lot of history in Ireland," Aunt Annie said, "a lot of bad experiences and bad feelings. It's a pain in the butt sometimes." She came up with a spatula. "Do you want onions?"

"Sure," Nita said.

Her aunt found a knife and handed it to Nita, then found an onion in a bin by the door and put it on the counter. "Hope you don't mind crying a little," she said.

"No problem."

They puttered about the kitchen together, talking about this and that: family gossip, mostly. Aunt Annie was Nita's father's eldest sister, married once about twenty-five years ago, and divorced about five years later. Her ex-husband was typically referred to in Nita's family as "that waste of time," but no one at home had ever been too forthcoming about just why he was a waste and Nita had decided it was none of her business. Aunt Annie had three kids, two sons and a daughter, all grown up now and moved out: Two of them now lived in Ireland, one in the States. Nita had met her two male cousins some years back, when she was very young, and remembered Todd and Alec only dimly as big, dark-haired, booming shapes that gave her endless piggyback rides.

Her aunt had moved with her kids to Ireland after the divorce, and had busied herself with becoming a successful farmer and stable-manager. Now she had other people to manage her stables for her: She saw to the finances of the farm, kept an eye on the function of the riding school that also was based on her land, and otherwise lived the life of a moderately well-to-do countrywoman.

They fried up hamburgers and onions. There were no buns: Her aunt took down a loaf of bread and cut thickish slices from it for both of them. "Didn't you have supper?" Nita said. "It's way past time."

"We don't have set mealtimes," Aunt Annie said. "My staff come in to get a snack when they can, and I tend to eat when I'm hungry. I was busy with the accounts for most of this evening—didn't notice I was hungry until just now. Unlike some," she said, looking ruefully down at the floor around the stove, which was suddenly littered with cats of various colors, "who are hungry whether they've just eaten or not."

Nita laughed and bent down to scratch the cats: the black-and-white one, again—Bronski—as well as a marmalade-colored cat with golden eyes; a tiny, delicate, white-bibbed tabby; and another black-and-white cat of great dignity, who sat watching the others, and Nita and her aunt, unblinking. "Bear," Aunt Annie said, "and Chessie, and Big Paws. All of you, out of here: You had your dinners! Now where's the mustard got to?"

She turned away to find it. Under her breath, Nita said hurriedly in the wizards' Speech, "You all get out of here and I'll see if I can liberate something for you later . . ."

They sat looking thoughtful—since almost everything that thinks can recognize and understand the Speech—then one by one got up and strolled off. Her aunt found the mustard and noticed the exodus. "Huh," she said. "Guess they don't like the smell of the onions."

"It's pretty strong," Nita said, smiled slightly, and started spreading mustard on bread.

When everything was ready, they sat down and ate. "I hope you don't mind being a little on your own tomorrow," Aunt Annie said. "You hit us at kind of a busy time. There's going to be a hunt here in a few days, and we have to start getting ready for it."

"You mean like a foxhunt?" Nita said.

"That's right. Some of the local farmers have been complaining about their chicken flocks being raided. Anyway, some of our horses are involved, so the vet has to certify them fit, and then the farrier is coming in tomorrow to do some reshoeing. It's going to be pretty hectic. If you want to be around here, that's fine. Or if you think you'll be bored, you might want to go down to Greystones—it's a pretty easy bike ride from here. Or take the bus over to Bray and look around."

"OK," Nita said. "I'll see how I feel . . ."

"Traveling eastbound takes it out of you," Aunt Annie said. "It won't be so bad going back."

You said it, Nita thought. *And the sooner the better.* But she smiled anyway and said, "I hope not."

They finished up and cleared the table. "If you want to watch TV late, forget about the ground-based stations," her aunt said. "All but one of them shut down around midnight, and the one that's left mostly just shows old movies. There's a fair amount of stuff on the satellite channels, though."

"Uh, thanks. I thought I might read for a while. After that I may just go to sleep again . . . I'm still kind of tired."

"That's fine. You make yourself completely at home." Her aunt looked at Nita with an expression as thoughtful, in its way, as the cats'. "It must have been a bit of a wrench, just being shipped off like that."

What did they tell you, I wonder? Nita thought. "It was," she said after a moment. "But I'll cope."

Her aunt smiled. "Typical of our side of the family," she said. "There's a long history of that. Well, if you get hungry or something later, just come on in and take what you need. Use the back door, though: I'm going to lock the front now and turn in. I'll leave a light on for you in here. You know where everything is, the bathroom and so forth?"

"Yeah, Aunt Annie. Thanks."

Her aunt headed off. Nita looked around the kitchen to see if there was anything else that needed cleaning up. Her mother had drummed into her that she should make sure she returned hospitality by helping out in the kitchen: Her aunt hated doing dishes above almost anything else, her mother had said. But there was nothing left to do.

Except something that needed a wizard to do it, and Nita set about that straight-away.

She headed out the back door, out through a little archway into the concrete yard again. The only light was the one she had left on in the trailer, and it was dim. She paused outside the door and looked up. Even now, past midnight, the sky wasn't completely black. Nevertheless, it was blanketed with stars, much brighter than she was used to seeing through the light pollution of the New York suburbs. And there was no sound here but the faintest breath of wind. No sound came, even from the dual carriageway a mile away. It was as if everyone in this part of the country had gone to bed and turned out the lights all at once. There was only one light visible, about a mile away across the fields: someone's house light. For some-one who had always lived in places where streetlights glowed all night, this utter darkness was a shock.

But the stars, she thought. The Milky Way was clearly visible, even bright. At home it was almost impossible to see it at all. *At least there's one thing worth seeing here.*

She shivered hard then, and ducked back into the trailer to get her jacket, and her manual.

Once she had them she headed out across the yard, making for the log fence that separated the land immediately around Aunt Annie's house from the fields beyond it. The closest field was planted with oilseed rape, or "canola," as they call it in the States—tall green plants with flowers at the top so extremely yellow that they had made Nita's eyes hurt when she looked at them in the sunshine that morning. The field beyond that was clean pasture, grassland left fallow this year. That was what Nita wanted, for there was a thick strip of woodland at the far side of it.

She made her way through the oilseed rape, enjoying the fragrance of it, and on to the next fence. This was barbed wire: She climbed one of the fence posts carefully, so as not to tear anything. Cautiously, for the ground over here wasn't as even as it had been in the rape field, Nita made her way into the center of the field, and opened her manual.

She said the two words that would make the pages generate enough light to read by, though not enough to mess up her night vision. Normally she wouldn't have needed the manual for this spell, which was more a matter of simple con-versation than anything else; but she didn't know the name she needed to call and had to look it up. The manual's index was straightforward, as usual. "*Canidae*," she said under her breath. "Here we go."

The spell was a calling, but the kind that was a request, not a demand. She hoped there would be someone to respond. She recited the standard setup, the request for the universe to hear. Then, "*Ai mathrára*," she said in the Speech, "if any hear, let them speak to me, for there's need."

And then she put the book down and sat there in the quiet, and waited.

It seemed to take a long time before she heard the soft sound of something rustling in the grass, about a hundred yards away. Normally she would never have heard it, but her ears were sharpened by sitting in total silence. The noise stopped.

"*Mathrára*," she said then, very quietly, "if that's you, then I'm here."

Another rustling, another silence.

"You speak it with an accent," said a voice in a series of short, soft barks, "but well enough. Let me see you."

Nita saw the long, low, sharp-nosed shape come toward her. The dog-fox had a tail bigger and bushier and longer than she would have thought possible. Only the faintest firefly gleam from the manual's pages silvered his fur, giving him enough of an outline to see, and glinted in his eyes.

"So," the fox said.

"What accent?" Nita asked, curious. As far as she knew, her accent in the Speech was quite good.

"We wouldn't say '*mathrára*' here. '*Madreen rua*,' that would be it." And Nita chuckled, because that meant "the little red dog" in the Speech.

"Local customs rule," Nita said, smiling. "As usual. I have a warning for you, *madreen rua*. There's a hunt coming through here in a few days."

The fox yipped softly in surprise. "They are early, then."

"Maybe," Nita said. "But if I were you, I'd spread the word to keep your people well out of this area, and probably for about five miles around on all sides. Maybe more. And you might lay off the chickens a little."

The fox laughed quietly, a panting sound. "They've poisoned almost all the rats: What's a body to eat? But for the moment . . . as you say. I am warned, wizard. Your errand's done." It looked at her thoughtfully.

"So then," the fox said. "Go well, wizard." And it whisked around and went bounding off through the pasture grass without another word.

Nita shut her manual and sat there in the quiet for a while more, getting her breath back. Talking to animals differed in intensity depending on how smart the animal was and how used to human beings it was. Pets like cats and dogs tended to have more fully humanized personalities, and could easily be made to understand you; but they also tended to be short-spoken—*possibly*, Nita thought, *because, being domesticated and more or less confined to a daily routine, they have less to talk about*. Wilder animals had more to say, but it was often more difficult to understand them, the message being colored with hostility or fear, or plain old bewilderment. The fox lived on the fringes of human life, knew human ways, but was wary, and so there was a cool tinge, a remoteness, about the way it came across.

At any rate, she had fulfilled her responsibilities for the evening. A wizard had a duty to prevent unnecessary pain, and foxhunting did not strike Nita as particularly necessary, no matter what farmers might say about the need to exterminate vermin. If a fox was stealing someone's chickens, let the farmer shoot it cleanly, rather than chasing it in terror across half the countryside and getting dogs to rip it to shreds.

Meanwhile, there were other concerns.

Kit? she said in her head.

Yeah!

She paused a moment. *What's that noise?*

I'm chewing, Kit said.

Oh no, you're eating dinner!

It's not such a fascinating experience that I can't take a few minutes out to talk to you, he said. Nita got a distinct impression of slightly lumpy mashed potatoes, and restrained herself from swallowing. *What's happening?* Kit asked.

This, she said, and gave him a series of pictures of the day as quickly as she could, ending with the fox. *Great, huh?*

Bored with me already, Kit said. *I knew it.*

Kit—! She would have punched him hard, had he been in range. As it was, he flinched a little from what he felt her fist and arm wanting to do. *Look*, she said, *I'm wiped. I'll talk to you more in the morning.*

He started to nod and stopped himself. She had to laugh a little. *Have a good night*, Kit said.

Will do.

She let the contact ebb away, then got up and started carefully walking back the way she had come. Behind her, from the woodland, a fox was barking; another, perhaps a mile away, answered it.

Nita smiled to herself and headed for the trailer.

As she had thought, she wasn't able to stay up very late that night. She tried to watch some television, but even the sixty-odd satellite channels were fairly dull, showing either old movies that she wasn't interested in or foreign-language material that was a strain for even a wizard to follow. Finally she turned off the TV and went back to the trailer to read, though not before opening a small can of cat food on the sly and parceling it out to the cats. They accepted this with great pleasure, purring and rubbing and making their approval known: But none of them spoke to her.

She went to bed and slept some more, but her dreams were not entirely pleasant. In one of them, she thought she felt the earth move, but it was probably just the wind shaking the trailer. When she woke up everything was quite still. It was early morning, how early she couldn't tell anymore without her watch: The different sunrise time here had her thoroughly confused. She found her watch and saw to her surprise that, even though the sun was well up the sky, it was only 7:00 A.M.

She got up and dressed in yesterday's clothes, slipped into the house, took a quick shower, dressed again in clean clothes, and went to see what there was for breakfast. There were already several people in the kitchen, two of whom Nita had been introduced to the previous day. One was Joe, the stable master, a tall, lean young man with a grin so wide Nita thought his face was in danger of cracking. Another was Derval, the head trainer, a tall, curly haired woman, eternally smoking a hand-rolled cigarette. She had a drawly accent that made her sound almost American.

"There y'are then," Derval said. "You want some tea?"

Nita was beginning to think that every conversation in Ireland began this way. "Yes, please," she said, and rooted around in the big ceramic crock for the bread. "Where's Aunt Annie?"

"Down at the riding school, waiting for the farrier. She said to tell you to come on down if you want to."

"OK," Nita said, and cut herself a slice of bread and put it in the toaster. The butter was already out on the counter, along with a basket of eggs from the farm's hens; various packages of bacon and a gruesome-looking sausage called "black pudding"; more toast, some of it with bites out of it; boxes of cereal; and spilled sugar. Breakfast was a hurried business in this house, from the look of things.

Nita sat down with her tea and toast and pulled over the local weekly paper, the *Wicklow People*. Its front-page story was about someone's car catching on fire in the main street of Wicklow town, and Nita sat there paging through it in total wonder that anyplace in the world should be so quiet and uneventful that a story like that would make the front page. Derval looked over her shoulder and pointed with one finger at an advertisement in the classifieds that said BOGS FOR SALE. Nita burst out laughing.

"If you're going to be around the stable block," Derval said to her, going to get another piece of bread out of the toaster, "just one thing. Watch out for the horse in number five. He bites."

"Uh, yeah," Nita said. She had been wondering when she was going to have to mention this. "I'm a little scared of horses . . . I hadn't been planning to get too close to them."

"Scared of horses!" Joe said. "We'll fix that."

"Uh, maybe tomorrow," Nita said. She had been put up on a horse once, several years ago on vacation, and had immediately fallen off. This had colored her opinions about horses ever since.

Joe and Derval finished their breakfasts and headed out, leaving Nita surrounded by cats eager to shake her down for another handout. "No way, you guys!" she said. "Once was a special occasion. You want more, you'd better talk to your boss."

They looked at her with thinly disguised disgust and stalked off. Nita finished her tea and toast, washed her cup and plate, and then wandered out into the concrete yard. There was a path past the back of her trailer into the farm area proper, and the road that wound past the front of the house curved around to meet it. Here there was another large concrete area with two or three big, brown, metal-sided, barnlike buildings arranged in a loose triangle around it. The field on the right-hand side was full of horse-jumping paraphernalia, jumps and stiles; all around the edge of the field ran a big track covered with wood shavings and chips for the horses to run on. Farther down and to her right was the stabling barn, and beyond it was what Derval had referred to as "the riding school," a big covered building with nothing inside except a floor thickly covered with the same chips as on the track outside. This was where the riders practiced when the weather was bad.

Nita took a little while to look around in there, found nothing of interest, and made her way back to the stables. There were about fifteen box stalls with various horses looking out over the doors, or eating their breakfasts, or standing there with vaguely bored expressions. She looked closely at the horse in number five, which was a big handsome black stallion. But he had a bad look in his eye, and when she greeted him in the Speech (since there were no humans around to hear), he eyed her coldly, laid his ears back, and snorted, "Bugger off, little girl, or I'll have your arm off."

Nita shrugged and moved on. Other horses were more forthcoming. When she spoke to them in the Speech, they answered, asking her for a sugar cube or if she would please take them out. A few just tossed their heads, blinked lazily, and went back to their eating.

At the end of the stable barn was an extremely large pile of hay, kept under cover so that the rain couldn't get at it and the horses could be given it easily. Nita was looking at it when something small and black—*A rock*, she thought— fell down from the top of it. It tumbled down the hay, and even though Nita sidestepped, the black thing fell crookedly and landed on one of her sneakers.

She looked down in shock. It was a kitten, its body no bigger than one of her hands. It more or less staggered to its feet, looked up at her, and meowed, saying, "Sorry!"

"Don't mention it," Nita said.

The kitten, which was already scampering away after a windblown straw, stopped so suddenly that it fell over forward. Nita restrained herself from laughing. The kitten righted itself, washed furiously for a second, then looked at her. "Another one," it said. "The wind *does* blow, doesn't it?"

"Another what?"

"Another wizard. Are you deaf?"

"Uh, no," Nita said. "Sorry, I'm new here. Who are you?"

"I am Tualha Slaith, a princess of the People," she said, rattling it all off in a hurry, "a bard and a scholar. And who are you?"

"I'm Nita Callahan."

"Nita?" said the kitten. "What kind of name is that?"

Nita had to stop for a moment. She was amazed to be getting this much conversation out of a domestic cat, let alone a kitten that barely looked old enough to be weaned. "I think it was Spanish, originally," she said after a second or so. "Juanita is the long form."

"Aha, a Spaniard!" the kitten said, her eyes wide. " 'There's wine from the royal Pope / Upon the ocean green: / And Spanish ale shall give you hope, / My dark Rosaleen!' "

"You lost me," said Nita. "Anyway, I'm not a big ale fan . . ."

The kitten looked at Nita as if she were a very dim bulb indeed. "It's going to get crowded in here shortly," the kitten said. "Let's go out." She scooted out the barn door, and Nita followed her, feeling rather bemused, out the back into the area between the riding school and the stable block. The path led toward the field where the jumping equipment was. No one was there at the moment.

The kitten stopped several times in her run to crouch down, her butt waggling, and pounce on a bug, or leaf, or stalk of grass, or blown bit of hay. She always missed. Nita was having trouble controlling her reaction to this, but if there was one thing a wizard had practice in being, it was polite: So she managed. A little dusty whirlwind passed them as they walked between the riding school and the stable block, and Tualha paused to let it go by. "Good day," she said.

"Do you usually talk to wind?" Nita asked, amused.

Tualha eyed her. "That's how the People go by," she said. "The People of the Air. You *are* new here." She scuttled on.

They came to the fence. Tualha made a mighty leap halfway up onto the fence post, hauled herself up claw over claw, and sat at the top, where she washed briefly.

Nita sat down on the fence next to her. "Aren't you a little young to be a bard?" she asked.

The kitten looked Nita up and down. "Aren't you a little young to be a wizard?"

"Well, no, I'm fourteen . . ."

"And that's what percentage of your life span?"

"Uh—" Nita had to stop and figure it out.

"You can't even tell me right away? Poor sort of *ban-draoia* you'd make over here. Maths are important."

Nita flushed briefly. Whatever a *ban-draoia* might be, math had never been one of her favorite things. "And you of Spanish blood," Tualha said, "and you don't know that song, about how the Spanish came to Ireland first? What *do* you know?"

"Not much, sometimes," Nita said, suspecting that here, at least, that was probably going to be true. "I know about the Spanish Armada, a little." *Very little*, she added to herself. Social studies had never been a favorite with her, either, but she was beginning to suspect that was going to have to change.

"That was *only* the fifteenth invasion," Tualha said. "The real causes of things go back much further. The wind moves, and things move in it. Now, in the beginning—"

"Do we have to go back *that* far?" Nita asked drily.

The kitten glared at her. "Don't interrupt. How do you expect to become wise?"

"How did you do it?"

Tualha shrugged. "I've been in the hills. But also, I had to be a bard: I was found in a bag. It's traditional."

Nita remembered her aunt saying something the previous night about one of the farm cats having been found in a sack by the roadside, abandoned and starving. The starving part, at least, had been dealt with: Tualha was fat as a little ball. "Anyway," Tualha said, glaring at Nita again, "it's all in the *Book of Conquests* and the *Book of Leinster* and the *Yellow Book of Lecan.*"

"I doubt I could just go get those out of the library where I come from," Nita said, "so perhaps you'll enlighten me." She grinned.

"It's all in the wizards' Mastery anyway," Tualha said, "if you'd bothered to look. But grow wise by me. In the beginning there was no one in this island; it was bleak and bare, nor was it an island at all. The Flood rose and covered it, and fell away again. Then two hundred and sixty-four years later came twenty-four men and twenty-four women: Those were Partholon and his people. At that time in Ireland was only one treeless and grassless plain, three lakes and nine rivers, so they built some more."

" 'Built—' " Nita said. "When was this?"

"Four hundred thousand years ago. Didn't I mention? Now, do stop interrupting. They built mountains and carved valleys, and they fought the Fomori. The monster people," Tualha said in obvious annoyance at Nita's blank look. "The Fomori made a plague, the sickness that makes those who catch it hate and fight without thought; and the plague killed Partholon's people. So the island that was not an island was empty. Then, after another three thousand years, the people of Nemed came. They settled here and dug rivers and planted forests, and they met the Fomori and caught their plague—fought with them, and lost, and in the great strife of the battle the land was broken away from the greater land, and drowned in ice, and then water. When the ice melted and the water drew back, another people came: the Fir Bolg. They brought new beasts and birds into the land, and there was song in the air and life in the waters."

"When did the cats get here?" Nita asked.

"Later. Shush! The Fomori came to the Fir Bolg, too, with gifts and fair words, and married with them, and darkened their minds; and the Fir Bolg caught the battle-sickness from the Fomori, and most died of it, as all the others had. And the ones who were left had the bad blood of the Fomori in them and became half-monstrous, too. Are you getting all this?" Tualha asked.

"I think so." Nita resolved to have a look at her manual later, though, to see if, as Tualha said, all this information was in there. It might have been in a form that made sense to a cat, but Nita was a little uncertain about it all, particularly about some of the dates.

"Well. After this, the One grew angry that Its fair land was being ruined and sent another people to live here. That was the Tuatha de Danaan, the Children and People of the Goddess Danu. They tried to parley with the Fir Bolg, but the Fir Bolg were sick with the battle-sickness of their Fomori blood, and would make no parley. So there was a great fight at the Plain of the Towers, Moytura. The battle came out a draw, and both sides drew apart and waited for a sign. And the sign came, sent by the One: the young hero-god Lugh the Allcrafted. He told the Tuatha to bring the Four Treasures of the People of Danu, the cup and stone and sword and spear they had brought with them when they first came here from the Four Oldest Cities. Seven years he reforged those treasures with the power that was in him. Then the Children of Danu went forth to battle once more at Moytura. Lugh went forward with the spear called Luin, and with it destroyed Balor of the Deadly Eye, and the Fomori."

Tualha stopped, panting a little. Nita made a list in her head. "That's, let's see," she said, "six invasions. If you count the Tuatha."

"It's *all* invasions," said Tualha, "from the land's point of view."

Nita thought about that for a moment. "You may have something there. So then who threw the Tuatha out?"

Tualha laughed at her. "Sure, you're joking me," she said. "They're still here."

"Say what?" Nita said.

A leaf went by Tualha on the breeze. She jumped at it, missed spectacularly, and came down on the ground so hard that Nita could hear the breath go out of her in a squeak. Nita couldn't help it anymore: She burst out laughing. "I'm sorry, I really am," she said, "but I think you need some practice."

Tualha looked at her scathingly. "When you're a cat-bard," she said, "you get to choose. You get to be fast, or you get to be smart. And no offense, but I prefer smart. Not sure what you prefer, *Shonaiula ni Cealodhain*," she muttered, and scurried off.

Nita chuckled a little, then got up and made her way back the way Tualha had gone, between the riding school and the stable. As she went she noticed a sort of burning smell and put her head quickly into the stable block to make sure that something flammable hadn't fallen into the hay. She couldn't see anything but one of the grooms leading out a chestnut horse.

Out in the concrete yard she found the source of the burning. A small pickup truck was there, and a square steel box about two feet on each side had been unloaded from it. *It's a forge*, Nita thought, as the woman standing by it pulled at a cord hanging out of one side, and pulled at it again and again, like someone trying to start a lawn mower.

The comparison was apt, since a moment later a compressor stuttered and then roared to life. *That pushes air into it*, Nita thought, *and then—* The woman went around to one side of the portable forge and applied a blowtorch to an aperture there. *How about that*, Nita thought. *Portable horseshoeing—*

Nita went to have a look as the chestnut horse was led up to be re-shoed. The woman by the forge had to be about sixty. She was of medium height, with short, close-cropped white hair and little wire-rimmed glasses, and she was wearing jeans and boots and a T-shirt. Her face was very lined and very cheerful, and her accent was lighter than a lot of the accents Nita had heard so far: She sounded like someone half-trying to speak with an American accent. "Ah, you again," she said to the chestnut as the groom led it up and fastened its reins to a loop on the back of the truck's tailgate. "We'll do better than we did last time. Ah," the farrier said then, looking up immediately as Nita wandered over. "You'll be Miz Callahan's niece."

"That's right," Nita said, and put her hand out to shake. She was getting used to the ritual by now, and was becoming relieved that no one was in a position to offer her any tea.

The farrier held up her hands in apology for not shaking hands: They were covered with grime. "Sorry," she said. "I'm Biddy O Dalaigh. How are you settling in?"

"Pretty well, thanks."

"Have you seen this done before?"

"Only on TV," Nita said. "And never out of the back of a truck."

Biddy laughed. "Makes it easier to get a day's work done," she said, rooting around in a box in the truck and coming out with a horseshoe. She looked critically from it to the horse's feet, then bent down to push it into the aperture of the furnace-box. "Used to be that all the farms had their own farriers. No one can afford it now, though. So I go to my work, instead of people bringing it to me."

Nita leaned against the truck to watch. "You must travel a lot."

Biddy nodded and walked around to the front of the horse, stroking it and whistling to it softly between her teeth. "All over the county," she said. "A lot of horse shows and such." With her back to the horse's nose, she picked up its right forefoot and curled it around and under, grasping it between her knees. With a tool like a nail-puller, she loosened the nails around the horse's hoof and pried them up one by one. Then she changed her leverage and knocked the shoe completely up and off. With another tool, a smaller one with a sharp point, Biddy began trimming down the rough edges of the hoof. "Tell Derval," Biddy said to Aisling, the blond groom handling the chestnut, "that he won't be needing the orthopedic any more; the hoof's cleared up."

Nita was surprised. "Orthopedic horseshoes?"

"Oh yes," Biddy said. "Horses have problems with their feet the same as people do. Tango here has been wearing a booster until this hoof grew back in straight—he hurt the foot a few months ago, and that can make the hoof go crooked. It's just an overdeveloped toenail, after all." She patted Tango as she got up. "We're all better now, though, aren't we, my lad? And you'll have a nice run tomorrow." She reached into the truck and came up with a pair of tongs.

"He's in the hunt?" Nita asked.

Biddy nodded. "He belongs to Jim McAllister up on the hill." She rooted around in the forge, stirring and rearranging the coals.

Nita peered into the opening. "Lava rocks?"

"Oh, aye, like in the barbecues. They work as well as charcoal unless you're doing drop-forging or some such."

Biddy turned her attention back to the hoof, scraping its edges a bit more. Then she picked up the tongs again. "Here we go, now," she said, and took hold of the hoof. With her free hand she used the tongs to pluck the horseshoe from the furnace and slap it hard against the hoof, exactly where she wanted it. There was a billow of smoke, and a stink like burned hair or nails.

Nita waved the smoke away.

"Foul, isn't it," Biddy said, untroubled. After removing the shoe from the hoof and dunking it in a bucket of cold water, she dropped the tongs, took a hammer out of a belt loop, reached into a pocket for nails, replaced the shoe on the hoof, and began tapping the nails in with great skill, each nail halfway in with one tap, all the way in with the next.

Nita watched Biddy do Tango's three other shoes. Then another horse was led out, and Nita turned away: This kind of thing was interesting enough, once. *Maybe I'll go down to Greystones*, she thought. Aunt Annie had told her that the bike was in the shed behind the riding school, if she wanted to use it and no one else had it. *Or maybe I won't.* It was strange, having nowhere familiar to go and no one familiar to go with. Being at loose ends was not a sensation she was used to, but she didn't feel quite bold enough at the moment to just go charging off into a strange town.

I wouldn't mind if Kit were here, though . . .

Nita wandered back the way she had come, back to the field where the jumping equipment lay around. She climbed over the fence and walked out into the field to look at it all: the odd candy-cane-striped poles, the jumps and steps and stiles, some painted with brand names or names of local shops.

The wind began to rise. From this field, which stood at the top of a gentle rise, Nita could see the ocean. She stood there and gazed at it for a while. The brightness it had worn this morning, under full sunlight, was gone. Now, with the sun behind a cloud, the ocean was just a flat, silvery expanse, dull and pewter-colored. Nita smelled smoke again, and idly half-turned to look over her shoulder, toward the farrier's furnace.

And was shocked not to see it there at all . . . or anything else. The farm was gone.

The contour of the land was still there—the way it trended gently downhill past where the farm buildings should stand, and then up again toward the dual carriageway and the hills on its far side. But there were no buildings, no houses that she could see. The road was gone. Or not gone: reduced to a rutted dirt track. And the smoke—

She looked around her in great confusion. There was a pillar of black smoke rising up off to one side, blown westward by the rising wind off the sea. Very faintly in the silence she could hear cries, shouts. Something white over there was burning. It was the little white church down the road, St. Patrick's of Kilquade, with its one bell. She stood there in astonishment, hearing the cries on the wind and then a terrible metallic note, made faint by the distance: the one bell blowing in the wind, then shattering with heat and the fall of the tower that housed it. A silence followed the noise . . . then faint laughter and the sound of glass exploding outward with the force of the fire.

And a voice spoke, down by her feet. "Yes, they have been restless of late, those ghosts," said Tualha, looking where Nita looked, at the smoke. "I thought I might find you here. It's as I said, *Shonaiula ni Cealodhain*. The wind blows, and things get blown along in it. Bards and wizards alike. Why would you be here, otherwise? But better to be the wind than the straw, when the Carrion-Crow is on the wing. It always takes *draoiceacht* to set such situations to rights."

Nita gulped and tried to get ahold of herself. This was a wizardry, but not one of a kind she had ever experienced. Worldgating, travel between planes, she knew. But those required extensive and specific spelling. Nothing of the sort had happened here. She had simply turned around . . . and been here. "Where are we?" she said softly. "How did we get here?"

"You went *cliathánach*," Tualha said. " 'Sideways,' as I did. True, it's not usually so easy. But that's an indication that things are in the wind indeed."

"Sideways," Nita breathed. "Into the past—"

"Or the future," Tualha said, "or the never-was. All those are here. You know that."

"Of course I know it," Nita said. It was part of a wizard's most basic knowledge that the physical world coexisted with hundreds of thousands of others, both like and very unlike it. No amount of merely physical travel would get you into any of them. With the right wizardry, though, you had to move no more than a step. "It shouldn't be anything *like* this easy, though," she said.

Tualha looked up at her with wide, bland eyes. "It is easier here," she said. "It always has been. But you're right that it shouldn't be *this* easy. There's danger in it, both for the daylight world and the others."

Nita looked at the smoke, shaking her head. "What was it you said? . . . The wind blows, and things get blown along with it?"

Tualha said nothing. Nita stood there and thought how casually she had said to her mother, *"If I go on call in Ireland, I go on call, and that's it."* It was not simply her mother's idea that she come here, after all. One of the Powers That Be had sent her here to do a job. She knew when she got back to the farmhouse—*if* she got back to the farmhouse—and opened her manual, she would find she was on active status again. And here she was, without her partner, without her usual Senior Wizards' support—for their authority didn't reach here: Europe had its own Seniors. Alone, and with a problem she didn't understand—she was going to have to get caught up on her reading.

Tualha crouched and leaped at a bit of ash that the wind sailed past her. She missed it. Nita sighed. "How do we get back?"

"You haven't done this before?" Tualha asked. "Where were you looking when it happened?"

"At the ocean."

"Look back, then."

Nita turned her back on the smoke and the cries and the brittle music of breaking glass, and looked out to the flat, gray sea, willing things to be as they had been before.

"There you are, then," Tualha said. Nita turned again. There was the farm, the riding school, the farmhouse—and the field, full of its prosaic jumping equipment, all decals and slightly peeling paint. "But indeed," Tualha said, "it's as I told you. Something must change. Get about it, before it gets about us."

Brí Cualann

Bray

THE NEXT MORNING NITA did what she usually did when she was confused—the thing that had made her a wizard in the first place. She went to the library.

She caught the bus to Bray, a green double-decker that stopped at the end of her aunt's road, and climbed up to the top level. There was no one at all there, so she took the seat right in front, its window looking directly forward and twelve feet down to the ground. It was interesting to ride along little country lanes and look down onto the sheep and the hedges and the potholes from such a height.

But she didn't let it distract her for very long. The section on Ireland in her wizard's manual was quite long. This did not surprise her, since at the moment the section on the United States was quite short . . . most likely since she wasn't there. The manual tended to have as much information as you needed on any particular subject, and simply waited for you to look for it.

She immediately found that she had been correct to be a little suspicious of Tualha's numbers. The things she had discussed as happening four hundred thousand years before had actually happened four hundred *million* years before. This didn't surprise Nita, either; she remembered her aunt Annie saying yesterday that as far as she knew, the only times cats were really concerned about were their mealtimes.

The manual told her of the formation of Ireland some four hundred million years earlier; of the pushing up of the great chain of mountains that it shared with Newfoundland, and the Pyrenees. A hundred and fifty million years later, Greenland began to move away from the ancient European continent, creating a huge gap in what was to become the northern Atlantic. The great island that had been both England and Ireland was flooded, as the waters of other seas flowed into the gap, and then split; and the ice came down and tore at it, leaving the terrible glacial valleys of the western Irish coast that Nita had seen when she flew in.

That was just the science of it, of course. Science may accurately reveal the details about concrete occurrences, the "what"s and "how"s of life, but a wizard knows to look further than science for the "why"s. And wizards knew that the world was *made*: not created in some disinterested abstract sense, like an assembly line of natural forces stamping out parts, but made, stone by stone, as an artist makes, or a craftsman, or a cook: with interest, and care. The One—the only name wizards have for that Power which was senior to the Powers That Be and everything else—like a good manager, had delegated many of its functions to the first-made creatures, the Powers, which some people in the past had called gods and others had called angels. The Powers made different parts of the world and became associated with them simply because they loved them, as people who make tend to love what they've made.

But something had gone wrong in Ireland's making. Someone had been—it was tempting to say "interfering." The manual said nothing specific about this. It tended to let one draw one's own conclusions on the more complex ethical issues. But several times the Makers had begun to make the island, and several times something had gone wrong: cataclysms, a glacial movement that happened too quickly, a continental plate ramming another faster than had been intended. A misjudgment? A miscalculation? Nita thought not. She thought she saw here the interference of her old enemy, the Lone Power, the One that (for good or evil) invented death and later went through the world seeing what It could destroy or warp.

It seemed that the Bright Powers, the Makers and Builders, had not seen, or suspected, the flaws inserted in their building by the Lone Power's working. So Ireland had come undone several times, and had had to be patched. Indeed, the top part of it had been welded on about two hundred and fifty million years after the original complex began to be formed—after other land that should have been Ireland was drowned beneath the sea.

The Bright Powers made two or three attempts to form Ireland, were frustrated two or three times by the Lone Power . . . and then, as Tualha had said, the One had intervened. It sent a new group of Makers into the world to shape Ireland: Makers with greater powers and more seniority, more central, than those who had worked here before. They would set it right.

They tried. Nita understood, from the manual and from what Tualha had told her, that just as the One had increased Its response, so had the Lone Power. The Fomori had been growing more powerful each time they had been challenged. Each time they were put down, they came back more powerful yet. And then came the first battle of Moytura.

The version that Tualha had told Nita turned out to be much romanticized and classicized. Moytura itself was a great strife of forces over many centuries, as mountains were raised and thrown down, river valleys were carved and choked, and the ice rose and fell. You could still see the evidence in places in Ireland—rock more warped and twisted than could be explained by any mere geological uprising or subsidence; places where fires had fallen and melted the stone in ways that geologists could make nothing of. Nita could make something of it. The weapons used to wage war in heaven had been brought to bear on Ireland. The battle went on for a good while.

And then—Nita turned a page over, scanning down it. She was beginning to get the drift of this. Here was the arrival of Lugh the Allcrafted. She thought she knew this particular Power. She had met It once or twice. A young warrior, fierce, kindly, a little humorous, liable to travel in disguise: a Power known by many names in many places and times. Michael, Athene, Thor—It was the One's Champion, one of the greatest of all creatures: definitely a Power to be reckoned with. As Lugh, that Power had come and poured his virtue into the great Treasures that the Tuatha de Danaan had brought from the Four Oldest Cities.

Then he and the Tuatha had gone out with those weapons against Balor of the Evil Eye. *Who was he?* Nita wondered. *The Lone Power Itself? Or some unfortunate creature that It corrupted and inhabited?* That was one of the Lone Power's favorite tactics. Either way, Balor had held the humans of the island; his twisted creatures, the Fomori; and the other, lesser Powers in great terror for thousands of years. But then came the second battle of Moytura, as Tualha had said, and all that changed. War came from heaven to earth with a vengeance. The Champion, in the form of Lugh, struck Balor down.

Nita turned another page. After putting down Balor, the Powers That Be had gotten busy finishing Ireland. They raised the mountains and smoothed them down, made the plains and the forests and lakes. And they fell more completely in love with the beautiful, marred place than any of their more junior predecessors had.

This was more common in the Old World, Nita read, than in the New. In places like North America, where the native human peoples had stories not of specific gods but instead about heroes and the One, it indicated that the Makers of that place had gone away, well-satisfied with their work. In some places in the world, though, the satisfaction took longer—places like Greece and Rome. Their Makers loved them too much to leave for a long while, though finally they did let go. But there were still a few places in the world where the Powers had never let go. This was one of them.

I bet this is why Ireland has so much trouble, one way and another, Nita thought. *The Powers won't move out and let the new tenants be there by themselves*. Like most wizards, Nita knew quite well that the Powers might indeed be good, but that didn't make them safe. Even the best of the Powers That Be could be affected by too much commerce with humans and physical reality.

Nita read that the Tuatha de Danaan, as the Irish had come to call the Builder-Powers, had never left. And when the human people, the "Milesians," came at last, the Powers struck a bargain with them, agreeing to relinquish the lands and vanish into the hills. At least, that was how it looked to the humans. They knew that some hills in Ireland, at the four great feasts of the year, became more than hills. The nonphysical then became more solid, more real, and the physical, if it was wise, would stay out of the way of what was older, stronger, and harder by far.

They had gone "sideways," had the Tuatha. They could not bear to leave Ireland, and so they had gone just one universe over—or two, or five. It was still Ireland, but it was also a little bit closer to the depths of reality, where, as Nita knew, Timeheart lay. She had been there several times, for brief periods. It had different appearances, depending on where and when you were. She had seen it look like a city, like the ocean, like the depths of space. What it always *was*, regardless of your viewpoint, was that place where the physical universe was as it would have been, had the Lone Power not taken exception and created something that the other Powers had not intended: entropy . . . death. The Powers simply moved into a universe near Timeheart that to them looked most like Ireland.

But much coming and going between Ireland and the alternate universe had forged a link, broadening the road from a little track into a highway easy to stumble onto. All of Ireland had become a place where one could suddenly go sideways. This to-ing and fro-ing of the greater and lesser Powers between the Ireland that was and their version of Ireland—Tir na nOg, as they called it, the Land of the Ever-Young—was very dangerous. But it wasn't a thing a lone wizard could just stop. At least, Nita couldn't stop it.

And *she* had gone sideways, and it hadn't hurt her . . . but then she was a wizard. If something like that started happening to regular people, though, people in the street who were standing waiting for a bus and suddenly found themselves in the middle of a Viking invasion—or something worse . . . Nita shuddered.

The problem with being sent somewhere by the Powers That Be to do a job is that, frequently, they leave it to you to find out what the job is. Nita flipped through the book to the directory pages and saw that, yes indeed, she was on active status, and her aunt's address was listed. There were local addresses for Senior wizards as well, asterisked with a note saying, "Consult in case of emergency."

Well then, Nita thought, *if they've put me on my own on this one, I guess that's what it is. Must be something that having Kit around wouldn't help.* The thought made her ache. Were the Powers trying to break up their partnership? Or, on the other hand, was this just the kind of solo work that even a partnered wizard had to do every now and then? Well, either way, she was not going to refuse the commission. She shut the book as the bus bounced into Bray.

Bray was not a very big town, its main street about half the length of the main street at home. As usual, everything continued to look small and cramped and a little worn-out by Nita's standards. She berated herself inwardly. *Just because you're used to everything looking slick and neat and new doesn't mean that it has to be that way here.* Aunt Annie had mentioned to her that Ireland had been in economic trouble for a while, and there just wasn't the money to spend on things that Nita took for granted.

She got off in the middle of town, across from the big Catholic church, and had a look around. There was a sign that said LEABHLAIR POBLACHTA, "public library." She grinned. Finding libraries had never been one of her problems.

The library was two buildings—the older one, which had been a schoolhouse once, a big, square, granite building, very solid and dependable looking, all on one story; and the newer annex, built in the same stone but in a slightly more modern style. She spent a happy two or three hours there, browsing. Nita had had no idea there was so much written in the Irish language—so many poems, by so many poets, humor, cartoon books, all kinds of neat things. And structurally the language looked, and occasionally sounded, very much like the Speech. But she tried not to be distracted from what she was there for.

She picked out several large books on Irish mythology and began going through them in hopes of correlating what Tualha had told her with what she had read in the manual. Mostly she found confirmation for Tualha's version—the terrible eye of Balor that burned everything it saw; many strange tales of the old "gods and goddesses," the greater and lesser Powers That Be. As usual, the Powers had their jobs divided up. Among many others, there were Govan, the smith and beer brewer; Diancecht, the great physician of the gods; and Brigid of the Fires, hearth goddess and beast goddess, artificer and miracle worker; bard gods and carpenter gods; builders; charioteers; cooks; and warriors.

There were also tales of the "little people." Nita had to smile at that. World-gating did odd things to the density and refractive index of air. Something near, seen through air whose structure was disturbed by wizardry, might seem far away, or small. But this was an effect of diffraction, not magic. The "little people" were little only to human perceptions, and only occasionally.

And then there were the stories of the saints. Bridget, for example. When the saints came to Ireland, so many miracles attended them that Nita seriously wondered whether the stories she was reading were not in fact new versions of the tales about the Powers, transferred to the saints to make them respectable to the new religion. Bridget's stories in particular were interesting, though there was confusion over whether the person involved was the old goddess in disguise or the new, mortal saint. Her miracles seemed to be of a friendly, homey sort, more useful than spectacular: She fixed broken things and fed people, and she said that her great wish was that everyone should be in heaven with God and the angels, and should have a nice meal and a drink.

There was a lot more material, and Nita did her best to digest it. And then the topic of digestion came to be considered seriously, since she hadn't had any breakfast. It was partly out of cowardice; she had awakened afraid to hang around the farm for long, lest she should look at some common thing and abruptly find herself back in time, or sideways in it. *I'm really no safer here, though*, she thought, as she stepped out of the library, looking up and down the little road that ran parallel to Bray's main street. This calm-looking landscape—with its brownstone houses and the truck unloading groceries for the supermarket around the corner, and the cars all double-parked on the yellow lines—all this could shift in a moment. A second, and she might find herself outside the Stone Age encampment that was here once long ago; or the little row of wattled huts that the Romans came to visit once and never left—their bones and coins had been found down by Bray Head; or the great eighteenth-century spa where people from Britain came on their vacations, promenading up and down the fine seafront, a second Brighton. No, there was nowhere she could go to get away from going sideways.

Nita went up to the main street and looked around for somewhere to eat. There were some tea shops, but at the moment she felt like she had had enough tea for a lifetime. Instead, near the bridge over the Dargle, she saw a restaurant with a sign that said AMERICAN-STYLE FRIED CHICKEN. *Hmm*, Nita thought, her mouth watering as she made for it, *we'll see about that.*

She went in. As she ordered, she saw a few heads turn among the kids who were sitting there, probably at her accent. She smiled. They were going to have to get used to the look of her for the little while she was going to be here.

She got a Coke and settled down to wait for her chicken, gazing idly over at the kids sitting at the other table. They were stealing glances back at her, boys and girls together: a little casual, a little shy, a little hostile. In that way, they looked almost exactly like everyone she knew at home. They *did* dress differently. Black seemed to be a big favorite here, as did a kind of heavy boot that she had never seen before. Everyone seemed very into tight, torn jeans, or just tight jeans, or very tight short skirts, all black again; and black leather seemed popular. She felt a little out of place in her down vest and her faded blue jeans, but she grinned at the other kids and paid attention to her Coke again.

A couple of minutes later, two of them came over. She looked up. One of them was a boy, very tall, with very shaggy dark hair, a long nose, dark eyes set very close together, and a big wide mouth that could have been very funny or very cruel depending on the mood of its owner. The girl could have been his twin, except that she was shorter, and her hair was teased and ratted out into a great black mane. At least parts of it were black; some were stunningly purple or pink. She was wearing a khaki T-shirt with a wonderfully torn and beat-up leather jacket over it—black again—black jeans, and those big heavy boots of which Nita was becoming envious.

"You a Yank?" said the boy. It wasn't entirely a question. There was something potentially a little nasty on the edge of it.

"Somebody has to be," Nita said. "Wanna sit down?"

They looked at her and shuffled for a moment. "You staying in town?"

"No, I'm out in Kilquade."

"Relatives?"

"Yeah. Annie Callahan. She's my aunt."

"Woooaaa!" said the boy in a tone of voice that was only slightly mocking and only slightly impressed. "Rich relatives, huh?"

"I don't know if *rich* is the right word," Nita said.

"You here looking for your roots?" the girl asked.

Nita looked at a lock of her own hair, then at the girl's. "Still attached to them, as far as I can tell. Though finding them around here doesn't seem to be a big problem."

There was a burst of laughter over this. "Come on and sit with us," the boy said. "I'm Ronan. This is Majella."

"OK."

Nita went with them. She was rapidly introduced to the others, who seemed to alternate between being extremely interested in her and being faintly scornful. The scorn seemed to be because she was an American, because they thought she had a lot of money, because they thought she thought they were poor, and various other reasons. The admiration seemed to be because she was American, because they thought she had a lot of money, and because she could see the big movies six months earlier than everyone else.

"Uh," Nita said finally, "my folks don't let me go see that many movies. I have to keep up my schoolwork all the time or they don't let me go out."

There was a general groan of agreement over this. "There's no escape," said Ronan.

More detailed introductions ensued. Most of the kids lived in Bray. One of them lived as far out as Greystones, but said she took the bus in "for the crack." Nita blinked until she discovered that *crack* was not a drug here, but a word for really good conversation or fun. Nita was immediately instructed about all the nightclubs and all the discos she should go to. "How many discos do you have here?" she asked, in some surprise. It then turned out that *disco* was not a word for a specific kind of building, or a specific kind of music, as it was in the States, but a dance that various pubs or hotels held once or twice a week. Several of them were no-alcohol kids' discos, highly thought of by this group, who went off into an enthusiastic discussion of what they would wear and who they would go with.

"You got somebody to go with?" said Ronan.

"Uh, no," Nita said, thinking regretfully of Kit. He loved to dance. "My buddy's back in the States."

"Oooh, she's got a *buddyyyyyy!*" Nita grinned a little: She was now beyond the blushing point. Her sister had been teasing her about Kit for so long that this was a very minor salvo by comparison.

"Aren't you a little young for that?" one of the girls said, clearly teasing, to judge by the young guy massaging her shoulders at the moment.

Nita arched her eyebrows. "Let's just say that in my part of the world we make up our minds about this kind of thing early."

"Whooooaaaaa!" said the group, and started punching one another and making lewd remarks, only about half of which Nita understood.

"So if your buddy's there, what are you doing here?" said Ronan.

"I know!" said Majella. "Her folks sent her away to separate them because they were—*ahem*!" And she shook her hand in a gesture intended to be slightly rude and slightly indicative of what they were doing.

Nita thought about this for a moment, and thought that the simplest way to manage things was to let them think exactly this. "Well, yeah," she said. "Anyway, I'm stuck here for six weeks."

"Stuck here! Only stuck here! In the best part of the earth! Well, excuse *us*!" they said, and began ragging her shamelessly, explaining what a privilege it was that she should be among them, and telling her all the wonderful places there were to see, and things to do. She grinned at this at last, and said, "I bet none of you do those things."

"Oh, well, those are *tourist* things," Ronan said.

"Thanks a lot," said Nita.

They chatted about this and that for a long while. Nita found herself oddly interested in Ronan, despite his looks—maybe *because* of his looks. She didn't know anyone at home who managed to look so dark and grim, no matter how punk he dressed. And there was an odd, cheerful edge to his grimness that kept flashing out, a certain delight in having opinions, and having them loudly, in hopes that someone would be shocked. Their conversation ranged through music ("Mostly junk except for the Cranberries") and art ("All bollocks"—Nita kept her mouth shut and made a note to find out what bollocks were), and quite a bit about politics, especially Irish politics, much of which left Nita completely in the dark. Ronan's opinions of anyone who wanted to colonize Ireland, from the English on back, were scathing. So were his views on people who thought they were Irish and weren't really, or who weren't Irish and thought they should have something to do with running the country, or thought that the Irish needed any kind of help with anything at all. The others tended to nod in agreement with him, or if they disagreed, to keep fairly quiet about this. Nita noticed this in particular, and suspected that they had felt the edge of his temper once or twice. She grinned to herself, thinking that he would have a slightly hotter time if he tried his temper on *her*. She sort of hoped he would.

It was amazing how long a couple of pieces of chicken and a few Cokes could be made to last; fortunately, the people running the shop didn't seem to care how long they stayed. Eventually, though, everybody had to leave: buses to catch, people to meet. One by one they said good-bye to Nita and headed off; Ronan was last. "Don't get lost looking for leprechauns, now, Miss Yank," he shouted to her over his shoulder as he made his way down Bray's main street.

She snickered and turned away, looking at the 45 bus pulling up across the street, and thought, *Naah . . . I'll walk home*. It was only eight miles, and the walk would take her through extremely pretty countryside.

Except for the first part—the climb up one side of Bray Head—it was an easy walk down, taking her about an hour to get to Greystones. She strolled into the town. It was more villagey-looking than Bray, smaller: a couple of banks, a couple of food stores, two small restaurants, a newsstand where you could get magazines' and cards and candy. Various other small shops . . . a dry cleaner. And that was it.

After that, the street was lined with big old houses and estates of smaller ones. And then the fields began again—in fact, they began almost as soon as she left the town. Nita strolled by the tiny golf course, looked down to Greystones's south beach beyond it; she walked past a cow who was chewing its cud with a blank expression. *"Dai,"* she said to it. It blinked at her and kept chewing.

The road climbed again, winding up through Killincarrig. *Everything does have a name here*, Nita thought. *It's amazing. I really should get a map. There may be one in the manual . . .*

There was. She consulted it as she went up the road. At the top of the hill, the road ended in a T-intersection: She turned left. That way led toward Kilquade and Kilcoole and Newcastle with its little church.

This road climbed and dipped over a little bridge that crossed a dry river, then rose between high hedges. Birds dipped and sang high in the air. The sun was quite hot: There was no wind.

There came a point where there was a right turn, and a signpost pointing down between two more high hedges, toward Kilquade. Nita took it, making her way down the narrow road. The houses here were built well away from one another, even though they were small. Some were larger, though.

The road dipped and broadened, curving around in front of Saint Patrick's. Nita stopped and looked at it for a moment. It was quite normal, a little white-painted church, with the tower off to one side of the building and the bell with a pulley-and-gear to make it ring. There was a big field on one side, and visible behind it a hedge, and beyond that some of Aunt Annie's land: another field planted with oilseed rape and those bright yellow flowers. The hum of bees came from it, loud. Nita stood still and listened, smelled the air. No broken stained glass, no fire, no blackening.

She turned and looked off to her right. She could see Little Sugarloaf, which she had passed on her walk, well behind her. And just beyond it, Great Sugarloaf, a perfect cone, standing straight, a sort of russet and green color this time of year, for in this heat the bracken was beginning to go brown already. *I wonder*, she thought. *Sideways . . .*

She had done it without wizardry yesterday. She stood there for a moment, and just looked. Not at Sugarloaf as it was, but as it could be; not this brown, but green.

Nothing.

Nothing . . .

. . . But it was green.

Her eyes widened a little. She looked at the nearby hedge. There were no flowers. She looked over her shoulder in panic at the church. The church looked just the same, but it was earlier in the year, much earlier. *I wonder*, she thought. *How far can I take it? Do I have to be looking for anything in particular?* Most wizardries required that you name the specifics that you wanted. . . . *All right. What does it look like?* she thought. *What could it look like?*

She looked at Sugarloaf again. *What does it look like? Show me. Come on, show me . . .*

There was no ripple, no sense of change, no special effects. One minute it was Sugarloaf, green as if with new spring. The next minute—it was a city.

There *were* no such cities. No one had ever built such towers, such spires.

Glass, it might have been, or crystal: a glass mountain, a crystal city, all sheen and fire. It needed no sunlight to make it shine. It shed its light all around, and the hills nearby all cast shadows away from it. Nita was not entirely sure she didn't see something moving in some of those shadows. For the moment, all she could see was the light, the fire; Sugarloaf all one great mass of tower upon tower, arches, architraves, buttresses, leaping up; an architecture men could not have imagined, since it violated so many of their laws. It was touched a little with the human idiom, true; but then those who had built it and lived in it—were living in it—had been dealing with the human idiom for a while and had become enamored of it. "They're still here," Tualha had said, and laughed.

Nita blinked, and let it go. And it was gone. Brown bracken appeared again, and a plain granite mountain with its head scraped bare. She let out a long breath and went walking again, to the last hill that would lead her up to her aunt's driveway. *That simple*, she said to herself. *That easy . . .* For wizards, at least. At the moment. *But it shouldn't be that easy . . .*

Something had better be done.

If only I could find out what!

She headed back to the farm.

The next morning was the foxhunt. Nita slept in and missed the earliest part of the operation, having been reading and chatting with Kit until late the night before. He hadn't been able to throw much light on anything, except that he missed her.

Kit, she had said, *I don't know how much more of this I can take.*

You can take it, he said. *I can take it, too. I saw your folks the other day.*

How are they?

They're fine . . . They're going to call you tonight. They said they were going to give you a couple of days to get acclimated before they bothered you.

Fine by me, Nita said. *I've had enough to keep me busy.*

She had felt Kit nod, thirty-five hundred miles away. *So I see*, he said. *I'd watch doing that too much, Neets.*

Hm?

I mean, it makes me twitch a little bit. You didn't do any specific wizardry, but with that result—makes you wonder what's going on over there.

Yeah, well, it can't be that bad, Kit. Look, you come back as easily as you go—

I sure hope *you do*, he said.

The conversation had trailed off after that. It was odd how it was becoming almost uncomfortable to talk to Kit, because their conversation couldn't run in the same channels it usually did, the easy, predictable ones. For the first time, she had things to tell him that he hadn't participated in. *How's Dairine?* she asked.

She's been busy with something . . . I don't know what. Something about somebody's planet.

Oh lord, not again, Nita said. *Sometimes I think she should be unlisted. She's never going to have any peace, at least not while she's in breakthrough . . . and maybe not later.* They chatted a while more, then grew silent.

Nita was thinking about this in the morning as she got her breakfast. The kitchen was in havoc. Many of the riders who were picking up their horses from the stable had come in for "a quick cup of tea." Nita was learning that there was no such thing in Ireland as a quick cup of tea. What you got were several cups of tea, taking no less than half an hour, during which every manner of interesting local news was passed on. "A quick cup of tea" might happen at any hour of the day or night, might include any number of people, male or female, and always turned into a raging gossip session with hilarious laughter and recriminations.

Finally the kitchen began to clear out. The people in the hunt were splendidly dressed, all red coats and black caps and beige riding britches and black shiny boots. They were discussing the course they would ride—a mean one—from Calary Upper behind Sugarloaf, down through various farmers' lands, straight to Newcastle. The thing that concerned them was that, suddenly, there were no foxes anywhere. Nita smiled to herself. Everyone was bemused by the situation. Some people blamed hunt protesters; others blamed the weather, crop dusting, sunspots, global warming, or overzealous shooting by local farmers. Nita grinned outright, and had another cup of tea. She was beginning to really like tea.

"Well, that's all we'll see of *them*," said her aunt Annie, pouring herself a cup as well and then flopping down in one of the kitchen chairs in thinly disguised relief.

"I thought they were coming through here," Nita said.

"Oh, they will, but that's not until this afternoon."

"No foxes, huh?" Nita said, in great satisfaction.

"Not a one." Her aunt looked over at her and said, "Personally, I can't say that I'm exactly brokenhearted."

"Me, either," said Nita.

"Doesn't matter. They'll hunt to a drag—it's just an old fox skin that leaves a scent for the dogs. They drag it along the ground. They'll have a good time."

Nita nodded and went back to her reading, half-thinking of going down to Bray again that afternoon, to see if Ronan or Majella was around. Then she talked herself out of it. It was too nice a day; the sun was hot. . . . There was no reason to go into a smelly town and suffocate herself with the bus fumes and traffic. She would put a towel down outside, lie in the sun, and pretend it was the beach. She missed the beaches back home: The water here was much too cold to swim in.

So that was what she did. And at about two-fifteen, she heard the cry of the hounds. She got up and pulled a T-shirt on over her bathing suit, put the manual in the trailer, and went to lean on the fence by the back field and see what she could see. She almost missed seeing the first horseman go by. He was about a half mile away across the field, thundering through the pasture: one rider with a long rope dragging behind him, and something dragging at the end of the rope.

There was a long pause. And then the note of the hounds came belling up over the fields, followed by the hounds themselves, woofing, lolloping, yipping. Then, over the rise behind them, came a splendid pouring of horses of all kinds—chestnut, brown, dapple, black—galloping down the hill; and a horn going *tarantara*! And the riders, hallooing and riding as best they could after the hounds.

It took them about a minute and a half to go by. There were about fifty people, all in their red jackets and their beige breeches and not-so-black boots. Then they were gone. The sounds of the hounds and the horses' hooves faded away over the next hill, south of the potato field, and were gone. Nita listened to the last cries fade out, then went back to lie in the sun.

*   *   *

The horses started coming back to the farm, some of them trucked in by trailer from Newcastle, about three hours later. There was much talk of rides and falls and jumps and water barriers, and a lot of other stuff that Nita didn't particularly understand. But everyone seemed to have had a good time. Nita was very glad that it had been able to happen without any foxes being ripped up.

Dinner that evening was replaced by a marathon "quick cup of tea," as the grooms from the stables got together with the stable-manager and the trainers. It was at least eleven-thirty or twelve before the last of them left, having been given wine and whiskey and everything else that Aunt Annie had.

Nita escaped to her trailer about eight, having had enough of the horsey talk, but came back later and helped her aunt do the dishes, or at least rinse them and put them in the dishwasher. "There's that done with for this year," said her aunt. She rolled her eyes at the ceiling. "The way they eat!"

"Yeah. You need anything else, Aunt Annie?"

"No, I think we're OK for the night. You ready to turn in?"

"I'm going to take a little walk first."

"OK. Just watch out for those holes in the pasture. It's pretty torn up out there, what with the neighbor's cows."

"Right."

Nita got her jacket and went out into the night. It was twelve-thirty by now, but it still wasn't fully dark; in fact, it was beginning, in the northeast, to slowly brighten again. Nita cast an eye up at the sky. There was a canopy of thin clouds, enough to obscure all but the very brightest stars and the occasional planet. Jupiter was high, as was the moon.

She wandered into the pasture, into the total dark and the quiet, and just stood there and listened. It was the first time she had really felt relaxed since she had come here. She was beginning to feel a little more in control of things: She had done enough reading to at least be able to go and see a Senior and tell him or her what she thought her problem was, and to be able to discuss it in terms that made some kind of sense to someone who lived here and was familiar with this kind of situation. In the great quiet she heard birds crying, somewhere a long way away. It might have been a rookery. She had heard that creaky, cawing sound a couple of times now, when the rooks were settled down for the night and some late noise disturbed them.

She stood there under the stars, waiting for the silence to resume. It didn't resume. The cawing got louder.

More rooks. Or no—what was that?

The hair stood straight up all over her as she heard the howl. *There are no wolves in Ireland!* she told herself. The wolfhounds had been bred specifically to deal with them, and there hadn't been wolves in Ireland since the late 1700s.

But that howl came shuddering out of the night, and several others behind it, followed by yips and barks. And the sound of hooves—not many sets of them, but just one, a long way off. One animal, galloping. *What in the worlds—? Have I gone sideways again?*

She strained to see in the moonlight. It was hard. Through the thin clouds, the moon was only at first quarter, and it was hard to see anything but a vague bloom of light over the cropland, black where it struck trees and hedgerows, the dimmest silver where it struck anything else. The hoofbeats got louder; and the howls got louder, too.

Nita hurriedly said the first five words of a spell that had proved very handy to her in other times and places. It was a simple force-field spell, which made a sort of shell around the wizard who spoke it. Blows went sideways from it; physical force stopped at it and just slid off. One word would release it if she needed to— and she had a feeling she would.

In the dark, not too far away, Nita saw something moving. There were spells that would augment a wizard's vision, but she didn't have any of them prepared at the moment. Now, though, she could just begin to see the faint silvering of moonlight on the big thing galloping toward her.

It was not a horse. No horse ever foaled was that tall. It went by a tree she knew the height of, at the edge of the field, and then by a fencepost she knew was only about six feet high. The top of the post came to just below its shoulder as the massive four-legged creature sprinted toward her. It definitely was not a horse, not with those antlers, six feet across at least; not with that skull, a yard and a half long; and no horse had such a voice, trumpeting, desperate, a sound like the night being torn edge to edge. She had seen its picture. It was an elk, but not like any elk that walked the earth these days; it was the old Irish elk, extinct since the ice came down.

It went by her like a piece of storm, its breath like a blast of fog. It shook the ground as it ran, and its feet went deep into the soft pasture, churning up great chunks of grass. It flew past her and gave her never a look. Bellowing, on it went, with a great roar, a trumpeting like an elephant's. And behind it came the wolves.

They were not normal wolves. All the wolfhounds in Ireland could not have done anything about *these*. These were the wolves that had hunted the Irish elk when they still walked this part of the world. They were four feet high at the shoulder, easily. She saw them come past the fencepost, too. They were rough-coated, their eyes huge and dark except when the moon glinted in them as one or another threw up its head to howl as it ran. A faint mist of light clung to them that had nothing to do with the mist on the field, or the moonlight. Their teeth were longer than a regular wolf's; their feet were bigger; their heads were heavier and more brutish. They were dire wolves, the wolves of the Stone Age or earlier, *Canis lupus dirus*. They were hunting the elk.

It suddenly occurred to Nita that there might be someone following behind this pack, as there had been someone behind the dogs this morning . . . and she did *not* want to meet that someone.

The wolves tore forward. There were about twenty of them. More than half of them held the main course, on the elk's track: The rest saw or scented her, she had no idea which, and angled toward her. Nita said the sixth word of the spell, felt the shield wink into place around her. Hurriedly she said the first eighteen words of another spell she knew, a killing spell she was very reluctant to use; but she had no weapon spell handy that was less dangerous, and frankly she was more willing to see the wolves dead than herself. *If they can be killed at all. Are they even real . . . ?*

Nita braced herself as best she could, and waited. The first wolf hit her shield— and didn't bounce; it knocked her down. Nita got a horrible glimpse of fangs trying desperately to break through to her—failing for the moment—

In shock, she fumbled for the last word of the killing spell but couldn't remember it. Those fangs knocked against the shield, right in front of her face, bending the shield in toward her—

Suddenly, hooves came down from above and broke the wolf's head, and kicked its body aside, and smashed its spine into the ground. Other wolves bit and hung onto the great dark shape that was rearing above Nita, while it smashed at more of the wolves with its hooves. The elk had bought her the second she needed; she remembered the nineteenth word. She said it.

Nita did not enjoy the sound that followed, but the spell worked, even though the shield hadn't. The wolves were flesh and blood enough that when you suddenly removed all the membranes from between their cells, the result was emphatic. It rained blood briefly. Nita looked at another of the wolves near her and said the nineteenth word. The wolf turned in mid-leap and showered down in gore. She said the nineteenth word again, and again, and she kept saying it, having no weapon more merciful, until there was nothing left but a sickly black wet patch in the field, gleaming dully in the moonlight . . . and the Irish elk, standing with its head down, panting, looking at her with great, dumb, understanding eyes.

Nita let the shield spell go, staggered to her feet, and tottered over to the elk. Its flanks and shoulders were torn where the dire wolves' teeth had met. "Brother," she said in the Speech, "let me see to those before you go."

"Hurry," said the elk. "The loss of the pack has slowed him. But he's coming."

He, Nita thought, and broke out in a cold sweat.

Fortunately, there was plenty of blood around, blood being what you needed for almost all the healing spells. Nita had some experience with those. She called her manual to her and it came, hurriedly. She started turning pages, not worrying where the blood that she was smeared with went. "Here," she said, and began reading the quickest of the healing spells, a forced adhesion that would not require her own blood and would cause the damaged tissue to at least hold together long enough for the knitting process to start. The spell was little more than wizardly Krazy Glue, but Nita was satisfied that the elk's body would be able to manage the rest of the business itself; the wounds weren't too serious.

It took about five minutes' recitation before the last of the wounds shut itself. The elk stood there shivering in all its limbs, as if expecting something to come after it out of the night. Nita was shivering, too; the healer always partook of the suffering of the healed—that was part of the price paid.

"Go now," she said. "Get out of here!"

The elk tossed its head and leaped away, galloping across the field. Nita stood there, panting, and wondering. *"Get out of here." Where is "here" anymore? Did I go sideways . . . or did they?*

She stood for a moment, listening. The silence reasserted itself, deep and whole, and the moon came out from behind a cloud.

Nita looked up at it and sighed, then turned and started making her way back to the farm. *I'm going to have to do something about these clothes before morning,* she thought. *I suppose the book has some laundry spells . . .* But she couldn't push the bigger problem out of her mind.

Without any spell worked by me, something came through from sideways. A lot of somethings.

I'm in deep, deep trouble . . .

Ath na Sceire

Enniskerry

THE NEXT MORNING NITA decided she would need expert help, and fast.

She pulled out her manual and began going through it looking for the names and addresses of the local Seniors. There were four Seniors for Ireland—one was on retirement leave, two were on active assignment and hence not available for consults, and one, the Area Senior, was located in a place called Castle Matrix. This impressed Nita, though not as much as it would have a couple of weeks before, when she had thought that probably half the people in Ireland lived in old castles. Now she hoped her business would take her that way . . . but you didn't go bothering the Area Advisory with a problem if you weren't sure it couldn't be handled at a less central level.

She therefore concentrated on the addresses of wizards in the Bray and Greystones area. There were about forty of these, which surprised her—she had been expecting fewer. Wizards on active status usually are only about one percent of the population, though in some places it can run as high as ten.

She looked the list up and down in mild perplexity. There was a problem in this part of the world; people tended not to use street numbers unless they lived in a housing estate. Sometimes they didn't even have a street, so that you might see an address that said, "Ballyvolan, Kilquade, County Wicklow"—and if you didn't know where Kilquade was, or what Ballyvolan was, or what road it was on, you were in trouble.

She sighed, ticked off a couple of names in Bray that did have street numbers. That done, she went to find her aunt Annie.

"Going out, are you?" Annie asked.

"Yeah. Aunt Annie, can you tell me where Boghall Road is?"

"The Boghall Road? That's, um, just off the back road between Greystones and Bray. What for?"

"Oh, I met somebody in one of the cafés in Bray yesterday, and I thought I might go over that way and see if I can find them." This was not entirely a fib— the sound and feel of Ronan's lean, edged, angry humor had kept coming back to her for the past day or so. It was just that the two phrases had nothing to do with each other, and if Aunt Annie thought they did, well . . . that was just fine.

Her aunt said, "Here, let me draw you a map."

"Oh, thank you!" Nita said with considerable gratitude. Her aunt sat down, sketched her a thumbnail map, and said, "If you get off the 45 bus here, at the top of Boghall, it's not a long walk to wherever you're going. That sound all right?"

"Fine, Aunt Annie . . . thanks."

"What time will you be back?"

"Not real late."

"All right. Call if you run into any problems. And take an umbrella or something: The weathermen have been predicting thundershowers."

"Will do." And she headed out.

She took the bus as far as a handy bit of woodland she had spotted not too far away from where the road from Greystones to Bray started downhill toward the town, just outside of the big Kilruddery estate. Nita had noticed it the other day—a stand of five cypresses, very big, very old. Generally the only people who walked up that way were the traveling people who lived in their trailers by the side of the road there.

So Nita popped into that grove of trees, looked around her, and paused for a moment. It was a matter of curiosity. Though you might have a sense of how many wizards were working in the area, there was one quick way to find out. It was difficult for a wizard to spend as much as a day without doing some wizardry, the Art being its own delight. She opened her manual, as she stood there under the trees in the summer sun, and quickly did the spell that showed one whatever active wizardries were working in an area. Ideally what happened was that the world blanked out and you were presented with a sort of schematic—points of light in a field—on which the real world was dimly overlaid. She did not get what she was expecting. Nita staggered back against one of the trees, half blinded. It was not just points of light that she was perceiving, but fields of it, whole patches of it—great tracts of residual wizardry that just had not gone away.

It's not supposed to do that! Nita thought. In theory the traces of a wizardry were gone by at least forty-eight hours later. *But this—!* It looked as if either the biggest wizardry on earth had been done here about two days ago, or else—and this concerned Nita more—all the wizardries done here in the past were still here, in residue.

She shut down the spell and stood there shaking. That last thought was not a good one. Doing a wizardry over another one, overlaying an old magic, was extremely dangerous. The two spells could synergize in ways that neither the wizard who wrought the original spell nor the one presently working could have expected. The results could be horrendous.

No wonder, she thought. *If that's the reason for last night, something like that— Was I working in an overlay area?* She called up the spell in memory for a moment more to look at it. All of Kilquade was covered by one big patch of residual wizardry; all of Bray was covered by another. There was, in fact, very little open space in this area that had not had a wizardry done on it at one time or another. She thought with horror of what might have happened had she done a teleportation spell closer to a more heavily overlaid area, like Bray. It was not a pleasant prospect at *all*.

She walked down the Boghall Road. It was a suburban street, with a church and a school at one end, a computer factory at the other end, and a baker's, little shops, and more houses and housing estates scattered along it or branching off from it. Mothers were out walking their babies in buggies; kids were out kicking soccer balls around.

Nita made her way to the address she was looking for, on a street called Novara Court, which branched off Boghall Road. All the houses here were very much the same. There was not much in the way of trees, as if people didn't want to block the view of Sugarloaf to the west or Bray Head immediately to the east. It was a handsome view.

Nita found the house but had an attack of shyness before she reached the doorstep. *How can I just go up and knock on the door and ask if there are wizards there?* But that was exactly what she needed to do, and there was no way out of it. Nita went up and rang the bell.

There was a long, long wait. *Oh good*, Nita was just thinking, *no one's home—* when the door was abruptly pulled open.

It was Ronan, from the chicken place.

He looked at her in astonishment.

She looked at him in much the same mood. Once again she was on the end of one of those coincidences of which wizards' lives are made, and which normal people (incorrectly) never take too seriously. A wizard, though, knows there are no coincidences. And she *had* told her aunt that she was coming to see him. *I've got to watch what I say around here!* And there was something else. An odd tremor—anticipation, a shiver down her back at the sight of him scowling at her, tall and dark, that she didn't quite know what to make of. . . .

"R. Nolan?" she asked. "Junior?"

"Yeah," he said, perplexed. "You're from—"

"I'm on errantry," Nita said, "and I greet you."

He stared at her with his mouth open. *"You?"* he asked.

"Me."

"You mean *you're* one of *us?*"

"Um." Nita made a wry face at him, and lowered her voice. "I've been places where the people had tentacles and more eyes than you have hairs," she said, "and they didn't make *this* much fuss about it. Can we talk? I require an advice."

It was the formal phrasing for a wizard on assignment who needed technical information. Ronan stared at her and said, "Just a minute. I'll get my jacket."

The door shut in her face, and Nita stood there on the doorstep, feeling like an idiot. After a moment Ronan came out again, and they walked. "Let's get out of here," he said. "I don't want to be seen."

Nita had to laugh at that, though she got an odd twinge of pain when he said it. *Not seen with me? Or what?* "What, am I contagious or something?" she asked, as they made their way down to the Boghall Road.

"No, it's just—" He didn't say what it was just. "Never mind. You mean *you're* a—"

"Can we stop having this part of the conversation?" Nita said, both irritated and amused. "There's more stuff to talk about. Listen. This going sideways thing—"

"What?"

"Going sideways," Nita said, getting a little more irritated. "I assume you know about it. Well, it's happened to me twice in the past three days, and I don't mind telling you that I don't like it very much—"

"You went *sideways?"* Ronan asked. "We're not *allowed* to go sideways—"

"Listen," Nita said, "maybe *you're* not allowed to go sideways, fine, but *I* did it, and not on purpose, let me tell you. Now I need to talk to someone and find out what's going on here, because last night I was almost eaten by wolves and nearly stepped on by an Irish elk!"

"Jeez," said Ronan, almost in awe.

Nita smiled slightly. "My feelings exactly," she said. Carefully she told him how things had been going for her since she arrived.

"You could have been killed!" Ronan said.

"Tell me something I don't know," Nita said. "And I would like to avoid being killed in the future! Is this kind of thing normal?"

"Not really," Ronan said. "At least, not for us. We're not supposed to be doing that kind of thing. This whole area is badly overlaid."

"I saw that," Nita said. "But look . . . this kind of thing isn't safe."

"You got *that* in one," Ronan said, looking grim. "Jeez, Kilquade, *Kilquade* was supposed to be comparatively quiet. Not like Bray—"

"Things have gotten very unquiet up that way," Nita said. "Do you have a Senior around here that we can go talk to? This is not good at all."

"Sure. She's up in Enniskerry."

"Then let's get up there. I'm on active, and I don't know what for, and if I can't do wizardry for fear of overlays I am going to have a nasty problem on my hands. Have you got your manual?"

He looked at her. "Manual?"

"You know. Your wizard's manual, where you get the spells and the ancillary data."

"You get them out of a *book*?"

Nita was confused. "Where else would you get them?"

Ronan looked at her as if she were very dim indeed. "The way we always have—the way the druids and bards did it for two, three thousand years, maybe more. We do it by memory!"

Now Nita's mouth fell open. "You learn the whole manual *by heart*? The whole body of spells?"

"Well, the basic stuff. You have to learn the basic incantations that make more detailed information available. But mostly, mostly you learn it by heart—the area restrictions, the address list—if a change happens, you usually just wake up knowing about it one morning—and you make sure you remember it." He shook his head. "Why? You mean you get it written down?"

Nita pulled out her manual and showed it to him. Ronan paged through it with a mixture of fascination and disgust. "I can't believe this. This makes it too easy!"

"Are you kidding? Do you have any idea how thick this thing can get sometimes? I think we have a little more information to deal with than you do over here."

"Don't be so sure," Ronan said, handing the manual back to her in some irritation. "We may be a smaller place than you Yanks have to deal with, but it's a lot more complicated."

They walked down the street, each in a state of mild annoyance with the other. "Look," Nita said, "let's not fight over details. Are there a lot of you working around here? How many of you are there?"

Ronan shook his head. "Not a lot, really. We don't seem able to keep a lot of our wizards after eighteen or so."

"Why? What happens?"

"Emigration," Ronan said. "To England and the States. There's not much work here. You may be a wizard, but you've got to have a job, too. You can't make food or money out of nothing . . . The universe doesn't allow it."

"No," Nita said.

Ronan looked at her with more annoyance. "But there are still a fair number of locals. Can't understand why they should put *you* on active all of a sudden."

"Mmmh," Nita said. "Possibly past experience." She didn't feel like going into much more detail. "Never mind that. Let's go and see your Senior."

"We'll have to take the bus," Ronan said.

Enniskerry was about four miles away. Their bus crossed the dual carriageway and then went up a twisty, turny route the locals called "the thirteen-bend road." It paralleled the Glencree River as it poured down through beautiful woodland. Occasional old houses were scattered along the way, but mostly the road was bounded by hedges on one side and walls on the other, and the river chattering on the far side of the hedge.

They sat in the top of the bus. "I can't believe it," Ronan kept saying. "I mean, a *Yank*—!"

"Some of us have to be wizards," Nita said, rolling her eyes. "You know that. We can't function *entirely* with immigrants from Ireland." She grinned at him wickedly.

"Well, I suppose. But books!"

"You should see my sister," Nita said. "She gets hers out of a computer."

"Jeez," Ronan said in wonder and disgust.

They arrived at Enniskerry village. It was a pretty place; there was a handsome little red-and-white hotel with peaked roofs, a pub, some small antique stores, a food shop, and a florist. In the middle of the town's triangular "square" was a wonderful Victorian clock tower with a domed top and a weathervane. "Do we get off here?" Nita asked.

"Not unless you want to spend ten minutes climbing the steepest hill you've ever seen."

"Noooo . . . I'll pass."

The bus paused in the square for a few minutes, then continued up the winding road, which led westward. Where the road topped out, near another housing estate and a little store, they got off. Ronan turned and began to walk back down the hill. "It's over here," he said.

They walked partway down the hill and crossed the road to a pair of wooden gates between two pillars, one of which had the words KILGARRON HOUSE painted on it. "Wow," Nita said.

There was a little side gate; Ronan opened it for her, and they stepped through. Inside was a curving driveway leading to a large two-story house. Square and blocky, it might have been a farmhouse once. It had a beautiful view of the Dargle Valley, leading down toward Bray, and also of the church and water meadow just down the hill.

They went up to the door and knocked. There was a long pause, and then a little old lady came to the door. She was fresh faced and smooth skinned, and only the fact that her hair was quite silver really gave away much about her age. She was a bit stocky, with sharp, intelligent eyes. "Morning, Mrs. Smyth," said Ronan.

"And good morning to you," she said in a faintly Scots accent. "Are you on business or pleasure?"

"Business," Ronan said, nodding at Nita. "She's on errantry."

"I greet you, ma'am," Nita said, as she would have said to an American Senior she was being introduced to. The lady blinked at her.

"Are you on active status?"

"Yes'm. At least the manual says so."

"Then you'd better come in and have a cup of tea, and tell me what it's all about."

Nita rolled her eyes slightly at the prospect of yet another cup of tea, and resigned herself to the inevitable.

They were made comfortable in the sitting room, and the tea was brought out, and Mrs. Smyth poured it formally for them, and gave them cookies and sandwiches and cakes, and encouraged them to eat more before she would let them tell her anything about what was going on. Then Nita began to explain, as she had to Ronan. When she mentioned Tualha, and a few of the things the kitten had talked about, Mrs. Smyth's eyes widened. When Nita mentioned going sideways, Mrs. Smyth's jaw almost dropped. "My dear," she said. "I hope you understand that you must not do that again."

"Ma'am, I didn't do it on purpose the first time. Or the third. The only time I did it on purpose was when I looked at Sugarloaf. I won't do it again."

"I wonder . . ." Mrs. Smyth said. "Well. Something is certainly in the wind. We're coming up on Lughnasád; I'd be surprised if it didn't have something to do with that."

Ronan bit his lip. Nita looked from one of them to the other. "I hope you'll forgive me if I don't know what's going on here," she said, "but if I'm going to be on active status . . ."

"No, indeed. Lughnasád is one of the four great holidays—with Beltain, Samhain, and Imbolc. It used to be the harvest festival, a long time ago: People would celebrate the first crops coming in. And it also celebrated the turning of the heat of the summer toward the cooler weather."

"The heat of the summer?" Nita said, mildly skeptical. So far it had only gotten up into the high seventies.

Mrs. Smyth blinked at her. "Oh, you're used to it warmer where you live? We're not, though. I think the drought is just about official now, isn't it, Ronan?"

"They said they were going to start water rationing," Ronan said.

"So," said Mrs. Smyth. "I suppose that's another indication as well. Anyway, Nita's quite right; if this is allowed to continue, even the nonwizardly will start to notice it . . . and be endangered by it. This is, mmm, an undesirable outcome."

Nita couldn't help but laugh at that. "But what are you going to do about it?"

"Well, I think we're going to have to get together and discuss the matter."

"But if you don't *do* something—"

"My dear," Mrs. Smyth said, "you come from a very . . . energetic . . . school of wizardry. I appreciate that. But we do things a little more slowly here. No, we need to call the local wizards and the Area Supervisors together, and discuss what needs to be done. It'll take a day at least."

Nita chafed at that. It seemed to her that a day might be too long. But she was a stranger here, and theoretically these people knew best. "What do you think they'll decide?" Ronan said.

Mrs. Smyth shook her head. "It's hard to say. If we have here a rising of the old sort—a reassertion of the events associated with this holiday—then normally one would also have to reassert, reenact, the events that stopped whatever thing it was that happened."

"But what was it that happened?" Nita said.

"The second battle of Moytura," Ronan said. "I suppose you won't have heard about it—"

"I've heard about it," Nita said. "A little cat told me. In considerable detail."

"A cat told you?"

"Yeah. She said she was a bard, and—"

Mrs. Smyth looked at Nita in surprise. "You mentioned this before, but we didn't pursue it. How old was this cat?"

"She's a kitten. Not very old . . . maybe ten weeks." Nita told them, as well as she could remember, everything Tualha had told her.

"That is interesting," Mrs. Smyth said. "Normally cat-bards aren't born unless there's about to be some change in the ruled world, the animal world—as well as the human one. And she mentioned the Carrion-Crow, did she?"

Nita nodded. "I get a feeling that's not good?"

Ronan made a face. "The Morrigan is trouble," he said. "She turns up in the old stories, sometimes as a war goddess, or sometimes as three of them."

"It's the usual problem," Mrs. Smyth said, "of the language not being adequate to describe the reality. The Morrigan is one of the Powers, a much diminished one . . . though even the lesser Powers were often mistaken for gods in the ancient times. She has become, or made herself, the expression of change and violence. There was a lot of that around here in the old days," she said, and sighed. "And now. But she's also the peace afterward . . . if people will just let it be. Carrion-Crow she might be, but the crows are the aftermath of the battle, nature's attempt to clean it up . . . not the cause of it." Mrs. Smyth turned her teacup around. "It's dangerous to see her . . . but not always bad. She shows herself as a tall, dark woman, a fierce one. But she almost always smiles. She *is* Ireland, in some ways: one of its personifications. Or its hauntings."

She looked up at Ronan again. "So, the Morrigan . . . and the Hunt. Some very old memories are being resurrected. The foxhunt's running must have reminded the world of an older hunt over the same ground."

"What were those animals?" Nita said. "They looked like dire wolves, but they had some kind of werelight around them."

"They were faery dire wolves," Mrs. Smyth said, "from one of the companion worlds."

"Who was following them?" Nita said.

Mrs. Smyth looked at her. "I see by the Knowledge," she said, "that you've had a certain amount of dealing with the Other. The head of the Fomori—the Lone Power. I should say, a dangerous amount of dealings with It."

"I don't deal *with* It," Nita said. "Against It, possibly." She began to get angry. "I don't think you need to doubt which side I'm on. Are you saying that you think I'm attracting this trouble?"

Wizards do not tell white lies to make people feel better. Mrs. Smyth said nothing.

"Well, if I'm here for that purpose," Nita said, "I'm here because the Powers That Be sent me. If I'm a trigger, it's Their finger that's on me, not the Lone One's. The Lone One can't move wizards . . . you know that."

"I do know that," Mrs. Smyth said. "There have been changes in the Lone One recently, and you had something to do with those."

"Something," Nita said.

Ronan looked at her, and then back at Mrs. Smyth. "Her?"

"She was involved just now in the Song of the Twelve," Mrs. Smyth said. Ronan looked at her wide-eyed. "She was also involved in—Well, never mind. It's a distinguished start—if you and your partner survive, of course. Wizardly talent is usually tested to destruction. Your sister," Mrs. Smyth said, "where is she now? Did she come with you?"

"No, she's back in New York."

"Pity," Mrs. Smyth said. "At any rate, I advise you to keep your use of wizardry to the minimum. Ronan, you'll want to speak to your friends among the locals, especially the young ones. If anyone finds themselves going sideways, tell them not to meddle."

"What kind of reenactment were you thinking of doing?" Nita said.

"Well, my dear," Mrs. Smyth said, "we have a problem. If there's a reenactment of Moytura to be done, we don't have anything to do it *with*, even though three of the Treasures still exist."

"What do you mean, you don't have anything to do it with?"

"Nita," Mrs. Smyth said, "it took one of the Powers That Be a very long time to invest those objects with strength enough to function against the Lone Power in the form It took. The legend says that anything that the Lone One in Balor's form beheld with his eye open burst straightaway into fire and fell as ash, and poisoned the ground for leagues around so that nothing would grow there, and men who walked that ground died."

"Sounds nuclear," Nita said.

"So it might have been," Mrs. Smyth said. "The Lone One has never minded using natural phenomena for Its own ends. But Its power was so terrible that only an army of all the wizards in Ireland—for that's what the druids were—could even think about going up against It; and without the Treasures to protect them, they all would have been destroyed. The cup, known as the Cauldron of Rebirth, raised up their fallen; the sword, Fragarach the Answerer, held off Balor's creatures; and the Stone of Destiny kept the ground of Ireland whole and rooted when Balor's dark ships would have dragged it off its foundations and overturned the whole island into the deep. All the Treasures' power together, and all the wizards', was just enough to buy the time for the Spear of Lugh to pierce Balor's fire and quench it at last."

She took a sip of her tea. "Now, three of the four Treasures we still have—at least one of them is in the National Museum in Dublin. But they have no virtue anymore. No one *believes* that the gold-and-silver cup they have there, the Ardagh Chalice, is actually the Well of Transformations, the Bottomless Cauldron. No one really *believes* that the poor old notched bronze blade in the glass case is Fragarach, even though the legends say so. Its virtue has long since ebbed away as a result:

The soul in it, if you like, has departed. And the Lia Fail is now just a cracked stone half-buried in the ground somewhere up north, with an iron picket fence around it, and tourists come and take its picture because it's supposed to be Saint Patrick's gravestone or some such. Not because of what it really is, or was." Her smile was rueful. "The thousands of years and the loss of true *knowledge* of the nature of the Protectors have taken them and made them just a cup, just a sword, and a rock."

"What about the spear?"

"Its soul was the strongest of all of the Treasures," Mrs. Smyth said. "It should be the easiest to find . . . but it's nowhere in the world that we can feel. No, what we're going to do—if a reenactment—" She sighed. "I'd say we might have to wake up what's left of the Treasures. We're going to have to work something out from scratch. In the meantime, if I were you, I would step lightly. And thank you for coming to me. Where are you staying?"

"With my aunt, Anne Callahan, at Ballyvolan."

"Right," said Mrs. Smyth, and made a note. "Now then, another cup of tea?" Nita groaned.

Nita and Ronan went down to the little tea shop in Enniskerry and had a Coke to kill the time until the bus was ready to leave. "She's not much like the Seniors at home," Nita said, thoughtful, "except she's as tough."

Ronan was sitting slumped in his chair, his legs crossed, scowling out at her from under those black brows. The hair rose a little on Nita's neck, and she started to blush, and felt extremely stupid. "Just because she's not like your precious Seniors," he said.

"Ronan, just shut your face. You think you're the hottest thing on wheels, don't you?" And Nita scowled back at him, mostly to cover her own confusion at her anger. "You've got a chip on your shoulder the size of a two-by-four, and you'd better do something about it before it ruins your wizardry. And I'm not one of your little herd of head-nodders, so don't waste your dirty looks on me. You don't like the news, that's just tough."

He stared at Nita, and his expression had changed slightly when she dared to look at him again. He looked a little shocked, still angry; but there was an odd thread of liking there. "No," he said softly, "you're not one of them, are you? Girls have mean mouths where you come from."

She blushed again, feeling more like an idiot than ever, not understanding her own discomfort. "Wizards tell the truth where I come from," she said, annoyed. "I wasn't criticizing your Senior, as you would have discovered if you'd let me finish. Your manners need work, too."

"And what else needs work?" he said, that same odd soft tone.

She just looked at him, and her insides roiled. That dark regard was disconcerting when it was bent hard on you—worse still when he was smiling. *He really is pretty cool*, she thought, somewhat to her own horror. She wondered for a moment what some of the girls at school would think of this guy if they had a chance to see him. She knew what they would think, and what they would say. He was the kind of guy who gets notes passed about him all day, the kind that girls look at from the safety of groups, stealing glances, laughing softly together at their shared thoughts about him. *What would you do if you got him alone . . . ?*

And she *was* alone with him.

"Hulloooo!" he said to her, waving a hand in front of her face. "Earth to Nita!"

"Uh, what?" she said hurriedly. She finished her Coke in one gulp. "Listen, the bus is starting up."

"What's the hurry? I don't hear—" From outside there came a roar of diesel engine. Ronan looked at Nita oddly, then grinned. She flushed again and inwardly swore at herself. *Oh, he is cute. This is awful!*

"Can't keep the man waiting," Ronan said, and got up. "You going to come with?"

"Uh, no, I'll walk it. Fresh air," she said, mortified at the feebleness of the excuse. "Exercise."

"As far as the bus stop, then."

Reluctantly she walked out to see him that far.

"Do you have my number?" Ronan said as he got on. "Call me if you have any problems."

Problems! Do I have problems! Sweet Powers That Be . . . "I'll do that," Nita said. "You're in the book."

Ronan made an annoyed face. "I can't *believe* this," he said, and the bus doors shut in front of him.

Nita started home to Kilquade. It was a longish walk, but she was really beginning to enjoy the walking. This was one of the prettiest places she had ever been, and the quiet and the sound of the wind and the warm, fair weather were all conspiring to make it very pleasant.

She couldn't get rid of the look of Ronan's face, the whole feel of him, the uneasy, uncomfortable sense of—power: There was no other word for it. Add to that the fact that he was good-looking, and funny, when he wasn't angry—even then—Nita smiled grimly at herself, annoyed: It was funny to want someone to whom she also wanted to give a few good kicks.

Heaven help me, that's what it is. I've got a crush on him.

The admission made her nervous. Neither her parents nor the sex education classes at school ever told her anything really useful about how to *handle* this kind of thing. Oh, the mechanics of it, body changes and so forth, and how not to catch diseases, and responsibility, and family planning. Not important stuff, like kissing—how do you do it and still breathe? Is not wearing a bra a come-on? Is it worth it to chase someone, or will that just make you look stupid? And if you catch him, what do you do then?

Or what do you do if you get caught?

Nita heard something stirring in the hedge off to the right. At first she thought it was a bird—lots of birds nested in these hedges, encouraged by the thorns—but this sounded too loud. Nita paused, and saw a flash of color, a soft, russet red.

"Ai elhua," whispered a voice in the Speech, "I have a word for you."

Nita's eyebrows went up. She hunkered down by the hedge. The red dog-fox was deep inside it, curled up comfortably in a little niche in the wall the hedge grew against.

"Madreen rua!" she said. "Are you all right?"

"Oh yes. But that *you* may be—" The fox glanced around, a shifty, conspiratorial look. "And that I may repay a debt and all things be even again. There are wizardries afoot."

"No kidding."

"Then you should get help for those wizardries. One of the Ard-Tuatha de Danaan is in hide, not half a mile from here."

Nita was confused: There were several different ways to translate the term. "*Ard*—You mean, one of the Powers That Be? *Here*?"

"In truth. We are bound, we are all bound not to say exactly where, or who. But It is one of the Old Ones. Catch It at Its work, and It must help you, yes?"

"That's one way to put it." Nita frowned. The Powers That Be were required to assist wizards when requested to do so. But you had to catch Them first . . . and They usually made that difficult, preferring to do Their work in secret. That made it harder for the Lone Power to sabotage Them.

"Well," she said. "I am warned, *madreen rua*. My thanks."

"All's even," the fox said, and in the tiny space where it lay, it somehow managed to get up, turn around, and vanish back through a dark hole under the wall.

Nita got up and went on, trying to make sense of what the fox had told her. *It's hard to believe. Why would one of the Powers be hanging around* here?

She made her way down the little lane to her aunt's driveway and the farm. In the field to the right, Aunt Annie was heading off with a rake over her shoulder, probably to do something about the new potatoes she had just planted. They were a rare breed, something called fir-apple potatoes, and Aunt Annie raked and weeded them herself every day and wouldn't let anyone near them.

Nita grinned at this and went inside. She was making herself a sandwich in the kitchen when the phone began to ring. Nita ran for it, picked it up, and as she had heard others do, said, "Ballyvolan."

"Is Mrs. Callahan there?"

"No, she's not . . . Can I take a message for you?"

"Yes, please. Tell her that Shaun O'Driscoll called, and ask her to call back immediately; it's very urgent."

"All right." Nita scribbled down the message and said, "I'll see if I can catch her; she just went out. Bye." And she ran out across the gravel yard, vaulted the fence, and headed into the field.

Far away, over the hill of the second field, she could see her aunt walking toward the little rise in the middle of it. Yelling at her seemed ridiculous at this point, so Nita just ran after her as quickly as she could, puffing.

She was rather surprised to see her aunt take the rake off her shoulder and bang the wooden end of it on the ground.

She was even more surprised when the little hill split open and her aunt walked into the fissure.

Nita stopped and stood very still for a moment, and her mouth fell open.

Oh no! she thought. And she remembered Tom, her local Senior wizard, saying to her father, "Well, you know, Ed, it's *your* side of the family that the wizardry comes down from . . ."

My dad's sister . . .

My aunt's a wizard!

Nita ran after her, toward the gaping darkness in the side of the hill.

Faoin gCnoc

Under the Hill

THE FISSURE WAS DEEPER and wider than it looked. *Is this happening in my world?* Nita thought, and paused for a moment to try to see with double vision, as she had the other day. True enough, mere daylight vision showed her a smooth hill, no crack, nothing. But then no one in the house had seen her aunt . . . and *she* had. Nita was seeing sideways where her aunt was, and this was sideways, too. Not as sideways as it might have been, of course.

"Aunt Annie," she said, not loud, but urgently and with enough volume to carry. Ahead of her, her aunt stopped in shock, standing there with the rake.

She looked back at Nita and said, "Oh no."

"Aunt Annie," Nita said, grinning a little in spite of herself, "what *did* they tell you about why they'd sent me here?"

Aunt Annie's mouth opened and shut, and then she said, "When I get my hands on Ed . . . I'm going to pull his head off and hand it to him."

"They couldn't exactly tell you," Nita said, immediately wanting to defend her father. "It's not his fault."

"Maybe not," Aunt Annie said, "but, Nita! I had no idea!"

"Actually, I was hoping you wouldn't," Nita said, wryly. "I don't usually try to advertise it."

"But how can you *be* here?" Aunt Annie said. Then she shook her head. "Never mind that now. That you're here means you're intended to be. I've got business. Let's go see them."

"Them?"

"Be polite," Aunt Annie said. "And follow my lead."

Nita was entirely willing. She followed her aunt into the hill.

It was not a hill. It was a city. It was like the one that Nita had seen crowning Sugarloaf, but smaller, more intimate. It could not, of course, be inside the hill. It was two, three—ten? fifty?—universes over from Nita's world: broad streets, airy shade, the sound of running water, stone as fluidly formed as if it had been clay once, or flesh—but paused in mid-movement, possibly to move again someday. The buildings showed hints of thatched houses and old castles and castles no human being could have imagined, hints of architecture Nita recognized as extraterrestrial from her travels: Apparently the builders had had connections elsewhere.

The light was different, too: harder, somehow clearer than the light that rested on the fields around Aunt Annie's farm. Things seemed to have sharper edges, more weight, more meaning. Nothing here needed to glow with magical light or anything so blatant. Things here were too busy being *real* . . . more real even than the "real world." It was a slightly unnerving effect.

"Oh, and one other thing," her aunt said. "Don't eat or drink anything here."

Nita burst out laughing. "There had to be *one* place in Ireland where no one was going to make me drink tea or eat anything," she said.

Her aunt looked at her cockeyed, then laughed. "Well, you keep thinking of it that way."

They walked on among the high houses. "Where are we going?" Nita asked.

"To talk to the people who live here," said her aunt. "I do have certain rights. This is my land—I am the landowner—" She chuckled then. "As if anyone in Ireland can really *own* land. We all just borrow it for a while." She glanced at Nita. "Where were you last night?"

"I was out with some very, very large things that should have been wolves, but weren't," Nita said. "Oh, by the way. There was a phone call for you. A Shaun O'Driscoll—"

"I just bet," said Aunt Annie. "The Area Senior. Well, we'll see him shortly, but I need to deal with these first."

"These people—"

"You know the name," her aunt said. "We don't usually say it; it's considered impolite. Like shouting at someone, 'Hey, human!' "

The Sidhe, Nita thought. *The people of the hills . . . the not-so-little little people.* "You see them often?" Nita said.

"Often enough. 'Good fences make good neighbors,' as the poet says. However, every now and then, when you share common ground, you need to have a good long chat over the fence. That's what this is about."

They came to the heart of the city. There were twelve trees in a circle, and three bright chairs under the trees, seemingly resting on the surface of a pool of water. Or rather, the chairs on either side of the central one were true chairs; the central one was a throne. The trees moved in the wind, and the shadows thrown by their branches wove and shifted on the surface of the bright water in patterns that seemed to Nita to be always on the edge of meaning. People stood around and watched from under the shade of those trees: tall people, fair people, with beautiful dogs at heel. Handsome cats sat here and there, watching; unconcerned birds sang rainbows in the trees. Nita tried to look at a few of the people and found it difficult. It wasn't that they were indistinct. They were almost too solid to bear, and their clothes and weapons, in an antique style, all shone with certainty and existence.

The chairs on either side of the throne were filled; a man sat in one, a woman in the other. The throne was empty. Aunt Annie walked straight toward the three seats, across the water. Nita watched with professional interest. She knew several ways to walk on water, but she felt safe in assuming that the water here was more assertive and didn't mind being walked on without more active spelling. She headed out after her aunt.

Aunt Annie stopped about ten feet away from the central throne, acknowledged it with a slight nod, and then looked at the person sitting in the right-hand chair. "The greeting of gods and men to you, Amadaun of the Queen of the Hill in Cualann. And to you, Lady of this Forth."

The lady bowed her head. "To you also, *Aoine ni Cealodhain,* greeting," said the man in the right-hand chair. "And greeting to you, *Shonaiula ni Cealodhain.*"

Nita was slightly out of her depth, but she knew how to be polite. She bowed slightly and said, "I am on errantry, fair people, and the One greets you by me."

"This we had known," said the woman in the chair.

"Then perhaps you will explain to me," said Aunt Annie, "why my niece was chased halfway across my field last night by *that one's* hunt. I thought we had an agreement that if you saw any power of that kind waking, you would warn me so that I could take appropriate action."

"We had no warning ourselves, *Aoine*," said the woman.

"I would then appreciate your view of what's happening here. It's most unusual for you to have no warning of so major an intrusion. That you didn't means we have trouble on our hands."

"Trouble rarely comes near us, *Aoine*. But it would be true to say that the past is becoming troublesome. We have had a messenger at our gates . . . one of the Fomori."

"And what did this messenger say?"

"That the old shall become new in our fields, and yours. He offered us . . . what we were offered once before: the end of your kind, once and for all."

Aunt Annie said nothing. The young man, the Amadaun, looked at Nita and said, "You must understand that the children of the Milesians are not looked upon with favor in some of the Fifth House."

"If you mean that some of the nonhuman species think humans were a dumb idea," Nita said, "yes, I've heard that opinion before."

"There are those Powers in this part of the world, and children of the Powers— Powers fallen lower than we—who never looked kindly on human folk and would be glad to see them all dead. At their own hands, or by the hands of other humans— so that old angers are inflamed, and old hatreds seem to live uncannily long."

"Yes," Nita said, "I've noticed that."

"It is the land, of course," said the fair young woman. "The land remembers too well. It saw Partholon come; it saw Nemed; it saw us, and the Fir Bolg, and the hosts of man. It threw us off, one after the other, in its way, having been taught to do so by the Lone One, and was given a memory that other lands don't have—a sense of injury. Long time we've tried to heal that, but there is no healing it now. The old angers waken again and again."

"There must be something that could be done," Nita said.

"If there is an answer, we do not have it," said the Lady of the Forth, "and the Fomori are at our gates. Soon enough they'll be at yours."

"They have been at *our* gates, they and their children, for a long while," said Aunt Annie, "under various names. We do what we can, as do you. What are the Fomori threatening you with this time?"

"Nothing concrete as yet. Of course they demanded tribute. They have done that before. We will, of course, refuse to give it; we have done that before, too. And then they will begin to strike, here and there, at the innocent, the ones who have no defense."

"That too we know about," said Aunt Annie, "for a long time now. Nonetheless, something needs to be done. I think all the wizards will now be called together. Probably there should be another meeting between us once that has happened. Doing seems to have passed into our hands, these days, and out of yours."

"That seems to be true," said the Amadaun. "Advise us what you do. We will back you as far as possible. Meantime, rain has not fallen here for too long. We seem to be losing the ability to order our world as we used to. Something outside is becoming very strong . . . and Lughnasád is coming, when old battles are remembered. Even with the power of the Treasures, it was very close. We almost lost last time. Without the Treasures—" The form on the left shook her head. "There is no saying. We need your help."

"Keep your people in, then, if you would," said Aunt Annie. "Sideways and the not-sideways parts of the world are getting too close together at the moment; we need to part them until this is resolved."

"We will do that. And you"—the Amadaun looked at Nita—"what would you say to us?"

Nita looked at the shining forms all around her and shook her head. "I think you owe me one," she said. "For the other night. If your carelessness let that happen, I think you owe me a favor one of these days."

There were shocked looks at her boldness, and Aunt Annie looked at her askance. But there was a wry smile from the Amadaun. "Our people have long known that a favor given must be returned, and a wrong done must be avenged," he said. "Come here, then, and let me speak a word in your ear."

Nita stepped up to him, wondering. The Amadaun leaned over and whispered; and the hair stood up all over Nita. It was a word in the Speech, a name . . . but not the kind of name mortals had. There was too much power in it, and too much time. She glanced at the Amadaun in shock, met his eyes, and found no relief there: The time was in them, too.

"Should you need help," the Amadaun said, "name that name."

"Thank you," Nita said, trying to get some of her composure back. "I'll do that. Meanwhile, I hope you do well and that things are quiet for you."

"A mortal wishes what we wish," said the Lady of the Forth, smiling. "There's a change."

"Thank you," said Aunt Annie.

Nita rejoined her, and together they walked out the way they had come. The sunlight looked thin and wan when they came out, when it should have looked golden; everything seemed a little unreal, a little fake, compared with the way it had looked earlier.

Nita looked at Aunt Annie and was a little surprised to find that she had sweat standing out on her forehead. "Are you OK?" she said. "You look pale."

"I'm all right," said Aunt Annie. "It's just a strain talking to those people. They don't see time the way we do."

"I kind of liked it in there," Nita said.

Her aunt looked at her. "Yes, I thought you might. They prefer the young; the younger wizards have always bent a little more easily to their ways. I make *them* uneasy, too; I'm a little too close to mortality for their liking . . . But anyway, I still can't believe it. You're a wizard!"

"At times I find it hard to believe myself," Nita said. "Like last night. My wizardry was not working terribly well."

"Yes, it's a problem we have around here," said her aunt. "The overlays . . . If I'd known, I could have warned you."

"How could you have known? How was I supposed to tell you?" She broke out laughing. "What *did* they tell you when they sent me out here?"

Her aunt shook her head. "They said you were getting too involved with your friend Kit. He's your partner, I take it."

"Yeah. They're really nervous about it, Aunt Annie. I try to calm them down . . ."

"Listen, you're lucky. At least you were able to tell your folks. I was never able to tell your grandma and grandpa."

"Even when they know," Nita said drily, "it doesn't always make for the best of times. But Aunt Annie, look, what are we going to *do*?"

"We can't do anything just yet."

Nita groaned. Her aunt looked at her with a sympathetic expression. "Look, honey, I know. But the tradition of wizardry is different in this part of the world. They've been doing it for thousands of years before there even *were* American wizards. And don't forget that at home you're working in a relatively clean environment; the magic of the Native American wizards was of a much more naturalistic kind. There was practically no overlay, since their wizardry worked so completely in conjunction with nature and the environment. Over here we're dealing with the equivalent of wizardly toxic waste . . . the accumulation of thousands of years of buildup. No, we take our time. We need to get everyone together to talk."

"When is this Lughnasád thing?"

"It starts tomorrow, really—"

"Tomorrow?!"

"It goes on for two weeks . . . don't panic. The first week is the beginning of it; August fifteenth is the end. It's the end that we have to worry about. Things will be building up; forces will have to be released. It's going to be like a dam breaking. If we can dig a channel somehow, something for the power, the flow, to run off into . . . Otherwise—"

"Otherwise even the nonwizards are going to notice."

Her aunt laughed. "Nita, nonwizards have been noticing for *years*. Fortunately, Ireland just has a reputation for being a strange place. So when people hear these weird stories, they discount them . . . It's not always a bad thing: For example, this is one of the only places in Europe where there were almost no witch trials. People were simply so used to bizarre things happening that there didn't seem any point . . . *Everyone* knew someone who was a little strange . . . But, meantime, we'll get the wizards together and talk to them. Until then, try to restrain yourself. I know the urge to do wizardry all the time is very strong, especially at your age. But don't—you know—just *don't*."

And that was the last that was said about it for a while. Aunt Annie went into the farm office, shut herself in, and started making phone calls. Nita returned to her trailer to do some more reading from the manual.

As she turned the corner, she froze in surprise: The trailer shifted slightly as she looked at it. Someone was in there. She paused and tried to see through the window before going any closer. Inside, someone bent forward into the light: A shadow moved—

She ran to the trailer door and threw it open. On the bed, Kit looked up in surprise, blinked at her. "Hi, Neets. What's the scoop?"

Nita stood there with her mouth working and nothing coming out. "What are you *doing* here?" she said finally.

Kit opened his mouth, too, and closed it, and then said, "I thought you'd be glad to see me."

"You turkeybrain, I *am* glad to see you! But what are you doing *here*? I thought—"

"Oh." Kit turned red, then started laughing. "Neets, uh, I feel like a dork."

She withheld comment for the moment. "Oh?"

"Well, I mean, you promised your folks that *you* wouldn't come back to see me. But *I* never said anything of the kind. No one asked me. So I said to my mom, 'I have to go out for a while, I'll be back for dinner.' And she said, 'Fine, have a nice time . . .' "

Nita climbed into the trailer, sat down on the bed and began laughing. "You're kidding."

"Neets," Kit said, "I think they still don't get it about me being a wizard. Not really. But who cares? As long as I come home on time for dinner, no one minds me being here."

"Great! Come meet my aunt."

She dragged him inside. Her aunt had taken a break from phone calls to feed the cats, and now stood there looking at Kit with a can of cat food in her hand. "Aunt Annie," Nita shouted, "this is Kit!"

"Ah." Her aunt blinked. "Half a second, then, and I'll feed him, too."

Nita snickered, sat Kit down at the table, and started making tea. Out of the tangle of mewing and hollering cats, one detached itself and strolled over to the kitchen table, jumped up on it, and regarded Kit with big eyes. It was Tualha. "And who is this?" she said.

Nita had to laugh a little at Kit's expression. "Kit, Tualha. She's a bard. Tualha, Kit Rodrigues. He's a wizard."

"*Dai stihó,*" said Kit.

"*Slán,*" said the cat, looking him up and down. To Nita she said, "I see the Spanish have finally arrived."

"What?"

"Kit, don't get her started. She'll be reciting poetry at you in a minute."

"I don't mind that."

"So listen," Nita's aunt said, coming over to the table and sitting down as she dried her hands on a dishcloth. "Kit, you're welcome here, but one question. Do your parents know you're a wizard?"

"Oh yeah."

She shook her head. "It's getting easier these days than it used to be." She looked at Nita, and then at Kit, and at Nita again. "Listen," she said, "I want the straight word from you on this. You two aren't doing what your mom and dad were concerned you were doing—I mean, what they told me they thought you were doing? Are you?"

She had the grace to look embarrassed as she said it. Nita and Kit could do nothing but look at each other and then burst out laughing. "Why does everyone think that?" Kit said, sounding momentarily aggrieved. "Do we go around panting at each other or something?" Then he lost it and cracked up again.

"No," Nita said to Aunt Annie. "We're not."

"Well," said her aunt, "never mind, then. It's matters here that really concern me, and I've got enough on my plate at the moment. You know anything about it?"

"There was a précis in the manual of what's been going on here," Kit said. He sighed. "We've got problems."

That *we* was one of the nicest things Nita had heard in a long time. She had had enough of working by herself. "Yeah. Well, the Seniors here seem to have at least a handle on what to do. I just hope it works. Did you read about that?"

"Yeah. It seems they've already made some progress. There's a stone—is it?— that they had to wake up—"

"It was half awake already," Nita said. "It's the other three objects that are going to be a problem."

"Yeah. They said one of the objects was 'dormant,' and another was 'unaccounted for.' That doesn't sound terrific."

"Nope."

"Listen," Aunt Annie said, "I'll leave you two to chat. I've got to get back on the phone." She smiled at them and headed out of the room.

"Phone? What for?"

"Other wizards," Nita said.

Kit looked mystified. "To just talk to them? Why don't they—"

"NO, DON'T DO THAT!" she yelled, sitting bolt upright as she felt him casually starting to line up the beam-me-up spell in his head. "You can't do that here!"

"Why not?"

"Feel around you for the overlays! They're all over the place! And you better watch how you go home, too."

He paused a moment, and then looked surprised. "Wow, you're not kidding. How do you get around here?"

"I walk. Or there's a bike to ride."

"Well, let's go do that, then. Sounds like I've got a lot of catching up to do."

Nita slipped into the office, bent over Aunt Annie at her desk, scribbled a note on her pad: *Going out bike riding, OK?* Her aunt nodded and went right on with her conversation about spell structure.

They were out for a long time . . . partly because Kit was rubbernecking at the scenery while they walked and talked. But part of it was the weather turning odd. The thunderstorms the weathermen had been predicting materialized, but they dropped hail rather than rain. Nita and Kit had to take shelter from several of the showers, and when they finally got down to the dual carriageway again, they found hailstones as big as marbles lying on the road, steaming bizarrely in the bright sunshine. The sound of thunder rumbled miles away, sporadic but threatening, all through the ride.

They had been taking turns riding, or sometimes Kit would ride and Nita would sit on the handlebars, or the other way around. At the moment Kit was walking the bike beside Nita, looking around appreciatively. "This is great," he said. "I guess if you had to be sent someplace, this is as good as any."

"Huh," Nita said. "I don't remember you being real excited about it at first."

He colored somewhat. "Yeah, well."

Nita grinned. "Listen, how's Dairine doing?"

"OK, as far as I can tell. I think she may be on assignment; she doesn't seem to have been around your place much in the past few days. Busy."

"I bet. Wizards all over the place are real busy around now." Nita shook her head. The oppressive, thunderstorm-about-to-happen feeling had not stopped.

"Here it comes," Kit said, looking up at a thundercloud they had been watching. It was drifting halfway between them and the sea as they turned down the Kilquade road. Almost as soon as he spoke, Nita saw the bolt of lightning lance down and strike one of the hills behind the farm. Silently she started counting seconds, and had barely gotten to two before the crack of thunder washed over them. "A little too close," said Kit. "Let's get inside."

They headed down the driveway in a hurry, and came to the gravel yard in front of the house. Nita was heading for the front door when Kit looked around him with a sudden surprised expression. "Wait a minute. What's that?" he said.

"That *what*?" Nita was feeling a little cross. She could feel the rain coming in the air and didn't want to stand around outside waiting for it, after all she'd been through today.

"That," Kit said, swinging around as if looking for something. "Can't you feel it? Inanimate. Strong."

Nita shook her head, wondering what he was talking about. Kit was staring down toward the farmyard, between the buildings. "There's something going on down there," he said. "Something alive."

"This place is full of horses and sheep and cows," Nita said. "Kit—"

"No," he said. "Not something that's usually alive. It's inanimate, it's a thing, it's—come on!"

He started down that way. There was another roll of thunder. Nita didn't see the lightning stroke this time. She went after Kit, muttering to herself. Kit frequently sensed things she didn't, just as she sensed things he didn't. They had areas where their talents overlapped, certainly, but Nita's specialty was live things; Kit had always been more for inanimate objects. And if he really felt he was on the trail of something important—

"It's really weird," he said as she caught up with him. "It's nothing—I've never felt one that alive before."

"One *what*?"

He looked into the farmyard and shook his head and gestured. "That," he said.

Nita looked. There was nothing in the farmyard but Biddy's pickup truck, with its forge on the back. *"That?"*

"It's not the truck itself," Kit said. "That's a little more awake than usual, but nothing really strange. It's the thing in back. That box. What is that?"

"It's a forge, a portable forge," Nita said, mystified. "It belongs to the lady who shoes the horses."

Right then, Biddy came out of the hay barn, shrugging into a windbreaker. She looked up at the sky, pausing for a moment, then headed toward the truck.

"Uh-oh," Kit said, looking up with a panicked expression.

Nita felt the electrical potential in the air become suddenly unbearable, not just a prickling but a pain all over her. It took Nita only a second to put up a shield spell around herself and Kit. She saw Biddy look up; she saw the lightning lance down at the truck. The breath went right out of Nita in horror, for there was simply no way she could quickly extend her shield so far—

Biddy lifted her hand abruptly—

—and the lightning simply went elsewhere. It didn't strike anything else, it didn't miss; it just stopped. And went away. There was not even a thunderclap.

And Biddy stood there, looking up at the sky, and glanced around, looking to see whether anyone had been watching. Seeing no one, she smiled very slightly, and got into the truck.

"Now what was that?" Kit whispered.

Nita pulled him behind the nearby smoking shed, out of sight of the truck as it turned, heading for the driveway. He barely noticed; he was watching the truck. "Who is that?" he said. "Is that your aunt?"

"No. I told you, that's the lady who puts the horseshoes on. Biddy."

"She's a wizard!"

"She's not," Nita said. "She can't be." It just didn't feel right. "That wasn't a wizardry. Wizards can hide . . . but the magic still feels like magic, whatever."

Kit shook his head. "Then how do you explain that? She swatted a lightning bolt away like a bug. And her truck, or that forge in her truck anyway, is alive. That *I* can feel."

"I don't know," Nita said. "Things are getting weird around here . . ."

" 'Getting!' " Kit laughed, then looked thoughtful. "You going to tell your aunt about this?"

"I don't know," Nita said. "I think . . . I think I want to talk to Biddy first."

"Makes sense," Kit said. "Then what?"

"Check with the Seniors. They seem to be running this show."

"OK," Kit said. "You're on."

They talked until nearly midnight. The last thing Kit said was, "You been meeting a lot of people around here? Kids, I mean?"

"Some. They're OK."

"Are they nice to you?"

Nita thought of Ronan and immediately flushed. How was she supposed to explain this to Kit? *Explain what?* some part of her mind demanded. *Heaven only knows what Ronan thinks about you: If anything, he probably thinks you're too young for him.* "They're fine," she said after a moment. "They're not geeky, the ones I've met."

"Some of the kids back home," Kit said, "are saying that I 'got you in trouble.' "

She burst out laughing. "No wonder you jumped when Aunt Annie poked you. Idiots." She punched him. "Go on home, it's your dinner time."

"Oh, crud, I forgot!" He got up hurriedly and started riffling through his manual.

"Don't forget the overlays!" Nita said. "If you leave them out of your calculations, you'll wind up in the middle of the Atlantic."

"So? We have friends there." He found the page he was looking for.

"Kiiiiiit!" Nita said, annoyed, until he looked at her. "Just be *careful*."

He nodded, and started reading the transposition spell under his breath. At the very end of it, on the last word, he looked back up at her.

"See you in a couple days," Nita said quietly.

He nodded and grinned, and the air slammed into the space where he had been. Nita went to bed.

Baile atha Cliath

Dublin

THE NEXT MORNING, WHEN Nita came into the kitchen, Aunt Annie was sitting at the table with a portable phone and a cup of tea, going through the yellow pages. She looked up and said, "Want to go into town?"

"Bray?"

"No, Dublin—"

The phone rang again. It had been doing that all morning: Nita had been able to hear it even out in the trailer. Aunt Annie sighed and picked up the receiver. Nita turned to get herself a cup of tea.

After a while Aunt Annie hung up and looked over at Nita. "We'll be meeting at a pub in town tonight," she said, starting to dial another number. "This should be fun for you; you haven't been in a pub yet."

Nita blinked at that. "Am I allowed?"

"Oh yes, they're not like bars in the States. You can't drink, of course, but you can be in a pub all right, as long as you're over a certain age and it's earlyish. Different pubs have different policies. But you'll have no problems." Aunt Annie chuckled, then, and said into the phone, "Doris? Anne. Johnny says tonight at nine, in the Long Hall. Will you call Shaun and Mairead? Right. Yes, we are. Right. Bye."

"How are we going into town?" Nita said. "Driving?"

"No, we'll take the train," Aunt Annie said. "Doris will give us a ride back; we're more or less on her way. Have your breakfast and we'll go. We can slouch around and do tourist things."

Nita grinned and went to get her jacket.

It turned out that she didn't need it. It was another hot day, up in the eighties now. They drove into Greystones to catch the shuttle train to Bray—the line was only electrified from Bray to Dublin—and stood on the platform, looking out toward Greystones's south beach. Dogs ran and barked, and there were even a few people in the water, which astonished Nita; she had felt the water while down by the seafront in Bray, and it was some of the coldest water she had ever experienced. Most of the people were out in the sun on the sand, turning very pink.

"Most of the time you can tell right away in the summer when someone is from Ireland," Aunt Annie said, "especially when the sun's been out. It doesn't seem to occur to people here to use sunblock, since they see the sun so rarely . . . They all turn into lobsters, the poor things." She shook her head. "Not this year, though. People are actually getting tans."

Nita looked toward the big orange and black diesel train that was pulling in. "Global warming?" she asked.

Aunt Annie just shook her head. "Take one of the right-hand seats," she said. "You'll get a better view of the water as we go in."

Nita did. The train pulled out, and Nita looked out at the north beach as they passed it: more sunbathers and someone riding a horse at a gallop.

"Aunt Annie," she said, "you know something? Why didn't I see your name when I went through the manual and looked in the wizards' directory?"

"Confidentiality," her aunt said. "I wasn't known to you yet. The manual senses such things." She looked at Nita thoughtfully. "I suppose I really should have anticipated it; my kids came out nonwizardly, after all. But anyway, I was looking at my manual this morning . . . You've been busy."

"You've got that right," Nita said.

Aunt Annie smiled. "Not unusual. Things quiet down, though, after you get to be my age. I remember when I first got my manual, I had about three years when I hardly had a moment to myself. Then things got calm when I went off to college."

"Did you have a partner?"

The train went abruptly darkish, lit only by the feeble ceiling lights, as it passed into the tunnel bored through Bray Head. "I did for a while," she said. "But she and I parted company eventually. It happens," she said, at Nita's stunned look. "You grow apart . . . or one partner finds something more important than the magic . . . or you start disagreeing about how to work."

Nita shook her head. She couldn't imagine not agreeing with Kit on a plan or course of action within a matter of seconds; and indeed, there had been times when if they hadn't been able to agree that fast, they would have been dead. "Do you still talk?" she asked.

"Oh yes, pretty often. We're friendly enough."

The train burst out into the light again, revealing the beach on the other side of Bray Head, and the iron-railed Promenade with its hotels and arcade, and the new aquarium. "Don't worry," said Aunt Annie. "I think maybe you and your partner have been through enough trouble together that you'll be working together for a long while."

They pulled into Bray station and changed to the sleek little bright green Dublin Area Rapid Transit train waiting at the next platform over. About half an hour later, the train slid into Tara Street station. Nita and her aunt got out and made their way beneath the skylights and down the escalator, out into the streets of Dublin.

It was a fascinating combination of old and new, and Nita was rather bewildered by it all at first. There were tiny cobbled alleys that looked as if they hadn't been repaved in a hundred years, or maybe two, right next to broad streets roaring with traffic and alive with lights and shoppers; old, old churches caught in the middle of shiny new shopping centers; noisy, cheerfully messy street markets in the shadow of big department stores.

"It takes a little while to get used to," her aunt said as they crossed the street south of O'Connell Bridge and headed past the stately fronts of Trinity College and the Bank of Ireland, on the way to the pedestrian precinct at Grafton Street. "If you come from one of the big cities in the States, Dublin can seem very small at first, sort of caught in a time warp, slower, more casual about things. Later—"

she chuckled—"you wonder how you ever put up with a place where people are in such a hurry all the time. And you find that life can go along very well without all the conveniences you were used to once." She smiled. "It's the people here: They make the difference."

They turned left at the corner of Grafton Street, heading for the National Museum. It was next to the Dail, the Irish houses of parliament, and Aunt Annie clearly knew her way around it. As soon as they had paid their admission fees, she led Nita down a flight of stairs, past a sign that said TREASURY. "There are a lot of gorgeous things here," she said, "but this is probably the most famous of them."

They stopped in front of a glass case that was thicker than any of the others scattered around the big room. No one else was nearby. Nita moved close to look at it. The cup inside sat on a big Lucite pedestal; a bright spotlight was trained on it from above. Nita thought this might have been unnecessary . . . since she suspected the cup might be able to glow by itself.

"The Ardagh Chalice," her aunt said softly. Nita looked at it, not just with her eyes, but with a wizard's senses. She looked as hard as she could. The chalice was about two feet high and a foot wide, mostly gold, with elaborate and beautiful spiral patterns worked on its sides in silver, and ornamented with rubies and topazes. The jewels were lovely enough, but Nita had more of an eye for the engraved and inlaid knotwork ornamentation on the sides. They were spell diagrams in a very antique style, and though they looked simple, that was an illusion created by the extreme skill of whoever had designed them. They were subtle, and potentially of huge power; but they were now quiescent, emptied of their virtue.

"It's not really very old," Nita said.

"The physical aspects of it, no." Her aunt looked at it. "This chalice was made in the second century."

"Not the Holy Grail, then," Nita said.

Her aunt smiled slightly. "No. And yes. The Treasures might have been made by gods, but they were made of mortal matter . . . and matter passes. The problem is, of course, that the power put in them—the *soul* of the Treasures, more or less— is as immortal as the Powers that made them. The soul passes on when the envelope wears out—reincarnates, finds another body that's suitable. This cup was a vessel for a while. But not anymore, I think. Do you feel anything different?"

Nita looked at the cup again, longer this time. Finally she said, "I don't know. It's as if . . . if you knew how to shake this awake, this soul, you might do it. But you'd have to know how."

Her aunt nodded. "We may have to figure out how. Come and see the sword." They went up a flight of stairs and through another room or two. They finally stopped in a room full of ancient goldwork: torques and stickpins and necklaces and bracelets of gold, beads and bangles, carved plates linked together.

"Gold used to be mined in Wicklow," her aunt said, "not too far from us. But by the fourth century most of it was gone. Anyway, *this* is worth more than any of them, if you ask me."

The central case held the sword. It lay there very plain against red velvet, long and lean, shaped like a willow leaf, with no gold or jewel anywhere about it—a plain bronze blade, notched, scraped, somewhat withered-looking. Nita bent close to it, feeling with all of her. "Now *this* is old," she said.

"Older than the cup," said Aunt Annie. "Bronze Age, at least."

Nita nodded. There was a faint feeling of purpose still in the old bronze, like a memory impressed on matter by a mind now gone, like the ghosts in Aunt Annie's backyard, a tape still replaying but heard very faintly. But there was no vigor in the sword, only recollection: wistful, mournful, feeble. . . . "It might have been the real sword once," Nita said. "But it's almost forgotten. There's not nearly as much there as in the cup. You're going to have a hard time waking it up."

Her aunt nodded. "That's what I think, too."

Nita shook her head. "And there's nothing else in the building that's even this much awake . . ." She sighed. "So we have the stone, and *maybe* the cup, and something that *might* work for the sword, but probably won't . . . and no spear."

"That about sums it up, yes. The wizards around the country will be looking for other swords that might work better. But the spirit of the Spear Luin seems to have passed completely. Either no body was strong enough to contain it . . . or it was just too powerful to be contained anymore in a universe that had no suitable envelope for it, and it passed out entirely."

Nita thought that it had passed. Spears were symbols of the element of fire, and fire was the most uncontainable of the five elements, next to plasma. Nita began to worry. Three of the Treasures would not be enough, to judge from what the Sidhe had hinted. But she was fresh out of ideas about what to do.

She looked at her aunt. "Are we done here?"

"I think so. Want to go over to Grafton Street?"

"Sounds good."

They spent the afternoon doing, as her aunt had promised, touristy things; touring the shopping center at Saint Stephen's Green, having tea in the Shelbourne Hotel, listening to the street performers playing on pipes and banjos and, occasionally, spoons. They walked over O'Connell Bridge to look up the river Liffey at the graceful curve of the Halfpenny Bridge, one of the trademarks of Dublin; and browsed through the shops on the south side of the Halfpenny Bridge, Dublin's so-called Left Bank. They sat by the statue of the goddess of the Liffey in her stone Jacuzzi and were grateful for the spray; it was hotter that afternoon than it had been all summer. Mothers put their little children in the fountain, and they splashed happily. The patrolling *Gardai*, the police, smiled and looked the other way.

About seven o'clock, Aunt Annie asked, "Dinner?" Nita agreed happily, and they went off to have a very New Yorkish pizza in a little restaurant on South Anne Street. Then they went a few blocks west, to the pub where that night's meeting would take place.

The Long Hall was a handsome place, fronted with windows of beveled and stained glass, arranged so that people standing inside, in front of the windows, couldn't quite be seen from outside. The glass in the tops of the windows was clear, showing the beautiful carved and painted plaster ceiling and the gas fixtures still hanging from it. Some of them had been converted for electricity; some hadn't.

Nita and Annie walked in, and Nita gazed admiringly at the huge polished hardwood bar and the antique mirrors, which reached nine feet up the wall at the back of the bar to the ceiling. Carved wood and beveled glass and brass railings were everywhere. So were many cheerful people, drinking, but talking more. The place was filled with the subdued roar of many conversations.

"We're in the back room. Hi, Jack," said Aunt Annie to one of the men behind the bar. He was busy filling a glass with creamy dark Guinness from one of the arched taps at the bar: He nodded to Aunt Annie but didn't say anything.

"Jack Mourne," Aunt Annie said to Nita, as they made their way through a low, carved archway into the back room. "He owns the place."

"Does he know what's going on?"

"I should think he does: He's one of the Area Advisory-Specialists. What would you like to drink, hon?"

"Can I get a Coke?"

"No problem. Be right back."

Nita found herself a seat at a small round wooden table with ornate iron legs and waited, fidgeting a little self-consciously. She had never been in a bar by herself, though Aunt Annie seemed to think that this wasn't quite the same. *She might have a point, though,* Nita thought. Here, the drinking looked almost incidental. People were shouting at each other across the back room, chatting, arguing, laughing, pointing, hollering.

"Here you go," Aunt Annie said, sitting down next to Nita with a relieved look. She handed Nita her drink and sipped briefly at her pint. "Perfect," she said. "Jack pulls the best pint in this part of town."

"Aunt Annie," Nita said, "if this is a wizard's meeting—how are you going to keep the regular people out of here?"

"Spell on the back-room archway," Aunt Annie said. "Look closely at the carving when you go to the rear ladies' room. Nonwizards hit it and decide they don't feel like going back there after all. On normal nights, Jack just takes the spell finial off: that little carved flower in the lower right-hand corner. And no one can hear us through all this din anyway; but there are voice scramblers on just in case. Jack makes anything wizardly come out sounding like an argument about football. It's a nice scrambler, took him a while to write. But he's one of our best writers. You need a custom spell in this part of the world, it's Jack you come to, or Marie Shaughnessy down in Arklow, or Charles and Alison Redpath up north in Aghalee."

"Then all these people back here are wizards?" Nita asked, looking around her in astonishment. She had never been in such a large gathering of her own before.

"Oh yes. All that could come on short notice, of course. Relax awhile; we can't do anything until Doris and Johnny get here."

So Nita drank her Coke and listened to the accents around her, and chatted every now and then with the people who came up to her aunt to say hello. If she had been mired in Irish accents before, the situation was much worse now: She heard about twenty different accents from as many different people, no two of them the same, and some very odd indeed. In addition, there were a lot of people from Northern Ireland down for this meeting, and their accents astounded her; they sounded more like New Yorkers than anything else, though more nasal. They all seemed like very open, friendly people, which to Nita seemed a little strange at first. Seeing what most Americans saw of Northern Ireland from the news, she half-expected them to be furtive and depressed, as if afraid a bomb might suddenly go off under them. But none of them was. One man in his thirties, a jocund young man in a leather jacket covered with patches, told Nita he had never seen a bomb or been within fifty miles of one, nor had anyone he knew. The peaceful, small-

town life he described seemed hard to reconcile with all the news photos Nita had
seen of shattered buildings and people with ski masks and rifles.

There was a slight commotion at the door as Mrs. Smyth came in through the
archway. "Hey, Doris, how they cuttin'?" someone shouted. Doris Smyth looked
at the speaker and said something clear and carrying in Irish that provoked a roar
of approval from the listeners, and caused the person who had asked the question
to be genially pummeled.

Behind Mrs. Smyth, someone else came in: a short man in a long overcoat and
plaid scarf. At the sight of him, many of the wizards in the room called "Johnny!"
or "Shaun!" and there was a general stir of approval through the back room. Nita
bent over to her aunt Annie and said, "Who's that?"

"Shaun O'Driscoll," said Aunt Annie. "Or Johnny, some people call him. He's
the Area Senior for Europe."

"Wow," Nita said, never having seen so high-ranked a wizard before. Area
Seniors answered only to Regional Seniors, and Regionals to the three Seniors for
Earth. When she had thought of the Senior in charge of all wizards from Shannon
to Moscow and Oslo to Gibraltar, she had imagined someone more imposing—not
a little man with thinning hair and (she saw as he took off his coat) a leisure suit.
He didn't seem very old. He had a fierce-looking mustache, and his eyes were very
cool; he gazed around the room and returned all the greetings without ever quite
smiling. It was the kind of effect, Nita thought, that made you want to try to get
him to smile. It would be worth seeing when it happened, for his face was otherwise
a nest of laugh lines.

Doris and Johnny were served pints by another of the gathered wizards, and
people started settling down, leaning against the walls when they ran out of seats.
Johnny didn't sit, but stood in the middle of the room, waiting for them to settle,
like a teacher with a big, unruly class.

"Thanks for coming," he said. "I know this was short notice, but we've had
some serious problems crop up in the past few days, and there was no way to hope
to manage them except by requiring an intervention meeting."

Some heads turned at this, and some murmuring was heard among the assembled wizards. "I know that wasn't the way it was announced," Johnny said, "but
it turns out we have less time for this discussion than was originally thought when
we organized this meeting last night and this morning. We have had serious transitional leakages all over the island, with some sympathetic transitionals in mainland Europe; and this condition has to be contained as quickly as possible. There
have been echoes and ripples as far away as China and Peru.

"Anyway," Johnny said, "I want to thank those of you who were in the middle
of other assignments and found them changed, or who were off active and were
suddenly reactivated. The Powers That Be may not thank you until later, but I like
to do it early. I also want to welcome those of you who have come unusual distances, including Nita Callahan. Stand up, love."

Nita flushed fiercely and hoped it didn't show too much in the pub's dim light.
She stood up.

"Nita has been reassigned here temporarily courtesy of North American Regional. She has blood affinities with this area and was involved in the New York
incursion, the Hudson Canyon intervention in June, and more recently, the Reconfiguration; Dairine Callahan is her sister."

There was a stir at this, which surprised Nita somewhat. She nodded and smiled a little uncertainly at Johnny; he gestured for her to sit down. "We're glad to have you," he said. "Bear with us: We do things a little differently here than you're used to, and if you think of anything that seems useful during this discussion, don't hesitate to sing out."

Huh, Nita thought, sitting down. *Reassigned courtesy of North American Regional? Who's that? Not Tom and Carl. Someone—or something—further in, or higher up?* But she put the thought aside for the moment.

"Over the past four nights we've had sideways leakages in thirty-three out of thirty-six counties," Johnny said, "and how Monaghan, Wexford, and Westmeath were missed is a mystery to us, especially since Westmeath contains the Hill of Tara. In the thirty-three counties, about ninety wizards have experienced timeslides, live remembrances of the so-called Mythological Period, solid remembrances that returned interactions, viewings of extradimensional objects without doing the wizardries required for such viewings, and even physical intervention by nonphysical entities or creatures not native to this reality, including physical attacks on occasion. One of us met Cuchullain in warp spasm, which is enough to turn anyone's hair: That it happened in the middle of the big shopping center in Tallaght didn't help, either. The Brown Bull of Cooley was seen crossing the dual carriageway north of Shannon; it wandered down onto the Iarnrod Eireann tracks and caused a derailment, though fortunately neither the train drivers nor any of the other people on the train saw it, and by great good luck no one was hurt. Possibly most to the point, there was an earthquake in the fields north of Naas, at the old site of the Battle of Moytura."

This caused some anxious looks and muttering. Johnny motioned for the crowd to quiet down. "It was only about three point one on the Richter scale, and nothing came of it but some broken china. The Lia Fail is still managing to hold this island in one place and one piece, no matter what the politicians say. But how long it can hold matters so stable is a good question. Much of its old virtue is gone, as you know. Another such attack will certainly be more effective, on both natural and supernatural levels."

"Johnny," said one of the wizards sitting back by the wall, a handsome little dark-haired woman with a sharp face, "these transitional leakages, are we sure that something else isn't causing them? Something European?"

Johnny shook his head. "I'd prefer to blame Local Europe myself, Morgan, but we're out of luck on this one. All indications point at us."

"Then what are we going to do?"

Johnny looked grim. "We're going to have to re-create Moytura, I think. Unless someone else can think of something better."

Half the room started muttering to the other half. Johnny waited for the house to settle down. "Re-create Moytura with *what*?" asked the Northern Ireland-based wizard Nita had been talking to, the young guy in the leather jacket.

"Good question," Johnny said. "Three of the Four Treasures are still with us, though diminished, as you know. In their present state, they're too weak to be of any use. But the souls of those Treasures are still in the world, or the Worlds, somewhere. We are going to have to recall those souls to suitable envelopes, and then take them out into battle against the Lone Power. We know that with them we have a chance. Without them . . ." He shrugged.

Relative silence fell for a few moments. "Who does the going-into-battle bit?" asked a voice from somewhere against the back wall.

"Lacking one of the Powers That Be, probably Doris and me to lead," Johnny said. "And all of you we can get together in one place."

"Where are you going to get suitable envelopes, then?" asked another.

"We'll try to use the old ones," Doris said. "They've worked before: With a little coercion, they'll work again . . . or so we hope. The Lia Fail is still working; the Ardagh Chalice we think we can reawaken."

"Don't you think the museum will miss it?" said the young wizard in the leather jacket.

Doris smiled slightly. "Not if a wizardry that looks and weighs exactly the same is sitting in the museum case," she said. "If the *Taoiseach* can borrow the Chalice just to show it off at a politicians' dinner party in Dublin Castle, I think *we* might take the loan of it for a night or so, for something important, and not feel too guilty afterward. But everything depends on the circumstances and the power of the ritual used to call the cup's soul back. Which is what we're going to have to work on. It's not just warriors we're going to need to make this work, but poets. Where are Charles and Alison?"

"Stuck in traffic," said someone from the bar side of the room.

Johnny grinned. "Ah, the real world. But at least Liam and Mairead and Nigel are here. I'll be wanting to talk to you three afterward. The rest of you: I want you all to talk to your Area Supervisors about your schedules for the next two weeks. Any one of you may have to drop everything at a moment's notice and lend a hand. Also, given the seriousness of the situation, travel restrictions on teleportation are off for the duration. Just use your judgment and be very careful about the overlays!"

More chatter erupted. In the middle of it, someone said, "But Johnny, wait a tick! Isn't this going to make things worse?"

Johnny waved for quiet. The room settled. "How do you mean?" he said.

"If you're going to call back the souls of the Treasures—if you can," said the speaker, a tall dignified-looking wizard with a mighty mustache, "isn't the land going to get even more awake and aware than it already is? I mean, the Treasures *are* the land, in some ways. At least that's what we were always told: four of the five elements, in their most personified forms. Air and water and earth and fire are going to wake up more than ever, until the situation is resolved and everything is laid to rest again."

Johnny nodded slowly. The room got quiet as people looked at his expression. "Yes," he said after a while. "It's going to get *much* worse. Which makes it to our advantage to get the situation resolved, as you say, as quickly as possible. Otherwise first Ireland, then the rest of Europe, and eventually all the other continents are going to be overrun with the past happening again, and the dead walking, and all kinds of other inconveniences. If we can't stop this, then the barriers between present and past will break down everywhere, and the physical world will be progressively overrun by the nonphysical: All the myths and truths that became myth, all the dreams and nightmares, all the more central and more peripheral realities will superimpose themselves on this one . . . inextricably."

"For how long?" asked a small voice out of the hush.

"If that level of imposition ever takes hold fully," Johnny said, "I don't see how the process could *ever* be reversed."

Silence, broken only by the noise of cheerful conversation in the frontmost, nonwizardly part of the pub. "Right," said the man with the mustache. "But in the meantime, while you Seniors are intervening, Ireland's dreams and nightmares are going to keep coming true—even more than they have been—and the past will keep happening, and the dead and the undead and the immortal will walk. And 'other inconveniences.' "

"That's exactly right, Scott," Johnny said.

There was another long silence. Then a voice said, "I need another pint."

A chorus of other voices went up in agreement. Nita noticed that her Coke was long gone, and she was very thirsty.

"I'll get you another," her aunt Annie said, and got up. "Anybody else? Katherine? Nuala? Orla? Hi, Jim—" She moved off.

Nita sat there feeling somewhat shaky. "Hey, you look like a sheet," said a voice by her. She looked up: It was Ronan.

She smiled faintly at him as he sat down and did her best to control herself. He looked even cuter than he had previously, if that was possible. Black leather suited him, and so did this subdued lighting. "I feel like one," she said. "How about you?"

"Sounds pretty bad," Ronan said. But he looked and sounded remarkably unconcerned. "Don't worry about 'auld Shaun' there, he just likes to sound like doom and destruction all the time. Comes of being Area Senior; they all sound like the world's ending half the time."

Probably because it is, Nita thought. It was only the sheer number of wizards in the world, and the sacrifices they kept making from week to week, that kept civilization on an even keel; or so it seemed to her. "Look, can I ask you something?"

"Sure."

"I'm just curious. Was your Ordeal bad?"

He looked peculiarly at her. "Almost got me killed, if that's what you mean."

"So will crossing O'Connell Street," Nita said. "Never mind . . . I don't know what I mean. I mean, it seemed to me that my Ordeal was pretty awful. I was just curious whether I was an exception, or whether everyone had that bad a time. My sister did, but she's not exactly a normal case. And I haven't had that many chances to discuss it with other wizards."

Ronan looked thoughtful and took a drink of his orange-and-lemon drink. "I got timeslid," he said.

Nita shrugged slightly. "We bought a timeslide from our local Seniors for ours," she said.

"I didn't buy mine," Ronan said. "I *got* it." He took another drink. "One day I took the Oath—the next I was walking up Vevay Road, you know, at the top of Bray by the Quinnsworth, the supermarket? Well, it stopped being Vevay Road. It was just a dirt track with some thatched huts down near where the school would be, at the bottom of the hill, and it was raining cats and dogs. Thunder and lightning."

Nita shivered: She disliked being caught out in the rain. "What did you do?"

"I went up Bray Head," Ronan said, bursting out in a laugh that sounded as if, in retrospect, he didn't believe his own craziness. "I wanted to see where everything was, you know? It was a mess. You know how the sea gets during a storm. Well, maybe you don't—"

"I live on Long Island," Nita said. "We get high-force gales on the Great South Bay, when the hurricanes come through. The whole sea is one big whitecap, spray so thick in the air you can't see—"

"Driving inland," Ronan said. "Between the rain and the spray, there was almost no difference between being in the water and being on the land. Well, I saw the boat come in, straight for the rocks. Little thing." He saw Nita's blank look and said, "The Romans."

That made her raise her eyebrows. She had seen the Roman coins that had been found at the base of Bray Head: She had seen a reconstruction of the archaeological site, with Roman bones. "They were going to try to set up a colony, weren't they?" she asked.

Ronan nodded. Nita watched him. She remembered that afternoon in the chicken place in Bray and the vehemence of Ronan's feelings about colonizers of any kind. But at the moment, Ronan just sat, and flushed a little, and looked away from Nita as he said, "Well, they were going to get killed, weren't they? Them and their little boat and all, in that sea. One of the lifeboats couldn't have stood it, let alone that little smack. So I 'took the sea in.' "

Nita stared at him. What Ronan was describing was temporary but complete control of a pure element: using the wizardly Speech to describe every molecule of an object or area so completely and accurately that for a short period you become it. *Control* was barely the word for it. It became as much a part of you as your body . . . for a while. Then came the backlash, for human beings are not really meant to have more than one physical body at a time. You might find the association impossible to break—and have to spend the rest of your life coexisting with what you had described, which would surely drive you insane. Or the strain of the wizardry itself might kill you. An adult wizard, full of experience, might have done such a wizardry once . . . and no other wizardry, ever again. A young wizard on Ordeal, or soon after, could have done it and lived . . . maybe. His head might never be entirely right again.

But here sat Ronan, still blushing slightly. He said, "It wasn't much of it I had to take, just the sea around Bray Head. The people in the boat jumped ship and made it ashore. I couldn't save the boat; it went all to pieces when I lost control. I must have passed out up there—the slide came undone after a while, and some tourists doing the cliff walk from the Greystones side found me slipping down the rocks on the seaward side, and they called the *Guardai*. I spent a few days in the hospital." He shrugged. "Hypothermia," he added, and laughed. "Too true—but they never knew from what."

"Wow," Nita said under her breath, almost lost in admiration of him. She was starting to blush, but she ignored it as she looked at him again. "But you knew," she said, "that there was just the one boat. The Romans never made it here except for those people. Britain was giving them too much trouble. You could have let them go under."

If there was a little challenge in her voice, Ronan didn't rise to it. "Could I?" he said. "I knew it was a timeslide. Would I have been changing history? Did I have any choice?"

"Damn straight you did," Nita said, again under her breath.

Ronan heard it. He looked up from under his brows at her, that familiar scowl. "That's as may be. What could I do? Seeing them waving their arms and trying to get off, and knowing they would drown if they tried it, in that water." He looked away again, as if slightly embarrassed. "Sure nothing came of it anyway. They were marooned; no one ever came after them. They settled down there, and married the people there, some of them. I'm related to them, for all I know."

Nita smiled slightly. "You didn't *know* that no one would come after them, though. Suppose you *had* changed history? Suppose you had just saved the lives of the people who were going to report back to Rome and bring in the conquerors?"

Ronan drank his drink and looked away.

Nita reached out and patted his arm—a casual enough gesture, she did it with Kit all the time, but as she did it to Ronan, the shock of it, the closeness of actually touching him, ran up her arm like fire and half wilted her. "Never mind," she said, trying to get some control back. The point of each wizard's Ordeal was always a private thing: That Ronan should share this much of it with her was more than he had to do. "You want another of those?" she said. "What do you call it?"

"A Saint Clements. 'Oranges and lemons, say the bells of Saint Clements—' " He burst out laughing at Nita's uncomprehending look. "Don't know that one, I take it. Not in America's top forty?"

Nita knew when she was being made fun of, and knew when not to take it seriously: Her heart warmed that he liked her enough to do it at all. "Eat turf and die, Paddy," she said, mocking, and got up, feeling in her pocket for change.

She got Ronan's drink, and when she got back, found her own waiting for her, and rather to her surprise, Johnny sitting in her seat chatting with Ronan. "Here," Johnny said, and got up; "I was holding it for you. Listen, dear, I have a message for you. Tom and Carl send their best."

"You know them? How are they?" Nita said, sitting right up. "Are they OK? It was them, then!"

"They're fine. I consult with them fairly often, especially Tom: He's an Advisory to the North American Regional for compositional spelling. *What* was 'them'?"

"I mean, it was them who sent me on assignment. They, I mean."

Johnny smiled very slightly, and all his wrinkles deepened. "Ahh . . . no. Not even a Regional Senior, or one of the Planetaries, can actually put a wizard on active assignment. No matter how certain we are that the world's ending." He shot a humorous look at Ronan, and Ronan looked like he was tempted to try to pull his head down inside his black turtleneck. "No, those decisions are made higher up. I might have mentioned North American Regional, but there are more than humans involved in that. Never mind for now. I take it Doris had a talk with you about our local problems."

Nita opened her mouth to answer, and was startled by a sudden shout from up front. "Last orders now, ten minutes, gentlemen. Last orders, please!"

Johnny laughed at the look her face must have been wearing. "All the pubs have to close at eleven-thirty this time of year," he said. "Anyway, Doris says she told you the ropes."

"If you mean she told me not even to sneeze in the Speech," Nita said, "yes."

Johnny laughed under his breath. "It must seem hard. Believe me, it's for the best . . . and there'll be enough magic around here for anybody, come the end of the month, if things keep going the way they've been going. We'll be in touch with you, of course."

"Johnny," Ronan said suddenly, "this may be out of turn—"

"Knowing you, my lad," Johnny said, "probably."

"Johnny—Look, it's nothing personal," Ronan said, glancing at Nita and blushing furiously. "But why can't this be handled locally? Why do we need blow-ins?"

Nita turned red, too, with annoyance. She thought of about six different cutting things to say, but kept her mouth shut on them all.

Johnny simply looked mildly surprised. "Self-sufficiency, is it?" he said. "Have you fallen for that one? It's an illusion, Ro. Why do we need the help of the Tuatha de Danaan? Why do we need the Powers That Be? Or even the Lone Power? For that One has a function in the Universe, too. You know that. The whole lot of us are interconnected, and there's no way we can get away from it, or any one group of us solve even the littlest problem entirely by ourselves. This matter *is* being handled locally. It's being handled on *earth.* Next thing, you're going to ask me what the Northern Irish wizards are doing here." His eyebrows went up and down. "You've been listening to too many politicians. Better apologize to her before she turns you into a soggy beer mat," Johnny said, patted Nita on the shoulder, and moved on.

"Time now, gentlemen, time now. Take those glasses away, Charlie!" Jack was shouting from the front of the pub. Nita did her best to keep her face still. She had gone hot and tight inside, and was holding onto herself hard; controlling her emotions had never been her strongest suit, and she had no desire to say something stupid here, where she was a guest and could make her aunt look bad. *Besides, I'm a wizard among wizards. It should take more than some provincial punk with a chip on his shoulder to get me annoyed!*

"Look, Nita," Ronan said. He sounded slightly desperate. "I didn't—"

"You bet you didn't," she said. And shut up. And then lost it again. "Look," she said, her voice low but fierce, "do you think this was *my* idea? Do you think I wouldn't rather be back home with my partner, taking care of business, than messing around in this dumb little place where you can't even twitch without permission? Do you think I don't have better things to do? 'Blowins,' " she said bitterly, and picked up her drink and began to swallow the whole thing at once, to shut herself up: At least she couldn't say what she was thinking while she was drinking something.

It was the wrong drink. In the middle of the second swallow she spluttered in shock at the alcoholic black-bread taste of it, and from beside her, Aunt Annie said, "You're going to get us thrown out of here, you know that? Here, have a napkin."

Nita gasped and choked and took the napkin gratefully, and began mopping Guinness off herself and the table. Ronan was leaning against the wall and laughing, soundlessly, but so hard that he was turning twice as red as he had been. Furious, Nita felt around in her head for the small simple spell that would dump his own drink in his lap. She then remembered where she was, and in rapid succession shoved the sodden napkin down the neck of his turtleneck and, while Ronan was fumbling for it, knocked his glass sideways with her elbow. "Oops," she said in utter innocence, as the drink went all over him.

"Come on now, gents, time now, time. Have you no homes to go to? You, too, ladies. No offense meant," Jack shouted from the front of the pub. The conversations were getting louder, if anything. Ronan sat and stared at his lap, and just as he lifted his eyes to Nita's, Johnny went by and patted him on the shoulder, and said, "I *told* you she was going to turn you into a soggy beer mat. No one ever listens to me. 'Night, Annie, give me a call in the morning . . ." And he was away.

"I guess we'd better go," Aunt Annie said, as the lights began flashing on and off to remind people that it was time to drink up and get out. "Doris is waiting. Ronan, do you need a ride home?"

"No, thank you, Mrs. Callahan," he said. "I came in with Barry."

"Right, then. Come on, Nita, let's call it a night."

Nita got up and looked down at Ronan. He was gazing back at her with an expression she couldn't interpret. Not anger, not amusement—what was it? She refused to waste her time trying to figure it out. "Keep your pants dry," she said to him, trying desperately to keep her face straight. Gratefully she followed Mrs. Smyth and Aunt Annie out, grinning to herself.

Blow-ins. Huh.

She grinned all the way home . . . and wasn't quite sure why.

Sliabh O Cualann

Great Sugarloaf Mountain

"WHAT'S GOING ON?" Kit asked the next afternoon. "How are things going with the Treasures?"

They were sitting around the kitchen table, looking at the papers. "Well," Nita's aunt said, "Doris and a couple of the other Seniors are going to go in today and lift the Ardagh Chalice. They'll leave a perfect copy in its place. They think they have a guess at how to make it wake up. Apparently whatever they did with the stone worked better than they expected; it seems your local Senior, Tom, is quite an asset," she said to Nita. "They were able to wake it up on the first try using the spell he wrote for them."

Nita nodded. "He says it's because he used to write so many commercials."

Aunt Annie chuckled. "I guess I can see the point. Well, anyway, it's awake. As you will have noticed, the land is getting, uh, restive . . . more than it was, anyway."

"Are they going to bring the stone here? Or somewhere special?" asked Kit.

"Oh no . . . there's no need for that. The stone *is* the earth of Ireland, in some ways; anywhere there is earth of Ireland, the stone is there in essence. The same way that the cup *is* the water of Ireland, and all wells and pools; the sword *is* the air of Ireland, the spear *is* the fire. The Treasures exist in essence in all the things they represent. But when they're awake, they coexist many times more powerfully than before. They themselves become weapons of considerable power; and the earth and air and water and fire themselves become weapons that we can turn to our advantage. We sincerely hope." She took a drink of her tea.

"What about the sword?" Kit said.

"It's hard to say," said Annie. "The cup is more awake than any of the envelopes they're thinking about using for the sword; so they're going to try the spell on the Chalice first and see how the reanimation works on that. If it does, they'll move on and try it on the sword in the museum."

"And the spear?" Kit said.

Aunt Annie shook her head. "No news. There are a lot of spears and pikes and whatnot lying around, but none of them seem ever to have been the Spear Luin. Which is a problem, for Luin was *the* weapon that overthrew Balor. The others were basically support for it."

Kit shrugged. "Well, something'll turn up. Something always does."

"I wish I had your confidence," Aunt Annie said, getting up to pour herself another cup.

"Something has to turn up," Kit said. "*We're* here."

Nita punched him lightly. "Something's always turned up before," she said. "This is not like before . . ."

Kit shrugged again. "Listen, if I can't keep your spirits up, you won't do good work."

"How can my spirits be other than wonderful when I have this to look at?" she said, pushing the paper at him.

The *Wicklow People* had come out that morning; the usual details of the fortunes and misfortunes of Wicklow people overseas, or the failure of the county council to do something about an urgent local problem, or the accusations of one of the local political parties about the purported bad behavior of one of the others had been forced off the front pages. Other people besides Nita had been having problems.

SILLY SEASON COMES TO NORTH WICKLOW, said the headline. Underneath it was the beginning of a three-page feature story concerning the bizarre occurrences in the county that week. The trouble had started in the country. A farmer had claimed that a dinosaur—a small one, but still plainly a dinosaur—had been eating his sheep. These claims had been greeted with amusement by his neighbors, some of whom had suggested that he had, in the local way of putting it, "drink taken."

The *Gardai* declined comment on this business, as they did about the reports of rocks rolling uphill at Ballywaltrim, or the problem incurred by the dairy-cattle farmer over by Kilmacanogue, who claimed his Guernsey herd was stolen—driven away across the dual carriageway by a man who said he was Finn MacCumhal, and was entitled to take any cattle that the owner was not strong enough to defend in battle. There was a chorus of noisy protests to Bray Urban District Council and Wicklow County Council about this—some people insisting that the psychiatric hospital at Newcastle needed to look into its security.

Matters were no better anywhere else in Ireland. There were reports from all over of people's lives being suddenly turned topsy-turvy by the appearance of ancient heroes, ancient villains, and ancient monsters, with which Ireland was well supplied. Several people dug up buried treasures after being told where to find them by kindly ghosts; unicorns were seen in Avonmore Forest Park; merfolk were heard singing off Howth. The *Gardai* had no comment on these matters, either.

Nita and Kit were perusing these accounts when Johnny O'Driscoll arrived. Nita put the newspaper aside and introduced Kit to him. "You're very welcome," Johnny said to him. "Your friend here will have warned you about the overlays, though."

"She mentioned them, yes."

"Well, be careful. We have enough problems at the moment."

Nita poured a cup of tea for Johnny; he took it, drank it with a thankful air, and said, "Everyone else I've talked to this morning has had a problem, so I might as well hear yours, too. What have you been up to?"

"Nothing really," she said. "But I did have an interesting conversation with a fox the other day." And she described her meeting with the dog-fox and the information he had given her.

Johnny looked thoughtful. "I have to say," he said, "that I'd suspected for some time that at least one of the Bright Powers was in the area, in human form. I had no solid confirmation. Normally, if one of Them is going to be in the area on business, the Knowledge gives warning of it, or the manual does, depending on which you use. But there's been no such warning. Then again, this isn't a normal situation. Anyway, I had other indications. Interesting to hear them confirmed."

Nita glanced over at Kit. "Why do They hide?" she said.

"To keep the other side from knowing that They're here. Except that the other side seems to know already, so that reason doesn't work in this case." He shook his head. "I don't know. The Powers are frequently beyond our ability to explain . . . but there's nothing strange about that. They're the next major level of creation up from us, after all. Should a rock expect to be able to explain a human being?"

"We have enough trouble with that ourselves," Kit said.

"Just so. Anyway, whatever Power It is doubtless has good reasons for wanting to stay hidden. I wouldn't want to break Its cover prematurely."

Kit and Nita looked at each other.

"Meanwhile," Johnny said, "Anne, if it's all right with you, Doris will be stopping in this afternoon with what she's picked up. The Enniskerry region is too badly overlaid for her to keep it up there for a few minutes without the area remembering all kinds of things that are better not roused. Down here is a little cleaner; you and I can do something to suppress those memories about the Church and Cromwell's people."

"No problem," said Aunt Annie. "We'll put it in the back office."

"Fine. Your staff doesn't usually go in there?"

"Only my secretary. I can ask her not to."

"Fine. These Treasures are proving a little more dangerous than we thought. Harry, who went up to do the work on the stone, did it all right . . . but I think he's probably not going to be worth much of anything for the next few days. We have to be very careful that we don't let people spend too much time near these things. If you show me where you want to put it, I'll build a warding for that room and see that it doesn't do anyone any damage."

"But how can the Treasures be hurting people?" Nita asked. "They're *good*!"

"Oh, absolutely," Johnny said. "There are probably no more powerful forces for good on the planet . . . except for human beings, naturally. But just because they're good doesn't mean they're *safe*."

"Listen, Shaun," Aunt Annie said then, "is there any plan yet for where we're going to do the big ceremony, the reenactment?"

"It'll have to start up at Matrix," Johnny said. "It has all the necessary equipment. That's right," he said to Nita, "you haven't seen my place yet, have you? Not really *my* place, of course. No one owns Castle Matrix but itself . . . and whatever's under it. You'll see." He got up. "Anyway, Matrix is where it'll start. But where it'll end . . ." He shook his head. "I have to go down to Bray. Either of you need a ride?"

"Thanks," Nita said. "We were going to take the bus, but if it's OK . . ."

"Sure, come on."

Johnny dropped them more or less in the center of town, where Herbert Road crosses Main Street. They waved good-bye to him as he drove off, and Kit said, "I didn't have any breakfast . . . I'm an empty shell. Is there anywhere to eat around here?"

"There's a chicken place over here that's not too bad," Nita said. "I've got some money. Let's go in there."

They walked in, went to the counter, and ordered. Nita took one quick glance at the back of the restaurant, and her stomach turned over inside her in nervous response. Ronan was sitting back there. He shot Nita one quick glance and then looked down again at the Coke he was busy with.

"You OK?" Kit asked, as they turned away with their drinks and went to a table. "Your face is all weird."

"Uh," Nita said. "I poured a drink over a guy last night."

"You were out with a guy?"

Nita blushed. "No, not me. A bunch of us were out."

"What, a bunch of the kids around here?"

"What is this, the Spanish Inquisition? I was out with my aunt. There was a big wizards' meeting in town."

"Oh," Kit said.

Nita rolled her eyes and said, "Spare me! Never mind that." She took a drink of her Coke—her mouth was suddenly dry—and said, "Half a second." Then she got up and went back to Ronan's table.

He looked up at her with an expression partly unease and partly annoyance, and he still managed to smile on top of it all. "You forgot your Coke," he said.

"No, it's back there."

"I mean, I thought you were going to pour it on me."

She looked at him ruefully. "Listen, Ronan, I'm sorry. Look, come on and sit with us, and meet my partner."

"That's him?" He craned his neck a little.

"Yeah, he's just in from the States. Come on and sit with us."

Somewhat reluctantly, Ronan got up, bringing his drink, and went and stood by the table. "Kit," she said, "this is Ronan. Ronan, Kit Rodrigues."

They shook hands, Kit willingly enough, Ronan with some reserve, and they looked at each other. *"Dai stihó,"* Kit said.

Ronan raised his eyebrows as he sat down. "You can tell?"

Kit looked surprised. "It sticks out all over you."

"Your partner couldn't."

Kit shrugged. "It's always easier for guy wizards to tell guys, and girls to tell girls. Anyway, Neets has other things to think about. And she's in a weird place: You get thrown off. I didn't know her aunt was one of us till she was pointed out to me."

There was tension in the air. Nita had thought this would be a good idea, at first; now she was beginning to regret it. "I was just telling Ronan," she said to Kit, "that I was sorry I dumped the drink on him last night."

Ronan looked bemused. "Watch out for her. She's got a temper."

"I've noticed," Kit said. "Just hope you never see her sister lose hers. Whoo! But Neets is no prize, either."

"Will you two stop talking about me as if I'm not here?" Nita said, annoyed. Then they both grinned at her, and she blushed. *Bad enough being teased from just one direction . . .*

"Scoot over, Kit," she said, sat down next to him, and started working on her Coke again. Then she said to Ronan, "How was *your* day?"

There was an abrupt sound of breaking glass from outside. All three of their heads jerked up at the same time. "What the heck—!" Kit said.

"Probably an accident," Ronan said, getting up hurriedly. "The corner next to here's a bad one; people are always coming around it too fast—"

The next sound of glass breaking was the shop's own window, and it was not a car that broke it. Something big, dark, and blunt slammed into it from outside, and plate glass rained in. The ladies behind the counter cried out in surprise and hurried to the back of the shop. The shop's three other patrons followed them, leaving Kit and Nita and Ronan standing there.

Something stepped in through the broken glass. If you had taken a human being, and coated it with tar, rolled it in gravel, and then turned it loose to walk around blindly smashing things, it might look something like the creature that appeared before them. At least, it would if it were about five feet tall and about four feet broad, with arms and thighs as thick as a man's waist, and a round ugly face like a boulder.

They looked at the creature in shock as it came toward them. "It's a drow," Ronan whispered. "Fomori . . ."

They could see others like it stalking past, out in the street. The sounds of breaking plate glass were spreading down the road. Cars screeched to a halt, horns blasted. There was one long screech followed by the sound of more breaking glass, and the crunch of metal, too, this time.

"Someone's hit one," Kit said.

"I feel sorry for their car," Ronan said. "Come on."

"How do you stop them?" asked Nita.

"Stop them?! You don't stop them. You run away!" Ronan said. He grabbed Nita's arm with one hand and Kit's with the other and hustled them out the back door.

They ducked into Castle Terrace behind the chicken place. Nita looked down to the end of the street, toward the remains of the old castle. Several of the drows were there, tearing the place up, or down. They appeared to be made of good Wicklow granite, and to dislike everything they saw. Several of them, down the street, were punching holes in the walls of the Bank of Ireland: Its alarm bell was ringing disconsolately. Another drow, in Herbert Road, was busy turning over a car, while people struggled and screamed and tried to get out of it.

"This is not good," Nita muttered. "We can't just leave these things running all over the place!"

"There's no wizardry that can deal with these," Ronan said, "not with overlays all over the place! You've just got to get away! If they—"

That was when the heavy hand fell on Ronan's shoulder. "No *way!*" Kit said. He then spoke three words, very short and sharp. The drow reeled back, mostly because it had no head left. Rock dust sifted down past Ronan as Kit pulled him away. "You were saying?" Kit said, breathing hard.

A great crack or fissure ran down the drow from its neck straight down its center. It staggered and the crack spread. But something else happened as well. The drow got wider. It seemed to grow two heads, then six arms, then eight. It fell to the ground with a terrible crash and broke in two; and got up . . . twice. It had twinned.

"I was saying *that*," Ronan said. "Run!"

Herbert Road was blocked by more drows. Nita, Kit, and Ronan dodged around the formerly single drow and ran into Main Street. People were running and screaming in all directions. Cars were being overturned; windows and walls were being bashed in or pulled down. Two drows were in the process of overturning the monument in front of the Royal Hotel. "What the heck is *this* supposed to be a reenactment of?" Nita asked, looking around in panic.

"It's not a reenactment. They're Fomori, doing what they always do . . . destroying everything in sight."

Nita looked up Main Street toward the old beam-and-plaster building that had been the town's market hall and was now the tourist center and museum. It was still fairly clear up there. "Come on," she said.

They ran up that way, accompanied by a lot of other people who apparently had the same idea. They didn't get much farther than the little arcade of shops in the middle of the street before they saw the first squat gray forms appearing down at the other end of the road. One of the drows began pulling at the gryphon-topped granite fountain in front of the Heritage Center.

They stopped. "No good," Nita said. "We don't dare use spells—they'll just backfire. We've got to do something else."

"Such as?" Ronan asked, desperate.

She smiled at him, rather crookedly. She was beginning to shake. "Let's try this," she said.

There was a format for these things. She swallowed, and called the name once; she called it twice. The second time it made her throat hurt—more in warning, she thought, than because of the sound of it. Something was saying to her, *Are you sure? Very sure?* She gulped, and said the name the third time. The word shook her and flung her down.

Nita sat up on the sidewalk, slightly dazed. It took a swallow or two to get her throat working again. Then she shouted in the Speech, "Pay me back what you owe me—and do it *now!*"

Because wizardry was involved, she expected immediate results. Because wizardry was involved . . . she got them.

Over the screams and the breaking glass, over the crashes of cars and the howling of the sirens of the *Gardai* came another sound: bells. Not church bells. It was as if someone had taken the sound of hoofbeats and tuned them, as if what came galloping did so on hooves of glass, or silver, a clangor of relentless and purposeful harmonies. Other bells were the sounds that bridles might make if each one were built like a musical instrument, made to be carried into battle and shaken to frighten the enemy—a sharp, chilly sound. The galloping and the sound of the bells came closer together and were joined by a third sound, a high, eerie singing noise, the sound that metal might make if you woke it up and taught it how to kill. The faces of the buildings near the Heritage Center flushed bright, as if a light came near them.

And then the tide of color poured itself down into Main Street from both sides of the Heritage Center, and the first of the drows fell away from the gryphon fountain, screaming as a crystal sword pierced it. The horses shone, the riders shone, but not with any kind of light; they were simply more *there* than the main street was, more *there* than the broken glass, and the crashed cars, and the gray things; more vivid, more real. Everything seen in the same glance with them went pallid or dull—the crimson of cloaks and banners that burned like coals, the blues and emerald greens like spring suddenly afire amid the concrete, the gold of torques and arm rings glowing as if they were molten, the silver of hair burning like the moon through cloud, the raven of hair burning like the cold between the stars. The riders poured down into Main Street, and the drows fled screaming before them— not that it helped. Two of them took refuge in the smoked-glass-and-aluminum phone booths down at one end of the street; the faery horses smashed the booths to splinters with their hooves, then smashed the drows. Down past the Chinese restaurant, down past the real estate agents and the appliance stores, the riders came storming between the cars, or through them, as if the cars were not real to them; and perhaps they were not. The riders' swords shone and sang where the sunlight fell on them, that high, inhumanly joyous keen of metal that will never know rust. The riders had spears like tongues of fire, and sickles like sharpened moons, and bows of glass that fired arrows that did not miss. The gray things went down like lumps of stone when the weapons struck them. They lay like stone and didn't move again. The only screams were those of the drows now; everything mortal was hiding or standing very still, hoping against hope it wouldn't be noticed by the terrible beauty raging through the main street of Bray.

The riders swept down the street to where Nita and Ronan and Kit stood, their backs against the wall next to the pub by the arcade, and swept on past them, toward the Dargle, driving a crowd of the drows before them. A *Garda* sergeant in his blue shirtsleeves stood astounded on the corner and watched them pass, too dumbfounded to do anything but cross himself; several of the riders bowed to him as they passed, and smiled as they did it.

One of the riders turned aside from the bright tide, and paused by the wizards, looking down at Nita. He said, "Are you repaid, then?"

Nita looked up at him, at the crimson and emerald and golden splendor of his clothing and the impossible handsomeness of his face, and she felt dingy and shopworn by comparison. Her heart ached in her with pity for the wretched ordinariness of life, seen next to this awful, assured beauty. But she said, "Yes, thank you. Thank you very much."

"I would have saved the favor, myself," said the black-haired rider, "for you'll need it more later. But what's done is done. And now get up and ride, for the Queen desires to speak with you."

"You mean the Lady of the Forth?" Nita said.

"No," said the rider. "The Queen of all the Forths of this land. The Queen in Cualann, whom it is unwise to refuse . . . as it is unwise to refuse her Fool."

"The Amadaun!" Ronan said, his eyes going wide. "Do what he says," he said to Nita. And she caught a flash of unnerved thought from him: *He can kill with a look or a touch, this one, if offended*—

"No problem with that," Nita said, at the moment having no time for Ronan's nervousness. "But one thing first." She looked around her in distress: the cars stopped or crashed in the street, the shattered glass, the stunned townspeople standing around. She beckoned Kit and Ronan off to one side a little and said, "We can't leave the place this way. Little hiccups in daily reality, people can deal with— but this? They'll never be able to explain it to themselves—"

"Or their insurance companies," Kit muttered.

Nita shook her head. "They'll lose their grip."

Ronan looked at them curiously. "What are you thinking of doing?"

Kit looked thoughtfully at Nita. "Patch it?"

Nita nodded. Ronan stared at her. " 'Patch it'? Patch *what*? With what?"

Nita bit her lip. "Time," she said. "With a spare piece. It's basic alternate-universe theory; you must know about this. Somewhere parallel to our universe, where this happened, there has to be one where this *didn't* . . . where the drows never popped out, where this damage wasn't done. You patch this timeline with an equivalent piece of that one." She looked around her, considering. "The area and the timespan's small enough not to have to get an authorization, the way you'd have to for a full timeslide. And the reason's good, which is the whole point."

"But the overlays—"

"Ronan," Kit said, holding his voice very steady in a way Nita knew meant he was fighting not to lose his temper, "we can't sit around debating this all day. A few minutes more, and what's happened will have printed itself too strongly on these people's minds to be patched over. We'll be careful of the overlays. You in or what?"

Ronan looked from him to Nita. She shrugged, nodded.

"All right—"

"Here it is," Kit said, riffling through his manual. "We're inside the time limit, we can do the short form. Ronan?"

"Yes," Ronan said, looking slightly off to one side like someone having an idea, "I see it. You start."

Kit and Nita started reading together: Ronan joined them. It was a little odd to hear the Speech for the first time in an Irish accent, but Nita didn't let that distract her, concentrating instead on the part of the spell that located and verified the piece of alternate spacetime they needed. They copied it into the spell buffer prepared for it and held it ready. Then they performed the second part of the spell, which bilocated the copied spacetime with the one presently proceeding locally.

Kit looked up after a moment, breathing hard. Everything around them suddenly looked a little peculiar, as if every object had two sets of outlines, which were vibrating, jarring against one another. "Come on," he said to Nita and Ronan, "let's get out of here and drop it in place."

"How are we going?" Nita said, glancing up at the Amadaun.

There were suddenly three more horses beside him, bridled and saddled, ready to go. "Can you ride?"

"I can be carried," Nita said, utterly unhappy about the idea.

"Up, then."

Kit helped her up. "Where is the Queen?" Nita asked the Amadaun. "Did she come out with you?"

"She did not: She goes not foraying anymore. Though because of you, that may change."

Nita thought about that for a minute. Ronan, meanwhile, swung up in his saddle with perfect ease, gathered up the reins, and sat there like a lord. Kit clambered up into his saddle, clutching the pommel.

"Don't fear," the Amadaun said. "You won't fall."

Nita desperately hoped that was true. "OK," she said to Kit. "As soon as we're clear, let it drop."

The Amadaun turned his mount and led them at a walk up Herbert Road. By the entrance to the church parking lot, Kit paused, looked over his shoulder, said one word. Looking back toward the main street with Ronan, Nita saw the outlines of everything tremble, then suddenly solidify. With that, the glitter of broken glass in the road was gone, and a sudden confused silence fell over the shouting that had started in the street.

"Good," Kit said. "It took, nice and solid. Let's go."

And they rode. Nita knew these horses from old stories, but she still was not prepared for how fast they went. One moment she was trying to find a way to sit so that she wouldn't slip off; the next, she was galloping. Though it physically felt as if she were trapped in a dream sequence in a movie, the horse moving in slow motion, everything else blurred past her with such speed that she could hardly tell which way they were going. Apparently the Good People's horses didn't care about roads; rough or smooth was all one to them, for they ran "sideways," across water or fetlock-deep through a hillside in their path. The country around them appeared as it had—how many hundreds of years ago?—before there were roads, or people, or anything else to trouble the serenity of the world. It was an Ireland of apple trees in flower, of long hillsides green with flowery meadows, deep forests, thickets of hazel and rowan.

They rode westward out of Bray and made for Sugarloaf.

In the sideways world, Sugarloaf was not a mountain, but a city that stood huge and golden, the towers lancing up as Nita had seen them from a distance back in Kilquade. The rider alongside them looked at Nita and at the view ahead and smiled slightly. "It is the chief of our *dúns* in these parts," he said. "And the fairest. Other mountains are higher, but none was so well shaped, we thought."

"I saw."

"So you did. You have the gift; it comes of the blood, I suppose." The Fool looked at her. "Not a safe gift, though."

"Neither is wizardry," Nita said.

The Amadaun nodded. "As you will no doubt keep discovering before the end. No matter. We're here."

They dismounted before the great gates. The horses tossed their heads, somehow losing their saddles and tack at the same time, and wandered off into the surrounding meadows. "Come then," said the Fool. "The Queen holds summer court."

They did not go though the gates. The Fool led them instead a short distance around the high, shining walls to where an open pavilion of white silk was pitched in the meadow. Inside it was a simple chair, surrounded by several young women. In the chair sat another woman, who watched them come.

The Fool led them just inside the pavilion, in front of the lady in the chair. Later, Nita would have trouble remembering the lady's face; what chiefly struck her was the woman's hair, masses of it, a beautiful mellow gold like the wheat ripening in Aunt Annie's third field over. The thick braids of it that hung down reached almost to the ground; the rest was coiled up, braided, and wound around her head, the only crown she wore. She was dressed all in a white silk much finer than that of the pavilion, and she held something wrapped in more silk in her lap.

"The greeting of gods and man to you, wizards," she said.

They all bowed. "And to you, madam," Ronan said, "our greeting and the One's."

She bowed her head in return. "I may not keep you long here," she said. "You are on errantry, and we respect that. But word has come to us of what the wizards are doing. We know a little of *draoiceacht* ourselves, and we have something here that may be of use to you."

She turned her attention to the bundle in her lap. "Madam," Kit said, "may I ask a question?"

She looked up, and her eyes glinted a little with merriment. "Could I stop you?"

"Who are you, please?"

She sat back in the chair at that. "Bold one," she said. "But the stranger in the gate has a right to ask. I am one who 'died into the hills.' " Ronan turned his face away. "Feel no shame," she said. "The name is long given to us by humans, and we are used to it. The first of us who lived here after the Making, and could not bear to leave, slipped sideways here, by what art you know; it is part of wizardry. We took ourselves to live outside of the world's time, and exiled ourselves as a result; we cannot go back except for a little while, every now and then. A night of moon to dance in; a morning, or an afternoon, on each of the four great turning-days of the year, when the hills stand open, and there is easy commerce between this world and yours. We are near one of those days now, which is why you can be here at all."

She turned back a bit of the silk of the wrapped thing in her lap, toying with it. "Now and then, the desire for the physical world becomes too much for us, and one or another of us crosses back into it—to live the lives of human beings, in a world where things are definite and deadly, and what one does matters forever. We age swiftly when we do that, and our passions rule us; we do terrible deeds sometimes, forgetting the calm of the slower-running time outside the world. I have been back several times, and returned here after each visit, which makes me un-usual . . . for many of us have gone over to try death and have not come back from it. Your world would know me by several names. I was called Aoife, and Fand, and Macha, and other names besides. But most important at the moment, I was called Emer, the wife of Cuchullain mac Sualtim, who was Hero of Ulster. And that is how I come by this."

She looked down at the bundle in her lap and slowly unfolded the wrappings around it. "After Cuchullain died," she said, "I gave it to Conall of the Hundred Battles. It passed from him, eventually; he could not bear the spirit that was in the thing. It was in pain, because there was no hand mighty enough to wield it anymore, and no mind that understood its power. Our wise folk thought at last that it ought to be brought out of the world, and 'into the hills,' to spare its pain. And so it was. See—"

She slipped the silk aside, and held up what had been in it. It was a sword. There were no jewels on it; the hilt was plain gold, riveted with silver, and the blade was a long graceful willow-leaf curve of mirror-polished steel, about two and one-half feet long, coming to a "waist" about a foot above the hilt, then flaring slightly outward again. There was a wavy pattern in its steel, but more than that, the blade itself seemed to waver slightly, as if seen through a heat haze. Even in this golden light, with the summer of the Otherworld all around them, the Queen looked pale and plain as she held it up; the sword made whatever was seen with it seem less than real, as the Sidhe had done in Bray.

"Cruaidin Cailidcheann, he called it, the Hard, Hard-Headed. But it had another name first. Cuchullain's true father was not Sualtim, but Lugh the Allcrafted; and this is Fragarach, the Answerer, the Sword of Air, which Lugh sent to him. Take it."

Nita put her hand out to it, and felt a cold fire burning, and a pressure of wind forcing her hand away. "It doesn't want me," she said.

"No. It has its own desires, and I can hold it only because I am one of the Undying. One of you," she said to Kit and Ronan.

Ronan put a hand out, then snatched it back, and scowled. "It doesn't want me, either."

"You then," she said to Kit. "Take it, young wizard, and give it to the Senior, with my blessing. He will be the one to wield it, I think. Say also to him," she said, turning to Ronan, "that I ask him again the question I have asked him before, and ask whether he has any new answer for me."

"I will," Ronan said, but his eyes slid to Fragarach.

Kit bowed slightly. "And I'll deliver this." He took the sword, and apparently had no trouble with it.

"Go, then. The Amadaun will see you home. And have a care, for the One-Eyed is very strong. He is not as strong as he was once . . . but neither are the Treasures." The Queen's green eyes were troubled. "Nonetheless, they may serve. They must serve."

The three nodded.

"Go now."

The horses were brought for them, and they rode back to Nita's aunt's. The dual carriageway wasn't there, but they could recognize the Glen of the Downs as the Good People's horses left it swiftly behind them. The sea glinted before them with colors they had never seen before, under the Otherworld's sun, as they rode down the hill toward Kilquade; then the new colors faded, and there was nothing shining on the sea but mundane sunlight. The road faded into visibility around them at the end of Aunt Annie's driveway.

"Go well," said the Amadaun as they dismounted, and their three horses faded away. "We can do no more for you. One Treasure from the land itself; one from the hand of the People; one from humankind. The fourth must come from elsewhere: from one of the Powers, or not at all."

"You say you're a Fool," Nita said. "Are you making a joke?"

"Always. But the jokes are always true. Beware," he said. "And the One go with you."

He faded away as well. They turned and headed down the driveway, Kit carrying the sword across his hands and looking extremely nervous.

"You said things around here are *getting* weird?" he said to Nita.

She sighed. "Don't ask me for hints that they might get *less* weird," she said. "My money says things get worse yet."

Cheárta na Chill Pheadair

Kilpedder Forge

THERE IT LAY IN the middle of the kitchen table, along with old Lotto tickets and a tea-stained copy of the *Wicklow People,* on top of the place mats, next to a plastic cookie tray with nothing but crumbs left in it, and the milk jar and sugar bowl: Fragarach the Answerer, shining under the light that hung down from the ceiling. They sat around it, nursing their tea, and looking at it. It was hard to look at anything else. The cats sat up on the kitchen counter, the way they did when waiting to be fed, and stared at it, too, big-eyed.

"And that was it," Kit said to Nita's aunt. "They said we would have to come up with the fourth one ourselves, somehow."

"Did they give you any hints?" Aunt Annie said.

Nita shook her head. "Unless you caught something that I didn't, Ronan. I can't always understand the way people talk around here."

Ronan shook his head. "I heard what you heard, more's the pity. I was hoping they might come up with the spear, too."

"You and me both," said Aunt Annie. She stretched, and slumped in her chair. Nita noticed how tired she looked and felt sorry for her.

"Did you do the warding you were going to do?" she said.

Her aunt nodded. "The back office is ready for the cup," she said. "Johnny went to help Doris with it; apparently it's more alive than they had expected and it was causing them trouble. They should be here in a while. Anyway, when you're in the back of the house, watch out for the office door. I had to draw the spell pattern partway up the inside of it to miss the rug in there, and if you open the door, it'll break the circuit. Just reach in through the door if you need something."

They nodded. "Aunt Annie," Nita said, "I was going to ask you. Where does Biddy the farrier live?"

She tried to make it sound nonchalant and had no idea whether she had succeeded. Her aunt looked at her a little curiously. "Just up the road in Kilpedder," she said. "Next to the shop across the dual carriageway. She has her regular forge there. Why?"

Nita tried not to squirm. "I had a couple of questions I wanted to ask her," she said.

"About her forge," Kit said. "It's really neat. I hadn't seen a portable one like that before."

"Oh. Well, it's getting close to teatime: You should be able to find her up there in a while—her work rarely keeps her out much later than this."

Nita became aware of a low buzzing and looked around her. "Is that the oven timer?" she said.

Aunt Annie looked bemused. "No, the oven's not on."

They looked at each other as the buzzing got louder. Some of the spoons on the table began to vibrate gently, moving along the table a little.

"Look at the sword!" Kit said. "It's vibrating."

It was. The low humming sound that Nita had mistaken for the oven timer was coming from it, and it was getting louder. "It sounds a little like feedback," she said.

A faint *beep-beep* sound came from outside. The sword's hum got louder, and (Nita thought) more threatening. "Ohmigosh," her aunt said, "it's Doris and Johnny, and they've got the cup!"

"Neat!" Kit said, and got up. "Let's go see!"

"No!" Aunt Annie said, sounding panic-stricken. "We don't have the place prepared to have *two* of the Treasures here at once! Put two of these things together without adequate preparation, and you're going to get something that makes atomic critical mass look like a wet firecracker!" She looked around hurriedly. "Crikey, I can't leave now! Kit, quick, take it and get out of here!"

He picked it up, rather nervously. It jumped and jittered in his hands, and the hum started to scale up into a howl. "Where?"

"Anywhere! Somewhere far! More than fifty miles. I'll cover you for the overlays, just *go*!"

He looked at Nita. "Copernicus," he said, and said three words, and vanished. The air went *whoomf* into where he had been, not the usual explosion.

Outside, car doors slammed. "Here, let me get that for you, Doris," they heard Johnny say.

They all went to the door. Johnny was pulling the glass sliding door aside. Behind him came Doris Smyth, holding something wrapped in a pastel-striped pillowcase. The something shone through the pillowcase as if it were on fire: a still, cool, changeless fire that nonetheless rippled and wavered on everything it touched, like the sun looked at from underwater. "Back office, Anne?" said Doris, sounding strained but cheerful.

"Right. Don't open the door, just walk through it."

"Certainly. Johnny, you handle that; I have my hands full."

There was no room for them all down that narrow hall. Nita and Ronan stood there and watched as the three older wizards walked past the bookshelves and turned the corner, out of view. Except that they weren't entirely out of view at all; they were faintly visible in the reflected light from the cup, even through the intervening walls. Nita shook her head.

"Don't do things like this at home, do you?" Ronan asked.

She grinned at him and headed back into the kitchen. "Neither do you, buster. Not as a rule, anyway."

She went to fill the kettle for the next inevitable round of tea. "Where's Copernicus?" Ronan said.

"On the moon. Southern hemisphere."

"The moon?"

Nita shrugged. "She said more than fifty miles. That should be enough." Then she looked at Ronan's face as she plugged the kettle in. "Haven't you been there?"

"To the moon? No!"

"Why not? It's neat." He opened his mouth, and Nita suddenly felt annoyed at herself. "The overlays, I guess. I'm sorry. Look, there have to be some places you can teleport from safely. If you can find one, and hop over and see us, we'll run the wizardry through for you and show you around. It's no big deal."

"I'd like that," he said, and smiled slightly. It was a look Nita hadn't seen on him often: the chip off the shoulder for the moment and just a touch of wistfulness. "It must be grand," he said, "being where you don't have to be afraid to do all the wizardries you know can be done."

She laughed a little, and leaned against the counter, waiting for the kettle to boil. "It has its downside—you wouldn't believe the trouble you can get into. Remind me to tell you about the shark who almost ate me . . ."

"Want a look?" Aunt Annie said, coming back into the kitchen with Johnny and Doris behind her.

"Yeah!" Nita said. She headed down the hall, with Ronan behind her.

There was no need to do anything special. Walls meant nothing to the light of the Chalice—or rather the light of what was inside it. The Chalice sat on its pillowcase, with the gold inlay on the outside of the bowl, and in the spirals and curves that ran down its stem and massive foot, all burning as if molten and ready to flow off the cup at a moment's notice. The burning came from the blue-white light filling the Chalice's foot-and-a-half-wide bowl, a light that was liquid, and still trembling slightly from having been moved. It shone through the metal as if it were glass, and through everything else it reached. Nita looked at her hands, and saw through them as if they were a sketch held up to sunlight: an incomplete and smudgy sketch, possibly in need of revision.

She looked at Ronan, and away again, shaking her head. Words seemed inadequate and out of place. But at the same time she couldn't help noticing his expression, like that of someone struggling with a memory and, oddly, not trying to remember, but to forget—

Maybe he felt her eyes on him: He turned his gaze away from the cup and looked at her with a troubled expression. "Let's get together sometime soon," he said. "I need to talk."

Nita suddenly found herself afraid to find out what he wanted to talk about. She nodded and went away hurriedly, back to the kitchen.

The three older wizards were sitting around the kitchen table, waiting for the tea to finish brewing. "There's a message for you from the Queen," Nita said to Johnny. He looked at her questioningly, and Nita repeated the message.

He smiled very slightly, and it was a sad look. "She's asking," Johnny said, "whether there's any hope that the world they have chosen to live in will ever come any closer to Timeheart. They love Ireland, make no mistake; but, at the same time, they're of the Powers, and they long for Timeheart, where they were created. But the legends say they must stay in the world they have chosen until the One's Champion comes back with his spear and they lose the world of their desire." He shook his head. "A while yet, I think . . ."

"Do you want Kit back?" Nita asked.

Johnny passed a hand over his forehead, smoothing his hair back. "Where is he?"

"The moon."

"That's all right, then. Wait a few minutes before you bring him back here. I can add a limiter to the binding on the cup that'll make it at least safe for the sword to be here with it. But the sword will need its own binding."

Doris poured the tea. "That's one less problem," she said. "Now if we just knew what to do about the spear, we'd be fairly ready."

There was silence around the table at that, and some hopeless looks. "You couldn't find anything that would work?" Nita said, as Ronan came in and sat down again.

"My dear," said Doris, "we have the original stone awake again, and what seems to be the original sword. The cup has ensouled very emphatically indeed. We dare not try to conjoin an inferior or weak spear to them. They would blast it out of existence. The resouled spear must be at least as strong as they—preferably much stronger. But we have no proper envelope. It's not strictly a change that a physicist would understand, but matter is not quite the robust stuff it was at the beginning of the world, when Creation as an art was young and the energies of it dwelt new and hot in the nucleus of every atom. As gravity and other forces have declined over many millions of years, so has the basic . . . selfness . . . of matter. You see how the resouled Treasures make everything around them look insubstantial and unreal. The souls in them are reminding the matter they embody how matter was then. It was much closer to being alive."

"But then the spear's soul will remind the matter it's in. Won't it?"

"Not if the matter is simply unable to hold the soul long enough in one place for the change to take," Johnny said. "It'd be like trying to hold a burning coal in a tissue. The spear's soul is the fiercest of them all. I had hoped I was wrong about this, but the research I've been doing over the past couple days indicates that no spear on earth would be strong enough now to contain the soul for long enough to do the trick, whether it had contained the soul before or not."

"Off the earth, then," Nita suggested.

Johnny cocked his head. "It's a thought that occurred to me. But the changes in matter that have happened here have happened everywhere else, too. And we keep coming back to the problem"—he smoothed his hair again—"that we don't have much time."

Ronan sighed and sat back. "It's a pity we can't just make a new one," he said.

Aunt Annie sighed, too. "Even if we had uncontaminated matter from the beginning of time," she said, "we wouldn't have the expertise to do anything with it. I think we're just going to have to keep looking for some other kind of answer." She glanced over at Johnny and Doris. They nodded.

Nita got up. "I'll go get Kit," she said. "Fifteen or twenty minutes be long enough?"

"Fine."

She looked at her aunt, who nodded. "The overlay buffer is still in place. Go ahead."

Nita said the transport spell quickly in her head, considering how much air she would need, doubling it as usual, and arranging the spell intake so that it would take the air from outside the house rather than inside—the memory of the last time she had done such a spell in her own house, without stopping to consider that her father's desk was covered with paperwork, was still with her. She vanished.

She found Kit sitting on his favorite rock—a pumice boulder on which he had been using a sharp piece of granite to whittle the crude likeness of a human face, for the bemusement of future lunar photographic surveys. The sword lay across his lap.

She climbed up beside him. "Johnny said he should be ready for you to come back in a little while."

"I don't want to go right back there," Kit said, turning the sword over in his lap and looking at it. "There's someone I want to have a talk with first."

"Biddy," Nita said.

Kit nodded. "Remember what the fox said to you," he said.

"Listen," Nita said. "You remember how you told me that you felt her forge was alive?" He nodded. Nita started to tell him what Doris had said about the relative liveness of matter at the beginning of time.

He stopped her. "It's OK, I heard it. I used your ears."

She punched him. "Illegal brain-tapping! You didn't even ask me! What if you had overheard something I was thinking?"

"What, about Ronan?"

She blushed and punched him again, much harder, so that in the low gravity he fell off the boulder and bounced a couple of times in the moondust. "Great," he said, as he got up and dusted himself off. "This stuff is all down my shirt. Now I'm going to itch all night."

"Serves you right. Eavesdropper!"

"Still," he said, and looked thoughtful. "He's sharp, your buddy Ronan. Why *shouldn't* they make another one?"

"Because they don't know how. Whaddaya mean, 'my buddy'?" She started heading around the rock to punch him again, far gone in embarrassment.

"Hmm," Kit said. "Neets, forget it, I'll lay off."

"Promises, promises."

"Look, let's go see Biddy."

"What are we going to say to her?"

He shook his head. " 'Come out with your hands up'? I don't know. But if one of Them is here, They need to be giving us a hand. Do you know where we're going?"

"Yeah. I'll pass you the coordinates."

Nita pictured the place in her head—she had seen it often enough when riding past it on the farm's bike—and translated the image quickly into coordinates that could be plugged into a transport spell. "Got it," Kit said. "Just change that bit there. Got it? Go."

They made the jump. Air slid out and away from them, and they were standing by the dual carriageway, near the pub that stood there. It was getting dark.

"Over here," Nita said, and led the way over to the right, where a small group of whitewashed buildings stood near the Kilpedder shop. There was a low iron gate at the entrance to them, covered with ornate and graceful wrought-iron work. A sign hanging on a nearby wall said B.O DALAIGH, I.F.A.

Carefully and quietly Nita unlatched the gate and swung it inward. There were no lights showing in any of the buildings, though Biddy's truck was parked in front of one of them.

"Maybe she went out," Nita said.

Kit shook his head and went slowly to the truck. He put one hand up against the forge-box at the back. "Feel this," he said.

Nita laid her hand against it, and snatched it back with the shock. Life, for a wizard, is something that can be felt like the warmth from a radiator. This was not just a warmth, but a burning—and totally unlike the kind of low-level awareness that inanimate objects normally manifested.

"I can't believe you didn't feel it the first time," Kit said.

"Different specialties, different sensitivities," said Nita. "Besides, I never touched it. But look at that."

She nodded at Fragarach. The dusk was falling all around them, but it had no power over the sword; Fragarach shone as if it lay out in full sunlight, though the waning moon was high and the bats were out.

"It knows," Kit said. " 'Uncontaminated matter from the time of Creation,' did they say?" He chuckled. "Let's see if we can find her."

He went off around one of the outbuildings. Nita leaned against the forge, and breathed out.

"Looking for somebody?" Biddy said from the shadows.

Nita jumped, then laughed a little nervously. *Get a grip on yourself,* she thought. *Now what was the wording?* She didn't move, just watched Biddy head over toward her. "Elder sister," Nita said, "in the One's name, honor and greeting."

"Now what do you mean by—" She stopped, as Kit came around the corner, with the sword in his hand. It had been bright enough. Now, in Biddy's immediate presence, it blazed.

Biddy looked at it and her face altered. Recognition and affection and surprise all appeared in it. "Now I thought that had been put away somewhere safe," she said in her soft drawl.

"It was," Nita said. "But nothing much is going to be safe anymore, unless it gets used."

"It knows you," Kit said. "I can feel that. It just about shouts that it knows you." There was an odd exultation in his face; Nita felt inclined to keep her distance for the moment. "And it knows your forge, there. I think maybe you made this." He hefted the sword, but there was something in the gesture that also looked as if the sword had moved itself, a small leap of excitement. "Or someone using the metal that's been built into that forge made this. Probably both."

Biddy looked at them thoughtfully and leaned against the wall, folding her arms.

"Cutlery isn't usually my stock in trade," Biddy said. "Pretty, though."

"Oh, come *on,*" Kit said. And Nita added, "I wish you'd ditch the accent. It's really bad."

"What?" Biddy said.

Nita had to laugh. "I'm sorry. It's probably good enough to fool the people around here, but it wouldn't fool a real American for very long. The morning I met you, I was wondering why you sounded so weird. Now I know." She laughed again. "You may be one of the Powers That Be, but you're no more perfect than we are. Especially not at sounding like you've lived somewhere you've never been!"

Biddy looked faintly shocked. Then she leaned back again, and she, too, laughed a little, then fell silent, looking at the sword.

"Well?" Kit said.

"Well," said Biddy. "May I see it, then?"

Kit went to her and handed her the sword hilt-first. She took it and held it up to examine it, laying it for a moment across the flat of her forearm. "Not much changed," she said. "Though it's more tired than I remember."

"You can do something about that," Nita said.

Biddy glanced over at her with a humorous look. "You have a lot of confidence in my abilities," she said.

"You'd better believe we do," Kit said. "We've worked with the Powers before."

"Not all of us are of equal ability," Biddy said. "And spending time in a physical body tends to affect one's ability to do one's job."

"The last Power we worked with took on the Lone One after spending ten years in the shape of a macaw, sitting on a perch and eating sunflower seeds," Kit said dryly, "so I wouldn't sell myself short if I were you."

Biddy sighed and looked at the sword. "How long have you been here?" Nita said.

"Since the beginning," Biddy said. She turned the sword over again and looked at Fragarach's flat, as if searching for flaws. "I never left. Couldn't bear to."

Nita boosted herself up onto the fence rail. "You were one of the ones who made Ireland, then."

Biddy nodded, turning Fragarach over again. "The first of the blow-ins," she said, and smiled slightly. "Here." She handed Fragarach back to Kit.

"The stories say that the Tuatha de Danaan came bringing the Treasures from the Four Cities," Kit said. "Those are just parts of Timeheart, aren't they? And you were one of the ones who made the Treasures in the first place."

"I was the Smith of Falias," said Biddy, "among others. I made Fragarach . . . yes."

"And then the stories tell about Govan, the Smith of the Gods, who came to Lugh the Allcrafted," Nita said, "and how they went away together and took the Spear of Victory, Luin, and forged it full of fire and a fierce spirit . . ."

She looked at Nita and nodded slowly. "That was me as well."

"You could do that again," Kit said.

Biddy frowned. "I doubt it," she said. "The worlds aren't what they used to be, and neither is matter."

"The anvil in your forge is," Kit said.

"That can't be used as anything but an anvil," Biddy said. "Its nature is set, from time's beginning almost."

"But if you could get some more of that old original matter—you could do it. You could make another spear!"

"What do you take me for?" Biddy asked, laughing hopelessly. "You really didn't understand me. When you live in the physical world, you have to do it in a physical body. Those are the rules. And if you're going to spend as long in a mortal form as I have, you give up a lot of your power by necessity. It would burn the body out, otherwise, and the brain; physicality just isn't robust enough to bear our state of being for very long. The memories all ebb away after a while. And why shouldn't they? I did my work well—too well." She laughed, with some bitterness in the sound. "I fell in love with what I made and couldn't leave it.

You're quite right that we're not perfect, especially that way. Once I had finished my part in making this place, I didn't want anything more but to be here in peace, forever. The One released me to do that—just to be here, and be useful in my small way, until I'm required to give my power back at the end of things. I do my forge work and live in the place I love."

"Then make yourself useful," Kit said, sounding grim. "Otherwise this place you love is going to be nothing but a big pile of cinders, after Balor gets through with it."

Biddy was shaking her head. "This is one use I can't be. I haven't the power to pull matter here from the heart of time, or its beginning, either! And wizards or not, not even the Seniors have that kind of power!"

"I know someone who does," Nita said, "at the moment, anyway." Kit glanced at her, uncomprehending for a moment—then he got it, and his eyes glittered. "Never mind that now. The memories may ebb—but you can't have forgotten how you made that."

Biddy's eyes lingered on Fragarach. "No," she said. "That I remember very well."

"And the spear?" Kit said.

"I remember some of the details," Biddy said softly. "But I had that other Power to help me, the one they called Lugh the Allcrafted."

"I can't get you someone who knows how to do everything," Nita said, grinning, "but I can sure get you someone who *thinks* she does. Second best, maybe. But take it or leave it."

Biddy stood there, her eyes downcast, irresolute.

"Come on," Nita said. "We could require it of you, in the One's name. Once a Power, always a Power, regardless of how much or little of it you have left. Those are the rules, as you say. But—" She broke off.

Nita and Kit stood quiet. Biddy stared at the ground.

She looked up, then. "It's better than doing nothing, I suppose. Tell me what you want of me."

"Come have some tea at my aunt's," Nita said.

Kit groaned.

Some hours later almost all the free chairs in Aunt Annie's kitchen were full of wizards, all talking hard. Most of them there knew Biddy, and there had been some shock at Nita's announcement of who else she was besides the local farrier, but Fragarach's response to Biddy couldn't be explained in any other way. Shock had been quickly put aside in favor of planning.

"It was Ronan's idea," Nita said, and Ronan blushed right out to his ears. "We can make another. We can!"

"I'll entertain explanations of how," Johnny said, sitting back and stroking his mustache. "Don't tell me you're thinking of pinching some ur-matter from Timeheart, either, because it won't work. Matter there is structured differently from the way matter was at the beginning of time in this universe."

"Timeslide, then," Kit said.

Johnny shook his head. "We would need a wizard with enough power to drive that kind of a slide back far enough. You're talking billions of years."

Kit bent over to Nita and said, "Should I?"

"I think you'd better," Nita said, and sighed. It had been so quiet until now, relatively speaking. "It's after lunch. See if you can do it without raising the alarm, if you know what I mean."

Kit nodded and went out. "It might help," Aunt Annie said to Johnny, "if we understood a little more about exactly what kind of matter's needed."

"Well, you've got a bard around here somewhere, haven't you?" he said. "Let's hear the authorized version first, and then Biddy can give us what she remembers of the technicalities so that we can work on the spelling proper."

"Hmm," Aunt Annie said. She went to the door. "Tualha! Kitty, kitty, kitty! Tuna!"

The kitchen immediately began to fill with meowing cats. "Do you really think this will work, Shaun?" Doris asked.

He stretched, then shrugged. "It's our best chance, I think, considering that no envelope presently extant seems to be suitable. It seems as if the spear's soul burns out its containers the way—well . . ." He looked at Biddy, then away.

The kitty door flapped as Tualha scrambled in through it. She stood there, very small and black, with her tail pointing straight up in the air, and said, "Mew."

Nita burst out laughing. "Cut us some slack, Tualha. It's the Senior for Europe, and he wants your advice."

"Oh, well, that's different," Tualha said. She looked up at Aunt Annie and said, "First things first. What about that tuna?"

"There was a time," Johnny said, "when bards performed first, and *then* the lord of the hall gave them largesse."

Tualha looked disdainfully at him. "Welcome to the twentieth century. Tuna," she said to Nita's aunt. "And then cream, please."

Annie raised her eyebrows, and went to get it. It was astounding how fast such a small kitten could eat, especially in contrast to all the other cats, who had to be fed, too, so that they wouldn't steal Tualha's food. Eventually she was lifted up on the table and given her saucer of cream there, and she lapped it with a thoughtful air, burping occasionally, while the human wizards sat around and nursed their tea.

"Now then," Johnny said.

Tualha sat down and began washing her face. "What do you want to know?" she said.

"Tell us if you would, o bard, of the forging of the Spear Luin."

Tualha began washing behind one ear. "The Spear of Victory itself came from the city Falias; Arias the poet-smith, whom some called Govan, made it there. The song says that Arias took a star and hammered it on the anvil, and so made the blade of the spear. Then the Tuatha de Danaan brought it with them through the air and the high air when they came to Ireland. And with them it stayed, and gave light to any place it was in, for the burning that was in it."

Tualha stopped, yawned, and then started in on the other ear. "Then came Balor, and made a tower of glass for himself and his creatures in the sea near Ireland. Balor's likeness was that of a human, but gross and misformed, and one eye squinted away almost to nothing for the hugeness and horribleness of the other. So great was it that it took four Fomori with forks of iron to pull the eyelid up when Balor wanted it so. And when it opened, what its glance fell on scorched and burned and was poisoned, and blasted off the world and out of it."

Glances were exchanged around the table. "It was foretold by other wizards," said Tualha, "that only fire and the spirit of fire would end Balor, and that one would come who had all skills, and was kin to Balor, and would make that end of him. So the Tuatha waited, looking for that one to come."

"Another of the Powers," Aunt Annie said, "by the sound of it. And a fairly central one, if Balor is another version of the Lone Power."

Johnny nodded. Tualha had tucked herself down into meat-loaf shape. "Nuada the King did not know who that one might be," she said, "so he gathered to him all the great Powers that were in Ireland in those days: Diancecht the Physician, and Badb the Lady of Battles, and the Morrigan, the Great Queen; he gathered in Govan the Smith, and Luchtar the Builder, and Brigit whose name meant the Fiery Arrow, who was healer and smith and poet all together; and cupbearers and druid-wizards and craftsmen of all kinds. And one day they were feasting when a young man came to the door of their great *rath* and asked to come in. The doorman asked what skill he had. He said he was a warrior, and a harper, and a storyteller, too, and a champion in the fight, and a smith, and a cupbearer and a doctor and a wizard and a poet. And when the Powers heard that, they said, 'This must be Lugh the Allcrafted, our deliverer. Let him in so that we can test his power.' They did that, and the young man could do everything he said he could: And the Ildánach, the Allcrafted, is what the Powers nicknamed him. Then they started their plan to drive Balor and the threat of his eye, and his creatures, the Fomori, from Ireland forever."

Tualha looked thoughtfully at the saucer, then at Aunt Annie. Aunt Annie poured her some more cream. "Thirsty work," Tualha said, and had a brief drink. "Then," she said, licking cream off her whiskers, "Lugh went off in private for a long time with Govan the Smith; they took counsel and made a plan, and Lugh had the Spear of Victory brought to him. In secret Lugh and Govan labored for three years, or some say seven, forging the spear anew. Unquenchable fire they forged into it, and a fierce spirit—" Tualha yawned, and crouched down in meat-loaf shape again. "Then when they were done Lugh returned to the great *rath* of the Tuatha de Danaan with the spear, just in time to meet a party of the Fomori that had been sent there by Balor to demand a tribute of slaves from the Tuatha. Lugh unwrapped the spear and called on the Tuatha to cover their eyes, and the spear roared with rage and blasted the Fomori to ash on the instant, all but one that Lugh sent back to Balor to tell what had happened, and bring the message of Lugh's defiance to him." Tualha rolled over on her side and yawned again, blinking at them. "Then the war starts. Did you want anything else?"

"No, that'll do for now. Thank you."

Something went *POW!* out in the front yard. All heads turned at that, and there were some concerned expressions; but a moment later they heard the front door slide open, and Kit walked in.

"Noisy, that," Johnny said. "You weren't so loud when you left."

"Not my fault," Kit said, jerking his thumb over his shoulder.

Behind him, Nita's sister, Dairine, walked into the kitchen: twelve years old, small, skinny, and bright-eyed, with a shock of red hair, wearing shorts and sneakers and a Batman T-shirt three sizes too large for her—one of Nita's, actually. Nita started to fume slightly—Dairine had started borrowing her clothes lately, and returning them in less than pristine condition—but there were more important things to be concerned about at the moment; she kept her annoyance to herself.

Dairine glanced around the kitchen with interest, then said, "Hi, Neets. Hi, Aunt Annie!" And she put down the portable computer she was carrying, and went and gave her aunt a hug.

Johnny and Doris and Biddy and Ronan all watched this with some amusement. "My sister," Nita said to Johnny. "Dairine."

Johnny blinked. "*This* is the Dairine Callahan who—" He paused, then, and laughed at himself. "It would be, wouldn't it? The youngest ones are always the strongest, after all. They're just getting a lot younger these days . . ."

Another chair was pulled in from the living room while introductions were made. Nita had to smile as she watched the portable computer unlean itself from against the table leg, flop down flat on the floor, grow short spidery legs, and wander over to the cat food dish where Bronski was still eating. Bronski hissed at the computer, hit it hard with one paw, and when that didn't do any good, went out the cat door in a hurry.

Nita looked over at Kit, and said, "Any problems?"

"Nothing significant," he said. "She'd had her lunch, so we have a few hours."

"You brief her?"

"I know what you're trying to do, more or less," Dairine said, reaching out to take a cookie from the fresh package their aunt had brought out. "Mmm." She chewed for a few seconds, then said, "It's all been updating itself in the précis in my manual for the past few days." She nodded over at the computer, which was still examining the cat food dish with interest.

"The language is interesting," Johnny said, leaning back in his chair. " 'Took a star and hammered it on the anvil—' "

"When I was in Timeheart, I used meteoric iron," Biddy said quietly. "There seemed to be a certain . . . appropriateness to it."

"There's plenty of that around," Kit said. "Not all in museums, either."

"But not ur-matter," Doris said. "You would need meteoric iron from around the time of the birth of the universe."

Dairine shook her head. "It wouldn't be meteoric," she said. "That early in the physical universe, there weren't any planetary bodies to shatter and turn into meteors yet, not even in the oldest galaxies." She looked at Nita for confirmation: Nita nodded. "You're going to have to get real starsteel."

The older wizards looked at her. "From the nucleus of a *star*?" Johnny asked.

Dairine looked at him with interest. "Plenty of iron inside stars, especially the type As and Fs."

Biddy stared at Dairine. "You're suggesting that someone should put one end of a timeslide into the center of a star light-years away and millions of years back in time, and fasten the other end *here*? And then do what?"

"Forge what comes out at this end," Dairine said. "That's your department, though. You did that—" She glanced over into the next room where Fragarach lay on a sideboard with several layers of spell-warding glowing around it to keep its power from combining disastrously with that of the cup in the back office. "The techniques shouldn't be so different."

"You really think you can do this?" Doris asked Dairine.

"You mean, can I get you what you need?" Dairine said. She sat back in her chair and let her eyes drop closed a little, and then began to speak in the Speech. It was not exactly a spell, but the schematic for one, the outline, with certain key words and phrases left out so that nothing untoward would start to happen just yet. Nita lost the thread of it after about a minute: She had never heard any spell so complex in her life, and the several parts of it that she *did* understand—the power control parameters and the description of the matter that would be conducted down the timeslide, along with several names to be invoked—all rattled her badly. Nita knew that her sister had, in some ways, *become* the manual since her own Ordeal; and by way of semi-parenthood, Dairine had the power of a whole race of sentient computer wizards to draw on. But Nita had not had those facts brought home to her quite so definitely as they were being brought home now. She shivered; it was a little like being big sister to a nuclear explosion that could pick its own time to go off and was thinking of doing so soon.

Dairine stopped and opened her eyes again. "That's the procedure," she said. "It won't be easy, but at least it's not too complicated. When do you want to do it?"

Doris was shaking her head. " 'Forged fire into it,' " she said. "That spell would certainly produce *that* result. Shaun?"

Johnny was looking very thoughtful. "If the other end of the slide were to slip out of place in either location or time," he said to Dairine, "it could annihilate the earth. You realize that, of course."

Dairine shrugged. "At the rate things are going, people might be thankful for something like that shortly. If I were you, I'd take the chance you've got. I can do this now, but whether I'll have the power next week, or next month, is a good guess. If the world still *exists* next week or next month."

There was a silence. "Well, Shaun?" Doris said. "You're the Supervisor."

He sat and stared into his teacup and then said, "I guess we haven't any choice. Tomorrow night, then? At Matrix. Assuming the other Planetaries concur."

Doris nodded, and Ronan, and Nita's aunt. "Will the Treasures be all right here tonight, Johnny?" Aunt Annie asked.

"I should think so. Let's meet at Matrix around eight-thirty in the evening; that'll give us plenty of time to get ready. This ought to be done at about sunset, so that the spear knows what it's for."

Everyone nodded and pushed their chairs back. Nita looked over at Dairine. "You came a long way for just this," she said.

Dairine stretched and grinned. "It was worth it to see the expression on your face when I outlined that spell. What a look! I thought you were gonna—"

"Never mind," Nita said. Becoming a wizard had mostly changed her sister for the better, but it also seemed to have increased some of Dairine's more annoying traits, like the bragging and teasing. "Listen, runt," she said, "I missed you, too. How are Mom and Dad?"

Dairine shrugged. "Mom keeps going on about 'her baby.' Dad looks depressed all the time. They're fine." Then she chuckled. "They'll never try a stunt like *this* on you again."

"Oh?"

"Uh-huh. I heard them arguing about it the other day. Went on for about an hour, and finally Mom said, 'If she wants to be a wizard, fine, let her. Better to have a daughter who's a wizard than not have a daughter.' "

"*Awright,*" Nita said softly. "When can I—" She was about to say *go home*, except that it occurred to her that she didn't want to go home right this minute.

Not until after the business with the spear was settled, anyway. And besides, I'm on assignment . . . I'd have to see it through anyway. "Never mind," she said again. "Did you tell them where you were going?"

"What, and get them all crazed again? No way. Mom hasn't figured out a way to get any promises out of *me* yet, and that's the way it's going to stay. For the time being, anyhow. What time is it at home when it's eight-thirty in the evening here?"

"Three-thirty in the afternoon."

"No sweat," Dairine said. "I don't have to be home for dinner until seven our time. Yes, I know where we're going; it's in the manual. See you tomorrow. Bye, Kit. Spot, heel!"

The computer scuttled over to her; cats hissed and bristled at it as it went by. Dairine vanished, and not one of the various papers on the table moved.

"Hey, pretty slick," Kit said.

Nita laughed to herself for a second. "Look," she said, "you'd better get back, too. Your folks are going to start wondering."

"Let 'em wonder," Kit said. But he started heading for the door. Nita followed and said, "Make sure you get your sleep."

Kit laughed, too, a rueful noise. Excitement sometimes made it hard for him to sleep the night before a big wizardry, and Nita was used to teasing him about the circles under his eyes. "I'll try," he said. "Take it easy, huh?"

"Yeah."

Kit vanished, too; Johnny and Doris and Ronan headed out past Nita to Johnny's car, saying their good nights as they went. As Ronan passed her, he said, "That was your sister?"

"Uh-huh."

"You poor thing," said Ronan.

Nita nodded in complete agreement. "She has her uses, though," she said. "See you later."

Ronan chuckled and went out.

Nita went back into the kitchen, where she found her aunt staring moodily at a sink full of teacups. "They breed," she said, "I swear they do."

Nita laughed and reached up to the shelf that held the dishwashing liquid.

Casleán na mBroinn/ Caher Matrices

Castle Matrix

SLEEP REFUSED TO COME easily to Nita that night. Finally about midnight she got up and struggled back into her clothes, thinking that she would see if there was anything worth watching on TV, even if it was some boring movie on satellite or the twenty-four-hour news channel.

She never made it past the backyard. It was a clear night, while the last few had been misty, and the Milky Way hung overhead, nothing subtle about it: the galaxy seen edge-on and for once looking it, ridiculously bright. Nita climbed up on the fence between the yard and the riding ring and just sat there and stared at the stars for a long time. Only a month or so ago she had been out that way, among thousands of alien creatures—and she still felt stranger here than she had there. . . .

The crunch of the gravel down the drive got her attention. Nita held very still and listened, finding herself getting very tense. Who knew what kind of people went sneaking around farms when everyone was in bed . . .

She knew, though. The tension got worse . . . not to say that it was entirely unpleasant.

By the time the dark shape turned the corner of the house and paused, looking around, Nita's sight was so adjusted to the night that he might as well have been spotlit. And there were other indications, to another wizard, anyway. Very quietly she said, *"Dai."*

He said nothing for the moment, just came over to where she sat on the fence. His head was on a level with hers; very faintly, the starlight caught in Ronan's eyes. *"Dai,"* he said. It came out as more of a growl.

She laughed at him, very softly so as not to attract any attention from the house. "You sound angry all the time," she said, "you know that? Doesn't it run you down?"

He turned away from her a moment, leaning against the fence next to her and looking up at the sky. "I couldn't sleep," he said.

Nita grunted softly and looked up herself. "And you walked all the way up here from Bray? I'm glad I didn't bother going in to look at the TV. There must *really* be nothing on."

This time she actually felt him getting angry, sensed it rising off him like steam off a hard-ridden horse. "Look," she whispered as he opened his mouth, "just spare me, OK? *Everything* somebody says to you, you find a reason to get ticked off about it. It's a wonder anyone even talks to you anymore. Except you're so—" Words jostled in her head. She shut up. *Cute. Sensitive. Helpless . . .*

He opened his mouth again, shut it, and then opened it again and started to laugh, almost soundlessly. "Yeah. I guess. I've always been this way. But lately it's been getting worse. Like whatever causes it is getting closer."

Ronan looked at her sidewise—a sort of wry expression, clearly visible even in this dimness. "Funny. I thought you were pretty different when I met you first—"

"And now you think I'm pretty normal?" Nita asked. "Thanks a lot."

"No," Ronan said, sounding annoyed. "I think you're more different than anybody around here. Especially the other girls." He sounded less annoyed. "A lot of them talk tough all the time, but if you push them, they give. You, though, you don't talk tough—mostly. When you do, you're scary." He shrugged. "And as for pushing—you just fall all over whoever does it, like a brick wall."

Nita blushed at this, not sure what to make of it. "Well, you're sure different from everyone else *I* know," she said, and then shut her mouth again lest the confusion inside find its way out and make her look like a total dork.

But Ronan just laughed again. "You think loud, too," he said.

The last blush was nothing compared to this one, but Nita fought it down, starting to get annoyed herself. That broke off, though, when she saw the way he was looking at her. For once, there was no anger about it. Bizarrely, the look made her start to shake a little. Then it occurred to her that there was nothing bizarre about it, for it was not her own physical excitement she was feeling. She knew what *that* felt like.

There was nothing in the manual about this. *Or is there?* Nita thought. *Have I ever looked? It's not as if the subject has ever come up, working with Kit—*

Then abruptly she knew, or started to know, more about it. Nita sat there in the starlight and swallowed, getting her first taste of what it was like for a native wizard to experience the Knowledge, the direct input from the wizardly database, which was the way Irish wizards experienced the information. *Would it keep getting this way for me if I stayed here longer?* she wondered. But that was hardly important just now: There was other information to consider. Of course wizards got physical with each other sometimes, just the same as other human beings did. But they experienced it somewhat differently. It had to do with the Speech, which had physical components as well as verbal and mental ones—and when two people fluent in the Speech were attracted, they were likely to overhear each other's bodies as well as their minds—

Nita broke out in a sweat. *Not mine,* she thought, fascinated. She looked at Ronan, and for a long few moments her thoughts chased themselves unintelligibly through her head. Only one finally made itself plain:

Well, heck, I guess you have to start somewhere. And I do like him—otherwise I wouldn't even be thinking *about this . . .*

Ronan looked away. And Nita said, "You're not going to get any pushing out of me on this one." She was still shaking, but it was her own nervousness this time.

She just sat there and waited.

He leaned back on the fence. His face was quite close to hers: She caught the starlight in his eyes one more time before he bent in to kiss her.

She spent the first two seconds trying to figure out what to do with her nose. After that Nita was simply lost in sensation: the kiss itself, and what underlay it, the rush and pour of thought and emotion that was both of their minds getting tangled together. She was nervous about it at first, but after a moment it seemed completely natural, that odd, fresh scent of his mind—*Green*, she thought, *of course*, and was tempted to laugh—and behind it, another sensation, something faint but familiar; she couldn't place it. . . .

The kiss broke. She blinked at him. Her heart was racing.

The second kiss went on for a lot longer. This time, as the sweetness built in her body, Nita went shouldering through that welcoming greenness in his mind, touching it, but curiously hunting that sense of something else. And there in the dark was some of that anger, quite a bit of it, actually, fretting, churning against itself. There was something down in the warm dark here, an irritant, a scent or color that she knew, that made Ronan keep lashing out at everything: some kind of energy looking to be properly expressed. Not mere rage, but a righteous anger, turning on itself, without an outlet, impotent at the moment, straining to get out and be put to the right purpose. Nita blinked in the middle of the kiss. A flash of scarlet, an impression of something swift and fierce and full of temper, and utterly good—

Her eyes flew open and she broke off the kiss in shock as she recognized the mind-sense of what was struggling down inside of Ronan. *"Peach!"* she whispered. But that had been only one of that creature's names. It had many others. Without her being able to prevent it, she felt Ronan's thought follow hers, down to the image of how she had seen Peach last—moulted out of its old body, now superb, immortal, unconquerable, one of the Powers That Be, the one with many names, the One's Champion—

"No," Ronan gasped. *"No!"*

And he was gone now, running, the sound of his going frantic on the gravel. Fading. Gone. Nita sat there on the fence, shaking, half in tears, half too amazed to cry.

The night fell silent again around her.

She went back to bed, but it was a long time before she could sleep.

The next evening she and her aunt and Kit got into the car together at about eight. The shadows were just getting long: Sunset was not until nine-thirty that night, and it wouldn't be completely dark until maybe eleven.

Castle Matrix was eastward from Greystones and Kilquade, in the mountains beyond Sugarloaf. They drove down many small narrow roads, which got smaller and narrower and bumpier all the way, until finally they came to a driveway with two huge trees at the end of it, each one beginning to be covered with a great mass of red berries.

"Rowan," Nita's aunt said.

"I know," Nita said. "I have a friend at home who's a rowan tree."

Her aunt chuckled. "It's still so funny to hear things like that come out of one of my relatives . . ."

"There it is," said Kit. They turned out of the driveway into an open graveled area. Off to one side, Castle Matrix rose. The main part of it was a plain square tower, about a hundred and twenty feet tall and fifty feet on a side, of light gray granite. To Nita's intense delight, it actually had battlements on top. There were narrow arrow-slit windows here and there up and down the face of the tower, and a huge iron-bound oaken door at the bottom. Off to one side, an additional wing had been added. It was about fifty feet high, with diamond-paned windows. A low fieldstone wall ran around the graveled area. She wandered over to it after they got out of the car. Biddy's truck was parked by that wall, and the forge was missing from the back of it.

The oak door swung open for them. There was Johnny in his leisure suit, looking very ordinary except for what he held in one hand. It was a rod that burned with light. Nita recognized it as a tool she had used once before herself, a rowan wand that had spent time out in moonlight: a potent weapon for a lower-level wizard, though she couldn't imagine what Johnny needed one for. "Come on in," he said.

Nita and Kit went in behind Annie, looking around in curiosity. About six feet inside the door was a long, heavy, wine-colored brocade curtain. "Drafts," Johnny said, pushing it aside; "you wouldn't believe the drafts we get in here in winter."

They passed through the curtain and looked around, and up, and up. This was the castle's main hall, about fifty feet across; it had whitewashed walls, black-and-white-tiled floors, and big, handsome polished wooden tables. Immediately to their left was a huge fireplace with a strange sort of grate that seemed to be designed to hold the fire's coals vertically rather than horizontally; a big iron spit and a crank to turn it stood in front, and there were smaller fireplaces, grills actually, on either side of the main grate. Tall arched windows, about five feet wide, were set into the west and south walls. The wooden tables had been pulled off to the sides of the big room, and in the middle of the floor, where all the tiles were dark, a very elaborate spell diagram was being laid out in white. Nita sniffed, and recognized the sweetish smell of water-based acrylic paint from her art classes.

"Doesn't scuff off in the middle of a spell," Johnny said, picking up a brush. "Anyway, welcome to Matrix."

"Have you always lived here?" Kit said, looking around in admiration. "Did you inherit it?"

"Oh no," Johnny said. "I found this place in ruins. A big tree growing through what was left of the roof, right about here"—he pointed to the center of the room, where the spell diagram was. "We had it removed when we started to renovate the place, my wife and I. She's in London at the moment with our son. But the Normans built the place, originally, sometime in the eleven hundreds, when they were trying to subdue Ireland." He chuckled and looked down at his work. "They fell in love with it and got 'more Irish than the Irish,' as the saying goes."

"Seems to be a lot of that going around," Kit said.

Johnny nodded. "They built this place on the site of an old holy well . . . It's still here. But there's more than that. Matrix had been a center for a lot of kinds of faith, or power, over the years. The Mother Goddesses were honored here first . . . That's where its first name came from. *Matrix* means *womb*, but the older form was probably *matricis*—the Castle of the Mothers. Then for a while, I think, the well was sacred to Brigit, the old fire goddess; and later to Saint Bridget, the Mary of the Gael as they called her. Other mysteries were here later. There was some connection with the Knights Templars; some of them said this was one of the Grail Castles. But all those came later. We have older business tonight . . ."

"Are you about ready?" Aunt Annie asked.

"Just about. Waiting on Biddy and Dairine. Ronan's in the back with Doris, making tea."

"Where else?" Kit muttered.

"Give it time, you'll get used to it," Nita said. She wandered over to the diagram that Johnny was working on, noticing the elegance and cleanness of it. Half the figures in the Speech that she was used to tracing out laboriously and in whole here were only hinted at; a single graceful stroke held the place for a figure or diagram much more complex. *I guess when you're Senior for a continent, though, you get enough practice to be able to do that . . .* It was a big five-noded diagram, with a separate circle for each of the existing three Treasures—each written around with the reinforcing and warding spells that each specific Treasure would need—and a fourth circle for the starsteel that would become the spear. That fourth circle was particularly densely written in, and Nita could understand why. The spell there was for the magnetic bottle that would be needed to confine the starsteel and cool it down until it was safe to work; for in its native condition inside the star the starsteel would not be solid metal, or even molten, but iron plasma at something more than seven thousand degrees Kelvin. If there was any specific part of the spell diagram Nita would have been interested in double-checking, that was it. But again the shorthand that Johnny was using was a little beyond her. . . .

Nita stopped then, suddenly, and looked down as Johnny finished one character and touched it with the rowan rod. The acrylic flared briefly bright, then died down again.

Nita stared at the floor.

"Something wrong?" Johnny asked.

"There's something down there."

She was aware of Kit looking at her uncomprehendingly from off to one side, where he had been examining a set of old pikes mounted against the wall. "Yes, there is," Johnny said. "I didn't expect you to feel it, but then a lot of wizards older and more experienced than you don't. There's a power in the earth here, not the earth itself, though. The water table runs fairly high here, and this castle's element is water. No surprise, since the place is more or less haunted by the 'female principle,' and water and femaleness are associated. You saw the little stream that runs down by the forge, out by where you parked? We'll be doing work down there later."

Nita stood there just feeling it—a long, slow swelling, biding its time, caring nothing for the flash and dazzle and busyness of life, but only for slow nourishment, things growing, things prospering, birth, being. She glanced up at Johnny and said, "This is the only place where we could do what we have to, isn't it?"

"To keep fire from getting out of hand," he said, "water, always. One way or another, we have plenty of it here."

Doris came in, followed by Ronan with the tea tray. He put it down on one of the tables and joined Nita and Kit as they looked at the diagram. Johnny finished one last figure, then stood up. "Tidy enough?" he asked. "Did I miss anything?"

Nita shook her head in complete helpless ignorance. Kit said, "Don't look at me," and moved off to pour himself a cup of tea. Doris came to stand by Johnny and look over the diagram.

"All names seem to be in place," she said. Her gaze dwelt particularly on one spot, which Nita had noticed earlier and not known what to make of. While the rest of the spell was written in shorthand, the names of the participants were all written out in full, which was vitally necessary. Your name in the Speech was meant to describe you completely, and to work with a shortened version of your name was to dangerously shortchange yourself of your own potential power. The name written in the spot Doris and Nita were examining, though, was not the complex, fussy thing that most human names were. It was simple, just six curves and a stroke. Names that short tended to be like short words in the dictionary— the shorter they are, the more meanings they tend to have—and mortals did not have names like *that* one, all power and age. But then again, one of them spelling tonight was not mortal. *Still—there's something odd about it. The usual continuation curve is cut off awful short—*

"Hi, y'all," said Dairine as she swung in through the brocade curtain. "What's shakin'? All set? Oh," she said, stopping at the edge of the diagram and taking a long look at it.

"Does it meet with your approval?" Johnny asked.

"Looks fine to me. Yo, Spot!" she called, looking over her shoulder. The laptop computer came scuttling in and sat down under a table.

"You picked out a star yet?" Nita asked Dairine, as her sister paused beside her.

Dairine shook her head. "Can't predict the positions that accurately from this end," she said. "We're just going to have to wait until the time-slide's fastened, and then take a look around and pick one that looks good."

"Just make sure you pick a star that's not scheduled to have inhabited planets later," Kit said from the other side of the spell diagram.

Dairine looked at him with mild amusement. "Kit, from that end of time, it's already happened. There never *was* a star to have planets."

"You hope," Kit said. "If it didn't work, back then, then the star's either still just fine, or it's long since gone nova from its core being tampered with . . . and we're all going to be so much plasma in about fifteen minutes."

Dairine grinned at him. "Adds spice to life, doesn't it? Don't worry, Kit. I'm here."

Kit looked at Nita with an expression that was eloquent of what he thought that was worth. Nita shrugged at him. *She* is *pretty hot stuff at the moment*, she said privately.

If she screws this up, we all will be, Kit replied. *Oh, well . . . we've been in worse spots.*

That was true enough. Nita had never had a Senior spelling with her, let alone the Senior for a whole continent. In the past it would have lent her a lot of peace of mind. At the moment, though, it didn't seem to be helping much.

Pre-spell nerves, Kit said. *Me, too.*

It was small consolation. Nita sat down for a moment, watching Johnny go over the last few details of the spell diagram with the rowan wand to activate and check the separate character groups. The curtain to the kitchen wing stirred, and Biddy came in slowly, carrying what looked like a long, wide, rectangular piece of metal.

She placed the object inside the node of the spell diagram that was meant to contain the iron plasma, and then stood up, massaging her back. It was a bar of metal all right, about six inches thick and six inches wide, and about two feet long. The bar had a long, deep groove in it, about three inches wide and three inches deep, right down the length of it, to within about an inch of either end.

"There," she said to Johnny. "That's the casting mold I use for fireplace tools. The best I could come up with."

Dairine wandered over and looked at it. "How much does it hold?" she asked. "Molten metal, I mean."

"About twenty pounds."

"I mean in volume."

Biddy looked surprised. "I don't usually think of it in those terms. About a liter, I'd say."

"Hmm." Dairine looked at the mold, then glanced at the laptop computer. It got up from under the table, came over, and looked at the mold itself; then it and Dairine seemed to exchange glances, though how the computer did that with no eyes was a good question.

"Yeah," she said to it. To Biddy she said, "What's the melting temperature of the mold? I don't want to mess it up."

"It's case-hardened," she said. "About eight hundred degrees Fahrenheit."

"OK." Dairine looked thoughtful. "You want some carbon in with the iron?"

"About one and a half percent."

"Gotcha." Dairine looked at the computer for a moment; it made a soft disk-drive thinking noise, which amused Nita, since she could see that both its drives were empty. "OK," Dairine said to Johnny. "I'm ready when you are."

He took one last long look at the spell diagram as he stepped into the middle of it. "I know that in group spellings people usually divide the work up evenly among them," he said, "but if it's all right with you all, I'd sooner handle everything but the actual timeslide, and leave that part of things to Dairine. The Treasures themselves are going to need watching to make sure that they don't interfere, and I would prefer that each of you in the active diagram concentrate on that. Does that seem appropriate to you?"

Everyone nodded or muttered agreement.

"All right, let's get to it. Doris, the cup—"

"Right," she said, and went into the kitchen. A moment later, light swelled behind the brocade curtain, and she elbowed it aside and carried in the Ardagh Chalice. The whole thing blazed, and the knotwork designs running around its bowl and foot were so bright that to Nita's dazzled eyes they looked as if they were moving. Doris carefully bent down to place the cup in the center of its circle. It burned even brighter, and the light-liquid inside moved gently and threw ripples of brightness on the high ceiling.

"Water knows its own," Johnny said. "Doris, keep an eye on it. If any of these things is likely to get out of hand here, it's the cup."

"Oh, I'll mind it all right, don't you worry about that."

"We needn't do anything about the stone," Johnny said, glancing at the circle next to that of the cup. "We couldn't be much more in contact with the earth if we tried, and it's here already. Kit—"

Kit brought in Fragarach and laid it carefully in the circle waiting for it. Its light was burning low, but a breath of wind stirred the door curtains and the banners hanging from the ceiling as he put it in place.

"Air is ready," Johnny said. "One element only remaining, and that's the one we need. Ready, Dairine?"

She stepped into the circle for fire, next to the steel mold, and said, "Let's do it."

Johnny put his hands behind his back, bent over a little the way someone might bend over to read a newspaper lying on the ground, and began to speak, reading the spell from the diagram. Things had seemed quiet before—here, far from any town or road, close to sunset, that was hardly surprising—but the silence that shut down around them now, and into which the Speech began to fall, was more than natural. Nita felt her hair stand up on end, the old familiar excitement and nervousness of the start of a spell combining with the effect of the wizardry itself on the space and matter within its range of influence. Under the silence Nita could hear, or sense, a constant slow rush and flow of water—or the essence of it—welling up and sinking away again, taking all dangerous influences away with it.

That was something of a problem, of course, for that same flow was likely to perceive the building energies of the wizardry itself as a dangerous influence, and try to carry it away as well. Nita had particularly noticed the careful reinforcement that Johnny had done around the edges of the spell to prevent this. But all the same, the soft rushing sound that she more felt than heard was washing against the boundaries of the wizardry, becoming more insistent as the spell progressed, like waves pushing harder and harder against a coastline as the storm comes up behind them.

The spell was taking. It was always a sure sign when you began to perceive it as a physical thing, rather than just words spoken: Reality was being affected by it. Nita put up a tentative hand to the air in front of her and felt smooth, cool stone, though the air was clear and empty before her, or seemed that way. The Lia Fail was performing its function, holding the boundaries closed against whatever forces might come loose inside them.

The darkness was slowly falling outside, but not in the hall where they stood. Fragarach and the cup blazed, throwing long shadows back and up onto the walls from everyone who stood there—a clear, warm, pale light from the sword; a bluer, cooler burning from the cup. One moment the cup was brighter, the next the sword; Nita could hear Johnny's voice straining a little as his mind worked to keep them in balance until the symmetries of the first part of the spell were complete. There was no telling how long it would take. One moment he seemed to have been speaking forever, and the next, only for a few seconds. It was the usual confusion about time when you were in the middle of a spell. The world seemed to hold still while you redescribed it.

His voice stopped. Johnny looked over at Dairine.

She nodded, folded her arms, and began speaking. And if Nita's hair had stood up before, now she felt as if every hair had turned into a pin and was sticking her. Dairine was building the timeslide, the long pipeline through spacetime that would conduct the starsteel to where they needed it. The timeslide would not, of course, actually exist *in* space or time, but would circumvent them both. Normal matter disliked such circumventions of the rules and complained bitterly during the process. Nita looked at Kit and saw him nearly in the same distress, his jaw clenched to help bear it. Ronan looked no better, nor did any of the grown-ups. But Dairine looked completely unaffected. She paused for a moment, examined the spell diagram, and then said five words, carefully, a second or so between them. She waited again.

Abruptly they were no longer in a room. They stood, all of them, on or around a glowing webwork in the middle of nothingness, but a nothingness that was strewn with stars, cluttered with them, crowded with them. *They're too close together!* was Nita's first panicked thought. Not even in the hearts of young galaxies or new globular clusters was there stellar density like this; these stars were so close that some of their coronae were mingling. In other spots, three or four stars were pulling matter out of one another in bizarrely warped accretion disks. New stars were forming all over the place, or trying to, as they stole matter from one another, swirled, kindled as she watched. This was the view from the other end of the timeslide that Dairine had constructed.

She's crazy, Nita thought. *We're barely out of the big bang here—the universe can't be more than a few hundred thousand years old!* But if Dairine heard Nita's thought, she gave no sign of it. One after another of the stars nearby seemed to veer close, then away again, as Dairine considered it, rejected it. For a few seconds the sunspotted globes of stars seemed to pour past them, twisting and skewing. Then one loomed up close, a big white star with a tinge of gold.

Dairine closed her eyes and spoke one more word.

It was as if the world had caught fire. Nita was frozen as much by her own horror as by the spell itself. With her outward senses, she knew that everything was fine, that the darkness of Matrix and the light of the Treasures was all around her; but her mind saw nothing but annihilation. A ravening light so desperately destructive as to make the thought of physical existence seem ridiculous in the face of it, pressure and heat beyond anything she could imagine—she saw straight into the heart of this, and could not look away. Vaguely she could feel Dairine doing something, speaking again, naming in the Speech the amount and type of matter she wanted, the form, the place of delivery—all as casually as if she were filling out an order form. Dairine came to the end of her specifications, and was about to sign her name—

The rushing sound suddenly became deafening, and the perception of unquenchable fire was suddenly invaded by something: that cooler, bluer light, the feeling of liquid, quelling and subduing. Then, for the first time, Nita felt something from Dairine: panic, just barely controlled. The cup had sensed fire, and was trying to put it out—the essence of all quenchings was trying to flow up the timeslide, into the core of a live star. The *least* that could happen was that the timeslide would be deranged, and the whole energy output of that star would backfire down it—

Two more voices were raised then, in the Speech, quite suddenly—Doris's and Aunt Annie's—and their tone was astonishing. Nita almost burst out laughing, despite her terror, as the two of them scolded one of the elements of the universe as if it were an unruly child. They sounded as if they intended to send it to bed without dinner. Funny it might have been, but if the two of them had anything, they had certainty. The cup struggled, the blue light washed higher—then abruptly fell away.

Nita sagged with relief. Dairine had calmed down from her bad moment and was completing her end of the spell. Through the blinding images still in her mind, Nita could see Dairine look carefully at the metal mold resting on the floor, then crouch down and poke her finger very carefully at a spot in the air about a foot above it. She lowered her finger carefully to the mold, and said another word.

Fire followed her gesture. It paused in the spot where Dairine's finger had first paused, and Nita smelled ozone as the tiny spark of plasma took shape at this end of the timeslide and destroyed the air molecules in the spot where it had arrived. That one pinpoint of light drowned out even the fire of the Treasures and threw back shadows from everyone as stark as if they had been standing on the moon. Then the light began to flow down in a narrow incandescent pencil-line, cooling rapidly out of the plasma state into iron vapor and then into a molten solid again, as Dairine let it pass out of the small magnetic-bottle part of the spell and into the mold.

Slowly the mold filled, the steel of it smoking. All the air began to smell of burnt metal. Nita looked over at Dairine; she was turned into a white-and-black paper cutout by the ferocity of the light hanging a foot away from her nose, but she seemed not to be bothered by it. Nita could see her beginning to shake, though—even Dairine couldn't hold a wizardry like this in place for long. *Come on, Dari*, she thought. *Hang in there—*

The mold kept filling. Nita could feel the cup trying to get out of hand again, and her aunt and Doris holding it quiet by sheer skill in the Speech and calculated bad temper. Dairine was wobbling where she crouched, and put one hand behind her to steady herself, and sat down on the floor, but never once took her eyes off that spot in the air where the plasma was emerging—her end of the timeslide. If it moved, if it got jostled—

Come on, come on! Nita thought. *How long can it take? Oh, please, God, don't let my sister get fried! Or the rest of us*, she added hurriedly, as that possibility suddenly occurred to her. *Come on, Dari, you little monster, you can do it!*

The light very suddenly went out, with a noise like a large short circuit happening. Dairine fell over sideways. Everyone blinked; nothing was left but the light of the three Treasures—now looking very pale to their light-traumatized eyes—and one other light. The steel mold was full of it: iron, still liquid and burning red, skinning over and going dark, like cooling lava. Just the sight of it unnerved Nita and filled her with awe and delight. It somehow looked more definite and real than anything else in the area . . . anything else but Fragarach and the cup.

Nita went over to help Dairine up. Her sister tried to stand, couldn't, and sagged against Nita.

"What's this 'little monster' stuff?" Dairine whispered. "It never even got really tough." And she passed out.

"Here," Johnny said from above Nita, and bent down to pick Dairine up. "I'll put her in on the couch. She's going to be out of it for a while. Biddy—"

Biddy was standing there looking at the mold and shaking all over. Nita glanced at Kit, who had noticed this as well. He shook his head, said nothing.

"I think we're going to have a late night," Johnny said. "You're all welcome to stay. We've got room for you. I think we should all take a break for an hour or so. Then—we've got a spear to forge."

He looked at Biddy. She was still trembling, as if with cold.

She looks worse than Dairine did, Kit said to Nita privately.

Nita glanced over at him. *If she pulls her bit off that well, we'll be in good shape.*

If, Kit said. *But why am I getting nervous all of a sudden?*

Nita shook her head and went to find something to drink. She agreed with Kit. The problem was, wizards rarely got hunches that didn't have meaning, sooner or later.

She had a feeling it would be sooner.

Lughnasád

NITA WENT AND TOOK a nap immediately. What she had seen had worn her out; and she had been drawn on for general energy assistance during the spell, too, so it was only understandable that she would feel a little wiped out afterward.

When she got up, it was two in the morning. Everything was very still except for a faint clanging sound, soft and repetitive, that wouldn't go away. She had an idea what it might be.

She got off the ancient bed in the upstairs bedroom Johnny had shown her and wandered down into the great hall. It was empty now: The spell diagram had been carefully scraped off, and the floor scrubbed. The clanging was closer.

She went gently out the front door of the hall and stood there, in the night, listening. Far off on a hill, a sheep went "baa." There was a faint hint of light about the far northeastern horizon, an indication that the sun was already thinking about coming up again and would do so in a couple of hours. *If it's like this now*, Nita thought, *what must it be like around midsummer? It must hardly even get dark at all . . .*

The sound was coming from off to her left. She followed a little path around the edge of the castle toward where the drystone wall ran. The sound of water came chuckling softly up the riverbed beneath it, and the clanging continued, louder.

She made a small wizard-light to help her go. It sprang out of the air beside her, a small silver spark, and lit her way down the rough stone steps that went toward the water.

The clanging paused, then resumed. Ahead of her was a small, low building with a rough doorway. There was no door in it, just an opening surrounded by stones. She paused there and looked in.

The castle's forge was larger than it had seemed from outside in the dark. Biddy's steel-walled portable forge had been carried in and set up on one side; her anvil stood in the middle of the floor on a low stone table there. There was a stone trough, like a watering trough for horses, off to one side, full of cold water that ran in and out from a channel to the river outside. Something else was there as well: the Ardagh Chalice, sitting all by itself on another stone sill, shining. Its light was quiet at the moment, though it flickered ever so slightly in time with Biddy's hammer blows, when the sparks flew up.

Biddy kept hammering—not a simple single stroke, but a *clang-tink, clang-tink*, doubled with the rebound of the hammered ingot on the anvil; a sound like a heartbeat, but metallic. Biddy's shirt sleeves were rolled up, her shirt was soaked with sweat, and sweat stood out on her forehead. Johnny was leaning against a wall, watching; Kit was sitting on the edge of the trough, swinging his legs. He raised his eyebrows at Nita as she came in.

"I couldn't sleep," he said. "Even after I went home. So I came back. My folks think I'm still in bed . . . It's not a problem."

"What about Dairine?"

"I saw her home. If she needs to come back tomorrow, she can."

"I don't think we'll be needing her anymore at this point," said Johnny. "Also, I wouldn't like to put all my eggs in one basket. Some of us might not come back from this intervention, and the newer talents like Dairine may be needed for defenses elsewhere if we can't pull this off."

Nita came in close enough to see what Biddy was doing, while at the same time staying out of her way so as not to spoil her concentration. The bar of starsteel had now been hammered out flat. As Nita watched, Biddy paused and picked up the hot steel in her tongs, shoving it back into the furnace. She turned up the feed to the propane bottle, and the steel began to glow cherry red, and brighter. "When are you going to do it?" Nita asked Johnny.

He sighed and leaned back. "I think we have to make our move tomorrow. May as well be: It's Lughnasád. A good day for it."

"But you can't have the spells ready by then," Biddy said to him. "You can't possibly—"

"They're ready enough," Johnny replied. "We can't wait for the poetry of them to be perfect. It's not the old days anymore, unfortunately. Brute force and the Treasures are going to have to carry the day . . . or nothing."

Biddy looked with a critical eye at the steel. It was getting crocus yellow. She pulled it out hurriedly, put it back on the anvil and began beating it with the hammer in such a way that it folded over. Nita looked at the lines running up and down the length of the spear blank and realized that she had already done this many times. This would strengthen the metal and give it a better edge. "When does the 'forging in the fierce spirit' bit start?" Nita asked.

Johnny laughed. "Oh, the re-ensoulment? As soon as Biddy's done. We can't wait any longer. Fortunately we don't have to do what the Power that worked with her the first time did, and actually call that spirit out of timelessness. It's here already, somewhere. All it needs is to be slipped into this body."

"It seems strange, sometimes," Kit said, leaning back and taking a drink out of a Coke he had with him. "The idea of weapons having souls . . ."

"Oh, it was common in the older days. It was a rare sword that wouldn't tell you its history when you picked it up—and verbally, not just the way one would do it these days, to a wizard sensitive to such things. That may be our problem today . . . that our weapons don't nag us anymore, or tell us what they think of what we're doing with them . . . just let themselves be used. But then they take their example from us. And bigger things than just people have lost their spirits over time: planets, nations . . ."

Nita looked at him curiously. "Nations have souls?"

"With so much life concentrated in them, how could they not? You must have seen how certain images, personifications, keep recurring. All our countries have their own hauntings, good and bad. The bad ones get more press, unfortunately." He shifted against the stone of the wall. "But the good ones do keep resurfacing . . ."

Nita looked at the steel, cooling now on the anvil as Biddy rested for a moment. "How much longer do you need to fold it?"

Biddy shook her head. "It's had enough. There are maybe twenty thousand layers in there now, if I've done my figuring right."

"It's not the hardness of the steel itself that's going to make it useful as a weapon," Johnny said, "but you're right; something useful should be beautiful, too . . . Let me know when you're ready."

"Not too long now," Biddy said. She put the spear blank in the fire one last time, and turned the gas up. The length of metal got hotter and hotter, reaching that crocus yellow shade again and getting brighter still. She watched the color critically. "About seven hundred degrees," Biddy said then. "That's all it needs. Kit, you want to move out of the way?"

Kit hopped down and moved hurriedly to the side as Biddy plucked the steel out of the fire and came past him. It was radiating such heat that Nita could feel it from where she stood clear across the room. But Biddy seemed not to mind it. To Nita's surprise, Biddy headed, not to the water trough, but straight for the Chalice.

"Straight in," Johnny said.

Nita opened her mouth to say, *You're nuts, that won't fit in there!* But Biddy, holding the length of metal by one end, eased it straight down into the light-liquid in the cup—and in, and in, and in, far past the point where it should have come out the bottom of the Chalice, if the Chalice had been any ordinary kind of vessel. She held the metal there. A roar and a bubbling went up, and the light of the Chalice rose and fell; but none of its contents flowed over the edge, and finally the bubbling died away and the roaring got quiet. Biddy pulled the metal up and out. It was dark again, almost a dark blue on its surface.

"So how exactly are we going to do this, Shaun?" Biddy said, as she laid the metal on the anvil again and reached for a file.

"Well. All the Dark Power's forays so far have been into our own world— twistings of our reality. We're just a beachhead, of course; it's Time-heart that's really being attacked. It's true, we have had some limited successes against it here, because we're fighting on our own ground, so to speak. But we can't hope to prosper if we stay merely on the defensive. We'll take it over into the Lone One's reality, into one more central. What happens there will affect what happens here."

"And what will happen here?" Kit said.

Johnny shook his head. "There's going to be a lot more trouble, and it can't be avoided. We'll move as fast as we can, try to finish the battle fast by forcing a fight with Balor immediately. I have a few ideas about how we can do that." He laughed ruefully. "Unfortunately, the only way I can test those ideas is to try them. If they don't work—" He shrugged.

"Then we're no worse off than we were," Nita said, "because the world looks like it's going to pieces at the moment anyway."

Johnny laughed softly. "The directness of the young. But you're right." He looked over at Biddy. "Let's finish this first. We can't do anything until it's done."

Biddy had been filing at the length of metal while they talked. The bar was now looking much more like a spear blade and less like a long, flat piece of metal. The steel shone, even in that dim place where the only light was from the coals in the forge and the camp lantern on the shelf, and the cup standing nearby. It glinted the way Fragarach did—as if it lay in sunshine that the rest of them couldn't see.

Biddy kept working on the blade with file and polishing wheel and cloth, and then after about twenty minutes held it up for them to see. "Sloppy but fast," she said. Nita shook her head; she didn't see anything sloppy about it. The flat of the blade gleamed, and the point of it looked deadly, a wicked needle.

"OK," Johnny said. "Let's get it mounted. Then around dawn we'll finish the job."

"Dawn will be fine. Then what?"

"Then this afternoon we go to war."

" 'We'?" Nita asked. "I take it you don't mean just us."

"No," Johnny said. "Wizards on active assignment will be helping . . . some just along for the ride, but they live here, and they feel involved. And when everybody's together, we go have us a fight."

He headed off. Biddy was still standing by the anvil, looking at the head of the spear, her expression very still. She looked up after a little while to gaze over at Nita.

"Do you know what I've forged here?" she asked.

Nita looked at the spearhead, and found that there were two answers to that question. One of them had something to do with Ronan and the way he had run from her after she had seen the Champion buried in him the other night. That answer was still partially obscure. But as for the other—The edge of the spearhead glinted in the low light, and Nita suddenly remembered the way Johnny had written Biddy's name in the circle and the way it seemed to be cut off—

"Your death," Nita said, or rather the answer spoke itself.

Biddy folded her arms and leaned back against the stone wall of the forge. "I gave up making," she said after a while. "At least, the kind of making that I used to do. Can you have any idea"—she shook her head, smiling a little: a hopeless look—"what it's like to ensoul your consciousness in a mountain range while it's still molten, and spend a century watching every crystal form? And to plan the long slides of strata, the way erosion wears at your work, even the scrape of glaciers? To *be* what you make . . ." Biddy sighed. "And to know what it'll become? You can't do that in one of these bodies. And I said I would do so no more, and that rather than ever do so again I would give myself back to the One—"

Nita threw a glance at Kit. She had been there: She knew the sound of the kind of promise that means one thing when you make it . . . and then later you find that the meaning has changed, but you are going to be held to the promise nonetheless. Or you hold to it. . . .

"And now," Nita said, "you *have* made something again. And you will have to do what you said. Become part of the making, as the Powers do . . ." But the Powers existed partly outside of time. One living *in* time, in a human body, might not find that body working too well after it came back from such an act of making. Nita shivered.

"I may not," Biddy said. But her voice was still full of doubts.

This tone of mind Nita knew as well. Her heart turned over inside her with pity and discomfort. Any advice would sound hollow to someone in Biddy's position, poised between sacrifice and refusal. But Nita thought of how it must have felt to the wizards who had advised *her* at one point or another. Still, they never shirked from reminding her of what she needed to do, though their hearts bled from it. It was the basic courtesy one wizard owed another—not to lie. How much more did a wizard owe that courtesy to one of the Powers?

"You can't very well get out of it at this point," Nita said. "Your name in the Speech is bound into the spelling we did yesterday. The name says who and what you are . . . and for how long." She swallowed. "Change the truth of that now, and the whole spell is ruined. You know that. No spear . . . no chance of ensouling it. No chance of saving Ireland."

Not to mention the rest of the world, Nita thought. But that would hardly seem germane to Biddy at the moment. "There it is, though," Nita said. "Refuse this making and you'll be part of the destruction of your first one . . . But you of all people should know what to do to keep this island healing, I would have thought."

Biddy looked at her and said nothing.

Nita was immediately mortified. She had completely screwed it up. "Sorry," she said, "sorry, never mind, forget I said anything—" She went out of the forge hurriedly, feeling totally hopeless and ineffective.

Kit came along after her. He said nothing to her until they were about halfway up to the house. "You sounded a little rattled back there, Neets," Kit said then. "Is there anything—"

"No," she said, and regretted it instantly. "Yes, but you can't do anything. Oh, Kit!—" *So how do I tell him about last night? About what I saw inside Ronan?* And the sight of that cool, sharp metal on the anvil had given her something else to think about. Its image resounded against the image of Ronan in her mind, leaving her with a feeling bizarrely compounded of disaster and triumph. But the resonance was incomplete. *It must be finished*, something—the Knowledge, perhaps—said to her. *It has to be fully forged. Otherwise—*

Nita breathed out. "I can't," she said, and she wasn't even sure who she was saying it to, or about what, anymore.

Kit punched her lightly in the arm a couple of times and said nothing.

They went back up to the upstairs bedroom together. Dawn wasn't that far away.

"It's not like the last time," Kit said, "or the time before."

The room had big overstuffed chairs in it, and a big glass case full of books. "Look at this," Kit said, reaching up for one. *"How to Build Your Own Staircase . . ."* He started leafing through it.

"How do you mean, 'not like the last time'?" Nita asked, getting up on the bed and leaning back against the big headboard.

"We've always been doing our stuff pretty much by ourselves," he said. "This is different. We don't have a lot of say about what's going on." Kit looked over at her. "I don't know if I like it."

Nita knew what he meant. "Maybe this is more what it's like for grown-ups," she said. "I guess this is what it'll be like when we're older. If we survive."

"You think we might not?" asked Kit.

"I don't know. We've been in a lot of situations we thought might kill us. Or that looked bad for part of a continent, part of an ocean . . ."

"Sometimes part of a universe."

"I know. But this time it just seems more . . . It seems bigger this time, even though it's smaller. You know what I mean?"

"It means you're away from home," Kit said. "I feel it, too, a little."

Nita yawned.

"But among other things," Kit added, "it means that if we get killed, it's not our fault."

"Oh, great," said Nita. "You find the strangest ways to be positive . . ."

"The only thing I don't understand," Kit said, and then stopped. A moment later he said, "I think we're missing somebody."

"Like who?"

"I don't know. But there's something we're missing."

"Well, I hope you figure out who it is pretty quick," Nita said. "Tomorrow . . ."

"Today," Kit said.

Nita yawned at him again.

"Neets," Kit said. "What happens if we do die?"

"We get yelled at," Nita said, and then burst out laughing at herself. "I dunno."

"Timeheart?"

"I suppose." She shook her head. "I mean, you know it's going to happen someday . . . but I don't think I've ever thought it would happen today." She thought a moment, then said, "Well, maybe once or twice. Why? You got a bad feeling?"

"No. That's sort of what worries me. All the times we've been in real big trouble and come through, I've had awful bad feelings. But this time, nothing." He leaned back in the big fat chair and stared at the ceiling. "I keep wondering if that means something . . ."

Nita looked at him. "Would it be so bad?" she said. "I mean, if you know you're going to die anyway. Might as well go down fighting as die in a bed somewhere, or a car crash or something. It's more useful."

"You sound like Dairine," Kit mumbled.

"Insults," Nita said. "Not very mature of you. I do *not*."

He fell asleep as she watched him. He had always had a gift for that, except on the night before a wizardry. He was feeling as wiped out as she was, though; or else he considered himself off duty at the moment. Nita sighed, and leaned back herself. . . .

She woke very suddenly indeed, and with that feeling of having pins stuck into her all over. She swung herself off the bed. Kit was sitting in the chair with his mouth open; she nudged him with her foot. His eyes flew open, and she said, "Kit—"

He felt it. He spared himself just time for one long stretch, then bounced up and headed out of the room. "They're doing it—"

She followed him around the upper gallery and down a tightly spiraling staircase in a corner tower of the castle. They came out on the bottom level, peered into the great hall, and saw nothing.

They're out in the forge, Kit said in her head. The predawn stillness was too much for even him to break. *Come on—*

They slipped out the front door; the squeak of it opening seemed as loud as a scream in that great quiet. Nothing spoke; outside, no bird sang; there was only that pale hint of light, high all around in the sky, omnidirectional, bemusing—

morning twilight, with thin cloud over everything and mist clinging low, running along the ground, hanging in wisps and tatters from bushes, hovering over trees.

The top of the drywall was just visible. Nita and Kit paused by it and looked down to the forge: There was no one there. *Out in the field*, Nita said. *That way—*

They turned and made their way through the dew-wet grass, quietly, toward the shadow that lay beneath a nearby oak tree. They heard voices ahead of them, speaking in unison in the Speech. There was no light, there was no diagram drawn—just four people standing there at the cardinal points of a circle. Nita could just make out where the circle had been trodden down in the long grass of the pasture: a dark curve where everything else was pale with dew. Struck down into the center of the circle, on a long shaft, was the spear. The shaft was very plain: some light-colored wood—ash, maybe. The blade of the spear, almost three feet long, had been socketed into the shaft and bound with more of the starsteel. Very plain, it was; there it stood, pale shaft, paler blade, with wizards around it, setting up the spell. Nita's aunt stood at one quarter of the circle, Doris Smyth at the second, Johnny at the third. The fourth was wrapped in shadow—a thin shape, wearing a long, dark cloak: Biddy. Only above the thrown-back hood did anything show: a faint gleam of silver hair, cropped short. Nita swallowed at the sight of her, kept quiet, watching.

The spell was about half built, to judge by the feeling of anticipation in the air. More than anticipation—it was a sort of insistent calling. Nita's nerves were jangling at the edges with it, even though she knew perfectly well that the call wasn't meant for her. Something very powerful was being called, something that lived in her in some small way, and that fragment or fraction was responding.

The long chorus in the Speech went on, the sound of the wizards' voices twining together, building, insistent, demanding that something, some great Power, should come here, come bind itself, come be in the world, be physical, real as this world counts reality. . . .

Nita listened to them and heard the wizardry begin to fold in on itself: the knot being tied, the insistence growing that something from outside the world, outside time, should wake up, heed the call, come here *now*! All four voices ended on that tone of command, and the silence fell; and they waited.

Everything waited.

In the east the sky was going gold, and low clouds were beginning to catch the fire of the sun that had not yet risen. The spear stood there in the cool light, still as a tree. Nita stood there watching it, holding her breath, not knowing what to expect.

Then it moved. It leaned, ever so slightly, eastward, leaned like a branch of a tree being blown that way in a wind. Leaned further. And it was beginning to make a sound as well. *No*, Nita thought then. *It's not making the sound itself.* But the sound was certainly happening around it, a low vibration that sounded like the noise that there ought to be just before an earthquake: a low rumble in the bones and the blood. It wasn't audible to the ears. The mind heard it, though—the fabric of things, the structure of spacetime all around, rumbling, being pushed up from under, or down from above. The feeling of some immense pressure being brought to bear on this spot—

Nita looked at Kit, and with him put her back up against a tree.

The sense of pressure got stronger. And the benevolence—that was the strange part. What was coming definitely meant well . . . maybe a little too well for mortals to bear. It wanted all things healed, everything made well, no matter what pains it cost: *everything* being put right, straightened, filled. Nita held onto the tree as she felt that down-pressing force trying to tamper with her, with the cells of her body, her mind. They resisted, in their dumb way, and so did she, thinking, *Leave me the way I am! Leave me alone! I know you want—I know—*

And that was exactly it. It wasn't a pressure, it was a being; not a thing, but a person; not just a person, but a Power. Coming down, here, now, swift to answer the call, fiercer than even Nita had thought, unstoppable now that it had heard the summons—and with a frightful violent strength, because it wasn't embodied, not chained by entropy and the other forces that work on matter, not yet.

Get in there, she thought, clinging to the tree as if she might be swept away. *Get in there!* The spear trembled, the blade of it shook on its shaft, a faint creaking sound of the wood betraying the strain as the metal binding tried to break, as the Power they had called tried to pour itself into this thing of wood and metal. For all the trouble that had gone into making it strong, the spear suddenly seemed to Nita to be very fragile in the face of this awful strength trying to inhabit it. The metal began to glow, the same cherry red that Nita had seen in the furnace, getting hotter and looking more real—more solid and concrete than anything in this world should look—as that Power pressed down into it, making it real, making it alive, waking it up—

Expressions were visible now in this light, but the only one Nita could look at, though she could hardly bear to, was Biddy's. Biddy's eyes were fixed desperately on the spear, as if it were some truth she wanted to see denied; an awful look of anticipation, potentially of horror, was on her face. But there was something else there as well: plain determination.

The metal was golden now, a hot, bright gold that didn't bear looking at, and scaling up past it toward white, almost the color of the star it had come from. White now, that blinding color of plasma new-plucked from the core. But not just metal anymore: alive, awake, and aware, *looking* at Nita.

That light fell on her. She hid her eyes and buried her face against the tree. It was useless. The light struck through everything. No escaping it—it would pierce through you, shake you apart—

And then it stopped.

She rubbed her eyes. They were useless for a few moments. Afterimages danced in them. Nita smelled burning. Wincing, squinting, she glanced around her.

The first light of the sun was coming up between two hills to the east. It fell on grass that was scorched in a great circle. She could see the little flakes of ash going up from where leaves of the tree had been burned. And in the middle of the circle, where the four wizards stood, something stood and looked back at them. It was shaped like a spear, but this fooled no one. They knew they were watched and considered, cheerfully, gravely, by something that would kill any one, or all, of them to do Its job—to find the darkness, pierce it, and be its end.

The socket and binding of the spear had held. Only the wood of the shaft was scorched black, but it was otherwise sound. Above it, the spearhead stood plain and cool and silvery—but there was something moving in the blade. The lines of layered metal that Biddy had hammered in, black once, now wavered and twisted, needle-thin lines of fire, white and yellow-white, swirling and writhing in the metal.

The air above the spear wrinkled and wavered the way air does above hot pavement in the summer, and the ozone smell was thick.

"It's awake," Kit said, softly, as if afraid of being overheard. "It worked!" And he looked over at Biddy just in time to see her collapse.

They hurried to her. Nita looked helplessly at Johnny as he came over, hoisted Biddy up. Her eyes were closed. Her breathing was so shallow it was hardly to be seen. He shook his head.

"What's wrong with her?" Nita said.

"I'm not sure . . . We'll take her inside and find out. Meanwhile—" He glanced over at the spear, gleaming crimson where the early sun was catching it. "We're ready," he said. "It's Lughnasád. This evening we move."

Nita nodded and looked across the field. Dark in his denims, Ronan was standing there. He had no eyes for anything but the spear. He was wearing an expression like that of someone who finds something that's lost, something he has been wanting for a long time, something without which he's not complete. It was a frightened look, and a frightening one.

What unnerved Nita even more was the way she could feel the spear looking back at Ronan. The spear considered him to be just such a lost object, recovered after a long time: that which completes.

She turned and walked away, hurriedly, before the spear started to get any such ideas about *her*.

ag na Machairi Teithra

The Plains of Tethra

ALL THAT DAY CARS came and went at Matrix. People coming to stay were being dropped off; other people were heading out to pick up more people from the train station. The castle got full. All the wizards Nita had seen in the Long Hall were there, as were many she had never seen before. The gravel parking lot out front got full, and people started parking among the sheep. Everyone had tea. Nita made it several times (as did everyone else). People went out to town for fast food and brought it back, and a lot of baking and cooking went on back in the kitchen; Doris made soda bread seven or eight times, smiling more and more as the compliments got louder. But Nita had noticed that there was a certain desperate quality to the conversations; it was the kind of talk meant to keep people from noticing that they themselves were nervous.

Not only the Junior wizards were nervous. Nita had watched Johnny that morning as he carried the spear in from the field. He was wincing as he carried it. "Are you all right?" she asked him.

"Yes," he said, and put the spear down to lean it against the doorpost—*hurriedly*, Nita thought, *and rather gratefully*. Johnny rubbed his hands together. "Well, no. It really is hard to hold for even a little while . . . It burns." He laughed. "It can hardly help it—we went to enough trouble to make it do that! But there's someone else it wants."

"We could all take turns carrying it."

"No, I think it's made its choice. He just has to stop fighting it . . ." Johnny shook his head. "I think he will."

Nita was confused. "Is there something the matter with it, that it hurts to carry it?"

"The matter? Nothing! The matter's with us, I'm afraid. We called the Spirit of Fire, and we got it—the essence of purification, and triumph . . ." He trailed off, then said, "Patience isn't one of its attributes. It sees the dross in us . . . and wants to see it burned away, and us made perfect, *now*. That's not possible, of course. It's not easy, meeting one of the cardinal virtues face to face . . ."

He picked up the spear again and went off in a hurry.

She could feel it looking at her, though, and she understood now what Johnny had said about some weapons being able to speak. She knew what this one wanted.

She looked over her shoulder and was not even slightly surprised to find Ronan there, looking after Johnny. "Hey, Paddy," she said softly.

"Hey, Miss Yank." But there was none of the good old abrasiveness in his voice now, nothing but soft fear. He was quiet for a moment, and then said, "I hear it calling all the time now. Not just calling me, either. *Him*."

For a moment Nita wasn't sure what Ronan meant—until the flash of scarlet, of wings or a sword that burned, flickered in her mind's eye. "Oh," she said, and laughed slightly. "Sorry. I usually think of Him as a Her. That's how we saw—"

"*Her?*" Ronan sounded outraged, as if this was one shock too many.

Nita burst out laughing: For the moment, at least, Ronan sounded normal. "Give me a break! As if the Powers care about something like gender. They change names and shapes and sexes and bodies the way we change T-shirts." She rubbed one ear. The One's Champion, in the last shape She commonly wore, had bitten Nita there several times. "It doesn't make Them any less effective on the job."

They wandered off into the field a little way, absently. "He's in there, all right," Ronan said. He sounded like a man admitting he had cancer. "I hear this other voice—not mine—He wants the spear. It's His, from a long way back. Lugh." He coughed slightly. Nita realized then, blushing with embarrassment for him, that he was trying to control the thickening in his throat, the tears. "Why *me?*" he asked softly.

"You're related," Nita said.

He stared at her.

It was true, though: The Knowledge made at least that much plain. "You've got some of His blood," she said, "from a ways back. You remember what the Queen said, about the Powers dipping in from outside of time and getting into relationships with people here for one reason or another. So He loved somebody when He was here physically, once. Maybe even as Lugh himself. Does it matter? When He finished the other job He was on, the One sent Him—or Her, whatever— another one. Busy guy. But as soon as He could, He came hunting—a suitable vessel. Like the spear did." And Nita smiled at him slightly. "Would you rather a blow-in got the job?"

Ronan smiled, but it was a weak smile. After a moment he said, "You knew Him. What's He like?"

She shook her head, not sure how to describe anything to Ronan that that flicker of scarlet across a dark mind didn't convey in itself. "Tough," she said. "Cranky, sometimes. But kind, too. Funny, sometimes. Always—very fierce, very—" She fumbled for words for a moment. "Very strong, very certain. Very right—"

Ronan shook his head. "It's not right for *me*," he said. "Why don't I get any say in this?"

"But you do," Nita said.

He didn't hear her. "I don't want certainty!" Ronan said softly. "I don't want answers! I don't even know what the *questions* are yet! Don't I get *any* time to find things out for myself, before Saint bloody Michael the Archangel or whatever else He's been lately moves in upstairs in my head and starts rearranging the furniture?"

Nita shook her head. "You can throw Him out, all right," she said. "You know the saying: 'Power will not live long in the unwilling heart.' Goes for the Powers, too, I think. But first you'd better see what you've got to replace Him with that will be able to use the spear to cope with Balor, 'cause *I* can't think of anything offhand."

"If I once let Him run me," Ronan said, bitter in this certainty at least, "He's in to stay."

Nita shook her head. She could think of nothing useful to say.

"Miss Tough Mouth," Ronan said softly. "Ran out of smart lines at last. It had to happen eventually."

"If the advice was any good before it ran out," Nita said, halfway between annoyance and affection, "better make the most of it."

Ronan was quiet for a breath. Then he said, "The other night . . ."

Nita held very still.

Ronan looked away from her, toward the castle. After a moment he headed off that way.

Nita stood and watched him go. A few moments later, Kit said from behind her, "He's in a nasty bind."

Nita nodded. "It's a real pain," she said softly. "What happens if he's right?"

"Let's just hope he's saved everybody in the meantime," Kit said.

They went back to the castle to get ready and meet the many new arrivals. By three o'clock, there were some three hundred wizards there; by eight perhaps another two hundred had arrived from all over. "What are all those things they're carrying?" Kit asked Aunt Annie during one quiet moment outside.

"Johnny told everybody to come armed," her aunt said. They had, though they made a most peculiar-looking army. There were a lot of rakes and shovels. Some people actually had swords, and there were many wands and rods in evidence, of rowan and other woods; there were staves of oak and willow and beech. One wizard, for reasons Nita couldn't begin to guess, was carrying an eggbeater. Another one, the dark-haired sprightly lady that Nita had seen in the Long Hall, had a Viking axe of great beauty and age, and she was stalking around looking most intent to use it on something.

" 'It is a great glory of weapons that is in it,' " said a voice down by Nita's foot, " 'borne by the fair-haired and the beautiful; all mannerly they are as young girls, but with the hearts of boon-comrades and the courage of lions; whoever has been with them and parts from them, he is nine days fretting for their company—' "

"Tualha," Nita said, bending down to pick her up, "you're really getting off on this, aren't you?"

"A bard's place is in battle," Tualha said, perching on Nita's shoulder uncertainly and digging in her claws. "And a cat-bard's doubly so, for we have an example of fortitude and of boldness and of good heart to set for the rest of you."

Kit looked at her with amusement. "What would *you* do in a battle?" he said.

"What she's doing to me now wouldn't be bad," Nita said, gritting her teeth.

Tualha ignored her. "I would make poems and satires on the enemy," she said, "so that they would curl up and die of shame; and welts would rise up all over them if they did not die straightaway, so that they would wish they were dead from that out. And those that *that* did not work on—" She displayed her claws.

"You'd give *them* cat scratch fever," Kit said, and laughed. "Remind me to stay on your good side."

Tualha started scrambling up and over into the backpack Nita was now wearing. "Annie, what about this one?" someone shouted from the castle. Nita's aunt sighed and said, "I'll see you two later."

"Aunt Annie," Nita said, "have you seen Biddy since this morning?"

"Huh? Yes." Her aunt's face looked suddenly pinched.

"She's not any better," Nita said, her heart sinking.

"One of us who's a doctor had a look at her." Aunt Annie shook her head. "The body—well, it's comatose. No surprise. What lived in it has gone elsewhere." She sighed. "It'll wind up in the hospital in Newcastle, I would guess, and hang on a little while before giving up and dying. Bodies tend to do that . . ."

She shook her head and went off toward the wizard who was calling her.

From the door of the castle, Johnny shouted, "Can people start coming into the big hall? As many of you as can fit, anyhow."

Not everyone could, though they spent a while trying. Many wizards lined the gallery above, or stood and listened in the outer halls and corridors. Others hung about outside in the parking lot, eavesdropping with their wizardry. Not that the ones closest to the door couldn't hear Johnny anyway. The acoustics in the great hall were very crisp, and Johnny's sharp voice echoed there as he stood in the center of the floor, his arms folded.

"We're about ready to go," Johnny said when the assembled wizards had quieted. "I take it you're all as ready as you can be." The crowd shifted slightly. "I can't tell you a great deal about what to expect, except that we're going into what is, for us, the country of myth . . . so expect to see even more of the old stories coming true, the legends that have been invading our world over the past few weeks. They'll be real. Just don't forget"—he smiled—"that we are the myths to them. In the Plains of Tethra, *we* are what they tell stories about, around the fire at night. So don't be afraid to use your wizardry; there aren't any overlays where we're going, or none that matter to what we're doing. At some point we'll be faced by an army. I don't know what it's going to look like. We've seen all kinds of Fomori over here in the last couple of weeks. I don't know how they'll appear on their own ground, but the important thing is not to be fooled by appearances. Anything can look like anything . . . so feel for essence and act accordingly. Don't forget that the People of the Hills, and the other nonphysicals who live over on that side, are as much oppressed by the Fomori and Balor as we have been in our world . . . maybe more so, and whether they actively come to our assistance or not, they're on our side. Be careful not to mistake them for Fomori and harm them. Don't get carried away in the excitement of things; remember your Oaths: no destruction that's not necessary."

Johnny paused. "One last thing," he said. "Most of us have never been in an intervention this crucial, or this dangerous. The odds against us are extremely high. Some of us"—and his glance swept across the group with great unease—"will not come back. It's a certainty. Please, please, *please* . . . be careful with your choice. One thing a wizard cannot patch, as you know, is any situation in which his or her own death occurs . . . so any of you with dependents, or responsibilities that you think may supersede this one, *please* think about whether you want to cross over. We'll need guardians on this side, too, to keep an eye on the worldgate in case the Fomori try to stage a breakthrough behind the main group. Bravery is valuable, but irresponsibility will doom us. Later, if not now. So *think*."

The crowd was silent. Nita looked at Kit and saw him swallow.

"Those of you who need to excuse yourselves, just remain here when we pass through," Johnny said. "Meanwhile, let's open the gate."

He turned to Nita's aunt. "Anne? This was always one of your specialties. You want to do the honors?" He reached over to the table, lifted the sword Fragarach, and handed it to Nita's aunt.

She took it. A breath of wind went through the hall; the hangings whispered and rustled. Then Aunt Annie laid the sword over her shoulder and headed up the narrow spiral stairway to the top of the castle.

The wizards in the hall began to filter out into the graveled parking lot in front. Nita and Kit went along. Nita was curious to see what would happen. Gatings were an air sorcery; the business of parting the fabric of spacetime was attached to the element of air, with all those other subtle forces that a wizard could feel but not see. Nita paused in the parking lot and craned her neck.

Against the low, golden sunset light, her aunt's silhouette appeared at the top of the tower, between two of the battlements. It was incongruous; a slightly portly lady with her hair tied back, in jeans and sneakers and a baggy sweatshirt, lifting up the Sword of Lugh with her two hands. She said, just loud enough to be heard down below, "Let the way be opened."

That was all it took; no complex spelling was needed, not tonight. The barriers between things were worn too thin already. A wind sprang up behind the assembled wizards. It was light at first, so that the trees merely rustled, then harder, and leaves began to blow away, and the cypresses down by the water moaned and bent in the wind. Hats blew off; people's clothing tried to jump off them. Nita hugged herself; the wind was cold. Beside her, Kit zipped up his windbreaker, which had been flapping around him like a flag. He stared back into the teeth of the wind. "Here it comes," he said.

Nita turned to look over her shoulder. It looked like a rainstorm coming, the way she had seen them slide along the hills here; it was the darker kind of light: wispy, trailing from sky to earth, sweeping down on them. Behind it the landscape darkened, silvered, muted, as if someone had turned down the brightness control on a TV. Everything went vague and soft. The effect swept toward them rapidly, swallowing the edges of the horizon, and then passed over them, roiling like a thundercloud. The wind dropped off as the effect passed.

Everything had become subdued, quiet; the warm light of sunset was now a dull, livid sort of light. The only bright thing to be seen was Fragarach, which had its own ideas about light and shining, and scorned to take the local conditions into account.

Aunt Annie lowered her arms, looked around her, and disappeared from the battlements. Nita glanced around and saw that everything in sight was muted down to this pallid, threatening twilight. The sunset was a shadow, fading away. Overhead was only low cloud and mist—no stars, no moon.

"That's it," Johnny said. "Someone get the spear. Doris, the cup—"

"Which way do we go?" asked one of the wizards.

"East, toward the sea, and the dawn. Always toward the east. Don't let yourselves get turned around."

Kit looked around. "There are a lot more trees here than there were before . . ."

"Yeah," said Nita. The only thing that was about the same was Castle Matrix, which surprised her. She had thought it would take some other shape here, as Sugarloaf had. But it looked like itself, with no change. The cars in the parking lot were gone, though, and so was the parking lot itself. There was nothing but longish grass stretching away to a ride between the trees of the forest and out into a clearing on the far side. It was still a beautiful place, but it now had a grimness about it.

The wizards began moving out. "It was a lot brighter the last time we were here," Nita said to Kit, thinking of Sugarloaf.

He nodded. "The people here are under attack." *So will we be*, she heard him think, but not say out loud for fear of unnerving her. Nita laughed softly; she could hardly be much more unnerved than she was at the moment.

Nita caught sight of Aunt Annie off to one side, carrying Fragarach. Some ways ahead of her, Doris Smyth walked with the cup still in its pillowcase. Nita and Kit passed her, and Nita couldn't help looking at the striped pillowcase quizzically. Doris caught the look and smiled. "Can't have it getting scratched," she said. "They'd ask questions when we bring it back."

Nita laughed, turned to say something to Kit, and stopped. Ahead of them she saw Ronan, stalking along in his black jeans and boots and leathers, carrying what looked like a pole wrapped in canvas. Except that she knew perfectly well that it wasn't a pole. She got the clear feeling that from inside the wrappings something was looking at her hard. *I think he'll stop fighting it*, Johnny had said.

"Come on," she said to Kit.

They made their way over to Ronan. "You OK?" Nita asked.

Ronan looked at her. "What a daft question. Why shouldn't I be OK?"

"The, uh—" Nita almost didn't like to say the spear's name in front of it. "Your friend there. Don't you have trouble carrying it? Johnny was having a real hard time."

"No. Should I? Is the wrapping coming undone?"

"Oh no," Nita said. "Never mind . . ." She particularly noticed, though, a slightly glazed look in Ronan's eyes, as if he was seeing something other than what the rest of them were seeing; it was an abstracted expression. Could the spear make it easier for the person it wanted to carry it, by dulling or numbing that person's own sense of it?

Or was it something else?

Nita shook her head, having no way to work out what was going on, and went on with Kit and all the others through the silvery twilight. It seemed to get a little less gloomy as they went on, though Nita suspected this was just because she was getting used to it. Then the darkness seemed to increase suddenly, and a shadow passed over them. Nita's head jerked up. Something big and winged flew over, cawing harshly, as the wizards passed through the space between two tongues of forest.

The bird came to rest on one of the tallest of the trees and looked down at them. The tree shuddered and all its leaves fell off on the spot. The crow laughed harshly. It was one of the gray-backed ones called hoodie-crows; Nita had seen her aunt shoot at them, and swear when she missed, since hoodies attacked lambs during the lambing season—killing them by pecking out their eyes and going straight through their skulls. There was muttering among the crowd as everyone looked at the crow.

Johnny, up near the front of the group, called, "Well, Scaldcrow? Smell a battle, do you?"

"Have I ever failed to?" said the bird in a scratchy, cawing voice; it was a woman's voice, and a nasty one, rich with wicked humor over some private joke.

"I see it all red; a fierce, tempestuous fight, and great are its signs; destruction of life, the shattering of shields; wetting of sword-edge, strife and slaughter, the rumbling of war chariots! Go on then, and let there be sweet bloodshed and the clashing of arms, the sating of ravens, the feeding of crows!" And she laughed again.

"Yes, you *would* like that part," Johnny said, not sounding particularly impressed. "The rumbling of chariots, indeed! You've been picking up roadkills by the dual carriageway again, Great Queen."

"Go your ways," Doris said beside Johnny. "There'll be a battle right enough. But we'll need you at the end, so don't go far."

The crow looked down at them, and the light of the cup caught in her eyes. She was quiet for a moment, then laughed harshly and vaulted up out of the tree, flapping off eastward. "I'll tell *him* you said so," she said, laughing still, and vanished into the mist.

Nita looked over at Ronan. "Now who was that?"

"It's just the Morrigan," he said.

Nita blanched. "Just!" said Kit. Apparently he had been researching matters in the manual as well. But Ronan just shrugged again.

"Oh, She's in a lot of the old stories," he said, "the chief of the battle goddesses; She loves to stir up troubles and wars." Nita shivered a little: She saw something more than the recitation of myth in Ronan's eyes. That dazzled look was about him again, but it was an expression of memory this time. He knew the Morrigan personally, or something looking through his eyes did . . . "But She can be good, too. She's one of the Powers that can go either way without warning."

"Well, She doesn't look real friendly at the moment," Kit said. "I'd just as soon She stayed out of this."

They walked on. Distances seemed oddly telescoped here. The landmarks were the same as they were in the real world, and Nita was already seeing things that had taken them half an hour to reach in the car. She was just pointing out Three Rock to Kit when they heard the first shouts of surprise from the wizards in front. And then the first wave of the Fomori hit them.

The Fomori ran at the wizards, screaming, from the shelter of the trees. Nita and Kit, being well off to one side and their view not blocked, had a chance to look the situation over before it got totally incomprehensible. There were a lot of the same kind of drow that they had seen in Bray; some of them were riding black creatures, which were horselike but fanged like tigers. There were strange headless humanoid creatures with eyes in their chests, and scaly wormlike beasts that flowed along the ground but were a hundred times the size of any snake. That much Nita could make out before the front line of the Fomori smashed in among the leading wizards, and battle broke out.

The wizards counterattacked: Spells were shouted, and weapons alive with wizard-light struck. And the fight started to be a very uneven one, so much so that Nita was surprised by it. The drows, at least, had seemed much stronger in her own world. But here they went down quickly under the onslaught of the wizards. Many of the drows not directly attacked turned and ran wailing into the woods, and some of those who had been resisted simply fell down dead after a simple stunning-spell or in the backlash of a stasis or rebound wizardry.

"It's just a feint," said Kit, shaking his head in disbelief. "That can't be the best they've got."

"I hope you're right," Nita muttered.

"Oh no," Kit said softly. "Not already."

She looked where he was looking. Off to their left a young woman was lying, loose-limbed and pale, like a broken doll thrown down. There were several drows lying in pieces by her, but it was no consolation, seeing they were spattered with that shade of red so bright, even in this dim light, that it looked fake. Nita shuddered, for experience had shown her that the fake look was a sure sign it was the real thing.

"Two more over that way," Kit muttered. "I thought there was supposed to be safety in numbers, Neets."

She shrugged. Two other wizards had gone over to check the young woman: Now one of them came back to Johnny, shaking her head.

"They'll have to be left here for now," Johnny said. "We'll see to them later . . . We can't wait. Come on."

There were a few moments of confusion while the wizards got themselves back in order. Then they headed out again.

"It's getting darker," Kit said, looking ahead. "Is that where we're supposed to be going? Downhill there?"

"I think so."

"Great," Kit said. "By the time we get down there, we won't be able to see anything."

That thought had occurred to Nita; it was getting hard enough to see their footing as it was, and since there were no roads here, this was a problem. She had made a small wizard-light to bob along in front of her, like an usher's flashlight in a movie theater, to help her see where to put her feet. "You got anything ready to hit these things with?" Nita asked Kit.

He looked sideways at her and smiled very slightly. "Well," he said. "There's always the beam-me-up spell. If you just leave the locus specification for the far end of the spell blank—or if you specify somewhere, say, out in deep space—"

Nita shuddered. "Yecch."

Kit shrugged. "Better them than me."

The wizards were heading downhill now, on a path paralleling the way the road ran in the real world, down onto the little twisty ridge of Kilmolin and then farther down into Enniskerry village. As they went down, there seemed to be some confusion among the front ranks; they were milling around, and the wizards following were pushing up close behind them.

"Hmf," said the young wizard in the leather jacket as they came up abreast of him. "Not the best of positions. Look at that." He pointed down the valley. "All strung out like this, if anything should come at us from the sides, it'd break us in two. No, Johnny's doing the right thing, gathering us together. That way if anything happens—"

And then it *did* happen. The Fomori forces came down out of the trees again; they came from both sides in great crowds, hitting the group of wizards in the middle. From where they stood, Nita and Kit could see the crowd being shoved together, in danger of being pinched apart into two groups that couldn't help each other. The fighting broke out in earnest now: flashes of wizard-fire repeating, a low sound of angry and startled cries beginning to ricochet up the valley. "Here we go," said the young wizard, and he was gone, off into the press.

Nita looked at Kit and asked, "Should we hold off—wait till it gets at us?" And then of course it *was* at them, as another attacking force hit the group up on the hill from both sides, and everything went crazy.

Nita had a great deal of difficulty remembering the fighting later. The one thing she did remember, rather to her horror, was that she enjoyed it a great deal. It helped a lot, knowing you were on the right side; though several times she wondered, as a drow or one of those black tiger-horse-looking things came at her, whether *they* knew that they were on the wrong side, and whether it affected them much. It didn't seem to. Everything turned into a wild confusion of waving arms and hands, shouting, being jostled and bumped. That was the worst of it, really; you could never tell what was going to bump into you, friend or enemy, and it kept you from reacting as quickly to enemies as you might—or else you accidentally hit a friend. Several times Nita was aware of not-so-accidentally elbowing other wizards, just in case they were something that was about to attack her— better to throw them a little off balance than to take the chance—and then of course she was embarrassed afterward. She did it to Kit once, knocking him right over, and was mortified.

The other thing she remembered vividly was the screaming. At the time it didn't bother her particularly; later on she found herself wondering whether too much television had somehow dulled her reactions to the pain of others. Everything seemed remote, like something in the crowd scene from a movie. Nita remembered one moment with particular clarity, of seeing a drow come at her, and saying the spell that had not worked on Main Street in Bray, and seeing the spell then work entirely too well as the drow exploded into fragments and splinters of stone that bled hot and splattered her with ichor that burned like drops of lava. Her wizard's shield took most of it, but a few drops got through, probably because she was distracted, and burned right through her clothes to her skin.

She wasn't able to keep track of what Kit was doing, but for the length of that strange battle, she didn't really care. She had her hands full. The screaming from all sides got louder, as beasts of the Fomor kind came at the wizards to savage them, sometimes missing, sometimes succeeding. That was when it began to come home to Nita that this was *not* a movie. One wizard went by her staggering and white-faced with shock and blood loss, one arm so badly torn that it seemed to be just barely hanging from his shoulder by a string. Another wizard, a young woman in jeans and a sweatshirt, hurried to help, and carried him away. It was not a movie. People were getting killed here. *And what happens next?* Nita thought, during one lull when the fighting seemed to be happening somewhere else and she had lost sight of Kit. *What happens if you die when you're not in the real world? Where does your soul go? Does it know where to go when you die?* But it seemed unwise to push that issue too far.

After a long while, there came another lull. Nita looked down the hill and saw nothing but human wizards milling around; there seemed to be no more drows, no more of the horse-things—just quiet. A lot of wizards, maybe ten percent of the whole group, had been hurt and were sitting or lying down on the ground while others tended to them. Nita didn't feel so wonderful herself; she sat down to rest on a log under the eaves of the forest, gasping for air.

After a while Kit found her. His clothes were spattered with burn holes, apparently from the hot lava-blood that lived in the drows, and he was limping as he came toward her. Nita staggered to her feet at the sight of him, but he shook his head and waved at her. "No, it's OK. I just turned my ankle."

"Well, come here, you can't just walk on it like that; it'll get worse. You won't be able to run anywhere if you have to."

He sat down on the log beside her. "Your specialty."

She nodded. She had always had a knack for the fixing and healing spells for either animate or inanimate objects. Spells for the living usually required the wizard's own blood, but there was no shortage of that; Nita had bashed herself pretty thoroughly trying to get loose from one drow that had caught hold of her. Now the memory made her shiver, but at the time it had seemed simply an annoyance and had made her angrier. She had blown up that drow while it was still holding her.

Nita shook her head and set to work. She spent five minutes or so working on Kit's leg. It was a strained tendon, and she talked it out of the strain and gave it the equivalent of several days' rest in several minutes. The spell seemed to come harder to her than usual, though, and at the end of it Nita was panting even harder than she had been from the exertion of the battle. "Something's not right," she said to Kit when she got her breath back. "It shouldn't take that much energy."

Kit was looking vaguely gloomy. "I think that's the catch," he said. "Wizardry works better here, but it takes more out of us—we can do less of it." He shook his head. "We'd better get this over with fast. In a few hours we won't be worth much."

She was too nervous to sit there much longer. Nita got up and dusted herself off. "Have you seen my aunt?" she said.

"She was down in front with Johnny, last I saw her. That was before the fighting started, though."

"Tualha," Nita said, turning to look over her shoulder at the backpack, "you any good at finding people? There's quite a crowd down there."

The kitten's head emerged cautiously. Tualha looked around quickly, then said, "In this case it won't be hard. I should look for Fragarach's light, or the cup's."

It was as good a hint as any. After about twenty minutes' walking, Kit and Nita found Aunt Annie, and Tualha had been right: She was with Doris Smyth, and it was the blue-green fire of the cup that gave away their location. Doris was working with one of the more seriously wounded people. Two of the larger and more muscular wizards were easing a young woman with a torn leg down into the cup. She seemed no smaller than she should have been, and the cup seemed no larger, but nevertheless the woman was lost from the waist down in that cool light, and a few moments later, when the other wizards helped her to her feet again, the leg was whole.

Doris was looking wobbly. "I'll not be doing much more of this," she said to Nita's aunt. "The cup's able enough for it, but it's just a tool; it can't work by itself without someone to tell it what to do. And not I nor anyone else will be able to keep doing this again and again—not here. Not today." She looked over at Nita and Kit as if seeing them there for the first time, and her face was very distressed. "Away with you, out of here," she said, "you shouldn't be seeing things like this at your age." And she turned her attention away to another hurt wizard who was being brought over.

Nita looked at Kit; his expression was a little sad. He motioned Nita over to one side, where her aunt was looking nearly as pale as Doris. "You OK, Aunt Annie?" Nita asked anxiously.

Her aunt nodded. "What about you?"

Annie was understandably preoccupied. She was looking off down the hillside, toward the place where Enniskerry would have been and past it. "It's awfully dark down there," she said softly.

Nita looked down the slope, past where the valley fell away along either side of the thirteen-bend road. Down where Bray and Shankill should have been, there was a wall of blackness, so opaque as to seem nearly solid. Just looking at it gave Nita a bad feeling.

"Something's on the other side of that," Kit said. "And it's watching us."

Her aunt looked at Nita regretfully. "I'm beginning to wish I'd left you home."

"You couldn't have. I would have found a way to come along, and you know it."

Her aunt suddenly reached out and hugged her. "Don't do anything stupid," she said.

"Listen, I was going to ask you about that—"

"Anne," Johnny said from one side. "Can I have a word?"

Feeling slightly embarrassed, Nita brushed herself off and was a little amused to see her aunt doing the same thing. "Look," Johnny said, "we can't have another set-to like that. Too many people got killed." It was then that Nita noticed the tears running down his face, incongruous with his calm voice. "I think we're going to have to play our aces a little early."

Nita's aunt hefted Fragarach. Or was it the sword itself that rose eagerly in her hand? Nita had trouble telling. "If we use them too early," her aunt said slowly, "we won't have them for later. You've seen the way wizardry is behaving here."

"That's precisely the problem. First of all, the sword, the cup, and the stone were never much good against Balor the last time. And second, if we're all killed or driven off by his creatures before we get to him—or if they delay us past the point where our wizardry, or even that of the Treasures, still works, then all of this will have been for nothing. I want you to use Fragarach on the next lot—because they're out there waiting for us, under cover of those next two patches of woodland. If we get hit again after that, Doris will use the cup. And I can use the stone the same way, if there's need." He paused and looked at her. "Something wrong? You look a little pale."

She shook her head. "Shaun," she said, "I just don't know if I can do this."

"Not lack of power, surely."

"Oh no. It's just—" She held up Fragarach. "Shaun, we speak so lightly of re-ensouling these things. The trouble is, it *worked*. There's a soul in this, and an intelligence and a *will*—one much older and stronger than mine, one that considers me mainly a form of transportation. Once I actually start to use it"—she laughed a little—"which is going to be the tool and which the user? I don't know how much of me is going to be left afterward; even now I can feel it pushing, pushing at my mind all the time. I don't know if you get the same sense from your rapport with the stone—it's earth, after all, and mostly passive. But if air, the lightest and most malleable of the elements, behaves this way—" She shook her head. "And what about fire, then? I have some experience, some ability to resist. But what's going to come of that poor child? What happens when the Power that comes with the spear puts forth Its full force—?"

She mentioned no names. Johnny shook his head. "Anne," he said, "we'd better just hope that it does; otherwise we're lost. Meanwhile, can you do your part? If not, I'll look for someone else. But you do have the rapport."

She looked at him. "I'll manage," she said.

Johnny headed off. "Get yourselves together," he said to the wizards he passed. "We're moving out, and the Fomori are going to come after us again."

Nita's aunt went after him. Nita watched her go and stood thinking a moment about Ronan. *He doesn't have her experience,* she thought. *But he has the power.*

Not as much, she heard Kit thinking. *Not as much as he might if he were younger . . . What's this going to do to him?*

She glanced over at Kit, unnerved. They tended not to accidentally hear each other thinking anymore, but evidently this Otherworld had more effects than those on active wizardry.

A shout went up from the wizards down the slope. Nita saw a mass of dark forms come charging at them, out of the trees again.

There were a few more moments of confusion, milling around, screams. Then Kit grabbed her arm, and pointed. Down the slope, she saw it, the upraised little line of red light that grew from a spark to a tongue of fire, and from a tongue to a lance of it that arrowed up into the threatening sky. The wind began to rise behind them, moaning softly. Then it became louder, a chorus of voices in the trees, uncertain at first, then threatening, long howls of rage. The wind rose and rose, bending the trees down before it, whipping leaves and dirt through the air so that it became hard to see. The wizards staggered against the blast of it, but even as she fought to stay upright, Nita had a feeling that the wind was avoiding her, and the threat in it was for someone else.

She and Kit headed downhill, because that was the way the wind was pushing them; but the great mass of wizards was pushing down that way, too, their cries mingling with the wind's. The two fronts of Fomori that had struck them from either side were staggering back and away, farther down the slope, blown that way, forced down by the raging wind that blew them over and over, that dropped trees on them and tossed logs from the woods after them like matchsticks. The Fomori were almost at the bottom of the hill now, in the little dell where Enniskerry village would have stood. There was no bridge over the Glencree River in this world; everyone would have to ford it. The wizards and the relentless wind pushed the Fomori down into the dell.

The wind rose to a scream then, and there were more sounds in it than screams: an odd sound of bells, which Nita recognized, and the sound of hooves, like glass ringing on metal. Nita looked up and saw what few mortals have seen and lived to tell about: the Sluagh Ron, the Dark Ride of the Sidhe. The People of the Hills leave their anger at home when they ride—their day is done, and their anger is a matter of the songs their bards sing to wile away the endless afternoon. But that afternoon was broken now, and the legendary past had come haunting them as surely as it had come after the mortals. The Sidhe rode in anger now, as the People of the Air, in the whirlwind, with a clashing of spears that shone with the pale fire that flickers around the faery hills on haunted nights. Their horses burned as bright and as dark as storm clouds with the sun behind them as they came galloping down the air. There was no more chance of telling how many riders there were than there was of counting the raindrops in a downpour. But two forms stood out at the head of them: the Queen with her loosened hair flying wild, on a steed like night, and the Fool on a steed like stormy morning, with their spears in their hands and a wind and a light of madness about them.

At the sight of them, a great shriek of despair and terror went up from the Fomori. The Sidhe cried out in answer, a cry of such pure, delighted rage that Nita shuddered at the sound of it, and the Sluagh Ron hit the great crowd of Fomori from the south. The wizards parted left and right to let them through, and the Sidhe drove the Fomori straight downward into the Glencree ford and up against the ridge on the far side of the river. Wailing, the Fomori went, and the press of riders and the darkness borne on the wind hit them and hid them from sight.

After what seemed a very long while, the wind died down, leaving the riders waiting there and the wizards looking at them, among the dead bodies of Fomori, and the twitching, witless ones, driven mad by the sight of the onslaught. Johnny went from where he had been talking to Nita's aunt, who held a Fragarach much damped-down and diminished-looking, and stood by the tallest of the riders, taking the bridle of her horse. "Madam," he said, "we hadn't looked to see you here."

"We were called by our own element," the Queen said, looking down at Nita's aunt and Fragarach. "Besides, it has been too long since I went a-foraying; and since our world seems like enough to die here, this is a good time to ride out again. We have not done badly. But I think we may not be able to do much more. All magics are diminishing in the face of our enemy's *draoiceacht*, and I feel the weariness in my bones. Do not you?"

Johnny nodded. "Nevertheless, we will press on," he said.

"We will go with you and look on this ending," said the Amadaun, and paused. "If an ending is indeed what we are coming to."

"One way or another," Johnny said.

Tir na nOg

JOHNNY WAVED THE WIZARDS forward, and they started down the winding way that paralleled the river and led toward Bray.

"Did you hear that?" Kit asked.

Nita shook her head; she was very tired. "Hear what?"

"What the Queen said. 'The weariness.' "

She had to laugh at that. "After what we've been through today, you'd be nuts not to be tired."

"Yeah, but that's not it. Don't you feel more tired than you did when we were up at the top of the hill?"

Nita blinked. "You're right."

Kit nodded down at the darkness in front of them. "That," he said. "There's some kind of energy-sapping spell tied up with it. Don't exert yourself if you can avoid it—you may need that energy for later."

She looked at him with very mild annoyance; sometimes Kit's practical streak came close to getting him hit. "What I *really* need right now in terms of energy is a candy bar," she said, "but the only thing I've got left in my backpack is a cat. And I can't eat that." She made an amused face. "Too many bones."

Tualha poked her head from the backpack and hissed, not amused. Kit grinned and produced a candy bar from one pocket. Nita took it, squinted at it in the dimness. "It's got peanuts in it!" she said. "I hate peanuts!"

"Oh, OK," Kit said, grabbed it back, and started to unwrap it.

Nita grabbed it away from him, scowled at him, and began eating. Tualha snickered at her, then disappeared into the pack.

They kept walking along the course of the river: It was the route of the thirteen-bend road in the real world. Trees arched close overhead in the gloom, and the sound of the river down in its stony watercourse was muted. *If something should hit us here, we'd have nowhere to go*, Nita thought as she took another bite of the candy bar. And then the screaming began again, very close. *It's not fair!* she thought, as she saw the drows and pookas come crashing in among them from down the steep slope to their right. At that point she also discovered something else: A wizard with a mouthful of caramel and peanuts is not much good for saying spells, even the last word of one that's already set up. She pushed backward out of the way while trying to swallow, managed it, and shouted the one word she needed just in time to blow away the drow that was heading for Kit's blind side, while he did the same to a pooka.

Something grabbed Nita from behind by her throat and chest, choking her. Nita fought to turn, for you can't blast what you can't see, but the stony hands held her hard and she couldn't get her breath; her vision started to blur.

Then there was a roaring noise behind her, the pressure released suddenly, and Nita fell, sprawling and gasping. She levered herself up, looking around her. "Kit—," she said, "did you—" And she ran out of words. All around them, the path through the forest was awash in blue-green light that rolled and flowed like water; and off to one side the river was climbing up out of its banks in response and running up onto the path. Both flows, of light and water together, were rushing with increasing speed eastward, leaving the wizards untouched but washing away the drows and pookas and other monsters like so much flotsam. Nita struggled to her feet again, against the flow. To Kit she said, "Looks like Doris is using the cup."

Kit nodded. "Come on, we should be breaking out into the open pretty soon. This path comes out in that flat ground by the freeway, doesn't it?"

"The dual carriageway, yeah . . . Tualha? You OK?"

From inside the backpack, a small, annoyed voice said, "Ask me again later."

Several more bends of the watercourse brought them out into the open ground. There was a great scattering of drows there, half-buried in the earth as if about a year's worth of mud had covered them there; many others, dealt with by the wizardry of individuals, lay broken or helpless. The last traces of the blue-green light of the cup's wizardry were sinking into the ground like water, along with the real water, which was running down into the watercourse of the Dargle, which the Glencree stream had just met. Kit and Nita splashed across the ford and up the other side, looking around them.

Nita sagged against Kit as she looked northward along the floodplain of the Dargle toward Bray. The darkness was getting more and more solid, and she felt about ready to collapse.

You and me both, Kit said in her head. She could feel the fatigue in the thought, and Nita looked around at the other wizards and saw that they were suffering, too. Some of them had to be helped along by others, and not because of injuries. And far down the floodplain, a long line of darkness hugged the ground, coming slowly toward them. It was bigger than all three of the previous forces that had attacked them put together.

Oh no, Nita thought. *I can't. And neither can a lot of the rest of us . . .*

"There never was any counting them, even in the old days," Tualha said. "It seems nothing has changed."

There was an awful silence. Many of the wizards looked at each other helplessly, hefted their weapons, and watched the Fomori come. Nita looked over at Johnny, who was off to the side of one small crowd, frowning, with his arms folded.

The ground began to shake.

The stone, Kit said silently, immediately doing the smartest thing: He looked up and around to make sure no tree or rock was likely to fall on him, and then he sat down. Nita followed suit. All around them, the earth groaned alarmingly as it was held still where they were but encouraged to move, and move violently, half a mile away. Down by that advancing line of darkness, trees toppled over and huge boulders of Wicklow granite rolled down the hillsides toward the ranks of the Fomori. They broke, screaming and running in all directions. It did them little good. One of the hillsides shrugged itself up and up until it fell over on the Fomori vanguard. Behind it, the rest milled about in confusion between the two ridges that paralleled the open ground where it sloped gently toward Bray.

The thunder of the quaking ground suddenly became a roar. Nita clutched at the earth as a single awful shock went through it—not one of the rippling waves they had been feeling, but a concussion like two huge rocks being struck together.

Toward Bray, the horde of dark Fomori was abruptly missing from the ground. Nothing could be seen but smoke and dust rising in the gloom.

"Let's go," Johnny said quietly, and started forward.

No one had much to say as they passed the great smoking chasm that had been a green meadow between two hills. One of the hills was flat now; the other had great cracks in it, and from far down among the rock-tumble in the chasm, as the wizards passed slowly by it, faint cries could be heard. Nita shuddered as she followed Kit; they had to squeeze their way along the side of the meadow—or what was left of it. The ground tilted dangerously toward the chasm. The riders of the Sidhe paced casually along the air above the huge smoking hole, but it occurred to Nita that the wizards might have a slightly harder time of it if they had to leave the area suddenly.

The gloom about them grew, and Nita's tiredness got worse and worse, so that it was almost as much as she could do just to drag herself along. Only the sight of Kit in front of her, doggedly putting foot in front of foot, kept her doing the same. *At least they're leaving us alone now*, she thought. *Or maybe there are none of them left.*

We hope, Kit said silently. *Hang in, Neets. Look, Johnny's stopped up at the top of that hill there.*

They went up after him, paused at the hillcrest and looked down over where Bray would have been had they been in the real world. In this Otherworld, they beheld a great flowery plain, but the darkness that lay over everything had shut the flowers' eyes. The plain was a featureless place, flat as heartbreak, right up to where Bray Head *should* have been visible—but a wall of black cloud rose there, shutting out the sight.

Nita squinted along the coastline, looking for some sight of the sea. That wall of blackness prevented her, though. *Is it clouds, or some other kind of storm? Why isn't it moving?*

But it was not cloud, as Nita had thought. There were shapes pushing through in the darkness. It was a line of dark ships—but ships like none she had ever imagined before, ships with hulls the size of mountains, with sails like thunderheads. She could see the chains of pallid lightning that held them to the shore. This was the black wizardry that would drag this alternate Ireland from its place in the sea up into the regions of eternal darkness and cold, into another ice age perhaps. What would happen to the real Ireland, and the rest of the world after it, Nita had no idea.

And under that wall of darkness . . .

Nita's mind was dulled with that awful weariness, and at first she thought she was looking at a hill standing between them and the sea. *Funny about that*, she thought. *That almost looks like a sort of squashed head, there.* But no head could be that ugly. It had huge twisted lips and a face that looked as if someone had purposely malformed it. It looked like a sculptor's model of a gargoyle's head, all squashed down, the nose pushed out of place. One eye squinted away to nothing; the other was abnormally huge, bulging, the lid a thin, warty skin over it. The smashed face sat on the great rounded shoulders of a crouching shape, with great flabby arms and thighs and a gross bulging belly—all the size of a hill. Face and body together combined into an expression of sheer spite, of long-cherished grudges and self-satisfied immobility. The look of it made Nita feel a little sick.

And then she saw it breathe.

And breathe again.

Loathing, that was almost all she could feel. She was afraid, too, but her fear seemed to take too much energy. *So this is Balor.*

It was not the way she had expected the Lone One to appear. Always before she had seen It as young and dynamic, dangerous, actively evil. Not this crouching, lethargic horror, this lump of inertia, of blindness and old, unexamined hates. Before, when confronted by the rogue Power that wizards fight, she had always wanted to fight It, too, or else run away in sheer terror. This made her simply want to sneak away somewhere and throw up.

But this was what they had to get rid of; this was going to destroy this island, and then the world.

It's really gross, came the thought from Kit, tired too, but not as tired as she was. *They'd better get rid of it quick.*

Nita agreed with him. Off to one side she saw Johnny, looking almost too tired for words. But Johnny's back was straight yet. "Lone One," he said, his voice calm and clear, "greeting and defiance, as always. You come as usual in the shape you think we'll recognize least. But this one of our hauntings we know too well, and we intend to see the back of it. Your creatures are defeated. Two choices are before you now: Leave of your own will or be driven out by force. Choose now!"

There was no answer, just that low, thick breathing, unhurried, untroubled.

"Ronan," Johnny said quietly. "The spear."

Ronan moved up, but he looked uneasy. The spear seemed heavy in his hands, and Johnny looked at him sharply. "What's the matter?" he said.

"It— I don't know. It's not ready."

Johnny looked at Ronan with some concern, and then said, "Well enough. Anne—"

Nita's aunt came up, carrying Fragarach, which looked dulled and tired. She glanced at Johnny, looking slightly confused. Johnny shook his head.

"Don't ask me," he said. "I think we've got to play this by ear. Do what you did before."

She held up Fragarach and said the last word of the spell of release. The wind began to blow again, but there was a tentative feel to it this time, almost uncertain. The gross, motionless figure did nothing, said nothing. The wind rose and rose, but there was still that feeling of a hollowness at the heart of it; and when it fell on Balor at last, there was no destroying blast, no removal. It might have been any other wind blowing on a hill, with as much result. It died away at last, with a moan, and left Fragarach dark.

"Doris," Johnny said.

Doris came up holding the cup. She spoke the word of release and tilted the cup downward. The blue-green light rose and flowed out of it, washing toward Balor. But it lost momentum and soaked into the muddy ground around the Balor-hill and was swallowed up. Afterward the cup was pallid and cold, just a thing of gold and silver, indistinct in the shadows.

"All right," Johnny said, sounding, for the first time since Nita had met him, annoyed. "Ronan, ready or not, you'd better use that thing."

Ronan looked unnerved, but he lifted the spear. The fires twisted and writhed in the metal of its head. Ronan leaned back, balanced the spear, and threw.

The spear flew like an arrow, struck Balor—

—and bounced, and fell like a dead thing; then, after a moment, it leaped into the air and flew, whining, back to Ronan's hand.

Silence. The wizards looked at each other.

And the laughter started. It was very low, hardly distinguishable as laughter at all at first. It sounded as if the ground should have trembled with it, and with malice, and amusement. *It's invulnerable*, Nita thought. *It's not fair. He could be stopped, the last time. Lugh put that spear right through His eye.* Nothing *should be able to stop the spear*—

Another sound began, a shadow of the first: rocks grating against rocks, a low tortured rumbling that grew louder and louder. With it, the earth really did start to tremble. People fell over in all directions, tried to find their footing, lost it, and fell again. Nita was one of them; when she got up, she noticed a particular feeling of insecurity, as if something she had been depending on had suddenly vanished.

Johnny was standing up again, having fallen himself. He looked at Nita's aunt in shock and said, "That was the stone going. The linkage to it is dead."

Nita's aunt looked at the shadows down by the seashore and said softly, "Then there's nothing to prevent . . . *that*."

Johnny shook his head. "And what happens here . . ."

Nita swallowed.

The groaning of the earth subsided; many who had fallen managed to get back on their feet. But there was no relief, for unchanged before them squatted the huge, dark, immobile form with its spiteful, pleased look. A soft protesting noise of distress and anger went up all around.

"It's *enjoying* this," Kit muttered. "We've lost, and It knows it, and It's prolonging it for *fun*."

"That's as much fun as it's going to have, then," came a sudden small voice: Tualha. She struggled out of the backpack and jumped to the ground, then climbed hurriedly onto a nearby stone. She panted a little, paused, and then her little voice rang out in that sick silence, louder than Nita had ever heard it before:

See the great power of Balor, lord of the Fomor!
See the ranks of his unconquerable army!
See how they parade in their pride before him!
See how they trample the earth of Eriu!

Nita stared at first, wondering what Tualha was up to. But the irony and sarcasm in the kitten's small voice got thicker and thicker, and she stared at Balor in wide-eyed amusement, the way Nita had seen her stare at captive bugs.

Is it not the way of his coming in power?
His splendor is very great; he bows down all resistance!

Never was a better way for the conqueror to come here;
May all who follow him fare just the same way!

See how the children and beasts flee before him,
And their elders, just hoary old men and women,
With their few bits of rusty ironmongery,
And a crock and a stone, that's all they have with them!

Can it really be so, what we see before us—
or is it a trick of the Plains of Tethra,
where everything seems otherwise than it is,
and night might be day, if one's will was in it?

Is it truly what we see, the mighty conqueror,
with his armies ranged and his ships all ready?
Or something much less, just a misconception,
a fakery made of lying and shadows?

No army here, just some shattered stonework,
some poor bruised goblins, all running away?
No ships at all, but just the old darkness,
the kind that used to scare children at bedtime?

And no mighty lord, no mastering horror,
just a bad dream left over from crazier times,
a poor ghost, wailing for what's lost forever?
Some run-down spook complaining about hard times,

and what he can't keep? Can it be that mortals
are too strong for him even here, on his own ground?
—that accountants and farmers, housewives and shopkeepers,
and children and *cats* are even too mighty?

Then all hail the ragged lord of the Fomor,
a power downthrown, a poor weak specter
that ought to take himself off to the West Country
and haunt some castle for American tourists!

Be off somewhere and beg your bread honestly,
and don't come around our doors with your threats,
you shabby has-been! Just slouch yourself off,
crooked old sloth-pile: Show some initiative!

Get up and—

The voice that spoke then made the earth shake again, and a violent pain went
right through Nita at the sound of it, as if she had been stabbed to the heart with
something not only cold, but actively hateful.

"Let me see this chatterer who makes such a clever noise," the voice said,
hugely, slowly, with infinite malice.

Tualha stood her ground. "Get up and do something useful, if you dare—"
It got up.

The terrified screams of many of the wizards made this seem to take much longer than it did; seconds dragging out to minutes of horror as the huge shape began to tear itself up out of the ground, bulking up against the darkening sky. Not just the ugly warped man-shape rose, but a steed for it as well—black as rotting earth, eyes filled with the decaying light of marshfire, fanged, taloned, breathing corruption. Above it, its rider rose, and Nita heard Its breathing and knew her old enemy again, knew by sight the One that she had been desperately afraid would catch her on the night of the wolves. Its pack was gathering to It out of the shadows now, ready to hunt the wizards' souls out into everlasting night and tear them to shreds like coursed hares, screaming. In the pack's longing thoughts, dangerously close to becoming real in this Otherworld, the shrieks could be heard, the blood could be smelled already. But at the moment she could do nothing but look at Balor's dark face, and see his bitter smile. As yet, though, no glance fired from his eye. The Balor-shape still bound It to that shape's rules.

Lugh put the spear right through Its eye, Nita thought abruptly. *That's it! It has to open Its eye first—*

Here it comes, Kit said to Nita. *This had better work!*

Off to one side, Ronan was holding the spear. It was immobile no longer; it was shaking in his hands, its point leaning toward the terrible dark shape before them, the fires writhing in its point. "Not yet," Nita said under her breath, "Ronan, not yet!"

She knew he couldn't hear her; even if he could, Nita didn't know if the being he was becoming would recognize her as someone it might be useful to listen to. Ronan was wrestling with the spear, holding it back as it pulled and strained in his hands.

A bare slit of light opened in the dark face of the bulk before them, like the first sliver of the sun coming up over a hill. It hit Nita in the eyes and face like thrown acid, searing. She cried out, fell down and crouched in on herself, trying to make herself as small as possible, as the light hit her all over and burned her. All around her she could hear the screams of others going down, and right next to her, on top of her, she thought, the sound and feel of Kit crying out hoarsely and rolling over in agony. It was worse than almost anything she could remember, worse than the time the dentist was drilling and the novocaine wore off and he couldn't give her any more. The pain scraped down her nerves and burned in her bones, and no writhing or crying helped at all. The tears ran out and mixed with the mud that her face was grinding into.

But at the same time, something in her refused to have anything to do with all this, and was embarrassed, and angry—the same kind of anger that had awakened in her while she was fighting and liking it. Shaking her head in that anger, Nita pushed herself up on her hands and knees, even though it felt like she would die doing it, and squinted ahead of them. Through the mud and her tears of pain she could just make out Ronan, still struggling with the spear. Farther ahead, the darkness was broken only by that awful sliver of evil light, getting wider now as Balor's eye opened.

"And if it had opened all the way, all Ireland would have burned up in that one flash," she heard Tualha half singing, half saying. *But it has to be open enough for him to get a clean shot. If he screws it up again, it'll all have been for nothing. Ronan, Ronan, don't let it go yet!*

Tualha yowled and fell off the stone onto Nita. She scooped the kitten up, fumbled for her backpack, couldn't reach it, and stowed Tualha, writhing, inside her shirt, where her clawing made little difference against the storm of pain Nita was already feeling. It could be fought, but not much longer; she could feel the onslaught of the light increasing, its power building. Soon it would be ready. Beside her, Kit stirred and bumped up against her. "Come on," she moaned, grabbed him by one arm and tried to get him up at least to his hands and knees. "Come on. Oh, God, Kit, *Ronan!*"

She looked over and saw that Balor's eye was open enough. But Ronan was still holding the spear, despite its struggles. It was roaring now, a desperate noise, trying to get loose. *What's the matter?* Nita thought. "Ronan!"

He was nothing but a silhouette against that light, writhing himself, kept on his feet by the Power that had been dwelling in him more and more since they came here. "Ronan, *let it go!*" she cried. "Kit, he has to—he won't—"

Their minds fell together, as they had before. That reassuring presence: frightened, as she was, but also perturbed, looking for an answer. *What's the matter with him?* she heard Kit think. *With me, Neets. RONAN!*

Their minds hit him together, fell into his. Only for a second, for something larger than both of them was fighting for control, and losing. Ronan was holding that Power off, and he had only one thought, all fear and horror: *If I let it go now, if once I throw the spear, I become the Power, become Lugh, become the Champion. Never mortal again—*

Make him do it, Kit cried, frantic, to the Other who listened. *He's going to get the whole world killed!*

No! It doesn't work that way! Nita was equally frantic. *He has to do it himself! Ronan*—and she gulped—*go on!*

Silence—

—and then Ronan lifted the spear. It shouted triumph as Ronan leaned back, and then it leaped out of his hands, roaring like the shock wave of a nuclear explosion, trailing lightning and a wild wind behind it as it went. That terrible eye opened wide in shock as a fire more terrible than its own hurtled at it. In the instant of the eye's opening the pain increased a hundred times over. Nita screamed and fell

—and then came the piercing. Nothing alive on that field failed to feel it, for everything alive had entropy in its bones; all cries went up together as the essence of all burning ate the darkness to its heart, and however briefly, to each of theirs. It was painful, but a terrible relief: terrible because the mortals present knew that, once they returned to the real world, that small personal darkness would be back with them again.

Something else, though, did not find it a relief; something that had almost nothing but entropy about it. The scream of the Lone Power in Its shape as Balor went up, and up, and would have torn the sky if the sky were made of anything more solid than air. It took a long time to die away.

The pain was gone at least. Nita got to her knees and looked around her, blinded no longer, though her ears were ringing. Kit was just getting up next to her. She helped him up and hugged him. "Are you all right?"

"I'll live," he said, sounding dazed, and hugging back. "Where's Ronan?"

He was standing not too far away, looking confused. The spear was back in his hand again, but quiet now, not straining to go anywhere. Ronan was leaning on it, panting, his forehead against the shaft of it, so he did not see the tall shadow rising up over him, towering higher and higher; the immense shape of a woman dressed in black, but with light flickering in the folds of the darkness like a promise, and long dark hair stirring in the wind that had begun to come down from the heights, blowing the blackness of the clouds out over the sea, so that high up the sky began to show again, dark blue, with, here and there, a star.

Against the growing light and the clean darkness, that woman raised her arms, and her voice went up into the silence like thunder. *"Let the hosts and the royal heights of Ireland hear it,"* the Morrigan cried, and even Ronan looked up now in terror and wonder, "and all its chief rivers and invers, and every rock and tree; victory over the Fomori, and they never again to be in this land! Peace up to the skies, the skies down to the earth, the earth under the skies; power to every one!"

The wizards and the Sidhe shouted approval. The wind rose and took the clouds away, and the Morrigan's great shape bent sideways in that wind and dissipated like a mist, though Nita particularly noticed how her eyes seemed to dwell on Ronan before they vanished completely.

You know, Kit said in Nita's head, *it's funny, but She looks kind of like Biddy . . .*

Nita shook her head, and she and Kit went over to Ronan. He was looking up at the sky, still leaning on the spear. But when he looked down at last, and saw them coming, he straightened up slightly and smiled. Nita was very relieved; his abstracted, inhuman look was gone completely.

"The spear came back," he said to Nita, sounding very bemused. "By itself."

"You put too much English on it," she said, and grinned.

He winced slightly. "Ooh. No puns, please." He looked ahead of him. The great bulk that had been Balor was nothing but a hill now; there was only the vaguest shape about it that suggested that awful bloated bulk. Grass grew on it, and as they looked a rabbit hopped out of cover from under a thornbush growing on it and began to graze.

"I didn't dare let it go," Ronan said.

Nita nodded. "I know. But you're OK—aren't you?"

He looked at her. *"He's* still in there, if that's what you mean."

Kit shook his head. "I think you may be stuck with Him," he said. "But remember which side He's on. I think He'll behave . . . if you do. If you're lucky, you'll never hear from Him again."

"And if I'm not lucky?" Ronan said.

" 'Those who serve the Powers,' " said the small voice from down by their feet, " 'themselves become the Powers.' It's usually the way."

"You," Nita said, picking up Tualha. "I didn't know you knew language like that—that last bit."

"I got carried away," Tualha said, her ears going flat.

"Not good technique for a bard," Kit said. Tualha scowled at him, and he laughed and began scratching behind her ears until finally she gave up and purred.

All around them the light was growing. Nita looked up and around, watching the clouds retreating and the brightness growing still, though there was no sun now, but a soft violet evening all around them. Everything was beginning to burn with a certainty surpassing anything Nita had seen even in the *dúns* of the Sidhe.

Beside her, one of the wizards, the handsome woman with the dark hair and the Viking axe, said with a chuckle, "Ah . . . the Celtic twilight." But Nita knew a joke when she heard one, and also knew that excellent clarity drawing itself about them; she had seen it before. All around them, the wizards gathered there began to shine in that light, seeming more perfectly themselves than ever before; the Sidhe, already almost too fair to bear, began to acquire a calmer beauty, more settled, older, deeper.

Johnny was standing by the Queen's steed. He looked up at her now and said, "Well, madam, you asked me a question once. Would your world ever draw closer to Timeheart and end your exile? And I could give you only the answer that the bards gave us long ago. The Champion must come with His spear, and the world of your desire be lost." He laughed softly. "But then the fulfillment of a prophecy rarely looks like our images of it. Will this do?"

She bowed her head. "This will do, Senior. Do swiftly take your people home, for shortly this world will perfect itself beyond their ability to bear it . . . at least, just yet. And we . . ." She looked toward the sunset, and said, "We will prepare for the dawn."

Johnny looked at Nita's aunt. "We've got a dawn of our own waiting for us," he said. "Do the honors?"

She lifted Fragarach. With Balor's power passed, it burned like a star in her hands, and the other Treasures blazed in answer as the wind rose in the east and blew into the opening gap in the air before her. The dark outline of Castle Matrix grew in the early morning of their own world, and the song of a single early blackbird drifted through it.

As one, the People of the Hill turned toward that thin, sweet music. But then one by one they looked toward the light slowly growing in their own northeastern sky; sunrise following hard on the heels of sunset, as was normal in this part of the world in the heart of summer. The splendor of morning in a world growing ever nearer to Timeheart began to swell in the sky, blinding, glorious—

The wizards looked around them with regret and moved through the doorway in the air. Nita and Kit and Tualha, followed by Ronan, were near the rear of the group; they turned, there in the parking lot of Castle Matrix, and looked through the gateway back into Tir na nOg.

"I am sorry," Nita's aunt said softly to Johnny, "to have to leave our dead there. Another world, so far away . . ."

Johnny looked sorrowful as well—but there was a strange edge of thoughtfulness to the look, an expression of mystery, almost of joy. "Yes, but . . . look what's happening to the place. It won't be just another world for long . . . It's being drawn into the very center of things. Can you really be dead if you're in Timeheart?" he asked. "Can *anything*?"

In the northeast, over the sea, a line of light, blinding, brighter than a sun, broke over the water. The Spear Luin in Ronan's hands flamed at the touch of that light on its steel. All that country on the other side of the gateway flushed with a light more powerful, seemingly more solid than the solid things it fell on, and burned, transfigured—

The gateway closed.

"So," Johnny said, turning away. "Little by little, we make the Oath come true . . ."

Nita and Kit and Ronan looked at each other. Behind them the blackbird sang again—and they heard the young wizard in the leather jacket sigh and say, "Oh, well. What's for breakfast?"

They went to find out.

"Now that things have quieted down somewhat," Johnny was saying to Nita's aunt two days later in her kitchen, "the Chalice goes back to the museum, obviously. And the stone naturally stays where it is. But Fragarach . . ."

"You take it," Aunt Annie said. "The neighbors would talk if they saw something like that in here. You've got a castle . . . Hang it on the wall there someplace."

Johnny chuckled. Nita pulled the newspaper in front of him toward her, also moving Tualha, who was dozing on the paper, and put the teapot down. STRANGE OCCURRENCES END? asked the *Wicklow People,* in large, somewhat relieved letters. It had indeed quieted down a lot, all over the world. "The spear," Johnny said, "will stay with Ronan, naturally."

"*I* wouldn't try to take it away from him," Kit said from the living room, where he was playing with the teletext functions of the TV set. "It'd probably eat me alive."

"Quite." He chuckled. "And I see that we're losing you two."

"My mom," Nita said, "says they can change my flight home after all." She grinned slightly. "So I go home over the weekend. Not that it hasn't been fun . . . but every wizard knows her own patch of ground best." And she smiled at Ronan.

He smiled back and said nothing that the others could hear.

"Well, you come back anytime," her aunt said, and grabbed her and hugged her with one arm. "She always does the dishes," she said to Johnny. "And without wizardry, even."

"Impressive," Johnny said. "But there was something else I was meaning to tell you—" He sipped his tea. "Oh, that was it. I'd say the odd things aren't quite done happening yet."

"Oh?" Everyone at the table looked at him.

"No. I was out for a walk after things settled down last night, and I saw the strangest thing. A party of cats carrying a little coffin. I stopped to watch them go by, and one of them said to me, 'This is Magrath. Magrath na Chualainn is dead.' And they walked off—"

Tualha's eyes flew open at that. "What?" she cried. "What? Did you say Magrath?"

"Why, uh, yes—" Johnny said, sounding uncertain and concerned. "If it's a relative, I'm—"

"Relative, never mind that, *what* relative! Great Powers about us, if Magrath is dead, *then I'm the Queen of the Cats!*"

She leaped off the table and tore into the living room. There was a brief sound of scrabbling, and then from the living room, Kit said, "Uh, Annie, your cat just went up the chimney . . ."

There was a moment of silence in the kitchen. "Ahem," Nita's aunt said to her after a breath or two. "Welcome to Ireland."

"Are you sure you don't want to stay another couple of weeks?" Johnny asked.

Nita smiled at him and went out to the trailer to start packing.

A Small Glossary

Amadaun (pronounced AM-ah-dawn)*: Irish word for "fool." In Irish legend, the Amadaun was the fool or court jester of a court of the Sidhe: sometimes employed as a messenger and often as an adviser. Though a servant of the King or Queen of the faery court, the Amadaun was a dangerous one—he could kill a mortal with a casual blow or a word, sometimes even with a thought. Like mortal court jesters, the Amadaun was often thought to be the repository of unusual wisdom and could be prophetic.

Baile atha Cliath (pronounced BAL-ly uh-CLEE-uh): Dublin. "The City of the Ford of the Reed Hurdles," the pre-Viking name of the city: The "hurdles" were barriers woven of reeds and staked out in the river to catch salmon. The name is older than *Dubh linn*, "the Black Pool," which was the Vikings' nick-name for the city. Both the ford and the pool are on the river Liffey.

Balor: The King of the Fomori, also known as Balor of the Evil Eye, variously described as an archdemon, a fallen god, or an avatar of the Lone Power, depending on who is telling his story. One version says that Balor began as a mortal Fomor, the son of their king, but he passed too close to a place where his father's druids were making a cauldron full of death-magic and the fumes of the evil potion got into his eye. After that, the eye would destroy or strike dead whatever Balor looked at. Whether he started out as a mortal or not, the form of Balor that went up against the Tuatha de Danaan was described as "huge as a hill," and his eyelid so huge and heavy over the deadly eye that it took four men with forked sticks to lift the lid so that it could look at his enemies and destroy them. Lugh killed him by throwing the Spear of Destiny at that eye when it was still in the process of opening, before it could destroy the Tuatha. *See also* Fomor(i).

Ban-draoia (pronounced ban-DROY-uh): A female sorcerer or wizard. Originally "she-druid."

Ban-gall (ban-GALL): Gall-woman. Possibly an insult, depending on who says it and how they feel about *gallain* (i.e., anyone not of Gaelic extraction).

Blow-in: A foreigner who settles in Ireland and is presumed to be likely to leave suddenly (no matter how long he's been there); not seen as being seriously attached to the place as it really is but "in love" with some romanticized and inaccurate version of it.

Cuchullain (pronounced cuh-HULL-in): The young hero of Ulster (later, part of Northern Ireland). Son of the Power Lugh and a mortal woman, Dechtire:

*All pronunciations of Irish words are approximate.

raised by Dechtire and her husband, Sualtim. The boy was originally called Setanta. After (as a child) accidentally killing a watchdog belonging to a northern lord named Culann, Setanta volunteered to take the watchdog's place and acquired the nickname *cu Chullain*, "the Hound of Culann" (later, because of this, he was also called "the Hound of Ulster"). When Cuchullain was a teenager and considered old enough to go to war, his father, Lugh, appeared to him and gave him the sword Fragarach. He married Emer, described (as usual) as the most beautiful woman in Ireland, and also (not so usually) as a woman so wise that there were very few people except for Cuchullain who could always understand what she was talking about. Cuchullain fought in many battles against monsters and evil powers—and against warriors from the southern three parts of ancient Ireland—and finally died in battle against the Morrigan, who was his great enemy and had been trying to kill him almost since his birth. Emer died soon afterward, though some at the time felt that she might actually have been a queen of the Sidhe who had been "passing" as a mortal for love of Cuchullain, and who passed on to Tir na nOg after her husband's death. *See also* Fragarach.

Cup: The "Cauldron of Rebirth." Not specifically named in Irish, though in Welsh called *Pair Cadeni:* one of the Four Treasures of Ireland, identified over many years with various chalices (including the Ardagh Chalice in the National Museum) and even with the Holy Grail. Water was its element: It could heal the sick and (some said, in the right hands) even raise the dead. It could also produce food enough to feed great multitudes with whatever food they liked best, so that "no one ever went from it unsatisfied."

Draoiceacht (pronounced DROY-ki'cht): Wizardry. In its original usage, "druid-craft."

Drow: A stone monster of the Fomori, similar to the Scandinavian troll.

Dún (rhymes with "put"): Used interchangeably in early times for a castle, fortified house, or other strong place. The word persists in many Irish place names, such as Dún Laoghaire.

Faery: One of the inhabitants of the Otherworlds, in this case particularly Tir na nOg, or something that has to do with them. The word is also used by some writers to mean the place itself. Originally derived from the Latin *fatae* or "fates," *faery* means the Powers that involve Themselves in the destinies of living things. Unfortunately the term has been corrupted by various storytellers, so that it now summons up ludicrous and unrealistic imagery of tiny flying beings who ride butterflies, live in flowers, etc., *ad nauseam*. True faery is beautiful, but extremely dangerous; the casualty rate of those who interact willingly with it is high, even among wizards.

Fomor(i) (foe-MOR-ee): The early monster people of Ireland. No specific time is assigned to their coming. In the old stories they are treated more as a recurring plague that is repeatedly defeated and then reasserts itself after a period of peace and recovery. Both evil-intentioned humans and various kinds of monsters are included in the term, including pookas, drows, lindworms, and other supernatural creatures. It usually required magic as well as physical force to kill them.

Fool, the. *See* Amadaun.

Forth: An ancient or prehistoric hill-fort, also a small hill presumed to be the former site of a hill-fort (whether it actually was or not). Irish tradition in the second half of this millennium often assumed forths to have been built by the Sidhe. Many country people assumed that the Good People were still living in them and treated their local forths with caution or avoided them entirely.

Fragarach (pronounced FRAG-uh-rack): One of the Four Treasures of Ireland— the Sword of the Air, forged by one or another of the gods (or Powers That Be) in the ancient time, and given to Cuchullain by Lugh. It later passed to Conall of the Hundred Battles, and then was taken out of the world and held in trust by the Sidhe, in the understanding that mortals might need it later. Fragarach was said to have power over the winds when in hands that knew how to use it properly.

Garda: The *Garda Siochona* (pronounced GAR-da shi-KOH-na) or Civil Guards. The Irish equivalent of police. Found as *Garda* (one policeman) or *ban Garda* (policewoman), though the latter is no longer used as an official title for policewomen.

Gardaí (pronounced Gar-DEE): Plural of *Garda*.

Lia Fail (pronounced LEE-uh FOYLE): The Stone of Destiny, one of the Four Treasures of Ireland, originally supposed to be located near the Hill of Tara in County Meath, now sometimes identified with a different stone near Armagh. Legend had it that the stone would shout aloud when the rightful High King of Ireland stood on it at his elevation to the throne. Its element was carth: Some stories claimed that if the Lia Fail were ever removed from Ireland, the island would sink into the sea.

Lugh (pronounced loo): A god of ancient Ireland, identified with that particular member of the Powers That Be who holds the position of the One's Champion—the great warrior against the Lone Power, sometimes identified in other cultures with divine or semi-divine figures like Athene, Thor, and Saint Michael the Archangel. Lugh led the gods' fight against Balor by helping forge the Spear of Destiny, which he used to destroy Balor at the Battle of Moytura. Lugh was secretly the father of Cuchullain, having earlier caught away his mother, Dechtire, into Tir na nOg to live with him. He also appears in Welsh mythology as the young sun god Llew.

Pooka (originally *púca*): An Irish demon that tends to manifest as an evil-looking goat or (more recently) as a small black horse that entices people to ride on its back and then throws itself and its rider into a lake or river, where the rider always drowns. There are also reports of pookas appearing as menacing-looking black dogs, which tend to attack lonely travelers at crossroads in the middle of the night. Pookas can sometimes be merely mischievous—misleading or frightening travelers—but are more often deadly.

Rath (rhymes with "author"): A hill-fort. Sometimes the term includes whatever buildings (halls, towers, etc.) are built into or on the rath.

Sidhe (pronounced shee): The faery people of Ireland. A short version of *Daoine Sidhe*, the People of the Hills. Sometimes (most inaccurately) confused with elves. Usually considered to be the Tuatha de Danaan, the original children of the goddess Danu, one of the mother-goddesses of Ireland; or descendants of those children. Some legends identify them with weak-minded fallen angels, too good to be damned, but too fallible for heaven. Considered by wizards to be descendants of those of the Powers That Be who could not bear to leave the place They had built under the instruction of the One. They are deathless except by violence, and are expert in some forms of wizardry, especially music, shapechange, illusion, and the manipulation of time. They are always referred to by the Irish by euphemistic names like "the Good Folk," "the Good People of the Parish," "the Gentry," or other nicknames meant to avoid offending them by using their real names directly. (In Irish magical tradition, as elsewhere in the world, to name a name directly is to control, or attempt to control, the thing named.)

Spear of Destiny: Also known as "the Spear Luin" (originally *luisne,* "flaming, glaring") and as the *Gae Bolg* (under which name Cuchullain was supposed to have used it briefly). One of the Four Treasures of Ireland, it was forged originally by Lugh for use against Balor of the Evil Eye. Its element was fire, and it was so dangerously hot that it had to be kept point-down in a huge barrel of water so that it could not burn down the place where it was being kept. It never missed the target it was thrown at, infallibly destroyed the target, and always returned to the hand that had thrown it.

Stone. *See* Lia Fail.

Sword. *See* Fragarach.

Taoiseach (pronounced TEE-shock): The prime minister of Ireland. Leader of the political party presently in power. Has legislative and political powers somewhat like those of the president of the United States or the prime minister of the United Kingdom. By contrast, the presidency of Ireland is largely a ceremonial position and is considered to be above politics.

Tir na nOg (pronounced TEER na-NOHG): The Land of Youth (or of the Ever-Young), the alternate universe or other-Ireland inhabited by the Sidhe. Time runs at a different rate in this universe, or rather entropy does: Experience continues unabated while bodily aging proceeds at an infinitesimal fraction of its usual speed, if at all. Humans who venture there frequently experience untoward side effects on attempting to return to universe with different time/entropy rates. See the legend of the hero Oisín for an example.

The Wizard's Dilemma

For Jason Gamble,
the favorite nephew,
and
for Sam's friend's daughter . . .
both members of the next generation

Contents

Friday Afternoon
567

Friday, Early Evening
576

Friday Evening
584

Friday Night
598

Saturday Morning and Afternoon
606

Saturday Afternoon and Evening
624

Saturday Evening
630

Sunday Morning
638

Sunday Afternoon and Evening
649

Monday Morning and Afternoon
654

Monday Night, Tuesday Morning
660

Tuesday Morning and Afternoon
669

Tuesday Evening
677

Late Tuesday Evening
685

Late Tuesday Night,
Wednesday Morning
694

Wednesday
707

Thursday
720

Friday Morning
725

Friday Afternoon
736

Dawn
755

The revelation of some uneasy secrets
would move most anything, even pigs and fishes,
to lift their heads and speak: and at such times
it furthers one to cross the great dark water
and learn the truth its silent shadows hide.

In the wet, reedy evening, birdsong echoes,
old calling young, eventually answered;
while another stands in the dark and calls its fellow,
hearing for answer only the ancient silence
in which tears fall, under a moon near-full.
The lead horse breaks the traces and goes astray
to cry its clarion challenge harsh at heaven.
Understandably. But can it understand in time
the danger that dogs immoderate success? . . .

—hexagram 61
"a wind troubles the waters"

If Time has a heart, it is because other hearts stop.

—Book of Night with Moon
9.v.IX

Friday Afternoon

"HONEY, HAVE YOU SEEN your sister?"

"She's on Jupiter, Mom."

There was no immediate response to this piece of news. Sitting at a dining-room table covered with notebooks, a few schoolbooks, and one book that had less to do with school than the others, Nita Callahan glanced over her shoulder just in time to catch sight of her mother looking at the ceiling with an expression that said, *What have I done to deserve this?*

Nita turned her head back to what looked like her homework, so that her mother wouldn't see her smile. "Well, yeah, not *on* Jupiter; it's hard to do that . . . She's on Europa."

Her mother came around and sat down in the chair opposite Nita at the table, looking faintly concerned. "She's not trying to create life again or something, is she?"

"Huh? Oh, no. It was there already. But there was some kind of problem."

The look on her mother's face was difficult to decipher. "What kind?"

"I'm not sure," Nita said, and this was true. She had read the mission statement, which had appeared in her copy of the wizard's manual shortly after Dairine left, but the fine print had made little sense to her—probably the reason why she or some other wizard had not been sent to deal with the trouble, and Dairine had. "It's kind of hard to understand what single-celled organisms consider a problem." She made an amused face. "But it looks like Dairine's the answer to it."

"All right." Her mom leaned back in the chair and stretched. "When will she be back?"

"She didn't say. But there's a limit to how much air you can carry with you on one of these jaunts if you're also going to have energy to spare to actually get anything done," Nita said. "Probably a couple of hours."

"Okay . . . We don't have to have a formal dinner tonight. Everyone can fend for themselves. Your dad won't mind; he's up to his elbows in shrubs right now, anyway." The buzz of the hedge trimmer could still be heard as Nita's dad worked his way around the house. "We can take care of the food shopping later . . . There's no rush. Is Kit coming over?"

Nita carefully turned the notebook page she'd been working on. "Uh, no. I have to go out and see him in a little while, though . . . Someone's meeting us to finish up a project. Probably it'll take us an hour or two, so don't wait for me. I'll heat something up when I get home."

"Okay." Her mother got up and went into the kitchen, where she started opening cupboards and peering into them. Nita looked after her with mild concern when she heard her mom's tired sigh. For the past month or so, her mom had been alternating between stripping and refinishing all the furniture in the house and leading several different projects for the local PTA—the biggest of them being the effort to get a new playground built near the local primary school. It seemed to Nita that her mother was always either elbow deep in steel wool and stain, or out of the house on errands, so often that she didn't have a lot of spare time for anything else.

After a moment Nita heaved a sigh. *No point in trying to weasel around it, though*, she thought. *I've got problems of my own.*

Kit . . .

But it's not his fault . . .

Is it?

Nita was still recovering from an overly eventful vacation in Ireland, one her parents had planned for her, to give Nita a little time away from Kit, and from wizardry. Of course, this hadn't worked. A wizard's work can happen anywhere, and just changing continents couldn't have stopped Nita from being involved in it any more than changing planets could have. As for Kit, he'd found ways to be with Nita regardless—which turned out to have been a good thing. Nita had been extremely relieved to get home, certain that everything would then get back to normal.

Trouble is, someone changed the location of "normal" and didn't bother sending me a map, Nita thought. Kit had been a little weird since she got home. Maybe some of it was just their difference in age, which hadn't really been an issue until a month or so ago. But Nita had started ninth grade this year and, to her surprise, was finding the work harder than she'd expected. She was used to coasting through her subjects without too much strain, so this was an annoyance. Worse yet, Kit wasn't having any trouble at all, which Nita also found annoying, for reasons she couldn't explain. And the two of them didn't see as much of each other at school as they'd used to. Kit, now in an accelerated-study track with other kids doing "better than their grade," was spending a lot of his time coaching some of the other kids in his group in history and social studies. That was fine with her, but Nita disliked the way some of her classmates, who knew she was best friends with Kit, would go out of their way to remind her, whenever they got a chance, how well Kit was doing.

As if they're fooling anyone, she thought. *They're nosing around to see if he and I are doing something else . . . and they can't understand why we're not.* Nita frowned. Life had been simpler when she'd merely been getting beaten up every week. In its own way, the endless sniping gossip—the whispering behind hands, and the passed notes about cliques and boys and clothes and dates—was more annoying than any number of bruises. The pressure to be like everyone else—to do the same stuff and think the same things—just grew, and if you took a stance, the gossip might be driven underground . . . but never very far.

Nita sighed. Nowadays she kept running into problems for which wizardry either *wasn't* an answer, or else was the wrong one. And even when it was the right answer, it never seemed to be a simple one anymore.

As in the case of this *project, for example.* Nita looked down at the three notebook pages full of writing in front of her. *If I didn't know better, I'd think it was turning into a disaster.* Nita knew that wizards weren't assigned to projects they had no hope of completing. But she also knew that the Powers That Be weren't going to come swooping in to save her if she messed up an intervention. She was expected to handle it: That was what wizards were for . . . since the Powers couldn't be everywhere Themselves.

This left Nita staring again at her original problem: how to explain to Kit why the solution he was suggesting to their present wizardly project wasn't going to work. *He's so wrong about this,* she thought. *I can't believe he doesn't see it. I keep explaining it and explaining it, and he keeps not getting it.* She sighed again. *I guess I just have to keep trying. This isn't the kind of thing you can just give up on.*

Her mother plopped down beside her again with a pad of Post-it notes and peeled one off, sticking it to the table and starting to jot things down on it. "The sticky stuff on those is getting old," Nita said, turning to a clean page in her notebook. "It doesn't stick real well anymore."

"I noticed," her mother said absently, repositioning the note. "Milk, rye bread—"

"No seeds."

"Your dad likes caraway, honey. Humor him."

"Can't you just get me one of the little loaves without the seeds, Mom?"

Her mother gave her a sidelong look. "Can't *you* just . . . you know . . ." She attempted to twitch her nose in the manner of a famous TV "witch" of years past, and failed to do anything much except look like a rabbit.

Nita rolled her eyes. "Probably I could," she said, "but the trouble is, that bread was made *with* the seeds, and it thinks they belong there."

"Bread *thinks*? What about?"

"Uh, well, it— See, when you combine the yeast with the flour, the yeasts—" Nita suddenly realized that if this went on much longer, she was going to wind up explaining some of the weirder facts of life to her mother, and she wasn't sure that either she or her mother was ready. "Mom, the wizardry would just be a real pain to write. Probably simpler just to take the seeds out with my fingers."

Her mother raised her eyebrows, let out a breath, and made a note. "Small loaf of nonseeded rye for daughter whose delicate aesthetic sensibilities are offended by picking a few seeds out of a slice of bread."

"Mom, picking them out doesn't help. The *taste* is still there!"

"Scouring pads . . . chicken breasts . . ." Her mom gnawed reflectively on the cap of the pen. "Shampoo, aspirin, soup—"

"*Not* the cream-of-chemical kind, Mom!"

"Half a dozen cans of nonchemical soup for the budding gourmet." Her mother looked vague for a moment, then glanced over at what Nita was writing. She squinted a little. "Either I really *do* need reading glasses or you're doing math at a much higher level than I thought."

Nita sighed. "No, Mom, it's the Speech. It has some expressions in common with calculus, but they're—"

"What about your homework?"

"I finished it at school so I wouldn't keep getting interrupted in the middle of it, like I am here!"

"Oh dear," her mother said, peeling off another note and starting to write on it. "No seedless rye for *you*."

Nita immediately felt embarrassed. "Mom, I'm sorry—"

"We all have stress, honey, but we don't have to snap at each other."

The back door creaked open, and Nita's father came in and went to the sink.

Nita's mother glanced up. "Harry, I thought you said you were going to oil that thing. It's driving me nuts."

"We're out of oil," Nita's father said as he washed his hands.

"Oil," her mother said, and jotted it down on the sticky note. "What else?"

Her father picked up a dish towel and stood behind her mother's chair, looking down at the shopping list. "Lint?" he said.

This time her mother squinted at the notepaper. "That's 'list.' "

"Could have fooled me."

Nita's mom bent closer to the paper. "I see your point. I guess I really should go see the optometrist."

"Or maybe you should stop using the computer to write everything," her dad said, going to hang up the towel. "Your handwriting's going to pot."

"So's yours, sweetheart."

"I know. That's how I can tell what's happening to yours." Her father opened the refrigerator, gazed inside, and said, "Beer."

"Oh, now *wait* a minute. You said—"

"I lost ten pounds last month. The diet's working. After a hard day in the shop, can't I even have a cold beer? Just one?"

Nita put her head down over her notebook and concentrated on not snickering.

"We'll discuss that later. Oh, by the way, new sneakers for *you*," her mother said, giving her father a severe look, "before your old ones get up and start running around by themselves, without either of our daughters being involved."

"Oh, come on, Betty, they're not that bad!"

"You put *your* head in the closet, take a sniff, and tell me that again . . . assuming you make it out of there alive . . . If you can even *tell* anymore. I think all those flowers you work with are killing your sense of smell—"

"You don't complain about them when I bring home roses."

"It counts for more when somebody brings roses home if he's not also the florist!"

Nita's dad laughed and started to sing in off-key imitation of Neil Diamond, "Youuu don't bring me floooooowerrrs . . . ," as he headed for the back bedroom.

Nita's mom raised her eyebrows. "Harold Edward Callahan," she said as she turned her attention back to her list making, "you are potentially shortening your lifespan . . ."

The only answer was louder singing, in a key that her father favored but few other human beings could have recognized. Nita hid her smile until her mother was sufficiently distracted, and then went back to her own business, making a few more notes on the clean page. After some minutes of not being able to think of anything to add, she finally closed the notebook and pushed it away. She'd done as much with the spell as she could do on paper. The rest of it was going to have to wait to be tested out in the real world.

She sighed as she picked up her copy of the wizard's manual and dropped it on top of her notebook. Her mother glanced over at her. "Finished?"

"In a moment. The manual's acquiring what I just did."

Her mother raised her eyebrows. "Doesn't it go the other way around? I thought you got the spells out of the book in the first place."

"Not all of them. Sometimes you have to build something completely new if there's no precedent spell to help you along. Then when you test the new spell out and it works okay, the manual picks it up and makes it available for other wizards to use. Most of what's in here originally came from other wizards, over a lot of years." She gave the wizard's manual a little nudge. "Some wizards don't do anything much *but* write spells and construct custom wizardries. Tom, for example."

"Really," Nita's mother said, looking down at her grocery list again. "I thought he wrote things for TV."

"He does that, too. Even wizards have to pay the bills," Nita said. She got up and stretched. "Mom, I should get going."

Her mother gave her a thoughtful look. "You know what I'm going to say . . ."

" 'Be careful.' It's okay, Mom. This spell isn't anything dangerous."

"I've heard *that* one before."

"No, seriously. It's just taking out the garbage, this one."

Her mother's expression went suddenly wicked. "While we're on the subject—"

"It's Dairine's turn today," Nita said hurriedly, shrugging into the denim jacket she'd left over the chair earlier. "See ya later, Mom . . ." She kissed her mom, grabbed the manual from on top of her notebook, and headed out the door.

In the backyard, she paused to look around. Long shadows trailed from various dusty lawn furniture; it was only six-thirty, but the sun was low. The summer had been short for her in some ways—half of it lost to the trip to Ireland and the rush of events that had followed. Now it seemed as if, within barely a finger-snap of summer, the fall was well under way. All around her, with a wizard's ear Nita could hear the murmur of the birches and maples beginning to relax toward the winter's long rest, leaning against the earth and waiting with mild expectation for the brief brilliant fireworks of leaf-turn; the long lazy conversation of foliage moving in wind; and the light of sun and stars beginning to taper off to silence now, as the hectic immediacy of summer wound down.

She leaned against the trunk of the rowan tree in the middle of the backyard and looked up through the down-drooping branches with their stalks of slender oval leaves, the green of them slowly browning now, the dulled color only pointing up the many heavy clusters of glowing BB-sized fruit that glinted scarlet from every branch in the late, brassy light. "Nice berries this year, Liused," Nita said.

It took a few moments for her to hear the answer: Even with the Speech, there was no dropping instantly into a tree's time sense from human life speed. *Not bad this time out . . . not bad at all,* the tree said modestly. *Going on assignment?*

"Just a quick one," Nita said. "I hope."

Need anything from me?

"No, that last replacement's still in good shape. Thanks, though."

You're always welcome. Go well, then.

She leaned for a moment more to let her time sense come back up to its normal speed, then patted the rowan tree's trunk and went out into the open space by the birdbath. There she paused for a little to just listen to it all: life, going about its business all around her—the scratchy self-absorbed noise of the grass growing, the faint rustle and hum of bugs and earthworms contentedly digging in the ground, the persistent little string music of a garden spider fastening web strand to web strand in a nearby bush—repetitive, intense, and mathematically precise. Everything was purposeful . . . everything was, if not actually intelligent, then at least aware—even things that science didn't usually think were aware, because science didn't yet know how to measure or overhear the kinds of consciousness they had.

Nita took a deep breath, let it out again. This was the core of wizardry, for her: hearing it all going, and keeping it all going—putting in a word in the Speech here or a carefully constructed spell there, fixing broken things, helping what was hurt to heal and get going again . . . and being astonished, delighted, sometimes scared to death in the process, but never, ever bored.

Nita said a single word in the Speech, at the same time stroking one hand across the empty air in search of the access to the little pinched-in pocket of time space where she kept some of her wizardly equipment.

Responsive to the word she'd spoken, a little tab of clear air went hard between her fingers: She pulled it from left to right like a zipper, and then slipped her hand into the opening and felt around. A second later she came out with a piece of equipment she usually kept ready, a peeled rod of rowan wood that had been left out in full moonlight. She touched the claudication closed again, then looked around her and said to the grass, "Excuse me . . ."

The grass muttered, unconcerned; it knew the drill. Nita lifted the rod and began, with a speed born of much practice, to write out the single long sentence of the short-haul transit spell in the air around her.

The symbols came alive as a delicate thread of pale white fire, stretching around her from the point of the rowan wand as she turned: a chord of a circle, an arc, then the circle almost complete as she came to the end of the spell, writing in her "signature," her name in the Speech, the long chain of syllables and symbols that described who and what she was today.

With a final figure-eight flourish, she knotted the spell closed, pulled the wand back, and let the transit circle drop to the grass around her, an arabesqued chain of light. Turning slowly, Nita began to read the sentence, feeling the power lean in around her as she did so, the pressure and attention of local space focusing in on what Nita told it she wanted of it, relocation to *this* set of spatial coordinates, life support set to planet-surface defaults—

The silence began to build around her, the sound of the world listening. Nita read faster, feeling the words of the Speech reach down their roots to the Power That had first spoken them and taught them what they meant, till the lightning of that first intention struck up through them and then through Nita, as she said the last word, completed the spell, and flung it loose to work—

Wham! The displacement of transported air always sounded loud on the inside of the spell, even if you'd engineered the wizardry to keep it from making a lot of noise on the outside. The crack of sound, combined with the sudden blazing column of light from the activated transit, left Nita momentarily blind and deaf.

Only for a moment, though. A second later the light died back, and she was standing near the end of a long jetty of big rough black stones, all spotted and splotched with seagull guano and festooned with washed-up seaweed in dull green ribbons and flat brown bladdery blobs. The sun hung blinding over the water to the west, silhouetting the low flat headlands that were all she could see of the

Rockaway Beach peninsula from this angle. Somewhere beyond them, lost in mist and sun glare and half submerged beneath the horizon line, lay the skyline of New York.

Nita pulled her jacket a little more tightly around her in the chilly spray-laden wind and turned to look over her shoulder. Down at the landward end of the quarter-mile-long jetty, where it came up against the farthest tip of West End Beach, was a squat white box of a building with an antenna sticking up from it: the Jones Inlet navigational radio beacon. Beyond it there was no one in sight— the weather had been getting too cool for swimming, especially this late in the day. Nita turned again, looking southward, toward the bay. At the seaward end of the jetty was the black-and-white painted metal tower that held up the flashing red Jones Inlet light, and at its base a small shape in a dark blue windbreaker and jeans was lying flat on the concrete pediment to which the tower was fastened, looking over the edge of the pediment, away from Nita.

She headed down the jetty toward him, picking her way carefully over the big uneven rocks and wondering at first, *Is he all right?* But as she came near, Kit looked up over his shoulder at her with an idle expression. "Hey," he said.

She climbed up onto the cracked guano-stained concrete beside him and looked down over the edge, where the rocks fell steeply away. "What're you doing?" Nita said. "The barnacles complaining about the water temperature again?"

"Nope, I'm just keeping a low profile," Kit said. "I don't feel like spending the effort to be invisible right now, with work coming up, and there've been some boats going through the inlet. Might be something happening at the Marine Theater later. It's been a little busy."

"Okay." She sat down next to him. "Any sign of S'reee yet?"

"Nothing so far, but it's only a few minutes after when we were supposed to meet. Maybe she got held up. Whatcha got?"

"Here," Nita said, and opened her manual. Kit sat up and flipped his open, too, then paged through it until he came to the "blank" pages in the back where research work and spells in progress stored themselves.

Nita looked over his shoulder and saw the first blank page fill itself in with the spell she had constructed that afternoon, spilling itself down the page, section by section, until that page was full, and the continued-on-next-page symbol presented itself in the lower right-hand corner, blinking slowly. "I had an idea," she said, "about the chemical-reaction calls. I thought that maybe the precipitates weren't going to behave right—"

"Okay, okay, give me a minute to look at it," Kit said. "It's pretty complicated."

Nita nodded and looked out to sea, gazing at the blinding golden roil and shimmer of light on the Great South Bay. These waters might *look* pretty, but they were a mess. New York and the bedroom communities around it, all up and down Long Island and the Jersey shore, pumped terrible amounts of sewage into the coastal waters, and though the sewage was supposed to be treated, the treatment wasn't everything it was cracked up to be. There was also a fair amount of illegal dumping of garbage and sewage going on. Various wizards, independently and in groups, had worked on the problem over many years; but the nature of the problem kept changing as the population of the New York metropolitan area increased and the kinds of pollution shifted.

Nita and Kit were more than usually concerned about the problem, as they had friends who had to live in this water. Since shortly before Nita had had to go away for the summer, they'd been slowly trying to construct a wizardry to take the pollution out of the local waters on an ongoing basis. If it worked, maybe the scheme could be extended up and down the coast. But the problem was getting it to work in the first place. Their efforts so far hadn't been incredibly successful.

Kit was looking at the second full page of Nita's work. Now he turned it over and looked at the third page, the last one. "This," he said, tapping a section near the end, "is pretty slick."

"Thanks."

"But the rest of this—" Kit shook his head, turned back to the first two pages, and touched four or five other sections, one after another, so that they grayed out. "I don't see why we need these. This whole contrareplication routine would be great—if the chemicals in the pollution knew how to reproduce themselves. But since they don't, it's a lot of power for hardly any return. And implementing these is going to be a real pain. If you just take this one—" he touched another section and it brightened—"and this, and this, and you—"

Nita frowned. "But look, Kit, if you leave those out, then there's nothing that's going to deal with the sewer outfall between Zachs Bay and Tobay Beach. That's tons of toxic sludge every month. Without those routines—"

Kit closed his eyes and rubbed the bridge of his nose in a way Nita had seen Tom, their local advisory wizard, do more than once when the world started to get to him. "Neets, this is all just too involved. Or involved in the wrong way. You're making it more complicated than it needs to be."

Oh no . . . here we go again. I thought he was going to get it this time, I really did . . . "But if you don't name all the chemicals, if you don't describe them accurately—"

"The thing is, you don't *have* to name them all. If you just take a look at the spell I brought with—"

"Kit, *look*. That stripped-down version you're suggesting isn't going to do the job. And the longer we don't *do* something, the worse the problem gets! Everything that lives along this shoreline is being affected . . . whatever's still alive, anyway. Things are *dying* out there, and every time we go back to the drawing board on this, *more* things die. Getting this wizardry running has taken too long already."

"Tell me about it," Kit said in a tone that struck Nita as a lot more ironic than it needed to be.

And after all the work I did! she thought. Nonetheless she tried to calm down. "All right. What do *you* think we should do?"

"Maybe," Kit said, and paused, "maybe it would be good if we let S'reee take a look at both versions. If she thinks—"

Nita's eyes widened. "Since when do we need a third opinion on something this straightforward? Kit, it'll either do what it's supposed to or it won't. Let's test it and find out!"

He took a deep breath and shook his head. "I can tell already, it's not going to do what we need."

She stared at Kit, not knowing what to say, and then after a moment she got up and stared down at him, trying to keep from clenching her fists. "Well, if you're so sure you're right, why don't you just do it yourself? Since my advice plainly isn't worth jack to you."

"It's not that it's not worth anything, it's that—"

"Oh, *now* you apologize."

"I wasn't apologizing."

"Well, maybe you need to!"

"Neets," Kit said, also frowning now, "what do you want me to do? Tell you that I think it's gonna be fine, when I don't really think so?"

Nita flushed. When you were working with the Speech, in which what you described would come to pass, lying could be fatal . . . and you quickly learned that even talking *about* spells less than honestly was dangerous.

"Energy is precious," Kit said. "Neither of us can just throw it around the way we used to a couple years ago. It's a nuisance, but it's something we have to consider."

"Do you think I wasn't considering it? I took my time over that. I didn't even put it through the spell checker. I checked all the syntax, all the balances, by hand. It took me forever, but—"

"Maybe the 'forever' was a hint, Neets," Kit said.

She had been trying to hang on to her temper, but now Nita got so furious that her eyes felt hot. "Fine," she said tightly. "Then you go right ahead and handle this yourself. And just leave me out of it until you find something you feel is simplistic enough to involve me in."

Kit's expression was shocked, and Nita didn't care. *Who needs this?* she thought. *No matter what I try to do, it's not good enough! So maybe it's time I stopped trying. Let him work it out himself, if he can.*

Nita turned and made her way back down the jetty, her eyes narrowed in annoyance as she slapped her claudication open and pulled out the rowan wand. In one angry, economical gesture, she whipped the wand around her, dropping her most frequently used transit circle to the stones, the one that would take her home. It was a little harder to speak the spell than usual. Her throat was tight, but not so much so that she couldn't say the words that would get her out of there. In a clap of imploding air, she was gone, and spray from a wave that crashed against the jetty went through the place where she had been.

Friday, Early Evening

KIT RODRIGUEZ JUST SAT there on the concrete platform at the bottom of the Jones Inlet light tower for some minutes, looking at the spot where Nita had vanished, listening to the hiss of the surf, and trying to work out what the heck had just happened.

What did I say? Kit went over their conversation a couple of times in his head and couldn't find any reason for her to have gotten so upset. *What is her* problem *these days? It can't be school. Nobody bothers her anymore; she does okay.*

It was a puzzle, and one he'd been having no luck solving. Maybe it was because he'd been so busy . . . and not just during the last couple of months, either. Granted, lately he'd been spending a lot of time on the bottom of the Great South Bay. And over the past couple of years, he'd also been to Europe, and had stopped off on or near most of the planets in the solar system, though only on the way to places much farther out, including some places that weren't exactly planets. Even Kit's mother, who initially had been really nervous about his wizardry, had eventually started to admit that all that travel was probably going to be educational, and theoretically ought to make him, if not smarter, at least more mature. But Kit was beginning to have his doubts. For the past few weeks, when he hadn't been in school, in bed, or a few hundred feet deep in water, he'd been spending a lot of his spare time sitting on a particular rock in the Lunar Carpathians, looking down on the green-blue gem that was Earth from three hundred thousand kilometers out, and coming back again and again to the question, *Are girls another species?*

The first time the thought had occurred to him, he'd felt embarrassed. He had been in places where members of other species had been present in their hundreds—sometimes in their thousands—tentacles and oozy bits and all. None of them had at the time struck him as all that alien; they were, when you got right down to it, just people. And though their differences from human beings were tremendous, sometimes making them completely incomprehensible, that still didn't undermine his affection for them. He liked the aliens he met, even when they were weird. *Come to think of it, I like them* because *they're weird.* But Nita, who theoretically was just as human as Kit was, had been pushing the weirdness-and-incomprehensibility envelope pretty hard lately. Her behavior was hard to understand, from someone who was usually so rational—

Something dark broke the dazzle of the water about a quarter mile away. Kit cocked an ear and heard a long high whistle, slightly muffled, and after that first shape—a short stumpy barnacle-pocked dorsal fin—came the sleek dark shining shape of the back of a humpback whale, rolling in the water as she breached and blew. One small eye set way down at the end of the long, long jaw regarded Kit as S'reee slid toward the jetty, back-finning expertly to keep from coming to grief on the rocks. "*Dai stihó,* K!t," she whistled and clicked in the Speech. "Sorry I'm late. Traffic . . ."

Uneasy as he was, Kit had to chuckle. "I know. I can hear it even up here." The main approaches to New York Harbor ran straight through this part of the Great South Bay, and for a whale, keeping clear of the ever-increasing number of ships—not so much the ships themselves but the inescapable sound of their engines and machinery, always a nuisance for a creature that worked extensively with sonar—was a problem and made getting around quickly a lot more trouble than it used to be. Noise pollution in the bay was as much a problem for the many species who lived there as was the sewage, and would probably be a more difficult problem to solve. It was one of a number of projects S'reee had been forced to tackle since her abrupt promotion to the position of senior cetacean wizard for these waters.

S'reee rolled idly in the water, looking down the jetty. "It's my fault; I should have left the Narrows earlier. But never mind. Where's hNii't?"

"I don't think she's going to be with us today," Kit said.

S'reee didn't reply immediately, but that thoughtful little eye dwelt on Kit. As whales went, S'reee wasn't that much older than Kit or Nita, but the increased responsibilities she'd been pushed into had been making her perceptive—maybe more perceptive than Kit exactly cared for right now, especially since he still wasn't sure that he hadn't misstepped somehow.

"Well," S'reee said after a moment, "is that a problem? Can we manage, or should we reschedule?"

Kit thought about that. "I've got something that might be worth looking at," he said. "We may as well lay it out in place and have a look at it."

"All right."

Kit reached into the pocket of his jeans, which was also the way into his own storage pocket of space, and came out with a little ball of light, a spell in compacted form, which he dropped to the concrete he was standing on. As the compaction routine came loose and let the spell expand, he shoved his manual down into the pocket, then picked up the spell and shook it out.

It was a webwork of interconnected statements in the Speech, all of which briefly flared bright and then, dimming, settled and spread themselves into a form that could have been mistaken for a cloak made of plastic wrap. Kit whirled it around him, then held still while the spell sealed itself shut all about him and completed its access to its air supply, also tucked away in the spatiotemporal claudication in his pocket. Normally this spell was used as a space suit, for occasions when moving or working in a large "bubble" of air wasn't desirable, but Kit had adapted it for use as a wet suit. He glanced back at the beach to make sure no one was watching—the last thing he wanted was for someone to think some kid out here was suicidal—and jumped well away from the rocks, into the water next to S'reee.

The two of them submerged. Kit took a moment to adjust the wizardry he was wearing, to add weight as necessary so that it would counteract the buoyancy of the air in the wet suit and his lungs, then he took hold of S'reee's dorsal fin, and she towed him away from the jetty, southward.

The waters were getting murky this time of year, but not murky enough to hide something that Kit was beginning to get tired of looking at: an irregular cluster of humped, sinister shapes, half buried in sludge, not far from where the sewerage outfall from Tobay Beach tailed off. Half a century ago, some ship had dropped or dumped a cargo of mines on the bottom, in about fifty fathoms of water. But as far as Kit was concerned, that wasn't half deep enough.

"We really need to do something about that," Kit said, glancing at the mines as they passed them by. "Somebody seriously exceeded their recommended stupidity levels the day they dumped *those* here."

"I wouldn't argue the point," S'reee said as they headed out to the point where they had been preparing to anchor their wizardry. "But one thing at a time, cousin. Do you really think you have a solution for our present problem?"

"I've got *something*," Kit said. "You tell me."

"Shortly."

It took them a few minutes more to reach the spot, due south of Point Lookout, where the three of them had been contemplating anchoring the wizardry once they'd settled on what it was going to be. Here the tides came out of Jones Inlet with most force, helping keep the dredged part of the ship channel clean; but here also the pollution from inside the barrier islands came out in its most concentrated form, and this, Kit and Nita had thought, would be a good place to stop it. "The day before yesterday, I spent a little while checking the currents here," S'reee said, as she paused to let Kit slip off, "and I'd say you two were right about the location. Also, the bottom's pretty bare. There isn't too much life to be inconvenienced by tethering a spell here, and what there is won't mind being relocated. Let's see what you've got."

Kit pulled out his manual, turned to the workbook section, and instructed it to replicate the structure of the proposed spell in the water, where they could see it. A few seconds later he and S'reee were looking together at the faintly glowing schematic, a series of concentric and intersecting circles full of the "argument" of the wizardry.

S'reee swam slowly around it, examining it. "I have to confess," she said at last, "this makes more sense than what the three of us were looking at earlier. All those complex chemical-reaction subroutines . . . they'd have taken us weeks to set up, and exhausted us when we tried to fuel them. Besides, it was too much of a brute-force solution. It's no good shouting at the Sea, as our people say; you won't hear what it has to say to you, and it won't listen until you do."

"You think it'll listen to this?"

S'reee swung her tail thoughtfully. "Let's find out," she said. "If nothing else, it's going to be quicker to test to destruction, if it fails at all. And between you and me—and I hate to say it—it's a more elegant solution than what Nita was proposing."

Kit felt uneasy agreeing with her. "Well," he said, "if it doesn't work, it won't matter how elegant it is. Let's get set up."

He started laying out the spell for real. It contained a simplified version of one of the circles he and Nita had been arguing about two days before—there was no point in wasting a perfectly good section of diagram that could be tied into the revision. Kit drew a finger through the water, and the graceful curves and curlings of the written Speech followed after as he drifted around in a circle about twenty yards across, reinstating the first circle as he'd held it in memory.

"Is this how the second great circle looks?" S'reee said, describing the circle with a long slow motion of body and tail. Fire filled the water, following her gesture, writing itself in pulsing curls and swirls of light—all the power statements and the conditionals that were secondary parts of the spell.

"You've got it," Kit said. "One thing, though . . ." He looked ruefully at the place where Nita's name was written. Carefully he reached out and detached the long string of characters in the Speech that represented Nita's wizardly power and personality, and let it float away into the water for the time being. A wizard doesn't just casually erase another wizard's name, any more than you would casually look down the barrel of a gun, even when you were sure that the chamber was empty. Changing a name written in the Speech could change the one named. Erasing a name could be more dangerous still.

"You'll need to knit that circle in a little tighter to compensate," S'reee said.

"Taking care of that now."

It took only a few moments to finish tightening the structure. Kit looked it over one more time; S'reee did the same. Then they looked at each other. "Well?" Kit said.

"Let's see what happens," said S'reee.

Together they began to recite—Kit in the human, prose-inflected form of the Speech; S'reee in the sung form that whale-wizards prefer. Kit stumbled a couple of times until he got the rhythm right—though the pace was quicker than that at which whales sing their more formal and ritual wizardries, it was still fairly slow by human standards. *One word at a time,* he thought, resorting to humming the last syllables when he needed to let S'reee catch up with him; and as they spoke together and fed power to it, the wizardry began to light up around them like a complex, many-colored neon sculpture in the water, a hollow sphere of curvatures and traceries, at the center of which they hung, waiting for the sense of the presence they were summoning.

And slowly, as the wizardry came alive around them, the presence was there, making itself felt more strongly each passing moment as Kit and S'reee worked together toward the last verse—the wizard's knot, in this case a triple-stranded braid, which would seal together three great circles' worth of spell. The pressure came down around them, the weight of tons of water and millions of years of time, hard to bear; but Kit hunched himself down a little, got his shoulders under the weight and bore it up. The water went from the normal dusky green of these depths to a flaring blue-green, like a liquid set on fire. All around them, if it was possible for water to feel wetter than water already was, it did. The personality of the local ocean, partly aware, washed through both Kit and S'reee, intent on washing away resistance over time, as it always had.

Kit had no intention of being washed anywhere. Slowly and carefully he and S'reee started to put their case, defining a specific area on which they desired to operate, telling the ocean what they wanted to do and why it was going to be a good thing.

They were reminding the ocean how things had once been: a long discussion, setting aside for the moment its outrage over having been systematically polluted. But then the local waters were a different issue from the greater, world-girdling Sea, which was a whole living thing, a Power in its own right and the conduit through which the whales' own version of wizardry came to them.

The Sea stood in the same relationship to the ocean as the soul stood to the body, and the ocean, merely physical as it was, had its own ideas about the creatures that had come over the long ages to populate it. To the ancient body of water, which had suddenly found itself playing host to the first and simplest organisms, everything biological looked suspiciously like pollution. The merely physical ocean, remembering that most ancient, blood-saline water, had for a long time resisted the idea of anything living in it. Many times life had tried to get started as the seas cooled, and many times it had failed before the one fateful lightning strike finally lanced down and stirred the reluctant waters to life.

Now, Kit was suggesting—with S'reee, a recently native form of "pollution," to back him up—a possible compromise. Here in this one place, at least, the ocean had an opportunity to return to that old purity, to water in which any chemical except salt was foreign. Maybe in other places this same intervention could be brought about, with wizards to power it and the ocean's permission. But first they had to get this initial permission granted.

It was a long argument, one which the ocean was reluctant to let anyone else win, even though it stood to benefit. Kit knew from his research in the manual and from a number of conferences with S'reee that there was always difficulty of this kind with oceanic wizardries. The waters themselves, far from being fluid and pliant to a wizard's wishes, could be as rigid as berg ice or as hostile as hot pillow lava to action from "outside." The discussion had to be most diplomatic.

But Kit and S'reee had done their homework, and they didn't have to hurry. They just kept patiently putting their case in the Speech, taking their time. And Kit thought he started to feel a shift. . . .

I think it's starting to listen! S'reee said privately to Kit.

Kit swallowed and didn't respond . . . just kept his mind on the argument. But now he was becoming certain that she was right. Just this once, persistence was winning out. They'd both been hoping for this, for though the waters had flinched under those early lashes of lightning, they also had conceived a certain sneaking fascination for the wild proliferation of life that had broken loose in them over a mere few thousand millennia. Now, as Kit and S'reee hung in the center of the spell sphere they had constructed, they saw the light of the Sea around them start slowly, slowly to shift in color and quality as it began to accept the spell.

The shimmer of the wizardry's outer shell began to dissolve into splashes of green and gold brilliance, the catalytic reactions that would make the pollutants snow down as inert salts onto the ocean bottom as fast as they built up. That inert "garbage" would still have to be cleaned up, but the Sea itself had routines for that, older than human wizardry and just as effective for this particular job.

Kit and S'reee watched the wizardry spread away in great ribbony tentacles, diffusing itself, dissolving slowly into the water—one long current drifting away southward, another running up the channel, with the rising flood tide, toward the inland waters and the main sources of the pollution. After three or four minutes there was nothing left to be seen but the most subtle shimmer, a radiance like diluted moonlight.

Then even that was gone, leaving the waters nearly dark, but someone sensitive to the power they had released could still have felt it, a tingle and prickle on the skin, the feel of advice taken and being acted upon. The silence faded away, leaving Kit and S'reee listening to the wet-clappered *bonk, bonk* of the nun buoy half a mile away, the chain-saw ratchet of motorboat propellers chopping at the water as they passed through Jones Inlet.

Kit, hovering in the water, looked over at S'reee. The dimly seen humpback hung there for a long moment, just finning the water around her, then dropped her jaw and took a long gulp of the water, closing her mouth again and straining it back out through the thousands of plates of baleen.

"Well?" Kit said.

She waved her flukes from side to side, a gesture of slow satisfaction. "It tastes better already," she said.

"It *worked*!"

S'reee laughed at him. "Come on, K!t, a spell always works. You know that."

"If you mean a spell always does *something*, sure! It's getting it to do what you *originally* had in mind that's the problem."

"Well, this one did. It certainly discharged itself properly. If it hadn't, the structure of it would still be hanging here, complaining," S'reee said. "But I think we've done a nice clean intervention." She chuckled, a long scratchy whistle, and finned her way over to Kit, turning a couple of times in a leisurely victory roll.

Kit high-fived one of her ventral fins as it waved past him, but the gesture brought him around briefly to where he saw Nita's name, detached from the spell, still hanging there, waving like a weed in the water and glowing faintly. Kit sighed and grabbed the string of symbols, wound them a few times around one hand, and stuffed them into his "pocket," then grabbed hold of that ventral fin again and let S'reee tow him back to the surface.

They floated there for a few minutes in the twilight, getting their breath again as the reaction to the wizardry began to kick in. "How long was that?" Kit said, looking at the shore, where all the streetlights down the parkway had come on and the floodlights shone on the brick red of the Jones Beach water tower and picked out its bronze-green pyramidal top.

"Two hours, I'd guess," S'reee said. "As usual it seems like less when you're in the middle of it. Maybe you should get yourself back onto land, though, K!t. I'm starting to feel a little wobbly already."

Kit nodded. "I'll go in a few minutes," he said, and looked around them. They were about three miles off Jones Beach. He looked eastward, to where a practiced eye could just make out the takeoff lights of planes angling up and away from Kennedy Airport. "I wonder, how soon could we expand the range of this closer to the city? There's a whole lot of dirty water coming from up there. Even though they don't dump raw sewage in the water anymore, the treatment plants still don't do as good a job as they should."

"You're right, of course," S'reee said. "But maybe we should leave the wizardry as it is for a while, and see how it behaves. After that, well, there's no arguing that the water around here can still use a lot more work. But we've made a good start."

"Yeah, the oysters should be happy, that's for sure," Kit said. There hadn't been shellfish living off the south shore of Long Island for many years now. After this piece of work, that would have a chance to change. Certainly the oystermen would be happy in ten or twenty years, and the fish who ate oysters would be, too, a lot sooner.

"True. Well, I don't see that we can do much more with this at this point," S'reee said, "except to say, well done, cousin!"

"Couldn't have done it alone," Kit said. But something in the back of his mind said, *But you* did *do it alone. Or not with the usual help . . .*

"Come on," S'reee said, "you've got to be feeling the reaction. We're both going to need a rest after that. I'll swim you back."

As they got close to the jetty, Kit said, "We should have another look at the wizardry again . . . When, do you think?"

"A week or so is soon enough," S'reee said, standing on her head in the water and waving her flukes meditatively in the air as Kit let go of her and clambered up out of the water onto the lowest rocks. "No point in checking the fueling routines any sooner; they're too charged up just now."

"Okay, next Friday, then. And I want to think about what we can do about those explosives down there, too."

"You're on, cousin. *Dai stihó.* And when you see hNii't' . . ." S'reee paused a moment, then just said, "Tell her we all have off days; it's no big deal."

"I will," Kit said. "*Dai, S'reee.*"

The humpback slid under the water without so much as a splash. Kit spent a moment listening to the high raspy whistle of S'reee's radar-ranging song dwindling away as she navigated out of the shallows, heading for the waters off Sandy Hook. Then, in the flashing crimson light of the jetty's warning beacon, he unsealed the wet-suit spell, shook it out, wrapped it up tight, and shoved it back into his pocket along with Nita's written name and his manual. He shivered then, feeling a little clammy. *It's the interior humidity of the suit,* he thought, frowning. *I forgot to adjust the spell after I noticed the problem the last time.*

Kit grimaced, toying with the idea of doing a wizardry to dry his clothes out, and then thought, *Probably by the time I get home they'll be dry from my body heat already. No point in wasting power.*

He reached into the back of his mind and felt around behind him for his own preset version of what he referred to as the beam-me-up spell, found the one that was set for home, and pulled it into reality, shook it out in one hand, like a whip: a six-foot chain of multicolored light, a single long sentence in the Speech, complete except for the wizard's knot at the end that would set it going. He said that one word, and the wizardry came alive in his hand, bit its own tail. Kit dropped the chain of fire on the worn wooden decking of the fishing platform and stepped into it. . . .

The blaze of the working spell and the pressure-and-noise *whoomp!* of displaced air blinded him briefly, but it was a result Kit was used to now. He opened his eyes again and saw streetlight-lit sidewalk instead of planking. Kit bent over, picked up the wizardry again, undid the knot and shook it out, then coiled it up and stuffed it into his pocket, and down still farther into the pocket in his mind, while simultaneously bracing himself for what he knew was going to hit him in a few seconds. Wobbly as he, too, was starting to feel now, he might not be able to keep it from knocking him over. . . .

But nothing happened. Kit glanced around and then thought, *Whoops! Wrong destination*, for he was standing not outside his own house but two and a half blocks away. It was Nita's house he was looking at: He had grabbed the wrong spell, the only other one in his mind that got as much use as the take-me-home one. Nita's house's porch light was off; there were lights in the front windows, but the curtains were drawn.

I should go see if she wants to talk, he thought.

But her mood had been so grim, earlier . . . and now he'd found that he'd underestimated the dampness of his clothes. They were chilly, and he was getting still chillier standing here.

I really don't feel like it, Kit thought. *Let it wait until tomorrow. She'll be in a better mood then.*

He walked away into the dusk.

Friday Evening

Kit walked a couple of blocks down Conlon Avenue to his own house, the usual kind of two-story frame house typical of this area. It was strange that he and Nita had lived so close together for so long and had never run into each other before becoming wizards; just one of those things, Kit guessed. Or maybe there was some reason behind it. But the Powers That Be were notoriously closemouthed about Their reasons. *Whatever. We both know where we are now.* Then Kit breathed out, amused. *Or at least most of the time we do . . .*

As Kit headed up the driveway to his house, he heard the usual *thump, wham-wham-wham-wham-wham* of paws against the back door, and he grinned and stopped. *CRASH* went the screen door, flying open, and a bolt of black lightning— or something moving nearly as fast as lightning might if it had four legs and fur— came hurtling out, leaped over the steps to the driveway without touching them, hit the ground with all legs working at once, like something out of a cartoon, and launched itself down the driveway at Kit. He had just enough time to brace himself before Ponch hit him about chest high, barking.

Kit laughed and tried to hold Ponch's face away from his, but it didn't work; it never worked. He got well slobbered, as Ponch jumped up and down on his hind legs and scrabbled at Kit's chest with his forepaws. The barking was as deafening as always, but there was, of course, more to it than that. Anyone who knew the Speech could have heard Kit's dog shouting, "You're late! You're late! Where were you? You're late!"

"Okay, so I'm late," Kit said. "What're you complaining about? Didn't anyone feed you?"

You smell like fish, Ponch said inside his head, and licked Kit's face some more.

"I just bet I do," Kit said. "Don't avoid the question, big guy."

I'm hungry!

Kit snickered as he pushed the dog down. Ponch was very doggy in some ways—loyal, and (as far as he knew how to be) truthful. He was also devious, full of plots and tricks to get people to feed him as many times a day as possible. *I should be grateful that that's as devious as he gets*, Kit thought as he made his way to the back door. "Come on, you," he said, and pulled open the screen door.

Inside was a big comfortable combined kitchen and dining room, where his mama and pop usually could be found this time of night. The only thing that happened in the living room at Kit's house was TV watching and the entertainment of family friends and guests—when that didn't drift into the kitchen as well. There was a big couch off to one side, under the front windows, with a couple of little tables on either side, one of which had a small portable TV that was blaring the local news; in the middle of the room was the big oval dining table, and on the other side of the room were the cooking island and, beyond it, the fridge and sink and oven and cupboards. On the cooking island was a pot, boiling, but as Kit went by he peered into it and saw nothing but water. He chucked his book bag over the back of one of the dining-room chairs and sidestepped neatly as Ponch, running in the slowly closing screen door after him, hit the tiled floor and skidded halfway across it, almost to the door that led to the living room. "Hey, Mama," Kit called, "I'm home. What's for dinner?"

"Spaghetti," his mother called from somewhere at the back of the house. "It would have been meatballs as well, but we didn't know which planet you were on."

Kit let out a small breath of relief, for spaghetti was not one of the things his mother could ruin, at least not without being badly distracted. She was one of those people who do a few dishes really well—her *arroz con pollo* was one of the great accomplishments of civilization on Earth, as far as Kit was concerned—but beyond those limits, his mama often got in trouble, and there were times when Kit was incredibly relieved to find his pop cooking. *Especially since it means I don't have to interfere . . .* He smiled ruefully. The last time he tried using wizardry to thicken one of his mama's failed gravy recipes had been memorable. These days he stuck to flour.

Kit's father came up the stairs from the basement into the kitchen—a big brawny broad-shouldered man, dark eyed, and dark haired except around the sideburns, where he claimed his work as a pressman at a Nassau County printing plant was starting to turn him gray. "He's gonna take that screen door off its hinges some day, son," Kit's father said, watching Ponch recover himself and start bouncing around the kitchen.

"Might not be a bad idea," said Kit's mother from the next room. "It's as old as the house. It looks awful."

"It's not broken yet," Kit's father said. "Though every time that dog hits it, you get your hopes up, huh?"

Kit's mother came into the kitchen and didn't say anything, just smiled. She was taller than Kit's dad, getting a little plump these days, but not so much that she worried about it. Her dark hair was pulled back tight and bunned up at the back, and Kit was slightly surprised to see that she was still in one of her nurse's uniforms—pink top and white pants. *Though maybe it's not "still,"* he thought as she paused to give Kit a one-armed hug and sat down at the end of the table.

"You have to work night shift tonight, Mama?"

She bent over to slip one of her shoes onto one white-stockinged foot, then laced the shoe up. "Just evening shift," she said. "They called from work to ask if I could swap a shift with one of the other nurses in the med-surg wing; he had some emergency at home. I'll be home around two. Popi'll feed you."

"Okay. Did anybody feed Ponch?"

"I did," said Kit's mother.

"Thanks, Mama," Kit said, and bent over to kiss her on the cheek. Then he looked down at Ponch, who was now sitting and gazing up at Kit with big soulful eyes and what was supposed to pass for a wounded look. *You didn't believe me!*

Kit gave him a look. "You," he said. "You fibber. You need a walk?"

"YEAH-YEAH-YEAH-YEAH-YEAH-YEAH!"

His mother covered her ears. "He's deafening," she said. "Tell him to go out!"

Kit laughed. "*You* tell him! He's not deaf."

"I'm glad for him, because *I* will be shortly! Pancho! Go *out!*"

Delighted, Ponch turned himself in three or four hurried circles and launched himself at the screen door again. *Thump, wham-wham-wham-wham-wham, CRASH!*

"I see," Kit's father said as he paused by the spaghetti pot, "that he's figured out how to push the latch with his paw."

"I noticed that, too," Kit said. "He's getting smart." And then he made an amused face, though not for his father to see. *Smart* didn't begin to cover the territory.

"So how did your magic thing go tonight?" his dad said.

Kit sat down with only about half a groan. "It's not magic, Pop. Magic is when you wave your hand and stuff happens without any good reason or any price. Wizardry's the exact opposite, believe me."

His father looked resigned. "So my terminology's messed up. It takes a while to learn a new professional vocabulary. The thing with the fish, then, it went okay?"

Kit started to laugh. "You call S'reee a fish to her face, Pop, you're likely to remember it for a while," he said. "It wasn't the fish; it was the water. It was dirty."

"Not exactly news."

"It's gonna start getting cleaner. *That*'ll be news." Kit allowed himself a satisfied grin. "And you heard it here first."

"I imagine Nita must be pleased," his mother said.

"I imagine," Kit said, and got up to go to the fridge.

He could feel his mother looking at him, even without turning to see. He could hear her looking at his pop, even without so much as a glance in her direction. Kit grimaced, and hoped they couldn't somehow sense the expression without actually seeing it themselves. The problem was that they were parents, possessed of strange unearthly powers that even wizards sometimes couldn't understand.

"I thought maybe she was going to come over for dinner," said his pop. "She usually does, after you've been out doing this kind of work."

"Uh, not tonight. She had some other stuff she had to take care of," Kit said. *Like chewing the heads off her unsuspecting victims!*

The sudden image of Nita as a giant praying mantis made Kit snicker. But then he dismissed it, not even feeling particularly guilty. "Where's Carmela?"

"Tonight's a TV night for her," Kit's pop said. "A reward for that math test. I let her take the other portable and the VCR; she's upstairs pigging out on Japanese cartoons."

Kit smiled. It was unusual for things to be so quiet while his sister was conscious, and the thought of sitting down and letting the weariness from the evening's wizardry catch up with him in conditions of relative peace and quiet was appealing. But Ponch needed walking first. "Okay," Kit said. "I'm gonna take Ponch out now."

"Dinner in about twenty minutes," his dad said.

"We'll be back," Kit said. As he went out the back door, he took Ponch's leash down off the hook where the jackets hung behind the door. Out in the driveway he paused and looked for Ponch. He was nowhere to be seen.

"Huh," Kit said under his breath, and yawned. The post-wizardry reaction was starting to set in now. If he didn't get going, he was going to fall asleep in the spaghetti. Kit went down to the end of the driveway, looked both ways up and down the street. He could see a black shape snuffling with intense interest around the bottom of a tree about halfway down Conlon.

Kit paused a moment, looking down where Conlon Avenue met East Clinton, wondering whether he might see a shadow a little taller than him standing at the corner, looking his way. But there was no sign of her. He made a wry face at his own unhappiness. *Just a fight.* Nonetheless, he and Nita had had so few that he wasn't really sure about what to do in the aftermath of one. In fact, Kit couldn't remember a fight they'd had that hadn't been over, and made up for, in a matter of minutes. This was hours, now, and it was getting uncomfortable. *What if I really hurt her somehow? She's been so weird since she got back from Ireland. What if she's so pissed at me that she—*

He stopped himself. *No point in standing here making it worse. Either go right over there now and talk to her or wait until tomorrow and do it then, but don't waste energy obsessing over it.*

Kit sighed and turned the other way, toward the end of the road that led to the junior-senior high school. He saw Ponch sniffing and wagging his tail near the big tree in front of the Wilkinsons' house. Ponch cocked a leg at the tree and, after a few seconds' meditation, bounded off down the street. Kit went after him, swinging the leash in the dusk.

From farther down the street came a sound of furious yapping. It was the Akambes' dog, whose real name was Grarrhah but whose human family had unfortunately decided to call her Tinkerbell. She was one of those tiny, delicate, silky-furred terriers who looked like she might unravel if you could figure out which thread to pull, but her personality seemed to have been transplanted from a dog three or four times her size. She was never allowed out of the backyard, and whenever one of the other neighborhood dogs went by, she would claw at the locked gate and yell at them in Cyene, "You lookin' at me? I can take you! Come over here and say that! Stop me before I tear 'im apart!" and other such futile provocations.

Kit sighed as Ponch went past and as he followed, and the noise scaled up and up. There was no point in going over and talking to Grarrhah. She took her watch-dog role terribly seriously, and would work herself into such a lather that she would already be lying there foaming at the mouth from overexcitement and frustration by the time you got to the gate. Making a poor creature like this more crazy than she was already was no part of a wizard's business, so Kit just walked by as Grarrhah shrieked at him from behind the gate, "Thief! Thief! Burglars! Joyriders, ram raiders, walk-by shooters; lemme at 'em, I'll rip 'em to shreds!"

Kit walked on, wondering if there was something he could do for her. Then he grinned sourly. *What a laugh! I don't even know what to do about Neets.*

All at once he changed his mind about letting things wait until the next day. Kit reached into his pocket and pulled out the manual. Among many other functions, it had a provision for print messaging for times when wizards were having trouble getting in touch with each other directly—a sort of wizardly pager system. He flipped to the back pages where such messages were written and stored. "New message," he said. "For Nita—"

The page glowed softly in the dusk and displayed the long string of characters in the Speech that was Nita's name, and the equivalent string for her manual.

There the book sat, ready to take down his message . . . and Kit couldn't think what to say. *I'm sorry? For what? I didn't run her down. I told her what I thought. I don't think I was nasty about it. And I was right, too.*

He was strongly tempted to tell her so, but then Kit came up against a bizarre notion that doing that under the present circumstances would be somehow unfair. He spent another couple of minutes trying to find something useful to say. But he wasn't sure what was bothering Nita, and he was still annoyed enough at the way she'd behaved to feel like it wasn't his job to be the understanding one.

Kit frowned, opened his mouth . . . and closed it again, discarding that potential message as well. Finally all he could find to say was, "If you need some time by yourself, feel free."

He looked at the page as the words recorded themselves in the Speech.
More?
"No more," Kit said. "Send it."
Sent.

He stood there for a moment, half hoping he would get an answer right back. But there was no response, no hint of the subtle fizz or itch of the manual's covers that indicated an answer. *Maybe she's out. Maybe she's busy with something else.*

Or maybe she just doesn't want to answer . . .

He closed the manual and shoved it back into his pocket. Then Kit started walking again. When he reached the streetlight where Jackson Street met Conlon, he looked around. "Ponch?" he said, then listened for the jingle of Ponch's chain collar and tags.

Nothing.

Now where'd he go? Sweat started to break out all over Kit at the thought that Ponch might have gotten into someone's backyard and caught something he shouldn't have. Ponch's uncertain grasp of the difference between squirrels—which he hunted constantly with varying success—and rabbits—which he chased and almost always caught—had made him disgrace himself a couple of months back when one of the neighbor's tame rabbits had escaped from its hutch and wandered into Kit's backyard. Ponch's enthusiastic response had cost Kit about a month's allowance to buy the neighbor a new rabbit of the same rare lop-eared breed . . . a situation made more annoying by the fact that wizards are enjoined against making money out of nothing except in extreme emergencies connected with errantry, which this was not. Kit had yelled at Ponch only once about the mistake; Ponch had been completely sorry. But all the same, every time Ponch's whereabouts couldn't be accounted for, Kit began to twitch.

Kit started to jog down the street toward the entrance to the school, where Ponch liked to chase rabbits in the big fields to either side. But then he stopped as he heard a familiar sound, claws on concrete, and the familiar jingle, as Ponch came tearing down the sidewalk at him. Kit had just enough warning to sidestep slightly, so that Ponch's excited jump took him through air, instead of through Kit. Ponch came down about five feet behind where Kit had been standing, spun around, and started jumping up and down in front of him again, panting with excitement, "Come see it! Come see, look, I found it, c'mon c'mon c'mon c'mon, comesee-comeseecomesee!"

"Come see *what?*" Kit said in the Speech.

"I found something."

Kit grinned. Normally, with Ponch, this meant something dead. His father was still getting laughs out of the story about Ponch and the very mummified squirrel he had hidden for months under the old beat-up blanket in his doghouse. "So what is it?"

"It's not a *what*. It's a *where.*"

Kit was confused. There was no question of his having misunderstood Ponch; the dog spoke perfectly good Cyene, which anyone who knew the Speech could understand. And as a pan-canine language, Cyene might not be strong on abstract concepts, but what Ponch had said was fairly concrete.

"Where?" Kit asked. "I mean, *what* where?" Then he had to laugh, for he was sounding more incoherent by the moment, and making Ponch sound positively sophisticated by comparison. "Okay, big guy, come on, show me."

"It's right down the street."

Kit was still slightly nervous. "It's not anybody's rabbit, is it?"

Ponch turned a shocked look on him. "Boss! I promised. And I said, it's not a *what!*"

"Uh, good," Kit said. "Come on, show me, then."

"Look," Ponch said. He turned and ran away from Kit, down the middle of the dark, empty, quiet side street . . .

. . . and vanished.

Kit stared.

Uhhh . . . what the—!

Astonished, Kit started to run after Ponch, into the darkness . . . and vanished, too.

Nita had come back from the Jones Inlet jetty that evening to find that her mother had left to go shopping. Her dad was in the kitchen making a large sandwich; he looked at Nita with mild surprise. "You just went out. Are you done for the day already?"

"Yup," Nita said, heading through the kitchen.

"Kit coming over?"

"Don't think so," Nita said, dropping her manual on the dining-room table.

Her father raised his eyebrows and turned back to the sandwich he was constructing. Nita sat down in the chair where she'd been sitting earlier and looked out the front window. She was completely tired out, even though she hadn't done anything, and she was thoroughly pissed off at Kit. The day felt more than exceptionally ruined. Nita put her head down in her hands for a moment.

As she did, she caught sight of a sticky-note still stuck to the table. "Uh-oh—"

"What?"

"Mom forgot her list—"

"You mean her 'lint'?" Her dad chuckled.

"Yeah. It's still stuck here."

"She'll call and get me to read it to her, probably."

There was a soft *bang!* from the backyard—a sound that could have been mistaken for a car backfiring, except that there weren't likely to be cars back there. "Is that Dairine?" Nita's dad said.

"Probably," said Nita. It hadn't taken her parents long to learn the sound of suddenly displaced air—a sign of a wizard in a hurry or being a little less than slick about appearing out of nothing. At first it seemed to Nita as if her folks, after they'd found out she was a wizard, spent nearly all their time listening for that sound in varying states of nervousness. Now they were starting to get casual about it, which struck her as a healthy development.

But wait a minute. Maybe it's Kit, coming back to apologize— Nita started to get up.

The screen door opened and Dairine came in.

Nita sat down again. "Hey, runt," she said.

"Hey," said Dairine, and went on past.

Nita glanced after her, for this was not Dairine's normal response to being called runt. Her little sister paused by the table just long enough to drop her own book bag onto a chair, then went into the living room, pushing that startling red hair out of her eyes. It was getting longer, and, as a result, her resemblance to their mother was stronger than ever. *Has she started noticing boys?* Nita wondered. *Or is something else going on?*

Something scrabbled at the back door. Dairine sighed, came back through the dining room and the kitchen, went to the screen door, and pushed it open. A clatter of many little feet followed, as what appeared to be a little silvery-shelled laptop computer, about the size of a large paperback book, spidered into the kitchen on multiple spindly legs.

Nita peered at it as it followed Dairine back into the living room. "Am I confused," she said, "or is that thing getting smaller?"

"You're always confused," said Dairine as she headed for her room, "but yeah, he's smaller. Just had an upgrade."

Nita shook her head and went back to looking at her mom's list. Dairine's version of the wizard's manual had arrived as software for the household's first computer, and had been through some changes during the course of her Ordeal. Finally she'd wound up with this machine . . . if *machine* was the right word for something that was clearly alive in its own right. In the meantime the household's main computer continued to go through periodic changes, which made some of the neighbors suspect that Nita's father was making more money as a florist than he really was. For his own part, Nita's dad shrugged and said, "Your mom says it does the spreadsheets just fine. I don't want to know what else it might do . . . and as long as I don't have to pay extra for it . . ."

The phone on the wall rang. Her dad went over to it, picked it up. "Hello . . . Yes. Yes, you did, dopey . . . I am . . . Wait and I'll read it to you . . . Oh. Well, okay, sure . . . She just came in. No, both of them . . . Sure, I'll ask."

Nita's dad put his head around the corner. "Honey, your mom forgot a couple other things, too, so she's coming back. She says, do you want to go clothes shopping? They're having sales at a couple of the stores in the mall."

Nita couldn't think of anything else to do at the moment. "Sure."

Her dad turned his attention back to the phone. Nita went back to her room to change into a top that was easier to get in and out of in a hurry. From upstairs she could hear faint thumping and bumping noises. *What's she doing up there?* she thought, and when she finished changing, Nita went up the stairs to Dairine's room.

It was never the world's tidiest space—full of books and a ridiculously large collection of stuffed animals—but now it was even more disorganized than usual. Everything that had been on Dairine's desk, including chess pieces and chessboard, various schoolbooks, notebooks, calculators, pens, papers, paintbrushes, watercolor pads, compasses, rulers, a Walkman and its earphones, and much less classifiable junk, was now all over Dairine's bed. The desk was solely occupied by an extremely handsome, brushed stainless-steel cube, about a foot square, sitting on a clear Lucite base. Dairine looked over her shoulder at Nita as she came in. "Whaddaya think?" she said.

"I think it's gorgeous," Nita said, "but what is it?"

Dairine turned it around. There on one side was what could have been mistaken for the logo of a large computer company . . . but there was no bite out of the piece of fruit in question. The logo was inset into the side of the cube in frosted white and was glowing demurely. This by itself would not have been all that unusual, except that there was no sign of any cord plugged into any wall.

"You mean this is a *computer*? Is this what you're replacing the old downstairs one with?" Nita said, sitting down on the bed. "It looks really cool. One of your custom jobs?"

"Nope, it's their new one," Dairine said. "Almost. I mean, the newest one in the stores looks like this. But those don't do what *this* one does."

Nita sighed. "Internet access?"

Dairine threw Nita a *you-must-be-joking, of-course-it-has-that* look. Wizards had had a web that spanned worlds for centuries before one small planet's machine-based version of networking had started calling itself World Wide. But that didn't mean they had to be snobbish about it; and local technology, and ideas based on it, routinely got adapted into the business of wizardry as quickly as was feasible. "All the usual Net stuff, sure," Dairine said, "but there's other business . . . the new version of the online manual, mostly. I'm in the beta group." She glanced over fondly at her portable, which was sitting on the desk chair, scratching itself with some of its legs. "*They* voted me in."

Nita raised her eyebrows and leaned back. "Coming from the machine intelligences, that sounds like a compliment. Just make sure you don't mess up Dad's accounting software when you port it over." She cocked an eye at the portable, which was still scratching. "Spot here have some kind of problem?"

"If you're smart, you won't suggest he's got bugs!"

"No, of course not . . ."

Dairine leaned against the desk. "His shell's itching him from the last molt. But he's also been getting more like an organic life-form lately. I don't know whether it's a good thing or not, but there's nothing wrong with his processing functions, or his implementation of the manual, and he seems okay when we talk." Dairine looked at the laptop thoughtfully. "I thought Kit was going to be with you. He said he wanted to see the new machine when it came in."

"Huh?"

Nita's heart sank a little at the look Dairine was giving her. But her sister just picked the laptop up off the chair and put it on the desk. The laptop reared itself up on some of its legs and went up the side of the new computer's case like a spider, clambering onto the top and crouching there. Somehow it managed to look satisfied, a good trick for something that didn't have a face. Dairine sat on the end of the bed. "Something going on?"

Nita didn't answer immediately.

"Uh-huh," her sister said. "Neets, it's no use. Mom and Dad you might be able to hide it from for a while, but where I'm concerned, you might as well have it tattooed on your forehead. What's the problem?"

Nita stared at the bedspread, what she could see of it. "I had a fight with Kit. I can't *believe* him. He's gotten so—I don't know—he doesn't listen, and he—"

"Neets," Dairine said. "Level with me. By any chance . . . are you on the rag?"

Nita's jaw dropped. Dairine fell over laughing.

Nita gave Dairine an annoyed look until she quieted down. At last, when Dairine was wiping her eyes, she muttered, "I don't have that problem. Anyway, it's the wrong time."

"Well, you do a real good imitation of it," Dairine said. "If that's not it, what *is* the problem?"

Nita crossed her legs, frowning at the floor. "I don't know," she said. "Since I got back, it's like . . . like Kit doesn't trust me anymore. In the old days—"

"When dinosaurs walked the earth."

"Nobody likes a smart-ass, Dairine. Before I went away, if I'd given him the spell I gave him today, after all that work, he'd have said, fine, let's do it! Now, all of a sudden, everything's too much trouble. He doesn't even want to try."

"Maybe he doesn't want to blow energy on something that looks like it's going to fail," Dairine said.

"Boy, and I thought *he* was the winner of the tactlessness sweepstakes right now," Nita said. "You should call him up and offer to coach him."

"He'll have to make an appointment," Dairine said, pushing the pillows into a configuration she could lean on. "I've been busy." But her face clouded as she said it.

Aha, Nita thought. "I was going to ask you about that—"

The open window let in the sound of a car pulling into the driveway below. Dairine looked out the window. Below, a car door opened and shut, though the car's engine didn't turn off. "There's Mom," Dairine said.

Nita sighed and got up.

"But one thing," Dairine said. "Was Kit clear that the guy you were seeing over there—"

"I wasn't *seeing* him!"

"Yeah, right. Ronan. You sure Kit isn't confused about that?"

Nita stared. "Of course he isn't."

"You sure *you're* not confused about it?"

For that, Nita had no instant answer.

"Nita?" her mother called up the stairs.

"Later," Nita said to Dairine. "And don't think you're getting off easy. I want a few words with you about 'busy.' "

Dairine made a noncommittal face and got up to do something to the new computer as Nita went out.

In the darkness, Kit stood very still. He had never seen or experienced a blackness so profound; and with it came a bizarre, anechoic silence in which not even his ears rang.

"Ponch?" he said.

Or tried to say. No sound came out. Kit tried to speak again, tried to shout . . . and heard nothing, felt nothing. It was the kind of effect you might expect from being in a vacuum. But he knew that feeling, having been there once or twice. This was different, and creepier by far.

Well, hang on, Kit thought. *Don't panic. Nothing bad has happened yet.*

But that doesn't mean that it's not going to. Come to think of it, am I even breathing? Kit couldn't feel the rise of his chest, couldn't feel or hear a pulse. *What happens if there's nothing to breathe here? What happens if I suffocate?*

True, he didn't feel short of breath. *Yet*, said the back of his mind. Kit tried to swallow, and couldn't feel it happening. Slowly, old fears were creeping up his spine, making his neck hairs stand on end in their wake. It was a long time since Kit had gotten over being afraid of the dark . . . but no dark he'd had to cope with as a little kid had ever been as dark as *this*. And those darknesses had been scary because of the possibility that there was something hiding in them. This one was frightening, and getting more so by the minute, because of the sheer certainty that there was *nothing* in it. *I've had enough of this. Which way is out?!*

. . . *But no!* Kit thought then. *I'm not leaving without my dog. I'm not leaving Ponch here and running away!*

But how do you run away when you can't move? And how do you find something when you can't go after it? The horror of being trapped here, wherever *here* was, rose in him. *I'm not going to put up with this*, Kit thought. *I'm not going to just stand here and be terrified!* He tried to strain every muscle, tried to strain even *one*, and couldn't move any of them. It was as if his body suddenly belonged to someone else.

So I can't move. But I can still think—

There was a spell Kit knew as well as his transit spells, so well that he didn't even bother keeping it in compacted form anymore; he could say it in one breath. It was the spell he used to make a small light for reading under the covers at night. Kit could see the spell in his mind, fifty-nine characters in the Speech, twenty-one syllables. Kit pronounced them clearly in his mind, said the last word that tied the knot in the spell, and turned it loose—

Light. Just a single source of light, pale and silvery. There was no way to tell for sure if it was coming from near or far; it looked small, like a streetlight seen from blocks away. Just seeing it relieved Kit tremendously. It was the first change he had managed to make in this environment. And if he could do that, he could do something else. *Just take a moment and think* what *to do*—

Kit realized he was gasping for breath. He also realized that he was able to feel himself gasping. He tried to move his arms, but it was like trying to swim in taffy. As he concentrated on that light, he thought he saw a change in it. *The light's moving*— But that was wrong. Something dark was moving in front of it. *Oh no, what's that*—

Suddenly he could move his hand a little. He reached toward his pocket to fish out something he could use as a weapon if he had to protect himself. It was taking too long. The dark thing was blocking the light, getting closer. Kit strained as hard as he could to get his hand into his pocket, but there was no time, and the dark object got closer, flailing its way toward him. Kit felt around in his mind for one other spell he'd used occasionally when he had to. Not one that he liked to use, but when it came to the choice between surviving and going down without a fight . . .

The dark shape blotted out the light, leaving it visible only as a faint halo around whatever was coming. Kit said the first half of the spell in his mind and then waited. He wasn't going to use it unless he absolutely had to, for killing was not something a wizard did unless there was no choice.

The dark shape was closer. Kit felt the spell lying ready in his mind, turning and burning and wanting to get out and do what it had been built for. *But not yet*, Kit thought, setting his teeth. *Not just yet. I want to see—*

The black shape was right in front of him now. It launched itself at him. Kit got ready to think the last word of the spell—

—and the dark thing hit him chest high, and started washing his face as it knocked him over backward.

The two of them came down hard together on blacktop. Suddenly everything seemed bright as day in the single light of the streetlight down at the end of the side street. There Kit lay in the road, with a bump that was going to be about the size of a phoenix's egg starting to form on the back of his head, and on top of him Ponch washed his face frantically, saying, "Did you see it? Did you see what I found? Did you? Did you?"

Kit didn't do anything at first but grab his dog and hug him, thinking, *Oh, God, I almost blew him up; thank you for not letting me blow him up!* Then he sat up, looking around him, and pushed Ponch off with difficulty. "Uh, yeah," he said, "I think so . . . But why are you all wet?"

"It was wet there."

"Not where *I* was," Kit said. "But am I glad you came along when you did. Come on, let's get out of the street before someone sees us." Fortunately this was a quiet part of town, without much traffic in the evening, and the two of them had the additional protection that most people didn't recognize wizardry even when it happened right in front of them. Any onlooker would most likely just have seen a kid and his dog suddenly fall over in the middle of the street, where they'd probably been playing, unseen, a moment before.

Kit got up and brushed himself off, feeling weird to be able to move. "Home now?" said Ponch, bouncing around him.

"You better believe it," Kit said, and they started to walk back down the street.

"I'm hungry!"

"We'll see about something for you when we get in."

"Dog biscuits!" Ponch barked, and raced down the street.

Kit went after him. When he came in the back door, his father was just taking the spaghetti pot over to the sink to drain it. "Perfect timing," he said.

Kit looked in astonishment at the beat-up kitchen wall clock. It was only fifteen minutes since he'd left.

His father looked at him strangely. "Are you all right? You look like you've seen a ghost."

Kit shook his head. "Uh . . . I'm okay. I'll explain later. Leave mine in the pot for me for a few minutes, will you, Pop?" He headed into the living room and sat down by the phone.

That was when the shakes hit him. He just sat there and let it happen—not that he had much choice—and meanwhile enjoyed the wonderful normality of the living room: the slightly tacky lamps his mother refused to get rid of, the fact that the rug needed to be vacuumed. At least there *was* a rug, and a floor it was nailed to—not that terrifying empty nothingness under his feet. Finally Kit composed himself enough to pick up the phone and dial a local number.

After a few rings someone picked up. A voice said, "Tom Swale."

"Tom, it's Kit."

"Hey there, fella, long time no hear. What's up?"

"Tom—" Kit paused, not exactly sure how to start this. "I need to ask you something about your dogs."

"Oh no," Tom said, sounding concerned. "What have they done now?"

"Nothing," Kit said. "And I want to know how they do it."

There was a pause. "Can we start this conversation again?" Tom said. "Because you lost me somewhere. Like at the beginning."

"Uh, right. Annie and Monty—"

"You're saying they *didn't* do anything?"

"Not that I know of."

"Okay. This conversation now makes sense to Sherlock Holmes, if no one else. Keep working on *me*, though."

Kit laughed. "Okay. Tom, your dogs are always turning up in your backyard with . . . you know. Weird things."

"Including you, once, as I recall."

"Hey, don't get cute," Kit said.

He was then immediately mortified by the tone he had taken with his Senior wizard, a genuinely nice man who had a lot to do in both his jobs and didn't need thirteen-year-olds sassing him. But Tom simply burst out laughing. "Okay, I deserved that. Are you asking me how they do it?"

"Yeah."

"Then it's my reluctant duty to tell you that I'm not sure. Wizards' pets tend to get strange. You know that."

"But do they always?"

"Well, except for our macaw—who was strange to start with and who then turned out to be one of the Powers That Be in a bird suit—yes, mostly they do."

"Are there any theories about why?"

"Loads. The most popular one is that wizards bend the shape of certain aspects of space-time awry around them, so that we're sort of the local equivalent of gravity lenses . . . and creatures associated with us for long periods tend to acquire some wizardly qualities themselves. Is this helping you?"

There was a lot of barking going on in the background. "I think so."

"Good, because as you can probably hear, the nonweird part of our local canines' lifestyle has kicked in with a vengeance, and they say they want their dinners. But they can wait a few minutes. As far as wizards' dogs are concerned, the development of 'finding' behaviors seems to be relatively common. It may be an outgrowth of the retrieving or herding behaviors that some dogs have had bred into them. Does Ponch have any Labrador in him?"

"Uh, there might be some in there." This had been a topic of idle discussion around Kit's house for a long time, his father mostly referring to Ponch, when the subject came up, as "the Grab Bag." "But he's mostly Border collie. Some German shepherd, too."

"Sounds about right."

"But Tom—" Kit was wondering how to phrase this. "That the dogs might be able to find things, that I can understand. But how can they find *places*? Because Ponch has started finding them."

There was quite a long pause. "That could be interesting," Tom said. "Has he taken you to any of these places?"

"Just once. Just now."

"Are you all right?"

"Now I am. I think," Kit said, starting to shake again.

"You sure?"

"Yeah," Kit said. "It's all right. It was just . . . nothing. No sound, no light or movement. But Ponch got in there, and he knew how to get out again. He got *me* out, in fact, because I couldn't do much of anything."

"That's interesting," Tom said. "Would you consider going there again?"

"Not right now!" Kit said. "But later on, yeah. I want to find out where that was! And how it happened."

"Well, pack animals do prefer to work in groups. From Ponch's point of view, you two probably constitute a small pack, and maybe that's why he's able to share his new talent with you. But until now, to the best of my knowledge, no wizard's found out exactly where the dogs go to get the things they bring back, because no one's been able to go along. If you really want to follow up on this—"

"Yeah, I do."

"Then be careful. You should treat this as an unstable worldgating; you may not be able to get back the same way you left. Better check the manual for a tracing-and-homing spell to keep in place. And make sure you take enough air along. Even though Ponch seems unaffected after short jaunts, there's no guaranteeing that the two of you will stay that way if you linger."

"Okay. Thanks."

"One other thing. I'd confine the wizardry to just the two of you."

Kit was silent for a moment. Then he said, "You're saying that I should leave Nita out of this . . ."

Tom paused, too. "Well, it's possible that the only one who's going to be safe with Ponch as you start investigating this will be you. The semisymbiotic relationship might be what got you out of your bad situation last time. You don't want to endanger anyone else until you're sure what's going on."

"Yeah, I guess so."

"But there's something else," Tom said. "I just had a look at the manual. Nita's assignment status has changed. It says, 'independent assignment, indeterminate period, subject confidential.' You know what that's about?"

"I have an idea," Kit said, though he was uncertain.

"It sounds like she's chasing down something of her own," Tom said. "Usually when there's a formal status change like that, it's unwise to interrupt the other person unless you need their help on something critical to an ongoing project."

"Uh, yeah," Kit said. *Now, how much does he know?* "We just wound up a project, so nothing's going on." He felt guilty at the way he'd put that—but there were lots of things that "we" could mean.

"Okay. I saw the précis on that last one, though. Nice work; we'll see how it holds up. But as regards Ponch, let me know when you find something out. The manual will want an annotation from you on the subject, though it'll 'trap' the raw data as you go. And if you find anything in Ponch's behavior that has to do with more-normal worldgating, tell the gating team in New York—though the fact that a dog's involved is probably going to make them laugh, if it doesn't actually ruffle their fur . . ."

"So to speak. Okay, Tom. Thanks!"

"Right. Best to Nita." And Tom hung up, to the sound of more impatient barking.

Ouch, Kit thought. The last few words made him hurt inside.

But he took a moment to get over it, then got up and went back into the kitchen to see about some spaghetti.

Friday Night

AFTER DINNER KIT WENT upstairs to his bedroom, pausing by the door to Carmela's room, at the sound of a faint hissing noise coming from inside. He knocked on the door.

"Come in!" his sister shouted.

Slightly surprised, Kit stuck his head in the door. His sister was lying on her bed, on her stomach, and the source of the hissing was the earphones she was wearing. On the TV, it looked as if a young boy in a down vest and baseball cap was being electrocuted by a long-tailed yellow teddy bear. "Oh," Kit said, now understanding why Carmela had shouted.

"What?" His sister pulled one of the earphones out.

"Nothing," Kit said. "I heard something going *'sssssssss'* in here. Thought maybe it was your brains escaping."

His sister rolled her eyes.

"Isn't that kind of stuff a little below your age group?" Kit said.

Carmela ostentatiously put the earphone back in. "Not when you're using it to learn Japanese. Now go away."

Kit closed her door and, for once, did what she told him. Carmela was no more of a nuisance to Kit than she had to be at her age. She had even taken his wizardry pretty calmly, for an otherwise excitable fifteen-year-old, when Kit had told the family about it. After the shock wore off, "I always *knew* you were weird" had been Carmela's main response. Still, Kit kept an eye on her, and always put his manual away where she wouldn't find it; the thought of her turning into an older version of Dairine terrified him. *Still, wizardry finds its way. If it's gonna happen, there's no way I can stop it.* His older sister, Helena, seemed safe from this fate, being too old for even late-onset wizardry. She had just left for her first year of college at Amherst, apparently relieved to get out of what she described as "a genuine madhouse." Kit loved her dearly but was also slightly (and guiltily) relieved to be seeing less of her, for she was the only member of the family who seemed to be trying to pretend that Kit's wizardry had never really happened. *Maybe she'll sort it out over the next year or so.*

Meantime, I have other problems. . . .

He pushed his door open and looked around at his room. It was a welter of bookshelves; the usual messy bed; a worktable, where he made models; the desk, where his ancient computer sat; and some rock posters, including one from a hilariously overcostumed and overmade-up metal group, which had been a present from Helena when she cleared out her room—"a souvenir," she'd said, "of a journey into the hopelessly retro."

Kit tossed his jacket onto the bed and plopped down into the desk chair, where he put out his hand and whistled for his manual. It dropped into his hand from the little pouch of otherspace where he kept it. Kit pushed the PC's keyboard to one side and opened the manual.

First he turned to the back page, the messaging area. There was nothing there, but he'd known there wouldn't be; he hadn't felt the "fizz" of notification when he picked up the manual. Then Kit paged backward to the active wizards' listing for the New York area. Yes, there it was, between CAILLEBERT, ARMINA, and CALLANIN, EOIN:

> CALLAHAN, Juanita L.
> 243 E. Clinton Avenue
> Hempstead, NY 11575
> (516) 555-6786
> power rating: 6.08 +/−.5
> status: conditional active
> independent assignment / research:
>   subject classification withheld
> period: indeterminate

Apparently the Powers had something planned for her . . . or were maybe just cutting her some slack. *Sounds like she can use it, too,* Kit thought, feeling brief irritation again at the memory of the afternoon. *Well, okay.*

He paused and then flipped back to a spot a few pages after Nita's listing, running his finger down one column. There it was: RODRIGUEZ, CHRISTOPHER R. Address, phone number, power rating, status, last assignment, blah, blah, blah. . . . But there was something else after his listing.

> Notes: adjunct talent in training

Kit sat back. *Now what the heck does* that *mean?*

He heard thumping on the stairs down the hall and glanced up in time to see Ponch hit his door, push it open, and wander in, waving his tail. The dog turned around a few times in the middle of the floor, then lay down with a thump.

Kit looked at him thoughtfully. Ponch banged his tail on the floor a few times, then yawned.

"You tired, big guy?" Kit said, and then yawned as well. "Guess I am, too."

"It's like chasing squirrels when I do what we did," Ponch said. "I want to sleep afterward."

"I understand that, all right," Kit said. "Got a little while to talk?"

"Okay."

"Good boy. Ponch, just where exactly were we?"

"I don't know."

"But that wasn't the first time you did that, was it?"

"Uh . . ." Ponch looked as if he thought he was about to confess to something that would get him in trouble.

"It's okay," Kit said, "I'm not mad. How long have you been doing that?"

"You went away," Ponch said. "I went looking for you."

Kit sighed. When Nita had been in Ireland over the summer, he'd "beamed over" there several times to help her out. Once or twice he'd been there long enough to get a mild case of gatelag, and he remembered Ponch's ecstatic and relieved greetings when he came back. "So . . . when? End of July, beginning of August?"

"I guess. Right after you went the first time."

"Okay. But where *did* you go? Since you didn't find me."

"I tried, I really tried!" Ponch whimpered. "I missed you. You were gone too much."

"It's okay; I'm not mad that you didn't find me! It was just an observation."

"Oh." Ponch licked his nose in relief.

"So where did you go?"

"It was dark."

"You're right there," Kit said. "The same place we were together?"

"We weren't there together all the time," Ponch said. "You're not there until you *do* something."

Kit wasn't terribly clear about what Ponch meant. He was tempted to push for more information, but Ponch yawned at him again. "Can we go there another time?"

"Sure." Ponch put his head down on his paws. "Whenever you want. Can I go to sleep now?"

"Yeah, go ahead," Kit said. "I wish *I* could."

Shortly, Ponch had rolled over on his side and was emitting the tiny little snore that always sounded so funny coming from such a big dog. Kit stood up, yawning again. He couldn't put off the reaction to the evening's wizardry much longer, but first he wanted to look into a couple of things. Fortunately, tomorrow was Saturday, and he could sleep late. Kit sat down again, opened the manual once more, and soon found the section he wanted. *Tracking and location protocols . . . isodimensional . . . exodimensional . . .*

Kit found a pen and a pad and started making notes.

The mall was crowded that evening, but not so much so that Nita and her mother had any trouble getting their shopping done. The clothes came first, for Nita's mother was concerned that Nita didn't have anything decent to wear to school; and privately Nita agreed with her. At the first shop they went into, though, some differences emerged between their definitions of *decent.*

Nita's mom walked among the racks, shaking her head and trying to avoid looking at the two tops and three skirts Nita was carrying. "They're all so expensive," her mother said under her breath. "And they're not terribly well made, either. Such a rip-off . . ."

Nita knew this wasn't the problem. She trailed along behind, not saying anything. As she finished looking at the racks, her mother stopped and looked at Nita. "Honey, tell me the truth. Are the other girls really wearing stuff like this?" From the nearest rack, she picked up a black skirt identical to one of the ones Nita was carrying, holding it up with a critical expression.

"Stuff exactly like this, Mom. Some of them are shorter. This one's a little conservative." *Because I chickened out on the really short one.*

"And the principal hasn't been sending people home for wearing skirts this short? *Really?*"

"Really."

"You wouldn't be bending the truth in the service of fashion, here?"

Nita had to laugh at that. "If I was gonna lie to you about anything, Mom, don't you think I would have done it when it was about much bigger stuff? Great white sharks? Saving the world?" And she grinned.

"I begin to wonder," her mom said, putting the skirt back on the rack, "exactly how much you *aren't* telling me that I ought to know about."

"Tons of things," Nita said. "Where should I start? Did I tell you about the dinosaurs in Central Park?"

Her mother looked over her shoulder with one of those expressions that suggested she wasn't sure whether Nita was joking. But the expression shaded into one that meant her mom had realized this *wasn't* a joke and she didn't like the idea. "Is this something recent?"

"Uh, kind of. Except we made it so it never happened, and maybe *recent* isn't the right word."

Nita's mother frowned, perplexed. Nita ignored this; the translation of what she'd said was bothering her. "Potentially recent?" Nita said, to see how the substitution sounded. Unfortunately English lacked the right kind of verb tenses to describe a problem that could be easily expressed in the Speech. "No, it can't happen anymore, I don't think. At least, not that time, it can't. *Formerly* recent?"

"Stop now," Nita's mother said, "before this takes you, me, and the dinosaurs many places that none of us wants to go, and let's get back to the skirt." She picked it up again. "Honey, your poor old mom tries hard not to live entirely in the last century, but this thing's hardly more than a wide belt."

"Mom, remember when you trusted me about the shark?"

"Yeeees . . . ," her mother said, sounding dubious.

"So trust me about the skirt!"

Her mother gave her a cockeyed look. "It's not the sharks I'm worried about," she said. "It's the wolves."

"Mom, I promise you, none of the 'wolves' are going to touch me. I just want to look *normal*. If I can't *be* normal, let me at least simulate the effect!"

Her mother looked at her with mild surprise. "You're not having problems at school, are you?"

"No, I'm fine."

"The homework—"

"It's no big deal. There's more than there used to be, but so far I'm not overloaded."

"You *are* having problems, though."

"Mom—" Nita sighed. "Nobody beats me up anymore, if that's what you're worried about. They can't. But a lot of the kids still think I'm some kind of nerd princess." She grimaced. Once Nita had thought that when she got into junior high, reading would be seen as normal behavior for someone her age. She was still waiting for this idea to occur to some of her classmates. "It's nothing wizardry will cure. Just believe me when I tell you that dressing in style will help me blend in a little. I know I didn't care much about clothes in grade school, but now it's more of an issue. As for the length, if you're worried that moral rot will set in, I'll promise to let you know if I see any early warning signs."

Her mother smiled slightly. "Okay," she said, put back the skirt she'd been holding, and reached out to take the one Nita was carrying. "Moral rot hasn't been much of a problem with you. So this is an experiment. But if I hear anything from your principal, I'm going to make you wear flour sacks down to your ankles until you graduate. You and the dinosaurs better make a note."

"Noted, Mom," Nita said. "Thanks." She went off to put the other two skirts back where she'd found them. *This one's a start. She'll soften up in a couple of weeks, and we can come back for the other ones.*

They went to the cash register and paid for the skirt. Then Nita's mom drove them to the supermarket, and as they tooled up and down the aisles with the cart, Nita began to feel normal, almost against her will. But then, while standing there with a bottle of mouthwash in her hand and working out if it was a better bargain than other bottles nearby, Nita's mother suddenly turned to her and said, "What *kind* of dinosaurs?"

Boy, Nita thought, *maybe it's a good thing I didn't mention the giant squid!*

When Nita and her mom got home, Nita and Dairine helped put away the groceries (and Nita helped her mom keep Dairine out of them); so it was half an hour before she could get up to her room and fish out her manual. As she picked it up, she felt a faint fizz about the covers, a silent notification that there was a message waiting for her. Hurriedly she flipped it open to the back page. At the top of the page was Kit's name and his manual reference. In the middle of the page were the words: *If you need some time by yourself, feel free.*

Just that. No annotation, no explanation. Nita flushed hot and cold, then hot again.

Why, that little— He wouldn't even pick up the phone and call me!

Or else he's really, really mad, and he doesn't trust himself to talk to me.

Or maybe he just doesn't feel like it.

Nita felt an immediate twinge of guilt . . . and then stomped on it. *Why should I feel guilty when* he's *the one who's screwing up? And then can't take the heat when someone tries to straighten him out about it?*

Time by myself? Fine.

"Fine," she said to the manual.

Send reply?

"Yeah, send it," Nita said.

Her reply spelled itself out in the Speech on the page, added a time stamp, and archived itself. *Sent.*

Nita shut the manual and chucked it onto her desk, feeling a second's worth of annoyed satisfaction . . . followed immediately by unease. She didn't like the feeling. Sighing, Nita got up and wandered back out to the dining room.

Now that the groceries were gone, computer-printed pages were spread all over the dining-room table. While Nita looked at them, her mother came in from the driveway with a couple more folders' worth of paperwork, dropping them on top of one pile. "Stuff from the flower shop?" Nita said, going to the fridge to get herself a Coke.

"Yup," her mother said. "It's put-Daddy's-incredibly-messed-up-accounts-into-the-computer night."

Nita smiled and sat down at the table. Her father was no mathematician, which probably explained why he pushed her so hard about her math homework. Her mom went into the kitchen, poured herself a cup of tea, and put it into the microwave. "You should make *him* do this," Nita said, idly paging through the incomprehensible papers, a welter of faxes and invoices and Interflora order logs and many, many illegible, scribbly notes.

"I've tried, honey. The last time he did the accounts, it took me a year to get them straightened out. Never again." The microwave dinged; her mother retrieved the cup, added sugar, and came back in to sit at the end of the table, sipping the tea. "Besides, I don't like to nag your dad. He works hard enough . . . Why should I make it hard for him when he comes home, too?"

Nita nodded. This was why she didn't mind spending a lot of time at home; with the possible exception of Kit, she seemed to be the only person she knew who *had* an enjoyable home life. Half the kids in school seemed to be worrying that their parents were about to divorce, but Nita had never even heard her parents raise their voices to each other. She knew they fought—they would vanish into their bedroom, sometimes, when things got tense—but there was no yelling or screaming. That suited Nita entirely. It was possibly also the reason her present fight with Kit was making her so twitchy.

Her mother paged through the paperwork and came up with a bunch of paper-clipped spreadsheet printouts. "Though privately," she muttered as she took the papers apart and started sorting them by month, "there are times I wish I'd never given up ballet. Sure, you get sprains and strains and pulled muscles, and your feet stop looking like anything that ought to be at the end of a human leg, but at least there was never much eye-strain." She smiled slightly. "But if I ever went back to that, there would be all those egos to deal with again. 'Creative differences' . . . that being code for everybody shouting at one another all day." She shook her head. "This is better. Now where did the pen go?"

Nita fished it out from under the papers and handed it over. Her mother started writing the names of months on top of the spreadsheets. "How many days in May, honey?"

"Thirty-one." Nita started looking around under the papers and came up with another pen. "Mom . . ."

"Hmm?"

"If you had a fight with somebody . . . and they were incredibly wrong, and you were right . . . what would you do?"

"Apologize immediately," her mother said.

Nita looked at her in astonishment.

"If they mattered to me at all, anyway," her mother said, glancing up as she put one page aside. "That's what I always do with your dad. Particularly if circumstances have recently proved me to be correct."

"Uh . . . ," Nita said, seriously confused.

Her mom labeled another page and turned it over. "Works for me," she said. "I mean, really, honey . . ." She glanced at the next page, turned it over, too. "Unless it's about a life-and-death issue, why make a point of being right? Of getting all righteous about it? All it does is make people less likely to listen to you. Even more so if they're close to you."

Nita gave her mother a sidelong look. "But, Mom, if it really *is* a life-or-death issue—"

"Sweetie, at your age, a lot of things look like life-and-death. Don't get that look; I'm not patronizing you," her mother added. "Or what you do—I know it's been terribly important sometimes. But think of the problem as a graph, where you plot the intensity of experience against total time. You've had less total time to work with than, say, your dad or I have. Things look a lot more important when the 'spreadsheet' is only a page long instead of four or five."

Nita considered that to see if it made sense. To her annoyance, it did. "I *hate* it when you sneak up on me by being objective," she said.

Her mother produced a weary smile. "I'll take that as a compliment. But it's accidental, honey. It'll take me days to get this sorted out, and right now my whole life is beginning to look like a grid. I don't see why yours shouldn't, too."

Nita smiled and put her head down on her arms. "Okay. But, Mom . . . what do you do if you find out that you're *wrong?*"

"Same thing," her mother said. "Apologize immediately. Why change a tactic that works?"

"Because it makes you look like a wimp."

Her mother glanced up from the papers again, raising her eyebrows. "Excuse me, I must have missed something. It's *not* right to apologize when you're wrong?"

Nita saw immediately why Dairine refused to play chess with their mother anymore. She was cornered. "Thanks, Mom," she said, and got up.

Her mother let out a long breath. "Nothing worthwhile is easy, honey," she said, and looked down ruefully at the papers, rubbing her eyes. "This, either. Come to think of it, I could probably use an aspirin about now." And she got up and went to get one.

Nita was starting to feel like she could use one herself. *She's probably right.*

And something's got to be done. The water situation out there isn't going to just fix itself—

But what am I supposed to do? I can't work with Kit when I'm pissed off at him! It's going to have to wait. The Powers That Be understand that wizards need room to be human, too.

But even as she thought it, Nita felt guilty. A wizard knew that the energy had been running slowly out of the universe for millennia. Viewed in that context, no delay was worthwhile. Every quantum of energy lost potentially could have been used to make some fragment of the cosmos work better. A relationship, for example . . .

Nita got up and wandered back to her room, thinking about what she might do to make herself useful, besides the project she and Kit and S'reee had been working on in the bay. It wasn't as if there weren't projects she'd been interested in that Kit hadn't been enthusiastic about. This would be a good time to start one of those.

Yet as Nita shut the door of her room, Dairine's point came back to her. *Is it possible that Kit and I really* do *still have unfinished business about Ronan?* Before, Nita wouldn't have thought it likely. Now she wondered. Dairine could be cunning and sly, and a pain in the butt . . . but she was also a wizard. She wouldn't lie.

But why wouldn't Kit have told me?

Unless he thought the idea was stupid. Or unless he really didn't think it was a problem.

She sat down at the desk and put her feet up on it, and picked up the manual, hoping to feel that fizz . . . but there was nothing. Nita dropped it in her lap and stared at the dark window. *I was stupid with him*, she thought. *But he wasn't being terribly open-minded, either. Or real tactful.*

She opened the manual idly. Life had changed so much since she'd found it; it now seemed as if she'd had the manual within reach all her life—or all the life that mattered. In some ways it seemed to Nita as if all her childhood had simply been an exercise in marking time, waiting for the moment when this book would snag her hand as she trailed it idly down a shelf full of books in the children's library. It was always handy now, either in her book bag or tucked away in her personal claudication. A couple years' use had taught Nita that the manual wasn't the infallibly omniscient resource she'd taken it for at the beginning. It *did* contain everything you needed to know to do your work . . . but it left deciding what the work *was* to you. You might make mistakes, but they were yours. The manual made it all possible, though. It was compendium, lifeline, communications device, encyclopedia, weapon, and silent adviser all rolled into one. Nita couldn't imagine what wizardry would be like without it.

And there was something else associated with wizardry that she couldn't imagine being without, either.

She riffled through the pages, let her hand drop. The manual fell open at a spot near its beginning, and as Nita looked down, she wondered why she should even be surprised that she found herself looking at this particular page.

In Life's name, and for Life's sake, I assert that I will employ the Art, which is Its gift, in Life's service alone, rejecting all other usages. I will guard growth and ease pain. I will fight to preserve what grows and lives well in its own way; I will not change any creature unless its growth and life, or that of the system of which it is part, are threatened or threaten another. To these ends, in the practice of my Art, I will ever put aside fear for courage, and death for life, when it is right to do so—looking always toward the Heart of Time, where all our sundered times are one, and all our myriad worlds lie whole, in That from Which they proceeded. . . .

She let out a long unhappy breath as she gazed at the words. *I will ease pain. . . .*

Nita had made her share of mistakes during her practice, but if there was one thing she prided herself on, it was taking the Oath seriously. *But lately maybe I haven't been doing a very good job. On the large things, yeah. But have they been blocking my view of the small ones?*

And what makes me think that being friends with Kit is something small?

Nita closed the book, put it down on the desk, and pushed it away. *It's too late tonight. Tomorrow. I'll go over and see him tomorrow . . . and we'll see what happens.*

Saturday Morning and Afternoon

SLEEPING IN TURNED OUT to be an idle fantasy. Kit rolled over just after dawn, feeling muzzy and wondering what had managed to jolt him out of a peculiar dream, when suddenly he realized what it was. A cold wet nose had been stuck into his ear.

"Ohh, *Ponch* . . ." Kit rolled over and tried to hide his head under the pillow. This was a futile gesture. The nose followed him, and then the tongue.

Finally he had no choice but to get up. Kit sat up in bed, rubbing his eyes, while Ponch jumped up and washed the back of Kit's neck as if he hadn't a worry in the world. Kit, for his own part, ached as if someone had run him over lightly with a truck, but this was a normal side effect of doing a large, complex wizardry; it would pass.

"Awright, awright," Kit muttered, trying to push Ponch away. He glanced at the clock on his dresser—*Ten after six?! . . . What have I done to deserve this?*—and then looked over at the desk. His manual sat where he had left it, last thing. Closing it, finally getting ready to turn in, he had felt the covers fizz, had opened the book to the back page, and had seen Nita's response.

Fine.

He got up, went over to the desk, and opened the manual again. Nothing had been added since. Nita was plainly too pissed off even to yell at him. But Tom had been pretty definite about letting her be if she was working on some other piece of business. *Okay. Let her get on with it.*

He shut the manual and went to root around in his dresser for jeans and a polo shirt. Ponch was jumping for joy around him, his tongue lolling out and making him look unusually idiotic. "What're *you* so excited about?" Kit asked in the Speech.

"Out, we're gonna go out, aren't we?" Ponch said in a string of muffled woofs and whines. "We're gonna go *there* again, you can go with me, this is great, let's go out!" And Ponch abruptly sat down and licked his chops. "I'm hungry," he said.

There . . . , Kit thought, and shuddered. But now that the experience was half a day behind him, he was feeling a little less freaked out by it, and more curious about what had happened.

He put his head out his bedroom door. It was quiet; nobody in his house got up this early on a Saturday, unless it was his dad, who was an occasional surf-casting nut and would sometimes head out before dawn to fish the flood tide down at Point Lookout. No sign of that happening today, though.

"Okay," he said to Ponch. "You can have your breakfast, and then I want a shower . . . and then we'll go out. After I take care of something."

Ponch spun several times in a tight circle and then launched himself out into the hall and down the stairs.

Kit went after him, fed him, and then went back upstairs to take a shower and make his plans. When he came downstairs, Ponch was waiting at the side door to be let out.

"In a minute," Kit said. "Don't *I* get something to eat, too?"

"Oh."

"Yeah, 'oh.' You big wacko." Kit grabbed a quart of milk out of the fridge and drank about half of it, then opened one of the nearby cupboards and found a couple of the awful muesli-based breakfast bars that his sister liked. He stuck them in his pocket and then went to the write-on bulletin board stuck to the front of the fridge. The pen, as usual, wasn't in the clip where it belonged; Kit found it behind the sink. On the board he wrote: GONE OUT ON BUSINESS, BACK LATER. This was code, which Kit's family now understood. To Ponch he said, "You go do what you have to first . . . I have something to get ready."

Kit let the dog out and locked the door behind them. Then he and Ponch went out into the backyard. It wasn't nearly as tidy or decorative as Nita's. Kit's father wasn't concerned about it except as somewhere to sit outside on weekends, and so while the lawn got mowed regularly, the back of the yard was a jungle of sassafras saplings and blackberry bushes. Into this little underbrush forest Ponch vanished while Kit sat down on a creaking old wooden lounger and opened his manual.

He knew in a general way what he wanted—a spell that would keep him connected to Ponch in mind, letting him share the dog's perceptions. It also needed to be something that would keep them within a few yards of each other, so that if physical contact became important, Kit could have it in a hurry. He paged through the manual, looking for one particular section and finding it: *Bindings, ligations, and cinctures*—wizardries that dealt with holding energy or matter in place, in check, or in alignment with something else. *Simplex, multiplex . . . Here's one. First-degree complex aelysis . . . proof strength in m-dynes . . . to the minus four* . . . The original formula for the spell, Kit saw, had called for fish's breath, women's beards, and various other hard-to-find ingredients. But over many years the formula had been refined so that all you needed to build it now were knowledge, intention, a basic understanding of paraphysics, and the right words in the Speech.

Yeah, this is what I need. "All right," Kit said softly in the Speech. "This is a beta-class short-term interlocution." He pronounced the first few sentences, and the spell started to build itself in the air in front of him—a twining and growing chain of light, word linking to word in a structure like a chain of DNA, but with three main strands instead of two.

After a couple of minutes he was finished and the structure nearly complete. Kit plucked it out of the air, tested it between his hands. It looked faintly golden in the early morning light, and felt at least as strong as a steel chain would, though in his hands it was as light and fine as so much spun silk.

Not bad, Kit thought. But there was still one thing missing. The place down at one end of the spell where his own name and personal information went was now full; Kit had pasted it in from the wizardry he and S'reee had just done. But as for Ponch . . .

It embarrassed him to have to turn to his dog, who'd now returned from the bushes and was sitting and watching Kit with great interest. "Ponch," he said, "I can't believe I've never asked you this before. But what's your name?"

The dog laughed at him. "You just said it."

"But Grrarhah down the street uses a Cyene name."

"If the people you lived with named *you* Tinkerbell," Ponch said in a surprisingly dry voice, "so would *you.*"

Kit had to grin at that. "I don't mind the name you gave me," Ponch said. "I use that. It says who I am." He stuck his nose in Kit's ear again and started to wash it.

"Euuuu, Ponch!" Kit pushed him away . . . but not very hard.

"Okay, look, give it a rest," Kit said. "I have to finish something here."

"Let me see."

Kit showed him the wizardry. As Ponch watched, Kit pronounced the fifteen or sixteen syllables of the Speech that wound themselves into the visible version of Ponch's name, containing details like his age and his breed (itself a tightly braided set of links with about ten strands involved). Ponch nosed at the leash; it came alive with light as he did so. "There's the collar," Kit said, looping the end of the spell through the wizard's knot he had tied there, then holding the wide loop up. The similar loop at the other end, made up of Kit's name and personal information, would go around his wrist.

Ponch slipped his head through the wider of the two loops, then shook himself. The loop tightened down.

"That feel okay?" Kit said. "Not too tight?"

"It's fine. Let's go."

"Okay," Kit said, and stood up. He slipped his wrist through the other loop and pronounced the six words that got the environmental and tracking functions of the wizardry going, the parts that would snap them back here if anything life threatening happened. The "chain" flickered, showing that the added functions were working. "Right. Show me how."

"Like this—"

Ponch took no more than a step forward, and without a moment's hesitation that darkness slammed silently down around them again. This time at least Kit was sure he had air around him and Ponch, and he had oxygenation routines ready to kick in if their bodies were affected by any kind of paralysis. Nonetheless, Kit still couldn't move, couldn't see anything.

Or could he?

Kit would have blinked if he could have, or squinted. Often enough before, in very dark places, he'd had the illusion that he could see a very faint light when there was actually nothing there. This was like that—yet somehow different, not as diffuse. He could just make out a tiny glint of light, far away there in the dark, distant as a star. . . .

It faded. Or maybe it wasn't truly there at all. *Oh well.*

Ponch?

Here I am.

And abruptly Kit really could see something, though he still couldn't move. Down just out of range of his direct vision, though still perceptible as a dim glow, he could tell that the "leash" was there, the long chain structure of the wizardry glinting with life as the power ran up and down it. It was unusual to be able to see it doing that, instead of as a steady glow; there was something odd about the flow of time here. Maybe that was the cause of the illusion of breathlessness.

Kit tried to speak out loud but again found that he couldn't. It didn't matter; the leash wizardry would carry his thoughts to Ponch. *What do we do now?* Kit said silently.

Be somewhere.

Kit normally would have thought that that was unavoidable. Now he wasn't so sure. *Well, where did you have in mind?*

Here.

And something appeared before them. It was hard to make out the distance at first, until Kit saw what the thing was: a small shape, pale gray against that darkness, except for a whiter underbelly.

It was a squirrel.

This was so peculiar that even if he hadn't been frozen in place, Kit still wouldn't have done much but stand and stare. There it was, just a squirrel, sitting up on its hind legs and looking at them with that expression of interest-but-not-fear you get from a squirrel that knows you can't possibly get near it in time to do anything about it.

Okay, Kit said in his mind, completely confused. *Now what?*

Shhh.

The instruction amused Kit. He wasn't exactly used to his dog telling him what to do. But suddenly, a little farther away, there was another squirrel, rooting around in the grass, looking for something: a nut, Kit supposed.

And another squirrel . . . and then another. They were all doing different things, but each of them existed absolutely by itself, as if spotlighted on a dark stage. Next to him, Ponch shifted from foot to foot, whimpering in growing excitement.

There were more squirrels every moment . . . ten of them, twenty, fifty. But then something else started to happen. Not only squirrels, but other things began to appear. Trees, at first. *I guess that makes sense; where there are squirrels, there are always trees.* They were unusually broad of trunk, astonishingly tall, with tremendous canopies of leaves. And slowly, underneath them, grass began to roll out and away into what built itself into a genuine landscape—grass patched with sunlight, wavering with the shadows of branches. The sky, where it could be seen, came last, the usual creamy blue sky of a suburban area near a large city, spreading itself gradually up from horizon to zenith, as if a curtain were being lifted. Finally, there was the sun, and Kit felt a breeze begin to blow.

Ponch made a noise halfway between a whine and a bark and leaped forward, dragging Kit out of immobility, as he tore off toward the nearest squirrel. The whole landscape now instantly came alive around them like a live-action version of a cartoon: squirrels running in every direction, and some of them rocketing up the trees, all of them in frantic motion—especially the one that Ponch was chasing as he dragged Kit along. This was an experience Kit had had many, many times before in the local park, and all he could do now was try not to fall flat on his face as he was pulled along at top speed.

Kit laughed, finding that his voice worked again. Briefly he considered just letting Ponch off the spell leash. But then that struck Kit as a bad idea. He still had no sense of where they were, or what the rules of this place were. *Better just tell the spell to extend as far as it needs to, so he can run.*

It took a few seconds to change the loci-of-effect and extensibility variables—longer than it normally would have taken, but then, Kit thought he wasn't doing badly for someone who was being hauled along through a forest at what felt like about thirty miles an hour. Finally Kit was able to extend the leash, then slowed down from the run until he was standing there in the bright sun between two huge trees, watching his dog go tearing off across the beautiful grass, barking his head off with delight.

He's found Squirrel World, Kit thought, and had to laugh. There was seemingly infinite running room, there was an endless supply of squirrels, and there were trees for the squirrels to run up, because there had to be some challenge about this for it to be fun. *He's found dog heaven. Or maybe Ponch heaven . . .*

Ponch was far off among the trees now. Kit sat down on the grass to watch him. This space had some strange qualities, for despite the increased distance, Kit's view of Ponch was still as clear and sharp as if he were looking at him through a telescope. Ponch was closing on the squirrel he'd been chasing. As Kit watched, the squirrel just made it to the trunk of a nearby tree and went up it like a shot. Ponch danced briefly around on his hind legs at the bottom of the tree, barking his head off, then spotted another squirrel and went off after that one, instead.

Maybe this isn't exactly Ponch heaven after all, Kit thought. *Could this be the dog version of a computer game?* For there didn't seem to be instant wish fulfillment here. Ponch still wasn't catching the squirrels; he was mostly chasing them.

Kit watched this go on for a while, as his dog galloped around over about fifty acres of perfect parkland, littered with endless intriguing targets. *The question is, where* is *this? Somewhere inside his mind? Or is it an actual place? Though it's a weird one.* Their entry here hadn't been anything like a normal worldgating. Normally you stepped through a gate, whether natural or constructed, and found another place waiting there, complete. Or sometimes, as he'd seen happen in Ireland over the summer, that other place came sweeping over you, briefly pushing aside the one where you'd been standing earlier.

But this was different. *It's as if Ponch was* making *this world, one piece at a time . . .*

He gazed down at the grass. Every blade was perfect, each slightly different from every other. Kit shook his head in wonder, looked up and saw Ponch still romping across the grass. There was always another squirrel to chase, and Kit noticed with amusement that the ones that weren't being chased were actually following Ponch, though always at a discreet distance. *So he won't be distracted?* When Ponch managed to pursue one closely enough that it actually had to run up a tree, there were always others within range when he was ready for them.

How is he doing *this?* Kit wondered. "Ponch?"

Ponch let off a volley of frustrated barks at the squirrel he was chasing, which had gone halfway up one of the massive tree boles and was now clinging to it head down and chattering at him. Kit couldn't make out specific Skioroin words at this point, but the tone was certainly offensive. Ponch barked at the squirrel more loudly. "Yeah, okay, get over it," Kit yelled. "There are about five thousand more like him out there! Can you give it a rest so we can have a few words, please?"

Ponch came galloping back to Kit a few seconds later. "Isn't it great, do you like it, do you want to chase some, I can make some more for you . . ."

"Sit down. Your tongue's gonna fall off if it waves around much more than that," Kit said.

Ponch sat down beside him and leaned on Kit in a companionable manner, looking entirely satisfied with life, and panting energetically.

"Look," Kit said. "How are you doing this?"

"I don't know."

"You must know a little," Kit said. "You told me yesterday, 'You're not there until you do something.' What did you do?"

"I wanted you."

"Yes, but that was the first time."

"That's what I did."

Kit sighed and put his head down on his knees, thinking. "This," he said, "what you did just now. How did you do this? Where did all these squirrels come from?"

"I *want* squirrels."

"Yeah, and boy, have you got them," said Kit, looking around him in amusement. The two of them were completely surrounded by squirrels, an ever growing crowd of them, all sitting up on their little hind legs and staring at Ponch, all intent and quiet . . . as if someone in a whimsical mood had swapped them for the seagulls in *The Birds*. "Where did they all come from?"

Ponch sat quiet for a moment, and stopped panting as a look of intense concentration came over his face. Then he looked at Kit and said, "I wanted them here."

Suddenly Kit got it. The way Ponch used *wanted* was not the way it would have been used in Cyene; it was the form of the word used in the Speech. And in the wizardly language, the verb was not passive. The closest equivalent in English would be *willed*; in the Speech, the word implies not just desire but creation.

"You *made* them," Kit said.

"I wanted them to be here. And here they are." The dog jumped up and began to bounce for sheer joy. "Isn't it *great*?!"

Kit rubbed his nose and wondered about that. "What happens when you catch them?" he asked, to buy himself time.

"I shake them around a lot," Ponch said, "and then I'm sorry for them."

Kit grinned, for this was more or less the way things went in the real world. But then he paused, surprised. He'd slipped and spoken to Ponch in English, but the dog had understood him.

"Are you able to understand me when I'm *not* using the Speech?" Kit asked.

Ponch looked amused. "Only here. I made it so I would always know what you're saying."

"Wow," Kit said. He looked around him again at the patient squirrels. "Have you made anything else?"

"Lots of things. Why don't you make something?"

"Uh . . . ," Kit said, and stopped. The ramifications of this were beginning to sink in, and he wanted to make some preparations. "Not right this minute. Look, you wanna go see Tom and Carl?"

Ponch began to bounce around again. "Dog biscuits!"

"Yeah, probably they'll give you some. And if they have a spare clue for me to chew on, that wouldn't hurt, either." Kit got up. "You done with these guys?"

"Sure. They wait for me. Even if they didn't, I can always make more."

"Okay. Let's go home."

Ponch acquired a look of concentration. A second later, the landscape went out, as if a light had simply been turned off behind it, and Kit felt a tug on the leash. He followed it—

—and they stepped out again into early morning in Kit's backyard: birdsong, dew, the sound of a single station wagon going down the street in front of the house as the newspaper guy threw the morning paper into people's driveways . . .

Kit took a deep breath of the morning air and relaxed. From above them came an annoyed chattering noise. Ponch wheeled around and began dancing on his hind legs and barking.

"Didn't you just have enough of those?" Kit said. "Shut up; you're going to wake up the whole neighborhood! Come on . . . We need to go see Tom."

Nita rolled over in her bed that morning, feeling strangely achy. At first she wondered if she was catching a cold; but it didn't seem to be that. *Probably it's just from being upset*, she thought. *Hey, I wonder . . .*

She got up and padded over to the desk, where her manual lay. Nita picked it up and flipped to the back page, hoping to see some long angry rant from Kit. But there was nothing.

She broke out in a sweat at the sight of the page with not a thing on it but the previous two communications. *He must be completely furious*, she thought. *This is gonna be awful . . . and when Dairine hears about it, she's going to laugh herself sick. I'll probably have to kill her.*

Nita put the manual down, pulled open a drawer in her dresser and extracted a clean T-shirt, then pulled it on along with yesterday's jeans and turned back to the desk. *I wonder what he's up to, though. Maybe he's out working on the water with S'reee.*

Nita flipped through to Kit's listing in the directory and glanced at it. *Last project: mesolittoral water-quality intervention, for details see reference MSI-B14-/XIiii/βγ66384-67/1141-2211/ABX6655/3: other participants, Callahan, Juanita L., hominid / Sol III, S'reee a!hruuni-Aoul-mmeiihnhwiii!r, cetacean / Sol III; intervention status complete / functioning . . .*

Nita's mouth dropped open.

. . . anentropia rate 0.047255-E^8, effectiveness rating 3.5+/− .10; review scheduled Julian date 2451809.5—

Oh, my God. It's working!

The initial reaction of sheer delight at the solution of a problem that had had them all literally running in circles for so long was now drowned by a nearly intolerable wave of combined embarrassment and annoyance.

They got it working without me.

He was right.

I was wrong.

Nita sat there in shock.

I am so stupid!

Yet she couldn't quite bring herself to believe it. And she was still listed as a participant in the spell. Nita paged back to the section where intervention references were kept, and shortly found a copy of the spell diagram that Kit and S'reee had been using.

Nita traced the curves and circles of it, all apparent in an enlarged hologram-matic format when you looked at the page closely. The basic structure of the wizardry was derived broadly from the last pattern she and Kit had worked on together, before they started disagreeing about the details. It was missing any of the extra subroutines she had insisted were absolutely necessary to make the spell work right. The detailed versions of the effectiveness figures were at the bottom of the page, updating themselves as she watched, demonstrating that the water coming out of Jones Inlet was indeed getting cleaner by the second. . . .

Nita sat there in the grip of an attack of complete chagrin. *What an utter dork I've been*, she thought. *I'm going straight over there to apologize. No, I'm not going to wait even that long.*

She flipped back to the messaging pages, touched the message from Kit to wake up the reply function. "Kit?" she said in the Speech. "Can we talk?"

Send?

"Send it," Nita said.

Then she waited. But to her complete astonishment, the page just flashed once, leaving her message sitting where it was. *Message cannot be dispatched at this time. Please try again later.*

What?? "How come?"

The notification blanked out, replaced by the words: *Addressee is not in ambit. Please try again later.*

Nita stared. She had never seen such a description before and didn't have any idea what it meant.

She put the manual down on the desk. "Keep trying," Nita said, and went downstairs. It was quiet; there was no smell of anyone having been making break-fast down there. *I may be the only one up.*

Nita picked up the kitchen phone and dialed Kit's number. It rang a couple of times, then someone picked up. "Hello?"

It was Kit's sister. "Hola, Carmela!"

" 'Ola, Nita," said Carmela, in a somewhat odd voice—she had her mouth full. There was a pause while she swallowed. "You missed him; he's not here."

"Where'd he go, do you know?"

"Nope. He left a note on the fridge; must've been early . . . said he was going out to do some wizard thing and he'd be back later."

"Today, you think?"

"Oh yeah, today. If he was gonna be gone longer than tonight, he sure would have told Pop and Mama, and they would've screamed, and I would've heard it."

Nita had to chuckle. "Okay, Mela. If he comes in, tell him I called?"

"Sure, Neets. No problem."

"Thanks. Bye-bye."

"Byeeee . . ."

Nita hung up. *He's out on errantry . . . but where? I should have been able to find him. It shouldn't matter if he was on the Moon, or even halfway out of the galaxy. His manual still would have taken the message. It's not like the manuals care about light speed, or anything like that.*

After a few moments Nita went back upstairs to see what the manual might be showing. The last page still hadn't changed.

I don't believe this, Nita thought. *I ought to call Tom and Carl and see what they say. Where is he that the manual can't find him?!*

She picked up the manual and started to take it downstairs to the phone with her, then stopped. She would have to tell Tom and Carl what had been going on, and she was too embarrassed.

But *where* was Kit?

Down the hall Dairine's door opened, and her sister wandered down toward her in the direction of the bathroom, wearing nothing but a huge Fordham T-shirt of their dad's. She looked at Nita vaguely. "What's for breakfast?"

"Confusion," Nita said, rather sourly.

"What?"

"Nothing yet. Nobody's up. And I can't find Kit."

Dairine stopped and stared at her, pushing the hair out of her eyes and yawning. "Why? Where is he?"

"Somewhere the manual can't find him."

"What?"

"Look at this!" Nita was concerned enough to show Dairine her manual, even though it meant she would see the messages above the strange new notification. Dairine looked at the back page and shook her head.

"I've never seen *that* before," she said. "You sure it's not a malfunction or something?"

Nita snorted. "Have you ever seen a manual malfunction?"

"I have to admit," Dairine said slowly, "if I did, I'd get worried . . . considering What powers them. Come on, let's see if mine's doing the same thing."

Nita followed Dairine to her room and glanced at where the pile of stuff from yesterday had mostly been dumped on the floor. "You'd better take care of this before Mom gets up," Nita said. "She'll have some new and never-before-seen species of cow."

"Plenty of time for that," Dairine said, going over to her desk and knocking one knuckle on the outside of the laptop's case. "She was up till half past forever last night with Dad's stuff."

The laptop sprouted its legs again and stood up on them, stretching them one after another like a centipede that thought it was a cat. "Morning, Spot," Dairine said.

"Mrng," said the laptop in a small scratchy voice.

"Manual functions?"

"Spcfy."

"Messaging," Dairine said.

The laptop popped open its lid, and its screen flickered on, showing the usual apple-without-the-bite logo, then blanking down again. A moment later the operating system herald displayed, a stylized representation of a book open to a small block of text. This was then replaced by a messaging menu, overlaid on a shimmering blue background subtly watermarked with the manual logo. "Main address list," Dairine said. "Test message." The screen blanked. "To Kit Rodriguez. Where are you? Send."

The words displayed themselves on the screen exactly as they had in Nita's manual, blinked out, and then reappeared with a little blue box underneath them in which was written in the Speech, *Error 539426010: Recipient is not in ambit. Please resubmit message later.*

"Huh," Dairine said. "More information."

The blue box enlarged slightly. *No further information available.*

"We'll see about *that*," Dairine muttered. "Thanks, cutie."

"*Yr wlcm*," said the laptop, and sat down on the desk again, stretching out its legs.

"Doesn't waste his words, does he?" Nita said, smiling.

"He's shy," Dairine said, with a wry expression. "You should hear him when we're alone. Let's try this."

She went over to the sleek cube of the new computer and waved a hand over the top of it. The light behind the apple came on. Nita cocked an ear. "Is its fan broken?"

"No, it doesn't have one. There's just some kind of little chimney that convects out the heat, so it doesn't need a fan."

"Or a plug . . ."

Dairine grinned, and waved over the top of the silvery case again. A second later the monitor, a suitably slick flat-screen model on a Lucite base, appeared to one side of the main processor case. "Mom may have some problems with that," Nita said.

"Oh, it won't do that when I get all the normal software installed and put it out downstairs. Meantime, I don't see why it should have to sit on the desk when there's umpteen billion cubic parsecs of perfectly good otherspace to stick it in."

On the screen appeared a manual herald like the one that had been displaying on the laptop, but this one had a discreet Greek letter β blazoned across the image of the book. Dairine waved once more over the top of the processor case, and the keyboard, also in brushed stainless steel, appeared. "What do you need that for?" Nita asked.

"I type faster than I talk."

"Impossible."

Dairine gave Nita a dirty look and started typing, while Nita looked in interest at the keyboard, the standard North American QWERTY type. "Not much good for the Speech."

Dairine hit the carriage return and shook her head. "Come on, Neets, really." She flicked a finger in the air over the keyboard; the keyboard stretched, and the keys shimmered and reconfigured themselves to display the 418 characters of the Speech. "Eventually we won't need this, but the wireless transparent neurotranslation routines are still in pre-alpha." She looked at Nita with a mischievous expression. "Getting interested finally? I can copy Spot for you and give you his twin, if you like."

"Thanks, but I'll stick with the manual I know."

Dairine shook her head in poorly concealed pity. "Luddite."

"Technodweeb," Nita said. "Call me sentimental. I like books. They don't crash."

"Huh," Dairine said, as the monitor blanked and then brought up a long, long list. Dairine glanced over at Spot. "You wanna pass it that last error?"

A moment later that same little blue screen appeared on the monitor. "Right," Dairine said. She glanced over her shoulder at Nita. "Sometimes the beta shows background information that the normal release version doesn't have in it yet, or doesn't routinely release. Any additional information on this?" she said to the desktop machine.

The blue box was partly overlapped by another one, in a lighter shade of blue. It contained the words:

> For accurate and secure message storage and delivery, manual messaging functions require each party's manual to supply a coordinate based on the intersection between each wizard's personal description in the Speech and his present physical location in a given universe. Message dispatch and storage cannot be achieved when one or both addressees are in transit or experiencing transitory states between universes. Please remessage when the condition no longer obtains.

"Oh, well, I guess that's okay, then," Dairine said in astonishment heavily tinged with irony. She looked at Nita. "Another *universe*? That's normally not a transit you make without permission from seriously high up."

"Yeah," Nita said. She opened her manual again and paged through to where Kit's status report was.

Dairine hit a couple of keys; the monitor changed to show the same view. Under the listing for the water wizardry, Kit's status report said:

> Present project: access-routine investigation and stabilization, training assignment with adjunct talent; situation presently in development. Detail reference: in abeyance due to possible Heisenberg-related effects; update expected c. Julian day 2451796.6.

"*Adjunct*?" Dairine muttered.

The thought went through Nita like a spear: *He's working with someone else!* At first it seemed ridiculous. *But considering how I treated him . . . why* shouldn't *he want to work with other people? I've brought this on myself. Idiot! Idiot!*

"Whatever else is going on," Dairine said, "the Powers That Be know about it. Look, here's an authorization code. They must have some way of keeping tabs on him if They've even got a projected update time in there. Point six . . . that's after dinner, I guess. Try again then."

Nita closed her manual, feeling slightly relieved. "Yeah . . ."

"But Neets, look," Dairine said, "if you're worried, why not just try to shoot him a thought? No matter what the manual's doing, it's not like your brain is broken."

"Unusual sentiment from you," Nita said.

Dairine's smile was slightly sardonic. "So maybe I'm mellowing in my old age," she said. There was more of an edge than usual on the expression, but Nita got the feeling it wasn't directed at her . . . for a change.

She sat down on the bed, pushing the area rug around with her feet. "Never mind. If he's in another universe, I doubt I've got the range to reach him."

"Probably you're right," Dairine said. "But that's not the reason you're not going to try, is it?"

Nita looked at her sister and found Dairine regarding her with an expression that actually could have been described as *understanding*. "You're afraid you're gonna find that he's shut you out on purpose," Dairine said, "and you couldn't stand it."

Nita didn't say anything. Dairine glanced away, looking at the computer, and hit a key to clear the screen.

"Well . . . ," Nita said at last, "lately it's been harder than usual to hear him thinking, anyway. And he's been having the same trouble with me."

There were things that that could mean for wizards, especially if they'd been working closely together for some time . . . and Nita knew Dairine understood the implications. "Neets," Dairine said at last, "if you're really that worried, you should take the chance, anyway. It's better than sitting here busting a gut."

"I hate it when you're right," Nita said finally.

"Which is always," Dairine said, "but never mind; I'm used to it by now." She went back to tapping at the keyboard.

Nita let out a long breath and closed her eyes.

Kit?

Nothing.

Kit? Where are you?!

Still nothing. Nita opened her eyes, as upset with herself, now, as with the situation. She must have sounded completely pitiful and helpless, if he'd heard her.

But I don't think he did. And that by itself was strange. Even when you called someone mind to mind and they refused contact, there was always a sense that they were still *there*. This time there was no such sense. And the manual, as Nita opened it once more to the page she'd marked, and looked at it again, still reported Kit as out there, doing *something*. . . .

"Nothing?" Dairine said.

"Not a refusal," Nita said, trying to keep relief out of her voice. "Just . . . nothing. Maybe he really is just out of range."

Dairine nodded. "Just have to wait till he gets back, then."

Nita sighed and headed downstairs. As she came into the dining room, she heard someone in the kitchen. Turning the corner, she saw that it was her mother, standing there by the counter and looking bleary as she drank a mug of tea and gazed out the window.

"Mom, you look pooped!" Nita said.

Her mother laughed. "I guess. Even after I went to bed last night I had numbers going around and around in my head . . . Took me a while to get to sleep. Never mind, I'll have a nap before dinner. Speaking of which, where *has* Kit been the past day or so?"

Nita tried to think of what to say. Her mother glanced at her, glanced away again. "Just so I can keep the leftovers from piling up," her mother said. "I just like to know when I'm supposed to be cooking for five. You think he might be along tonight?"

"I don't know for sure," Nita said. "I'll tell you when I find out."

"Okay. I'm going to the shop later, if you want me." Her mom had another drink of tea, then put the mug aside. "Some paperwork was missing from what your dad gave me yesterday, and I need to go root around in what *he* calls a filing system. Did we miss anything from shopping last night?"

"I think we need more milk."

"I think we need to buy your sister a cow," her mother said, and went off to get dressed.

Nita went up to her room to kill some time until she could reach Kit. It was annoying to be mad at someone, but it was even worse to discover that you were wrong to be mad at them, and worse yet not to be able to apologize to them and get it over with. *I'm never gonna make* this *mistake again!*

Or at least I sure hope I won't . . . because it just hurts too much.

When Kit got over to Tom and Carl's place with Ponch, he wasn't surprised to find Tom already working—sitting out on the patio in jeans and T-shirt and a light jacket, typing away on his portable computer at the table next to the big square koi pond. "It's the only quiet time I get before the phone starts ringing," Tom said, letting Kit in the side gate. "Come on in, tell me what you found . . ."

Over a cup of tea, while Ponch sprawled under the table, Kit described what Ponch had been doing, and Tom looked at the "hard" report in his Senior's version of the manual, which was presently about the size of a phone book. Tom shook his head, turning over pages and reading what Kit could see even from across the table was a very abstruse analysis indeed, in very small print.

"This is a new one on me," he said at last. "I'll ask Carl to have a look later; the worldgating and timesliding end of things is more his specialty. But I'm not even sure that what Ponch is doing *is* either of those. And I can't find any close cognates to this kind of behavior in any other wizards' reports."

"Really?" Kit said. "How far does that go back?"

"All the way," Tom said absently. "Well, nearly. Some of the material before the first hundredth of a second of the life of this universe is a little sketchy. Privacy issues, possibly."

He shook his head and closed the book. "Kit, I'm not sure *where* you were. I'm not sure it can even be classified as a *where*, as a physical universe that, given the right geometries, can be described in terms of its direction and distance from other neighboring universes. Ponch's place might be another dimension, another continuum even, completely out of the local sheaf of universes. Or an entirely different state of being, not physical the way we understand it at all." He shrugged. "He's found something very unusual that's going to take some exploring before we begin to understand it. At least your whole experience is stored in the manual, and you'll want to add notes to it later. It'll help the other wizards who'll be starting analysis on it."

"I thought your version of the manual was going to be able to explain this."

Tom leaned back. "There's never any guarantee of that. We're told new things *about* the universe all the time. But we're not routinely told what they *mean*. Wizardry is like science that way. We're expected to figure out the meaning of the raw data ourselves."

"So what do I do?"

"Well, what were you thinking of doing?"

"What Ponch suggested," Kit said. "Going into that . . . that 'state,' I guess, and seeing if I could do what he was doing: make things."

"Probably not a bad idea," Tom said. "You seem to have come out of this all right . . . but don't get careless. Exploratory wizardry can be dangerous, even though you *are* working for the Good Guys."

The patio door slid open, and there was Carl, in jeans and flip-flops and an NYPD T-shirt. "I heard voices," he said.

"Sorry, we didn't mean to disturb you—"

"Not *your* voices," Carl said, rueful. "The voices of certain fur-bearing persons who're in the kitchen right now, eating anything that doesn't run away fast enough."

"Dog biscuits!" Ponch said, and immediately got up and went over to jump on Carl in a neighborly way.

"Go on in. They'll show you where the box is," Carl said, and Ponch ran into the house. "If there's anything they know, it's that."

"Where's *ours*?" came a chorus of voices from the koi pond.

"It's too early. And you're all overweight, anyway," Carl said, sitting down at the table.

A noise of boos and bubbly razzes came from the pond.

"Everybody's a critic," Carl said. "What have we got?"

"Take a look," Tom said, and pushed his copy of the manual over to Carl.

"Huh," Carl said after a moment's reading. Then he looked over his shoulder in the direction of the continuing racket. "Will you guys hold it *down*?" He glanced over at Kit. "See, if you'd waited half an hour, you could have had all the fish breath you wanted."

Kit laughed. "What do you make of this?" Tom said.

Carl shook his head. "Once again, the universes remind us of their most basic law; they're not only stranger than we imagine, they're stranger than we *can* imagine. Which is what makes them so much fun." He turned a page. "I really don't understand this, but there are a couple of people I can call later. You going to go back there?" he said to Kit.

"Yeah, when I get back home."

"All right. Try an experiment. Try to affect the space where you find yourself, the way Ponch did, and see how that works. But also, see if you can bring something back with you. It doesn't have to be anything big. A leaf, a pebble. But something to analyze might help us determine the nature of the space, or whatever, that it comes from."

"Just test it first to make sure it's not antimatter," Tom said.

"Uh, *yeah*," Kit said. He had no desire to be totally annihilated.

"It's just a thought," Carl said. "Antimatter universes are well outnumbered by orthomatter ones, but you can't tell just by looking."

"I'll make a note," Kit said.

"Anything from Nita?" said Tom.

"Uh . . . not yet," Kit said. "I think, besides whatever she's working on, she may be wanting to take a little holiday from group spelling. We were having a rough time there for a while."

"Happens all the time," Carl said, leaning back in his chair. "You get stuck at different stages of mastery, and things can get a little bumpy. It passes, as a rule. But it can be tough when one partner or member of a group is working faster than the other, or in a different paradigm."

Kit thought about that. "Look . . . do you guys ever fight?"

Carl and Tom looked at each other in astonishment, and then at Kit, and both laughed. "Oh, lord! Constantly!" Tom said. "And it's not just about the joint practice, either. There aren't enough hours in the day for all the stuff we have to deal with. Finding time just to be friends can be tough, but it has to be made . . . and when we don't make it, we get sore at each other more easily."

"It always came so naturally with Neets," Kit said. "I guess maybe I didn't think much about having to work on it."

"Believe it, you have to," said Carl. "And then we have what we laughably call 'normal lives' as well. I have a job and an office to go to, Tom has to sit here and hit his deadlines, and there are bills to pay and work to do around the house and everything else. But first and foremost comes the wizardry, and keeping it part of 'normal life' is always a challenge. Sure, we bite each other sometimes. Sometimes it takes a while to patch things up. Don't let it throw you. But don't let it take too long, either."

"No," Kit said. "It's funny. I'm glad I got this last job done. It's useful. But now I don't know what to do next. And Neets always knows; she always has an idea for something else that needs doing. Sometimes it drives me nuts. Now it feels weird not to have her bugging me about 'the next thing.' "

"You'll work it out," Carl said. "Sorting out the details of your practice in the early part of your wizardly career is the exciting part."

"Yeah." Kit got up. "I'll let you know how it comes out."

"Right."

He recovered Ponch from pigging out on dog biscuits and walked home from Tom and Carl's, giving Ponch a chance to run ahead and lose some of the excitement. The route took Kit past Nita's, not entirely accidentally. He knew that sometimes she got up early. But all the curtains at her house were still drawn, all the doors were closed, and the car was in the garage. Kit reached into his jacket pocket, slipped his hand around the manual. There was no fizz about its cover.

He sighed and went on by, and a few minutes later they were back at Kit's house. It was still quiet inside as he went down the driveway and into the back, and he and Ponch took themselves into the back of the yard, among the sassafras trees, where they were out of view from the Macarthurs' and Kings' houses.

"You ready?" Kit said to Ponch.

"Let's go!"

And they stepped together once more into the dark. . . .

For Nita, the afternoon took its own sweet time going by. There was still no sign of Kit. Her mother had gone off to the shop after lunch, and Dairine went off, too, and took Spot with her. Nita sighed and tried to watch TV, but there was nothing on. She tried to do some work with the manual, but every time she touched it, its cover was still and fizzless under her hands, and she put it down as quickly as she picked it up. She even dallied with the idea of doing some work on a science report that was due in a couple of weeks, but the thought of actually starting it before she needed to was repulsive. *When I first got into wizardry, I'd never have thought it was possible to be bored again*, Nita thought, *but it seems that a wizard really* can *do anything, given enough time.*

Around four o'clock she was back in her bedroom, having just finished a bologna sandwich, when she heard a *whoomp!* of displaced air in the backyard. Nita looked hurriedly out the back window but saw that it was only Dairine, with Spot spidering along behind her. She sighed, slumped a little, and took down a book to read.

She had read no more than a page or two when Dairine came in, looking out of sorts. "Where've you been?" Nita asked, chucking the book away, since it was obvious she wasn't going to get any reading done, either.

"Europa."

"Again?"

Dairine frowned. "Neets," she said wearily, and sat on her bed, "I'm having some problems."

"You?"

"Please," Dairine said. She was staring at the bedspread as if it were written over with the secrets of the universe instead of a slightly faded stars-and-moons pattern. After a while she said in a low voice, as if embarrassed, "I'm not getting the results I was getting a while ago."

Nita pushed back from her desk and folded her arms, putting her feet up. This was a problem she'd come to know all too well. "Dair, it happens to all of us. You get a little older . . . you lose your initial edge and your first big blast of power, and start feeling your way to where your specialty's going to be. It's not always what you first thought it'd be. Tom says it's real common for a first specialty to shift, and for your power levels to jump around a lot when you're new to the Art."

Her sister sat there, still staring at the quilt. This worn-down look wasn't something Nita was used to seeing in her sister. Dairine's energy levels were usually such that you wanted to hook her up to wires and make serious money by selling power to the electric company. "I don't care if it is normal," Dairine said. "I hate it."

"You think you're the only one? I wasn't wild about my first flush wearing off, either. But you get used to it."

"Why do we *have* to get used to it?" Dairine burst out. "What good am I if I'm not effective?"

"You mean, what good are you if you can't solve every problem you come up against in three seconds?" Nita said. "Well, obviously, none at all. Guess you'd better go straight to the bathroom and flush yourself."

Dairine stared at her sister. "Or find a black hole and jump in," Nita said, leaning back and closing her eyes. "Tom says there's a lot of interest in the time-dilation effects, especially on the middle-sized ones. Be sure to file a report with the Powers when you get back. Assuming this universe is still here."

Nita waited for the explosion. There wasn't one. She opened her eyes again to find Dairine staring at her as if she were something from Mars. Actually, Dairine had stared at things from Mars with a lot less astonishment.

"What?" Dairine said.

Nita had to smile, even though Dairine's whining was annoying her. "Sorry. I was going to say, you remind me of me when I was your age."

Dairine made a face. *"There's* a horrible thought." She wrapped her arms around her knees, and put her face down against them. "The last thing I want is to be that normal again." She produced an elaborate shudder, turning *normal* into a swear word.

"You want to watch that, Dari," Nita said. "Just because we're wizards doesn't mean we're any better than 'normal' people. The minute you start acting like there's a 'them' and an 'us,' you're in trouble. The only thing that makes wizards different is that we have the power to do more than usual to help. And helping other people, as part of keeping the world running, is the only reason the power exists in the first place." It was a lesson Nita had learned at some cost, having done enough dumb things in her time until she got it straight.

Dairine gave Nita a noncommittal look. "Edgy, aren't we? Still nothing from Kit?"

Nita made a face. "No. But just let it sit for the time being, okay? Meanwhile, what was their problem? The amoebas or whatever they are?"

"They call themselves *hnlt*," Dairine said. "And how they manage to do that when they've only got one cell each, I don't know."

" 'Life knows its way,' " Nita said, quoting a proverb commonplace to wizards in more than one star system. "And personality arrives right behind it. Sooner than you'd think, a lot of the time."

"Yeah. Well, they have this—I mean, there's a—" Then Dairine made a wry face at how ineffective English was for describing this kind of problem. She dropped into the Speech for a couple sentences' worth of description of something that seemed to be happening to the gravity on Europa. Apparently the sea bottom far down under the surface ice was being catastrophically shifted in ways that were destroying some of the *hnlt* habitats.

After a moment, Nita nodded. "That's a nasty one. So what did you do?"

Dairine looked glum. "I suggested they wait a little while and see what happens," she said. "The Sun's real active now, and the activity is pushing Jupiter's atmosphere around a lot harder than usual, even the densest parts down deep. That's what's causing the gravitational and magnetic anomalies. It'll probably quiet down by itself when the sunspot cycle starts to taper off."

"Makes sense. Good call."

"But Neets, what's the *point*? I couldn't do anything. I *couldn't*! Only a few months ago I could—I could do everything up to and including pushing planets around. And now, because I can't, a lot of the *hnlt* are going to die before the Sun quiets down. All I can do is help them relocate their habitats elsewhere on Europa. But those other places are going to be just as vulnerable. No matter what I do, I'm not going to be able to save them all . . ."

Nita shook her head; not that she didn't feel sorry for her sister. "Dari, it's just the way things go. You started at a higher-than-usual power level, so you're having a bigger-than-usual crash."

"Why don't you try finding some *more* awful way of putting that?" Dairine muttered. "Take your time."

Nita understood how Dairine felt; she'd been down this road herself. "You'll be finding your next few years' working-level in a while. But as for the way you were last month . . ." Nita sighed at the memory of the way *she'd* been when she got started. "Entropy's running. The energy runs out of everything . . . even us. We have to learn not to blow it all over the landscape, that's all."

Dairine was silent for a few moments. Finally she leaned against the wall and nodded. "I guess I'll just have to keep working on it. Where's Mom?"

"Late," Nita said. "She's probably still looking for Dad's paperwork. She said he started burying it all in those old carnation boxes in the back again."

"Uh-oh. And after she got him the new filing cabinets." Dairine snickered. "I bet he got yelled at."

They heard someone pulling into the driveway. Nita cocked an ear at her bedroom window, which was right above the driveway, and could tell from the sound that it was her dad's car. Her mom had walked to town. Nita glanced at the clock. It was a little before five, the time their dad usually shut the store on Saturdays. "There they are. Bet he closed up early to get her to stop giving him grief."

The back door opened, closed again. Nita got up, yawning; even after the sandwich, dinner was beginning to impinge on her mind, and her stomach was making sounds that could have passed for a polite greeting on Rirhath B. "Mom say anything to you about what she was going to make tonight? Maybe we can get a head start."

"I don't remember," Dairine said as they headed through the living room. This answer was no surprise; Dairine's normal response to food was to eat it first and ask questions later.

"Huh," Nita said. "Dad—"

She stopped. Her father stood in the kitchen, looking down at the counter by the stove as if he expected to find something there, but the counter was bare, and her father's expression was odd. "You forget something, Daddy?" Nita said.

"No," he said. And then Nita saw his face working not to show what it felt, his hands not so much resting on the edge of the counter as holding it, holding on to it, and heard his voice, which pushed its way out through a throat tight with fear.

"Where's Mom?" Dairine said.

Nita's stomach instantly tied itself into a horrible knot. "Is she all right?" she said.

"She's—" her father said. And then immediately after that, "No. Oh, honey—"

Dairine pushed her way up beside Nita, her face suddenly as pale as her father's. "Daddy, *where's Mom?!*"

"She's in the hospital." He turned to them, but he didn't let go of the counter, still hanging on to it. As his eyes met Nita's, the fear behind them hit her so hard that she almost staggered. "She's very sick, they think—"

He stopped, not because he didn't know what to say, but because he refused to say it, to think it—it was impossible. Nonetheless Nita heard it, as her dad heard it, repeating over and over in his head:

They think she might die.

Saturday Afternoon
and Evening

IN A PLACE WHERE directions and distances made no sense, Kit and Ponch stood in the endless, soundless dark, the leash spell hanging loose between them and glowing with silent power.

So here we are. You feel okay?

I feel fine.

So what should I make?

Anything, Ponch said, as he had before.

Kit thought about that . . . and discovered that he couldn't decide what to do first. *Typical,* he thought. *Presented with the possibility to create anything you can think of, your mind goes blank.*

He tried to take a breath and found that his breathing now seemed to be working properly. "Am I getting used to this place?" Kit said softly in the Speech, and found that he could actually hear himself.

No answer; but then if one *had* come, he'd have jumped out of his skin.

"Okay," he said then. "Lights . . ."

And suddenly Kit found himself standing unsupported in the midst of interstellar glory. "Wow," he said softly. He and Ponch were apparently somewhere in the fringes of a gigantic globular cluster, all the nearby darkness blazing with stars of every possible color—and the farther darkness was peppered with not just thousands but hundreds of thousands of galaxies, little globes and ovals and spirals everywhere, a megacluster of the kind that astronomers were sure existed but had never seen.

It's bright, Ponch said.

"No argument there," said Kit, as he wondered why producing all this had been so easy. He was used to wizardry taking a good deal more effort. Is *this even wizardry?* he wondered. It had needed no construction of spells, no careful and laborious plugging in of words and variables, and no sudden drain of energy after the wizardry was fueled from your own power and turned loose. That last factor was what made Kit mistrust this process. He was used to the concept that every wizardry had its price, and one way or another, you paid; and its corollary: that any wizardry that doesn't charge you a decent admission fee usually isn't worth anything.

All the same, it would be smart to play around in here a little and see what it *was* worth. Kit also thought he could guess why Carl wanted him to try to bring back some small physical artifact. It would confirm whether or not this space was simply some kind of illusion or mirage, amusing but otherwise not terribly useful.

"Okay," he said, "let's take this from the top. A sun, first . . ."

And one appeared, though he hadn't even asked for it in the Speech: a deep yellow-orange star, a vast, roiling, heaving landscape of blinding flame, directly below his feet. For a second Kit flinched at the roar and turmoil of burning gas beneath him, all dancing with prominences and loops and arches of radiant plasma—inexhaustible fountains of fire half a million miles high, leaping away from the star's seething limb and pouring themselves back into the surface again in slow-motion grace. *In vacuum you wouldn't normally get sound, I guess*, Kit thought. But he seemed to be in some kind of peculiar rapport with this space that let him sense things he ordinarily wouldn't, and the tearing basso wind-roar of superheated ions blasting upward past him was strangely satisfying. Ponch, sitting beside him, squinted down at the ravening brilliance but didn't comment.

"Not bad, huh?" Kit said.

Ponch yawned. "The squirrels are more fun."

"You've got a one-track mind," Kit said. "Okay, now we need a planet . . ."

And the star receded into the distance, reducing itself to proper sunlike size. Below Kit was his planet, all covered in cloud, muttering softly to itself as it rotated, already coasting away from them along its orbit. Kit thought he could actually feel the heat pouring off it, a feverish sensation. *A lot of heat trapped under those clouds*, he thought. *It's a "supergreenhouse," like Venus . . .* There was no telling how big this world was, without anything to give him a frame of reference. *Have to go down there and take a closer look*, Kit thought—

—and suddenly he was standing on a rocking, shaking, stony surface. All around him rocks tumbled down low cracked cliffs, and a wind as brutal as the solar one but laden with a stinging drizzle of acid instead of fire shrieked past him. In a more normal reality, Kit knew this terrible supersonic fog would have eaten the unprotected flesh off his bones in seconds, but here he seemed immune. *Because I imagined it?*

Kit grinned and waved one hand in front of him airily. "Lose the acid," he said, "lose the wind, lose the clouds." The instant he spoke, the air went clear, fell silent, and the dull, overarching, brassy canopy faded away to dark clarity. The stars showed through again, and the high, hot, golden sun. But sound vanished as well, and it started to get very cold.

"No, no; atmosphere is okay!" Kit said. "Something I can breathe. Landscape . . ."

Green rolling grassland spread itself away in every direction under a blue, blue sky. Ponch leaped up in delight. "Squirrels!"

"No squirrels," Kit said. "Don't overdo them or you'll get bored." He rubbed his hands together in delight. "You know what this is, Ponch? It's magic-crayon country."

"Crayons? Where?" Ponch had conceived a weird fondness for the taste of crayons when Kit was younger, and had always gone out of his way to steal and eat them.

"Not that way," Kit said, turning around and gazing all about him at the total wilderness. "But if I thought of an elephant with three hairs in its tail here— *Uh-oh.*"

Ponch began barking deafeningly. The elephant, large and purple-gray, as in the original illustration from that old children's book, looked around in surprise, then looked over at Ponch and said, a little scornfully, "Do you have a problem?"

"Sorry," Kit said. "Uh, can I do something for you?"

"Trees are generally better for eating purposes than grass," the elephant said. "A little more variation in the landscape would be nice. And so would company."

Kit thought about that. A second later the grassland looked much more like African veldt, with a scattering of trees and an impressive mountain range in the distance, and another elephant stood next to the first one. They looked each other up and down, twined their trunks together, and walked off into the long grass, swinging their three-haired tails as they went.

Kit paused then, wondering whether they were a boy and a girl, and then wondering whether it mattered. *Maybe it's better not to get too hung up on the minor details right now*, he thought.

He glanced down at Ponch. "Want to try another one?"

"You sure you don't want to think again about the squirrels?"

"Yes, I'm sure." Kit folded his arms, thinking. He took a step forward, opened his mouth to speak—

—and found he didn't have to do even that. The two of them were standing in a waste littered with reddish rocks; an odd springy green mosslike growth was scattered here and there around them. The strangely foreshortened landscape ran up to a horizon hazed in red-violet dust, where low mountains reared up jagged against an amethyst sky; and so did an outcropping of delicate towers, apparently built of green glass or metal, gleaming faintly in the setting of a small, remote-seeming, pinky-white marble of a sun.

"Yes," Kit said softly. It was Mars, but not the Mars of the real world, which nowadays, as he'd seen for himself, was unfortunately short on cities. This was the romantic Mars of stories written a hundred years ago, where fierce eight-legged thoats ran wild across dead sea bottoms, and displaced, sword-swinging warriors from Earth ran around after very, very scantily clad Martian princesses.

Ponch glanced around, looking for something.

"What?" Kit said.

"No trees."

"You can hold it in till we get home. Come on . . ."

He took another step forward, thinking. One step and he and Ponch were in the darkness; another, and they were in what looked like New York City but wasn't, because New York City was not under a huge glass dome, floating through space.

"Aha," Ponch said, immediately heading toward a fire hydrant.

"Uh-uh," Kit said. Another few steps and they were in darkness; another step after that, in a landscape all veiled in blowing white, whiteness crunching underfoot, and up against an indigo sky, great crackling curtains of aurora, green and blue and occasionally pinkish red, hissing in the ferociously cold air. Something shuffled past in the blowing snow, some yards away, paused to swing its massive head around toward Kit, looking at him out of little dark eyes: a polar bear. But a polar bear the size of a mammoth. . . .

Ponch jumped and strained at the leash, barking. "Oh, come on; let him live," said Kit, and he took another step, into the dark. Reluctantly, Ponch followed. Kit was getting the rhythm of it now. A few steps in darkness, to do a few moments' worth of thinking . . . and then one step out into light, into another landscape or vista or place. The last step, this time, and he and Ponch were wading up to Kit's knees and Ponch's neck in some kind of long, harsh-edged beach grass clothing a vista of endless dunes. Off to their right the sea rolled up to a long black beach in an endless muted roar. Kit looked up into the shadow of immense wings going over, ruffling his hair and making the grass hiss around him with their passing— one huge shape silhouetted against the twilight, then two, five, twenty, with wings that seemed to stretch across half the sky. They soared in echelon toward a horizon over which a long violet evening was descending, and beyond which the distant and delicate fire of a barred spiral galaxy, seen almost face on, was rising slowly behind a glittering haze of nearer, lesser stars.

He had the hang of it now. *Just let the mind run free, let the images flow.*

A few steps more and Kit came out into the middle of a vast plane of what looked like black marble, stretching away to infinity in all directions, and above it light glinted, reflected in the surface: not a sun or a moon, but an artificial light of some kind, almost like a spotlight. Far away, on a patterned place in the floor, small figures stood, some of them human, some not—some of them alien species that Kit had seen before in his travels, others of which he had never seen the like. One moved, then another. There was a pause, and then several moved at once, and one of them vanished. Kit started to go closer, until he saw the great shadowy shapes bending in all around him in the upward-towering dimness, to look more closely at the one piece that seemed to have escaped the game board.

Kit smiled slightly, waved at them, and took another step. The darkness descended, then rose once more on some long, golden afternoon on a rise of land overlooking a lake. A pointy-towered palace lay all sun gilded down by the water, banners flying from every sharp-peaked roof, and knights on horses clattered along a dusty road toward the castle gate, the late sun glittering sharp off lance heads and armor, the colors of the knights' surcoats as vivid as enamel. Another step, quicker, as Kit started pushing the pace: out into the aquamarine light of some underwater place, white sand under his feet, lightwaver playing in broad patterns across it, and an odder, bluer light glimmering against the depths ahead of him as the rippling, ribbony creatures of some alien abyss came up out of shadows ten miles deep to peer curiously at the intruder.

Kit found he could do without the darkness between worlds. It was a new vista at every step now, and Ponch padded along beside him on the wizardly leash as calmly as any dog being taken for a walk in the park. Forests of massive trees, all drowned in shadow, bare sand stretching away to impossible distances and suggesting planets much larger than Earth, gleaming futuristic cityscapes covering entire continents; a step, and night under some world's overarching greenish rings, a single voice chanting in the air, like a nightingale saluting them; a step, and the time before dawn in a vast waste of reedy waters reflecting the early peach-pink of the sky, everything still except for the flop of a fish turning, then putting its head up to look thoughtfully at them as they waded past; a step, and the blurring, whirling uncertainty of the vast space between an atom's nucleus and the silvery fog of its innermost electron shell—

—and a step out into a place where, if he had taken another step, Kit would have fallen some thousands of feet straight down. There, on the top of a mountain imperially preeminent among its fellows, Kit paused, looking down through miles of blue-hazed air at lakes held between neighboring peaks like silent jewels under a rosette of suns—three small pinkish stars riding high in a morning sky—and all the snow on all the mountains from here to the horizon stained warm rose, so they all looked lit from within. Kit breathed that high chill air—which no one besides him and Ponch had ever breathed before, the air of a world made new that moment—and shook his head, smiling the smallest smile.

He thought of the darkness. *What a place to play. Neets has got to see this.*

He stood there looking down on the immense vista for a few moments longer. "We should get back," he said.

"Why?"

"I'm not sure about the time difference yet," Kit said. "And I don't want to worry Mom."

Another thought niggling at the back of Kit's mind was: *If this . . . state . . . is as easy to shape and reshape as it seems, it'd be real easy to get hooked on it.* He'd had a phase, a couple years back, when he'd been hooked enough on a favorite arcade game to give himself blisters and blow truly unreasonable amounts of his allowance money in the process. Now Kit remembered that time with embarrassment, thinking of all the hours he'd spent on something that now bored him, and he watched himself, in a casual way, for signs that something similar might happen again.

But I almost forgot. Kit reached down and picked up something from the mossy rocks at his feet: a single flower, a little five-petaled thing like a white star. Kit slipped it into his pocket, and farther in, right down into the space-time claudication, sealing it there. Then he turned around to glance at Ponch—the top of the peak was so narrow that they hadn't had room to stand side by side. "Ready?"

"Yes, because I don't think I can hold it in much longer."

Together they stepped straight out into the air, out into the darkness—

—and out into Kit's backyard.

He looked around. Twilight was falling. *Guess I was right to be a little concerned about the time,* Kit thought. *Looks like it wasn't running at the same rate in all those places. Something else to tell Tom . . .*

He took the leash off Ponch, wound up the wizardry, and stuffed it into his pocket. Ponch immediately headed off toward the biggest of the sassafras trees to give it a good "watering."

Kit went into the house. His mother and father were eating; his dad looked up at Kit, raised his eyebrows, and said, "Son, can't you give us a hint on how long you're going to be when you go out on one of these runs? Tom couldn't tell me anything."

"Sorry, Pop," Kit said as he went past his dad, patting him on the shoulder. "I wasn't sure myself. I didn't think it'd be this long, though, and now I know what the problem is . . . I'll watch it next time."

"Okay. You want some macaroni and cheese?"

"In a minute."

Kit headed up the stairs in a hurry; Ponch hadn't been the only one with "holding it" on his mind. Then he went into his room to check his pocket and was delighted to find the flower right where he'd put it. Kit placed it carefully on his desk, traced a line around it with his finger, and said the six words of a spell that would hold the contents aloof from the local progress of time for twenty-four hours.

This was not a cheap spell, and the pang of the energy drain the spell cost him went straight through him. Kit had to sit down in his desk chair and get his breath back. While he sat there, he reached farther into his pocket, touched his manual . . . and felt the fizz.

He grinned, pulled it out, paged to the back of it . . . and let out a long breath. The manual was showing a message that had come in only a few minutes before. *I can't talk now. But can we talk later? I've got some apologizing to do.*

All right, Kit thought, relieved. *She's seen sense at last, and I'm not gonna rub her nose in it. There's too much serious neatness going on here.* "Reply," he said to the manual. "Call me anytime: I'm ready."

And he ran down the stairs, exhilarated, to feed Ponch and have his own dinner. *Just wait till she sees! Whatever's been going on with her, this is gonna take her mind off it.*

I can't wait.

Saturday Evening

HOW SHE AND DAIRINE got their dad into the dining room and sat him down, Nita couldn't afterward remember, except for a flash of horror at the awful topsy-turviness of things. It was the parents who were supposed to be strong when the kids were scared. But now there were just the three of them, sitting there close, all of them equally scared together. Her father was hanging on to his control, and Nita held on to hers as much out of her own fear as out of sympathy; if she broke down, he might, too.

"She collapsed as she was leaving the store," her father said, staring at the table. "I thought she was kneeling down to look at one of the plants in the window, you know how she would always fuss over the display not being just right. She just seemed to kneel down . . . and then she leaned against the doorsill. And she didn't get up."

"What was it?" Dairine cried. "What happened to her?"

"They're not sure. She just passed out, and she wouldn't wake up. The ambulance came, and we took her over to the county hospital. They did some physical tests, and then they X-rayed her chest and her head, and put her in the ICU . . ." Her father trailed off. Nita saw the frightened look in his eyes as he relived some memory that terrified him. "They said they'd call when they had some news."

"I'm not waiting for that!" Dairine said. "We have to go to the hospital. Right now!" She turned as if intending to go get her jacket.

Her father caught hold of her. "*Not* right now, honey. The doctor told me that they need a few hours to get her stable. She's okay, but they need to do some tests, and—"

"Dad," Nita said.

He looked at her.

The terror in his eyes was awful, worse than what Nita was feeling. She wanted to grab him and hold him and pat his back and say, "It's going to be all right." But she had no idea whether it was going to be all right or not. Nita settled for grabbing him and holding him, and Dairine, too.

Then they began to wait.

The time until they went to the hospital passed in a kind of horrible disturbed silence, most of the disturbance coming from the phone, as it rang and rang and rang again, and every time, Nita's father lunged for it, hoping it was the hospital, and every time, it wasn't. There were always people on the other end who'd heard from someone they knew about Nita's mom or had seen the ambulance at the shop. Every time Nita's dad had to explain to someone what had happened, he got more upset.

"Daddy, *stop answering it!*" Nita cried at one point.

"They're your mother's friends" was all he would say. "And mine. They have a right to know. And besides, what if the hospital calls?" And there was no arguing with that.

"Let us answer it," Dairine said.

"No," said their dad. "Things are hard enough for you two. You let me handle it." The phone rang again, and he went to answer it.

After that, it seemed that the phone just went on ringing all evening.

Nita was terrified. She wasn't used to not knowing what was happening, not being able to *do* anything—and her shock was such that she wasn't even able to make any kind of plan about what to do next. Dairine paced around the house like a caged creature, her face alternately frightened and furious, and she wouldn't talk to anybody, not even Spot, who crouched mutely near one of the chairs in the living room and simply watched her go back and forth. Nita felt actively sorry for it but didn't know what to do; Spot's relationship was exclusively with Dairine, and she didn't know how it would take to being comforted by someone else.

If comforted *is even the word*, Nita thought, *because I wouldn't know what to say or do to make it comfortable . . . any more than I know what to say to Dairine. Or Dad*. That was the worst of it: not being able to do anything for either of them. Again and again, after her dad hung up the phone, that deadly quiet would descend, emphasizing the voice that was *not* there, all of a sudden. And then the phone would ring into the silence again . . . and Nita felt certain that if it rang once more, she'd scream.

But finally the hospital called. Nita watched her father answer, his face naked in its changes, shifting every second between fear and uncertainty and greater fear. "Yes. This is he. Yes." He paused, turning away from where Nita sat at the dining-room table.

"She is?"

Nita's heart seized.

"Uh, good."

She breathed again. *And I don't even know why; I don't even know what's happening!*

"Yes . . . sure we can. About half an hour. Yes. Thanks."

He hung up, turned to Nita. Dairine was standing there by the living-room door, as intently as Nita had been. "She's still in intensive care," her dad said, "but they say she's stable now, whatever that means. Let's go."

Shortly, Nita found herself walking into a setting entirely too familiar to her from too many TV shows: all the people in pastel uniforms with stethoscopes hanging around their necks and shoved into their breast pockets, all the white jackets, the metal beds and the stretcher-trolleys in the corridors, people going places in a hurry and doing important but inexplicable things. What the TV shows had never gotten across, and what now struck itself deeply into Nita's mind, was the smell of the place. It wasn't a bad smell. It was clean enough . . . but that cleanliness was cold, a chilly distancing scent of disinfectant and other chemicals. The faces of the people working there were kind, mostly, but a lot of them had a strange preoccupied quality, unlike the faces of the actors on the TV shows. These people weren't acting.

Nita and Dairine stuck close to their father as they made their way through the hospital corridors and to the reception desk, where someone could tell them where to go. "They've moved her out of ICU, Mr. Callahan," the lady at the desk said. "She's over in Neurology now. If you go down that hall and turn right—"

Her father nodded and led them off down the hall. About three minutes' walking brought them through swinging doors and up to a nurses' station.

One of the nurses there, a large, cheerful-looking lady in a pink scrub-style uniform, with her brown hair pulled back tight in a bun, looked up as they approached. "Mr. Callahan?"

"Yes."

"The doctor would like to see you—that's Dr. Kashiwabara, she's the senior neurologist. If you can go into that room across the hall and wait for a few minutes, she'll be with you shortly."

They went into the plain little room—white walls, beige tile floor, noisy orange sofa that was also literally noisy, with plastic-covered cushions that wheezed when you sat down on them—and waited, in silence. Nita's dad put an arm around her and Dairine, and Nita hoped she didn't look as stiff with fear as she felt. *I can't believe this*, she thought, bizarrely angry with herself. *I'm so scared, I can't even think. I wasn't this afraid when I thought a* shark *might eat me! And this isn't even about* me. *It's someone else—*

But that makes it worse. That was true, too. There'd been times when Kit was in some bad spot, and the terror had risen up and had nearly choked the breath out of her. And that was just Kit—

Just! said the back of her mind in shock. Nita shook her head. Kit was so important to her . . . but he wasn't her mother.

The door opened, and the sound made them all jump. "Mr. Callahan?" said the little woman in the white coat who was standing there. She was extremely petite and pretty, with short black hair, and had calm, knowledgeable eyes that for some reason immediately put Nita more at ease. "I'm sorry to have kept you waiting. These are your daughters?"

"Nita," said Nita's dad, "and Dairine."

"I'm pleased to meet you." She shook their hands and sat down on the couch across from them.

"Doctor, how's my wife? Is she any better?"

"She's resting," said the doctor. "I don't want to alarm you, but she had several minor seizures after we admitted her, and sedation was necessary to break the cycle and allow us to find out what's going on."

"Do you know?"

The doctor looked at the chart she was carrying, though she didn't open it. "We have some early indications, but first I want to talk to you about some things we didn't have time to discuss while we were admitting Mrs. Callahan. Has she been having any physical problems lately?"

"Physical problems—"

"Double vision, or problems with her sight? Headaches? Any trouble with coordination—a little more clumsiness than usual, perhaps?"

"She's been saying she needed to get reading glasses," Dairine said softly.

Nita looked at her dad. "Daddy, she's been taking a lot of aspirin lately. I didn't realize until just now."

Their father looked stricken. "She hadn't mentioned anything to me," he said to the doctor. "The hours I've been working lately, sometimes the kids have been seeing more of her than I have."

Dr. Kashiwabara nodded. "All right. I'll be going over these issues with Mrs. Callahan myself when she's more lucid. But what you've told me makes sense in terms of what we've found so far. There's been time to do an X ray, anyway, and there seems to be a small abnormal growth at the base of one of the frontal lobes of her brain."

Nita swallowed.

"What kind of growth?" her dad said.

"We don't know yet," said Dr. Kashiwabara. "I've scheduled her for a PET scan this evening, and an MRI scan tomorrow morning; those should tell us what we need to know."

"This is a brain tumor we're talking about," said Nita's father, his voice shaking. "Isn't it?"

Dr. Kashiwabara looked at him, then nodded. "What we need to do is find out what kind it is," she said, "so that we can work out how best to treat it. What we do know at this point is that the tumor seems to have grown large enough to put pressure on some nearby areas of Mrs. Callahan's brain. That's what caused the seizures. We've medicated her to prevent any more. She's going to be pretty woozy when you see her; please don't be concerned about that by itself. For the time being, while we run the tests, she's going to have to stay very quiet to keep excess pressure from building up in her skull and brain. It means she needs to stay flat on her back in bed, even if she feels like she's able to get up."

"For how long?" Dairine said.

"Depending on how the tests go, it may be only a couple of days," Dr. Kashiwabara said. "We'll do the scans that I mentioned, and then there'll have to be a biopsy of the growth itself—we'll remove a tiny bit of tissue and test it to see what kind it is. After that, we'll know what our next move needs to be."

The doctor folded her hands and rubbed them together a little, then looked up. "I'll be doing that procedure myself," she said. "I don't want to trouble your wife about signing the permissions, Mr. Callahan. Maybe we can take care of that before you leave."

"Yes," Nita's dad said, hardly above a whisper, "of course."

"I want you to call me if you have any questions at all," Dr. Kashiwabara said, "or any concerns. I may not be able to get back to you immediately—I have a lot of other people to take care of—but I promise you I will always call you back. Okay?"

"Yes. Thank you."

"All right," said the doctor, and got up. "Why don't you go see her now? But, please, keep it brief. The seizures will have been very fatiguing and confusing for her, and she won't be fully recovered from them until tomorrow. Come with me; I'll show you the way."

They walked down the corridor together, and Dr. Kashiwabara led them into a room where there were four of those steel beds: two of them empty, the third with a cloth curtain pulled partway around it, under which they could see a nurse in white shoes and pink nursing sweats doing something or other. In the fourth bed, beyond the partway-pulled curtain, their mom lay under light covers, with one arm strapped to a board, and an IV running into that arm. She was in a hospital gown, and someone had tied her hair back and put it up under a paper cap. Her eyes suddenly looked sunken to Nita; it was the same tired look she had been wearing this morning, but much worse. *Why didn't I notice?* Nita's heart cried. *Why didn't I see something was wrong?!*

"Mrs. Callahan?" said Dr. Kashiwabara.

It took Nita's mom's eyes a few moments to open, and then they seemed to have trouble focusing. "What . . . oh." She moistened her lips. "Harry?"

It was as if she couldn't see him properly. "I'm here, honey," he said, and Nita was astonished at how strong he sounded. He took her hand and sat in the chair by the bed. "And the girls are here, too. How're you feeling?"

There was a long pause. "Like . . . bats."

Nita and Dairine looked at each other in poorly concealed panic. "Baseball bats," their mother said. "Very sore."

"Like somebody was hitting you with baseball bats, you mean?" Nita said.

"Yeah."

From the seizures, Nita thought. Her mother turned her head toward her, across from her dad. "Oh, honey . . . ," she said, "I'm sorry . . ."

"What're you sorry for, Mom? This isn't your fault!" Nita said. And even as she said it, she knew exactly whose fault it was.

There was only one of the Powers Who at the beginning of things had insisted on inventing something never contemplated before in the universe: entropy, disease . . . death. That Lone Power had been her enemy more than once, but suddenly it seemed to Nita that she hadn't done It nearly as much damage as she should have.

Dairine, next to Nita, leaned over the bed. "Mom, why didn't you tell us your head was hurting you?"

"Honey, I *did*." She shook her head on the pillow. "I thought . . . I thought it was stress." She smiled. "Seems I miscalculated . . ."

She drifted off then, her eyes closing. Nita and Dairine exchanged a glance. Nita took her mom's hand and closed her eyes, trying something she had never tried with her mother. She slipped her consciousness a little way into her mother's body, gingerly, carefully. Without a wizardry specifically built to the purpose, she could get nothing clear—just a fuzzy, muzzy feeling, a faint vague pain at the edge of things, an odd sense of dislocation . . .

. . . and one other thing. A small something. A *lot* of small somethings that were *not* her mom. They were all gathered together into something little and hot and strange, burning against the cooler, "normal" background: something alien . . . and malevolent.

Nita gulped, and opened her eyes. *I could be wrong. I didn't do that exactly by the book. But boy . . . will I, later.*

Her mother opened her eyes. "I don't want you to worry," she said, very clearly.

Her dad actually managed to laugh. "Listen to you," he said. "Worrying about *us*, as usual. You concentrate on getting rested up, and help these people do whatever they need to do."

"Don't have much choice," Nita's mother said. "Got me outnumbered." She closed her eyes again.

Nita met her dad's eyes across the bed. "We should go," he said softly. "Sleep's probably the best thing for her."

"Mom," Dairine said, "we'll see you tomorrow, okay? You have a nap."

" 'nt to extremes . . . to get one," her mother whispered. "Sorry."

They sat there for a few minutes more, saying nothing. Finally one of the nurses looked in the door at them, put his finger to his lips, then gestured out into the hall with his head and raised his eyebrows.

Nita got up, bringing Dairine with her. "Dad . . . ," she said.

His eyes had been only for their mother's face. Now he turned, saw the nurse, who looked at their dad and tapped his watch. Nita's father nodded, got up. It was hard for him to let go of their mom's hand. Nita had to look away from that, as she felt the tears welling up in her. *I'm not going to cry here*, she thought. *The whole world can hear me, and Dad—*

She headed for the door. Behind her came her dad and Dairine, and they stood lost for a moment in the hall. There was nothing they could do but go home.

It was dark, it was late, when they got back. *Where did the evening go?* Nita thought as her dad locked the back door. Somehow hours had fleeted by as if in a few minutes, leaving only pain and a feeling of having been cheated of time, somehow . . . not that Nita wanted *that* particular slice of time back. Going through it once was enough. Dairine apparently agreed; she went upstairs to her room, and Nita heard the door shut.

"Daddy," Nita said.

He was sitting in his chair in the living room, with only one lamp on, everything else in shadow, his face rigid and stunned-looking in the dim light. "What?"

"Daddy . . . what they told us," Nita said softly, "it's scary, yeah . . . but maybe it's not what you were thinking."

He didn't ask how she knew. "Nita," her father said, reluctant, "you didn't see them when they first brought her in, after the X ray, before I came back. I saw the doctor looking at the X ray. I saw her face . . . ."

Nita swallowed. Her dad put his face in his hands, then raised it again. His cheeks were wet. "They're being careful," he said. "They're right to be: They have to do the tests. But I saw the doctor's face." He shook his head. "It's not . . . it's not good."

Then he clenched his fists. "I shouldn't be frightening you," he said. "I could be wrong."

"You always say we have to tell each other when we're scared," she said. "You have to take your own advice, Dad."

He was silent for a long time. "It's stupid," he said. "I keep thinking, 'If I hadn't been working so hard, this wouldn't have happened. If she hadn't been working so hard on the accounts, this wouldn't have happened.' It's like it has to be all my fault, somehow. As if that would help." He laughed, a short, bitter sound. "And even when I know it's not . . . I *feel* like it is. Stupid."

Nita swallowed. "I keep thinking," she said, "I should have seen it, that she wasn't feeling okay."

"So do I."

Nita shook her head. "But I guess that . . . when someone's been there forever . . . you stop looking at them, some ways. It's dumb, but it's what we do."

Her father wiped his hands on his pants and looked up at her with an expression that was considering, and full of pain. "You know," he said, "you sound a lot like your mom sometimes."

It was the best thing he could have said to her. It was the worst thing he could have said to her. When the shock wore off, all that Nita could say was "You should try to get some sleep."

Her father gave her a look that said, *You must be kidding*. But aloud he said, "You're right."

He got up, gave her a hug. "Good night, honey," he said. "Get me up at eight." He went off to the back bedroom and closed the door.

Nita went to bed, too, but there was nothing good about her night at all. She lay awake for hours, rerunning in her mind all kinds of things that had happened the previous week, especially conversations with her mother—trying to see what had gone wrong, what could have gone differently, how she could have predicted what had happened today, how she could have prevented it somehow. It was torment—and she didn't seem able to stop doing it—but it was better than going on to the next set of thoughts that Nita knew was lying in wait for her. The past, at least, was fixed. The only alternative was the future, in which any horrible thing could happen.

The sound of a hand turning the knob of her bedroom door brought Nita sitting up straight in bed in absolute terror. *Of what?* she thought a second later, scornful and angry with herself, while also trying to breathe deeply and slow down her pounding heart, which seemed to be shaking her whole body. But she knew what she was afraid of. Of hearing the phone ring downstairs in the middle of the night, of having her father come in and tell her . . . tell her—

Nita gulped and struggled for control. In the darkness, she heard a couple of steps on the floor. "Neets," said a small voice. Then the bedsprings creaked a little.

Dairine crept into Nita's bed, threw her arms around Nita, buried her face against her chest, and began to sob.

Nita suddenly found herself looking at a moment long ago: a small Dairine, maybe five years old, running down the sidewalk outside the house, oblivious— then tripping and falling. Dairine had pushed herself up on her hands and, after a long pause, started to cry . . . but then came the laughter of the kids down the street, the ones toward whom she'd been running. Nita had been struck then by the sight of Dairine's face working, puckering, as she tried to decide what to do, then steadying into a downturned mouth and thunderous frown, a scowl of furious determination. Dairine got up, and said just one thing: *"No."* Knees bleeding, she wiped her face, and walked slowly back to the house, shoulders hunched, her whole body clenched like a small fist with resolve.

I don't think I've seen her cry since, Nita thought. And so Dairine had gone on, for so long, expressing herself almost entirely through that toughness. But now the shell had cracked, and who would have ever known that there was such pain and fear contained inside it?

But Nita knew now, and there was nothing she could do but hang on to her sister and let Dairine sob herself silent. *It's not fair*, Nita thought, the tears leaking out as she hugged Dairine to her. *Who do I get to cry on? Who's going to be strong for me?*

If any Power listened, It gave her no answer.

Sunday Morning

BEFORE DAWN NITA FOUND herself awake and sitting up in bed, looking at the faint blue light outside her window. There had been no transition from sleeping to waking: just that unsettling consciousness, and a feeling that the world was wrong, that *everything* was wrong. She had no idea how long it had taken her to get to sleep last night after Dairine, silent and drained, had finally slipped away.

Drained. That was the word for how Nita felt, too. But some energy was beginning to coil back into that void as the shock wore off. Nita looked at her manual, and saw the words in front of her eyes without even having to touch it: *I will fight to preserve what grows and lives well in its own way; I will not change any creature unless its growth and life, or that of the system of which it is part, are threatened—*

She swallowed. *I am a wizard. And if my mom's life isn't "threatened" right now, I don't know when it will be. There has to be another way to fight this than just what they've got in the hospital.*

And I'm going to find out what it is.

She got up, dressed, grabbed the manual, and took it back to bed with her. Its covers were fizzing. Nita settled herself up against the wall at the head of the bed and flipped the book open to read the message waiting for her, then glanced out the window at the bleak predawn light. *I'll get in touch with him later. No point in waking him up early just to get him upset. I've done enough stupid stuff to him lately.*

She paged through the manual to the section with information on the medical and healing-related wizardries. That section was much larger this morning than she had ever found it before. Nita began reading what was there with intensity and with a concentration she could hardly remember having expended since she first found this book and understood what it meant. She had a couple of hours to spare before the time her dad had told her to wake him up.

She used them, pausing only once, to go to the bathroom, taking the book with her when she did. To say that the subject was complex was understating badly. There was just too much information. She had the manual stop displaying everything that had to do with injuries and trauma, chronic diseases and afflictions . . . and though she narrowed and narrowed her focus, the section she was reading didn't get any thinner. Finally there was almost nothing between the covers except pages and pages of material concerning abnormal growths and lesions, and still she found more every time she targeted a specific condition. Nita also saw a lot of a word in the Speech that she didn't much like—a word that translated into English as *intractable.* There was a lot of discussion of theory here, but not many spells. Nita got nervous when she noticed that, but she didn't stop reading. There had to be a way. There was *always* a way, if you could just push through to the core of the matter. . . .

The light grew in her room; she hardly noticed. Birds began singing the restrained songs of early autumn, but Nita shut their voices out. She read and read . . . and suddenly her alarm clock went off, at eight-thirty.

Nita scrambled out of bed, shut the noisy thing off, and went to see if her dad was up yet. Pausing outside the master bedroom, listening, she couldn't hear any sound of anyone stirring in there.

She knocked softly on the door. No answer. "Dad . . ."

Still nothing. Nita eased the door softly open and peeked in.

Her father was asleep in the reading chair in the corner between the two bedroom windows. He sat slumped over, his mouth hanging open a little, a slight snore emitting from him—almost the same sound Ponch made when he lay on his back with his feet in the air and snored; the thought almost made her smile. But smiling about anything right now seemed like some kind of betrayal.

She glanced at the bed, which had not been slept in, and let out an unhappy breath, then went over to her dad and crouched down beside the chair. "Daddy," she said.

His eyes opened slowly; he looked at her as if he couldn't understand what he was doing here.

Then it all came back to him. She saw the pain fill his eyes. Nita clenched her jaw and managed to keep from getting any weepier than she already felt. "It's eight-thirty, Dad," she said. "You said we should go to the hospital in an hour or so."

"Yeah." He slowly sat upright and rubbed his face. "Yeah." He looked at her then. "How are you doing, honey?"

"Better. Maybe better," she said. "Daddy, I guess I was so scared, I forgot for a minute."

"Forgot what?"

"Maybe I can do something."

Her father looked at her, uncomprehending.

"Daddy," Nita said, "I *am* a wizard. In fact, we've got two of them in the house. And we know a bunch more of them, all over the place. Wizardry's *about* fixing broken things, healing hurt things . . . saving lives. We must be able to do *something*."

Her dad's expression went curiously neutral. "Honey," he said, sounding slightly embarrassed, "you know, that's the kind of thing I . . . try not to think about. It still seems like a fairy tale, sometimes. Even when everything's all right, I don't think about it much. And right now . . . now I'd be afraid it'll . . ."

Fail, Nita thought. It was the thought that had been nagging at her, too. "Dad, in Mom's case, it's really complicated. I've barely had time to start working out what to do. But there has to be *something*. I'm not going to do anything else until I find out what."

Her father rubbed his face again. "Well . . . all right. In the meantime, we'd better get ourselves over there. Have you had your shower?"

"Not yet."

"You go ahead. I'll make us some breakfast. Is Dairine up?"

"I don't know. She had trouble getting to sleep last night."

"She wasn't alone," her father said softly.

He reached out to Nita and hugged her. "Oh, honey . . ." He ran out of words for a few moments. Then he hugged her harder. "You hang in there. We'll all keep each other going somehow, and it'll be all right."

"Yeah," Nita said, hoping that it was true.

When they got to the hospital, Nita's mother was sleeping, having been up early for the MRI scan. "She was awake late last night," the head nurse, that large lady with the bun hairstyle, told Nita's dad, "and it seems like a good idea for her to get caught up on her sleep now. But her doctor's finishing another procedure, and she asked me if you could wait for half an hour or so. She'd like to see you."

"No problem," Nita's father said. In reality it wasn't even that long; after she and Dairine went up to take a quick look in at their mom, and Nita saw that she was indeed sleeping peacefully, Nita left Dairine there to have a moment with their mom by herself, and made her way back to the little waiting room, where she found her dad already talking to Dr. Kashiwabara. The doctor looked up as Nita came in.

"Good morning," she said as Nita sat down. "Well, your mom had a quiet night—except for the scans, of course. She's been doing the sensible thing, and sleeping when we weren't actually running her in and out of the machines. In fact, she fell asleep during the MRI this morning, which I wouldn't normally have thought possible; it's like sleeping in a garbage can while someone's banging on it."

"If you lived long with our daughters," Nita's dad said, "you'd be surprised what you'd learn to sleep through."

Dr. Kashiwabara smiled faintly. "Come to think of it," she said, "where's the younger one?"

Nita looked around in surprise. Dairine should have come back from their mom's room by now. "Be right back," she said.

Nita retraced her steps. Slipping quietly into the room, she found Dairine standing there, her back against the wall near the door, looking across the closer, empty bed at the curtained one where their mother lay. In her arms she was holding Spot—which Nita hadn't noticed Dairine bringing to the hospital in the first place—and the whole room was sizzling with the electric-air feel of a wizardry on the ebb, either newly dismantled or incomplete.

"What are you doing?" Nita whispered, and grabbed Dairine by the upper arm. "Come *on!*"

Dairine didn't resist her; she didn't have the energy. Nita was sure she knew why, but there was no dealing with it right now. She hustled Dairine back to the little conference room and sat her down.

Nita's father gave Dairine one of those looks that said, *Misbehaving again, I see*, but said nothing aloud. The doctor greeted Dairine, then turned back to their father.

"Well," she said, "Mrs. Callahan's status is pretty stable. And now we've had the scans that I wanted. I've had a chance to look at them, and this morning I had a couple of my colleagues look at the results. We're all in agreement."

She took a long breath. "Mr. Callahan," she said, "I don't know; you'll have to tell me whether you think it's better that you and I should discuss this alone first."

"Not a chance," Nita said. Dairine shook her head.

Her father swallowed. "They're both intelligent girls, Doctor," he said. "They're going to have to hear, anyway. Better they should get the explanation from you than secondhand from me."

The doctor nodded, then got up, shut the door to the corridor, and sat down again. "All right," she said. Her voice was measured, gentle. "Mr. Callahan, the growth in your wife's brain is definitely a tumor. We're ninety percent sure that it's a growth of a type called glioblastoma multiform. This kind of growth is very invasive, very fast growing. It invades nearby tissue quickly and destructively. And it is usually malignant."

They all sat still as statues.

"The only way we're going to be a hundred percent sure of the assessment is to do a biopsy," Dr. Kashiwabara said. "We'll do that in a day or two, so that we can determine our course of action. But I want to stress to you that the tumor itself can be removed. That will relieve the pressure on the surrounding structures."

"But that's not everything, is it?" Nita said.

The doctor shook her head. "I said that this kind of growth is invasive. It has a tendency to spread—to seed itself throughout the body, to other organs: the lymph nodes, the liver and spleen, the bone marrow. Because glioblastomas grow so quickly at this stage in their development, it's hard to tell how long the tumor may have been there in 'silent' mode, seeding itself. The important thing is going to be to start chemotherapy as soon as possible after the surgery to remove the tumor. Possibly radiotherapy as well."

Nita's father nodded. "Have you discussed this with my wife?" he said.

"Not yet," said the doctor. "That comes next. I wanted a chance to prepare you first, since you two will want to talk about it together, and it's important that you both have all the facts."

"The 'seeding,' " her father said. "It's cancer that you mean. Spreading."

"Yes," said Dr. Kashiwabara.

Nita felt as if she had been turned to ice where she sat. *Cancer* was a word that she had come across repeatedly in her reading that morning, but she had been trying to ignore it. Now she realized her folly, for the most basic tool of wizardry is words, and a wizard who ignores words willfully is only sabotaging herself.

"What are her chances?" Nita's father said.

"It's too soon to tell," said the doctor. "Right now our priority is to get that tumor out of there. Afterward there'll be time to look at the long-term options."

"Is the operation dangerous?" Nita said.

Dr. Kashiwabara looked at her. "There's a certain risk," she said. "As in any surgical procedure. But the tumor's in an area where it won't be too hard to get at, and for this kind of surgery, we use a technique that's more like the way we fix people's noses than anything else. It's not nearly as invasive or traumatic as brain surgery was years ago. I'll sit down with you and show you some diagrams, if you like."

"Thanks," Nita said. "Yes."

The doctor turned back to their dad. "Is there anything else you want to ask me?"

"Only when you think the surgery will be scheduled."

"As soon as possible. There's a team of local specialists that we put together for this kind of surgery. I'm getting everyone's schedules sorted out now. I think it'll be Wednesday or Thursday."

"Okay," Nita's dad said. "Thanks, Doctor."

The doctor went off, leaving them together. *I saw her face*, Nita remembered her dad saying. She was shaking. *He was right . . .*

"There's no point in us hanging around here," her father said. "Why don't we look at the diagrams Dr. Kashiwabara has for us. Then I'll drop you two home, and come back a little bit later, so I can talk to Mom."

"Daddy, no!" Dairine said. "I want to stay and—"

Dari, Nita said silently, *shut up. We need to see Tom, in a hurry. And you and I need to talk.*

"No, honey," their father said. "I want to see her first. Okay?"

"All right," Dairine said, subdued, but she shot Nita a rebellious look. "Let's go."

Nita held her fire until they were home, and all had had something to eat. When her father was getting ready to go out, she stopped him at the door and said, "We may be going out, Dad. Don't be surprised if we're not here when you get back. There are visiting hours tonight, right?"

"Yes, I think so. You can go then." Her dad exhaled. "I guess it's a good thing that the surgery will happen quickly. We can start . . . coping, I guess."

"Yeah. And we'll do more than that." She gave him a hug. "Give that to Mom for me."

"I will."

She watched him pull out of the driveway and drive off.

Nita started up the stairs and met Dairine halfway down them, shrugging into her jacket, with Spot under her arm. "Not so fast," Nita said. "I want you to tell me what you were doing in there."

"Something," Dairine said. "Which was more than *you* were."

Nita was tempted to hit her sister—to *really* hit her, which shocked her. Dairine brushed by her and headed for the back door. Nita grabbed her own jacket and her manual, locked the back door, and went after her.

Dairine was halfway down the driveway already. "Were you crazy, doing a wizardry right there?" Nita whispered as she caught up with her. "And you *bombed*, didn't you? You crashed and burned."

Dairine was walking fast. "I don't want to talk about it."

"You'd better talk about it! She's my mother, too! What were you trying to do?"

"What do you think? I was trying to cure her!"

Nita gulped. "*Just like that?* Are you *nuts*? Without even knowing exactly what *kind* of growth you were operating on yet? Without—"

"Neets, while I've still got the power, I've got to try to do something with it," Dairine said. "Before I lose the edge!"

"That doesn't mean you just do any old thing before you're prepared!" Nita said. "That wizardry just came *apart*! What if some piece of it got loose and affected someone else in there? What if—"

"It doesn't matter," Dairine muttered, furious. "It didn't work." Nita looked at her, as they crossed the street and headed down the road that led to Tom and Carl's, and saw the tears starting to fill Dairine's eyes again. "It didn't work," Dairine said, more quietly. *How can it not have worked?* This isn't even anything *like* pushing a planet around; this isn't even a middle-sized wizardry— It . . ." She went quiet.

Nita could feel the tension building all through Dairine, like a coil winding tighter and tighter. "Come on," she said.

When they rang Tom's doorbell, it was a few moments before he answered, and as he opened the screen door, Nita wasn't quite sure what to make of his expression. "It's Grand Central Station around here this morning," Tom said, "in all kinds of ways. Come on in."

"Is this a bad time?" Nita asked timidly.

"Oh, no worse than usual," said Tom. "Come on in; don't just stand there."

He quickly closed the front door behind Nita and Dairine as they went by, which was probably just as well, because otherwise a passerby might have seen the six-foot-long iridescent blue giant slug sitting in the middle of the living-room floor, deep in conversation with Carl. At least it would have looked like a giant slug to anyone who hadn't been to Alphecca VI, but slugs weren't usually encrusted with rubies of such a size. "Hey, ladies," Carl said as they passed, and then went back to his conversation with his guest.

Tom led them into the big combined kitchen–dining room. "Are you two all right?" Tom said. "No, I can tell you're not; it's just about boiling off you. What's happened?"

Briefly Nita told him. Tom's face went blank with shock.

"Oh, my God," he said. "Nita, Dairine, I'm so sorry. This started happening when?"

"Yesterday afternoon."

Tom sat down at the table. "Please," he said, gesturing them to seats across from him. "And you say they've got the scans done already. That helps." He looked up then. "It also explains something Carl noticed an hour or so ago . . ."

Carl had just said good-bye to the Alpheccan, who had vanished most expertly, without even enough disturbance of the air to rustle the curtains. "Yeah, I thought that was you earlier," Carl said, coming over to sit down at the table and looking at Dairine. "It had your signature, with that kind of power expenditure. But something went real wrong, didn't it?"

"It didn't work," Dairine said softly.

"There are only about twenty reasons why it shouldn't have," Carl said, sounding dry. "Inadequate preparation, no concrete circle when so many variables were involved, insufficiently defined intervention locus in both volume and tissue type, other unprotected living entities in the field of possible effects, inadequate protection for the wizardry against 'materials' memory of past traumas in the area; shall I go on? *Major* screwup, Dairine. I expect better of you." He was frowning.

Nita tried to remember if she'd ever seen Carl frown before, and failed, and got the shivers.

"I thought I could just *fix* it," Dairine said, looking pale. "I mean—I've done that kind of thing before."

Carl shook his head. "Yes, but you can't go on that way forever. Your power levels are down nine, maybe ten points from mid-Ordeal levels. That's just as it should be. But hasn't it occurred to you that there's another problem? You started very big. This is a small wizardry by comparison—and you haven't yet mastered the reduction in scale to make you much good at the small stuff. Sorry, Dairine, but that's the price you pay for such a spectacular debut. Right now Nita's the only one in your house who's got the kind of control to attempt any kind of intervention on your mother at all. You're going to have to let her handle it. And I warn you not to interfere in whatever intervention Nita may elect. It could kill all three of you. It's going to be hard for you to sit on your hands and watch, but that's just what you're going to have to do."

"It's not fair," Dairine whispered.

"No," said Tom. "So let's agree that it's not, then move past that to some kind of solution. If indeed there is one."

"If!" Nita said.

Tom looked at her steadily, an expression inviting her to calm herself down. "Maybe a Coke or something?" Carl said.

"Please," Nita said. Carl got up to get the drinks. To Tom, Nita said, "I was doing a lot of reading this morning. I kept running into references to spells that had to do with cancer being difficult because the condition is 'intractable,' or 'recalcitrant.' " She shook her head. "I don't get it. A spell *always* works."

"Except when the problem keeps reconstructing itself afterward," Tom said, "in a different shape. It's like that intervention you and Kit were working on, the Jones Inlet business. If the pollution coming out of the inner waters was always the same, the wizardry would be easy to build. But it's changing all the time."

Nita grimaced. "Yeah, well," she said, "I blew a whole lot of time on detail work on that one, and the spell worked just fine without it. I think I'm having a lame-brain week." She rubbed her face. "Just when I most seriously don't need one!"

"There's not much point in beating yourself up about that right now," Tom said. "The foundations of the wizardry were sound, and it did the job, which is what counts. And you may be able to recycle the subroutines for something else eventually."

Carl came back with four bottles of Coke, distributed them, and sat down. He exchanged glances with Tom for a second longer than absolutely necessary, as information passed from mind to mind.

"Oh boy," Carl said. "Nita, Tom's right. The basic problem is the structure of the malignancy itself—"

"Look, let's take this from the top," Tom said. "Otherwise there are going to be more misunderstandings." He held out his hand, and a compact version of his manual dropped into it. He put it down on the table and started leafing through it. "You've done some medical wizardry in the past," he said to Nita.

"Yeah. Minor healings. Some not so minor."

Tom nodded. "Tissue regeneration is fairly simple," he said. "Naturally there's always a price. Blood, either in actual form or expressed by your agreement to suffer the square of the pain you're intending to heal—that's the normal arrangement. But when you start involving nonhuman life in the healing, things get complicated."

Nita blinked. *"Excuse* me? My mother was human the last time I looked!"

Carl gave Tom an ironic look. "What my distracted colleague here means is that it's not just your mother you have to heal, but also whatever's attacking her. If you don't heal the *cause* of the tumor or the cancer, it just comes back somewhere else, in some worse form."

"What could be worse than a brain tumor?!" Dairine said.

"Don't ask," Tom said, still leafing through the manual. "There are too many ways the Lone Power could answer that question." He glanced up then. "Your main problem is that cancer cells are tough for wizards to treat because they're neither all inanimate nor all biological life. They're a hybrid . . . which causes problems when trying to write a spell that will eradicate them without hurting normal cells. It's exactly the same thing that makes chemotherapy slightly dangerous. It poisons the good cells as well as the bad ones unless it's very carefully managed."

"The other part of the problem," Carl said, "is that the viruses and malignant cells mutate as they spread. That makes cancer as intractable for wizards to treat as for doctors. Even if you could wave your hands in the air and say, 'Disease go away!' all you can do is make the disease go away that's there *today*. After that, all it takes is one virus that you missed, hidden away in just one cell somewhere, to start breeding again. They get smarter and nastier after an incomplete eradication. What comes back will kill you faster than what was there originally. Worse, you can never get them all. A spell complex enough to do that, accurately naming and describing each and every cell, and what you think might be hiding in it, would take you years to write. By which time . . ." He shook his head.

"I thought maybe *you* did spells like that," Nita said in a small voice.

Tom smiled, even though the smile was sad. "That's a much higher compliment than I deserve. No, a wizardry *that* complex is well beyond my competence . . . which is a shame, because if it wasn't, I wouldn't rest by day or night until I had it for you."

Nita gulped.

"A lot of wizards have spent a lot of time on this one, Nita," said Carl. "There are ways to attempt a cure, but the price is high. If it weren't, there wouldn't be much cancer; we'd be stomping it out with ease wherever we found it. As it is, look at the world around you, and see how far we've got."

That thought wasn't one she cared for. "You say there are ways to 'attempt' a cure," Nita said. "It sounds like it doesn't work very often."

"That's because of the most basic part of the problem," Carl said. "It leaves us, in some ways, even less able to do anything than the medical people. We're wizards. Viruses, though they're not exactly *organic* life, are life regardless. And we cannot just go around killing things without dealing with the consequences, at every level."

"Oh, come *on!*" Dairine said.

"Not at all," Carl said. "Where do you draw the line, Dairine? Where in the Oath does it say, 'I'll protect this life over here but not *that* one, which is just a germ and happens to be annoying me at the moment?' There's no such dichotomy. You respect *all* life, or none of it. Of *course*, that doesn't mean that wizards never kill. But killing increases entropy locally, and it's always to be resisted. Sometimes, yes, you must kill in order to save another life. But you must first make your peace with the life-form you're killing."

"If I'm just going to be killing a bunch of viruses," Nita said, "I should be able to manage that."

Carl shook his head. "It may not be so easy. Viruses have their own worldview: 'Reproduce at any cost.' Which also can mean 'kill your host.' In dealing with that kind of thing, a wizard is handicapped right from the start."

"Blame the Speech," Tom said. "It's the basis on which every wizardry is predicated . . . but here, it's also our weak spot, if this *is* a weakness. Everything that lives knows the Speech and can use it to tell you how life feels for it, how its universe makes it behave . . ."

Nita stared at the table, her heart sinking. Tom was right. It was hard to be angry at something—a rock, a tree—that you could hear saying to you, *This is how I'm made; it's not my fault; you see how the world is, the way things are; what else can I do?* And for the simplest things—and viruses are about as simple as things get—it would be hard to explain to them why they shouldn't be doing this, why they should all just stop reproducing themselves and essentially commit suicide so that your mother didn't have to die. Their world was such a simple one, it wouldn't allow for much in the way of—

Nita's eyes went wide.

She slowly looked up from the table at Tom. "What about—Tom, is it possible to change a cancer virus's perception of the world—change the way the universe seems for them, *is* for them—so that they're more sentient? So that a wizard *could* deal with them to best effect? Talk them out of being there . . . talk them out of killing? Something like that?"

Tom and Carl looked at each other. Tom's look was dubious. But Carl's expression was strangely intrigued. He nodded slowly.

"You know the rules," he said. " 'If they're old enough to ask . . .' "

" '. . . they're old enough to be told.' "

Tom folded his hands and looked at them. "Nita," he said, "I couldn't ask about this before. Who are you thinking of doing this wizardry for? Your mother or you?"

Nita sat silent, then she opened her mouth.

"Don't," Carl said. "You're still in shock; you can't possibly have a clear answer to the question yet. You're going to have to find out as you do your work. But the question matters. Wizardry, finally, is about service to other beings. Our own needs come second. If you start fooling yourself about that, the deception is going to go straight to the heart of any spell you write, and ruin it. And maybe you as well."

"Okay," Tom said. "Let that rest for the moment." To Nita he said, "Are you clear about what you're suggesting you want to do?"

"I guess it would mean changing the way things behave in the universe, locally," Nita said. "Inside my mom." And she gulped. When she put it that way, it suddenly became clear how many, many ways there were to screw it up.

"Changing the structure of the universe itself," Tom said. "Yes. You get to play God on a local level."

"You're going to tell me that it's seriously dangerous," Nita said, "and the price is awful."

"Anything worth having demands a commensurate price," Carl said. "What is your mother's life worth to you? . . . And yes, this option has dangers. But I see that's not likely to stop you in the present situation."

He leaned back a little in his chair, folding his arms, looking at Nita. "We have to warn you clearly," Carl said. "You think you've been through a lot in your career so far. I have news for you. You haven't yet played with *anything* like this. When you start altering the natural laws of universes, it's like throwing a rock into a pond. Ripples spread, and the first thing in the local system to be affected, the first thing the ripples hit, is *you*. You're going to need practice handling that, keeping yourself as you are in the face of *everything* changing, before trying it for real . . . and unfortunately, in this universe, everything *is* for real."

"I don't care," Nita said. "If there's a chance I might be able to save my mom, I have to try. What do I need to do?"

"Go somewhere it's *not* for real," Carl said. "One of the universes where you can practice."

Nita stared at him, confused. "Like learning to fly a plane in a simulator?"

"It wouldn't be a simulation," Tom said. "It'll be real enough. As Carl said, figures of speech aside, it's *always* for real. But if you have to make mistakes while you're learning how to manipulate local changes in universal structure, there are places set aside where you can make them and not kill anybody in the process."

"Or where, if you kill yourself making one of those mistakes, you won't take anyone else with you," said Carl.

There was a moment's silence at that.

"Where?" Nita said. "I want to go."

"Of course you do, right this minute," Carl said, rubbing his face. "It's going to take time to set up."

"There may not *be* a lot of time, Carl! My mom—"

"Is not going to die today, or tomorrow," Tom said, "as far as the doctors can tell. Isn't that so?"

"Yes, but—" Nita stopped. For a moment she had been ready to shout that they weren't being very considerate of her. But that would have been untrue. As her Senior wizards, their job was to be tough with her when she needed it. Anything else would have been *really* inconsiderate.

"Good," Carl said. "Get a grip. You're going to need it, where you're going. The aschetic continua, the 'practice' universes, are flexible places—at least the early ones in the sequence—but if you indulge yourself in sloppy thinking while you're in one, it can be fatal."

"Where are they?" Nita said. "How do I get there?"

"It's a worldgating," Tom said. "Nonstandard, but you'd be using existing gates." He glanced at Carl. "Penn Station?"

"Penn's down right now. It'd have to be Grand Central."

Nita nodded; she had a fair amount of experience with the worldgates there. "What do I do when I get there?"

"Your manual will have most of the details," Carl said. "You'll practice changing the natures and rules of the nonpopulated spaces that the course makes available to you. You'll start with easy ones, then move up to universes that more strenuously resist your efforts to change them, then ones that will be almost impossible to change."

"It's like weight lifting," Nita said. "Light stuff first, then heavier."

"In a way."

"When you finish the course," Tom said, "if you've done it correctly, you'll be in a position to come back and recast your mother's physical situation as an alternate universe . . . and change its rules. If you still want to."

If? Nita decided not to press the point. She'd noticed over time that sometimes Tom and Carl spent a lot of effort warning you about things that weren't going to happen. "Yes. I want to do it."

Tom and Carl looked at each other. "All right," Tom said. "You're going to have to construct a carrying matrix for the spells you'll take with you—sort of a wizardly backpack. Normally you'd read the manual and construct the spells you need, on the spot, but that won't work where you're going. In the practice universes, time runs at different speeds, so the manual can be unpredictable about updating . . . and you can't wait for it when you're in the middle of some wizardry where speed of execution is crucial. Your manual will have details on what the matrix needs to do. What it looks like is up to you."

"And one last thing," Carl said. He looked sad but also stern. "If you go forward on this course, there's going to come a time when you're going to have to ask your mother whether this is a price *she* wants you to pay."

"I know that," Nita said. "I'm used to asking my mom for permission for stuff. I don't think this'll be a problem." She looked up at them. "But what *is* the price?"

Tom shook his head. "You'll find out as you go along."

"Yeah," Nita said. "Okay. I'll get started as soon as I get home."

And then, to Nita's complete shock, she broke down and began to cry. Tom and Carl sat quietly and let her, while Dairine sat there looking stricken. After a moment Tom got up and got Nita a tissue, and she blew her nose and wiped her eyes. "I'm sorry," she said, "that keeps happening all of a sudden."

"Don't be sorry," Tom said. "It's normal. And so is not giving up."

She sniffed once or twice more and then nodded.

"Go do what you have to," Tom said.

She and Dairine got up. "And Nita," Carl said.

On her way to the front door, she looked back at him.

"Be careful," Carl said. "There are occupational hazards to being a god."

Sunday Afternoon
and Evening

NITA AND DAIRINE WALKED home, and Nita went up to her room and settled in to work. The moment she sat down at her desk, she saw that her manual already had several new sections in it, subsequent to the usual one that dealt with worldgatings and other spatial and temporal dislocations.

The first new section had general information about the practice universes: their history, their locations relative to the hundreds of thousands of known alternate universes, their qualities. *They're playpens*, Nita thought as she read. *Places where the structure that holds science to matter, and wizardry to both of them, has some squish to it; where the hard corners on things aren't so hard, so you can stretch your muscles and find out how to exploit the squish that exists elsewhere.* There was no concrete data about how the practice universes had been established, but they were very old, having apparently been sealed off to prevent settlement at a time almost too ancient to be conceived. *One of the Powers That Be, or Someone higher up, foresaw the need.*

While it was useful that no one lived in those universes to get hurt by wizards twisting natural laws around, there seemed to be a downside as well. You couldn't stay in them for long. The manual got emphatic about the need not to exceed the assigned duration of scheduled sessions—

> Universes not permanently inhabited by intelligent life have only a limited toleration for the presence of sentients. The behavior of local physics within these universes can become skewed or deranged when overloaded by too many sentient-hours of use in a given period. In extreme cases such over-inhabitation can cause an aschetic continuum to implode. . . .

Boy, there's *a welcome I won't overstay*, Nita thought, though not without a moment's curiosity about what it was like inside a universe when it imploded. *Something to get Dairine to investigate, maybe.* Nita managed just a flicker of a grim smile at the thought.

> Access scheduling is arranged through manual functions from the originating universe. Payment for the gating is determined by duration spent in the aschesocontinuum and deducted from the practitioner at the end of each session. Access is through local main-line gating facilities of complexity level XI or better; the gating type is a diazo-Riemannian timeslide, which, regardless of duration spent in the aschetic continuum, returns practitioners to the originating universe an average of +.10 planetary rotations along duration axis, variation +/− .005 rotation.

Nita did the conversion from the decimal timings, raised her eyebrows. *So you go in, then come out more or less two hours after you went . . . no matter how much time you spend there.*

Could get tiring.

Ask me if I care!

There were many other details. Nita spent the rest of an hour or so absorbing them, then passed on to what seemed the most important part of the work in front of her: constructing the matrix to hold the spells she'd be using in the practice universes. The matrix would hold a selection of wizardries ready for use until she could get back to where the manual could be depended on for fast use.

The thought of a place where you couldn't depend on the manual made Nita twitch a little. But that was where she had to go to do her mother any good, so she got over it and started considering the structure of the matrix. It was complex; it had to be in order to hold whole ready-to-run spells apart from one another, essentially in stasis, so that they couldn't get tangled. The matrix structure that the manual suggested was straightforward enough to build but fiddly—like putting chain mail together, ring by ring and rivet by rivet, each ring going through three others.

Nita cleared her desk and laid the manual out where she could keep her eye on the guide diagram it provided. Then she put out her hands and pronounced eighty-one syllables in the Speech. Once complete, the sentence took physical form, drifting like a glowing thread into her hands. She said the sentence again, and again, until she had nine of the strands. Then Nita wound them together and knotted the ends of the ninefold strand together with a wizard's knot, creating a single sealed loop, which she scaled down in size. The next loop of nine strands was laced through that one, as were the next two. When it was finished, there would be three-to-the-sixth links in the matrix: seven hundred twenty-nine of them. . . .

Nita didn't allow the numbers to freak her out. She kept at it, making each set of nine strands, winding them together, looping them, linking them through the other available links, and fastening them closed. The work was as hypnotic in its way as crocheting—a hobby that Nita had taken up a couple of years ago at her mother's instigation, then promptly dumped because the constant repetition of motions made her hands cramp. But this was not about making a scarf. This was about saving her mother's life . . . so Nita found it a lot easier to ignore the cramps.

Gradually the delicate structure began to grow. Several times Nita missed hooking one of the substructures into all the others it had to be connected to, and the diagram in the manual flashed insistently until she went back and fixed it. Slowly, though, she started to get the rhythm down pat, and the eighty-one syllables, repeated again and again, came out perfectly every time, though they started becoming meaningless with the repetition. *I'm going to be saying these things in my sleep*, Nita thought, finishing one more unit and moving on to the next.

About an hour into this work, Nita heard her dad come home. The back door shut, and she heard him moving around downstairs in the kitchen, but she kept doing what she was doing. A few minutes later there was a knock at her door, and he came in.

Nita looked up at him, grateful for the interruption, and flexed her hands to get rid of the latest bout of cramps. The steady energy drain that came with doing a repetitive wizardry like this was really tiring her out, but that couldn't be helped. "How's Mom?" she said.

"She's fine," her father said, and sat down wearily on her bed. "Well, not fine; of course not. But she's not in pain, and she's not so full of the drugs this afternoon . . . We talked about the surgery. She's okay about that."

"Really?" Nita said.

Her father rubbed his face. "Well, of course not, honey," he said. "Who *wants* anybody monkeying around with their brain? But she knows it's got to be done."

"And the rest of it?"

Her dad shook his head. "She's not exactly happy about the possibility that the cancer might have spread. But there's nothing we can do about that, and there's no point in worrying about it when there's something so much more important happening in a few days."

He looked at the faint line of light lying on Nita's desk. "What's that?"

She picked it up, handed it to him. "Go ahead," she said when he hesitated. "You can't hurt it."

He reached out and took the delicate linkage of loop after loop of light into his hands. "What's it for?"

"Helping Mom."

"You talked to Tom and Carl?"

"Yeah." Nita wondered whether to get into the details, then decided against it. *When he's ready to ask, I'll be ready to tell. I hope.* "There are places I can go," she said, "where I can learn the skills I need to deal with the . . . cancer." She had trouble saying the word. *I'm going to have to get over that.* "I won't be gone for long, Dad, but I'll be going to places where time doesn't run the same way. I may be pretty tired when I get back."

He handed back the partly made matrix. "You really think this has a chance of making a difference? Of making your mom well?"

"It's a chance," Nita said. "I won't know until I try, Daddy."

"Is Dairine going with you?"

Nita shook her head. "She's got to sit this one out."

Her father nodded. "All right. Sweetheart . . . you know what I'm going to say."

"Be careful."

He managed just the slightest smile. "When are you going to tell Mom about this?"

"When I've tried it once. After I see how it goes, I'll tell her. No point in getting her worried, or excited, until I know for sure that I *can* get where I have to go and do what I have to."

"One other thing, hon . . ."

Nita looked at her father with concern.

"For tomorrow and Tuesday, anyway, I think you and Dairine should go to school as usual. It's better for us all to stick to our normal routines than to sit around home agonizing over what's going on."

Nita wasn't wild about this idea, but she couldn't find it in her heart to start arguing the point with her father right now. "Okay," she said after a moment.

"Then I'll go get us something to eat," her father said, and went out.

Nita turned back to the desk, let out a long sad breath at the pain and worry in her dad's face, and said the eighty-one syllables one more time. . . .

Kit spent the day adding notes to his manual on where he had been. Once or twice during the process he checked the back of the book to see if there was anything from Nita but found nothing. At first he thought, *Maybe she's busy. It's not like she doesn't have her own projects to work on.* But as the evening approached, Kit began to wonder what she was up to. *I guess I could always shoot her a thought.*

He pushed back in his desk chair, leaned back—

"Ow!"

Kit turned around hurriedly and realized that Ponch was lying right behind him, half asleep . . . or formerly half asleep. He wasn't now; not with one of Kit's chair legs shoved into his gut. "Sorry," Kit said, pulling the chair in a little.

"Hmf," Ponch said, and put his head down on his paws again.

Kit sighed and closed his eyes once more. *Neets? . . .*

. . . Nothing. Well, not quite. She was there, but she wasn't in receiving mode right now, or just wasn't receptive. Additionally, coming from her direction, Kit could catch a weird sort of background noise, like someone saying something again and again—a fierce in-turned concentration he'd never felt in her before. *What's she doing? . . .* The noise had a faint taste of wizardry about it, but there was also an emotional component, a turmoil of extreme nervousness, but blocked, stifled— he couldn't make anything of it.

Weird, he thought. *Neets? Anybody home?*

Still no reply. Finally Kit sighed and leaned forward to his work again. The manual had presented him with a detailed questionnaire about his experiences in the places he'd been, and there were still a lot of sections to fill in. *I'll walk over there after I'm done and see what the story is.*

It was after eight before Kit got up. He went downstairs to get his jacket, for it was chilly; fall was setting in fast. As Kit went by, his pop looked up from the living-room chair where he was reading, and said, "Son, it's a school day tomorrow. Don't be out late."

"I won't," Kit said. "Just gonna drop in on Nita real fast."

With a scrabble of claws on the stairs, Ponch threw himself down them and turned the corner into the living room. "Whereyagoin'-whereyagoin'-whereyagoin'!"

"Mr. Radar Ears strikes again," Kit's father said. "Can't move around here without that dog demanding you take him out for a walk."

"He has his reasons," Kit said, amused, and headed out.

The streetlight at the corner was malfunctioning again, sizzling as its light jittered on and off. Kit didn't mind the "off"; as he crossed the street with Ponch, he could see more plainly the stars of autumn evening climbing through the branches of the trees. Already there were fewer leaves to hide them. At the rate this fall had been going, with sharp frosts every night, there would be few leaves, or none, left in a couple of weeks. Past the faint glints of Deneb and Altair in that sky were Uranus and Neptune. Kit couldn't see them with the naked eye, but to a wizard's senses they could be felt, even at this distance, as a distant tang of mass in the icy void. Kit smiled at the thought that they seemed even more like the local neighborhood than usual, compared to the places he'd been today.

He came to Nita's house and, to his surprise, found it dark and Nita's dad's car gone. *Maybe they all went out somewhere, to the movies or to visit somebody, something like that. Oh well, Mela said she called. And she got my message. She'll get back to me.*

Kit walked Ponch for a little while more, then went home and settled once again at his desk to finish that report in the manual, but first he used it to leave Nita another message. *Tried to reach you earlier, but you sounded busy. Call when you can.* He would have added *See you at school tomorrow*, except that this was less likely than it used to be. Their classes were all different, and at the moment they didn't even have the same lunch period.

He sent the message, then paged through the manual to finish his report. Ponch curled up behind Kit's chair, muttering a little to himself as he groomed his paws after their walk. "If you were going to tell someone your gut feeling about the places where we went yesterday," Kit said to Ponch, reading him one of the questions he still had to answer, "what would it be?"

"They smelled nice," Ponch said slowly. "But smell isn't everything . . ."

Kit raised his eyebrows, made a note of that, and went back to work.

Monday Morning and Afternoon

NITA SAW DAWN COME in again . . . this time because she hadn't bothered to go to sleep after coming back from the hospital. She had been too busy working on the spell matrix. Now, worn out, she sat at her desk in the vague morning light and looked at it as it lay in her hands.

To a wizard far enough along in her learning to think in the Speech, and used to seeing the underpinnings of power beneath mere appearance, it looked two ways. One was a complex, interwoven glitter and shimmer of strands of light with nine prominent "knots" showing, each one a receptor site into which a "free" wizardry could be offered up. But the other semblance, which had made it easier for Nita to work with the wizardry in its later stages, was a charm bracelet, though one with no charms on it as yet. The manual suggested it would take time for her to choose the spells she needed and mate them successfully to the matrix. Nita hoped it wouldn't take as long as the manual suggested it might. She needed to hurry.

She poured it through her fingers, feeling the virtual mass she had bound into the matrix's structure. It now looked and felt enough like an ordinary charm bracelet that no one would find it strange Nita was wearing it. It was also a convenient shape; she wouldn't have to keep it in a pocket.

"Didn't think you'd be done with it already," Dairine said from right behind her.

Nita started, nearly falling right out of her chair, then looked over her shoulder. "Yeah, well, think about that the next time you accuse me of not doing anything."

Dairine nodded. She looked wan, in that early light, and her dad's big T-shirt hanging off her made her look more waiflike and fragile than usual. Nita regretted having spoken sharply to her. "You okay?"

"No," Dairine said, "and why should I be? Terrible things are happening, and there's nothing I can do. Worse, I have to sit around and hope that *you* get it right." She glowered.

This, at least, was a more normal mode of operation for Dairine. Nita poked her genially. "We'll see what Carl says," she said. "Go on."

Dairine went off. Nita got up and opened a drawer, to choose her clothes for that day, picked up that new skirt and almost decided not to wear it. Then she thought, *Why not? If I get sent home, it'll just give Mom an excuse to feel like she was right. Probably cheer her up, too.* She fished around for a top to go with it, then went off for her shower.

Half an hour later, showered and dressed, Nita felt slightly better, almost as if she hadn't been up all night. She went downstairs to have a bite of breakfast and found her father finishing a bowl of cereal. He glanced at Nita as she rummaged in the fridge, and said, "Isn't that a little short?"

Nita snickered. "Mom bought it, Dad. It was long enough for *her.*"

Her father raised his eyebrows. He normally left this kind of issue to Nita and her mom to resolve; now he seemed to be having second thoughts. "Well, I suppose . . . Come by the store when you're out of school and we'll go straight over and see Mom."

"Okay." She put the milk down and hugged him. "See you later."

Her father went out, and Nita watched him get into the car and drive off. It felt to her as if he was just barely holding it all together, and that tore at Nita. *Well, if I can make this work, he won't need to be that way for long.*

Please, God, let it work!

She drank a glass of milk and then sat down at the kitchen table with her manual, flipping to the back of it. There she saw the new message from Kit and was immediately guilt stricken. *I'll catch up with him at school today,* she thought. *Right now, though, I've gotta take care of this first.* She opened a new message on a clean page. *Carl?*

The answer came straight back; he was using his manual, too. *Good morning. Got a moment?*

If it's just a moment, yes.

I'm done. Want to check it out?

Okay. Come on over.

Nita reached into her claudication-pocket, pulled out the transit spell she used for Tom and Carl's backyard, and tweaked the ingress parameters so that there'd be no air-displacement bang. Then she dropped it to the floor and stepped through.

Carl was standing in the doorway from the house to the patio, tying his tie and looking out at the garden. Nita paused for just a moment to admire him; she didn't often see him dressed for work. "Nice tie, Carl."

He glanced down at it. It was patterned all over with bright red chilies, a surprising contrast to the sober charcoal of the suit. "Yeah, it was a gift from my sister. Her ideas of business wear are unique. What've you got for me?"

"Here," Nita said, going over to hand him the charm bracelet. He raised his eyebrows, amused by the shape, and then dissolved the appearance to show the matrix itself, enlarged until it stretched a couple of feet in length, shimmering and intricate, between his hands.

"Yeah," Carl said, examining it section by section. "Right . . ." He showed her one spot where the linked strands didn't come together quite the same way they did elsewhere. "Open receptor site there . . ."

"I know. I left it that way on purpose, in case I need to expand it later." Nita pointed at the spell strands around the spot. "See, there's reinforcement around it, and a blocker."

"Hmm . . ." He looked at the rest of the matrix. "Yeah, I see what you've done; it makes sense. Okay, I'll sanction it."

Carl took the two ends of the matrix strand and knotted them with a slightly more involved version of the wizard's knot. The whole length of the matrix flashed briefly with white fire as Carl set his Senior's authorization into the structure of the wizardry. Though the flash died away quickly, for a few moments the whole backyard hummed with released and rebound power. Nita was distracted from the sight of a small, complex structure now hanging from the strand, like a tangled knot of light, by a sudden annoyed voice that said:

> *"Any chance you might*
> *hold it* down *out there? People*
> *in here are still sleeping."*

Nita looked around. One of the koi in the fishpond had put its head up out of the water and was giving them both a cranky look.

Carl sighed. "Sorry, Akagane-sama." He bowed slightly in the fish's direction.

The koi, a big handsome one spotted in dark orange-gold and white, rolled halfway over on the edge of the pool, and caught sight of Nita with one golden eye. It looked at her thoughtfully, then said:

> *"If half a loaf is better*
> *than no bread, then at least*
> *I want the crumbs now."*

"It's blackmail, that's what it is," Carl said, and vanished into the house. A few moments later he came back out and dropped some koi pellets and toast crumbs into the water.

The fish let out a bubble of breath, glancing at what Carl was holding. "All the drawing lacks," it said,

> *"is the final touch; to add*
> *eyes to the dragon . . ."*

Then it slipped back into the water with a small splash, and started eating.

Nita glanced at Carl. He shrugged. "Sometimes I don't know whether I have koi or koans," he said. "Anyway, you're all set now. The Grand Central gate will acknowledge this when it comes in range." He handed Nita the matrix, and it looked like a charm bracelet again. But there was something added: a single golden charm—a tiny fish. "So when're you going to start?"

"Uh, this afternoon, if I can stay awake that long."

"Go well, then," Carl said. "Speaking of which, I have to go, too." He patted her on the shoulder. "Good luck, kiddo." He went into the house.

Nita slipped the bracelet onto her wrist, and headed back to her transit circle.

Kit went to school that morning still excited about what he'd brought back from his dog walk. He'd transited the little flower, still in stasis, over to Tom's Sunday night, and he spent all his morning classes wondering what Tom would make of it. At lunchtime Kit managed to get out to where the pay phones were ranked in front of the Conlon Road entrance, and waited in line for nearly ten minutes before one was free.

Tom answered right away. "You get it okay?" Kit said.

"Yup. And I've been going through a précis of the raw data from your walk— the whole capture is about a thousand pages, maybe more. The really interesting thing about your jaunt, though, is that the places you went, the places you made, *are still there.*"

Kit wasn't sure what to make of that. "I thought they would just go away afterward."

"Seems not."

"What does that mean?"

"That I need an aspirin, mostly," Tom said. "Well, it means a few other things, too."

Kit glanced around—none of the other kids nearby was paying him the slightest attention—and whispered, "But . . . you can't just make things—planets, whole universes—out of *nothing!*"

"Strangely enough, that's how it was originally done. What's unusual is that it's not usually done that way any*more*. Received wisdom had it that the grouped khiliocosms, or 'sheaf of sheaf of universes,' the whole aggregate of physical existence, had a stable and unchanging amount of matter and energy. What you and Ponch have been doing would seem to call that into question."

"Uh, then I guess we're sorry," Kit said. "We didn't mean to make trouble for anybody."

Tom burst out laughing. "The only ones it's trouble for are the theoretical wizards, most of whom are probably now pulling out their hair, scales, or tentacles. You get transitory changes in the structure and nature of wizardry every now and then. Mostly they're situational ripples in the fabric of existence, and mostly they pass. But they're going to have a party explaining *this* one."

"Is it going to be a problem?" Kit said.

"For the average wizard in the street? No," Tom said. "But I think you should have a talk with Ponch to keep him from running off and creating universes on his own. We don't know how stable these universes are . . . and we don't know if they might not be able to proliferate."

"Proliferate?"

"Breed," said Tom.

Kit was taken aback. "Universes can *breed*?" he whispered.

"Oh yes. I could get into the geometries of it, the mechanics of isoparthenogenetic *n*-dimensional rotations and so on, but then I'd need *three* aspirins, and my stomach'll get upset. Just have a word with Ponch, okay? I'd rather not wake up and discover that one of Ponch's creations has self-rotated and left our home space hip-deep in squirrels. It would cause talk."

"Uh, yeah."

"Meanwhile, what you brought back is safe, and lots of people are going to want to look at it. So on behalf of research wizards everywhere, thanks a lot. What's the rest of your day look like?"

"Geometry, social studies . . . and gym." Kit made a face. He was not a big gym fan; wizardry can keep you from falling off the parallel bars, but it can't make you good at them.

"Uh-oh," Tom said, picking up on Kit's tone of voice. "Every now and then I think, *In the service of my Art I may accidentally drown in liquid methane or have my living-room rug slimed by giant slugs, but no one can ever make me climb one of those ropes again.*"

"Must be nice," Kit said.

"It will be, you'll see. Meanwhile, I think you've impressed Somebody with how you handled yourself out there. I was told to authorize you for further exploration. When you two go for your next walk, though, leave the manual on verbose reporting. It'll be useful for the researchers."

"No problem."

"Thanks again . . ." Tom hung up.

Then there was nothing to do with the rest of the day but go through classes as usual. While changing periods, Kit looked for Nita but didn't see her. Once, as he was just going into his math classroom before the bell rang, he caught sight of someone from behind, way down the hall, who he thought was her. But then Kit dismissed the idea; Neets didn't wear skirts that short. *And it's a shame,* said some unrepentant part of his mind.

Kit made an amused face. That part of his mind had been getting outspoken lately. His dad had reassured him that this was nothing to be concerned about— "revving up," he called it—but he wouldn't say much more. That made Kit want to laugh. His father, big and tough and worldly wise though he was, had a core of absolute shyness that few people outside the family recognized—but Kit knew it was the source of his own quiet side. He suspected that when it came to the facts of life, *he* was going to have to ask his dad to sit down and explain it all, to get the chore out of the way.

Kit went through the rest of the day, looking around for Nita again when school finished, but he couldn't find her. He went home, checked his manual, and found no new message from her, so he walked over to her house but found no one home. It made Kit want to laugh as he looked at the empty driveway. There'd occasionally been times when he didn't want to see Nita about anything specific, and she couldn't be avoided. Now, when he *did* want to talk to her, she couldn't be found. . . .

Kit went home, had dinner, and did his homework. By the time he was finished with the miserable geometry, he was ready to take all the blame for their fight, if only to get things back the way they ought to be—anything to distract himself from the horror of cosines and the Civil War. He pushed all the schoolbooks on his desk aside and shot her a thought: *Neets! Earth to Nita!*

Nothing. But this time it was a nothing he recognized—a faint mutter of distant low-level brain activity. Nita was deeply asleep. Kit glanced at the clock in mild bemusement. *At eight at night?!*

Never mind. Tomorrow morning early I'll meet her before she goes to school; we'll walk over together.

He wandered down the hall to his sister's room, peered in. Carmela was not there, but the TV and the tape deck were, and from the earphones lying on the bed, he could faintly hear someone singing in Japanese. The VCR was running, and on the TV, some kind of cartoon singing group—three slender young men with very long ponytails—seemed to be appearing in concert, while searchlights and lasers swept and flashed around them. *It's not like the house isn't full of her weird J-pop half the time to start with,* Kit thought, *but she's got* cartoon *J-pop, too? Oh well. It's an improvement on the heavy metal.*

Carmela emerged from the upstairs bathroom and brushed past him. "Looking lonely, little brother," she said, flopping down on her stomach and putting the earphones back in. "Where's Miss Juanita been lately?"

"Good question," Kit said, and headed down the stairs.

"Where ya goin'?" she shouted after him.

He smiled. "Out to walk the dog."

Monday Night,
Tuesday Morning

NITA WOKE UP AFTER midnight. She felt a flash of guilt for having fallen asleep straight after coming home from the hospital. But no matter how much she might have felt that precious time was slipping by, she'd been completely worn out, and there was no point in trying to do anything wizardly. Now the charm bracelet was satisfyingly heavy around her wrist, glinting in the light of the lamp on her desk, and she was rested and ready. *So let's get to work . . .*

She went downstairs to check where people were, and found that her dad had gone to bed. Nita made herself a sandwich and brought it back upstairs with her, pausing by Dairine's door to listen.

Silence. Softly Nita eased the door open, peered inside. In the darkness she could make out a tangle of limbs, pillows, and T-shirt on the bed—Dairine, in her usual all-night fight with the bedding. Nita shut the door and went into her room again.

She ate the sandwich with workmanlike speed and changed into jeans and sneakers and a dark jacket. Then she went to her desk to pick up the few small stand-alone wizardries that she thought would be useful for this exercise. One at a time she hooked each of them to a different link of the charm bracelet: a small gold house key, a little silvery disc with the letters *GCT* intertwined on one side and the number twenty-five on the other, a tiny stylized lightning bolt, a pebble, a little megaphone.

Nita pulled out her transit wizardry and changed its time-space coordinates, triggering the fail-safe features that would abort the spell if anyone was standing in the target area. Then she dropped the circle to the floor and stepped through, pulling it after her as she went.

The side doorway into which Nita stepped normally serviced one of the food stands in the Graybar Passage on one side of the terminal. Now there were only some black plastic garbage bags there, and Nita stepped over them and came out into the big archway dividing the passage from the Main Concourse. It would be a while before Grand Central shut down; a few trains were still moving in and out . . . and so was other traffic. Nita made her way to the right of the big octagonal brass information center, heading for the doorway that led to track twenty-five.

No train stood at the platform this late. Nita paused under the archway at the bottom of the platform, behind some iron racks and out of view of the control center far down the track on the right. She felt around in the back of her mind for another wizardry she'd prepared earlier, lying there almost ready to go. Nita said the thirty-fifth word, and the air around her rippled and misted over in a peculiar half-mirrored way. Whoever looked at her would see only what was directly behind her; she was effectively invisible now.

Nita walked on down the platform. Grand Central's most-used worldgate was down here, hanging in the space between tracks twenty-five and twenty-six, and accessible from either side for those who knew how to pull it over to the platform. Quite a few wizards used it for long-distance transport in the course of any one day—

Nita stumbled. *"Auuw!"* said someone down by her feet.

She recovered herself and stood still, looking around but unable to see what she'd tripped on. "Uh . . . sorry!"

"Oh," a voice said. "I see what you're doing. Wait a minute."

Suddenly there was a small black cat standing down by her foot, looking up at her. "Better," the cat said in the Speech. "Sorry about that. We were invisible two different ways."

"Dai, Rhiow," Nita said. Rhiow was the leader of the Grand Central worldgate supervision group, all of whose members were cats, since only feline wizards can naturally see the hyperstring structures on which worldgates are constructed. "I'm on errantry, and I greet you—"

"Aren't we all?" Rhiow said. "Nice to see you, too." She was looking at the opening in the air, filled with an odd shimmering darkness, which had manifested itself at Nita's approach. "Now, there's a configuration you don't see every day."

"Carl okayed it."

"Of course he did. It wouldn't be here otherwise. Good timing on your part, though." Rhiow looked back toward the scurrying people in the Main Concourse with a put-upon expression. "This gate's been getting three times the usual use while the others are moving around."

"Moving!" Nita's eyes widened. She'd seen more than once now what happened when a worldgate dislocated itself improperly. The results could vary from simply disastrous to extremely fatal.

"No, it's all right; it's our idea, not the gates'!" Rhiow said. "But Penn Station is being moved into a new building, across Eighth Avenue, and the gates have to go, too. We've had our paws full."

"It was nice of you to take the time to see me off."

"Not a problem, cousin," Rhiow said. "I wanted to make sure this behaved itself when you brought it online. Meanwhile, watch how you go, and watch how you handle what you find. We can bring danger with us even to a training session, so you be careful."

"I will."

"Dai stihó then, cousin."

"Dai . . ."

Manual in hand, Nita stepped through.

At first there was only a second's worth of darkness and the usual feel of the brushing of the worldgate across and through her, a feathers-on-mind feeling— strange as always but swiftly over. And then she broke out into light again, as if through the surface of water . . .

. . . and found herself on the opposite platform, next to track twenty-six.

Nita glanced around, confused. *Uh-oh. Am I still invisible?* She was. But then she realized that she needn't have worried. There was no one in sight at all.

She walked slowly back up the platform under the long line of fluorescent lights, going softly to avoid attracting any attention in this great quiet. *Now where'd Rhiow go?* Nita thought, glancing back at the platform to make sure she hadn't missed her somehow. But there was no sign of her, no movement, no sound anywhere—nothing but the soft cool breath of the draft coming up out of the dark depths of the tunnel through which the trains came into the station from under Park Avenue.

In the archway that led out into the Main Concourse, Nita paused, looking around her cautiously. There was no one out there, and all the lights were low. That was really bizarre, for even when the station was closed in the middle of the night, the lights were always up full, and there were always *some* people here: cleaners, transit police, workers doing maintenance on the trains and tracks. The lightbulb stars still burned, distant, up in the great blue backward sky of the terminal's ceiling, but below them the terminal was empty, drowned in a silence even more peculiar than the twilight now filling it.

Nita stood there and listened hard . . . not just with the normal senses, but with those that came with wizardry and were sharpened by its use. She tried to catch any hint of something wrong, the influence of the Lone Power or other forces inimical to a wizard. But there was no glimmer of danger to be sensed, no whisper of threat. *Okay*, she thought. *Mere weirdness I can handle.*

Softly Nita went out across the huge cream-colored expanse of the Main Concourse floor and up the ramp to the doors that led out onto Forty-second Street. She pushed one brass door open, stepped out onto the sidewalk.

There was no one here, either, and it wasn't one in the morning. It was mid-afternoon. The sun was angling westward, not even out of sight behind the skyscrapers yet.

Nita looked up and down Forty-second. No traffic, no cars, no people anywhere in sight; only the traffic lights hung out over the street, turning from red to green as she watched. A thin chill wind poured down the street past her, bearing no smells of hot-dog vendors, no voices, no honking horns . . . no sounds at all.

This was so creepy that Nita could hardly bear it. Once before she'd been in a New York that was nearly this empty . . . and she and Kit had had a bad time there. But here Nita got no sense of the Lone Power being in residence. She'd have instantly recognized that cold hostile tang in the air, the sense of being watched and overshadowed by something profoundly unfriendly.

Nita reached into her pocket of space, pulling out her manual and flipping it open to the new section about the practice universes. *Aschetic Spaces Habituation and Manipulation Routine*, it said: *Introduction:*

> You have now successfully entered the first of a series of "aschesis" or "live proof" continua that have been made available to you. Successful handling and manipulation of this continuum will result in your being offered the next one in the series.

> You are cautioned not to remain past your assigned time. Time warnings embedded in your manual may not function correctly.

A smaller block of text appeared underneath:

A timepiece based on the vibratory frequency of one or more crystalline compounds or elements has been detected on your person. Please use this timepiece for temporal measurements until further advice is given. Please do not change the vibratory frequency of [QUARTZ] in this universe.

"Gee, that was the first thing on my list," Nita muttered, glancing at her watch. She did a double take; the face of the watch, which until then had been plain white with black numerals, was now showing a red half-arc around the face, from the numbers 1 to 7. Nita glanced back at her manual.

Your total permitted time for this session has been marked.

YOUR GOAL:

Each universe or continuum possesses a "kernel," or core, which contains a master copy of its physical laws and the local laws of wizardry. This master copy is a single complex statement in the Speech that lists all properties of matter and energy in the local universe, and the values for which these properties are set. To manipulate physical law on a universal scale, whether temporarily or permanently, the universe- or continuum-kernel first must be located.

To avoid easy alteration of natural laws by local species, world-kernels are normally hidden. This universe's kernel has been concealed in a routine manner. You must find the kernel before your allotted time elapses. You must then use the kernel to change the local environment. If you cannot find the kernel within the time allowed, this assignment will be offered to you again in one planetary rotation of your home world or one idiopathic cycle appropriate to your species. . . .

Just once a day. Nita swallowed. Wednesday was coming fast. "All right," she said to the manual, "the meter's running; let's go!"

The red arc on her watch began to flash softly; as she watched, it subtracted a tiny bit of itself from the point at which it had started.

Okay, she thought, *where do you begin?*

Nita walked away from the terminal, down that empty street, to pause at the corner of Forty-second and Lexington, looking up and down the avenue. Nothing moved anywhere. She leaned her head back to look up at the spire of the Chrysler Building, glittering in the westering sun against an unusually clear blue sky.

If I were this universe's heart, where would I be?

If it was a riddle, it was one whose answer wasn't obvious. So for a long time Nita walked north on Lexington Avenue through the windy afternoon, looking, listening, trying to get the feel of the place. It was missing something basic that her own version of New York had, but she couldn't put her finger on what was missing. At Eighty-fourth Street, on a hunch, she turned westward, heading crosstown, and started to page through the manual again for some hint of what she was doing wrong. She found a lot of information about the structures of aschetic universes, and one piece of this caught her attention, for she'd been wondering about it.

Entire universes and continua are by definition too large and often too alien to allow quick kernel assessment and location while their genuine physical structures are displaying. Wizards on assessment/location duties therefore routinely avail themselves of a selective display option that screens out distracting phenomena, condenses the appearance and true distances of the space being investigated, and identifies the structure under assessment with a favorite structural paradigm already familiar to the wizard. Early assessment exercises default to this display option. . . .

So it gave me someplace I'm used to working, Nita thought. *Probably just as well.* She paused at the corner of Fifth Avenue and Eighty-fourth, looking across the street and downtown at the Metropolitan Museum of Art, and then went across the street and into Central Park, continuing to read through the manual. There were no more hints, and two hours were gone already. Nita looked at some of the spells she'd used for detection in the past, but they didn't seem much good for this. They were mostly for finding physical things, not other spells.

And the spells in the book don't seem to be working right, anyway, Nita thought as she came out at Eighty-sixth and Central Park West, turning south. She wasn't getting the usual slight tingle of the mind from the wizardries as she read. It was as she'd been warned: The manual's normal instant access to the fabric of wizardry didn't seem to be working here.

Either way, Nita started to feel that spells weren't the answer. *If that's not it, there has to be another way. Besides just wandering around!* But the silent streets in which nothing moved—no sound but the wind—made everything seem a little dreamlike, the stuff of a fairy tale, not a real place at all.

But it is *real. The only thing missing . . .*

. . . is the sound.

Nita stopped at the southwest corner of Central Park West and Eighty-first and thought. Then she went down the path from the corner to the planetarium doors, and cut across the dog run to go up the steps to the nearby terrace, where the "astronomical" fountain was. There she sat on a bench under the ginkgo trees, near where the water ran horizontally over the constellation-mosaicked basin, and looked at her watch. She had only two hours left. Part of her felt like panicking. *This isn't working; I don't have time to spend another day doing this; what about Mom!* But Nita held herself quiet, and sat there, and listened.

Water and the wind; nothing else. But even those sounds were superfluous. She could tune them out, the way she tuned out Dairine's CD player when she didn't want to hear it. That didn't take a spell.

And maybe I don't need to tune them out, anyway. For this place to be normal, for real, she needed to tune things *in*. She needed those sounds, the sounds that to her spelled out what life was like in the city, what made it its own self.

Traffic, for example. The horns that everybody honked even though it was illegal. The particular way the tires hissed on the road in hot weather, when the surface got a little sticky in the sun. The sound of trucks backing up and making that annoying high-pitched *beep-beep-beep*. Air brakes hissing. Car engines revving as the lights changed. Sirens in the distance. One by one, in her mind, she added the sounds to the silence. There was a kind of music to it, a rhythm. Footsteps on the road and on the sidewalks created some of that; so did the rattle of those bikes with the little wagons attached that the guys from the stores used to deliver groceries.

And so did the voices. People talking, laughing, shouting at one another in the street; those sounds blended with the others and started to produce that low hush of sound, like a river. It wasn't a steady sound. It ebbed, then flowed again, rising and falling, slowly becoming that long, slow, low, rushing throb that was the sound of the city breathing.

Not even breath. Something more basic. A pulse . . .

Nita held still. She could hear it now. It was not a pulse as humans thought of such things. It was much too slow. You would as soon hear a tree's pulse or breathing as this. But Nita was used to hearing trees breathe, and besides, their breath was part of this bigger one. Slowly and carefully, as if the perception was something she might break if she moved too suddenly, she turned her head.

The "sound" was louder to the south. If this place had a heart, it was south of her.

Nita got up carefully and, concentrating on not losing the way she was hearing things now, made her way back to the stairs and down from the fountain terrace, back toward Central Park West, then started heading south again. Within a block she knew she was going the right way. *It's stronger.*

Within another block she was so sure of what and how she was hearing that she didn't need to walk carefully anymore. Nita began to alternate jogging and walking, heading for the source of that heartbeat. Even in the silence, now that she'd let that recur, she could hear that slow rush of cityness underneath everything, like the sound she'd once heard of blood flow in an artery, recorded and much slowed down, a kind of windy growl. She got as far as Central Park South and realized that the source of the pulse was to her right and ahead of her: downtown, on the West Side somewhere.

Nita followed the pulse beat, feeling it get stronger all the time, as if it was in her bones as well as the city's. She went west as far as Seventh Avenue, then knew she was on the right track. The pulse came from her left, and it was much closer now. Another ten blocks maybe?

It turned out to be fifteen, but the closer Nita got, the less she cared about the distance, or the fact that she was dog tired. *I'm going to do it. It's going to be okay. Mom's going to be okay!*

She came out in Times Square, and smiled as she perceived the joke—there were lots of people who would have claimed that this was the city's heart. But her work wasn't done yet. The kernel was hidden here somewhere. Now that she knew what to listen for, Nita could feel the force of it beating against her skin, like a sun she couldn't see. Nita stopped there in the middle of a totally empty Times Square, all blatant with neon signs and garish, gaudy electric billboards along which news of strange worlds crawled and flashed in letters of fire, in the Speech and in other languages, which she didn't bother to translate. She turned slowly, listening, feeling . . .

There. A blank wall of a building. It was white marble, solid. But Nita knew better than to be bothered by mere physical appearance, or even some kinds of physical reality. She went to the wall, passed her hands over it.

It was stone, all right. But stone was hardly a barrier to a wizard. Nita jiggled the charm bracelet around on her wrist until it showed one spell she had loaded there, the charm that looked like a little house key. It was a molecular dissociator, a handy thing for someone who'd locked themselves out or needed to get into something that didn't have doors or windows. Nita gripped the charm; it fed the wizardry into her mind, ready to go. All she had to do was speak the words in the Speech. She said them, put her hands up against the stone, feeling the molecules slip aside . . . then reached her hands through the stone, carefully, since she wasn't sure if what she was reaching for was fragile.

She needn't have worried. Her first sense of it as her fingers brushed it was that it was not only stronger than the stone behind which it was hidden but stronger than anything else in this universe, which might reach who knew how many light-years from here in its true form rather than this condensed semblance-of-convenience. What Nita pulled out through the fog that she had made of the stone was a glittering tangle of light about the size of a grapefruit, a structure so complex that she could make nothing of it in a single glance . . . and that was just as it should be. This was a whole universe's worth of natural law—the description of all the matter and energy it contained and how they worked together—gathered in one place the same way that you could pack all of space into a teacup if only you took the time to fold it properly. The kernel burned with a tough, delicate fire that was beautiful to see.

But she didn't have time for its beauty right this moment. *Next time I'll have more time to just look at one of these*, Nita thought. *Right now I have to affect the local environment somehow.*

The longer she held the kernel in her hands, the more clearly Nita could begin to feel, as if in her bones, how this core of energy interacted with everything around it, was at the heart of it all. Squeeze it a little this way, push it a little that way, and this whole universe would change—

Nita squeezed it, and the sphere of light and power grew, and her hand sank into it a little, the "control structures" of the kernel fitting themselves to her. Her mind lit up inside with a sudden inrush of power, a webwork of fire—the graphic representation of the natural laws of this universe, of its physics, mathematics, and all the mass and energy inside it—and she knew that it was hers to command.

For a moment Nita stood there just getting the feel of it. It was almost too much. All that kept her in control was the fact that this was not a full-fledged universe but an aschetic one, purposely kept small and simple for beginners like her—a kindergarten universe with all the building blocks labeled in large bright letters, the corners on all the blocks rounded off so she couldn't hurt herself.

Still, the taste of the power was intoxicating. *And now to use it.* Through the kernel, Nita could feel the way all energy and matter in this universe interrelated, from here out to the farthest stars . . . and while she held what she held, she owned all that power and matter. She *ruled* it. Nita smiled and squeezed the kernel harder, felt her pulse increase as that of local space did—energy running down the tight-stranded web-work, obedient to her will.

In that clear afternoon sky, the clouds started to gather. The day went gray in a rush; the humidity increased, and the view of the traffic lights down the street misted, went indistinct. She felt the scorch and sizzle of positive ionization building in the air above the skyscrapers as the storm came rolling and rumbling in.

Nita held it in check for a while, let the clouds in that dark sky build and curdle. They jostled together, their frustrated potential building, but they couldn't do anything until Nita let them. Finally the anticipation and the growing sense of power was too much for her. *Do it!* she said to the storm, and turned it loose.

Lightning flickered and danced among the skyscrapers and from cloud to cloud as the rain, released, came instantly pouring down. The Empire State Building got hit by lightning, as it usually did, and then got hit several more times as Nita told the storm to go ahead and enjoy itself. Thunderclaps like gigantic gunfire crashed and rattled among the steel cliffs and glass canyons, and where Nita pointed her finger, the lightning struck to order. She made it rain in patterns, and pour down in buckets, but not a drop of it soaked through her clothes—the water had no power over *her*. And when some of the electrical signs started to jitter and spark because of all the water streaming down them, Nita changed the behavior of the laws governing electricity, so that current leaped and crept up the rain and into the sky, a slower kind of lightning, sheeting up as well as down.

In triumph Nita splashed and jumped in the flooding gutters, like a kid, then finally ran right out into the middle of the empty Times Square and whirled there in the wet gleam and glare all alone—briefly half nuts with the delight of what she'd done, as the brilliant colors of the lights painted the puddles and wet streets and sidewalks with glaring electric pigment, light splashing everywhere like Technicolor water. The feeling of power was a complete blast . . . though Nita reminded herself that this was just a step on the way to something much bigger. Curing her mother was going to be a lot more delicate, a lot more difficult . . . and the wizardry was going to cost her. But the innocent pleasure of doing exactly as she pleased with the power she'd come so far to find was something she badly needed.

The novelty took a while to wear off. Finally Nita banished the storm, sweeping the clouds away and right out of the sky with a couple of idle gestures—exactly the kind of thing a wizard normally couldn't do in the real world, where storms had consequences and every phrase of every spell had to be evaluated in terms of what it might accidentally harm or what energy it might waste. *It'd be great if wizardry were like this all the time,* Nita thought. *Find the heart of power, master it, and do what you like; just command it and it happens; just wish it and it's done . . .*

But that was a dream. Reality would be more work. And it would be more satisfying, though not all that different—for bioelectricity was just lightning scaled down, after all, and every cell in the body was mostly water. Now Nita stood there in the cool air, as the sun started to set in the cleared sky behind the skyscrapers, and looked again at the tangle of power that she held, this whole universe's soul. On a whim as she looked down at it, Nita altered its semblance, as she'd altered the look of the spell matrix she wore. Suddenly it wasn't a tight-packed webwork of light she was holding, but a shiny red apple.

Nita looked at it with profound satisfaction, and resisted the urge to take a bite out of it. *Probably blow me from here to the end of things*, she thought. She brought the kernel back over to where she'd found it, and held it up to the stone wall. It didn't leap out of her hand back to its place, as she'd half expected it would; it was reluctant. *It enjoys this kind of thing,* she thought. *It likes being mastered . . . being used.*

It likes not being alone.

Nita smiled. She could understand that. Carefully she said the words that would briefly dissolve the stone, and slipped the kernel back in.

Wait till Kit sees this, she thought, pulling her hands out of the stone and dusting them off, *when it's all over and Mom is better at last. He's gonna love it.*

She checked her watch. *Half an hour to spare; not too bad. I'll do better next time.* She turned the charm bracelet on her wrist to show the little disc that said GCT/25, her quick way back to the ingress gate. "Home," Nita said, and vanished.

She came out on the platform at Grand Central, invisible again; a good thing, for just as she stepped out of the gate, a guy went by driving a motorized sweeper, cleaning the platform for the rush hour that would start in just a couple of hours. Nita glanced at her watch. It was three in the morning; as predicted, the return gating routine had dropped her here two hours after she'd left. But she was six hours' worth of tired. She fished around in her pocket and came up with her transit circle . . .

. . . and couldn't bear to use it for a second or so yet. Nita walked off the platform out into the Main Concourse—where a guy with a wide pad-broom was pushing some sweeping compound along the shiny floor—and out past him, invisible, and up the ramp, to push open the door and stand on Forty-second street again. *This* time there was traffic, and garbage in the gutter, and horns honking; this time the streetlights were bright; this time the sidewalks were full of people, hurrying, heading home from clubs or a meal after the movies, hailing cabs, laughing, talking to each other. As Nita dropped her transit circle onto the sidewalk, out of the way of the pedestrians, the wind coming down Forty-second flung a handful of rain at her, like a hint of something happening somewhere else, or about to happen.

Nita grinned, stepped through her circle, and came out in her bedroom. She pulled the circle up after her, and had just enough energy to pull her jeans off, crawl into bed, and pull the covers up before the darkness of sheer exhaustion came down on her like a bigger, heavier blanket.

"Nita?"

"Huh?!" She sat up in bed, shocked awake. Her father stood in the doorway, drying his hands on a dish towel, looking at her with concern.

"Honey, it's eight-thirty."

"Omigosh!!" She leaped out of bed, and a second later was amazed at how wobbly she felt.

"Don't panic; I'll drive you," her dad said. "But Kit was here ten or fifteen minutes ago. I thought you'd gone already—you don't usually oversleep—and then he went so he wouldn't be late." Her dad looked at her alarm clock. "Didn't it go off? We'll have to get you another one."

"No, it's okay," Nita said, rummaging hurriedly in her drawer. "What time are we going to see Mom today?"

"When you get back from school."

"Good. I've got something to tell her." And Nita smiled. It was the first time in days that she'd smiled and it hadn't felt wrong.

It's going to work. It's going to be okay!

Tuesday Morning
and Afternoon

NITA'S FATHER TOOK THE blame for her lateness when he delivered her to the school's main office, and when her dad left, Nita went to her second-period social studies class feeling more or less like she'd been rolled over by a steam shovel—she was nowhere near recovered from the previous night's exertions. She waved at Jane and Melissa and a couple other friends in the same class, sat down, and pulled out her notebooks, intent on staying awake if nothing else.

This was going to be a challenge, as the Civil War was still on the agenda, and the class had been stuck in 1863 for what now seemed about a century. Mr. Neary, the social studies teacher, was scribbling away on the blackboard, as illegibly as ever. *He really should have been a doctor*, Nita thought, and yawned.

Neets?

She sat up with a jerk so sudden that her chair scraped on the floor, and the kids around her looked at her in varying states of surprise or amusement. Mr. Neary glanced around, saw nothing but Nita writing industriously, and turned back to the blackboard, talking about Abraham Lincoln at his usual breakneck speed while he wrote.

Nita, for her own part, was bending as far over as she could while she wrote, trying to conceal the fact that she was blushing furiously. *Kit—*

I was starting to think you were avoiding me!

No, I—

Where've you been*? Don't you answer your manual anymore?*

She could have answered him sharply . . . then put the urge aside. That was what had started this whole thing. *Look*, she said silently. *I'm really sorry. It was all my fault.*

All of it? Kit said. *Wow. Didn't think you were gonna go* that *far. The Lone Power's gonna be real surprised when It finds out you let It off the hook.*

His tone was dry but not angry . . . as far as she could tell. *Please*, Nita said. *I'd like to be let off it, too.*

There was a pause at Kit's end. *Where've you been? I've got some stuff to show you.*

It's, uh, it's been busy. I—

Look, Kit said, *save it for later. Wait for me after school, okay?*

Okay.

She felt him turn away in mind to become engrossed in the test paper that had just been put down in front of him. Nita turned her attention back to what her social studies teacher was doing at the blackboard . . . and was astonished to find that she *could*. Just that brief contact had suddenly lifted from her mind a kind of grayness that had been hanging over it since before her mom went into the hospital. *And now*, she thought, *even if Dairine can't help, maybe Kit can.*

But could he? *And what even makes me think that after the pain in the butt I've been, he's going to want anything to do with what I'm planning?* She desperately wanted to believe that he *would* want something to do with it, but she'd been pretty good at being wrong about things lately. *And even if I asked him, would he think I was just asking because—*

"Nita?"

Her head jerked up again. This time there was some subdued laughter from the kids around her. "Uh," she said, "sorry . . . what was the question?"

"Gettysburg," said Mr. Neary. "Got a date?"

"Yeah, but he'll have to stand on a box to reach," said a voice in the back of the room, just loud enough for Nita to hear, and for the kids around her to snicker at.

"July first through July third, eighteen sixty-three," Nita said, and blushed again, but more in annoyance this time. There were a number of guys in her classes who thought it weird or funny that Nita hung around with a boy younger than she was, and Ricky Chan was the tallest and handsomest of them. His dark good looks annoyed her almost as much as his attitude, and Nita couldn't think which satisfied her more: the fact that everyone around her knew she thought he was intellectually challenged—which drove Ricky nuts—or that if he ever *really* annoyed her, she could at any moment grab him by his expensive black leather jacket and dump it, and him, into one of several capacious pockets of otherspace that numerous alien species were presently using as a garbage dump. *Except that wizards don't do that kind of thing.*

But boy, wouldn't it be fun to do it just once!

Mr. Neary turned his attention elsewhere, and Nita went on taking notes. That class, and the rest of the day, passed without further event; and when the last bell rang at three-thirty and she went out into the parking lot, Nita saw Kit loitering by the chain-link fence near the main gate.

Nita headed for the gate, ignoring the voices behind her, even the loudest one: "Hey, Miss *WAH*-Neeta, where'd you send away for those legs?"

"Yeah, nice butt, nice face . . . shame about the giant bulging brain!"

The usual laughter from behind ensued. Nita began to regret her belief that changing out of jeans was going to make the slightest difference to her life at school.

Do you want to, or should I?

Want to what? Nita asked silently. *We're supposed to be above this kind of thing.*

Kit's expression, as she caught up with him, was neutral. *There are species who would love these guys,* he said. *As a condiment.*

She made a face as they walked up to the corner together, turning out of sight and out of range of the guys behind them. "Yeah," she said, "I was thinking about that. Among other things. Such as that I'm a complete idiot."

Kit waved the sentiment away.

"No," Nita said, "I mean it. You're not supposed to make this easier for me."

"Oh," Kit said. "Okay, suffer away."

She glared at him. Then when Kit turned an expression on her of idiot expectancy, like someone waiting to see a really good pratfall, she managed to produce a smile—yet another one that to her surprise didn't feel somehow illegal. "You won't even let me do *that* right," Nita said.

"My sister won't let me do it, either," Kit said. "I don't see why *you* should get to." He lowered his voice. "Now, what the heck have you been *doing* that you're sound asleep at eight o'clock?"

All the things she'd been intending to say when this subject came up now went out of her head. "My mother has a brain tumor," Nita said.

Kit stopped short. *"What?"*

She told him, fighting to keep her face from crumpling toward tears as she did so. She'd meant to keep walking while she told him, but she found it impossible. Everything came out in a rush that paradoxically seemed to take her entire attention. Kit just stood there staring at Nita until she ran down.

"Oh, my God," he said in a strangled voice.

"Hey, lookit, he's not wasting any time," said a voice from down the street behind them.

Other voices laughed. "Yeah, where's the box for him to stand on?" said one. The laughter increased.

Kit frowned. The laughter suddenly broke off in what sounded like a number of simultaneous coughing fits.

"Kit!" Nita said.

Kit didn't stop frowning, just took Nita discreetly by the elbow and started to walk. "If they're gonna sneak out behind the bleachers in the field at lunchtime and smoke," he said, "it's not *all* my fault if it starts catching up with them. Come on— Neets, why didn't you *tell* me?"

"I just did," she said, confused.

"I mean, when you found out!"

"Uh—"

"God, you weren't kidding; you *are* an idiot! Why didn't you *call* me? Even if you were mad at me!"

"I *wasn't* mad at you! I mean—"

"Then, why didn't you—"

"I didn't want to call you just because I *needed* you!"

Then Nita stopped. Earlier that had seemed to make some kind of sense. Now it seemed inexpressibly stupid.

"You're right," she said then. "I've been having a complete brain holiday. Sorry, sorry—"

"No," Kit said. They turned the next corner, into Kit's street, and he shook his head, looking more furious than before. "They didn't tell me. They didn't even *tell* me. I'm gonna—"

"Who?"

"Tom and Carl. I'm gonna—"

"Gonna *what*?" Nita said, exasperated. "They're our Seniors. They *couldn't* tell you anything. It was private stuff; you know that has to be kept confidential, and they can't even deal with it at all unless it affects a wizardry. They didn't tell me what *you* were doing, either. So forget it."

Kit was silent as they walked down the street. Finally he said, "What're we going to do?"

We.

Nita held out her arm to show him the charm bracelet. Kit looked at it, seeing what was under the semblance. "That's what I heard you making. How'd you get it done so fast?"

Fear, Nita thought. "You need it for the practice universes," she said, "and I don't have much time. They operate tomorrow, or Thursday at the latest. That's the best time to do the wizardry, when she's not awake—"

"You're going to need someone to backstop you," Kit said.

That thought had been on Nita's mind. Strange, though, how she now felt some resistance to the idea. "Look, if I can just—"

"Neets." Kit stopped, looked at her. "This is your *mom*. You can't take chances. You're gonna have to spend almost all your free time in those other universes, and you're gonna be wrecked. And I bet Tom and Carl told Dairine to butt out, didn't they?"

"Uh, yeah."

"Well?"

"Yeah, of course . . . yeah." *What was I going to do, tell him I don't* want *his help? What's the matter with me?* "Thanks."

Suddenly Nita felt more tired than she'd been even in school. "Look, we're going to the hospital to see her as soon as I get home. You want to come to the hospital with us?"

Kit looked stricken. "I can't today. We have to go clothes shopping; can you believe it? Dad says we absolutely have to. But you'll go tomorrow, right?"

"Yeah, we go every day. Dad goes a couple of times."

"So I'll go with you then. It'll give me time to read up on what you've been doing." They stopped outside Kit's house. "As long as it's okay with you," he said suddenly.

"Huh? Yeah," Nita said.

"Okay. You going to go straight off and practice when you get back?"

"Yeah, I have to."

"All right. Just *call* me when you get back in, okay? Don't forget." He punched her in the arm.

"Ow! I won't forget."

"Then tell your mom I'll see her tomorrow."

And Kit headed up the driveway and vanished into the house.

Nita let out a long breath of something that was not precisely relief, and went home.

Her dad was hanging up the phone in the kitchen. He looked unhappy. "Daddy," Nita said, "are you okay?"

Dairine came around the corner as her dad got his jacket off one of the dining-room chairs. "Yes," he said, "but I could be happier. That was Dr. Kashiwabara. She says they're going to have to reschedule Mom's surgery for Friday or Saturday. One of the specialists they need—the doctor who does the imaging—had some kind of emergency and had to fly to Los Angeles." He sighed. "He'll be back in a day, they said, but I'm not wild about the idea of your mother being operated on by someone who might be jetlagged."

Nita threw a look at Dairine, who just nodded once. There were ways to add so much energy to another human being that they might have a whole solar system's worth of lag and not be affected. This was one of the simplest wizardries, and not beyond Dairine's abilities right now, no matter what else might be going on. "I think it'll be okay, Daddy," Nita said, dumping her schoolbooks on the table. "Let's go see Mom."

They drove to the hospital and found her mother, surrounded by a large pile of paperbacks, talking brightly to the lady in the next bed. "The only good thing about this," her mom said as they pulled the curtain around her bed for some privacy, "is that I'm really getting caught up on my reading."

Nita was about to throw a small silence-circle around them all, until she noticed that Dairine was walking quietly around the bed, doing it already. She made a mental note to herself to let Dairine do everything wizardly that she was capable of right now. As her dad pulled a chair over to the bed, Dr. Kashiwabara stuck her head in past the curtain and greeted them all, and Nita's dad immediately went out into the hall with her.

Nita sat down in the chair, looking idly at the books as she took her mom's hand. Many of them were of a type of techno-thriller that her mother didn't usually read. "Your tastes changing, Mom?"

"No, honey." Her mother's smile was a little rueful. "I just read the parts with all the shooting and blowing things up, and then I imagine doing that to the tumor . . . when I'm not hitting it with lightning bolts and setting it on fire. Guided imagery's a good tool to use to help deal with this, they say. Whether it actually makes it go away or not, it's a way to constructively use the tension. One of the therapists has been coaching me in how to do it. It gives me something to do when my eyes give out."

Nita nodded, feeling her mom's pulse as Dairine sat down on the other side of the bed. There was a faint resonance to that other pulse she'd felt and heard in the practice universe, not merely a sound or sensation but a direct sensation of the inner life—under threat, but still strong. "So what have you been doing?" her mother said.

"A lot." Nita explained to her mother as quickly and simply as she could about the practice universes, and the work she was doing there so that she could learn how to rewrite the rules inside the mini-universe that was her mom's body, and then talk the cancer cells out of what they were doing. Her mother nodded as she listened.

"In a way it sounds like what the therapist's been showing me how to do," said Nita's mom. "Though your version might be more effective. Okay, honey, I don't see that it can hurt . . . You go ahead. But you realize that they're still going to have to operate."

"Yeah, I know. I thought about trying to take the tumor out, but it makes more sense to let the doctors do it. They've had more practice."

Her mother gave her a slightly cockeyed look. "Well, I think it's considerate of you to let them do something." She reached over to the other side of the bed and ruffled Dairine's hair. "Are you helping with this, sweetie?"

"No," Dairine said, and abruptly got up and went out through the curtain.

Her mother looked after Dairine with concern. "Oh no . . . what did I say?"

"Uhm," Nita said. "Mom, she can't help." Softly she explained the problem. "She's really upset; she feels useless. And helpless."

"*That* I can sympathize with," Nita's mother said, squirming a little in the bed. "Poor baby." She sighed. "I guess it's tougher to deal with than running around from planet to planet, having fun."

Nita found this idea more than usually exasperating. "Uh, excuse me . . . 'fun'? Mom, I've nearly had a ton of bricks dropped on me by a white hole, I've nearly been eaten by a great white shark, and the Lone Power's nuked me, dropped a small star on me, and tried to have me ripped apart by perytons. And Dairine may have had even more 'fun' than I have, not that I'd admit it to her. Wizardry has its moments, but it's not just fun. So gimme a break!"

Nita's mother looked at her thoughtfully. "If I haven't been taking it seriously enough, I'm sorry. It's still kind of hard to get used to. But, honey . . . if wizardry is so scary for you, so painful . . . why do you keep on *doing* it?"

Nita shook her head, not knowing where to begin. The rush you got from talking the universe out of acting one way and into acting another, with only the Speech and your intention for tools; to know what song the whales sing, and to help them sing it; to stand in the sky and look down on the world where you worked, and to be able to make a difference to it, and to *know* that you did—even in the Speech there were no words for that. And helping others do the same thing—particularly when spelling with a partner—"It doesn't always hurt," Nita said. "There's so much about it that's terrific. Remember when we took you to the Moon?"

Her mother's gaze went remote with memory. "Yes," she said. Her glance went back to Nita then. "You know, sweetie, sometimes I wake up and think I just dreamed that. Then Dairine comes in with that computer walking behind her . . ."

Nita smiled. "Yeah. There's a lot more like the Moon where that came from, Mom. And here, too. Life on Earth isn't a finished thing. New kinds of life keep turning up all the time. We have to be here for them, to help them get settled in."

"New kinds of life," her mother murmured.

"It just keeps on finding a way," Nita said.

And so does death, said a small cold voice in the back of her mind.

Nita gulped. "The hurt—I guess it balances out, even though you have to work at seeing it that way. But, Mom, a lot of energy goes into making wizards what they are. We have a responsibility to life, to What made it possible for us to be wizards in the first place. If you just take that power and use it while everything's going okay, and then, afterward, decide you don't like the hard part, and just dump it all and walk off—" She shook her head. "Things die faster if you do that. And it does happen. 'Wizardry does not live in the unwilling heart.' But sometimes . . . sometimes it's real hard to stay willing."

"Like now," her mother said.

"I am not going to just let this thing kill you without doing something to stop it," Nita said to her mother in the Speech, in which it is, if not impossible, at least most unwise to lie.

Her mother shivered. "I heard that. Good trick when it's not in a language I know."

"But you *do* know it," Nita said. "Everything knows it. On some level, even your cancer knows it . . . and I'm gonna do everything I can to talk it out of what it's doing to you." Nita tried hard to sound certain of what she was doing.

Her mother looked at her. "That's why you're looking so tired."

"Uh, yeah. You spend time in those other universes, which you don't spend here . . . and it wears you out a little."

"I suppose I shouldn't ask you if you've been doing your homework," her mother said.

Nita swallowed. "Mom, right now I'm doing the only homework that matters."

Her mother was silent. Then, softly, she said, "Honey, what if—what you're planning—"

Doesn't work? Nita couldn't bear to hear it, wouldn't have it said. "Mom, we won't know if that's a problem till I've done it. Meanwhile, let the doctors do their thing. If nothing else—"

"It might buy you some time?"

Nita's smile was slightly lopsided with pain. "I've bought too much time as it is," she said. "It's how I spend it that counts now."

Just then one of the nurses put her head in the door. "Mrs. Callahan, your medication . . ."

"Laura, can it wait half an hour? I still haven't seen my husband and my other daughter, and I'd like to be able to speak English to them, for a little while at least."

The nurse looked at her watch. "I'll check. I think that'll be all right." She went off.

"Is this the stuff to prevent the seizures?"

Her mother winced. "It's not just that now, honey. My eyes are bothering me, and the headaches are getting bad. They try to keep me from reading, but if I can't at least do that, I'll go completely nuts just lying here. Do me a favor? Go find Dairine and let me spend some time with her before Daddy comes back."

A nervous expression passed across her mother's face, which she wasn't able to hide.

"It's about the biopsy, isn't it?" Nita said.

Her mother closed her eyes, and Nita felt the fear that went right through her. "Yup," her mother said.

Nita didn't even have to ask, *Was it positive?* She knew. "I'll go find her," Nita said. But she didn't let go of her mother's hand. "Mom," she said, "I really hate this."

"I hate it, too."

"All I want is for you to be home again."

Her mother opened her eyes and gave Nita a sly look. "Yelling at you to clean your room?"

"Sounds like paradise."

"I'm going to remind you of that later."

Nita found a smile somewhere. "You do that."

"I will. Go on, sweetie. Do your work . . . and we'll see what happens."

Nita kissed her mom and got out of there in a hurry, before the mood changed. She went out into the hall and saw Dairine leaning in the doorway of a little alcove where there were some vending machines—her gaze trained on the floor, her arms folded.

Thanks for the circle, she said silently to Dairine as she went over to her. *You got a couple of minutes? Mom wants to talk to you.*

About what? I can't do anything. Dairine didn't look up. *All this power, and it's not enough.*

Nita leaned against the same wall, folded her arms, stared down at the same undistinguished gray linoleum. *I know,* she said. *It'd be nice to be able to just make this vanish . . . but . . .*

But what can I do?!

Don't let her go through this alone was all Nita could think of to say.

Dairine nodded and went off down the hall. Nita watched her sister go, small and quick and tense, shoulders hunched, into their mother's room.

Tuesday Evening

WHEN KIT GOT HOME at last and lugged his share of the shopping into the kitchen, it was nearly seven.

Neets? Kit said silently as he started unpacking the contents of too many plastic bags onto the sofa. There were some T-shirts and some new jeans, but mostly the contents of these bags seemed to be socks, socks, and more socks.

Nothing. *Nope, she's off doing her training-universe stuff already. Can't blame her.*

". . . and it's all got to be washed separately," his mother said, sounding less than enthusiastic, as she came in from the car. "Kit, honey, just make two piles, dark stuff and light stuff. This is going to take me forever."

Ponch came bounding in from outside, released from the backyard. "I think certain people want a walk," Kit's dad said as he entered and started unpacking another bag onto the kitchen table. "You go do that, son; I'll take care of these— Did you leave *any* socks in the store for the rest of humanity?" he called after Kit's mother.

"No. You're going to be wearing these till you die. Where did you hide the laundry basket?"

Kit gladly left his father in the company of all the world's socks, went to the back door, looked at the leash . . . then picked up the other one he'd left hanging beside it, invisible to nonwizardly eyes. "Ponch?"

"Yeah-yeah-yeah-yeah-yeah-yeah!"

They went down the street together, Ponch running ahead to take care of business while Kit went along behind him, paging through his manual as twilight deepened toward full dark. He found a good-sized section discussing the theory and structure of the practice universes but no information on how to get into them. *Access to the aschetic continua and to more detailed information is released on a need-to-go basis*, the manual said. *Consult your Area Advisory or Senior for advice and assessment.*

Yeah, and what if they say no? Kit closed the manual and shoved it into his "pocket." *And what if Nita gets pissed about my asking, because she thinks I think she can't handle it?*

Better not to get involved.

But I am involved.

It wasn't just that he liked Nita's mother. He couldn't imagine a world without her, and knew Nita couldn't, either. The shock of finding out what was happening was giving way to the fear of what life would be like afterward . . . after—

He didn't even want to think it. *And neither does Neets . . .*

Her fear was on Kit's mind. The two of them had been in some frightening situations. Mostly, though, these hadn't involved the kind of fear that lingered; they'd been over with in a hurry. What Kit had felt in Nita today, by contrast, had settled deep into her and made her something of a stranger. *And there's nothing I can do to help, really. She's got to get over it herself.*

If she can.

Ponch came running back to Kit. *Let's go!*

They headed down the street, to the side gate of the school. It was usually locked, but this was hardly a problem for Kit; he and the padlock through the gate's latch were old friends. As he reached the gate he reached out and held the padlock briefly. "Hey there, Yalie," he said in the Speech.

It wasn't as if inanimate objects were intelligent, as such, but they didn't mind being treated that way. *Who goes there?*

"Like you don't know."

The padlock popped open in his hand. Kit slipped it out, softly opened the gate and let himself and Ponch through, then locked up again. "You keep an eye on things now."

You can depend on me.

Kit smiled. Ponch had launched himself away across the grass, in the general direction of the school buildings. Kit let him run awhile, then whistled to call him back. All the lights in the school were off except for the exit lights at the ends of the hallways, and the houses nearby were all screened from the road and parking lot on this side by hedges. No one could see them in the near-darkness.

He shook out the wizardly leash and put the shorter loop around his wrist. Ponch ran back to him, jumped up, and put his forepaws against Kit; Kit braced himself and slipped the bigger loop around the dog's neck.

"Ready?"

"Ready."

Together they stepped into the deeper dark—

—and walked several steps more through it before breaking out into the light. There wasn't *much* light, though. A dim gray illumination inhabited the space, a thunderstorm twilight, with a greenish tinge like a bruise. A fog swirled around them, too, of the same color as the light. *Where is this?* Kit said silently to Ponch, down the leash. *I wasn't thinking of this.*

Neither was I. I don't always come out where I'd planned to.

They walked on through the grayness together. Ponch was sniffing at the featureless ground as they went. *Not very exciting*, Kit said. *How about if we—*

Not yet.

This assured tone from his dog was strange enough, but there was also something urgent about it. *You smell something?*

Always. But here—Ponch smelled the air, then went forward again with his nose to the ground—*it's something different.*

Like what?

Like— The light was getting dingier, fading away—an odd, slow effect, as if the universe were hooked up to a dimmer, and the whole thing were being turned slowly, slowly down. *It's you, but it's* not *you*, Ponch said, perturbed.

Dimmer and dimmer . . . and then Kit caught his first sight of them in the dark.

A rustling, a shifting in the shadowless light that was fading away all around him . . . and the sudden thought, as the hair went up on the back of his neck was: *I don't want to be in the dark with* them*!*

He had never really seen them, when he was little. *Well, of course not! I was imagining them.* But his early childhood had been haunted by these creatures themselves by night, and the fear of them by day. Kit took a step backward. Beside him Ponch held his ground, but he whimpered softly, the same eager sound he made when he had a squirrel in his sights.

The rustling sound got louder and seemed to come from all around him. Kit glanced about, getting more nervous by the minute. His childhood night fears hadn't been anything like what some adults seemed to expect: unlikely things hiding somewhere specific—under the bed, in the closet, or behind a dresser. They'd been nowhere near so easy to nail down, or to ridicule. Silly monster-shapes would have been infinitely preferable to his tormentors, which had had no shapes at all. Shadow had been their element, twilight their breeding place; and if summer had been Kit's favorite season when he was little, it was because in summer the nights were shortest and the twilight a long time coming. It had been years since he'd thought of these creatures. *But maybe they haven't forgotten me.* And now, in a place where things that weren't real could become that way, his fears had come looking for him.

But have they? Kit thought. *Or did I find them . . . make them . . . the way I made those other worlds?*

He clenched his jaw as the scrabbling sound of jaws munching and chewing around him got louder. *It doesn't matter*, he thought. *If I run away now, they win. No way I'm going to let that happen.* His eyes narrowed. *I'm a wizard. And more than that, I'm* thirteen*! I got over these things years ago!*

But would that make a difference? The shadows grew deeper, the scrabbling noises louder than before, closer. The thought of dead eyes staring at him out of the dark, no-color eyes that were black holes even in the night, brought the hair up on the back of his neck. Kit turned, thinking he saw something—the old familiar way the shadow turned and writhed against his bedroom wall when a car went by in the street, flinching from the headlights, then wavering up and out into the dark again when the lights died, the shape towering up against the wall and dissolving its features. Kit gasped, felt around in the back of his mind for a wizardry that would save him—

—then abruptly stopped, because nothing was towering up anywhere. The scrabbling noises were still going on all around him and getting louder, but whatever these things were, they weren't his night terrors. Now he caught the first real glimpse of one of them as it came close enough to be clearly seen through the dimness . . . and what Kit saw was something that looked more like a giant centipede than anything else. It didn't seem to have a front or back end, just a middle, and about a million legs, but that was all.

Millipede, Kit corrected himself, watching the shiny gray-black creature, about a yard long, come chittering and skittering along this space's streaky gray floor, at the head of a group of maybe twenty of them. This whole scenario was looking more and more like a bug's-eye view of a kitchen floor late in the day, before anyone turned the lights on. The surface on which he and Ponch and the millipedes stood even started to look like linoleum.

Kit listened to his pulse starting to go back to normal as the first millipede came cruising along toward him, all those little feet whispering against the floor—a completely innocuous sound, now that he knew what it was. Ponch looked suspiciously at the creature, and a growl stirred down in his throat.

No, it's okay, Kit said. *Let it go. It won't hurt us.*

Are you sure?

Kit had a spell ready just in case. *I think it's all right*, he said. *Just let it go. Unless—*

"I'm on errantry, and I greet you," Kit said in the Speech.

The millipede creature paused, reared half its body up off the ground, and faced the two of them, its little legs working in midair. But there was no sense of recognition, no reply. The creature dropped down again and went flowing on past him and Ponch, all those legs making a tickly shuffling sound as it went. All its friends went flowing away after it, the little legs rustling and bustling softly along on the floor. Kit watched them vanish into the still-growing shadows, and slowly relaxed.

Now why did you make those? Ponch said, looking after them with a disapproving expression.

Did I make them?

I know I didn't, Ponch said in a reproachful tone. *And I don't care for the way they smelled. Don't make any more, all right?*

I think we're in agreement on that. Kit went forward, walking but not with intention to make another universe, or anything else, right this second. He just wanted to recover a little.

Ponch padded along beside him, his tongue hanging out. *Those were like the things I see sometimes when I'm asleep and it doesn't go right.*

Kit knew that Ponch dreamed, but it hadn't occurred to him that dogs might have nightmares. *So what do you usually do when you see them?*

Bite them . . . and then run away.

Kit laughed. *I think if I bit one of those, it wouldn't have tasted real wonderful.* But once he'd seen the creature clearly, it hadn't seemed terribly threatening. In the past he'd seen aliens that had looked much more horrendous. *If it was a nightmare, it was someone else's.*

Though if things had gone a little differently, it could have been mine. If I'd run, for example. Kit was suddenly certain of that. *I need to watch what I think in here, not let my mind wander.*

He looked down at Ponch. *You want to make something first?*

Squirrels, Ponch said.

Kit rolled his eyes. *Look, I changed my mind. Let me go first. We can do the squirrels last, and you can have yourself a big run around while I rest.*

All right.

They walked through fifteen or twenty universes more. It was getting easier for Kit now to imagine them quickly, but despite that he spent a little more time in each one, making sure the small details looked correct. *After all, if these things are going to be here after I'm gone, I should take a little more care.* In one of them he spent a long while under that world's Saturn-like rings, watching to make sure they behaved as they really should when they rose and set. In another he stood on a long narrow spit of land pushing out into a turbulent sea, while the waves crashed all around him, and waited what seemed like nearly an hour for what he knew was coming: a fleet of huge-sailed ships that came riding up out of a terrible storm and with difficulty made landfall by that strange new shore.

As the last of the strangers came up out of the sea and into their new home, bearing their black banner with its single white tree, Kit glanced down at Ponch, who sat beside him, supremely unconcerned, scratching behind one ear.

The dog looked up as he finished scratching. *Aren't you done yet? Why don't you find one you like and* stay *there?*

Kit had to laugh. *Like* you *want to.*

Well, yes!

Come on, then. Squirrels . . .

Ponch leaped forward, and the sea and sky vanished as that universe flowed around them, full-formed—a great grove of those huge trees suddenly standing around the two of them as if it had been there forever. A veritable carpet of squirrels shrieked and leaped away as Ponch came plunging down into the middle of them.

Kit chuckled and went strolling off among the trees while the barking and squeaking and chattering scaled up behind him. *Maybe Neets'll be back by the time I get home*, he thought, heading into the depths of the green shade. *She's got to see this.*

The greenness went darker around him, the trees becoming fewer but much taller, and their high canopy becoming more solid. Kit stuffed his hands into his pockets and gazed down at the grass as he scuffed through it. He was feeling oddly uncomfortable. Until now any thought of Nita would have been perfectly ordinary. But now thinking about her unavoidably brought up the image of her mother. . . . It was as unavoidable as the idea of what might happen to her.

Imagine if it was my mama. Or my pop . . .

But Kit couldn't imagine it. His mouth went dry just at the thought. *It's no wonder she didn't call me. She's been completely freaked out.*

The shadows fell more deeply around him as he went, and though Kit could still feel the grass under his feet, he noticed that it was becoming indistinct. *At least Neets is working on an answer*, he thought. But there was no avoiding the thought that no matter what any of them did for Nita's mother, wizards or not . . . finally, there was always the possibility that *nothing* would work.

He passed the last of the trees and came to a place where there was only the vaguely seen grass left. Kit walked slowly toward the edge of this, and slowly the light around him faded down toward darkness again—a clean plain empty darkness, not like the place where the millipedes had been: simply space with nothing in it. He paused there, turned to look behind him. Distant, as if seen through a reducing lens, all the trees were gathered together in their little halo of sunlight and glowing green grass, and Kit could just make out a small black shape running back and forth and being avoided, and then chased, by many little gray forms.

Kit turned around and looked out into the dark again. Now it was just an innocent void—no millipedes, and no ghosts of childhood fears, either. *I wonder how I got so scared of the dark, anyway?* It all seemed such a long time ago, and that phase of his life had come to an end, without warning, when he was eight. He could remember it vividly, those first heady nights when he *realized* that he wasn't afraid anymore and could lie there in the dark and stare at the ceiling of his room and not be afraid of falling asleep—not have to lie there shaking at the thought of what lay waiting for him on the other side of dream.

Before that, the sight of this would have left me scared to death. But now there was something intriguing about this imageless emptiness. Kit stood there for a long while, and then felt something cold and wet touch his hand. He looked down. Ponch was sitting there beside him, gazing up at him.

Bored already?

Bored? Oh, no. But it isn't good to leave you by yourself a long time. It's rude.

Kit smiled. *It's okay . . . I coped.* He looked back toward the trees. There was a gray line beneath the nearest trees: the squirrels, looking for Ponch.

Ponch looked back, too. *It happened faster that time*, Ponch said, *this world.*

Yeah, Kit said.

I think it was because you'd seen it before.

Kit looked down at his dog, briefly distracted. It wasn't as if Ponch wasn't normally fairly smart. But this kind of thought, or interaction, even when the Speech was involved, wasn't exactly what Kit would have expected. *Is he getting smarter? Or am I just getting better at understanding him?*

Or is it a little of both?

There was no telling. Now Kit looked back into the darkness again and found not even the shadows of fear in it. The only things that now seemed to lie hidden there were wonder and possibility. What Kit found inexpressibly sad, considered together with this, was the thought of what was happening to Nita's mother, the limits of possibility in his own world all too clearly delineated.

Are we done? Ponch asked after a moment.

Not just yet, Kit said. *I think I want to take it a little further.*

What will you make?

Kit thought about that, and then, for no particular reason, about the millipedes. *If I can make fears real . . .*

. . . could I make hopes real, too?

He looked out into the dark, and found nothing there for the moment but uncertainty.

Kit shook his head. *I don't want to make anything just yet*, he said to Ponch. *Let's just walk.*

They headed into the darkness. Kit let the light fade slowly behind them, until the two of them went forward together in utter blackness. There was no way to judge how far they went except by counting paces. Kit soon lost count, and stopped caring about it. There was something liberating about not knowing where you were going, just surrendering yourself to the night—and not making anything, either, but just being there, and letting the darkness be there, too, not trying to fill it with form but letting it exist on its own terms.

The blackness pressed in around them until it seemed to Kit to almost have a texture, like water, becoming a medium in its own right—not something unfriendly, just something *there*. It slowly became enjoyable. *If I had any scared-of-the-dark left in me*, Kit thought, *it's definitely cured now.* But after a while he began to lose interest, and once again he prepared to say good-bye to the dark for the time being.

Then Kit paused, for he thought he saw something.

Often enough, on this trip and the last, he'd had the illusion of seeing something in the blackness when nothing was there. Now Kit tried to see more clearly, and couldn't get that tiny glitter of light—for it *was* light—to resolve. *Not in front of us, though.*

Under us?

He couldn't be sure. *Ponch, you smell anything?*

No. What is it?

Look down there.

Kit got down on his hands and knees. This brought him closer to the minuscule glint of light, but not close enough. He passed his hands over the surface he'd been walking on. The light was underneath it . . . inches down, or miles, he couldn't tell.

I wonder . . .

Kit pressed against the surface. Did it give a little? It hadn't ever actually felt springy under his feet, but now Kit found himself wondering if this was because he'd been taking it for granted as a hard surface, and it had accommodated him.

He pressed harder against it. A strange feeling, as if the surface was giving under his hands, or under his will. *Let's see . . .*

Slowly, slowly Kit's hands sank into the darkness as he pushed. He slipped one out, rested it where the surface was still hard, and concentrated on the other hand, sliding it further and further down into that cool, resistant darkness. Faintly he could see the glow from that tiny spark or grain of light silhouetted against his fingers. He reached even further down, having to lie flat on the surface now, pushing his arm in up to the shoulder.

Got it—

Kit closed his fist on the light, started to withdraw his arm. It was difficult. The blackness resisted him. As he exerted himself, beginning to breathe hard, he felt a faint stinging sensation between two of his fingers. Looking down, he saw the spark escape between them and slip down into the dark again.

He pushed his hand down into the darkness once more, recovering the spark. It did sting, a sharp little sizzle like licking the end of a battery. Kit closed his hand again, pulled upward. Once more the spark slipped free, drifting lower, out of his reach.

Kit took a deep breath, not sure why he had to have this thing . . . *but I'm going to, and that's all there is to it.* He reached down as far as possible, but couldn't quite reach it. Finally he took a breath, held it, and pushed his face and upper body right down into that cool liquid blackness. By stretching his arm down as far as it would go, Kit just managed to get his hand underneath the spark. This time he didn't try to grasp it, just cupped it in his palm, and slowly, slowly brought his hand up through the pliant darkness. After a few seconds Kit dared to lift his face out, gasping, and pushed himself to his knees, while ever so slowly lifting his cupped hand.

The little glint of light almost slipped out of his hand, just under the surface. Kit stopped, let it settle, then slowly pulled his hand up toward him. The liquid darkness drained out of his hand, pouring away, and abruptly the spark flowed away with it . . .

. . . into Kit's other hand, which he'd put under the one that had the spark in it. As the last ribbons of darkness flowed away, there that tiny glint of light remained.

Kit sat down on the dark surface, getting his breath back. He could feel Ponch's breath on his neck as the dog looked curiously over his shoulder. *What is it?*

I don't know, Kit said. *But I'm going to take it home.*

They both gazed at it. It was not bright: an undifferentiated point source of light, faint, with a slight cool green cast to its radiance, like that of a firefly. Kit was briefly reminded of an old friend, and smiled at the memory. On a whim, he leaned in close to the little spark, breathed on it. It didn't brighten, as a spark of fire would have, but it stung his hand more emphatically.

Kit reached sideways to his claudication, pulled it open, and with the greatest care slipped the little spark in. When he was sure it was safe, he closed the pocket again and got to his feet, wobbling.

You all right, boss?

I think so. That took a lot out of me. Let's go home.

All right. The leash wizardry tightened as Ponch pulled Kit forward. *What was that about?*

Kit shook his head. *I'm not sure*, he said. The light of the normal world, nearly blinding by contrast to where they'd been, broke loose around them. *I think it was because it was . . . all alone.*

They stood there under the streetlight, and then Kit undid the leash and let Ponch go sprinting down the road. A late blackbird repeated a few solitary notes up in a tree. *Just me*, it sang, *just me.*

Kit stood listening in the dark . . . then went after Ponch.

Late Tuesday Evening

IT WAS A QUIET drive home from the hospital for Nita and Dairine and their dad. It was as if they'd all been hoping that when the tumor was removed, a closer look at it would prove the diagnosis wrong. But it wasn't going to happen that way. *I can't waste a minute, now*, Nita thought. *Every second I'm not working on this, those things are multiplying inside her. Kit'll understand. I've got to get going . . . and I can't wait for him.*

Nonetheless she tried to contact Kit before she left. She couldn't find him; the manual gave her the same subject-is-not-in-ambit message as before. *He never did get a chance to tell me just where he was, or how he's doing that*, she thought, dropping her transit circle to the floor and watching it flare with the brief shiver of life and light that meant the spell was ready. *Gotta find out . . .*

Along with several other wizardries, Nita had added her invisibility spell to her charm bracelet, as a small dangling ring with nothing inside it. Now she activated it and a moment later stepped through the transit ring, popping out once more in that vacant doorway in Grand Central. This time of day there were a lot more people around, and a fair number of trains coming in and out. It took Nita some minutes to get down to the worldgate end of the platform, as she had to sidestep in one direction or another about every three paces to keep from being run over by commuters who couldn't see her. At least the gate was idle and ready for her when she reached it. She went through in a hurry.

On the other side she found the platform empty again, and everything quiet. Nita walked down to the gateway on the Main Concourse and paused there to look at the painted sky. The figures of all the constellations were strange—the center of the "sky" not a bull, here, but a strange cat-shape, like a jaguar leaping with outstretched paws. Other odd forms shared the ecliptic with it: lizards and frogs and birds with long curling tails. Even this sky's color was different, a deep violet blue rather than the creamy Mediterranean color of the ceiling that Nita was familiar with.

She went up the ramp across the empty, shining floor and past the information booth—which was a brass ziggurat here—and came out into what at first she took for early evening. Then Nita got a glimpse of the sun and realized that it was afternoon . . . but in a Manhattan that was definitely not her usual one.

The skyscrapers all around were capped with stepped pyramids of the kind she had just seen substituted for the usual information booth inside the terminal. Uniformly the buildings seemed to be made of a golden stone—or maybe this was just the effect produced by that strange sun, which was bigger than it should have been, and was orange gold, though it stood at a height more like that of noon than sunset.

Down the center of the street ran a green strip of grass that reminded Nita of the built-up flower beds running down the middle of each block of Park Avenue. She looked across the street, and up; from high on the tops of some of the buildings south of Forty-second, Nita saw blinding orange light reflecting back. *Mirrors?* she thought. And the sky was very dark blue, almost a violet color. She was reminded of the way the sky looked on Mars. *Maybe not as much oxygen in the atmosphere?* Nita thought. *An old Earth, maybe; a tired one . . .*

It didn't matter. Her job was to find the place's kernel. And it would be better hidden, here.

She sat down on the curb of that empty Forty-second Street and listened. A slower pulse this time, fainter . . . like a place running down, a heart beating more out of habit than from any desire to go on living. Resignation? Could a whole universe feel resigned, ready to let go of life? It was an odd sensation. *But ours is old, too. Does* it *feel that way?*

After a few seconds she put the thought aside. There was something about the light here that was affecting her, maybe, or just the influence of this place's great age. But the realization itself could be useful. She'd listen for a slower pulse, a more leisurely beat . . .

Nita closed her eyes, held still, and felt for the kernel, the heart. She had no idea what this city sounded like when it was inhabited. But the wind, breathing down between the skyscrapers, didn't change. She listened to it, and let it give her hints.

Very slowly, they came. Strange hornlike sounds, not the wind but something else . . . also the muted cries of birds and animals, the clatter of machinery. Nita put her hands flat down on the sidewalk on either side of her, feeling it, listening through the touch.

The sidewalk was stone, not concrete. Its gray-black basalt was quarried out of the island itself—brought here in great slabs by mechanical means of which Nita got glimpses—then carved to size, set in place, and fastened by some physical process that she didn't understand, again sensed only obscurely and at a great distance in time. There was a characteristic scent to the stone, sharp, hot—*They used lasers on it, maybe?*—then a glimpse of some kind of crystal, maybe not exactly the lasers Nita understood but similar enough.

She started to think that this approach might have been typical of the people who built this place, simple techniques and very advanced ones combined—an "old science," more like wizardry than anything else, and a "new science," far ahead of anything her own world had. And this world would have been that way because of the way its own universal law ran, a combination of some kind of science actually left over from some other universe—*That's weird!*—with something newer, homegrown: the two sorts of law tangled together but never perfectly melded, the ancient tension between them defining a particular feeling, unique to this world, a vibration like what a wizard could hear in a crystal's heart, a pulse not slow but actually very fast—

Then Nita heard it, a buzz, a faint whine like a bee going by. *Got it!*

She opened her eyes and turned slowly where she sat, checking what she "heard" and felt against the evidence of her other senses—

—and caught a sudden motion of something down the street. Nita stared in surprise. Something moved there, going across Forty-second Street and heading uptown; crossing the street, low . . .

. . . *rolling* across the street? Nita stood up to see better but got only a glimpse as whatever it was went up Lexington Avenue and vanished behind the building at the corner. If what she'd seen was a machine, it was one the likes of which Nita had never seen before. And while there *was* some machine-based life that had become sentient, this didn't look like any member of the various mechlife species with which Nita was familiar. From where she'd been sitting, this looked more like a long stretched-out Rollerblade—

Weird, but it can wait. Nita stood still and listened again, shutting everything out but this place's own pulse. *Uptown . . .* The sense was fainter this time, which didn't surprise her; she knew the tests would be getting harder. Nonetheless, it was clear enough to follow, and whatever Nita had seen down the road was heading in the same direction.

She went after it, not with any concern for her safety—after all, the practice universes were limited to wizards—but with considerable curiosity. As she came around the corner of Forty-second and Lex, Nita looked uptown, where the ground rose slightly, and saw something rolling up the sidewalk on the left-hand side of the avenue. It wasn't a single object at all, but a number of them, rolling away from her in a loose cluster. In this strange, rich light, they gleamed a dark bluish metallic color. Most of them looked about the size of tennis balls, at this distance, but there were two or three of them that were larger, maybe soccer-ball size. They were approaching the corner of Forty-fourth and Lex. As Nita watched, they rolled out onto the ornate pavement of Lexington Avenue, here all covered up and down its shining white length with characters in some alien language, then crossed the avenue and headed east down the side street.

Nita began to jog after them, crossing Lexington and looking down as she did at the huge colored characters inlaid in slabs of stone into the surface of the street. The workmanship was beautiful; you couldn't see so much as a crack between the inlay and the road itself, all done in a pearly white stone like alabaster. *I wonder what this looks like from a height*, she thought. *And what the letters say . . .* She grinned as she headed toward the corner where the blue spheres had turned. *Be funny if it wasn't some incredibly significant message, but just the name of the street.* She came to the corner of Forty-fourth, headed around it at a run—

—and instantly found herself tripping over several perfectly spherical shiny blue objects, which had been in the act of rolling back up the sidewalk toward her.

Nita spent the next three seconds trying not to fall, trying not to bang into the beautifully and bizarrely carved wall of the building to her left, and trying not to step on the spheres, several of which were still rolling toward her. She finally got her balance back and stood there bracing herself against the wall and breathing hard for a few seconds, while the five spherical things, like blue-metal ball bearings of various sizes, rolled around her and then paused, one after another.

"*Dai stihéh,*" they said to her, five times over.

Nita's jaw dropped.

"Uh, *dai,*" she said.

The giant blue ball bearings looked at her with mild interest. At least Nita *felt* that she was being looked at, but with exactly what, there was no telling. The spheres had no features of any kind; the only thing she could see in them was the reflection of the skyscrapers behind her, the sky, and her own face, wearing an embarrassed expression.

"Where's the rest of you?" said one or another of the ball bearings.

Confused, Nita looked around her. " 'The rest'? There's just one of me. I mean, I have a—I mean, there's another wizard I work with, but he's—"

" 'He'? There's just one of them?" The ball bearings sounded disappointed.

"Uh, yeah," she said. "We come in ones, where I come from."

The ball bearings seemed to be regarding her with faint disappointment. "But there *are* more of you," one said.

Nita hadn't previously heard the Speech spoken with nothing but plural endings, even on the adjectives, and she was getting more confused every moment. "Well, in general, yes."

"Look, it's another singleton, that's all," one of them said to the others. "Looks like we're unusual in this neighborhood; the rest of us need to get used to it. It doesn't matter, anyway. We're all wizards together . . . that's the important thing."

"Uh, yes," Nita said. "Sorry, but what exactly *are* you?"

"People," said the blue ball bearings, in chorus.

Nita smiled. "Something else we have in common. Do you have something that other people call you?"

The spheres bumped into one another in sequence, and with their striking produced a little chiming chord, like a doorbell saying hello.

Nita took a breath and tried to sing it back at them. After a pause the spheres bumped together again, creating a soft jangling noise, which Nita realized was a regretful comment on her accent. "Sorry," she said. "Sometimes I'm not much good at staying in one key."

The spheres jangled again, but there was a humorous sound to it. "So call us Pont," one of them said.

Nita grinned a little; in the Speech it was one of the adjectival forms of the word for the number five. "Sure. It's nice to meet you. I'm Nita."

The spheres bumped themselves cordially into her ankles. "You guys here to practice looking for the kernel?" she said.

"Yes," one of them said.

"Well, no," said another.

"What we mean is, we've done this one already," said a third. "But the others have a head start, and they're running against time, so if you want to get in on it, you'd better hurry."

Pont started to roll down the street, and Nita followed them. "Others? How many more people are here?"

"Oh, just a few on this run," Pont said. "Some of them are repeating a secondary exercise—their time wasn't good enough the last cycle out."

"I haven't done this one before," Nita said. "Is it hard?"

The spheres looked at her. Two of them, to Nita's surprise, melded into one, running together exactly the way two drops of water become one, without even ceasing to roll. "How many of these have you done before?"

"Just one."

"Huh," Pont said. Nita couldn't repress a snort of laughter; the spheres' tone of voice was almost identical to one of Dairine's. "That's not bad. Usually you get a couple between this one and the starter scenario. You must have found the first one pretty quickly."

"I don't know," Nita said. "The manual was vague about the projected solution times—"

"Oh, the manuals," they said, and a couple of them bounced up and down in midroll, a shrug. "They're not much good in these spaces . . . and even outside them, they don't always correctly predict what's going to happen in here. You learn not to pay too much attention to them in testing mode. And you figure things out yourselves . . . but you're doing that already." They were looking up at Nita's charm bracelet, she could tell.

They paused at the corner of Third and Forty-fourth, and Nita looked up and down the street, listening. That high whining buzz was still perfectly audible if she stopped to listen for it, and still coming from the north, but also east a little more. "At least another block over," she said.

"Lead the way."

She trotted across Third and looked down at the patterns in the pavement again. "You know what these mean, Pont?"

"Not a clue," Pont said as they rolled across the avenue after her. "I think we're lacking the necessary cultural referents."

"You're not alone." They headed northward again, past the sleek, polished goldstone frontages of the buildings. It was odd that though these had doorways every now and then, there were no windows at street level, or lower than about thirty feet off the ground. This feature was doubtless expressive of some truth about this universe, but Nita didn't have the slightest idea what that might be.

"This is definitely one of the odder practice universes," Pont said as they made their way across Forty-fifth and on past more blind walls.

Nita raised her eyebrows. "Oh? What makes you say that?"

"Well, the way the space here is curved is unusually acute. The lack of entasis makes it—"

"Oh, come on, the entasis level is fine. It's just that everything looks odd to *you*," said another of the balls.

"It does not. It's perfectly obvious that *you* just don't know—"

"You're both crazy," yet another of the balls chimed in. "If you just—"

Nita had had plenty of arguments with herself in her head, but now she thought she was hearing one in a form she'd never imagined. "Look, don't fight about it," she said. "It wastes time. Pick just *one* of you to tell me, or something."

This astonished Pont so much that they stopped rolling and stared at one another. Nita stood still and waited for them to sort themselves out, while making a mental note that when she got back to where the manual worked at its normal speed, she was going to look up this life-form in a hurry.

"Well?" Nita said.

One of the five—the two who had combined themselves had come apart again as they were all crossing Forty-fifth—now said, "You could put it this way—"

Its surface shimmered. Without any warning at all, Nita found herself seeing the world the way Pont, or one of it, did—a landscape so alien that she could make almost nothing of it. Everything had a metallic sheen to it, and everything was fluid and in constant motion, running or rolling down one surface or another. And every surface was curved. It was like a world made of mercury, not just silvery but in a hundred different colors. Every single thing Nita could see was shaped like some version of a sphere, tiny or massive, everything either already perfectly spherical or working hard to get that way. There were no straight lines anywhere. Where it could be seen, even the horizon was curved.

Nita blinked. More than mere vision was involved in what she was perceiving. This space was acutely curved, so that its sky seemed to bend down and cover you like an umbrella. It was a perspective both claustrophobic and oddly big, giving you the illusion that you could wrap that universe around you like an overcoat, an absolutely huge one.

"Wow," Nita said. At first she was eager to break out of this way of seeing things. But then she caught herself, and looked a little harder. *This is weird, but—I wonder . . .* She held still, watched, and listened. Listening didn't do much good in this worldview; all the motion happened in silence. But the motion had a trend in one general direction. Everything Nita could see, everything that slid or rolled or pulsated around her, had a slight drift toward the direction in "front" of her—northward and eastward, though a little more eastward than the way she'd originally been heading.

Aha, Nita thought. *One point of view is good, but a second one from another mind helps you fine-tune your first one. It's like triangulating.* "Okay, okay," Nita said, and the image of the world-as-mercury oozed and flowed away, leaving her looking around her again, with relief, at edges and straight lines. She listened again for that buzz, heard it, and put it together with the direction in which things had been slipping and oozing.

"Are you all right?" Pont asked, sounding anxious.

Nita smiled; the "you" was plural. "I'm okay. Come on; you helped. We're closer than I thought—"

She headed down Forty-fifth at a trot and turned the corner onto Second Avenue, and paused there. All of Pont ran into her ankles, she'd stopped so suddenly. "What?"

Nita looked up and down Second, perplexed, for she hadn't expected it to be a canal. Where the curb would normally have been was now a sheer drop, and water reflecting that dark blue sky ran down between the white stone walls of the two sides of the avenue.

"We could roll across," said one of Pont.

"No, we couldn't. We left the wizardry home," said another.

"I told you we should have brought it," said the third.

"*You* said we should bring the multistate compressor," said the fourth, "and so we did. *We* were the one that wanted to bring the solidifier, but—"

Nita began to wonder what these creatures' family life was like. Just by *themselves*, if that was the right term, they seemed to have trouble getting along. "Look, guys," she said, "there's a bridge across at Forty-second."

"We'll have to go all the way down there and retrace our tracks."

"Better than going all the way up to Fifty-seventh," Nita said, peering up the avenue-cum-canal, "because that's the next one. Or we could swim."

Pont looked at her with all of itself. " 'Swim'?"

She looked at the spheres. They lacked anything to swim with. "Okay, maybe not. Come on."

Nita jogged downtown as far as Forty-second, with Pont rolling after her, fast.

The bridge arched up in a smooth ramp across the water, coming down on the opposite sidewalk, and they all headed north again. Nita could hear the little buzzing whine at the back of her mind getting stronger and stronger and followed it more quickly, while checking her progress against her memory of Pont's view of the world. Pont rolled along behind, arguing genially about their last timing in "the exercise" and how it might have been improved.

Just north of Fifty-fourth, Street Nita realized that she had come a little too far north. "East from here," she said to Pont, as they came up behind her.

The spheres looked at themselves, and made a little musical sound that translated itself, via the Speech, into "Uh-oh."

"What's the matter?" Nita said. She backtracked to the corner of Fifty-fourth, and headed east toward First Avenue.

"Nothing."

"That's easy for *you* to say," said another of Pont.

"Yes, well, you didn't like it much last time," said a third.

"And we don't like it much now, either," said the fifth one, which surprised Nita; she'd been starting to think of it as the quiet one. "We thought they would have moved it significantly. It almost always gets moved for a redo. But it looks like somebody has a little surprise for us."

Nita gave up trying to figure out what they were talking about, and headed toward First Avenue. She stopped at the corner, Pont rolling up alongside her. Nita's sense of the location of the kernel placed it right out in front of her, near where the block of Fifty-fourth between First and York should have been. But here there were no more streets at all. Directly in front of them was a huge stepped pyramid of golden stone, incomplete at its top, and behind it the East River flowed by. Sticking out into the river from one side of the pyramid was a long jetty or pier of that white stone.

"There they are," Pont said. "They didn't waste their time."

Nita squinted down at the jetty, bright in the sun, and saw down near the end of it what appeared to be a woolly mammoth, a second object of roughly cylindrical shape that wavered oddly around the edges, and a third small shape, elongated and six-legged, which was heading toward the end of the jetty while the other two faced off against each other.

"It's down there," Nita said. "Down in the water."

"We *told* you we should have left the compressor home," said Pont to one of themselves.

"And what we said was—"

"Come on, guys," Nita said. "Give it a rest. I can do water." She headed past the pyramid, toward the jetty.

The smallest of the creatures was slipping into the water. Nita jogged down the jetty, and saw that the bigger of the two creatures looked like a woolly mammoth only in terms of the bulk of its body. Seen up close, it looked much more like a giant three-legged football with green-and-brown shag carpeting stapled to it. Its companion, which faced it silently, was a bundle of bright purple tentacles about six feet high, waving gently, and changing colors as they did.

"*Dai stihó*, guys," Nita said as she went by the two wizards. They gazed at her as she passed—the tentacly wizard with one of several stalked eyes attached to the top of it, and the furry football apparently with its fur, which "followed" Nita as she went by.

She went to the end of the jetty, where the other wizard had vanished, and looked down at the water. Down there she could clearly feel the kernel's tight small buzz of power. It wasn't even all that far down. *No point in floating*, Nita thought. She flicked the charm bracelet around on her wrist, came up with the charm that was shaped like a little glass bubble, took hold of it, and jumped in.

As Nita sank, the air-and-mass spell came to life around her, holding the water away but at the same time counteracting the buoyancy of the air she'd brought with her to breathe. Because it was so compact, the spell's validity was limited, but she was sure she'd have time to do what she needed to do. *It's almost right underneath me. All I have to do is—*

—and then she saw, right under her, the sleek form swimming up toward her. Her first thought was *It's an otter*—and indeed it looked like one. But otters have fewer legs. This creature, golden-pelted, was stroking strongly along toward Nita with its front and back paws; and in the middle ones it held a tangle of light and power, small and bright, from which came the singing whine she'd been tracking.

As the creature flashed past, dark cheerful eyes blinked at her, and it grinned. Then it was heading toward the blue-lighted roil of surface. Nita let out a breath of slight annoyance and went after it, bobbing up to the surface in her bubble of air.

The other wizard was already clambering up out of the water with the kernel. This it showed to the other wizards, and one of them said, "All right, you've proved your point."

"Twenty-four minutes," the otter creature said to the furry three-legged wizard. "But it nearly didn't do me any good!" It turned its long sleek head to look at Nita as she climbed up onto the jetty and banished the bubble wizardry. "Look what I passed on the way up!"

"Dai stihó," Nita said. "Hey, you beat me fairly. I just got here late."

"Didn't think They were going to let anybody else in here, this cycle," said the furry creature. "Oh well. *Dai*, cousin!"

"Here's Pralaya," said Pont, indicating the "otter." "And that's Mmemyn"— one of Pont rolled over to the massive three-legged creature with the strange fur— "and here's Dazel. What was the matter with you two?" Pont said to them. "Why'd you just let Pralaya take the kernel?"

I did not wish to dissolve, said a slow silent voice that seemed to come from Mmemyn in a diffuse sort of way. *I did not anticipate the replay of this scenario putting the kernel under water.*

Nita realized that Mmemyn's voice came from the weird patchy fur that mostly covered it.

"Neither did I," said Dazel. "But it was plain by the time I got here that no effort would have brought me to the kernel before Pralaya got to it. Next time out, though, the outcome will be different."

"It will if Nita here does as well next time as they did on this run," Pont said. "They got the scent of that kernel right away and went straight across the city—a downhill roll all the way. Very direct."

"In this continuum, that's not easy," Pralaya said, putting down the kernel on the stone, where it lay glowing. "You've made a good start, cousin! What project are you working on that They've let you in for practice?"

"I'm . . . I'm trying to save my mother's life," Nita said. And suddenly the strangeness of it all caught up with her, as it hadn't done almost since she first became a wizard—the alien feel of another space and creatures all around her who were strangers to her in a way that few humans ever had to deal with. She found it hard to look at them; she couldn't do anything but stand there, trying to hang on to her composure.

The other wizards looked at one another, silent. Pont said, "In the Five's names, why are we keeping them standing here like this when they're distressed? It's all too new for them! Come on, everyone—if this run's done, let's go to the playpen for a while. We can show them the rest of us, and replay a couple of other runs, and let them get a feel for how it's done."

Pont bumped against Nita's legs. She looked down. They said, "Come with us, Nita. There's more to this sheaf of universes and dimensions than just places to play hunt-the-kernel. Come relax; tell us the why of what you're hunting, and maybe we can help with the how."

Pont are right, said Mmemyn. *Will you come?*

"Uh, yes," Nita said. "Sure, let's go."

And instantly the world faded around them all and vanished.

Late Tuesday Night, Wednesday Morning

NITA BLINKED AND LOOKED around her. It was dark.

Not entirely dark, though. It was as if she and Pont and the others were standing on a shining white dance floor—one that was miles and miles from one side to the other. If the curvature of the last space had surprised Nita, this place had a similar effect, but exactly in reverse. You could feel the flatness of this place in the air, on your skin, in your bones. You could practically see the ruler lines embedded in everything.

Next to her, sitting up on his hind legs, Pralaya made a little raspy chuckle. "Yes, it's a good thing it never rains here," he said, glancing around. "You'd go crazy waiting for the water to run off."

"Don't know what *you're* complaining about," Pont said, rolling past them toward a light source off to one side, where Nita could see shapes silhouetted. "Lovely place, this: no ups, no downs. Paradise." The rest of Pont went past Nita, making a feeling like a shrug. "You always could find a square thing where a round one should be, Pralaya."

"Just a natural talent," Pralaya said, looking after Pont with amusement. He gave Nita a wry look.

The two of them went after Pont, Dazel and Mmemyn bringing up the rear. "You two obviously have history," Nita said.

"Oh, some," Pralaya said, pattering along six-footedly beside Nita as they made their way toward the light. "We're neighbors. Their home universe isn't too far from mine, the way the local sheaf of worlds is presently structured. We started running into one another pretty frequently in here when I began this series of workouts. If you're here more than once or twice, you'll start recognizing the present batch of regulars pretty quickly."

"I think it's going to be more than once or twice," Nita said. "I don't have much time left, and I'm a long way from where I need to be."

"You're new at this, to be so sure," Pralaya said, as they got closer to the light. "Feel the kernel?"

"Huh?" Nita paused. She hadn't realized this was another practice universe.

"Don't stop," Pralaya said. "Some places you're not going to have the leisure. You have to learn to sense on the move. Come on!"

Nita tried "listening" as they went. It was hard to do while your other senses were interfering, but this discovery obscurely annoyed her; she could just hear Dairine saying, *Can't walk and chew gum at the same time, huh?*

The annoyance focused her just enough to let Nita "hear" the kernel, just for a second, as a sort of difference in texture in the feel of the local space. "It's right there in front of us," Nita said, surprised. "Right in the middle of everybody."

"Not bad," Pralaya said. "This kernel's tough to sense; it's a fairly low-power one. We usually keep it locked in one spot—there are so many of us in and out of this space that no one feels like hunting for it every time."

"I thought everybody's time here was really limited."

"Oh, in the aschesis-universes proper, of course it is," Pralaya said. He paused for just a moment to scratch behind his ear with the middle set of paws, bending himself nearly into a half circle as he did so, then picked up the pace again. "But this isn't one of those. This is a pocket of space pinched off from the main aschesis sheaf. The Powers let us use it to relax in between finishing up a seeking run and going home again. It's useful, since sometimes when you finish a run, you're almost too tired to gate straight . . ."

They came to the fringes of the lighted area. Fifteen or twenty creatures of various sorts were standing or sitting around on what would have passed for nice furniture on several planets Nita knew. On one piece of furniture, an ordinary-looking occasional table done in shiny metal, sat this space's kernel, a brilliant and compact little webwork of light about the size of a baseball. Pont were presently rolling under that table toward a group standing together and talking on the far side of the table, and the wizards assembled there had turned toward them and were greeting them.

"We've got more victims," Pont were saying to them. "Look, all; here's Nita."

All those strange eyes turned on her, and there were polite bows and limbs waving and wings flapping and a lot of voices saying "*Dai stihó*, cousin!"

"Uh, I'm on errantry, and I greet you," she said.

A chorus of replies, mostly amused variants on the theme "So are we!" went up around the group. Pont came rolling back to her and said, "You're in luck: a lot of the present class of practicers are here. Here are Lalezh; they're from Dorint. And that's Nirissaet; they're from Algavred XI—watch the tails! And that's Buerti, they're from Ilt. And this is Kiv . . ."

It went on that way for a while, and Nita despaired of remembering more than a few of the wizards' names, let alone those of planets or universes. But shortly she was surrounded by people talking in the Speech and arguing amiably about the best way to find a world kernel in a hurry, and someone brought her what she at first thought was a glass of water, except that there was no glass involved—just the water, holding a tumbler shape by itself. Pralaya raised his eyebrows in amusement as he caught her glance, waggling them in the general direction of the kernel where it sat on the coffee table. Apparently the kernel in the playroom often was used for just that: play.

While Nita was working out where the rim of her invisible glass was, she heard a lot of information and gossip from the alien wizards around her, and she quickly realized that in even a fairly short time she could find out all kinds of useful things, any one of which could possibly help her save her mother. Nita actually had worked up her courage enough to ask a few questions of the most senior of the group that had collected around her—a wizard called Evrysss, who looked more like a giant spiny python than anything else—when her attention was suddenly grabbed by someone walking by at the edge of the group. But what really got Nita's attention was that it wasn't an alien. It was a pig. It wasn't one of the spotty breeds, but plain pink-white, with bristles that looked slightly silvery in this light, so that it glinted a little.

"—and so I said to Hvin, 'Now, just look here, if you keep straining your shael out of shape trying to get the kernel to deform its laws like that, you're never going to—' " Evrysss blinked at Nita's sudden astonished look. "Oh, haven't you been introduced? Chao?" The pig stopped, looked at the group, glanced up at Nita. "He'neet', this is the Transcendent Pig."

Nita's eyes opened wide as the pig stepped toward her, and she saw that little shining ripples seemed to spread out in the floor from where it stepped, as if solid things went briefly uncertain where it trod. About six possible responses to what Evrysss had said now went through Nita's head, but fortunately, before she blurted one of them out, she remembered the right one. She looked down at the Pig, and said, "What's the meaning of life?"

The other wizards chuckled, or hissed or bubbled with laughter, and the Pig gave Nita a wry look out of its little piggy eyes. "I'll tell you the meaning of my life," it said, "if you'll tell me the meaning of yours."

"Uh . . . that might take a while. Even assuming I knew."

"It would for me, too," said the Pig, "so let's put it aside for the moment. Come on, sit down, make yourself comfortable."

She did, settling onto a nearby chromy framework that looked more or less like a human chair. Nita had first come across a reference to the Transcendent Pig when she was doing her earliest reading in the manual, just before she went on Ordeal. The Pig was classified as one of the "insoluble enigmas," a sort of creature that fell somewhere between wizards and the Powers That Be. Indeed the term *creature* was possibly inaccurate, for (so the manual said) no one responsible for creation could exactly remember *having* created it in the first place. At least the Pig's motives appeared to be benign, and it had been proved again and again to be immensely and inexplicably knowledgeable. Nita thought this was why the manual insisted that every wizard immediately ask the meaning-of-life question when meeting the Pig. There was always a chance the Pig might slip and actually answer it.

Well, not this time, she thought. "Do you come here often?" Nita said, and then cracked up at herself; hearing it, it seemed like about the most witless thing she could have found to say.

"Don't feel too silly," the Pig said dryly. "Everybody tends to concentrate so hard on the mandated question that their minds go blank on anything else. But I wander in and out of here every now and then. I like being at the cutting edge, and out here where no one has to be too afraid of making a mistake, some interesting work's being done. Not all of it as personal as yours, maybe, but it's all valuable."

"You mean you know?" Nita suddenly felt slightly embarrassed.

"Knowing is most of my job," the Transcendent Pig said. "But then there's a long tradition of oracular pigs. I should know: I started it." It paused. "That is, assuming you're into sequential time."

"It works all right for me," Nita said, rather cautiously.

"Well, preference is everything, as far as time's concerned; you can handle it however you like."

Nita had to smile at that. "*You* can, maybe. But you're built to be everywhen at once."

It gave her a sly look. "I suppose you might be right," the Pig said. "If everyone started to believe they could handle it the way I do, everywhen might get crowded."

Nita laughed. There was something about the Pig that put her at her ease—one thing being that, to her astonishment, it had a New York accent. She spent a while chatting with it about Earth and then about various other planets where her errantry had taken her, and soon realized there was absolutely nowhere she'd been that the Pig didn't know—it had been there, seen that, and left the T-shirt behind. "Or, rather, I'm there now," it said. "Or *have* been there now."

Nita smiled, reminded of trying to explain the tenses of conditional time to her mother. "My own language isn't much good for this kind of thing. Guess we should keep it in the Speech."

"No problem. Who did you come in with?"

"A bunch of people," Nita said. "Mostly Pralaya and, uh, Pont."

The Pig smiled at Nita's slightly embarrassed look as she used the "slang" version of Pont's name. "Oh," the Pig said, "you're another one who can't manage the music of the spheres? Don't worry about it, cousin. No one expects anybody else to handle home languages perfectly. The Speech is all anyone here really needs."

Nita nodded. "You hear that word so much around here," she said then, "and with wizards generally: *hrasht . . .*" It was the word in the Speech that translated as "cousin."

"Oh, the term's accurate enough," the Pig said. "We're all children of brothers and sisters, of kindred creatures who're children of that odd couple Life and Time. All related, mostly by just trying to live our lives and get by in the face of tremendous odds. But in a lot of cases, trying to do *more* than just get by." The Transcendent Pig looked around. "This is one of the places where you come to push past the usual definitions of what's possible." It gave her a thoughtful look. "And if you're lucky, you both pull off what you're seeking and get to enjoy it afterward."

"That's what I'm here for," Nita said.

"Trying to save a life is always worthwhile," said the Pig. "But the bigger work can be a lot easier sometimes. Nonetheless, I'd say you're in the right place for advice." It looked over at the wildly assorted group of beings standing around a tall table, all in the light, waving their manipulatory appendages at one another and talking at high speed.

"Got any to spare?" Nita said.

The Transcendent Pig waggled its eyebrows at her. "Not for free. You know the price."

"Uh, yeah. I'll pass." Nita still wasn't completely clear about the price she would pay for *this* particular work of wizardry. Taking on another obligation seemed unwise, especially when it was known to be—in wizardly terms—an extremely expensive one.

"So will we all," the Pig said, and got up, quirking its tail at her. "Keep your ears open, all the same. You never know what one of your cousins'll mention that could turn out to be really useful later on."

The Transcendent Pig wandered off. In her turn Nita got up off the more-or-less chair she'd been sitting on and went over to listen again to some of the other wizards who were talking in a group. What she had come to think of as "the kernel," they were calling by as many other names as there were species in the group: the World-Soul, the Cosmic Egg, the Shard, and numerous others. Some of the wizards were knowledgeable about the structure of the kernel itself, in ways Nita was certain she would never have time to master. Pont, in particular, were in the midst of a long talk with one of the other wizards—a storklike alien about six feet tall who seemed to have had some kind of accident in a paint store, one where they sold iridescent paint that didn't keep the same color for more than a minute. "If you're having so much trouble dealing with the place's kernel," Pont were saying, "you should get help. Go in as a team! It's always an option for any of us, once we're done with the orientation runs."

The other wizard, Kkirl, stretched her wings in a sudden blaze of scarlet and green, then folded them again. "I have concerns," she said. "The kernel of the planet in question is unstable. It won't stay where it's put; whether the turmoil on that world is itself a reflection of the kernel's instability, or the other way around, I cannot tell, though I have been working with it for many cycles now—"

"*Planets* have kernels?" Nita said.

"Not of the same power and complexity you would find in a universe-type kernel," Kkirl said, "but much smaller, more delicate ones, easily deranged if mishandled. I've spent as long as I dare assessing the situation and trying to make small adjustments. There's no more time, for the planet is inhabited by some hundreds of thousands of my people, and if that world's destruction by earthquakes and crustal disturbances is to be avoided, something must be done now. In the past two cycles, the quakes have become severe enough to threaten large parts of the surface of the planet. The Powers sanctioned an intervention that would deal with the kernel itself, and I was here to prepare one final test sequence. I don't really need it. But I'm still not sure it's safe to go on with the intervention by myself, let alone with—"

"Kkirl, what use is a meeting like this unless you use it to your advantage?" Pont said. "The Powers Themselves might have thrown us in your way. Let us— some of us, anyway—help you out! You can tell us how to proceed, and we'll be guided by you. Or, if nothing else, we can just lend you power. These aren't circumstances where anyone would be tempted to improvise."

Kkirl looked around, her feathers a little ruffled, uncertain. Several other wizards had been listening to their conversation, Pralaya among them. Now Pralaya stood up on its hindmost legs in order to look Kkirl in the eye more easily, and said, "Cousin, if your people's lives are in danger, letting your uncertainty hobble you is playing right into the Lone Power's desires. And delay could be fatal. Judging from what you've told us, it's becoming fatal already. You have to move past the uncertainty. What else are we all here for?"

Kkirl stood there silent. Finally she looked up, rustled her wings, and said, "You're right. I see no other way. And there's no point putting it off anymore. Who will come?"

"We will," Pont said. "What about you others?"

"I'll come," Pralaya said. "Of course. Who else?"

Mmemyn said, *I am free to come*; and another wizard that Nita had met only briefly, a long graceful silvery fishlike creature in a bubble of water, said, "I, too."

"Well enough. I'll draw up the transit circle, then," Kkirl said. "You will want to plug in your names and bring appropriate breathing media: The atmosphere is a reducing one, and there's a lot of oxygen." She glanced over at the "fish." "Not a problem for you, Neme, except for the acid in the air."

The various wizards started to get ready, adjusting their life-support wizardries, and Nita was surprised when one of Pont rolled over to her. "You know," it said, "you might come along as well."

Nita looked down at it, and over at the others, surprised. "Me? I'm just getting started. I didn't even get the kernel this time."

"Just an accident of timing," Pralaya said, glancing up.

Kkirl paused in the act of starting to pace out the circle. "And you're probably the youngest of us here," said Kkirl, "so that whatever you might lack in expertise, you'd surely make up in power. Do come, hNeet. The kernel won't be where I left it in any case; looking for it will be extra practice for you."

Her mother's predicament went through Nita's mind. But these people were trying to help her, to help her mom. It was the least she could do to help them. "Yeah," she said. "Sure, I'll come."

Kkirl went back to pacing out her transit circle, and it appeared on the floor before them. The wizards who were going produced their names in the Speech and started plugging them into the spell, in the empty spots Kkirl was now adding for them.

Nita looked over the diagram carefully as it completed itself. The coordinates for the solar system in question had an additional set of vector and frame coordinates in front of it, which Nita thought must be the determinators for an entirely different universe. Otherwise the diagram made perfect sense, and the long-form description of the planet itself made it plain why Kkirl was working on it. *It's tearing itself apart*, Nita thought, bending down to look at it closely. *The planet was big to start with, and then it captured all these moons, even a little "wandering planet" passing through its solar system . . . and now the gravitational stresses from some of the more massive moons have thrown everything out of whack.* This was a problem of the same kind as Dairine's, just as insoluble by brute force. Inherent in the transit circle, though, and written as an adjunct to it, Nita could see Kkirl's intended solution. The planet itself was going to have both its crust structure and its gravitational and magnetic fields reorganized and rebalanced. That could be done only by using the kernel, which when itself rewritten would in turn rewrite the whole under-crust stucture of the planet. *It's like the kernel is the master copy of a DNA molecule. Rewrite it and turn it loose, and every other molecule in a body gets changed in response.* This was fairly close to what Nita had in mind for her mother, and her heart leaped as she saw from Kkirl's diagram that she'd been on the right track, and began to see how she could implement a similar solution herself.

"See something that doesn't work?" Kkirl said, coming around behind her and looking over Nita's shoulder at the diagram.

"No," Nita said. "It looks fine."

"I'm glad. It's taken awhile. But the conditional statements there were the worst part. Fortunately the solution is adjudged to be ethical—see the GO/NO GO toggle down at the end? If that one tiny little knot won't knot, you might as well give up and go home."

Nita nodded. "Okay," she said, and reached into the back of her mind to pull out the constantly updated graphic version of her personal description. It manifested itself in the usual long graceful string of glowing writing in the Speech, but as she ran it briefly through her hands, Nita noticed some changes here and there, particularly in the sections that had to do with family and emotional relationships. *Mom . . .* , she thought. She let the written version of her name slide glowing to the floor and snug itself into the spot waiting for it in Kkirl's wizardry.

Then, suddenly getting the feeling that someone was behind her, Nita looked over her shoulder. Dazel was towering up behind her and leaning over her, looking down at her with a number of its eyes, while its many, many pink and dark-violet tentacles wreathed slowly in the air. It said nothing. The rest of its eyes were arching down over her to look carefully at her name in the Speech.

"Uh, hi," Nita said.

"Yes," Dazel said. It said nothing further, but more and more of its eyes curled down in front of her to look at her name, where it lay glowing against the white floor, until only eye was left still looking at Nita, hanging there on its thin, shiny pink stalk about three inches in front of her nose. The eye's pupil was triangular, and the rest of the eye was bloodshot, if blood were purple.

"Uh, right. Excuse me," Nita said, and slowly and carefully edged sideways out from underneath all those overarching eyes, trying hard not to make it look as if she was creeped out.

The eyes watched her go, but otherwise Dazel didn't move, except for those tentacles, which never seemed to stop their silent wreathing and twisting in the air. Nita made her way over to where Pralaya and Pont were settling some final details with Kkirl and a couple of other wizards, and sat down on a little stepstool-looking piece of furniture near Pralaya. As several of Pont rolled off to say something to a couple of wizards on the other side of the gathering, Nita bent over with her elbows on her knees and looked sideways at Pralaya. "Is it just me," Nita said softly, "or is there something a little . . . I don't know . . . *unusual* about him?" She glanced at Dazel.

Pralaya looked casually over his shoulder, then back toward Nita, scrubbing his face thoughtfully with one paw. "I don't really know," he said. "He does have this way of just standing there and looking at you with all those eyes for minutes on end. I mean, it's not as if there's anything *wrong* with lots of eyes. Or none, for that matter. Maybe it's the multiple brains." Pralaya started scrubbing the other side of his face. "I did ask him once if there was something bothering him, but the answer didn't make much sense."

Nita shook her head. "But the Speech *always* makes sense."

"If you're using it with the intent to be understood, yes," Pralaya said. He waggled his whiskers, an expression Nita took as a shrug. "Whatever; it's not my business."

Nita was starting to feel boorish at having even mentioned it. These people were, after all, wizards, except for the Pig, and had all been extremely kind to her. "Never mind," she said, "probably it *is* just me. So much has been happening—"

"Now what was *that* about?" said one of Pont, rolling out from under another of the tables.

"*That* what?" Nita said.

"Dazel there," said Pont, and a couple of them split apart in an uneasy way and then recombined, while "looking" across at Dazel. "They're leaving, apparently. We said to them, 'Go well,' and they said, 'Some of us may, but one of us will not.' "

Nita and Pralaya and all of Pont looked across at Dazel. It gazed back at them with some of those waving eyes, and then vanished.

"Ready now," Kkirl said, straightening up from checking the wizardry one last time. "Shall we?"

They all stepped into position, each into his, her, or its allotted place in the diagram. Nita gulped as she realized she was about to do a wizardry with almost no preparation, with beings she'd met hardly an hour before. But it was too late now. There were Pont, in their part of the circle, their five spheres bumping into one another and chiming a little nervously; Pralaya, sitting up on his haunches, his four other paws with their delicate little fingers now folded, expectantly, over his tummy; Neme, the fish-wizard, hanging in its globe of water like a Siamese fighting fish in a bowl, all gauzy silver fins and big eyes; Mmemyn, standing there seemingly eyeless and expressionless, like a giant, badly upholstered gymnastics horse; and Kkirl, her wings spread a little as she stepped into the control circle of the transit wizardry and began reciting the triggering sequence in the Speech, the words drowning out all other sound, including the tiny hissing feel of the playroom space's own kernel.

Nita took a breath, made sure her own personal atmosphere was in place around her and secured by the wizardry attached to her charm bracelet. Then she joined in the chorus of other voices, birdlike, moaning, chiming, growling. The sound of the Speech rose up in their conjoined voices and leaned in close around them, pressing in on all of them as the power built, down on them, squeezing them out of this space and, with a sudden explosive release, into another—

The sourceless radiance of the playroom space vanished, replaced by the high, hard, bright light of a sun high in a pale blue sky, all streaked with wind-torn, sulfurously yellow cloud. Nita and the other wizards stood in a saffron-stained wilderness of ice and blowing snow. Around them blasted a screaming wind that would have been not only bitterly cold—if a temperature-opaque forcefield hadn't been holding Nita's air around her—but also unbreathable, laden with a stinging acid sleet.

The other wizards looked around with dismay. "There has been a lot of discharge of poisonous gas into the atmosphere because of the earthquakes," Kkirl said. "It's getting worse all the time."

"This isn't the seismically active area," Pont said, their spheres dividing up into numerous smaller ones and rolling out of the diagram.

"No, this is where I left the kernel," Kkirl said. "I was hoping it would stay anchored near the planet's magnetic pole. But as you see, it's gone again."

Nita looked out into that snow and listened once more. The wind was screaming in her ears, distracting her, and she wasn't perceiving this universe as artificially compressed, like the ones she'd practiced in. It stretched out all around her, vast to both her normal and her wizardly senses, real and challenging. At the same time, Nita was aware of Pralaya's eyes on her, thoughtful but also a little impatient and challenging, and she was reminded of Dairine again. Nita concentrated on listening. In the shriek of the wind, or behind it, something caught Nita's ear, and she looked over at Kkirl in confusion.

"Are you *sure* it's not here?" Nita shouted over the wind.

"What?"

"There's— I don't know, it's kind of an echo. Can you hear it?"

Kkirl listened. "No . . ."

Nita turned, looking all around her. There was nothing to see in this howling wilderness, but she could hear it now, she was sure. "Pont," she said, "can you give me a— Can you help me out here?" for Pont were short of hands. "Do what you did before?"

"What? Oh—"

Pont's surface shimmered. Suddenly overlying Nita's own perceptions was that odd, tightly curved view of the world: downcurving sky, the golden-hued ice curving away and down all around them, the wind blasting the snow past the wizards and away from them in great chilly clouds. Nita didn't fight the perception but leaned into the curvatures, staring around her, listening.

All the others were doing so, too, Nita could tell, though her perceptions of them were conditioned by Pont's. All the other wizards looked spherical, though all in different ways, as distinctive as basketballs from soccer balls from baseballs. Some hint of Kkirl's flamboyant colors showed, in the tight and elegant way she curved space around her; as did Mmemyn's slightly slow and scattered personality, in a sphere that was a little diffuse in the way it reflected its surroundings; as did Pralaya's, in a neat and compact roundness. Nita could sense everyone using their own wizardry-altered senses to search through the space around them for the kernel, as she was doing. Again Nita thought she felt a prickling tangle of unseen power rolling away from her, not far away, in a slow twisting path, downward—

Is it moving? Pralaya said in her mind.

That's what I thought, Nita said. *Pralaya, can you do what Pont's doing here? If three of us, or you and I and however many of Pont there are, all look at the same time—*

Yes.

And the look of the world changed again. The icy golden surface underneath them was still the same, as was the wind howling past, but now the wind had a voice, eloquent, upset. Nita's companions were once more wearing forms that looked much like Nita's own way of seeing them, but with something added. Now there were depths of texture and mind that hadn't been there before, as if you could put out a hand and feel thought, warm like fur—a livelier, more animate sense of the others than Pont's slightly chilly perception. *Maybe it's because Pralaya and I are both mammals*, Nita thought. *Or something like mammals . . .*

In the moment it took her to see through Pralaya's eyes and mind, Nita perceived many things quickly: glimpses of a blue-green forested home world with much water running under the shadows of the trees, a golden-eyed mate with an amused look, pups tumbling and squeaking in some dimly lighted den—a warm and affable outlook on a world that felt challenging and complex but basically friendly. Then everything steadied down to ice and snow and complaining wind again, and one more sense of the kernel, sharper and more precisely targeted: something trickling, running, down under the ice, where it was warmer and liquid was possible, where heat and other energy channeled narrowly up through veins in the crust, and that fizzing, writhing, unbalanced knot of local law was burrowing down in deep—

Down! Nita said.

The others looked down with her, inside the glacier on which they all stood, through it to the underlying stone, through that to the first boundary layer where the stone changed—and Kkirl laughed angrily, and said, *Powers' names, trust it to more or less stay put this one time! Come on, cousins, if it gets itself down into the mantle in this state, it'll derange the whole place before we can operate on it!*

They all knew the Mason's Word spell. That word gives new life to stone, but the more complex version of the spell reminds stone of previous states of being, times when the fourth element was mostly air or fire, or stone in some other phase—dust floating in space before coalescing into a planet, only an atom or two sticking together here and there. Nita used that spell now, pulling the words out of storage in the "pebble" charm on her bracelet, telling the ice and stone beneath her that their atoms were far enough apart for hers to slip between with no trouble.

The ice rose past Nita and swallowed her up like a blur of fog, and the stone like darker fog, hotter, resisting a little, as the whole group dropped down in pursuit of the kernel. Further down they plunged, the shadowy mist of stone rushing up past Nita as if she'd jumped feet first into dark water. But it wasn't happening fast enough; the kernel was well ahead.

Nita turned herself, swimming through the stone, diving through it as if it were the water off Jones Inlet, where she'd spent so much time lately. Far behind, she could sense the kernel more clearly, dropping toward the discontinuity level, where the crust became the mantle and the lava under the planet's skin seethed. *Can't let it get in there!* Nita laid her arms back along her sides and let the increasing pull of gravity take her, worked to make an arrow or torpedo of herself. She was the smallest, the lightest of the pursuing wizards—*Or maybe just being the youngest is enough,* she thought, as slowly, slowly she got closer to the kernel's tangle of light. It was losing speed, as if the stone through which it sank was getting denser. It felt that way to Nita now, the stone more like water than mist, and then more like mud than water, but she didn't let that stop her. The kernel was just ahead of her now, just out of reach. The others were nowhere near it. *Don't wait for them; they're not going to be here in time, just get it!*

With difficulty, as she arrowed down through the seething, thickening, darkening fire, Nita got her arms down and in front of her again, reached out. The kernel was slowing more . . . but so was she, and then the shock waves started to hit her. She'd known the boundary between crust and mantle would be like a wall, but she hadn't expected it to be as much a wall of violent vibration as one of heat. Now Nita could feel how the world shook where the rotating stony liquid of the upper core dragged itself against the underside of the relatively static crust in small rotating storms of liquid fire, like the spots in the atmosphere of Jupiter, just as dense, just as furious. The worst earthquakes imaginable were just the side effects of these, and Nita went straight through one after the kernel, blinded by the roaring swirling tumult of the fire.

Something caught her from behind, braced her for just a precious moment and lent her power. The world went clear and hard and sharp as it had done earlier, and so did the kernel, a bright fierce tangle of power, just long enough for Nita to grab it in both hands. It fought her, unstable and willful as Kkirl had warned her, jumping and bucking and stinging in her hands as if trying to get away. Nita wouldn't let it, wouldn't drop it.

Pralaya, Nita thought, knowing where that jolt of power had come from and not sure whether there was another one available. *Where's Kkirl? What does she want to do with this thing?*

Hang on. She's coming.

Together they hung on, though the storm of molten fire tore at them and tried to blow them around like leaves in a wind. Pralaya was feeding her strength, and Nita was glad of it. She wasn't sure how much longer she could hold on to the kernel, but abruptly the fire around her was disturbed by another presence, a swirl of color that wasn't so blinding, and the crooked little claw fingers hidden under the bends of Kkirl's wings caught hold of Nita's hands and the kernel, both at once.

An eyeblink later Nita was seeing the kernel as Kkirl saw it, complex and dangerous, yes, but not too much so to never be mastered. Kkirl had been studying this problem for a long time, and she was ready. Those delicate little claws sank deep into the force-crackling knot of that world's heart and froze the kernel's processes in place for just the few seconds it would take to enact what Kkirl had been planning all this while.

Nita could see and feel how she was doing it, how Kkirl was reshaping the way the kernel called for the planet's upper mantle and lower crust to interact— thinning out some of the more massive areas near the core, redistributing the mass so that the planet's continental plates would move more slowly and evenly and resist the uneven tidal effects of the planet's moons. Nita watched what Kkirl was doing—manipulating the kernel like a Rubik's Cube and setting in place the changes she wanted, one after another, but not actually triggering them until they were all set up. Nita realized this technique was what she would need for her mom—using the kernel inside her mother to reshape the cancer viruses and render them harmless, or maybe even helpful. *I'm so glad I came.*

Kkirl, better get on with it! Nita heard Pralaya thinking. He was running out of power to feed them.

Ready in a moment, Kkirl said.

I don't think we have that long! Nita said. She was still hanging on to the kernel along with Kkirl, but just barely; the thing was jerking and shaking in their hands and claws like a live thing, trying to tear free, resisting what was being done to it—

Now!

Kkirl turned loose the changes she had set into the kernel. A roar, a rumble all around as the old structures and energy flows tried to hang on just a little longer, as the new ones, shaky at first, started to assert themselves—then a terrible sudden shudder of that world, from the heart out, as everything started to fall into place. *Let's get out of here!* Pralaya shouted from behind them, and Nita let go of the kernel and started to struggle back up through the fire toward the surface, as the planet began restructuring itself.

Getting up and out of the fiery turmoil seemed to take infinitely longer than getting down into it. The smoky fog of molten stone gradually lightened, then abruptly vanished as Nita broke up out of the ice and back into normal physical form, and her normal life-support sphere reasserted itself around her. She collapsed to her knees, gasping for air. The other wizards erupted out of the ice around her, each doing the same, as the reaction to the wizardry hit. Underneath them the ground shook, and the air was full of the groans, shrieks, and crashing noises of ice shattering for miles in every direction. Nita saw Kkirl stagger to her long thin feet, fling her wings up, and shout into the snowy air one long sentence in the Speech.

The ground reared up, and Nita found herself sliding sideways down a slab of ice. Everything went dark, then bright again, the recall spell grabbing Nita and all the others and dumping them unceremoniously back onto the floor of the playroom. There they all slumped, lay, sloshed, or rolled gently from side to side for some moments, until one by one they started to recover.

Kkirl was a bright, collapsed bundle of feathers, rising and falling gently in the middle with her breathing, but not moving otherwise. Nita managed to get to her feet, and went shakily over to put an arm around Kkirl. "You all right?"

A faint squeaking noise was all that came from inside the feathers, as Nita was joined by Pralaya, who put out a paw to one of Kkirl's splayed-out wings. "Thanks," Nita said to him. "I'd have dropped the kernel back there if you hadn't helped."

"At least you caught it before it fell straight down into the core," Pralaya said.

Kkirl's head came up on its long neck out of the huddle of bright feathers; she was blinking.

"I don't know if that went the way it was supposed to . . . ," Nita said, uncertain.

"Oh, it did! It did!" Kkirl said, staggering to her feet again. She shook her feathers out and back into place, looking unsteady but cheerful. "It's going to take some hours for the planet's crust to quiet down; it was never going to start looking better right away. But the intervention worked; that world's saved at last! Thank you, cousins," she said, turning to all the others. "Thank you all!"

There was a gradually rising hubbub of voices as the group who'd gone out with Kkirl recovered from what they'd done and other wizards still in the playroom came over to congratulate them. Nita, standing next to Pralaya, said to him, "I should head home . . . They're gonna be wondering what happened to me."

"Don't be a stranger, cousin," Pralaya said. "We haven't had much time to deal with *your* problem today, after all."

"Don't worry about that," Nita said. "I'll be back here tomorrow . . . I want to try out what I saw Kkirl do. I think it may work for my mom."

"Then maybe I'll see you," Pralaya said, patting her with one of the middle paws. "Go well . . . and I hope you find her better."

Nita nodded, shook out her transit-circle spell, and took herself home.

After what she'd been through, her bedroom looked almost too ordinary and normal to be believed—so much so that tired and hungry as she was, and though she plopped right down onto her bed, she couldn't go to sleep. She tried briefly to get in touch with Kit but found that he was asleep. Then, out of curiosity, Nita paged through the manual to see what the listings on the other wizards looked like. They were all interesting enough—she had a brief chuckle over the concept of Pralaya having had thirty-six pups with his mate, nine at a time. But even after twenty minutes or so of reading, she didn't feel sleepy.

Finally, still feeling listless and jangly, Nita got up again and went downstairs to get something to drink. As she turned the corner into the dining room, she was unnerved to find her dad sitting in a dining-room chair, in the dark, with the phone's receiver in his hand. It was beeping disconsolately, in the manner of a phone that should have been hung up a long time before.

Nita swallowed hard with sudden fear, took the receiver away from him, and hung it up. "Daddy, what is it?"

He looked up at her, as scared as she was. "It was the hospital." Nita's stomach instantly tied itself into a knot. "Mom had some more seizures after we left," her father said.

"Oh no," Nita said. Whatever small feelings of success she had had after the long evening's work had run out of her in about a second, leaving her completely terrified again. "Is she okay?"

"They got them to stop, yeah," her father said. "But it took longer this time. Honey, she's got to have that surgery as soon as she can."

"It's still going to be Saturday?"

"Yes. But is that going to be soon enough?"

Nita didn't know what to say. Her father looked up at her. "How was . . . whatever you were doing?"

"It was pretty good," Nita said, but now she wasn't so sure. "I need some more practice before Saturday, but I think I'm going to be able to help."

Her father didn't answer, just rubbed his face with both hands. *He doesn't believe me*, Nita thought. *But he doesn't want to say so.* "Daddy," she said, "you should go to bed. If Mom sees you're tired out, it's gonna get her worried."

He sighed, looked up at her. "You really do remind me of her sometimes," he said. "You two nag in exactly the same way."

"Thanks loads," Nita said. "Go on, Dad. Get some sleep. We'll go see her tomorrow afternoon."

He nodded, got up, went off to bed. *But he won't sleep*, Nita thought.

And for a long time, neither did she.

Wednesday

Nita more or less sleepwalked through school the next day. She got spoken to several times for not paying attention. All she could really think about during school was seeing her mom in the hospital that afternoon, and then getting back into the practice universes and following up on what she'd seen Kkirl do with the kernel the day before.

She looked for Kit during the day but didn't see him, and there was no sign of him at the school gates when she started for home, and no note for her in the manual. *Maybe he's at the other gates*, Nita thought, and retraced her steps to the gates on the north side of the school. But he wasn't there, either. She'd tried shooting him a thought earlier, without response; now she tried it again. Still nothing. . . .

For a change of pace, and on the off chance she might find Kit coming back from one of his other friends' houses, Nita went home the back way. It was a slightly longer route than her usual one, but it gave her a little time to mull over what she'd seen and felt Kkirl doing with the kernel. *But there's no way to tell if Mom's kernel is going to behave like that one did*, Nita thought. She really hoped it wouldn't. Without Pralaya's help and Kkirl's, she wouldn't have been able to hold the kernel for long—and Kkirl had had lots of time to plan what she was going to do. *Help is going to be a real good idea on this*, she thought. *Glad Kit's gonna be there.*

Yet she remembered Kkirl's initial reluctance to let the other wizards help with her own intervention, and Nita could understand where it had come from. *Suppose the one helping you messes up somehow?* It would be awful being in a situation where you might wind up blaming someone you knew well for . . . for—

She wouldn't even think it. *But it would be better if there was no one to blame but yourself if something went wrong. Or no one you were close to . . .*

Nita paused at the corner, gazing across the street while waiting for traffic to pass. *Pralaya wanted to help*, Nita thought. And Pralaya's entry in the manual, when she'd taken a look at it, had been impressive. He was old as wizards went—a part-time local Advisory on his planet, with a lot of experience. *But still . . .* It was hard to let anybody else get involved in this, whether she knew them or not. There was so much riding on it, so much that could go wrong.

She let out a long breath. There was no more traffic, and across the street from her was the church where Nita's mom went on Sundays.

Nita paused, then crossed the street. When she and Dairine had been much younger, they had routinely been dragged here. Then Nita's mother had had some kind of change of heart and had stopped insisting the kids go. "I don't think it's right to try to make you believe what I believe just because *I* believe it," she'd said. "When you're old enough, I want you to make up your own minds." And so church had become a matter of choice in the years that followed. Sometimes Nita didn't go to church with her mom, and sometimes, for reasons she found hard to describe to herself, she did—possibly it was exactly *because* her mother had made it optional. The things she heard in church sometimes seemed exactly right and true to Nita, and sometimes seemed so incredibly stupid and wrong that she was tempted to snicker, except that she knew better. And also, she had no desire for her mother, when they got home, to pull her head off and beat her around the shoulders with it for acting so rude. But by and large the issue of belief or disbelief in what went on in church didn't seem as important to Nita as the issue of just sometimes being there with her mom. It was simply part of the way they were with each other.

As a result of this Nita didn't go to the church by herself all that often. Now, though, as she came down the sidewalk in front of it, she stopped and stood there.

Why not, Nita thought. *After all, it's the One.* And no wizard worthy of the name could fail to acknowledge his or her most basic relationship with the utter-most source of wizardry, the Power most central to the Powers, Their ancient source.

She went in. She was half terrified that she would run into somebody her family knew or that, indeed, she would run into anybody at all. But there was no one there this time of the afternoon.

The place was fairly modern: high white ceiling, stained glass with a modern-art look to it, simple statues, and an altar that was little more than a table. Generally Nita didn't pay much attention to the statues and pictures; she knew they were all just symbols of something bigger, as imperfect as matter and perception were liable to make such things. But today, as she found a pew near the back and slipped into it, everything seemed, somehow, to be looking at her.

Nita pulled down the kneeler and knelt, folding her hands on the back of the pew in front of her. Then after a moment, she put her head down against her hands.

Please, please, *don't let my mother die. I'll do whatever it takes.*

Whatever.

But if You do let her die—

She stopped herself. Threatening the One was fairly stupid, not to mention useless, and (possibly worst of all) rude. Yet her fear was slopping back and forth into anger, about once every five minutes, it seemed. Nita couldn't remember a time when her emotions had seemed so totally out of her control. She tried to get command of herself now. It was hard.

Just . . . please. Don't let her die. If You don't, I'll do . . . whatever has to be done. I don't care what it is. I'm on Your side, remember? I haven't done so badly before. I can do this for her. Let what I'm going to do work . . . let me help her. Help me help her.

I haven't asked You for much, ever. Just give me this one thing. I'll do whatever it takes if You just let me save her, help me save her, let her live!

The cry from her heart left her trembling with her emotion. But the silence around her went on, went deep, continued. No answers were forthcoming.

And I was expecting what, exactly? Nita thought, getting angry—at herself, now—and getting up off her knees. A wave of embarrassment, of annoyance at her own gullibility and hopelessness, went through her.

She got up and went out the front door . . . and stopped. A long black hearse had driven up and was now parking down at the end of the church sidewalk. Someone was getting ready for a funeral.

For a moment Nita stood there transfixed with horror. Then she hurried away past the hearse, refusing to look at it more than once, and more determined than ever to make all of this work.

That afternoon when she and her dad and Dairine got to the hospital, they made it no farther than the nursing station. The head nurse there, Mrs. Jefferson, came out from behind the desk and took them straight into that little room across the hall, which Nita irrationally was now beginning to fear.

"What's the matter?" Nita's father said, as soon as the door was closed.

"Your wife's had another bout of seizures," Mrs. Jefferson said. "About an hour ago. They were quickly controlled again—no damage was done as far as we can tell—but she's exhausted. The doctor wanted her kept sedated for the rest of the day, so she's sleeping again. She'll be better tomorrow."

"But she won't be *that* much better until the surgery happens," Nita's dad said, sounding bleak.

Mrs. Jefferson just looked at him. "It's been scheduled for Friday now," she said. "Did Dr. Kashiwabara get through to you?"

"About that? Yes." Nita's father swallowed. "But between now and then—"

"We're keeping a close eye on her," Mrs. Jefferson said. "One of us was with her when it started this morning, which is why we were able to stabilize her so quickly." She paused. "She'd been hallucinating a little . . ."

Nita's dad rubbed his eyes, looking even more stricken. "Hallucinating how?"

The nurse hesitated. "Is Mrs. Callahan interested in the space program? Or astronomy?"

"Uh, yes, somewhat," Nita's father said warily.

"Oh, good." The nurse looked slightly relieved. "She was talking about the Moon a lot, when she first came to, after the seizures last night. Something about walking on the Moon. And she also kept repeating something about looking for the light, needing to use the light, and how 'all the little dark things' were trying to hide the light from her. That seems to have something to do with some of the guided imagery work that her crisis counselor was doing with her, or it may have been a response to some of the optical symptoms she's been having." The nurse shook her head. "Anyway, it's common enough for people to be confused afterward. I wouldn't worry too much about it."

Nita's heart was cold inside her.

"Can we sit with her for just a few minutes?" Nita's father said. "We won't try to wake her up."

The head nurse was about to say no . . . but then she stopped. "All right," she said. "Please keep it brief; if the doctor finds out that I let you . . ."

"We won't be long."

The three of them slipped into the room where Nita's mom was staying. Her roommates were gone; there was just the single bed now that had its curtains drawn around it. They slipped in through the curtains, stood there quietly.

Nita looked silently at her mom and thought about how drawn her face looked, almost sunken in; there were circles under her eyes. It was painful to see her like this. *Got to hurry with what I'm doing*, Nita thought, though she felt as tired as her mother looked. *Got to.*

Her dad was looking down at her mom as if she was the only thing in the world that mattered. Her mom and dad had known each other for a long time before they got married; apparently it had been a joke among their friends, that all of them knew her mom and dad were an item long before they knew it themselves. Here were two old friends, and suddenly one of them was really sick, might even—

Nita forcibly turned away from the thought and looked at her father's face. *No*, she thought.

No.

She was back in the practice universes almost as soon as she could get upstairs to her room and through her transit circle to Grand Central. Now that she knew where the playroom was, too, she made that space her first stop. On her next-to-last chance to practice, having another wizard along to give her a few last-minute pointers would be welcome.

But the playroom was empty when she got there. The central area still shone with that sourceless pale radiance, and the assorted alien furniture still sitting around glinted in the light. As she walked, Nita felt around her for the kernel and sensed it immediately. It had wandered away from the seating area, rolling out into the huge white expanse of the floor.

Nita went after it, only partly to have a little more practice in manipulating it. The glance she had had at her manual before leaving had made it plain that the next practice universe she encountered was going to be much more difficult, more closely tailored to her own problem. Whatever Power handled access to the practice universes had noticed Nita's looming deadline and was forcing the pace . . . and she was feeling the tension. She was also aware that she was stalling. *But only a little*, she thought, as she spotted the kernel's vague little star of light, maybe a quarter mile away.

Nita hiked toward it, hearing nothing but its faint buzz in all that great, flat empty space. In this darkness, bare of the sounds of fellow wizards, it was all too easy to hear other things: the machines around her mother's bed in the hospital, the whisper of the nurses saying things to each other that they thought—incorrectly—Nita and Dairine couldn't hear. Nita reached the kernel, picked it up, and turned it over in her hands, holding it carefully; for all its power, it looked like such a fragile thing. Holding it she could feel how every little detail of this "pocket" universe was anchored in it, endlessly malleable. The more you believed in that malleability, the more easily the kernel could be changed. *That's something I've got to exploit*, she thought. *Not be afraid to improvise.*

But she *was* afraid. *It'd be dumb not to admit that*, Nita thought. *All I have to do is push through the fear. And at least Kit'll be there to help.*

The kernel in her hands sang softly, like a plucked string, as someone else came into the playroom. She turned to see who it was. Way back among the furniture, a golden-furred form sat up on its haunches and peered around. "Pralaya?" Nita called.

Abruptly he was right beside her. "That was quick," Nita said.

"Microtransit," Pralaya said, dropping down on all six feet again. "When you know a kernel's signature, if it's not too complex or unstable, you can home on it. Most of us learn this one pretty quickly; it's fairly simple." He yawned.

"You sound tired," Nita said as they started to walk back toward the furniture.

"I just finished a next-to-last workout," Pralaya said. "Shortly I'll have to do the real piece of work, but not right this moment. I'm considering a few last options. What about you?"

"I've got to do my next-to-last, too," Nita said. "Or I think it will be. There's not much time left. They're going to be operating on my mom the day after tomorrow."

"How are you holding up?"

There were moments when the darkness here seemed to press in unusually closely around Nita. This was one of them. "Not so well," she said. "I'm scared a lot of the time. It makes it hard to work." She made a face. "Just another of the Lone One's favorite tactics—to use your own fear to make what you do less effective."

"It's a tactic that has another side, though," Pralaya said. "One you can use to your advantage. Fear can keep you sharp and make you sensitive to solutions you might not have seen otherwise."

"I guess. But I could do without Its tactics, at the moment, or Its inventions. Especially the first one It came up with."

"Death . . . ," Pralaya said, musing. "Well, it's struck me that the Powers have been fairly philosophical about Their dealings with death and entropy. What They can't cure, we must endure, or so They say."

Nita nodded. "I guess we all wonder about *why* sometimes. Why the Powers That Be didn't just reverse what the Lone Power had done. Or trash everything and start all over if They couldn't repair the damage."

They got back to the furniture, and Nita dropped the kernel to its more usual place on the table. "Well," Pralaya said, "the manual is sparing with the details. But I think the other Powers had only a limited amount of energy left to Them afterward. The Lone One wasn't just another Power; It was first among equals, mightiest of all the Subcreators. Terrible energies were entrusted to It when things got started, and when It had expended those energies, they weren't available for use elsewhere by the Others."

Nita looked down at the kernel. "The Lone Power's changing now, though," she said. "Ever so slowly . . ."

"So they say. Not that that does us much good, here and now. Falling's easy. Climbing's hard, and It has a long climb ahead. And meantime, we have to keep on fighting Its many shadows among the worlds, and in our own hearts, as if no victory'd been won."

"The shadows in our hearts . . . ," Nita said softly. She'd had too close a look at her own shadows when Dairine passed through her Ordeal, and since then she had wished often enough that there were some way to get rid of them. But there wasn't; not even wizards can make things happen just by wishing.

"I've got to get going," she said. "I'll stop in when I've finished my run."

"I'll probably still be here," Pralaya said. "I wanted to talk to Pont about a couple of things."

"Or . . ." Nita hesitated. "No, never mind; you're tired."

Pralaya gave her an amused look. "You're thinking that another point of view to triangulate with might not be a bad idea."

"Seriously, if you're tired, though—"

"You are, too," Pralaya said, "and you're not letting it stop you." He got up. "Why not, if you like? I may as well spend the time, till Pont shows up, doing something useful."

Nita hesitated just a moment more, then smiled. "Yeah," she said. "Let's go."

She got her transit circle ready. *Lucky he was here*, she thought. While Pont was friendly enough, there was a congenial quality about Pralaya that made him easier to work with, and the sharpness of his mind and the way he saw the aschetic universes were advantages.

Luck, though? said something at the back of her mind, something faintly uneasy. *Is there really such a thing?*

"Ready?" Pralaya said, dropping his own transit circle to the ground.

"Ready," Nita said.

They vanished.

Two hours by the playroom's time, much later by Nita's watch, she and Pralaya returned to the playroom—and Nita was never so glad to see such a boring, bland worldscape in her life, after the turbulent one she and Pralaya had just come out of. And that one had been, so her manual had warned her, more like the inside of a human body than anything else she'd worked with.

"I still feel silly for having expected to see tubes and veins and things," Nita said, as she flopped down into one of the chairs, which, though made for a hominid, had legs that bent in different places than hers did.

Pralaya reached over to the table, picked up the kernel in two paws, and tossed it to her. Nita turned it over in her hands, found the mass-manipulation part of the construct, and twiddled with it until the chair changed shape beneath her. "And I wasn't expecting all that sand," she said.

"The symbolism's a good-enough reflection of how a malignant illness like your mother's works," Pralaya said, curling up on the lounger next to Nita's chair. "Scrape it away in one place . . . the cells just keep breeding, filling in the gaps. And as for the tubes and organs and so on, working with them as such wouldn't help you. It's not your mother's tubes you're trying to cure; it's all of her. A big job."

Nita nodded, and rubbed her eyes. Finding the kernel had not been difficult, much to her relief, though it had been hidden in what seemed a world's worth of desert, with only the occasional eroded skyscraper-peak sticking up out of the sand.

But the practice malignancy that the aschetic universe had created for her had been much more than she could handle. She had managed to get rid of the viruses in a large area of it, but only by brute force, rather than talking them out of what they were doing. There had been billions of them, as many of them as there had been grains of sand, and their response to Nita had been furious, a storm of self-preservation. More than once they had almost buried her under dune after rolling dune . . . and when she had run out of both energy and time that could be spent in that universe, even after blasting clean a large part of that huge waste, she could feel the rest of it lying under the scorching, unfriendly sky, simply waiting for her to leave so that it could get on with what it had been doing . . . killing someone.

I can't give up now, Nita thought. Yet the thought of her mother's situation was really starting to scare her.

What if it's all for nothing? she thought. *What if even this—*

She hadn't wanted to say it to her mother, hadn't wanted to hear it said. But half the power inherent in wizardry lay in telling the truth about things. To deny the truth was to deny your own power.

"Problems?" Pralaya said quietly.

Nita paused, then nodded.

"I'm getting scared," Nita said. "I'm beginning to think . . . think that if what's wrong with my mom is as bad as things were in that last universe, then I may not be able to do it." It was hard to say, but it had to be said.

Pralaya made a little sideways tilt of his sleek head, which Nita had started to recognize as the way his people nodded.

"And willpower may not be enough," Nita said softly. "Trying my best . . . still may not be enough." She swallowed hard. "Loving her . . . no matter how much . . . it doesn't matter. It still may not be enough."

There was a long silence. In a slightly remote-sounding voice, Pralaya said, "Running into that hard wall of impossibility is something we all do eventually."

"It hurts," Nita said softly. "Knowing there's wizardry . . . knowing that it can do so much . . . but not this. It would almost have been better not to know at all."

"That can happen," Pralaya said to her.

She looked up, shocked, for his tone was not precisely cautionary.

"Wizardry doesn't live in the unwilling heart," Pralaya said, again with that slightly remote tone, "as you know. If it starts to hurt too much, you can always give it up."

Nita sat silent in the unchanging radiance. "If I do that," she said, "then what's been given to me's been wasted. The universe would die a little faster because I threw away what the Powers gave me to work with."

"Of course, you're the only one who can say whether it's worth it," Pralaya said. "And afterward, you wouldn't know. Forgetfulness would come soon enough. Your mother might still die, but at least you wouldn't feel guilty that you couldn't stop it."

Nita didn't answer. She was beginning to hear more clearly something in Pralaya's voice that she hadn't been able to identify, really, until now, when they were alone here, in the quiet.

"But also," Pralaya said, "you're acting as if your mother was doing something she wasn't going to do, anyway."

"What?"

"Die," Pralaya said.

Nita just looked at him. *There's something about his eyes*, she thought. At first she had dismissed it as just another part of his alienness. Now, though . . .

"We're all mortal," Pralaya said. "Even the longest lived of us. Sooner or later, the bodies give up, wear out, run down. Matter-energy systems have that problem, in the universes where living beings reside. I don't know of any solutions for that problem that are likely to do your species—or mine, for that matter—much good."

"But it wasn't supposed to happen *now*!" Nita cried. "I'm just a kid! My sister's even more of one! She's going to be . . ." She trailed off. It was indeed going to be worse for Dairine, as if Nita could even imagine, yet, how bad it was going to be for *her*. "She's going to be completely miserable," Nita said.

" 'Wasn't supposed to happen'?" Pralaya said. "According to whom?"

Nita couldn't think of an answer to that.

"Twist and turn as we may," Pralaya said softly, "sooner or later we all come up against it. We do our service to the Powers That Be . . . but They do not always treat us in return as we feel we deserve to be treated. And then . . . then we look around us and begin to consider the alternatives."

Nita looked at Pralaya, uneasy again. He looked at her with those great dark eyes, and Nita saw a change in expression, as if someone else was looking out at her.

And suddenly she knew, understood, and her mouth went dry.

"I know who you are," Nita said, not caring now whether she was wrong or would feel stupid about it afterward.

"I thought you'd work it out eventually," the Lone One said.

They sat there in the silence for a few moments. "So that's it?" the Lone One said after a long pause. "You're not going to go all hostile on me?"

Nita's mind was in a turmoil. She knew her enemy . . . and at the same time, she'd never seen It like this before. *It* has *been changing*, she thought. *We gave It the chance to do that, right from the start*. But there was more to her reaction than just that realization. She had to admit that even through her fear and unease she was curious.

"Not right this minute," Nita said. "Not until I understand some things. I was in Pralaya's mind, once or twice. He's a real wizard. He has a real life. He has a mate, and pups, and . . ." She shook her head. "How can you be *you* . . . and Pralaya, too?"

It looked at her with mild amusement in those big dark eyes. "The same way I do it with you," the Lone One said.

Nita gulped.

"You know the rule: 'Those who resist the Powers . . . yet do the will of the Powers. Those who serve the Powers . . . themselves become the Powers.' And if you serve Them . . . then, if you're not careful, you also sometimes may serve me. I'm still one of Them, no matter what They say."

Nita didn't move, didn't say anything. She was remembering some more of the stricture It had quoted: *Beware the Choice! Beware refusing it!* She hadn't been quite clear about what that had meant before. Now she was beginning to get an idea.

"Sooner or later," It said, "every wizard leaves me a loophole through which I can enter. Sooner or later every wizard just wants to make a deal, just one time. Sooner or later every wizard gets tired of always having it go the way the Powers That Be—the *other* Powers, I mean—insist it has to go. No room for flexibility in Their way of thinking. No room for compromise. So unreasonable of Them. But wizards have free will, and they don't always see things the Powers' way. When they come around to that line of thinking, I'm always here."

It stretched and scratched Itself. "For Pralaya, the loophole was curiosity. It still is; we've coexisted for some time. His people's minds are constructed differently from yours. They don't see an inexorable enemy when they see me, but part of the natural order of things. They've learned to accept death. Very civilized people."

Nita had her own ideas about that.

"He's useful," the Lone One said. "Pralaya is a very skilled, experienced wizard. He's had a long life; during it, various troubles have avoided him. That's been my doing. In return, occasionally I can exploit his acceptance of me, to slip in when he lets his guard down, and handle some business of my own."

"Like dealing with me," Nita said.

She was controlling herself as tightly as she could, waiting for any sense that her mind was being overshadowed by the Lone One's power against her will. But she couldn't feel any such thing.

"Among other things," the Lone Power said. "And if there's going to be a deal, the structure of it is simple enough. One less wizard in the world is worth something to me. Your mother's life is worth something to you." Pralaya shrugged. "Over your short career, you've been something of an irritant to me. But not so much so that I'm not willing to do you a favor in order to get rid of you."

Nita stared at it. "You're telling me that if I give up my wizardry . . . you'll save my mother's life."

"Yes."

Nita swallowed. "Why do I have a real hard time believing you?"

It gave her a whimsical look. "So I bend the truth sometimes. One of the minor uses of entropy. What do you expect of me? I use what tools I've been left . . . and the one I invented always works the best. It's working here and now, while we sit here talking. The cancer cells are spreading all through your mother's body right this minute, eating her alive." It smiled slightly. "Cute little machines that they are. Life thinks it can overcome everything . . . but in some ways, it's too strong for its own good. This is one of them."

Nita's mouth was bone-dry with fear. "Why should you keep your word once you've given it?"

It laughed. "Why shouldn't I? You think one ordinary mortal's life means that much to me? But a wizard . . . that's another story. You people cause me no end of grief, even over your little lifetimes. I run around and try again and again to kill you, or just to keep you from undoing my best work. It takes up too much of my time. Now here's a thing that's easy for me to do. You come to terms with me, and I call off the viruses. Because you've willingly, consciously come to terms with me, by the Oath you swore, you then lose your wizardry. One less problem for me in the universe, afterward. Maybe more than just one less."

"It's a trick," Nita said.

"Not at all," the Lone Power said. "You don't believe me? Fine. You go right on inside your mother as planned. Take Pralaya with you, even; he'll be glad to help. But I'm telling you, you're still going to find it too much for you. The viruses will win in the end." The Lone One shrugged again. "But I'm even willing to let you try to beat me fair and square, and fail, and I'll *still* do you that last favor afterward . . . if you agree to the price."

The price. The words echoed. Suddenly Nita found herself wondering whether this encounter itself was the price that the manual had so far failed to specify.

And she was becoming cold inside at the thought that perhaps just by sitting here this long and listening to the Lone One, she had already paid it.

"What if I refuse?" Nita said.

"I couldn't care less," the Lone Power said. "Stretch your power to the uttermost. It won't help. The operation will end, and the doctors will get that tumor out, all right. But even in the short run it won't matter, because the viruses in your mother's body won't have listened to anything *you* have to say, and the secondary tumors will already be forming in her bone marrow and her pancreas and her liver. You'll have maybe a few more weeks with her. Or maybe you'll overextend yourself in the wizardry and leave your mother having to deal with the reality of *your* death, while her own is creeping up on her. Nice going-away present, that."

If Nita had felt cold before, it was nothing to how she felt now. She could find nothing to say.

"Don't make up your mind right away," the Lone Power said. "Think about it. You've got plenty of time . . . until the morning after next, at least. And then you can slip inside your mother, find her kernel, the software of her soul, and do your best."

"And you'll make sure I fail!"

"Far be it from me to be so unfair," the Lone Power said, and folded Pralaya's middle arms, leaning back in the lounger. "There's, oh, a chance in a million or two that you can save her . . . but your inexperience means that you'll have to do it by brute power, fueled by despair . . . and you'll almost certainly die, either doing it or trying to."

Nita was silent.

"It'll be a lot easier my way," the Lone Power said. "You go in, you fail . . . and then you agree to my price and I call off my little friends. Spontaneous remission, the doctors will all say afterward. Miracle cure. Everybody will be happy . . . most especially your dad." Nita gulped again. "And as for you, you just don't do any more wizardry. Your mother doesn't even have to know about it. Or you can tell her that you had to use up all the wizardry in you for this one big job, while you still remember what you were, anyway. And you'll be amazed how soon she stops bringing up the subject at all."

Pralaya scratched his tummy with his middle legs. "But then mortals always get so twitchy about magic, anyway. No matter what you've told your mother since she found out about it, she's never been entirely sure that you didn't get the wizardry somewhere . . . let's just say, somewhere unhealthy." It smiled at her, and the look was supremely ironic. "You'll be able to relieve her and your father of their concerns once and for all. And indirectly, their concerns about your little sister. I doubt even Dairine is going to rub their noses in her continued practice of wizardry when *you've* forgotten all about it. She'll go undercover and you'll all be just a normal happy family again."

Except for all the things that will never again be right . . . *no matter how normal we seem.*

Nita sat there feeling numb. "Just how are the other Powers letting you get away with this kind of thing?" she asked at last.

"They can't stop me," It said. "Not without undoing all of creation. And They're not willing to do that. Oh, there are some pocket universes where They have one or another of my aspects bound. You've seen one of those—on your Ordeal." It shrugged. "But I can't be confined to such places. The power of creation was given into my hands, once, and the willing gifts of Gods cannot be taken back after they are given . . . so I am still part of everything created, one way or another. And will be, until it all ends. But that's a long way ahead of us." It stretched. "There are more immediate concerns. You'll let me know what you decide, sooner or later . . . and if you pay my price, your mother will live."

It got up and stretched again. "I'll take my host home," the Lone One said. "It doesn't do for me to overshadow him for too long at a time; he might get suspicious. You'll decide what to do. And when you head out to do your final intervention, you'll find Pralaya waiting for you, ready to help you out—one way or the other."

Pralaya's transit circle appeared at his feet. "But one way or another," the Lone Power said, "I suggest you make your peace with the other Powers That Be. Your relationship with them isn't likely to last in its present form for much longer."

And Pralaya stepped through his circle, and vanished.

Nita sat there alone in stunned silence for a long, long while, thinking. Finally she got up and prepared her own transit circle, wanting more than anything else just to go home, where things would seem normal again, where she could get a little rest and try to work out where the truth lay.

But the image of her mother lying pale and stricken in the hospital bed kept coming before her eyes, and Nita was afraid that she had already made up her mind.

It was late when she got back, and the sight of her darkened bedroom seemed to suck the energy out of her. Nita fell onto the bed and lay there in desperate weariness, while her mind raced. For what seemed like hours, though it was probably only a few minutes, she tried to find a way out of the bargain she was being offered . . . *any* way out.

She couldn't find one. *I need another viewpoint*, she thought. But it was too late to talk to Kit.

And I need Pralaya, she thought. *That extra dose of ability, his talent at seeing and analyzing the alternate universes.* He was good at it, there was no question of that. She was going to need all the help she could get.

But Kit is going to want to come, she thought. *I can't stop him. And, oh, I do need his help.*

But he was even less experienced at this business of manipulating kernels than she was. *And if he* does *come along, when he sees Pralaya, what if he realizes who's hiding inside him?*

The details of this bizarre relationship were still making her head go around in circles. Up until now the Lone Power usually had manifested itself in displays of brutal and destructive power. Nita knew perfectly well that It could be subtle when It pleased. But she hadn't pictured anything like *this*. And regardless of the mechanism by which It had subverted this wizard, if Kit recognized Its presence in Pralaya, he was going to be furious that Nita was still working with him. *He's not going to understand what I'm up against here*, she thought.

He will if you explain it to him, said the back of her mind.

But Nita was already beginning to try to frame that explanation in her head, and the more she tried, the more it sounded like something that would simply make Kit think she had sold out to the Lone Power.

And what if he's right?

She turned over and stared at the ceiling, her mind noisy with tentative dialogue, and with anguish.

To save her mother . . . and lose her wizardry.

Was it worth it? Once, when Nita's wizardry was new, maybe she would have said *No!* right away. The Oath seemed so clear-cut then, the lines between good and evil very thickly drawn.

But now . . .

Her mother.

She simply could not imagine a life without that serene, dancing presence sailing through it. Her mother was always there, behind everything, involved in everything. The idea of a life without her, of an emptiness where she had been: never again to hear her voice, joking, yelling, singing to herself, never again.

Not this side of Timeheart, anyway.

Normally it was a comfort thinking of Timeheart, where everything that existed was preserved in perfection, close to the center of things. But the Heart of Time was remote—a remote certainty at best, a remote possibility when you were in a more cynical or suspicious mood. It was an abstract, nothing like the concrete reality of the woman who had been genially cursing at her Cuisinart just a week or so ago. The woman who had always been there with a hug for Nita, who had been able to understand about everything—about being bullied, about doing well or badly at school—even, to a certain extent, about wizardry itself.

And now . . . if I do this . . . I'll have to give that up.

But she would still be here.

Yet . . . to give it up— The idea was bitter. A window on a hundred thousand other worlds, and a most intimate window on this one, closed forever—even the memory of it slowly ebbing away until there was just a small nameless ache at the bottom of her that she would learn to ignore with time, the place where wizardry had been and wasn't anymore. So many people had that ache and thought it was normal. Eventually Nita would be just one more of them. She would remember—if she remembered anything—"those great games she used to play with Kit." That was all they would be: memories of childhood fantasies.

And *he* would still remember the reality, while Nita would pass him on the street, maybe, or in school, and not know what he had been to her . . . not *really*.

But at least nobody would be dead.

Except the part of you that the Powers gave the wizardry to, Nita thought. *Murdered, just as if you'd shot it with a gun.* How could it possibly be a good thing to do that, no matter *whose* life it saved?

She put her face in her hands. It was a dilemma.

But, then, that's what a dilemma is, Nita thought. *A two-horned problem.*

A thing split in two.

Like me.

Like me and Kit, whispered a thought that had been lying unspoken in the back of her mind for a while now, for fear that speaking it might make it come true.

She moaned out loud with the sheer unfairness of it. Yet what use was keeping wizardry and partnership, and all the rest of it, when her mother wouldn't be there to see it and roll her eyes and insist that she do her homework? All the hospital talk of chemotherapy and radiotherapy and so on, after the surgery, could not hide from her what it took no wizardry at all to see: the looks on the faces of the doctors and nurses who were caring for her mom. They usually would not even say the name of the thing that had attacked her mother from within. They merely said "C.A." or used long Latin and Greek words, all of which had the ominous "oma" ending clinging to them, like a dark shadow trailing away behind. The doctors were as afraid of what was going to happen to her mom as Nita was. For all the magic that was medical science, there was precious little hope in their eyes.

If anything's going to save her, Nita thought, *it's going to have to be something I do.*

But which *something?*

The weariness was beginnning to catch up with her. Nita put her face into her pillow. She wanted to cry, but she felt too tired to do even that.

Mom. Kit. Her mind went back and forth between the two of them.

I'm just going to have to go ahead and get what help I can get out of Pralaya. And then . . . if it doesn't work . . .

She was afraid now to try to see that far ahead in her life. But she was considering the options—and the idea of what Kit would think of this scared Nita. Yet she knew that keeping her options open was the right thing.

Like you were right about Jones Inlet? said another small voice in the back of her mind.

She gripped the pillow with both hands and ground her face into it. *Tell me what to do!* she begged whoever might be listening. *Give me a hint!*

But the night was silent around her, and no answers came. And the only Power That had spoken to her so far had been the One she had sworn never to deal with.

Finally sleep took her. But her dreams were all bad, and even in the midst of them, she knew that when she woke up, things would be no better.

Thursday

THE AWAKENING WAS SUDDEN, and Nita lay there with her heart pounding, knowing something was wrong but unable to work out what it was. Finally her eyes focused as she looked over at her alarm clock, and she realized it was eleven-thirty in the morning.

Didn't it go off? What happened? she thought, sitting bolt upright in bed.

"Dad called school," Dairine's voice said. Nita looked up and saw Dairine sitting in her chair with her feet up on Nita's desk, wearing nothing but one of her dad's T-shirts, and looking small and miserable. "He asked them to let us both off today because of the operation tomorrow."

Nita lay down again, wishing that she could just go back to sleep . . . except that it was hardly any better than being awake.

"Dair," she said, "if giving up your wizardry would make Mom better, would you do it?"

Her sister looked at her in complete shock and didn't say anything for at least a minute. For Dairine this was something of a record.

"Is that what you're going to have to do?" she said at last.

"I don't know."

"I'd . . . ," Dairine said. "I'd . . ." And she trailed off, her eyes going haunted.

Nita nodded.

"Are you sure it would work?" Dairine said after a while.

Nita shook her head. "Nothing's sure," she said.

Dairine pulled her knees up under the baggy T-shirt and hugged them to her for a long time. Then she looked up.

"And then it would all be gone?"

"Everything," Nita said. "All the magic, gone forever."

Dairine sat with her forehead on her knees, minute after minute. When she looked up, her face was wet. "If you were sure . . ."

Nita shook her head again.

"I'd miss you," Dairine said.

"I wouldn't be gone," Nita said.

"You know what I mean."

Nita nodded. "Yeah," she said. "I'd miss you, too."

And Dairine got up and went out of Nita's room, heading downstairs.

Nita could do little else that day but work with the manual, trying to evaluate the effectiveness of her work with the kernels and fine-tuning the spells she would have with her while working on her mother. But the problem that she could not solve kept intruding itself between her and her preparation, and there was no respite from it, nowhere to hide.

The sound of the discreet *bang!* in the backyard brought Nita's head up— almost a welcome distraction. But then her heart went cold. *Kit. How am I going to explain this to him?*

It just isn't fair, she thought. *What's happened to Mom has spoiled everything. Even things I should be glad about hurt now.*

She heard the back door open and the faint sound of Kit saying something to Dairine in the kitchen, then his footsteps on the stairs, and a scrambling noise behind him as Ponch ran up. The dog was first into her room; he burst past Kit and ran up to Nita and put his forepaws up on her. "We went bang!" he said.

"Yeah, I heard you, big guy," Nita said, and looked at Kit as he came in and sat down on the bed.

"How'd it go?" Kit said. "You get your practice done?"

"Yeah . . . the last one, I think."

He looked concerned. "Is that going to be enough? Are you ready?"

At that she had to put her face in her hands, rubbing her eyes in an attempt to keep from looking like she was hiding her face. "I don't know," she said. "But it can't wait any longer."

"I guess you couldn't really put it off," Kit said, sounding like he could tell perfectly well that Nita wanted to.

"No," she said, unhappy. "When Mom's anesthetized is the best time to do this; even during sleep there's a chance she could be conscious enough to get caught up in what's going on, and that'd be a problem."

"Well," Kit said, "if you've done all the preparation you can . . . I guess there's nothing to do now but wait."

"Yup," she said.

"And while we're doing that, we can talk about exactly what you want me to be doing to help."

She didn't answer right away. Kit looked at her sharply, and she noticed Ponch's eyes on her, too, an expression more subtle and considering than you usually got from him. "Neets," Kit said, "why're you so twitchy all of a sudden?"

"Well, why on Earth wouldn't I be twitching!" Nita said.

Kit and Ponch just looked at her. "Neets," Kit said, "give me a break. This is *me*, remember? You're twitching more than usual. More than makes sense even for what you're going through, not that it's not awful enough. What's *happened* to you since we talked last?"

"Kit . . . ," Nita said at last. "We've saved a lot of lives in our time. A *lot*."

"Millions," Kit said. There might have been some pleasure in the way he said it, but no pride.

"So how come I may not be able to save the one who matters?"

"Like those other times didn't matter, really," Kit said, with mild scorn. "But Neets, the key word here is *we*. You don't have to go through this alone."

She didn't say anything for a long while. "You don't understand," Nita said at last. "This time, I think I *have* to do it alone." And she tightly controlled her mind so that he wouldn't hear her thought: *Because I couldn't stand it if somehow you wound up paying the same price I might have to . . . and losing your wizardry, too!*

Kit's look got suddenly even more concerned. "Neets. Tell me what you've been doing. I don't want a précis. I want the details. All of them."

She was silent for some moments. Then Nita told him.

It took a while, though doing some of the explaining mind to mind sped things up. But toward the end of it, as she began telling him about Pralaya, Kit's expression turned grave. When she told him about that last conversation she and Pralaya had had, Kit's eyes went cold. He didn't say anything for a good while.

"I'm still not sure how He was doing that," Nita said.

"As an avatar," Kit said. "Neets, *all* the Powers That Be can do that when They need to, when They're on the job. For cripes' sake, if the One's Champion can live inside a macaw for years at a time, why should it surprise you that the Lone Power can pull the same stunt every now and then?"

Slowly she nodded, feeling cold inside.

"Neets, I hate to say it, but this really looks like the Lone One's been getting at you. Even before It fell, It preferred to work by Itself. Then It got isolated and proud, and after that came the Fall . . . and now that pride is still Its favorite way of tripping people up. It makes them think they can handle everything by themselves."

"Kit, in this case there's actually something to it! You just don't have the experience at what I'm going to have to be doing—"

"As if that matters! Neets, you're not thinking straight right now. You even missed something as simple as the mechanism the Lone One's using to hide inside Pralaya. How can you be so sure about your thinking on everything else?"

That was something she couldn't bear to hear. Followed to its logical conclusion, that line of reasoning would suggest that everything Nita had been planning was possibly useless, doomed to failure from the start.

"If you accept Its help," Kit said, "you're probably going to lose your wizardry! But what's more important is that doing that is just *wrong*."

Now she did hide her face in her hands. "Kit," she said softly, "it looks more and more like, to save my mom, I'm going to lose it no matter what I do. Or die trying. But I have to *try*."

"Not alone," Kit said. "And not this way, Neets! You come to any kind of deal with that One, it's gonna backfire somehow. Believe me!"

"All this is real easy for *you* to say, but *your mother's not dying*!"

Kit's expression was pained, but he just shook his head. "You think I haven't imagined about a hundred times how this must be for you? But it doesn't change the rights and wrongs of it, Neets. It says right there in the Oath, 'I will defend life *when it is right to do so*.' It's *never* right to do it on the Lone Power's terms, and if you let It sucker you into this—"

"Kit, you've got to believe me. It's not like that. You don't really understand what's going on here."

"I understand that you're messing around with the Lone Power, and you're going to get burned! What makes you think It has the slightest intention of doing what It says It's going to? It's gonna find some loophole to exploit, just the way It always does, and leave you out in the cold."

He stopped. There was a long, long silence as he and Ponch watched her.

Nita discovered that she was actually starting to shake. *He's right. But I'm right, too. What do I do—?* "Look," she said. "I can't take much more of this right now. Tomorrow morning is getting closer every minute, and I'm not sure I'm ready yet."

"When are you going to start work in the morning?" Kit said.

Nita rubbed her eyes again. "Around eight. The doctors said that's when they're starting."

"I'll be here," Kit said. "Neets, please . . . Get some rest. Get your brains straightened out. *You're not going to do this alone.*"

He got up and headed out hurriedly, almost as if something was making him nervous. Ponch licked her hand and trotted out after Kit.

Nita sat there for a long while. *There's no way I'm going to be able to keep him from coming along . . .*

. . . if I wait for him.

But Nita *did* want to wait for him. She knew his help would be invaluable. At the same time, she knew that the minute Kit set eyes on Pralaya, there would be trouble. She would lose Pralaya's help. And she needed that, too, regardless of who might live inside Pralaya from time to time.

And at the end of it all, if she could not cure her mother herself, then Pralaya had to be there to implement the bargain.

There were no answers, and time was running out. The only consolation was for Nita to keep telling herself that tomorrow around this time, it would all be over. Her mother would have been saved or else she wouldn't have been, and if she hadn't, Nita wouldn't be in any position to worry about anything else.

It was not much consolation at all.

The rest of the day was a waking nightmare. Nita was tempted to go back into the practice universes one last time, but she wasn't sure what difference that would make—and she was tired, tired. She needed her rest but couldn't seem to get any. Details of the spells she would need to take with her, last-minute ideas, and the constantly returning thought that Kit might be right and she might be completely wrong kept going around and around in her head, and gave her no peace.

It seemed like about five minutes after Kit had come over that Nita's dad came home from work, and they all went to the hospital together. Her mother hadn't had any more seizures, for which Nita was profoundly thankful. Except the thought kept creeping in: *Is this the Lone One just giving me more time to think . . . and to be grateful to It?* The idea made her shudder.

When they went into Nita's mom's room, Nita saw that a number of machines had been moved in by the bed. One apparently was to make sure there was warning if she had any more seizures—there were ugly little pink and blue contact pads glued all over her head, with the hair held down around them in a hopeful sort of way by one of the "turbans" Nita had seen some of the nurses wearing. Her mom looked unnatural, drawn, more tired than ever, and her smile was wearing thin at the edges.

"Oh, honey, don't look at me like that," her mom said, seeing Nita's expression. "I look like the bride of Frankenstein, I know that. It's all right. I was due for another haircut, anyway."

Two things hit Nita at once. The first thing was that, as always, her mother was trying to take care of her, even when she herself was sick. The second, which struck Nita with a terrible inevitability, was that what her mother was saying was not true: It would never be all right, never again. Her mom was really going to die.

For several long seconds, Nita could find nothing at all to do or say, and she didn't dare look her mom in the eye; she knew her mother would see instantly what was the matter. Fortunately, Dairine got between her and her mom, and Nita disentangled herself and turned away, never more grateful for her sister's inborn ability to get in the way.

But the moment decided her. Kit or no Kit, Lone One or not, she would do anything she had to do to save her mother: give up her wizardry, agree to whatever had to be agreed to. She was lost.

But at least I know now, she thought. The rest of the visit passed in a kind of cheerful fog of small talk, all of it forced; none of them felt much like discussing what was going to happen the next day. After a while Nita's dad asked Nita and Dairine to give him a few moments alone with their mom.

Nita went down the hall, down by the soft-drink machine, and Dairine followed her slowly.

"Is it gonna be all right?" Dairine said. Suddenly she didn't sound like her usual competent self. Suddenly she sounded very young and scared, really wanting her older sister to tell her that things were going to work.

"Yeah," Nita said. "One way or another."

And there was nothing else to say and nothing else to do but wait for the morning.

Friday Morning

HOW NITA SLEPT THAT night she never knew; she assumed it must have been exhaustion. At six that morning, her dad, fully dressed and ready to leave, awakened her.

"Dad," Nita said, and got out of bed.

He looked at her with a terrible stillness. She would almost have preferred him to cry or yell; but he was now reduced to simply waiting.

"Are you ready?" he said.

There was almost no way to answer him and still tell the truth. "I'm going to start work when they do," Nita said. "It may take me as long as Mom spends in the OR, or even longer, so don't panic if I'm not here when you get home."

"All right," her father said.

He reached out and put his arms around her. All Nita could do was bury her face in his shoulder and hang on, hang on hard, trying not to cry, much though she wanted to; she was sure it would frighten him if she lost her control now.

"Be careful, honey," he said, still with that terrible control. "I don't want to—" He stopped. *Lose you both*, she heard him think.

"I'll be careful," Nita said. "Go on, Daddy. I'll see you later."

She let go of him and turned away, waiting for him to leave. He went out the back door; a moment later, Dairine came into her room.

"Did you hear from Kit?" she asked.

Nita nodded. *Oh, please, don't ask me any more.*

Dairine didn't say anything. "Look," she said then, as outside, their dad started the car. "Come back," Dairine said. *"Just come back."*

Nita was astonished to see tears in her sister's eyes. For a split second she wanted desperately to tell Dairine that she was afraid she might not come back . . . or that she might come back and not be a wizard anymore—and Nita wasn't sure which possibility was more awful. But she didn't dare say anything. If Dairine got any real sense of what was going on inside Nita's head, there was too much of a danger that she might interfere . . . and Tom and Carl had been emphatic about what would happen then.

Nita just nodded and hugged Dairine. "You ready to give the surgeons whatever energy they need?"

"All set."

"Then go on," she said. "Dad's waiting. Keep an eye on him, Dari." She swallowed. "Keep him from getting desperate. It's going to matter."

Dairine nodded and went downstairs.

*   *   *

Nita waited to hear the car drive away. Then she got herself ready, checking the charm bracelet one last time for the spells stored there. A couple of openings remained, and she spent a few minutes considering what she might add. Finally, thinking of that first meeting with Pont and the other wizards, she added the subroutine that let the wizard using it walk on water. *If there was ever a day I needed to believe I could do that*, she thought, *it's today*.

Then she opened her manual to the pages involving access to the practice universes.

Let's go, she said to the manual. *The playroom first . . . and then the main event*.

The page she was looking at shimmered, and then the print on it steadied down to a new configuration, a more complex one than she'd seen so far. It flickered, and then said: *Secondary access to nonaschetic "universe" analog has been authorized. Caution: This "universe" is inhabited. Population: 1.*

Nita pulled her transit-circle spell out of the back of her mind, dropped it to the floor, took one last deep breath, and stepped through.

At seven-fifteen that morning, Kit was sitting on the beat-up kitchen sofa, eating cornflakes out of an ancient beat-up Scooby-Doo bowl in a studied and careful way. It was partly to steady his stomach—cornflakes were comfort food for him, inherently reassuring on some strange level—and partly his standard preparation for a wizardry. All your power wouldn't do you much good if your brains weren't working because your blood sugar was down in your socks somewhere.

He finished the bowl he was working on, contemplated a second one, and decided against it. Kit took his mom's favorite bowl to the sink and washed it out carefully, going over his preparations one last time in his head. He knew as much about the aschetic universes as the manual would tell him without approval from a Senior. He knew that Nita's authority and agreement would be enough to get him inside her mother with her; and beyond that, he had every power-feeding technique he could think of ready to go in the back of his head.

"I want to come along," Ponch said from behind him.

Kit sighed as he finished washing the spoon, and he put it in the rack, too. "I don't think you can," he said. "It's going to be complicated enough as it is."

"I want to be with you. And I want to see her."

Kit sighed again. Ponch had caught some of his boss's nervousness about what Nita had gotten herself into. "Look," Kit said. "You can come over and see her off, okay? Then you have to go home and wait for me."

Ponch wagged his tail. "And *no* coming after me once I've left you," Kit said. "You have to stay here."

Ponch drooped his head, depressed that Kit had anticipated what he'd been thinking.

Kit went to get his jacket from the hooks behind the door. He checked his jacket pocket for his manual, though he wasn't sure how useful it would be inside Nita's mom. *Better to have it, though*. As he was running through his checks one last time, his mom, wearing what his dad referred to as the "Tartan Bathrobe of Doom," wandered into the kitchen, looked back at Kit and Ponch, and caught the dog's sad expression. "He hasn't been bad again, has he?" she said.

Ponch drooped his head some more and wagged his tail again, an abject look that fooled Kit not at all. "Not in any of the usual ways, Mama," he said. "Look, I'm going to help Nita, and this is a serious one. I may not be back for a while."

"Okay, *brujito*."

He had to smile at that. His mom had taken longer than his father to come to terms with Kit's wizardry; his father had been surprisingly enthusiastic about it, once he got over the initial shock. "Hey, my son's a *brujo*," he started saying to Kit's mother. "What's the matter with that?" His pop wore his pride in a way that seemed to suggest that he thought he was somehow responsible for Kit's talent. *Maybe he is*, Kit thought. So far he didn't have any data on which side of the family his wizardly tendencies descended from; he'd been much too busy lately to look into it.

At least the situation was presently working in his favor. "Come on," Kit said to Ponch. As they went out into the backyard together, Kit glanced over in the general direction of Nita's house and in thought said, *Neets?*

There was no answer.

Kit stood still, hoping against hope that she was just distracted for a moment. *Nita!*

Nothing.

It was the matter of a second to throw a transit circle around himself and Ponch, and it took no more than another second to make sure it would be silent in operation. A moment later Kit and Ponch were standing in Nita's bedroom.

It was empty. Kit stood there, listening to the sounds of an empty house, feeling for the presence of other human beings, and knowing immediately that Nita was already gone.

He felt just a flash of anger, replaced almost immediately by fear. *She left early because she was afraid for me*, he thought.

One more error in judgment. *Now what?* Kit thought, going cold with fear. *Go over to see Tom and Carl, get permission to follow her—*

Why? I can find her, Ponch said in Kit's head.

Kit looked at Ponch in astonishment. *How?*

The way I found the squirrels.

"But that was making a new universe," Kit said. "Neets is in an old one, a universe that exists already!"

"We can make some of *that* one as if it's new," Ponch said, in a tone of voice suggesting that he was surprised this wasn't obvious. "The part *she's* in."

Kit couldn't think of anything to say.

"I know her scent," Ponch said, impatient. "We can be where she's gone. Let's go!"

Kit was uncertain, but time was short. He reached into his claudication and rummaged around it to find the wizardly leash, then slipped it around Ponch's neck and said, "Okay, big guy, give it your best shot."

Ponch stepped forward, and together they vanished.

They walked for a long time in the dark, an experience Kit was glad no longer unsettled him. Every now and then would come a flicker of light, and he could just see, or sense, Ponch putting his head out into that light and sniffing, the way he might have put his head out a dog door, then pulling back again, turning away. *Having trouble?* Kit asked silently, the third or fourth time this happened.

No. The world just twists, is all. And something doesn't want us to be where she is.

Kit swallowed. But finally they came out into the light and stayed there, and Kit looked around him in surprise, even though his experience of alternate universes had been expanded a lot lately. It was a huge place, a flat space, and its emptiness made it seem to echo in the mind. The sourceless lighting and the shining floor with the assortment of weird chairs, beds, hammocks, frames, and tables in the middle of it made it all look much like a furniture showroom.

Ponch pulled Kit toward the furniture, still sniffing. There were some people there: aliens, which didn't surprise Kit particularly—hominids were not at all in the majority in his home universe. As he approached, a few of them looked at him with slight surprise, and one of them pointed a greater than usual number of eyes at him. It was a Sulamid, Kit noticed, an alien native to the far side of his own galaxy, one of a people who—unusually—were almost all wizards, a fact that apparently had something to do with the way their brains were divided.

The looks they were giving him—furred people, one tall cadaverous hominid, a four-legged alien, another one that looked like five or six oversized blue ball bearings in company, and the Sulamid with its many stalky eyes—were speculative. "I'm on errantry," Kit said, "and I greet you."

Ponch barked. To Kit's bemusement, every wizard present looked in what seemed to be surprise at Ponch. The Sulamid bent over in half and then straightened up again, its eyes and various of its tentacles tying themselves in graceful knots.

"I'm looking for another of my species," Kit said. "My colleague thinks she was just here. Have you seen her?"

Various looks were exchanged. "You just missed them," said the ball bearings. "They were here with more of us: Pralaya. They just left. They were on an intervention. Pralaya was going to assist them."

The whole group of them were still looking at him. Kit started to feel uneasy, for he thought he knew what they were thinking: *This other wizard is trying to interfere somehow.* "Did she say anything about what she was going to be doing?" Kit said, somehow knowing that it was useless to do so. These other wizards were not going to help him; they were uncertain why he was here, uncertain whether he might somehow foul an intervention in progress.

"No," said first the ball-bearing wizard and then the others.

"She has gone into the dark," said the Sulamid, "all too accompanied. And her destination is an unknown."

The other wizards threw the Sulamid an odd look and began, one after another, to vanish. Shortly the space was empty except for Kit and Ponch and the Sulamid, which was standing not far away, its tentacles wreathing gently, looking at Kit with a lot of its eyes.

"How do you know?" Kit said after a moment.

"Vision is useless without comprehension," said the Sulamid. "Comprehension is bootless without compassion."

"Uh, yeah," Kit said.

The Sulamid bowed once again, if a bow was what it was. It was not directed at Kit but at Ponch. "Pathfinder, seer for the seer in the dark," said the Sulamid, "tracker in the night-places, wait."

And it vanished, too.

Kit could only stand there and look around him at the light and the empty furniture. "Well, thanks loads, guys," he said. *Why were they all so freaked out? What's the matter with them?*

But he and Ponch were not quite alone; not everyone who'd been there originally had left. Behind Kit someone coughed, or maybe it was more like a snort. He and Ponch both turned.

Behind them, looking at them thoughtfully, was what Kit had initially mistaken for a four-footed alien of some kind. But it was actually a pig.

Kit looked at it in astonishment. Ponch instantly barked once, excitedly, and started to run toward the pig, possibly thinking that it could be chased like a squirrel. Kit hurriedly grabbed Ponch by the collar and made him sit down. And to the Pig he said, "What's the meaning of life?"

"You know, a friend of yours was asking me the same thing the other day," said the Transcendent Pig, ambling over, sitting down, and looking Ponch over in an amiable way. "*Is* asking," it added.

The statement was slightly confusing, even taking into account the multidirectional time tenses in the Speech. At least Kit knew that he wasn't the only one confused by the Pig. Every other wizard was, too, and even the Powers That Be weren't sure where the Pig had come from, and tended to describe it as a concrete expression of the universe's innate sense of humor, a sort of positive chaos.

"Is she?" was all Kit could think to say.

"Yes. And you know," said the Pig, "it's all just a big plot, isn't it? You're all just hoping that I might actually slip and answer the question, and *tell* one of you."

Kit blinked at that. "Uh, well—"

"Or else it's a practical joke planted by Someone high up," the Pig muttered, settling down with its trotters under it, a position that made it look peculiarly like a cat. "Wouldn't put it past Them. *Or* Their Boss."

Kit gave the Pig a look. "Oh, come on! The Powers . . ." His voice trailed off as the Pig gave him the same look right back. "I mean, the One . . . wouldn't play *jokes*—"

"Wouldn't It?" said the Transcendent Pig. "Been out in the real world lately?"

"Uh . . ."

"Right. Life being all the other things it is, if it's not funny sometimes, what's it worth? But you changed the subject."

"No, I didn't."

"Maybe you didn't," the Pig said. "I'll allow you that one. You were saying?"

Kit took a long breath. Beside him Ponch lay down but never took his eyes off the Pig. "You're really well traveled," Kit said.

"Omnipresence will do that for you," said the Pig, and it yawned.

"You said you'd seen Nita—" Kit wondered why such simple terms as *my friend* and *my* partner kept sticking in his throat. *What's the matter with me?*

Because one might not be true anymore. And— He absolutely refused to deal with the thought that the other might not be, either.

"Yes. I'm with her now, in fact."

"You are?"

The Pig gave Kit a wry look. "It wouldn't be a terribly useful kind of transcendence if I *wasn't*. Being everywhere at once is part of the job description."

"Where is she? What's she doing?" Kit said after a moment.

The Pig gave him another of those long dry looks. "Oh, come on, now. You know the drill, or you should. You tell me three truths that I don't know, and I tell you one."

Kit raised his eyebrows. "That doesn't sound real fair."

"If you knew how much trouble a human being can get into with just one truth," the Pig said, "you wouldn't be asking for more."

"Got a point there," Kit said. In a flash the thought went through his head that it was possible he didn't need to venture his time or his power on this gamble. Yet somehow he felt that the time spent would be worth his while. "So let's get going."

"An admirable attitude," said the Transcendent Pig. "First truth."

"I'm looking for the wizard who's meant to be my partner," Kit said.

"The first part I know perfectly well. The second part is conditional. 'Meant'? What exactly would it be that's doing the meaning?"

"I think the day we find that out for sure," Kit said, only half joking, "it might all be over."

The Pig raised its eyebrows. "I'm tempted to give you that one," it said. "From a member of Homo sapiens, the secondary insight is relatively unusual these days." It acquired a considering look. "But a half-truth is a half-truth. Give me a whole one this time."

Kit thought for a little while more, wondering what he would add on at the end of all this to make an extra half-truth. *Worry about it shortly.* He said, "My dog makes alternate universes, ones that no one's ever seen before. They're new."

The Pig blinked. "That *is* news. Continuous creation?"

"You've got me."

"Yes, but let's leave that issue out of it for the moment."

Kit blinked, too. "I thought continuous creation had been discredited, though."

The Pig smiled. "The moment any scientist says anything's impossible, you should start wondering. Science, like life, finds ways. But, anyway, you own a brain, and you still think continuous creation's been discredited? So where did *your* last bright idea come from?"

"Uh . . . ," Kit said.

"Right," said the Pig. "Next truth."

"I think," Kit said, with the utmost reluctance, "that my partnership with Nita is about to get totally screwed up if I don't do something, and I'm not sure what to do. I have to find her, I know that. It's vital. But after that—"

"I'll grant you that," the Pig said. "So that's two and a half. What else have you got?"

Kit sat there scouring his mind for some moments, unable to think of even one truth, let alone two. The Pig started to get up.

"Wait a minute!" Kit said, and the Pig looked at him.

It was a desperate move, but it was all Kit could think of. "Here," Kit said.

He looked all around then. For some reason he felt like he didn't want anyone but the Pig to see this.

"It's all right," said the Transcendent Pig. "We're alone. Yes, I'm sure; don't give me that look. What is it?"

Kit pulled his personal claudication open, slipped his hand into it, and came out with that little spark, carefully cupped in both hands. He held the hands just a little bit apart so that the Pig could see in.

It peered between his fingers, and looked at Kit with an odd, speculative expression. "Now, isn't that something," it said. "A glede."

"A what?"

"A glede. Or a dragon's eye, it's called sometimes." The Pig turned its head this way and that, looking at the little spark. "The idea was, you might draw a dragon, but the eyes were where the soul was—some people thought—and the drawing wouldn't come to life until the eyes were added."

The Pig let out a thoughtful breath. "Fine, put it away. Where'd you find it?"

"In the dark," said Kit. "When I stopped making things, and just let the night be what it was." He tucked the glede away.

When he finished doing that, Kit found the Pig watching him closely. "Over time," the Pig said, "and outside it, too, other beings have moved over and through that darkness one way or another. Some of them have found or brought back . . . objects like that—what the void brings forth in silence. The question, afterward, has always been what to do with them."

"What *do* I do with it?" Kit said.

The Transcendent Pig shrugged a transcendently porcine shrug, glancing away. "That's hardly one of the traditional questions."

Kit snorted. "Don't you get *tired* of the traditional questions?"

It glanced back at him, its eyes squinted closed a little in what Kit realized was the beginnings of a smile. "Tired? I can't get tired," the Pig said. "But bored? *Hoo*boy."

"So?"

The Pig was quiet for a little while. "Now, if I was a stinker," it said at last, "I would demand a whole third truth from you, and then tell you one of the truths you originally asked for: where she is. But there's the glede to consider; things like that don't turn up often. And besides, I've always been a sucker for young— well, for people in your situation."

Kit waited, not able to make much of this.

The Pig raised its eyebrows. "You got lucky today, but don't try to take advantage. So think for a moment, and then ask your question."

Kit thought for what seemed to him like hours but was probably no more than a matter of minutes. Finally he looked up and said, "How can I save her?"

The Pig rolled its eyes. "*Her* her, or *her*, her mother?"

Kit merely smiled.

The Transcendent Pig let out an exasperated breath. "The last time someone asked me a question phrased that way," said the Pig, "Atlantis sank. You know that story?"

"Several versions of it. And don't change the subject!" Kit said, severe.

The Pig gave him a shocked look, and then laughed out loud. "You simian-descended, equivocating, pronoun-starved little mortal twerp," it said. "Maybe the universe does favor young wizards because they haven't properly mastered the Speech's plurals yet. We really have to look into that."

It chuckled briefly, then composed itself. "All right. As you know," the Pig said, "Nita is attempting an intervention to save her mother's life. Unfortunately that intervention has been contaminated by the Lone Power from the start and therefore has little chance of succeeding, and much chance of backfiring. With results such as you should be able to imagine."

Kit swallowed, or tried to; his mouth had suddenly gone dry. "Oh, my God," Kit said.

"Yes," the Pig said.

Then all of a sudden something boiled over in the back of Kit's head. "Now just *wait* a minute," he said, annoyed. "First of all, I knew that. And second, you *knew* the Lone One was talking to her? And you didn't *tell* her?"

"She didn't ask," the Pig said. "Questions are important, and there's not a lot I can do without them. Don't look so shocked! The Powers That Be have the same problem. But it wasn't *my* business to tell her. For one thing, on some level, she *knows*. That One can never make Itself *completely* unrecognizable . . . and that's Its own fault. You set yourself apart from all previous creation, fine, but you're going to look and feel different to all creation afterward. What's more important is that the way she deals with the realization, when she comes up with it herself, is likely to be crucial to what she's working on. *That* I wouldn't interfere with, even if I could." It gave Kit a look. "And if you were smart, neither would you."

"So?" Kit said.

The Pig lay down with a thoughtful air. "Well," it said, "if I were you—which could happen, transcendence being what it is—I'd listen carefully to my hunches, when everything goes dark. You never know, you might hear something useful."

"Okay," Kit said. "Thanks."

"That's *it*?" the Pig said.

"Thanks a *lot*," Kit said.

"Well, I can't fault your manners," the Pig said. "Be being you, youngster. Go well!" And it got up and wandered away, the floor rippling uncertainly after it as it went. A moment or so later it was simply gone, without doing a transit or gating as such.

I guess if you're transcendent, you don't need to, Kit thought. He looked down at Ponch. "What do you make of that?" he said.

Ponch produced a feeling like a shrug. "I think maybe it's cheating. It shouldn't be *that* easy."

"I wish I felt better," Kit said. Yet there was something about what the Pig had said, something that was eluding him. . . .

"It's all right," Ponch said. "I know her scent. I got it fresh yesterday; it hasn't changed that much. And the trail is fresh. I can track her."

Changed, Kit thought, confused. *How could it change?*

"Come on!" Ponch said. "The longer we stand here, the farther away she goes."

"Let's go," Kit said. "There's not much time."

The leash was still around Ponch's neck. Kit picked it up and wound it around his wrist. The two of them stepped into the darkness and were gone.

Grand Central was in shadow as Nita came out of the gate by track twenty-four, and as she put her foot down, she heard a splash. There was so little light in the space around her that Nita spent some power to produce a small wizard's candle, a glimmer of light that rode above her shoulder as she looked around.

The tracks were all under water, and water lapped at the piers that held up the platforms—a bizarre sight. Even the platforms were an inch deep or so in water, like black glass, the surface of it rippling gently, silent and intimidating. Beside her, Pralaya slipped into the water, ducking under it, and coming up again down by the place where the platforms tapered in, down where the tracks ducked more deeply under Forty-sixth Street. "This would be a wonderful swimmery," she heard him say from down in the darkness, "but I think perhaps it shouldn't be this way?"

"You got that in one," Nita said. Already she was trying to sense around her for this micro-universe's kernel, and she couldn't feel anything. *What's the matter? I should be able to at least get a hint. It's my mother, after all!* But it felt wrong somehow; she couldn't hear that faint buzz or whine that she'd learned to associate with a kernel, the sound of life doing its business. "Can you feel anything?" she said.

Pralaya surfaced in front of her, twisting and rolling in the dark water. "I'm not sure," he said. "There's . . . a darkness . . ."

Nita was all too aware of this darkness. Listening, watching, she could feel it all around her. It bent in; it pressed against her; and worst of all was the sense that at any moment Pralaya's innocent, merry personality could be twisted out of shape by the Lone Power suddenly looking out of his eyes at her, offering her the bargain she could not refuse.

It's here, she thought, feeling that heavy, dark presence leaning in all around her. *It's waiting for me to make a mistake.* And maybe she already had.

"Come on," she said to Pralaya, "let's get out into the open."

Together they made their way toward what would have been the Main Concourse in her own world. "What does this look like to you?" Nita said to Pralaya as they made their way through the wet.

"In my world? This is the Meeting of the Waters," Pralaya said. "The place where the rivers come together before they run to the Sea."

Nita thought of the Sea and immediately was sad, seeing in her mind's eye Jones Inlet, and the Sun over the water, leaning westward in the afternoon, and the long, broad golden sunset light over the Great South Bay, where she had screwed things up so seriously with Kit. But now they came out under what should have been the ceiling of the Main Concourse. . . .

Nita stood there and took in a long breath of shock, and let out another long one of sorrow. The whole place was under water, five feet deep, and the beautiful cream-colored stone walls of the terminal, to the four compass points, were striped with green-brown tide-marks of high water from other times, and still flooded deep in an unhealthy dark water that lapped and sucked at the walls. The whole place smelled of damp and cold and weed and chilly pain, and Nita shuddered as she splashed out of the platform arcade into the center of the terminal. She looked up at what should have been a warm, summery, Mediterranean-sky ceiling, and instead saw nothing but watery stars and autumn constellations, all fish and dolphins and sea serpents—not to mention poor Andromeda shackled to the rock, waiting to be eaten by the monster from the waves. It was not a view that filled Nita with confidence.

"Is it always so dark here?" Pralaya said.

Nita thought of fire gaping out of the depths of this space, not so long ago; yet now that scenario seemed positively preferable, for it had put only her own life at stake, not her mom's. "Not usually," she said, and led Pralaya up out of the Main Concourse, up the ramp to what normally would have been the street.

It was no improvement. The sky was clouded, dark and heavy; this was a city in shadow and under threat, with the waters rising all around. Some of the sky-scrapers around them were in good-enough shape, but many of them were crumbling. *Too many*, Nita thought, knowing that she was seeing what her own mind could most effectively make of her mother's physical condition. Things were already going wrong here, and her doubt rose up and choked her.

"We have to go where it's worst, don't we?" Nita said.

Pralaya nodded. "It would be the only way."

They stood there in the thunder-colored water, in the flooded street, and gazed up and down it. All of Forty-second Street was a river, and no traffic light, or any other light, burned on it anywhere; buildings cliffed out above the street, dark and forbidding, their lower stories wet and scummed with mold, their upper windows dulled with the residue of recent storms. Overhead, the roiling gray sky was like an unhealed wound, uncomfortable, unwell, unresolved. Nita closed her eyes and swallowed. Somewhere here was the kernel, the software of her mother's soul.

She held still and listened, listened.

"Do you have time for this?" said the voice behind her, a little provocative.

"Yup," Nita said, fierce. "Don't joggle my elbow, Pralaya, or I'll chew one of your legs off."

There was a pause. In a hurt voice Pralaya said, "I wouldn't have thought I'd have deserved that from you, Nita."

"Yeah, well," Nita said. "Sorry, cousin." *Assuming you're really my cousin at the moment, and not That One.*

The trouble was, there was no telling. . . . *Never mind that.* Nita held still and listened with all of her. *It's my* mother, *for heaven's sake! I should be able to hear her.* But it was hard, suddenly.

And who's making *it hard? Or is it just tough to sense your own mother when you're on business, as opposed to when you're at home? She becomes like water, like air, like anything else you get used to and take for granted.*

Beside her, in the water, Pralaya paddled along as they worked their way down Forty-second Street. "Sorry," Nita said again. She would have said, *I didn't mean that*, except at the time she *had* meant it, cruel as it was, and a wizard did not lie in the Speech—that was fatal. *More fatal than what I'm about to do?*

Nita stood at the spot where Forty-second normally crossed the Vanderbilt Avenue underpass, saw the drowned canal that the under-running road had become, and wished that Kit were here. It seemed to her that if only he were here, everything would be all right.

Yet she had constructed the circumstances in which he *couldn't* be here. She stood there in the muddy, westward-flowing water . . .

. . . and something bit her in the leg.

Nita yelped and jumped. "What was *that*?" she said.

Pralaya had already clambered up onto a pillar of the west side of Grand Central, sticking up out of the water. "We're not alone here," he said. "What would these be? They have teeth—"

"Cancer viruses," Nita said. "I wouldn't let them get too friendly with your extremities, if I were you."

Peering down into the muddy water, Nita could see them: little dark blocky hexagonal shapes with fierce straight little tails or stingers, cruising around. The water was teeming with them, large and small, like the little dark minnows in one of the local freshwater creeks. *So many!* Nita thought. *How am I going to persuade all* these *things to do anything? The Lone Power was right. It was right.*

She considered using the spell that would let her walk on water . . . but that took more energy than she now felt like using. *I'm going to need everything I can possibly save for later*, Nita thought. *Better use the low-power one I tailored earlier.* "I have a spell against these," she said to Pralaya. The spell would at least protect the two of them from the stings, but it couldn't stop the viruses from doing what they pleased with her mother.

She pulled the spell off her charm bracelet. With a little effort, she pulled the charm in two. It stretched like taffy then parted with a snap, leaving her holding two identical versions of the spell. Nita tossed Pralaya the clone, then dropped her version of it into the water.

Pralaya stretched out his version of the spell, adjusted it, and dropped it around him. Nita saw this happening and could not avoid thinking, *Here is the Power That invented these things, indirectly; and I'm protecting Its servant against them.*

Not that he knows . . .

Nita held still then, again, and listened. In this threatening light it was hard to think clearly. Everything seemed geared to leave you frightened, chilled, cowed, as slowly the livid sunset light behind those clouds shut down toward some final night.

Nita knew that day was waiting back there somewhere. If she could just find it, sense it, hear it. The sound of morning, of a dawn past all this leaden twilight. If she could just find it. If she could, it wouldn't matter if her wizardry departed her forever; it would be worth it.

And at the same time . . . She sloshed up Forty-second in the general direction of Fifth, listening with all of her, not hearing anything, and beginning, as predicted, to despair. *Kit . . .*

The bleak wind blew over the gray waters, and Nita walked on through it all, with Pralaya swimming beside her, and knew true desperation's colors at last.

Friday Afternoon

"I THOUGHT YOU SAID you were going to be able to find her."

"I should have been able to. But the scent's changed again."

"What?" Kit was confused, and stood still in the utter darkness where they had been walking. "How?"

Beside him Kit could feel Ponch gazing around him. "The One who doesn't want us to find Nita has changed it. The world she's gone to is twisted out of orientation with the usual ones."

Kit tried to put his own concerns aside; there was something more on his mind. "So where are they?" he said.

"Elsewhere."

"Thanks loads."

"You don't have the words for it," Ponch said, a little sharply. "You can't smell what's happening the way I do. We have to backtrack. There's a scent . . . but there's also trouble."

"What kind?"

Ponch shook himself. "Since we're not with Nita, it's going to be hard to convince the ones who guard the borders to let us in."

Kit let out a long nervous breath. "Never mind. Let's just keep going."

Nita and Pralaya kept making their way along through the dark waters, southward along Fifth Avenue. Nita had only a hunch to go on now, only the faintest sense of where her mother's kernel lay. Pralaya paused with her at the corner of Fifth and Fortieth, putting his head up out of the water and peering about him, while all around the two of them, the viruses darted and poked at their defense shields like angry little bees.

"Should we try it again?" Pralaya said.

Nita looked up and down the street—or rather the river, which the street had become—and nodded. "Yeah . . ."

She let her mind fall toward Pralaya's again, adding his viewpoint of this place to hers. Everything quivered, changed.

The darkness around them became even more oppressive, an inward-leaning, watching, sullen nest of shadows. Nita could feel how the place was full of death and the anticipation of death, and wanted them out of there.

But if Pralaya is the Lone One, why is It finding this so scary and upsetting? Nita thought. That was a question that she wasn't going to ask him out loud, though. She put it aside and did her best to feel around them for the kernel, listening.

A stronger hint this time. *South and west; and not too far.*

Nita let her mind drop away from Pralaya's again. He was lying there in the water, shivering. "You okay?" she said.

"Yes," he said, and shook himself all over, those big dark eyes troubled. "But, Nita, this is a terrible place. I wonder that you can bear it here."

She was shaking, too, but she couldn't let it stop her. "It's the one place I've been working to be," Nita said. "Let's go."

She set off westward, toward Sixth Avenue—splashing through water that was deeper and deeper—and Pralaya followed her, slowly, almost as if reluctant. Nita refused to spend any time trying to figure this out. She was tired, and very scared—both for herself and for her mother—and she simply wished that all this was over. The thought came to her: *You are now so tired, you will make some terrible mistake.*

And she was too tired even to care about *that*.

In the darkness between worlds, Kit felt Ponch pause and look at something. "This is interesting," the dog said.

Kit couldn't see anything. "What is it?"

"Home," Ponch said in surprise.

"What?" Kit said, bemused. "Show me!"

"Here."

Suddenly they stepped out into Kit's backyard . . . except that the place had the feel of the universes that Kit and Ponch had been creating when Ponch first started taking Kit along on his walks—like something that Kit had made just now with whatever power lay between the worlds, ready to be used if you knew it was there. Kit looked around him in surprise at an utterly perfect summer day. Everything he could have wanted was there: the knowledge that school was out for the summer, the sound of Carmela's stereo blasting upstairs, his mother laughing with loving scorn at something his father was doing in the kitchen. The sky was flawlessly blue, the air just hot enough to make one think about going to the beach, but not having to *do* anything. The locusts were beginning to say *zzzeeeeeeee* in the trees. And just over there, the sudden *whoomp!* of air as Nita appeared out of nothing, turned toward him, grinning with excitement, her manual in her hand—

"Stop it right there," Kit said to the world. The image froze.

He stood there, now the only thing that could move in that whole still reality, and turned slowly, taking it all in: weeds and flowers, summer sunshine, peace. It was perfection, of a kind. The moment, held captive—heart's desire, caught in one place and unable to escape.

But moments aren't meant to be held captive. They're meant *to escape. That's what makes them matter.*

But I could make perfection, anyway, Kit thought as he turned, seeing a passing white cabbage butterfly caught in midair, in midstroke of its wings, trapped there as if in amber clearer than water. *I could go to live in it, if I wanted—the world where everything worked. I could even use this power to make myself believe that was where I'd always lived, the way things had always been.*

He swallowed. *I could* make *Timeheart. Another* one.

Kit held that moment for a long, long while, trapped in the grip of his mind, like a butterfly in his hand. He kept turning. The backyard with its backyard sassafras jungle, the long grass to lie in all through this lazy afternoon, looking up at the clouds—and standing there, frozen, but laughing, ready for anything: Nita. Not angry at him, not afraid, not troubled by any dark shadow hanging over her. Here it need never have happened. Here it was fine, had always been fine. He could be here the rest of his life if he liked, and everything, always, would be fine.

And if he could make that, then he could make anything. *Anything.*

Maybe this was how it had all started. The manual was "sketchy on the first hundredth of a second," Tom had said. "Privacy issues." Was it possibly something as simple as this—that in some other region of spacetime, some other being, no more or less powerful than Kit, had stumbled across a spark such as the one he held now, and had created?

If it had happened that way, maybe it could happen that way again?

Here he was. Here was the power. All Kit had to do . . . was use it, and get everything right this time. Everything: a whole universe of universes, innumerable, unfolding themselves as he watched—the essence of creation running riot, running rampant, life exploding through it. For a single moment that included and encompassed all moments, stretching out endlessly around him, time without beginning or end; Kit was lost in the vision—

—and then he had to laugh. He started to laugh so hard, he could hardly stand it; his sides started to hurt.

Oh, yeah, he thought. *Nice try. Gimme a break!*

When he was able to breathe again, Kit straightened up and gazed around him. No matter how he created such a perfect place—or had this one been left for him to find?—no matter that he might even be able to delude himself into believing that it was reality, the truth was that it *wouldn't* be. Elsewhere the real world would go on, people would hurt, life would be alternately happy and miserable . . . in the real places where wizards were needed to fight the fight, even if they might never see it won. And *this . . . This isn't real enough for me*, Kit thought. *I want the kind of reality that surprises me. And, anyway, wizardry isn't for getting out of reality, out of the world. It's for getting further* into *it.*

He gave that frozen pseudo-Nita one last glance, then turned away, back to the butterfly, embedded in air—and turned it loose.

The moment resumed. "Kit," Nita said, "Hey, whatcha—"

Kit squeezed his eyes shut and erased it all. A moment later he was standing in the darkness again, listening only to the silence . . . and having a little trouble breathing. *This isn't going to stop us*, he thought. *I know what the Lone Power trying to stop me feels like. We'll go all the way through. One way or another, we'll do what's necessary.*

They came to where the corner of Sixth and Thirty-eighth would have been if it hadn't been just an intersection of two muddy, rushing rivers, and stopped there. Nita could feel the kernel more clearly now; it wasn't too far away. But somehow this wasn't making her feel any better. The darkness, that watching presence hidden in it, and the little swarming, biting viruses were all beginning to wear her down. Pralaya was always there, companionable enough, but not really that much help. And again and again the words of the Wizard's Oath kept coming back to Nita, as she slogged her way along through the dark, resisting water: *"I will guard growth and ease pain."*

But does there come a time when you stop *growing?*
And when you and the universe agree *that you're going to stop?*
"*I will ever put aside fear for courage, and death for life, when it is right to do so.*"
Was there the slightest possibility, here and now, that it *wasn't* right?
How could you tell, without being one of the Powers?
And if people can't tell, then the game just isn't fair!
But that didn't matter right now. Nita stopped at the corner and looked down Sixth Avenue. The water seemed a little less deep down there; but that over-shadowing dark presence seemed much stronger. "The kernel's there," she said to Pralaya. "I'm sure of it."
"I think you're right," he said. "What is that—that tallest building there?"
"The Empire State," Nita said. It struck her as a poor place to hide anything. *But then, Its purpose isn't to keep the kernel hidden. It's to let me find it and use it and fail. So that I'll agree to the bargain—*
"Come on," she said, and splashed down Sixth Avenue with Pralaya swimming along beside her, uncertainty in his dark eyes.

Kit and Ponch were moving once more through the darkness. "It fooled us that time," Ponch said. "But not twice." The dog was angry.
"It's not your fault," Kit said. "It was after me."
"I should have expected it. But now we know something."
"What?"
"That you have something that can stop It."
Kit took a couple of long breaths. That thought had occurred to him.
"I'm telling the darkness," Ponch said, "to take us to where we'll learn best what to do to find Nita, to help her."
Kit's mouth was dry; he was getting more nervous by the moment. "Are we going to have time for this?"
"All the time we need."
How much longer they spent in the darkness, he wasn't sure. Kit could feel in Ponch a terrible sense of urgency, of the darkness resisting, pushing against him, trying to slow him down. But Ponch wasn't letting it stop him. He was pushing back, fierce, unrelenting. They slowed down, finally stopped, and Kit could feel Ponch pushing, pushing with all his strength against whatever was fighting him—
—until without warning they broke through into the light. Ponch surged forward, the leash wizardry extending away in front of Kit, while Kit stood still and rubbed his eyes, which were watering in the sudden brilliant light.
It was a beach. He was standing at the water's edge, and turning, he could see Jones Inlet behind him.
Is this another of Its tricks? Kit thought, confused. *Another place where I'm supposed to get distracted by what could have been?*
But somehow he knew it wasn't so. Though this was Jones Inlet, it was also something else.
Kit turned, looking south again. It was the Sea: darkness and light under the Sun, Life and the home of Life—all potential, lying burning and swirling under the dawn. "The Sea," Ponch was barking, shouting, as he ran down the beach and fought with the waves. "The Sea!" And it wasn't just what dogs always said—*Oh*

boy, the water!—but something else, both a question and an answer, a reference to the beginning of things, the oldest Sea from which Life arose. *And our blood's like that Sea*, Kit thought. *The same salinity. The same—*

His eyes went wide. Ponch had been right. Here was the solution . . . the one that the Lone Power was counting on Nita not seeing, because she had messed it up so badly before.

"You're right!" Kit yelled to Ponch. "You're right! Come on, we've got to find her, before she starts!"

Ponch came running back, bounced around him a last few times, and then they leaped forward into the darkness together and vanished from the beach, leaving only footprints, which were shortly washed away.

Nita stood at the base of the Empire State Building and looked up at it. In this version of New York, there was a great flight of steps up to it, up from the water level, and she immediately went about halfway up them, glad to get out of the water, where the viruses were swarming and snapping more thickly than they had anywhere else. Pralaya came flowing up the stairs along with her, shaking the water out of his golden fur and scratching himself all over. "Those things," he said, "even though they didn't really bite me, they make me itch."

"Me, too," Nita said. She stood there and craned her neck upward, looking at the terrible height of the tower. Even in her own New York, when you were this close to it, the Empire State always looked as if it was going to fall on you. But here, she wasn't sure that it might not somehow be possible. And all around them was that terrible shadowy darkness, thicker in the air here than anywhere else, pressing in on them, looking at them.

"Let's go in," Nita said. She could hear the kernel now without actually having to listen to it: a buzz, that familiar fizz on the skin. Part of her was afraid; it shouldn't have been this easy to find. And she knew why it had been so easy. . . .

They went in through the doors at the top of the steps and found themselves in a vast gray hall full of shadows. Standing up, here and there in the dimness, were many banks of steely doored elevators, which Nita saw were intended to go in only one direction: down. All around the great floor of the place were a number of square pools, and Nita looked at them and decided not to step into any of them. They had that black-water depth that suggested they had no real bottoms.

"Right," Nita said. She glanced once at her charm bracelet, made sure that the spells on it were active, and began walking through the place, listening.

Pralaya followed, pausing by each of the elevator banks and cocking his head to listen. "I'm not sure," he said.

"I am," Nita said. "Not up, but down." She paused by one of the pools, listening.

"Not here," she said softly. "But this is the right direction." She passed between two more of the great square pools, listening again. That faint fizz on her skin got more pronounced.

"That one," she said softly, and walked over to it. She knelt by the edge of the water, listening, then got up again and moved around to the other side of the pool. *Right there*, she thought. The kernel was well down in the black water, but not out of reach. Nita shook the charm bracelet around to check the status of her personal shields again, twiddled with one charm to adjust the shield just slightly, and then with the other arm reached down into the water.

It was freezing cold, so cold she could hardly breathe, and she could feel her fingers going numb. But she groped, and reached deeper, though she felt the buzzing and stinging of little dark lancets against her skin. None of them was getting through . . . yet.

There.

Slowly she reached under what she'd felt—the jabbing of the little black needles against her skin increased, but Nita forced herself not to rush—slowly she closed her fingers around what was waiting there for her. Slowly she drew it up.

It was an apple.

Nita stood up with it in her hands. It dripped black water, and as that water fell into the pool, the pool's surface came alive with more of the ugly little hexagonal virus shapes that had swarmed around her and Pralaya outside. These, though, were bigger, and somehow nastier. They had no eyes, but they were nonetheless looking at her and seeing prey, the kind they already knew the taste of.

"Okay," she said softly, and turned the "apple" over in her hands, feeling for the way its control structures were arranged. She found the outermost level quickly, let her hands sink into what now stopped being an apple and started being that familiar tangle of light.

All around, the shadows leaned in to watch what she was doing. Nita gulped and looked down into the pool, where those awful little black shapes had now put their "heads" up out of the water and were looking at her, hating her.

Guys, Nita said, *I'd like you to stop doing what you're doing to my mother.*

The buzzing, snarling chorus said, *No! We have a right to live!*

I mean it, Nita said. *It's really got to stop. It's* going *to stop, one way or another. It can be with your cooperation, or without it.*

No! they snarled. *We are her. We are of her. We live in her. She gave us birth.*

Not on purpose!

That does not matter. We have rights here. We were born. We have a right to do what we were created to do. The snarling was getting louder, more threatening. *You are also of her. What we do to her, we can do to you, given time.*

Nita didn't like the sound of that. *Guys*, she said, *last chance. Agree to stop doing what you're doing, or I must abolish you.* It was the formal phrasing of a wizard who, however reluctantly, discovers that he or she must kill.

The snarling scaled up; the waters in the pools all around her roiled. Shaking, Nita squeezed and manipulated the power-strands in the kernel until she found the one control sequence that managed the shapes of proteins in this internal space. She stroked it slowly and carefully into a shape that would forbid this kind of viral shape to exist in the local space-time.

One last chance, guys, she said.

The snarling only got louder.

Nita took a deep breath, flicked the charm bracelet around to bring the power-feed configuration she'd designed into place, then brought it together with the kernel. *I'm sorry!* she said, and pushed the power in . . .

And nothing happened.

Nita stared at the kernel, horrified. She tried feeding the necessary power into the kernel again, twisted that particular strand of power until it bit into her fingers—

But that spell is now invalid, said a dark voice inside her. *It uses a version of your name that is no longer operational. Your name has changed; you have changed. When you were looking at your mother in the hospital last night, you made up your mind to pay my price, and therefore the spell cannot work.*

Nita stood still in utter shock and terror. She wanted to shout *No!* but she couldn't, because she was suddenly horribly certain that, just this once, the Lone Power was telling the truth. The fact that the spell hadn't worked simply confirmed it.

And because I agreed, I'm going to lose my wizardry . . . and my mom will die.

Standing there with the kernel, realizing once and for all that she'd done everything she could and there was nothing else she knew that would make the slightest difference, Nita's world simply started to come undone. She could do nothing to stop the tears of fear and grief and frustration that began to run down her face.

It told me it wouldn't work. What made me think I might somehow be able to manage it anyway?

"Pralaya," she said.

"This is beyond my competence," Pralaya said. "I wish I could help you, but . . ."

Nita nodded once, and the grief started to give way to anger. "Just what I thought," she said. "So much for any help from *you!*"

He looked shocked.

"But that would hardly be the Lone One's preferred method," she said. "No way It's going to give me any help at all, if it can be avoided."

Pralaya looked more stunned than before, if possible. "What are you talking about?"

"You don't know what's living inside you," Nita said. "Well, I bet you're about to find out. Come on," she said to the One she knew was listening. "This is the moment you've been waiting for, isn't it?"

"Not with any possible doubt of the outcome," said that huge dark satisfied voice.

The Lone Power was standing there looking at her; and for just the briefest second, Pralaya coexisted with Its newly chosen form. It looked human, like a young man—though an inhumanly handsome one—and shadows wrapped around It like an overcoat, shadows that reached out and now wrapped themselves around Pralaya, dragged him, struggling and horrified, into themselves, and hid him away.

"Now, you shouldn't really have said that," said the young man. "While he didn't actually know what was happening, I could have let him live. But you had to come right out and tell him, at which point his usefulness to me vanished."

Nita stood there horrified. "You just *killed* him!"

"No," the Lone One said, "*you* did. Not a bad start, but then you were intent enough on killing *something*." All around Nita, the snarling of the viruses was getting louder and louder. "Anyway, don't be too concerned about Pralaya; I'll find another of his people to replace him if there's need. Now, though, matters stand as I told you they stood. All we need is your conscious answer to the question. Can we do business?"

Nita stood there, frozen.

And another voice spoke out of the darkness.

"Fairest and Fallen," Kit said, "one more time . . . greeting and defiance." Beside him, Ponch just bared his teeth and growled.

Nita stared in astonishment at Kit and Ponch. The Lone Power gave them an annoyed look.

"*You* again," the Lone One said. "Well, I suppose it was to be expected. You'll do anything to try to run her life for her, won't you?"

Nita's eyes widened in shock. "The chance that she might possibly pull something off without your assistance drives you crazy," the Lone Power said conversationally. "Well, fortunately you're not going to see anything like that today. She's decided to turn to someone else for her last gasp at a partnership." Its smile made it plain Who that was meant to be.

"We *know* better, so don't try this stuff on us," Kit said.

"*You* think you know better," It said.

It looked at Nita. "Does he?" It said. "Or are you perhaps a little tired of him ordering you around?"

Nita stood silent, trembling.

"Might you possibly, just this once, know better? Know best? Actually make the sacrifice?"

"Neets, don't pay any attention to It," Kit said. "You know why I came—"

"To keep her Oath from being contaminated," said the Lone One dryly. "Too late for that. The deal is done, and she's made her choice at last. Without *you*."

Nita saw Kit flinch at that, but he straightened up again. "I wouldn't write me off as useless just yet," Kit said. "And I wouldn't bet that Neets is just going to dump me."

"I would," the Lone One said. "I hold the only betting token that matters at all in the present situation. Only with my help can she save her mother's life."

"It's not true, Neets!" Kit shouted. "It tried pretty hard to keep Ponch and me from getting here. It must have a reason!"

"I can do without further interference," said the Lone One. "That's reason enough. Now, though, if I thought you might possibly accept a different version of the same bargain . . ." It stood musing. "Suppose Nita here keeps her wizardry—even despite the mistake she's just made. I even save her mother, in the bargain—"

Kit shook his head, and Ponch growled again. "I serve Life, and the Powers That Be That cast you out, and the One, the Power beyond Them. And so does Neets, whatever you've done to her. So just get used to it!"

The brief silence that followed was terrible. "I've been used to it for too long," said the Lone Power. "Here and there, I stop mortals from incessantly reminding me." The shadow wrapped around It, already huge, grew longer and darker; and inside it moved things that Nita emphatically did not want to see. It had been a long time since her bedroom shadows had been full of their little legs and their blind front ends, and their fangs, the little jaws that moved. . . .

Kit, though, laughed. "Been there, seen them," he said. "Millipedes? Is *that* all you've got? What a yawn."

His tone was astonishing. It banished the shadows, all by itself. Nita remembered how she had dreaded those things when she was little, and now found herself thinking, to her amazement, *Can someone else really show you how to kill the fears? Is it that easy? I thought they always said you had to do it yourself.*

But maybe there was more to it than that. Maybe others' strengths weren't their own property—

—if they offered . . .

"Kit," Nita said. "I know what you want to do, and after how stupid I've been with you, it's great that you even tried, but you've got to get out of here—"

"And leave you alone with *That*? Not a chance."

The Lone Power laughed. "Well, anyone can see where *this* is going. Unless you throw him out of here yourself, it looks like you're going to let someone else die for you again. I wouldn't have thought you were such a coward."

The flush of fury and embarrassment and pain struck through Nita like fire. She opened her mouth to say, *You think I* wanted *it that way the last time? You think I'm not brave enough to do it now? Okay, here—*

She didn't get a chance, for another shape leaped through the shadows and hit Nita about chest high. She came crashing down hard beside one of the pools. "Don't!" Ponch barked at her. "Don't do it!"

Nita rolled over and tossed Ponch off to one side. *Oh, the good pooch; I love him, but I can't let him stop me. There's still time, I can still save her.* Nita pushed herself up on her hands and knees, and opened her mouth again. But as she did, the greater darkness that had hung about her since she came to this place—that leaning, inward—pressing obscurity—came wrapping down around her, squeezing the breath right out of her, and it spoke.

Don't I get something to say about this?

That darkness leaned in ever closer around all of them, even the Lone One. It was a different kind of darkness than the Lone Power's enwrapping shadows. Nita stared up into it, confused, frightened . . .

. . . and then realized she had no reason to be. Nita knew this darkness . . . from a long time ago . . . from the inside. Some memories, she realized, are recovered only under very special circumstances. This dark, immense presence, completely surrounding her, owning the world, *being* the world . . .

"Mom?" Nita whispered.

"I *do* get something to say about this," said that voice, not just suspected now but actually heard.

"Nothing that matters," said the Lone Power, though it sounded just slightly uncertain.

"The *only* thing that matters," said her mother's voice.

"It's too late," the Lone One said. "She's made the bargain."

"She's made nothing," said Nita's mother's voice, "because this is *my* universe, and *I* say what goes here, and *she does not have my permission*."

And Nita's mother was standing there, in the dark, between Nita and the Lone Power, in her T-shirt and her denim skirt, with her arms folded, and her red hair a spot of brightness even in this gloom. "This is *my* body," said Nita's mother. "If this is going to be a battleground, *I* make the rules."

"For a mortal," said the Lone One, "you're unusually assured. With little reason. You believe everything some part-time psychologist tells you?"

"For an immortal," said Nita's mother, "you're unusually dumb. The therapist, as it happens, was plainly more right than she knew. There they are, the nasty little things, just the way I imagined them." She glanced at the shadowy pools, roiling full of viral death. "In here somewhere, to match the darkness, there has to be light

... and that's my weapon, for the darkness comprehendeth it not. On that point, I have sources of reassurance other than any therapist—much older ones. They say that you cannot command a soul that's firmly opposed to you."

"But bodies are not souls."

"At this level," Kit said, "just how sure are you?"

There was a slightly unnerved silence at that.

Nita's mother looked over her shoulder at Nita. "My daughter and I," she said, "are fighting the same battle. Maybe I do it in more ordinary ways. But we're on the same side. And you, if I recognize you correctly, are no friend of mine. *Get off my turf!*"

She talks a good fight, Kit thought. *But it's gonna take more than that.*

Nita was almost breathless with tension, yet she suddenly realized that this was the first time in a good while that she'd overheard Kit think. In any case, she had to agree with him. *She's tougher than she looks,* Nita thought. *But then she was a dancer. Dancers are tough. Maybe what we need to be doing is feeding* her power—

"You have no power to order me around," said the Lone One. "I've been part of 'your turf' since the beginning of things. I have my own rights here."

"I've heard that line before," Nita's mother said. "I reject it. *I* choose who shares my body with me . . . as I chose my children . . . and my husband. *I* choose! You think you have any rights here that I don't grant you? Maybe you can live inside people who don't look at themselves closely. But those who fight with you every day and have an idea of what they're wrestling with? Let's just find out."

She stood up tall. Nita gulped. She had seen her mother looking ethereal, in her tutu and swan feathers and dinky little crown, in the poster from a Denver Opera Ballet production—looking like something you could break in two. But looking over her shoulder one day and seeing Nita eyeing dubiously that old framed poster, her mother had said, "Honey, take my advice. Don't mess around with swans. One of those pretty white wings could break your leg in three places." And off she had gone with the laundry basket, sailing past, graceful and strong, with the danger showing only around the edges of the chuckle.

But just bravery isn't going to be enough. Not here—

"And just what do you plan to fight me with?" the Lone One said. "You have no weapons to equal my power. Not even the diluted form of it that's killing you now."

"She may not have anything but guts and intention," Kit said, "but that's half of wizardry to start with. And *we're* carrying." He reached into his claudication and came up with a long string of symbols in the Speech.

Nita looked at it, uncomprehending. The Lone One laughed.

"That won't work," It said. "Certainly not for *her.* And not even for Nita anymore, as you've seen. You think that by plugging an older version of Nita's name into this spell, she will no longer be mine? It won't work. It takes more power than either of you have to reverse the kind of changes she's been through. She knows me now. She's willing to pay my price to keep her mother alive . . . and, sorry, Mom, but permission or no permission, it's Nita's choice that finally counts."

"Oh yeah?" Kit said. "Neets," he said to her then, holding out his hand, looking at her urgently. "Quick—"

"Oh, of course, give him all your power, why don't you." The Lone One laughed. "So much for your doing anything useful by yourself."

Nita swallowed. In Its voice she heard too many thoughts of her own, roiling in its darkness the way the viruses were boiling around in the pools.

Can't cope.

No independence.

Scared to make a move without her partner.

Doesn't have the nerve to strike out on her own—

Nita swallowed . . . and took off the charm bracelet.

—going to let him do all the dangerous stuff.

Going to prove him right again, and you wrong—

She hesitated one last time . . .

. . . and then threw the bracelet to Kit.

Kit caught it and quickly attached the old version of Nita's name he'd saved from the Jones Inlet wizardry. Then he reached into the air beside him and brought something else out.

A small pale spark of light—

The light it gave at first seemed little, but swiftly it lit up all that place, and even chased the shadows briefly from the Lone One's face . . . a sight that made Nita turn away—for the terror of It, to some extent, she could stand, but the beauty of It, seen together with that ancient deathliness, was difficult to bear. Around the Lone One, the darkness hissed with Its alarm, as if suddenly full of snakes. *A glede—*

"The dragon's eye," Kit said as he hooked the glede into an empty link of the charm bracelet, and the whole chain came alive with sudden fire. "Something brand new, something you've never touched. Something born after the change happened to *you*, the chance to be otherwise. Something you can't affect—"

"Not true!" It cried. "All creation, even the void from which things are created anew, has my power at the bottom of it."

"Not here, it doesn't! Not in this! Whether you like it or not, even while you're killing people, the world is starting to heal . . . *and so are you!*"

Nita swallowed hard, watching Kit and suddenly remembering Tom and Carl's backyard and a fish looking up out of the water at her.

> *All the drawing lacks*
> *is the final touch: to add*
> *eyes to the dragon—*

She desperately wanted to shout to Kit that yes, this had to be the answer—but she didn't dare. She'd been wrong about so many things lately. What if her certainty, her desperation, got Kit killed, too? *And the Lone One's right, that's not who I am anymore—*

—but the other memory that came back to her, the amused piggy voice saying, "That is, assuming you're into sequential time . . . you can handle it however you like . . ."

That blazing spark of light on the bracelet Kit held glittered at her like possibility made visible.

Why in the world not*?!* Nita thought. *If you can't put together what you were* *with what you are now—so you can make up for your mistakes and not make the same ones again—then what's the point? This isn't about reversing anything. It's about going forward!*

"Kit!" she cried.

He threw her the charm bracelet. Nita snatched it out of the air, and almost dropped it as the added power of the glede jolted up her arm like an electric shock.

"I wouldn't do that if I were you!" the Lone One cried. "You'll destroy your mother, and yourself, here and now!"

Nita hesitated for just a second . . . then put the charm bracelet back on, taking hold of the two versions of her name that hung from it, side by side. "Well, guess what?" she said. "You're *not* me!" And in the single quick gesture she'd had entirely too much practice with lately, she knotted the names tight together with the wizard's knot.

The blast of power that went through her was like being hit by lightning. Whether because of her remade name or the presence of the glede, suddenly Nita could comprehend all those little darknesses in the water much more fully than just by using the kernel. Those stinging, buzzing little horrors were right about being, in their own twisted way, part of her mother. But now she could see exactly what to do about them. The solution was the same as what she had been trying to do with Kit and S'reee at Jones Inlet . . .

. . . except that, where she'd been wrong about how to use her part of the wizardry before, here and now she was right. Her wizardly fix for Jones Inlet had been too complicated. "This whole contrareplication routine would be great," Kit had said, "if the chemicals in the pollution knew how to reproduce themselves." Of course, they hadn't. But viruses were just very smart chemicals in a protein shell that *did* know how to reproduce themselves . . . which made the solution perfect for her mother.

It set me up, Nita thought in growing fury. *The Lone One made sure I came up against a problem where my solution would fail—and fail painfully—and where I fought with Kit. So that when I came to this moment, I'd be too hurt, too scared to try this solution again, too scared even to see it!*

She trembled with rage. But to waste time on being angry now would only play into Its hands. Nita's eyes narrowed in concentration as she channeled the power from the glede through both the kernel and her memory of her part of the Jones Inlet wizardry, and into the dark waters around her . . .

Every pool around them roiled in agitation as all the viruses thrust their heads up out of the lapping darkness, like blind fish gasping in the air, desperately crying *no!*

For many of them it was already too late. All around them, the sea of her mother's blood was churning as if in a storm with the power that washed through it—and from all around came countless little dark explosions as the viruses' shells unraveled. The wizardry was reminding the human blood of how it had once been part of an older, purer, uncontaminated Sea, one that was the outside of a world rather than the inside.

Yet Nita could feel through the kernel that there were some places where, for all the glede's power, that cleansing Sea didn't, couldn't quite reach. Scattered through her mother's inner world, little knots of darkness still lay, waiting . . . and there were many, many of them.

Too many . . .

Nita fell to her knees, defeated.

All for nothing . . .

"I told you," the Lone One said. "You should have done it my way. Too late now—" And it began to laugh.

Nita began to cry. It was all over . . . all over . . .

A deathly silence fell.

And an angry whisper broke it.

"With me," it said, "you can do what you like. *But not with my daughter!*"

And then another whisper.

"Mrs. Callahan—"

A moment later, someone took hold of Nita's bracelet. Nita looked up, gasping.

"You need this, sweetie," her mother said, her voice controlled despite her anger as she turned the bracelet past the new-made version of Nita's name. "But Kit's right. This is what I've been looking for!"

With a roar of fury, the Lone One moved toward the three of them, a terrible wave of shadow rearing up above It, ready to break. All around them, the waters of the pools rose up, to drown them, to destroy . . .

. . . and then suddenly fell back as if they had struck a wall. Everything kindled to blinding fire around them, the water glittering as it splashed away, the walls of the great hall shining, the Lone One standing there aghast in the blaze and terror of that light as Nita's mother pulled the glede free of Nita's bracelet, stood up, and squeezed the glede tight in her upheld fist, a gesture both frightened and fierce.

She was lost in the resultant violent blast of fire, and Nita tottered sideways and clutched at Kit, watching her mother in amazement and terror: a goddess with a handful of lightning, imperial and terrible, rearing up into the darkness and towering over them all, even over the Lone One, and—to Nita's astonishment and concern—paying It no mind at all. All her mother's attention now was on what she gripped in her hand, a writhing struggling knot of lightnings growing and lashing outward all the time, until it crowned her with thunder and robed her in fire, and there were no shadows left to be seen anywhere.

The fear and pain in her face were awful to see, as Nita's mother struggled with the glede, trying to keep from being consumed by its power as other mortal women had been consumed, in old stories, by fire from beyond the worlds. But her eyes were ferocious with concentration, and the look of terror and anguish slipped away as she started to get the better of the Power she held.

Slowly she straightened, looking down at all of them—a woman in a T-shirt and a faded denim skirt, blazing with the fire from heaven, and with sudden certainty.

"*The Light shone in the darkness,*" she said softly, and the whole little universe that was Nita's mom shook with it. "*And the darkness comprehended it not.* This *light!* But you never learn, do you? Or only real slowly."

The Lone Power stared at her with at least as much incredulity as Kit and Nita. After a second, It turned away.

"*Oh*, no you don't," Nita's mother said. And the lightning blasted out from her, and struck It down into the nearest pool.

Nita's mother looked at the Lone Power dispassionately as it struggled in the water. "If I am going to go anywhere," she said, "first *you're* going to find out up

close and physical what the things you've done to me all this while have felt like."
It struggled to get up out of the water. Nita's mom flung out her hand, and the
lightning knocked It back in again.

"Having fun with *that*?" her mother said. "Doesn't feel like so much fun from
inside my body, does it? You should have thought of that before you came in here.
Just feel all those broken bones and strains, those six weeks off for tendonitis, the
bruises and infections and herniated muscles and all the rest of it. Oh, we knew
about pain, all right! Dance is two hours' worth of childbirth every weekday evening at eight, and a Saturday matinee!"

The Lone Power writhed and splashed in the water, stricken with the experience of her agony.

"And then how about this?" her mother said. "Now that I've got your attention—"

Nita flinched, for this was the phrase that most often preceded the tongue-
lashing you got when you hadn't cleaned your room properly—and to a certain
extent she could feel what her mother was imposing on the Lone One. Here the
experience inflicted on It was all the more intense for being recent, fresh in the
sufferer's mind—the blurred vision, the growing pain, the uncomfortable and unhappy sense that, hey, this isn't supposed to be happening, what's the matter with
me?—the loss of control, of mastery over a body that was always precisely mastered in the old days; the slowly growing fury, inexpressible, bottled up, that things
weren't working the way they should.

In fact, that nothing *was working the way it should.*

For in this place, under these circumstances, Nita's mother now knew that if
matters had somehow gone otherwise, death itself wouldn't have happened. It was
an additive, an afterthought, somebody's "good idea." And here was the somebody,
right here, within reach . . . and available, just this once, for spanking.

Not liking it, either, Nita thought.

"Fun, huh?" Nita's mother said softly. "But even with your inventions, this
Life that you hate so much is still too much for you. It was always too much for
you. Whatever you do, it just keeps finding a way. Maybe even this time."

The Lone One writhed and floundered in the water, and couldn't get away.
Nita's mom looked down at It from what seemed a great distance. Under that
majestic regard, as It finally managed to drag itself out of the pool, the Lone One
seemed crumpled into a little sodden shape of shadow, impotent in this awful blaze
of wrathful fire. *Beaten*, Nita thought, and her heart went up in a blaze of triumph
to match the blinding light.

"But no," said her mother then, in a much more mortal voice, and hearing it,
Nita's heart fell from an impossible height, and kept on falling. "That's what you're
expecting, isn't it? You want me to win this battle. And after that, when we're all
off our guard, comes the betrayal."

The light began to fade. *No*, Nita thought. *No, not like this! Mom!*

But her mother had her own ideas . . . as usual. There was no longer any great
distance between her and the much diminished darkness that was now the Lone
Power in what she had made of her interior world. "No," Nita's mother said, "not
even at *that* price. You've really been stuck playing this same old game for a long
time, haven't you? And you just don't believe a mortal could refuse the opportunity."

From that sodden darkness there now came no answer. Nita's mother stood there looking down at the Lone Power as if at a daughter who'd turned up in particularly grimy clothes just after the laundry had all been done.

"No," Nita's mother said. "I can guess where this is going. How many times have I heard my daughters wheedle me to let them stay up late, just this once? It starts there, but that's never where it stops. And if I was firm with *them*, I have to be the same way with myself when my turn comes, too." She was looking entirely less like a furious goddess, entirely more like a slightly tired woman. "Because I'm up against my own time limit, now, aren't I? Override the body now, and we'll all be sorry for it later. If not personally, then in the lives of the people around us."

Nita was horrified. "Mom, *no!*"

"Honey." Nita's mother chucked the lightning away, careless, and came over to her. The lightning hit the floor, lay there burning, and then came slowly humping back toward Nita's mom, like some animate and terrible toy. "Believe me, if there was ever a time for the phrase 'Don't tempt me,' this is it."

"But, Mom, we're *winning!*"

"We're supposed to think so," she said. "Look at It there; what a great 'beaten' act." She gave the Lone Power a look that was both clinical and thoroughly unimpressed. "The point being to encourage us to go home in 'triumph,' and to distract me, at any cost, from doing what I know is right. If It can't ruin my life, and yours, straightforwardly, by killing me, It'll try it another way."

She walked a little way over to It, the lightning following her. "Can't you see it, honey? If we carry this to its logical conclusion, I live, all right. I survive this—and what the things in my body are doing to me now—because of what you kids have done here. And then I live and live, and live some more, and I get to like it so much that my whole life becomes about *not dying*. What kind of life is *that* going to be? Because sooner or later, no matter what any of us do, it's going to happen anyway. Finally—who knows how many years from now—I get to die, all bitter and furious and scared, and doing everything I can to make everybody around me miserable—including you, assuming you *are* still around, and I haven't driven you and Dairine and your dad away with the sheer awfulness of my wanting to keep on living. *That's* what that One has in mind. Well, I won't do it, sweetie. Not even for this." The persistent tangle of lightning was rubbing against her leg like a cat; she gave it a sideways nudge with her foot, and turned away from the Lone One, coming back toward Nita and Kit. "Not even because I love you, and I'm afraid to leave your dad and you and Dairine, and I don't know what comes afterward for me, and I love my life, and I hate the thought of leaving all of you alone, in pain, and I'm not ready, *and I just don't want to go!*"

It was a cry of utter anguish, and the air all around them trembled with it, rent as if by thunder. That shadow, crouched down off to the side, stirred just slightly, crouched down further. "Not even for that," her mother said, a lot more quietly, unclenching her fists. "It is not going to happen."

"Mom . . . ," Nita said, and could find no other words.

Her mother just shook her head. For a moment, she seemed too choked up to speak. She pulled Nita close and held her, and then, her voice rough, she said, "Sweetie, I may not be what you are, but this I know. There's a power in what we are as mortal beings that even *that* One can't match. If we throw it away, we stop being human. I won't do it. And certainly not when doing it plays into the enemy's hands."

She let go of Nita and turned around. "So as for *you*," Nita's mother said to the Lone Power, her eyes narrowing in what Nita recognized as her mother's most dangerous kind of frown, "you'll get what you incorrectly consider your piece of me soon enough. But in the meantime, I'm tired of looking at you. So you just take yourself straight on out of here before I kick your poor deluded rear end from here to eternity."

The Lone Power slowly picked Itself up, towered up before them all in faceless darkness . . . and vanished without a sound.

"Mom . . ." Nita shook her head, again at a loss for words.

"Wow," Kit said. "Impressive."

Her mother smiled slightly, shook her head. "It's all in the documentation, honey," she said to Nita. "It says it plain enough: 'Have I not said to you, "you are gods"?' So we may as well act like them when it's obviously right to and the power's available."

They all turned to look around at the sound of a splash. Ponch had jumped into one of the now-cleansed pools and was paddling around.

Nita's mom smiled, then looked at the surroundings, once again dark and wet, then she glanced down at what Nita still held in her hands. "Is that what I think it is?"

Nita nodded and handed it over. Her mother tossed the apple in her hand, caught it again, looking at it thoughtfully, and polished it against her skirt. "Are we done here?" she said.

Nita looked around her sorrowfully. "Unless you can think of anything to add."

Her mother shook her head. "No point in it now," she said. She looked at the apple with an expression of profound regret, turning it over in her hands. For a moment Nita saw through the semblance, saw the kernel as it was, the tangle of intricate and terrible forces that described a human body with a human mind and soul inside it, infinitely precious, infinitely vulnerable. Then her mother sighed and chucked the apple over her shoulder into one of the nearby pools. It dropped into the waters and sank, glowing, and was lost.

Nita let out a long breath that became a sob at the end. There was no getting it back now, nothing more that could be done.

"Better this way," her mother said, sounding sad. "You don't often get a chance like this; be a shame to ruin it. Come on, sweetie." She looked around at the darkness and the water. "We should either call the plumber or get out of the basement. How do we do that, exactly?"

"I don't think you have to do anything but wake up," Kit said. "But Nita and I should go."

"Don't forget Ponch," Nita's mother said, as the dog clambered out of the pool he'd been swimming in and came over to the three of them. "If I come out of the anesthesia barking, the doctors are going to be really confused."

Ponch shook himself, and all three of them got splattered. "Kit needed me to get in," Ponch said. "Without me, I don't think he can get out. I'll see him safely home."

Nita's mother blinked at that. "Sounds fair," she said. "Meantime, what about this?" She bent over to pick up the dwindling knot of lightning that was all that was left of the glede.

The question answered itself, as it faded away in her hands. "One use only, I think," Kit said.

"I think I got my money's worth," Nita's mother said. "But thanks for the hint, Kit; you made the difference."

"Just a suggestion someone gave me," Kit said. "To listen to my hunches when it all went dark . . ."

"That one sure paid off. Go on, you kids, get out of here."

Nita hugged her mom while Kit put the leash on Ponch. Then Kit offered Nita his arm. She paused a moment, took it, and they stepped forward into the darkness.

The two of them came out in Kit's backyard. Nita saw Kit looking around him with an odd expression. "Something wrong?" she said. "Or is it just that reality looks really strange after what we've been through?"

"Some of that, maybe," he said. He took the leash off Ponch and let the dog run toward the house.

"Kit—"

He looked at her.

"You saved my butt," she said.

Kit let out a breath. "You let me."

She nodded.

"Anyway," Kit said, "you've saved mine a few times. Let's just give up keeping score, okay? It's a distraction."

Nita nodded. "Come on," she said. "Let's go to the hospital."

Between transit circles and the business of appearing far enough away from the hospital not to upset anybody, it took them about fifteen minutes to get there. Down in that awful little waiting room, Nita found her dad and Dairine—and the look on her father's face nearly broke Nita's heart. There was hope there, for the first time in a long, long week.

Nita sat down while Kit shut the door. "Are they done?" Nita said.

Her father nodded. "They got the tumor out," he said. "All of it. It went much better than they hoped, in fact. And they think . . . they think maybe it hasn't spread as far as they thought. They have to do some tests."

"Is Mom awake yet?"

"Yeah. The trouble with her eyes is clearing up already, the recovery room nurses said, but they want us to leave her alone till this evening; it's going to take her a while to feel better. We were just waiting here for you to catch up with us." He looked at her. "What about you?"

Nita swallowed. "I think we did good," she said, "but I'm not sure how good yet. It's gonna take a while to tell."

Her dad nodded. "So let's go home . . . and we'll come back after dinner."

As much as Nita felt like she really needed a nap, she couldn't sleep. Kit went home for a while, but when Nita's dad was starting the car, Kit appeared again in the backyard, and Nita went downstairs to meet him.

As she was walking across the yard, there was another bang, less discreet:

Dairine. She stalked out of the air with an annoyed expression. "Where've you been?" Nita said.

"The hospital."

"You weren't supposed to go yet!"

"I know. I sneaked in. They just found me and threw me out."

She looked at the two of them. "Have you seen the précis in the manual?" she said.

Nita shook her head.

"I have," Dairine said softly. "I owe you guys one."

Kit shook his head. "Dari, if you read the précis, then you know—"

"I know what's probably going to happen to her," Dairine said. "Yeah. But I know what you guys did. You gave it your best shot. That's what matters."

She turned and went into the house.

"She's mellowing," Kit said quietly.

"She's in shock," Nita said. "So am I. But, Kit—Thanks for not letting me go through it alone." She gulped, trying to keep hold of her composure. "I'm not—I mean, I'm going to need a lot of help."

"You know where to look," Kit said. "So let's get on with it."

In the hospital they found Nita's mother already sitting up in bed. She had a blackening eye and some bruising around her nose, but that was all; and the sticky contacts and wires and machines were all gone, though she now had an IV running into her arm. Nita thought her mom looked very tired, but as they came in, her face lit up with a smile that was otherwise perfectly normal.

She looked at Kit. "Woof," she said.

Kit cracked up.

"Does this have some profound secret meaning," Nita's dad said, sitting down and taking his wife's hand, "or is it a side effect of the drugs?"

Nita's mother smiled. "No drug on the planet could have produced the trip I've just been through," she said.

There was a long silence. "Did it work?" Nita's father said then.

"In the only way that matters," her mother said. "Thank you, kids."

Nita blinked back tears. Kit just nodded.

The head nurse came in and stood by the bed. "How're you feeling?"

"Like someone's been taking out pieces of my brain," Nita's mother said, "but otherwise, just fine. When can I go home?"

"The day after tomorrow," said the nurse, "if the surgeons agree. It's not like the surgery itself was all that major, and you seem to be getting over the post-op trauma with unusual speed. If this keeps up, we can send you home and have a private-duty nurse keep an eye on you for the first few days. After that, there'll be other business, and we'll be seeing a fair amount of each other. But there's time for you to deal with that when you're feeling better and the surgery's healed."

"You're on," Nita's mother said. "Now let me talk to you about dinner."

"No dinner tonight," said the nurse. "Just the bottle, until tomorrow."

"I want a second opinion," Nita's mother said, unimpressed.

The nurse laughed, and went out.

"And a cheeseburger!" Nita's mother called after her.

Nita chuckled; her mother got junk food cravings at the oddest times. Then she caught herself chuckling, and stopped abruptly.

"No," her mother said. "Don't. You're right; it's disgusting, and there's no reason you shouldn't laugh." This she said as much to Nita's dad as to Nita.

Her father didn't say anything.

"Would you two excuse us a second?" Nita's mother said to Kit and Nita.

They went out. "Back in a moment," Kit said, and walked away down toward the vending machine and the rest rooms—a little too quickly, Nita thought. She watched him turn the corner. *It didn't occur to me how much this was hurting him, too. If he's going to be watching out for me, I'd better keep a close eye on him. Might get to be a full-time occupation.*

Nita leaned against the wall outside the room. She should not have been able to hear anything from where she was, but she could.

"Harry," she heard that soft voice say. "Cut it out and look at me. We've bought me some time. We have time to say our good-byes—enough for that, at the least. Beyond that, it's all a gamble. But it always has been, anyway."

Nita could hear her dad breathing in the silence, trying to let it in.

"But one thing, before I forget. You don't need to waste any more time worrying about Kit."

"No?"

"No."

I shouldn't be able to hear this, Nita thought. She closed her eyes and concentrated on not listening. It didn't work. *It has to have something to do with where I've just been.*

"But enough of that. We've got things to do. Listen to me! I don't want you to start treating me like someone who's about to die. I expect to spend every remaining moment *living*. There's little enough time left, for any of us."

Nita could have sworn she heard her father gulp. "Oh, God, sweetheart, don't tell me there's going to be some kind of . . . of disaster!"

"What? Of course not." Her voice went soft and rough again, in a way that Nita had last heard just after her mom had dropped a handful of lightning. "But, Harry, being where I've just been, do you think that sixty years looks any longer to me than six months? Or that anything that's just *time* looks like it's going to last? So shut up and kiss me. We've got a lot to do."

There was only silence then. Nita took herself away as quietly as she could. Down the corridor and around the corner, she found Kit leaning against the wall, his arms folded, waiting for her.

"What are they up to in there?" he asked after a moment.

"Don't ask." She gave him a thoughtful look. He didn't ask. *And I bet he doesn't have to.*

"So, what now?"

"Just for a little while," Nita said, "we leave them alone."

Kit nodded. Together, they headed out.

Dawn

NITA WENT HOME AFTER that, and slept the clock around. They would only need to go to the hospital once or twice more to pick up equipment that the visiting nurse would need, and to talk to the doctors about chemotherapy and so on. Nita was glad enough to let her dad take care of all that. For her own part, she and Dairine mostly just sat and held her mom's hands, and listened to her complain about the hospital food, which she had been allowed to start eating that morning. It was a peculiar kind of happiness that Nita and Dairine were experiencing, and Nita was being careful to say nothing that might break it. Just under the surface of it lay a lot of pain. But right now, the simple joy of knowing that her mom would be home the next day was more than enough for Nita . . . and she knew Dairine agreed.

They went home that evening, and Nita went off to her room and went straight to sleep again. She was getting caught up a little on her own weariness, enough to dream again, but the realization that she *was* dreaming coincided with a certain amount of confusion. The mountainous landscape towering all around her in a misty early morning sun wasn't anyplace she recognized. Neither were the forests running up and up those slopes, all golden, or—as she turned, and paused, amazed—the vast, glittering, many-spired city that was looming out of the mist a mile or so away from her. Beyond it was a faint glimmer, as of the sea unseen in the overshadowing light. Nita thought of the roil and shimmer of the light on Jones Inlet, and let out a long breath of wonder. "Where *is* this?" she said aloud.

"The inside, honey," Nita's mother said. "The heart of things . . . what's at the core. Don't you ever dream about this?"

"Uh . . . yeah, sometimes. But it never looked exactly like this."

"Oh, well, this is my part of the territory. That's yours over there; of course, it'd be here, too. It's part of me, like you are." Her mother, in that beat-up denim skirt and T-shirt again, waved a hand back at the glittering towers, half veiled in radiant mist. "I know you'll live there, eventually. Have your own children there." She smiled slightly. "What is it they say? Your grandchildren are your revenge on your kids?" And Nita's mother laughed. "Well, at least you'll know what to expect from them. Partly. But this . . ." She turned her back on the towers, looking toward the mountains. "This is mine. When you grow up at the edge of the Continental Divide, there's always this wall towering up over you . . . and when you're little, you look at it and say, 'I'm going to go there someday. Right to the top of that mountain.' Or else you imagine mountains that don't have any top. The places that just go right up and up, into the center of things . . . forever."

"Yeah," Nita said.

They stood there a while together, looking at those mountains, and then began to walk slowly down through the flower-starred meadow below where they'd been standing. "It's not fair," Nita said softly. "How come I only get to really know you now, when I'm going to lose you?"

"I don't know if you can ever lose me, honey. I'm your *mother*. There's a bond neither of us can break unless we want to. And it doesn't have to hurt."

Nita wasn't sure about that as yet. But still, there was no lying here. . . .

"So this is it?" Nita's mother said, gazing around her with a look of awe and appreciation. "What you told me about: Timeheart?"

"Uh," Nita said. "I'm not sure. I'm not sure how nonwizards see it."

"After all *that*," Nita's mom said, "am I a nonwizard?"

Nita had no answer for her, but her heart lifted, and she felt a twinge of something that until now she had been afraid to feel: hope.

And it wasn't even hope that her mother would somehow miraculously survive. Nita would hurt for a long while every time she remembered all those dark little creatures dying, and the feeling of many of them *not* dying, hidden away where even the flush of power from the glede couldn't reach. But Nita had reason to believe that she and her mom would have enough time to get to know each other very well before the hardest moment—the moment of final parting—had to be faced.

And when that came . . .

. . . there would, eventually, be Timeheart, where no matter what you dreamed might await you, there was always more.

If she could just last through the testing that would follow, just keep faith long enough to find out *what* that more would be.

"I could definitely get used to this," her mother said.

You will, Nita thought . . . or heard. With the words came a pang of relief mingled with pain, the two impossible to separate. It would be a long time before Nita would get used to the pain, she knew. But the relief was there regardless, and here, in this place, there was no matching echo of grief to suggest that the relief was somehow false or illusory. Nothing that happened here could fail to be real. If she felt relief here, it was justified.

"No," Nita's mother said, "I don't think I'm going to let anyone throw me out of here."

"I don't think they can," Nita said, the tears coming to her eyes, even here. She knew, as all wizards know if they know nothing else, that in Timeheart everything worth having, everything that is loved, or of love, is preserved in perfection.

And everyone? . . .

As usual there were no concrete answers; the place was itself an answer before which all questions faded. Except, suddenly, one.

"Honey," her mother said, "not that I object to the idea, or anything. But can you tell me why there would normally be pigs in heaven?"

"Uh, Mom, this isn't—" But Nita stopped herself; she wasn't sure. And then there was still the question of the Pig, wandering along through the meadow not too far from them and gazing, as they did, at the mountains. The Pig looked, if anything, more transcendent than usual; it did not so much glow as seem to illuminate everything around it, if indeed the luminous surroundings could be anymore illuminated than they already were.

"You're here, too?" Nita said to the Transcendent Pig.

"The annoying thing about omnipresence," the Pig said, "is that everybody keeps asking you that question. At least you didn't ask me what was the meaning of life."

Nita made a face. "I forgot."

It chuckled. "You're *here* and you need to ask?"

She smiled then. "Mom, this is the Transcendent Pig. Chao, this is my mother."

"We've met," said the Pig, nodding in a friendly way to Nita's mom.

Nita's mother smiled back. "You know, we have," she said, "but for the life of me I can't remember when."

"You will," said the Pig. It glanced at Nita. "She has a lot of remembering to do. Not right away . . . but soon."

Nita's mother nodded as well, gazing at the Pig with an odd expression of slowly dawning recognition. It glanced at Nita. "They all remember me eventually," it said. "The way they all remember the Lone One. We have history."

The three of them walked along through the meadow together for a little ways. "Mom," Nita said, "I really don't want to lose you."

"I don't think we get much choice on this one," Nita's mother said. "Honey, our ways are going to part, one way or another." She looked at Nita with an expression that was sorrowful but tender. "Parents and kids do it all the time, as they both grow up. You and I are just going to have to do it faster than we planned . . . and more permanently. Since there's no way out of it, let's enjoy every day. Heaven only knows what may happen afterward, but they can't take away from us what we make, one day at a time, just all of us together. That, we keep . . . and anything else . . ." Her mother looked up at the mountains. "We'll find out soon enough."

Nita nodded. "But oh, Mom . . . I'm going to miss you so much! Always!"

"I'm going to miss you too, honey. But it won't be forever . . . not the kind of forever that matters. If this is where I'm going to be, I think everything will be just fine."

"It won't be the same, though," Nita said softly. "It won't be like being able to talk to you."

"You'll usually know what I would have said, if you think about it," her mother said. "We know each other that well, at least. Other than that, I'll always be around, even though you won't hear much from me. I mean, sweetheart, you started out inside me . . . Don't you think at the end of the process, things sort of go the other way around?"

Nita wiped her eyes and looked over at the Pig, which was looking at her mother with quiet approval. "Can't add much to that," it said.

Nita just hugged her mom; it was all she could do. "Go well," she said.

"As long as you do, sweetheart . . . I always will."

Nita's mother slowly let her go, then looked over her shoulder, up at those mountains, towering skyward into another kind of eternity, and began to walk toward them, through the mist.

Nita stood there with the Pig and watched her mom vanish, shining, into the mist. "What happens now?" Nita said.

"What usually does. Life . . . for a while. Then the usual brief defeat," said the Pig. "But victory's certain. Never think otherwise. There *is* loss, and there *is* pain, and in your home frame of reference, they're real enough, not to be devalued. But today the energy's running out of things just a little more slowly . . . for those who trust their hearts as a measure."

Nita swallowed hard. "You'll keep an eye on her," she said.

"Of course I will. I always do. But somehow," said the Pig, looking at Nita's mother, who was moving higher and higher up the hillside, almost lost in the ever-growing light, "I don't think she'll need it."

. . . The light on the bedroom ceiling woke Nita, glinting through her window from a car pulling into the driveway below. Nita sat up in bed, wiped her face, and tried on a smile. To her astonishment, it didn't feel like such a terrible fit.

She got up, threw on jeans and a T-shirt, and went downstairs to tell her mom hello.